# 30 Stories to Remember

# 30

# STORIES TO

# REMEMBER

SELECTED BY

## Thomas B. Costain

AND

## John Beecroft

DOUBLEDAY & COMPANY, INC.

*Garden City, New York*

# PERMISSIONS

# Contents

# 30 Stories to Remember

# The Split Second

## DAPHNE DU MAURIER

M RS. ELLIS was methodical and tidy. She disliked disorder. Unanswered letters, unpaid bills, the litter and rummage of a slovenly writing desk were things that she abhorred.

Today, more than usual, she was in what her late husband used to call her "clearing" mood.

She had wakened to this mood; it remained with her throughout breakfast and lasted the whole morning.

Besides, it was the first of the month, and as she ripped off the page of her daily calendar and saw the bright clean 1 staring at her, it seemed to symbolise a new start to her day.

The hours ahead of her must somehow seem untarnished like the date; she must let nothing slide.

First she checked the linen. The smooth white sheets lying in rows upon their shelves, pillow slips beside, and one set still in its pristine newness from the shop, tied with blue ribbon, waiting for a guest that never came.

Next, the store cupboard. The stock of homemade jam pleased her, the labels, and the date in her own handwriting.

There were also bottled fruit, and tomatoes, and chutney to her own recipe. She was sparing of these, keeping them in reserve for the holidays when Susan should be home, and even then, when she brought them down and put them proudly on the table, the luxury of the treat was spoilt by a little stab of disappointment; it would mean a gap upon the store-cupboard shelf.

When she had closed the store cupboard and hidden the key (she could never be quite certain of Grace, her cook), Mrs. Ellis went into the drawing-room and settled herself at her desk.

She was determined to be ruthless. The pigeonholes were searched, and those old envelopes that she had kept because they were not torn and could be used again (to tradesmen, not to friends) were thrown away. She would buy fresh buff envelopes of a cheap quality instead.

Here were some receipts of two years back. Unnecessary to keep them now. Those of a year ago were filed, and tied with tape.

A little drawer, stiff to open, she found crammed with old counterfoils from her chequebook. This was wasting space.

Instead, she wrote in her clear handwriting, "Letters to Keep." In the future, the drawer would be used for this purpose.

She permitted herself the luxury of filling her blotter with new sheets of paper. The pen tray was dusted. A new pencil sharpened. And steeling her heart, she threw the stub of the little old one, with worn rubber at the base, into the wastepaper basket.

She straightened the magazines on the side table, pulled the books to the front on the shelf beside the fire—Grace had an infuriating habit of pushing them all to the back—and filled the flower vases with clean water. Then with a bare ten minutes before Grace popped her head round the door and said, "Lunch is in," Mrs. Ellis sat down, a little breathless, before the fire, and smiled in satisfaction. Her morning had been very full indeed. Happy, well spent.

She looked about her drawing-room (Grace insisted on calling it the lounge and Mrs. Ellis was forever correcting her) and thought how comfortable it was, and bright, and how wise they had been not to move when poor Wilfred suggested it a few months before he died. They had so nearly taken that house in the country, because of his health, and his fad that vegetables should be picked fresh every morning and brought to the table, and then luckily—well, hardly luckily, it was most terribly sad and a fearful shock to her—but before they had signed the lease, Wilfred had a heart attack and died. Mrs. Ellis was able to stay on in the home she knew and loved, and where she had first gone as a bride ten years before.

People were inclined to say the locality was going downhill, that it had become worse than suburban. Nonsense. The blocks of flats that were going up at the top end of the road could not be seen from her windows, and the houses, solid like her own, standing in a little circle of front garden, were quite unspoilt.

Besides, she liked the life. Her mornings, shopping in the town, her basket over her arm. The tradesmen knew her, treated her well.

Morning coffee at eleven, at the Cosy Café opposite the bookshop, was a small pleasure she allowed herself on cold mornings—she could not get Grace to make good coffee—and in the summer, the Cosy Café sold ice cream.

Childishly, she would hurry back with this in a paper bag and eat it for lunch; it saved thinking of a sweet.

She believed in a brisk walk in the afternoons, and the heath was so close to hand, it was just as good as the country; and in the evenings she read, or sewed, or wrote to Susan.

Life, if she thought deeply about it, which she did not because to think deeply made her uncomfortable, was really built round Susan. Susan was nine years old, and her only child.

Because of Wilfred's ill-health and, it must be confessed, his irritability, Susan had been sent to boarding school at an early age. Mrs. Ellis had passed many sleepless nights before making this decision, but in the end she knew it would be for Susan's good. The child was healthy and high-spirited, and it was impossible to keep her quiet and subdued in one room, with Wilfred fractious in another. It meant sending her down to the kitchen with Grace, and that, Mrs. Ellis decided, did not do.

Reluctantly, the school was chosen, some thirty miles away. It was easily reached within an hour and a half by a Green Line bus; the children seemed happy and well cared for, the principal was grey-haired and sympathetic, and as the prospectus described it, the place was a "home from home."

Mrs. Ellis left Susan, on the opening day of her first term, in agony of mind, but constant telephone calls between herself and the headmistress during the first week reassured her that Susan had settled placidly to her new existence.

When her husband died, Mrs. Ellis thought Susan would want to return home and go to a day school, but to her surprise and disappointment the suggestion was received with dismay, and even tears.

"But I love my school," said the child; "we have such fun, and I have lots of friends."

"You would make other friends at a day school," said her mother, "and think, we would be together in the evenings."

"Yes," answered Susan doubtfully, "but what would we do?"

Mrs. Ellis was hurt, but she did not permit Susan to see this.

"Perhaps you are right," she said. "You are contented and happy where you are. Anyway, we shall always have the holidays."

The holidays were like brightly coloured beads on a frame and stood out with significance in Mrs. Ellis' engagement diary, throwing the weeks between into obscurity.

How leaden was February, in spite of its twenty-eight days; how blue and interminable was March, for all that morning coffee at the Cosy Café, the choosing of library books, the visit with friends to the local cinema, or sometimes, more dashing, a matinee "in town."

Then April came, and danced its flowery way across the calendar. Easter, and daffodils, and Susan with glowing cheeks whipped by a spring wind, hugging her once again; honey for tea, scones baked by Grace ("You've been and grown again"), those afternoon walks across the heath, sunny and gay because of the figure running on ahead. May was quiet, and June pleasant because of wide-flung windows, and the snapdragons in the front garden; June was leisurely.

Besides, there was the school play on Parents' Day, and Susan, with bright eyes, surely much the best of the pixies, and although she did not speak, her actions were so good.

July dragged until the twenty-fourth, and then the weeks spun themselves into a sequence of glory until the last week in September. Susan at the sea . . . Susan on a farm . . . Susan on Dartmoor . . . Susan just at home, licking an ice cream, leaning out of a window.

"She swims quite well for her age," thus casually, to a neighbor on the beach; "she insists on going in, even when it's cold."

"I don't mind saying," this to Grace, "that I hated going through that field of bullocks, but Susan did not mind a scrap. She has a way with animals."

Bare scratched legs in sandals, summer frocks outgrown, a sun hat, faded, lying on the floor. October did not bear thinking about. . . . But, after all, there was always plenty to do about the house. Forget November, and the rain, and the fogs that turned white upon the heath. Draw the curtains, poke the fire, settle to something. The *Weekly Home Companion*. Fashions for Young Folk. Not that pink, but the green with the smocked top, and a wide sash would be just the thing for Susan at parties in the Christmas holidays. December . . . Christmas . . .

This was the best, this was the height of home enjoyment.

As soon as Mrs. Ellis saw the first small trees standing outside the florist and those orange boxes of dates in the grocer's window, her heart would give a little leap of excitement.

Susan would be home in three weeks now. Then the laughter and the chatter. The nods between herself and Grace. The smiles of mystery. The furtiveness of wrappings.

All over in one day like the bursting of a swollen balloon; paper ribbon, cracker novelties, even presents, chosen with care, thrown aside. But no matter. It was worth it.

Mrs. Ellis, looking down upon a sleeping Susan tucked in with a doll in her arms, turned down the light and crept off to her own bed, sapped, exhausted.

The egg cosy, Susan's handiwork at school, hastily stitched, stood on her bedside table.

Mrs. Ellis never ate boiled eggs, but, as she said to Grace, there is such a gleam in the hen's eye; it's very cleverly done.

The fever, the pace of the New Year. The Circus, the Pantomime. Mrs. Ellis watched Susan, never the performers.

"You should have seen her laugh when the seal blew the trumpet; I have never known a child with such a gift for enjoyment."

And how she stood out at parties, in the green frock, with her fair hair and blue eyes. Other children were so stumpy. Ill-made little bodies, or big shapeless mouths.

"She said, 'Thank you for a lovely time,' when we left, which was more than most of them did. And she won at Musical Chairs."

There were bad moments, too, of course. The restless night, the high spot of colour, the sore throat, the temperature of 102.

Shaking hands on the telephone. The doctor's reassuring voice. And his very footsteps on the stairs, a steady, reliable man.

"We had better take a swab, in case."

A swab? That meant diphtheria, scarlet fever?

A little figure being carried down in blankets, an ambulance, hospital . . . ?

Thank God, it proved to be a relaxed throat. Lots of them about.

Too many parties, keep her quiet for a few days. Yes, Doctor, yes.

The relief from dread anxiety, and on and on without a stop, the reading to Susan from her *Playbook Annual*, story after story, terrible and trite, "and so Nicky Nod *did* lose his treasure after all, which just served him right, didn't it, children?"

"All things pass," thought Mrs. Ellis, "pleasure and pain, and happiness and suffering, and I suppose my friends would say my life is a dull one, rather uneventful, but I am grateful for it, and contented, and although sometimes I feel I did not do my utmost for poor Wilfred—his was a difficult nature, luckily Susan has not inherited it—at least I believe I have succeeded in making a happy home for Susan." She looked about her, that first day of the month, and noticed with affection and appreciation those bits and pieces of furniture, the pictures on the walls, the ornaments on the mantelpiece, all the things she had gathered about her during ten years of marriage, and which meant herself, her home.

The sofa and two chairs, part of an original suite, were worn but comfortable. The pouf by the fire, she had covered it herself. The fire irons, not quite so polished as they should be, she must speak to Grace. The rather melancholy portrait of Wilfred in that dark corner behind the bookshelf, he looked at least distinguished. And was, thought Mrs. Ellis to herself, hastily. The flower picture showed more to advantage over the mantelpiece; the green foliage harmonised so well with the green coat of the Staffordshire figure who stood with his lady beside the clock.

"I could do with new covers," thought Mrs. Ellis, "and curtains too, but they must wait. Susan has grown so enormously the last few months. Her clothes are more important. The child is tall for her age."

Grace looked round the door. "Lunch is in," she said.

"If she would open the door outright," thought Mrs. Ellis, "and come right into the room, I have mentioned it a hundred times. It's the sudden thrust of the head that is so disconcerting, and if I have anyone to lunch . . ."

She sat down to guinea fowl and apple charlotte, and she wondered if they were remembering to give Susan extra milk at school this term, and the Minidex tonic; the matron was inclined to be forgetful.

Suddenly, for no reason, she laid her spoon down on the plate, swept with a wave of such intense melancholy as to be almost unbearable. Her heart was heavy. Her throat tightened. She could not continue her lunch.

"Something is wrong with Susan," she thought; "this is a warning that she wants me."

She rang for coffee and went into the drawing-room. She crossed to the window and stood looking at the back of the house opposite. From an open window sagged an ugly red curtain, and a lavatory brush hung from a nail.

"The district *is* losing class," thought Mrs. Ellis. "I shall have lodging-houses for neighbors soon."

She drank her coffee, but the feeling of uneasiness, of apprehension, did not leave her. At last she went to the telephone and rang up the school.

The secretary answered. Surprised, and a little impatient, surely. Susan was perfectly all right. She had just eaten a good lunch. No, she had no sign of a cold. No one was ill in the school. Did Mrs. Ellis want to speak to Susan? The child was outside with the others, playing, but could be called in if necessary.

"No," said Mrs. Ellis, "it was just a foolish notion on my part that Susan might not be well. I am so sorry to have bothered you."

She hung up the receiver, and then went to her bedroom to put on her outdoor clothes. A good walk would do her good.

She gazed in satisfaction upon the photograph of Susan on the dressing table. The photographer had caught the expression in her eyes to perfection. Such a lovely light on the hair too.

Mrs. Ellis hesitated. Was it really a walk she needed? Or was this vague feeling of distress a sign that she was overtired, that she had better rest?

She looked with inclination at the downy quilt upon her bed. Her hot-water bottle, hanging by the washstand, would take only a moment to fill.

She could loosen her girdle, throw off her shoes, and lie down for an hour on the bed, warm with the bottle under the downy quilt. No. She decided to be firm with herself. She went to the wardrobe and got out her camel coat, wound a scarf round her head, pulled on a pair of gauntlet gloves, and walked downstairs.

She went into the drawing-room and made up the fire, and put the guard in front of it. Grace was apt to be forgetful of the fire. She opened the window at the top so that the room should not strike stuffy when she came back.

She folded the daily papers ready to read when she returned, and replaced the marker in her library book.

"I'm going out for a little while. I shan't be long," she called down to the basement to Grace.

"All right, ma'am," came the answer.

Mrs. Ellis caught the whiff of cigarette, and frowned. Grace could do as she liked in the basement, but there was something not quite right about a maidservant smoking.

She shut the front door behind her, and went down the steps, and into the road, and turned left towards the heath.

It was a dull, grey day. Mild for the time of year, almost to oppression. Later, there would be fog, perhaps, rolling up from London the way it did, in a great wall, stifling the clean air.

Mrs. Ellis made her "short round," as she always called it. Eastward, to the Viaduct ponds, and then back, circling, to the Vale of Health.

It was not an inviting afternoon, and she did not enjoy her walk. She kept wishing she was home again, in bed with a hot-water bottle, or sitting in the drawing-room beside the fire, soon to shut out the muggy, murky sky, and draw the curtains.

She walked swiftly past nurses pushing prams, two or three of them in groups chatting together, their charges running ahead. Dogs barked beside the ponds. Solitary men in mackintoshes stared into vacancy. An old woman on a seat threw crumbs to chirping sparrows. The sky took on a darker, olive tone. Mrs. Ellis quickened her steps. The fairground by the Vale of Health looked sombre, the merry-go-round shrouded in its winter wrappings of canvas, and two lean cats stalked each other in and out of the palings.

A milkman, whistling, clanked his tray of bottles and, lifting them to his cart, urged the pony to a trot.

"I must," thought Mrs. Ellis inconsequently, "get Susan a bicycle for her birthday. Nine is a good age for a first bicycle."

She saw herself choosing one, asking advice, feeling the handle bars. The colour red perhaps. Or a good blue. A little basket on the front and a leather bag, for tools, strapped to the back of the seat. The brakes must be good, but not too gripping, otherwise Susan would topple headfirst over the handle bars and graze her face.

Hoops were out of fashion, which was a pity. When she had been a child there had been no fun like a good springy hoop, struck smartly with a little stick, bowling its way ahead of you. Quite an art to it too. Susan would have been good with a hoop.

Mrs. Ellis came to the junction of two roads, and crossed to the opposite side; the second road was her own, and her house the last one on the corner.

As she did so she saw the laundry van swinging down towards her, much too fast. She saw it swerve, heard the screech of its brakes. She saw the look of surprise on the face of the laundry boy.

"I shall speak to the driver next time he calls," she said to herself. "One of these days there will be an accident."

She thought of Susan on the bicycle, and shuddered.

Perhaps a note to the manager of the laundry would do more good.

"If you could possibly give a word of warning to your driver, I should be grateful. He takes his corners much too fast."

And she would ask to remain anonymous. Otherwise the man might complain about carrying the heavy basket down the steps each time.

She had arrived at her own gate. She pushed it open, and noticed with annoyance that it was nearly off its hinges. The men calling for the laundry must have wrenched at it in some way and done the damage. The note to the manager would be stronger still. She would write immediately after tea. While it was on her mind.

She took out her key and put it in the Yale lock of the front door. It stuck. She could not turn it. How very irritating.

She rang the bell. This would mean bringing Grace up from the basement, which she did not like.

Better to call down, perhaps, and explain the situation.

She leant over the steps and called down to the kitchen.

"Grace, it's only me," she said, "my key has jammed in the door; could you come up and let me in?"

She paused. There was no sound from below. Grace must have gone out. This was sheer deceit. It was an agreed bargain between them that when Mrs. Ellis was out Grace must stay in. The house must not be left. But sometimes Mrs. Ellis suspected that Grace did not keep to the bargain. Here was proof.

She called once again, rather more sharply this time.

"Grace?"

There was a sound of a window opening below, and a man thrust his head out of the kitchen. He was in his shirt sleeves. And he had not shaved.

"What are you bawling your head off about?" he said.

Mrs. Ellis was too stunned to answer. So this was what happened when her back was turned. Grace, respectable, well over thirty, had a man in the house. Mrs. Ellis swallowed, but kept her temper.

"Perhaps you will have the goodness to ask Grace to come upstairs and let me in," she said.

The sarcasm was wasted, of course. The man blinked at her, bewildered. "Who's Grace?" he said.

This was too much. So Grace had the nerve to pass under another name. Something fanciful, no doubt. Shirley, or Marlene.

She was pretty sure now what must have happened. Grace had slipped out to the public house down the road to buy this man beer. The man was left to loll in the kitchen. He might even have been poking his fingers in the larder. Now she knew why there was so little left on the joint two days ago.

"If Grace is out," said Mrs. Ellis, and her voice was icy, "kindly let me in yourself. I prefer not to use the back entrance."

That would put him in his place. Mrs. Ellis trembled with rage. She was angry seldom; she was a mild, even-tempered woman. But this reception, from a lout in shirt sleeves, at her own kitchen window, was rather more than she could bear.

It was going to be unpleasant, the interview with Grace. Grace would give notice in all probability. But some things could not be allowed to slide, and this was one of them.

She heard shuffling footsteps coming along the hall. The man had mounted from the basement. He opened the front door and stood there, staring at her.

"Who is it you want?" he said.

Mrs. Ellis heard the furious yapping of a little dog from the drawing-room. Callers . . . This was the end. How perfectly frightful, how really overwhelmingly embarrassing. Someone had called, and Grace had let them in, or, worse still, this man in his shirt sleeves had done so. What would people think?

"Who is in the drawing-room, do you know?" she murmured swiftly.

"I think Mr. and Mrs. Bolton are in, but I'm not sure," he said. "I can hear the dog yapping. Was it them you wanted to see?"

Mrs. Ellis did not know a Mr. and Mrs. Bolton. She turned impatiently towards the drawing-room, first whipping off her coat and putting her gloves in her pocket.

"You had better go down to the basement again," she said to the man, who was still staring at her; "tell Grace not to bring tea until I ring. These people may not stay."

The man appeared bewildered.

"All right," he said, "I'm going down. But if you want Mr. and Mrs. Bolton again, ring twice."

He shuffled off down the basement stairs. He was drunk, no doubt. He meant to be insulting. If he proved difficult, later in the evening, after dark, it would mean ringing for the police.

Mrs. Ellis slipped into the lobby to hang up her coat. No time to go upstairs if callers were in the drawing-room. She fumbled for the switch and turned it, but the bulb had gone. Another pinprick. Now she could not see herself in the mirror.

She stumbled over something, and bent to see what it was. It was a man's boot. And here was another, and a pair of shoes, and beside them a suitcase and an old rug. If Grace had allowed that man to put his things in her lobby, then Grace would go tonight. Crisis had come. High crisis.

Mrs. Ellis opened the drawing-room door, forcing a smile of welcome, not too warm, upon her lips. A little dog rushed towards her, barking furiously.

"Quiet, Judy," said a man, grey-haired, with horn spectacles, sitting before the fire. He was clicking a typewriter.

Something had happened to the room. It was covered with books and papers; odds and ends of junk littered the floor. A parrot, in a cage, hopped on its perch and screeched a welcome.

Mrs. Ellis tried to speak, but her voice would not come. Grace had gone raving mad. She had let that man into the house, and this one too, and they had brought the most terrible disorder; they had turned the room upside down; they had deliberately, maliciously, set themselves to destroy her things.

No. Worse! It was part of a great thieving plot. She had heard of such things. Gangs went about breaking into houses. Grace, perhaps, was not at fault. She was lying in the basement, gagged and bound. Mrs. Ellis felt her heart beating much too fast. She also felt a little faint.

"I must keep calm," she said to herself, "whatever happens, I must keep calm. If I can get to the telephone, to the police, it is the only hope. This man must not see that I am planning what to do."

The little dog kept sniffing at her heels.

"Excuse me," said the intruder, pushing his horn spectacles on to his forehead, "but do you want anything? My wife is upstairs."

The diabolic cunning of the plot. The cool bluff of his sitting there, the typewriter on his knees. They must have brought all this stuff in through the door to the back garden; the french window was ajar. Mrs. Ellis glanced swiftly at the mantelpiece. It was as she feared. The Staffordshire figures had been removed, and the flower picture too. There must be a car, a van, waiting down the road. . . . Her mind worked quickly. It might be that the man had not guessed her identity. Two could play at bluff. Memories of amateur theatricals flashed through her mind. Somehow she must detain these people until the police arrived. How fast they had worked. Her desk was gone, the bookshelves too, nor could she see her armchair.

But she kept her eyes steadily on the stranger. He must not notice her brief glance round the room.

"Your wife is upstairs?" said Mrs. Ellis, her voice strained, yet calm.

"Yes," said the man, "if you've come for an appointment, she always makes them. You'll find her in the studio. Room in the front."

Steadily, softly, Mrs. Ellis left the drawing-room, but the wretched little dog had followed her, sniffing at her heels.

One thing was certain. The man had not realised who she was. They believed the householder out of the way for the afternoon, and that she, standing now in the hall, listening, her heart beating, was some caller to be fobbed off with a lie about appointments.

She stood silently by the drawing-room door. The man had resumed typing on his machine. She marvelled at the coolness of it, the drawn-out continuity of the bluff.

There had been nothing in the papers very recently about large-scale house robberies. This was something new, something outstanding. It was extraordinary that they should pick on her house. But they must know she was a widow, on her own, with one maidservant. The telephone had already been removed from the stand in the hall. There was a loaf of bread on it instead, and something that looked like meat wrapped up in newspaper. So they had brought provisions. . . . There was a chance that the telephone in her bedroom had not yet been taken away, nor the wires cut. The man had said his wife was upstairs. It may have been part of his bluff, or it might be true that he worked with a woman accomplice. This woman, even now, was probably turning out Mrs. Ellis' wardrobe, seizing her fur coat, ramming the single string of cultured pearls into a pocket.

Mrs. Ellis thought she could hear footsteps in her bedroom.

Her anger overcame her fear. She had not the strength to do battle with the man, but she could face the woman. And if the worst came to the worst, she would run to the window, put her head out, and scream. The people next door would hear. Or someone might be passing in the street.

Stealthily, Mrs. Ellis crept upstairs. The little dog led the way with confidence. She paused outside her bedroom door. There was certainly movement from within. The little dog waited, his eyes fixed upon her with intelligence.

At that moment the door of Susan's small bedroom opened, and a fat elderly woman looked out, blowzy, and red in the face. She had a tabby cat under her arm. As soon as the dog saw the cat it started a furious yapping.

"Now that's torn it," said the woman. "What do you want to bring the dog upstairs for? They always fight when they meet. Do you know if the post's been yet? Oh, sorry. I thought you were Mrs. Bolton."

She brought an empty milk bottle from under her other arm and put it down on the landing.

"I'm blowed if I can manage the stairs today," she said, "somebody else will have to take it down for me. Is it foggy out?"

"No," said Mrs. Ellis, shocked into a natural answer, and then, feeling the woman's eyes upon her, hesitated between entering her bedroom door and withdrawing down the stairs. This evil-looking old woman was part of the gang and might call the man from below.

"Got an appointment?" said the other. "She won't see you if you haven't booked an appointment."

A tremour of a smile appeared on Mrs. Ellis' lips.

"Thank you," she said, "yes, I have an appointment."

She was amazed at her own steadiness, and that she could carry off the situation with such aplomb. An actress on the London stage could not have played her part better.

The elderly woman winked and, drawing nearer, plucked Mrs. Ellis by the sleeve.

"Is she going to do you straight or fancy?" she whispered. "It's the fancy ones that get the men. You know what I mean!"

She nudged Mrs. Ellis and winked again.

"I see by your ring you're married," she said. "You'd be surprised, even the quietest husbands like their pictures fancy. Take a tip from an old pro. Get her to do you fancy."

She lurched back into Susan's room, the cat under her arm, and shut the door.

"It's possible," thought Mrs. Ellis, the faint feeling coming over her once again, "that a group of lunatics have escaped from an asylum, and in their terrible, insane fashion, they have broken into my house not to thieve, not to destroy my belongings, but because in some crazed, deluded fashion they believe themselves to be at home."

The publicity would be frightful once it became known. Headlines in the papers. Her photograph taken. So bad for Susan. Susan . . . That horrible, disgusting old woman in Susan's bedroom.

Emboldened, fortified, Mrs. Ellis opened her own bedroom door. One glance revealed the worst. The room was bare, was stripped. There were several lights at various points of the room, flexes attached, and a camera on a tripod. A divan was pushed against the wall. A young woman, with a crop of thick fuzzy hair, was kneeling on the floor, sorting papers.

"Who is it?" she said. "I don't see anyone without an appointment. You've no right to come in here."

Mrs. Ellis, calm, resolute, did not answer. She had made certain that the telephone, though it had been moved like the rest of her things, was still in the room.

She went to it and lifted the receiver.

"Leave my telephone alone," cried the shock-haired girl, and she began to struggle to her knees.

"I want the police," said Mrs. Ellis firmly to the exchange, "I want them to come at once to 17 Elmhurst Road. I am in great danger. Please report this message to the police at once."

The girl was beside her now, taking the receiver from her.

"Who's sent you here?" said the girl, her face sallow, colourless, against the fuzzy hair. "If you think you can come in snooping, you're mistaken. You won't find anything. Nor the police, neither. I have a trade license for the work I do."

Her voice had risen, and the dog, alarmed, joined her with high-pitched barks. The girl opened the door and called down the stairs.

"Harry?" she shouted. "Come here and throw this woman out."

Mrs. Ellis remained quite calm. She stood with her back to the wall, her hands folded. The exchange had taken her message. It would not be long now before the police arrived.

She heard the drawing-room door open from below, and the man's voice called up, petulant, irritated.

"What's the matter?" he shouted. "You know I'm busy. Can't you deal with the woman? She probably wants a special pose."

The girl's eyes narrowed. She looked closely at Mrs. Ellis.

"What did my husband say to you?" she said.

"Ah!" thought Mrs. Ellis triumphantly. "They are getting frightened. It's not such an easy game as they think."

"I had no conversation with your husband," said Mrs. Ellis quietly; "he merely told me I should find you upstairs. In this room. Don't try any bluff with me. It's too late. I can see what you have been doing."

She gestured at the room. The girl stared at her.

"You can't put any phony business over on me," she said; "this studio is decent, respectable, everyone knows that. I take camera studies of children. Plenty of clients can testify to that. You've got no proof of anything else. Show me a negative, and then I might believe you."

Mrs. Ellis wondered how long it would be before the police came. She must continue to play for time. Later, she might even feel sorry, perhaps, for this wretched, deluded girl who had wrought such havoc in the bedroom, believing herself to be a photographer; but this moment, now, she must be calm, calm.

"Well?" said the girl. "What are you going to say when the police come? What's your story?"

It did not do to antagonize lunatics. Mrs. Ellis knew that. They must be humoured. She must humour this girl until the police came.

"I shall tell them that I live here," she said gently; "that is all they will need to know. Nothing further."

The girl looked at her, puzzled, and lit a cigarette.

"Then it is a pose you want?" she said. "That call was just a bluff? Why don't you come clean and say why you're here?"

The sound of their voices had attracted the attention of the old woman in Susan's room. She tapped on the door, which was already open, and stood on the threshold.

"Anything wrong, dear?" she said slyly to the girl.

"Push on out of it," said the girl impatiently, "this is none of your business. I don't interfere with you, and you don't interfere with me."

"I'm not interfering, dear," said the woman, "I only wanted to know if I could help. Difficult client, eh? Wants something outsize?"

"Oh, shut your mouth," said the girl.

The girl's husband, Bolton or whatever his name was, the spectacled man from the drawing-room, came upstairs and into the bedroom.

"Just what's going on?" he said.

The girl shrugged her shoulders and glanced at Mrs. Ellis.

"I don't know," she said, "but I think it's blackmail."

"Has she got any negatives?" said the man swiftly.

"Not that I know of. Never seen her before."

"She might have got them from another client," said the elderly woman, watching.

The three of them stared at Mrs. Ellis. She was not afraid. She had the situation well in hand.

"I think we've all become a little overwrought," she said, "and much the best thing to do would be to go downstairs, sit quietly by the fire, and have a little chat, and you can talk to me about your work. Tell me, are you all three photographers?"

As she spoke, half of her mind was wondering where they had managed to hide her things. They must have bundled her bed into Susan's room; the wardrobe was in two parts, of course, and could be taken to pieces very soon; but her clothes . . . her ornaments . . . these must have been concealed in a lorry. Somewhere, there was a lorry filled with all her things. It might be parked down another road, or might have been driven off already by yet another accomplice. The police were good at tracing stolen goods, she knew that, and everything was insured; but such a mess had been made of the house; insurance would never cover that, nor would her fire policy, unless there was some clause, some proviso against damage by lunatics; surely the insurance people would not call that an act of God. . . . Her mind ran on and on, taking in the mess, the disorder, these people had created, and how many days and weeks would it take for her and Grace to get everything straight again?

Poor Grace. She had forgotten Grace. Grace must be shut up somewhere in the basement with that dreadful man in shirt sleeves, another of the gang, not a follower at all.

"Well," said Mrs. Ellis with the other half of her mind, the half that was acting so famously, "shall we do as I suggest and go downstairs?"

She turned, and led the way, and to her surprise they followed her, the man and his wife, not the horrible old woman. She remained above, leaning over the banisters.

"Call me if you want me," she said.

Mrs. Ellis could not bear to think of her fingering Susan's things in the little bedroom.

"Won't you join us?" she said, steeling herself to courtesy. "It's far more cheerful down below."

The old woman smirked. "That's for Mr. and Mrs. Bolton to say," she said, "I don't push myself."

"If I can get all three of them pinned into the drawing-room," thought Mrs. Ellis, "and somehow lock the door, and make a tremendous effort at conversation, I might possibly keep their attention until the police arrive. There is, of course, the door into the garden, but then they will have to climb the fence, fall over that potting shed next door. The old woman, at least, would never do it."

"Now," said Mrs. Ellis, her heart turning over inside at the havoc of the drawing-room, "shall we sit down and recover ourselves, and you shall tell me all about this photography."

But she had scarcely finished speaking before there was a ring at the front door, and a knock, authoritative, loud.

The relief sent her dizzy. She steadied herself against the door. It was the police. The man looked at the girl, a question in his eye.

"Better have 'em in," he said, "she's got no proof."

He crossed the hall and opened the front door.

"Come in, officer," he said. "There's two of you, I see."

"We had a telephone call," Mrs. Ellis heard the constable say, "some trouble going on, I understand."

"I think there must be some mistake," said Bolton. "The fact is, we've had a caller and I think she got hysterical."

Mrs. Ellis walked out into the hall. She did not recognise the constable, nor the young policeman from the beat. It was unfortunate, but it did not really matter. Both were stout, well-built men.

"I am not hysterical," she said firmly, "I am perfectly all right. I put the telephone call through to the exchange."

The constable took out a notebook and a pencil.

"What's the trouble?" he said. "But give me first your name and address."

Mrs. Ellis smiled patiently. She hoped he was not going to be a stupid man.

"It's hardly necessary," she said, "but my name is Mrs. Wilfred Ellis of this address."

"Lodge here?" asked the constable.

Mrs. Ellis frowned. "No," she said, "this is my house, I live here." And then because she saw a look flash from Bolton to his wife, she knew the time had come to be explicit. "I must speak to you alone, Constable," she said, "the matter is terribly urgent; I don't think you quite understand."

"If you have any charge to bring, Mrs. Ellis," said the officer, "you can bring it at the police station at the proper time. We were informed that somebody lodging here at Number 17 was in danger. Are you, or are you not, the person who gave that information to the exchange?"

Mrs. Ellis began to lose control.

"Of course I am that person," she said. "I returned home to find that my house had been broken into by thieves, these people here, dangerous thieves, lunatics, I don't know what they are, and my things carried away, the whole of my house turned upside down, the most terrible disorder everywhere."

She talked so rapidly, her words fell over themselves.

The man from the basement had now joined them in the hall. He stared at the two policemen, his eyes goggling.

"I saw her come to the door," he said; "I thought she was balmy. Wouldn't have let her in if I had known."

The constable, a little nettled, turned to the interruption.

"Who are you?" he said.

"Name of Upshaw," said the man, "William Upshaw. Me and my missus has the basement flat here."

"That man is lying," said Mrs. Ellis, "he does not live here; he belongs to this gang of thieves. Nobody lives in the basement except my maid—perhaps I should say cook-general—Grace Jackson, and if you will search the premises you will probably find her gagged and bound somewhere, and by that ruffian."

She had now lost all restraint. She could hear her voice, usually low and quiet, rising to a hysterical pitch.

"Balmy," said the man from the basement, "you can see the straw in her hair."

"Quiet, please," said the constable, and turned an ear to the young policeman, who murmured something in his ear.

"Yes, yes," he said, "I've got the directory here. It's all in order."

He consulted another book. Mrs. Ellis watched him feverishly. Never had she seen such a stupid man. Why had they sent out such a slow-witted fool from the police station?

The constable now turned to the man in the horn spectacles.

"Are you Henry Bolton?" he asked.

"Yes, officer," replied the man eagerly, "and this is my wife. We have the ground floor here. This is my wife. She uses an upstairs room for a studio. Camera portraits, you know."

There was a shuffle down the stairs, and the old evil woman came to the foot of the banisters.

"My name's Baxter," she said, "Billie Baxter they used to call me in my old stage days. Used to be in the profession, you know. I have the first-floor back here at Number 17. I can witness this woman came as a sort of Paul Pry, and up to no good. I saw her looking through the keyhole of Mrs. Bolton's studio."

"Then she doesn't lodge here?" asked the constable. "I didn't think she did; the name isn't in the directory."

"We have never seen her before, officer," said Bolton. "Mr. Upshaw let her into the house through some error; she walked into our living-room, and then forced her way into my wife's studio, threatened her, and in hysterical fashion rang for the police."

The constable looked at Mrs. Ellis.

"Anything to say?" he said.

Mrs. Ellis swallowed. If only she could keep calm, if only her heart would not beat so dreadfully fast, and the terrible desire to cry would not rise in her throat.

"Constable," she said, "there has been some terrible mistake. You are new to the district, perhaps, and the young policeman too—I don't seem to recognise him—but if you would kindly get through to your headquarters, they must know all about me; I have lived here for years. My maid Grace has been with me a very long time; I am a widow; my husband, Wilfred Ellis, has been dead two years; I have a little girl of nine at school. I went out for a walk on the heath this afternoon, and during my absence these people have broken into my house, seized or destroyed my belongings—I don't know which—the whole place is upside down; if you would please get through immediately to your headquarters . . ."

"There, there," said the constable, putting his notebook away, "that's all right; we can go into all that quietly down at the station. Now, do any of you want to charge Mrs. Ellis with trespassing?"

There was silence. Nobody said anything.

"We don't wish to be unkind," said Bolton diffidently; "I think my wife and myself are quite willing to let the matter pass."

"I think it should be clearly understood," interposed the shock-haired girl, "that anything this woman says about us at the police station is completely untrue."

"Quite," said the officer. "You will both be called, if needed, but I very much doubt the necessity. Now, Mrs. Ellis"—he turned to her, not harshly in any way, but with authority—"we have a car outside, and we can run you down to the station, and you can tell your story there. Have you a coat?"

Mrs. Ellis turned blindly to the lobby. She knew the police station well; it was barely five minutes away. It was best to go there direct. See someone in authority, not this fool, this hopeless, useless fool. But in the meantime, these people were getting away with their criminal story. By the time she and an additional police force returned, they would have fled. She groped for her coat in the dark lobby, stumbling again over the boots, the suitcases.

"Constable," she said softly, "here, one minute."

He moved towards her.

"Yes?" he said.

"They've taken away the electric bulb," she said rapidly in a low whisper; "it was perfectly all right this afternoon, and these boots, and this pile of suitcases, all these have been brought in, and thrown here; the suitcases are probably filled with my ornaments. I must ask you most urgently to leave the policeman in charge here until we return, to see that these people don't escape."

"That's all right, Mrs. Ellis," said the officer. "Now, are you ready to come along?"

She saw a look pass between the constable and the young policeman. The young policeman was trying to hide his smile.

Mrs. Ellis felt certain that the constable was *not* going to remain in the house. And a new suspicion flashed into her mind. Could this officer and his subordinate be genuine members of the police force? Or were they, after all, members of the gang? This would explain their strange faces, their obvious mishandling of the situation. In which case they were now going to take her away to some lair, drug her, kill her possibly.

"I'm not going with you," she said swiftly.

"Now, Mrs. Ellis," said the constable, "don't give any trouble. You shall have a cup of tea down at the station, and no one is going to hurt you."

He seized her arm. She tried to shake it off. The young policeman moved closer.

"Help," she shouted, "help . . . help . . ."

There must be someone. Those people from next door, she barely knew them, but no matter, if she raised her voice loud enough . . .

"Poor thing," said the man in shirt sleeves, "seems sad, don't it? I wonder how she got like it."

Mrs. Ellis saw his bulbous eyes fixed on her with pity, and she nearly choked.

"You rogue," she said, "how dare you, how dare you!" But she was being bundled down the steps, and through the front garden, and into the car, and there was another policeman at the wheel of the car; and she was thrust at the back, the constable keeping a steady hold upon her arm.

The car turned downhill, past the stretch of heath; she tried to see out of the windows the direction, but the bulk of the constable prevented her.

After twisting and turning, the car stopped, to her great surprise, in front of the police station.

Then these men were genuine, after all. They were not members of the gang. Stupefied for a moment, but relieved, thankful, Mrs. Ellis stumbled from the car. The constable, still holding her arm, led her inside.

The hall was not unfamiliar; she remembered coming once before, years ago, when the ginger cat was lost; there was somebody in charge always, sitting at a sort of desk, everything very official, very brisk. She supposed she would stop here in the hall, but the constable led her on to an inner room, and here was another officer seated at a large desk, a more superior type altogether, thank heaven, and he looked intelligent.

She was determined to get her word in before the constable spoke.

"There has been great confusion," she began. "I am Mrs. Ellis, of 17 Elmhurst Road, and my house has been broken into, robbery is going on at this moment on a huge scale; I believe the thieves to be very desperate and extraordinarily cunning; they have completely taken in the constable here, and the other policeman . . ."

To her indignation this superior officer did not look at her. He raised his eyebrows at the constable, and the constable, who had taken off his hat, coughed and approached the desk. A policewoman, appearing from nowhere, stood beside Mrs. Ellis and held her arm.

The constable and the superior officer were talking together in low tones. Mrs. Ellis could not hear what they were saying. Her legs trembled with emotion. She felt her head swim.

Thankfully, she accepted the chair dragged forward by the policewoman, and in a few moments, too, she was given a cup of tea. She did not want it though. Precious time was being lost.

"I must insist that you hear what I have to say," she said, and the policewoman tightened her grip on Mrs. Ellis' arm. The superior officer behind the desk motioned Mrs. Ellis forward, and she was assisted to another chair, the policewoman remaining beside her all the while.

"Now," he said, "what is it you want to tell me?"

Mrs. Ellis gripped her hands together. She had a premonition that this man, in spite of his superior face, was going to prove as great a fool as the constable.

"My name is Ellis," she said, "Mrs. Wilfred Ellis, of 17 Elmhurst Road. I am in the telephone book. I am in the directory. I am very well known in the district, and have lived at Elmhurst Road for ten years. I am a widow, and I have one little girl of nine years at present at school. I employ one maidservant, Grace Jackson, who cooks for me and does general work. This afternoon I went for a short walk on the heath, round by the Viaduct and the Vale of Health ponds, and when I returned home I found my house had been broken into; my maid had disappeared; the rooms were already stripped of my belongings, and the thieves were in possession of my home, putting up a stupendous act of bluff that deceived even the constable here. I put the call through to the exchange, which frightened the thieves, and I endeavoured to keep them pinned in my drawing-room until help arrived."

Mrs. Ellis paused for breath. She saw that the officer was paying attention to her story, and kept his eyes fixed upon her.

"Thank you," he said, "that is very helpful, Mrs. Ellis. Now, have you anything you can show me to prove your identity?"

She stared at him. Prove her identity? Well, of course. But not here, not actually on her person. She had come away without her handbag, and her calling cards were in the writing desk, and her passport—she and Wilfred had been to Dieppe once—was, if she remembered rightly, in the left-hand pigeonhole of the small writing desk in her bedroom.

But she suddenly remembered the havoc of the house. Nothing would be found. . . .

"It's very unfortunate," she said to the officer, "but I did not take my handbag with me when I went out for my walk this afternoon. I left it in the chest of drawers in the bedroom. My calling cards are in the desk in the drawing-room, and there is a passport—rather out of date; my husband and I did not travel much—in a pigeonhole in a small desk in my bedroom. But everything has been upset, taken by these thieves. The house is in utter chaos."

The officer made a note on a pad beside him.

"You can't produce your identity card or your ration book?" he asked.

"I have explained," said Mrs. Ellis, governing her temper, "my calling cards are in my writing desk. I don't know what you mean by ration book."

The officer went on writing on his pad. He glanced at the policewoman, who began feeling Mrs. Ellis' pockets, touching her in a familiar way. Mrs. Ellis tried to think which of her friends could be telephoned to, who could vouch for her, who could come at once by car and make these idiots, these stone-witted fools, see sense.

"I must keep calm," she told herself again, "I must keep calm."

The Collins were abroad; they would have been the best, but Netta Draycott should be at home; she was usually at home about this time because of the children.

"I have asked you," said Mrs. Ellis, "to verify my name and address in the telephone book, or the district directory. If you refuse to do that, ask the postmaster, or the manager of my bank, a branch of which is in the High Street, and where I cashed a cheque on Saturday. Finally, would you care to ring up Mrs. Draycott, a friend of mine, 21 Charlton Court, the block of flats in Charlton Avenue, who will vouch for me?"

She sat back in the chair, exhausted. No nightmare, she told herself, could ever have the horror, the frustrated hopelessness, of her present plight. Little incident piled on little incident. If she had only remembered to bring her handbag, there was a calling-card case in her handbag. And all the while those thieves, those devils, breaking up her home, getting away with her precious things, her belongings . . .

"Now, Mrs. Ellis," said the officer, "we have checked up on your statements, you know, and they won't do. You are not in the telephone book, nor in the directory."

"I assure you I am," said Mrs. Ellis with indignation; "give me the books and I'll show you."

The constable, still standing, placed the books before her. She ran her finger down the name of Ellis to the position on the left-hand page where she knew it would be. The name Ellis was repeated, but not hers. And none with her address or number. She looked in the directory and saw that beside 17 Elmhurst Road were the names of Bolton, of Upshaw, of Baxter. . . . She pushed both books away from her. She stared at the officer.

"There is something wrong with these books," she said, "they are not up to date, they are false, they are not the books I have at home."

The officer did not answer. He closed the books.

"Now, Mrs. Ellis," he said, "I can see you are tired, and a rest would do you good. We will try to find your friends for you. If you will go along now, we will get in touch with them as soon as possible. I will send a doctor along to you, and he may chat with you a little and give you a sedative, and then, after some rest, you will feel better in the morning and we may have news for you."

The policewoman helped Mrs. Ellis to her feet.

"Come along now," she said.

"But my house?" said Mrs. Ellis. "Those thieves, and my maid Grace, Grace may be lying in the basement; surely you are going to do something about the house; you won't permit them to get away with this monstrous crime; even now we have wasted a precious half hour——"

"That's all right, Mrs. Ellis," said the officer, "you can leave everything in our hands."

The policewoman led her away, still talking, still protesting, and now she was being taken down a corridor, and the policewoman kept saying: "Now, don't fuss, take it calmly; no one's going to hurt you," and she was in a little room with a bed; heavens . . . it was a cell, a cell where they put the prisoners, and the policewoman was helping her off with her coat, unpinning the scarf that was still tied round her hair, and because Mrs. Ellis felt so faint the policewoman made her lie down on the bed, covered her with the coarse grey blanket, placed the little hard pillow under her head.

Mrs. Ellis seized the woman's hands. Her face, after all, was not unkind.

"I beg of you," she said, "ring up Hampstead 4072, the number of my friend Mrs. Draycott, at Charlton Court, and ask her to come here. The officer won't listen to me. He won't hear my story."

"Yes, yes, that will be all right," said the policewoman.

Now somebody else was coming into the room, the cell. Clean-shaven, alert, he carried a case in his hands. He said good evening to the policewoman, and opened his case. He took out a stethoscope and a thermometer. He smiled at Mrs. Ellis.

"Feeling a little upset, I hear," he said. "Well, we'll soon put that to rights. Now, will you give me your wrist?"

Mrs. Ellis sat up on the hard narrow bed, pulling the blanket close.

"Doctor," she said, "there is nothing whatever the matter with me. I admit I have been through a terrible experience, quite enough to unnerve anyone; my house has been broken into; no one here will listen to my story, but I am Mrs. Ellis, Mrs. Wilfred Ellis, of 17 Elmhurst Road; if you can possibly persuade the authorities here . . ."

He was not listening to her. With the assistance of the policewoman he was taking her temperature, under her arm, not in the mouth, treating her like a child; and now he was feeling her pulse, dragging down the pupils of her eyes, listening to her chest. . . . Mrs. Ellis went on talking.

"I realise this is a matter of routine. You are obliged to do this. But I want to warn you that my whole treatment, since I have been brought here, since the police came to my house before that, has been infamous, scandalous. I don't personally know our M.P., but I sincerely believe that when he hears my story he will take the matter up, and someone is going to answer for the consequences. Unfortunately I am a widow, no immediate relatives, my little daughter is away at school; my closest friends, a Mr. and Mrs. Collins, are abroad, but my bank manager . . ."

He was dabbing her arm with spirit; he was inserting a needle, and with a whimper of pain Mrs. Ellis fell back on to the hard pillow. The doctor went on holding her arm, her wrist, and Mrs. Ellis, her head going round and round, felt a strange numb sensation as the injection worked into her blood stream. Tears ran down her cheeks. She could not fight. She was too weak.

"How is that?" said the doctor. "Better, eh?"

Her throat was parched, her mouth without saliva. It was one of those drugs that paralysed you, made you helpless.

But the emotion bubbling within her was eased, was still. The anger, the fear and frustration that had keyed her nerves to a point of contraction seemed to die away.

She had explained things badly. The folly of coming out without her handbag had caused half the trouble. And the terrible, wicked cunning of those thieves. "Be still," she said to her mind, "be still. Rest now."

"Now," said the doctor, letting go her wrist, "supposing you tell me your story again. You say your name is Mrs. Ellis?"

Mrs. Ellis sighed and closed her eyes. Must she go into it all again? Had not they got the whole thing written down in their notebooks? What was the use, when the inefficiency of the whole establishment was so palpable? Those telephone books, directories, with wrong names, wrong addresses. Small wonder there were burglaries, murders, every sort of crime, with a police force that was obviously rotten to the core. What was the name of the Member? It was on the tip of her tongue. A nice man, sandy-haired, always looked so trustworthy on a poster. Hampstead was a safe seat, of course. He would take up her case . . .

"Mrs. Ellis," said the doctor, "do you think you can remember now your real address?"

Mrs. Ellis opened her eyes. Wearily, patiently, she fixed them upon the doctor.

"I live at 17 Elmhurst Road," she said mechanically. "I am a widow, my husband has been dead two years. I have a little girl of nine at school. I went for a short walk on the heath this afternoon after lunch, and when I returned——"

He interrupted her.

"Yes," he said, "we know that. We know what happened after your walk. What we want you to tell us is what happened before."

"I had lunch," said Mrs. Ellis; "I remember perfectly well what I ate. Guinea fowl and apple charlotte, followed by coffee. Then I nearly decided to take a nap upstairs on my bed, because I was not feeling very well, but decided the air would do me good."

As soon as she said this, she regretted it. The doctor looked at her keenly.

"Ah!" he said. "You weren't feeling very well. Can you tell me what the trouble was?"

Mrs. Ellis knew what he was after. He and the rest of the police force at the station wanted to certify her as insane. They would make out she had suffered from some brain storm, that her whole story was fabrication.

"There was nothing much the matter," she said quickly. "I was rather tired from sorting things during the morning. I tidied the linen, cleared out my desk in the drawing-room—all that took time."

"Can you describe your house, Mrs. Ellis?" he said. "The furniture, for instance, of your bedroom, your drawing-room?"

"Very easily," she answered, "but you must remember that the thieves who broke into the house this afternoon have done what I begin to fear is irreparable damage. Everything had been seized, hidden away. The rooms were strewn with rubbish, and there was a young woman upstairs in my bedroom pretending to be a photographer."

"Yes," he said, "don't worry about that. Just tell me about your furniture, how the various things were placed, and so on."

He was more sympathetic than she had thought. Mrs. Ellis launched into a description of every room in her house. She named the ornaments, the pictures, the position of the chairs and tables.

"And you say your cook is called Grace Jackson?"

"Yes, Doctor, she has been with me several years. She was in the kitchen when I left this afternoon; I remember most distinctly calling down to the basement and saying that I was going for a short walk and would not be long. I am extremely worried about her, Doctor. Those thieves will have got hold of her, perhaps kidnapped her."

"We'll see to that," said the doctor. "Now, Mrs. Ellis, you have been very helpful, and you have given such a clear account of your home that I think we shan't be long in tracing it, and your relations. You must stay here tonight, and I hope in the morning we shall have news for you. Now, you say your small daughter is at school? Can you remember the address?"

"Of course," said Mrs. Ellis, "and the telephone number too. The school is High Close, Bishops' Lane, Hatchworth, and the telephone number is Hatchworth 202. But I don't understand what you mean about tracing my home. I have told you, I come from 17 Elmhurst Road."

"There is nothing to worry about," said the doctor; "you are not ill, and you are not lying, I quite realise that. You are suffering from a temporary loss of memory that often happens to all sorts of people, and it quickly passes. We've had many cases before."

He smiled. He stood up, his case in his hand.

"But it isn't true," said Mrs. Ellis, trying to raise herself from the pillow. "My memory is perfectly all right. I have given you every detail I can think of; I have told you my name, where I live, a description of my home, the address of my daughter at school . . ."

"All right," he said, "now, don't worry. Just try to relax and have a little sleep. We shall find your friends for you."

He murmured something to the policewoman and left the cell. The policewoman came over to the bed and tucked in the blanket.

"Now, cheer up," she said, "do as the doctor said. Get a little rest. Everything will be all right, you'll see."

Rest . . . But how? Relax . . . But to what purpose? Even now her house was being looted, sacked, every room stripped. The thieves getting clear away with their booty, leaving no trace behind them. They would take Grace with them; poor Grace could not come down to the police station to give witness to her identity. But the people next door, the Furbers, surely they would be good enough; it would not be too much trouble . . . Mrs. Ellis supposed she should have called, been more friendly, had them to tea, but after all, people did not expect that unless they lived in the country; it was out of date. If the police officer had not got hold of Netta Draycott; then the Furbers must be got in touch with at once. . . .

Mrs. Ellis plucked at the policewoman's sleeve.

"The Furbers," she said, "next door, at number 19, they will vouch for me. They are not friends of mine, but they know me well by sight. We have been neighbors for quite six years. The Furbers."

"Yes," said the policewoman, "try to get some sleep."

Oh, Susan, my Susan, if this had happened in the holidays, how much more fearful; what would we have done? Coming back from an afternoon walk to find those devils in the house, and then, who knows, that dreadful photographer woman and her husband taking a fancy to Susan, so pretty, so fair, and wanting to kidnap her. Then what fear, what terror . . . At least the child was safe, knew nothing of what was happening, and if only the story could be kept out of the newspapers, she need never know. So shameful, so degrading, a night spent in a prison cell through such crass stupidity, through such appalling blunders . . .

"You've had a good sleep then," said the policewoman, handing her a cup of tea.

"I don't know what you mean," said Mrs. Ellis, "I haven't slept at all."

"Oh yes, you have." The woman smiled. "They all say that."

Mrs. Ellis blinked, sat up on the narrow bed. She had been speaking to the policewoman only a moment before. Her head ached abominably. She sipped at the tea, tasteless, unrefreshing. She yearned for her bed at home, for Grace coming in noiselessly, drawing the curtains.

"You're to have a wash," said the policewoman, "and I'll give you a comb through, and then you are to see the doctor again."

Mrs. Ellis suffered the indignity of washing under supervision, of having her hair combed; then her scarf and coat and gloves were given to her again, and she was taken out of the cell, along the corridor, back through the hall to the room where they had questioned her the night before. This time a different officer sat at the desk, but she recognised the police constable, and the doctor too.

The last came towards her with that same bland smile on his face.

"How are you feeling today?" he said. "A little more like your true self?"

"On the contrary," said Mrs. Ellis, "I am feeling very unwell indeed, and shall continue to do so until I know what has happened at home. Is anyone here prepared to tell me what has happened at 17 Elmhurst Road since last night? Has anything at all been done to safeguard my property?"

The doctor did not answer, but guided her towards the chair at the desk.

"Now," he said, "the officer here wants to show you a picture in a news-paper."

Mrs. Ellis sat down in the chair. The officer handed her a copy of *The News of the World*—a paper Grace took on Sundays; Mrs. Ellis never looked at it—and there was a photograph of a woman with a scarf round her head, and chubby cheeks, wearing some sort of light-coloured coat. The photograph had a red circle round it, and underneath was written:

"Missing from Home, Ada Lewis, aged 36, widow, of 105 Albert Build-ings, Kentish Town."

Mrs. Ellis handed the paper back across the desk.

"I'm afraid I can't help you," she said. "I don't know this woman."

"The name Ada Lewis conveys nothing to you?" said the officer.

"Nor Albert Court Buildings?"

"No," said Mrs. Ellis, "certainly not."

Suddenly she knew the purpose of the interrogation. The police thought that she was this missing woman, this Ada Lewis from Albert Buildings. Simply because she wore a light-coloured coat and had a scarf round her hair. She rose from the chair.

"This is absolutely preposterous," she said. "I have told you my name is Ellis, Mrs. Wilfred Ellis, of 17 Elmhurst Road, and you persist in disbeliev-ing me. My detention here is an outrage; I demand to see a lawyer, my own lawyer. . . ." But wait, she hadn't needed the services of a lawyer since Wilfred died, and the firm had moved or been taken over by some-body else; better not give the name; they would think she was lying once again; it was safer to give the name of the bank manager. . . .

"One moment," said the officer, and she was interrupted once again, be-cause somebody else came into the room, a seedy, common-looking man in a checked shabby suit, holding his trilby hat in his hand.

"Can you identify this woman as your sister, Ada Lewis?" asked the officer.

A flush of fury swept Mrs. Ellis as the man stepped forward and peered into her face.

"No, sir," he said, "this isn't Ada. Ada isn't so stout, and this woman's teeth seem to be her own. Ada wore dentures. Never seen this woman before."

"Thank you," said the officer, "that's all. You can go. We will let you know if we find your sister."

The seedy-looking man left the room. Mrs. Ellis turned in triumph to the officer behind the desk.

"Now," she said, "perhaps you will believe me?"

The officer considered her a moment, and then, glancing at the doctor, looked down at some notes on his desk.

"Much as I would like to believe you," he said, "it would save us all a great deal of trouble if I could, unfortunately I can't. Your facts have been proved wrong in every particular. So far."

"What do you mean?" said Mrs. Ellis.

"First, your address. You do not live at 17 Elmhurst Road because the house is occupied by various tenants who have lived there for some time and who are known to us. Number 17 is an apartment house, and the floors are let separately. You are not one of the tenants."

Mrs. Ellis gripped the sides of her chair. The obstinate, proud, and completely unmoved face of the officer stared back at her.

"You are mistaken," said Mrs. Ellis quietly. "Number 17 is not a lodging-house. It is a private house. My own."

The officer glanced down again at his notes.

"There are no people called Furber living at number 19," he went on. "Number 19 is also a lodginghouse. You are not in the directory under the name of Ellis, nor in the telephone book. There is no Ellis on the register of the branch of the bank you mentioned to us last night. Nor can we trace anyone of the name of Grace Jackson in the district."

Mrs. Ellis looked up at the doctor, at the police constable, at the police-woman, who was still standing by her side.

"Is there some conspiracy?" she said. "Why are you all against me? I don't understand what I have done. . . ."

Her voice faltered. She must not break down. She must be firm with them, be brave, for Susan's sake.

"You rang up my friend at Charlton Court?" she asked. "Mrs. Draycott, that big block of flats?"

"Mrs. Draycott is not living at Charlton Court, Mrs. Ellis," said the police officer, "for the simple reason that Charlton Court no longer exists. It was destroyed by a fire bomb."

Mrs. Ellis stared at him in horror. A fire bomb? But how perfectly terrible! When? How? In the night? Disaster upon disaster . . . Who could have done it, anarchists, strikers, unemployed, gangs of people, possibly those who had broken into her house? Poor Netta and her husband and children; Mrs. Ellis felt her head reeling. . . .

"Forgive me," she said, summoning her strength, her dignity, "I had no idea there had been such a fearful outrage. No doubt part of the same plot, those people in my house . . ."

Then she stopped, because she realised they were lying to her; everything was lies; they were not policemen; they had seized the building; they were spies; the government was to be overthrown; but then why bother with her, with a simple harmless individual like herself; why were they not getting on with the civil war, bringing machine guns into the street, marching to Buckingham Palace; why sit here, pretending to her?

A policeman came into the room and clicked his heels and stood before the desk.

"Checked up on all the nursing homes," he said, "and the mental homes, sir, in the district, and within a radius of five miles. Nobody missing."

"Thank you," said the officer. Ignoring Mrs. Ellis, he looked across at the doctor.

"We can't keep her here," he said; "you'll have to persuade them to take her at Moreton Hill. The matron *must* find a room. Say it's a temporary measure. Case of amnesia."

"I'll do what I can," said the doctor.

Moreton Hill. Mrs. Ellis knew at once what they meant by Moreton Hill. It was a well-known mental home somewhere near Highgate, very badly run, she always heard, a dreadful place.

"Moreton Hill?" she said. "You can't possibly take me there. It has a shocking reputation. The nurses are always leaving. I refuse to go to Moreton Hill. I demand to see a lawyer—no, my doctor, Dr. Godber; he lives in Parkwell Gardens."

The officer stared at her thoughtfully.

"She must be a local woman," he said; "she gets the names right every time. But Godber went to Portsmouth, didn't he? I remember Godber."

"If he's at Portsmouth," said Mrs. Ellis, "he would only have gone for a few days. He's most conscientious. But his secretary knows me. I took Susan there last holidays."

Nobody listened to her though, and the officer was consulting his notes again.

"By the way," he said, "you gave me the name of that school correctly. Wrong telephone number, but right school. Co-educational. We got through to them last night."

"I'm afraid then," said Mrs. Ellis, "that you got the wrong school. High Close is most certainly not co-educational, and I should never have sent Susan there if it had been."

"High Close," repeated the officer, reading from his notes, "is a co-educational school, run by a Mr. Foster and his wife."

"It is run by a Miss Slater," said Mrs. Ellis, "a Miss Hilda Slater."

"You mean it *was* run by a Miss Slater," said the officer; "a Miss Slater had the school and then retired, and it was taken over by Mr. and Mrs. Foster. They have no pupil there of the name of Susan Ellis."

Mrs. Ellis sat very still in her chair. She looked at each face in turn. None was harsh. None was unfriendly. And the policewoman smiled encouragement. They all watched her steadily. At last she said:

"You are not deliberately trying to mislead me? You do realise that I am anxious, most desperately anxious, to know what has happened? If all that you are saying is some kind of a game, some kind of torture, would you tell me so that I know, so that I can understand?"

The doctor took her hand, and the officer leant forward in his chair.

"We are trying to help you," he said; "we are doing everything we can to find your friends."

Mrs. Ellis held tight to the doctor's hand. It had suddenly become a refuge.

"I don't understand," she said, "what has happened. If I am suffering from loss of memory, why do I remember everything so clearly? My address, my name, people, the school . . . Where is Susan; where is my little girl?"

She looked round her in blind panic. She tried to rise from the chair.

"If Susan is not at High Close, where is she?" said Mrs. Ellis.

Someone was patting her on the shoulder. Someone was giving her a glass of water.

"If Miss Slater had retired to give place to a Mr. and Mrs. Foster, I should have heard, they would have told me," she kept repeating; "I only telephoned the school yesterday. Susan was quite well, and playing in the grounds."

"Are you suggesting that Miss Slater answered you herself?" inquired the officer.

"No, the secretary answered. I telephoned because I had . . . what seemed to me a premonition that Susan might not be well. The secretary assured me that the child had eaten a good lunch and was playing. I am not making this up. It happened yesterday. I tell you, the secretary would have told me if Miss Slater was making changes in the school."

Mrs. Ellis searched the doubtful faces fixed upon her. And momentarily her attention was caught by the large 2 on the calendar standing on the desk.

"I *know* it was yesterday," she said, "because today is the second of the month, isn't it? And I distinctly remember tearing off the page in my calendar, and because it was the first of the month I decided to tidy my desk, sort out my papers, during the morning."

The police officer relaxed and smiled.

"You are certainly very convincing," he said, "and we can all tell from your appearance, the fact that you have no money on you, that your shoes are polished, and other little signs, that you do definitely belong somewhere in this district; you have not wandered from any great distance. But you do not come from 17 Elmhurst Road, Mrs. Ellis, that is quite certain. For some reason, which we hope to discover, that address has become fixed in your mind, and other addresses too. I promise you everything will be done to clear your mind and to get you well again; and you need have no fear about going to Moreton Hill; I know it well, and they will look after you there."

Mrs. Ellis saw herself shut up behind those grey forbidding walls, grimly situated, frowning down upon the further ponds the far side of the heath. She had skirted those walls many times, pitying the inmates within.

The man who came with the groceries had a wife who became insane. Mrs. Ellis remembered Grace coming to her one morning full of the story, "and he says they've taken her to Moreton Hill."

Once inside, she would never get out. These men at the police station would not bother with her any more.

And now there was this new, hideous misunderstanding about Susan, and the talk of a Mr. and Mrs. Foster taking over the school.

Mrs. Ellis leant forward, clasping her hands together.

"I do assure you," she said, "that I don't want to make trouble. I have always been a very quiet, peaceable sort of person, not easily excited, never quarrelsome, and if I have really lost my memory I will do what the doctor tells me, take any drugs or medicines that will help. But I am worried, desperately worried, about my little girl and what you have told me about the school and Miss Slater's having retired. Would you do just one thing for me? Telephone the school and ask them where you can get in touch with Miss Slater. It is just possible that she has taken the house down the road and removed there with some of the children, Susan amongst them; and whoever answered the telephone was new to the work and gave you vague information."

She spoke clearly, without any sort of hysteria or emotion; they must see that she was in deadly earnest, and this request of hers was not wild fancy.

The police officer glanced at the doctor, then he seemed to make up his mind.

"Very well," he said, "we will do that. We will try to contact this Miss Slater, but it may take time. Meanwhile, I think it is best if you wait in another room while we put through the enquiry."

Mrs. Ellis stood up, this time without the help of the policewoman. She was determined to show that she was well, mentally and bodily, and quite capable of managing her affairs without the assistance of anybody, if it could be permitted.

She wished she had a hat instead of the scarf, which she knew instinctively was unbecoming, and her hands were lost without her handbag. At least she had gloves. But gloves were not enough.

She nodded briskly to the police officer and the doctor—at all costs she must show civility—and followed the policewoman to a waiting room. This time she was spared the indignity of a cell. Another cup of tea was brought to her.

"It's all they think about," she said to herself, "cups of tea. Instead of getting on with their job."

Suddenly she remembered poor Netta Draycott and the terrible tragedy of the fire bomb. Possibly she and her family had escaped and were now with friends, but there was no immediate means of finding out.

"Is it all in the morning papers about the disaster?" she asked the policewoman.

"What disaster?" said the woman.

"The fire at Charlton Court the officer spoke to me about."

The policewoman stared at her with a puzzled expression.

"I don't remember him saying anything about a fire," she said.

"Oh yes, he did," said Mrs. Ellis. "He told me that Charlton Court had been destroyed by fire, by some bomb. I was aghast to hear it because I have friends living there. It must surely be in all the morning papers."

The woman's face cleared.

"Oh, that," she said. "I think the officer was referring to some fire bomb during the war."

"No, no," said Mrs. Ellis impatiently. "Charlton Court was built a long time after the war. I remember the block being built when my husband and I first came to Hampstead. No, this accident apparently happened last night, the most dreadful thing."

The policewoman shrugged her shoulders.

"I think you're mistaken," she said; "there's been no talk of any accident or disaster here."

An ignorant, silly sort of girl, thought Mrs. Ellis. It was a wonder she had passed her test into the force. She thought they only employed very intelligent women.

She sipped her tea in silence. No use carrying on any sort of conversation with her.

It seemed a long while before the door opened, but when it did it was to reveal the doctor, who stood on the threshold with a smile on his face.

"Well," he said, "I think we're a little nearer home. We were able to contact Miss Slater."

Mrs. Ellis rose to her feet, her eyes shining.

"Oh, Doctor, thank heaven . . . Have you news of my daughter?"

"Steady a moment now. You mustn't get excited or we shall have all last night's trouble over again, and that would never do. I take it, when you refer to your daughter, you mean someone who is called, or was called, Susan Ellis?"

"Yes, yes, of course," said Mrs. Ellis swiftly. "Is she all right, is she with Miss Slater?"

"No, she is not with Miss Slater, but she is perfectly well, and I have spoken to her on the telephone myself, and I have her present address here in my notebook."

The doctor patted his breast pocket and smiled again.

"Not with Miss Slater?" Mrs. Ellis stared in bewilderment. "Then the school *has* been handed over; you spoke to these people called Foster. Is it next door? Have they moved far? What has happened?"

The doctor took her hand and led her to the seat once more.

"Now," he said, "I want you to think quite calmly and quite clearly and not be agitated in any way, and your trouble will be cleared up, and your mind will be free again. You remember last night you gave us the name of your maid, Grace Jackson?"

"Yes, Doctor."

"Now, take your time. Tell us a little about Grace Jackson."

"Have you found her? Is she at home? Is she all right?"

"Never mind for the moment. Describe Grace Jackson."

Mrs. Ellis was horribly afraid poor Grace had been found murdered, and they were going to ask her to identify the body.

"She is a big girl," she said, "at least not really a girl, about my own age, but you know how one is inclined to talk of a servant as a girl; she has a large bust, rather thick ankles, brownish hair, grey eyes, and she would be wearing, let me see, I think she may not have changed into her cap and apron when those thieves arrived; she was still probably in her overalls; she is inclined to change rather late in the afternoon; I have often spoken about it; it looks so bad to open the front door in overalls, slovenly, like a boardinghouse; Grace has good teeth and a pleasant expression, though of course if anything has happened to her she would hardly——"

Mrs. Ellis broke off. Murdered, battered. Grace would not be smiling.

The doctor did not seem to notice this. He was looking closely at Mrs. Ellis.

"You know," he said, "you have given a very accurate description of yourself."

"Myself?" said Mrs. Ellis.

"Yes. Figure, colouring, and so on. We think, you know, it is just possible that your amnesia has taken the form of mistaken identity and that you are really Grace Jackson, believing yourself to be a Mrs. Ellis, and now we are doing our best to trace the relatives of Grace Jackson."

This was too much. Mrs. Ellis swallowed. Outraged pride rose in her.

"Doctor," she said rapidly, "you have gone a little too far. I bear no sort of resemblance to my maid, Grace Jackson, and if and when you ever find trace of the unfortunate girl, she would be the first to agree with me. Grace has been in my employment seven years; she came originally from Scotland; her parents were Scottish, I believe—in fact, I know it, because she used to go for her holiday to Aberdeen. Grace is a good, hard-working, and I like to think honest girl; we have had our little ups and downs, but nothing serious; she is inclined to be obstinate; I am obstinate myself—who is not? —but . . ."

If only the doctor would not look at her in that smiling, patronising way.

"You see," he said, "you do know a very great deal about Grace Jackson."

Mrs. Ellis could have hit him. He was so self-assured, so confident.

"I must keep my temper," she told herself. "I must, I must . . ."

Aloud she said: "Doctor, I know about Grace Jackson because, as I have told you, she has been in my employment for seven years. If she is found ill or in any way hurt, I shall hold the police force here responsible, because in spite of my entreaties, I do not believe they kept a watch on my house last night. Now perhaps you will be good enough to tell me where I can find my child. She, at least, will recognise me."

Mrs. Ellis considered she had been very restrained, very calm. In spite of terrible provocation she had not lost control of herself.

"You insist that your age is thirty-five?" said the doctor, switching the subject. "And that Grace Jackson was approximately the same?"

"I was thirty-five in August last," said Mrs. Ellis; "I believe Grace to be a year younger, I am not sure."

"You certainly don't look more," said the doctor, smiling.

Surely, at such a moment, he was not going to attempt to appease her by gallantry?

"But," he continued, "following upon the telephone conversation I have just had, Grace Jackson should be, today, at least fifty-five or fifty-six."

"There are probably," said Mrs. Ellis icily, "several persons of the name of Grace Jackson employed as domestic servants. If you propose tracing every one of them, it will take you and the police force a considerable time.

I am sorry to insist, but I must know the whereabouts of my daughter Susan before anything else."

He was relenting; she could see it in his eye.

"As a matter of fact," he said, "it happens, very conveniently, that Miss Slater was able to put us in touch with the lady; we have spoken to her on the telephone, and she is only a short distance away, in St. John's Wood. She is not sure, but she thinks she would remember Grace Jackson if she saw her."

For a moment Mrs. Ellis was speechless. What in the world was Susan doing in St. John's Wood? And how monstrous to drag the child to the telephone and question her about Grace. Of course she would be bewildered and say she "thought" she would remember Grace, though goodness only knows it was only two months since Grace was waving her good-bye from the doorstep when she left for school.

Then she suddenly remembered the Zoo. Perhaps, if these changes at school were all being decided upon in a great hurry, one of the junior mistresses had taken a party of children up to London to the Zoo, to be out of the way. The Zoo or Madame Tussaud's.

"Do you know where she spoke from?" asked Mrs. Ellis sharply. "I mean, somebody was in charge, somebody was looking after her?"

"She spoke from 2a Halifax Avenue," said the doctor, "and I don't think you will find she needs any looking after. She sounded very capable, and I heard her turn from the telephone and call to a little boy named Keith to keep quiet and not make so much noise, because she couldn't hear herself speak."

A tremour of a smile appeared on Mrs. Ellis' lips. How clever of Susan to have shown herself so quick and lively. It was just like her, though. She was so advanced for her age. Such a little companion. But Keith . . . It sounded very much as though the school *had* suddenly become co-educational; this was a mixed party being taken to the Zoo or Madame Tussaud's. They were all having lunch, perhaps, at Halifax Avenue, relations of Miss Slater's, or these Fosters, but really the whole thing was most inexcusable, that changes should come about like this, and the children be taken backwards and forwards from High Close to London without any attempt to notify the parents. Mrs. Ellis would write very strongly to Miss Slater about it, and if the school had changed hands and was to be co-educational, she would remove Susan at the end of the term.

"Doctor," she said, "I am ready to go to Halifax Avenue at once, if the authorities here will only permit me to do so."

"Very well," said the doctor. "I am afraid I can't accompany you, but we have arranged for that, and Sister Henderson, who knows all about the matter, will go with you."

He nodded to the policewoman, who opened the door of the waiting room and admitted a severe middle-aged woman in nurse's uniform. Mrs. Ellis said nothing, but her mouth tightened. She was very sure that Sister Henderson had been summoned from Moreton Hill.

"Now, Sister," said the doctor cheerfully, "this is the lady, and you know where to take her and what to do; and I think you will only be a few minutes at Halifax Avenue, and then we hope things will be straightened out."

"Yes, Doctor," said the nurse.

She looked across at Mrs. Ellis with a quick professional eye.

"If only I had a hat," thought Mrs. Ellis, "if only I had not come out with nothing but this wretched scarf, and I can feel bits and pieces of hair straggling at the back of my neck. No powder compact on me, no comb, nothing. Of course I must look terrible to them, ungroomed, common . . ."

She straightened her shoulders, resisted an impulse to put her hands in her pockets. She walked stiffly towards the open door. The doctor, the Sister, and the policewoman conducted her down the steps of the police station to a waiting car.

A uniformed chauffeur was to drive, she was thankful to see, and she climbed into the car, followed by the Sister.

The awful thought flashed through her mind that there might be some charge for the night's lodging in the cell and for the cups of tea; also, should she have tipped the policewoman? But anyway, she had no money. It was impossible. She nodded brightly to the policewoman as a sort of sop, to show she had no ill feeling. She felt rather different towards the doctor. She bowed rather formally, coldly. The car drove away.

Mrs. Ellis wondered if she was expected to make conversation with the Sister, who sat stalwart and forbidding at her side. Better not, perhaps. Anything she said might be taken as evidence of mental disturbance. She stared straight in front of her, her gloved hands primly folded on her lap.

The traffic jams were very bad, worse than she had ever known. There must be a Motor Exhibition on. So many American cars on the road. A rally, perhaps . . .

She did not think much of Halifax Avenue when they came to it. Houses very shabby, and quite a number with windows broken.

The car drew up at a small house that had 2a written on the pillar outside. Curious place to take a party of children for lunch. A good Lyons Café would have been so much better.

The Sister got out of the car and waited to help Mrs. Ellis.

"We shan't be long," she said to the chauffeur.

"That's what you think," said Mrs. Ellis to herself, "but I shall certainly stay with Susan as long as I please."

They walked through the piece of front garden to the front door. The Sister rang the bell. Mrs. Ellis saw a face looking at them from the front window and then quickly dart behind a curtain. Good heavens . . . It was Dorothy, Wilfred's younger sister, who was a schoolteacher in Birmingham; of course it was, it must be. . . . Everything became clearer; the Fosters must know Dorothy; people to do with education always knew each other, but how awkward, what a bore. Mrs. Ellis had never cared for Dorothy, had stopped writing to her in fact; Dorothy had been so unpleasant when poor Wilfred died, and had insisted that the writing bureau was hers, and rather a nice piece of jewellery that Mrs. Ellis had always understood had been given by Wilfred's mother to her, Mrs. Ellis; and in fact the whole afternoon after the funeral had been spent in most unpleasant argument and discussion, that Mrs. Ellis had been only too glad to send Dorothy away with the jewellery, and the bureau, and a very nice rug to which she had no right at all.

Dorothy was the last person Mrs. Ellis wanted to see, and especially in these very trying circumstances, with this Sister at her side, and herself looking so untidy, without a hat or a bag.

There was no time to compose herself because the door opened. No . . . no, it was not Dorothy after all, but . . . how strange, so very like her. That same thin nose and rather peeved expression. A little taller, perhaps, and the hair was lighter. The resemblance, though, was really quite extraordinary.

"Are you Mrs. Drew?" asked the Sister.

"Yes," answered the young woman, and then because a child was calling from an inner room she called back over her shoulder impatiently, "Oh, be quiet, Keith, do, for heaven's sake."

A little boy of about five appeared along the hall dragging a toy on wheels. "Dear little fellow," thought Mrs. Ellis, "what a tiresome nagging mother. But where are all the children; where is Susan?"

"This is the person I have brought along for you to identify," said the Sister.

"You had better come inside," said Mrs. Drew rather grudgingly. "I'm afraid everything's in a fearful mess. I've got no help, and you know how it is."

Mrs. Ellis, whose temper was beginning to rise again, stepped neatly over a broken toy on the door mat and, followed by the Sister, went into what she supposed was this Mrs. Drew's living-room. It was certainly a mess. Remains of breakfast not cleared away—or was it lunch?—and toys everywhere, and some material for cutting out spread on a table by the window.

Mrs. Drew laughed apologetically.

"What with Keith's toys and my material—I'm a dressmaker in my spare time—and trying to get a decent meal for my husband when he comes home in the evening, life isn't a bed of roses," she said.

Her voice was so like Dorothy's. Mrs. Ellis could hardly take her eyes off her. The same note of complaint.

"We don't want to take up your time," said the Sister civilly, "if you will just say whether this person is Grace Jackson or not."

The young woman, Mrs. Drew, stared at Mrs. Ellis thoughtfully.

"No," she said at length, "I'm sure she is not. I haven't seen Grace for years, not since I married; I used to look her up in Hampstead occasionally before then; but she had quite a different appearance from this person. She was stouter, darker, older too."

"Thank you," said the Sister, "then you are sure you have never seen this lady before?"

"No, never," said Mrs. Drew.

"Very well then," said the Sister, "we needn't detain you any longer."

She turned, as though to go, but Mrs. Ellis was not to be fobbed off with the nonsense that had just passed.

"Excuse me," she said to Mrs. Drew, "there has been a most unfortunate misunderstanding all round, but I understand you spoke to the doctor at the police station at Hampstead this morning, or someone did from this house, and that you have a party of school children here from High Close, my child amongst them. Can you tell me if she is still here; is anyone from the school in charge?"

The Sister was about to intervene, but Mrs. Drew did not notice this, because the little boy had come into the room, dragging his toy.

"Keith, I *told* you to stay outside," she nagged.

Mrs. Ellis smiled at the boy. She loved all children.

"What a pretty boy," she said, and she held out her hand to him. He took it, holding it tight.

"He doesn't usually take to strangers," said Mrs. Drew, "he's very shy. It makes me wild at times when he won't speak and hangs his head."

"I was shy myself as a child, I understand it," said Mrs. Ellis.

Keith looked up at her with confidence and trust. Her heart warmed to him. But she was forgetting Susan. . . .

"We were talking about the party from High Close," she said.

"Yes," said Mrs. Drew, "but that police officer was rather an idiot, I'm afraid, and got everything wrong. My name was Susan Ellis before I married, and I used to go to school at High Close, and that's where the mistake came in. There are no children from the school here."

"What a remarkable coincidence," said Mrs. Ellis, smiling, "because my name is Ellis, and my daughter is called Susan, and an even stranger coincidence is that you are so like a sister of my late husband's."

"Oh?" said Mrs. Drew. "Well, the name is common enough, isn't it? The butcher is Ellis, down the road."

Mrs. Ellis flushed. Not a very tactful remark. And she felt suddenly nervous, too, because the Sister was advancing and was leaning forward as though to take her by the arm and walk to the front door. Mrs. Ellis was determined not to leave the house. Or at any rate, not to leave it with the Sister.

"I've always found High Close such a homey sort of school," she said rapidly, "but I am rather distressed about the changes they are making there, and I am afraid it is going to be on rather a different tone in the future."

"I don't think they've changed it much," said Mrs. Drew; "most small children are horrible little beasts, anyway, and it does them good not to see too much of their parents and to be thoroughly well mixed up with every sort of type."

"I'm afraid I don't agree with you on that," said Mrs. Ellis. So peculiar. The tone, the expression might have been Dorothy's.

"Of course," said Mrs. Drew, "I can't help being grateful to old Slaty. She's a funny old stick, but a heart of gold, and she did her best for me, I'll say that, and kept me in the holidays, even after my mother was killed in a street accident."

"How good of her," said Mrs. Ellis, "and what a dreadful thing for you." Mrs. Drew laughed.

"I was pretty tough, I think," she said. "I don't remember much about it. But I do remember my mother was a very kind person, and pretty too. I think Keith takes after her."

The little boy had not relinquished Mrs. Ellis' hand.

"It's time we were getting along," said the Sister. "Come now, Mrs. Drew has told us all we need to know."

"I don't want to go," said Mrs. Ellis calmly, "and you have no right to make me go."

The Sister exchanged a glance with Mrs. Drew.

"I'm sorry," she said in a low tone, "I shall have to get the chauffeur. I wanted them to send another nurse with me, but they said it wouldn't be necessary."

"That's all right," said Mrs. Drew. "So many people are bats these days, one extra doesn't make much difference. But perhaps I had better remove Keith to the kitchen, or she may kidnap him."

Keith, protesting, was carried from the room.

Once again the Sister looked at Mrs. Ellis.

"Come along now," she said, "be reasonable."

"No," said Mrs. Ellis, and with a quickness that surprised herself she reached out to the table where Mrs. Drew had been cutting out material, and seized the pair of scissors.

"If you come near me, I shall stab you," she said.

The Sister turned and went quickly out of the room and down the steps, calling for the chauffeur. The next few moments passed quickly, but for all this Mrs. Ellis had time to realise that her tactics were brilliant, rivalling the heroes of detective fiction.

She crossed the room, opened the long french windows that gave on to a back yard. The window of the bedroom was open; she could hear the chauffeur calling.

"Tradesmen's entrance is ajar," he shouted; "she must have gone this way."

"Let them go on with their confusion," thought Mrs. Ellis, leaning against the bed. "Let them. Good luck to them in their running about. This will take down some of that Sister's weight. Not much running about for her at Moreton Hill. Cups of tea at all hours, and sweet biscuits, while the patients were given bread and water."

The movement went on for some time. Somebody used the telephone. There was more talk. And then, when Mrs. Ellis was nearly dozing off against the bed valance, she heard the car drive away.

Everything was silent. Mrs. Ellis listened. The only sound was the little boy playing in the hall below. She crept to the door and listened once again. The wheeled toy was being dragged backwards and forwards, up and down the hall.

And there was a new sound coming from the living-room. The sound of a sewing machine going at great speed. Mrs. Drew was at work.

The Sister and the chauffeur had gone.

An hour, two hours must have passed since they had left. Mrs. Ellis glanced at the clock on the mantelpiece. It was two o'clock. What an untidy, scattered sort of room, everything all over the place. Shoes in the middle of the floor, a coat flung down on a chair, and Keith's cot had not been made up; the blankets were rumpled, anyhow.

"Badly brought up," thought Mrs. Ellis, "and such rough, casual manners. But poor girl, if she had no mother . . ."

She took a last glance round the room, and she saw with a shrug of her shoulder that even Mrs. Drew's calendar had a printing error. It said 1952 instead of 1932. How careless . . .

She tiptoed to the head of the stairs. The door of the living-room was shut. The sound of the sewing machine came at breathless speed.

"They must be hard up," thought Mrs. Ellis, "if she has to do dress-making. I wonder what her husband does for a living."

Softly she crept downstairs. She made no sound. And if she had, the sound of the sewing machine would have covered it.

As she passed the living-room door it opened. The boy stood there, staring at her. He said nothing. He smiled. Mrs. Ellis smiled back at him. She could not help herself. She had a feeling that he would not give her away.

"Shut the door, Keith, *do*," nagged his mother from within. The door slammed. The sound of the sewing machine became more distant, muffled. Mrs. Ellis let herself out of the house and slipped away. . . . She turned northward, like an animal scenting direction, because northward was her home.

She was soon swallowed up in traffic, the buses swinging past her in the Finchley Road, and her feet began to ache, and she was tired, but she could not take a bus or summon a taxi because she had no money.

No one looked at her; no one bothered with her; they were all intent upon their business, either going from home or returning, and it seemed to Mrs. Ellis, as she toiled up the hill towards Hampstead, that for the first time in her life she was friendless and alone. She wanted her house, her home, the consolation of her own surroundings; she wanted to take up her normal, everyday life that had been interrupted in so brutal a fashion.

There was so much to straighten out, so much to do, and Mrs. Ellis did not know where to begin or whom to ask for help.

"I want everything to be as it was before that walk yesterday," thought Mrs. Ellis, her back aching, her feet throbbing. "I want my home. I want my little girl."

And here was the heath once again. This was where she had stood before crossing the road. She even remembered what she had been thinking about.

She had been planning to buy a red bicycle for Susan. Something light, but strong, a good make.

The memory of the bicycle made her forget her troubles, her fatigue. As soon as all this muddle and confusion were over, she would buy a red bicycle for Susan.

Why, though, for the second time, that screech of brakes when she crossed the road, and the vacant face of the laundry boy looking down at her?

# The Theft of the Mona Lisa

## KARL DECKER

FOR twenty-one years the story of the world's greatest single theft has been kept "under the smother." Until now there has been not even a hint of the tangled and intricate plot of which it was the mainspring. Da Vinci's Mona Lisa was stolen from the Louvre on August 21, 1911. The picture was valued at $5,000,000 in itself. Just how many millions it put into the pockets of the clever thieves who took it never will be known. It made them all rich enough to retire. But, you protest, the picture was recovered two years later, still in the hands of the thief, who, instead of profiting, went to jail for three years.

That, of course, is the story of record. The picture was recovered, the actual thief went to prison and the French were content to get La Joconde back in her old place on the wall of the Salon Carré without investigating too deeply. Back, however, of this record of futile, foolish theft lies the true story, a tale of underworld high finance known only to those who were concerned in it, and to the writer, to whom it was told with the understanding that it was not to be divulged until permission was given or until the narrator had died.

With that strange quirk of vanity characteristic of the creative crook, the author and director of the plot volunteered the story, and told it to me with gusto and infinite detail and the pride of the artist in his work. He regarded it as a crime unapproached in insolence and ingenuity, and the world will agree with him.

Briefly, they did not steal the Mona Lisa to sell it. Its taking was an exciting necessity, but only as a means to an end. They cared not what happened to it, so long as it remained lost for a reasonable time. They knew even better than the police how embarrassing a white elephant the stolen goods would be. So they hid it and would have returned it voluntarily to the Louvre in time, had not a minor member of the cast idiotically run away with it. To his elementary mind, it followed that the painting itself must be the prize. His treachery had no effect whatever on the real plans of the gang. They were annoyed, because such a fool would sooner or later fall into the hands of the police, and when he did he would blab. To have grabbed him and recovered the picture, however, would have exposed themselves to police attention, so they let him go.

I first heard the story one shivering January day in 1914 in Casablanca. If you believe the tourist literature, Morocco is a child of the sun. Morocco believes it itself and is without stoves. Where there is no artificial heat, any temperature below fifty can be extremely uncomfortable; and that winter, snow had covered the south of Europe and an occasional blast had blown across the Mediterranean to North Africa. A boom such as Florida knew after the war was roaring in Morocco in those days, just before the war, with Casablanca trumpeted as the coming metropolis of Africa. Lots along the Place de la République, miles from the city walls, were selling for nine hundred francs a square meter and rising with each sale. Every other Frenchman one met was selling real estate, and the Spanish and English were scrambling to get in. A deal had just been completed out near Roches Noires that popped the eyes of the colonial government, trying to hold the game level for the French alone.

## Going After the Big Money

Into the midst of this dirt selling turmoil strolled an old acquaintance—strolled with the elegance and insouciance that always marked him. The chances for turning a dishonest penny had brought him there and he was already up to his armpits in options and had organized a company to take over all the hotels in Morocco, selling stock by the bale throughout Morocco and France. His was a blithe unscrupulousness based upon his amused contempt for what he called "the squirming hordes of saps in the world." There was hardly a trick known that he hadn't worked in his time, but he had set a mark in his later years below which he never dropped. Less than fifty thousand dollars was piker money and he scorned it. Excepting a casual and brief meeting in Mexico, the last time I had seen much of him had been in Buenos Aires several years earlier. Later he had left Buenos Aires hurriedly. The estimate of the loot he took with him was more than a quarter of a million dollars in gold.

Legitimately, he owned a name that, in the republics south of the Tropic of Cancer, is at once so rare and so highly respected among Spanish patronymics that merely to identify himself by it would have meant unlimited opportunities, but he never used it and none of his lighter companions ever knew it. He had used a dozen of the commoner Spanish names, but one alias that clung to him had been the bright thought of a humorous friend. To those who trained with him he was always the Marques de Valfierno—that is, the Marquis of the Vale of Hell. He looked the *marques*, if not the rest. His admiring associates declared that "his front was worth a million dollars." White mustache and imperial, and a leonine mass of waving white hair, gave Eduardo a distinction that would have taken him past any royal-palace gate in Europe without the troubling necessity of giving his name.

## Crossing Trails in Casablanca

Though my principles permitted me to extend nothing of approval to his life and methods, there was, nevertheless, an old friendship based upon the fact that he was one of the few I have known who never bored me. There was nothing in our meeting to suggest that we were seeing each other for the first time in years, but then we had been running into each other in out-of-the-way corners of the earth frequently. We met in front of the tiny restaurant that in those days marked the angle of the junction of the main street of the town that wandered from the seaside to the old clock tower in the city hall, and a smaller street that crooked its way off into the Arab quarter. Here, hunting the sun, we sat on the narrow cobbled terrace babbling of this 'n' that.

I had just come down from Fez over roads that were swamps; a trip marked by a series of misadventures. In the Foreign Legion post at Ain Hammam the dozen of us making up the party had been shot over for three hours on New Year's Eve by rebel tribesmen, and later, bogged down to the axles in a swamp nine miles from K'nitra, we had been forced to make a long walk through mud at times to our knees to reach that crude village.

In telling the *marques* of our trip I had mentioned the names of those in the party, most of them coming down from Fez, others picked up at Meknes, and included among them was W. E. Perugia, representing a Manchester cotton house.

"Italian?" asked Eduardo.

"Probably his father was Italian, but his mother must have been English, for he was as strikingly British as pressed cabbage on a London menu," I told him. "He lives in Higher Crumpsall, Manchester, if you can think of anything more English."

"Just wondering about that name," said Eduardo. "Same as that of the simp that helped us get the Mona Lisa."

And then I sat up and began to take notice.

"Poor old Perugia was picked up in Florence with the Mona Lisa in his trunk, and is due for a stretch," said the Marques de Valfierno.

"Meaning," I asked, "that La Joconde has been rescued from the kidnapers?"

"Where have you been hibernating?" asked Eduardo. "Mona Lisa is smirking that 'enigmatic smile' of hers in the Salon Carré again and Perugia is in jail. They caught him and got the picture on the eleventh of last month."

All news to me. I had been upcountry for three months, and in that time had never seen a newspaper or heard from the outside world. Later I checked up and found the *marques* had his date right. Perugia had been taken with the painting on December 11, 1913.

In the open space in the terrace on which we sat, a Chinese kid, hardly bigger than a drink of whisky, had set up his show and was tossing a handful of drumsticks into the air in a juggling act and tapping a tiny tambour that hung at his waist. We tossed him a couple of coins, and Eduardo said:

"I'll give you what you, in your vulgar misuse of the English language, call the lowdown on that little trick in Paris, if you agree to put the smother on it until I'm ready to give you the go-ahead signal, or until I am dead."

I verified the news of the death of the Marques de Valfierno months ago.

"The clamor that followed the disappearance of La Joconde created an impression that it was a lone, single exploit," said Eduardo. "Everyone believed that one big chance had been taken for a single great stake. As a matter of fact, that coup was merely the climax of a series of operations that had been carried on for three years. Familiar as you are with my shady past, you know that I have always been deeply interested in art. I always felt that the man who made two great pictures bloom where there had been only one before was a benefactor of mankind. You remember my little plant in Buenos Aires?"

### Making Murillos to Order

I had spent several days in that art factory in Buenos Aires where the *marques* had gone into quantity production of Murillos. It was one of the busiest places in the Argentine. Yves Chaudron, a pale wisp of a Frenchman, almost a skeleton in his skinniness, was Eduardo's *alter ego* in those days. Chaudron's skill was of that uncanny sort that breaks the heart of the collector. For years a picture restorer, he had drifted naturally into picture falsification. An artist without a touch of the creative instinct, he was the most masterly imitator of others France had ever developed. Placed before a painting to be copied, he drove at his work like a madman, catching every little trick of the artist who had painted it, duplicating his brush strokes, matching colors so perfectly that copy and original were indistinguishable.

Here his work merely began, however. As a restorer he had learned every little trick of the game. In the factory in B. A. there were whirling electric fans turned upon the freshly varnished canvases, breaking the surfaces into thousands of tiny cracks; vacuum cleaners reversed to toss clouds of dust upon the varnish, finely ground coffee to be scattered over the picture to reproduce the fly specks with which old pictures are defaced.

The factory specialized in Murillos. They were sold by scores to rich widows to be given to the churches of the Argentine. That country today has more Murillos than it has cows. Every day the Marques de Valfierno went through the newspapers looking for those heavy black crosses and the words, "Ha Fallecido," that announced the deaths of leading Argentinos. The larger the cross and the greater the space taken, the more important the late deceased, and from these the list of prospects was compiled. Widows grasped at the chance to buy a Murillo and give it to a favorite church as a memorial to the dead husband.

"Chaudron and I enriched the Argentine," said Eduardo. "I shall always contend that a forged painting so cleverly executed as to puzzle experts is as valuable an addition to the art wealth of the world as the original. The æsthetic impression created is the same, and it is only the picture dealer, always a creature of commerce, as is a hardware salesman, or the pseudo art lover who wants a picture because of its dollar value, who is really hurt when an imitation is discovered. The bargain-hunting art lover differs in no fashion from the collector of relics who steals a brick from the birthplace of a famous writer. Beauty means nothing to him. He is collecting relics. If the beauty be there in the picture, why cavil at the method by which it was obtained?"

One never accused the *marques* of sophistry. He was sensitive and it hurt his feelings.

"In Buenos Aires, Chaudron developed and grew in power," continued the *marques*, "but after a short time there was nothing more for me to learn. It was too simple and easy a method. I finally left the work of pullulating Murillos to subordinates and went into finance on a grand scale, and, as a result, it became necessary for me to leave B. A. expeditiously. Chaudron— though in no fashion connected with the 520 per cent syndicate I was running—followed me to the Mexican city, where you and I so felicitously met again. I think I told you there, at dinner one night, of my activities in that town. There I was graduated in sap psychology."

### With the Guidebooks as a Selling Agent

"I was still specializing in Murillo, but with a difference. I was engaged in selling a famous Murillo that hung in that city. As a Murillo it was a pleasant and affable jest, but it had authority. Guidebooks said it was a Murillo and everyone in Mexico was convinced of its authenticity, so that half the sales work was done before I started.

"It was in selling that Murillo, sometimes several times a week, that I learned of that queer quirk in the brain of the collector that will cause him to buy what he can never sell again; what he can never exhibit and that will have to be kept hidden at all times.

"Selling that Murillo was simple. I lived at that time in a huge hotel where I found my saps. The fish swam right into my net. I learned to distinguish the type I dealt with at a glance; learned to feel them out and start the fire burning.

"I never took that painting out of its frame. It was not necessary. The sap always knew that I'd had that painting, however. The trick was a clever one, if I do say it myself. The buyer was always told to mark the back of the canvas in any way he pleased, so that he could distinguish it. They always fell for that. Frequently they used fountain pens, writing their initials, or a cipher they regarded as ingenious, inconspicuously in a corner of the canvas. Sometimes the clever ones snipped a few threads in a certain fashion. Within less than a week the painting they had marked was delivered to them on the other side of the Rio Grande, with the mark they had placed upon the back of the canvas clear and distinct, the canvas itself showing jagged edges where it had been cut from the frame.

"Also I always sent them a batch of clippings, some in Spanish and some making pretense of having been printed in an English-language newspaper. I had plenty of these always on hand, ready to ship with the painting. They were not dated, merely reading that yesterday an infamous outrage had been committed and that the priceless Murillo had been ripped from its frame by some *Yanqui* vandal. If any buyer ever returned to the city and saw the Murillo still in its place, he took it for granted that it was a copy substituted for the original. The trick by which the umpchay got the painting he marked was foolishly simple.

"When we had a fish frying we would simply drop into the building where the Murillo was hanging and slip inside the stretcher of the original another stretcher with the copy painted on its canvas. The face of the copy was flat against the back of the original in its frame; and as the Murillo was in a poorly lighted place, the two stretcher frames were never noticed. When the sap marked what he thought was the back of the original, he was really marking the back of the copy, and that's what he got. When the fake was taken down, it was cut around the edges to lend an air of verisimilitude to the whole transaction, and there you were."

### Cramping an Artist's Style

"Chaudron made the copies at first, but after a while, as business waxed, we had to get two or three assistants, which was bad for our game. The only way to keep a Mexican from talking is to decapitate him. Rumors began to rumble about us. Chaudron grew captious, complaining that copying the same old Murillo week after week was cramping his style and spoiling his art. Grafters and crooks tried to cut in on our game, and the town began to pall upon me; so we tossed up that enterprise and, filthy with money, sailed for Paris.

"And all this prolix introduction is intended to make you understand clearly just how and why Leonardo da Vinci's Mona Lisa came to be stolen. Others had fattened and battened upon credulous visitors to Paris, but in other ways. Thousands of Corots, Millets, even Titians and Murillos, were being sold in the city every year, all of them fakes, but from my peak of ultrasophistication in the game, this trade seemed cheap and unworthy.

"I knew Paris as I knew all the capitals of Europe, as I knew New York and every large city where money accumulates. I knew every workman in my own line of any importance and it was not long before I had gathered under my flag three of the keenest. One was English, and wore a monocle with a nonchalance that conveyed the impression that it must have been discovered in its place by the midwife who ushered him into the world. Another was a Frenchman. The third was an American. He was our ace, for his acquaint-

ance included those who have had their family names in the Social Register
since the days when Delmonico's was at Fourteenth Street."

### Leading Lambs to the Slaughter

"We campaigned from the hotels around the Étoile, but we also had our
own establishment; and the dinners we gave and the wines and liquors and
liqueurs we served are still lovingly remembered. Our attitude toward our
lambs being prepared for the sacrifice was that of men who knew Paris so
intimately that there was nothing that could be asked of us, from the wield-
ing of influence at the Quai d'Orsay to the piloting of a party through the
haunts of Les Apaches or conducting the grand ducal tour that could not be
arranged. So, when we gathered about our little lamb at a specially arranged dinner in our own villa, the stage-set was perfect. After the Chamber-
tin, the champagne; and after the champagne, the Napoleon brandy in huge
sniffing glasses and the lamb bleating rapturously. Then the intimation, the
innuendo, the braggadocio and the inevitable, 'Why not?' The lamb was
psychologically incapable of reasoning by this time, and if we had told him
that we could get the Cathedral of Notre Dame and set it up in his back
yard for him, he would have believed us. Thus we sold 'treasures from the
Louvre' for three years.

"We never took anything from the Louvre. We didn't have to. We sold
our cleverly executed copies, and instead of sending the sap clippings, we
sent him forged documents we pretended we had pilfered from the files of
the various departments—documents marked 'confidential' and fixed up with
seals and blue-and-red ribbons until they looked more authentic and important than a peace treaty. These documents told of the mysterious disappearance from the Louvre of some gem of painting or world-envied *objet
d'art* unique of its kind. The documents always stated that in order to avoid
scandal a copy had been temporarily substituted by the museum authorities.

"We never reached the top in our flight, however, until we sold La
Joconde for the first time. That took an enormous amount of negotiation,
but we were perfect in our parts by then; and when the multimillionaire we
had picked was properly framed for the killing, we found that nothing we
had ever attempted was easier.

"I had sold the Murillo of the Mexican to horny-handed and well-heeled
men lacking in any background of culture or knowledge of art, and found
them many times as difficult to prepare mentally as the really notable col-
lectors I encountered in Paris. The collector knows much more about art
and much less about men, which was useful to me. Instead of blanching at
the cool suggestion that we steal the true Mona Lisa and sell it to him, our
first quarry as coolly asked, 'Why not? It has never been done, but that is no
reason why it could not be done, and knowing Paris as you do, you should
be able to manage it.'

"After that, it was merely a question of how much and when. This was

May of 1910. He got the picture in June, just a month later. The portrait of Lisa Gherardini, wife of Francesco di Bartolomeo di Zanobi del Giocondo, painted by Leonardo da Vinci within the first five years of the sixteenth century, known to many generations of French as La Joconde and to the rest of the world as Mona Lisa, or La Gioconda, continued in the Louvre, naturally.

"Our client was told that a copy had been substituted, and was satisfied at first; but he must have talked, for the rumor got into a little weekly, Le Cri de Paris, and the authorities and a flock of experts assured the world that La Joconde, then on the wall of the Salon Carré, was the same that had always been there, made lots of trouble for us. Later it was squared. Two or three amenable journalists in Paris kept the fires burning by printing stories about the substitution of a copy and kidding the experts. Our American millionaire preferred to believe the rumor.

"What we had learned, however, was worth all the bother this near fiasco caused us. We knew now that we could sell La Joconde. The next trip, we decided, there must be no chance for recriminations. We would steal—actually steal—the Louvre Mona Lisa and assure the buyer beyond any possibility of misunderstanding that the picture delivered to him was the true, the authentic original."

### The Mona Lisa Sold Six Times

"Surely I do not have to tell you that we never intended that we should get the stolen picture. The original would be as awkward as a hot stove. To go hawking it about or even to try to sell copies after the bomb had burst would have been primer stuff.

"Obviously, the thing to do was to deliver the copy in the United States before the theft. The customs would pass it without a thought, copies being commonplace and the original still being in the Louvre, though even a manifest copy would attract attention once the theft of the original was known. We began our selling campaign, and the first deal went through so easily that the thought, 'Why stop with one?' naturally arose. There was no limit in theory to the fish we might hook. Actually, we stopped with six American millionaires. Six were as many as we could both land and keep hot. The earlier victims might have cooled off, had we been too greedy. Chaudron made the copies as fast as we cabled the orders. When all had passed the New York customs, we stole the Mona Lisa.

"Stealing La Joconde was as simple as boiling an egg in a kitchenette," said Eduardo, tossing a silver gersh to the juggling Chinese kid, who was now keeping three knives in the air. "It was a psychological *tour de force*. Our success depended upon one thing—the fact that a workman in a white blouse in the Louvre is as free from suspicion as an unlaid egg. Just that. No one ever questioned what a white-bloused workman did, for that white blouse was a uniform that gave him all the rights and privileges of the museum. If I, dressed as I am at this moment, should go into the Louvre and attempt to take a picture from the wall, there would be shrieks and outcries from all directions. If, however, I wore a white blouse over my clothes, I could take down any picture, pick up any small piece of sculpture, grab me a priceless Renaissance antique and carry them where I pleased, so long as I didn't attempt to leave the building. That was the gimmick in the trick.

"Perugia did not take that picture by himself. Just toss that bit of French-made history into the can. He needed help and he had it. You know the Louvre, of course, but there are parts of it you don't know. It was Perugia's knowledge of all the little secret hideaways in the place that made him invaluable. Without him we'd have had a hard time placing the two men who helped him where they could remain unseen during Sunday afternoon and night.

"As you know, the picture was taken on Monday morning. That's clean-up day and the public is barred. The Louvre was closed to the public on the day before—Sunday, August 20, 1911—at four o'clock in the afternoon. Perugia was there that Sunday afternoon with the two men who had been picked to help him. On Sunday there are no copyists in the building, for the crowd is usually too great to give a painter a chance to swing an arm. It made it possible to put our three men under cover."

### Looters in the Louvre

"Perugia had worked in the Louvre for three years. He knew, for instance, of the narrow little room with the secret doorway between the Galerie d'Apollon and the Salle Duchâtel. That little room was used for storing easels and camp stools used by the copyists, though the copyists knew nothing of its location. Their truck was always gathered up by the attendants and stuck in there after the Louvre had been closed. That room was large enough to hide Perugia and the two men who helped him. There they stayed after the Louvre was closed on Sunday afternoon.

"Perugia, of course, could have gone back on the Louvre pay roll and had his little blouse and identification card issued to him, but it would have taken some time to arrange and it would have marked him when any investigation started. He had worked for me before and that connection might be traced.

"The three men were all there in the Louvre and all set when the mob of workmen began flocking in at half-past six o'clock Monday morning. They slipped into the white blouses they had concealed under their clothes, oozed out of the alcove and bustled about the place, pretending to be busy. The head workman, Picquet, had started a group at work on some repairs in the Grande Galerie, which opens into the Salon Carré. He was constantly in and out, and it was not until he had taken himself off into another part of the building that my men dared attempt anything.

"Picquet stated, under investigation later, that at 7:20 precisely, he entered the Salon Carré with two of his workmen, who corroborated him, and pointed out La Joconde. 'That,' he told the two with him, 'is the most valuable picture in the Louvre' and babbled on about the great price it would bring if France ever had to sell it. Monsieur Picquet seems to have been a great hand with a watch, for he testified that at 8:35, precisely, he passed through the Salon Carré again and called attention to the fact that the picture was no longer there.

"The picture, as a matter of fact, was taken five minutes after he passed around into the other part of the building. The three men had some trouble in getting the painting down from the wall, for it weighed, panel, cradle, frame, shadow box and glass, nearly two hundred and twenty pounds. This was the first thing that should have been remembered when Perugia was captured with the picture and regarded by the French authorities as the only one engaged in that theft. What Perugia had told us had caused us to give him the help he needed. He had been present when the picture was taken down to be placed in the magnificent Renaissance frame given to the museum by the Countess of Béarn about three years before, and he knew it was a piano-mover's job."

### Getting Away With La Joconde

"There's a foolish general notion that the Mona Lisa is painted on canvas, and several stories got into print telling how the picture was cut from its frame and wrapped around the body of the man who stole it. One story told of its being rolled up and thrust into a metal cylinder that was tossed out of a window to a confederate. It would have been as easy to roll up the cover of a tomb. Da Vinci painted it on a wooden panel, a heavy block made of three slabs of close-grained Italian walnut an inch and a half thick. The panel measures 30.32 inches by 20.86 inches. The panel itself weighed eighteen pounds and was braced and guarded against warping by a massive heavy cradle of close-grained, seasoned ebony, and that cradle alone weighed one hundred and ten pounds. The Renaissance frame weighed twenty-five pounds and the shadow box fifteen pounds. The heavy plate glass in the shadow box, and not in the frame itself, weighed twenty-five pounds.

"Three men in blouses carrying a painting through the halls of the Louvre on cleaning day would interest no one except Head Workman Picquet, and he was not there. Even Picquet would be unlikely to ask any questions, for it was the habit of the Louvre photographers to order pictures taken to their studio at any time, and any workman about the place was likely to be called on to do the job. There was no arrangement requiring orders, requisitions or anything of that sort. 'Hey, you, Jacques; La Joconde to the studio'—and that was that.

"The disappearance of the painting from its place in the Salon Carré did not interest anyone during Monday. Picquet noticed it, but it was no skin off his knuckles. That sort of thing was happening all the time. He took it for granted that it had been sent to the photographers a short distance away. There is a plain-clothes-detective service in the Louvre under former Commissioner of Police de Mauroy, but the few men patrolling the place are never on duty at night or on cleaning days. It is taken for granted that thieves are to be found only among the visitors.

"Picquet commented on the fact that La Joconde was missing when he passed through the Salon Carré at 8:35 that morning, wisecracking to the workmen with him that it had probably been taken away because the authorities thought he might steal it, as he testified later at the investigation conducted by M. le Drioux, *juge d'instruction*, who had the case before him. It was just this attitude on the part of the head workman and the authorities that made it possible for us to snatch their greatest treasure. Not until three o'clock on Tuesday afternoon did anyone think it worth while to wonder what had become of the Louvre's most famous painting. More than twenty-four hours in which to make a get-away!"

### When Lady Luck Smiled

"Perugia and the two lumps with him had a bad five minutes with that picture. It was not so hard getting it down from the wall, but getting the shadow box and frame off was a job that had them sweating. They carried La Joconde, frame and all, out of the Salon Carré, into the Grande Galerie, and turned sharply to the right about two yards from the entrance of the Salon Carré and into the Salle de Sept-Mètres, where the Italian primitives hang, and then whipped through the door in the right-hand corner. Here there is a small, cramped stairway, used only by employes and attendants, leading to the floor below. There was no one about and here they removed the wooden panel, leaving frame and shadow box on the stairway.

"Then for the first time our beautiful scheme failed to click. Perugia had failed to carry out my orders and the duplicate key I had had made for the door at the bottom of the staircase had never been tried in the lock. It had been made by my own locksmith from a wax impression, and he had hammered into me the necessity of trying it out before the big coup was to be pulled off. Perugia was too lazy or too careless to attend to this in time, and that one little lapse nearly ruined us.

"But Lady Luck was hovering around us throughout the entire affair. Perugia had with him a screw driver and he worked rapidly getting the lock off. He had taken off the bronze knob and had taken one screw out of the lock when he got the whistle from one of the aides on guard in the Salle de Sept-Mètres. He stepped back, dropping the wooden panel behind him and hiding it with his blouse skirt.

"The man who came down the stairs was the official plumber of the Louvre, a man named Sauvet. When Perugia called out peevishly to him that he couldn't get the door open because the knob was gone, Sauvet graciously thrust his own key into the lock, turned the knob bar with a pair of pliers in his kit and helped the thief of the Mona Lisa out of his hole.

" 'Better leave the door open so it won't bother anybody else,' Sauvet suggested. Everybody tried to make it easy for us. It may all seem like pure dumb luck, but what helped us was as much dumbness as luck.

"Sauvet passed through the door and went on his way while the two helpers ran rapidly down the stairs and followed Perugia. They were not out of the Louvre yet, however, for the door opened into the Cour du Sphinx; but this was crossed in a flash, one of the aides carrying the picture under his blouse. From the Cour du Sphinx they entered the Cour Visconti, with a door opening into the street. That door was wide open. The guard stationed there was washing the vestibule and, as was brought out at the subsequent investigation, had gone off to get a bucket of water. Lady Luck caressing us again. My three men slipped out into the Quai du Louvre, and *voilà!* That was the last ever seen of any of them until Perugia was picked up in Florence last month.

"Perugia led the way, almost running, and was seen by a passer-by, who reported this incident later, and also told of seeing Perugia throw some shining object into the ditch that runs alongside the street. He also reported that the man looked like a shopkeeper and carried an oblong package wrapped in a white cloth under his arm. That oblong package was the grotesquely mistreated Mona Lisa and the white cloth was Perugia's blouse, which he had slipped off in the vestibule of the Cour Visconti, taking the picture from the helper who was carrying it. The shining object Perugia was seen to throw away was the bronze door knob, afterward found in the ditch at the side of the Quai du Louvre."

## The Greatest Theft in History

"There was an automobile waiting for Perugia. He was hustled into it, and within fifteen minutes he was at our headquarters on the Left Bank. We were waiting for him with a razor-edged anxiety, you can appreciate. None of us except Perugia and the two utterly unimportant assistants assigned to help him had gone anywhere near the Louvre and had perfect alibis for that morning and the day and night before.

"And then, of course, the wild burst of elation. We gave ourselves up to a quality of hilarious enjoyment for which we were well-fitted and educated. The big job was finished; the great coup had been pulled off. The most magnificent single theft in the history of the world had been accomplished and we were proud and happy.

"The six copies were in the United States. It had been easy to get them past the customs, one at a time. Each was a masterpiece. Chaudron almost died of joy and pride when he learned the priees his work had brought. He never after that regretted his lack of creative ability. Yves retired to a country place near Paris and only occasionally does a piece of work for some really great worker in the field of fake-art salesmanship.

"An old Italian bed, an antique almost priceless in itself, was sacrificed to make the panels Chaudron used. The wood was Italian walnut, seasoned by time to the identical quality of that on which La Joconde was painted. Copyists are not allowed to paint reproductions of any work of art in the Louvre of the same size as the original, but this meant nothing to Chaudron. From the smaller copy he made in the Louvre he threw up his master copy, and the creation of the others was child's play to him."

## Cleaning Up on the Coup

"Perugia wasn't taken into account in our arrangements. He was paid handsomely—enough to take care of him for the rest of his days if he had taken his good fortune with ordinary intelligence. He had no intelligence, however, and as soon as the chance occurred he stole the picture from its hiding place and scurried out of the country with it. The poor fool had some nutty notion of selling it. He had never realized that selling it, in the first place, was the real achievement, requiring an organization and a finesse that was a million miles beyond his capabilities.

"Whether he ever offered it for sale before he was caught, I don't know, but I do know that he rambled along the Riviera squandering the money we had given him. We never troubled to grab him, for it would simply have meant exposing ourselves to wholly unnecessary chances of detection. We paid off in Paris—Chaudron, Perugia, half a dozen small fish and some dealers who had helped us out—and then we hurried over to the United States. There we cleaned up. Delicately and with infinite finesse we got into touch with each of the nervously hopeful dealers who were waiting for us, delivered those beautifully executed copies to them and took their money. It was a bagful. We disbanded our organization and went our several ways. I have never seen any of my worthy pals since. Any work along the lines we had been doing would have seemed anticlimactic after the grand coup, and I think the others all dropped into respectable and respected paths of life. As for me, inaction is impossible. I am at work again.

"Eventually all those Mona Lisa copies will come to light. Without those, there are already thirty Mona Lisas in the world. That in the Prado Museum is, if anything, superior to the one in the Louvre. Every now and then a new one pops up. I merely added to the gross total."

"As you tell it," I remarked, "there was no theft of the Mona Lisa in 1910, and yet the story won't down that the picture in the Louvre was under suspicion in July of that year and an anonymous writer in that same Cri de Paris you have quoted insisted that the painting on exhibition in the Salon Carré was a copy he had seen in the hands of Louis Heuzy, a dealer in antiques at St. Etienne, and had been identified as that copy by two spots of green paint he had accidentally splashed on the left upper corner of the painting when he had restored it for Heuzy in 1902. He asserted that these two dots of green paint could be quite clearly seen by anyone looking at the painting in the Louvre. I happened to be in Paris that summer and distinctly recall that newspaper discussion."

"Maybe yes and maybe no," said Eduardo. "What I can tell you is that I did not take the Mona Lisa from the Louvre in 1910. If the painting were stolen that year, it was someone stealing my act. I certainly had no part in any theft of any work of art from the museum during that year, although I pretended to have stolen quite a number.

"But here is a simple little method of determining the authenticity of the famous Da Vinci painting. Let them procure a photograph known certainly to have been taken in the early years of the century, say 1901, and another of the early part of the year 1910, and a third, taken this year, of the painting now in the Louvre. Let them submit these photographs to any great authority on questioned documents or a committee of scientific experts, and let them decide.

"Men who have spent years in working over questioned documents could take those photographs and, by submitting them to their microscopes and micrometers, decide beyond any possible doubt whether those photographs were all photographs of the same painting or of two or of three different paintings.

"No artist copying a painting free hand could possibly reproduce every line, every angle and every dimension without showing hundreds of deviations. These variations would not affect the appearance as a whole, but they would certainly be there to be detected by a close scientific examination.

"Let the Louvre turn from art experts to the scientific experts. This, of course, is merely a suggestion, and you may take it from me the Louvre is not likely to act on it. There is too much at stake."

It was growing late. The Chinese kid had gathered up his drumsticks and knives, and had disappeared into the Arab quarter. A string of grunting camels toiled up from the water front and a group of Englishmen in tweeds followed after them on the way to the Anfa Club for a brandy peg before dinner. The mueddin in the minaret of the mosque was chanting the sunset call to prayer, and Arabs, French civilians and Foreign Legionnaires, Berbers, and Spanish dock wallopers, daintily gowned Frenchwomen and the waterport scum of Maltese, Egyptians and Chinese were jostling past or hunting tables on the little terrace.

"Time for a cocktail, or two, or three, before dinner," said the Marques de Valfierno.

# The Soldiers' Peaches

## STUART CLOETE

MRS. BRENNEN took snuff. She got it out of her grandson's store; going in and helping herself from the big tin on the second shelf. It was a habit her family deplored. Mrs. Brennen did not like snuff much. It was one of the things she had got over. It made her cough. But the fact that her family deplored her taking it prevented her from giving it up completely. She drank a little too. Not much; just enough to get "tiddly." That was what she called it, "I'm a little tiddly to-day," she'd say, and the family didn't like that either. Nor did she, save for the fun of shocking them and the interest outwitting them gave her.

An old woman did not have much fun, and she had her reputation as a character to keep up. Sometimes she wished she was not a character. "Mad," people called her behind her back; "eccentric," to her face. "Dear Mrs. Brennen, you would do that. You are so eccentric." "Mad" she would not agree to; "eccentric," yes; if it was eccentric to like sitting on the stoep in the sun and only talking when you wanted to. There was too much talk in the world. Sometimes she would go for days without talking. "One of her spells," they called it. Oh, yes, she knew what they said: "Old Mrs. Brennen is having one of her spells." But she was too busy thinking to worry about what people thought. "Let 'em talk," she said. "If they'd seen what I've seen, they'd stay silent. If they'd seen what I've seen, they'd have something to think about. Lot of damned old women! That's what they are, men and all." Her family made her laugh with their goings-on. When they reached her age, if they ever did, they'd know that nothing mattered very much. She took another pinch of snuff. Some of it slipped between her fingers on to her black alpaca dress. She flicked it off with the back of her fingers and turned to watch a span of oxen pull up to the store.

The *voorloper* bent down to pick up some clods to throw into the faces of the oxen. The driver whistled and turned the handle of the brake. The big wheels locked, dragged on a yard or two and stopped. Taking off his hat, the driver went into the store. The *voorloper* sat in the dust under the horns of the leaders.

Mrs. Brennen wondered how many wagons she had seen pull up like that since she had come to Brennen's Store as a bride. Thousands and thousands of wagons. Thousands of men, too—white men, Kaffirs, men on foot, in Cape carts, in spiders, or riding, and now they came in motor-cars. Mrs. Brennen did not like motor-cars. Of course they saved time. But what did one do with the time one saved? No one could tell her that. She chuckled. They couldn't tell her, because they didn't know.

She had seen two wars and some native troubles. Once when Brennen was away, the store had been burned by Kaffirs. She had just escaped. A friendly native had warned her. She had hidden in the bush. She had taken Susie with her—a sweet little dog. She had never had another dog like Susie— black and white, as soft to touch as silk, with a wet pink nose. Generally, black-and-white dogs had black noses, but Susie's had been pink. As she crouched among the rocks, the Kaffirs had come quite near her. Susie had tried to bark and she had held her between her knees and strangled her. Then the Kaffirs had gone and she had buried Susie. The road had been moved since then, and the new store built. Susie was buried about where the wagon stood now. She looked at her hands. They were very frail, veined, knotted and lumpy with gout. Once they had been beautiful. Brennen had said she had beautiful hands. Once they had strangled a pet dog while wild Kaffirs swarmed round her.

They were off-loading the wagon. Mealies. Her grandson, George, was buying them, then. He would pay too much for them. He always paid too much for everything. She thought of a horse he had bought once. That must have been twenty years ago. Like all horses said to be salted, it had died of horse sickness. She had told him it wasn't salted. Anyone could see it was not salted. A salted horse had a look. You couldn't explain it. You just knew the look it had.

George came out of the store now. A stupid boy. He always had been stupid.

"Don't pay ten shillings a bag!" she shouted. "Don't pay more than eight; and sample them!" *If it wasn't for me, I don't believe he'd sample them,* she thought. She watched him drive a knife with a hollow groove into the bags, emptying the pips into his hand. Some chickens ran out to pick up the fallen mealies. One of them picked a tick from the heel of the near wheeler—a big red and white ox that was chewing its cud.

Mrs. Brennen closed her eyes. Sometimes they forgot who she was. Yes, sometimes they forgot that it was still her store. That she was Cecelia Brennen, the mother of them all. The mother of a multitude of fools. Children, grandchildren, great-grandchildren. It was hard to keep track of them now. Each year they came to show her the new babies they had bred. She thought of her first grandson. She had been so pleased with him. She looked at George; he had been the first grandson. He was leaning against the door of the store. Babies were like everything else; when there were so many of them, they became commonplace. It was hard to remember their names or even their mothers' names. She liked the Kaffir babies best—black like puppies, and pleasantly nameless. The Kaffir women who brought them to her to admire did not expect her to remember anything; all they wanted was a smile and a present. But that was what most people wanted, when you came to think of it—a smile and a present.

She nodded her head. They thought her memory had gone; but she knew more than the whole pack of them put together. Knew everything that was worth remembering. Ninety-three, and the pattern of her life trailed out like a cloak behind her—her loves and hates, that had once been so hot and cold, all meaningless now—just part of the fabric; brilliant threads that had been woven through it. Remember—she remembered all right. The things she forgot, like the names of her great-grandchildren, and of the women her grandsons had married, were not important. What did it matter if she did not recognise them all, so long as they knew her? Besides, women all looked the same now. They had no character—short curly hair, red lips, red nails and no shape.

She watched the wagon go. The driver shouted and clapped his whip. The *voorloper* trotted in front of the running oxen. The hind wheels were still locked, and dragged. That was like a Kaffir, to start his span with the brake on. The driver clapped his whip again and took off the brake, then he ran forward and jumped on to the disselboom. She remembered a man being brought into the store who had been run over that way. He had slipped and the wheels had gone over his legs. Empty of ballast, the wagon moved noisily. One wheel let out piercing squeaks. *Grease*, Mrs. Brennen thought. *George should have noticed it and sold him some grease.*

She stared down the road. It was red, unmetalled, dusty, and wide enough to turn a span. Part of it was bordered with big blue gums; grey foliaged untidy trees whose bark hung in torn white ribbons from the trunks. There was the bottle store, the chemist's, the Standard Bank, the coolie store, and the usual white houses with red roofs that got smaller and more disreputable as the road went on. The best part of the dorp was behind her. That was where the doctor lived, and the bank manager, and Mr. Fairburn. No one knew quite what Mr. Fairburn did or where he got his money. That was where George wanted to live. He thought it was common to live opposite the store. He wanted to drive down to it in his new car each day, as if he was a professional man.

She laughed. Perhaps that was it, or perhaps he wanted her tucked away safely where she could not see everything that went on. But the store was her life. It did not change, like the children. It did not die. It did not go away. It grew, but it grew slowly and precisely. You knew which way it was going to grow. Seventy years was a long time to sit in one place. She had been asked why she did not travel! Travel. Why go and look for life when it was going on all around you if you had eyes to see and waited long enough? She thought of the story of the two hunters. One had walked for miles, looking for game. The other had sat near a water-hole. The first had killed nothing. The second had taken what he wanted. It was better and less exhausting to let things come to you than to go and search for them. The store was like a water-hole—everyone had to come to it in the end. If they wanted a needle or a plough, they came to Brennen's.

She saw a car. What a dust it threw up! It came from Pretoria. It was many years since she had been there. They said Church Square was now a garden. It had been the outspan. They had often outspanned there in the old days. Sometimes there had been two hundred wagons, lying wheel to wheel. But the great days were gone, and where were the men to-day who could compare with the men she had known then? Men like the old president, Joubert, De Wet, De la Rey, Cecil Rhodes, or Doctor Jim. Men like Brennen her husband. That was another reason she sat in the store all day. Brennen was with her. She could feel his company.

She looked at George. He had not moved. George was fat. She hated fat men. A fat woman was comfortable, but a fat man an abomination.

The car stopped at the store. A young man got out; he had a letter in his hand. He looked at the notice outside the store. Then he went up to George and gave him the letter. She would find out what was in it later. A man in a car bringing George a letter.

George was bringing him over. He looked like an Englishman. There was even something familiar about him. The turn of his head or the way he walked.

"She may know," she heard George say, "but she's difficult. She has spells."

That was another of George's delusions—that she was deaf. She hated being shouted at, but it was worth letting them think it for the asides she heard.

"This is Mr. Vane," George said, putting his mouth to her ear. "He has come from England, *Ouma*."

She put out her hand. "I can see he comes from England," she said. "Look at his boots." Mrs. Brennen wondered if she would take snuff now or later. He seemed a nice young man, fresh complexioned, very clean and shiny, with reddish hair.

"Sit down," she said.

He sat down.

"How much did you pay for those mealies, George?" she asked.

"Nine shillings."

He would go in a minute and leave her with the young man. George got up.

"I said you weren't to pay more than eight."

She looked him up and down. Once she had had great hopes of George.

"I'll be going," George said. "See you later."

"Thank you," the Englishman said. "I do hope I'm not being a nuisance, Mrs. Brennen."

"Nothing is a nuisance now," she said.

She got her snuff-box. "Take snuff?" she asked.

"No, thank you."

"Quite right, young man. A filthy habit. He"—she pointed to George's back—"thinks I am a disgrace to the family." She chuckled. "But I bred them. If it wasn't for me, there'd be no family—and the store is mine. That's what they don't like. They'd like to sell the store and go into something else—too grand for Brennen's general store. Ride round in motor-cars. That's what they want to do—just ride round and round. There's no sense in riding round and round." She looked at her visitor. He seemed a little bewildered. *Never seen anyone like me before,* she thought.

"Never seen anyone like me, have you?" she asked. "And you won't again, young man; I'm one of the last of them. Real people, we were. Men and women. Real," she said. She closed her eyes. "What do you want?" she asked. "Why did you come here? Who gave you a letter to George? No good having a letter to George. He's a fool. He's my grandson, and I know."

"It's a long story." Francis Vane lit a cigarette. He wondered how to begin. "It's my father," he said. "You see, his father—my grandfather—was killed near here with the Three Hundred and First, and I wondered if any-one could tell me about it. They sent me to George Brennen. I had a letter to him."

"No good sending anyone to him," Mrs. Brennen said.

"Do you remember them coming here?" Vane asked. "It was in Novem-ber 1880."

"Of course I remember," Mrs. Brennen said. "John—that's George's father—was ill then. We thought he would die, and then they came. 'Kiss me, Mother . . . kiss your darling daughter'—that's the tune they played as they marched in. They had a doctor with them—a Captain Bull. He saved John's life and we gave him a cage of wild birds. . . . But what do you want to know?" she asked.

"I want to know how it happened. You see, my grandfather commanded the Three Hundred and First. He was killed. They said it was his fault. That he was incompetent. My father is very old now and he broods about it. He wants to know where his father is buried. He wants to know what happened. He's very old," he said again.

"I'm very old," Mrs. Brennen said, "and I know; I brood too. Thinking, I call it. Your grandfather. Then that's it. That's why I thought I'd seen you before. I danced with him that night. He danced well. We gave them a dance in the old store." She nodded to the warehouse behind the present building. "We cleared everything out. Ploughs, harrows, soft goods and all. We put buck sails over them and gave the officers a dance. They had come from Lydenburg and were going to Pretoria. They didn't think there'd be a war. They said it would be a massacre if it came—Boers against trained troops like them. The Three Hundred and First," Mrs. Brennen said. "Yes, the Three Hundred and First."

Francis Vane leaned forward.

Mrs. Brennen saw it all. She saw them march in. "Kiss me, Mother . . . kiss your darling daughter." The drum-major tossed his stick, caught it, twirled it; men in red—an endless stream of sunburnt young men in red—mounted officers, rumbling transport, mules, baggage, wagons drawn by oxen, dogs that followed the battalion with lolling tongues.

For a day Brennensdorp had been gay, populated with soldiers. They had swarmed everywhere—walking about in pairs, standing in groups, or lying on their backs in the shade of the gum trees—they had been small then and their shade thin. She saw them washing in buckets, their young chests bare, their hair wet, their eyes wrinkled against the soapy water. She had propped Johnny up so that he could see the soldiers. And it had been hot. It was not hot like that now. It had been so hot that the sheets of corrugated iron on the roof cracked as they pulled at the nails. The trees had danced up and down on the veld and the road was wet with mirage water. The red jackets of the troops had made it seem hotter. Wherever you looked there were red jackets. How they worked to empty the store! Everyone had helped. They had thrown mealie meal on the floor to make it fit for dancing.

The colonel had come to thank her. "Thank you, Mrs. Brennen," he had said. "It is very kind of you to entertain us like this."

Colonel Vane had admired her. She had seen it in his eyes. "I hear your little boy is ill," he said. "Perhaps we can help you. Would you like to see Captain Bull, our doctor?"

She had seen him. A kindly man. He had come at once in his dusty boots. Brennen had given him beer. The bottles were kept cool in a canvas bucket that hung from the roof. "I'll stay with him, Mrs. Brennen," the doctor said, and he had stayed watching at the bedside.

The dance had been an event. Boys had been sent out to call in the countryside—all that were loyal, that is—and they had come, every man and woman and girl for miles round. Both sides of the street had been full of their Cape carts and buggies. The regimental band played tune after tune. The doorway was filled with watching Tommies. The dust and mealie flour had risen off the floor in clouds. It clung to the dresses of the girls, to the clothes and moustaches of the men. Music, laughter and some kissing.

There was a tale she had heard about a clown who had made jokes while his little son was dying. She felt like that clown. She kept going in to look at Johnny. The doctor put his finger to his lips and motioned her away. She had gone away. . . .

"May I have the pleasure of this dance, Mrs. Brennen?"

"Delighted."

"How well you dance, Mrs. Brennen."

"How light you are, Mrs. Brennen."

What did they expect, she wondered. It was strange how one could go on saying and doing all the right things when one was feeling nothing. It was as if one stood some way off watching oneself. She had noticed this, time and again. *That cannot be me. This cannot be me.* Cecelia Brennen could not be doing this. But Cecelia Brennen was doing it. Her place was with her son; her place was at the dance. She was Mrs. Brennen, the wife of John Brennen, of Brennensdorp. It was her place to entertain the soldiers of the Queen.

There had been a great killing of beasts and fowls, a great baking, a great emptying of casks of wine and brandy. She had seen to it all, and to her sick child as well. She had worn cyclamen taffeta with a bustle and hoops.

Her hair hung in ringlets round her neck. A pretty young thing—the belle of the ball and the mother of a dying child. But he had not died. *If only Johnny can grow up strong and healthy, like these officers,* she thought. *If only—* Excusing herself, she ran to see him. Captain Bull was asleep; the child slept, too, his hand in that of the soldier. How tired he looked!

In the morning Johnny was better. "He'll come through," the doctor said. He made up medicine for him in a whisky bottle. She and Brennen had wondered what they could give him. They could not give money. "Give him my cage of birds," Johnny said. They were beautiful birds; little finks of every colour—*rooibekkies, blouvinks, kingvinks.* They were all tame, and sang and twittered on their perches. She had taken them to Captain Bull. "A present from Johnny," she said. Brennen had come at that moment with a Kaffir carrying a case of champagne. The champagne and the birds had been stowed in the doctor's cart. The case of wine on the bed, and the cage slung from the roof and lashed to the sides, so that it should not swing.

"Good morning, Mrs. Brennen." Colonel Vane rode up. "I am glad to hear your little boy is better."

Behind the colonel there was a donkey wagon loaded with yellow peaches. It had just come in and the soldiers were crowded round it, eating peaches and stuffing them into their haversacks to eat on the march. The colonel was laughing.

"Fruit's good for them," he said.

"It's a good year for peaches. All the trees in the district are weighed down with them," she said.

Then the bugles sounded. The colour-sergeants shouted, "Fall in." The markers were waiting. The men, fully accoutred, ruddy with sleep, ran out. Transport drivers cursed as their hubs bumped. The Three Hundred and First was going. They had come and they were going.

"Kiss me, Mother . . . kiss your darling daughter"—the band struck up again. Like a red snake the regiment swung out of the dorp in a cloud of dust. Then the dust fell. To-night they would lie in Pretoria.

The Three Hundred and First had gone and Johnny would get well. She was sitting with Johnny when it happened. A man came galloping down the street. A private soldier, wounded, riding an officer's charger. It was streaked with sweat, its chest splashed with foam, its eyes were wild. She recognised the horse. It was Colonel Vane's horse. The big bay she had patted as he said good-bye.

The soldier pulled up and almost fell from the saddle.

"What is it?" she said. "Oh, what is it?" She knelt beside him in the dust.

"The doctor sent me to get help! They are all finished!" he said. "They're cut to hell—the whole bloody lot! We walked into it! The colonel's dead! I took his horse!" He began to cry. "They got us—they got us fair! It was murder!"

He was only a boy. She held him in her arms and the blood from the wound in his neck ran on to her shoulder. Suddenly he sat up. "Bandages," he said, "and brandy . . . and food! That's what the doctor said! We've got no bandages! They're all bleeding, and nothing to stop it! Oh, God, Mrs. Brennen, nothing to stop it! I must get back!" He dragged the horse towards him and tried to mount.

"What are you going to do?" she asked.

"I don't know, but I must go back. I can't stay here."

"Where is it? Where did it happen?"

"At the little river—they were all round us."

"The Spruit?"

"That's what they call it."

Brennen was inspanning already, loading up the Cape cart. That would be the quickest; the wagons could follow. It was not very far. She ran into the house for sheets, towels, bedding, mattresses, blankets, brandy; the house and store were emptied of everything that might be useful.

She climbed into the cart beside her husband. He had put in four horses instead of two.

"Trot the oxen, Jan!" he shouted to the driver who was inspanning.

"They cannot trot so far, baas!"

"Trot them and be damned!" Brennen said.

And then they were off at a gallop, rocking first on one wheel and then on the other as they hit the bumps in the road. Hardly checking for the drift, they splashed through the water. Brennen hit the horses as they slowed up to pull out of it. She had never seen him hit a horse before. They sprang into the traces again with such a jerk that she thought the swingletree would break loose. She looked at the pole. Brennen had tied it with a double riem. They were on the flat now. The horses were bolting. Let them bolt. Nothing could go wrong with a strong cart and good gear on a straight road unless one of the horses fell. The whip clapped like a pistol as Brennen urged them to greater speed. The four reins were like live things in his hands as he cried out the horses' names: "Bles! Charlie! Klinkie! Chaka!" Chaka was a new black horse. Brennen had put him on the off lead, where he could get at him best with his whip. "Come, Bles! . . . Come, Charlie!" She gripped the arms of her chair. What a drive it had been. She smelt the dust in her nostrils.

The road was always dusty, but now it had been made worse by the passing of a thousand men and their transport. The dust rose in clouds, obliterating everything, so that sometimes she could see only the horses' ears and their tossing manes. The reins went down to nothing. They disappeared into the dust. She could see no road. That they kept on it was a miracle.

And then they got there. The horses shied and pulled across the road as the leaders almost ran into an overturned wagon.

The dust fell slowly.

"You've come." It was the boy on the colonel's horse. "I was coming back to find you," he said.

They got out of the cart. Some soldiers took the horses out. She saw it all—the undulating ground, the bush, the trees by the road—many of them scored by bullets. There was blood everywhere. It ran down the sloping road into pools.

They helped the doctor to move the men, to bandage, to cut more bandages. Tents were pitched, food cooked, great cauldrons of hot water got ready to dress the wounded. She had gone in to Colonel Vane. His legs were off. While she was with him, Frantz Joubert, the Boer commandant, had come in.

"Will you drink with me, Commandant?" the colonel said. "And you, too, Mrs. Brennen." It was the champagne her husband had given the doctor. They drank. Joubert said, "Here's to Queen Victoria. May she live long and take her soldiers from the Transvaal."

They had wrapped the dead in blankets and buried them where they fell along the side of the road, on the veld where they had taken up their positions. Beside almost every body there were peaches; they had fallen from the hands of the men as they were ambushed. Their pipe-clayed haversacks still bulged with them. The dead of the Three Hundred and First were buried with their peaches where they lay.

She saw Johnny's cage of birds. It was broken and the birds were free. The wild birds were free once more and the men were dead.

"Yes," she said, looking up, "that's what happened to the Three Hundred and First. The birds were free and the men were dead, and buried where they fell."

"But——" Vane said.

She had not spoken. She had sat for nearly half an hour with her head sunk on her breast.

She looked accusingly at her grandson. "And they think I can't remember. I can remember everything. I can even remember the names."

"That's what I was afraid of," George Brennen said—"one of her spells."

They were silent, staring at the old woman; her head was lowered again.

Suddenly, from the next house, a woman screamed at a child.

"Didn't I tell you not to eat so many peaches? Peaches—you guzzle peaches all day, and then bring them home at night, so that you can eat more. You'll be sick, I say. Where did you get them? Did you steal them?"

"I didn't steal them, Mother. They're the soldiers' peaches. We drove over there to get them. They're wild peaches." The child was crying.

Mrs. Brennen got up. "Let her have the peaches. Let her have all she wants. The soldiers' peaches never hurt anyone." Mrs. Brennen sat down again. "The soldiers' peaches," she said—"that grew out of their pockets."

Tears ran down her cheeks. They followed the lines of her face and dripped on to the snuff-stained alpaca dress. She made no effort to stay them.

"Out of their pockets?" Vane said.

"She means their haversacks."

"Then there are peach trees?"

"Yes, there are trees—plenty of them."

"And they buried them where they fell? Do you know the place well?" Vane asked.

"Everyone knows it well. All the children get peaches from them. They grow like this." George Brennen traced a pattern on the dust of the stoep with his finger. "Here is where there are the most. . . . That was where the main body got it. . . . They were buried on both sides of the road . . . and out here is where the scouts fell." He made scattered dots.

"Then there were scouts out," Vane said. "And it wasn't my grandfather's fault."

"It was nobody's fault," Brennen said. "The Boers were hidden and they held their fire."

Vane laughed. "Can we go over there to-morrow?" he asked. "I'll make a map of it for my father. Poor father," he said. "If only he had known this years ago! He nearly came once, and then he was afraid to come—afraid of what he'd find."

"We call them the soldiers' peaches," George Brennen said. "And I wish she had told you the story—I have heard it hundreds of times—but she's old; she has spells."

His grandmother looked up. "I remember as well as anyone," she said. She pointed to Vane. "I remember his grandfather. A fine man. There were some fine men in those days."

Brennen took Vane's shoulder. "Come along to my place. Spend the night and we'll drive over there to-morrow."

# A Night to Remember

(an extract from the book)

## WALTER LORD

### 1. "Another Belfast Trip"

HIGH in the crow's-nest of the new White Star Liner *Titanic*, Lookout Frederick Fleet peered into a dazzling night. It was calm, clear and bitterly cold. There was no moon, but the cloudless sky blazed with stars. The Atlantic was like polished plate glass; people later said they had never seen it so smooth.

This was the fifth night of the *Titanic's* maiden voyage to New York, and it was already clear that she was not only the largest but also the most glamorous ship in the world. Even the passengers' dogs were glamorous. John Jacob Astor had along his airedale Kitty. Henry Sleeper Harper, of the publishing family, had his prize Pekingese Sun Yat-sen. Robert W. Daniel, the Philadelphia banker, was bringing back a champion French bulldog just purchased in Britain. Clarence Moore of Washington also had been dog-shopping, but the 50 pairs of English foxhounds he bought for the Loudoun Hunt weren't making the trip.

That was all another world to Frederick Fleet. He was one of six lookouts carried by the *Titanic*, and the lookouts didn't worry about passenger problems. They were the "eyes of the ship," and on this particular night Fleet had been warned to watch especially for icebergs.

So far, so good. On duty at 10 o'clock . . . a few words about the ice problem with Lookout Reginald Lee, who shared the same watch . . . a few more words about the cold . . . but mostly just silence, as the two men stared into the darkness.

Now the watch was almost over, and still there was nothing unusual. Just the night, the stars, the biting cold, the wind that whistled through the rigging as the *Titanic* raced across the calm, black sea at 22½ knots. It was almost 11:40 P.M. on Sunday, the 14th of April, 1912.

Suddenly Fleet saw something directly ahead, even darker than the darkness. At first it was small (about the size, he thought, of two tables put together), but every second it grew larger and closer. Quickly Fleet banged the crow's-nest bell three times, the warning of danger ahead. At the same time he lifted the phone and rang the bridge.

"What did you see?" asked a calm voice at the other end.

"Iceberg right ahead," replied Fleet.

"Thank you," acknowledged the voice with curiously detached courtesy. Nothing more was said.

For the next 37 seconds Fleet and Lee stood quietly side by side, watching the ice draw nearer. Now they were almost on top of it, and still the ship didn't turn. The berg towered wet and glistening far above the forecastle deck, and both men braced themselves for a crash. Then, miraculously, the bow began to swing to port. At the last second the stem shot into the clear, and the ice glided swiftly by along the starboard side. It looked to Fleet like a very close shave.

At this moment Quartermaster George Thomas Rowe was standing watch on the after bridge. For him too, it had been an uneventful night—just the sea, the stars, the biting cold. As he paced the deck, he noticed what he and his mates called "Whiskers 'round the Light"—tiny splinters of ice in the air, fine as dust, that gave off myriads of bright colors whenever caught in the glow of the deck lights.

Then suddenly he felt a curious motion break the steady rhythm of the engines. It was a little like coming alongside a dock wall rather heavily. He glanced forward—and stared again. A windjammer, sails set, seemed to be passing along the starboard side. Then he realized it was an iceberg, towering perhaps 100 feet above the water. The next instant it was gone, drifting astern into the dark.

Meanwhile, down below in the First Class dining saloon on D Deck, four other members of the *Titanic's* crew were sitting around one of the tables. The last diner had long since departed, and now the big white Jacobean room was empty except for this single group. They were dining-saloon stewards, indulging in the time-honored pastime of all stewards off duty—they were gossiping about their passengers.

Then, as they sat there talking, a faint grinding jar seemed to come from somewhere deep inside the ship. It was not much, but enough to break the conversation and rattle the silver that was set for breakfast next morning.

Steward James Johnson felt he knew just what it was. He recognized the kind of shudder a ship gives when she drops a propeller blade, and he knew this sort of mishap meant a trip back to the Harland & Wolff shipyard at Belfast—with plenty of free time to enjoy the hospitality of the port. Somebody near him agreed and sang out cheerfully, "Another Belfast trip!"

In the galley just to the stern, Chief Night Baker Walter Belford was making rolls for the following day. (The honor of baking fancy pastry was reserved for the day shift.) When the jolt came, it impressed Belford more strongly than Steward Johnson—perhaps because a pan of new rolls clattered off the top of the oven and scattered about the floor.

The passengers in their cabins felt the jar too, and tried to connect it with something familiar. Marguerite Frolicher, a young Swiss girl accompanying her father on a business trip, woke up with a start. Half-asleep, she could think only of the little white lake ferries at Zurich making a sloppy landing. Softly she said to herself, "Isn't it funny . . . we're landing!"

Major Arthur Godfrey Peuchen, starting to undress for the night, thought it was like a heavy wave striking the ship. Mrs. J. Stuart White was sitting on the edge of her bed, just reaching to turn out the light, when the ship seemed to roll over "a thousand marbles." To Lady Cosmo Duff Gordon, waking up from the jolt, it seemed "as though somebody had drawn a giant finger along the side of the ship." Mrs. John Jacob Astor thought it was some mishap in the kitchen.

It seemed stronger to some than to others. Mrs. Albert Caldwell pictured a large dog that had a baby kitten in its mouth and was shaking it. Mrs. Walter B. Stephenson recalled the first ominous jolt when she was in the San Francisco earthquake—then decided this wasn't that bad. Mrs. E. D. Appleton felt hardly any shock at all, but she noticed an unpleasant ripping sound . . . like someone tearing a long, long strip of calico.

The jar meant more to J. Bruce Ismay, Managing Director of the White Star Line, who in a festive mood was going along for the ride on the *Titanic's* first trip. Ismay woke up with a start in his de-luxe suite on B Deck—he felt sure the ship had struck something, but he didn't know what.

Some of the passengers already knew the answer. Mr. and Mrs. George A. Harder, a young honeymoon couple down in cabin E-50, were still awake when they heard a dull thump. Then they felt the ship quiver, and there was "a sort of rumbling, scraping noise" along the ship's side. Mr. Harder hopped out of bed and ran to the porthole. As he looked through the glass, he saw a wall of ice glide by.

The same thing happened to James B. McGough, a Gimbels buyer from Philadelphia, except his experience was somewhat more disturbing. His porthole was open, and as the berg brushed by, chunks of ice fell into the cabin.

Like Mr. McGough, most of the *Titanic's* passengers were in bed when the jar came. On this quiet, cold Sunday night a snug bunk seemed about the best place to be. But a few shipboard die-hards were still up. As usual, most were in the First Class smoking room on A Deck.

And as usual, it was a very mixed group. Around one table sat Archie Butt, President Taft's military aide; Clarence Moore, the traveling Master of Hounds; Harry Widener, son of the Philadelphia streetcar magnate; and William Carter, another Main Liner. They were winding up a small dinner given by Widener's father in honor of Captain Edward J. Smith, the ship's commander. The Captain had left early, the ladies had been packed off to bed, and now the men were enjoying a final cigar before turning in too. The conversation wandered from politics to Clarence Moore's adventures in West Virginia, the time he helped interview the old feuding mountaineer Anse Hatfield.

Buried in a nearby leather armchair, Spencer V. Silverthorne, a young buyer for Nugent's department store in St. Louis, browsed through a new best seller, *The Virginian.* Not far off, Lucien P. Smith (still another Philadelphian) struggled gamely through the linguistic problems of a bridge game with three Frenchmen.

At another table the ship's young set was enjoying a somewhat noisier game of bridge. Normally the young set preferred the livelier Café Parisien, just below on B Deck, and at first tonight was no exception. But it grew so cold that around 11:30 the girls went off to bed, and the men strolled up to the smoking room for a nightcap. Most of the group stuck to highballs; Hugh Woolner, son of the English sculptor, took a hot whisky and water; Lieutenant Hokan Bjornstrom Steffanson, a young Swedish military attaché on his way to Washington, chose a hot lemonade.

Somebody produced a deck of cards, and as they sat playing and laughing, suddenly there came that grinding jar. Not much of a shock, but enough to give a man a start—Mr. Silverthorne still sits up with a jolt when he tells it. In an instant the smoking-room steward and Mr. Silverthorne were on their feet . . . through the aft door . . . past the Palm Court . . . and out onto the deck. They were just in time to see the iceberg scraping along the starboard side, a little higher than the Boat Deck. As it slid by, they watched chunks of ice breaking and tumbling off into the water. In another moment it faded into the darkness astern.

Others in the smoking room were pouring out now. As Hugh Woolner reached the deck, he heard a man call out, "We hit an iceberg—there it is!"

Woolner squinted into the night. About 150 yards astern he made out a mountain of ice standing black against the starlit sky. Then it vanished into the dark.

The excitement, too, soon disappeared. The *Titanic* seemed as solid as ever, and it was too bitterly cold to stay outside any longer. Slowly the group filed back, Woolner picked up his hand, and the bridge game went on. The last man inside thought, as he slammed the deck door, that the engines were stopping.

He was right. Up on the bridge First Officer William M. Murdoch had just pulled the engine-room telegraph handle all the way to "Stop." Murdoch was in charge of the bridge this watch, and it was his problem, once Fleet phoned the warning. A tense minute had passed since then—orders to Quartermaster Hitchens to turn the wheel hard a-starboard . . . a yank on the engine-room telegraph for "Full Speed Astern" . . . a hard push on the button closing the watertight doors . . . and finally those 37 seconds of breathless waiting.

Now the waiting was over, and it was all so clearly too late. As the grinding noise died away, Captain Smith rushed onto the bridge from his cabin next to the wheelhouse. There were a few quick words:

"Mr. Murdoch, what was that?"

"An iceberg, sir. I hard-a-starboarded and reversed the engines, and I was going to hard-a-port around it, but she was too close. I couldn't do any more."

"Close the emergency doors."

"The doors are already closed."

They were closed, all right. Down in boiler room No. 6, Fireman Fred Barrett had been talking to Assistant Second Engineer James Hesketh when the warning bell sounded and the light flashed red above the watertight door leading to the stern. A quick shout of warning—an ear-splitting crash

—and the whole starboard side of the ship seemed to give way. The sea cascaded in, swirling about the pipes and valves, and the two men leaped through the door as it slammed down behind them.

Barrett found things almost as bad where he was now, in boiler room No. 5. The gash ran into No. 5 about two feet beyond the closed compartment door, and a fat jet of sea water was spouting through the hole. Nearby, Trimmer George Cavell was digging himself out of an avalanche of coal that had poured out of a bunker with the impact. Another stoker mournfully studied an overturned bowl of soup that had been warming on a piece of machinery.

It was dry in the other boiler rooms further aft, but the scene was pretty much the same—men picking themselves up, calling back and forth, asking what had happened. It was hard to figure out. Until now the *Titanic* had been a picnic. Being a new ship on her maiden voyage, everything was clean. She was, as Fireman George Kemish still recalls, "a good job . . . not what we were accustomed to in old ships, slogging our guts out and nearly roasted by the heat."

All the firemen had to do was keep the furnaces full. No need to work the fires with slice bars, pricker bars, and rakes. So on this Sunday night the men were taking it easy—sitting around on buckets and the trimmers' iron wheelbarrows, shooting the breeze, waiting for the 12-to-4 watch to come on.

Then came that thud . . . the grinding, tearing sound . . . the telegraphs ringing wildly . . . the watertight doors crashing down. Most of the men couldn't imagine what it was—the story spread that the *Titanic* had gone aground just off the Banks of Newfoundland. Many of them still thought so, even after a trimmer came running down from above shouting, "Blimey! We've struck an iceberg!"

About ten miles away Third Officer Charles Victor Groves stood on the bridge of the Leyland Liner *Californian*, bound from London to Boston. A plodding 6000-tonner, she had room for 47 passengers, but none were being carried just now. On this Sunday night she had been stopped since 10:30 P.M., completely blocked by drifting ice.

At about 11:10 Groves noticed the lights of another ship, racing up from the east on the starboard side. As the newcomer rapidly overhauled the motionless *Californian*, a blaze of deck lights showed she was a large passenger liner. Around 11:30 he knocked on the Venetian door of the chart room and told Captain Stanley Lord about it. Lord suggested contacting the new arrival by Morse lamp, and Groves prepared to do this.

Then, at about 11:40, he saw the big ship suddenly stop and put out most of her lights. This didn't surprise Groves very much. He had spent some time in the Far East trade, where they usually put deck lights out at midnight to encourage the passengers to turn in. It never occurred to him that perhaps the lights were still on . . . that they only seemed to go out because she was no longer broadside but had veered sharply to port.

## 2. *"There's Talk of an Iceberg, Ma'am"*

Almost as if nothing had happened, Lookout Fleet resumed his watch, Mrs. Astor lay back in her bed, and Lieutenant Steffanson returned to his hot lemonade.

At the request of several passengers Second Class Smoking Room Steward James Witter went off to investigate the jar. But two tables of card players hardly looked up. Normally the White Star Line allowed no card playing on Sunday, and tonight the passengers wanted to take full advantage of the Chief Steward's unexpected largesse.

There was no one in the Second Class lounge to send the librarian looking, so he continued sitting at his table, quietly counting the day's loan slips.

Through the long white corridors that led to the staterooms came only the murmurs of people chatting in their cabins . . . the distant slam of some deck-pantry door . . . occasionally the click of unhurried high heels —all the usual sounds of a liner at night.

Everything seemed perfectly normal—yet not quite. In his cabin on B Deck, 17-year-old Jack Thayer had just called good night to his father and mother, Mr. and Mrs. John B. Thayer of Philadelphia. The Thayers had connecting staterooms, an arrangement compatible with Mr. Thayer's position as Second Vice-President of the Pennsylvania Railroad. Now, as young Jack stood buttoning his pajama jacket, the steady hum of the breeze through his half-opened porthole suddenly stopped.

One deck below, Mr. and Mrs. Henry B. Harris sat in their cabin playing double Canfield. Mr. Harris, a Broadway producer, was dog-tired, and Mrs. Harris had just broken her arm. There was little conversation as Mrs. Harris idly watched her dresses sway on their hangers from the ship's vibration. Suddenly she noticed they stopped jiggling.

Another deck below, Lawrence Beesley, a young science master at Dulwich College, lay in his Second Class bunk reading, pleasantly lulled by the dancing motion of the mattress. Suddenly the mattress was still.

The creaking woodwork, the distant rhythm of the engines, the steady rattle of the glass dome over the A Deck foyer—all the familiar shipboard sounds vanished as the *Titanic* glided to a stop. Far more than any jolt, silence stirred the passengers.

Steward bells began ringing, but it was hard to learn anything. "Why have we stopped?" Lawrence Beesley asked a passing steward. "I don't know, sir," came a typical answer, "but I don't suppose it's much."

Mrs. Arthur Ryerson, of the steel family, had somewhat better results. "There's talk of an iceberg, ma'am," explained Steward Bishop, "and they have stopped, not to run over it." While her French maid Victorine hovered in the background, Mrs. Ryerson pondered what to do. Mr. Ryerson was having his first good sleep since the start of the trip, and she hated to wake him. She walked over to the square, heavy glass window that opened directly on the sea. Outside, she saw only a calm, beautiful night. She decided to let him sleep.

Others refused to let well enough alone. With the restless curiosity that afflicts everyone on board ship, some of the *Titanic's* passengers began exploring for an answer.

In C-51 Colonel Archibald Gracie, an amateur military historian by way of West Point and an independent income, methodically donned underwear, long stockings, shoes, trousers, a Norfolk jacket, and then puffed up to the Boat Deck. Jack Thayer simply threw an overcoat over his pajamas and took off, calling to his parents that he was "going out to see the fun."

On deck there was little fun to be seen; nor was there any sign of danger. For the most part the explorers wandered aimlessly about or stood by the rail, staring into the empty night for some clue to the trouble. The *Titanic* lay dead in the water, three of her four huge funnels blowing off steam with a roar that shattered the quiet, starlit night. Otherwise everything normal. Toward the stern of the Boat Deck an elderly couple strolled arm in arm, oblivious of the roaring steam and the little knots of passengers roving about.

It was so bitterly cold, and there was so little to be seen, that most of the people came inside again. Entering the magnificent foyer on A Deck, they found others who had also risen but preferred to stay inside where it was warm.

Mingling together, they made a curious picture. Their dress was an odd mixture of bathrobes, evening clothes, fur coats, turtle-neck sweaters. The setting was equally incongruous—the huge glass dome overhead . . . the dignified oak paneling . . . the magnificent balustrades with their wrought-iron scroll work . . . and, looking down on them all, an incredible wall clock adorned with two bronze nymphs, somehow symbolizing Honor and Glory crowning Time.

"Oh, it'll be a few hours and we'll be on the way again," a steward vaguely explained to First Class passenger George Harder.

"Looks like we've lost a propeller, but it'll give us more time for bridge," called Howard Case, the London manager of Vacuum Oil, to Fred Seward, a New York lawyer. Perhaps Mr. Case got his theory from Steward Johnson, still contemplating a sojourn in Belfast. In any event, most of the passengers had better information by this time.

"What do you think?" exclaimed Harvey Collyer to his wife, as he returned to their cabin from a tour around the deck. "We've struck an iceberg —a big one—but there's no danger. An officer told me so!" The Collyers were traveling Second Class, on their way from Britain to a fruit farm just purchased in Fayette Valley, Idaho. They were novices on the Atlantic, and perhaps the news would have roused Mrs. Collyer, but the dinner that night had been too rich. So she just asked her husband if anybody seemed frightened, and when he said no, she lay back again in her bunk.

John Jacob Astor seemed equally unperturbed. Returning to his suite after going up to investigate, he explained to Mrs. Astor that the ship had struck ice, but it didn't look serious. He was very calm and Mrs. Astor wasn't a bit alarmed.

"What do they say is the trouble?" asked William T. Stead, a leading British spiritualist, reformer, evangelist and editor, all rolled into one. A professional individualist, he seemed almost to have planned his arrival on deck later than the others.

"Icebergs," briefly explained Frank Millet, the distinguished American painter.

"Well," Stead shrugged, "I guess it's nothing serious; I'm going back to my cabin to read."

Mr. and Mrs. Dickinson Bishop of Dowagiac, Michigan, had the same reaction. When a deck steward assured them, "We have only struck a little piece of ice and passed it," the Bishops returned to their stateroom and undressed again. Mr. Bishop picked up a book and started to read, but soon he was interrupted by a knock on the door. It was Mr. Albert A. Stewart, an ebullient old gentleman who had a large interest in the Barnum & Bailey Circus: "Come on out and amuse yourself!"

Others had the same idea. First Class passenger Peter Daly heard one young lady tell another, "Oh, come and let's see the berg—we have never seen one before!"

And in the Second Class smoking room somebody facetiously asked whether he could get some ice from the berg for his highball.

He could indeed. When the *Titanic* brushed by, several tons of ice crumbled off the berg and landed on the starboard well deck, just opposite the foremast. This was Third Class recreation space, and the ice was soon discovered by steerage passengers coming up to investigate. From her cabin window on B Deck, Mrs. Natalie Wick watched them playfully throwing chunks at each other.

The ice soon became quite a tourist attraction. Major Arthur Godfrey Peuchen, a middle-aged manufacturing chemist from Toronto, used the opportunity to descend on a more distinguished compatriot, Charles M. Hays, President of the Grand Trunk Railroad. "Mr. Hays!" he cried, "have you seen the ice?"

When Mr. Hays said he hadn't, Peuchen followed through—"If you care to see it, I will take you up on deck and show it to you." And so they went all the way forward on A Deck and looked down at the mild horseplay below.

Possession of the ice didn't remain a Third Class monopoly for long. As Colonel Gracie stood in the A Deck foyer, he was tapped on the shoulder by Clinch Smith, a New York society figure whose experiences already included sitting at Stanford White's table the night White was shot by Harry K. Thaw. "Would you like," asked Smith, "a souvenir to take back to New York?" And he opened his hand to show a small piece of ice, flat like a pocket watch.

The same collector's instinct gripped others. Able Seaman John Poingdestre picked up a sliver and showed it around the crew's mess room. A steerage passenger presented Fourth Officer Boxhall with a chunk about the size of a small basin. As Greaser Walter Hurst lay half-awake, his father-in-law—who shared the same quarters—came in and tossed a lump of ice into Hurst's bunk. A man entered the stewards' quarters, displaying a piece about as big as a teacup, and told Steward F. Dent Ray, "There are tons of ice forward!"

"Ah, well," Ray yawned, "that will not hurt." And he prepared to go back to sleep.

A little more curious, First Class Steward Henry Samuel Etches—off duty at the time of the crash—walked forward along the alleyway on E Deck to investigate, ran into a Third Class passenger walking the other way. Before Etches could say anything, the passenger—as though confronting Etches with irrefutable evidence about something in dispute—threw a block of ice to the deck and shouted, "Will you believe it *now?*"

Soon there was far more disturbing evidence that all was not as it should be. By 11:50—ten minutes after the collision—strange things could be seen and heard in the first six of the *Titanic's* 16 watertight compartments.

Lamp Trimmer Samuel Hemming, lying off duty in his bunk, heard a curious hissing sound coming from the forepeak, the compartment closest to the bow. He jumped up, went as far forward as he could, and discovered that it was air escaping from the forepeak locker where the anchor chains were stowed. Far below, water was pouring in so fast that the air rushed out under tremendous pressure.

In the next compartment aft, containing the firemen's quarters and cargo hatch No. 1, Leading Fireman Charles Hendrickson was also aroused by a curious sound. But here it was not air—it was water. When he looked down the spiral staircase that led to the passageway connecting the fireman's quarters with the stokeholds, he saw green sea water swirling around the foot of the grated, cast-iron steps.

Steerage passenger Carl Johnson had an even more disturbing experience in the third compartment aft. This contained the cheapest passenger accommodations—lowest in the ship and closest to the bow. As Johnson got up to see what was causing a mild commotion outside his cabin, water seeped in under the door and around his feet. He decided to dress, and by the time his clothes were on, the water was over his shoes. With a detached, almost clinical interest, he noticed that it seemed to be of very even depth all over the floor. Nearby, steerage passenger Daniel Buckley was a little slower to react, and when he finally jumped out of his bunk, he splashed into water up to his ankles.

Five postal clerks working in the fourth compartment were much wetter. The *Titanic's* post office took up two deck levels—the mail was stacked, along with First Class luggage, on the Orlop Deck and was sorted just above on G Deck. The two levels were connected by a wide iron companionway, which continued up to F Deck and the rest of the ship. Within five minutes water was sloshing around the knees of the postal clerks, as they dragged 200 sacks of registered mail up the companionway to the drier sorting room.

They might have spared themselves the trouble—in another five minutes the water reached the top of the steps and was lapping onto G Deck. The clerks now abandoned the mail room altogether, retreating further up the companionway to F Deck.

At the top of the stairs they found a married couple peering down at them. Mr. and Mrs. Norman Campbell Chambers of New York had been attracted by the noise, while returning to their cabin after a fruitless trip to the Promenade Deck. Now, the Chambers and the postal clerks watched the scene together, joking about the soaked baggage and wondering what might be in the letters they could see floating around the abandoned mail room.

Others joined them briefly from time to time—Fourth Officer Boxhall . . . Assistant Second Steward Wheat . . . once even Captain Smith. But at no point could the Chambers bring themselves to believe that anything they saw was really dangerous.

The fifth watertight compartment from the bow contained boiler room No. 6. This was where Fireman Barrett and Assistant Second Engineer Hesketh jumped through the watertight door just as it slammed down after the collision. Others didn't make it and scrambled up the escape ladders that laced their way topside. A few hung on, and after a moment some of the others came down again.

Shouts of "Shut the dampers!" and then "Draw the fires!" came from somewhere. Fireman George Beauchamp worked at fever pitch as the sea flooded in from the bunker door and up through the floor plates. In five minutes it was waist deep—black and slick with grease from the machinery. The air was heavy with steam. Fireman Beauchamp never did see who shouted the welcome words, "That will do!" He was too relieved to care as he scurried up the ladder for the last time.

Just to the stern, Assistant Second Engineer Hesketh, now on the dry side of the watertight door, struggled to get boiler room No. 5 back to normal. The sea still spouted through a two-foot gash near the closed door, but Assistant Engineers Harvey and Wilson had a pump going, and it was keeping ahead of the water.

For a few moments the stokers stood by, aimlessly watching the engineers rig the pumps; then the engine room phoned to send them to the Boat Deck. They trooped up the escape ladder, but the bridge ordered them down again, and for a while they milled around the working alleyway on E Deck—halfway up, halfway down—caught in the bureaucracy of a huge ship and wondering what to do next.

Meanwhile the lights went out in boiler room No. 5. Engineer Harvey ordered Fireman Barrett, who had stayed behind, to go aft to the engine room for lanterns. The connecting doors were all shut; so Barrett had to climb to the top of the escape ladder, cross over, and go down the other side. By the time he retraced his steps, the engineers had the lights on again and the lanterns weren't needed.

Next, Harvey told Barrett to shut down the boilers—the pressure, built up while the ship was at full steam, now lifted the safety valves and was blowing joints. Barrett scrambled back up the ladder and drafted 15 or 20 of the stokers wandering around E Deck. They all clattered down and began wetting the fires. It was back-breaking work, boxing up the boilers and putting on dampers to stop the steam from rising. Fireman Kemish still remembers it with feeling: "We certainly had one hell of a time putting those fires out . . ."

Clouds of steam gushed through the boiler room as the men sweated away. But gradually order returned. The lights burned bright, the place was clear of water, and, in No. 5 at any rate, everything seemed under control. There was an air of cheerful confidence by the time word spread that the men on the 12-to-4 watch were dragging their beds to the recreation deck because their rooms were flooded. The men on the 8-to-12 watch paused in their work, thought this was a huge joke, and had a good laugh.

Up on the bridge, Captain Smith tried to piece the picture together. No one was better equipped to do it. After 38 years' service with White Star, he was more than just senior captain of the line; he was a bearded patriarch, worshiped by crew and passengers alike. They loved everything about him— especially his wonderful combination of firmness and urbanity. It was strikingly evident in the matter of cigars. "Cigars," says his daughter, "were his pleasure. And one was allowed to be in the room only if one was absolutely still, so that the blue cloud over his head never moved."

Captain Smith was a natural leader, and on reaching the wheelhouse after the crash, he paused only long enough to visit the starboard wing of the bridge to see if the iceberg was still in sight. First Officer Murdoch and Fourth Officer Boxhall trailed along, and for a moment the three officers merely stood peering into the darkness. Boxhall thought he saw a dark shape far astern, but he wasn't sure.

From then on all was business. Captain Smith sent Boxhall on a fast inspection of the ship. In a few minutes he was back: he had been as far forward in the steerage as he could go, and there was no sign of damage. This was the last good news Captain Smith heard that night.

Still worried, Smith now told Boxhall, "Go down and find the carpenter and get him to sound the ship." Boxhall wasn't even down the bridge ladder when he bumped into Carpenter J. Hutchinson rushing up. As Hutchinson elbowed his way by, he gasped, "She's making water fast!"

Hard on the carpenter's heels came mail clerk Iago Smith. He too pushed on toward the bridge, blurting as he passed, "The mail hold is filling rapidly!"

Next to arrive was Bruce Ismay. He had pulled a suit over his pajamas, put on his carpet slippers, and climbed to the bridge to find whether anything was happening that the President of the line should know. Captain Smith broke the news about the iceberg. Ismay then asked, "Do you think the ship is seriously damaged?" A pause, and the Captain slowly answered, "I'm afraid she is."

They would know soon enough. A call had been sent for Thomas Andrews, Managing Director of Harland & Wolff Shipyard. As the *Titanic's* builder, Andrews was making the maiden voyage to iron out any kinks in the ship. If anybody could figure out the situation, here was the man.

He was indeed a remarkable figure. As builder, he of course knew every detail about the *Titanic*. But there was so much more to him than that. Nothing was too great or too small for his attention. He even seemed able to anticipate how the ship would react to any situation. He understood ships the way some men are supposed to understand horses.

And he understood equally well the people who run ships. They all came to Andrews with their problems. One night it might be First Officer Murdoch, worried because he had been superseded by Chief Officer Wilde. The next night it might be a couple of quarreling stewardesses who looked to Andrews as a sort of Supreme Court. This very evening Chief Baker Charles Joughin made him a special loaf of bread.

So far, Andrews' trip had been what might be expected. All day long he roamed the ship, taking volumes of notes. At 6:45 every evening he dressed for dinner, dining usually with old Dr. O'Loughlin, the ship's surgeon, who also had a way with the stewardesses. And then back to his stateroom A-36, piled high with plans and charts and blueprints. There he would assemble his notes and work out his recommendations.

Tonight the problems were typical—trouble with the restaurant galley hot press . . . the coloring of the pebble dashing on the private promenade decks was too dark . . . too many screws on all the stateroom hat hooks. There was also the plan to change part of the writing room into two more staterooms. The writing room had originally been planned partly as a place where the ladies could retire after dinner. But this was the twentieth century, and the ladies just wouldn't retire. Clearly, a smaller room would do.

Completely absorbed, Andrews scarcely noticed the jar and stirred from his blueprints only when he got Captain Smith's message that he was needed on the bridge.

In a few minutes Andrews and the Captain were making their own tour —down the crew's stairway to attract less attention . . . along the labyrinth of corridors far below . . . by the water surging into the mail room . . . past the squash court, where the sea now lapped against the foul line on the backboard.

Threading their way back to the bridge, they passed through the A Deck foyer, still thronged with passengers standing around. Everybody studied the two men's faces for some sign of good news or bad; nobody could detect any clue.

Some of the crew weren't so guarded. In D-60, when Mrs. Henry Sleeper Harper asked Dr. O'Loughlin to persuade her sick husband to stay in bed, the old doctor exclaimed, "They tell me the trunks are floating around in the hold; you may as well go on deck."

In C-91 a young governess named Elizabeth Shutes sat with her charge, 19-year-old Margaret Graham. Seeing an officer pass the cabin door, Miss Shutes asked him if there was any danger. He cheerfully said no, but then she overheard him further down the hall say, "We can keep the water out for a while."

Miss Shutes glanced at Margaret, who was uneasily nibbling at a chicken sandwich. Her hand shook so badly the chicken kept falling out of the bread.

No one was asking questions along the working alleyway on E Deck. This broad corridor was the quickest way from one end of the ship to the other—the officers called it "Park Lane," the crew "Scotland Road." Now it was crowded with pushing, shoving people. Some were stokers forced out of boiler room No. 6, but most were steerage passengers, slowly working their way aft, carrying boxes, bags, and even trunks.

These people didn't need to be told there was trouble. To those berthed far below on the starboard side, the crash was no "faint grinding jar." It was a "tremendous noise" that sent them tumbling out of bed.

Mrs. Celiney Yasbeck—a bride of 50 days—ran out into the corridor with her husband. Instead of making the long hike to the deck, it was easier to look below for trouble. In their night clothes they walked along to a door leading down to the boiler rooms and peeked through. Engineers were struggling to make repairs and get the pumps going. The Yasbecks needed no second glance—they rushed back to their cabin to dress.

Far above on A Deck, Second Class passenger Lawrence Beesley noticed a curious thing. As he started below to check his cabin, he felt certain the stairs "weren't quite right." They seemed level, and yet his feet didn't fall where they should. Somehow they strayed forward off balance . . . as though the steps were tilted down toward the bow.

Major Peuchen noticed it too. As he stood with Mr. Hays at the forward end of A Deck, looking down at the steerage passengers playing soccer with the loose ice, he sensed a very slight tilt in the deck. "Why she is listing!" he cried to Hays. "She should not do that! The water is perfectly calm and the boat has stopped."

"Oh, I don't know," Mr. Hays replied placidly, "you cannot sink this boat."

Others also felt the downward slant, but it seemed tactless to mention the matter. In boiler room No. 5, Fireman Barrett decided to say nothing to the engineers working on the pumps. Far above in the A Deck foyer, Colonel Gracie and Clinch Smith had the same reaction. On the bridge the commutator showed the *Titanic* slightly down at the head and listing 5 degrees to starboard.

Nearby, Andrews and Captain Smith did some fast figuring. Water in the forepeak . . . No. 1 hold . . . No. 2 hold . . . mail room . . . boiler room No. 6 . . . boiler room No. 5. Water 14 feet above keel level in the first ten minutes, everywhere except boiler room No. 5. Put together, the facts showed a 300-foot gash, with the first five compartments hopelessly flooded.

What did this mean? Andrews quietly explained. The *Titanic* could float with any two of her 16 watertight compartments flooded. She could float with any three of her first five compartments flooded. She could even float with all of her first four compartments gone. But no matter how they sliced it, she could not float with all of her first five compartments full.

The bulkhead between the fifth and sixth compartments went only as high as E Deck. If the first five compartments were flooded, the bow would sink so low that water in the fifth compartment must overflow into the sixth. When this was full, it would overflow into the seventh, and so on. It was a mathematical certainty, pure and simple. There was no way out.

But it was still a shock. After all, the *Titanic* was considered unsinkable. And not just in the travel brochures. The highly technical magazine *Shipbuilder* described her compartment system in a special edition in 1911, pointing out, "The Captain may, by simply moving an electric switch, instantly close the doors throughout and make the vessel practically unsinkable."

Now all the switches were pulled, and Andrews said it made no difference.

It was hard to face, and especially hard for Captain Smith. Over 59 years old, he was retiring after this trip. Might even have done it sooner, but he traditionally took the White Star ships on their maiden voyages. Only six years before, when he brought over the brand-new *Adriatic*, he remarked:

"I cannot imagine any condition which would cause a ship to founder. I cannot conceive of any vital disaster happening to this vessel. Modern shipbuilding has gone beyond that."

Now he stood on the bridge of a liner twice as big—twice as safe—and the builder told him it couldn't float.

At 12:05 A.M.—25 minutes after that bumping, grinding jar—Captain Smith ordered Chief Officer Wilde to uncover the boats . . . First Officer Murdoch to muster the passengers . . . Sixth Officer Moody to get out the list of boat assignments . . . Fourth Officer Boxhall to wake up Second Officer Lightoller and Third Officer Pitman. The Captain himself then walked about 20 yards down the port side of the Boat Deck to the wireless shack.

Inside, First Operator John George Phillips and Second Operator Harold Bride showed no sign that they realized what was happening. It had been a tough day. In 1912 wireless was still an erratic novelty; range was short, operators were inexperienced, and signals were hard to catch. There was a lot of relaying, a lot of repeats, and a lot of frivolous private traffic. Passengers were fascinated by the new miracle, couldn't resist the temptation of sending messages to friends back home or on other ships.

All this Sunday the messages had piled up. It was enough to fray the nerves of any man working a 14-hour day at 30 dollars a month, and Phillips was no exception. Evening came, and still the bottomless in-basket, still the petty interferences. Only an hour ago—just when he was at last in good contact with Cape Race—the *Californian* barged in with some message about icebergs. She was so close she almost blew his ears off. No wonder he snapped back, "Shut up, shut up! I am busy; I am working Cape Race!"

It was such a hard day that Second Operator Bride decided to relieve Phillips at midnight, even though he wasn't due until 2:00 A.M. He woke up about 11:55, brushed by the green curtain separating the sleeping quarters from the "office," and asked Phillips how he was getting along. Phillips said he had just finished the Cape Race traffic. Bride padded back to his berth and took off his pajamas. Phillips called after him that he thought the ship had been damaged somehow and they'd have to go back to Belfast.

In a couple of minutes Bride was dressed and took over the headphones. Phillips was hardly behind the green curtain when Captain Smith appeared: "We've struck an iceberg and I'm having an inspection made to see what it has done to us. You better get ready to send out a call for assistance, but don't send it until I tell you."

Then he left but returned again in a few minutes. This time he merely stuck his head in the doorway:

"Send the call for assistance."

By now Phillips was back in the room. He asked the Captain whether to use the regulation distress call. Smith replied, "Yes, at once!"

He handed Phillips a slip of paper with the *Titanic's* position. Phillips took the headphones from Bride, and at 12:15 A.M. began tapping out the letters "CQD"—at that time the usual international call of distress—followed by "MGY," the call letters of the *Titanic*. Again and again, six times over, the signal rasped out into the cold, blue Atlantic night.

Ten miles away, Third Officer Groves of the *Californian* sat on the bunk of Wireless Operator Cyril F. Evans. Groves was young, alert, and always interested in what was going on in the world. After work he liked to drop by Evans' wireless shack and pick up the latest news. He even liked to fool with the set.

This was all right with Evans. There weren't many officers on third-rate liners interested in the outside world, much the less wireless telegraphy. In fact, there weren't any others on the *Californian*. So he used to welcome Groves' visits.

But not tonight. It had been a hard day, and there was no other operator to relieve him. Besides, he had been pretty roughly handled around 11:00 when he tried to break in on the *Titanic* and tell her about the ice blocking the *Californian*. So he lost no time tonight closing down his set at 11:30, his scheduled hour for going off duty. Now—dead-tired—he was in no mood for shooting the breeze with anybody. Groves made a brave try: "What ships have you got, Sparks?"

"Only the *Titanic*." Evans scarcely bothered to glance up from his magazine.

This was no news to Groves. He recalled that when he showed Captain Lord the strange liner that had just stopped nearby, the Captain told him, "That will be the *Titanic* on her maiden voyage."

In search of something more interesting, Groves took the headphones and put them on. He was really getting quite good, if the message was simple enough. But he didn't know too much about the equipment. The *Cali-*

*fornian's* set had a magnetic detector that ran by clockwork. Groves didn't wind it up, and so he heard nothing.

Giving up, he put the phones back on the table, and went below to find livelier company. It was just a little after 12:15 A.M.

### 3. *"God Himself Could Not Sink This Ship"*

The door to the cook's quarters whacked open against the iron cot of Assistant Baker Charles Burgess. He woke up with a start and stared at Second Steward George Dodd standing in the doorway. Normally a rotund, jolly man, Dodd looked serious as he called, "Get up, lads, we're sinking!"

Dodd moved forward to the waiters' quarters, where Saloon Steward William Moss was trying to rouse the men. Most of them were laughing and joking, when Dodd burst in, shouting, "Get every man up! Don't let a man stay here!"

He moved on with Moss toward the stewards' quarters. Just outside, Smoking Room Steward Witter was already getting some disturbing news from Carpenter Hutchinson: "The bloody mail room is full." Moss came up and added, "It's really serious, Jim."

The wisecracks that greeted the first warnings faded, and the crew tumbled out of their berths. Still half-asleep, Baker Burgess pulled on pants, a shirt, no lifebelt. Walter Belford wore his white baker's coat, pants, didn't stop to put on his underdrawers. Steward Ray took more time; he wasn't worried—nevertheless he found himself putting on his shore suit. Steward Witter, already dressed, opened his trunk and filled his pockets with cigarettes . . . picked up the cowl from his first child, which he always carried with him . . . then joined the crowd of men now swarming out into the working alleyway and up toward the boat stations.

Far forward, away from the uproar, Trimmer Samuel Hemming climbed back into his bunk, satisfied that the hissing sound in the forepeak didn't mean very much. He was just drifting off to sleep when the ship's joiner leaned in, saying, "If I were you, I'd turn out. She's making water one-two-three, and the racket court is getting filled up." An instant later the boatswain appeared: "Turn out, you fellows. You haven't half an hour to live. That is from Mr. Andrews. Keep it to yourselves and let no one know."

Certainly no one knew in the First Class smoking room. The bridge game was going full blast again. Lieutenant Steffanson was still sipping his hot lemonade, and another hand was being dealt, when a ship's officer suddenly appeared at the door: "Men, get on your lifebelts; there's trouble ahead."

In her A Deck stateroom, Mrs. Washington Dodge lay in bed, waiting for Dr. Dodge, Assessor for San Francisco, to dig up some news. The door opened and the doctor came in quietly: "Ruth, the accident is rather a serious one; you had better come on deck at once."

Two decks below, Mrs. Lucien Smith—tired of waiting for Mr. Smith to finish exploring—had gone back to sleep. Suddenly the lights snapped on,

and she saw her husband standing by the bed, smiling down at her. Leisurely he explained, "We are in the north and have struck an iceberg. It
does not amount to anything but will probably delay us a day getting into
New York. However, as a matter of form, the Captain has ordered all ladies
on deck."

And so it went. No bells or sirens. No general alarm. But all over the
*Titanic*, in one way or another, the word was passed.

It was very bewildering to eight-year-old Marshall Drew. When his aunt
Mrs. James Drew woke him and said she had to take him on deck, he sleepily protested he didn't want to get up. But Mrs. Drew paid no attention.

It was no less bewildering to Major Arthur Peuchen, despite his sight-
seeing expedition to look at the ice. He heard the news on the grand staircase and could hardly believe it. Completely stunned, he stumbled to his
cabin to change from evening dress to something warm.

For many, first word came from their stewards. John Hardy, Second
Class Chief Steward, personally roused 20 to 24 cabins. Each time he threw
the door open wide, shouting "Everybody on deck with lifebelts on, at
once!"

In First Class it was more polite to knock. These were the days when a
steward on a crack liner didn't have more than eight or nine cabins, and he
was like a mother hen to all the passengers he served.

Steward Alfred Crawford was typical. He had spent 31 years handling
difficult passengers, and now he knew just how to coax old Mr. Albert
Stewart into a life jacket. Then he stooped and tied on the old gentleman's
shoes.

In C-89, Steward Andrew Cunningham helped William T. Stead into his
lifebelt, while the great editor mildly complained that it was all a lot of
nonsense. In B-84, Steward Henry Samuel Etches worked like a solicitous
tailor, fitting Benjamin Guggenheim for his lifebelt.

"This will hurt," protested the mining and smelting king. Etches finally
took the belt off altogether, made some adjustments, put it on again. Next,
Guggenheim wanted to go on deck as he was, but Etches was adamant—it
was much too cold. Ultimately Guggenheim submitted; Etches pulled a
heavy sweater over him and sent him packing off topside.

Some of the passengers were even more difficult. At C-78, Etches found
the door locked. When he knocked loudly with both hands, a man inside
asked suspiciously, "What is it?" and a woman added, "Tell us what the
trouble is." Etches explained and again tried to get them to open the door.
He had no luck, and after a few minutes' pleading he finally passed on to the
next cabin.

In another part of the ship a locked door raised a different problem. It
was jammed, and some passengers broke it down to release a man inside.
At this point a steward arrived, threatening to have everybody arrested for
damaging company property when the *Titanic* reached New York.

At 12:15 it was hard to know whether to joke or be serious—whether to chop down a door and be a hero, or chop it down and get arrested. No two people seemed to have the same reaction.

Mrs. Arthur Ryerson felt there wasn't a moment to lose. She had long since abandoned the idea of letting Mr. Ryerson sleep; now she scurried about trying to keep her family together. There were six to get ready—her husband, three children, governess, and maid—and the children seemed so slow. Finally she gave up on her youngest daughter; just threw a fur coat over her nightgown and told her to come on.

There seemed all the time in the world to Mrs. Lucien Smith. Slowly and with great care she dressed for whatever the night might bring—a heavy woolen dress, high shoes, two coats, and a warm knitted hood. All the while Mr. Smith chatted away about landing in New York, taking the train south, never mentioning the iceberg. As they started for the deck, Mrs. Smith decided to go back for some jewelry. Here Mr. Smith drew the line. He suggested it might be wiser not to bother with "trifles." As a compromise Mrs. Smith picked up two favorite rings. Closing the door carefully behind them, the young couple headed up toward the Boat Deck.

The things people took with them showed how they felt. Adolf Dyker handed his wife a small satchel containing two gold watches, two diamond rings, a sapphire necklace, and 200 Swedish crowns. Miss Edith Russell carried a musical toy pig (it played the *Maxixe*). Stewart Collett, a young theological student traveling Second Class, took the Bible he promised his brother he'd always carry until they met again. Lawrence Beesley stuffed the pockets of his Norfolk jacket with the books he had been reading in bed. Norman Campbell Chambers pocketed a revolver and compass. Steward Johnson, by now anticipating far more than "another Belfast trip," stuck four oranges under his blouse. Mrs. Dickinson Bishop left behind 11,000 dollars in jewelry, then sent her husband back for her muff.

Major Arthur Peuchen looked at the tin box on the table in C-104. Inside were 200,000 dollars in bonds, 100,000 dollars in preferred stock. He thought a good deal about it as he took off his dinner jacket, put on two suits of long underwear and some heavy clothes.

Then he took a last look around the little cabin—the real brass bed . . . the green mesh net along the wall for valuables at night . . . the marble washstand . . . the wicker armchair . . . the horsehair sofa . . . the fan in the ceiling . . . the bells and electrical fixtures that on a liner always look as if they were installed as an afterthought.

Now his mind was made up. He slammed the door, leaving behind the tin box on the table. In another minute he was back. Quickly he picked up a good-luck pin and three oranges. As he left for the last time, the tin box was still on the table.

Out in the C Deck foyer, Purser Herbert McElroy was urging everyone to stop standing around. As the Countess of Rothes passed, he called, "Hurry, little lady, there is not much time. I'm glad you didn't ask me for your jewels as some ladies have."

Into the halls they poured, gently prodded along by the crew. One room steward caught the eye of Miss Marguerite Frolicher as she came down the corridor. Four days before, she had playfully teased him for putting a life-belt in her stateroom, if the ship was meant to be so unsinkable. At the time he had laughed and assured her it was just a formality . . . she would never have to wear it. Remembering the exchange, he now smiled and re-assured her, "Don't be scared; it's all right."

"I'm not scared," she replied, "I'm just seasick."

Up the stairs they trooped—a hushed crowd in jumbled array. Under his overcoat Jack Thayer now sported a greenish tweed suit and vest, with an-other mohair vest underneath. Mr. Robert Daniel, the Philadelphia banker, had on only woolen pajamas. Mrs. Turrell Cavendish wore a wrapper and Mr. Cavendish's overcoat . . . Mrs. John C. Hogeboom a fur coat over her nightgown . . . Mrs. Ada Clark just a nightgown. Mrs. Washington Dodge didn't bother to put on stockings under her high-button shoes, which flopped open because she didn't stop to button them. Mrs. Astor looked right out of a bandbox in an attractive light dress, Mrs. James J. Brown—a colorful Denver millionairess—equally stylish in a black velvet two-piece suit with black and white silk lapels.

Automobiling, as practiced in 1912, affected the attire of many ladies—Mrs. C. E. Henry Stengel wore a veil tightly pinned down over her floral hat, Madame de Villiers a long woolen motoring coat over her nightgown and evening slippers.

Young Alfred von Drachstedt, a 20-year-old youth from Cologne, settled on a sweater and a pair of trousers, leaving behind a brand-new 2133-dollar wardrobe that included walking sticks and a fountain pen, which he some-how felt was a special badge of distinction.

Second Class was somewhat less elegantly disarrayed. Mr. and Mrs. Al-bert Caldwell—returning from Siam, where they taught at the Bangkok Christian College—had bought new clothes in London, but tonight they dressed in the oldest clothes they owned. Their baby Alden was wrapped in a blanket. Miss Elizabeth Nye wore a simple skirt, coat, and slippers. Mrs. Charlotte Collyer didn't bother to put up her hair, just tied it back with a ribbon. Her eight-year-old daughter Marjory had a steamer rug around her shoulders. Mr. Collyer took little trouble dressing, because he expected to be back soon—he even left his watch lying on his pillow.

The scene in Third Class was particularly confusing because the White Star Line primly quartered the single men and single women at opposite ends of the *Titanic*. Now many of the men—who slept toward the bow—hurried aft to join the girls.

Katherine Gilnagh, a pert colleen not quite 16, heard a knock on the door. It was the young man who had caught her eye earlier that day playing the bagpipes on deck. He told her to get up—something was wrong with the ship. Anna Sjoblom, an 18-year-old Finnish girl bound for the Pacific North-west, woke up when a young Danish swain came in to rouse her roommate. He also gave Anna a lifebelt and urged her to come along. But she was too seasick to care. Eventually there was so much commotion that she went up after all, even though she still felt awful. She was quickly helped into a lifebelt by Alfred Wicklund, a schoolfriend from home.

Among these young men, Olaus Abelseth was especially worried. He was a 26-year-old Norwegian heading for a South Dakota homestead, and an old family friend had put a 16-year-old daughter in his care until they reached Minneapolis. As he pushed his way aft along the E Deck working alleyway, Minneapolis seemed a long way off.

Abelseth found the girl in the main steerage hallway on E Deck. Then, along with his brother-in-law, a cousin and another girl, they all climbed the broad, steep Third Class stairs to the poop deck at the very stern of the ship.

Into the bitter night the whole crowd milled, each class automatically keeping to its own decks—First Class in the center of the ship, Second a little aft, Third at the very stern or in the well deck near the bow. Quietly they stood around waiting for the next orders . . . reasonably confident yet vaguely worried. With uneasy amusement they eyed how one another looked in lifebelts. There were a few half-hearted jokes.

"Well," said Clinch Smith as a girl walked by carrying a Pomeranian, "I suppose we ought to put a life preserver on the little doggie too."

"Try this on," a man told Mrs. Vera Dick as he fastened on her life jacket. "They are the very latest thing this season. Everybody is wearing them now."

"They will keep you warm if you don't have to use them," Captain Smith cheerfully explained to Mrs. Alexander T. Compton of New Orleans.

At about 12:30 Colonel Gracie bumped into Fred Wright, the *Titanic's* squash pro. Remembering he had reserved the court for 7:30 in the morning, Gracie tried a little joke of his own: "Hadn't we better cancel that appointment?"

"Yes," replied Wright. His voice was flat and without enthusiasm, but the wonder is he played along at all. He knew the water was now up to the squash-court ceiling.

In the brightly lit gym, just off the Boat Deck, Mr. and Mrs. Astor sat side by side on a pair of motionless mechanical horses. They wore their lifebelts, and Mr. Astor had an extra one in his lap. He was slicing it open with his penknife, whiling away the time by showing his wife what was inside.

While the passengers joked and talked and waited, the crew moved swiftly to their stations. The Boat Deck teemed with seamen, stewards, firemen, chefs, ordered up from below.

A curiously late arrival was Fifth Officer Harold Godfrey Lowe. A tempestuous young Welshman, Lowe was hard to suppress. When he was 14, his father tried to apprentice him to a Liverpool businessman, but Lowe said he "wouldn't work for nobody for nothing." So he ran away to sea and a life after his own heart—schooners . . . square-riggers . . . five years steaming along the West African coast.

Now, at 28, he was making his first trip across the Atlantic. This Sunday night he was off duty and slept right through the collision. Voices outside his cabin on the Boat Deck finally woke him up. When he looked out the porthole and saw everybody in lifebelts, he catapulted out of bed, into his clothes, and rushed on deck to help. Not exactly an auspicious start, but then, as Lowe later explained to U. S. Senator Smith, "You must remember that we do not have any too much sleep, and therefore when we sleep we die."

Second Officer Charles Herbert Lightoller was late too, but for an entirely different reason. Like Lowe, he was off duty in his bunk when the *Titanic* hit, but he woke up instantly and, in his bare feet, ran out on the Boat Deck to see what was up. Nothing could be seen on either side of the ship, except on the starboard wing of the bridge, where he dimly made out Captain Smith and First Officer Murdoch. They too were peering into the night.

Lightoller returned to his cabin and thought it over. Something undoubtedly was wrong with the ship—first that jar, now the silent engines. But he was *off* duty, and until called, it was no business of his. When they needed him, they would send for him. When this happened, he should be where they'd expect to find him. Lightoller got back into bed and lay awake waiting . . .

Five, 15, 30 minutes went by. He could now hear the roar of the funnels blowing off steam, the rising sound of voices, the clanking of gear. But still, his duty was to be where they'd expect to find him.

At 12:10 Fourth Officer Boxhall finally came bursting in: "You know we have struck an iceberg."

"I know we have struck something," Lightoller replied, getting up and starting to dress.

"The water is up to F Deck in the mail room," continued Boxhall, by way of a little prodding. But no urging was needed. Lightoller was already well on the way. Cool, diligent, cautious, he knew his duty to the letter. He was the perfect Second Officer.

On the Boat Deck men began to clear the 16 wooden lifeboats. There were eight on each side—a cluster of four toward the bow, then an open space of 190 feet, then another four toward the stern. Port boats had even numbers, starboard odd. They were numbered in sequence, starting from the bow. In addition, four canvas collapsible lifeboats—known as Englehardts—were stowed on deck. These could be fitted into the empty davits after the two forward boats were lowered. The collapsibles were lettered A, B, C and D.

All the boats together could carry 1178 people. On this Sunday night there were 2207 people on board the *Titanic*.

This mathematical discrepancy was known by none of the passengers and few of the crew, but most of them wouldn't have cared anyhow. The *Titanic* was unsinkable. Everybody said so. When Mrs. Albert Caldwell was watching the deck hands carry up luggage at Southampton, she asked one of them, "Is this ship really nonsinkable?"

"Yes, lady," he answered, "God Himself could not sink this ship."

So now the passengers stood calmly on the Boat Deck—unworried but very confused. There had been no boat drill. The passengers had no boat assignments. The crew had assignments, but hardly anybody bothered to look at the list. Now they were playing it strictly by ear—yet somehow the crew seemed to sense where they were needed and how to be useful. The years of discipline were paying off.

Little knots of men swarmed over each boat, taking off the canvas covers, clearing the masts and useless paraphernalia, putting in lanterns and tins of biscuits. Other men stood at the davits, fitting in cranks and uncoiling the lines. One by one the cranks were turned. The davits creaked, the pulleys squealed, and the boats slowly swung out free of the ship. Next, a few feet of line were paid out, so that each boat would lie flush with the Boat Deck . . . or, in some cases, flush with Promenade Deck A directly below.

But the going was slow. Second Officer Lightoller, in charge of the port side, believed in channels, and Chief Officer Wilde seemed quite a bottleneck. When Lightoller asked permission to swing out, Wilde said, "No, wait." Lightoller finally went to the bridge and got orders direct from Captain Smith. Now Lightoller asked Wilde if he could load up. Again Wilde said no; again Lightoller went to the bridge; again Captain Smith gave him the nod: "Yes, put the women and children in and lower away."

Lightoller then lowered Boat 4 level with A Deck and ordered the women and children down to be loaded from there. It seemed safer that way—less chance of falling overboard, less distance to the water, and it helped clear the Boat Deck for hard work ahead. Too late he remembered the Promenade Deck was closed here and the windows were shut. While someone was sent to get the windows open, he hastily recalled everybody and moved aft to Boat 6.

With one foot in No. 6 and one on deck, Lightoller now called for women and children. The response was anything but enthusiastic. Why trade the bright decks of the *Titanic* for a few dark hours in a rowboat? Even John Jacob Astor ridiculed the idea: "We are safer here than in that little boat."

As Mrs. J. Stuart White climbed into No. 8, a friend called, "When you get back you'll need a pass. You can't get back on tomorrow morning without a pass!"

When Mrs. Constance Willard flatly refused to enter the boat, an exasperated officer finally shrugged, "Don't waste time—let her go if she won't get in!"

And there was music to lull them too. Bandmaster Wallace Henry Hartley had assembled his men, and the band was playing ragtime. Just now they stood in the First Class lounge, where many of the passengers waited before orders came to lower the boats. Later they moved to the Boat Deck forward, near the entrance to the grand staircase. They looked a little nondescript— some in blue uniform coats, some in white jackets—but there was nothing wrong with their music.

Everything had been done to give the *Titanic* the best band on the Atlantic. The White Star Line even raided the Cunarder *Mauretania* for Bandmaster Hartley. Pianist Theodore Brailey and cellist Roger Bricoux were easily wooed from the *Carpathia*. "Well, steward," they happily told Robert Vaughan who served them on the little Cunarder, "we will soon be on a decent ship with decent grub." Bass-violist Fred Clark had never shipped before, but he was well known on the Scotch concert circuit, and the line bought him away too. First violinist Jock Hume hadn't yet played in any concerts, but his fiddle had a gay note the passengers seemed to love. And so it went—eight fine musicians who knew just what to do. Tonight the beat was fast, the music loud and cheerful.

On the starboard side things moved a little faster. But not fast enough for President Ismay, who dashed to and fro, urging the men to hurry. "There's no time to lose!" he urged Third Officer Pitman, who was working on Boat 5. Pitman shrugged him off—he didn't know Ismay and he had no time for an officious stranger in carpet slippers. Ismay told him to load the boat with women and children. This was too much for Pitman: "I await the Commander's orders," he announced.

Suddenly it dawned on him who the stranger might be. He eased down the deck, gave his hunch to Captain Smith, and asked if he should do what Ismay wanted. Smith answered a crisp, "Carry on." Returning to No. 5, Pitman jumped in and called, "Come along, ladies!"

Mrs. Catherine Crosby and her daughter Harriet were firmly propelled into the boat by her husband, Captain Edward Gifford Crosby, a Milwaukee shipping man and an old Great Lakes skipper. Captain Crosby had a way of knowing things—right after the crash he scolded his wife, "You'll lie there and drown!" Later he told her, "This ship is badly damaged, but I think the watertight compartments will hold her up." Now he was taking no chances.

Slowly others edged forward—Miss Helen Ostby . . . Mrs. F. M. Warren . . . Mrs. Washington Dodge and her five-year-old son . . . a young stewardess. When no more women would go alone, a few couples were allowed. Then a few single men. On the starboard side this was the rule all evening —women first, but men if there still was room.

Just aft, First Officer Murdoch, in charge of the starboard side, was having the same trouble filling No. 7. Serial movie star Dorothy Gibson jumped in, followed by her mother. Then they persuaded their bridge companions of the evening, William Sloper and Fred Seward, to join them. Others trickled in, until there were finally 19 or 20 in the boat. Murdoch felt he could wait no longer. At 12:45 he waved away No. 7—the first boat down.

Then he ordered Pitman to take charge of No. 5, told him to hang around the after gangway, shook hands, and smiled, "Good-by, good luck."

As No. 5 creaked downward, Bruce Ismay was beside himself. "Lower away! Lower away! Lower away! Lower away!" he chanted, waving one arm in huge circles while hanging on to the davit with the other.

"If you'll get the hell out of the way," exploded Fifth Officer Lowe who was working the davits, "I'll be able to do something! You want me to lower away quickly? You'll have me drown the whole lot of them!"

Ismay was completely abashed. Without a word he turned and walked forward to No. 3.

Old-timers in the crew gasped. They felt Lowe's outburst was the most dramatic thing that could happen tonight. A Fifth Officer doesn't insult the President of the line and get away with it. When they reached New York, there would be a day of reckoning.

And nearly everyone still expected to reach New York. At worst, they would all be transferred to other ships.

"Peuchen," said Charles M. Hays as the Major began helping with the boats, "this ship is good for eight hours yet. I have just been getting this from one of the best old seamen, Mr. Crosby of Milwaukee."

Monsieur Gatti, *Maître* of the ship's *à la carte* French restaurant, was equally unperturbed. Standing alone on the Boat Deck, he seemed the picture of dignity—his top hat firmly in place, grip in hand, and a shawl traveling blanket folded neatly over his arm.

Mr. and Mrs. Lucien Smith and Mr. and Mrs. Sleeper Harper sat quietly chatting in the gym just off the Boat Deck. The mechanical horses were riderless now—the Astors had moved off somewhere else. And for once there was no one on the stationary bicycles, which the passengers liked to ride, pedaling red and blue arrows around a big white clock. But the room with its bright, blocked linoleum floor and the comfortable wicker chairs was far more pleasant than the Boat Deck. Certainly it was warmer, and there seemed no hurry.

In the nearly empty smoking room on A Deck, four men sat calmly around a table—Archie Butt, Clarence Moore, Frank Millet, and Arthur Ryerson seemed deliberately trying to avoid the noisy confusion of the Boat Deck.

Far below, Greaser Thomas Ranger began turning off some 45 electric fans used in the engine room, and he thought about the ones he had to repair tomorrow. Electrician Alfred White, working on the dynamos, brewed some coffee at his post.

At the very stern of the *Titanic*, Quartermaster George Thomas Rowe still paced his lonely watch. He had seen no one, heard nothing since the iceberg glided by nearly an hour ago. Suddenly he was amazed to see a lifeboat floating near the starboard side. He phoned the bridge—did they know there was a boat afloat? An incredulous voice asked who he was. Rowe explained, and the bridge then realized he had been overlooked. They told him to come to the bridge right away and bring some rockets with him. Rowe dropped down to a locker one deck below, picked up a tin box with 12 rockets inside, and clambered forward—the last man to learn what was going on.

Others knew all too well by now. Old Dr. O'Loughlin whispered to Stewardess Mary Sloan, "Child, things are very bad." Stewardess Annie Robinson stood near the mail room, watching the water rise on F Deck. As she puzzled over a man's Gladstone bag lying abandoned in the corridor, Carpenter Hutchinson arrived with a lead line in his hand—he looked bewildered, distracted, wildly upset. A little later Miss Robinson bumped into Thomas Andrews on A Deck. Andrews greeted her like a cross parent:

"I thought I told you to put your lifebelt on!"

"Yes," she replied, "but I thought it mean to wear it."

"Never mind that. Put it on; walk about; let the passengers see you."

"It looks rather mean."

"No, put it on . . . Well, if you value your life, put it on."

Andrews understood people very well. A charming, dynamic man, he was everywhere, helping everyone. And people naturally looked to him. He handled them differently, depending on what he thought of them. He told garrulous Steward Johnson that everything would be all right. He told Mr. and Mrs. Albert Dick, his casual dinner companions, "She is torn to bits below, but she will not sink if her after bulkheads hold." He told competent Stewardess Mary Sloan, "It is very serious, but keep the bad news quiet, for fear of panic." He told John B. Thayer, whom he trusted implicitly, that he didn't give the ship "much over an hour to live."

Some of the crew didn't need to be told. About 12:45, Able Seaman John Poingdestre left the Boat Deck to get his rubber boots. He found them in the forecastle on E Deck forward, and was just starting up again when the wooden wall between his quarters and some Third Class space to starboard suddenly gave way. The sea surged in, and he fought his way out through water up to his waist.

Further aft, Dining Saloon Steward Ray went to his quarters on E Deck to get a warmer overcoat. Coming back up, he went forward on "Scotland Road" toward the main staircase. The jostling firemen and Third Class passengers were gone now. All was quiet along the broad working alleyway, except for water sloshing along the corridor from somewhere forward.

Still further aft, Assistant Second Steward Joseph Thomas Wheat dropped down to pick up some valuables from his room on F Deck, port side. It was right next to the Turkish bath, a gloriously garish set of rooms that formed a sort of bridge between the Victorian and Rudolph Valentino eras of interior decoration. The mosaic floor, the blue-green tiled walls, the gilded beams in the dull red ceiling, the stanchions encased in carved teak—all were still perfectly dry.

But when Wheat walked a few yards down the corridor and started back up the stairs, he saw a strange sight: a thin stream of water was flowing *down* the stairs from E Deck above. It was only a quarter-inch deep—just about covered the heel of his shoe—as he splashed up the steps. When he reached E Deck, he saw it was coming from the starboard side forward.

He guessed what had happened: water forward on F Deck, blocked by the watertight compartment door, had risen to E Deck, where there was no door, and now was slopping over into the next compartment aft.

Boiler room No. 5 was the only place where everything seemed under control. After the fires were drawn, Lead Fireman Barrett sent most of the stokers up to their boat stations. He and a few others stayed behind to help Engineers Harvey and Shepherd with the pumps.

At Harvey's orders he lifted the iron manhole cover off the floor plates on the starboard side, so Harvey could get at the valves to adjust the pumps.

The boiler room was now clouding up with steam from the water used to wet down the furnaces. In the dim light of their own private Turkish bath, the men worked on . . . vague shapes moving about through the mist.

Then Shepherd, hurrying across the room, fell into the manhole and broke his leg. Harvey, Barrett, and Fireman George Kemish rushed over. They lifted him up and carried him to the pump room, a closed-off space at one end of the boiler room.

No time to do more than make him comfortable . . . then back into the clouds of steam. Soon orders came down from the bridge for all hands to report to boat stations. As the men went up, Shepherd still lay in the pump room; Barrett and Harvey kept working with the valves. Another 15 minutes and both men were beginning to cheer up—the room was still dry, the rhythm of the pumps was fast and smooth.

Suddenly the sea came roaring through the space between the boilers at the forward end of the room. The whole bulkhead between No. 5 and No. 6 collapsed.

Harvey shouted to Barrett to make for the escape ladder. Barrett scrambled up, the foam surging around his feet. Harvey himself turned toward the pump room where Shepherd lay. He was still heading there when he disappeared under the torrent of rising water.

The silence in the Marconi shack was broken only by the rasping spark of the wireless, as Phillips rapped out his call for help and took down the answers that bounced back. Bride was still struggling into his clothes, between dashes to the bridge.

So far the news was encouraging. First to reply was the North German Lloyd steamer *Frankfort*. At 12:18 she sent a crisp "OK . . . Stand by"— but no position. In another minute acknowledgments were pouring in—the Canadian Pacific's *Mt. Temple* . . . the Allan liner *Virginian* . . . the Russian passenger steamer *Birma*.

The night crackled with signals. Ships out of direct contact got the word from those within range . . . The news spread in ever-widening circles. Cape Race heard it directly and relayed it inland. On the roof of Wanamaker's department store in New York, a young wireless operator named David Sarnoff caught a faint signal and also passed it on. The whole world was snapping to agonized attention.

Close at hand, the Cunarder *Carpathia* steamed southward in complete ignorance. Her single wireless operator, Harold Thomas Cottam, was on the bridge when Phillips sent his CQD. Now Cottam was back at his set and thought he'd be helpful. Did the *Titanic* know, he casually asked, that there were some private messages waiting for her from Cape Race?

It was 12:25 when Phillips tapped back an answer that brushed aside the *Carpathia's* courteous gesture: "Come at once. We have struck a berg. It's a CQD, old man. Position 41.46 N 50.14 W."

A moment of appalled silence . . . then Cottam asked whether to tell his captain. Phillips: "Yes, quick." Another five minutes and welcome news —the *Carpathia* was only 58 miles away and "coming hard."

At 12:34 it was the *Frankfort* again—she was 150 miles away. Phillips asked, "Are you coming to our assistance?" *Frankfort:* "What is the matter with you?" Phillips: "Tell your captain to come to our help. We are on the ice."

Captain Smith now dropped into the shack for a firsthand picture. The *Olympic*, the *Titanic's* huge sister ship, was just chiming in. She was 500 miles away; but her set was powerful, she could handle a major rescue job, and there was a strong bond between the two liners. Phillips kept in close touch, while urging on the ships that were nearer.

"What call are you sending?" Smith asked.

"CQD," Phillips answered noncommittally.

Bride had a bright idea. While CQD was the traditional distress call, an international convention had just agreed to use instead the letters SOS— they were easy for the rankest amateur to pick up. So Bride suggested, "Send SOS; it's the new call, and it may be your last chance to send it."

Phillips laughed at the joke and switched the call. The clock in the wireless shack said 12:45 A.M. when the *Titanic* sent the first SOS in history.

None of the ships contacted seemed as promising as the light that winked ten miles off the *Titanic's* port bow. Through his binoculars Fourth Officer Boxhall saw clearly that it was a steamer. Once, as he tried to get in touch with the Morse lamp, he felt he saw an answer. But he could make nothing of it and finally decided it must be her mast light flickering.

Stronger measures were necessary. As soon as Quartermaster Rowe reached the bridge, Captain Smith asked if he brought the rockets. Rowe produced them, and the Captain ordered, "Fire one, and fire one every five or six minutes."

At 12:45 a blinding flash seared the night. The first rocket shot up from the starboard side of the bridge. Up . . . up it soared, far above the lacework of masts and rigging. Then with a distant, muffled report it burst, and a shower of bright white stars floated slowly down toward the sea. In the blue-white light Fifth Officer Lowe remembered catching a glimpse of Bruce Ismay's startled face.

Ten miles away, Apprentice James Gibson stood on the bridge of the *Californian*. The strange ship that came up from the east had not moved for an hour, and Gibson studied her with interest. With glasses he could make out her side lights and a glare of lights on her afterdeck. At one point he thought she was trying to signal the *Californian* with her Morse lamp. He tried to answer with his own lamp, but soon gave up. He decided the stranger's masthead light was merely flickering.

Second Officer Herbert Stone, pacing the *Californian's* bridge, also kept his eye on this strange steamer. At 12:45 he saw a sudden flash of white light burst over her. Strange, he thought, that a ship would fire rockets at night.

#### 4. *"You Go and I'll Stay a While"*

Second Class passenger Lawrence Beesley considered himself the rankest landlubber, but even he knew what rockets meant. The *Titanic* needed help —needed it so badly she was calling on any ship near enough to see.

The others on the Boat Deck understood too. There was no more joking or lingering. In fact, there was hardly time to say good-by.

"It's all right, little girl," called Dan Marvin to his new bride; "you go and I'll stay a while." He blew her a kiss as she entered the boat.

"I'll see you later," Adolf Dyker smiled as he helped Mrs. Dyker across the gunwale.

"Be brave; no matter what happens, be brave," Dr. W. T. Minahan told Mrs. Minahan as he stepped back with the other men.

Mr. Turrell Cavendish said nothing to Mrs. Cavendish. Just a kiss . . . a long look . . . another kiss . . . and he disappeared into the crowd.

Mark Fortune took his wife's valuables, as he and his son Charles saw off Mrs. Fortune and their three daughters. "I'll take care of them; we're going in the next boat," he explained. "Charles, take care of Father," one of the girls called back to her brother.

"Walter, you must come with me," begged Mrs. Walter D. Douglas.

"No," Mr. Douglas replied, turning away, "I must be a gentleman."

"Try and get off with Major Butt and Mr. Moore," came a final bit of wifely advice; "They are big, strong fellows and will surely make it."

Some of the wives still refused to go. Mr. and Mrs. Edgar Meyer of New York felt so self-conscious arguing about it in public that they went down to their cabin. There, they decided to part on account of their baby.

Arthur Ryerson had to lay down the law to Mrs. Ryerson: "You must obey orders. When they say 'Women and children to the boats,' you *must* go when your turn comes. I'll stay here with Jack Thayer. We'll be all right."

Alexander T. Compton, Jr., was just as firm when his mother announced she would stay rather than leave him behind: "Don't be foolish, Mother. You and Sister go in the boat—I'll look out for myself."

Mr. and Mrs. Lucien Smith were having the same kind of argument. Seeing Captain Smith standing near with a megaphone, Mrs. Smith had an inspiration. She went up to him, explained she was all alone in the world, and asked if her husband could go along with her. The old Captain ignored her, lifted his megaphone and shouted, "Women and children first!"

At this point Mr. Smith broke in: "Never mind, Captain, about that; I'll see she gets in the boat." Turning to his wife, he spoke very slowly: "I never expected to ask you to obey, but this is one time you must. It is only a matter of form to have women and children first. The ship is thoroughly equipped and everyone on her will be saved."

Mrs. Smith asked him if he was being completely truthful. Mr. Smith gave a firm, decisive, "Yes." So they kissed good-by, and as the boat dropped to the sea, he called from the deck, "Keep your hands in your pockets; it is very cold weather."

Sometimes it took more than gentle deception. Mrs. Emil Taussig was clinging to her husband when No. 8 started down with her daughter. Mrs. Taussig turned and cried, "Ruth!" The brief distraction proved enough: two men tore her from Mr. Taussig and dropped her into the lowering boat.

A seaman yanked Mrs. Charlotte Collyer by the arm, another by her waist, and they dragged her from her husband Harvey. As she kicked to get free, she heard him call, "Go, Lottie! For God's sake, be brave and go! I'll get a seat in another boat!"

When Celiney Yasbeck saw she had to go alone, she began yelling and crying to rejoin Mr. Yasbeck, but the boat dropped to the sea while she tried in vain to get out.

No amount of persuasion or force could move Mrs. Hudson J. Allison of Montreal. A little apart from the rest, she huddled close to Mr. Allison, while their small daughter Lorraine tugged at her skirt.

Mrs. Isidor Straus also refused to go: "I've always stayed with my husband; so why should I leave him now?"

They had indeed come a long way together: the ashes of the Confederacy . . . the small china business in Philadelphia . . . building Macy's into a national institution . . . Congress . . . and now the happy twilight that crowned a successful life—advisory boards, charities, hobbies, travel. This winter they had been to Cap Martin, and the *Titanic's* maiden voyage seemed a pleasant way to finish the trip.

Tonight the Strauses came on deck with the others, and at first Mrs. Straus seemed uncertain what to do. At one point she handed some small jewelry to her maid Ellen Bird, then took it back again. Later she crossed the Boat Deck and almost entered No. 8—then turned around and rejoined Mr. Straus. Now her mind was made up: "We have been living together for many years. Where you go, I go."

Archibald Gracie, Hugh Woolner, other friends tried in vain to make her go. Then Woolner turned to Mr. Straus: "I'm sure nobody would object to an old gentleman like you getting in . . ."

"I will not go before the other men," he said, and that was that. Then he and Mrs. Straus sat down together on a pair of deck chairs.

But most of the women entered the boats—wives escorted by their husbands, single ladies by the men who had volunteered to look out for them. This was the era when gentlemen formally offered their services to "unprotected ladies" at the start of an Atlantic voyage. Tonight the courtesy came in handy.

Mrs. William T. Graham, 19-year-old Margaret, and her governess Miss Shutes were helped into Boat 8 by Howard Case, London manager of Vacuum Oil, and young Washington Augustus Roebling, the steel heir who was striking out on his own as manager of the Mercer Automobile Works in Trenton, New Jersey. As No. 8 dropped to the sea, Mrs. Graham watched Case, leaning against the rail, light a cigarette and wave good-by.

Mrs. E. D. Appleton, Mrs. R. C. Cornell, Mrs. J. Murray Brown and Miss Edith Evans, returning from a family funeral in Britain, were under Colonel Gracie's wing, but somehow in the crowd he lost them, and it wasn't until much later that he found them again.

Perhaps the Colonel was distracted by his simultaneous efforts to look after Mrs. Churchill Candee, his table companion in the dining saloon. Mrs. Candee was returning from Paris to see her son, who had suffered the novelty of an airplane accident, and she must have been attractive indeed. Just about everybody wanted to protect her.

When Edward A. Kent, another table companion, found her after the crash, she gave him an ivory miniature of her mother for safekeeping. Then Hugh Woolner and Bjornstrom Steffanson arrived and helped her into Boat 6. Woolner waved good-by, assuring her that they would help her on board again when the *Titanic* "steadied herself." A little later Gracie and Clinch Smith dashed up, also in search of Mrs. Candee, but Woolner told them, perhaps a little smugly, that she had been cared for and was safely away.

It was just as well, for the slant in the deck was steeper, and even the carefree were growing uneasy. Some who left everything in their cabins now thought better of it and ventured below to get their valuables. They were in for unpleasant surprises. Celiney Yasbeck found her room was completely under water. Gus Cohen discovered the same thing. Victorine, the Ryersons' French maid, had an even more disturbing experience. She found her cabin still dry, but as she rummaged about, she heard a key turn, suddenly realized the steward was locking the stateroom door to prevent looting. Her shriek was just in time to keep him from locking her in. Without stretching her luck any further, she dashed back on deck empty-handed.

Time was clearly running out. Thomas Andrews walked from boat to boat, urging the women to hurry: "Ladies, you *must* get in at once. There is not a moment to lose. You cannot pick and choose your boat. Don't hesitate. Get in, get in!"

Andrews had good reason to be exasperated. Women were never more unpredictable. One girl waiting to climb into No. 8 suddenly cried out, "I've forgotten Jack's photograph and must get it." Everybody protested, but she darted below. In a moment she reappeared with the picture and was rushed into the boat.

It was all so urgent—and yet so calm—that Second Officer Lightoller felt he was wasting time when Chief Officer Wilde asked him to help find the firearms. Quickly he led the Captain, Wilde, and First Officer Murdoch to the locker where they were kept. Wilde shoved one of the guns into Lightoller's hand, remarking, "You may need it." Lightoller stuck it in his pocket and hurried back to the boat.

One after another they now dropped rapidly into the sea: No. 6 at 12:55 . . . No. 3 at 1:00 . . . No. 8 at 1:10. Watching them go, First Class passenger William Carter advised Harry Widener to try for a boat. Widener shook his head: "I think I'll stick to the big ship, Billy, and take a chance."

Some of the crew weren't as optimistic. When Assistant Second Steward Wheat noticed Chief Steward Latimer wearing his lifebelt over his greatcoat, he urged the Chief to put it under the coat—this made swimming easier.

On the bridge, as Fourth Officer Boxhall and Quartermaster Rowe fired off more rockets, Boxhall still couldn't believe what was happening. "Captain," he asked, "is it *really* serious?"

"Mr. Andrews tells me," Smith answered quietly, "that he gives her from an hour to an hour and a half."

Lightoller had a more tangible yardstick—the steep, narrow emergency staircase that ran from the Boat Deck all the way down to E Deck. The water was slowly crawling up the stairs, and from time to time Lightoller walked over to the entrance and checked the number of steps it had climbed. He could see very easily, for the lights still gleamed under the pale green water.

His gauge showed time was flying. The pace grew faster—and sloppier. A pretty French girl stumbled and fell as she tried to climb into No. 9. An older woman in a black dress missed No. 10 entirely. She fell between the bow and the side of the ship. But as the crowd gasped, someone miraculously caught her ankle. Others hauled her into the Promenade Deck below, and she climbed back to the Boat Deck for another try. This time she made it.

Some of them lost their nerve. An old lady made a big fuss at No. 9, finally shook off everybody, and ran away from the boat altogether. A hysterical woman thrashed about helplessly, trying to climb into No. 11. Steward Witter stood on the rail to help her, but she lost her footing anyway, and they tumbled into the boat together. A large fat woman stood crying near No. 13: "Don't put me in the boat. I don't want to go into the boat! I have never been in an open boat in my life!"

Steward Ray brushed aside her protests—"You've got to go, and you may as well keep quiet."

A plan to fill some of the boats from the lower gangways went completely haywire. The doors that were to be used were never opened. The boats that were to stand by rowed off. The people who were to go were left stranded. When the Caldwells and several others went all the way down to a closed gangway on C Deck, somebody who didn't know about the plan locked the door behind them. Later some men on the deck above discovered the group and lowered a ladder for them to crawl back up.

A shortage of trained seamen made the confusion worse. Some of the best men had been used to man the early boats. Other old hands were off on special jobs—rounding up lanterns, opening the A Deck windows, helping fire the rockets. Six seamen were lost when they went down to open one of the lower gangways; they never came back . . . probably trapped far below. Now Lightoller was rationing the hands he had left—only two crewmen to a lifeboat.

No. 6 was halfway down when a woman called up to the Boat Deck, "We've only one seaman in the boat!"

"Any seamen there?" Lightoller asked the people on deck.

"If you like, I will go," called a voice from the crowd.

"Are you a seaman?"

"I am a yachtsman."

"If you're sailor enough to get out on that fall, you can go down." Major Arthur Godfrey Peuchen—vice-commodore of the Royal Canadian Yacht Club—swung himself out on the forward fall and slid down into the boat. He was the only male passenger Lightoller allowed in a boat that night.

Men had it luckier on the starboard side. Murdoch continued to allow them in if there was room. The French aviator Pierre Maréchal and sculptor Paul Chevré climbed into No. 7. A couple of Gimbels buyers reached No. 5. When the time came to lower No. 3, Henry Sleeper Harper not only joined his wife, but he brought along his Pekingese Sun Yat-sen and an Egyptian dragoman named Hamad Hassah, whom he had picked up in Cairo as a sort of joke.

On the same side, Dr. Washington Dodge was standing uncertainly in the shadow of No. 13, when Dining Room Steward Ray noticed him. Ray asked whether the doctor's wife and son were off, and Dodge said yes. Ray was relieved, because he took a personal interest in them. He had served the Dodges coming over on the *Olympic*. In fact, he had persuaded them to take the *Titanic* back. In a way, he was why the Dodges were on board . . . It was no time for philosophy—Ray called out, "You had better get in here," and he pushed the doctor into the boat.

The scene was almost punctilious at No. 1. Sir Cosmo Duff Gordon, his wife and her secretary Miss Francatelli—whom Lady Duff Gordon liked to call Miss Franks—asked Murdoch if they could enter.

"Oh certainly do; I'll be very pleased," Murdoch replied, according to Sir Cosmo. (On the other hand, Lookout George Symons, standing near, thought Murdoch merely said, "Yes, jump in.") Then two Americans, Abraham Solomon and C. E. H. Stengel, came up and were invited in too. Stengel had trouble climbing over the rail; finally got on top of it and rolled into the boat. Murdoch, an agile terrier of a man, laughed pleasantly, "That's the funniest thing I've seen tonight."

Nobody else seemed to be around—all the nearby boats were gone and the crowd had moved aft. When the five passengers were safely loaded, Murdoch added six stokers, put Lookout Symons in charge and told him, "Stand off from the ship's side and return when we call you." Then he waved to the men at the davits, and they lowered No. 1—capacity 40 persons—with exactly 12 people.

As the boat creaked down, Greaser Walter Hurst watched it from the forward well deck. He remembers observing somewhat caustically, "If they are sending the boats away, they might just as well put some people in them."

Down in Third Class there were those who didn't even have the opportunity to miss going in No. 1. A swarm of men and women milled around the foot of the main steerage staircase, all the way aft on E Deck. They had been there ever since the stewards got them up. At first there were just women and married couples; but then the men arrived from forward, pouring back along "Scotland Road" with their luggage. Now they were all jammed together—noisy and restless, looking more like inmates than passengers amid the low ceilings, the naked light bulbs, the scrubbed simplicity of the plain white walls.

Third Class Steward John Edward Hart struggled to get them into life jackets. He didn't have much luck—partly because he was also assuring them there was no danger, partly because many of them didn't understand English anyhow. Interpreter Muller did the best he could with the scores of Finns and Swedes, but it was slow going.

At 12:30 orders came down to send the women and children up to the Boat Deck. It was hopeless to expect them to find their way alone through the maze of passages normally sealed off from Third Class; so Hart decided to escort them up in little groups. This took time too, but at last a convoy was organized and started off.

It was a long trip—up the broad stairs to the Third Class lounge on C Deck . . . across the open well deck . . . by the Second Class library and into First Class quarters. Then down the long corridor by the surgeon's office, the private saloon for the maids and valets of First Class passengers, finally up the grand stairway to the Boat Deck.

Hart led his group to Boat No. 8, but even then the job wasn't over. As fast as he got them in, they would jump out and go inside where it was warm.

It was after one o'clock when Hart got back to E Deck to organize another trip. It was no easier. Many women still refused to go. On the other hand, some of the men now insisted on going. But that was out of the question, according to the orders he had.

Finally he was off again on the same long trek. It was 1:20 by the time he reached the Boat Deck and led the group to No. 15. No time to go back for more. Murdoch ordered him into the boat and off he went with his second batch at about 1:30.

There was no hard-and-fast policy. One way or another, many of the steerage passengers avoided the *cul de sac* on E Deck and got topside. There they stood waiting, nobody to guide or help them. A few of the barriers that marked off their quarters were down. Those who came across these openings wandered into other parts of the ship. Some eventually found their way to the Boat Deck.

But most of the barriers were not down, and the steerage passengers who sensed danger and aimed for the boats were strictly on their own resources.

Like a stream of ants, a thin line of them curled their way up a crane in the after well deck, crawled along the boom to the First Class quarters, then over the railing and on up to the Boat Deck.

Some slipped under a rope that had been stretched across the after well deck, penning them even further to the stern than the regular barrier. But once through, it was fairly easy to get to the Second Class stairway and on up to the boats.

Others somehow reached the Second Class promenade space on B Deck, then couldn't find their way any further. In desperation they turned to an emergency ladder meant for the crew's use. This ladder was near the brightly lit windows of the First Class *à la carte* restaurant, and as Anna Sjoblom prepared to climb up with another girl, they looked in. They marveled at the tables beautifully set with silver and china for the following day. The other girl had an impulse to kick the window out and go inside, but Anna persuaded her that the company might make them pay for the damage.

Many of the steerage men climbed another emergency ladder from the forward well deck, and then up the regular First Class companionway to the boats.

Others beat on the barriers, demanding to be let through. As Third Class passenger Daniel Buckley climbed some steps leading to a gate to First Class, the man ahead of him was chucked down by a seaman standing guard. Furious, the passenger jumped to his feet and raced up the steps again. The seaman took one look, locked the gate and fled. The passenger smashed the lock and dashed through, howling what he would do if he caught the sailor. With the gate down, Buckley and dozens of others swarmed into First Class.

At another barrier a seaman held back Kathy Gilnagh, Kate Mullins and Kate Murphy. (On the *Titanic* all Irish girls seemed to be named Katherine.) Suddenly steerage passenger Jim Farrell, a strapping Irishman from the girls' home county, barged up. "Great God, man!" he roared. "Open the gate and let the girls through!" It was a superb demonstration of sheer voice-power. To the girls' astonishment the sailor meekly complied.

But for every steerage passenger who found a way up, hundreds milled aimlessly around the forward well deck . . . the after poop deck . . . or the foot of the E Deck staircase. Some holed up in their cabins—that's where Mary Agatha Glynn and four discouraged roommates were found by young Martin Gallagher. He quickly escorted them to Boat 13 and stepped back on the deck again. Others turned to prayer. When steerage passenger Gus Cohen passed the Third Class dining saloon about an hour after the crash, he saw quite a number gathered there, many with rosaries in their hands.

The staff of the First Class *à la carte* restaurant were having the hardest time of all. They were neither fish nor fowl. Obviously they weren't passengers, but technically they weren't crew either. The restaurant was not run by the White Star Line but by Monsieur Gatti as a concession.

Thus, the employees had no status at all. And to make matters worse, they were French and Italian—objects of deep Anglo-Saxon suspicion at a time like this in 1912.

From the very start they never had a chance. Steward Johnson remembered seeing them herded together down by their quarters on E Deck aft.

Manager Gatti, his Chef and the Chef's Assistant, Paul Maugé, were the only ones who made it to the Boat Deck. They got through because they happened to be in civilian clothes; the crew thought they were passengers.

Down in the engine room no one even thought of getting away. Men struggled desperately to keep the steam up . . . the lights lit . . . the pumps going. Chief Engineer Bell had all the watertight doors raised aft of Boiler Room No. 4—when the water reached here they could be lowered again; meanwhile it would be easier to move around.

Greaser Fred Scott worked to free a shipmate trapped in the after tunnel behind one of the doors. Greaser Thomas Ranger turned off the last of the 45 ventilating fans—they used too much electricity. Trimmer Thomas Patrick Dillon helped drag long sections of pipe from the aft compartments, to get more volume out of the suction pump in boiler room No. 4.

Here, Trimmer George Cavell was busy drawing the fires. This meant even less power, but there must be no explosion when the sea reached No. 4. It was about 1:20 and the job was almost done when he noticed the water seeping up through the metal floor plates. Cavell worked faster. When it reached his knees, he had enough. He was almost at the top of the escape ladder when he began to feel he had quit on his mates. Down again, only to find they were gone too. His conscience clear, he climbed back up, this time for good.

Most of the boats were now gone. One by one they rowed slowly away from the *Titanic*, oars bumping and splashing in the glass-smooth sea.

"I never had an oar in my hand before, but I think I can row," a steward told Mrs. J. Stuart White, as No. 8 set out.

In every boat all eyes were glued on the *Titanic*. Her tall masts, the four big funnels stood out sharp and black in the clear blue night. The bright promenade decks, the long rows of portholes all blazed with light. From the boats they could see the people lining the rails; they could hear the ragtime in the still night air. It seemed impossible that anything could be wrong with this great ship; yet there they were out on the sea, and there she was, well down at the head. Brilliantly lit from stem to stern, she looked like a sagging birthday cake.

Clumsily the boats moved further away. Those told to stand by now lay on their oars. Others, told to make for the steamer whose lights shone in the distance, began their painful journey.

The steamer seemed agonizingly near. So near that Captain Smith told the people in Boat 8 to go over, land its passengers, and come back for more. About the same time he asked Quartermaster Rowe at the rocket gun if he could Morse. Rowe replied he could a little, and the Captain said, "Call that ship up and when she replies, tell her, 'We are the *Titanic* sinking; please have all your boats ready.'"

Boxhall had already tried to reach her, but Rowe was more than eager to try his own luck; so in between rocket firing he called her again and again. Still no answer. Then Rowe told Captain Smith he thought he saw another light on the starboard quarter. The old skipper squinted through his glasses, courteously told Rowe that it was a planet. But he liked the eagerness of his young Quartermaster, and he lent Rowe the glasses to see for himself.

Meanwhile Boxhall continued firing rockets. Sooner or later, somehow they would wake up the stranger.

On the bridge of the *Californian*, Second Officer Stone and Apprentice Gibson counted the rockets—five by 12:55. Gibson tried his Morse lamp again, and at one o'clock lifted his glasses for another look. He was just in time to see a sixth rocket.

At 1:10 Stone whistled down the speaking tube to the chart room and told Captain Lord. He called back, "Are they company signals?"

"I don't know," Stone answered, "but they appear to me to be white rockets."

The Captain advised him to go on Morsing.

A little later Stone handed his glasses to Gibson, remarking: "Have a look at her now. She looks very queer out of the water—her lights look queer."

Gibson studied the ship carefully. She seemed to be listing. She had, as he called it, "a big side out of the water." And Stone, standing beside him, noticed that her red side light had disappeared.

## 5. "I Believe She's Gone, Hardy"

The other ships just didn't seem to understand. At 1:25 the *Olympic* asked, "Are you steering south to meet us?" Phillips patiently explained, "We are putting the women off in the boats."

Then the *Frankfort*: "Are there any ships around you already?" Phillips ignored this one. Again the *Frankfort*, asking for more details. This was too much. He jumped up, almost screaming: "The damn fool! He says, 'What's up, old man?'" Then he angrily tapped back: "You fool, stand by and keep out."

From time to time Captain Smith dropped in—once to warn that the power was fading . . . again to say she couldn't last much longer . . . later to report that the water had reached the engine room. At 1:45, Phillips begged the *Carpathia*: "Come as quickly as possible, old man; engine room filling up to the boilers."

Meanwhile Bride draped an overcoat over Phillips' shoulders, then managed to strap a lifebelt on him. The problem of getting him into his boots was more complicated. Phillips asked whether any boats were left— maybe the boots wouldn't be needed.

Once he turned the set over to Bride and went out to see what was happening. He returned shaking his head: "Things look very queer."

They looked queer indeed. The sea now slopped over the *Titanic's* forward well deck . . . rippled around the cranes, the hatches, the foot of the mast . . . washed against the base of the white superstructure. The roar of steam had died, the nerve-racking rockets had stopped—but the slant of the deck was steeper and there was an ugly list to port.

About 1:40, Chief Officer Wilde shouted, "Everyone on the starboard side to straighten her up!" Passengers and crew trooped over, and the *Titanic* swung sluggishly back on even keel. The work on the boats resumed.

As No. 2 prepared to cast off at 1:45, Steward Johnson, his pockets bulging with oranges, yelled up to the Boat Deck for a razor to cut the falls. Seaman McAuliffe dropped one down, calling, "Remember me at Southampton and give it to me back!" McAuliffe was probably the last man on the *Titanic* so sure of returning to Southampton.

First Officer Murdoch knew better. As he walked along the deck with Chief Steward Hardy of Second Class, he sighed, "I believe she's gone, Hardy."

There was no longer any difficulty persuading people to leave the ship. Paul Maugé, the chef's assistant, jumped 10 feet into a dangling boat. Somebody on a lower deck tried to drag him out, but he squirmed free and was safe.

Third Class passenger Daniel Buckley—safely through the broken gate and onto the Boat Deck—took no more chances. With several other men he jumped into a boat and huddled there crying. Most of the men were hauled out, but somewhere he got a woman's shawl. He said Mrs. Astor put it over him. In any case, the disguise worked.

Another young man—no more than a boy, wasn't as lucky. Fifth Officer Lowe caught him under a seat in No. 14, begging that he wouldn't take up much room. Lowe drew his gun, but the boy only pleaded harder. Then Lowe changed tactics, told him to be a man, and somehow got him out. By now Mrs. Charlotte Collyer and other women in the boat were sobbing, and her eight-year-old daughter Marjory joined the uproar, tugging at Lowe's arm and crying, "Oh, Mr. Man, don't shoot, please don't shoot the poor man!"

Lowe paused long enough to smile and nod at her reassuringly. The boy was out now, anyhow, lying face down near a coil of rope.

But No. 14's troubles weren't over. Another wave of men rushed the boat. Seaman Scarrott beat them back with the tiller. This time Lowe pulled his gun and shouted, "If anyone else tries that, this is what he'll get!" He fired three times along the side of the ship as the boat dropped down to the sea.

Murdoch barely stopped a rush at No. 15. He yelled at the crowd, "Stand back! Stand back! It's women first!"

All the way forward, there was more trouble at Collapsible C, which had been fitted into the davits used by No. 1. A big mob pushed and shoved, trying to climb aboard.

Two men dropped in. Purser Herbert McElroy fired twice into the air. Murdoch shouted, "Get out of this! Clear out of this!" Hugh Woolner and Bjornstrom Steffanson—attracted by the pistol flashes—rushed over to help.

Yanking the culprits by arms, legs, anything, they cleared the boat. The loading continued.

Jack Thayer stood off to one side with Milton Long, a young shipboard acquaintance from Springfield, Massachusetts. They had met for the first time this evening over after-dinner coffee. Following the crash, Long—who was traveling alone—attached himself to the Thayer family, but he and Jack lost the older Thayers in the crowd on A Deck. Now they were alone, debating what to do, supposing the rest of the family was already off in the boats. They finally decided to stay clear of Boat C. With all the uproar, it seemed bound to tip over.

But they were wrong. Things gradually straightened out, and finally Boat C was ready for lowering. Chief Officer Wilde shouted to know who was in command. Hearing him, Captain Smith turned to Quartermaster Rowe—still fiddling with the Morse lamp—and told him to take charge. Rowe jumped in and got ready to lower.

Close by, President Bruce Ismay stood, helping get the boat ready for lowering. He was calmer now than in those early moments when Lowe had bawled him out—in fact he seemed every inch an accepted member of the Titanic's crew.

This was a frequent role for Ismay, but by no means his only one. Sometimes he preferred the role of passenger. So far during the voyage he had shifted back and forth several times.

At Queenstown he was a sort of super-Captain. He told Chief Engineer Bell the speed he wanted for various stages of the voyage. He also set the New York arrival time at Wednesday morning, instead of Tuesday night. He didn't consult Captain Smith on this.

Later, at sea, Ismay was mostly a passenger, enjoying the fine cuisine of the à la carte restaurant . . . shuffleboard . . . bridge . . . tea and scones in his deck chair on the port side of A Deck.

This Sunday he was enough of a member of the crew to see the ice message that arrived from another ship. In the bright, sunny Palm Court—just as the bugler sounded lunch—Captain Smith gave him a warning from the Baltic. During the afternoon Ismay (who liked to remind people who he was) fished it out of his pocket and waved it at Mrs. Ryerson and Mrs. Thayer. In the smoking room before dinner, while the twilight still glowed through the amber-stained windows, Captain Smith sought and got the message back. Then Ismay walked down to the restaurant, immaculate in his dinner jacket, very much a First Class passenger.

After the crash he went back to being in the crew—up with the Captain on the bridge . . . consulting with Chief Engineer Bell . . . and now, despite the tongue-lashing from Fifth Officer Lowe, shouting orders about the boats.

Then came another switch. At the very last moment he suddenly climbed into Boat C. Down it dropped, with 42 people including Bruce Ismay—just another passenger.

Most of the passengers were different. William T. Stead, independent as ever, sat reading alone in the First Class smoking room. To Fireman Kemish passing by, he looked as though he planned to stay there whatever happened.

Reverend Robert J. Bateman of Jacksonville stood outside, watching his sister-in-law Mrs. Ada Balls enter a boat. "If I don't meet you again in this world," he called, "I will in the next." Then as the boat jerked down, he took off his necktie and tossed it to her as a keepsake.

George Widener and John B. Thayer leaned against the Boat Deck rail, quietly talking things over. Contrary to young Jack's guess, his father wasn't safe in a boat and, in fact, didn't have any idea of entering one. A little way off, Archie Butt, Clarence Moore, Arthur Ryerson and Walter Douglas stood silently together. Major Butt was very quiet, had no pistol, took no active part, despite the stories later told that he practically took charge.

Further aft, Jay Yates—described as a gambler hoping to make a maiden-voyage killing—stood alone and friendless. To a woman entering a boat, he handed a page torn from his appointment book. Signed with one of his aliases, the note read, "If saved, inform my sister Mrs. F. J. Adams of Findlay, Ohio. Lost. J. H. Rogers."

Benjamin Guggenheim had a more detailed message: "If anything should happen to me, tell my wife I've done my best in doing my duty."

Actually Guggenheim almost outdid himself. Gone was the sweater that Steward Etches made him wear. Also his lifebelt. Instead he and his secretary now stood resplendent in evening clothes. "We've dressed in our best," he explained, "and are prepared to go down like gentlemen."

There were a few couples too. The Allisons stood smiling on the Promenade Deck, Mrs. Allison grasping little Lorraine with one hand, her husband with the other. The Strauses leaned against the Boat Deck rail, their arms about each other's waist. A young Western couple waited nearby; when Lightoller asked the girl if he could put her in a boat, she told him cheerfully, "Not on your life. We started together and, if need be, we'll finish together."

Archibald Gracie, Clinch Smith, a dozen other First Class men worked with the crew, loading the last boats. As they helped Miss Constance Willard of Duluth, Minnesota, they smiled and told her to be brave. She noticed great beads of sweat stood out on their foreheads.

Lightoller was sweating too. He peeled off his greatcoat. Even in sweater and pajamas, he was wringing wet from hard work. He looked so odd on this bitter-cold night that Assistant Surgeon Simpson, always a wag, called out, "Hello, Lights, are you warm?"

The Assistant Surgeon was with old Dr. O'Loughlin, Purser McElroy, and Assistant Purser Barker. Lightoller joined them for a moment. They all shook hands and said, "Good-by."

No time for more. A glance down the emergency stairway told Lightoller the water was now on C Deck . . . rising fast. But the lights were still bright . . . the music still ragtime . . . the beat still lively.

Only two more boats. One of them, No. 4, had been a headache all night. Over an hour ago Lightoller lowered it to A Deck, planning to fill it from there, but the windows were all closed. Then, someone noticed the *Titanic's* sounding spar stuck out directly below the boat. Seaman Sam Parks and Storekeeper Jack Foley went down to chop it away, but they had trouble finding an ax. Time was wasting. Lightoller hurried on to the other boats—he'd load this one later.

Meanwhile the passengers waiting to go in No. 4 cooled their heels. And they were very prominent heels. The Astors, Wideners, Thayers, Carters and Ryersons were sticking pretty much together. When Lightoller first ordered the boat loaded, wives, children, maids, and nurses went down to the Promenade Deck to get in as a group. When they found they couldn't, they just stayed put.

Eventually most of the husbands turned up, and for over an hour the cream of New York and Philadelphia society just waited around while the windows were opened and the sounding spar chopped away. Once they were ordered back up to the Boat Deck, but then Second Steward Dodd sent them right down again. Exasperated, Mrs. Thayer exclaimed, "Just tell us where to go and we will follow! You ordered us up here and now you're sending us back!"

It was 1:45 when Lightoller returned. Now he stood—one foot in No. 4, the other on an open window sill. Somebody put deck chairs against the rail to serve as steps. The men stood by to pass the women and children through the windows.

John Jacob Astor helped Mrs. Astor across the frame, then asked if he could join her. She was, as he put it, "in delicate condition."

"No, sir," Lightoller replied. "No men are allowed in these boats until the women are loaded first."

Astor asked which boat it was, and Lightoller said, "Number 4." Colonel Gracie was sure Astor merely wanted to locate his wife later. Lightoller was sure he planned to make a complaint.

Then came the Ryersons' turn. Arthur Ryerson noticed their French maid Victorine had no lifebelt. Quickly he stripped off his own and buckled it on her. When Mrs. Ryerson led her son Jack to the window, Lightoller called out, "That boy can't go!"

Mr. Ryerson indignantly stepped forward: "Of course that boy goes with his Mother—he is only 13." So they let him pass, Lightoller grumbling, "No more boys."

At 1:55, No. 4 dropped to the sea—just 15 feet below. Mrs. Ryerson was shocked to see how far the ship had sunk. She watched the water pour in the big square ports on C Deck, sweep around the period furniture of the de-luxe suites. Then she looked up at the Promenade Deck. Mr. Ryerson was still standing by the rail with Mr. Widener, looking down at the boat. They seemed very quiet.

Only one boat left. Collapsible D had now been fitted into the davits used by No. 2 and was ready for loading. There was no time to spare. The lights were beginning to glow red. Chinaware was breaking somewhere below. Jack Thayer saw a man lurch by with a full bottle of Gordon's gin. He put it to his mouth and drained it. "If I ever get out of this," Thayer said to himself, "there is one man I'll never see again." (Actually, he was one of the first survivors Thayer met.)

Lightoller took no chances. Most of the passengers had moved aft, but still—one boat . . . 47 seats . . . 1600 people. He had the crew lock arms in a wide ring around Boat D. Only the women could come through.

Two baby boys were brought by their father to the edge of the ring, handed through, and placed in the boat. The father stepped back into the crowd. He called himself "Mr. Hoffman" and told people he was taking the boys to visit relatives in America. His name really was Navatril and he was kidnaping the children from his estranged wife.

Henry B. Harris, the theatrical producer, escorted Mrs. Harris to the ring, was told he couldn't go any further. He sighed, "Yes, I know. I will stay."

Colonel Gracie rushed up with Mrs. John Murray Brown and Miss Edith Evans, two of the five "unprotected ladies" whom he had offered his services on the trip. He was stopped by the line but saw the women through. They reached Boat D just as it was starting down the falls. Miss Evans turned to Mrs. Brown: "You go first. You have children waiting at home."

Quickly she helped Mrs. Brown over the rail. Then someone yelled to lower away, and at 2:05 Collapsible D—the last boat of all—started down toward the sea—without Edith Evans.

Directly below, Hugh Woolner and Bjornstrom Steffanson were standing alone by the rail. It had been a hard night—helping Mrs. Candee . . . trying to save the Strauses . . . dragging those cowards out of Boat C. Now they were on A Deck trying to find someone else to help, but the deck was absolutely deserted. The lights had a reddish glow.

"This is getting rather a tight corner," Woolner remarked; "let's go through the door at the end." They walked forward to the open end of the Promenade Deck. As they came out, the sea poured onto the deck, over their evening pumps and up to their knees. They hopped on the railing. Nine feet away they saw Boat D sliding down the side of the ship. It was now or never.

"Let's make a jump for it!" cried Woolner, "there's plenty of room in her bow!" Steffanson hurled himself out at the boat, landing head over heels up front. The next second Woolner followed, falling half in, half out. In another instant Collapsible D hit the water and cast off. As it pulled away, Seaman William Lucas called up to Miss Evans still standing on deck, "There's another boat going to be put down for you."

## 6.  *"That's the Way of It at this Kind of Time"*

With the boats all gone, a curious calm came over the *Titanic*. The excitement and confusion were over, and the hundreds left behind stood quietly on the upper decks. They seemed to cluster inboard, trying to keep as far away from the rail as possible.

Jack Thayer stayed with Milton Long on the starboard side of the Boat Deck. They studied an empty davit, using it as a yardstick against the sky to gauge how fast she was sinking. They watched the hopeless efforts to clear two collapsibles lashed to the roof of the officers' quarters. They exchanged messages for each other's families. Sometimes they were just silent.

Thayer thought of all the good times he had had and of all the future pleasures he would never enjoy. He thought of his father and his mother, of his sisters and brother. He felt far away, as though he were looking on from some distant place. He felt very, very sorry for himself.

Colonel Gracie, standing a little way off, felt curiously breathless. Later he rather stuffily explained it was the feeling when *"vox faucibus haesit,* as frequently happened to the old Trojan hero of our schooldays."  At the time he merely said to himself, "Good-by to all at home."

In the wireless shack there was no time for either self-pity or *vox faucibus haesit.* Phillips was still working the set, but the power was very low. Bride stood by, watching people rummage the officers' quarters and the gym, looking for extra lifebelts.

It was 2:05 when Captain Smith entered the shack for the last time: "Men, you have done your full duty. You can do no more. Abandon your cabin. Now it's every man for himself."

Phillips looked up for a second, then bent over the set once more. Captain Smith tried again, "You look out for yourselves. I release you."  A pause, then he added softly, "That's the way of it at this kind of time . . ."

Phillips went on working. Bride began to gather up their papers. Captain Smith returned to the Boat Deck, walked about speaking informally to men here and there. To Fireman James McGann, "Well, boys, it's every man for himself."  Again, to Oiler Alfred White, "Well, boys, I guess it's every man for himself."  To Steward Edward Brown, "Well, boys, do your best for the women and children, and look out for yourselves."  To the men on the roof of the officers' quarters, "You've done your duty, boys. Now, every man for himself."  Then he walked back on the bridge.

Some of the men took the Captain at his word and jumped overboard. Night Baker Walter Belford leaped as far out as he could, cannon-balled into the water in a sitting position. He still shudders and sucks his breath sharply when he thinks of the stabbing cold. Greaser Fred Scott, just up from Boiler Room 4, tried to slide down an empty fall, missed, and took a belly-flopper into the sea. He was picked up by Boat 4, still standing by the ship but trying to row clear of the barrels and deck chairs that were now hurtling down. Steward Cunningham made a hefty leap and also managed to reach No. 4.

But most of the crew stuck to the ship. On top of the officers' quarters, Lightoller noticed Trimmer Hemming at work on one of the tangled collapsibles . . . yet Hemming should have gone long ago as part of the crew in No. 6.

"Why haven't you gone, Hemming?"

"Oh, plenty of time yet, sir."

Not far away two young stewards idly watched Lightoller, Hemming and the others at work. In the fading light of the Boat Deck, their starched white jackets stood out as they leaned against the rail, debating how long the ship could last. Scattered around the Boat Deck, some 15 First Class bellboys were equally at ease—they seemed pleased that nobody cared any longer whether they smoked. Nearby, gymnasium instructor T. W. Mc-Cawley, a spry little man in white flannels, explained why he wouldn't wear a life jacket—it kept you afloat but it slowed you down; he felt he could swim clear more quickly without it.

By the forward entrance to the grand staircase, between the first and second funnel, the band—now wearing life jackets on top of their overcoats—scraped lustily away at ragtime.

The passengers were just as calm, although they too had their jumpers. Frederick Hoyt saw his wife into Collapsible D, leaped and swam to where he thought the boat might pass. He guessed well. In a few minutes Boat D splashed by and hauled him in. For the rest of the night he sat soaked to the skin, rowing hard to keep from freezing.

But for the most part the passengers merely stood waiting or quietly paced the Boat Deck. New York and Philadelphia society continued to stick together—John B. Thayer, George and Harry Widener, Duane Williams formed a little knot . . . lesser luminaries like Clinch Smith and Colonel Gracie hovering nearby. Astor remained pretty much alone, and the Strauses sat down on a deck chair.

Jack Thayer and Milton Long debated whether to jump. The davit they were using as a gauge showed the *Titanic* was going much faster now. Thayer wanted to jump out, catch an empty lifeboat fall, slide down and swim out to the boats he could dimly see 500 to 600 yards away. He was a good swimmer. Long, not nearly as good, argued against it and persuaded Thayer not to try.

Further forward, Colonel Gracie lent his penknife to the men struggling with the collapsibles lashed to the officers' quarters. They were having a hard time, and Gracie wondered why.

Some of the Third Class passengers had now worked their way up to the Boat Deck, and others were drifting toward the gradually rising stern. The after poop deck, normally Third Class space anyhow, was suddenly becoming attractive to all kinds of people.

Olaus Abelseth was one of those who reached the Boat Deck. Most of the evening he had been all the way aft with his cousin, his brother-in-law, and the two Norwegian girls. With other steerage men and women, they aimlessly waited for someone to tell them what to do.

Around 1:30 an officer opened the gate to First Class and ordered the women to the Boat Deck. At 2:00 the men were allowed up too. Many now preferred to stay where they were—this would clearly be the last point above water. But Abelseth, his cousin and brother-in-law went up on the chance there was still a boat left. The last one was pulling away.

So they just stood there, as worried about being in First Class as by the circumstances that brought them there. Abelseth watched the crew trying to free the collapsibles. Once an officer, searching for extra hands, called, "Are there any sailors here?"

Abelseth had spent 16 of his 27 years on the sea and felt he should speak up. But his cousin and brother-in-law pleaded, "No, let us just stay here together."

So they did. They felt rather awkward and said very little. It was even more awkward when Mr. and Mrs. Straus drew near. "Please," the old gentleman was saying, "get into a lifeboat and be saved."

"No, let me stay with you," she replied. Abelseth turned and looked the other way.

Within the ship the heavy silence of the deserted rooms had a drama of its own. The crystal chandeliers of the à la carte restaurant hung at a crazy angle, but they still burned brightly, lighting the fawn panels of French walnut and the rose-colored carpet. A few of the little table lights with their pink silk shades had fallen over, and someone was rummaging in the pantry, perhaps for something to fortify himself.

The Louis Quinze lounge with its big fireplace was silent and empty. The Palm Court was equally deserted—one passerby found it hard to believe that just four hours ago it was filled with exquisitely dressed ladies and gentlemen, sipping after-dinner coffee, listening to chamber music by the same men who now played gay songs on the Boat Deck above.

The smoking room was not completely empty. When a steward looked in at 2:10, he was surprised to see Thomas Andrews standing all alone in the room. Andrews' lifebelt lay carelessly across the green cloth top of a card table. His arms were folded over his chest; his look was stunned; all his drive and energy were gone. A moment of awed silence, and the steward timidly broke in: "Aren't you going to have a try for it, Mr. Andrews?"

There was no answer, not even a trace that he heard. The builder of the Titanic merely stared aft. On the mahogany-paneled wall facing him hung a large painting called, "The Approach of the New World."

Outside on the decks, the crowd still waited; the band still played. A few prayed with the Reverend Thomas R. Byles, a Second Class passenger. Others seemed lost in thought.

There was much to think about. For Captain Smith there were the five ice messages received during the day—the last told exactly where to expect the berg. And there was the thermometer that fell from 43 degrees at seven o'clock to 32 degrees at 10 o'clock. And the temperature of the sea, which dropped to 31 degrees at 10:30 P.M.

Wireless Operator Jack Phillips could ponder over the sixth ice warning—when the Californian broke in at 11:00 P.M. and Phillips told her to shut up. That one never even reached the bridge.

George Q. Clifford of Boston had the rueful satisfaction of remembering that he took out 50,000 dollars' extra life insurance just before the trip.

For Isidor Straus there was the irony of his will. A special paragraph urged Mrs. Straus to "be a little selfish; don't always think only of others." Through the years she had been so self-sacrificing that he especially wanted her to enjoy life after he was gone. Now the very qualities he admired so much meant he could never have his wish.

Little things too could return to haunt a person at a time like this. Edith Evans remembered a fortuneteller who once told her to "beware of the water." William T. Stead was nagged by a dream about somebody throwing cats out a top-story window. Charles Hays had prophesied just a few hours earlier that the time would soon come for "the greatest and most appalling of all disasters at sea."

Two men perhaps wondered why they were there at all. Archie Butt didn't want to go abroad, but he needed a rest; and Frank Millet badgered President Taft into sending Butt with a message to the Pope—official business but spring in Rome, too. Chief Officer Wilde didn't plan to be on board either. He was regularly on the *Olympic*, but the White Star Line transferred him at the last minute for this one voyage. They thought his experience would be useful in breaking in the new ship. Wilde had considered it a lucky break.

In the wireless shack Phillips struggled to keep the set going. At 2:10 he sounded two V's—heard faintly by the *Virginian*—as he tried to adjust the spark for better results. Bride made a last inspection tour. He returned to find a fainting lady had been carried into the shack. Bride got her a chair and a glass of water, and she sat gasping while her husband fanned her. She came to, and the man took her away.

Bride went behind the curtain where he and Phillips slept. He gathered up all the loose money, took a last look at his rumpled bunk, pushed through the curtain again. Phillips still sat hunched over the set, completely absorbed. But a stoker was now in the room, gently unfastening Phillips' life jacket.

Bride leaped at the stoker, Phillips jumped up, and the three men wrestled around the shack. Finally Bride wrapped his arms about the stoker's waist, and Phillips swung again and again until the man slumped unconscious in Bride's arms.

A minute later they heard the sea gurgling up the A Deck companionway and washing over the bridge. Phillips cried, "Come on, let's clear out!" Bride dropped the stoker, and the two men ran out onto the Boat Deck. The stoker lay still where he fell.

Phillips disappeared aft. Bride walked forward and joined the men on the roof of the officers' quarters who were trying to free Collapsibles A and B. It was a ridiculous place to stow boats—especially when there were only 20 for 2207 people. With the deck slanting like this, it had been hard enough launching C and D, the two collapsibles stowed right beside the forward davits. It was impossible to do much with A and B.

But the crew weren't discouraged. If the boats couldn't be launched, they could perhaps be floated off. So they toiled on—Lightoller, Murdoch, Trimmer Hemming, Steward Brown, Greaser Hurst, a dozen others.

On the port side Hemming struggled with the block and tackle for Boat B. If he could only iron out a flutterfoot in the fall, he was sure it could still be launched. He finally got the lines working, passed the block up to Sixth Officer Moody on the roof, but Moody shouted back, "We don't want the block; we'll leave the boat on the deck."

Hemming saw no chance of clearing Boat B this way; so he jumped and swam for it. Meanwhile the boat was pushed to the edge of the roof and slid down on some oars to the deck. It landed upside down.

On the starboard side they were having just as much trouble with Boat A. Somebody propped planks against the wall of the officers' quarters, and they eased the boat down bow first. But they were still a long way from home, for the *Titanic* was now listing heavily to port, and they couldn't push the boat "uphill" to the edge of the deck.

The men were tugging at both collapsibles when the bridge dipped under at 2:15 and the sea rolled aft along the Boat Deck. Colonel Gracie and Clinch Smith turned and headed for the stern. A few steps, and they were blocked by a sudden crowd of men and women pouring up from below. They all seemed to be steerage passengers.

At this moment Bandmaster Hartley tapped his violin. The ragtime ended, and the strains of the Episcopal hymn "Autumn" flowed across the deck and drifted in the still night far out over the water.

In the boats women listened with wonder. From a distance there was an agonizing stateliness about the moment. Close-up, it was different. Men could hear the music, but they paid little attention. Too much was happening.

"Oh, save me! Save me!" cried a woman to Peter Daly, Lima representative of the London firm Haes & Sons, as he watched the water roll onto the deck where he stood.

"Good lady," he answered, "save yourself. Only God can save you now."

But she begged him to help her make the jump, and on second thought he realized he couldn't shed the problem so easily. Quickly he took her by the arm and helped her overboard. As he jumped himself, a big wave came sweeping along the Boat Deck, washing him clear of the ship.

The sea foamed and swirled around Steward Brown's feet as he sweated to get Boat A to the edge of the deck. Then he realized he needn't try any longer—the boat was floating off. He jumped in . . . cut the stern lines . . . yelled for someone to free the bow . . . and in the next instant was washed out by the same wave that swept off Peter Daly.

Down, down dipped the *Titanic's* bow, and her stern swung slowly up. She seemed to be moving forward too. It was this motion which generated the wave that hit Daly, Brown, and dozens of others as it rolled aft.

Lightoller watched the wave from the roof of the officers' quarters. He saw the crowds retreating up the deck ahead of it. He saw the nimbler ones keep clear, the slower ones overtaken and engulfed. He knew that this kind of retreat just prolonged the agony. He turned and, facing the bow, dived in. As he reached the surface, he saw just ahead of him the crow's-nest, now level with the water. Blind instinct seized him, and for a moment he swam toward it as a place of safety.

Then he snapped to and tried to swim clear of the ship. But the sea was pouring down the ventilators just in front of the forward funnel, and he was sucked back and held against the wire grating of an air shaft. He prayed it would hold. And he wondered how long he could last, pinned this way to the grating.

He never learned the answer. A blast of hot air from somewhere deep below came rushing up the ventilator and blew him to the surface. Gasping and sputtering, he finally paddled clear.

Harold Bride kept his head too. As the wave swept by, he grabbed an oarlock of Collapsible B, which was still lying upside down on the Boat Deck near the first funnel. The boat, Bride and a dozen others were washed off together. The collapsible was still upside down, and Bride found himself struggling underneath it.

Colonel Gracie was not as sea-wise. He stayed in the crowd and jumped with the wave—it was almost like Newport. Rising on the crest, he caught the bottom rung of the iron railing on the roof of the officers' quarters. He hauled himself up and lay on his stomach right at the base of the second funnel.

Before he could rise, the roof too had dipped under. Gracie found himself spinning round and round in a whirlpool of water. He tried to cling to the railing, then realized this was pulling him down deeper. With a mighty kick he pushed himself free and swam clear of the ship, far below the surface.

Chef John Collins couldn't do much of anything about the wave. He had a baby in his arms. For five minutes he and a deck steward had been trying to help a steerage woman with two children. First they heard there was a boat on the port side. They ran there and heard it was on the starboard side. When they got there, somebody said their best chance was to head for the stern. Bewildered, they were standing undecided—Collins holding one of the babies—when they were all swept overboard by the wave. He never saw the others again, and the child was washed out of his arms.

Jack Thayer and Milton Long saw the wave coming too. They were standing by the starboard rail opposite the second funnel, trying to keep clear of the crowds swarming toward the stern. Instead of making for a higher point, they felt the time had come to jump and swim for it. They shook hands and wished each other luck. Long put his legs over the rail, while Thayer straddled it and began unbuttoning his overcoat. Long, hanging over the side and holding the rail with his hands, looked up at Thayer and asked, "You're coming, boy?"

"Go ahead, I'll be right with you," Thayer reassured him.

Long slid down, facing the ship. Ten seconds later Thayer swung his other leg over the rail and sat facing out. He was about ten feet above the water. Then with a push he jumped as far out as he could.

Of these two techniques for abandoning ship, Thayer's was the one that worked.

The wave never reached Olaus Abelseth. Standing by the fourth funnel, he was too far back. Instead of plunging under, this part of the ship was swinging higher and higher.

As she swung up, Abelseth heard a popping and cracking . . . a series of muffled thuds . . . the crash of glassware . . . the clatter of deck chairs sliding down.

The slant of the deck grew so steep that people could no longer stand. So they fell, and Abelseth watched them slide down into the water right on the deck. Abelseth and his relatives hung on by clinging to a rope in one of the davits.

"We better jump or the suction will take us down," his brother-in-law urged.

"No," said Abelseth. "We won't jump yet. We ain't got much show anyhow, so we might as well stay as long as we can."

"We must jump off!" the cry came again, but Abelseth held firm: "No, not yet."

Minutes later, when the water was only five feet away, the three men finally jumped, holding each other's hands. They came sputtering to the surface, Abelseth hopelessly snarled in some rope from somewhere. He had to free his hands to untangle the line, and his cousin and brother-in-law were washed away. Somehow he got loose, but he said to himself, "I'm a goner."

In the maelstrom of ropes, deck chairs, planking, and wildly swirling water, nobody knew what happened to most of the people. From the boats they could be seen clinging like little swarms of bees to deck houses, winches and ventilators as the stern rose higher. Close in, it was hard to see what was happening, even though—incredibly—the lights still burned, casting a sort of murky glow.

In the stories told later, Archie Butt had a dozen different endings—all gallant, none verified. According to one newspaper, Miss Marie Young, music teacher to Teddy Roosevelt's children, remembered him calling, "Good-by, Miss Young, remember me to the folks back home." Yet the papers also reported Miss Young as saying she saw the iceberg an hour before the crash.

In an interview attributed to Mrs. Henry B. Harris, Archie Butt was described as a pillar of strength, using his fists here—a big brother approach there—to handle the weaklings. Yet Lightoller, Gracie and the others working on the boats never saw him at all. When Mrs. Walter Douglas recalled him near Boat 2 around 1:45, he was standing quietly off to one side.

It was the same with John Jacob Astor. Barber August H. Weikman described last moments with the great millionaire. It was a conversation full of the kind of small talk that normally takes place only in the barber's chair. And even more trite: "I asked him if he minded shaking hands with me. He said 'With pleasure' . . ." Yet, Barber Weikman also said he left the ship at 1:50, a good half-hour earlier.

Butt and Astor's endings were parlayed in a single story attributed to Washington Dodge, the San Francisco Assessor: "They went down standing on the bridge, side by side. I could not mistake them," the papers had him saying. Yet Dr. Dodge was in Boat 13, a good half-mile away.

Nor did any one really know what happened to Captain Smith. People later said he shot himself, but there's not a shred of evidence. Just before the end Steward Edward Brown saw him walk onto the bridge, still holding his megaphone. A minute later Trimmer Hemming wandered on the bridge and found it empty. After the *Titanic* sank, Fireman Harry Senior saw him in the water holding a child. Pieced together, this picture, far more than suicide, fits the kind of fighter who once said: "In a way, a certain amount of wonder never leaves me, especially as I observe from the bridge a vessel plunging up and down in the trough of the sea, fighting her way through and over great waves. A man never outgrows that."

Seen and unseen, the great and the unknown tumbled together in a writhing heap as the bow plunged deeper and the stern rose higher. The strains of "Autumn" were buried in a jumble of falling musicians and instruments. The lights went out, flashed on again, went out for good. A single kerosene lantern still flickered high in the after mast.

The muffled thuds and tinkle of breaking glass grew louder. A steady roar thundered across the water as everything movable broke loose.

There has never been a mixture like it—29 boilers . . . the jeweled copy of the Rubáiyát . . . 800 cases of shelled walnuts . . . 15,000 bottles of ale and stout . . . huge anchor chains (each link weighed 175 pounds) . . . 30 cases of golf clubs and tennis rackets for Spalding . . . Eleanor Widener's trousseau . . . tons of coal . . . Major Peuchen's tin box . . . 30,000 fresh eggs . . . dozens of potted palms . . . 5 grand pianos . . . a little mantel clock in B-38 . . . the massive silver duck press.

And still it grew—tumbling trellises, ivy pots and wicker chairs in the Café Parisien . . . shuffleboard sticks . . . the 50-phone switchboard . . . two reciprocating engines and the revolutionary low-pressure turbine . . . 8 dozen tennis balls for R. F. Downey & Co., a cask of china for Tiffany's, a case of gloves for Marshall Field . . . the remarkable ice-making machine on G Deck . . . Billy Carter's new English automobile . . . the Ryersons' 16 trunks, beautifully packed by Victorine.

As the tilt grew steeper, the forward funnel toppled over. It struck the water on the starboard side with a shower of sparks and a crash heard above the general uproar. Greaser Walter Hurst, struggling in the swirling sea, was half blinded by soot. He got off lucky—other swimmers were crushed under tons of steel. But the falling funnel was a blessing to Lightoller, Bride and others now clinging to overturned Collapsible B. It just missed the boat, washing it 30 yards clear of the plunging, twisting hull.

The *Titanic* was now absolutely perpendicular. From the third funnel aft, she stuck straight up in the air, her three dripping propellers glistening even in the darkness. To Lady Duff Gordon she seemed a black finger pointing at the sky. To Harold Bride she looked like a duck that goes down for a dive.

Out in the boats, they could hardly believe their eyes. For over two hours they had watched, hoping against hope, as the *Titanic* sank lower and lower. When the water reached her red and green running lights, they knew the end was near . . . but nobody dreamed it would be like this—the unearthly din, the black hull hanging at 90 degrees, the Christmas card backdrop of brilliant stars.

Some didn't watch. In Collapsible C, President Bruce Ismay bent low over his oar—he couldn't bear to see her go down. In Boat 1, C. E. Henry Stengel turned his back: "I cannot look any longer." In No. 4, Elizabeth Eustis buried her face.

Two minutes passed, the noise finally stopped, and the *Titanic* settled back slightly at the stern. Then slowly she began sliding under, moving at a steep slant. As she glided down, she seemed to pick up speed. When the sea closed over the flagstaff on her stern, she was moving fast enough to cause a slight gulp.

"She's gone; that's the last of her," someone sighed to Lookout Lee in Boat 13. "It's gone," Mrs. Ada Clark vaguely heard somebody say in No. 4. But she was so cold she didn't pay much attention. Most of the other women were the same—they just sat dazed, dumbfounded, without showing any emotion. In No. 5, Third Officer Pitman looked at his watch and announced, "It is 2:20."

Ten miles away on the *Californian*, Second Officer Stone and Apprentice Gibson watched the strange ship slowly disappear. She had fascinated them almost the whole watch—the way she kept firing rockets, the odd way she floated in the water. Gibson remarked that he certainly didn't think the rockets were being sent up for fun. Stone agreed: "A ship is not going to fire rockets at sea for nothing."

By two o'clock the stranger's lights seemed very low on the horizon, and the two men felt she must be steaming away. "Call the Captain," Stone ordered, "and tell him that the ship is disappearing in the southwest and that she has fired altogether eight rockets."

Gibson marched into the chart room and gave the message. Captain Lord looked up sleepily from his couch: "Were they all white rockets?"

Gibson said yes, and Lord asked the time. Gibson replied it was 2:05 by the wheelhouse clock. Lord rolled over, and Gibson went back to the bridge.

At 2:20 Stone decided that the other ship was definitely gone, and at 2:40 he felt he ought to tell the Captain himself. He called the news down the speaking tube and resumed studying the empty night.

## 7. *"There Is Your Beautiful Nightdress Gone"*

As the sea closed over the *Titanic*, Lady Cosmo Duff Gordon in Boat 1 remarked to her secretary Miss Francatelli, "There is your beautiful nightdress gone."

A lot more than Miss Francatelli's nightgown vanished that April night. Even more than the largest liner in the world, her cargo, and the lives of 1502 people.

Never again would men fling a ship into an ice field, heedless of warnings, putting their whole trust in a few thousand tons of steel and rivets. From now on Atlantic liners took ice messages seriously, steered clear, or slowed down. Nobody believed in the "unsinkable ship."

Nor would icebergs any longer prowl the seas untended. After the *Titanic* sank, the American and British governments established the International Ice Patrol, and today Coast Guard cutters shepherd errant icebergs that drift toward the steamer lanes. The winter lane itself was shifted further south, as an extra precaution.

And there were no more liners with only part-time wireless. Henceforth every passenger ship had 24-hour radio watch. Never again could the world fall apart while a Cyril Evans lay sleeping off duty only ten miles away.

It was also the last time a liner put to sea without enough lifeboats. The 46,328-ton *Titanic* sailed under hopelessly outdated safety regulations. An absurd formula determined lifeboat requirements: all British vessels over 10,000 tons must carry 16 lifeboats with a capacity of 5500 cubic feet, plus enough rafts and floats for 75 per cent of the capacity of the lifeboats.

For the *Titanic* this worked out at 9625 cubic feet. This meant she had to carry boats for only 962 people. Actually, there were boats for 1178—the White Star Line complained that nobody appreciated their thoughtfulness. Even so, this took care of only 52 per cent of the 2207 people on board, and only 30 per cent of her total capacity. From now on the rules and formulas were simple indeed—lifeboats for everybody.

And it was the end of class distinction in filling the boats. The White Star Line always denied anything of the kind—and the investigators backed them up—yet there's overwhelming evidence that the steerage took a beating: Daniel Buckley kept from going into First Class . . . Olaus Abelseth released from the poop deck as the last boat pulled away . . . Steward Hart convoying two little groups of women topside, while hundreds were kept below . . . steerage passengers crawling along the crane from the well deck aft . . . others climbing vertical ladders to escape the well deck forward.

Then there were the people Colonel Gracie, Lightoller and others saw surging up from below, just before the end. Until this moment Gracie was sure the women were all off—they were so hard to find when the last boats were loading. Now, he was appalled to see dozens of them suddenly appear. The statistics suggest who they were—the *Titanic's* casualty list included four of 143 First Class women (three by choice) . . . 15 of 93 Second Class women . . . and 81 of 179 Third Class women.

Not to mention the children. Except for Lorraine Allison, all 29 First and Second Class children were saved, but only 23 out of 76 steerage children.

Neither the chance to be chivalrous nor the fruits of chivalry seemed to go with a Third Class passage.

It was better, but not perfect, in Second Class. Lawrence Beesley remembered an officer stopping two ladies as they started through the gate to First Class. "May we pass to the boats?" they asked.

"No, madam; your boats are down on your own deck."

In fairness to the White Star Line, these distinctions grew not so much from set policy as from no policy at all. At some points the crew barred the way to the Boat Deck; at others they opened the gates but didn't tell anyone; at a few points there were well-meaning efforts to guide the steerage up. But generally Third Class was left to shift for itself. A few of the more enterprising met the challenge, but most milled helplessly about their quarters—ignored, neglected, forgotten.

If the White Star Line was indifferent, so was everybody else. No one seemed to care about Third Class—neither the press, the official Inquiries, nor even the Third Class passengers themselves.

In covering the *Titanic*, few reporters bothered to ask the Third Class passengers anything. The New York *Times* was justly proud of the way it handled the disaster. Yet the famous issue covering the *Carpathia's* arrival in New York contained only two interviews with Third Class passengers. This apparently was par for the course—of 43 survivor accounts in The New York *Herald*, two again were steerage experiences.

Certainly their experiences weren't as good copy as Lady Cosmo Duff Gordon (one New York newspaper had her saying, "The last voice I heard was a man shouting, 'My God, My God!'"). But there was indeed a story. The night was a magnificent confirmation of "women and children first," yet somehow the loss rate was higher for Third Class children than First Class men. It was a contrast which would never get by the social consciousness (or news sense) of today's press.

Nor did Congress care what happened to Third Class. Senator Smith's *Titanic* investigation covered everything under the sun, including what an iceberg was made of ("Ice," explained Fifth Officer Lowe), but the steerage received little attention. Only three of the witnesses were Third Class passengers. Two of these said they were kept from going to the Boat Deck, but the legislators didn't follow up. Again, the testimony doesn't suggest any deliberate hush-up—it was just that no one was interested.

The British Court of Enquiry was even more cavalier. Mr. W. D. Harbinson, who officially represented the Third Class interests, said he could find no trace of discrimination, and Lord Mersey's report gave a clean bill of health—yet not a single Third Class passenger testified, and the only surviving steward stationed in steerage freely conceded that the men were kept below decks as late as 1:15 A.M.

Even the Third Class passengers weren't bothered. They expected class distinction as part of the game. Olaus Abelseth, at least, regarded access to the Boat Deck as a privilege that went with First and Second Class passage . . . even when the ship was sinking. He was satisfied as long as they let him stay above decks.

A new age was dawning, and never since that night have Third Class passengers been so philosophical.

At the opposite extreme, it was also the last time the special position of First Class was accepted without question. When the White Star Liner *Republic* went down in 1908, Captain Sealby told the passengers entering the lifeboats, "Remember! Women and children go first; then the First Cabin, then the others!" There was no such rule on the *Titanic*, but the concept still existed in the public mind, and at first the press tended to forestall any criticism over what a First Class passenger might do. When the news broke that Ismay was saved, the New York *Sun* hastened to announce, "Ismay behaved with exceptional gallantry . . . no one knows how Mr. Ismay himself got into a boat; it is assumed he wished to make a presentation of the case to his company."

Never again would First Class have it so good. In fact, almost immediately the pendulum swung the other way. Within days Ismay was pilloried; within a year a prominent survivor divorced her husband merely because, according to gossip, he happened to be saved. One of the more trying legacies left by those on the *Titanic* has been a new standard of conduct for measuring the behavior of prominent people under stress.

It was easier in the old days . . . for the *Titanic* was also the last stand of wealth and society in the center of public affection. In 1912 there were no movie, radio or television stars; sports figures were still beyond the pale; and café society was completely unknown. The public depended on socially prominent people for all the vicarious glamour that enriches drab lives.

This preoccupation was fully appreciated by the press. When the *Titanic* sailed, the New York *Times* listed the prominent passengers on the front page. After she sank, the New York *American* broke the news on April 16 with a lead devoted almost entirely to John Jacob Astor; at the end it mentioned that 1800 others were also lost.

In the same mood, the April 18 New York *Sun* covered the insurance angle of the disaster. Most of the story concerned Mrs. Widener's pearls.

Never again did established wealth occupy people's minds so thoroughly. On the other hand, never again was wealth so spectacular. John Jacob Astor thought nothing of shelling out 800 dollars for a lace jacket some dealer displayed on deck when the *Titanic* stopped briefly at Queenstown. To the Ryersons there was nothing unusual about traveling with 16 trunks. The 190 families in First Class were attended by 23 handmaids, eight valets, and assorted nurses and governesses—entirely apart from hundreds of stewards and stewardesses. These personal servants had their own lounge on C Deck, so that no one need suffer the embarrassment of striking up a conversation with some handsome stranger, only to find he was Henry Sleeper Harper's dragoman.

Or take the survivors' arrival in New York. Mrs. Astor was met by two automobiles, carrying two doctors, a trained nurse, a secretary and Vincent Astor. Mrs. George Widener was met not by automobile but by a special train—consisting of a private Pullman, another car for ballast, and a locomotive. Mrs. Charles Hays was met by a special train too, including two private cars and two coaches.

It was a reception in keeping with people who could afford as much as 4350 dollars—and these were 1912 dollars—for a de-luxe suite. A suite like this had even a private promenade deck, which figured out at something like 40 dollars a front foot for six days.

This kind of life, of course, wasn't open to everybody—in fact it would take Harold Bride, who made 20 dollars a month, 18 years to earn enough to cross in style—so those who enjoyed it gradually became part of a remarkably tightly-knit little group, which also seemed to vanish with the *Titanic*.

There was a wonderful intimacy about this little world of the Edwardian rich. There was no flicker of surprise when they bumped into each other, whether at the Pyramids (a great favorite), the Cowes Regatta, or the springs at Baden-Baden. They seemed to get the same ideas at the same time, and one of these ideas was to make the maiden voyage of the largest ship in the world.

So the *Titanic's* trip was more like a reunion than an ocean passage. It fascinated Mrs. Henry B. Harris, wife of the theatrical producer, who certainly wasn't part of this world. Twenty years later she still recalled with awe, "There was a spirit of camaraderie unlike any I had experienced on previous trips. No one consulted the passenger list, to judge from the air of good fellowship that prevailed among the cabin passengers. They met on deck as one big party."

This group knew the crew almost as well as each other. It was the custom to cross with certain captains rather than on particular ships, and Captain Smith had a personal following which made him invaluable to the White Star Line. The Captain repaid the patronage with little favors and privileges which kept them coming. On the last night John Jacob Astor got the bad news direct from Captain Smith before the general alarm, and others learned too.

But the other end of the bargain was to respect the privilege. Nobody took advantage of the Captain's confidence—hardly a man in the group was saved.

The stewards and waiters were on equally close terms with the group. They had often looked after the same passengers. They knew just what they wanted and how they liked things done. Every evening Steward Cunningham would enter A-36 and lay out Thomas Andrews' dress clothes just the way Mr. Andrews liked. Then at 6:45 Cunningham would enter and help Andrews dress. It happened all over the ship.

And when the *Titanic* was going down, it was with genuine affection that Steward Etches made Mr. Guggenheim wear his sweater . . . that Steward Crawford laced Mr. Stewart's shoes . . . that Second Steward Dodd tipped off John B. Thayer that his wife was still on board, long after Thayer thought she had left. In the same spirit of devotion, Dining Room Steward Ray pushed Washington Dodge into Boat 13—he had persuaded the Dodges to take the *Titanic* and now felt he had to see them through.

The group repaid this loyalty with an intimacy and affection they gave few of their less-known fellow passengers. In the *Titanic's* last hours men like Ben Guggenheim and Martin Rothschild seemed to see more of their stewards than the other passengers.

The *Titanic* somehow lowered the curtain on this way of living. It never was the same again. First the war, then the income tax, made sure of that.

With this lost world went some of its prejudices—especially a firm and loudly voiced opinion of the superiority of Anglo-Saxon courage. To the survivors all stowaways in the lifeboats were "Chinese" or "Japanese"; all who jumped from the deck were "Armenians," "Frenchmen," or "Italians."

"There were various men passengers," declared Steward Crowe at the U. S. inquiry, "probably Italians, or some foreign nationality other than English or American, who attempted to rush the boats." Steward Crowe, of course, never heard the culprits speak and had no way of knowing who they were. At the inquiry things finally grew so bad that the Italian Ambassador demanded and got an apology from Fifth Officer Lowe for using "Italian" as a sort of synonym for "coward."

In contrast, Anglo-Saxon blood could do no wrong. When Bride described the stoker's attack on Phillips, some newspapers made the stoker a Negro for better effect. And in a story headlined, "Desirable Immigrants Lost," the New York *Sun* pointed out that, along with the others, 78 Finns were lost who might do the country some good.

But along with the prejudices, some nobler instincts also were lost. Men would go on being brave, but never again would they be brave in quite the same way. These men on the *Titanic* had a touch—there was something about Ben Guggenheim changing to evening dress . . . about Howard Case flicking his cigarette as he waved to Mrs. Graham . . . or even about Colonel Gracie panting along the decks, gallantly if ineffectually searching for Mrs. Candee. Today nobody could carry off these little gestures of chivalry, but they did that night.

An air of *noblesse oblige* has vanished too. During the agonizing days of uncertainty in New York, the Astors, the Guggenheims and others like them were not content to sit by their phones or to send friends and retainers to the White Star Line offices. They went themselves. Not because it was the best way to get information, but because they felt they ought to be there in person.

Today families are as loyal as ever, but the phone would probably do. Few would insist on going themselves and braving the bedlam of the steamship office. Yet the others didn't hesitate a minute. True, Vincent Astor did get better information than the rest—and some even spoke to General Manager Franklin himself—but the point is that these people didn't merely keep in touch—they were *there*.

Overriding everything else, the *Titanic* also marked the end of a general feeling of confidence. Until then men felt they had found the answer to a steady, orderly, civilized life. For 100 years the Western world had been at peace. For 100 years technology had steadily improved. For 100 years the benefits of peace and industry seemed to be filtering satisfactorily through society. In retrospect, there may seem less grounds for confidence, but at the time most articulate people felt life was all right.

The *Titanic* woke them up. Never again would they be quite so sure of themselves. In technology especially, the disaster was a terrible blow. Here was the "unsinkable ship"—perhaps man's greatest engineering achievement—going down the first time it sailed.

But it went beyond that. If this supreme achievement was so terribly fragile, what about everything else? If wealth meant so little on this cold April night, did it mean so much the rest of the year? Scores of ministers preached that the *Titanic* was a heaven-sent lesson to awaken people from their complacency, to punish them for top-heavy faith in material progress. If it was a lesson, it worked—people have never been sure of anything since.

The unending sequence of disillusionment that has followed can't be blamed on the *Titanic*, but she was the first jar. Before the *Titanic*, all was quiet. Afterward, all was tumult. That is why, to anybody who lived at the time, the *Titanic* more than any other single event marks the end of the old days, and the beginning of a new, uneasy era.

# Aerial Football: The New Game

### GEORGE BERNARD SHAW

(*From the Neolith of November 1907*)

IS she dead?" said the motor bus driver, looking very sick, as the medical student from the Free Hospital picked up Mrs. Hairns in the Gray's Inn Road.

"She smells frightfully of your petrol," said the student.

The driver sniffed at her. "That's not petrol," he said. "It's methylated spirit. She's been drinking. You'll bear me witness that she smells of drink."

"Don't you know all you've done yet?" said the policeman. "You've killed his lordship."

"What lordship?" said the driver, changing from tallow color to green.

"The back end of the bus swung right into the carriage," panted the footman. "I heard his lordship's neck crack." The footman wept, not because he loved his late employer, but because sudden death affected him that way.

"The Bishop of St. Pancras," said a boy, in explanation.

"Oh, my good Lord!" said the motorman, in great trouble. "How could I help it?" he added, after wiping his brow, appealing to the crowd, which seemed to have been in solution in the air, so suddenly had it precipitated round the accident. "The bus skidded."

"So would any bus skid in this mud, going at that rate," said an indignant bystander.

And immediately the crowd began to dispute as to whether the bus had been going too fast or not, with the motorman passionately maintaining the negative against the affirmative of the whole Gray's Inn Road.

Mrs. Hairns certainly did smell of drink. She had done so more or less for forty years whenever she had twopence to spare. She had never been a nice looking woman nor a cleanly dressed one; and the passage of the crowded motor bus over her ribs had made surprisingly little difference in her appearance. A little more mud ground into her garments could make them no worse than they were; and the change from being drunk and able to shuffle home and being drunk and incapable was not startling.

As to the bishop, there was not a scratch nor a speck of mud on him. He had not been touched. He had been boyishly proud of being a bishop, and had expressed his pride by holding his neck very stiff. Consequently it broke when the carriage was stopped suddenly by the swinging round of the tail of the bus.

Mrs. Hairns was taken aback when the bus suddenly swooped round at her. That made no difference, because no presence of mind on her part could have saved her. It did not hurt her at all. A single broken rib touching a lung is painful; but when an overwhelming shock annihilates your nerves, and an overwhelming weight makes bone dust of all your ribs, and wraps them up in a squash with your heart and lungs, sympathy becomes ridiculous. The game is up. The remediable has become irremediable: the temporal, eternal. A really flexible mind accepts the situation and thinks a great deal about it before there is time even to die. The suddenest death is a long business compared with the lightning work of imagining an experience of, say, a thousand years.

Mrs. Hairns was squashed clean out of the Gray's Inn Road on to the foot of a hill with a city on the top. It was rather like Orvieto, of which city there was a photograph in the drawing room of the Vicar of St. Pancras, who employed Mrs. Hairns as a charwoman whenever he attempted to reclaim her, and was beaten every time by her acquired taste for methylated spirits, which enabled her to drink furniture polish with avidity, though you could trust her with untold dozens of mere hock. Beyond getting the photograph focussed on her retina occasionally whilst dusting, Mrs. Hairns knew nothing about Orvieto. A place so unlike Pentonville Hill suggested dread and discomfort to her. She felt sure it must be almost as bad as heaven, which she associated with teetotalism, cleanliness, self-control, being particular, and all sorts of horrors. Now that she found herself actually on the road to it, she looked up at it with the utmost misgiving until a superior voice behind her made her start and attempt a shambling curtsey. It was the bishop.

"Can I obtain a conveyance anywhere here," he said, "to take me up to the gate?"

"I can't say, I'm sure, sir," said Mrs. Hairns: "I'm a stranger here."

The bishop passed on the moment she said "can't say," taking no further interest in her, and resigned himself to walk up.

There was a horse grazing a little way off. As Mrs. Hairns noticed it, a faint ray of heavenly comfort stole into her soul. Though for many years—ever since the passing away of the last rays of her youth at twenty-four or thereabouts—she had been interested in nothing but methylated alcohol, she had been born with an unaccountable fancy, not for horses exactly, but, as she put it, for a horse. It was an unintelligent and innocent fancy; but it had won her hand in marriage for the late Alfred Hairns, normally and by economic necessity a carman, but by natural vocation a poacher. This rude fancier of the equine was too poor to afford a horse. But after all he was too poor to afford a residence in London, or a double bed, or even a suit of clothes. Yet he always had a London address; he never appeared in the streets naked; and neither he nor Mrs. Hairns slept on the floor. Society had convinced him that the lodging, the bed, and the clothes were indispensable, whether he could afford them or not: accordingly, he had them. The conviction that a horse was equally indispensable was idiosyncratic with him; so he always kept a horse, even when he could by no means afford to keep himself, maintaining that a horse made no difference—that it even paid its way. The same view has been taken of 80 h.p. motor cars.

Bonavia Banks was attracted by his idiosyncrasy, which was also her own. She easily persuaded him that a wife was as indispensable as a horse, and equally made no difference. She became Mrs. Alfred Hairns, and bore thirteen children, of whom eleven died in infancy owing to the malversation of their parental care by the horse. Finally the horse died; and the heartbroken Hairns was tempted to buy a magnificent thoroughbred for four pounds from the widow of a gentleman who had paid two hundred and thirty for him only three days before. Hairns, whilst leading his bargain home, was savaged by him so that he died of lockjaw the day after the horse was shot. Thus perished miserably Alfred Hairns, the victim of the bond between man and beast which proclaims that all life is one.

The horse raised its muzzle from the grass; looked at Mrs. Hairns carelessly; switched its tail; moved on a few steps to an uncropped patch of verdure; and was about to continue its repast when, as if some fibre of memory had suddenly vibrated, it erected its ears; raised its neck; and looked more attentively at her. Finally it came to her, stopping only once on the way absent-mindedly to graze, and said, "Don't you remember me?"

"Chipper!" exclaimed Mrs. Hairns. "It can't be."

"It *is*," said Chipper.

Chipper conversed after the manner of Balaam's ass. That is, Mrs. Hairns knew what he was saying too well to notice that he did not actually utter any sound. But for the matter of that neither did she, though she did not notice that also. Conversation in this Orvietan region was wholly telepathic.

"Have I got to walk up that hill, Chipper?" said Mrs. Hairns.

"Yes," said Chipper, "unless I carry you."

"Would you mind?" said Mrs. Hairns shyly.

"Not at all," said Chipper.

"Ain't there a vehicle?" said Mrs. Hairns. "I can't ride barebacked. Not that I can ride anyhow."

"Then you must walk," said Chipper. "Hold on to my mane; and I'll help you up."

They got up somehow, and were close to the gate before it occurred to Mrs. Hairns to ask what place it was, and to ask herself why she was going there.

"It's heaven," said Chipper.

"Oh Lord!" said Mrs. Hairns, stopping dead. "Why didn't you tell me before? I never done anything to get me into heaven."

"True," said Chipper. "Would you rather go to hell?"

"Don't be so silly, Chipper," said Mrs. Hairns. "Ain't there nothin' between hell and heaven? We ain't all saints; but then we ain't all devils neither. Surely to gracious there must be a place for everyday sort of people that don't set up to be too particular."

"This is the only place I know," said Chipper; "and it's certainly heaven."

"Belike there might be some kitchens in it," said Mrs. Hairns. "You won't let on that I used to get a bit overcome once in a way, Chipper, will you?"

Chipper snuffed up a noseful of Mrs. Hairns's aura. "I should keep on the lee side of St. Peter," he said. "That's Peter," he added jerking his head in the direction of an elderly gentleman with a pair of keys of XII century design.

The keys were more for ornament than use, apparently; for the gate stood wide open; and a stone placed against it to keep it from blowing-to was covered with moss, and had evidently not been moved for centuries. This surprised Mrs. Hairns, because it had been strongly impressed on her in her childhood on earth that the gates of heaven were always shut tight, and that it was no end of a business to get them opened.

A group of angels stood in the carriage way. Their wings, purple and gold, heliotrope and silver, amber and black, and all sorts of fine colours, struck Mrs. Hairns as lovely. One of them had a sword with a blade of lambent garnet-colored flame. Another, with one leg naked from the knee down, and a wading boot on the other, had a straight slender trumpet, which seemed long enough to reach to the horizon and yet was as handy as an umbrella. Through the first floor window of one of the turrets of the gate Mrs. Hairns saw Matthew, Mark, Luke, and John in bed with their breeches on according to the old rhyme. Seeing that, she knew this was really the gate of heaven. Nothing else would have quite convinced her.

Chipper addressed himself to Peter. "This woman is drunk," said Chipper.

"So I see," said St. Peter.

"Ow Chipper!" said Mrs. Hairns reproachfully. "How could you?" They all looked at her; and she began to cry. The angel with the sword of flame drew it across her eyes and dried her tears. The flame did not hurt, and was wonderfully reviving.

"I'm afraid she's hopeless," said Chipper. "Her own children will have nothing to do with her."

"Which planet?" said the angel with the trumpet.

"Tellus," answered Chipper.

"What am I to tell them?" said Mrs. Hairns.

The angels laughed. Peter roared. "Come!" said the trumpet angel: "she can make puns. What's wrong with her?"

"She's a liar and a thief," said Chipper.

"All the inhabitants of Tellus are liars and thieves," said the trumpet angel.

"I mean she is what even they call a liar and a thief," said Chipper.

"Oh!" said the sword angel, looking very grave.

"I'm only making it easy for you," said Chipper to Mrs. Hairns; "so that they shan't expect too much." Then, to Peter, "I brought her up because she once got out and walked on a hot Sunday when I was dragging her up a hill with her husband, three of his friends, their wives, eight children, a baby, and three dozen of beer."

"Fancy your remembering!" said Mrs. Hairns. "Did I really?"

"It was so unlike you, if I may say so," said Chipper, "that I have never forgotten it."

"I dessay it *was* silly of me," said Mrs. Hairns apologetically.

Just then the bishop arrived. He had been energetically climbing the hill by the little foot tracks which cut across the zig-zags of the road, and had consequently been overtaken by Chipper, who knew better.

"Is this the gate of heaven?" said the bishop.

"It is," said Peter.

"The *front* gate?" said the bishop suspiciously. "You are sure it is not the tradesman's entrance?"

"It is everybody's entrance," said Peter.

"An unusual arrangement, and in my opinion an inconvenient one," said the bishop. He turned from Peter to the angels, "Gentlemen," he said. "I am the Bishop of St. Pancras."

"If you come to that," said a youth in a dalmatic, putting his head out of one of the turret windows, "I am St. Pancras himself."

"As your bishop, I am glad to meet you," said the bishop, "I take a personal interest in every member of my flock. But for the moment I must ask you to excuse me, as I have pressing business at court. By your leave, gentlemen"—and he shouldered his way firmly through the group of angels into heaven and trotted sturdily up the street. He turned only once, for a moment, to say, "Better announce me," and went his way. The angels stared after him quite dumbfounded. Then the trumpet angel made a post horn of his trumpet, and first root-a-tooted at the sky, and then swept the trumpet downwards like the ray of a searchlight. It reached along the street to the bishop's coat tails; and the next blast swept him like a dry leaf clean round a corner and out of sight.

The angels smiled a beautifully grave smile. Mrs. Hairns could not help laughing. "Ain't he a tease!" she said to Chipper, indicating the trumpet angel.

"Hadn't you better follow the bishop in?" said Chipper.

Mrs. Hairns looked apprehensively at Peter (she was not afraid of the angels), and asked him might she go in.

"Anybody may go in," said Peter. "What do you suppose the gate is for?"

"I didn't understand, sir," said Mrs. Hairns. And she was approaching the threshold timidly when the bishop came back, flushed and indignant.

"I have been through the whole city in a very high wind," said the bishop; "and I cannot find it. I question whether this is really heaven at all."

"Find what?" said Peter.

"The Throne, sir," said the bishop severely.

"*This* is the throne," said St. Pancras, who was still looking out of the window, with his cheeks on his palms and his palms propped on his elbows.

"*This!*" said the bishop. "Which?"

"The city," said St. Pancras.

"But—but—where is He?" said the bishop.

"Here, of course," said the sword angel.

"*Here!* Where?" said the bishop hurriedly, lowering his voice and looking apprehensively round from one to the other until he finished with the trumpet angel, who had sat down to take off his wading boot and shake a stone out of it.

"He is the presence in which we live," said the sword angel, speaking very harmoniously.

"That is why they are angels," St. Pancras explained.

"What are you looking about for?" said the trumpet angel, standing up with his boot comfortable again. "Did you expect to see somebody in a shovel hat and apron, with a nose, and a handkerchief to blow it with?"

The bishop reddened. "Sir," he said, "you are profane. You are blasphemous. You are even wanting in good taste. But for the charity my profession imposes on me I should be tempted to question whether you are in the truest sense of the word a gentleman. Good morning." And he shook the dust of heaven from his feet and walked away.

"Ain't he a cure!" said Mrs. Hairns. "But I'm glad there's no throne, nor nobody, nor nothin'. It'll be more like King's Cross." She looked at them rather desolately; for something in the sword angel's voice had made her feel very humble and even ashamed of being drunk. They all looked back at her gravely; and she would have cried again, only she knew it would be of no use after the sword had touched her eyes: her tears were dried for ever. She twisted a corner of her jacket—a deplorable jacket—in her restless fingers; and there was a silence, unbroken until the snoring of Matthew, Mark, Luke, and John became painfully audible, and made her look forlornly up at their common little wooden beds, and at the flyblown illuminated text on the wall above them: "A broken and a contrite heart, O Lord, thou wilt not despise."

"I wonder," she said, "would one of you gentlemen say a prayer for a poor drunken old charwoman that has buried eleven, and nobody's enemy but her own, before I offer to go in."

Suddenly she sat down stunned in the middle of the way; for every angel threw up his hands and wings with an amazing outcry; the sword flamed all over the sky; the trumpet searched the corners of the horizon and filled the universe with ringing notes; and the stars became visible in broad daylight and sent back an echo which affected Mrs. Hairns like an enormous draught of some new and delightful sort of methylated spirit.

"Oh, not such a fuss about me, gentlemen," she said. "They'll think it's a queen or a lady from Tavistock Square or the like." And she felt shyer than ever about going in. The sword angel smiled, and was going to speak to her when the bishop came back, pegging along more sturdily than ever.

"Gentlemen," he said: "I have been thinking over what passed just now; and whilst my reason tells me that I was entirely justified in acting and speaking as I did, still, your point of view may be a tenable one, and your method of expressing it, however unbecoming, effective for its purpose. I also find myself the victim of an uncontrollable impulse to act in a manner which I cannot excuse, though refraint is unfortunately beyond my powers of self-inhibition."

And with that speech he snatched off his apron; made a ball of it; stuffed it into his shovel hat; and kicked the hat into space. Before it could descend, the sword angel, with a single cut of his wings, sprang into the air whooping with ecstasy, and kicked it a mile higher. St. Pancras, who had no wings, but shot up by mere levitation, was on it in a second and was shooting off with it when the trumpet angel collared him and passed it to the amber and black angel. By that time Matthew, Mark, Luke, and John were out of bed and after Peter into the blue vault above, where a football match was already in full swing between the angels and the saints, with Sirius for one goal and the sun for the other. The bishop looked in amazement for a moment at the flying scrum; then, with a yell, sprang into the air and actually got up nearly fifty feet, but was falling from that dangerous height when the saint he patronized swooped and caught him up into the game. Twenty seconds later his hat was halfway to the moon; and the exultant shouts of the angels had dwindled to mere curlew pipings, whilst the celestial players looked smaller than swifts circling over Rome in summer.

Now was Mrs. Hairns's opportunity to creep in through the gate unnoticed. As her foot approached the threshold the houses of the heavenly street shone friendly in the sunshine before her; and the mosaics in the pavement glowed like flower beds of jewels.

"She's dead," said the student from the Free Hospital. "I think there was a spark left when I took hold of her to straighten her out; but it was only a spark. She's dead now all right enough—— I mean poor woman!"

HAFOD Y BRYN,
*July 31, 1907.*

# Courtship of My Cousin Doone

## WALTER D. EDMONDS

WE were sitting side by side on the rails of the training-track fence: John Callant with his long upper lip moving up and down over his chew of tobacco, Doone's gold watch in his fist, and his impudent blue eyes following the prances of Blue Dandy as Doone limbered him up along the back stretch; and myself, a boy of twelve, bare-legged, dividing my attention between the horse and John Callant's mouth, for he had a neat way of spitting that some day I intended to master, just as I dreamed of being old enough some day to hold the lines over the back of one of Uncle Ledyard's trotters.

It was a broiling hot, early August morning, and Doone had already had out Maidy and Arrogance, and had left Blue Dandy for the last. Uncle Ledyard had watched the mares at their training and had then gone back to the house to wait for the mailman. In some way he had conceived a dislike for the gray horse, and he never had a good word to say for him, but Doone and John Callant, and, therefore, myself, believed in the animal's great future.

From where I sat I could see the broad low house under the elms, and Uncle Ledyard in his chair on the back veranda, tilted backward against the wall, his wide hat on the table, his beard bent against the open collar of his gray-flannel shirt, and beyond him the paddock, placed at the edge of the flatland over our Black River Valley, so that the colts looking over the fence seemed to be pricking their ears at the old man from the sky.

Blue Dandy came up to us on springing feet, his head up against the check, and Doone said over his shoulder, "I'm going to start him this time."

We watched him take the horse along to the gate, swing him neatly and bring him back. Blue Dandy went up on his toe calks and tossed the bit and eyed us as he went past, knowing he was going to start. Doone was settling his feet in the racks of the sulky and drawing the loops back to his hands. And I watched him with affection; for, excepting my own father, I thought Doone the finest man in the universe.

He was past thirty then, a black Boyd like Uncle Ledyard, but taller and smooth shaven. He had a straight nose, rather long, and a thin long jaw, and a mouth that closed itself firmly when he had nothing to say. Others of us used to wonder what would become of him, living alone with his

father at Boyd House, training his horses, or going fishing or shooting, according to the season. But I had no doubts about him, for I knew that before
he got through he would win all the great stakes of America with Blue
Dandy.

"He's turning," said John, round his cud of tobacco, and he lifted the
watch and fastened his eye on the wire.

Doone had wheeled the horse again, and before I knew it—for I had been
watching the mailman out of the tail of my eye—they were by us and spinning out the dust for the first turn. John's lips made a note of the seconds
on the watch, but he stopped chewing to follow the horse's head along the
rails into the back stretch, and suddenly he began to whistle.

I could see Doone leaning back against the reins with the wind lifting
his black hair and his mouth talking to the horse round the stem of his
short pipe. Blue Dandy was arching his neck against the rails and fighting
off from them as if he was bothered by the way they slid back of him. He
had always been shy of the rail; but his action was fine to watch, putting
down his feet as if his pride was in them and lifting his knees like the wind
in November. He was a big beast, three years old, coarser than the painting
of Greybriar over the mantel in the old house, but with the same searching
eye, and his head put on right. He hadn't shown speed enough in his second
year to be raced even at Boonville, and it was only Doone's patience and
the belief he and John Callant had in the horse that kept them after him.

He came by us again with the wonderful, deep, even blasts of his breathing like a great bellows, and he seemed that morning to cock his eye at us as
much as to say, "You poor fools," and then he was making his usual wide
sweep on the turn again, in spite of all Doone could do with him. It was so
still as they swung into the back stretch that we could hear Doone's voice
cursing him gently over the roll of his hoofs against the hard dirt. And all
of a sudden John's free hand lit on my knee and he stopped his whistling to
say, "Oh, Mary," and I felt a shiver go through me, though the sun was
broiling the back of my neck; for I saw that Blue Dandy was forgetting
about the rails and putting his head out against the bit, and I realized that
at last he had got the balance of the sulky under his tail. And John's whistle
turned mournful on one note, as it did when he was happy.

"Watch him, Teddy," he said. "He's roused."

It looked to me as if the horse had stepped clean out of the thills and
skipped three posts when he did it. Doone's face was skimming lower to
the rail, his arms were flat along the topsides of the lines and his eyes half
shut against the wind; and as they straightened into the stretch I saw him
leaning far inwards, the way he did when he was finishing the third heat,
and the tire of the nigh wheel was carving a line in the dirt to edge the
grass, and the horse's head was out in front of him; his nostrils were the
color of poppies, and the breath came out of them like the breath of victory.

I heard Doone crying, "So-o-o-o! So-o-o-o!" like the sound of the wind
against his teeth, but the horse was round the far bend and going down the
back stretch before he began to get back his stature and come up on his

pasterns, and he turned as if he was dancing on a spring bed, putting his head up, fluttering the dust out of his nostrils, and tossing out his mane. When he came back to us on the rail, he didn't come in for his sugar loaf, but swung away as if he scorned John Callant and me, and he had to toe around the track for a lap before he stopped and put out his ears and remembered that he was a lad again.

Doone was laughing.

"What did he make, John?"

"Two-seventeen," said John.

Doone whistled.

"I knew he was tearing into the last bend. And he wasn't fighting me either."

"He was running," said John. "I thought he might break, but he went off as smooth as a feather, the rascal."

"He was smooth," said Doone, and he put his legs out of the racks and swung himself off the seat. "You'd better take him in now."

John gave him back his watch and hopped over the seat, and we watched them jouncing down the track, and John's legs made me think of a frog's, the way they hung down with the toes turning out.

"Good morning, Teddy," said Doone. "Did you like him today?"

"He's a promising youngster," said I, wishing I could spit the way John did.

Doone grinned at me, and then we heard a deep snort.

"Promise!" said my Uncle Ledyard. "Well, he may have it, but if he's got anything else, you'll have to show it to me."

He had come across from the house and was leaning on the rail with his short beard broken on his forearms and the hat back on his head. His face was red with anger as Doone said, "I'll show it to you, dad," but his eyes were miserable. And it suddenly occurred to me why he didn't like the horse. He must have seen the promise in him from the beginning, and he was jealous of the memory of Greybriar. For to some men the horse is very much the same as a woman, for though he may own many in his lifetime, it is rarely that he is privileged to love more than one.

Uncle Ledyard was a massive man, with hard, heavy legs and broad hands and wrists powerful from training many horses. Though he was past seventy, he would still take his turn at driving the two mares if Doone was away; but he had become too heavy for racing. He showed his age nowhere else, unless it was in the badger hairs coming into his short beard and long, heavy eyebrows. It was odd to see the resemblance between him and Doone; the eyebrows on Doone not yet so long, but the eyes and nose the same—the eyes dark-brown and silent, but with a light of the devil in them when they were angry with each other. And they both smelled of horses and tobacco and clean hay.

"I'll grant you he's not so pretty as Greybriar," Doone said, "but he's going to have speed that the old one never got even a smell of."

"He would do very well in the milk wagon," said Uncle Ledyard.

They were both looking at him now in the door of the horse barn, where John Callant was combing the sweat off him with bright showers from the edge of the stick. And Doone looked bitter, for he loved the gray horse, and it hurt him not to have a good word for him from his father.

But the old man would never give it to him. Now he said, "You needn't think I've come over to look at the brute, Doone." He held up a blue letter in his fist. "Here's the devil to pay," he said.

"Is it from the admiral?" Doone asked.

"It is. He writes me he's coming up from Long Island," said Uncle Ledyard, "and he says he ought to get here tomorrow afternoon. And now he wants to know if it's going to be convenient, the damned old rip."

Doone sucked in his breath, and I knew why. They had just barely enough money to run the stable, and they let the house go; so when the admiral was coming for a visit, everything had to be turned out, the silver polished, the house cleaned, the harness shined for the carriage team, and the wagonette waxed, for the admiral lived in a grand way and moved in the high society of Long Island, and Uncle Ledyard didn't like to be ashamed of anything that belonged to him.

"What train is he coming on?" asked Doone, and I knew he was calculating the time he would have.

Uncle Ledyard gave a snort that sounded like Ajax, the black Percheron stud horse, when little Ralph Amber leads him into the horse barn.

"Train! Train! The old devil has got beyond any trains. He writes me he's coming in his automobile!" His eye rolled murderously, until it came over the paddock and he saw the colts pricking their ears at the sound of his voice. "The damned old jackass thinks he's going to drive in here and disturb the country with his dirty engine, roaring and spitting out his stinking smoke and sounding his horn at the hogs down at Meecher's Crossing —and I wish to God he would run over them, or I will myself some day, and bring that crummy loafer Meecher into court for damage to my disposition."

Doone grinned at him, and seeing me with my eyes sticking out on sticks, Uncle Ledyard grinned himself and asked me whether I knew what a motor car was. I told him I had seen them in New York City in the winter, but I had never ridden in one.

"Well," said Uncle Ledyard, "I'll ask him to give you a ride in his, if he doesn't wreck the thing getting here."

I could see that he was mightily pleased at the notion of the admiral's visit. The admiral was one of the few friends he had left—they had gone to college together—and with Doone not caring for people around, or indeed anything but training the horses, the old man must have found the place lonesome, for though my father often came to see him, they could never agree on the matter of a Royal Coachman as against my father's favorite red-and-white fly, which was a trouble to them both.

"There's another thing, Doone," said Uncle Ledyard. "It'll give you something to think about. He's bringing the girl along."

Doone looked up.

"Kathy?" he asked.

"Yes," said Uncle Ledyard. "And you'll have to look out for her."

"I'm busy," said Doone. "Let her run around with Teddy."

"I'll not let her," said I. "I don't want any girls interfering with my business."

Uncle Ledyard grinned at the two of us.

"Maybe you'll find her changed, Doone."

"She used to be a damned nuisance," Doone said. "Running around the horses in her bare legs almost as dirty as Teddy is now."

Uncle Ledyard shrugged his shoulders.

"It is a damned nuisance," he said. But he didn't mean it. He was thinking of the afternoons he would have with the admiral on the back veranda over their long glasses, both of them remembering the old days together. It was a pleasant place, that back veranda, for the flatland carried your eye out straight into the sky, with the paddock fence and the neat heads of the two-year-olds against it. Even under the shadow of the broad roof, you had a feeling of the sky over you, the run of the clouds, the hot, still heat of the sun, with the bees drowsing in the weed-grown borders, or the wrens in the lilac hedge, or the drumming of the colts' feet against the sod. I used to like lying in the old red-and-purple-tasseled hammock and hearing the admiral swearing in the heat of the afternoon, his silver hair carefully combed, his mustache right to the last hair, the dew of Highland whisky on his red cheeks, and his stock white under his chin, and his blue coat, cut by a tailor from London, outlandish opposite Uncle Ledyard's loose corduroy. I began to think about it with a kind of luxury in my nostrils, for the admiral always brought with him the scent of a strange, elegant world. But a slap on my rear brought me to.

"Wake up," said Doone. "Get over to John and tell him I want to have him in the house as soon as he's finished Blue Dandy."

They went off for the house side by side, Doone to get after Mrs. Callant, who managed the house in her own way that made all the women of our valley rail against her—maybe from envy—and Uncle Ledyard to frame a telegram to the admiral that the telegraph company would be willing to accept.

"John," I said, walking into Blue Dandy's stall and sitting down in the straw under the horse's nose, "Doone wants you in the house directly you're through here."

"He does, does he?" said John, finishing off the quarters with a stick. Then he drew on the light burlap blanket and began rubbing down Blue Dandy's legs with his bare hands. The horse niddled my hair with the tip of his tongue—a trick I never saw in any other horse—until I made a snatch for it and he tossed his head.

"So, there!" said John, but Blue Dandy paid no attention to him and began again to niddle me with his tongue tip. "What does he want me for now, anyway?"

"He's got some work for you."

"Don't I know that?" said John. "Well, he can wait till I finish the horse."

I shivered under the tongue tickle and then made another grab, and this time he let me catch it in my fingers. For some reason, it pleased him, and he dropped his nose closer while I held the tongue, and closed his eyes and drooped his ears in a way that made John spit out his quid for disgust. "The old mule," he said.

I sank back on my back, with the horse over me, and looked up at the wet curve of his belly, seeing the clean way his legs were put into his body. The stall was right beside the door and, the door to the stall being open, the sun came in around me where I lay in the deep straw. I could see the motes lazy in the sunlight, and smell the fresh timothy overhead in the loft, and listen to the teeth whistle of John on one note, and the fine hot smell of Blue Dandy covered us both.

"John," I said, "when do you suppose I'll be let to drive Blue Dandy?"

"Oh, I guess in a while. You've got some growing to do."

"I'm pretty stout, John."

"Not enough. I'll tell you, though. When you meet with a bee that has the thirteenth stripe on his back, come and ask me again."

"Oh," I said.

John picked up the nigh hind hoof and looked at the plate, tapped it with his finger nail and let it fall. I watched him lazily, my fingers mechanically twitching the warm tongue.

"John," I said, "what kind of a girl was Kathy?"

"The admiral's girl?" John asked absently.

"The same," said I—for when we were alone together, my tongue always followed the twists of John's speech.

"Well," he said, "she used to be a coltish creature. A bit of a harridan in her, I think, as is in the admiral himself."

"What did she look like?"

"She was a lean little fidget, black as a Boyd, but her eyes gray. And she had good legs and a long black braid on her back, and she was always pestering Doone to take her in the sulky with him, to ride in his lap with her hands on the reins behind his. She had some promise as a mare."

"John!" I said. "What are you talking about?"

John turned an impudent eye on me.

"Sure you was asking about her."

"She isn't a horse," I said.

"I didn't say she was. No doubt she's growed into a fine lady. I think Doone was partial to her some way. But she hasn't been back. And anyway, he don't have no interest in girls at all."

"I haven't," I said. "Why should he?"

"Well, well," said John. "Maybe he shouldn't. But if I was a handsome gentry and all the girls asking under their eyelids, I wouldn't be speaking to my horse alone when I saw a good-looking piece bugging potatoes alone in the field, unless I said 'Whoa.'"

I looked at John for a while.

"But what was Kathy like?" I demanded.

"Amn't I telling you? She used to bedevil me all day long, running into the horse barn in her bare legs and her pinafore up behind, and no decent sight, and sitting down in the straw under my feet, and asking John-this and John-that, till my poor noddle rocked with the blather, for all the world like yourself."

"Oh," said I haughtily, "I was just asking because the admiral's coming tomorrow afternoon, and I think that's what Doone wants you for—to clean the silver."

John gave me a grim, hurt look, but I was not sorry for him. If there was one job he hated beyond ordinary work, it was cleaning the silver, for his wife put him out on the porch in plain view of the road, with an apron round his middle and eau de Cologne in his hair to keep off the barn smell.

I had been asked to stay to lunch, so I stayed. In any other house, even a twelve-year-old boy would have felt in the way, but Uncle Ledyard took me into the office with himself, and I sat down on the floor beside the gun case, where Artemis, the Gordon-setter bitch, had her bed, and looked up at the deer heads on the walls and the stuffed bass that had been caught in the big hole in the canal and that weighed six pounds and a quarter. Uncle Ledyard sat in his leather chair in front of the stove and lit his cigar and let the thunder of housecleaning racket over his head.

For like all dirty people, Mrs. Callant made a great noise about cleaning, and after she had served us our lunch we could hear her voice screeching from all parts of the house at once, for Minna, for Mrs. Toidy, who did the heavy cleaning, or for John. Her feet would bang down the stairs, her strong hands would shake the bedding from the windows, her impulsive fingers drop a glass with a crash. She was always asking what Mrs. Phœbe would say to this mopping, that dusting, for Mrs. Phœbe Boyd could not bear the dirt in Uncle Ledyard's house and made a yearly attempt, with three pairs of white cotton gloves, to show her she was a lazy slattern. But Mrs. Callant only succeeded in raising the dust and making an unholy turbulence. The trouble was that she was a born cook, and Uncle Ledyard took her food for the stuff of heaven it was and accepted her airs and her racket along with it, as he was doing now.

I do not know what he was thinking about, but he must have known I was looking at the bass, for he said suddenly, "I caught him on a Royal Coachman, which is the best fly in the universe. So the next time your father offers you one of his crazy red-and-white contraptions, ask him for a Royal Coachman."

I looked up at the bass and grew cold, because that was a point I knew my father was right on, and it seemed an injustice in God for Uncle Ledyard to have caught the fish.

But I said, "If father had been fishing there that evening, he'd have caught him too."

"Would he?" asked Uncle Ledyard, putting his hand in his beard and peering down at me. "And what does that prove, Teddy, since he wasn't?"

"Why," said I, "that bass would have weighed seven pounds instead of six."

The process of cleaning stopped over our heads while Uncle Ledyard laughed, and hearing it, John Callant, with a fork in his hand, stuck his face in at the door to see what was up.

"And Callant," Uncle Ledyard said to him, "do you know, I think the boy is right at that!"

Just then we heard Mrs. Callant clattering down the stairs and her voice on the edge of screeching, "Oh, Misther Boyd!" Her red Hibernian face appeared in the door, and she saw John.

"Get back to yer silver, you idle, lazy loafer! Wasting your time in the house!"

John gave her a dirty look, and she lifted her damp cleaning cloth to slap him, when my Uncle Ledyard said, "Susanna!" with all the harshness of his heavy voice.

Immediately her hand dropped in front of her apron, and she put the other in it, and her bold eyes grew round and amazed. She jerked her heels for a curtsy and said, "Yis, your honor."

There was a great silence in the house, with only the distant noise of the reaper in the oats.

"John," said Uncle Ledyard, "that's all."

John grinned at his wife as he went out, and I could see her memorizing the dirty look she wanted to give him, but she stood there very meekly in front of Uncle Ledyard. He looked at her a while before he spoke:

"Haven't I told you time and again to come to my door gently and to knock on it, and to come in if I say, 'Come in,' and to go away quietly if I don't?"

"Yes, your honor."

"And if I say, 'Come in,' what are you to do?"

"I'm to come in quietlike, your honor, and tell you what it is that's bedeviling me."

"And do you call this coming in quietly, you noisy, roaring beasey?" thundered Uncle Ledyard. "Do I want to be screeched at by you to come running all over the house? I'd like to put my belt across your backside to make you remember your place!"

"Yes, your honor," Mrs. Callant said, curtsying again.

Uncle Ledyard breathed hard in his nose and stared at her from under his shaggy brows with a hard stare which seemed, to me, to please her unaccountably.

"Now tell me decently what it is that's on your brain, if you've got one."

"Oh, sir," said Mrs. Callant, in a desperate kind of whispering voice. "It's just that it's come into my head, where we are to put Miss Kathy, now she's a fine lady."

"What's the matter with the room she used to have?"

"It was all right for a little girl," said Mrs. Callant. "But it doesn't seem daintified now, and besides, it's all full of mice."

Uncle Ledyard swore.

"Why is it full of mice? Why haven't you cleared them out, you loafing Irishwoman? What do I hire you for to take care of my house, if you let the mice eat it out from under my feet?"

Mrs. Callant seemed momentarily at a loss. Then her eyes fell on Artemis beside me on the floor, and a glance of hatred was exchanged between them.

"Sure and I think it's that bitch has been killing the cat, your honor."

Uncle Ledyard swore at her again, and she seemed quite contented.

"You're right, Susanna," he said. "She's been to a finishing school and run the admiral's big house on Long Island for him, and we must do better for her than her old room."

"Yes, your honor; that's just what was in my head too."

"Be quiet, can't you?"

"Yes, sir, that's what I'm trying to do."

"Be still!" roared Uncle Ledyard.

"Yes, your honor."

"The admiral has the guest room next the withdrawing room, for he doesn't like the stairs."

"No, they're bothersome to a gentleman going to bed."

Uncle Ledyard gave her a glare.

"What's the matter with the other room downstairs?"

"It smells of the bats," said Mrs. Callant.

"Why does it?" asked Uncle Ledyard, scowling threateningly.

"Sure, it's the bats that smell, not the room," said Mrs. Callant. "And I can't be forever chasing them out, the nasty creatures."

"Then I don't see where we're going to put her," said Uncle Ledyard.

Both Mrs. Callant and I knew there was the room Doone's mother used to have, but the old man would let nobody into it from the day she died. It was a queer thing about him, but there it was, and nobody could decently suggest his giving it to Kathy.

There was a long pause.

"Haven't you any ideas at all?" asked Uncle Ledyard.

"No, Misther Boyd, unless it's yourself that has one. But I was just thinking, couldn't we put her into Misther Doone's room?"

"What'll we do with Doone?"

"He won't be minding the bats."

"I don't think he'll like it," said Uncle Ledyard, "but call him."

Doone came in from the horse barn in answer to the bell which Mrs.

Callant swung brawnily from the back porch. He hardly seemed to be listening to Uncle Ledyard.

"It's a nuisance, Doone, but you see how it is."

Doone seemed annoyed, but he took it good-naturedly.

"So long as I don't have to do the moving," he said. "I'm worried about Pansy, dad. She looks to me as if she'd foal early."

"No," said Uncle Ledyard.

"She does."

"I'll ask John Callant."

"He doesn't know."

"Poor fool that he is," said Mrs. Callant. . . . "Shall I change the rooms, then, your honor?"

"Yes, yes."

Doone went out, and Mrs. Callant after him. She closed the door with great caution and then shrieked for Minna and Mrs. Toidy at the top of her lungs. We heard them come running, talk excitedly, and then all three mounted the stairs to gather Doone's few clothes.

"I wish that Doone had something in his head besides the horses," Uncle Ledyard said, after a time.

"He likes fishing," I said.

"I know that, Teddy. But it's not what I'm thinking."

He lit his cigar again and puffed on it, and under cover of the smoke I saw him eying the miniature of Doone's mother that hung under the picture of Greybriar over the mantel.

When I came over the river the next morning, I brought a letter for Uncle Ledyard from my mother. And as I approached Boyd House in the early-morning sunlight, it seemed to me that the old house was wearing a new shine, for the light glistened on the warm old yellow of its clapboards, and the dew still lay on the shady side of the roof that came down from the peak of the house in a slow curve, clear out to the veranda eaves.

It was the oldest house in our part of the valley, and I always thought that the Boyd who built it must have been a shortish man, because the rooms had such low ceilings that Doone always had to bend his head in going through a door. The grant to the land was to Julian Boyd from King George, and that deed with the royal seal of England and a bill of sale signed by Mr. Boyd and sixteen Indians in council, and marking the transfer of two thousand acres for a rifle, a set of razors, a quilted dressing gown and two barrels of whisky, was all the title they needed to show so long as they kept up the back pages of the family Bible, that ended with Doone's name.

Minna was mopping the back porch, making a smell of suds against the smell of asters, and I passed her with a nod and went through the dining room.

It was a small room, as a dining room should be, so that a man could feel himself in close communion with his dinner, and the furniture was beautiful old Hepplewhite in Domingan mahogany, almost golden with age, that made eating there a time of dignity. And I found Uncle Ledyard having a cup of coffee with the sun about his plate.

"Good morning, Teddy," he said, and accepted my mother's letter.

I watched him while he read it, his eyebrows drawn low, his eyes concentrated on my mother's even handwriting. Then he looked up at me and said, "I'm sorry your mother's sister is ill, Teddy. I hope it's not so bad as it sounds. Of course, you can stay with us. We'll be glad to have you, for with the admiral here, and Kathy, Doone will be needing an extra hand with the horses."

"I'm willing to help him out," I said as calmly as any man could, for all the way over it had seemed the most fortunate thing in the world that my aunt should be ill and my mother have to go to her, so that I could come over to Boyd House.

"Have you had your breakfast, Teddy?"

"Yes, thanks," said I. "Where's Doone?"

"He's out with Pansy. He doesn't fancy the way she's behaving."

"I'll run over," I said.

"I wish you'd come back," he said, "and help me bring up some stuff from the cellar."

"I will."

But Doone was coming out of the stable and met me in the yard.

"How's Pansy?" I said.

"I guess I was wrong. She's all right for the time."

Pansy was a small black creature with a two-seven mile on the books. She was bred to The Earl, a horse that had done some great trotting the last year on the Grand Circuit.

"You'd better not go in now," said Doone. "I don't want her disturbed."

"How's Blue Dandy?" I asked.

"He's fine."

"Aren't you going to work him today?"

"I have. Before you came, Teddy. But now we'll have to make ready for the admiral."

"Well," I said, "I'm staying here now, so I'll be able to help you out. And if you want," I added, with my heart pumping up against my windpipe, "I can take Blue Dandy round for you now and then."

His hand dropped on my shoulder.

"I guess we'll make out together," he said.

"Can't I please drive him, Doone?"

"Do you know how old I was before dad let me trot in the sulky?"

"No."

"Fifteen."

"But I'm big for my years."

He gave me a pat, but I wouldn't go into the house with him, for I was afraid I might cry, but instead I went out to the asters to see if there were any bees with thirteen stripes on their backs. I had never counted the stripes on a bee before, and after a while it looked hopeless, because I saw none with more than seven. But by twelve o'clock I was getting too hungry to keep to myself, and I found them at lunch together.

"When will they come, dad?" Doone asked.

"About four o'clock," Uncle Ledyard said.

In spite of myself, I was excited. And by three o'clock, with the fidgety waiting, I had forgotten all about Blue Dandy. For in our back country there had never been an automobile.

Doone had put on his black coat and Mrs. Callant had pressed Uncle Ledyard's pepper and salt, and I had put on my stockings and shoes.

There was a table on the veranda with bottles on it, and glasses, and mint in a white bowl with ice floating in the water, and raspberry vinegar for Kathy and myself. Uncle Ledyard looked hot as tomatoes, and Doone was long-faced, and I lay in the hammock, curled up, for there was a tickle in the bottom of my insides.

You couldn't hear a sound in the house behind us, except for Minna's giggling now and then. The men were bringing the oats in from the eight-acre piece, but their voices sounded far away and less articulate than the groans the reach made under the heavy load as the horses hauled from shock to shock. I thought I couldn't bear sitting still another minute, when Doone lifted his head.

"Listen, dad."

The old man threw up his chin. I held my breath. There was a clicking of toenails through the withdrawing room, the screen door opened, and the thin black-and-red shape of Artemis toed over the porch. Her tail was stiff as a rod with a three-pound bass making a long run, and she growled softly.

"Shut up, girl," said Uncle Ledyard.

In the field the team stopped in a turn, and Adam Fuess, on the load, shaded his eyes and looked for where the road opened from the woods. Then one of the two-year-olds whinnied and there was a spatter of hoofs for the corner of the paddock, and then far away we heard the noise, like the noise a goose makes, flying in the fall against a high wind.

"Is it the horn?" asked Uncle Ledyard.

"It doesn't sound like cursing," said Doone.

"Then it isn't Jim," said Uncle Ledyard.

Doone got slowly to his feet. Artemis looked up at him and gave a wave of her tail, and then stared out again and growled. Uncle Ledyard got up, too, and I followed him and Doone and the dog to the carriage circle, and we stood between the tubbed geraniums, myself on the carriage block, and stared at the woods.

Then we heard the engine running with a noise like firecrackers strung very tight together. The horn sounded again, like a man who has swallowed too large from his glass, and there it was, coming out of the woods with its brass front and the brass rails running down to it from the bit of glass and a great roll of dust hiding all its back end.

There was a chap in the front seat bending his belly over a wheel, with glasses over his eyes like the goggles you drive in a horse race with. And the admiral was standing up and leaning over the chap's shoulder with his hat in his hand and his white hair shining and his face red from shouting. And beside him was a woman sitting very straight. I noticed that even as far away as she was, the straight, graceful way she sat the jounces of the motor car. She had on a soft, whitish-yellow coat and a hat of the same color; but there was a bright green veil tied over it and round her neck, and the ends reached straight out behind her like the tail of a flying bird.

We could hear the engine picking up in the noise it made, and the dust rose higher, and then the car brayed like a jackass, and we saw that it was the admiral punching the horn. Uncle Ledyard caught me up on his shoulder and roared, "Hurray, boy, hurray!" Doone waved his hand, and I screamed, "Hurray, hurray!"

Mrs. Callant and John came running out of the house, and Minna sidled out behind them, and I caught a glimpse of Mrs. Toidy's face peering from the upstairs window. In the field, Adam Fuess was waving his hat from the top of the load, and the big team had their heads up and were lifting their feet and snorting. And we all shouted again, for in truth it was a marvelous and heroic thing to think of that coughing contrivance traveling by itself all the two hundred and ninety miles from New York City to Boyd House.

The driving chap leaned over, turning the wheel in his hands, and the front wheels of the car turned toward us, and the car came after them, whirling round the corner, whirling back to make the circle, and as the driver chap pulled at a rod outside, the door stopped right in front of the block as neatly as John Callant would have wheeled up the wagonette behind the bays. Then the driving chap pushed a button in front of him and the engine ceased coughing and the body shaking. There was a moment's silence and then there was a report like a twelve-gauge shotgun that has gone off in both barrels when nobody was expecting it.

I jumped, and Uncle Ledyard swore, and behind us Minna squealed and Mrs. Callant crossed herself with her hand under her apron. But the admiral was roaring with laughter.

"Only a back fire," he said off-hand. "How are you, my boy?"

He stood up in the tonneau and looked down at us, just a little condescending from the pride of his new car. But Uncle Ledyard was grinning up at him and saying, "Get out of your bread box, Jim, and let me shake hands with you."

The driver chap had got out, looking rather cramped in the knees, and opened a door in the side of the car, and the admiral got down.

"It's good to see your old face again," he said, pumping Uncle Ledyard's hand and giving it the grip that I had always tried to see. But I never did, though I knew when they were giving it, because they looked solemn and stiff and happy like two dogs at a new post. Then the admiral turned to Doone and shook hands with him, saying, "How are you, Doone?" And

Doone thanked him. But I saw that he was looking past the admiral at the lady in the back seat, so I looked too.

The admiral and the driver chap were gritty beyond belief, but no dust showed on her whitish coat, and the green of her scarf was too bright to be dimmed by it, and as she rose from the seat her cheeks looked fresh in the shade of her hat. Her color was high from the long drive. She was very lovely as she hesitated in the tonneau, for she stood gracefully and easily, and the coat fitted her nicely, showing her slimness from the hem of her skirts to her eagerly lifted chin.

Then she got down through the door and came over to us, and she walked well, with her feet sure of the ground. Uncle Ledyard took off his hat, and so did the admiral. He said, "This is Kathy," with pride.

But Doone was bareheaded. He took her hand and bowed. His voice sounded strange to me as he said, "Hello, Kathy."

"Hello, Doone."

Her voice was low, strong and cordial, but there was hint of reserve in it, too, as there had been in Doone's—as if each had found a strength in the other they had not been looking to find, and they were surprised and on guard. But there was no mistaking the look in Doone's eyes. I had seen them once look like that when he first put his hands over a filly.

Then Uncle Ledyard was booming, "Well, well, Kathy," and she was giving a little cry and running into his arms, and his stiff short beard was bending against the fresh skin of her cheek. And Adam Fuess in the oat field might have heard his smacking kisses.

She stood back laughing softly and holding both his big hands in her slim, gloved ones.

"Dear nunky," she said.

He beamed all over, with his eyes, his mouth; his whole self seemed to be smiling at her.

"My Lord, Kathy," he said. But her eyelids drooped in front of his stare and she made a curtsy as she held his hands, and then she rose with the most graceful gesture in the world, as if we were all of us in a play, and her eyelids swept up from her eyes and I saw the color of them for the first time under her thick black lashes.

John had said they were gray, but they were beyond any gray that I ever saw, for now they seemed blue, and now green, and now almost hazel, like the colors one finds in silver.

But now her eyes caught sight of him and she cried, "John!" and then, "Mrs. Callant!" And John came grinning up to her, his face like a frog, eyes popping and mouth going round his face like the hoop on a silo.

"Bedevil and all——" he began but Mrs. Callant pushed him aside.

"Always a-swearing, you damned fool," she said. Then she made a curtsy to Kathy and said, "Pleased and honored we are, Miss Kathy, and hope to entertain you comfortably. You're to have Misther Doone's room and he's to sleep with the bats."

Kathy laughed and turned to look gayly at Doone, who was flushing a little, and the admiral roared and cursed, and said with a laugh, "Hard bedding, Doone."

Uncle Ledyard said, "Stop the racket, you fool," to Mrs. Callant, and then to John, "Help with the bags, John. And dust them off carefully."

"That's right," said the admiral, his blue eyes sticking out boldly. "I'm dry as feathers with all the dirt of your dirty back roads, Leddy. . . . Joe"— and he spoke to the driver chap—"get out the bags. And then John Callant here can show you where to put the car and where to sleep."

"Put the car?" said John, turning a disfavorable eye on the driver.

"Do as you're told," said Uncle Ledyard.

"Sure and where am I told to put it? In the barn?" asked John in the rhetorical voice he used when he was offended.

"In the barn? Do you want to scare the living wits out of Pansy?"

"Who's Pansy?" Kathy asked.

"She's the black mare," I said. "She's going to foal."

That made Kathy look at me, and she smiled.

"Who are you?" she asked, for they were all tossing about with the bags, of which there were more than you could believe possible, since the admiral never moved anywhere without all his forty pairs of shoes. "I'm Kathy O'Chelrie," she said.

"I know you're Kathy," said I. "But I thought your name was Porter like the admiral's."

She did not take offense, seeing how surprised I was.

"No," she said, "my father was O'Chelrie, and my mother married the admiral as a young widow."

"Oh, I see," I said. "Well, my name's Teddy Armond, and I've heard of you from Uncle Ledyard and from John Callant."

She gave me a little bow.

"May I call you Teddy, like the others?"

I do not know why, but her words put a small shiver in the hollow of my back and I felt that if she kissed me I shouldn't mind this time; but I respected her more for not doing it. And then I remembered something, and I looked at her again.

"Haven't I seen you before somewhere?"

"I don't believe so," she said. "The last time I was here, Teddy, you hadn't been born."

"I have, though," I said, getting more and more sure of myself. "I've seen a picture of you."

She smiled again. It was a lovely smile. She had a beautiful, wide, generous mouth and her teeth were white and strong. She looked like a person who had never been tired in her whole life. And then I remembered, and the little chill went all over, and in the quiet sunlight, with the bustle of getting out the bags all round us, I caught a vague and sweet scent from her. It was not like perfume such as ladies put on their handkerchiefs; it was light and bright and a little intoxicating, and it lay between us like our understanding. I forgot even my excitement about the auto, for Kathy was Kathy

O'Chelrie, of New York, who was in the play that had the whole city agog.

Then Doone came over to us, and I said, "Do you know who she is, Doone?"

"What do you mean?"

The admiral looked up at me, red in the face, with his white mustache stiff as a bull's horns, but I didn't heed his annoyance. And I would have told Doone, if Kathy had not met my eyes again. The corners of her mouth twitched to a smile, but her eyes were serious and made me feel great pride in myself.

"I've promised not to tell," I said. "You'll have to find it out for yourself."

"What is he talking about, Kathy?" asked Doone.

She looked at him and smiled. I think even then she was in love with him, and I thought, "If I were Doone, I would be with her."

"Don't you know?" she said. "I'm Kathy. You used to call me a damned nuisance, Doone. I remember once I stole your trousers and you had to chase me for them." The devil in her eyes made me laugh. Doone flushed.

"I remember," he said. "And I gave you a proper lambasting."

The color waved in her cheeks. She had plenty of temper. And they stared at each other, a quick, hard meeting of eyes.

Then the admiral swore.

"A damned nuisance is right. . . . Ledyard, do you realize we've come three hundred miles in the last two days and you haven't offered me a drink yet?"

## II

It was the strangest thing in the world how Kathy's entrance changed the very breath in that old, man's house. It was something I noticed when she passed over the threshold. The sunlight seemed to come with her.

She stood in the living room that occupied the center of the house and drew herself up with a deep breath.

"It hasn't changed. It hasn't changed at all, nunky. I love it."

His voice sounded hoarser than usual as he put his arm round her slim, long waist. "It hasn't looked the way it does now for a good many years, Kathy."

"What'll I do with that engine, Misther Ledyard?" John Callant whispered.

"Put it in the woodshed, John," whispered my uncle.

But the admiral heard him.

"You can't treat it that way, Leddy, you old coper! Don't you realize that automobile cost more than three of your horses put together?"

"Did it, Jim? You'd do better to deal with me then, I think."

The admiral drew a shivering breath and his eyes swelled. And I waited expectantly for the bursting dams of his profanity. But John said, "The lad out there wants a garridge for it."

"Put it there," said the admiral quite calmly.

"But there isn't anny such thing," said John, scratching his head. "I can put a rick cover over it, if you like."

"No!" roared the admiral.

"Would it take cold, then?" asked John.

"You blasted, impudent rogue!" said the admiral.

"Sure the reaper's out. Maybe we could put it alongside the manure cart."

"Get out of here," said Uncle Ledyard. "And take care of it properly."

John went out grumbling, and we heard him say to the chauffeur, "Wind up the trinket, me boy, and bring it along afther me." He wasn't taking any chances of a ride.

The car coughed and roared, and then went off.

Kathy smiled.

"Nothing's changed."

"It'll seem a rough place," said Uncle Ledyard.

"No, it won't. It's lovely. I don't think I've been in real country since I was here—oh, years and years ago."

"There's no other real country," said Uncle Ledyard. "Maybe you'll want to get washed. Mrs. Callant'll show you Doone's room."

We four men went out on the porch and the admiral sat down in the high-backed rocker as if he hadn't come farther than a trip to the village, and he and Doone and Uncle Ledyard fixed their own glasses and drank good health to one another. I poured myself some raspberry vinegar and put in the mint, and went over to the hammock. Then Doone excused himself to go look at Pansy, and the two old men sat still for a long moment, smiling at each other.

It was then that I knew really of the change in the house. It wasn't dead behind us the way it was when the admiral and Uncle Ledyard used to sit on the veranda. Then everything about it seemed to look out at the men in the fields, or the colts in the paddock, at Doone on the track, with John Callant and the sulky behind one of the racers, at Artemis coming in from a stroll.

Now the house had an inward life, and it had a voice.

It was the light, quick feet of Kathy I heard, moving back and forth in Doone's room over our heads. The splash of the water into the basin. Her voice humming on the edge of song. The noise her slippers made as she took them from the bag and dropped them on the floor. They were delicate sounds, and hearing them made me sink lower in the old, tasseled hammock and wonder at the way I felt my hands at the end of my wrists, and tightened the muscles in my legs.

"Well, Jim," said Uncle Ledyard, "you look pretty hearty."

"I'm all right, Leddy," said the admiral, combing the Bourbon out of his mustache. "I can't run around as fast, maybe. But, thank God, my digestion's all right."

"It's a pleasure to have you, then," said Uncle Ledyard. "You and Kathy. Do you realize, you damned sailor, that she's a beautiful piece of it?"

"Why shouldn't I, being a damned sailor? And with a hundred people a day to tell me, if I couldn't see it for myself. Even Teddy has eye enough for that."

"I hope she won't get bored here, grown up as she is. It's different from your place."

"A lot she sees of that," snorted the admiral.

"What do you mean, Jim?"

"Well, she's gone on the stage now. That's what I brought her up here for. To get her away from all the puppies that paw around after her. They'd follow her to hell, but they wouldn't come here. I wouldn't myself, if you weren't here and didn't have the best whisky in America."

"There's plenty of that," said Uncle Ledyard. "Why don't you marry her off?"

"I could marry her in a minute to Rowland Atterbury or any other man you'd care to name," said the admiral. "But she won't stand for them. Girls have got their heads nowadays, and ten to one she'd make me a scandal. Now, in France they do it decently. A father can see to breeding his own line. You keep them at home and marry them off and they have a child, and that's the end of the contract. After that there's nobody responsible."

Uncle Ledyard tilted back his chair.

"I wish Doone would get married."

The admiral cocked his eye.

"Do you mean him and Kathy?"

"Well, I wouldn't say no."

"Lord!" said the admiral. "Doone couldn't get her."

"It's the other way round, Jim. He won't look at a girl."

The admiral stuck his red nose into his glass.

"He was looking at her pretty hard when we got here. Ten to one she turns him down."

"All right," said Uncle Ledyard. "Fifty dollars."

"Good," said the admiral. "That's easy money for me."

"He won't do it," said Uncle Ledyard, "but if he did go after her, I'll bet a hundred dollars that he'll bring her back."

"You poor fool," said the admiral, "I'll take it." He took a long drink from his glass. "I like Doone, you know. Even though he's a queer, solitary man like yourself, I've nothing against him. They won't think he's much of a match at home, for he hasn't the money. And that's one thing she has to have or she'll die."

"He's better-blooded than any of your Long Island pups," said Uncle Ledyard.

"I won't say yes or no," said the admiral. "But she has money enough for the two of them in her own name, and she'll have more from me."

"What's money got to do with it?" demanded my uncle.

"Well, I won't try to stop it."

"You'd be cheating on our bet if you did."

The admiral opened his mouth.

"So I would, you old fox."

"Have a drink," suggested Uncle Ledyard.

"Thanks, I will. I'll drink against my possible expenses. And I've bought a new boat."

"Curse your boats," said Uncle Ledyard. "I'm expecting a foal by The Earl out of Pansy. He's by Circumstance out of Fancy Girl. I'll show her to you tomorrow."

"Tomorrow," said the admiral, "you're going to have the thrill of your life, Ledyard. I'm taking you out in the car."

We heard Kathy coming down the stairs, and in a moment she was walking through the withdrawing room and at the door, and we were all on our feet.

She didn't want anything to drink.

"Minna brought me some water fresh from the spring," she said. "It's made me feel clean."

Uncle Ledyard smiled at her with his eyes from under the long hairs of his eyebrows, and the admiral said very soberly, "I believe it is good water, though I've never tasted it myself."

"Don't stand up for me," she said. "Please."

We all sat down again and watched her. She had leaned against a veranda post, with her hands holding it behind her. Her back rested against it so straight that there was no daylight showing between, and she had thrown back her head to rest her cheek against the white paint. The afternoon sunlight slanted across her, leaving one shoulder in the shadow and making a sculpture of the fine bones in her face. She seemed half asleep there, with her eyes veiled, as if she could never move again, as if her body was drinking the secrets of the house and the meadows.

The two old men sat solemnly looking at her and not saying a word through her silence, though the admiral's breath was beginning to rasp at the edges of his nostrils.

As the sun sank, the light warmed on her face, showing the details that I did not know, at that time, a woman had—the fine down under the brows and on the upper cheeks, like a bloom on fruit, it was so fine; the small way her nostrils were set, and the sensitiveness of her upper lip. It was short and curling—a light and beautiful thing. But the lower lip was strong and round and full, and her mouth in the sunlight was dark and red. She did not make me think of the wood blooms, for all the mystery in her body; nor of the strong, open field flowers, for the strength in her long hands. No, she did not make me think of flowers at all, though I could think of everything that lived and bloomed and grew and moved and had wings. The spirit in her was her own. She drew in her breath sharply, and her breast sprang, and she opened her eyes.

I was startled to find them looking straight at me.

"It's so good, nunky," she said to Uncle Ledyard. "I feel the way I used to the first day I got here. I can't sit down with you. I must see it all."

"Shall I take you around?" asked Uncle Ledyard.

"No, you stay here with Jim. I've got to go round everything till it's dark. I've got to get tired—all tired out tonight—or I won't sleep, nunky."

Uncle Ledyard smiled.

"Run along then," he said, "and mind you come in when Mrs. Callant rings the supper bell."

"I will—I promise I will."

They smiled at each other. Then she was looking at me again.

"Will you come with me, Teddy?"

"If you like."

"Come on, then."

She swung away from the post as if her feet were released, and I scrambled out of the hammock. I was surprised when she went into the withdrawing parlor, and more so when she stopped in it for a minute. For it was a strange and, to me, a disagreeable room.

It had rose-pink walls and fine old lyre-backed chairs, and brass lamps with etched-glass globes. The seats of the chairs were of brocade so faded that they were snuff color. There was a stove with Corinthian columns and much brass, and a harpsichord with rosewood inlay, and a small grand piano, of which I had never heard the voice, and a lady's secretary the glass doors of which were lined with old-rose silk. It was a room half dead, in which there was an old scent that might be forgotten perfume or decaying hopes. And there was only one picture on the walls—an engraving of a picture called Sacred and Profane Love. Some former Boyd lady must have bought it for that room and her successors must have approved of it. Though you could scarcely see it in the shadows, Kathy stopped in front of it. When I stopped next to her, she took my hand. And I felt her touch to be the only warm, living thing in the room. Then she tilted her head and looked up at the ceiling.

There was a small trapdoor just over her head.

"Do you know what that is, Teddy?"

"No. I've never bothered to notice it," I said.

"Doone's mother had it made, so after dinner she could come in here and he could say his prayers to her through it. She was a delicate lady, I believe. She was very beautiful. I wonder if she was happy."

"Why shouldn't she be?"

"That's what a man would ask, Teddy." Then she seemed to forget me for a while. I tried to think of Doone's face, as a little boy, with the candle on the floor in his room while he knelt, and his dark face like a gypsy's, saying "Our Father——" I must have said it aloud, for suddenly Kathy squeezed my hand tighter and looked down at me. I could not see her face in the shadow, but the bend of her neck was so gracious that my heart stopped. Then she laughed.

"Come, Teddy. Let's go outdoors."

"Where?" I asked.

"Everywhere."

We went out, and we went everywhere.

The sky was vast and crimson; there were fleece clouds overhead that caught the light against their breasts and turned it down. The two of us walking through it were like small things caught in a great flame. The buildings looked stiff and small and square, and the trees were like black torches.

We went to the garden where the rose beds of Doone's mother lifted pale globes of fragrance over the pigweed, and the white phlox shone silver like things drifting. We skirted the glen, looking down at the pool from which the house water was pumped, and in which, when Uncle Ledyard had it dug, the men found two skeletons and a dozen silver buttons and an Indian tomahawk. He had had them buried together in the burying ground, for he said there was no way of telling which was the Indian—a matter much better left for God to decide for Himself. We went over to the dairy barn, where Adam Fuess was weighing the last milk and pouring it into the cheese-factory cans for hauling in the morning. And we stood by the door as the cattle came out, with their bells and their warm grass breaths in our faces. We went up into the haymow and Kathy listened to see if there were any kittens, and when we heard them and found them, yellow and white, with their eyes not open, she nearly cried. She caught up her skirts and jumped with me clean to the mow floor, and we laughed breathlessly and ran outdoors.

It was darker now. The light was nearly off the flatland; the valley was in shadow. I pointed out to her the lights from our own place. And we heard a boat horn sounding from the canal towpath. Then we came to the back of the horse barn and heard Doone saying something to John Callant and the rumble of trolleys on the door. I showed Kathy how I had learned to lift the hook on the manure door and we went in. It was almost dark, but Pansy was standing in her box stall at the back, and she did not seem afraid of Kathy. Then we stopped while Blue Dandy put out his head and I showed Kathy how to tickle his tongue for him. Maidy and Arrogance wouldn't speak to us, so we came back to him. He looked fine and tall in the dark. Like the ghost of a horse.

No one saw us come out, and we went down by the canal with the bridge over us, and saw the boat's light at the bend and heard the horn. I put out my hand in the dark and touched Kathy. She was trembling a little.

"It looks cool, doesn't it, Teddy?"

Then we heard the clang of the house bell and we went back up the glen. And at the top we met Doone.

"I was looking all over for you," he said. "Where have you been?"

"All over," I said, as Kathy did not answer. "We found kittens and looked at Pansy."

"You're not supposed to go in there," he said.

"Why not?" It was Kathy that asked.

"She's due to foal soon and she's nervous."

"We didn't disturb her," said Kathy.

"She was quiet, Doone," I said. "I showed Kathy Blue Dandy. He gave her his tongue."

"Did he?" Doone sounded pleased, though I expected him to be jealous, as I should have felt if it had been my horse, and he said nothing more as we walked back to the lights of the house.

We had dinner that night as I had never seen it in the old house. The heavy silver was out on the sideboard and there were candles all over, and Minna, in a clean dress, looked quite smart. We had a soup made of green beans, light and creamy, and broiled small trout, and a saddle of lamb, and two kinds of wine, and a salad of cucumbers and icicle radishes, and a currant pastry. It was a fine sight to see the admiral eating of everything and looking over the top of his glass and then into the bottom of it and smoothing his white mustache. Uncle Ledyard was stiff and broad at the end of the table as he carved the saddle, and Doone looked handsome in his black coat with his black hair and dark face. And Kathy at the end of the table laughed with them all and talked to Doone and sometimes to me. She made him tell her about the horses—about Blue Dandy in particular—till the admiral grunted and wanted to know how anybody could have a liking for horse racing, now that automobiles were to be bought for money.

"You can travel all day."

"And walk up the hill," said Uncle Ledyard.

"You needn't in my car," said the admiral. "It'll take you thirty-five miles an hour on a decent road and swoop you up the hill like a sloop on a wave. I could mount to heaven's gates and make it in top gear, or maybe second, and you with your Blue Dandys would be eating my dust."

"I shouldn't think of that," said Uncle Ledyard. "I'd look to your brakes, if I were you, Jim. You might make the wrong turn at that speed."

The admiral growled.

In the living room, John Callant opened the cellar trap, and a smell of hams hanging there, and tarragon in vinegar, and lavender, came up about us. And then John Callant came up again with a bottle of the old port.

"Oil your machinery with that, my boy," said Uncle Ledyard, "and maybe you'll convince me with your talk."

"I will," said the admiral.

So we all rose and Kathy went out of the room, and because I couldn't have the port, Uncle Ledyard sent me after her.

I thought she would stop in the living room where the fire was crackling, and sit on the great red-leather couch, but she went on into the withdrawing room, and when I had followed her there I was amazed. The candles were lighted in the lamps and the room was glowing softly, and Kathy was sitting at the old yellow keys of the piano. She began to play.

It needed tuning, but she did simple things with it so that there were just a few notes to come through her voice, and she sang for me very softly. I do not know what the song was, because I did not catch the words, she was so near to humming it, but her voice was soft and almost small. I looked at her with her dark hair and her red dress and her round, slim, bare arms.

And she said through her humming, "It's a queer old room, Teddy. It's rather pathetic. It's full of Boyd women. Here's their piano I'm playing on, and its voice is small; and the harpsichord has lost all its voice. Outside the door of this room is their big living room with its big furniture and its smell of men and tobacco. And on the other side is their veranda, where the men drink. The roof throws a shadow on the light in this room. They are all surrounded by the Boyd men—all big black men. I wonder if they were afraid of them. But the most pathetic thing of all, Teddy, is that there are no more Boyd men but Doone. Have you ever thought of that?"

"What's the matter with Doone?" I asked.

But she did not hear me.

"All around this room is the talk of horses. The men went all around this room, and if they came into it, it was to go to the veranda or to come in from it to the living room. They were always passing through it with their strong voices and the smell of horses on their trousers. But, Teddy, you could smell every one of those chair seats and you wouldn't find the smell of horse on any one of them. Even the piano has a small voice."

Her voice was deeper, and it made me shiver and feel sorry for the Boyd women—though I did not see why—and angry against them, too—though I did not see why for that, either.

"The Boyds have always married fair-haired women. Pale creatures, I should believe. I don't know why. They were very good to them and treated them like ladies. And there's no lady for Doone."

Her fingers flashed on the keys, and a mocking trill came from the piano. "And there's no lady for Doone," it said.

"And there's no place for a lady in this house," continued Kathy in her strangely electric voice; "no place except this room. Be damned to it! I want a drink!"

"What for?"

But she had swung off the stool and stepped out on the porch. I heard the bottle click once against the tumbler rim and I saw her, outside, down a swallow of Bourbon. She looked at me in the door, and I suppose I looked afraid, and white.

"Come out of there, Teddy. Let's not feel sorry for the Boyd ladies in their little rose-colored room, or glad for the Boyd women in the countryside anywhere you fancy. The room is pathetic, it seems to me, because it was built by the men for their ladies, and preserved. It's the Boyd mausoleum, though they don't know it. Tell me, does Doone ever run after the country girls?"

I was shocked. But I tried not to show it. My voice must have been stiff as I answered, "John Callant says not," for she laughed and kissed me, holding me tight against her, and as I wriggled I smelled the perfume in the lace yoke of her dress.

She put me down again, saying, "Poor Doone, it's a curse on him. He's lost even that. All his heart is in the horses. Damn them! Damn them!"

"Wait till you see Blue Dandy," I said, "and you won't damn them any more."

"Let's go into the living room."

She looked almost hoydenish as we passed through the rose room now. All the sweet sadness was out of her. Her voice was ready to laugh. Her color was high. And she moved with scorn in her hips, as if with her skirts she stirred aside the ghosts.

She leaned against the hearth, supple as a wild vine, and I lay down in a corner of the red-leather couch. Then, as swift as a seed dropping, she was herself again, and the men were coming into the room.

The admiral looked redder than ever behind his white mustache, and his eyes were bulging a little, like blue marbles, and he was tremendously polite in calling John Callant to place a chair for Kathy. Doone looked solemn and ready to laugh at him. Uncle Ledyard said to Kathy, with that smile he had for her only, "Did I hear you singing in the rose room, Kathy?"

"Not a tune," she said, laughing. "The piano's too far off."

He looked wounded. "I'll have the tuner tomorrow," he said.

And suddenly Kathy's lip trembled and her silver eyes flashed towards me, and I saw they were full of tears. She put her arm over his shoulder and kissed him.

"That would be lovely, nunky. I'll play to you then."

"Will you, Kathy?"

"Whatever song you like."

She was looking at Doone now, and her eyes were a challenge even I could read.

But the admiral, who had fallen into a doze, jumped and swore at a knot bursting in the fire.

"A clean miss!" he roared. "My God, mister, this isn't target practice!"

### III

August is apt to bring us fine weather. The meadows are sultry, but there is a wind in the sky and the clouds are great and dignified as they march against the mountains. It was clear the next morning when we sat at breakfast with the farm sounds spreading into the fields. And as we finished, John Callant put his nose against the screen door and said, "Misther Ledyard."

"Yes," said Uncle Ledyard.

"It's this feller that says he's chauffeur wants to ask the admiral does he want the car."

"Yes, I do," said the admiral. "I want it in half an hour."

"And what shall I tell him?"

"What I said," said the admiral, staring up coldly.

"Very well," said John. "But he's a queer chap."

"What do you mean?" Kathy asked.

"Well, Miss Kathy, he said he couldn't sleep at all last night."

"What did you do with him?" Uncle Ledyard asked threateningly.

"Sure we gave him the corner room. It wasn't the bedding, I'm sure. And my missus was keeping her eye on Minna that's taken a fancy to his elegance. He said it was the silence kept him awake."

"Silence?"

"That's what I said. He said it kept dinging in his ears. It's very queer," said John, shaking his head. "I wouldn't thrust a man like that, myself."

"Never mind," said the admiral. "Tell him to be prompt. We'll have a spin before it gets hot. . . . You're coming, Leddy. It'll show you what the world's doing while you stifle up here. . . . How about you, Kathy?"

Kathy glanced at Doone.

"I think I won't, Jim."

"Nor I," said Doone. "I'm busy this morning with Blue Dandy."

"All right," said the admiral. "Then Leddy and I will go. I'll take you the loop round Hawkinsville."

"Let's arrange to come down the hill," suggested Uncle Ledyard.

"No, we'll go up," said the admiral. "With just three aboard, she'll do it easy. We'll go down by Meecher's Crossing and then we'll get a good run at it."

Uncle Ledyard was silent. He didn't like the notion, that was plain, but he had the look of a man who has made up his mind to die game.

The car came rattling over from the machine shed on the minute and whirled round the carriage circle on its little wheels. The chauffeur had polished off all the dust, but I could see the admiral sniffing at it when he got in, to see if John had put it beside the dung cart. Uncle Ledyard got in and closed the door and said, "Good morning," to the chauffeur like a man saying good morning to Charon. Then the chauffeur got into the front seat and sat still, waiting for orders. I thought he did look like a man who hasn't slept well—there was an edgy expression about the eyes.

"Drive ahead," said the admiral, "and when we come to the turns, I'll tell you which way to put her."

The chauffeur yanked at some rods and the car started. The admiral waved his hat very gallantly and the dust rose up and they turned down the glen. We did not see them again all morning.

"It's a wonderful sight, to be sure," said John.

I agreed.

"I'd like to drive it myself," I said.

Doone threw me a hard look, but Kathy smiled.

"I'll show you if you like, some day, Teddy."

"Can you drive it?"

"Yes, but Jim won't let me."

I thought about it for a moment, and then I said, "I won't do it, though, till after I've driven Blue Dandy."

I thought that would be a long time off.

Kathy and I went over to the track and watched Doone bring out the gray horse. He was going to travel again—you could see it in his eye. As he entered the track, Kathy drew her breath in.

"He's beautiful!"

Doone heard her and his smile flashed for her. But he didn't speak, except to the horse, and Kathy might have been myself, for all the attention he paid her till he had finished the first heat. He made it in 2:10. I have never seen a horse come along so quickly as Blue Dandy did once he started really to trot—but then he was three years old.

As he went under the wire, I asked Kathy, "Can your automobile move like that?"

"It isn't a comparison," she said with a small smile. "That's a machine and this is a horse."

"Just the same," Doone said, as he swung off the sulky, "I would bet that Blue Dandy could run down that motor."

Kathy flashed.

"What would you be willing to bet, Doone?"

"Anything in the world."

"Would you really?" she asked.

He said, "Yes," but his eyes were on Maidy coming out with John. "Put her round," he said, and he held the watch.

The mare was a leggy black thing, with a racking stride. You could see she was fast, but she wasn't thunder like Blue Dandy.

He watched the colt again, and then Kathy went back to the house to wait for the mailman. Inside the rose room sounded the slow tinkle of the piano as the tuner worked over it. Mrs. Callant was scolding Mrs. Toidy in the kitchen and Minna was making the beds.

There was a letter for Kathy which she read twice over before she said to me, "I'm offered a new part in the fall. A leading part."

She was leaning her chin on her hand and staring out at Doone on the track behind Arrogance.

"Does he do that all day, Teddy?"

"He has to bring them into shape for Syracuse," I said. "He hasn't much time."

"What would he make if he won, I wonder?"

"I don't know," I said. "But he needs the money."

"And what will he do if he doesn't make it?"

"Oh, I don't know. He'll get along, I guess."

Mrs. Callant came out on the porch behind us, hiding her floury hands in her apron.

"Good morning, Miss Kathy. It's sorry I am to disturb you, but it's the piano man wants to know would you run your hand over the keys."

"Yes, of course."

The rose room had a faint, musty, morning smell, as it always did. With the lights gone out of it, it seemed just a place again. But Kathy sat down at the piano and ran off the scales.

"It's fine," she said to the tuner.

He bowed and knelt down to pick up his tools. He fumbled a little to find the fork.

"It's right there beside you," said Kathy impatiently. "At your right hand."

He said, "Thank you," found it and picked it up.

"It costs five dollars," he said.

"The fork?"

"No, the tuning. And there's five dollars for the last time."

"You'll have to see Mr. Ledyard," Kathy began. Then she asked, "When was the last one?"

"I tuned it for Mrs. Boyd a week before she died," he said.

"Hasn't my uncle paid you yet?"

"He wouldn't speak to me."

Kathy's color flared up. Her hands pulled some harsh, angry chords from the keys; she rose and swept out of the room. When she came back, she had ten dollars in her hand.

"Thank you," said the tuner.

"Don't thank me," she said sharply.

He picked up his bag and bumped against a chair. She didn't say anything at his clumsiness, but she was breathing angrily.

"What makes him so clumsy?" she asked when he was gone.

"He's nearly blind," I said.

"Then why didn't you help him, Teddy? Aren't you ashamed? Haven't any of you any feeling for people?"

Her anger swept over me; then she went out of the room.

"I'm sorry," I said. "Aren't you going to play some music?"

"I couldn't touch it," she said.

She watched Doone from the porch and her eyes looked, to me, as if she wanted to hurt him. I could not understand her at all. She was fidgeting. She couldn't be still.

She came in again with long, angry steps and sat down in the cool, dark living room. The windows seemed to make a visible barrier against the sunlight. It lay just outside the frames, but it would not come in; and yet the sounds of the horse's hoofs came in, and the steady "So-o-o! So-o-o!" of Doone's voice.

As she listened to it, the stiffness seemed to slip out of her. She quivered under it. She was like a horse afraid of the whip. Then she said, "For God's sake, shut that window."

I closed it.

"Please go away, Teddy."

I went out of the room. I went onto the porch, but Doone was through. He was walking with easy strides across the grass, and the scent of sweat was on the knees of his trousers and his hair was tangled from the wind. He nodded to me and went into the house to the bathroom, and I heard him washing. I stayed outside wondering what was the matter with Kathy and feeling lonesome and shut off both from her and from Doone. And after a while I let myself quietly into the office and sat down beside Artemis on the rug in front of the gun case.

The living-room door was open and the house was still. I could not hear a sound.

Then I heard Doone coming through the dining room, and a faint smell of horse reached me. He stopped in the shadow of the door as if he were looking. Then he came forward into the middle of the room. I knew in some way that he was not looking for me, and I did not move. Then Kathy's voice said, "Aren't you going to speak to me, Doone?" and I knew he was looking at her, and that she must be lying on the red-leather sofa. He didn't answer her. In the dining room the clock could be heard tick-tocking, and Mrs. Callant's feet moved about in the kitchen.

"Have you ever wanted to kiss a girl, Doone?"

I cannot describe the note there was in her voice. I know it made me go cold, and I dropped my hand on Artemis' nose and it felt cold as my hand.

"Why?" he said. And there was something strange in his voice also.

She waited a while before she spoke.

"Because," she said, "the way you were standing there wondering if I was asleep made me wonder."

"It's a queer question, anyway."

"It's a queer question for me to ask a man," Kathy said.

"I don't doubt that, Kathy."

It seemed to me as if they were speaking with swords.

"Doone, what was your mother like?"

"To people, or to me?"

"Oh, to you, Doone."

"She was a very lovely person to me. I don't think I ever loved anyone in the world like her. That's all I can tell you or will tell you, Kathy."

"Were you sorry for her?"

"Why do you ask that?"

"I've felt sorry for her," Kathy said.

"I think other people were too. I used to hate my father before she died. But there was no reason for it."

"Was he so good to her?"

"He gave her everything he had."

"What was that?" Kathy asked. And when he did not answer, she went on, "I suppose he saw that she didn't take cold, and brought her dress goods, and took her driving on Sunday, and kept her in her fine room out of the sun."

"Yes, he did all that," Doone said slowly. "I never heard him curse in front of her."

"Oh, Lord!" Kathy fell silent. "She must have been pretty."

"She was," said Doone. "But she was a sad person. There was something, I think, not right about her life."

I heard Kathy sit up on the sofa.

"Doone, why do you keep yourself like an anchorite?"

"I don't know. I keep myself busy. I like my horses. There is nothing like a horse. And there'll be no horse like Blue Dandy when I'm done with him." His voice warmed. It was like his own again. But Kathy said something.

"What's that, Kathy?"

"I was saying that horses had taken the soul out of you Boyds."

"I don't see what cause you have to say that," he said seriously. "There is no better friend than an honest horse, or an honest mare either. They give you all there is in them. They teach you to use your hands and your eyes, and to govern your temper."

"You poor fools! Govern your tempers like Ledyard! Doone, are you blind?"

"No, Kathy, not blind, quite."

"If you treated your women the way you do your horses, they'd give you something, Doone. 'All there is in them.' Poor things, they've never had the chance. By not hurting them, you've let them hurt you, but you've tortured them to death. I know it. Every last one. Wake up, Doone! For God's sake, wake up! Look at me!"

"I've been looking at you, Kathy."

"For a while you used to be friends with me. We used to pretend we were married, bare-legged little devils that we were. And you were twice the man then that you are now." Her voice softened. "Look at me, Doone? Why do you suppose I came up here?"

"I don't know."

"Kiss me, Doone."

I heard Doone breathing in the quiet of the house.

"Kiss me, you poor blind boy."

I held quite still, not drawing a breath. It was not a kiss I heard, only silence.

Then Kathy's voice was very low:

"Do you see now?"

"Yes," he said harshly. "How can I marry you?"

"Don't bother about that, Doone."

"Do you think I'm a fool? Do you want to be like the girls in the fields that they're always whispering about behind our backs?"

"Why not? I'm alive, Doone."

"So am I! Kathy, you wouldn't stand it a week, living here. You'd be lonesome for your friends—all your glad friends in their glad clothes. You'd miss the handclapping."

"Oh, so you know about that?"

"Yes, I do."

"So you think I'm not the proper wife for a Boyd. You want them like flowers—bleeding hearts, I suppose."

"I think you are rich and on the way to be famous."

"Damn you, Doone. Then why did you kiss me?"

He chuckled suddenly, and I let out my breath, knowing he was all right. And he rolled a brogue like John Callant.

"Sure and didn't you ask for it?" He turned to the window. "What do you suppose has happened to dad and the admiral, Kathy?"

Then we heard the admiral swearing.

I slipped in behind them and I saw Kathy standing up at his side, and her face was fiery and her eyes cold, and she was trembling.

"You've no heart in you, Doone."

We all looked out of the window, and Doone began to laugh. I laughed, too, and then Kathy could not stop herself from joining us.

For the swearing was coming round the corner of the glen. It came behind a gaunt brown farm team.

"That's Meecher's," said Doone, and there was Meecher walking beside them, his face solemn and virtue in his walk, as if he were the twelve apostles. He had a rope hitched from his team's eveners and to the front axle of the car. And sitting on the front seat, the sweat rolling off his brow and the profanity rolling under his mustache, was Admiral Porter, doing his damndest to keep the front wheels of the car behind the horses. My Uncle Ledyard was sitting back against the cushions of the back seat as solemn as a circuit judge. But of the chauffeur there wasn't a sign at all. They drove up to the carriage block and the admiral put on the brake before the team stopped and the car slid along like a stone bolt. Then the admiral got out.

"Here's your ten-dollars salvage!" he said, and paid Meecher. "Now go home and be damned to you and your dirty pigs!"

He yanked off his hat and stamped into the house. He stopped in the dining room.

"John!" he shouted in his foghorn voice. "John! John! John Callant! Come here!"

There was a great to-do in the kitchen and John looked through the door.

"For God's sake, John, bring me some hot whisky and lemon to my room."

"Is it your honor's had an accident?" said John.

"Blast your impudence! Do what I tell you!"

"Sure and is it sick you are, sir?"

The admiral paused and put his hand on his waistcoat. His voice became hollow.

"Yes," he said. "I'm sick. Hurry up, John."

"What is it, Jim?" Kathy asked.

"Shut up, girl. . . . Teddy, come and untie my shoes. I'm tired and I want to sleep."

He went to bed, drank his toddy, closed his eyes.

Uncle Ledyard came in laughing.

"We got to Meecher's, and coming round the corner," he said, "we ran into the white sow. She was farrowing right in the road. We couldn't get by her. We couldn't back up out of the ditch. We had to wait until she was through.

" 'What are you doing there, sitting and doing nothing, you lazy pup?' said Jim to the driver chap. 'Get out and move those pigs.'

" 'I'll not,' said the driver. 'I hired on for a shoffer, and not to be moving your pigs.'

" 'My pigs,' roared Jim, and he went on for a while. 'Get out before I throw you out.'

" 'I will not,' said the driver.

" 'Do you know this is mutiny?' asks Jim.

" 'For two cents I'd spit in the eye of the whole damned Navy,' said the driver; 'and as for you, you old billy goat, if you come out here in the road I'll knock you down.'

"I think the driver was a city fellow and he didn't like the look of this country from the first. But Jim wasn't waiting. He got out of the car so fast I could hardly keep up with him, and I thought I'd better be handy."

Kathy and Doone threw up their chins and howled, and I laughed, too, seeing in my own mind the two old gentlemen scrambling out into the dusty white road to trample the driver together. But Uncle Ledyard went on, with a drink and a long breath:

"I don't think the driver chap had his stomach in it. 'I'll not fight two old roosters like you,' he said. 'I'm through with you.'

" 'You're not, you're fired,' yelled Jim, and he started at him.

"The driver turned his back on us and walked off for Boonville, and I don't doubt he's made the twelve-o'clock train for New York. And we had to get Meecher and hire him to draw us back, because Jim didn't know what to do with the engine, and I'm glad he didn't, for he was in a mood to drown us all."

"Poor Jim," said Kathy, bubbling with laughter. "He won't be able to tour in his car, because he won't let me drive him."

"I'm glad of that," said Uncle Ledyard. "I think I got a touch of the sun. It was a very hot place for a while."

We sat still at last, listening to the admiral groaning in his sleep. But he got up for luncheon, and beyond a little excursion into the breeding of the chauffeur he seemed fairly normal. After the meal he and Uncle Ledyard were very companionable on the veranda, and about four o'clock they collected some men and had the car pushed into the machine shed and the door closed upon it. It didn't move again till Kathy took it out on her flight for New York and we went after her.

When we had dinner that night, I felt a strange tension in the room. And yet it was all soft with candlelight and the reflections of them in the wax on the mahogany, and Minna dropped only a fork. Nor was there anything the matter with Uncle Ledyard. He cut into the Tamworth ham as if it were butter against the edge of his knife, and his big hands cut slices fine as paper. The admiral wasn't saying a great deal, to be sure, but his hot whisky and the whisky he'd had in the afternoon were making him sleepy.

And I don't think there was anything wrong with Doone—at least, he didn't show it.

But Kathy had been late in coming downstairs. Whether she did it on purpose, I don't know; but there was mischief in her that night. She had put on a dress of a strange, burning orange, and she stopped on the stairs as she came down, so that the candle lamp on the newel post shone up against her and put reflections of the dress in her black hair. Doone stopped in a sentence to John Callant, who had come in from the barn, and he never took it up again. And John's lower jaw gapped enough to show his missing teeth, and I saw that against explicit orders he had his quid stowed away in the gap. It came loose while he stared and he had to leave the room.

"I'm sorry I kept you waiting," said Kathy in her deep voice, and it was so natural that it shocked us.

As she moved, the light played over the orange dress, making flame of it. It was cut very low and square in front, and fitted her tightly, and her skin looked so white that I couldn't take my eyes off it. She came over the dark floor with the little toes of her dark shoes moving as light as apple seeds and her body like a gypsy dancer's. And Uncle Ledyard bowed to her and offered his arm.

"The lads must wait a while longer, Kathy."

She tilted her chin to him as they swept into the dining room, but out of the tail of her eye she looked back at Doone. He was like an amazed man before the fire, and he did not move until the admiral struggled with the arms of his chair.

All through dinner she was bright at talking. She spoke about the stage, and of the contract she had been offered that morning by the mail. She described dressing in the windy, dark rooms back of the stage when snow was whistling outside, and hearing the sound of it on the other side of the wall and the sound of her audience clapping their hands. It was peculiar how vividly she brought another phase of life through the faint horse smell in that old house. Glasses tinkled through her words when she described after-theater suppers, and the young gentlemen attending her, stiff with eagerness or weak with too much wine.

She was talking at Doone; the admiral never heard a word, and Uncle Ledyard was always too fond of his food. But Doone talked back at her so naturally and seemed so polite in wanting to know what she had to tell, that I took no notice of him. I could not take my eyes off her. For tonight truly she had the scent of the other world in her.

And she wasn't through with it at dinner. Whatever she was trying to get out of Doone and had so far failed to get, she would not give up her game yet.

She went into the rose room when they stayed for their port, and she sat down at the piano. As she passed the door and her orange dress came against the rose walls, it was as if someone had screamed. But there wasn't a sound except the arrogant tapping of her heels and the swift scrape of the bench as she drew it up under her. Then she played.

I do not come from a musical family, and I do not know whose was the music. But it was strong, stormy stuff, with long rolls like thunder, and swift, sharp, petulant dancing of the trebles. The small room she played in was too small to hold the vastness of a sound that seemed to set the candle-lights swimming. It flowed in waves through the door until it filled the living room, and it went on into the dining room. I heard the cautious feet on gravel and saw the servants standing out on the drive in the moon-light.

Doone could not stand it, sitting in the dining room. He came into the living room and sat beside me. He would not go to the door of the rose room and she would not stop her playing. It was not until the admiral stamped uncertainly in upon us and roared, "For God's sake, Kathy, stop that noise!" that she banged to a stop.

We were dizzy with the silence. Then she stood in the door, one hand against the lintel by her cheek, and smiled sweetly at us.

Uncle Ledyard's voice said, "Now play us something simple, Kathy. Please."

She smiled at him sadly and disappeared, and the piano began to sing little tunes—of Tom Moore's: "I knew by the smoke that so gracefully curled——"

And her voice was small and low, and Uncle Ledyard looked very much moved, like a man dreaming of his good digestion, but Doone's face became haggard.

She played on for a little while; then she stopped altogether, and we saw that the admiral had fallen asleep.

"Perhaps," said Kathy, coming softly into the room, "I'd better follow his example."

She said good night and went slowly up the stairs, and as she rose from sight the beam cut off the orange dress. I never saw it again.

We called John Callant, who took the admiral away with a kind of pity. Uncle Ledyard climbed heavily to his room. Doone disappeared through his door, and I went up to the little room that had been Kathy's. I tried to sleep, but the music was swinging my bed. And finally I heard John Callant returning from the admiral, and his voice talking to Mrs. Callant:

"Stand over, Susie."

The bed creaked.

### IV

The moon was well on in the sky when I woke again. And I was broad awake. I knew something was happening.

The night was warm and still, and the crickets were making a tremendous threeping out in the oat stubble. When I went to the window, my first look was toward the horse barn, and sure enough there was John with a lantern, running for the house. His bare feet slapped onto the porch and he went through the dining room. I pulled on a sweater, opened my door stealthily, and stood in the hall.

I could hear him knocking gently on Doone's door.

The back hall was dark except for the crack of light coming from the Callants' room, and I stepped over that. The kitchen was still thick with the dinner scents as I went through it. In the dining room a dim sheen of moon glow lay on the mahogany.

I could see Doone's door open and John Callant standing in it with the lantern.

"She's coming, Misther Doone. She's been at it a while, I'm thinking, but it's a bad position. It's the front feet and her head turned, surely."

"I'll want my bag," Doone said. "Get it out of the office."

John slipped like a bat across the living room and rummaged through the office. Then he returned empty-handed.

"It's not there, Misther Doone. I can't find it. Oh, glory, what have you been doing with it?"

"Be still, you fool. I haven't been doing anything with it. I told Mrs. Callant to put it there when she moved the things out of my room."

"That woman," hissed John.

"Go ask her," said Doone.

John scurried past me with righteousness glaring from his eye. The lantern light he carried was sucked up the stairway and he went to his bedroom door.

"What have you been doing with Misther Doone's bag?" he demanded.

Mrs. Callant creaked the bed.

"What do you mean, blathering at me? Sure, I don't know which case it is you're racketing over."

"The case with the tools in it," said John. "Pansy's took now, and if it's dying she is because you've lost the case with the tools in it, it's skinning the hide off your back Misther Ledyard will be, if I don't myself."

"I don't know——" began his wife shrilly.

"And be still, can't you? Would you be waking the house? Now tell me where it is, or I'll put my own belt acrosst you."

"Where would it be but in Misther Doone's room where it always is?" demanded Mrs. Callant. "Sure isn't he always telling me not to handle his dirty things?"

"Bring me my pants to the kitchen," said John severely, "so I can leap into them as I pass. It's the straw in the stall that bothers me."

He came hurrying by me again with a breath of the stable, and Doone met him in the living room.

"Where is it?"

"It's in your room," said John. "I'm ashamed of her myself, the idle loafer; too lazy to touch it, as yourself told her."

Doone swore.

"Get me a pan of hot water. Hot, John."

John passed me once more—this time for the kitchen, where his wife met him, rubbing the sleep from her eyes with the leg of his trousers.

"Give them here," he ordered, "and heat me a pan of wather, quick. And hot, me girl, or Misther Doone will be enraged with us both."

As they stuffed the stove with kindling, I stole into the living room and lay down on the deep sofa. Doone was standing undecidedly by the door to the rose room, when his name was called softly. He hesitated, then went into the room, and the walls shone pink in the lantern light.

"What is it, Doone?" Kathy whispered.

"Pansy's foal," he said softly. "I'm sorry to have waked you, Kathy, but Mrs. Callant has left my case of instruments in your room. Can you find it?"

"Yes. Where is it, Doone?"

"It ought to be in the washstand back of the crockery."

I could see him standing still and dark in his shirt and trousers, and his bare feet in slippers. He was in front of the picture of Sacred and Profane Love and looking up at the little prayer door. Kathy's feet made no sound, but I heard the chink of crockery, and then I saw the bag being lowered. Her bare arm gleamed white in the lantern light, slim and quick.

"Can't I help, Doone?"

"No, thanks. Just drop the bag."

Her fingers were reluctant in unbending. He caught the bag in one hand and tucked it under his arm.

"I wish you'd let me help."

"It's no place for you, Kathy."

He came past me swiftly, without looking left or right. As the lantern swung through the dining-room door, an eddy of darkness flowed over the living room, and in it I smelled the cigar smoke of the evening, and a bit of wood smoke from the fireplace, and the faint, dew-damp grass smell. Then I heard John Callant saying on the porch, "Sure and I think it's hot enough. The kettle was steaming."

Their feet and their voices died over the grass.

As my eyes became accustomed to the darkness, I saw that the light in the rose room had not quite gone. Color had left, but the shapes of the stairs and the piano were dimly visible, and the brass candle brackets on the music rack had threads of gold. I got up softly to look in the door.

The light came from the prayer door, which was still open. Kathy was kneeling beside it. She must have had the candle on the floor, for there was a soft upward luminance on her face. I had never seen her so. She seemed hushed. Her lips were fuller and the eyelids were darkened. Her dark hair was hanging all around her, but one shoulder broke through. It was white and curved from the limpness of her hand.

Though my heart was bursting to call her name, I did not even stir until her eyelids lifted. A slight shiver possessed her, and she said, "Oh, it's you, Teddy."

The clock ticking in the dining room measured time from a great distance. She said again, "What are you doing up, Teddy?"

"I'm going out to the horse barn," I whispered. "Do you want to come with me?"

She said "Yes," at once, and I went back into the living room to wait for her. She was like a ghost coming down the stairs; her feet seemed timid of the stair treads. All I could see of her was the white of her nightgown, and, as she passed the door, a touch of moon glow on her breast.

"You aren't coming out that way, are you?"

"I forgot," she said. I thought she was still asleep. "I'll get a coat, Teddy."

"Here," I said. "Take Doone's."

I was in a hurry, and Doone's long driving coat hung behind the door. She slipped it on without a word; it hung loosely from her shoulders, inclosing the nightgown. It made her seem smaller as she stepped with me onto the damp grass.

We did not speak as we went along the drive. The threeping of crickets seemed to accompany our steps. A few fireflies were playing patterns among the trees of the glen. And before us, the hay-scented door of the barn loomed, with a nebule of brown light far in.

Kathy's hand dropped to my shoulder as we stole through the door, and through our slippers we felt the knots and splinters of the rough planks. Pansy's stall was at the back, and there, against the wall, we saw the black shadows of Doone and John bending their heads together.

There wasn't a sound in the barn but their muttering voices and the soft breathing of the horses as they stood with their heads over the doors. Then John grunted and Doone said, "It's all right now," in a deep, strong voice. And at the sound of it, the pricked ears of the horses relaxed.

Kathy and I stole forward together. We stood at the edge of the door looking into the stall. And we saw Doone kneeling, and the black mare still lying in the mussed straw, with John Callant squatting at her loins, his lumpy hand resting lightly on her side. They were both looking down at the foal.

"A fine foal," Doone was saying. "He shows his bone already."

He gave the mare a pat and drew himself erect on his knees.

"He's the incarnate spit of The Earl," said John. "He'll be a fine horse, I'm telling you."

Doone turned suddenly to the pan and rinsed his hands. He washed them with entire preoccupation, taking each finger in turn, cleaning between them. When he was satisfied he dried them on a meal sack.

"You'd better sit up with her a while, John. And I'll take the pan back to the kitchen. Tell Susanna to boil it in the morning."

"Yes, Misther Doone."

I felt Kathy's hand draw at my shoulder, and together we slipped out of the barn with only the eyes of the horses following our passage.

We did not speak at all, going back to the house, but in the dining room Kathy pressed my shoulder again.

"Good night, Teddy," she said. "You'd better go to bed now."

"Good night, Kathy."

I went upstairs slowly. At the landing I looked back. She was hanging up Doone's coat behind the door. I listened to her feet gently passing into the living room, then I heard the faint creak of the sofa. And I knew she was going to wait for Doone.

But I was sleepy. As soon as my head touched the pillow I forgot everything in the wide world.

What Kathy said to Doone when he found her waiting for him, or what he said to her, or whether they said anything at all, they know best themselves. But that she had waited for him, I discovered at breakfast when Uncle Ledyard said:

"We'll have to go out and look at the foal."

"Did Pansy foal last night?" I asked as innocently as I knew how.

"Yes, Teddy. And Doone says he's a beauty."

I glanced at Doone and found him staring sternly at me across the table. But when he did not give me away I knew that he had found Kathy, and I glanced quickly at her.

She was eating her raspberries so naturally, and she looked so fresh in her green dress, with its short, puffy sleeves, and she seemed so peaceful and contented, that I could hardly believe she had been up at all the night before. But when she smiled at me she gave me a pleasant feeling of secrets shared between us.

We finished breakfast leisurely, and then the four of us went out to the barn. The admiral was not interested. Horses were nothing in his life. I don't think he ever took notice of an animal before the morning he met Meecher's sow.

John Callant had cleaned out the stall and Pansy was standing in the far corner with her nostrils flaring gently in the fresh straw. Doone went in to her and stood her over, and we looked together at the foal.

He was black as she, and still shining, and he lay with his chin out and his eyes closed.

We stood together a moment without speaking and then moved off, and Doone came out and closed the stall door.

John Callant came out of the harness room with the harness slung on his arms and went in to Blue Dandy. Uncle Ledyard watched him.

"That new boy's going to show you something real, Doone. I fancy his breeding."

Doone laughed.

"I'll keep my money on Dandy," he said.

And he wheeled out the sulky. So quickly had he stepped back into the routine of training.

Kathy stood by as they put in the gray horse, but she did not say anything. And Doone scarcely noticed her. Her face showed nothing of her thoughts. She seemed very still and reserved, but she watched him till he had gone through the gate to the track. Then she went quietly back to the house. Later in the morning, when Doone had brought Blue Dandy out for his third mile, I heard the piano faintly from the open window of the rose room.

With the automobile out of action the old, familiar life of the farm laid its hand on us all. The cowbells passed back and forth from the pasture at sunrise and sunset, Doone trained his horses morning and afternoon, the mailman came at ten o'clock behind the old white horse, we ate breakfast and lunch and dinner, and the admiral and Uncle Ledyard sat together on the deep veranda at the back of the house and talked about their college days and Mr. McKinley and that wild, wonderful man Bryan who held out a cloven silver hoof with the innocent smile of an angel. It was wonderful to hear the admiral mention Bryan.

But in the dusk of the evening, before dinner, Doone and Kathy began to take walks together. Sometimes they would meet at the veranda steps, sometimes they would wander off separately, and now and then Doone would take his rod and Kathy would carry the landing net, and they would go down by the canal to try for a big one in the shallows.

When the admiral saw that for the first time, he opened his eyes, set down his glass and took hold of both ends of his mustache.

"By the Lord, Leddy, did you see that?"

"I've been expecting to see that," said Uncle Ledyard.

"I'm shocked," said the admiral. "As long as she showed her mother's wild Irish, I wasn't afraid. But that makes me feel five hundred dollars fluttering to get out of my pocket."

"Don't get too worried yet, my boy," said Uncle Ledyard. "She always did go fishing when she was little."

The admiral snorted.

"You can't tell me that when a woman offers to carry a man's net for him and sit by the shore and be bitten with bugs just to watch him do a namby-pamby business like that, that she isn't in love with him."

Uncle Ledyard looked thoughtful.

"I never thought of it that way," he said.

"She's sold her soul to him," said the admiral. "He's got her in his hip pocket. If she was just for making love with him, she wouldn't be hampered with fly-fishing outfits. Not Kathy."

He took a long drink.

"Maybe," he said, "the poor fool won't be able to see his chance."

I wasn't invited on these evening strolls of Kathy's and Doone's, and when I invited myself I was firmly discouraged. And I wouldn't have gone at all if Doone had not come home one night with the story of a big bass rising. I made up my mind to catch that bass. And the next evening I was on the other side of the canal, casting with my own rod and one of my father's red-and-white flies.

It was nearly dusk when they came along the towpath, and they came so quietly that I had no chance to reel in or to do more than flop down in the grass and let my fly trail in the currents, praying that Doone wouldn't see it.

He was out to do business that night. He didn't linger an instant on the bank, but whipped the fly from his reel and waded in to cast. By parting the grass with my hand, I could see him fifty feet from where I lay, getting a beautiful length, his mind lost in the water and the black current collaring at his knees. Kathy was sitting on the steep bank with the handle of the net between her feet and the hoop over her shoulder. There was thoughtfulness in the level black line of her brows and a strange sort of wistfulness in her mouth.

It was a perfect evening for bass—the moon not yet up and the water gray with a very slight ripple; but bass are a queer fish, and not one broke the water.

Twilight surrounded us, and the occasional whine of the reel as Doone stripped off some line, the suck of the water at his legs as he gradually worked down to the edge of the shoal, and the rhythmic rising of the line, looping and shooting, seemed only a part of its stillness. It was a long while before Kathy said: "You won't catch any fish tonight, Doone."

"It looks that way," he said, but he went on casting.

She drew a little breath, and it was so still that I could hear the quiver of it plainly.

"Doone," she asked, "when are we going to get married?"

His line faltered in the back cast, and his fly splashed heavily. I thought he would swear at her for disturbing him so, but he acted as if he had not heard her at all or noticed his own bad cast. Only he seemed to put viciousness into the next cast or two, and the rod whistled to itself.

"I don't know," he said over his shoulder.

His fishing changed entirely as he spoke. It wasn't a sport any more; the rod was like a whip in his hands that he was using mercilessly against her. But she would not allow it.

Her voice was full and vibrant and compelling:

"Can you doubt after this week that I'm in love with you?"

"How can I answer that?" he asked.

"I've done my best to prove it to you, Doone." Her voice had dropped, and I saw her as I never saw her again. Humble before him.

He wasn't entirely graceless. He said, "I'll always thank you for that, Kathy."

It seemed to me that she leaped against his words.

"I don't want thanks, Doone."

"Do you claim a debt?" There was something in his voice that made me think of Uncle Ledyard.

"No," she said, throwing up her chin. "It's a debt I've paid to myself."

She rose to her feet, dangerously swift, and her voice was stormy:

"Do you think I would come dunning you, Doone? Like a country girl. I wouldn't dun a Boyd—it wouldn't pay."

I could see her trembling. But she had got what she was after. He dropped the point of his rod, letting his line trail, and turned to her.

"Kathy?"

"Curse you and your thanks, Doone Boyd, and be damned to you!"

She lifted the net over her shoulder and threw it as far as she could into the canal. It dove in with a splash just beyond him, stood upright for an instant, and teetered slowly into the current. Before he could snatch it, it was out of his reach and settling in the deep water.

Bass are a queer fish. The big one took that moment to rise. He rolled like a whale and the sound of his splash was as if a sack of potatoes had gone over the side of a boat. The line sang through my fingers and the rod bucked. I yanked up the tip and jumped up in the grass like a wild Indian.

"Doone," I yelled, "I've got him!"

I did not look to see how he took my appearance. But I heard the splash of his legs. In a moment he was beside me, and his voice was steadying.

"Easy, Teddy. Keep up the tip of that rod. That's it. Use both your hands. Don't be ashamed of it. You've got a man's bass at the end of your line. Now begin wading out with me. You've got to fetch him into the current. Down with the tip! He's breaking!"

I had lost all thought, and my hand did as he said, and true enough, the bass came out, the whole length of him, a black shape in the middle of foam, and he fell back on his side like a cannon bursting.

My little rod pumped like my heart and I waded out along with Doone into the cold water and braced my back to fight him.

Doone was saying, "Oh, God, Kathy! Why did you have to throw in that net?"

"I'll lose him without a net!" I cried.

"We'll beach him some way," said Doone. "Start backing up the current. There's a bad log out there. We'll get him into the current and tire him. Put down that tip, for God's sake!"

The fish leaped again, turned over on his nose and went up the stream like an express. I stripped in my line as hard as I could.

Then Kathy said from the shore close to us, "Will he stay up there for a minute, Doone?"

"He will for a minute."

I heard a soft splashing, like an otter sliding into a brook, but I didn't dare lift my eyes from the faint white spot of froth where my line cut into the water. He jumped high in the black shadow.

"He's turned again," said Doone, and I began pulling the line in. Then we heard Kathy draw a gasping breath, and she splashed up beside us.

"Here's the net."

My heart sang at her words, but Doone said, "Give it to me, quick."

And he had it in his right hand and was dousing the mud from it. He seemed to reach over a mile of water, and as the bass came down past us he thrust it like a sword. It was a beautiful piece of judgment, perfectly calm, and I knew he wouldn't miss. As he lifted the net I saw his wrist buck to the flopping of the bass.

"He's a dandy, Teddy," he said quietly.

I sighed, and the rod seemed to ache in my hand. I turned around then and saw Kathy. She was standing between us and she was bare as the fish. Strings of water were dripping out of her black hair and making a silvery sheen on her skin in the gray twilight.

"He is a beauty, Teddy; you played him well."

"It was Doone," I said, as modestly as I could.

He was thumping the bass with the back of his knife and now he dropped him on the grass. I reeled in toward him and looked down.

"That's the biggest one I've caught, Doone. Will he weigh as much as the one in the office?"

"I'm afraid not, but he's over four pounds or John Callant is a Frenchman. We'd never have got him without the net. Good girl, Kathy."

She was slipping into her clothes on the bank above us.

"You needn't say that, Doone. . . . I'm glad you got it, Teddy."

I paid no attention to her, for the fish was filling me, and Doone was cutting a forked stick for me to carry it by. When we picked up our things to start back to dinner, Kathy had gone. But as we walked along the towpath, Doone seemed to me to be unkindly silent about the fish.

We had a great to-do weighing the fish before dinner, and Uncle Ledyard poured me a glass of port after dinner and I had to tell how he jumped, how he ran up the current and how Doone got him with the net. I said that the net had been dropped in the current and I made a story of Kathy's diving for it in the darkness in the black water; and she smiled at me; but both she and Doone were very still. And after that I had to go out on the kitchen porch while John skinned the fish and we opened his stomach to see what a fish of that size might have been eating.

"It looks like a crayfish," said John, poking the bit with the point of his knife. "There's two of them in it."

"Glory be!" exclaimed Mrs. Callant. "Who would suppose a living creature could eat such a thing?"

"It's the powers of their digestion," said John.

So I saw the fish put into the ice chest on a white kitchen plate, a trivial remnant of the fierce thing I'd caught, and I went back to the living room and catalogued his contents. It made a grand evening for me.

And I was sleepy with the port, sleepy and comfortable through and through, so that as my voice petered out, I became aware of the silence of the others, and particularly of Kathy, who had curled herself in a corner of the red-leather sofa and stared steadily into the fire. She would not play, when Uncle Ledyard asked her. She said it was my evening and that a woman should not butt into it. And even when I said I didn't mind her music, she wouldn't play. And Doone sat at the side of the hearth, and he, too, looked into the fire.

They sent me to bed when the admiral went, but I woke up again in a dream of the fish and remembered that I had left the fly that had caught him on the mantelpiece. I had a thought that it would be comforting to have that fly stuck in the frame of the mirror against the wall, and once I'd thought of it, it seemed to me that I couldn't possibly sleep unless I had it there. So I slipped out of my room and went downstairs.

I stopped in the door, for the lights were burning, and I saw Kathy standing on the stairs.

"Good night, Doone," she was saying lightly. "I am going to bed."

"Why do you go so soon?"

" 'You used to come at ten o'clock.' "

I thought she seemed silly. Her voice was brittle.

"It's past for us both. I'll forget all about it, Doone, and so will you. Good night."

"I shan't forget it, Kathy."

"You don't need me any more than I need you. As you say, we're different. I'm not a Boyd lady by instinct; though apparently I've made another Boyd woman. But you shan't have my name to rust in your Bible. Put me in the Apocrypha if you must put me down somewhere, again. I'd rather be there."

"You've lost your temper, Kathy. It'll be different tomorrow."

"I have not lost my temper. I don't even feel hurt any more. If you put my money before me, that's your prerogative—or your taste. As you please."

"Oh, can't you see, Kathy?"

"Or is it because you've had enough of me now?"

"That's a cruel speech."

"You didn't hesitate to take it when I offered it to you," she said, and she bent for a moment over the rail. "Perhaps you are wise, Doone, at that. You knew what you wanted. But you don't know. None of you Boyds ever did. Poor devils."

She smiled very sweetly and genuinely when she said that, and kissed her hand to him so debonairly that he had nothing to say.

"Good night, Doone."

Her skirts rustled lightly as she went out of sight.

I heard Doone poking the logs, and then sitting down, and I slipped back to my room, knowing he might stay that way for an hour.

A thunderstorm was brewing beyond the flats. When I looked from my window I saw its head rising up black in the moonlight. It had a heavy voice, and the old house shivered under it. I got into bed and lay still to listen to the gathering of wind.

The still curtains lifted over my window when it came with its cool breath. And then the rain was on the roofs, the gutters ran full, and the lightning danced on the plaster of my wall, and the thunder was bearing down upon us, blow after blow.

I could not sleep till it was over, and as it died beyond the valley, half an hour later, I decided that I might as well get my fly anyhow.

In the living room I found Doone. He was just coming down the stairs from Kathy's room, and his face was troubled.

"Hello," he said to me, and I saw that he was still dressed. "What are you doing down here?"

"I was after the fly, Doone."

"What fly?" he asked irritably.

"The one I caught the fish on."

"Oh, that one." He stood still for a moment by the fire, with his head cocked toward Kathy's room. "Have you seen Kathy in your midnight wanderings?" he asked.

"No," I said. "Isn't she in bed?"

He gave me a black look. But at that instant, John Callant came in to us.

"Misther Doone," he said, "what's up?"

"What do you mean?"

"Is the admiral all right?" asked John.

"What do you mean?"

"I heard a racket in the storm," said John, "and I went out to see if it was the horses, but what it was was the engine."

"What are you talking about?"

"The Packyard, the automobile, to be sure," said John, with the wind whistling in his teeth. "It's gone!"

"By God, that's it!" cried Doone. "She's jumped off the porch roof and taken it out."

"What's that about my motor?" demanded a sepulchral voice.

"Motor!" exclaimed John. "The words was in me mouth."

The admiral's door opened and he stood there in his flannel gown and carpet slippers with the blue nightcap's tassel dancing first over one eye and then over the other.

"Kathy's skipped in the motor," said Doone.

"Damn it!" roared the admiral. "She'll kill herself and smash it to bits! She drives like the devil!"

By this time Uncle Ledyard had waked and come to the head of the stairs.

"What's the racket for?"

"Kathy's stolen my motor!" roared the admiral.

"Where's she going?" asked Uncle Ledyard, hurrying down with his nightshirt open to show the black hair on his chest, curly as the forehead of a bull.

"To New York, I suppose. She got another letter from that manager chap who's always after her. I suppose she got bored."

Doone turned on John.

"Put Blue Dandy in the runabout."

"Yes, your honor."

John scurried away like a rabbit.

"Where are you going, boy?" asked Uncle Ledyard.

"I'm going to catch her," said Doone.

"Catch her?" scoffed the admiral. "With a horse?"

"With Blue Dandy," Doone corrected him.

"How long is she gone?" asked Uncle Ledyard.

"She can't have more than half an hour's start."

Uncle Ledyard grasped his beard.

"Half hour's handicap. Twenty-five miles to Deerfield Hill. You'll have to catch her on that, Doone."

"I will," said Doone.

"The devil you will!" cried the admiral.

"The devil he won't," said Uncle Ledyard. "That horse is my own breeding. He's the stuff of a king in him."

"He might if it wasn't Kathy in the car," said the admiral stubbornly.

"We made a bet on it," cried Uncle Ledyard. "Remember, Jim?"

"A hundred dollars," said the admiral.

"I'll double it," said Uncle Ledyard.

"You poor fool," said the admiral.

I could hear them talking back and forth as I ran to my room and yanked on some clothes. I hadn't been asked to go, but I was going anyhow. In two minutes I was down again, crouching in the shadow of the carriage block. John was bringing Blue Dandy along the drive at a walk, as if going to chase a girl in an auto in the middle of a black night were the most natural thing in the world. The big gray pricked his ears at me, his nostrils flared but John was watching the windows of the office, through which he saw Doone taking money from the desk. He stopped the runabout just beyond the block, sprang out and stood to Blue Dandy's head. I could just see the red shine of his bat ears between me and the light, and I took that chance to climb over the back and crawl under the seat.

Then Doone came with his long strides and jumped over the wheel. I saw the two old gentlemen crowding through the door in their nightshirts and stand together, the admiral holding the tassel of his nightcap from his eyes with a steady hand.

"Bring her back, boy!" roared my Uncle Ledyard.

Doone gathered the reins and John sprang back from the horse's head.

"Hold him down to his wind, Misther Doone."

"He's off!" cried Uncle Ledyard as the wheels turned deliberately out of the circle.

"Make it three hundred dollars," suggested the admiral.

Then the wheels swung into the high road, and I dared raise my head over the side to take a last view of the flat lights of the house. I saw the two old gentlemen standing with John on the lawn. Uncle Ledyard was waving his hand. And I saw Mrs. Callant leaning from an upstairs window. She was screeching—something, I think, about wanting to know was it the house on fire.

Over my head, Doone spoke to Blue Dandy.

V

I have no very clear idea about those first three miles and a half. For, though we spun along easily and smoothly through the Boyd woods, Doone swung off the Forestport road at the Corners and took the lane short cut to Alder Creek, and through the lane the runabout bucked like a mule and I was sore before we had gone a hundred yards. But I didn't dare crawl out until we had come onto the Utica road, for I knew that Doone would send me home afoot.

I lay on my side with my head toward the back and watched the tree tops sweep the stars, and saw the lantern light travel along the bushes, and listened to the steady mushy thud of Blue Dandy's hoofs in the muddy road. The rubber tires made no sound, even in striking the stones, but the water ran off the spokes when we slid through a puddle and the brown roil of it sprayed from the tire level with my eyes.

It was a good thought of Doone's to take the lane; he wanted to go slow, anyway, at that early stage and the roughness of the narrow track need not steal from his pace. And as Kathy must have gone round by Forestport, we gained nearly a mile and cut her lead several minutes.

But it was a painful journey for me, and as soon as the wheels spun out on the hard surface of the main highway, I kicked round and stuck my head under the seat flap and said, "Doone."

He did not speak, but his hand closed on my neck and he lifted me out like a rat.

"Don't make me walk back, Doone. Please."

"You have the damndest way of turning up, Teddy," he said. His voice was perfectly calm. He wasn't angry with me. He was surprised and he was thinking. But he never stopped driving, and that, I thought, was a good sign for me.

"Please, Doone," I said. "I want to come along with you."

"You're that much extra for the horse to drag," he said grimly.

"Only seventy-five pounds," I said. "And he doesn't know I'm here."

"You little fool. You may make just the difference."

"Not to Blue Dandy," I said, with complete confidence. "And besides, I love her just as much as you do."

He didn't answer that. He was still holding me by the neck and steadying me on the short footboard. Then he pushed me into the seat.

"Sit down," he said.

I knew it was all right, then. I braced myself against the back rest and put my eye on Blue Dandy.

Something—whether it was Doone's hand on the reins, or the new road, or a word from John Callant—must have told the horse that he had a long trip before him, for he had settled himself in a long stride. He wasn't straining himself. He was just trotting, and the lantern on my left sent a glimmer forward along his side and I saw his head up and his ears pricked against the stars. His head swayed a little to the trotting, but his withers went straight as an arrow away from us and his quarters drove his hind hoofs against the road with the smooth strokes of pistons. No matter how you looked at that horse, he gave you a sense of his power and his great heart.

"Aren't we going a bit too fast?" I asked Doone.

His eyes were dark under his hat brim, but the lantern put a faint gleam on his closed lips and his chin.

"Do you think so, Teddy?" he said. And he considered it. His voice was full of passion as he made up his own mind. "I think the boy knows what's up. He's got his eye on the road ahead of him. He's not after Kathy or anything alive. It's the car he's chasing. It's his own race, really, and he knows it."

After that we didn't say anything, but I watched the road coming back at us through the light, a running ribbon, with the wet of the rain still on it. There was little mud, for the road was shouldered and ditched and beaten hard with the summer's travel. But it must have felt cool and welcome to Blue Dandy's hoofs. The beat of them was proud as a great drum.

The air was cool, too, and fresh from the storm, and there wasn't any wind. I could see the stars clearly, a great arch of them over the open fields. They did not move, nor did we seem to move, either, when my eye was on them; only the trees marched backward against us and the breast of the earth rose and fell with the grade of the road as if it were breathing.

The farms lay silent on each side, lightless and sleeping. The cows were still in the low mist of the low pastures, black shapes like floating black boats. The oak shocks stood like tepees on the hillside lots. But the fields were still, for the crickets were yet knuckled down in their shapes after the heavy rain. There were only three sounds in the world as we crossed it—the clink of a cowbell as the cow lifted her head to see us go past; the barking of a dog as he ran to the road and watched our lantern come down on his property; the everlasting beat of Blue Dandy's hoofs.

We had passed the high ground by the Hurley House and were coming down the long grades when Doone suggested a little more speed, and we made the run into Remsen in under the hour. The village was dark and had a little cold wind of its own against our faces, and the walls of the houses beat back the sound of our passage, and long after we had rolled by the smithy, I thought I could hear the sound of hoofs behind us going back and forth between the houses.

Doone slowed Dandy on the two short hills between there and Barneveld, but we made the downward curve into that town flying, and in that run the lather came out on the horse and the scent of him was strong against our faces. He was lifting his hoofs and setting them down as if he flung the road back on his calks.

But Doone stopped him at the water trough and wet his handkerchief and cleaned his head and took him out at a walk.

In all that time we had seen no living man. And in Barneveld only the doctor lifted his window. Maybe he was expecting a call that night.

Then we went through the underpass of the railroad and had the long level stretches ahead of us to Nine Mile Creek. Blue Dandy took up his speed again, and I began to nod sleepily to the shuttle of the wheels. I scarcely noticed Doone's arm pulling me over to him, but I leaned against his coat and smelled the tobacco smell of it and closed my eyes.

His body was still and hard as a rock. His wrist took up the play of Blue Dandy against the reins. But it seemed to me, as I fell asleep, that I heard his heart beating; though it might have been the steady drumming of the horse's hoofs.

It was the sudden leap of his chest that woke me.

"There she is," he said quietly.

And I sat up and rubbed at my eyelids. For a time I could make out nothing but the fences flying back at me and the surge of the gray quarters of the horse. Then far away ahead, coming out from some trees, I saw two short beams of light. They went on for a way and then vanished. But they came out again and I saw that they had passed behind a barn.

"She's on the edge of the hill," said Doone.

And as he said that, the lights dipped over.

"How far ahead is she, Doone?"

He glanced aside for a bearing and said, "Half a mile maybe."

He lifted the reins and felt of the horse.

"We're going fine. He's seen the lights, I think, and marked them down."

In truth, the horse was traveling now. The wheels of the runabout were humming in their pointed boxes, the whiffletree cheeped hungrily, the tires whimpered against the road. The sound of speed was in them, and to me it seemed that a wind was freshening from the south.

"She won't see us yet a while," Doone said. "She's been over the road only once and her eyes will be stuck to it."

We went over the hill like a breaking wave and swept down so fast that I thought Blue Dandy was bound to break and gallop. Doone was talking, "So-o-o-o, boy—so-o-o-o," over and over, a steadying sound. And the horse laid back his ears to it and kept his breast up to the collar and his head high. He blew out a great blast from his nostrils that shuddered the runabout under us, and his deep, even panting was a sound to smother the noise of a hundred autos.

I could not see that we lost any pace as we drew out of the shallow valley and took the level to the first dip before the road climbs Deerfield Hill. But Doone had the reins in both hands. He was not watching for the lights of the car; his eyes were on the horse with his heart. I think for that last wild stretch he forgot all about Kathy, and his soul, like the horse's, was in beating the automobile.

It was I who saw the lights turn on the sharp bend ahead and made out Kathy's head bent back to us. Her hat had come off or she had thrown it away, and her hair was loose on the back of her neck. She saw us. She must have guessed who we were. Maybe she could make out the gray shine of the horse's hide. But she didn't falter. Her eyes returned to the road, and the car picked up speed.

I felt Doone crowding me over to the left. Then he was on his feet and leaning across me, and Blue Dandy was taking the curve, and the trees tilted away from us, and a barn wall leaned back from the road like an old woman lifting her hands for horror. Our off wheels slid clear to the edge of the ditch and the tires squeaked frantically against a patch of broken stone, and then we had the straight ahead of us and Doone sat down.

Kathy was going like lightning. We could see the lights pulling farther and farther off. But Doone laughed.

"There's the hill!" he shouted. "She'll have to change her gears, and we haven't got to bother about that!"

Blue Dandy snorted again as we took the right curve to the dell. The car had gained a hundred yards going down there and was rocketing up the beginning of the grade.

"She'll not make those turns!" cried Doone.

And as we came to each of them, I stared ahead to see the car on its back with its wheels spinning. But each turn of the woods unfolded and swam back, and the road was bare, and we came to the long, straight, upward slant and saw the car.

It was marvelous courage in the horse, feeling the ground rising against his feet, but his stride never wavered. The wind was coming out of him at each breath, and his hide was black with his sweat. His head was out against the bit hard. And even I could see he was slowing. But I saw that the auto was slowing also. And the auto had no heart—only a kind of oil. For a moment it almost stopped, and I saw Kathy pushing desperately against the brass rod. The gears grunted and ground. We gained so fast for an instant that it seemed that the auto was rolling back down the hill to us. But then a cloud of smoke burst from it, and it picked up again noisily, and for a long time we held even, not gaining, not losing.

But at last, as we saw the road stretching out of the trees to the sky at the crest of the hill, Doone gave a shout.

"Now, boy!"

He did not reach for his whip, because he had no need of a whip; and besides, the race was Blue Dandy's. I felt a last burst of power in the traces, and then the auto began to come back to us.

Doone swung the horse left. We crawled up abreast and I saw Blue Dandy putting his eye on the auto. The engine missed a beat. Kathy's chin dropped, and all of a sudden she threw out the gear and yanked at the brake. The car stopped swiftly, and Blue Dandy hauled up so they stood side by side— auto and horse. The auto was quivering from the idling engine, but the horse shook from the beating of his great heart. And anyone could have seen which was the better.

Doone passed me the reins.

He climbed down over the wheel slowly and walked up to her. But she didn't get out of the car. She leaned her chin on her hand and her elbow on the edge of the seat and bent down to him.

"Doone!" she exclaimed prettily. "What on earth brings you here?"

"Can you ask, Kathy?"

Deliberately she turned her eyes to the horse, and I saw that they were still shining.

"He is a beauty, Doone! No wonder you're proud of him."

"He's the finest horse in the universe," I said.

"Don't butt in," Doone said to me. And now I saw he had forgotten the horse entirely. "Do you think I'd let you go off like a thief, Kathy? Without a word to me? In the middle of the night?"

"Thief, Doone!"

"You know very well. You've got my pride in your hand, and Lord knows what you've done with my heart."

"Have I?" asked Kathy.

"It was gone, and that's how I found you missing."

"What shall we do about it, Doone?"

She had folded both hands on the edge of the seat and was leaning far out to him, and her eyes were soft for him.

"I've brought along the stable money," said Doone. "Are you going to New York?"

"I was," she said soberly.

"I'll get in with you then," said Doone. "We'll get married in Utica. Let people talk if they want to. I've lost my pride, but I don't give a damn."

"Maybe," said Kathy, and her eyes twinkled—"maybe you've found it."

"Can I have it, then?"

"You've had it all the time, Doone. But if you want legal title, I don't mind."

Doone said no more. But his face was sober as he passed through the lights of the auto lamps. And Kathy turned round as he got in and lifted her chin at him and smiled.

"Aren't you going to kiss each other?" I asked, for I had my own proper ideas on such subjects.

But they did not need to kiss each other. They smiled at me rather vaguely. And Kathy said in a low voice, "We'll get married in Utica, but I don't want to go to New York. We'll go to the hotel—I think it's exciting for new-married people to go to a hotel, probably, and sign Mr. and Mrs. in public, don't you, Doone?"

"I think," said Doone, "anything I do with you now will be exciting."

She gave a little husky laugh.

"We've got to pretend, you see, Teddy?"

"I see," I said.

"We'll spend the night there and tomorrow we'll come home in the evening."

"Don't you want to go home to New York?" Doone asked.

"I want to go home," she said. "I've wanted to for a long time now. But, Doone, I thought you were putting me out of Boyd House."

"Let's get on, then," said Doone.

Kathy bent her head obediently and put in the gears. Then she looked up in dismay.

"But Blue Dandy, Doone!"

"Oh," I said, "don't bother about him! I'll get him home all right. That's what I came along for."

My heart was in my mouth as I said that, but I looked straight at Doone. And he looked back.

"Of course," he said, "Teddy can take care of him."

He put his hand on her arm, and still looking at him, she put in the gear and started the car. It made a great noise of moving, but it went. I thought Dandy might put up a show, but he merely eyed the thing and pricked his ears once at Doone. Then I turned him.

I walked him all the way back to Barneveld and put him up at the livery for a feed, which I charged to Uncle Ledyard. I slept for an hour in the next stall and then took him on. It was the grandest day of my life. The horse was tired and we took it very easy, and it was nearly noon when we got through the Boyd woods. But Blue Dandy put on a fine show in that last half mile. We came home at a ringing trot, and I held the whip on my knee and said "So, boy, so" as deep as I could. They saw us coming.

Uncle Ledyard came out to meet me, and the admiral was with him, and John Callant ran over from the barn. I tossed the reins to him as I got out.

"You'd better take him in, John."

His mouth gaped at me.

"Where did you catch them, Teddy?" Uncle Ledyard asked.

"On Deerfield Hill," I said. "We took our time."

"Where are they now?" demanded the admiral.

"I should think," I said, "that they're getting married."

The admiral did not swear very long, but it was handsomely loud.

"You'd better have a drink, Jim," said Uncle Ledyard.

"I'm all right. But it beats me how she cranked the car in the first place," he said.

"Sure, I did that for her," said John. "I wound it up myself in the dark."

"You pup," said Uncle Ledyard. "Why didn't you tell us sooner?"

"Sure, she needed a sporting chance," said John. "A girl against that horse."

"John," I said sternly, "you'd better take him in right away."

"Yes, your honor," said John.

# Hotel Room

## (from the book of that title)

### CORNELL WOOLRICH

### The Night of June 20th, 1896

THE lights were going on in the St. Anselm Hotel for the first time. The last mason had left a week ago. The last painter and carpenter had left two days ago. The last decorators were still busy, in some of the rooms on some of the floors, working overtime, working like mad, unrolling carpets, tacking up drapes, unpacking mirrors. Everyone was new at his job, from the manager down to the merest bellboy; everyone was confused, highly excited, uncertain just what was expected of him, and how to go about what was expected of him. Everyone was asking the personnel member just over him what to do and how to do it, and then getting it wrong because he'd been told wrong. The bellboys were asking the bell captain, the bell captain was asking the desk clerk, the desk clerk was asking the manager. It stopped there; the manager had no one higher than himself to ask. So he passed the blame in reverse direction, and it started down the line again: to desk clerk, to bell captain, to bellboy. Then, when it got there, it had to stop once more and start up-rank again. But everyone was making allowances, so there was no great harm done, except to nervous energy. Everyone knew no one could be expected to be letter-perfect. Everyone knew they'd do better in a day or so, or a week. Everyone knew things would calm down and straighten out.

This was opening day, and the hotel had been in business for exactly six hours, ever since high noon.

Now room by room the lights were going on. Window after window bloomed yellow, against the outer presummer darkness, as the rooms were taken. Not in direct order, one after the next, of course. Haphazardly; but still the desk clerk was working his registrations upward pretty much floor by floor, from lower to higher. It was simpler that way. The second and third had been all gone even days before the opening, by premature reservation. The fourth and fifth were sold out by midafternoon, and by nightfall he was already as high as the ninth, with just a scattering of back singles on the two immediately below. And a completely booked hotel in those days was no mean feat.

The carriage arrived a little before ten. Carriages had been arriving all day in unending succession, rolling up in an almost unbroken line, so no one gave it a second look. It was a hired carriage, not a private one. There were telltale grains of rice sprinkled on its black felt flooring. There was a fairly sizable amount of hand-luggage on the seat beside the driver. At the back some mischievous person had affixed a placard reading "Just Married." There was also an empty soup can and an old shoe trailing along behind it at the end of a string, and clattering considerably over the pavement.

A young man alighted, rather nervously. He had on a starched collar the height of his neck. He had on a dark-blue jacket, pinched-in at the back and secured by a halfbelt that ended at the sides. He had on white duck trousers, this being the beginning of the warm season. A flower from some recent function decorated the buttonhole of his lapel. He was about twenty-four.

He looked at the blazing hotel entrance. He looked extremely frightened. Then he turned back toward the carriage, and removed the flat-crowned, rigidly stiff straw hat he wore. This had a tricolored band of blue, white and green around it, and was secured to one of the buttons of his jacket by a black cord. He held out his hand toward the carriage, and, rather strainedly, forced a smile of reassurance. A reassurance that it was obvious he didn't feel himself at the moment, much less being able to pass it on to someone else.

A smaller hand reached out to take his, and its owner followed him down.

She was about eighteen. Perhaps not even that. She had dark-brown hair, piled high atop her head and drawn back from her face in what was called a pompadour. She wore a hat that went high up on one side and far down on the other. It stayed that way through the aid of numbers of pins. It had willow plumes on the side that was up, it had roses and green leaves on the side that was down. A collar as high as his gripped her throat. However, it was not starched linen, but lace, stiffened with whalebone ribs. She held the bottom of her dress up from the ground with one hand. This was highly necessary, for it not only touched the ground, it *lay* over it for quite a few inches on all sides of her when at rest.

But in spite of all this she would have been beautiful in any generation.

They stood there terrified together, hand clasping hand low at their sides, as if trying to hide this bond from the world.

One of the peripatetic bellboys appeared. "Take your luggage in, sir?" he inquired.

The boy could only nod mutely, too stricken to speak. He paid and tipped the coachman, with considerable agitated fumbling of hands.

"Thank you kindly," the coachman said. "Lots of luck to the two of you." He touched whip to horse-flank. "And may all your troubles be little ones," he added.

"I wonder how he could tell about us so easy?" the girl whispered with a nervous titter.

"They like to tease a lot," he said soothingly. He curled her hand protectively about his arm. "Shall we go in?"

They went up the still-new entrance steps of the St. Anselm and into a marble-floored lobby that had, for the present occasion, been turned into almost a jungle of potted palms, ferns, and floral good-luck offerings. Most of these would be removed within a day or two, but at the moment it was almost like picking your way through a hothouse greenery.

"This way, sir, if you'd care to register," the bellboy called helpfully to them. He was visible only above the waist, where he stood, and their baggage, presumably on the floor, had disappeared completely.

They approached the desk.

"Mr. Graham, please!" the bellboy called, addressing banked flowers.

Mr. Graham, the desk clerk, peered out at them from one side of a huge horseshoe of pink roses that partially screened his domain. They shifted over to the side he was on, since they had been erroneously standing over at the other side of the obstacle until then. Mr. Graham, however, had sought to adjust himself to them at the same moment as they did to him, so he had shifted back to the first side, by the time they left it and reached the second. Immediately, both parties corrected their mistake. Mr. Graham returned to the second side, his left; they returned to the first, their right.

Mr. Graham found a way of stopping the pendulum-like fluctuation at last, before it continued any further and died down of its own momentum. "Just stand there where you are now and wait for me," he suggested wearily. "I'll be right over."

"I made a reservation," the young man said timidly, when equipoise had been re-established. "John Compton." He corrected himself. "Mr. Compton." He corrected himself a second time, and far more all-embracingly. "Mr. and Mrs. John Compton."

The girl dropped her eyes for a moment at this point, both pleased and shy.

The young man leaned forward. "The—er—the special suite," he said diffidently.

"Oh, the bridal suite," blurted out the insensitive Mr. Graham. "Yes, of course. We received your reservation. I have it right here."

The girl picked at one of the marginal roses on the horseshoe as a cover for her self-consciousness.

"I'm terribly sorry," Mr. Graham said. "If we'd only known where to reach you in time—"

"Why? Is something wrong?" the young groom demanded tautly.

"There was a hitch," Mr. Graham apologized. "We've been doing everything we can to be ready on time, but those things will happen. Well, the fact of the matter is, Mr. Compton, it's not quite finished yet. I wouldn't feel right about putting you in there, on an—on an occasion such as this." He bestowed a glance on the dewy-eyed bride, which sent her back to roseleaf plucking again in a hurry. "Won't you let me put you elsewhere just for tonight, and then I promise you the suite will be yours, without fail, tomorrow?"

The young pair looked at one another.

"Do *you* mind?" he murmured.

"Do *you*?" she breathed back.

The two deferring questions should have neutralized one another and brought them right back where they were, but he already seemed to be able to translate her meanings without any difficulty, inexperienced husband though he was. "Well, all right," he said, "if you're sure we can have the other tomorrow."

"I give you my word," Mr. Graham promised. He turned to the rack behind him. "I have a lovely room, up on the ninth. I'm sure you'll find it satisfactory." He handed a key to the bellboy. "Nine-twenty-three for Mr. and Mrs. Compton, Richard. Will you sign here, please, Mr. Compton?"

The groom bent over and wrote: "Mr. and Mrs. John T. Compton, Indiana." He looked at it tenderly when he'd finished. Then he looked at her lovingly. "First time together—on paper," he whispered.

She nodded eagerly, and clung closer to his arm, both her hands now clasped around it.

They went over and joined their waiting luggage and the bellboy in the brand-new elevator, its trellis-like ironwork still glistening with freshly applied gold-leaf.

The boy ushered them off at the ninth floor, stopped at a door, keyed and opened it, reached in. Some brand-new electric lights went on in bright welcome.

*And at this point the story of Room 923 begins.*

They followed him in and looked around.

"Oh, it's nice, isn't it?" she said.

"Yes, it is, isn't it?" he agreed.

The bellboy bustled around, trying to make unnecessary actions look like highly necessary ones. Then he retired to the door and came to the crux of the matter. "Will there be anything else, sir, for now?"

"No, thank you." Young Compton put something in his hand a little self-consciously.

The boy eyed it with widening eyes. "Thank you. Thank you very *much*, sir." He backed out, closed the door, and they were alone.

The slightest of pauses followed.

Then she asked, "Did he bring everything up?"

"Yes," he said. Then he contradicted himself by amending, "Wait, I'll count," and told off each separate piece with outpointed finger. "One, two, three—and that little one. Yes, he brought everything up."

Another sliver of pause came between them; under other circumstances it would have been scarcely noticeable as such, but now they were acutely aware of every momentary silence that occurred between them.

"Don't you want to take off your hat?" he suggested with an odd mixture of intimacy and abashed formality.

"Yes, I guess I may as well," she assented.

She crossed to the dressing-table and seated herself at the glass. He remained where he was, watching.

"Gee, I always *did* think you had such pretty hair!" he blurted out suddenly with boyish enthusiasm. "The very first time I met you, I noticed that about you."

She turned her head and smiled at him, equally girlish to his boyishness for an unguarded moment. "I remember, I'd just washed it that day. And Mamma had helped me put it up afterward. I told her that night how lucky it was we had."

She turned back to the glass and looked at it intently in there. "It must be terrible to grow old and have it turn gray. I can't picture that; the same hair, like it is now, should turn gray and still be on *me*."

"But everyone's does when they get old enough."

"Yes, other people's; but to have it happen to *you!*" She peered at herself more closely. "I can't imagine it ever happening to *me*. But when it does, it won't be me any more. It'll be somebody else." She touched her fingers to the sides of her face. "An old lady looking out of my eyes," she said wonderingly. "A stranger inside of me. She won't know me, and I won't know her."

"Then I'll be a stranger too," he said thoughtfully. "Two strangers, in a marriage that was begun by two somebody-elses."

For a moment they were both frightened by this thing their nervously keyed prattle had conjured up. Then they both laughed, and the imminent fright went away.

He went over to her and touched his lips to the piled hair on the top of her head. She acknowledged the caress by placing her hand atop his, where it rested lightly on her shoulder.

"Are you tired?" he murmured close to her ear.

"Yes. Not—too much, though. Just from all the excitement."

"Should we unpack our things?"

She welcomed the offered distraction. "All right, let's. Because tomorrow we'll be doing so much."

"Want me to help you?"

"No, I can manage. I know which key belongs to which."

He opened a door in the wall. "Look at the size of this closet."

She came over beside him to look. "I want a closet that big when we have our own place. I love the way they smell when they're new, don't you? All clean wood-shavings and cedar. Just think, our things will be the first that were ever hung up in it. We sort of christen it."

They smiled at each other. For a moment they were more like children playing house than two slightly bewildered, slightly frightened people about to enter on the most momentous stage of their personal lives.

"How'll we do it?" he asked. "Should I take half, and you half?"

"I guess that's what they—do," she concurred vaguely.

"Which side do you want?" he invited.

"It doesn't make any difference. I'll take from here over, and you take from there over."

He was already over at one of the valises, squatted down on his heels before it, applying himself perseveringly first to one lock, then the other. "My brother gave me this one," he said, in apology for its recalcitrance. "I never can quite get it the first time, as long as I've been using it. There it is." The lid went back and over.

She darted a quick glance of curiosity at the contents. "Oh, how many neckties! Does everybody have that many?"

"I've kept every one I ever owned, I guess," he admitted. "I've never thrown one away, from the very first one I wore when I first put on long pants."

"That's a pretty one there, on top. The one with the blue. Wear that one tomorrow. I'd like it on you."

"Ma gave me that on my birthday, when I was twenty-one. The last birthday—she was with us."

"Oh, well, then maybe—" she said with quick compunction.

"No, I like to wear it. I've worn it lots of times, since. That's what she wanted me to do. She bought it for me to wear." He extricated it from under the straps with a zigzag sawing motion. "I'll take it out now, and leave it on top here. So I'll remember in the morning."

He spread it flat along the top of the dresser. She stepped over after him and evened out, with her finger tips, a slight ripple that had remained in the topmost fold, as though the tie now belonged to the two of them alike, and must be cherished equally by both. "The bees are raised in it," she said with proprietary approval. "I like that."

They went back to their unpacking. They were not exactly with their backs to one another, but each with one shoulder given to the other, due to the position of the two pieces of luggage.

He glanced around after a moment. "It smells nice in there," he complimented her.

"Mamma put in two little bags of sachet, one in each corner, before I left."

Again they both returned to their unpacking.

With a double armful of fuming cambric layers, like someone holding newly trapped snow in her arms, she crossed to the dresser, opened the drawer, carefully put them in. She carried the fleecy articles turned toward the side, away from him, so that he wouldn't get too close a look at them. Within a day or two it wouldn't matter, they would be as one about such things, but at the moment modesty still claimed her, for these were articles of under-apparel.

When he in turn made a trip to the bureau with a double armful from his own receptacle, he likewise held it turned away from her to conceal it from view as much as possible.

Self-consciousness, which had more or less glazed the two of them during those few moments, thawed away again now that that was done. Smiling across-shoulder at one another, he closed down his suitcase, she closed down hers. She brushed off her finger tips against their opposites, but to indicate completion rather than that the task had been dusty. "Well, that much is finished," she said with satisfaction.

"Yes," he agreed. "We won't have to do that now." Then he suggested, "Why don't you sit down? No sense standing."

She selected an armchair, deposited herself into it with a little bounce of possessiveness, due in part no doubt to the newness of the springs. She said again, as she had about the closet, "Oh, I'd love to have a chair like this when we have our own home."

He slung himself down beside her on one arm of the chair, and tucked his arm around her to her further shoulder, and feeling it there, she allowed her head to pillow back against it.

They were quiet for some moments, utterly, blissfully content. No need to talk, nor even to caress. Their being together like this, close like this, was in itself one big caress. He allowed his head to incline toward hers at last, that was the only thing, and remain there, cheek pressed to the top of her head.

Their eyes looked out straight ahead, into the distance, into the future, into a from-now-on, that was in the same place for the two of them. Golden future, peach-bloom future, impossible to capture, and even had it been possible to capture, impossible to hold. And even had it been possible to hold, impossible to bear, to endure. Not of this world at all, a future without a cloud, without a pain, without a spiteful word; without a wrinkle, without a gray hair, without a stiffening bone. A dream within a dream within a dream. The Great Shortchange practiced on youth since time immemorial. The boy, the girl, and the Great Untruth, blinding them all alike, two by two, down the countless generations. The bait that traps them together. A Christmas-tree bauble that, when they try to touch it, let alone hold onto it, crumples into a thousand tinseled fragments. And when they look, they hold nothing in their hands, only silvery dust. Like when you pinch a moth by the wings. But even the moth at least is there, for the moment you pinch it. This other thing isn't.

Once during his double revery she said softly, "I can't believe it even yet, can you?"

He understood the unexpressed thought. "No," he said. "Me either."

"That there was a time, only a little while ago, when there wasn't any you yet, just me. By myself, alone."

"And now there's you and me, both."

"It must be terrible to be alone."

"Like we were a couple months ago."

"I can't remember it any more, can you? But it must be terrible. To go through each day without any—you."

"But now we don't have to any more," he said. "From now on, each day has you in it."

He took out a watch. She'd seen it before. It had been given to him on his graduation from high school. He'd told her so. It was gold-plated. He'd told her so. It had a fob of two little pennants of black moiré ribbon. They hung from an inch-wide bar. That was gold-plated too. It was the only watch they had with them, but one was enough. They had no separate needs of time; there was no time apart from one another. There was only time together.

He opened the lid with a spunky little click. She loved to look at the lid. It was bright as a mirror. It had on it: "To John, from Mother and Dad."

He said, "I guess we better think about—" And then he stopped, because he hadn't been ready in time with the right last word. The sentence really called for the terminal phrase "—going to bed," but he didn't want to use that. She didn't want him to either.

He only stopped a moment; you could hardly notice it. Then he didn't go back over the first part again. He only said "—retiring."

"I guess we better," she assented.

He got off the arm of the chair.

Then he said, "I guess I better go downstairs a minute—first." Somebody must have told him this was the considerate thing to do. Maybe his father, maybe one of his friends.

"All right," she said tractably.

She had stood up, too, now.

He came close and he kissed her.

His face didn't have the handsome regularity of a Greek statue. But a Greek statue couldn't smile, couldn't show light in its eyes.

He went nearly as far as the door, but not quite.

Then he touched his pockets exploratively. His wallet, with his—their—money in it.

"I don't need this," he said. "I'll leave it up here."

He went over and he put it on the dresser-top. Not too far from where the necktie was, tomorrow's necktie.

Then he did go to the door, all the way this time.

And he turned and looked at her so tenderly, so softly, that the look was a caress in itself. With just a touch of rue in it.

"Are you afraid?" he said.

"You mean now, about your going downstairs awhile?"

"No, I mean after—when I come back again."

She dropped her eyes only momentarily. Then she quickly raised them again, and they looked directly into his, candidly and confidently. "No, because I know you love me. And even if part of love is strange, if the rest of it is good, then all of it has to be good. And soon there *are* no different parts to it, it is all just one love. Those are the words my mother told me, when she kissed me good-bye."

"I love you," he said, as devoutly as when you're in a church saying a prayer meant only for God and yourself to hear. "So don't be afraid." Then he said only one thing more. "I'll be back in just a little bit."

Then he closed the door. But for a minute or two his face seemed to glow there where it had been. Then it slowly wore thin, and the light it had made went away.

Like the illusion of love itself does.

In a prim little flurry now she started disrobing. Intent on having it complete before she should be interrupted.

At the moment of passing from chemise to nightrobe, quite instinctively and without knowing she did it, she briefly closed her eyes. Then as the gown rippled downward to the floor, she opened them again. It was not, she had learned or been cautioned when still quite a little girl, nice to scrutinize your own body when it was unclothed. The gown was batiste, a trousseau gown, with eyelet embroidery and a bertha—that is to say, an ample capelike flap covering both shoulders; it was bluish in the shadows where it fell hollowed, pink where her body touched against it, but its actual color was snowy-white.

She had always brushed her hair before retiring. She did it now, for there was something comforting about the sense of normalcy it gave to do it; it was like something familiar to cling to in an eddy of imminent strangeness. She counted each stroke to herself, up to fifty; she longed to go past there, up to a hundred, for it would have seemed to help to arrest time, not allow it to go forward, but she conscientiously curbed herself and refrained.

Then she gave a look around the room, inquiringly and still with that flurried intensity. There was nothing left to do now, no remaining detail unattended.

She went to the bed, turned her back to it, and entered it.

She drew the covers up tightly about one shoulder—the other was turned inward to the pillow.

She gave a little sigh, of finality, of satisfaction, of when there is utterly nothing left to do and one is content there isn't.

Her eyes remained fixed on the door. Not in a hard stare, but in soft expectancy. Nothing tenderer in this world, the eyes of youth looking for its love.

It tires you to look too long at any one object, no matter how gently. Her eyes left the door at last, and went over to the window. That didn't hold them nearly as long, for there was nothing to be expected of it. Love wouldn't enter through there. Then they went to the chair. There she made a discovery that cried for immediate reparation. One lace-cuffed leg-opening of her foreshortened pantaloons was hanging down in full, indelicate sight, escaping perversely from under everything else. It must have freed itself later, for she had painstakingly folded that particular article scrupulously from sight; it was the one thing of all she wished to have remain unnoticed.

"Will I have time to get over there and back before—?" she asked herself, appalled.

But it couldn't be allowed to remain that way; it was more than indelicate, it was almost brazen, rakish, the way it flaunted itself.

She suddenly braved the risk. The covers flew back, she gave a sprightly little vault out of the bed, reached the chair, interred the offending garment, and returned to the bed. The way a child steals from its bed for a moment and scrambles back again undetected by its parents.

Reinstated, again she watched the door.

Now this time it was her hands that tired first, and not her eyes. They tightened in their hold of one another. Soon they grew taut, almost strained; were crushing against one another. She straightened them out. Almost at once they crept toward one another again, crooked, interlocked; clung desperately together, as though each without the other would die.

At last she took them away from one another altogether, seeing she could do nothing with them. One sought out her hair, and nervously felt at it here and there to see if it was in order. It was left, for that matter, in less order than it had been at first. The other sought the shoulder of her gown and twisted that about a little.

Perhaps he was standing just outside the door, uncertain whether to come in. Perhaps young men had trepidations at such a delicate time as this, just as she—just as girls—did. Perhaps if she were to go to the door, open it, that would resolve his irresolution for him.

The decision to go to the door, open it and look out, far more daring than the sortie to the chair had been, grew on her for many minutes before she found the courage to carry it out. At last, pinning her underlip beneath her teeth as if to steel herself to the act, she emerged from the bed once more. Because this was a door, and outside was a public corridor, she put on her wrapper first and gathered it tight. Then she went over to it, the door, and stood there by it, summoning up fresh reserves of courage, sorely needed. She put her hand out gingerly toward the knob, the way you reach for something very hot that you're afraid will burn you.

Then she hesitated there like that, hand on knob.

If he didn't discover her in the act of doing this, she wouldn't tell him —later—that she had done it. It smacked a little too much of boldness, or, what was equally as bad, impatience.

Now she touched the door with her other hand, and inclined her head closer toward it, as if trying not so much to listen but rather to divine by some other subtle sense whether he was present there on the other side of it—or not.

She opened the door and looked, and he wasn't; it was empty there on the other side.

She sighed, and the attentive forward-lean her body had taken relapsed into a backward inert slump of disappointment.

Perhaps he was further down the corridor, walking to and—? She tightened further her already tightened wrapper, and like an aerialist walking on a single wire, advanced through the door-opening and out to the corridor proper, one foot keeping in a straight line behind the other.

It was empty from end to end. Just carpeting, and light bulbs looking so lonely against the wall, like forgotten little orphan suns. She remembered the hall from before, from when they'd first come in, but it hadn't looked so lonely then. Maybe because she hadn't been so lonely then either.

She stood there long, long moments. But nothing, no one, came into sight. The emptiness stayed as empty as before. She re-entered the room at last, closed the door, and mournfully inclined her head against it on the inside in a desolate sort of way. Then that ended too, presently, as all attitudes and postures must sooner or later.

She moved away from there and roamed the room, without a destination, deep in thought, absently touching things as she went, to guide herself. He could not mean to stay away this long. He had lost track of the time. That must be it. That must be the explanation, there could be no other.

Perhaps if she called down, he would understand. Yes, but what genteel way was there to convey the message? "Would you ask my husband to come up, please?" She shuddered at that. It was so unthinkable it made her squeeze her eyes tightly shut for a moment. No, she couldn't say anything like that. The man at the phone—

She tried out several other phrases in her mind, and rejected them as being almost as indelicate if not equally so. "Could you tell me what the time is, please? Our watch has stopped up here." But the mere fact that she was watching the watch; he'd read between the lines—"Could you please arrange to have us called at such-and-such an hour?" But that was unsatisfactory from another point of view; that was almost too neutral. The man down there might take the request literally, and while accepting it, fail entirely to convey it to her husband, in which case nothing would have been solved.

She had stopped meanwhile by one of the valises, her own, and this finally, as she glanced down and noticed it, gave her the sought-after inspiration. The perfect phrasing in which to imbed her unspoken message. Completely neutral, and yet personal enough to require his participation. She rehearsed it to herself, in order to have the wordage arranged right and not be caught faltering at the moment of pronouncing it. Then, letter-perfect, she went to the wall telephone and brought down the corded earpiece from it. She wound the little crank and the connection was established.

A man's voice, frighteningly immediate and immediately frightening, the gruffest voice a man had ever used in the whole world before, the harshest, the raspiest, said: "Yes, please? Can I be of service?"

She began too low, and had to start over at once.

"Beg pardon?"

"I said, I can't seem to open one of our suitcases. My husband—" She swallowed hard, and almost spoiled it, but recovered in time. "Would you ask him if he has the key with him, please?"

"I will without fail, madam, just as soon as I see him."

She'd had the same sensation once years before, when a small boy in a tree had dropped a soft splashy snowball on her as she passed below and it had struck and disintegrated at the nape of her neck.

"Oh, isn't he—? I thought he was—"

"He went out of the building, madam. I saw him as he went past."

"But are you sure it was—?"

"The night bellboy told me it was the young man from '23."

She didn't speak any further. She hadn't strength enough to hang up, she hadn't fortitude enough to continue listening.

He must have sensed an urgency she hadn't wanted to show. "Shall I send out and see if he's outside by the entrance?"

She didn't say anything. Her breath was too much in the way, rising up again before it had even finished going down, leaving no passage clear.

The wait was cruel and long. And this had nothing to do with measured time, for even had it been of no duration whatever, an immediate turn-about, it would have been no less cruel, no less long. The heart cannot measure, it can only feel; in a single instant it can feel as much as in a long slow hour, it cannot feel more than that.

There was a background murmur soon, as of tidings being brought, and then a clear-spoken address directly to her: "He doesn't seem to be out there right now, madam. He may have taken a short stroll away from the hotel. Just as soon as he returns I'll notify him that you—"

She heard him go, at the other end, and what was there to stay for anyway? But she stayed; just stayed there, on and on, through long slow minutes that never seemed to pass away.

At last she came away from there, a thin shining line down each cheek like silver threads unraveling from her eyes. She was cold suddenly, in mid-step, in mid-room, with a knifelike instantaneousness that temperature alone could never have brought about. Quivering spasmodically, with clenched teeth and rigidity of movement. Clutching for the warmest thing she could lay hands on, a woolen bathrobe, she encased herself in it like a cocoon, muscles too chill-bound to allow her to insert arms through sleeves. Covered up to her very eyes, she huddled in the chair they had once shared, feet folded up, a lumpy little woolen mound of misery.

The chill soon stopped. Only misery went on; whether warm blood or cold, the same misery. Her eyes stared hauntedly, fixedly, from just above the upended robe-collar; darkly shadowed now by long strain, perhaps darkly shadowed too by the fact that they were so recessed within the sheltering robe. Her mouth was hidden, and most of her nose. Only the eyes, like low-burning lamps of despair. Never wavering, scarcely blinking. Duller now than they had been before. Tearless too, for grief was past its early weeping stage; had become a deeper, unseen thing.

The night wore on, with a hush like funeral velvet draperies.

When she was a little girl, she had feared the night, as most small children do. Once, awakening too early and in the dark, she had cowered there uneasy and sent up a little plea: "Make the light come soon; make the night go away." Now, it was the day she feared, the coming of light. For while the night still lasted, it might yet return him. But when the day came, she would have lost him altogether. She knew that well, knew that well. It was in the night that he had gone, and if the night did not bring him back to her, the day never would. His absence would be sealed forever. So now she prayed for darkness, prayed for night, the punishing night, to last beyond its span.

"Don't let the day come. Don't let it come yet. Wait till he's back first. Then let it come."

But mercilessly the night thinned away, as if there were a giant unseen blackboard eraser at work, rubbing it out. And in the new light he didn't come, just as he hadn't in the former dark. Still her eyes stared out over the woolen folds, looking nowhere, seeing nothing now. Duller than dull, hopelessly opaque.

She must have slept, or dozed awake at least. Her head went over a little to the side at last, became more inert. The eyes never fully closed, but lost some of their haunted fixity. The lids did not drop over them the whole way, but sagged to a somnolent meridian.

The fidgeting of the knob must have been hours after. No hope came with its fluttering, somehow. Hope would not come back; it had been dead too long perhaps. It didn't even stir, strangely enough. Nor when the questioning tap came. Nor when it parted at the seams and a gap was made, empty the first few instants. Then an errant flounce of skirt peered momentarily, showing hope it had been right to lie there dead.

Above, a head looked cautiously in, everything else kept back.

The woman was in maid's headgarb, ruched cap atop a massive pillow of upturned red hair, kept walled in by barrettes. She was buxom, florid, maternal in every respect. Save perhaps the actuality.

"Did I come too soon, now?" she murmured softly.

The eyes just looked at her.

"They told me one of the rooms around here was a bride and groom, but sure it's the first day for all of us, and I would be getting mixed up like this."

The eyes just looked.

"Shall I step out and be coming back a little later then?"

A voice like the echo of far-off sound said: "It doesn't matter."

"Did the young man step out for a minute?"

The far-off voice said: "He's gone."

She advanced more fully into the room now, concerned. "What's the matter, darlin'? What ails—?"

The bunched-up robe suddenly exploded like an overstuffed pod, lay there flaccid, the chair was empty, and she was clinging to her, and being clung to. Someone of one's own kind, another woman. Someone like your mother, someone like your sister. Someone like—you.

The maid held her, and patted her, and coaxed her. "Sh, darlin'. Sure and he'll be back before you know it. Any minute now, through the door he'll be coming."

"He won't. He won't. He never will again."

"How lang ago did he leave? How lang is it he's gone?"

"At twelve. I think it was at twelve. But I don't know any more. I can't remember any more."

"But sure, darlin', it's only a little after two o'clock now."

"At twelve last night."

The ruddy face whitened. For a moment *her* eyes were frightened too, then she covered it up. She patted the girl some more, she held her to her. Then she left her briefly, saying she'd be back. The girl just stood there exactly where she'd left her, like someone deprived of her own powers of locomotion.

When the maid came back she held a thick crockery mug of steaming tea. She led her, like an automaton, to the chair and into it, and held the mug up to her lips.

"Come, now. This'll do you good. They have a little closet on each floor at the back of the hall, with a gas-ring in it, so we maids can brew ourselves a cup of tea at noon." She stroked her hair a little as the girl tasted of it. She finally left the mug in her hands altogether. Then she turned to make the bed, from habit that was already fixed by morning-long practice. When she saw she had no need to, she drew in her lips in unspoken commiseration, and quickly turned away again with an almost pirouette-like rapidity.

She sat down herself then, in solacing camaraderie, but on the very edge of the chair, to show that her stay was stolen and had to be a short one.

She asked what her name was, the girl's. This brought on pain again, but the mug was there to conceal the flickering her lips made. "It was to have been Compton."

The maid quickly spoke of her own, to snare her mind away. "Mine's Ann, spelt shart, without the e. I don't know why they left it aff, but as long as they did, I might as well keep it that way. Ye can write it quicker that way."

She rose soon and had to leave her, telling her she had half the floor still to do, but promising to look in on her a little later. "I'll be right out there somewhere. Cahll me if you want anything, and I'll drop the broom and dustpan and come to you in a minute. Don't you want to get a little rest now."

The girl averted her eyes from the bed almost in horror. "I couldn't get in there. I couldn't."

"Let me fix you in the chair, then." She put a pillow behind her head and, daring the official wrath, for all the bedding was new, slipped another to the floor underneath her feet. She took one of the blankets and deftly spread it over her. She stroked her hair soothingly, before turning to go. "Is there no one ye want me to tell, for you, now?"

The girl said plaintively, "There was only he. Who else could there be?"

She left as she had entered the first time, gradually; her face remaining to peer back after the rest of her was already hidden.

"Come back soon, Ann," the girl whispered.

A flirt of skirt in the door-seam, just like the first time, and she was gone.

She had left the chair when Ann next entered. This was quite some hours later, and she was crouched on the floor, head and shoulder supported upright against the dresser. One of the drawers peered open. Against her she held pressed a man's white shirt, still buttoned in a flat oblong. One empty papery sleeve she had drawn up around her own shoulder, as if seeking a phantom embrace. She was awake.

Ann said nothing, drew it subtly away from her, and it deftly vanished from sight. She got her back to the chair again. She had brought more tea, and this time slabs of buttered white bread. The tea she got her to take, the bread she couldn't.

"And is there no one you're going to tell about this, darlin'?" she breathed coaxingly.

"I have no one. Who is there?"

Then, belatedly, she noticed a change in her comforter's appearance. "You're going away. You're going to leave me."

Ann had on a short pinched-in jacket, a bell-shaped ground-trailing skirt, and on her head a flat saucer-like straw hat from which looped three cherries, one of them on a broken stem. "I have to, darlin'. Sure I finished up lang ago. I hung behind all I could. I even asked the housekeeper could I be staying with you in here tonight. 'An employee in one of the guest-rooms? Out of the question!' You know how *they* talk."

The girl wrung her hands, and bowed her forehead against them. "Oh, what'll I do? All night in here, alone."

"I'll be here bright and early. I'll look in at you the first thing." She drew her from the chair, and tried to guide her across the room.

At the last minute the girl noticed the destination, shrank back. "I can't. Don't ask me to. I'll keep staring at the door, and the door'll keep staring at me. Like last night."

"Is it the door that bothers you, now?"

"All night long I'll watch it, waiting for it to open."

"If I cover it so ye can't see it, then will ye try to sleep?"

"But how can you?"

The purposeful Ann looked about, for a daring moment even eyed the drapes. Then, discarding such a job-risking choice, came to a heroic decision. Modestly she turned away from her protégée. Up, in bunchy awkwardness, went the ground-trailing skirt. Down, in sudden release, came a petticoat. Not new, not even whole perhaps, but her own, all she had to give. She stepped clear, the skirt subsided, and the diminution could not have been detected.

She picked it up, went to the door, and held it outspread against it in measurement. It was inadequate.

"Wait, now," she said determinedly, though nothing had been said.

Her arms came close together, widened with a rending noise, and the petticoat had opened from waist to hem into twice its former area.

"Oh, no!" the girl protested too late. "Your petticoat— How'll you get home?"

"Sure and many's the time I hadn't one to my name, and I still moved about. It's June."

She slipped out, came back with a palmful of thumbtacks filched from the supply room at the end of the hall. Using only the toil-toughened heel of her hand to drive them home, she obliterated the door for at least two-thirds of the way down with a sort of diagonal slipcover effect. The bottom third could not be seen from a prone position in the bed.

"There, darlin'," she said, "it won't hurt you anny more."

"Now when I look at it," the girl mused, "I'll think of you, not of—"

Ann was able now to lead her docilely to the bed, help her in, and prod and plump the covers about her. The girl lay with her head flat on the pillow, staring straight up at the ceiling overhead. Ann stood there by her a moment, placed her hand on her forehead in consolation; looked down considering, decided, and finally put her lips to the girl's forehead in a sisterly kiss of sympathy.

"Rest, now," she coaxed her. "Till the marning, darlin'. We've been told to get here by seven, but I'll make sure I'm here by six, so I can be with you a little bit." She moved on toward the door, the ex-petticoat bellied out hugely for a moment, there was a smothered latch-click, and she was gone.

The girl's eyes kept staring straight up at the ceiling overhead. Not right away, not soon even, but after a lengthy while they flickered closed, reopened briefly once or twice, and then at last she slept.

Her sleep was not without the continuing thoughts and images of her waking, however; its stresses and its longings kept on uninterrupted. And, as in most such dreams, there was a magic formula by which she could recover him, bring him back. Waiting there for her to use, if only she could. So easy that it tantalized, so simple that it tortured, made her twitch upon the bed. It was: just to speak his name, just to say it. That was all she had to do.

Other names like meteors flashed by, lighting up momentarily the black skies of her sleep, but always the wrong ones. "Arthur." "Wallace." And the strange name of a little boy she had once schooled with: "Ansel." While he waited patiently just out of sight to appear when she would have pronounced his own, the right one.

Faster and faster her head rolled to and fro on the pillow. She even arched her back clear of the bed time after time, to fall back again frustrated every time.

And suddenly, as she seized upon it at last, the effort of doing so shattered the dream like a dark-glass casing, too much violence for its fragile texture, and her eyes flew open and she awoke.

Saying it low first, then louder, louder still, then screaming it out, in vain effort to stay the dream and have it fulfill its promise. "Johnny! John-eee!"

But the dream wouldn't come back, and the magic formula was no good now.

Over and over she screamed it, hoping against hope that it would work. "John-eee! John-eee!" Then stopped at last only because she had no more breath to spend.

In a moment or so someone tapped tentatively on the other side of the door. She seized a corner of the pillow and stuffed it into her mouth, and closed her teeth on it, to keep from screaming any more.

Then the voice of a man said, speaking to someone beside him: "Nobody in there. It must have come from somewhere else, I guess." And they went away again.

She whimpered awhile, and lay awake awhile, in the silence of the coffin-like night.

Then again she slept, and then again she dreamed. But the new dream was less exacting, producing him without requiring of her any magic formula.

The petticoat vanished and the naked door was there again.

Then it opened, and she knew he was there, just back out of sight. Her heart could feel his presence salving its hurt.

Then his head appeared, timorously. She had to call out, to reassure him: "It's all right, Johnny. It's all right."

Then at last all of him, and there he was. The tie he'd worn, the suit. Even to his hat, thrown back upon his head, as she had seen him once do on the train, to relieve heat and haste.

He came all the way in, as far as the foot of the bed. As though he were *staying* now, as though he were *staying* now. He even rested both hands on the footrail of the bed. He was so near her now, and she to him. Almost she thought she could feel the warmth of his breath carried to her on the cold barren air. Almost she thought she could see those little glints of topaz, like spinning pinwheels, in his dark-brown eyes.

"I can explain," he said. "I can explain why I stayed so long."

"I know you can," she said docilely. "I know you can, Johnny."

"But only if I have time enough. If they don't give me time enough—"

"Hurry, Johnny! Hurry, while you still have time—!"

But just as he started to, it was already too late. Time, the mysterious enemy, overtook him. Three cherries sprouted from the top of his head, and dangled over sideward, one on a broken stem.

His face got redder than it had been, and broader, and he was Ann the chambermaid, leaning over the foot of the bed and crooning pleadingly: "Don't you know me, now? Don't you remember me from yesterday?"

The girl murmured softly, but wistfully rather than with resentment, "Now he'll never come. Now you've made him go away forever. And just when I almost had him."

Ann stayed with her awhile, and gave her tea again. Then she left, promising, "I'll be back soon, dear. As soon as ever I can."

When she came it was several hours later, and she had someone else with her. She stood back by the doorway in deference, and let the other come forward alone and take command of the visit. The newcomer was a woman.

She wore pince-nez glasses. She wore a dress of sleek bronze-colored bombazine, iridescent like the breast feathers of a pouter pigeon, and at her waist a black alpaca apron with two pockets. In one was a writing-tablet, in the other a great mass of keys, resembling a porous chunk of ore that has been imperfectly smelted and failed to fuse properly. From her bosom hung an open-face gold watch, suspended upside-down so that it could be lifted and read with a single move of the hand. A lead pencil was thrust raffishly (but no doubt the raffishness was not intended) through one of the "rats" at the back of her head.

She patted the girl's hand. It was meant kindly, but it was a perfunctory pat. She exuded no warmth, such as Ann breathed with every breath she drew. "Now, dear," she said, "what is it?"

"Nothing," the girl said. She could think of no other answer to make to a question like that.

"Now, dear," the housekeeper said again, "what do you want us to do?"

"Nothing," the girl said. She could think of no other answer to make to that question either.

"Is there nothing you would like us to do?"

This time the girl looked up at her with the plaintiveness of a sick child coaxing for a drink of water. "Can I have Ann back?"

The woman turned her head to where Ann stood. "Ann has her duties," she replied disapprovingly. "She must not stay away from them too long."

As though she understood the hint, Ann immediately slithered out the door and was gone.

The housekeeper gave the girl's hand one more perfunctory pat, turned to go herself. At the open door she said, "Mr. Lindsey will have to be notified. He will have to decide what is to be done." Then she closed the door after her.

The girl remained alone.

Some time after, a knock again interrupted her solitude. The knock did not wait for a response, but the door was opened immediately on its heels, and a dignified and well-dressed gentleman entered, with the air of someone who did not need to ask permission but was free to enter a room like this at any time he chose.

He was about her father's age, and dressed somewhat as she had seen her father dressed; but not at ordinary times, only on rare occasions, such as churchgoing on an Easter Sunday morning. He had a very heavy down-turned mustache, glistening with wax, and wore a small flower, she did not know its name, in the buttonhole of his swallowtail coat.

"My poor child," was his greeting to her. "I've come to see what can be done about this." Then, after having already seated himself, he asked, "May I sit down a moment and have a little chat with you?"

Her face flickered briefly as the sympathy in his voice revived her grief. She nodded mutely; he made her feel less lost and lonesome.

"I'm Mr. Lindsey, dear," he introduced himself; and though he didn't add that he was the manager, somehow she knew that he must be. He had too much of an air of habitual authority about him.

"Tell me about yourself," he said artlessly.

And, hesitantly and awkwardly at first, but soon without any self-consciousness whatever or even awareness that she was doing so, she was answering the sprinkling of guiding questions that he put to shape the course of her talk. She did not even know that they were questions, they were so deftly inserted. She did not even know, in telling him about their house at home, that she had told him what street it was on, or what its number was, or of course what town it was situated in. Sitting back at ease in his chair, one knee crossed above the other, nodding benignly, he skillfully slanted the conversation.

Then almost in mid-word—hers, not his own—his knees had uncoupled, he was on his feet taking leave of her, and the refreshing little flow of confidence had ended. Mouth still open on an unfinished sentence, she watched him go to the door and open it, with a soothing "Forgive me, my child; I must hurry. There's an awful lot to do here today."

"Good-bye, Mr. Lindsey," she said forlornly, eyes hopeful to the end that he might change his mind and remain.

Just as he closed the door she heard him say, in a tactfully lowered voice to someone who must have remained out there waiting for him: "They must be sent for. She can't remain here alone like this."

He returned in about two hours' time—or perhaps it was even three; her standards of time were all awry now—and now there was another man with him. He opened the door on the concluding words of something they had just finished discussing, and she caught the tail-end of it. "—might be better, as you say. The sight of it might frighten her." He entered alone first; the second person lingered outside the door an additional moment or two. She had a vague impression, she didn't know why, that he was disencumbering himself of something. She even glimpsed a stiffly outthrust arm for an instant, held as when one shucks a sleeve off it.

Then the other man came in at last. He was older than Mr. Lindsey. He could almost have been her Grandpa, if her Grandpa had still been alive. He came in smoothing down his mop of snowy-white hair, as if he had just finished removing something from his head. His attire was incomplete almost to the point of freakishness. She had never seen anyone dressed like that before, except in their own home. He had on dark-blue trousers, an undershirt with elbow-length sleeves, suspenders over this, and pinned to the undershirt as one would wear a medal, some sort of a shield or badge. Still, everything was so unreal to her now, so strange, that this one little bit of added strangeness held no meaning, glided by her almost unnoted.

He seated himself and promptly began to talk to her. Mr. Lindsey remained standing in the background, attentive but taking no part.

Like Mr. Lindsey, his whole conversation was in the form of questions. Unlike Mr. Lindsey, they were all about Johnny, not herself. About his family, about where he had come from, about how long she had known him. She found it very difficult to talk to him, mainly because the subject-matter held so much pain in it for her. It hadn't been painful to talk about herself; it was painful to talk about Johnny. And some of the questions were so extremely private, that she could scarcely answer them at all. Questions such as only her own mother would have asked her—and even she had not. Did she know whether he had gone with girls at all before their engagement?

"I don't know. I think he must have. All boys do." And then, completely unsure of herself, she in turn transformed it into a question. "Don't they?"

Had she any way of knowing whether he had ever kissed any girl, before he had kissed her?

Her eyes pleaded with Mr. Lindsey over her interlocutor's shoulder, and his in turn tried to reassure her.

Her face felt warm and her voice was low. "He told me—when WE first did—he never had before."

"Did he tell you why?"

He had to lean forward to catch the whispered thread of sound. "He said he never liked anyone—enough to—until he knew me."

Then at last he let her be, and rose, and went and stood beside Mr. Lindsey, and they spoke together for a long while. She could hear some of it, but it held little meaning for her. It seemed to be on some general topic, rather than on herself and Johnny. One of those dry general topics, like politics, that grown-up men always seemed to discuss when they got together.

"Too little general education on the subject. Everything's kept hushed up, in this day and age of ours—"

"But you can't shout those things out loud," protested Mr. Lindsey.

"The girls grow up knowing nothing, and half of the boys grow up and what little they know is wrong, all wrong. Then we throw them at each other's heads, and many times this is what happens."

"But I'm a married man myself," she heard Mr. Lindsey tell him. "And I don't think anyone knew less than I did when I got married, and yet my marriage has turned out very happily."

"Don't doubt it," said the other man obdurately. "But it's still blind luck. Other things enter into it too. If a boy is brought up in a strict, religious household, and trained to believe all that is sinful—then his conscience will trouble him about it later on. The more decent the boy, the more his conscience will trouble him. You can't break away from your early training, you know. Never altogether. And I think something like that is what's at the bottom of this. I think this boy ran away because he loved her, not because he *didn't* love her. He wanted to keep himself from doing something that he thought was sinful to her—"

Now they were talking about Johnny himself, she could tell. "Johnny wouldn't have done anything that was sinful to me," she wanted to say, but she couldn't, she was too ashamed. She covered up her reddened face with both her hands, and tried to hide it.

For the first time the other man turned and glanced over to her. "He certainly wasn't waylaid, or it would have been reported to us by this time.

The same if he'd been injured in an accident. That leaves just this, what we've been discussing, and one other possibility—which I don't think is very likely at his age. A sudden complete loss of memory. I'm not a doctor, so I can't think what they call it. But there is such a thing; very rare though. Anyway, if it were that, I think he would have come to us of his own accord for help by now. We'll keep looking—and waiting—and I'm afraid that's all we *can* do. What'd you say his name was, again?" He moved toward the dresser, where the billfold lay, and reached out a hand toward it.

She sprang up with a quickness they hadn't known she was capable of, and lunged between him and the dresser like the sideward thrust of a knife, shielding it—the billfold—with her back. Or rather, shielding its exact position, for this was fetishism, though the word had not been born yet.

"No," she pleaded wildly, "don't touch it! Don't move it! It's right where his fingers left it, right in the exact place. If it stays there, then he'll come back. If you move it, then he never will."

The man gave Mr. Lindsey a look and withdrew his seeking hand.

She turned and let her own fingers hover lovingly above the article, without, however, touching it. "His hand was the last one touched it," she said. "His hand put it down right here. It's like a magic spell, and it mustn't be broken." She gestured as if patting the air above it. "It means that he'll come back."

"Did he go out without his tie too?" the man asked, noticing the necktie placed neatly folded beside it.

"No, that was the one he put out to wear for tomorrow." She stopped a moment, thought about it, pensively stroking her cheek with just two fingers. "But now tomorrow's yesterday." She turned to him bewilderedly, as if seeking his help. "Oh, what happened to tomorrow? Who took it away?" And turned to look, as if seeking it about the four corners of the room. "Who took tomorrow away?" And even took him by the sleeve and tugged at it repeatedly, like a small child demanding an answer to its question. "It was *there*. It was to have come. It never did. Yet now it's gone. Who took it? Who?"

A thin haze of grayish smoke seemed to begin rising all about, until she couldn't see him clearly any longer, nor Mr. Lindsey, nor the room itself. It didn't make her cough, though, like real smoke does. Just hampered her vision. The floor tipped up and nudged her knees. It didn't hurt though. She put her palms against it, to keep it from her face.

"You're the very one should know," she murmured. "You *are* a policeman. I understand that now; I didn't when you first came in— That's why you wear that little thing—there—" She toppled over on her side, and shielded her eyes with one best forearm. "Please Mr. Policeman. Catch them, make them give tomorrow back."

And then somebody's strong arms went around her and gently lifted and held her. The strong arms carried her and placed her on something soft that sank a little under her. And the gray smoke rolled in like a blanket and covered her all up. She could even *feel* it being tucked in around her chin.

When the haze that had misted her eyes had cleared away again, as at last it did, Papa was there in the room with her; he was the first one she saw. He was standing, back from the bed a little, beside a chair. In the chair sat Mamma, pressed close against him, his arm consolingly about her shoulder. Within her clenched hand, raised to just below her face, she held a tiny balled-up handkerchief, and from time to time would press it to her nose. But she was not crying now, though just previously she evidently had been. This was just the leftover corrective from when she had been crying. Both their faces were haunted with concern, their eyes were fixed troubledly on her, with a steadfastness which indicated they had been gazing at her like this for a long time past. They did not smile at her, seemed too deeply troubled to be able to, even when they saw that she recognized them. Papa's mustache even seemed to droop, for it was so heavy that it took whatever shape his mouth took under it, and his mouth therefore must have been turned deeply down.

Nearer at hand was someone else. She only noticed him last, for his head had been bent down low, listening to her breathing. She knew him to be a doctor, for she felt the tiny coolness his instrument made, moving here and there about her chest. She wasn't afraid; she had had doctors do this before with a stethoscope, for a bad cold in the chest, perhaps. This was *home*, a part of home; a part of being with Papa and Mamma, a part of being safe, of being cared for.

His face was wise and grave as a doctor's should be, as he righted his head at last. Glasses with a black cord at the side, and a trim, neat beard, not allowed to grow too long, and eyes that sympathized and gave you confidence.

"There, dear," he said, and patted her shoulder, and made a gesture to reclose the open neck of her gown, which, however, he did not complete. She did it herself, her attention attracted to it by his gesture.

He put away his stethoscope, and turned to them, to Mamma and Papa, and said, "She is sound physically. There is no need for worry on that score. But—" And then he didn't finish it.

Mamma's face tightened up even more than it was already. "What is it, Doctor?" she said in a whisper that was almost superstitiously fearful.

"She has suffered great shock," he said, and he rose now to finally face them in entirety, so that she could see only his back. He crossed the room before speaking further, and then, trickling water into a tumbler, said, "And those things sometimes take long to wear off." Then bringing the tumbler back to her side, he took from his bag which sat open on the floor a neat little oblong paper packet, and deftly unfolded it to make a little trough of it, and from this allowed a white powder to sift into the water and cloud it to the hue of diluted milk. "And sometimes never," he said, concluding at last his sentence.

Mamma gave a start and cried, "Oh, Doctor— Oh, no—!"

He stirred the dose by hand-motion alone, without the aid of any spoon, by giving his wrist a rotary motion. Then passed it to her and said, "Drink this, dear. Right down."

She knew the taste, she'd experienced it before. Calomel.

"Now lie back and rest," he said, when he'd taken the empty tumbler back from her, and gently placed his hand upon her forehead, again more as a gesture of what he wanted her to do than by exerting any actual pressure upon her.

She lay back and watched and listened, while he gave them his undivided attention at last.

Mamma said pleadingly, "What shall we do, Doctor? Doctor, what shall we do?"

"There is nothing you *can* do, except wait and see. Nothing I can do, nothing anyone can do. Except let time go by."

"Shall we take her back with us now, Doctor?" Mamma asked.

"Is it far?" he said.

She told him where it was, in Indiana. He closed his eyes briefly, as though he would have preferred it to be not that far. Then he said, "Yes, it's better if you do, even if the trip is a tiring one. The sooner you take her out of this terrible room and what it spells for her, the better off she'll be."

Mamma got up at once, and went forthwith to the bureau drawers, almost briskly, as though the mere act of starting preparations eased her distress somewhat.

Papa looked out into the hall and called to someone unseen: "Will you send the porter up?" Then came back and reached into his pocket for his billfold.

The doctor took up his hat, and went to shake hands with Papa. Mamma quickly let the drawer be momentarily, to go and join in the leave-taking.

Someone knocked on the door, and the doctor went to it and looked out. He stood there awhile, just his back showing, while someone spoke to him.

When he had closed the door again, he motioned them to come nearer. "They've found him," he breathed.

"Is he—?" Papa whispered.

"They found his body," the doctor said. "The pockets were all inside out. He didn't have his wallet with him. Maybe if he had had it on him, he wouldn't have been killed."

Mamma wrung her hands.

Papa looked down at the floor.

"I leave it up to you whether to tell her or not," the doctor said. He sighed and shook his head. "Keep her to yourselves a lot. All you can. Don't let people hurt her."

Mamma said, "Who would want to hurt her, Doctor? Our little girl."

"Nobody will want to. But everyone will. Every time she sees a boy holding a girl by the hand. Every time she sees a couple dancing. Every time she sees a baby roll by in its carriage— Keep her to yourselves a lot. All you can, all you can."

"But after we're gone, Doctor?"

"Maybe it won't matter any more by then. That would be the kindest thing. Hope for that, pray for that. Maybe it won't matter any more by then."

Then he patted Mamma on the shoulder, as one who tries to give solace where none can be given; then he shook Papa's hand. Then he was gone.

Mamma returned to her, and kissed her on the forehead, but dry-eyed and calm and wise and strong now, as she had always been when her girl was a little girl; her tears and fears no more to be seen. She helped her from the bed and stood her there before her, and dressed her as she used to when she was small. From the inside to the out, button by button, and hook-and-eye by hook-and-eye. The only difference was—she, Mamma, no longer needed to bend down on the point of her knee as she had when she was six or seven, for she was taller now, a full-grown height, not a child's height any more.

Papa in the meanwhile moved about in the background, his back to them; all the things were gone from the drawers. But on the top of the bureau his tie for tomorrow still lay, untouched, just where he had put it. She wanted to go over to it and stroke it, but Mamma, with a quick glance to see what drew her, turned her gently, ever so gently, the other way. So gently that she could not be resisted, for there was no force there to resist, only gentleness and that is stronger than force.

A porter came in and took the valises out, but she was only dimly aware of that, for Mamma was standing before her blocking her view.

Mamma put her hat on for her last of all, and adjusted it, and thrust the pins through it. The hat that went way up on one side, way down on the other.

Then Mamma placed an arm about her waist, and kissed her once again on the forehead, the kiss that she remembered so well from her childhood, the kiss of security, the kiss of consolation, the kiss of belonging to someone, of being a part of them; the kiss of home. And Mamma murmured gently beside her ear, "Come, our little girl is coming home with us."

Step by step, with her arm about her, she led her over to the door, then out past it to where Papa stood waiting, and reaching behind her, started to draw it tactfully closed after them.

But just as it was closing, the girl herself gave an abrupt turn, and pleading, "Just one moment—! Only one—!" stepped back to it and looked in once more, while Mamma's arm still held her around the waist.

And staring around at the emptiness, as if seeking him everywhere and finding him nowhere, she called out with whispered intensity: "Good-bye, Johnny! Good-bye! And good-bye to me too. For we both died in here the other night."

## The Night of September 30th, 1957

She arrived at about nine, that last night. That last night of the hotel. She came alone in a taxi. It had to take its place in what almost amounted to a conveyor-belt of taxis, each stopping in turn at the entrance, then drawing away again. There was this difference: hers was bringing its fare to the hotel, the rest were all taking theirs from it.

She was very frail and very old, and looked very small the way she sat there in the exact center of the broad rear seat. Her face looked unlined and peaceful, as though care had passed over it lightly.

The driver stopped at the entrance, his car grazing the one ahead as it drew away, the one just in back grazing his as it closed in to wait its turn.

She leaned forward a trifle and asked, "Is it that now?"

He looked at his watch and said, "Yes, ma'am, exactly that."

She nodded, gratified. "I wanted it to be that exactly."

"It's a hard thing to do," he said. "Let you out somewhere at an exact certain minute. I had to take you around the block three times. That made the meter climb up."

"I don't mind," she reassured him quickly. "I don't care." She paid him, and then when he turned in the seat to try and pass the change back to her, she put the flat of her hand up against it. "No, I don't want anything back," she said.

"But that was a five," he said.

"I know it was," she said imperturbably. "My sight is good." Then she added, as though that explained her generosity, "I don't ride in taxis very often."

He got out and opened the rear door for her and helped her down. She looked smaller than ever standing beside him there on the sidewalk and with two tremendous walls of baggage towering on both sides of her. He got her bag out. She only had one, a very small one, lightweight and old-fashioned. It too looked small, just as she did.

"The place is coming down, you know," he told her.

"I know it is," she said. "I can read the papers." But it wasn't said with asperity.

"They're putting up a twenty-six-story office building on the site."

"Twenty-eight," she corrected him. Then she gave a contemptuous sniff, presumably intended for office buildings in general and not just the difference of two floors.

She left him and went inside, carrying the bag herself. She stopped at the desk. "I have a reservation for Room 923," she said. "I engaged it several weeks ago."

He scanned some sort of a chart he had tacked up there off to one side. "I believe that floor's already been closed off," he said. "Won't one of the lower floors do?"

She was firm. "No. I specified that room, and my reservation was accepted. I had it confirmed. I won't take any other."

He went off and spoke to somebody about it. Then he came back and said, "You can have that room." He presented the register to her for her signature. It was open very far to the back, at the last few of its pages. She fingered the thick bulk of its preceding ones.

"How far back does this go?" she asked him.

He had to look at the opening page to find out. "Nineteen forty."

"And what happened to the old ones? There must have been others before this. What happened to the very first one of all?"

"I haven't the faintest idea," he admitted. "Probably done away with long ago. Thrown out."

"Thrown out!" she said with severity. "Things like that shouldn't be thrown out." She shook her head with disapproval. "Very well, I'll sign," she said. She wrote "Mrs. John Compton" in a wavering spidery hand, almost ghostly compared to some of the firm, fullbodied signatures that had gone before it.

He had to keep palming the bell repeatedly before he could attract any attention. The staff had already been skeletonized. Finally a harried bellboy appeared, picked up her bag, and mechanically started toward the street entrance with it. A sharp clang of the bell brought him around in his tracks.

"Show this lady to 923."

The bellboy showed undisguised astonishment for a minute. "You mean the lady's coming *in? Now?*"

"The lady's checking in, not out."

The elevator was empty on the up-trip, they and the operator were the only ones in it, though a moment before it had brought down fully twenty people.

He took her to the door of the room, opened it for her, put on the light. She looked around, first from the threshold, then timorously step by step as she advanced further into it. "They changed it," she said ruefully.

"No, ma'am," he said. "It hasn't been changed in years. It's been like it is now ever since I can remember it."

She smiled knowingly, as if to herself, but didn't contradict him any further. "He said this floor was already shut off. Now see that I have everything."

"Oh, you'll be taken care of, ma'am," he assured her earnestly. "I'll send the maid from one of the lower floors right up to you. And don't be nervous, ma'am. You'll be safe. The building is still fully protected."

"It never even occurred to me," she said almost indifferently.

When he'd gone, the chair seemed to cause her some dissatisfaction. She kept giving it small nudges, until the sum total of them had altered its position very considerably, particularly as to the direction in which it faced.

"*This* was where it was," she declared contentedly when she'd done. She even gave it a pat of commendation, as if to show how much better pleased with it she now was.

A maid tapped and came into the room. She was elderly, but still held herself straight. Her hair had grayed only to an intermediate salt-and-pepper, and then refused to whiten any further. Her figure was spare, in spite of her age. Or possibly because of it. Her eyes were sprightly, and the blue was very little dulled, behind the old-fashioned metal-rimmed spectacles she wore. Only her fingers, over-large at the joints, spindly between, betrayed the lifetime of hard work.

"Good evening," she said.

"Good evening," the other old woman replied.

Then she looked at her and asked, "What's your name?"

"Ann," the maid said. "Spelt the short way, without the 'e.'"

"Well, it's just as good that way as the other way," the old lady told her.

"I've stayed with it this long, what would be the sense of changing it now?" the maid agreed.

They smiled at each other, the way two affable strangers do, who know they have never met before, and presume they will never meet again, but for the moment take a polite interest in their mutual conversation.

"Ann," the old lady said. "Could I ask you to do something for me?"

"Sure, if I can."

"This dresser. I don't want it over there. I want it over here. This wall." She went over and showed her.

"Well, it's just for one night—" the maid said doubtfully.

"Doesn't matter," the old lady declared flatly. "Here's where it belongs. Not there. I can't do it by myself, or I would."

"I'll do it for you," the maid relented good-naturedly. "All right, I'll do it." She trundled it about and over without too much difficulty. "That right?" she asked.

"There. Now. That's more like it." Again the old lady gave it a pat, as she had the chair before, as though its misplacement had been due to willfulness on its own part that it now repented of. "Now'd you bring me everything I need?" she asked.

"Everything. Towels, soap. I even brought you an extra blanket, although I don't suppose at this time of year—"

"At my age," said the old lady almost vaingloriously, "you feel chilly at *any* time of the year."

"That's right too," said the maid reflectively. "I've noticed that myself for some time now." She backed toward the door. "I'll look in on you in the morning, just before we're all dismissed for the last time. The few of us there's left."

The old lady eyed her piercingly. "You're not crying, are you?"

The maid gave a shamefaced little smile. "Well, after all, it's like losing an old friend. So many years of my life—"

"You mustn't cry in here," the old lady reprimanded her quite severely. "This is a room of happiness. No tears in here." And she even shook her finger at her to add emphasis.

"I won't," the maid promised. "Good night. Sleep well."

"I intend to. I know that I will," declared the old lady staunchly. "I'm sure of it."

And as she closed the door and turned away from it, she repeated what she had just said. "This is a room of happiness. This is a room of reunion."

She began to unpack her bag now. From it she took a wafer-flat oblong white cardboard box, fastened with white paper tape.

"He didn't even want to put it in a box for me. I *told* him it was for a gift," she complained aloud, as if at the memory of some recent disputation. "Nowadays everything's too much for them."

She removed the bow-tied tape and the lid, peeled open the two inter-locking leaves of crisp tissue paper, and took out a necktie, bright and new. She went to the dresser top with it and laid it down there, painstakingly choosing a certain exact spot to place it in, measuring it off almost, moving it a little, smoothing it a little, until she had attained the desired accuracy of position.

"Johnny, this is for you. For you to wear tomorrow. They lost your other one, that night. And I don't want my Johnny to be without a necktie."

Then she lowered her face, touched her lips to it, and said with old-fashioned formality, "Wear it in good health, dear."

She returned to the bag, and as she took from it still something else, turned her head once more toward the dresser, as if addressing an after-remark to someone standing there unseen. "Luckily I didn't have to buy you one of these. I don't know much about picking them out." She opened a packet of yellowed tissue and from it took a wallet, worn with much handling and giving at the seams. "I've kept it for you all these years. Just the way it was. Thirty-nine dollars and eighty-five cents. Perhaps the money will come in handy to you. You might want us to go sightseeing tomorrow, on our first day together."

She placed it close to the tie, in just a certain place upon the dresser, and adjusted it too as she had the tie, as if fitting it to some invisible guide lines.

Returning to the opened bag a third and final time, she took out a neatly folded nightgown, and holding it up at shoulder-height, allowed it to fall open of its own weight. It was old-fashioned yet not old-fashioned, for fash-ion had come full circle again and its voluminous width and full-length sleeves were newer than the scantiness of intervening decades. It was old rather than old-fashioned, of finest batiste, with eyelet embroidery and a bertha, all handwork, the way a bridal gown should be, but citron-color with long existence. And the ghosts of hundreds of successive little bags of sachet still clung to it, even though they were gone now.

She disrobed now and put it on. It took on bluish hollows where it fell away from her body, yellow opacity where it clung close. It detracted from her age. She did not look like a young girl in it. Not even like a young woman. She looked like a wizened child, parading around in one of its elder's garments.

She loosened and brushed her hair now, with a brush that came from the bag. And that done, she went to the light switch and darkened the room. Then she went to the bed and got into it, but not with a complete absence of any effort. Lying there, she stirred awhile until she had attained the de-sired comfort, and then lay there awhile longer after that, in repose, mur-muring to herself. Aloud but softly. Just over her breath, as when one says a prayer.

"Good night, my Johnny. Good night, my love. We'll see each other tomorrow. And tomorrow *will* come. Oh, I know it will. I've never doubted that it will for a single moment.

"And thank you for so many things. So many, many things. As I've thanked you for them so many times before. Thank you for a perfect marriage. The most perfect a marriage could be. Never an angry word, never a sullen silence; never a quarrel, never a jealous stab, never a drunken stumble. Never the fright of illness, nor the ignominy of nursing and watching some of its more ignoble symptoms. Never the strife of lack of earning power, nor the bitter recriminations of failure and mistake and final ill-fortune. And above all, for not slowly aging before my eyes, as I would have slowly aged before yours, until finally neither of us was what the other had married, but somebody else entirely. Some unknown old man. Some unknown old woman. Thank you for staying young. And for letting me stay young along with you. A lifetime of youth. Eternal spring. Thank you for always being the bridegroom of our first night, romance blazing in your eyes. Thank you for all this. For all this, thank you forevermore. Good night, my beloved, my only, only love, my lifetime's love. Good night—the word I like to call you best of all: my husband. Your wife is wishing you good night."

In the morning, after her first discovery, the maid came back in a few minutes bringing the manager with her this time. They both looked at her, first, from where they stood. Then the manager went over closer to her and gently touched her forehead.

He turned around and said, "She's gone."

"I knew she was," the maid whispered. "I could tell even from the doorway."

He came back to where the maid was standing, and they both continued to look at her from there, the serene figure in the bed.

"That smile," he said under his breath. "Did you ever see anyone look so perfectly at rest, with such a peaceful, contented smile on their face?"

"She looks so happy," the maid concurred. "More like a—like a new bride than an old lady whose time has come to die."

"I guess she was one once," he mused. "Just like this room was brand-new once. And then they both got older—the two of them—slowly, slowly, over the years. A little bit at a time, and then they got—like they both are now. Done with. People are a lot like hotel rooms, when you come to think of it."

"And hotel rooms," amended the maid, "are a lot like people."

# Two Soldiers

## WILLIAM FAULKNER

ME and Pete would go down to Old Man Killegrew's and listen to his radio. We would wait until after supper, after dark, and we would stand outside Old Man Killegrew's parlor window, and we could hear it because Old Man Killegrew's wife was deaf, and so he run the radio as loud as it would run, and so me and Pete could hear it plain as Old Man Killegrew's wife could, I reckon, even standing outside with the window closed.

And that night I said, "What? Japanese? What's a pearl harbor?" and Pete said, "Hush."

And so we stood there, it was cold, listening to the fellow in the radio talking, only I couldn't make no heads nor tails neither out of it. Then the fellow said that would be all for a while, and me and Pete walked back up the road to home, and Pete told me what it was. Because he was nigh twenty and he had done finished the Consolidated last June and he knowed a heap: about them Japanese dropping bombs on Pearl Harbor and that Pearl Harbor was across the water.

"Across what water?" I said. "Across that Government reservoy up at Oxford?"

"Naw," Pete said. "Across the big water. The Pacific Ocean."

We went home. Maw and pap was already asleep, and me and Pete laid in the bed, and I still couldn't understand where it was, and Pete told me again—the Pacific Ocean.

"What's the matter with you?" Pete said. "You're going on nine years old. You been in school now ever since September. Ain't you learned nothing yet?"

"I reckon we ain't got as fer as the Pacific Ocean yet," I said.

We was still sowing the vetch then that ought to been all finished by the fifteenth of November, because pap was still behind, just like he had been ever since me and Pete had knowed him. And we had firewood to git in, too, but every night me and Pete would go down to Old Man Killegrew's and stand outside his parlor window in the cold and listen to his radio; then we would come back home and lay in the bed and Pete would tell me what it was. That is, he would tell me for a while. Then he wouldn't tell me. It was like he didn't want to talk about it no more. He would tell me to shut up because he wanted to go to sleep, but he never wanted to go to sleep.

He would lay there, a heap stiller than if he was asleep, and it would be something, I could feel it coming out of him, like he was mad at me even, only I knowed he wasn't thinking about me, or like he was worried about something, and it wasn't that neither, because he never had nothing to worry about. He never got behind like pap, let alone stayed behind. Pap give him ten acres when he graduated from the Consolidated, and me and Pete both reckoned pap was durn glad to get shut of at least ten acres, less to have to worry with himself; and Pete had them ten acres all sowed to vetch and busted out and bedded for the winter, and so it wasn't that. But it was something. And still we would go down to Old Man Killegrew's every night and listen to his radio, and they was at it in the Philippines now, but General MacArthur was holding um. Then we would come back home and lay in the bed, and Pete wouldn't tell me nothing or talk at all. He would just lay there still as a ambush, and when I would touch him his side or his leg would feel hard and still as iron, until after a while I would go to sleep.

Then one night—it was the first time he had said nothing to me except to jump on me about not chopping enough wood at the wood tree where we was cutting—he said, "I got to go."

"Go where?" I said.

"To that war," Pete said.

"Before we even finish gittin' in the firewood?"

"Firewood, hell," Pete said.

"All right," I said. "When we going to start?"

But he wasn't even listening. He laid there, hard and still as iron in the dark. "I got to go," he said. "I jest ain't going to put up with no folks treating the Unity States that way."

"Yes," I said. "Firewood or no firewood, I reckon we got to go."

This time he heard me. He laid still again, but it was a different kind of still.

"You?" he said. "To a war?"

"You'll whup the big uns and I'll whup the little uns," I said.

Then he told me I couldn't go. At first I thought he just never wanted me tagging after him, like he wouldn't leave me go with him when he went sparking them girls of Tull's. Then he told me the Army wouldn't leave me go because I was too little, and then I knowed he really meant it and that I couldn't go nohow noways. And somehow I hadn't believed until then that he was going himself, but now I knowed he was and that he wasn't going to leave me go with him a-tall.

"I'll chop the wood and tote the water for you-all then!" I said. "You got to have wood and water!"

Anyway, he was listening to me now. He wasn't like iron now.

He turned onto his side and put his hand on my chest because it was me that was laying straight and hard on my back now.

"No," he said. "You got to stay here and help pap."

"Help him what?" I said. "He ain't never caught up nohow. He can't get no further behind. He can sholy take care of this little shirttail of a farm while me and you are whupping them Japanese. I got to go too. If you got to go, then so have I."

"No," Pete said. "Hush now. Hush." And he meant it, and I knowed he did. Only I made sho from his own mouth. I quit.

"So I just can't go then," I said.

"No," Pete said. "You just can't go. You're too little, in the first place, and in the second place——"

"All right," I said. "Then shut up and leave me go to sleep."

So he hushed then and laid back. And I laid there like I was already asleep, and pretty soon he was asleep and I knowed it was the wanting to go to the war that had worried him and kept him awake, and now that he had decided to go, he wasn't worried any more.

The next morning he told maw and pap. Maw was all right. She cried.

"No," she said, crying, "I don't want him to go. I would rather go myself in his place, if I could. I don't want to save the country. Them Japanese could take it and keep it, so long as they left me and my family and my children alone. But I remember my brother Marsh in that other war. He had to go to that one when he wasn't but nineteen, and our mother couldn't understand it then any more than I can now. But she told Marsh if he had to go, he had to go. And so, if Pete's got to go to this one, he's got to go to it. Jest don't ask me to understand why."

But pap was the one. He was the feller. "To the war?" he said. "Why, I just don't see a bit of use in that. You ain't old enough for the draft, and the country ain't being invaded. Our President in Washington, D.C., is watching the conditions and he will notify us. Besides, in that other war your ma just mentioned, I was drafted and sent clean to Texas and was held there nigh eight months until they finally quit fighting. It seems to me that that, along with your uncle Marsh who received a actual wound on the battlefields of France, is enough for me and mine to have to do to protect the country, at least in my lifetime. Besides, what'll I do for help on the farm with you gone? It seems to me I'll get mighty far behind."

"You been behind as long as I can remember," Pete said. "Anyway, I'm going. I got to."

"Of course he's got to go," I said. "Them Japanese——"

"You hush your mouth!" maw said, crying. "Nobody's talking to you! Go and get me a armful of wood! That's what you can do!"

So I got the wood. And all the next day, while me and Pete and pap was getting in as much wood as we could in that time because Pete said how pap's idea of plenty of wood was one more stick laying against the wall that maw ain't put on the fire yet, maw was getting Pete ready to go. She washed and mended his clothes and cooked him a shoe box of vittles. And that night me and Pete laid in the bed and listened to her packing his grip and crying, until after a while Pete got up in his nightshirt and went back there, and I could hear them talking, until at last maw said, "You got to go, and so I want you to go. But I don't understand it, and I won't never, and so don't expect me to." And Pete come back and got into the bed again and laid again still and hard as iron on his back, and then he said, and he wasn't talking to me, he wasn't talking to nobody: "I got to go. I just got to."

"Sho you got to," I said. "Them Japanese——" He turned over hard, he kind of surged over onto his side, looking at me in the dark.

"Anyway, you're all right," he said. "I expected to have more trouble with you than with all the rest of them put together."

"I reckon I can't help it neither," I said. "But maybe it will run a few years longer and I can get there. Maybe someday I will jest walk in on you."

"I hope not," Pete said. "Folks don't go to wars for fun. A man don't leave his maw crying just for fun."

"Then why are you going?" I said.

"I got to," he said. "I just got to. Now you go on to sleep. I got to ketch that early bus in the morning."

"All right," I said. "I hear tell Memphis is a big place. How will you find where the Army's at?"

"I'll ask somebody where to go to join it," Pete said. "Go on to sleep now."

"Is that what you'll ask for? Where to join the Army?" I said.

"Yes," Pete said. He turned onto his back again. "Shut up and go to sleep."

We went to sleep. The next morning we et breakfast by lamplight because the bus would pass at six o'clock. Maw wasn't crying now. She jest looked grim and busy, putting breakfast on the table while we et it. Then she finished packing Pete's grip, except he never wanted to take no grip to the war, but maw said decent folks never went nowhere, not even to a war, without a change of clothes and something to tote them in. She put in the shoe box of fried chicken and biscuits and she put the Bible in, too, and then it was time to go. We didn't know until then that maw wasn't going to the bus. She jest brought Pete's cap and overcoat, and still she didn't cry no more, she jest stood with her hands on Pete's shoulders and she didn't move, but somehow, and just holding Pete's shoulders, she looked as hard and fierce as when Pete had turned toward me in the bed last night and tole me that anyway I was all right.

"They could take the country and keep the country, so long as they never bothered me and mine," she said. Then she said, "Don't never forget who you are. You ain't rich and the rest of the world outside of Frenchman's Bend never heard of you. But your blood is good as any blood anywhere, and don't you never forget it."

Then she kissed him, and then we was out of the house, with pap toting Pete's grip whether Pete wanted him to or not. There wasn't no dawn even yet, not even after we had stood on the highway by the mailbox awhile. Then we seen the lights of the bus coming and I was watching the bus until it come up and Pete flagged it, and then, sho enough, there was daylight—it had started while I wasn't watching. And now me and Pete expected pap to say something else foolish, like he done before, about how Uncle Marsh getting wounded in France and that trip to Texas pap taken in 1918 ought to be enough to save the Unity States in 1942, but he never. He done all right too. He jest said, "Good-by, son. Always remember what your ma told you and write her whenever you find the time." Then he shaken Pete's hand, and Pete looked at me a minute and put his hand on my head and rubbed my head durn nigh hard enough to wring my neck off and jumped into the bus, and the feller wound the door shut and the bus began to hum; then it was moving, humming and grinding and whining louder and louder; it was going fast, with two little red lights behind it that never seemed to get no littler, but jest seemed to be running together until pretty soon they would touch and jest be one light. But they never did, and then the bus was gone, and even like it was, I could have pretty nigh busted out crying, nigh to nine years old and all.

Me and pap went back to the house. All that day we worked at the wood tree, and so I never had no good chance until about middle of the afternoon. Then I taken my slingshot and I would have liked to took all my bird eggs, too, because Pete had give me his collection and he holp me with mine, and he would like to git the box out and look at them as good as I would, even if he was nigh twenty years old. But the box was too big to tote a long ways and have to worry with, so I just taken the shikepoke egg, because it was the best un, and wropped it up good into a matchbox and hid it and the slingshot under the corner of the barn. Then we et supper and went to bed, and I thought then how if I would 'a' had to stayed in that room and that bed like that even for one more night, I jest couldn't 'a' stood it. Then I could hear pap snoring, but I never heard no sound from maw, whether she was asleep or not, and I don't reckon she was. So I taken my shoes and drapped them out the window, and then I clumb out like I used to watch Pete do when he was still jest seventeen and pap held that he was too young yet to be tomcatting around at night and wouldn't leave him out, and I put on my shoes and went to the barn and got the slingshot and the shikepoke egg and went to the highway.

It wasn't cold, it was jest durn confounded dark, and that highway stretched on in front of me like, without nobody using it, it had stretched out half again as fer just like a man does when he lays down, so that for a time it looked like full sun was going to ketch me before I had finished them twenty-two miles to Jefferson. But it didn't. Daybreak was jest starting when I walked up the hill into town. I could smell breakfast cooking in the cabins and I wished I had thought to brought me a cold biscuit, but that was too late now. And Pete had told me Memphis was a piece beyond Jefferson, but I never knowed it was no eighty miles. So I stood there on that empty square, with daylight coming and coming and the street lights still burning and that Law looking down at me, and me still eighty miles from Memphis, and it had took me all night to walk jest twenty-two miles, and so, by the time I got to Memphis at that rate, Pete would 'a' done already started for Pearl Harbor.

"Where do you come from?" the Law said.

And I told him again. "I got to get to Memphis. My brother's there."

"You mean you ain't got any folks around here?" the Law said. "Nobody but that brother? What are you doing way off down here and your brother in Memphis?"

And I told him again, "I got to get to Memphis. I ain't got no time to waste talking about it and I ain't got time to walk it. I got to git there today."

"Come on here," the Law said.

We went down another street. And there was the bus, jest like when Pete got into it yestiddy morning, except there wasn't no lights on it now and it was empty. There was a regular bus dee-po like a railroad dee-po, with a ticket counter and a feller behind it, and the Law said, "Set down over there," and I set down on the bench, and the Law said, "I want to use your telephone," and he talked in the telephone a minute and put it down and said to the feller behind the ticket counter, "Keep your eye on him. I'll be back as soon as Mrs. Habersham can arrange to get herself up and dressed." He went out. I got up and went to the ticket counter.

"I want to go to Memphis," I said.

"You bet," the feller said. "You set down on the bench now. Mr. Foote will be back in a minute."

"I don't know no Mr. Foote," I said. "I want to ride that bus to Memphis."

"You got some money?" he said. "It'll cost you seventy-two cents."

I taken out the matchbox and unwropped the shikepoke egg. "I'll swap you this for a ticket to Memphis," I said.

"What's that?" he said.

"It's a shikepoke egg," I said. "You never seen one before. It's worth a dollar. I'll take seventy-two cents fer it."

"No," he said, "the fellers that own that bus insist on a cash basis. If I started swapping tickets for bird eggs and livestock and such, they would fire me. You go and set down on the bench now, like Mr. Foote——"

I started for the door, but he caught me; he put one hand on the ticket counter and jumped over it and caught up with me and reached his hand out to ketch my shirt. I whupped out my pocketknife and snapped it open.

"You put a hand on me and I'll cut it off," I said.

I tried to dodge him and run at the door, but he could move quicker than any grown man I ever see, quick as Pete almost. He cut me off and stood with his back against the door and one foot raised a little, and there wasn't no other way to get out. "Get back on that bench and stay there," he said.

And there wasn't no other way out. And he stood there with his back against the door. So I went back to the bench. And then it seemed like to me that dee-po was full of folks. There was that Law again, and there was two ladies in fur coats and their faces already painted. But they still looked like they had got up in a hurry and they still never liked it, a old one and a young one, looking down at me.

"He hasn't got a overcoat!" the old one said. "How in the world did he ever get down here by himself?"

"I ask you," the Law said. "I couldn't get nothing out of him except his brother is in Memphis and he wants to get back up there."

"That's right," I said. "I got to git to Memphis today."

"Of course you must," the old one said. "Are you sure you can find your brother when you get to Memphis?"

"I reckon I can," I said. "I ain't got but one and I have knowed him all my life. I reckon I will know him again when I see him."

The old one looked at me. "Somehow he doesn't look like he lives in Memphis," she said.

"He probably don't," the Law said. "You can't tell though. He might live anywhere, overhalls or not. This day and time they get scattered overnight from he—— hope to breakfast; boys and girls, too, almost before they can walk good. He might have been in Missouri or Texas either yestiddy, for all we know. But he don't seem to have any doubt his brother is in Memphis. All I know to do is send him up there and leave him look."

"Yes," the old one said.

The young one set down on the bench by me and opened a hand satchel and taken out a artermatic writing pen and some papers.

"Now, honey," the old one said, "we're going to see that you find your brother, but we must have a case history for our files first. We want to know your name and your brother's name and where you were born and when your parents died."

"I don't need no case history neither," I said. "All I want is to get to Memphis. I got to get there today."

"You see?" the Law said. He said it almost like he enjoyed it. "That's what I told you."

"You're lucky, at that, Mrs. Habersham," the bus feller said. "I don't think he's got a gun on him, but he can open that knife da—— I mean, fast enough to suit any man."

But the old one just stood there looking at me.

"Well," she said. "Well. I really don't know what to do."

"I do," the bus feller said. "I'm going to give him a ticket out of my own pocket, as a measure of protecting the company against riot and bloodshed. And when Mr. Foote tells the city board about it, it will be a civic matter and they will not only reimburse me, they will give me a medal too. Hey, Mr. Foote?"

But never nobody paid him no mind. The old one still stood looking down at me. She said, "Well," again. Then she taken a dollar from her purse and give it to the bus feller. "I suppose he will travel on a child's ticket, won't he?"

"Wellum," the bus feller said, "I just don't know what the regulations would be. Likely I will be fired for not crating him and marking the crate Poison. But I'll risk it."

Then they were gone. Then the Law come back with a sandwich and give it to me.

"You're sure you can find that brother?" he said.

"I ain't yet convinced why not," I said. "If I don't see Pete first, he'll see me. He knows me too."

Then the Law went out for good, too, and I et the sandwich. Then more folks come in and bought tickets, and then the bus feller said it was time to go, and I got into the bus just like Pete done, and we was gone.

I seen all the towns. I seen all of them. When the bus got to going good, I found out I was jest about wore out for sleep. But there was too much I hadn't never saw before. We run out of Jefferson and run past fields and woods, then we would run into another town and out of that un and past fields and woods again, and then into another town with stores and gins and water tanks, and we run along by the railroad for a spell and I seen the signal arm move, and then I seen the train and then some more towns, and I was jest about plumb wore out for sleep, but I couldn't resk it. Then Memphis begun. It seemed like, to me, it went on for miles. We would pass a patch of stores and I would think that was sholy it and the bus would even stop. But it wouldn't be Memphis yet and we would go on again past water tanks and smokestacks on top of the mills, and if they was gins and sawmills, I never knowed there was that many and I never seen any that big, and where they got enough cotton and logs to run um I don't know.

Then I seen Memphis. I knowed I was right this time. It was standing up into the air. It looked like about a dozen whole towns bigger than Jefferson was, set up on one edge in a field, standing up into the air higher than ara hill in all Yoknapatawpha County. Then we was in it, with the bus stopping ever few feet, it seemed like to me, and cars rushing past on both sides of it and the streets crowded with folks from ever'where in town that day, until I didn't see how there could 'a' been nobody left in Mis'sippi a-tall to even sell me a bus ticket, let alone write out no case histories. Then the bus stopped. It was another bus dee-po, a heap bigger than the one in Jefferson. And I said, "All right. Where do folks join the Army?"

"What?" the bus feller said.

And I said it again, "Where do folks join the Army?"

"Oh," he said. Then he told me how to get there. I was afraid at first I wouldn't ketch on how to do in a town big as Memphis. But I caught on all right. I never had to ask but twice more. Then I was there, and I was durn glad to git out of all them rushing cars and shoving folks and all that racket fer a spell, and I thought, It won't be long now, and I thought how if there was any kind of a crowd there that had done already joined the Army, too, Pete would likely see me before I seen him. And so I walked into the room. And Pete wasn't there.

He wasn't even there. There was a soldier with a big arrerhead on his sleeve, writing, and two fellers standing in front of him, and there was some more folks there, I reckon. It seems to me I remember some more folks there.

I went to the table where the soldier was writing, and I said, "Where's

Pete?" and he looked up and I said, "My brother. Pete Grier. Where is he?"

"What?" the soldier said. "Who?"

And I told him again. "He joined the Army yestiddy. He's going to Pearl Harbor. So am I. I want to ketch him. Where you-all got him?" Now they were all looking at me, but I never paid them no mind. "Come on," I said. "Where is he?"

The soldier had quit writing. He had both hands spraddled out on the table. "Oh," he said. "You're going too, hah?"

"Yes," I said. "They got to have wood and water. I can chop it and tote it. Come on. Where's Pete?"

The soldier stood up. "Who let you in here?" he said. "Go on. Beat it."

"Durn that," I said. "You tell me where Pete——"

I be dog if he couldn't move faster than the bus feller even. He never come over the table, he come around it; he was on me almost before I knowed it, so that I jest had time to jump back and whup out my pocket-knife and snap it open and hit one lick, and he hollered and jumped back and grabbed one hand with the other and stood there cussing and hollering.

One of the other fellers grabbed me from behind, and I hit at him with the knife, but I couldn't reach him.

Then both of the fellers had me from behind, and then another soldier come out of a door at the back. He had on a belt with a britching strop over one shoulder.

"What the hell is this?" he said.

"That little son cut me with a knife!" the first soldier hollered. When he said that, I tried to git at him again, but both them fellers was holding me, two against one, and the soldier with the backing strop said, "Here, here. Put your knife up, feller. None of us are armed. A man don't knife-fight folks that are barehanded." I could begin to hear him then. He sounded jest like Pete talked to me. "Let him go," he said. They let me go. "Now what's all the trouble about?" And I told him. "I see," he said. "And you come up to see if he was all right before he left."

"No," I said. "I came to——"

But he had already turned to where the first soldier was wropping a handkerchief around his hand.

"Have you got him?" he said. The first soldier went back to the table and looked at some papers.

"Here he is," he said. "He enlisted yestiddy. He's in a detachment leaving this morning for Little Rock." He had a watch stropped on his arm. He looked at it. "The train leaves in about fifty minutes. If I know country boys, they're probably all down there at the station right now."

"Get him up here," the one with the backing strop said. "Phone the station. Tell the porter to get him a cab. And you come with me," he said.

It was another office behind that un, with jest a table and some chairs. We set there while the soldier smoked, and it wasn't long; I knowed Pete's feet soon as I heard them. Then the first soldier opened the door and Pete come in. He never had no soldier clothes on. He looked jest like he did when he got on the bus yestiddy morning, except it seemed to me like it was at least a week, so much had happened and I had done had to do so much traveling. He come in and there he was, looking at me like he hadn't never left home, except that here we was in Memphis, on the way to Pearl Harbor.

"What in durnation are you doing here?" he said.

And I told him, "You got to have wood and water to cook with. I can chop it and tote it for you-all."

"No," Pete said. "You're going back home."

"No, Pete," I said. "I got to go too. I got to. It hurts my heart, Pete."

"No," Pete said. He looked at the soldier. "I jest don't know what could have happened to him, lootenant," he said. "He never drawed a knife on anybody before in his life." He looked at me. "What did you do it for?"

"I don't know," I said. "I jest had to. I jest had to git here. I jest had to find you."

"Well, don't you never do it again, you hear?" Pete said. "You put that knife in your pocket and you keep it there. If I ever again hear of you drawing it on anybody, I'm coming back from wherever I am at and whup the fire out of you. You hear me?"

"I would pure cut a throat if it would bring you back to stay," I said. "Pete," I said. "Pete."

"No," Pete said. Now his voice wasn't hard and quick no more, it was almost quiet, and I knowed now I wouldn't never change him. "You must go home. You must look after maw, and I am depending on you to look after my ten acres. I want you to go back home. Today. Do you hear?"

"I hear," I said.

"Can he get back home by himself?" the soldier said.

"He come up here by himself," Pete said.

"I can get back, I reckon," I said. "I don't live in but one place. I don't reckon it's moved."

Pete taken a dollar out of his pocket and give it to me. "That'll buy your bus ticket right to our mailbox," he said. "I want you to mind the lootenant. He'll send you to the bus. And you go back home and you take care of maw and look after my ten acres and keep that durn knife in your pocket. You hear me?"

"Yes, Pete," I said.

"All right," Pete said. "Now I got to go." He put his hand on my head again. But this time he never wrung my neck. He jest laid his hand on my head a minute. And then I be dog if he didn't lean down and kiss me, and I heard his feet and then the door, and I never looked up and that was all, me setting there, rubbing the place where Pete kissed me and the soldier throwed back in his chair, looking out the window and coughing. He reached into his pocket and handed something to me without looking around. It was a piece of chewing gum.

"Much obliged," I said. "Well, I reckon I might as well start back. I got a right fer piece to go."

"Wait," the soldier said. Then he telephoned again and I said again I better start back, and he said again, "Wait. Remember what Pete told you."

So we waited, and then another lady come in, old, too, in a fur coat, too, but she smelled all right; she never had no artermatic writing pen nor no case history neither. She come in and the soldier got up, and she looked around quick until she saw me, and come and put her hand on my shoulder light and quick and easy as maw herself might 'a' done it.

"Come on," she said. "Let's go home to dinner."

"Nome," I said. "I got to ketch the bus to Jefferson."

"I know. There's plenty of time. We'll go home and eat dinner first."

She had a car. And now we was right down in the middle of all them other cars. We was almost under the busses, and all them crowds of people on the street close enough to where I could have talked to them if I had knowed who they was. After a while she stopped the car. "Here we are," she said, and I looked at it, and if all that was her house, she sho had a big family. But all of it wasn't. We crossed a hall with trees growing in it and went into a little room without nothing in it but a nigger dressed up in a uniform a heap shinier than them soldiers had, and the nigger shut the door, and then I hollered, "Look out!" and grabbed, but it was all right; that whole little room jest went right on up and stopped and the door opened and we was in another hall, and the lady unlocked a door and we went in, and there was another soldier, a old feller, with a britching strop, too, and a silver-colored bird on each shoulder.

"Here we are," the lady said. "This is Colonel McKellogg. Now, what would you like for dinner?"

"I reckon I'll jest have some ham and eggs and coffee," I said.

She had done started to pick up the telephone. She stopped. "Coffee?" she said. "When did you start drinking coffee?"

"I don't know," I said. "I reckon it was before I could remember."

"You're about eight, aren't you?" she said.

"Nome," I said. "I'm eight and ten months. Going on eleven months."

She telephoned then. Then we set there and I told them how Pete had jest left that morning for Pearl Harbor and I had aimed to go with him, but I would have to go back home to take care of maw and look after Pete's ten acres, and she said how they had a little boy about my size, too, in a school in the East. Then a nigger, another one, in a short kind of shirttail coat, rolled a kind of wheelbarrer in. It had my ham and eggs and a glass of milk and a piece of pie, too, and I thought I was hungry. But when I taken the first bite I found out I couldn't swallow it, and I got up quick.

"I got to go," I said.

"Wait," she said.

"I got to go," I said.

"Just a minute," she said. "I've already telephoned for the car. It won't be but a minute now. Can't you drink the milk even? Or maybe some of your coffee?"

"Nome," I said. "I ain't hungry. I'll eat when I git home." Then the telephone rung. She never even answered it.

"There," she said. "There's the car." And we went back down in that 'ere little moving room with the dressed-up nigger. This time it was a big car with a soldier driving it. I got into the front with him. She give the soldier a dollar. "He might get hungry," she said. "Try to find a decent place for him."

"O.K., Mrs. McKellogg," the soldier said.

Then we was gone again. And now I could see Memphis good, bright in the sunshine, while we was swinging around it. And first thing I knowed, we was back on the same highway the bus run on this morning—the patches of stores and them big gins and sawmills, and Memphis running on for miles, it seemed like to me, before it begun to give out. Then we was running again between the fields and woods, running fast now, and except for that soldier, it was like I hadn't never been to Memphis a-tall. We was going fast now. At this rate, before I knowed it we would be home again, and I thought about me riding up to Frenchman's Bend in this here big car with a soldier running it, and all of a sudden I begun to cry. I never knowed I was fixing to, and I couldn't stop it. I set there by that soldier, crying. We was going fast.

# How We Kept Mother's Day

### STEPHEN LEACOCK

OF all the different ideas that had been started lately, I think that the very best is the notion of celebrating once a year "Mother's Day." I don't wonder that May the eleventh is becoming such a popular date all over America and I am sure the idea will spread to England too.

It is especially in a big family like ours that such an idea takes hold. So we decided to have a special celebration of Mother's Day. We thought it a fine idea. It made us all realize how much Mother had done for us for years, and all the efforts and sacrifice that she had made for our sake.

So we decided that we'd make it a great day, a holiday for all the family, and do everything we could to make Mother happy. Father decided to take a holiday from his office, so as to help in celebrating the day, and my sister Anne and I stayed home from college classes, and Mary and my brother Will stayed home from high school.

It was our plan to make it a day just like Xmas or any big holiday, and so we decided to decorate the house with flowers and with mottoes over the mantelpieces, and all that kind of thing. We got Mother to make mottoes and arrange the decorations, because she always does it at Xmas.

The two girls thought it would be a nice thing to dress in our very best for such a big occasion, and so they both got new hats. Mother trimmed both the hats, and they looked fine, and Father had bought four-in-hand silk ties for himself and us boys as a souvenir of the day to remember Mother by. We were going to get Mother a new hat too, but it turned out that she seemed to really like her old grey bonnet better than a new one, and both the girls said that it was awfully becoming to her.

Well, after breakfast we had it arranged as a surprise for Mother that we would hire a motor car and take her for a beautiful drive away into the country. Mother is hardly ever able to have a treat like that, because we can only afford to keep one maid, and so Mother is busy in the house nearly all the time. And of course the country is so lovely now that it would be just grand for her to have a lovely morning, driving for miles and miles.

But on the very morning of the day we changed the plan a little bit, because it occurred to Father that a thing it would be better to do even than to take Mother for a motor drive would be to take her fishing. Father said that as the car was hired and paid for, we might just as well use it for a drive up into hills where the streams are. As Father said, if you just go out driving without any object, you have a sense of aimlessness, but if you are going to fish, there is a definite purpose in front of you to heighten the enjoyment.

So we all felt that it would be nicer for Mother to have a definite purpose; and anyway, it turned out that Father had just got a new rod the day before, which made the idea of fishing all the more appropriate, and he said that Mother could use it if she wanted to; in fact, he said it was practically for her, only Mother said she would much rather watch him fish and not try to fish herself.

So we got everything arranged for the trip, and we got Mother to cut up some sandwiches and make up a sort of lunch in case we got hungry, though of course we were to come back home again to a big dinner in the middle of the day, just like Xmas or New Year's Day. Mother packed it all up in a basket for us ready to go in the motor.

Well, when the car came to the door, it turned out that there hardly seemed as much room in it as we had supposed, because we hadn't reckoned on Father's fishing basket and the rods and the lunch, and it was plain enough that we couldn't all get in.

Father said not to mind him, he said that he could just as well stay home, and that he was sure that he could put in the time working in the garden; he said that there was a lot of rough dirty work that he could do, like digging a trench for the garbage, that would save hiring a man, and so he said that he'd stay home; he said that we were not to let the fact of his not having had a real holiday for three years stand in our way; he wanted us to go right ahead and be happy and have a big day, and not to mind him. He said that he could plug away all day, and in fact he said he'd been a fool to think there'd be any holiday for him.

But of course we all felt that it would never do to let Father stay home, especially as we knew he would make trouble if he did. The two girls, Anne and Mary, would gladly have stayed and helped the maid get dinner, only it seemed such a pity to, on a lovely day like this, having their new hats. But they both said that Mother had only to say the word, and they'd gladly stay home and work. Will and I would have dropped out, but unfortunately we wouldn't have been any use in getting the dinner.

So in the end it was decided that Mother would stay home and just have a lovely restful day round the house, and get the dinner. It turned out anyway that Mother doesn't care for fishing, and also it was just a little bit cold and fresh out of doors, though it was lovely and sunny, and Father was rather afraid that Mother might take cold if she came.

He said he would never forgive himself if he dragged Mother round the country and let her take a severe cold at a time when she might be having a beautiful rest. He said it was our duty to try and let Mother get all the rest and quiet that she could, after all that she had done for all of us, and he said that that was principally why he had fallen in with this idea of a fishing trip, so as to give Mother a little quiet. He said that young people seldom realize how much quiet means to people who are getting old. As to himself, he could still stand the racket, but he was glad to shelter Mother from it.

So we all drove away with three cheers for Mother, and Mother stood and watched us from the verandah for as long as she could see us, and Father waved his hand back to her every few minutes till he hit his hand on the back edge of the car, and then said that he didn't think that Mother could see us any longer.

Well, we had the loveliest day up among the hills that you could possibly imagine, and Father caught such big specimens that he felt sure that Mother couldn't have landed them anyway, if she had been fishing for them, and Will and I fished too, though we didn't get so many as Father, and the two girls met quite a lot of people that they knew as we drove along, and there were some young men friends of theirs that they met along the stream and talked to, and so we all had a splendid time.

It was quite late when we got back, nearly seven o'clock in the evening, but Mother had guessed that we would be late, so she had kept back the dinner so as to have it just nicely ready and hot for us. Only first she had to get towels and soap for Father and clean things for him to put on, because he always gets so messed up with fishing, and that kept Mother busy for a little while, that and helping the girls get ready.

But at last everything was ready, and we sat down to the grandest kind of dinner—roast turkey and all sorts of things like on Xmas Day. Mother had to get up and down a good bit during the meal fetching things back and forward, but at the end Father noticed it and said she simply mustn't do it, that he wanted her to spare herself, and he got up and fetched the walnuts over from the sideboard himself.

The dinner lasted a long while, and was great fun, and when it was over all of us wanted to help clear the things up and wash the dishes, only Mother said that she would really much rather do it, and so we let her, because we wanted just for once to humour her.

It was quite late when it was all over, and when we all kissed Mother before going to bed, she said it had been the most wonderful day in her life, and I think there were tears in her eyes. So we all felt awfully repaid for all that we had done.

# The Witness for the Prosecution

## AGATHA CHRISTIE

MR. MAYHERNE adjusted his pince-nez and cleared his throat with a little dry-as-dust cough that was wholly typical of him. Then he looked again at the man opposite him, the man charged with willful murder.

Mr. Mayherne was a small man, precise in manner, neatly, not to say foppishly dressed, with a pair of very shrewd and piercing gray eyes. By no means a fool. Indeed, as a solicitor, Mr. Mayherne's reputation stood very high. His voice, when he spoke to his client, was dry but not unsympathetic.

"I must impress upon you again that you are in very grave danger, and that the utmost frankness is necessary."

Leonard Vole, who had been staring in a dazed fashion at the blank wall in front of him, transferred his glance to the solicitor.

"I know," he said hopelessly. "You keep telling me so. But I can't seem to realize yet that I'm charged with murder—*murder*. And such a dastardly crime too."

Mr. Mayherne was practical, not emotional. He coughed again, took off his pince-nez, polished them carefully, and replaced them on his nose. Then he said:

"Yes, yes, yes. Now, my dear Mr. Vole, we're going to make a determined effort to get you off—and we shall succeed—we shall succeed. But I must have all the facts. I must know just how damaging the case against you is likely to be. Then we can fix upon the best line of defense."

Still the young man looked at him in the same dazed, hopeless fashion. To Mr. Mayherne the case had seemed black enough, and the guilt of the prisoner assured. Now, for the first time, he felt a doubt.

"You think I'm guilty," said Leonard Vole, in a low voice. "But, by God, I swear I'm not! It looks pretty black against me, I know that. I'm like a man caught in a net—the meshes of it all round me, entangling me whichever way I turn. But I didn't do it, Mr. Mayherne, I didn't do it!"

In such a position a man was bound to protest his innocence. Mr. Mayherne knew that. Yet, in spite of himself, he was impressed. It might be, after all, that Leonard Vole was innocent.

"You are right, Mr. Vole," he said gravely. "The case does look very black against you. Nevertheless, I accept your assurance. Now, let us get to facts. I want you to tell me in your own words exactly how you came to make the acquaintance of Miss Emily French."

"It was one day in Oxford Street. I saw an elderly lady crossing the road. She was carrying a lot of parcels. In the middle of the street she dropped them, tried to recover them, found a bus was almost on top of her and just managed to reach the curb safely, dazed and bewildered by people having shouted at her. I recovered her parcels, wiped the mud off them as best I could, retied the string of one, and returned them to her."

"There was no question of your having saved her life?"

"Oh, dear me, no! All I did was to perform a common act of courtesy. She was extremely grateful, thanked me warmly, and said something about my manners not being those of most of the younger generation—I can't remember the exact words. Then I lifted my hat and went on. I never expected to see her again. But life is full of coincidences. That very evening I came across her at a party at a friend's house. She recognized me at once and asked that I should be introduced to her. I then found out that she was a Miss Emily French and that she lived at Cricklewood. I talked to her for some time. She was, I imagine, an old lady who took sudden and violent fancies to people. She took one to me on the strength of a perfectly simple action which anyone might have performed. On leaving, she shook me warmly by the hand, and asked me to come and see her. I replied, of course, that I should be very pleased to do so, and she then urged me to name a day. I did not want particularly to go, but it would have seemed churlish to refuse, so I fixed on the following Saturday. After she had gone, I learned something about her from my friends. That she was rich, eccentric, lived alone with one maid and owned no less than eight cats."

"I see," said Mr. Mayherne. "The question of her being well off came up as early as that?"

"If you mean that I inquired——" began Leonard Vole hotly, but Mr. Mayherne stilled him with a gesture.

"I have to look at the case as it will be presented by the other side. An ordinary observer would not have supposed Miss French to be a lady of means. She lived poorly, almost humbly. Unless you had been told the contrary, you would in all probability have considered her to be in poor circumstances—at any rate to begin with. Who was it exactly who told you that she was well off?"

"My friend, George Harvey, at whose house the party took place."

"Is he likely to remember having done so?"

"I really don't know. Of course it is some time ago now."

"Quite so, Mr. Vole. You see, the first aim of the prosecution will be to establish that you were in low water financially—that is true, is it not?"

Leonard Vole flushed.

"Yes," he said, in a low voice. "I'd been having a run of infernal bad luck just then."

"Quite so," said Mr. Mayherne again. "That being, as I say, in low water financially, you met this rich old lady and cultivated her acquaintance assiduously. Now if we are in a position to say that you had no idea she was well off, and that you visited her out of pure kindness of heart——"

"Which is the case."

"I dare say. I am not disputing the point. I am looking at it from the outside point of view. A great deal depends on the memory of Mr. Harvey. Is he likely to remember that conversation or is he not? Could he be confused by counsel into believing that it took place later?"

Leonard Vole reflected for some minutes. Then he said steadily enough, but with a rather paler face:

"I do not think that that line would be successful, Mr. Mayherne. Several of those present heard his remark, and one or two of them chaffed me about my conquest of a rich old lady."

The solicitor endeavored to hide his disappointment with a wave of the hand.

"Unfortunate," he said. "But I congratulate you upon your plain speaking, Mr. Vole. It is to you I look to guide me. Your judgment is quite right. To persist in the line I spoke of would have been disastrous. We must leave that point. You made the acquaintance of Miss French, you called upon her, the acquaintanceship progressed. We want a clear reason for all this. Why did you, a young man of thirty-three, good-looking, fond of sport, popular with your friends, devote so much of your time to an elderly woman with whom you could hardly have anything in common?"

Leonard Vole flung out his hands in a nervous gesture.

"I can't tell you—I really can't tell you. After the first visit, she pressed me to come again, spoke of being lonely and unhappy. She made it difficult for me to refuse. She showed so plainly her fondness and affection for me that I was placed in an awkward position. You see, Mr. Mayherne, I've got a weak nature—I drift—I'm one of those people who can't say 'No.' And believe me or not, as you like, after the third or fourth visit I paid her I found myself getting genuinely fond of the old thing. My mother died when I was young, an aunt brought me up, and she too died before I was fifteen. If I told you that I genuinely enjoyed being mothered and pampered, I dare say you'd only laugh."

Mr. Mayherne did not laugh. Instead he took off his pince-nez again and polished them, a sign with him that he was thinking deeply.

"I accept your explanation, Mr. Vole," he said at last. "I believe it to be psychologically probable. Whether a jury would take that view of it is another matter. Please continue your narrative. When was it that Miss French first asked you to look into her business affairs?"

"After my third or fourth visit to her. She understood very little of money matters, and was worried about some investments."

Mr. Mayherne looked up sharply.

"Be careful, Mr. Vole. The maid, Janet Mackenzie, declares that her mistress was a good woman of business and transacted all her own affairs, and this is borne out by the testimony of her bankers."

"I can't help that," said Vole earnestly. "That's what she said to me."

Mr. Mayherne looked at him for a moment or two in silence. Though he had no intention of saying so, his belief in Leonard Vole's innocence was at that moment strengthened. He knew something of the mentality of elderly ladies. He saw Miss French, infatuated with the good-looking young man, hunting about for pretexts that would bring him to the house. What more likely than that she should plead ignorance of business, and beg him to help her with her money affairs? She was enough of a woman of the world to realize that any man is slightly flattered by such an admission of his superiority. Leonard Vole had been flattered. Perhaps, too, she had not been averse to letting this young man know that she was wealthy. Emily French had been a strong-willed old woman, willing to pay her price for what she wanted. All this passed rapidly through Mr. Mayherne's mind, but he gave no indication of it, and asked instead a further question.

"And you did handle her affairs for her at her request?"

"I did."

"Mr. Vole," said the solicitor, "I am going to ask you a very serious question, and one to which it is vital I should have a truthful answer. You were in low water financially. You had the handling of an old lady's affairs—an old lady who, according to her own statement, knew little or nothing of business. Did you at any time, or in any manner, convert to your own use the securities which you handled? Did you engage in any transaction for your own pecuniary advantage which will not bear the light of day?" He quelled the other's response. "Wait a minute before you answer. There are two courses open to us. Either we can make a feature of your probity and honesty in conducting her affairs whilst pointing out how unlikely it is that you would commit murder to obtain money which you might have obtained by such infinitely easier means. If, on the other hand, there is anything in your dealings which the prosecution will get hold of—if, to put it baldly, it can be proved that you swindled the old lady in any way, we must take the line that you had no motive for the murder, since she was already a profitable source of income to you. You perceive the distinction. Now, I beg of you, take your time before you reply."

But Leonard Vole took no time at all.

"My dealings with Miss French's affairs were all perfectly fair and above board. I acted for her interests to the very best of my ability, as any one will find who looks into the matter."

"Thank you," said Mr. Mayherne. "You relieve my mind very much. I pay you the compliment of believing that you are far too clever to lie to me over such an important matter."

"Surely," said Vole eagerly, "the strongest point in my favor is the lack of motive. Granted that I cultivated the acquaintanceship of a rich old lady in the hopes of getting money out of her—that, I gather, is the substance of what you have been saying—surely her death frustrates all my hopes?"

The solicitor looked at him steadily. Then, very deliberately, he repeated his unconscious trick with his pince-nez. It was not until they were firmly replaced on his nose that he spoke.

"Are you not aware, Mr. Vole, that Miss French left a will under which you are the principal beneficiary?"

"What?" The prisoner sprang to his feet. His dismay was obvious and unforced. "My God! What are you saying? She left her money to me?"

Mr. Mayherne nodded slowly. Vole sank down again, his head in his hands.

"You pretend you know nothing of this will?"

"Pretend? There's no pretense about it. I knew nothing about it."

"What would you say if I told you that the maid, Janet Mackenzie, swears that you *did* know? That her mistress told her distinctly that she had consulted you in the matter, and told you of her intentions?"

"Say? That she's lying! No, I go too fast. Janet is an elderly woman. She was a faithful watchdog to her mistress, and she didn't like me. She was jealous and suspicious. I should say that Miss French confided her intentions to Janet, and that Janet either mistook something she said, or else was convinced in her own mind that I had persuaded the old lady into doing it. I dare say that she herself believes now that Miss French actually told her so."

"You don't think she dislikes you enough to lie deliberately about the matter?"

Leonard Vole looked shocked and startled.

"No, indeed! Why should she?"

"I don't know," said Mr. Mayherne thoughtfully. "But she's very bitter against you."

The wretched young man groaned again.

"I'm beginning to see," he muttered. "It's frightful. I made up to her, that's what they'll say, I got her to make a will leaving her money to me, and then I go there that night, and there's nobody in the house—they find her the next day—oh! my God, it's awful!"

"You are wrong about there being nobody in the house," said Mr. Mayherne. "Janet, as you remember, was to go out for the evening. She went, but about half-past nine she returned to fetch the pattern of a blouse sleeve which she had promised to a friend. She let herself in by the back door, went upstairs and fetched it, and went out again. She heard voices in the sitting-room, though she could not distinguish what they said, but she will swear that one of them was Miss French's and one was a man's."

"At half-past nine," said Leonard Vole. "At half-past nine. . . ." He sprang to his feet. "But then I'm saved—saved——"

"What do you mean, saved?" cried Mr. Mayherne, astonished.

"By half-past nine I was at home again! My wife can prove that. I left Miss French about five minutes to nine. I arrived home about twenty past nine. My wife was there waiting for me. Oh, thank God—thank God! And bless Janet Mackenzie's sleeve pattern."

In his exuberance, he hardly noticed that the grave expression on the solicitor's face had not altered. But the latter's words brought him down to earth with a bump.

"Who, then, in your opinion, murdered Miss French?"

"Why, a burglar, of course, as was thought at first. The window was forced, you remember. She was killed with a heavy blow from a crowbar, and the crowbar was found lying on the floor beside the body. And several articles were missing. But for Janet's absurd suspicions and dislike of me, the police would never have swerved from the right track."

"That will hardly do, Mr. Vole," said the solicitor. "The things that were missing were mere trifles of no value, taken as a blind. And the marks on the window were not at all conclusive. Besides, think for yourself. You say you were no longer in the house by half-past nine. Who, then, was the man Janet heard talking to Miss French in the sitting-room? She would hardly be having an amicable conversation with a burglar?"

"No," said Vole. "No——" He looked puzzled and discouraged. "But, anyway," he added with reviving spirit, "it lets me out. I've got an alibi. You must see Romaine—my wife—at once."

"Certainly," acquiesced the lawyer. "I should already have seen Mrs. Vole but for her being absent when you were arrested. I wired to Scotland at once, and I understand that she arrives back tonight. I am going to call upon her immediately I leave here."

Vole nodded, a great expression of satisfaction settling down over his face.

"Yes, Romaine will tell you. My God! it's a lucky chance that."

"Excuse me, Mr. Vole, but you are very fond of your wife?"

"Of course."

"And she of you?"

"Romaine is devoted to me. She'd do anything in the world for me."

He spoke enthusiastically, but the solicitor's heart sank a little lower. The testimony of a devoted wife—would it gain credence?

"Was there anyone else who saw you return at nine-twenty. A maid, for instance?"

"We have no maid."

"Did you meet anyone in the street on the way back?"

"Nobody I knew. I rode part of the way in a bus. The conductor might remember."

Mr. Mayherne shook his head doubtfully.

"There is no one, then, who can confirm your wife's testimony?"

"No. But it isn't necessary, surely?"

"I dare say not. I dare say not," said Mr. Mayherne hastily. "Now there's just one thing more. Did Miss French know that you were a married man?"

"Oh, yes."

"Yet you never took your wife to see her. Why was that?"

For the first time, Leonard Vole's answer came halting and uncertain.

"Well—I don't know."

"Are you aware that Janet Mackenzie says her mistress believed you to be single, and contemplated marrying you in the future?"

Vole laughed.

"Absurd! There was forty years' difference in age between us."

"It has been done," said the solicitor drily. "The fact remains. Your wife never met Miss French?"

"No——" Again the constraint.

"You will permit me to say," said the lawyer, "that I hardly understand your attitude in the matter."

Vole flushed, hesitated, and then spoke.

"I'll make a clean breast of it. I was hard up, as you know. I hoped that Miss French might lend me some money. She was fond of me, but she wasn't at all interested in the struggles of a young couple. Early on, I found that she had taken it for granted that my wife and I didn't get on—were living apart. Mr. Mayherne—I wanted the money—for Romaine's sake. I said nothing, and allowed the old lady to think what she chose. She spoke of my being an adopted son to her. There was never any question of marriage—that must be just Janet's imagination."

"And that is all?"

"Yes—that is all."

Was there just a shade of hesitation in the words? The lawyer fancied so. He rose and held out his hand.

"Good-bye, Mr. Vole." He looked into the haggard young face and spoke with an unusual impulse. "I believe in your innocence in spite of the multitude of facts arrayed against you. I hope to prove it and vindicate you completely."

Vole smiled back at him.

"You'll find the alibi is all right," he said cheerfully.

Again he hardly noticed that the other did not respond.

"The whole thing hinges a good deal on the testimony of Janet Mackenzie," said Mr. Mayherne. "She hates you. That much is clear."

"She can hardly hate me," protested the young man.

The solicitor shook his head as he went out.

"Now for Mrs. Vole," he said to himself.

He was seriously disturbed by the way the thing was shaping.

The Voles lived in a small shabby house near Paddington Green. It was to this house that Mr. Mayherne went.

In answer to his ring, a big slatternly woman, obviously a charwoman, answered the door.

"Mrs. Vole? Has she returned yet?"

"Got back an hour ago. But I dunno if you can see her."

"If you will take my card to her," said Mr. Mayherne quietly, "I am quite sure that she will do so."

The woman looked at him doubtfully, wiped her hand on her apron and took the card. Then she closed the door in his face and left him on the step outside.

In a few minutes, however, she returned with a slightly altered manner. "Come inside, please."

She ushered him into a tiny drawing-room. Mr. Mayherne, examining a drawing on the wall, started up suddenly to face a tall, pale woman who had entered so quietly that he had not heard her.

"Mr. Mayherne? You are my husband's solicitor, are you not? You have come from him? Will you please sit down?"

Until she spoke he had not realized that she was not English. Now, observing her more closely, he noticed the high cheekbones, the dense blueblack of the hair, and an occasional very slight movement of the hands that was distinctly foreign. A strange woman, very quiet. So quiet as to make one uneasy. From the very first Mr. Mayherne was conscious that he was up against something that he did not understand.

"Now, my dear Mrs. Vole," he began, "you must not give way——"

He stopped. It was so very obvious that Romaine Vole had not the slightest intention of giving way. She was perfectly calm and composed.

"Will you please tell me about it?" she said. "I must know everything. Do not think to spare me. I want to know the worst." She hesitated, then repeated in a lower tone, with a curious emphasis which the lawyer did not understand: "I want to know the worst."

Mr. Mayherne went over his interview with Leonard Vole. She listened attentively, nodding her head now and then.

"I see," she said, when he had finished. "He wants me to say that he came in at twenty minutes past nine that night?"

"He did come in at that time?" said Mr. Mayherne sharply.

"That is not the point," she said coldly. "Will my saying so acquit him? Will they believe me?"

Mr. Mayherne was taken aback. She had gone so quickly to the core of the matter.

"That is what I want to know," she said. "Will it be enough? Is there anyone else who can support my evidence?"

There was a suppressed eagerness in her manner that made him vaguely uneasy.

"So far there is no one else," he said reluctantly.

"I see," said Romaine Vole.

She sat for a minute or two perfectly still. A little smile played over her lips.

The lawyer's feeling of alarm grew stronger and stronger.

"Mrs. Vole——" he began. "I know what you must feel——"

"Do you?" she asked. "I wonder."

"In the circumstances——"

"In the circumstances—I intend to play a lone hand."

He looked at her in dismay.

"But, my dear Mrs. Vole—you are overwrought. Being so devoted to your husband——"

"I beg your pardon?"

The sharpness of her voice made him start. He repeated in a hesitating manner:

"Being so devoted to your husband——"

Romaine Vole nodded slowly, the same strange smile on her lips.

"Did he tell you that I was devoted to him?" she asked softly. "Ah! yes, I can see he did. How stupid men are! Stupid—stupid—stupid——"

She rose suddenly to her feet. All the intense emotion that the lawyer had been conscious of in the atmosphere was now concentrated in her tone.

"I hate him, I tell you! I hate him. I hate him. I hate him! I would like to see him hanged by the neck till he is dead."

The lawyer recoiled before her and the smoldering passion in her eyes. She advanced a step nearer, and continued vehemently:

"Perhaps I shall see it. Supposing I tell you that he did not come in that night at twenty past nine, but at twenty past ten? You say that he tells you he knew nothing about the money coming to him. Supposing I tell you he knew all about it, and counted on it, and committed murder to get it? Supposing I tell you that he admitted to me that night when he came in what he had done? That there was blood on his coat? What then? Supposing that I stand up in court and say all these things?"

Her eyes seemed to challenge him. With an effort, he concealed his growing dismay, and endeavored to speak in a rational tone.

"You cannot be asked to give evidence against your husband——"

"He is not my husband!"

The words came out so quickly that he fancied he had misunderstood her.

"I beg your pardon? I——"

"He is not my husband."

The silence was so intense that you could have heard a pin drop.

"I was an actress in Vienna. My husband is alive but in a madhouse. So we could not marry. I am glad now."

She nodded defiantly.

"I should like you to tell me one thing," said Mr. Mayherne. He contrived to appear as cool and unemotional as ever. "Why are you so bitter against Leonard Vole?"

She shook her head, smiling a little.

"Yes, you would like to know. But I shall not tell you. I will keep my secret. . . ."

Mr. Mayherne gave his dry little cough and rose.

"There seems no point in prolonging this interview," he remarked. "You will hear from me again after I have communicated with my client."

She came closer to him, looking into his eyes with her own wonderful dark ones.

"Tell me," she said, "did you believe—honestly—that he was innocent when you came here today?"

"I did," said Mr. Mayherne.

"You poor little man," she laughed.

"And I believe so still," finished the lawyer. "Good evening, madam."

He went out of the room, taking with him the memory of her startled face.

"This is going to be the devil of a business," said Mr. Mayherne to himself as he strode along the street.

Extraordinary, the whole thing. An extraordinary woman. A very dangerous woman. Women were the devil when they got their knife into you.

What was to be done? That wretched young man hadn't a leg to stand upon. Of course, possibly he did commit the crime. . . .

"No," said Mr. Mayherne to himself. "No—there's almost too much evidence against him. I don't believe this woman. She was trumping up the whole story. But she'll never bring it into court."

He wished he felt more conviction on the point.

The police court proceedings were brief and dramatic. The principal witnesses for the prosecution were Janet Mackenzie, maid to the dead woman, and Romaine Heilger, Austrian subject, the mistress of the prisoner.

Mr. Mayherne sat in court and listened to the damning story that the latter told. It was on the lines she had indicated to him in their interview.

The prisoner reserved his defense and was committed for trial.

Mr. Mayherne was at his wits' end. The case against Leonard Vole was black beyond words. Even the famous K.C. who was engaged for the defense held out little hope.

"If we can shake that Austrian woman's testimony, we might do something," he said dubiously. "But it's a bad business."

Mr. Mayherne had concentrated his energies on one single point. Assuming Leonard Vole to be speaking the truth, and to have left the murdered woman's house at nine o'clock, who was the man Janet heard talking to Miss French at half-past nine?

The only ray of light was in the shape of a scapegrace nephew who had in bygone days cajoled and threatened his aunt out of various sums of money. Janet Mackenzie, the solicitor learned, had always been attached to this young man, and had never ceased urging his claims upon her mistress. It certainly seemed possible that it was this nephew who had been with Miss French after Leonard Vole left, especially as he was not to be found in any of his old haunts.

In all other directions, the lawyer's researches had been negative in their result. No one had seen Leonard Vole entering his own house, or leaving that of Miss French. No one had seen any other man enter or leave the house in Cricklewood. All inquiries drew blanks.

It was the eve of the trial when Mr. Mayherne received the letter which was to lead his thoughts in an entirely new direction.

It came by the six o'clock post. An illiterate scrawl, written on common paper and enclosed in a dirty envelope with the stamp stuck on crooked.

Mr. Mayherne read it through once or twice before he grasped its meaning.

"DEAR MISTER:

"Youre the lawyer chap wot acts for the young feller. If you want that painted foreign hussy showd up for wot she is an her pack of lies you come to 16 Shaw's Rents Stepney to-night It ull cawst you 2 hundred quid Arsk for Missis Mogson."

The solicitor read and reread this strange epistle. It might, of course, be a hoax, but when he thought it over, he became increasingly convinced that it was genuine, and also convinced that it was the one hope for the prisoner. The evidence of Romaine Heilger damned him completely, and the line the defense meant to pursue, the line that the evidence of a woman who had admittedly lived an immoral life was not to be trusted, was at best a weak one.

Mr. Mayherne's mind was made up. It was his duty to save his client at all costs. He must go to Shaw's Rents.

He had some difficulty in finding the place, a ramshackle building in an evil-smelling slum, but at last he did so, and on inquiry for Mrs. Mogson was sent up to a room on the third floor. On this door he knocked, and getting no answer, knocked again.

At this second knock, he heard a shuffling sound inside, and presently the door was opened cautiously half an inch and a bent figure peered out.

Suddenly the woman, for it was a woman, gave a chuckle and opened the door wider.

"So it's you, dearie," she said, in a wheezy voice. "Nobody with you, is there? No playing tricks? That's right. You can come in—you can come in."

With some reluctance the lawyer stepped across the threshold into the small dirty room, with its flickering gas jet. There was an untidy unmade bed in a corner, a plain deal table and two rickety chairs. For the first time Mr. Mayherne had a full view of the tenant of this unsavory apartment. She was a woman of middle age, bent in figure, with a mass of untidy gray hair and a scarf wound tightly round her face. She saw him looking at this and laughed again, the same curious, toneless chuckle.

"Wondering why I hide my beauty, dear? He, he, he. Afraid it may tempt you, eh? But you shall see—you shall see."

She drew aside the scarf and the lawyer recoiled involuntarily before the almost formless blur of scarlet. She replaced the scarf again.

"So you're not wanting to kiss me, dearie? He, he, I don't wonder. And yet I was a pretty girl once—not so long ago as you'd think, either. Vitriol, dearie, vitriol—that's what did that. Ah! but I'll be even with 'em——"

She burst into a hideous torrent of profanity which Mr. Mayherne tried vainly to quell. She fell silent at last, her hands clenching and unclenching themselves nervously.

"Enough of that," said the lawyer sternly. "I've come here because I have reason to believe you can give me information which will clear my client, Leonard Vole. Is that the case?"

Her eyes leered at him cunningly.

"What about the money, dearie?" she wheezed. "Two hundred quid, you remember."

"It is your duty to give evidence, and you can be called upon to do so."

"That won't do, dearie. I'm an old woman, and I know nothing. But you give me two hundred quid, and perhaps I can give you a hint or two. See?"

"What kind of hint?"

"What should you say to a letter? A letter from *her*. Never mind how I got hold of it. That's my business. It'll do the trick. But I want my two hundred quid."

Mr. Mayherne looked at her coldly, and made up his mind.

"I'll give you ten pounds, nothing more. And only that if this letter is what you say it is."

"Ten pounds?" She screamed and raved at him.

"Twenty," said Mr. Mayherne, "and that's my last word."

He rose as if to go. Then, watching her closely, he drew out a pocketbook, and counted out twenty one-pound notes.

"You see," he said. "That is all I have with me. You can take it or leave it."

But already he knew that the sight of the money was too much for her. She cursed and raved impotently, but at last she gave in. Going over to the bed, she drew something out from beneath the tattered mattress.

"Here you are, damn you!" she snarled. "It's the top one you want."

It was a bundle of letters that she threw to him, and Mr. Mayherne untied them and scanned them in his usual cool, methodical manner. The woman, watching him eagerly, could gain no clue from his impassive face.

He read each letter through, then returned again to the top one and read it a second time. Then he tied the whole bundle up again carefully.

They were love letters, written by Romaine Heilger, and the man they were written to was not Leonard Vole. The top letter was dated the day of the latter's arrest.

"I spoke true, dearie, didn't I?" whined the woman. "It'll do for her, that letter?"

Mr. Mayherne put the letters in his pocket, then he asked a question.

"How did you get hold of this correspondence?"

"That's telling," she said with a leer. "But I know something more. I heard in court what that hussy said. Find out where she was at twenty past ten, the time she says she was at home. Ask at the Lion Road Cinema. They'll remember—a fine upstanding girl like that—curse her!"

"Who is the man?" asked Mr. Mayherne. "There's only a Christian name here."

The other's voice grew thick and hoarse, her hands clenched and unclenched. Finally she lifted one to her face.

"He's the man that did this to me. Many years ago now. She took him away from me—a chit of a girl she was then. And when I went after him—and went for him too—he threw the cursed stuff at me! And she laughed—damn her! I've had it in for her for years. Followed her, I have, spied upon her. And now I've got her! She'll suffer for this, won't she, Mr. Lawyer? She'll suffer?"

"She will probably be sentenced to a term of imprisonment for perjury," said Mr. Mayherne quietly.

"Shut away—that's what I want. You're going, are you? Where's my money? Where's that good money?"

Without a word, Mr. Mayherne put down the notes on the table. Then, drawing a deep breath, he turned and left the squalid room. Looking back, he saw the old woman crooning over the money.

He wasted no time. He found the cinema in Lion Road easily enough, and, shown a photograph of Romaine Heilger, the commissionaire recognized her at once. She had arrived at the cinema with a man some time after ten o'clock on the evening in question. He had not noticed her escort particularly, but he remembered the lady who had spoken to him about the picture that was showing. They stayed until the end, about an hour later.

Mr. Mayherne was satisfied. Romaine Heilger's evidence was a tissue of lies from beginning to end. She had evolved it out of her passionate hatred. The lawyer wondered whether he would ever know what lay behind that hatred. What had Leonard Vole done to her? He had seemed dumbfounded when the solicitor had reported her attitude to him. He had declared earnestly that such a thing was incredible—yet it had seemed to Mr. Mayherne that after the first astonishment his protests had lacked sincerity.

He did know. Mr. Mayherne was convinced of it. He knew, but he had no intention of revealing the fact. The secret between those two remained a secret. Mr. Mayherne wondered if some day he should come to learn what it was.

The solicitor glanced at his watch. It was late, but time was everything. He hailed a taxi and gave an address.

"Sir Charles must know of this at once," he murmured to himself as he got in.

The trial of Leonard Vole for the murder of Emily French aroused widespread interest. In the first place the prisoner was young and good-looking, then he was accused of a particularly dastardly crime, and there was the further interest of Romaine Heilger, the principal witness for the prosecution. There had been pictures of her in many papers, and several fictitious stories as to her origin and history.

The proceedings opened quietly enough. Various technical evidence came first. Then Janet Mackenzie was called. She told substantially the same story as before. In cross-examination counsel for the defense succeeded in getting her to contradict herself once or twice over her account of Vole's association with Miss French; he emphasized the fact that though she had heard a man's voice in the sitting-room that night, there was nothing to show that it was Vole who was there, and he managed to drive home a feeling that jealousy and dislike of the prisoner were at the bottom of a good deal of her evidence.

Then the next witness was called.

"Your name is Romaine Heilger?"

"Yes."

"You are an Austrian subject?"

"Yes."

"For the last three years you have lived with the prisoner and passed yourself off as his wife?"

Just for a moment Romaine Heilger's eyes met those of the man in the dock. Her expression held something curious and unfathomable.

"Yes."

The questions went on. Word by word the damning facts came out. On the night in question the prisoner had taken out a crowbar with him. He had returned at twenty minutes past ten, and had confessed to having killed the old lady. His cuffs had been stained with blood, and he had burned them in the kitchen stove. He had terrorized her into silence by means of threats.

As the story proceeded, the feeling of the court which had, to begin with, been slightly favorable to the prisoner, now set dead against him. He himself sat with downcast head and moody air, as though he knew he were doomed.

Yet it might have been noted that her own counsel sought to restrain Romaine's animosity. He would have preferred her to be more unbiased.

Formidable and ponderous, counsel for the defense arose.

He put it to her that her story was a malicious fabrication from start to finish, that she had not even been in her own house at the time in question, that she was in love with another man and was deliberately seeking to send Vole to his death for a crime he did not commit.

Romaine denied these allegations with superb insolence.

Then came the surprising denouement, the production of the letter. It was read aloud in court in the midst of a breathless stillness.

"Max, beloved, the Fates have delivered him into our hands! He has been arrested for murder—but, yes, the murder of an old lady! Leonard, who would not hurt a fly! At last I shall have my revenge. The poor chicken! I shall say that he came in that night with blood upon him— that he confessed to me. I shall hang him, Max—and when he hangs he will know and realize that it was Romaine who sent him to his death. And then—happiness, Beloved! Happiness at last!"

There were experts present ready to swear that the handwriting was that of Romaine Heilger, but they were not needed. Confronted with the letter, Romaine broke down utterly and confessed everything. Leonard Vole had returned to the house at the time he said, twenty past nine. She had invented the whole story to ruin him.

With the collapse of Romaine Heilger, the case for the Crown collapsed also. Sir Charles called his few witnesses, the prisoner himself went into the box and told his story in a manly straightforward manner, unshaken by cross-examination.

The prosecution endeavored to rally, but without great success. The judge's summing up was not wholly favorable to the prisoner, but a reaction had set in and the jury needed little time to consider their verdict.

"We find the prisoner not guilty."

Leonard Vole was free!

Little Mr. Mayherne hurried from his seat. He must congratulate his client.

He found himself polishing his pince-nez vigorously, and checked himself. His wife had told him only the night before that he was getting a habit of it. Curious things, habits. People themselves never knew they had them.

An interesting case—a very interesting case. That woman, now, Romaine Heilger.

The case was dominated for him still by the exotic figure of Romaine Heilger. She had seemed a pale, quiet woman in the house at Paddington, but in court she had flamed out against the sober background, flaunting herself like a tropical flower.

If he closed his eyes he could see her now, tall and vehement, her exquisite body bent forward a little, her right hand clenching and unclenching itself unconsciously all the time.

Curious things, habits. That gesture of hers with the hand was her habit, he supposed. Yet he had seen someone else do it quite lately. Who was it now? Quite lately——

He drew in his breath with a gasp as it came back to him. The woman in Shaw's Rents. . . .

He stood still, his head whirling. It was impossible—impossible—— Yet, Romaine Heilger was an actress.

The K.C. came up behind him and clapped him on the shoulder.

"Congratulated our man yet? He's had a narrow shave, you know. Come along and see him."

But the little lawyer shook off the other's hand.

He wanted one thing only—to see Romaine Heilger face to face.

He did not see her until some time later, and the place of their meeting is not relevant.

"So you guessed," she said, when he had told her all that was in his mind. "The face? Oh! that was easy enough, and the light of that gas jet was too bad for you to see the make-up."

"But why—why——"

"Why did I play a lone hand?" She smiled a little, remembering the last time she had used the words.

"Such an elaborate comedy!"

"My friend—I had to save him. The evidence of a woman devoted to him would not have been enough—you hinted as much yourself. But I know something of the psychology of crowds. Let my evidence be wrung from me, as an admission, damning me in the eyes of the law, and a reaction in favor of the prisoner would immediately set in."

"And the bundle of letters?"

"One alone, the vital one, might have seemed like a—what do you call it?—put-up job."

"Then the man called Max?"

"Never existed, my friend."

"I still think," said little Mr. Mayherne, in an aggrieved manner, "that we could have got him off by the—er—normal procedure."

"I dared not risk it. You see you thought he was innocent——"

"And you knew it? I see," said little Mr. Mayherne.

"My dear Mr. Mayherne," said Romaine, "you do not see at all. I knew—he was guilty!"

# The Incredible Journey

## SHEILA BURNFORD

### 1

THIS journey took place in a part of Canada which lies in the north-western part of the great sprawling province of Ontario. It is a vast area of deeply wooded wilderness—of endless chains of lonely lakes and rushing rivers. Thousands of miles of country roads, rough timber lanes, overgrown tracks leading to abandoned mines, and unmapped trails snake across its length and breadth. It is a country of far-flung, lonely farms and a few widely scattered small towns and villages, of lonely trappers' shacks and logging camps. Most of its industry comes from the great pulp and paper companies who work their timber concessions deep in the very heart of the forests; and from the mines, for it is rich in minerals. Prospectors work through it; there are trappers and Indians; and sometimes hunters who fly into the virgin lakes in small amphibious aircraft; there are pioneers with visions beyond their own life span; and there are those who have left the bustle of civilization forever, to sink their identity in an unquestioning acceptance of the wilderness. But all these human beings together are as a handful of sand upon the ocean shores, and for the most part there is silence and solitude and an uninterrupted way of life for the wild animals that abound there: moose and deer; brown and black bears; lynx and fox; beaver, muskrat and otter; fishers, mink and marten. The wild duck rests there and the Canada goose, for this is a fringe of the central migratory flyway. The clear tree-fringed lakes and rivers are filled with speckled trout and steelheads, pike and pickerel and whitefish.

Almost half the year the country is blanketed with snow, and for weeks at a time the temperature may stay many degrees below zero; there is no slow growth of spring, but a sudden short burst of summer when everything grows with wild abandon; and as suddenly it is the fall again. To many who live there, fall is the burnished crown of the year, with the crisp sunny days and exhilarating air of the Northland; with clear blue skies, and drifting leaves, and, as far as the eye can see, the endless panorama of glorious rich flaming color in the turning trees.

This is the country over which the three travelers passed, and it was in the fall that they traveled, in the days of Indian summer.

John Longridge lived several miles from one of the small towns in an old stone house that had been in his family for several generations. He was a tall, austerely pleasant man of about forty, a bachelor, and a writer by profession, being the author of several historical biographies. He spent much of his time traveling and gathering material for his books, but always returned to the comfortable old stone house for the actual writing. He liked the house to himself during these creative periods, and for many years had enjoyed an ideal arrangement whereby his domestic wants were cared for by a middle-aged couple, Mrs. Oakes and her husband Bert, who lived in a small cottage about half a mile away. Mrs. Oakes came in every day to look after the house and cook the main meals. Bert was in charge of the furnace, the garden and all the odd jobs. They came and went about their business without disturbing Longridge, and there was complete accord among them all.

On the eve of the incredible journey, towards the end of September, Longridge sat by a crackling log fire in his comfortable library. The curtains were drawn and the firelight flickered and played on the bookshelves and danced on the ceiling. The only other light in the room came from a small shaded lamp on a table by the deep armchair. It was a very peaceful room and the only sound was the occasional crackling from the logs or the rustling of a newspaper, the pages of which Longridge turned with some difficulty, for a slender wheat-colored Siamese cat was curled on his knee, chocolate-colored front paws curved in towards one another, sapphire eyes blinking occasionally as he stared into the fire.

On the floor, his scarred, bony head resting on one of the man's feet, lay an old white English bull terrier. His slanted almond-shaped eyes, sunk deep within their pinkish rims, were closed; one large triangular ear caught the firelight, flushing the inside a delicate pink, so that it appeared almost translucent. Anyone unaccustomed to the rather peculiar points of bull terrier beauty would have thought him a strange if not downright ugly dog, with the naked, down-faced arc of his profile, his deep-chested, stocky body and whip-tapered tail. But the true lover of an ancient and honorable breed would have recognized the blood and bone of this elderly and rather battered body; would have known that in his prime this had been a magnificent specimen of compact sinew and muscle, bred to fight and endure; and would have loved him for his curious mixture of wicked, unyielding fighter yet devoted and docile family pet, and above all for the irrepressible air of sly merriment which gleamed in his little slant eyes.

He twitched and sighed often in his sleep, as old dogs will, and for once his shabby tail with the bare patch on the last joint was still.

By the door lay another dog, nose on paws, brown eyes open and watchful in contrast to the peacefulness radiated by the other occupants of the room. This was a large red-gold Labrador retriever, a young dog with all the heritage of his sturdy working forebears in his powerful build, broad noble head and deep, blunt, gentle mouth. He lifted his head as Longridge rose from the chair, depositing the cat, with an apologetic pat, on the floor, and carefully moving his foot from under the old dog's head before walking across the room to draw one of the heavy curtains and look out.

A huge orange moon was rising just above the trees at the far end of the garden, and a branch of an old lilac tree tap-tapped in the light wind against the window pane. It was bright enough outside to see the garden in clear detail, and he noticed how the leaves had drifted again across the lawn even in the short time since it had been raked that afternoon, and that only a few brave asters remained to color the flower beds.

He turned and crossed the room, flicking on another light, and opened a narrow cupboard halfway up the wall. Inside were several guns on racks and he looked at them thoughtfully, running his fingers lovingly down the smooth grain of the hand-rubbed stocks, and finally lifted down a beautifully chased and engraved double-barreled gun. He "broke" it and peered down the gleaming barrels; and as though at a signal the young dog sat up silently in the shadows, his ears pricked in interest. The gun fell back into place with a well-oiled click and the dog whined. The man replaced the gun in sudden contrition, and the dog lay down again, his head turned away, his eyes miserable.

Longridge walked over to make amends for his thoughtlessness, but as he bent down to pat the dog the telephone rang so suddenly and shrilly in the quiet room that the cat jumped indignantly off the chair and the bull terrier started clumsily to his feet.

Longridge picked up the receiver, and presently the breathless voice of Mrs. Oakes was heard, accompanied by a high-pitched, whining note in the distance.

"Speak up, Mrs. Oakes—I can hardly hear you."

"I can hardly hear you either," said the breathless voice distantly. "There, is that better? I'm shouting now! What time are you leaving in the morning, Mr. Longridge? What's that? Could you talk louder?"

"About seven o'clock. I want to get to Heron Lake before nightfall," he shouted, noting with amusement the scandalized expression of the cat. "But there's no need for you to be here at that time, Mrs. Oakes."

"What's that you said? Seven? Will it be all right if I don't come in until about nine? My niece is coming on the early bus and I'd like to meet her. But I don't like to leave the dogs alone too long. . . ."

"Of course you must meet her," he answered, shouting really loudly now as the humming noise increased. "The dogs will be fine. I'll take them out first thing in the morning and—"

"Oh, thanks, Mr. Longridge—I'll be there around nine without fail. What's that you said about the animals? (Oh, you pernickety, dratted old line!) Don't you worry about them; Bert and me, we'll see. . . . tell old Bodger . . . bringing marrow bone. Oh, wait till I give that operator a piece of my mi . . ."

But just as Longridge was gathering strength for a last bellow into the mouthpiece the line went dead. He put the receiver back with relief and looked across the room at the old dog who had climbed stealthily into the armchair and sat lolling back against the cushions, his eyes half closed, awaiting the expected reproof. He addressed him with the proper degree of ferocity, telling him that he was a scoundrelly opportunist, a sybaritic barbarian, a disgrace to his upbringing and his ancestors, "AND"—and he paused in weighty emphasis—"a very . . . *bad* . . . *dog!*"

At these two dread words the terrier laid his ears flat against his skull, slanted his eyes back until they almost disappeared, then drew his lips back over his teeth in an apologetic grin, quivering the end of his disgraceful tail. His parody of sorrow brought its usual reprieve: the man laughed and patted the bony head, then enticed him down with the promise of a run.

So the old dog, who was a natural clown, slithered half off the chair and stood, with his hindquarters resting on the cushions, waving his tail and nudging the cat, who sat like an Egyptian statue, eyes half closed, head erect, then gave a throaty growl and patted at the pink and black bull-terrier nose. Then together they followed the man to the door, where the young dog waited to fall in behind the little procession. Longridge opened the door leading on to the garden, and the two dogs and the cat squeeezd past his legs and into the cool night air. He stood under the trellised porch, quietly smoking his pipe, and watched them for a while. Their nightly routine never varied—first the few minutes of separate local investigation, then the indefinable moment when all met again and paused before setting off together through the gap in the hedge at the bottom of the garden and into the fields and woods that lay beyond. He watched until they disappeared into the darkness (the white shape of the bull terrier showing up long after Longridge was unable to distinguish the other two), then knocked his pipe out against the stone step and re-entered the house. It would be half an hour or more before they returned.

Longridge and his brother owned a small cabin by the shores of remote Heron Lake, about two hundred miles away; and twice a year they spent two or three weeks there together, leading the life they loved: spending many hours in companionable silence in their canoe, fishing in spring and hunting in the autumn. Usually he had simply locked up and left, leaving the key with Mrs. Oakes so that she could come in once or twice a week and keep the house warm and aired. However, now he had the animals to consider. He had thought of taking them all to a boarding kennel in the town, but Mrs. Oakes, who loved the assorted trio, had protested vigorously and assented that she herself would look after them "rather than have those poor dumb animals fretting themselves into a state in some kennel, and probably half starved into the bargain." So it had been arranged that she and Bert would look after the three animals. Bert would be working around the garden, anyway, so that they could be outside most of the time and Mrs. Oakes would feed them and keep her eye on them while she was working in the house.

When he had finished packing, Longridge went into the library to draw the curtains, and seeing the telephone he was reminded of Mrs. Oakes. He had forgotten to tell her to order some coffee and other things that he had taken from the store cupboard. He sat down at the desk and drew out a small memo pad.

*Dear Mrs. Oakes,* he wrote, *Please order some more coffee and replace the canned food I've taken. I will be taking the dogs (and Tao too of course!)* . . . Here he came to the end of the small square of paper, and taking another piece he continued: . . . *out for a run before I leave, and will give them something to eat, so don't let our greedy white friend tell you he is starving! Don't worry yourselves too much over them—I know they will be fine.*

He wrote the last few words with a smile, for the bull terrier had Mrs. Oakes completely in thrall and worked his advantage to the full. He left the pages on the desk under a glass paperweight; then opened the door in answer to a faint scratch. The old dog and the cat bounded in to greet him with their usual affection, bringing the fresh smell of the outdoors with them. The young dog followed more sedately and stood by, watching aloofly, as the other whipped his tail like a lash against the man's legs, while the cat pressed against him purring in a deep rumble; but he wagged his tail briefly and politely when the man patted him.

The cat walked into the library to curl up on the warm hearth. Later when the ashes grew cold he would move to the top of the radiator, and then, sometime in the middle of the night, he would steal upstairs and curl up beside the old dog. It was useless shutting the bedroom door, or any other door of the house for that matter, for the cat could open them all, latches or doorknobs. The only doors that defeated him were those with porcelain handles, for he found it impossible to get a purchase on the shiny surface with his long monkeylike paws.

The young dog padded off to his rug on the floor of the little back kitchen, and the bull terrier started up the steep stairs, and was already curled in his basket in the bedroom when Longridge himself came to bed. He opened one bright, slanted eye when he felt the old blanket being dropped over him, then pushed his head under the cover, awaiting the opportunity he knew would come later.

The man lay awake for a while, thinking about the days ahead and of the animals, for the sheer misery in the young dog's eyes haunted him.

They had come to him, this odd and lovable trio, over eight months ago, from the home of an old and dear college friend. This friend, Jim Hunter, was an English professor in a small university about two hundred and fifty miles away. As the university owned one of the finest reference libraries in the province, Longridge often stayed with him and was, in fact, godfather to the Hunters' nine-year-old daughter, Elizabeth. He had been staying with them when the invitation came from an English university, asking the professor to deliver a series of lectures which would involve a stay in England of nearly nine months, and he had witnessed the tears of his goddaughter and the glum silence of her brother, Peter, when it was decided that their pets would have to be boarded out and the house rented to the reciprocal visiting professor.

Longridge was extremely fond of Elizabeth and Peter, and he could understand their feelings, remembering how much the companionship of a cocker spaniel had meant when he himself was a rather lonely child, and how he had grieved when he was first separated from it. Elizabeth was the self-appointed owner of the cat. She fed and brushed him, took him for walks, and he slept at the foot of her bed. Eleven-year-old Peter had been inseparable from the bull terrier ever since the small white puppy had arrived on Peter's first birthday. In fact, the boy could not remember a day of his life when Bodger had not been part of it. The young dog belonged, in every sense of the word, heart and soul to their father, who had trained him since puppyhood for hunting.

Now they were faced with the realization of separation, and in the appalled silence that followed the decision Longridge watched Elizabeth's face screw up in the prelude to tears. Then he heard a voice, which he recognized with astonishment to be his own, telling everybody not to worry, not to worry at all—he would take care of everything! Were not he and the animals already well known to one another? And had he not plenty of room, and a large garden? . . . Mrs. Oakes? Why, she would just love to have them! Everything would be simply wonderful! Before the family sailed they would bring the dogs and the cat over by car, see for themselves where they would sleep, write out a list of instructions, and he, personally, would love and cherish them until their return.

So one day the Hunter family had driven over and the pets had been left, with many tearful farewells from Elizabeth and last-minute instructions from Peter.

During the first few days Longridge had almost regretted his spontaneous offer: the terrier had languished in his basket, his long arched nose buried in the comfort of his paws, and one despairing, martyred eye haunting his every movement; and the cat had nearly driven him crazy with the incessant goatlike bleating and yowling of a suffering Siamese; the young dog had moped by the door and refused all food. But after a few days, won over perhaps by Mrs. Oakes's sympathetic clucking and tempting morsels of food, they had seemed to resign themselves, and the cat and the old dog had settled in, very comfortably and happily, showing their adopted master a great deal of affection.

It was very apparent, however, how much the old dog missed children. Longridge at first had wondered where he disappeared to some afternoons; he eventually found out that the terrier went to the playground of the little rural school, where he was a great favorite with the children, timing his appearance for recess. Knowing that the road was forbidden to him, because of his poor sight and habit of walking stolidly in the middle, he had found a short cut across the intervening fields.

But the young dog was very different. He had obviously never stopped pining for his own home and master; although he ate well and his coat was glossy with health, he never maintained anything but a dignified, unyielding distance. The man respected him for this, but it worried him that the dog never seemed to relax, and always appeared to be listening—longing and waiting for something far beyond the walls of the house or the fields beyond. Longridge was glad for the dog's sake that the Hunters would be returning in about three weeks, but he knew that he would miss his adopted family. They had amused and entertained him more than he would have thought possible, over the months, and he realized tonight that the parting would be a real wrench. He did not like to think of the too quiet house that would be his again.

He slept at last, and the dreaming, curious moon peeped in at the window to throw shafts of pale light into the rooms and over each of the sleeping occupants. They woke the cat downstairs, who stretched and yawned, then leaped without visible effort onto the window sill, his gleaming eyes, with their slight cast, wide open and enormous, and only the tip of his tail twitching as he sat motionless, staring into the garden. Presently he turned, and with a single graceful bound crossed to the desk; but for once he was careless, and his hind leg knocked the glass paperweight to the floor. He shook the offending leg vigorously, scattering the pages of Longridge's note—sending one page off the desk into the air, where it caught the upward current of hot air from the wall register and sailed across the room to land in the fireplace. Here it slowly curled and browned, until nothing remained of the writing but the almost illegible signature at the bottom.

When the pale fingers of the moon reached over the young dog in the back kitchen he stirred in his uneasy sleep, then sat upright, his ears pricked —listening and listening for the sound that never came: the high, piercing whistle of his master that would have brought him bounding across the world if only his straining ears could hear it.

And lastly the moon peered into the upstairs bedroom, where the man lay sleeping on his side in a great four-poster bed; and curled against his back the elderly, comfort-loving white bull terrier slept in blissful, warm content.

2

There was a slight mist when John Longridge rose early the following morning, having fought a losing battle for the middle of the bed with his uninvited bedfellow. He shaved and dressed quickly, watching the mist roll back over the fields and the early morning sun break through. It would be a perfect fall day, an Indian summer day, warm and mellow. Downstairs he found the animals waiting patiently by the door for their early morning run. He let them out, then cooked and ate his solitary breakfast. He was out in the driveway, loading up his car when the dogs and cat returned from the fields. He fetched some biscuits for them and they lay by the wall of the house in the early sun, watching him. He threw the last item into the back of the car, thankful that he had already packed the guns and hunting equipment before the Labrador had seen them, then walked over and patted the heads of his audience, one by one.

"Be good," he said. "Mrs. Oakes will be here soon. Good-by, Luath," he said to the Labrador, "I wish I could have taken you with me, but there wouldn't be room in the canoe for three of us." He put his hand under the young dog's soft muzzle. The golden-brown eyes looked steadily into his, and then the dog did an unexpected thing: he lifted his right paw and placed it in the man's hand. Longridge had seen him do this many a time to his own master and he was curiously touched and affected by the trust it conveyed, almost wishing he did not have to leave immediately just after the dog had shown his first responsive gesture.

He looked at his watch and realized he was already late. He had no worries about leaving the animals alone outside, as they had never attempted to stray beyond the large garden and the adjacent fields; and they could return inside the house if they wished, for the kitchen door was the kind that closed slowly on a spring. All that he had to do was shoot the inside bolt while the door was open, and after that it did not close properly and could be pushed open from the outside. They looked contented enough, too—the cat was washing methodically behind his ears—the old dog sat on his haunches, panting after his run, his long pink tongue lolling out of his grinning mouth; and the Labrador lay quietly by his side.

Longridge started the car and waved to them out of the window as he drove slowly down the drive, feeling rather foolish as he did so. "What do I expect them to do in return?" he asked himself with a smile, "Wave back? Or shout 'Good-by'? The trouble is I've lived too long alone with them and I'm becoming far too attached to them."

The car turned around the bend at the end of the long tree-lined drive and the animals heard the sound of the engine receding in the distance. The cat transferred his attention to a hind leg; the old dog stopped panting and lay down; the young dog remained stretched out, only his eyes moving and an occasional twitch of his nose.

Twenty minutes passed by and no move was made; then suddenly the young dog rose, stretched himself, and stood looking intently down the drive. He remained like this for several minutes, while the cat watched closely, one leg still pointing upwards; then slowly the Labrador walked down the driveway and stood at the curve, looking back as though inviting the others to come. The old dog rose too, now, somewhat stiffly, and followed. Together they turned the corner, out of sight.

The cat remained utterly still for a full minute, blue eyes blazing in the dark mask. Then, with a curious hesitating run, he set off in pursuit. The dogs were waiting by the gate when he turned the corner, the old dog peering wistfully back, as though he hoped to see his friend Mrs. Oakes materialize with a juicy bone; but when the Labrador started up the road he followed. The cat still paused by the gate, one paw lifted delicately in the air—undecided, questioning, hesitant; until suddenly, some inner decision reached, he followed the dogs. Presently all three disappeared from sight down the dusty road, trotting briskly and with purpose.

About an hour later Mrs. Oakes walked up the driveway from her cottage, carrying a string bag with her working shoes and apron, and a little parcel of tidbits for the animals. Her placid, gentle face wore a rather disappointed look, because the dogs usually spied her long before she got to the house and would rush to greet her.

"I expect Mr. Longridge left them shut inside the house if he was leaving early," she consoled herself. But when she pushed open the kitchen door and walked inside, everything seemed very silent and still. She stood at the foot of the stairs and called them, but there was no answering patter of running feet, only the steady tick-tock of the old clock in the hallway. She walked through the silent house and out into the front garden and stood there calling with a puzzled frown.

"Oh, well," she spoke her thoughts aloud to the empty, sunny garden, "perhaps they've gone up to the school. . . . It's a funny thing, though," she continued, sitting on a kitchen chair a few minutes later and tying her shoelaces, "that Puss isn't here—he's usually sitting on the window sill at this time of the day. Oh, well, he's probably out hunting—I've never known a cat like that for hunting, doesn't seem natural somehow!"

She washed and put away the few dishes, then took her cleaning materials into the sitting room. There her eye was caught by a sparkle on the floor by the desk, and she found the glass paperweight, and after that the remaining sheet of the note on the desk. She read it through to where it said: "I will be taking the dogs (and Tao too of course!) . . .", then looked for the remainder. "That's odd," she thought, "now where would he take them? That cat must have knocked the paperweight off last night—the rest of the note must be somewhere in the room."

She searched the room but it was not until she was emptying an ash tray into the fireplace that she noticed the charred curl of paper in the hearth. She bent down and picked it up carefully, for it was obviously very brittle, but even then most of it crumbled away and she was left with a fragment which bore the initials J. R. L.

"Now, isn't that the queerest thing," she said to the fireplace, rubbing vigorously at the black marks on the tiles. "He must mean he's taking them all to Heron Lake with him. But why would he suddenly do that, after all the arrangements we made? He never said a word about it on the telephone—but wait a minute, I remember now—he was just going to say something about them when the line went dead; perhaps he was just going to tell me."

While Mrs. Oakes was amazed that Longridge would take the animals on his vacation, it did not occur to her to be astonished that a cat should go along too, for she was aware that the cat loved the car and always went with the dogs when Longridge drove them anywhere or took them farther afield for walks. Like many Siamese cats, he was as obedient and as trained to go on walks as most dogs, and would always return to a whistle.

Mrs. Oakes swept and dusted and talked to the house, locked it and returned home to her cottage. She would have been horrified to the depths of her kindly, well-ordered soul if she had known the truth. Far from sitting sedately in the back of a car traveling north with John Longridge, as she so fondly visualized, the animals were by now many miles away on a deserted country road that ran westward.

They had kept a fairly steady pace for the first hour or so, falling into an order which was not to vary for many miles or days; the Labrador ran always by the left shoulder of the old dog, for the bull terrier was very nearly blind in the left eye, and they jogged along fairly steadily together—the bull terrier with his odd, rolling, sailorlike gait, and the Labrador in a slow lope. Some ten yards behind came the cat, whose attention was frequently distracted, when he would stop for a few minutes and then catch up again. But, in between these halts, he ran swiftly and steadily, his long slim body and tail low to the ground.

When it was obvious that the old dog was flagging, the Labrador turned off the quiet, graveled road and into the shade of a pinewood beside a clear, fast-running creek. The old dog drank deeply, standing up to his chest in the cold water; the cat picked his way delicately to the edge of an overhanging rock. Afterwards they rested in the deep pine needles under the trees, the terrier panting heavily with his eyes half closed, and the cat busy with his eternal washing. They lay there for nearly an hour, until the sun struck through the branches above them. The young dog rose and stretched, then walked towards the road. The old dog rose too, stiff-legged, his head low. He walked toward the waiting Labrador, limping slightly and wagging his tail at the cat, who suddenly danced into a patch of sunlight, struck at a drifting leaf, then ran straight at the dogs, swerving at the last moment, and as suddenly sitting down again.

They trotted steadily on, all that afternoon—mostly traveling on the grassy verge at the side of the quiet country road; sometimes in the low overgrown ditch that ran alongside, if the acute hearing of the young dog warned them of an approaching car.

By the time the afternoon sun lay in long, barred shadows across the road, the cat was still traveling in smooth, swift bursts, and the young dog was comparatively fresh. But the old dog was very weary, and his pace had dropped to a limping walk. They turned off the road into the bush at the side, and walked slowly through a clearing in the trees, pushing their way through the tangled undergrowth at the far end. They came out upon a small open place where a giant spruce had crashed to the ground and left a hollow where the roots had been, filled now with drifted dry leaves and spruce needles.

The late afternoon sun slanted through the branches overhead, and it looked invitingly snug and secure. The old dog stood for a minute, his heavy head hanging, and his tired body swaying slightly, then lay down on his side in the hollow. The cat, after a good deal of wary observation, made a little hollow among the spruce needles and curled around in it, purring softly. The young dog disappeared into the undergrowth and reappeared presently, his smooth coat dripping water, to lie down a little way apart from the others.

The old dog continued to pant exhaustedly for a long time, one hind leg shaking badly, until his eyes closed at last, the labored breaths came further and further apart, and he was sleeping—still, save for an occasional long shudder.

Later on, when darkness fell, the young dog moved over and stretched out closely at his side and the cat stalked over to lie between his paws; and so, warmed and comforted by their closeness, the old dog slept, momentarily unconscious of his aching, tired body or his hunger.

In the nearby hills a timber wolf howled mournfully; owls called and answered and glided silently by with great outspread wings; and there were faint whispers of movement and small rustling noises around all through the night. Once an eerie wail like a baby's crying woke the old dog and brought him shivering and whining to his feet; but it was only a porcupine, who scrambled noisily and clumsily down a nearby tree trunk and waddled away, still crying softly. When he lay down again the cat was gone from his side —another small night hunter slipping through the unquiet shadows that froze to stillness at his passing.

The young dog slept in fitful, uneasy starts, his muscles twitching, constantly lifting his head and growling softly. Once he sprang to his feet with a full-throated roar which brought a sudden splash in the distance, then silence—and who knows what else unknown, unseen or unheard passed through his mind to disturb him further? Only one thing was clear and certain—that at all costs he was going home, home to his own beloved master. Home lay to the west, his instinct told him; but he could not leave the other two—so somehow he must take them with him, all the way.

## 3

In the cold hour before dawn, the bull terrier woke, then staggered painfully to his feet. He was trembling with cold and was extremely hungry and thirsty. He walked stiffly in the direction of the pool nearby, passing on his way the cat, who was crouched over something held between his paws. The terrier heard a crunching sound as the cat's jaws moved, and, wagging his tail in interest, moved over to investigate. The cat regarded him distantly, then stalked away, leaving the carcass; but to the terrier it was a disappointing mess of feathers only. He drank long and deeply at the pool and on his return tried the feathers again, for he was ravenous; but they stuck in his gullet and he retched them out. He nibbled at some stalks of grass, then, delicately, his lips rolled back over his teeth, picked a few overripe raspberries from a low bush. He had always liked to eat domestic raspberries this way, and although the taste was reassuringly familiar, it did nothing to appease his hunger. He was pleased to see the young dog appear presently; he wagged his tail and licked the other's face, then followed resignedly

when a move was made towards the direction of the road. They were followed a few moments later by the cat, who was still licking his lips after
his feathery breakfast.

In the gray light of dawn the trio continued down the side of the road
until they reached a point where it took a right-angled turn. Here they
hesitated before a disused logging trail that led westward from the side of
the road, its entrance almost concealed by overhanging branches. The leader
lifted his head and appeared almost as though he were searching for the
scent of something, some reassurance; and apparently he found it, for he led
his companions up the trail between the overhanging trees. The going here
was softer; the middle was overgrown with grass and the ruts on either side
were full of dead leaves. The close-growing trees which almost met overhead would afford more shade when the sun rose higher. These were all
considerations that the old dog needed, for he had been tired today even
before he started, and his pace was already considerably slower.

Both dogs were very hungry and watched enviously when the cat caught
and killed a chipmunk while they were resting by a stream in the middle of
the day. But when the old dog advanced with a hopeful wag of his tail, the
cat, growling, retreated into the bushes with his prey. Puzzled and disappointed, the terrier sat listening to the crunching sounds inside the bushes,
saliva running from his mouth.

A few minutes later the cat emerged and sat down, daintily cleaning his
whiskers. The old dog licked the black Siamese face with his panting tongue
and was affectionately patted on the nose in return. Restless with hunger, he
wandered up the banks of the creek, investigating every rock and hollow,
pushing his hopeful nose through tunnels of withered sedge and into the
yielding earth of molehills. Sadly he lay down by an unrewarding blueberry
bush, drew his paws down tightly over his blackened face, then licked the
dirt off them.

The young dog, too, was hungry; but he would have to be on the verge
of starvation before the barriers of deep-rooted Labrador heredity would be
broken down. For generations his ancestors had been bred to retrieve without harming, and there was nothing of the hunter in his make-up; as yet,
any killing was abhorrent to him. He drank deeply at the stream and urged
his companions on.

The trail ran high over the crest of this hilly, wooded country, and the
surrounding countryside below was filled with an overwhelming beauty of
color; the reds and vermilions of the occasional maples; pale birch, and yellow poplar, and here and there the scarlet clusters of mountain ash berries
against a rich dark-green background of spruce and pine and cedar.

Several times they passed log ramps built into the side of the hill, picking their way across the deep ruts left by the timber sleighs below; and sometimes they passed derelict buildings in rank, overgrown clearings, old stables
for the bush horses and living quarters for the men who had worked there a
generation ago. The windows were broken and sagging and weeds were
growing up between the floorboards, and even one old rusted cookstove had

fireweed springing from the firebox. The animals, strangely enough, did not like these evidences of human occupation and skirted them as far as possible, hair raised along their backs.

Late in the afternoon the old dog's pace had slowed down to a stumbling walk, and it seemed as if only sheer determination were keeping him on his feet at all. He was dizzy and swaying, and his heart was pounding. The cat must have sensed this general failing, for he now walked steadily beside the dogs, very close to his tottering old friend, and uttered plaintive worried bleats. Finally, the old dog came to a standstill by a deep rut half-filled with muddy water. He stood there as if he had not even the strength to step around it; his head sagged, and his whole body was trembling. Then, as he tried to lap the water, his legs seemed to crumple under him and he collapsed, half in and half out of the rut. His eyes were closed, and his body moved only to the long, shallow, shuddering breaths that came at widening intervals. Soon he lay completely limp and still. The young dog became frantic now: he whined, as he scratched at the edge of the rut, then nudged and pushed with his nose, doing everything in his power to rouse the huddled, unresponsive body. Again and again he barked, and the cat growled softly and continuously, walking back and forth and rubbing his whole length against the dirty, muddied head. There was no response to their attention. The old dog lay unconscious and remote.

The two animals grew silent, and sat by his side, disturbed and uneasy; until at last they turned and left him, neither looking back—the Labrador disappearing into the bushes where the crack of broken branches marked his progress farther and farther away; the cat stalking a partridge which had appeared at the side of the trail some hundred yards away and was pecking unconcernedly at the sandy dirt. But at the shrill warning of a squirrel, it flew off across the trail with a sudden whirr into the trees, while the cat was still some distance away. Undaunted, still licking his lips in anticipation, the cat continued around a bend in the trail in search of another, and was lost to sight.

The shadows lengthened across the deserted track, and the evening wind sighed down it to sweep a flurry of whispering leaves across the rut, their brown brittleness light as a benison as they drifted across the unheeding white form. The curious squirrel peered in bright-eyed wonder from a nearby tree, clucking softly to itself. A shrew ran halfway across, paused and ran back; and there was a soft sound of wings as a whisky-jack landed and swayed to and fro on a birch branch, tilting his head to one side as he looked down and called to his mate to come and join him. The wind died away—a sudden hush descended.

Suddenly, there was a sound of a heavy body pushing through the undergrowth, accompanied by a sharp cracking of branches, and the spell was broken. Chattering shrilly in alarm and excitement, the squirrel ran up the trunk of the tree and the whisky-jacks flew off. Now onto the trail on all fours scampered a half-grown bear cub, round furry ears pricked and small

deep-set eyes alight with curiosity in the sharp little face as he beheld the
old dog. There was a grunting snuffling sound in the bush behind the cub:
his mother was investigating a rotten tree stump. The cub stood for a moment and then hesitantly advanced toward the rut where the terrier lay.
He sniffed around, wrinkling his facile nose at the unfamiliar smell, then
reached out a long curved black paw and tapped the white head. For a
moment the mists of unconsciousness cleared and the old dog opened his
eyes, aware of danger. The cub sprang back in alarm and watched from a
safe distance. Seeing that there was no further movement, he loped back
and cuffed again with his paw, this time harder, and watched for a response.
Only enough strength was left in the old dog for a valiant baring of his
teeth. He snarled faintly with pain and hatred when his shoulder was raked
by the wicked claws of the excited cub, and made an attempt to struggle
to his feet. The smell of the drawn blood excited the cub further; he straddled the dog's body and started to play with the long white tail, nibbling
at the end like a child with a new toy. But there was no response: all conscious effort drained, the old dog no longer felt any pain or indignity. He
lay as though asleep, his eyes veiled and unseeing, his lip still curled in a
snarl.

Around the bend in the trail, dragging a large dead partridge by the
wing, came the cat. The wing sprang back softly from his mouth as he
gazed transfixed at the scene before him. In one split second a terrible
transformation took place; his blue eyes glittered hugely and evilly in the
black masked face, and every hair on the wheat-colored body stood upright
so that he appeared twice his real size; even the chocolate-colored tail puffed
up as it switched from side to side. He crouched low to the ground, tensed
and ready, and uttered a high, ear-splitting scream; and, as the startled cub
turned, the cat sprang.

He landed on the back of the dark furred neck, clinging with his monkeylike hind legs while he raked his claws across the cub's eyes. Again and
again he raked with the terrible talons, hissing and spitting in murderous
devilry until the cub was screaming in pain and fear, blinded with blood,
making ineffectual brushing movements with his paws to dislodge the unseen horror on his back. His screams were answered by a thunderous roar
as the huge black she-bear crashed through the bushes and rushed to the
cub. She swiped at the clinging cat with a tremendous paw; but the cat was
too quick for her and with a hiss of fury leaped to the ground and disappeared behind a tree. The unfortunate cub's head received the full force
of the blow and he was sent spinning across the track into the bushes. In
a blind, frustrated rage, maddened by the cries of her cub, the mother
turned for something on which to vent her fury, and saw the still figure
of the old dog. Even as she lumbered snarling towards him the cat distracted
her attention with a sudden leap to the side of the track. The bear halted,
then reared up to full height for attack, red eyes glinting savagely, neck
upstretched and head weaving from side to side in a menacing, snakelike
way. The cat uttered another banshee scream and stepped forward with a

stiff-legged, sideways movement, his squinting, terrible eyes fixed on his enormous adversary. Something like fear or indecision crept into the bear's eyes as the cat advanced; she shuffled back a step with lowered head. Slow, deliberate, purposeful, the cat came on—again the bear retreated, bewildered by the tactics of this terrible small animal, distraught by her cub's whimpering, slowly falling back before the relentless inch-by-inch advance. Now the cat stopped and crouched low, lashing his tail from side to side— the bear stopped too, shifting her weight uneasily before the spring that must follow, longing to decamp but afraid to turn her back. A sudden crackle of undergrowth turned the huge animal into a statue, rigid with apprehension—and when a great dog sprang out of the bush and stood beside the cat, teeth bared and snarling, every hair on his russet back and ruff erect, she dropped to all fours, turned swiftly and fled towards her cub. There was a last growl of desperate bravado from the bush and a whimpering cry; then the sounds of the bears' escape receded in the distance. Finally all was quiet again; the curious squirrel leaped from his ringside seat and scrambled farther down the trunk of the tree.

The cat shrank back to his normal size. His eyes regained their usual cool, detached look. He shook each paw distastefully in turn, glanced briefly at the limp, muddied bundle by his feet, blood oozing from four deep parallel gashes on the shoulder, then turned and sauntered slowly down the track towards his partridge.

The young dog nosed his friend all over, his lips wrinkling at the rank bear smell, then attempted to stanch the wounds with his rough tongue. He scratched fresh leaves over the bloodstained ones, then barked by the old dog's head; but there was no response, and at last he lay down panting on the grass. His eyes were uneasy and watchful, the hairs still stood upright in a ridge on his back, and from time to time he whined in perplexity. He watched the cat drag a large gray bird almost up to the nose of the unconscious dog, then slowly and deliberately begin to tear at the bird's flesh. He growled softly, but the cat ignored him and continued his tearing and eating. Presently, the enticing smell of raw, warm meat filtered through into the old dog's senses. He opened one eye and gave an appreciative sniff. The effect was galvanizing: his muddied half-chewed tail stirred and he raised his shoulders, then his forelegs, with a convulsive effort, like an old work horse getting up after a fall.

He was a pitiful sight—the half of his body that had lain in the rut was black and soaking, while the other was streaked and stained with blood. He looked like some grotesque harlequin. He trembled violently and uncontrollably throughout the length of his body, but in the sunken depths of the slanted black-currant eyes there was a faint gleam of interest—which increased as he pushed his nose into the still-warm bundle of soft gray feathers. This time there was no growling rebuff over the prey: instead, the cat sat down a few yards away, studiedly aloof and indifferent, then painstakingly washed down the length of his tail. When the end twitched he pinned it down with a paw.

The old dog ate, crunching the bones ravenously with his blunt teeth. Even as his companions watched him, a miraculous strength slowly seeped back into his body. He dozed for a while, a feather hanging from his mouth, then woke again to finish the last morsel. By nightfall he was able to walk over to the soft grass at the side of the track, where he lay down and blinked happily at his companions, wagging his pitiful tail. The Labrador lay down beside him, and licked the wounded shoulder.

An hour or two later the purring cat joined them, carelessly dropping another succulent morsel by his old friend's nose. This was a deer mouse, a little creature with big eyes and long hind legs like a miniature kangaroo. It was swallowed with a satisfying gulp, and soon the old dog slept.

But the cat purring against his chest and the young dog curled at his back were wakeful and alert most of the remaining night; neither moved from his side.

## 4

Hunger was now the ruling instinct in the Labrador and it drove him out to forage in the early dawn. He was desperate enough to try some deer droppings, but spat them out immediately in disgust. While he was drinking from a marsh pool still covered with lily pads, he saw a frog staring at him with goggle eyes from a small stone: measuring the distance carefully, he sprang and caught it in the air as it leaped to safety. It disappeared down his throat in one crunch and he looked around happily for more. But an hour's patient search rewarded him with only two, so he returned to his companions. They had apparently eaten, for there were feathers and fur scattered around and both were licking their lips. But something warned him not to urge his old companion on. The terrier was still utterly exhausted, and in addition had lost a lot of blood from the gashes suffered at the cub's claws the day before. These were stiff and black with blood, and had a tendency to open and bleed slightly with any movement, so all that day he lay peacefully in the warm fall sunshine on the grass sleeping, eating what the cat provided, and wagging his tail whenever one of the others came near.

The young dog spent most of the day still occupied with his ceaseless foraging for food. By evening he was desperate, but his luck turned when a rabbit, already changing to its white winter coat, suddenly started up from the long grass and swerved across his path. Head down, tail flying, the young dog gave chase, swerving and turning in pursuit, but always the rabbit was just out of reach of his hungry jaws. At last, he put all his strength into one violent lunge and felt the warm, pulsating prize in his mouth. The generations fell away, and the years of training never to sink teeth into feathers or fur; for a moment the Labrador looked almost wolflike as he tore at the warm flesh and bolted it down in ravenous gulps.

They slept in the same place that night and most of the following day, and the weather mercifully continued warm and sunny. By the third day the old dog seemed almost recovered and the wounds were closed. He had spent most of the day ambling around and sleeping, so that by now he seemed almost frisky and quite eager to walk a little.

So, in the late afternoon, they left the place which had been their home for three days and trotted slowly along the track together again. By the time the moon rose they had traveled several miles, and they had come to the edge of a small lake which the track skirted.

A moose was standing in the water among the lily pads on the far shore, his great antlered head and humped neck silhouetted clearly against the pale moon. He took no notice of the strange animals across the water but thrust his head again and again under the water, raising it high in the air after each immersion, and arching his neck. Two or three water hens swam out from the reeds, a little crested grebe popped up like a jack-in-the-box, in the water beside them, and the spreading ripples of their wake caught the light of the moon. As the three sat, ears pricked, they watched the moose squelch slowly out of the muddy water, shake himself, and turn, cantering up the bank out of sight.

The young dog turned his head suddenly, his nose twitching, for his keen scent had caught a distant whiff of wood smoke, and of something else— something unidentifiable. . . . Seconds later, the old dog caught the scent too, and started to his feet, snuffing and questioning with his nose. His thin whippy tail began to sweep to and fro and a bright gleam appeared in the slanted black-currant eyes. Somewhere, not too far away, were human be- ings—his world: he could not mistake their message—or refuse their invita- tion—they were undoubtedly cooking something. He trotted off determinedly in the direction of the tantalizing smell. The young dog followed somewhat reluctantly, and for once the cat passed them both; a little moon-mad per- haps, for he lay in wait to dart and strike, then streaked back into the shad- ows, only to reappear a second later in an elaborate stalk of their tails. Both dogs ignored him.

The scent on the evening breeze was a fragrant compound of roasting rice, wild-duck stew and wood smoke. When the animals looked down from a hill, tantalized and hungry, they saw six or seven fires in the clearing below —their flames lighting up a semicircle of tents and conical birch-bark shel- ters against a dark background of trees; flickering over the canoes drawn up on the edge of a wild rice marsh and dying redly in the black waters beyond; and throwing into ruddy relief the high, flat planes of brown Ojibway faces gathered around the centers of warmth and brightness.

The men were a colorful lot in jeans and bright plaid shirts, but the women were dressed in somber colors. Two young boys, the only children there, were going from fire to fire shaking grain in shallow pans and stirring it with paddles as it parched. One man in long soft moccasins stood in a shallow pit trampling husks, half his weight supported on a log frame. Some of the band lay back from the fires, smoking and watching idly, talking softly among themselves; while others still ate, ladling the fragrant contents of a black iron pot onto tin plates. Every now and then one of them would throw a bone back over a shoulder into the bush, and the watching animals gazed hungrily after. A woman stood at the edge of the clearing pouring grain from one bark platter to another, and the loose chaff drifted off on the slight wind like smoke.

The old dog saw nothing of this, but his ears and nose supplied all that he needed to know: he could contain himself no longer and picked his way carefully down the hillside, for his shoulder still pained him. Halfway down he sneezed violently in an eddy of chaff. One of the boys by the fire looked up at the sound, his hand closing on a stone, but the woman nearby spoke sharply, and he waited, watching intently.

The old dog limped out of the shadows and into the ring of firelight, confident, friendly, and sure of his welcome; his tail wagging his whole stern ingratiatingly, ears and lips laid back in his nightmarish grimace. There was a stunned silence—broken by a wail of terror from the smaller boy, who flung himself at his mother—and then a quick excited chatter from the Indians. The old dog was rather offended and uncertain for a moment, but he made hopefully for the nearest boy, who retreated, nervously clutching his stone. But again the woman rebuked her son, and at the sharpness of her tone the old dog stopped, crestfallen. She laid down her basket then, and walked quickly across the ring of firelight, stooping down to look more closely. She spoke some soft words of reassurance, then patted his head gently and smiled at him. The old dog leaned against her and whipped his tail against her black stockings, happy to be in contact with a human being again. She crouched down beside him to run her fingers lightly over his ears and back, and when he licked her face appreciatively, she laughed. At this, the two little boys drew nearer to the dog and the rest of the band gathered around. Soon the old dog was where he most loved to be—the center of attention among some human beings. He made the most of it and played to an appreciative audience; when one of the men tossed him a chunk of meat he sat up painfully on his hindquarters and begged for more, waving one paw in the air. This sent the Indians into paroxysms of laughter, and he had to repeat his performance time and time again, until he was tired and lay down, panting but happy.

The Indian woman stroked him gently in reward, then ladled some of the meat from the pot onto the grass. The old dog limped towards it; but before he ate he looked up in the direction of the hillside where he had left his two companions.

A small stone rebounded from rock to rock, then rolled into the sudden silence that followed.

When a long-legged, blue-eyed cat appeared out of the darkness, paused, then filled the clearing with a strident plaintive voice before walking up to the dog and calmly taking a piece of meat from him, the Indians laughed until they were speechless and hiccupping. The two little boys rolled on the ground, kicking their heels in an abandonment of mirth, while the cat chewed his meat unmoved; but this was the kind of behavior the bull terrier understood, and he joined in the fun. But he rolled so enthusiastically that the wounds reopened: when he got to his feet again his white coat was stained with blood.

All this time the young dog crouched on the hillside, motionless and watchful, although every driving, urgent nerve in his body fretted and strained at the delay. He watched the cat, well-fed and content, curl himself on the lap of one of the sleepy children by the fire; he heard the faint note of derision in some of the Indians' voices as a little, bent, ancient crone addressed them in earnest and impassioned tones before hobbling over to the dog to examine his shoulder as he lay peacefully before the fire. She threw some cattail roots into a boiling pot of water, soaked some moss in the liquid, and pressed it against the dark gashes. The old dog did not move; only his tail beat slowly. When she had finished, she scooped some more meat onto a piece of birchbark and set it on the grass before the dog; and the silent watcher above licked his lips and sat up, but still he did not move from his place.

But when the fires began to burn low and the Indians made preparations for the night, and still his companions showed no signs of moving, the young dog grew restless. He skirted the camp, moving like a shadow through the trees on the hill behind, until he came out upon the lake's shore a quarter of a mile upwind of the camp. Then he barked sharply and imperatively several times.

The effect was like an alarm bell on the other two. The cat sprang from the arms of the sleepy little Indian boy and ran towards the old dog, who was already on his feet, blinking and peering around rather confusedly. The cat gave a guttural yowl, then deliberately ran ahead, looking back as he paused beyond the range of firelight. The old dog shook himself resignedly and walked slowly after—reluctant to leave the warmth of the fire. The Indians watched impassively and silently and made no move to stop him. Only the woman who had first befriended him called out softly, in the tongue of her people, a farewell to the traveler.

The dog halted at the treeline beside the cat and looked back, but the commanding, summoning bark was heard again, and together the two passed out of sight and into the blackness of the night.

That night they became immortal, had they known or cared, for the ancient woman had recognized the old dog at once by his color and companion: he was the White Dog of the Ojibways, the virtuous White Dog of Omen, whose appearance heralds either disaster or good fortune. The Spirits had sent him, hungry and wounded, to test tribal hospitality; and for benevolent proof to the skeptical they had chosen a cat as his companion—for what *mortal* dog would suffer a cat to rob him of his meat? He had been made welcome, fed and succored: the omen would prove fortunate.

## 5

The trio journeyed on, the pattern of the next few days being very much the same, free of incident or excitement. Leaving their resting place at daylight, they would jog steadily along by day, their pace determined mainly by the endurance of the old dog. Their favorite sleeping places were hollows under uprooted trees where they were sheltered from the wind, and able to burrow down among the drifted leaves for warmth. At first there were frequent halts and rests, but daily the terrier became stronger; after a week he was lean, but the scars on his shoulders were healing, and his coat was smooth and healthy; in fact, he was in better condition and looked younger and fitter than at the outset of the journey. He had always had a happy disposition, and most of the time looked perfectly content, trotting along through the vast stillness of the bush with stolid, unalterable good humor. He was almost always hungry, but that skillful hunter the cat kept him provided with food which, while scarcely ever satisfying, was adequate by his new standard of living.

It was only the famished young dog who really suffered, for he was not a natural hunter, and wasted a lot of ill-afforded energy in pursuit. He lived mainly on frogs, mice, and the occasional leavings of the other two; sometimes he was lucky enough to frighten some small animal away from its prey, but it was a very inadequate diet for such a large and heavily built dog, and his ribs were beginning to show through the shining coat. He was unable to relax, his constant hunger driving him to forage even when the other two were resting; and he never joined in their amiable foolery, when sometimes the cat would skitter away in pretended fear from the growling, wagging white dog, often ending in being chased up a tree. Then the Labrador would sit apart, aloof and watchful, nervous and tense. It seemed as though he were never able to forget his ultimate purpose and goal—he was going home; home to his own master, home where he belonged, and nothing else mattered. This lodestone of longing, this certainty, drew him to lead his companions ever westward through wild and unknown country, as unerringly as a carrier pigeon released from an alien loft.

Nomadic life seemed to agree with the cat. He was in fine fettle, sleek and well groomed and as debonair as ever, and had adapted himself so well that at times it appeared as though he were positively enjoying the whole expedition. Sometimes he left the other two for an hour or so at a time, but they had ceased to pay any attention to his absence now, as sooner or later he always reappeared.

They traveled mostly on old abandoned trails, astonishingly plentiful in this virtually uninhabited region; occasionally they cut straight through the bush. It was fortunate that the Indian summer weather still continued, for the short thin coat of the bull terrier could not withstand low temperatures, and although a thicker undercoat was already growing in to compensate, it would never be adequate. The cat's coat, too, was thickening, making him appear heavier; the Labrador's needed no reinforcement and was already adapted to all extremes, the flat, thick hairs so close together that they made an almost waterproof surface. The short days were warm and pleasant when the sun was high, but the nights were cold: one night, when there was a sudden, sharp frost, the old dog shivered so much that they left the shallow cave of their resting place soon after a bright-ringed moon rose and traveled through the remainder of the night, resting most of the following morning in the warmth of the sun.

The leaves were losing their color rapidly, and many of the trees were nearly bare, but the dogwood and pigeonberry by the sides of the trail still blazed with color, and the Michaelmas daisies and fireweed flourished. Many of the birds of the forest had already migrated; those that were left gathered into great flocks, filling the air with their restless chatter as they milled around, the long drawn-out streamers suddenly wheeling to form a clamorous cloud, lifting and falling in indecision. They saw few other animals: the noisy progress of the dogs warned the shy natural inhabitants long before their approach; and those that they did meet were too busy and concerned with their winter preparations to show much curiosity. The only other bear that they had encountered was sleek and fat as butter, complacent and sleepy, his thoughts obviously already running on hibernation, and quite uninterested in strange animals. He was, in fact, sitting on a log in the sun when the animals saw him; after giving them a sleepy inspection from his little, deep-set eyes he yawned and continued the lazy scratching of his ear. The cat, however, growled angrily to himself for nearly an hour after this encounter.

The rabbits and weasels had changed to their white winter coats; a few snow buntings had appeared, and several times they had heard the wild, free, exultant calling of the wild geese, and had looked up to see the long black V-shaped skeins passing overhead on the long journey southwards. The visitors to the northlands were leaving, and those who remained were preparing themselves for the long winter that lay ahead. Soon the whole tempo, the very pulse of the North, would beat slower and slower until the snow fell like a soft coverlet; then, snug and warm beneath in dens and burrows and hollows, the hibernating animals would sleep, scarcely breathing in their deep unconsciousness, until the spring.

As though aware of these preparations and their meaning, the three adventurers increased their pace as much as was possible within the limits determined by the old dog's strength. On good days they covered as much as fifteen miles.

Since they had left the Indian encampment on the shores of the rice lake they had not seen any human beings, or any sign of human habitation, save once at nightfall when they were nosing around a garbage can outside the darkened cookhouse of a lumber camp deep in the very heart of the bush. Marauding bears had been there recently—their rank, heavy smell still hung on the air, and the cat refused to come nearer, but the old dog, watched by the other, tipped over the heavy can, then tried to pry off the lid with a practiced nose. The can rattled and banged loudly on some rocks and neither dog heard the door opening in the dark building behind. Suddenly a blast of shot ripped through the bottom of the can, blowing the lid off and strewing the contents all over the old dog. Deafened and stunned, he stood for a moment, shaking his head; a second shot clanged against metal and brought him to his senses—he grabbed a bone in passing from the plenty strewn all around, and dashed after the Labrador, running so fast that he outdistanced him. A spray of pellets followed, stinging into their hindquarters so that they leaped simultaneously and redoubled their speed. Soon they were in the shelter of the bush, but it was a long time before they halted for the night. The old dog was so exhausted that he slept until dawn. The pellets had been only momentarily painful, but the incident increased the young dog's wary nervousness.

However, a few days later, despite his care, they had another unexpected encounter. They were drinking at midday from a shallow ford crossing an overgrown track to a worked-out silver mine when a cottontail started up in the bracken across the water. The young dog sprang after, drenching the other two, and they watched the chase—the rabbit's head up, the dog's down, linked in a swerving, leaping rhythm of almost balletlike precision —until it disappeared among the trees.

The terrier shook his coat, spraying the cat again; furious, the cat stalked off.

Alone now, with a brief moment of freedom from the constant daytime urging, the old dog made the most of it. He pottered happily around the lichened rocks and mossy banks, savoring everything with his delicate connoisseur's nose; he flicked the caps of several large fawn mushrooms in some displeasure; a shiny black beetle received his keen attention for a while and he followed it like a bloodhound. Presently he lost interest and sat on it. He yawned, scratched his ear, then rolled lazily on a patch of dried mud. Suddenly he lay quite still, his paws dangling limply, his head turned back on the ground towards the trail: he freed a crumpled ear to listen more intently, then his tail registered his pleased anticipation—someone was walking through the bush towards him. He scrambled to his feet and peered shortsightedly down the trail, his tail curving his hindquarters from side to side in welcome. When an old man carrying a canvas bag appeared, talking quietly to himself, the bull terrier stepped out and awaited him. The old man did not pause: small and bent, he hobbled quickly past, lifting an ancient green felt hat from a crown of white hair as he went, and nodding to the dog with a brief smile of great sweetness. Two little gray-and-white chickadees preceded him, flitting from branch to branch over his head. The old dog fell in contentedly behind. Soon the cat appeared in the distance, running to catch up, his eyes on the chickadees; and far behind the cat again, his mouth framed around the dangling carcass of a rabbit, came the triumphant but deeply suspicious Labrador.

The straggling procession continued along the cool, green tunnel of the trail for half a mile, until the trees thinned out and they came upon a small cabin set back in a clearing within sight of the derelict mine workings. They passed, one after the other, through a small, neatly raked garden, between brown raspberry canes and leafless apple trees, and walked slowly up the few steps to the porch. Here the old man set his bag down, knocked on the green door, paused, then opened it, standing courteously aside to motion his following in before him. The old dog walked in, the cat closely by his shoulder, then the man. The young dog hesitated by the trail's side, his eyes round and distrustful above his burden, then, apparently reassured by the open door, he carefully laid the rabbit down behind a bush, scratching a layer of leaves over it, and, this done, followed the others. They stood in an expectant ring in the middle of the cabin, savoring a delicious, meaty smell.

They watched the old man brush the brim of his hat, hang it on a peg, then hobble over to a small, gleaming wood stove and thrust in another log, washing his hands afterwards in a basin filled from a dipper of water. He lifted the lid off a pot simmering on the stove, and the three watchers licked their lips in anticipation. As he took down four gold-rimmed plates from a dresser, a chipmunk appeared from behind a blue jug on the top shelf. Chattering excitedly he ran up the man's arm to his shoulder, where he sat and scolded the strangers with bright jealous eyes, his little striped body twitching with fury. Two gleaming lamps appeared in the darkness of the cat's face and his tail swished in response, but he restrained himself in deference to his surroundings.

The old man chided the chipmunk lovingly as he set four places at the table, handing it a crust which bulged its cheeks, then ladling four very small portions of stew onto the plates. The little animal's noise fell away to an occasional disgruntled squeak, but he ran from shoulder to shoulder to keep watch on the cat. The old dog edged nearer. Looking very small behind a high-backed chair, the old man stood for a moment with his clear, childlike blue eyes closed and his lips moving, then drew out his chair and sat down. He looked around the table, suddenly irresolute; then his brow cleared, and he rose to draw up the two remaining chairs and a bench. "Do sit down," he said, and at the familiar command the three animals behind him sat obediently.

He ate slowly and fastidiously. Two pairs of hypnotized eyes followed every movement of the fork to his mouth; the third pair remained fixed on the chipmunk. Presently the plate was empty, and the old man smiled around the table; but his smile turned again to bewilderment as he saw the three untouched plates. He considered them long and thoughtfully, then shrugged his shoulders and moved on to the next place. Soon that too came to its confusing end, and, sighing, he moved again. Spellbound, his visitors remained rooted to the floor. Even the old dog, for once, was nonplussed: although he shivered in anticipation and saliva ran from his mouth at the enticing smell, he remained sitting as custom and training decreed.

The old man sat on when the last plate was emptied, lost in his own world, his peaceful stillness diffusing through the little cabin so that the watchers sat graven in their places. A little wind stirred outside, swinging the door wide open on creaking hinges. A grosbeak flew in, to perch on the top, the mellow fall sunshine slanting on his brilliant plumage, and it seemed as though the living silence of the great forest around surged up and in through the open door with the bird's coming, so that the animals stirred uneasily, glancing behind them.

The chipmunk's shrill voice cut through the silence, and its claws scrabbled up the dresser as the cat half sprang—but recollected himself in time and slipped out of the door after the grosbeak instead. In a sudden awakening the old man had started to his feet; he looked around as though wondering where he was, his eyes lighting in surprise on the two dogs by the door. Slow recognition dawned on his face and he smiled down affectionately though his gaze looked through and beyond them. "You must come more often," he said; and to the old dog, who stood wagging his tail at the gentle warmth in the voice, "Remember me most kindly to your dear mother!"

He escorted the dogs to the door; they filed past him, their tails low and still, then walked slowly and with great dignity down the little winding path between the raspberry canes and the apple trees to the overgrown track. Here they waited for a moment while the young dog furtively uncovered his prize, and the cat joined them; then, without looking back, they trotted in close formation out of sight between the trees.

A quarter of a mile farther on the young dog looked carefully around before dropping his rabbit. He nudged it with his nose several times, then turned it over. A moment later its red-stained fur lay scattered and both dogs were eating ravenously, growling amicably as they crunched. The cat sat, flexing his claws as he watched. After a while he rose on his hind legs and stretched his forepaws to their full extent against a tree, then methodically sharpened their claws on the bark. His head turned sharply and he paused, still standing, at a rustle in the long dead grass: a split second later he pounced in a bounding arc; a paw flashed out, pinned down and held, his head bent down; and a small squeaking broke off abruptly. Before the dogs were even aware that he had gone he was back again by his tree, cleaning his whiskers with soft rounded paws.

The following day the travelers came down from the hills to find themselves on the banks of a river running north and south. It was about a hundred feet across to the far bank, and although shallow enough in the ordinary way, was far too deep for the animals to cross without swimming. The young dog led the way downstream for some distance looking for a means of crossing, as it was obvious that his companions would not even wet their feet if they could possibly help it, both sharing a great dislike of water. Once or twice he plunged in and swam around, looking back at the other two, obviously trying to entice them by showing them how easy it was, but they remained sitting close together on the bank, united in misery, and he was forced to continue trotting downstream, becoming increasingly worried as he went, aware that it was the wrong direction.

It was lonely, uninhabited country, so that there were no bridges, and the river if anything became wider as they trotted along the banks. After three or four miles the young dog could endure the frustration no longer; he plunged into the water and swam rapidly and strongly across to the far side, his tail streaming out behind like an otter's. He loved the water, and was as much at home in it as the other two hated and feared it. He stood on the far bank, barking encouragingly, but the old dog whined in such distress, the cat yowling in chorus, that he swam across again, paddling around in the shallows near the bank. The old dog walked gingerly into the shallow water, shivering and miserable, turning his head away. Once more the Labrador swam the river, climbed out on the far side, shook himself, and barked. There was no mistaking the command. The old dog took another reluctant step forward, whining piteously, his expressive tail tucked under. The barking continued; again the terrier advanced; again the Labrador swam across to encourage him. Three times he swam across, and the third time the old dog waded in up to his chest and started swimming. He was not a very good swimmer; he swam in jerky rapid movements, his head held high out of the water, his little black eyes rolling fearfully; but he was a bull terrier, a "white cavalier," and he kept on, following the wake of the other, until at last he climbed out on the far side. His transports of joy on reaching dry land were like those of a shipwrecked mariner after six weeks at sea on a raft: he rushed in circles, he rolled on his back, he ran along with alternate shoulders low in the long grass to dry himself, until finally he joined the Labrador on the bank to bark encouragingly at the cat.

The poor cat now showed the first signs of fear since leaving on his journey; he was alone, and the only way to rejoin his friends lay in swimming across the terrible stretch of water. He ran up and down the bank, all the time keeping up his unearthly Siamese wailing. The young dog went through the same tiring performance that he had used before, swimming to and fro, trying to entice him into the water; but the cat was beside himself with terror and it was a long long time before he finally made up his mind. When he did it was with a sudden blind desperate rush at the water, completely un-catlike. His expression of horror and distaste was almost comical as he started swimming towards the young dog who waited for him a few yards out. He proved to be a surprisingly good swimmer, and was making steady progress across, the dog swimming alongside, when tragedy struck.

Many years before a colony of beavers had dammed a small creek which had tumbled into the river about two miles upstream. Since the beavers had left, the dam had been crumbling and loosening gradually, until it had become just a question of time before it would give way altogether, and drain the flooded land behind. Now, by a twist of fate, a rotting log gave way and a large section bulged forward under the added strain. Almost as the two animals reached midstream the dam broke altogether. The pent-up force of the unleashed creek leaped through the gap in an ever-widening torrent, carrying everything before it and surging into the river, where it became a swift mountainous wave—carrying small trees, torn-away branches, pieces of riverbank and beaver dam before it on the crest. The young dog saw the onrushing wave several moments before it reached them, and frantically tried to swim into a position upstream of the cat, instinctively trying to protect him; but he was too late, and the great curling, crested wave surged over, submerging them in a whirling chaos of debris. The end of a log struck the cat full on the head; he was swept under and over and over until his body was finally caught on a half-submerged piece of the old dam, and was carried along on the impetus of the wave as it tore down the river bed.

The old dog, barking wildly in anxiety—for he had sensed the disaster although he could not see it—waded chest-deep into the churning water, but its force knocked him back again, breathless and choking; he was forced to retreat.

The other dog, strong swimmer though he was, made his way to the bank only with the greatest difficulty. Even then he was carried almost half a mile downstream before his feet were on firm ground. Immediately he set off, down the riverside, in pursuit.

Several times he saw the little figure of the cat, half under water, surging ahead on the swift white crest; but he was never near enough, except at one point where the partially submerged piece of beaver dam caught on an overhanging branch. He plunged in immediately; but just as he was nearly within reach it tore free and once more went whirling down the river until it was lost to sight.

Gradually the dog fell farther and farther behind. At last he was brought to a complete halt when the river entered a rocky gorge with no foothold on either side. He was forced to climb inland, and by the time he rejoined the river on the far side of the gorge there was no sign of the cat.

It was nearly dark when he returned to find the terrier, who was walking wearily towards him along the riverbank; the Labrador was exhausted, limping, and utterly spent and miserable—so much so that he barely returned the greeting of the bewildered and lonely old dog but dropped to the ground, his flanks heaving, and lay there until thirst drove him to the water's edge.

They spent that night where they were, by the bank of the river, peaceful at last after the violence of the afternoon. They lay curled closely together for comfort and warmth, and when a thin, cold rain fell as the wind rose they moved under the spreading branches of an old spruce for shelter.

In the middle of the night the old dog sat up, trembling all over with cold. He threw his head back and howled his requiem of grief and loneliness to the heavy, weeping sky; until at last the young dog rose wearily and led him away from the river, long before dawn broke, and over the hills to the west.

## 6

Many miles downstream on the side to which the dogs had crossed, a small cabin stood near the bank of the river, surrounded by three or four acres of cleared land, its solid, uncompromising appearance lightened only by the scarlet geraniums at the window sills and a bright blue door. A log barn stood back from it, and a steam-bath house at the side nearer the river. The patch of vegetable garden, the young orchard and the neatly fenced fields, each with their piles of cleared boulders and stumps, were small orderly miracles of victory won from the dark encroaching forest that surrounded them.

Reino Nurmi and his wife lived here, as sturdy and uncompromising as the cabin they had built with their own hand-hewn logs, their lives as frugal and orderly as the fields they had wrested from the wilderness. They had tamed the bush, and in return it yielded them their food and their scant living from trap lines and a wood lot, but the struggle to keep it in subjection was endless. They had retained their Finnish identity complete when they left their homeland, exchanging only one country's set of solitudes and vast lonely forests for another's, and as yet their only real contact with the new world that lay beyond their property line was through their ten-year-old daughter Helvi, who knew no other homeland. Helvi walked the lonely miles to the waiting school bus each day, and through her they strengthened their roots in the security of the New World, and were content meanwhile with horizons limited by their labor.

On the Sunday afternoon that the beaver dam broke, a day of some relaxation, Helvi was down by the river, skipping flat stones across the water, and wishing that she had a companion; for she found it difficult to be entirely fair in a competition always held against herself. The riverbank was steep and high here, so she was quite safe when a rushing torrent of water, heralded by a great curling wave, swept past. She stood watching it, fascinated by the spectacle, thinking that she must go and tell her father, when her eye was caught by a piece of debris that had been whirling around in a back eddy and was now caught on some boulders at the edge of the bank. She could see what looked like a small, limp body on the surface. She ran along by the boiling water to investigate, scrambling down the bank, to stand looking pityingly at the wet, bedraggled body, wondering what it was, for she had never seen anything like it before. She dragged the mass of twigs and branches further up on land, then ran to call her mother.

Mrs. Nurmi was out in the yard by an old wood stove which she still used for boiling the vegetable dyes for her weaving, or peelings and scraps for the hens. She followed Helvi, calling out to her husband to come and see this strange animal washed up by an unfamiliar, swift-surging river.

He came, with his unhurried countryman's walk and quiet thoughtful face, and joined the others to look down in silence at the small limp body, the darkly plastered fur betraying its slightness, the frail skull bones and thin crooked tail mercilessly exposed. Suddenly he bent down and laid his hand lightly on it for a moment, then pulled back the skin above and below one eye and looked more closely. He turned and saw Helvi's anxious, questioning face close to his own, and beyond that her mother's. "Is a drowned *cat* worth trying to save?" he asked them, and when her mother nodded, before Helvi's pleading eyes, he said no more, but scooped the soaking bundle up and walked back to the cabin, telling Helvi to run ahead and bring some dry sacks.

He laid the cat down in a sunny patch by the wood stove and rubbed it vigorously with sacking, turning the body from side to side until the fur stood out in every direction and it looked like some disheveled old scarf. Then, as he wrapped the sacking firmly around and her mother pried the clenched teeth open, Helvi poured a little warm milk and precious brandy down the pale cold throat.

She watched as a spasm ran through the body, followed by a faint cough, then held her breath in sympathy as the cat retched and choked convulsively, a thin dribble of milk appearing at the side of its mouth. Reino laid the straining body over his knee and pressed gently over the ribcage. The cat choked and struggled for breath, until at last a sudden gush of water streamed out, and it lay relaxed. Reino gave a slow smile of satisfaction and handed the bundle of sacking to Helvi, telling her to keep it warm and quiet for a while—if she was sure that she still wanted a cat.

She felt the oven, still warm though the fire had long died out, then placed the cat on a tray inside, leaving the door open. When her mother went into the cabin to prepare supper and Reino left to milk the cow, Helvi sat cross-legged on the ground by the stove, anxiously chewing the end of one fair braid, watching and waiting. Every now and then she would put her hand into the oven to touch the cat, to loosen the sacking or to stroke the soft fur, which was beginning to pulsate with life under her fingers.

After half an hour she was rewarded: the cat opened his eyes. She leaned over and looked closely into them—their blackness now contracted, slowly, to pinpoints, and a pair of astonishingly vivid blue eyes looked up instead. Presently, under her gentle stroking, she felt a throaty vibration, then heard a rusty, feeble purring. Wildly excited, she called to her parents.

Within another half-hour the little Finnish girl held in her lap a sleek, purring, Siamese cat, who had already finished two saucers of milk (which normally he detested, drinking only water), and who had groomed himself from head to foot. By the time the Nurmi family were eating their supper around the scrubbed pine table, he had finished a bowl of chopped meat, and was weaving his way around the table legs, begging in his plaintive, odd voice for more food, his eyes crossed intently, his kinked tail held straight in the air like a banner. Helvi was fascinated by him, and by his gentleness when she picked him up.

That night the Nurmis were having fresh pickerel, cooked in the old-country way with the head still on and surrounded by potatoes. Helvi ladled the head with some broth and potatoes into a saucer and put it on the floor. Soon the fishhead had disappeared to the accompaniment of pleased rumbling growls. The potatoes followed; then, holding down the plate with his paw, the cat polished it clean. Satisfied at last, he stretched superbly, his front paws extended so that he looked like a heraldic lion, then jumped onto Helvi's lap, curled himself around and purred loudly.

The parents' acceptance was completed by his action, though there had never before been a time or place in the economy of their lives for an animal which did not earn its keep, or lived anywhere else except the barn or kennel. For the first time in her life Helvi had a pet.

Helvi carried the cat up to bed with her, and he draped himself with familiar ease over her shoulder as she climbed the steep ladder stairs leading up to her little room in the eaves. She tucked him tenderly into an old wooden cradle, and he lay in sleepy contentment, his dark face incongruous against a doll's pillow.

Late in the night she woke to a loud purring in her ear, and felt him treading a circle at her back. The wind blew a gust of cold rain across her face and she leaned over to shut the window, hearing far away, so faint that it died in the second of wind-borne sound, the thin, high keening of a wolf. She shivered as she lay down, then drew the new comforting warmth of the cat closely to her.

When Helvi left in the morning for the long walk and ride to the distant school the cat lay curled on the window sill among the geraniums. He had eaten a large plate of oatmeal, and his coat shone in the sun as he licked it sleepily, his eyes following Mrs. Nurmi as she moved about the cabin. But when she went outside with a basket of washing she looked back to see him standing on his hind legs peering after, his soundless mouth opening and shutting behind the window. She hurried back, fearful of her geraniums, and opened the door—at which he was already scratching—half expecting him to run. Instead he followed her to the washing line and sat by the basket, purring. He followed her back and forth between the cabin and the wood stove, the henhouse and the stable. When she shut him out once by mistake he wailed pitifully.

This was the pattern of his behavior all day—he shadowed the Nurmis as they went about their chores, appearing silently on some point of vantage —the seat of the harrow, a sack of potatoes, the manger or the well platform —his eyes on them constantly. Mrs. Nurmi was touched by his apparent need for companionship: that his behavior was unlike that of any other cat she attributed to his foreign appearance. But her husband was not so easily deceived—he had noticed the unusual intensity in the blue eyes. When a passing raven mocked the cat's voice and he did not look up, then later sat unheeding in the stable to a quick rustle in the straw behind, Reino knew then that the cat was deaf.

Carrying her schoolbooks and lunch pail, Helvi ran most of the way home across the fields and picked up the cat as well when he came to meet her.

He clung to her shoulder, balancing easily, while she performed the routine evening chores that awaited her. Undeterred by his weight she fed the hens, gathered eggs, fetched water, then sat at the table stringing dried mushrooms. When she put him down before supper she saw that her father was right—the pointed ears did not respond to any sound, though she noticed that he started and turned his head at the vibration if she clapped her hands or dropped even a small pebble on the bare floor.

She had brought home two books from the traveling library, and after the supper dishes had been cleared away her parents sat by the stove in the short interval before bed while she read aloud to them, translating as she went. They sat, in their moment of rare relaxation, with the cat stretched out on his back at their feet, and the child's soft voice, flowing through the dark austerity of the cabin, carried them beyond the circle of light from the oil lamp to the warmth and brightness of strange lands. . . .

They heard of seafaring Siamese cats who worked their passages the world over, their small hammocks made and slung by their human messmates, who held them second to none as ship's cats; and of the great proud Siamese Ratting Corps who patrolled the dockyards of Le Havre with unceasing vigilance; they saw, with eyes withdrawn and dreaming, the palace watch-cats of long-ago Siam, walking delicately on long simian legs around the fountained courtyards, their softly padding feet polishing the mosaics to a lustered path of centuries. And at last they learned how these nobly born Siamese acquired the kink at the end of their tails and bequeathed it to all their descendants.

And as they listened, they looked down in wonder, for there on the rag rug lay one of these, stretched out flat on his royal back, his illustrious tail twitching idly, and his jeweled eyes on their daughter's hand as she turned the pages that spoke of his ancestors—the guardian cats of the Siamese princesses. Each princess, when she came down to bathe in the palace lake, would slip her rings for safekeeping on the tail of her attendant cat. So zealous in their charge were these proud cats that they bent the last joint sideways for safer custody, and in time the faithful tails became crooked forever, and their children's and their children's children. . . .

One after another the Nurmis passed their hands admiringly down the tail before them to feel the truth in its bent bony tip; then Helvi gave him a bowl of milk, which he drank with regal condescension before she carried him up the ladder to bed.

That night, and for one more, the cat lay curled peacefully in Helvi's arms, and in the daytime during her absence he followed her parents everywhere. He trailed through the bush after her mother as she searched for late mushrooms, then sat on the cabin steps and patted the dropped corn kernels as she shucked a stack of cobs. He followed Reino and his work horse across the fields to the wood lot and perched on a newly felled pungent stump, his head following their every movement, and he curled by the door of the stable and watched the man mending harness and oiling traps. And in the late afternoons when Helvi returned he was there waiting for her, a rare and beautiful enigma in the certain routine of the day. He was one of them.

But on the fourth night he was restless, shaking his head and pawing his ears, his voice distressed at her back. At last he lay down, purring loudly, and pushed his head into her hand—the fur below his ears was soaking. She saw their sharp black triangles outlined against the little square of window and watched them flicker and quiver in response to every small night sound. Glad for him in his newfound hearing, she fell asleep.

When she woke, later in the night, aware of a lost warmth, she saw him crouched at the open window, looking out over the pale fields and the tall, dark trees below. His long sinuous tail thrashed to and fro as he measured the distance to the ground. Even as her hand moved out impulsively towards him he sprang, landing with a soft thud.

She looked down and saw his head turn for the first time to her voice, his eyes like glowing rubies as they caught the moonlight, then turn away—and with sudden desolate knowledge she knew that he had no further need of her. Through a blur of tears, she watched him go, stealing like a wraith in the night towards the river that had brought him. Soon the low swiftly running form was lost among the shadows.

## 7

The two dogs were in very low spirits when they continued their journey without the cat. The old dog in particular moped badly, for the cat had been his constant close companion for many years—ever since the day when a small, furiously hissing kitten, with comically long black-stockinged legs and a nearly white body, had joined the Hunter family. This apparition had refused to give one inch of ground to the furious and jealous bull terrier, who was an avowed cat hater, and the terror of the nearby feline population; instead it had advanced, with every intention of giving battle evident in the tiny body. The dog, for the first and last time in his life, capitulated. That day a bond had been formed between them, and thereafter they had been inseparable. The kitten, surprisingly enough, had no love for cats either, so they formed a wickedly humorous partnership that waged unceasing war against them. When they sallied forth together the neighborhood emptied suddenly of not only cats but of dogs as well. They had mellowed with the years, however, and were now more tolerant, exacting only the dutiful homage they felt to be their due as conquerors. They had opened their ranks only to the gentle young dog when he arrived years later; but, fond as they were of him, the affection they bore for one another was something quite apart.

Now the dogs were thrown completely on their own resources. The Labrador did his best and tried to initiate the other into the art of frog and field mouse hunting, but the terrier's eyesight was too poor for him to have much success. But they were luckier than usual: once they surprised a large fisher in the very act of dispatching a porcupine. The shy fisher disappeared in one swift fluid movement at their approach, leaving the slain, outstretched porcupine, and the dogs enjoyed a feast that day such as they had never known before, the flesh being sweet and tender.

Another time the young dog caught a bittern, who had stood like a frozen statue on the edge of a lake, his long neck topped by the slim head flowing into a line down to the elongated body, and nothing moving but an apprehensive, blinking eye. He took off as the dog sprang, but his awkward clumsy flight, the long legs trailing, was not fast enough. The flesh was stringy and fishy, but it was all gobbled down voraciously, nothing remaining but the beak and feet.

One day they skirted a small farm, where, wary though he was of human beings, the young dog was hungry enough to cross an open field within sight of the farm and snatch one of a flock of chickens feeding there. They were still crouched over the mess of blood and scattered feathers, when they heard an angry shout, and saw the figure of a man at the far corner of the field, and a black collie running ahead, snarling as it came towards them.

The young dog braced himself for the inevitable attack; a few yards away the collie crouched low, lips drawn back, then sprang for the vulnerable throat before him. The young dog was a hopeless fighter, lacking both the instinct and the build; for, heavy and strong though he was, his mouth had been bred to carry game birds, and the jaw structure, with its soft protective lips, was a disadvantage. His only hope for survival against the razorlike slashing of the other dog's teeth lay in the thick protective folds of skin around his throat.

All too soon it was obvious that he was fast losing ground, and the effects of his inadequate diet were beginning to show in his endurance. He was on his back with the collie on top, ready to give the final slash, when the old dog took over. Up to now he had merely been an interested spectator, taking a keen interest from a professional point of view, for a good fight is meat and drink to a bull terrier. Now a look of pure, unholy joy appeared in the black-currant eyes, and he tensed his stocky, close-knit body, timing his spring with a mastery born of long practice. A white, compact bundle of fighting art shot like a steel projectile to the collie's throat. The impact knocked the black dog over as though he were a feather; the ecstatic bull terrier tightened his grip on the sinewy throat under him and began to shake his head; out of the corner of his eye he noticed that the Labrador was on his feet again. But the terrier's teeth were blunt nowadays, and with a tremendous effort the collie threw him off. The old dog's feet had barely touched the ground before he sprang again for that terrible throat grip, springing as if the years had dropped away and he were back in his fighting prime. Once more he brought the collie down, this time taking a firmer grip on the throat, shaking his powerful head until the dog below him was choking and strangling. The collie made a desperate, convulsive effort and rolled over, the silent white leech still hanging from his throat. He struggled to his feet: the terrier released his hold and walked away, his back turned arrogantly but his eyes slewed slyly in his flat head so that he looked almost reptilian. The collie stood shakily, blood dripping from his throat, awaiting the protection of his master. Normally he was a courageous dog, but he had never before encountered anything like these vicious, silent onslaughts.

The Labrador would have called it a day and left now, but the terrier was enjoying himself and still eyed the collie speculatively. Then his peculiar blend of bull terrier humor got the better of him, and he used an old fighting trick of his breed, which normally he kept, so to speak, up his sleeve, for those occasions when he intended not a killing, but merely punishment. He started to circle, faster and faster, almost as though he were chasing his own tail, and then, like a whirling dervish, he approached the bewildered collie and spun against him, knocking him several feet with the force of the impact, and following up his advantage with another crash at the end of each turn. Terrified at this unprecedented method of attack, bruised, bitter and aching, the enemy dog seized a split second between turns and fled, his tail tucked well between his legs, towards his master—who received him with a cuff on his already reeling head.

The farmer stared incredulously at the two culprits, who were now making off across the field to the cover of the bush, the young dog with a torn and bloodied ear, and several deep bites on his forelegs, but the happy old warrior jaunty and unscathed. When he saw the mass of feathers he flung his stick in sudden rage at the retreating white form, but so many sticks had been thrown after so many fights in the course of his long life that the bull terrier dodged it instinctively without even turning his head and continued at a leisurely trot, swinging his rounded stern with gay insolence as he went.

This battle did much to restore the morale of the old dog. That evening he even caught a field mouse for his supper, tossing it in the air with a professional flip which would have done credit to his ancestor who had killed sixty rats in as many minutes a hundred years ago.

Despite the stiffness and soreness from his wounds the young dog seemed happier too; perhaps because the west wind that blew that night brought a hint of remembered things, and stirred some deep awareness that every day, every hour brought them nearer to their destination; perhaps it was that the country they were crossing now was less rugged, less remote, and becoming more like the country in which he had been raised; perhaps it was just because his companion was so infectiously pleased with himself; but whatever it was, he seemed more at ease and less strained than he had been since the outset of the journey.

They slept that night in a dry shallow cave amongst the outcroppings of an abandoned molybdenum mine on the crest of a hill. Outside the cave was a large, sloping slab of exposed rock littered with discarded garter-snake skins, so light and dry yet supple that all night long they swayed and whispered to every small breath of wind as though repossessed.

The first pale streaks of dawn were barely showing across the sky when the young dog sat up alertly, hearing the shuffling approach of some animal through the dead leaves and twigs. He sat quivering, every nerve tense, recognizing the smell, and presently past the opening of the cave waddled a large porcupine, returning peacefully home from a night's foraging. Remembering the delectable meal the fisher had inadvertently provided for him, the young dog determined to repeat it. He sprang at the porcupine, intending first to overturn then kill it as he had seen the other animal do, but unfortunately he had not seen the patient preparatory work that the experienced fisher had put in before the kill—the relentless, cunning teasing, resulting in the harmless embedding of most of the quills into a fallen tree; then the quick, skillful flip at the base of the shoulder while the partially unarmed animal was still protecting its tender nose and throat under the tree. The porcupine turned at the instant of his spring, aware of the danger, and with incredible swiftness for such a clumsy-looking animal, spun round, whipping its terrible tail in the dog's face. The dog yelped and leaped back with the unexpected shock of pain, and the porcupine ambled away, looking almost outraged.

The Labrador was fortunate in that the tail had struck a sidewise, glancing blow, so that the quills had pierced only one side of his cheek, missing the eye by a fraction; but these quills were about two-and-a-half inches long, barbed at the piercing end, and were firmly and painfully embedded.

Try as he might the dog could do nothing to remove the pliant quills; he only succeeded in pushing them farther in. He tore at them with his paws; he scratched at the sites until they bled; he rubbed his head and cheek along the ground and against the trunk of a tree. But the cruel, stinging barbs dug in farther, and their stinging torture spread through his face and jaws. Eventually he abandoned the attempt to free them, and they journeyed on. But every time they paused the Labrador would shake his head, or scratch frantically with his hind leg, seeking release from the pain.

8

The cat by himself was a swift and efficient traveler. He had no difficulty at all in picking up the trail of the dogs from the point where they had turned off in a westward direction from the river, and the only thing that held him back was rain, which he detested. He would huddle miserably under shelter during a shower, his ears laid flat, his eyes baleful and more crossed than ever, waiting until the last drop had fallen before venturing out again. Then he would pick his way with extreme distaste through the wet grass and undergrowth, taking a long time, and stopping often to shake his paws.

He left no trace of his progress; branches parted slightly here and there, sometimes there was a momentary rustling of dried leaves, but never a twig cracked, and not a stone was dislodged from under his soft, sure feet. Without his noisier companions he saw everything and was seen by none, many an animal remaining unaware of the cold, silent scrutiny in the undergrowth, or from up a tree. He came within touching distance of the soft-eyed deer drinking at the lake's edge at dawn; he watched the sharp, inquisitive nose and bright eyes of a fox peer from the bushes; he saw the sinuous twisting bodies and mean vicious faces of mink and marten; once he looked up and saw the otterlike head of a fisher high above him, framed in the leafless branches of a birch, and watched the beautiful tail stream out behind when the animal leaped a clear fifteen feet through the air into the swaying green obscurity of a pine; and he watched with disdain the lean gray timber wolf loping quietly along the trail beneath him as he rested on the limb of a tree above. Those that he encountered face to face would not meet his eyes and turned away. Only the beaver went about their business and paid him no heed.

Age-old instinct told him to leave no trace of his passing; the remains of the prey he killed with such efficient dispatch were all dug into the ground and covered over; any excreta were taken care of in the same fashion, fresh earth being carefully scraped over. When he slept, which was seldom, it was a quick "cat nap" high in the thick branches of evergreens. He was infinitely cunning and resourceful always, and above all he feared nothing.

On the second morning of his travels he came down at dawn to drink at the edge of a reed-fringed lake; he passed within a hundred feet of a rough, concealing structure of reeds and branches on the lake shore, in which crouched two men, guns across their knees, and a Chesapeake dog. A fleet of decoy ducks bobbed realistically up and down in the water in front of them. The dog stirred uneasily, turning his head and whining softly when the cat passed by, silent and unseen, but one of the men bade him be quiet, and he lay down, ears pricked and eyes alert.

The cat stayed staring at him from behind some bulrushes for a while, then raised his tail so that it alone was in sight and twitched the end, enjoying the dog's silent frustration. He turned and stole silently down to the lake shore, where presently his long slim body, crouched on a rock, was seen in the binoculars of one of the men.

"Here, kitty, kitty!" called an uncertain voice, after a moment's silence. Then "Puss, puss . . . here, puss!" it tried, in gruff embarrassment—ignored by the cat, who curled his pink tongue down to the water and drank slowly and deliberately. Two voices called now, with an undertone of laughing disbelief. He raised his head and looked directly at the two figures standing up, black against the sky.

He heard their excited argument, and then, an intentional poseur, he shook each paw daintily in turn, stepped delicately down from the rocks, and vanished from the men's sight. Behind him he heard a burst of incredulous laughter, and continued on his way, well satisfied.

The cat went on through the early morning mists, still following the trail of the dogs; and here it could not have been very old, for he found a partly chewed rabbit-skin, and several other clues, near some rocks where they had evidently passed a night, and the scent was still quite sharp to his acute sense. They had cut across country at one point, through several miles of deep spruce and cedar swamp, so that the going was, alternately, soft and dry and strewn with needles, then damp and spongy. It was a gloomy place, and the cat appeared uneasy, frequently glancing behind him as if he thought he were being followed. Several times he climbed a tree and crouched on a branch, watching and waiting. But whatever it was he scented or imagined showed equal cunning, and never appeared.

But the cat remained wary and suspicious, and felt with every nerve in his body that something was following—something evil. He increased his pace, then saw with relief that the area of deep, gloomy bush was coming to an end: far ahead of him he could see patches of blue sky which meant more open country. An old fallen tree lay ahead of him on the deer trail he was following. He leaped onto the trunk to cross it, pausing for a brief second, then every hair on his back rose erect, for in that moment he heard quite distinctly and felt rather than saw the presence of the following animal—and it was not very far behind him. Without further delay the cat leaped for the trunk of a birch tree, and clinging with his claws looked back along the path. Into view, moving with a velvet tread that equaled his own, came what appeared to be a large cat. But it was as different from the ordinary domestic cat as the Siamese himself was different.

This one was almost twice as large, chunky and heavy, with a short bob-tail and thick furry legs. The coat was a soft gray, overlaid with a few darker spots. The head differed only from an ordinary cat in that it was framed in a ruff of hair, and the ears rose into tufted points. It was a wild, cruel face that the Siamese saw, and he recognized instinctively a wanton killer—and one that could easily outclass him in strength, ferocity and speed. He scrambled as far up the young birch as he could go, and clung there, the slender trunk swaying under his weight. The lynx stopped in the center of the trail, one heavy paw lifted, gazing up with gleaming malicious eyes; the Siamese flattened his ears and spat venomously, then looked quickly around, measuring his distance for escape. With a light bound the lynx landed on top of the fallen tree trunk, and for another endless moment the two pairs of eyes tried to outstare one another, the Siamese making a low eerie hissing noise, lashing his tail from side to side. The lynx leaped for the birch, straddling it easily with powerful limbs; then, digging in the long claws, he started up the trunk towards the cat, who retreated as far as was possible, and waited, swaying perilously now. As the heavy weight came nearer, the tree bent right over, and it was all that the cat could do to hold on. The lynx reached a paw out to its full length and raked at the cat, tearing a strip of the bark away. The cat struck back, but the tree was waving wildly, and he lost his grip with the movement, and fell. The tree was so far bent over that he had not too far to fall, but even in that short time he twisted in the air and landed on his feet, only to hear a heavier thud a few yards away; the tree, whipping back, had dislodged the lynx almost at the same time, but the heavier animal had fallen with more impetus and less agility; for a split second it remained where it was, slightly winded. The cat took his advantage of that second and was off like a streak, running for his life up the narrow deer trail.

Almost immediately he heard the other animal close behind. It was useless to turn and fight; this was no stupid bear who could be intimidated, but a creature as remorseless and cunning as the cat himself could be, to other smaller animals. Even as he ran he must have known that flight was hopeless too; for he leaped with desperation up the trunk of another tree; but they were all saplings and there was little length of trunk for him to climb. This time the enemy was more cunning: it followed only halfway up, then deliberately swayed the pliant young tree from side to side, determined to shake the cat off. The situation was desperate and the cat knew it. He waited until he was on the lowest arc of the swing, then, gathering up his muscles under him until he was like a coiled spring, he leaped for the ground. The lynx was almost as quick, but it missed by a hair's breadth when the cat swerved violently, then doubled on his tracks and shot like a bullet into a rabbit burrow that opened up miraculously in the bank before him. The terrible claws so close behind slashed harmlessly through empty air. The cat forced himself into the burrow as far as he could go, and crouched there, unable to turn and face what might come, for the burrow was very narrow. His pursuer, too, dropped to a crouching position, then pushed an exploratory paw into the burrow. The cat was fortunately out of reach, so the lynx lowered its head and rashly applied one malevolent green eye to the hole, withdrawing it quickly, however, and shaking the tawny ruffed head in baffled fury when a flurry of earth hit it full in the face— the cat's hind legs were working like pistons, hurling the earth back out of the hole.

The lynx drew back, to work out its next approach. Complete silence fell in the clearing, and all seemed peaceful and quiet in contrast to the wildly beating heart of the desperate, trapped cat.

Systematically the lynx began to dig away the earth around the entrance to the burrow with its powerful forepaws, and was so engrossed that it failed to hear, or to scent the soft downwind approach of a young boy wearing a bright red jacket and cap and carrying a rifle, who had entered the bush from the fields beyond. The boy was walking softly, not because he had seen the lynx, but because he was out after deer: he and his father, half a mile away, were walking in a parallel course, with prearranged signals, and the boy was very excited, for this was the first time his father had considered him responsible enough to accompany him with his own rifle. Suddenly he saw the infuriated animal scrabbling away at the earth, and heard it growling softly as a continuous hail of earth coming from an unseen source covered it. In that same instant the animal looked up and saw the boy. It crouched low, snarling, and no fear showed in his eyes, only pure hatred. In a split-second decision, whether for fight or flight, it sprang; and in the same instant the boy raised his rifle, sighted and fired, all in one quick motion. The lynx somersaulted in the air and fell, its breath expelled in a mournful whistle as it hit the ground; the forelegs jerked once, a last spasm of nerves flickered across the fur, and it lay dead.

The boy was trembling slightly as he approached the dead animal, unable to forget the look of evil, savage fury on the catlike face which now lay before him, lips still curled back over white, perfect fangs. He stood looking down at his unexpected victim, unwilling to touch it, waiting for his father, who presently came, panting and anxious, calling as he ran. He stopped, staring at the tawny body lying on the pine needles, and then at the white face of his son.

He turned the animal over and showed the boy the small neat hole where the bullet had entered.

"Just below the breastbone." He looked up, grinning, and the boy smiled shakily.

The boy reloaded his rifle and tied his red neckerchief on a branch, marking the entrance to the clearing for their return. Then they walked off down the trail together, still talking, and the hidden cat heard their voices receding in the distance.

When all was silent he backed out of his refuge, and emerged into the sun-dappled clearing, his coat covered with sandy dirt. Completely ignoring the dead body even though forced to step around it, he sat down within ten yards of it, coolly washing his fur from the end of his tail to the tip of his nose. Then he stretched himself luxuriously, and with a final gesture of contempt turned his back on the lynx and dug into the earth with his hind claws to send a last shower of dirt over the animal's face. That done, he continued on his way, cool and assured as ever.

Two days later he caught up with the dogs. He came out on the crest of a hill forming one side of a valley, where a small stream meandered between alder-grown banks. Across the valley, clearly discernible among the bare trees on the opposite slope, he saw two familiar and beloved golden and white figures. His tail switched in excitement; he opened his mouth and uttered a plaintive, compelling howl. The two figures on the hill opposite stopped dead in their tracks, listening to the unbelievable sound as it echoed around the quiet valley. The cat leaped on to an overhanging rock, and as the hollow, raucous howl went ringing back and forth again the dogs turned questioningly, their eyes straining to seek the reality of the call. Then the young dog barked frenziedly in recognition and plunged down the hillside and across a stream, closely followed by the old dog. Now the cat began to run too, bounding like a mad thing down the hill, and they met on the banks of the little stream.

The old dog nearly went out of his mind with excitement: he covered the cat with frantic licking; twice he knocked him over with his eager thrusting head; then, carried away with enthusiasm, he started on the same tight intricate circles that he had used on the collie, whirling nearer and nearer until he finally burst free from the circle and rushed at the cat, who ran straight up the trunk of a tree, twisted in his own length, then dropped on the back of the dog below.

All through this performance the young dog had stood by, slowly and happily swinging his tail, his brown eyes alight and expressive, until at last his turn came when the old white clown collapsed in an ecstatic panting heap. Then the Labrador walked up to the cat, who rose on his hind legs, placing black forepaws on the neck of the great dog who towered above him, gently questing at the torn ear.

It would have been impossible to find three more contented animals that night. They lay curled closely together in a hollow filled with sweet-scented needles, under an aged, spreading balsam tree, near the banks of the stream. The old dog had his beloved cat, warm and purring between his paws again, and he snored in deep contentment. The young dog, their gentle worried leader, had found his charge again. He could continue with a lighter heart.

9

Over two hundred miles now lay behind them, and as a group they were whole and intact, but of the three only the cat remained unscathed. The old dog, however, still plodded cheerfully and uncomplainingly along. It was the Labrador who was in really poor condition: his once beautiful gleaming coat was harsh and staring now, his grotesquely swollen face in horrible contrast to his gaunt frame, and the pain in his infected jaw made it almost impossible for him to open his mouth, so that he was virtually starving. The other two now allowed him first access to any newly killed and bleeding animal provided by the cat, and he lived solely on the fresh blood that could be licked from the carcass.

They had slipped into a steady routine during the day; the two dogs trotting along side by side, unconcerned and purposeful, might have seemed two family pets out for a neighborhood ramble.

They were seen like this one morning by a timber-cruising forester returning to his jeep along an old tote road deep in the Ironmouth Range. They disappeared round a bend in the distance, and, preoccupied with tree problems, he did not give them a second thought. It was with a considerable shock that he remembered them later on in the day, his mind now registering the fact that there was no human habitation within thirty miles. He told the senior forester, who roared with laughter, then asked him if he had seen any elves skipping around toadstools too?

But inevitably the time was drawing nearer when the disappearance of the animals must be uncovered, the hue and cry begin, and every glimpse or smallest piece of evidence be of value. The forester was able to turn the laugh a week later when his chance encounter was proved to be no dream.

At Heron Lake John Longridge and his brother were making plans for the last trip of the season. In England the excited Hunter family were packed in readiness for the voyage home. Mrs. Oakes was busy in the old stone house, cleaning and polishing, while her husband stacked the wood cellar.

Soon all concerned would be back where they belonged, like pieces of a jigsaw puzzle being fitted together; and soon it must be discovered that three of the pieces were missing. . . .

Sublimely unaware of the commotion and worry, tears and heartbreak that their absence would cause, the three continued on their way.

The countryside was less wild now, and once or twice they saw small lonely hamlets in the distance. The young dog resolutely avoided these, keeping always to the woods and dense bush wherever possible—much to the disgust of the old dog, who had implicit faith in the helpfulness and loving-kindness of human beings. But the young dog was the leader: however long-ingly the bull terrier looked towards a distant curl of smoke from a chimney he must turn away.

Late one afternoon they were followed for several miles by a single timber wolf who was probably curious about the cat and was no real menace: how-ever hungry, it would never have risked an encounter with two dogs.

Like all his kind, however, the young dog hated and feared the wolf with some deep primeval instinct which must have had its origin in those mists of time when they shared a common ancestor. He was uneasy and disturbed by the slinking gray shape that merged into the undergrowth every time he looked back to snarl at it.

Unable to shake off the hateful shadow, and aware that the sun was sink-ing, irritable and exhausted with pain, he chose the lesser of two evils—leaving the bush for a quiet country road with small farms scattered at lonely intervals along it. He hurried his companions on, seeking protection for the night in the form of a barn or even an open field near a farm, sensing that the wolf would not follow within sight of human habitation.

They approached a small hamlet at dusk, a few small houses clustered around a schoolhouse and a white frame church. When the young dog would have skirted this too, the old terrier suddenly turned mutinous. He was, as usual, hungry; and the sight of the warm lights streaming out from the houses convinced him that this evening there was only one sensible way of obtaining food—from the hand of a human being! His eyes brightening at the thought, he ignored the young dog's warning growl, and trotted on unheeding down the forbidden road towards the houses, his rounded porcine quarters swinging defiantly, his ears laid back in stubborn disregard.

The young dog offered no further resistance. His whole head was throb-bing violently with the pain of infection from the quills, and more than anything he wanted time to scratch and scratch, to rub the burning cheek along the ground.

The rebel passed the first few cottages, so snug and inviting to his comfort-loving soul—smoke rising in the still evening air, and the reassuring smell and sounds of humans everywhere. He paused before a small white cottage, snuffling ecstatically the wonderful aroma of cooking drifting out mingled with wood smoke. Licking his chops he walked up the steps, lifted a bold demanding paw and scratched at the door, then sat down, pricking his ears expectantly.

He was not disappointed. A widening stream of light from the opening door revealed a small girl. The old dog grinned hideously in pleasure, his slanted eyes blinking strangely in the sudden light. There is little to equal a bull terrier's grin, however charmingly presented, for sheer astonishing ugliness.

There was a moment's silence, followed by an urgent wail of "Dad. . . ." Then the door slammed shut in his face. Puzzled but persistent, he scratched again, cocking his head to one side, his big triangular ears erect, listening to footsteps scurrying around within. A face appeared at the window. He barked a polite reminder. Suddenly the door was thrown open again and a man rushed out, a bucket of water in his hand, his face convulsed with fury. He hurled the water full in the face of the astonished dog, then grabbed a broom.

"Get out! Get out of here!" yelled the man, brandishing his broom so menacingly that the terrier tucked his tail between his legs and fled, soaking and miserable, towards his waiting companions. He was not afraid, only deeply offended—never in his long life had human beings reacted in such a way to his friendly overtures. Justifiable fury he knew and expected when he had terrorized their pets in the old days; laughter, and sometimes nervousness—but never a crude, uncivilized reception like this.

Baffled and disappointed, he fell meekly in behind his leader.

Two miles along the road they came to a winding cart track leading uphill to a farm. They crossed the dark fields, startling up an old white horse and some cows, heading for a group of outbuildings clustered together some distance from the farmhouse. A thin curl of smoke rose from the chimney of one. It was a smokehouse, where hams were smoking over a slow hickory fire. Pressing against the faint warmth at the base of the chimney they settled down for the night.

The young dog spent a restless night. The running sores on his face had been extended, by his continuous frantic clawing, into raw inflamed patches over the glands on one side of his neck; and the spreading infection was making him feverish and thirsty. Several times he left the others to drink from a small lake a short distance away, standing chest-deep in the cool, soothing water.

When the old dog woke shivering with cold he was alone. The cat was some distance away, belly to ground and tail twitching excitedly, stalking his breakfast. Stealing through the morning air came a familiar smell of smoke and something cooking—beckoning irresistibly.

The mists were rolling back from the valley, and a pale sun was lightening the sky when the old dog came through the windbreak of tall Norway pines and sat down outside the farmhouse door. His memory was short; already human beings were back on their rightful pedestals, cornucopias of dog food in their hands. He whined plaintively. At a second, louder whine, several cats appeared from the barn nearby and glared at him with tiger-eyed resentment. At any other time, he would have put them to instant flight; now he had more pressing business and chose to ignore them. The door swung open, a wondrous smell of bacon and eggs surged out, and the terrier drew up all the heavy artillery of his charm: with an ingratiating wag of his tail he glued his ears back, and wrinkled his nose in preparation for his disastrous winning leer. There was an astonished silence, broken by the deep, amused voice of a man. "Well!" said the owner of the voice, surveying his odd visitor, whose eyes were now rolled so far back that they had almost disappeared into his head. He called into the house, and was answered by the pleasant, warm voice of a woman. There was a sound of footsteps. The tail increased its tempo.

The woman stood for a moment in the doorway, looking down in silent astonishment at the white gargoyle on the step, and when he saw her face break into a smile that past master in the art of scrounging proffered a civil paw. She bent down and shook it, laughing helplessly, then invited him to follow her into the house.

Dignified, the old dog walked in, and gazed at the stove with bland confidence.

He was in luck this time, for there could not have been pleasanter people or a more welcoming house for miles around. They were an elderly couple, James Mackenzie and his wife Nell, living alone now in a big farmhouse which still held the atmosphere of a large, cheerful family living and laughing and growing up in it. They were well used to dogs, for there had been eight children in that house once upon a time, and a consequent succession of pets who had always started their adopted life out in the yard but invariably found their way into the household on the wildest pretexts of the children: misunderstood mongrels, orphaned kittens, sad strays, abandoned otter pups—Nell Mackenzie's soft heart had been as defenseless before them then as it was now.

She gave their visitor a bowl of scraps, which he bolted down in ravenous gulps, looking up then for more. "Why, he's starving!" she exclaimed in horror, and contributed her own breakfast. She petted and fussed over him, accepting him as though the years had rolled back and one of the children had brought home yet another half-starved stray. He basked in this affection, and emptied the bowl almost before it reached the ground. Without a word Mackenzie passed over his plate as well. Soon the toast was gone too, and a jug of milk; and at last, distended and happy, the old dog stretched out on a rug by the warmth of the stove while Nell cooked another breakfast.

"What is he?" she asked presently. "I've never seen anything quite so homely—he looks as though he had been squeezed into the wrong coat, somehow."

"He's an English bull," said her husband, "and a beauty too—a real old bruiser! I love them! He looks as though he'd been in a fight quite recently, yet he must be ten or eleven if he's a day!" And at the unqualified respect and admiration in the voice, so dear to the heart of a bull terrier—but so seldom forthcoming—the dog thumped his tail agreeably, then rose and thrust his bony head against his host's knee. Mackenzie looked down, chuckling appreciatively. "As cocksure as the devil—and as irresistible, aren't you? But what are we going to do with you?"

Nell passed her hand over the dog's shoulder and felt the scars, then examined them more closely. She looked up, suddenly puzzled. "These aren't from any dogfight," she said. "They're *claw* marks—like the ones bears leave on fresh wood, only smaller—"

In silence they looked down at the dog by their feet, digesting the implication, the unknown story behind the sinister scars; and they saw now, for the first time, the gathering cloudiness in the depths of the humorous little eyes; the too-thin neck shamed by the newly distended belly; and they saw that the indefatigable tail which thumped so happily on the floor was ragged and old, with a broken end. This was no bold, aggressive adventurer—only a weary old dog; hungry not only for food but for affection. There was no shadow of doubt in either what they would do—keep him, if he would stay, and give him what he needed.

They searched unavailingly under the white coat and in the pink ears for an identifying registered tattoo, then decided that when Mackenzie went into Deepwater to fetch some new churns later in the day he would make some inquiries there, tell the Provincial Police, and possibly put an advertisement in a city paper. And if nothing came of that . . . "Then I guess we're landed with you for good, you disreputable old hobo!" said Mackenzie cheerfully, prodding his delighted audience with an experienced foot, so that the dog rolled over on his back with a blissful sigh and invited further attention under his forearms.

When he opened the door that morning Mackenzie had seen a flight of mallards going down in the direction of the small lake fed by the creek running through the farm. It was still early enough to walk over to see if they were still there, so he put a handful of shells in his pocket, took down an old pump gun from the wall and set off, leaving Nell stepping over and around the recumbent white form of their guest as she cleared the table. He noticed that an infinitesimal slit of eye followed her every movement.

Halfway over the still misty fields he stopped to load his gun, then walked quietly toward the cover of the alders fringing the little lake. Peering through the branches, he saw six mallards about halfway across, just out of range. With the wind the way it was he might wait all day for a shot, unless something startled them on the other side.

But even as he turned away he saw a disturbance in the reeds across the water. Simultaneously, quacking loudly in alarm, the mallards took off in a body. He fired twice as they came over, one bird plummeting into the water and the other landing with a thud on the shore nearby. He picked this one up, thinking that he would have to bring the light canoe for the other, when he saw to his astonishment a large head of a dog swimming towards it.

The sound of a shot and the splash of a duck had had the same effect on the Labrador as a trumpet call to an old war horse, and drew him as irresistibly. Without a second's hesitation he had plunged in for the retrieve, only to find that he was unable to open his mouth to grasp the heavy duck properly, and was forced to tow it ashore by a wingtip. He emerged from the water twenty feet from the man, the beautiful greenhead trailing from its outstretched wing, the sun striking the iridescent plumage. The Labrador looked doubtfully at the stranger, and Mackenzie stared back in open-mouthed amazement. For a moment the two were frozen in a silent tableau, then the man recovered himself.

"Good dog!" he said quietly, holding out one hand. "Well done! Now bring it to me." The dog advanced hesitantly, dragging the bird.

"Give!" said Mackenzie, as the dog still hesitated.

The dog walked slowly forward, releasing his hold, and now Mackenzie saw with horror that one side of his face was swollen out of all proportion, the skin stretched so tautly that the eyes were mere slits and one rigid lip pulled back over the teeth. Sticking out like evil little pins on a rounded cushion of raw skin were several quills, deeply embedded. Every rib showed up under the wet coat, and when the dog shook himself Mackenzie saw him stagger.

Mackenzie made up his mind quickly: no matter whose, this dog was desperately in need of urgent treatment; the quills must be extracted at once before the infection spread further. He picked up the ducks, patted the dog's head reassuringly, then "Heel!" he said firmly. To his relief the dog fell in behind unquestioningly, following him back to the farmhouse, his resistance weakened to the point where he longed only to be back in the well-ordered world of human beings, that solid world where men commanded and dogs obeyed.

Crossing the fields, the stranger padding trustingly at his heels, Mackenzie suddenly remembered the other dog, and frowned in bewilderment. How many more unlikely dogs in need of succor would he lead into the farmhouse kitchen today—a lame poodle this afternoon, a halt beagle to-night?

His long, early morning shadow fell over the woodpile, and the sleepy Siamese cat sunning himself there lay camouflaged by stillness as he passed, unobserved by the man, but acknowledged by the dog with a brief movement of his tail and head.

Mackenzie finished cleaning up the Labrador's face nearly an hour later. He had extracted the quills with a pair of pliers; one had worked its way into the mouth and had to be removed from within, but the dog had not growled once, only whimpering when the pain was most intense, and had shown pathetic gratitude when it was over, trying to lick the man's hands. The relief must have been wonderful, for the punctures were now draining freely, and already the swelling was subsiding.

All through the operation the door leading out of the kitchen to a back room had shaken and rattled to the accompaniment of piteous whining. The old dog had been so much in the way when Mackenzie was working, pushing against his hand and obviously worried that they were going to do his companion some harm, that Nell had finally enticed him out with a bone, then quickly shut the door on his unsuspecting face.

Now, still deeply suspicious of foul play, he was hurling himself against the door with all his weight, but they did not want to let him in yet until the other dog had finished a bowl of milk. Mackenzie went to wash his hands, and his wife listened to the anxious running feet and the thuds that followed until she could bear it no longer, certain that he would harm himself. She opened the door and the old dog shot out in a fury, prepared to do battle on behalf of his friend—but he drew up all standing, a comical, puzzled expression on his face as he saw him peacefully lapping up a bowl of milk. Presently they sat down together by the door and the young dog patiently suffered the attentions of the other.

It was evident by their recognition and devotion that they came from the same home—a home which did not deserve to have them, as Nell said angrily, still upset by the gaunt travesty of a dog that had appeared; but Mackenzie pointed out that they must have known care and appreciation, as both had such friendly, assured dispositions. This made it all the harder to understand why they should be roaming such solitary and forbidding country, he admitted. But perhaps their owner had died, and they had run away together, or perhaps they had been lost from some car traveling across country, and were trying to make their way back to familiar territory. The possibilities were endless, and only one thing was certain—that they had been on the road long enough for scars to heal and quills to work their way inside a mouth; and long enough to know starvation.

"So they could have come from a hundred miles away or more," said Mackenzie. "From Manitoba, even. I wonder what they can have lived on, all that time—"

"Hunting? Scrounging at other farms? Stealing, perhaps?" suggested Nell, who had watched with amusement in the kitchen mirror her early morning visitor sliding a piece of bacon off a plate after breakfast when he thought her back was turned.

"Well, the pickings must have been pretty lean," said her husband thoughtfully. "The Labrador looks like a skeleton—he wouldn't have got much farther. I'll shut them in the stable when I go to Deepwater; we don't want them wandering off again. Now, Nell, are you quite sure that you want to take on two strange dogs? It may be a long time before they're traced—they may never be."

"I want them," she said simply, "for as long as they will stay. And in the meantime we must find something else to call them besides 'Hi!' or 'Good dog.' I'll think of something while you're away," she added, "and I'll take some more milk out to the stable during the morning."

From his sunny observation post on the woodpile, the cat had watched Mackenzie cross the yard and usher the two dogs into a warm, sweet-smelling stable, shutting the door carefully behind him. Shortly afterwards the truck rattled down the farm road, then all was quiet again. A few curious farm cats were emboldened to approach the woodpile, resenting this exotic stranger who had taken possession of their favorite sunning place. The stranger was not fond of other cats at the best of times, even his own breed, and farm cats were beyond the pale altogether. He surveyed them balefully, considering his strategy. After two or three well-executed skirmishes the band dispersed, and the black-masked pirate returned to his lair to sleep.

Halfway through the morning he awoke, stretched, and jumped down, looking warily around before stalking over to the stable door. He bleated plaintively and was answered by a rustle of straw within. Leisurely, he gathered himself for a spring, then leaped effortlessly at the latch on the door. But he was not quite quick enough; the latch remained in position. Annoyed, unused to failure, he sprang again, this time making sure of success. For a split second, almost in the same impetus as the spring, one paw was curved around the wooden block handle supporting his weight, while the other paw released the latch above and the door swung open. Purring with restrained pleasure, the cat walked in, suffering a boisterous welcome from his old friend before investigating the empty bowl. Disappointed, he left the stable, the two dogs following him into the sunlit yard, and disappeared into the henhouse. Several enraged and squawking fowls rushed out as he made his way towards the nesting-boxes. Curving his paws expertly around a warm brown egg, he held it firmly, then cracked it with a neat sideways tap from a long incisor tooth, the contents settling intact on the straw. He had brought this art to perfection after years of egg stealing. He lapped with delicate unhurried thoroughness, helping himself to two more before retiring to his woodpile again.

When Mackenzie drove into the farmyard later on in the afternoon he was surprised to see the two dogs sleeping in the sun by the shelter of the cattle trough. They stood by the truck wagging their tails in recognition as he unloaded, then followed him into the farmhouse.

"Did you let them out of the stable, Nell?" he asked, opening a parcel at the kitchen table and sheepishly dropping a meaty bone into the shark-like mouth that had opened beside him.

"Of course not," she answered in surprise. "I took them out some milk, but I remember being particularly careful to close the door."

"Perhaps the latch wasn't down properly," said Mackenzie. "Anyway, they're still here. The Lab's face looks better already—he'll be able to eat a decent meal by this evening, I hope; I'd like to get some meat on those bones."

Nothing was known of the runaways in Deepwater, he reported, but they must have come from the east, for a mink breeder at Archer Creek had spoken of chasing a white dog off his doorstep the night before, mistaking it for a local white mongrel well known for his thieving ways. Most men thought the Labrador could have been lost from a hunting trip, but nobody could account for an unlikely bull terrier as his companion. The Indian

Agent had offered to take the Labrador if nobody turned up to claim him, as his own hunting dog had recently died. . . .

"Indeed he will not!" Nell broke in indignantly.

"All right," said her husband, laughing. "I told him we would never separate them, and of course we'll keep them as long as we can—I'd hate to think of one of my own dogs running loose at this time of year. But I warn you, Nell, that if they are heading somewhere with a purpose, nothing on earth will keep them here—even if they're dropping on their feet, the instinct will pull them on. All we can do is keep them shut in for a while and feed them up. Then, if they leave, at least we've given them a better start."

After supper that night the Mackenzies and their guests moved into the little back room: a cozy, pleasantly shabby place, its shelves still filled with children's books, tarnished trophies and photographs; while snowshoes, mounted fish and grandchildren's drawings jostled one another for space on the walls with award ribbons, pedigrees and a tomahawk. Mackenzie sat at a table, puffing peacefully on a pipe, and working at the minute, intricate rigging of a model schooner, while his wife read *Three Men in a Boat* aloud to him. The replete and satisfied Labrador had eaten ravenously that evening, cleaning up bowls of fresh milk and plates of food with a bottomless appetite. Now he lay stretched full length under the table in the deep sleep of exhaustion and security, and the terrier snored gently from the depths of an old leather sofa, his head pillowed on a cushion, four paws in the air.

The only disturbance during the evening was the noise of a tremendous cat battle out in the yard. Both dogs sat up immediately and, to the astonishment of the elderly couple watching, wagged their tails in unison, wearing almost identical expressions of pleased and doting interest.

Later on they followed Mackenzie out quite willingly to the stable, where he piled some hay in a corner of a loose box for them, filled the bowl with water, then shut the door firmly behind him—satisfying himself that the latch was down and firmly in place, and would remain so even when the door was rattled. Shortly afterwards the lights downstairs in the farmhouse went out, followed in a little while by the bedroom light upstairs.

The dogs lay quietly in the darkness, waiting. Soon there was a soft scrabbling of paws on wood, the latch clicked, and the door opened a fraction, just enough to admit the slight body of the cat. He trampled and kneaded the hay for a while, purring in a deep rumble, before curling up in a ball at the old dog's chest. There were several contented sighs, then silence reigned in the stable.

When the young dog awoke in the cold hour before dawn only a few pale laggard stars were left to give the message which his heart already knew —it was time to go, time to press on westwards.

The yawning, stretching cat joined him at the stable door; then the old dog, shivering in the cold dawn wind; and for a few minutes the three sat motionless, listening, looking across the still dark farmyard, where already they could hear the slight stirrings of the animals. It was time to be gone:

there were many miles to be traveled before the first halt in the warmth of
the sun. Silently they crossed the yard and entered the fields leading to the
dark, massed shadows of the trees in the farthermost corner, their paws
making three sets of tracks in the light rime of frost that covered the field;
and even as they turned onto a deer trail leading westward through the
bush, a light came on upstairs in the farmhouse. . . .

Ahead of them lay the last fifty miles of the journey. It was as well that
they had been fed and rested. Most of the way now lay through the Strellon
Game Reserve, country that was more desolate and rugged than anything
they had yet encountered. The nights would be frosty, the going perilous
and exhausting; there could be no help expected from any human agency.
Worst of all, their leader was already weak and unfit.

## 10

Pieces of a jigsaw puzzle were gradually joining together, and the picture
was taking shape. In eastern Canada a liner was steaming up the St. Lawrence River, the heights of Quebec receding in the distance as she made
her way to Montreal. Leaning against the railings on the upper deck, watching the panorama of the river, were the Hunters, returning from their long
stay in England.

The children, Peter and Elizabeth, were wildly excited, and had hardly
left the deck since the liner had entered the Gulf. Ever since they had
wakened that morning, they had been counting the hours until their arrival home. There was all the joy and excitement of seeing their own homeland again, and soon their friends, their home and possessions—and above
all they could not wait to see their pets. Over and over again Elizabeth had
discussed their first meeting, for she was secretly longing to be reassured
that Tao would not have forgotten her. She had bought him a red leather
collar as a present.

Peter was perfectly happy and not in any way doubtful about his reunion;
ever since he had been old enough to think at all he had known that, just
as surely as Bodger belonged to him and was always there, so did he belong
to the bull terrier—and his homecoming would be all the present that his
dog would need.

And their father, seeing the endless arrowheads of mallards in the Canadian dawn, knew that soon he and the eager Luath would see them again,
over the Delta marshlands and the stubble fields in the west. . . .

A thousand miles westward of the liner, John Longridge sat at his desk,
a letter from his goddaughter in his hand, his thoughts as bleak as the
empty, unresponsive house to which he had returned only a short while ago.
He read the excited plans for her reunion with Tao—and of course the dogs
—with a sinking heart, then laid the letter down unfinished, his despair
deepening as he looked at the calendar: if the Hunters caught an early

plane they would be home tomorrow night; in twenty-four hours' time he must give them his heartbreaking news—his charges were gone; and he had no idea where, or what had befallen them.

Mrs. Oakes was equally miserable. Between them they had pieced together the fate of his charred note, and the course of confusion which had enabled three disparate animals to disappear without trace, and with perfect timing and perception. It was this perfection which had convinced him that his charges had not run away—if they had been unhappy, they could have gone at any time during the months of their stay.

He had already considered every possible catastrophe that could have overtaken them—death on the road, poison, traps, theft, disused wells—but not by the wildest stretch of imagination could he make any one of them account for three animals of such different temperaments. Nor could he understand how such a distinctive trio could pass unremarked in this small community: he had already spoken to some of Bodger's friends at the school, and not one sharp-eyed child had seen them that last morning, or any strange car, or in fact anything out of the ordinary; and Longridge knew that the area covered by rural school children was immense. The vast network of the Provincial Police could report nothing, either.

And yet he must have something more concrete than this to offer the Hunters tomorrow—if not a hope, at least a clear-cut finality.

He pressed his aching head into his hands and forced himself to set his thoughts out rationally: animals just did not vanish into thin air, so there must be some reasonable explanation for their disappearance, some clue as obvious and simple as the day-to-day pattern of their lives. A half-buried recollection stirred uneasily in his memory, but he could not identify it.

It was growing dark, and he switched on a lamp and moved over to light the fire. The silence in the room was oppressive. As he put a match to the kindling and watched the flames leap up, he thought of the last time he had sat by it: saw again a pair of dreaming sapphire eyes in their proud masked setting; tenanted his armchair with a luxuriously sprawling white form; and returned to the shadowy corner its listening, grieving ghost. . . .

Again the half-submerged memory distracted him: Luath's eyes . . . some difference in the pattern of his behavior . . . Luath's behavior on the last morning, the gesture of his unexpected paw . . . With a sudden flash of insight, he understood at last.

The door opened and he turned to Mrs. Oakes. "I know now—I know where they have gone," he said slowly. "Luath has taken them home—he has taken them all back to his own home!"

Mrs. Oakes looked at him in incredulous silence for a moment, then "No!" she burst out impulsively. "No—they couldn't do that! It's not possible—why, it must be nearly three hundred miles! And someone would have seen them—someone would have told us . . ." She broke off, dismayed, remembering that neither dog wore a collar. The terrier would carry no identifying marks, either, as he had been registered in England.

"They wouldn't be where anyone would see them," said Longridge thoughtfully. "Traveling by instinct, they would simply go west by the most direct route—straight across country, over the Ironmouth Range."

"Over the Ironmouth?" echoed Mrs. Oakes in horror. "Then there's no use hoping any more, if you're right," she said flatly. "There's bears and wolves and all manner of things, and if they weren't eaten up the first day they'd starve to death."

She looked so stricken and forlorn that Longridge suggested there was a good chance that they had been befriended by some remote prospector or hunter; perhaps, he enlarged, even now making his way to a telephone. . . .

But Mrs. Oakes was inconsolable.

"Don't let's fool ourselves any more, Mr. Longridge," she broke in. "I daresay a *young* dog could cross that country, and possibly even a cat—for there's nothing like a cat to look after itself—but you know as well as I do that old Bodger couldn't last ten miles! He used to be tired out after I'd walked him to my sister's and back. Oh, I know that half of it was put on to get something out of me," she admitted with a watery smile, catching Longridge's eye, "but it's a fact. No dog as old as that could go gallivanting across a wilderness and live for more than a day or two."

Her words fell away into a silence and they both looked out at the ominous dusk.

"You're right, Mrs. Oakes," said Longridge wearily at last. "We'll just have to face it—the old fellow is almost certainly dead. After all, it's been nearly four weeks. And I wouldn't give a candle for Tao's chances either," he added, "if we're going to be honest. Siamese can't stand the cold. But if they *did* make for their own home there's a chance at least that a big powerful dog like Luath would get there."

"That Luath!" said Mrs. Oakes darkly. "Leading that gentle old lamb to his death! And that unnatural cat egging him on, no doubt. Not that I ever had any favorites, but . . ."

The door shut, and Longridge knew that behind it she wept for them all.

Now that Longridge had his conviction to work on he wasted no time.

He called the Chief Ranger of Lands and Forests, and received assurance that word would be circulated throughout the department, and the game wardens and foresters contacted—tomorrow.

The Chief Ranger suggested calling a local bush pilot, who flew hunters into the remoter parts of the bush and knew most of the Indian guides.

The pilot was out on a trip and would not return until tomorrow; his wife suggested the editor of the rural section of the local newspaper.

The editor was still not back from covering a plowing match; his mother said that the hydro maintenance crew covered a large area of the country. . . .

The Line Superintendent said that he would be able to get in touch with the crews in the morning; he suggested the rural telephone supervisor, who was a clearinghouse of information for miles around. . . .

Everyone was sympathetic and helpful—but he was no farther on. He postponed the probable frustration of hearing that the supervisor would not be back from visiting her niece across the river until tomorrow, or that a storm had swept all the rural lines down, and searched for a map of the area.

He found a large-scale one, then drew a connecting line between his own small township and the university town where the Hunters lived, marking down the place names through which it passed. He found to his dismay that there were few of these, the line passing mostly through uninhabited regions of lakes and hills. The last forty or fifty miles seemed particularly grim and forbidding, most of it being in the Strellon Game Reserve. His hopes sank lower and lower, and he felt utterly despondent, bitterly regretting his offer to take the animals in the first place. If only he had kept quiet and minded his own business, they would all be alive now; for he was convinced, after looking at the map, that death through exposure, exhaustion, or starvation must have been inevitable.

And tomorrow the Hunters would be home again. . . . Dejectedly he picked up the phone and asked for the rural supervisor. . . .

Late that night the telephone rang. The telephone operator at Lintola—Longridge glanced at the map to find Lintola a good many miles south of his line—had some information: the schoolteacher had mentioned that the little Nurmi girl had rescued a half-drowned Siamese cat from the flooded River Keg, about two weeks ago, but it had disappeared again a few days afterwards. If Mr. Longridge would call Lintola 29 ring 4 tomorrow at noon she would try and have the child there and he could talk to her himself. The supervisor had one other piece of information which she offered rather diffidently for what it was worth—old Jeremy Aubyn, who lived up at the Doranda mine, had talked about "visitors" when he came in for his monthly mail collection, whereas everybody knew that the last visitor who had made the twelve-mile walk through the bush to the mine had been his brother, who had been dead for the last three years—poor old man. His only elaboration had been that they were "delightful people." . . . Old Mr. Aubyn had lived so long with only wild animals for company that he might easily be confused, she added delicately.

Longridge thanked her warmly, and put the receiver back, picking up the map. He discounted the information about the old recluse at the Doranda mine—who had probably met some prospectors or Indians—and concentrated on Lintola. It looked as though he had been right, then—they were indeed making for their own home. Two weeks ago, he puzzled, the cat had been alive, and, according to Longridge's map, must have traveled over a hundred miles. But what had happened to the other two? Must he now face the probability that Luath, too, was dead? Drowned possibly, as the cat would surely have been except for a little girl. . . .

Lying awake in the dark that night, unable to sleep, he thought that he would have given anything to feel the heavy thud on the bed that used to announce the old dog's arrival. How extremely unloving and intolerant he had felt so often, waking in the middle of the night to the relentless shoving and pushing of his undesirable and selfish bedfellow.

"Tonight," he reflected wryly, "I'd give him the whole bed! I'd even sleep in the basket myself—if only he would come back!"

### 11

Longridge's hours of telephoning the night he returned had brought results; and in the following week he and the Hunters spent many hours patiently tracking down evidence which was sometimes so conflicting and confusing that it was useless, and sometimes so coincidental that it was difficult to believe. Sometimes they felt wearily that every man, woman or child who had seen a cat or a dog walking along a road in the last five years had called to tell them so. But on the whole everyone had been extraordinarily helpful and kind, and they had evidence of several genuine encounters. When the results had been sifted down, they bore out Longridge's original guess as to the line of travel—the dogs (nothing further had been heard of the cat) had taken an almost perfect compass course due west, and the line he had drawn on the map had been remarkably accurate.

The brother of one of the bush pilot's Indian guides had met a cousin recently returned from rice harvesting who had some wild story of a cat and dog appearing out of the night and casting a spell over the rice crop so that it multiplied a thousandfold; and the little girl called Helvi Nurmi, her voice distressed and tearful, had described in detail the beautiful Siamese cat who had stayed for so short a time with her. Somewhere in the Ironmouth Range a forester had reported seeing two dogs; and a surly farmer had been overheard in Joe Woods's General Store (Public Telephone), Philipville, saying that if he could lay hands on a certain white dog ("Ugly as sin he was—a great vicious powerful beast!") who had killed a flock of prize-winning chickens and savagely beaten up his poor peace-loving collie, he would break every bone in his body!

Peter had smiled for the first time on hearing this: it had conjured up for him a vivid picture of Bodger in his aggressive element, thoroughly enjoying himself in a fight, cheerfully wicked and unrepentant as ever. He would rather have heard this than anything, for he knew that his unquenchable, wayward old clown was not made for sadness or uncertainty. His deep grief he kept to himself, and would not undermine it now with this softening hope: Bodger was dead; Luath almost certainly so; and his conviction was steady and unalterable.

Elizabeth's attitude was the complete reverse of her brother's: she was completely and utterly convinced that her Tao was alive, and that sooner or later he would return. Nothing could shake her confidence, even though there had been no word of her cat since he had left the Nurmis' so long ago and so many miles away. She dismissed all tactful efforts to explain the odds against his return—someday, somehow, a penitent Siamese would reappear, and, after a scolding due a thoughtless truant, he would receive with pleasure and surprise his new red collar. . . .

But she was the only one who held this cheerful confidence. After the kindly James Mackenzie had telephoned with the news that both dogs had been alive ten days ago, the family had pored over the map and seen the barrier that stretched between them and any admitted hope: wild, lonely terrain, rugged and cruel enough to beat down the endurance of any fresh and powerful dog, let alone the sick, half-starved, exhausted one that Mackenzie had described, leader and part sight for another whose willing heart could not withstand for long the betrayal of his years. All that could be hoped for now was that the end of their long journey had come quickly and mercifully in that wilderness.

Longridge was visiting the Hunters; and, partly to get away from the depressing telephone calls from well-meaning but ill-informed people, and partly because it was Peter's twelfth birthday the following Sunday, he suggested that they all go and camp out in the Hunters' summer cottage on Lake Windigo. Even though it had been closed for the winter, they could take sleeping bags, using only the living room and kitchen which could be warmed by the Quebec heater.

At first there had been some qualms from Elizabeth about leaving the house in case Tao should choose that week end to return, but Longridge showed her that Lake Windigo lay on the direct westward route that he had traced on the map, and reminded her that Tao knew the surrounding area for miles from his many expeditions with the dogs. Elizabeth packed the red collar and seemed satisfied—too easily, he suspected, dreading her disillusionment.

The cottage was full of memories, but it was easier to accustom the mind to new ones and train it to the loss in surroundings that were so different at this time of year. It was as if they were discovering new land; a cold lake empty of boats, the few cottages nearby all blindly shuttered, locked and empty. Trails that they did not even know existed were apparent, now that the trees were bare and the undergrowth had died down. Peter had a new camera, and spent hours stalking chipmunks, squirrels and birds with it. Elizabeth spent most of the days in a precarious treehouse they had built the previous summer between three great birches on the lake shore.

On the last afternoon, the Sunday of Peter's birthday, they decided to make a last expedition, taking the old Allen Lake Trail, then cutting off up the face of the hill to Lookout Point, and returning by the lake shore. It was an exhilarating walk through the crisp, clear air, the leaves thick and soft along the quiet trails, and over everything the indefinable healing peace and stillness of the northland bush.

They walked for the most part in companionable silence, each busy with his own thoughts. To Jim Hunter a walk without a dog lacked savor—and he remembered other fall days when, gun in hand, he had walked through this same peaceful solitude, Luath ranging from side to side: the excited summons to a treed partridge, and the gentleness of his dog's mouth around the soft fallen bird; then dawns and dusks on Manitoba marshes and lakes crowded his memory—freezing hours of patient waiting shared in canoes and blinds and stubble fields. The thought of Luath's last retrieve as Mackenzie had described it affected Hunter more than anything else; for he knew the frustrated humiliation his dog would feel with a pain-locked mouth and a bird to be brought in.

Peter had taken a short cut up the steep rockbound side of the hill. He sat on a log, staring into space, and he too remembered this time last year —when he had tried to train Bodger as a gun dog by throwing a stuffed leather glove into the bush after firing a BB gun: the willing co-operation and eager retrieves the first day; then, increasingly limp-tailed boredom and sulky ears, followed by deepening deafness, limping paws, and an unbearable air of martyrdom; and terminated two days running so subtly, by Bodger's appearance out of the bush with a diligent, puzzled expression—but no leather glove. The corners of Peter's mouth lifted when he remembered the scene that followed—the third day's throw and shot; then his quiet stalk after his White Hope into the depths of the bush—and the wily Bodger furiously digging a third glove grave. . . .

He sighed now—in his sudden loneliness rubbing his eyes with the back of his hand—and picked up his camera, for he could hear his family coming.

They sat for a long time on the flat rocks of the Lookout Hill, where long ago the Indians had built their warning signal fires, looking across the endless chains of lakes and tree-covered hills to the distant blur that was the great Lake Superior. It was very peaceful and quiet: a chickadee sang his poignant little piece for them, and the inevitable whisky-jack arrived on soundless wings to pick up cooky crumbs from within a few feet. Everyone was silent and pre-occupied.

Suddenly Elizabeth stood up.

"Listen!" she said. "Listen, Daddy—I can hear a dog barking!"

Complete and utter silence fell as everyone strained their ears in the direction of the hills behind. No one heard anything.

"You're imagining things," said her mother. "Or perhaps it was a fox. Come along, we must start back."

"Wait, wait! Just one minute—you'll be able to hear it in a minute, too," whispered Elizabeth, and her mother, remembering the child's hearing was still young and acute enough to hear the squeaking noise of bats and other noises lost forever to adults—and now even to Peter—remained silent.

Elizabeth's tense, listening expression changed to a slowly dawning smile. "It's Luath!" she announced matter-of-factly. "I know his bark!"

"Don't do this to us, Liz," said her father gently, disbelieving. "It's . . ."

Now Peter thought he heard something too: "Shhh . . ."

There was silence again, everyone straining to hear in an agony of suspense. Nothing was heard. But Elizabeth had been so convinced, the knowledge written so plainly on her face, that now Jim Hunter experienced a queer, urgent expectancy, every nerve in his body tingling with certain awareness that something was going to happen. He rose and hurried down the narrow path to where it joined the broader track leading around the hill. "Whistle, Dad!" said Peter breathlessly, behind him.

The sound rang out piercingly shrill and sweet, and almost before the echo rebounded a joyous, answering bark rang around the surrounding hills.

They stood there in the quiet afternoon, their taut bodies awaiting the relief of suspense; they stood at the road's end, waiting to welcome a weary traveler who had journeyed so far, with such faith, along it. They had not long to wait.

Hurtling through the bushes on the high hillside of the trail a small, black-tipped wheaten body leaped the last six feet down with careless grace and landed softly at their feet. The unearthly, discordant wail of a welcoming Siamese rent the air.

Elizabeth's face was radiant with joy. She kneeled, and picked up the ecstatic, purring cat. "Oh, Tao!" she said softly, and as she gathered him into her arms he wound his black needle-tipped paws lovingly around her neck. "Tao!" she whispered, burying her nose in his soft, thyme-scented fur, and Tao tightened his grip in such an ecstasy of love that Elizabeth nearly choked.

Longridge had never thought of himself as being a particularly emotional man, but when the Labrador appeared an instant later, a gaunt, stare-coated shadow of the beautiful dog he had last seen, running as fast as his legs would carry him towards his master, all his soul shining out of sunken eyes, he felt a lump in his throat, and at the strange, inarticulate half-strangled noises that issued from the dog when he leaped at his master, and the expression on his friend's face, he had to turn away and pretend to loosen Tao's too loving paws.

Minutes passed; everyone had burst out talking and chattering excitedly, gathered around the dog to stroke and pat and reassure, until he too threw every vestige of restraint to the winds, and barked as if he would never stop, shivering violently, his eyes alight and alive once more and never leaving his master's face. The cat, on Elizabeth's shoulder, joined in with raucous howls; everyone laughed, talked or cried at once, and for a while there was pandemonium in the quiet wood.

Then, suddenly—as though the same thought had struck them all simultaneously—there was silence. No one dared to look at Peter. He was standing aside, aimlessly cracking a twig over and over again until it became a limp ribbon in his hands. He had not touched Luath, and turned away now, when the dog at last came over including him in an almost human round of greeting.

"I'm glad he's back, Dad," was all he said. "And your old Taocat, too!" he added to Elizabeth, with a difficult smile. Elizabeth, the factual, the matter-of-fact, burst into tears. Peter scratched Tao behind the ears, awkward, embarrassed. "I didn't expect anything else—I told you that. I tell you what," the boy continued, with a desperate cheerfulness, avoiding the eyes of his family, "You go on down—I'll catch up with you later. I want to go back to the Lookout and see if I can get a decent picture of that whisky-jack." There will never be a more blurred picture of a whisky-jack, said Uncle John grimly to himself. On an impulse he spoke aloud.

"How about if I came too, Peter? I could throw the crumbs and perhaps bring the bird nearer?" Even as he spoke he could have bitten back the words, expecting a rebuff, but to his surprise the boy accepted his offer.

They watched the rest of the family wending their way down the trail, Tao still clutched in Elizabeth's arms, gentle worshiping Luath restored at last to the longed-for position at his master's heels.

The two remaining now returned to Lookout Point. They took some photographs. They prised an odd-shaped fungus growth off a tree. They found, incredibly, the cylindrical core of a diamond drill. And all the time they talked: they talked of rockets, orbits, space; gravely they pondered the seven stomachs of a cow; tomorrow's weather; but neither mentioned dogs.

Now, still talking, they were back at the fork of the trail; Longridge looked surreptitiously at his watch: it was time to go. He looked at Peter. "We'd better g—" he started to say, but his voice trailed off as he saw the expression on the face of the tense, still, frozen boy beside him, then followed the direction of his gaze. . . .

Down the trail, out of the darkness of the bush and into the light of the slanting bars of sunlight, joggling along with his peculiar nautical roll, came —Ch. Boroughcastle Brigadier of Doune.

Boroughcastle Brigadier's ragged banner of a tail streamed out behind him, his battle-scarred ears were upright and forward, and his noble pink and black nose twitched, straining to encompass all that his short peering gaze was denied. Thin and tired, hopeful, happy—and hungry, his remarkable face alight with expectation—the old warrior was returning from the wilderness. Bodger, beautiful for once, was coming as fast as he could.

He broke into a run, faster and faster, until the years fell away, and he hurled himself towards Peter.

And as he had never run before, as though he would outdistance time, Peter was running towards his dog.

John Longridge turned away, then, and left them, an indistinguishable tangle of boy and dog, in a world of their own making. He started down the trail as in a dream, his eyes unseeing.

Halfway down he became aware of a small animal running at lightning speed towards him. It swerved past his legs with an agile twist and he caught a brief glimpse of a black-masked face and a long black tail before it disappeared up the trail in the swiftness of a second.

It was Tao, returning for his old friend, that they might end their journey together.

# The Catbird Seat

## JAMES THURBER

MR. MARTIN bought the pack of Camels on Monday night in the most crowded cigar store on Broadway. It was theatre time and seven or eight men were buying cigarettes. The clerk didn't even glance at Mr. Martin, who put the pack in his overcoat pocket and went out. If any of the staff at F & S had seen him buy the cigarettes, they would have been astonished, for it was generally known that Mr. Martin did not smoke, and never had. No one saw him.

It was just a week to the day since Mr. Martin had decided to rub out Mrs. Ulgine Barrows. The term 'rub out' pleased him because it suggested nothing more than the correction of an error—in this case an error of Mr. Fitweiler. Mr. Martin had spent each night of the past week working out his plan and examining it. As he walked home now he went over it again. For the hundredth time he resented the element of imprecision, the margin of guesswork that entered into the business. The project as he had worked it out was casual and bold, the risks were considerable. Something might go wrong anywhere along the line. And therein lay the cunning of his scheme. No one would ever see in it the cautious, painstaking hand of Erwin Martin, head of the filing department at F & S, of whom Mr. Fitweiler had once said, 'Man is fallible but Martin isn't.' No one would see his hand, that is, unless it were caught in the act.

Sitting in his apartment, drinking a glass of milk, Mr. Martin reviewed his case against Mrs. Ulgine Barrows, as he had every night for seven nights. He began at the beginning. Her quacking voice and braying laugh had first profaned the halls of F & S on March 7, 1941 (Mr. Martin had a head for dates). Old Roberts, the personnel chief, had introduced her as the newly appointed special adviser to the president of the firm, Mr. Fitweiler. The woman had appalled Mr. Martin instantly, but he hadn't shown it. He had given her his dry hand, a look of studious concentration, and a faint smile. 'Well,' she had said, looking at the papers on his desk, 'are you lifting the oxcart out of the ditch?' As Mr. Martin recalled that moment, over his milk, he squirmed slightly. He must keep his mind on her crimes as a special adviser, not on her peccadillos as a personality. This he found difficult to do, in spite of entering an objection and sustaining it. The faults of the woman as a woman kept chattering on in his mind like an unruly witness. She had, for almost two years now, baited him. In the halls, in the elevator, even in his own office, into which she romped now and then like a circus horse, she was constantly shouting these silly questions at him. 'Are you lifting the oxcart out of the ditch? Are you tearing up the pea patch? Are you hollering down the rain barrel? Are you scraping around the bottom of the pickle barrel? Are you sitting in the catbird seat?'

It was Joey Hart, one of Mr. Martin's two assistants, who had explained what the gibberish meant. 'She must be a Dodger fan,' he had said. 'Red Barber announces the Dodger games over the radio and he uses those expressions—picked 'em up down South.' Joey had gone on to explain one or two. 'Tearing up the pea patch' meant going on a rampage; 'sitting in the catbird seat' meant sitting pretty, like a batter with three balls and no strikes on him. Mr. Martin dismissed all this with an effort. It had been annoying, it had driven him near to distraction, but he was too solid a man to be moved to murder by anything so childish. It was fortunate, he reflected as he passed on to the important charges against Mrs. Barrows, that he had stood up under it so well. He had maintained always an outward appearance of polite tolerance. 'Why, I even believe you like the woman,' Miss Paird, his other assistant, had once said to him. He had simply smiled.

A gavel rapped in Mr. Martin's mind and the case proper was resumed. Mrs. Ulgine Barrows stood charged with willful, blatant, and persistent attempts to destroy the efficiency and system of F & S. It was competent, material, and relevant to review her advent and rise to power. Mr. Martin had got the story from Miss Paird, who seemed always able to find things out. According to her, Mrs. Barrows had met Mr. Fitweiler at a party, where she had rescued him from the embraces of a powerfully built drunken man who had mistaken the president of F & S for a famous retired Middle Western football coach. She had led him to a sofa and somehow worked upon him a monstrous magic. The aging gentleman had jumped to the conclusion there and then that this was a woman of singular attainments, equipped to bring out the best in him and in the firm. A week later he had introduced her into F & S as his special adviser. On that day confusion got its foot in the door. After Miss Tyson, Mr. Brundage, and Mr. Bartlett had been fired and Mr. Munson had taken his hat and stalked out, mailing in his resignation later, old Roberts had been emboldened to speak to Mr. Fitweiler. He mentioned that Mr. Munson's department had been 'a little disrupted' and hadn't they perhaps better resume the old system there? Mr. Fitweiler had said certainly not. He had the greatest faith in Mrs. Barrows' ideas. 'They require a little seasoning, a little seasoning, is all,' he had added. Mr. Roberts had given it up. Mr. Martin reviewed in detail all the changes wrought by Mrs. Barrows. She had begun chipping at the cornices of the firm's edifice and now she was swinging at the foundation stones with a pickaxe.

Mr. Martin came now, in his summing up, to the afternoon of Monday, November 2, 1942—just one week ago. On that day, at 3 P.M., Mrs. Barrows had bounced into his office. 'Boo!' she had yelled. 'Are you scraping around the bottom of the pickle barrel?' Mr. Martin had looked at her from under his green eyeshade, saying nothing. She had begun to wander about the office, taking it in with her great, popping eyes. 'Do you really need *all* these filing cabinets?' she had demanded suddenly. Mr. Martin's heart had jumped. 'Each of these files,' he had said, keeping his voice even, 'plays an indispensable part in the system of F & S.' She had brayed at him, 'Well, don't tear up the pea patch!' and gone to the door. From there she had bawled, 'But you sure have got a lot of fine scrap in here!' Mr. Martin could no longer doubt that the finger was on his beloved department. Her pickaxe was on the upswing, poised for the first blow. It had not come yet; he had received no blue memo from the enchanted Mr. Fitweiler bearing nonsensical instructions deriving from the obscene woman. But there was no doubt in Mr. Martin's mind that one would be forthcoming. He must act quickly. Already a precious week had gone by. Mr. Martin stood up in his living room, still holding his milk glass. 'Gentlemen of the jury,' he said to himself, 'I demand the death penalty for this horrible person.'

The next day Mr. Martin followed his routine, as usual. He polished his glasses more often and once sharpened an already sharp pencil, but not even Miss Paird noticed. Only once did he catch sight of his victim; she swept past him in the hall with a patronizing 'Hi!' At five-thirty he walked home, as usual, and had a glass of milk, as usual. He had never drunk anything stronger in his life—unless you could count ginger ale. The late Sam Schlosser, the S of F & S, had praised Mr. Martin at a staff meeting several years before for his temperate habits. 'Our most efficient worker neither drinks nor smokes,' he had said. 'The results speak for themselves.' Mr. Fitweiler had sat by, nodding approval.

Mr. Martin was still thinking about that red-letter day as he walked over to the Schrafft's on Fifth Avenue near Forty-Sixth Street. He got there, as he always did, at eight o'clock. He finished his dinner and the financial page of the *Sun* at a quarter to nine, as he always did. It was his custom after dinner to take a walk. This time he walked down Fifth Avenue at a casual pace. His gloved hands felt moist and warm, his forehead cold. He transferred the Camels from his overcoat to a jacket pocket. He wondered, as he did so, if they did not represent an unnecessary note of strain. Mrs. Barrows smoked only Luckies. It was his idea to puff a few puffs on a Camel (after the rubbing-out), stub it out in the ashtray holding her lipstick-stained Luckies, and thus drag a small red herring across the trail. Perhaps it was not a good idea. It would take time. He might even choke, too loudly.

Mr. Martin had never seen the house on West Twelfth Street where Mrs. Barrows lived, but he had a clear enough picture of it. Fortunately, she had bragged to everybody about her ducky first-floor apartment in the perfectly darling three-story red-brick. There would be no doorman or other attendants; just the tenants of the second and third floors. As he walked along, Mr. Martin realized that he would get there before nine-thirty. He had considered walking north on Fifth Avenue from Schrafft's to a point from which it would take him until ten o'clock to reach the house. At that hour people were less likely to be coming in or going out. But the procedure would have made an awkward loop in the straight thread of his casualness, and he had abandoned it. It was impossible to figure when people would be entering or leaving the house, anyway. There was a great risk at any hour. If he ran into anybody, he would simply have to place the rubbing-out of Ulgine Barrows in the inactive file forever. The same thing would hold true if there were someone in her apartment. In that case he would just say that he had been passing by, recognized her charming house, and thought to drop in.

It was eighteen minutes after nine when Mr. Martin turned into Twelfth Street. A man passed him, and a man and a woman, talking. There was no one within fifty paces when he came to the house, halfway down the block. He was up the steps and in the small vestibule in no time, pressing the bell under the card that said 'Mrs. Ulgine Barrows.' When the clicking in the lock started, he jumped forward against the door. He got inside fast, closing the door behind him. A bulb in a lantern hung from the hall ceiling on a chain seemed to give a monstrously bright light. There was nobody on the stair, which went up ahead of him along the left wall. A door opened down the hall in the wall on the right. He went toward it swiftly, on tiptoe.

'Well, for God's sake, look who's here!' bawled Mrs. Barrows, and her braying laugh rang out like the report of a shotgun. He rushed past her like a football tackle, bumping her. 'Hey, quit shoving!' she said, closing the door behind them. They were in her living room, which seemed to Mr. Martin to be lighted by a hundred lamps. 'What's after you?' she said. 'You're as jumpy as a goat.' He found he was unable to speak. His heart was wheezing in his throat. 'I—yes,' he finally brought out. She was jabbering and laughing as she started to help him off with his coat. 'No, no,' he said. 'I'll put it here.' He took it off and put it on a chair near the door. 'Your hat and gloves, too,' she said. 'You're in a lady's house.' He put his hat on top of the coat. Mrs. Barrows seemed larger than he had thought. He kept his gloves on. 'I was passing by,' he said. 'I recognized—is there anyone here?' She laughed louder than ever. 'No,' she said, 'we're all alone. You're as white as a sheet, you funny man. Whatever *has* come over you? I'll mix you a toddy.' She started toward a door across the room. 'Scotch-and-soda be all right? But say, you don't drink, do you?' She turned and gave him her amused look. Mr. Martin pulled himself together. 'Scotch-and-soda will be all right,' he heard himself say. He could hear her laughing in the kitchen.

Mr. Martin looked quickly around the living room for the weapon. He had counted on finding one there. There were andirons and a poker and something in a corner that looked like an Indian club. None of them would do. It couldn't be that way. He began to pace around. He came to a desk. On it lay a metal paper knife with an ornate handle. Would it be sharp enough? He reached for it and knocked over a small brass jar. Stamps spilled out of it and it fell to the floor with a clatter. 'Hey,' Mrs. Barrows yelled from the kitchen, 'are you tearing up the pea patch?' Mr. Martin gave a strange laugh. Picking up the knife, he tried its point against his left wrist. It was blunt. It wouldn't do.

When Mrs. Barrows reappeared, carrying two highballs, Mr. Martin, standing there with his gloves on, became acutely conscious of the fantasy he had wrought. Cigarettes in his pocket, a drink prepared for him—it was all too grossly improbable. It was more than that; it was impossible. Somewhere in the back of his mind a vague idea stirred, sprouted. 'For heaven's sake, take off those gloves,' said Mrs. Barrows. 'I always wear them in the house,' said Mr. Martin. The idea began to bloom, strange and wonderful. She put the glasses on a coffee table in front of a sofa and sat on the sofa. 'Come over here, you odd little man,' she said. Mr. Martin went over and sat beside her. It was difficult getting a cigarette out of the pack of Camels, but he managed it. She held a match for him, laughing. 'Well,' she said, handing him his drink, 'this is perfectly marvellous. You with a drink and a cigarette.'

Mr. Martin puffed, not too awkwardly, and took a gulp of the highball. 'I drink and smoke all the time,' he said. He clinked his glass against hers. 'Here's nuts to that old windbag, Fitweiler,' he said, and gulped again. The stuff tasted awful, but he made no grimace. 'Really, Mr. Martin,' she said, her voice and posture changing, 'you are insulting our employer.' Mrs. Barrows was now all special adviser to the president. 'I am preparing a bomb,' said Mr. Martin, 'which will blow the old goat higher than hell.' He had only had a little of the drink, which was not strong. It couldn't be that. 'Do you take dope or something?' Mrs. Barrows asked coldly. 'Heroin,' said Mr. Martin. 'I'll be coked to the gills when I bump that old buzzard off.' 'Mr. Martin!' she shouted, getting to her feet. 'That will be all of that. You must go at once.' Mr. Martin took another swallow of his drink. He tapped his cigarette out in the ashtray and put the pack of Camels on the coffee table. Then he got up. She stood glaring at him. He walked over and put on his hat and coat. 'Not a word about this,' he said, and laid an index finger against his lips. All Mrs. Barrows could bring out was 'Really!' Mr. Martin put his hand on the doorknob. 'I'm sitting in the catbird seat,' he said. He stuck his tongue out at her and left. Nobody saw him go.

Mr. Martin got to his apartment, walking, well before eleven. No one saw him go in. He had two glasses of milk after brushing his teeth, and he felt elated. It wasn't tipsiness, because he hadn't been tipsy. Anyway, the walk had worn off all effects of the whiskey. He got in bed and read a magazine for a while. He was asleep before midnight.

Mr. Martin got to the office at eight-thirty the next morning, as usual. At a quarter to nine, Ulgine Barrows, who had never before arrived at work before ten, swept into his office. 'I'm reporting to Mr. Fitweiler now!' she shouted. 'If he turns you over to the police, it's no more than you deserve!' Mr. Martin gave her a look of shocked surprise. 'I beg your pardon?' he said. Mrs. Barrows snorted and bounced out of the room, leaving Miss Paird and Joey Hart staring after her. 'What's the matter with that old devil now?' asked Miss Paird. 'I have no idea,' said Mr. Martin, resuming his work. The other two looked at him and then at each other. Miss Paird got up and went out. She walked slowly past the closed door of Mr. Fitweiler's office. Mrs. Barrows was yelling inside, but she was not braying. Miss Paird could not hear what the woman was saying. She went back to her desk.

Forty-five minutes later, Mrs. Barrows left the president's office and went into her own, shutting the door. It wasn't until half an hour later that Mr. Fitweiler sent for Mr. Martin. The head of the filing department, neat, quiet, attentive, stood in front of the old man's desk. Mr. Fitweiler was pale and nervous. He took his glasses off and twiddled them. He made a small, bruffing sound in his throat. 'Martin,' he said, 'you have been with us more than twenty years.' 'Twenty-two, sir,' said Mr. Martin. 'In that time,' pursued the president, 'your work and your—uh—manner have been exemplary.' 'I trust so, sir,' said Mr. Martin. 'I have understood, Martin,' said Mr. Fitweiler, 'that you have never taken a drink or smoked.' 'That is correct, sir,' said Mr. Martin. 'Ah, yes.' Mr. Fitweiler polished his glasses. 'You may describe what you did after leaving the office yesterday, Martin,' he said. Mr. Martin allowed less than a second for his bewildered pause. 'Certainly, sir,' he said. 'I walked home. Then I went to Schrafft's for dinner. Afterward I walked home again. I went to bed early, sir, and read a magazine for a while. I was asleep before eleven.' 'Ah, yes,' said Mr. Fitweiler again. He was silent for a moment, searching for the proper words to say to the head of the filing department. 'Mrs. Barrows,' he said finally, 'Mrs. Barrows has worked hard, Martin, very hard. It grieves me to report that she has suffered a severe breakdown. It has taken the form of a persecution complex accompanied by distressing hallucinations.' 'I am very sorry, sir,' said Mr. Martin. 'Mrs. Barrows is under the delusion,' continued Mr. Fitweiler, 'that you visited her last evening and behaved yourself in an—uh—unseemly manner.' He raised his hand to silence Mr. Martin's little pained outcry. 'It is the nature of these psychological diseases,' Mr. Fitweiler said, 'to fix upon the least likely and most innocent party as the—uh—source of persecution. These matters are not for the lay mind to grasp, Martin. I've just had my psychiatrist, Doctor Fitch, on the phone. He would not, of course, commit himself, but he made enough generalizations to substantiate my suspicions. I suggested to Mrs. Barrows, when she had completed her—uh—story to me this morning, that she visit Doctor Fitch, for I suspected a condition at once. She flew, I regret to say, into a rage, and demanded—uh—requested that I call you on the carpet. You may not know, Martin, but Mrs. Barrows had planned a reorganization of your department—subject to my approval, of course, subject to my approval. This brought you, rather than anyone else, to her mind—but again that is a phenomenon for Doctor Fitch and not for us. So, Martin, I am afraid Mrs. Barrows' usefulness here is at an end.' 'I am dreadfully sorry, sir,' said Mr. Martin.

It was at this point that the door to the office blew open with the sud-

denness of a gas-main explosion and Mrs. Barrows catapulted through it.
'Is the little rat denying it?' she screamed. 'He can't get away with that!'
Mr. Martin got up and moved discreetly to a point beside Mr. Fitweiler's
chair. 'You drank and smoked at my apartment,' she bawled at Mr. Martin,
'and you know it! You called Mr. Fitweiler an old windbag and said you
were going to blow him up when you got coked to the gills on your heroin!'
She stopped yelling to catch her breath and a new glint came into her
popping eyes. 'If you weren't such a drab, ordinary little man,' she said,
'I'd think you'd planned it all. Sticking your tongue out, saying you were
sitting in the catbird seat, because you thought no one would believe me
when I told it! My God, it's really too perfect!' She brayed loudly and
hysterically, and the fury was on her again. She glared at Mr. Fitweiler.
'Can't you see how he has tricked us, you old fool? Can't you see his little
game?' But Mr. Fitweiler had been surreptitiously pressing all the buttons
under the top of his desk and employees of F & S began pouring into the
room. 'Stockton,' said Mr. Fitweiler, 'you and Fishbein will take Mrs. Barrows to her home. Mrs. Powell, you will go with them.' Stockton, who had
played a little football in high school, blocked Mrs. Barrows as she made for
Mr. Martin. It took him and Fishbein together to force her out of the door
into the hall, crowded with stenographers and office boys. She was still
screaming imprecations at Mr. Martin, tangled and contradictory imprecations. The hubbub finally died out down the corridor.

'I regret that this has happened,' said Mr. Fitweiler. 'I shall ask you to
dismiss it from your mind, Martin.' 'Yes, sir,' said Mr. Martin, anticipating
his chief's 'That will be all' by moving to the door. 'I will dismiss it.' He
went out and shut the door, and his step was light and quick in the hall.
When he entered his department he had slowed down to his customary
gait, and he walked quietly across the room to the W20 file, wearing a look
of studious concentration.

# Act One

(an extract from the book)

## MOSS HART

WHEN they move at all, things move with the speed of light in the theatre. There was a message to call Max Siegel waiting for me when I awoke the next morning. "I have a telegram from Sam Harris," said the voice on the phone. "It says, 'Tell young author I will produce his play if George Kaufman likes it and agrees to collaborate. Is he willing to collaborate with Kaufman? Am sending play air mail to Kaufman direct.'"

"Do you mind reading that to me again, Mr. Siegel," I said. I knew very well what the telegram said, but I was sparring for a moment of time to make up my mind, and a moment was all that I needed. "Tell him yes," I said, almost before he had finished reading it again. "When will I know whether Mr. Kaufman likes it or not?" I asked.

"He usually reads a play the day he gets it," replied Max Siegel, "and I'll call you right away. He ought to have it by day after tomorrow, so I should think you'd have an answer by about Thursday. Okay?"

"Okay," I answered.

"I'm going to draw up the contracts now," he said. "That's how sure I am that he's going to like it. Don't write any musical comedies in the meantime!" His laugh came merrily over the phone. "Good-bye, playwright," he added, and the connection at the other end clicked off.

I could hardly wait for four o'clock that afternoon to break the news of what I had done to the group at Rudley's and most particularly to Lester. I thought I knew pretty well what their reaction would be, and if I was right it was the better part of valor, I thought, to brave Lester's wrath among the safety of numbers. I was correct on all counts. Lester's wrath was great, and if the argument about my tactics with Jed Harris had been loud and vehement, the debate on my willingness to collaborate with George Kaufman was now outraged and violent.

"It will be *his* play!" "No one will ever know *your* name is on the program!" "You might just as well say 'By George S. Kaufman' and leave it at that!" "He'll get *all* the credit!" "They won't even know you had anything to do with it!" "A first play is what you establish your reputation with!" "You're just handing your play over to Kaufman and saying good-bye to yourself!"

The voices around the table grew so loud that the manager, accustomed though he was to loud talk from that corner of the room, came over and asked us to quiet down or to leave. It did me no good to protest that I knew very well that all or a good part of what they were saying might more than likely be true, but that what I was seizing was the main chance—the golden opportunity of working with the Herr Professor himself. There would be other plays to write, I argued, and if I emerged with little personal recognition from this one, the apprenticeship was well worth it. My arguments had as little effect on them as theirs did on me. I finally took a cowardly refuge by stating flatly that all this bellowing was largely academic. George Kaufman might be thoroughly uninterested in *Once in a Lifetime*, and even if he was interested, I had not yet signed any contracts; when the moment came for that, there would still be time to reconsider.

This bit of subterfuge fooled nobody, of course, Lester least of all, and I carefully remained absent from Rudley's for the next three days. My mind was made up, and though I had every intention of sticking to my decision, I well knew that continued argument carried with it the danger of making the half-truth seem valid. Eddie in particular was a most convincing and persuasive talker, who could brilliantly pervert any discussion to his own ends, sometimes purely for the pleasure of winning the debate. I did not wish to be shaken, for the more I thought of it, the more certain I became that a chance to work in collaboration with George Kaufman would be of greater value to me in the end than even a production as sole author of the play, by Jed Harris or anyone else.

It seemed imperative that I acquaint Jed Harris with this fact as soon as possible, for so far as he was concerned, he must still believe he held the right to produce the play if he chose to do so. Nevertheless, I let two full days go by before I could summon up enough courage to put through a call to the Madison Hotel. Having seen him plain like Shelley—plainer, perhaps, than ever Shelley was seen—I was aware that his reception of the news that I was withdrawing the play might range anywhere from magnanimity to cold fury, with a likelihood of something fairly bloodcurdling in between. I called the hotel at the unlikely hour of nine o'clock in the morning in the hope that he could not be disturbed and I could leave a message, but to my horror the call was put through immediately.

The low but intensely alive voice of Jed Harris came over the wire with the same vibrant urgency and excitement that any kind of contact with him immediately generated. Even on the telephone that quiet voice contained all the power of his presence. Stumblingly, I blurted out my story. There was nothing but silence from the other end of the phone, while I awkwardly backed and filled and explained and excused, and I finally ground to a halt and waited. I gave thanks to Alexander Graham Bell for an invention that could put this much distance between me and the silence at the other end of the phone.

When he spoke at last, the tone was as hushed as ever, the voice even softer and more silken. "I think you're doing exactly the right thing," he said. "I'm going to do *Uncle Vanya* as my first production of the season.

Chekhov has never been produced well in this country, don't you agree?"
The question was asked respectfully, in the manner of one expert on the
Russian theatre consulting another expert on a point beyond the comprehension of the mere layman. My relief was so great that I could do nothing
more than grunt some sort of acknowledgment in reply.

There was another little silence and then the voice came softly through
again. "Do you know George Kaufman? Ever met him?" he asked.

"No," I replied.

"Has he read the play yet, do you know?" he inquired.

"He may be reading it today," I answered. "He should have gotten it by
this morning. That's why I wanted to call you before he read it, just in case
he liked it. And I want to thank you, Mr. Harris, for being so . . ."

"Listen," the voice cut in, "this is George Kaufman's home telephone
number. Put it down. You call him right away and tell him that Jed Harris
says that this is just the kind of play he ought to do. Good-bye."

And before I could utter a word, there was a click from the receiver at
the other end. I sat staring at the telephone, wondering anew at the un-
predictability of Jed Harris, and for a moment I had a strong impulse to
call him back immediately and thank him. I would drop him a note and
do it properly, I decided, after I talked to George Kaufman; and I picked
up the telephone again.

The number had barely buzzed once when a voice said, "Yes?" Not
"Hello"—just "Yes." "May I speak to Mr. Kaufman, please," I said. "This is
he," said the voice bluntly.

"Oh," I said and paused lamely. I had expected to give my name and state
my business to a secretary before being put through. I had always taken it
for granted that a secretary was as much a part of a famous playwright's
stock in trade as a typewriter and blank paper. It was disconcerting to find
myself talking to George Kaufman without that small moment of preparation beforehand.

"Yes?" said the voice again, this time quite testily.

There was nothing to do but speak up. "My name is Moss Hart," I said,
plunging. "You don't know me, Mr. Kaufman, but Sam Harris is sending
you a play of mine to read." I paused, suddenly overcome with timidity.

"I received it this morning," said George Kaufman. "I am reading it
tonight."

"Oh," I said again, and stopped, thereby reaffirming the impression, I
thought hopelessly, of what a brilliant conversationalist I was. There was
nothing but silence from the other end of the telephone, so I gulped and
continued. "Well," I said, "Jed Harris has read the play and he asked me to
give you a message. He said to tell you that this was just the kind of play
you ought to do."

Even as I spoke the words I was dimly conscious of their peculiar ring.
But I was so relieved to have it quickly over and done with, that for a brief
moment I did not realize no reply had come from the other end of the
wire, and for another moment I thought we had been disconnected.

"Hello? . . . Hello?" I said into the receiver two or three times. But we had not been disconnected. The voice of George Kaufman was glacial when it again sounded over the telephone. Each word seemed to be incrusted with icicles. "I would not be interested in anything that Jed Harris was interested in," he said and hung up.

I put down the telephone and stared stupidly at it in complete dismay.

Not until long afterward did I learn that George Kaufman and Jed Harris were at that particular moment at the climax of a corrosive theatrical quarrel, a quarrel of such bitterness that it has remained irreconcilable to this very day.

Obviously, the motive of that seemingly innocent message was to produce exactly the deplorable result that it had had. There could be only one explanation: If Jed Harris intended to punish me for withdrawing the play, he had deftly accomplished his purpose in the most stinging and hurtful way. It is the only conclusion I have ever come to on this ill-natured and wayward bit of wickedness, for when I next met Jed Harris some three or four years later, the trepidation that awesome gentleman still inspired in me precluded any kind of inquiry on my part. I was still not brave enough to cross swords with him, and by that time it no longer mattered.

It mattered very much indeed at the moment however. I remained sitting in the chair by the telephone, too numbed by the sudden collapse of my hopes of working with George Kaufman, to do anything more than stare out the window and perceive the full idiocy of my behavior. I briefly considered calling Lester, Miss Fishbein, and even Max Siegel, but I doubted if there was anything very much that Max Siegel could do now to repair the damage, and I was in no mood for either "I told you so" or the disclosure of what a complete fool I had been.

I finally went about my business and did nothing. The play might be sold elsewhere, of course, and I supposed that I would be consoled and even console myself with the idea that this had been a blessing in disguise, but I knew I would never believe it. The chance of working with George S. Kaufman was gone, and I could not take the loss of that opportunity lightly. I was then, and am still, all things being equal, a great believer in the element of luck in the theatre—in that strange alchemy of timing that seemingly by chance and little else brings together an admixture of talents which, working in combination, infuses the theatre with a magical alloy that blends it into a mosaic-like junction of play, playwright, actor and director. It was my deep-rooted and perhaps childish belief in the mystique of this process that had made me grasp so eagerly and so unhesitatingly at the chance of working with George Kaufman.

I had felt in that moment when Max Siegel read me Sam Harris' telegram that luck was running my way, and I felt just as strongly now that fortune's wheel had seemingly spun past me. It would be nonsense to suggest that a complete reliance on so dubious and uncertain an element as luck does not imply an evasion of the other substantial realities that go into the making of any career, theatrical or otherwise. But I have seen the element of luck operate conversely too often not to remain convinced that it plays an exceptional and sometimes absurd part in the precarious charting of that thin line that divides success from failure. I am not an optimist where fate is concerned. I do not believe that one's destiny is resolved beforehand. It is a doctrine I have always rejected as indicating a certain poverty of mind or as the excuse of the insolvent, for it is a dogma that allows inaction to become a virtue. Nevertheless, I could think of no action on my part that would retrieve the disaster of that morning, and I went through the rest of that day and evening in a state of real wretchedness.

I was asleep when the telephone rang the next morning, but contrary to my usual custom of putting the pillow over my head and turning over, I got out of bed and answered it myself.

"Is this the young author?" the voice of Max Siegel came cheerfully over the telephone.

"Yes," I answered, thoroughly wide awake in a moment and shaking a little with excitement.

"Can you meet George Kaufman here at the Music Box at three o'clock?" he went on.

"You mean he read it?" I asked incredulously.

"Certainly he read it," said Max Siegel. "That's what he wants the meeting for this afternoon. He likes it very much—I told you he would. What's the matter?" He laughed. "You sound like you don't believe it! It's true. You'll be here at three o'clock then?"

"Yes," I managed to reply. "Three o'clock, the Music Box."

I hung up, and startled my mother, who had just come into the room, by throwing my arms around her and kissing her three or four times soundly.

"We're going to be rich," I said gleefully. "This time next year we may not even be living in Brooklyn." She smiled, pleased at my good spirits, but refrained from asking if they were once again based upon my "homework." She had been through six years of varying forms and degrees of enthusiasm every time I finished a play, and I have no doubt she had heard a version of the same speech before.

"I'm going to work with George Kaufman, *that's* the difference *this* time," I said. "George S. Kaufman," I repeated, rolling out the name luxuriously.

She stared at me blankly, the name having registered nothing at all, and then added hastily, "That's very nice." It was the tone of voice and the expression she reserved, I remembered, for such moments as when I would rush to show her a new stamp I had garnered by barter in my stamp-collecting days.

"You go ahead and do your shopping." I laughed. "I'll make my own breakfast." She smiled encouragingly, obviously pleased that she had not deflated my good spirits by her unawareness of who George Kaufman was.

"If you're going to bring him home to work with you," she said politely,

"I hope you won't do it until after next week. We're having the painters next week."

"I'll explain that to him," I said carefully as I made my way toward the kitchen.

While the eggs fried, I composed in my mind a graceful little speech of gratitude I intended to deliver to Mr. Kaufman at the right moment after all the business details were out of the way. It sounded a shade too reverential even to my own ears, I decided, as I tried speaking it aloud while I waited for the coffee to boil, but there was no time to polish it up now. That could be done on the subway on the way into town.

I hurried through breakfast as quickly as possible and got to the telephone to acquaint Lester and Miss Fishbein with the happy trend of events, but more particularly to insist that for this first meeting I wanted to meet with George Kaufman alone. As I suspected, this did not sit any too well with either one of them, but I was firm, and at three o'clock I walked alone up the stairs of the Music Box Theatre to the mezzanine and knocked on the door of Sam Harris' office.

Max Siegel, smiling as usual, stood in the doorway, and behind him, slumped down in one of the large armchairs, I caught a glimpse of George Kaufman. That first glimpse of George Kaufman caught fleetingly over Max Siegel's shoulder made all the caricatures I had seen of him in the Sunday drama sections through the years come instantly alive. The bushy hair brushed straight up from the forehead into an orderly but somehow unruly pompadour, the tortoise-shell glasses placed low on the bridge of the rather large nose, the quick, darting eyes searching incisively over the rims, the full sensuous mouth set at a humorously twisted tilt in the descending angularity of the long face—each single feature was a caricaturist's delight. It was easy to understand why he had been caricatured so often. It was not a handsome face in the way the word handsome is generally used to describe men's looks, but it was an immensely attractive one. He had the kind of good looks that men as well as women find attractive.

Though it was rather a mild October day, he sat in the chair in his overcoat, and around his neck was wrapped a long blue woolen scarf that hung outside the coat and came almost to his knees. His legs were twisted or, rather, entwined one under the other in the most intricate fashion, so that one wondered how he would ever get out of the chair if he had to do so quickly, and one arm was stretched clear around the back of his neck to the opposite side of his head where it was busily engaged in the business of scratching the back of his ear.

"This is the young author, George," said Max Siegel, ushering me to the center of the room.

"Hi," said Mr. Kaufman wearily. He lifted in greeting one finger of the hand that was not engaged in scratching his ear, but he did not move otherwise. Even the one finger was lifted slowly and with infinite lassitude.

"Sit down," said Max Siegel, and smiled reassuringly at me. I retreated to the sofa at the other end of the room, but my eyes remained fastened and expectant on the figure slumped in the armchair.

"You want me to do the talking, George?" said Max Siegel after what seemed to me an unconscionably long time. Again the one finger of the disengaged hand rose slowly in assent. "Mr. Kaufman is willing to work with you on the play and he has suggested some terms for a division of the royalties," said Max Siegel, consulting a typewritten slip of paper on the desk. "Would you prefer to go over them with your agent?" he asked, coming over and handing me the paper. "I think you'll find they're very generous terms," he added.

"I'm sure there will be no difficulty," I said. I took the slip of paper from him and put it in my pocket without looking at it. My eyes were still riveted on the unmoving figure in the armchair. There was another long silence, and a long drawn-out and mournful sigh came from the depths of the chair, followed by a slight but unmistakable belch. It was a somewhat surprising sound—a cross between a prodigious yawn, a distant train whistle hooting over a lonely countryside, and the satisfied grunt of a large dog settling down in front of the fireplace. It was followed by still another silence while Mr. Kaufman's eyes restlessly searched for something they seemed to find missing on the ceiling. He had a perfect view of the ceiling, for he was now sunk so low in the chair that only the top of his head was visible from where I sat. The long legs wrapped one around the other in a tight sailor's knot obscured most of his face, but now the legs moved slightly and his voice issued clearly from behind them.

"When can we have a working session?" he said.

"Whenever you want to," I answered quickly. "Right away—any time—now." The words came out in too great a rush, but there was nothing I could do to stem my eagerness. Behind the legs the arms rose slowly and one hand reached into an inside pocket and withdrew an envelope, while the other hand found a pencil in the handkerchief pocket. I could not see his face, but he was holding up the envelope and evidently regarding some notations on the back of it.

"Would eleven o'clock tomorrow morning be all right?" he asked tiredly.

"Fine," I replied.

"My house," he said, "158 East 63rd Street." The envelope and pencil were moving down and going back into his pocket and one arm was going around the back of his neck again to scratch his ear. I waited and looked inquiringly across the room to where Max Siegel sat behind the desk.

Max Siegel winked at me and addressed the armchair. "Is that all you want of the young author now, George?" he said.

"That's all," came the answer, "except a second act."

Max Siegel made a slight gesture back to me, which seemed to say, Well, that's it, I guess. I cleared my throat and took a deep breath. It seemed that the moment for my graceful little speech had arrived. I had polished it up rather well in the subway, I thought smugly, and I knew it by heart. I rose from the sofa and stood in front of the armchair.

"Mr. Kaufman," I said, "I would like you to know how very much it means to me to . . ." and that was all I said. To my horror, the legs unwound themselves with an acrobatic rapidity I would not have believed possible, and the figure in the chair leaped up and out of it in one astonishing movement like a large bird frightened out of its solitude in the marshes. He was out of the chair, across the room, had opened the door and was flying down the stairs, the blue scarf whipping out behind him.

I stared dazedly after the retreating figure until it disappeared down the stairway. "What have I done?" I stammered. "What did I do?"

Max Siegel, to my intense relief, was shaking with laughter. "You haven't done anything," he answered. "Maybe I should have warned you. Mr. Kaufman hates any kind of sentimentality—can't stand it!" He started to laugh again, but controlled himself. "Maybe I should have told you about George over the phone, but it never occurred to me that you were going to make a speech at him. Did you actually prepare a speech of thanks?"

I nodded sheepishly.

"Well, no great harm done," he said. "He had a barber's appointment that he had to get to, and you saw to it that he got there on time." He handed me a sheet of paper with a check attached. "I'm certain Miss Fishbein will agree these are very generous terms, so you can just fill in the contracts and sign them. That's a check for five hundred dollars for your advance royalty. Congratulations." He held out his hand and smiled. "If you want to, you can make the speech to me so it won't be a total loss."

I smiled back and shook my head. "Is there anything else I ought to know about Mr. Kaufman?" I asked.

He hesitated and laughed again. "There is, but if I started you'd never make that eleven o'clock appointment tomorrow morning. Anyway, it's like marriage—nothing anybody tells you about it is really any help. You've got to live it out for yourself; and if I know George, you'll be living it out every day from now on. Get a good night's sleep—that's the best advice I can give you." We shook hands warmly and I walked out into the bright October afternoon.

I stood for a moment outside the Music Box and looked up at its columned façade with a new and proprietary interest, the contracts and the check rustling importantly in my pocket. There could be no doubt of it now; at last I was on my way.

The rest of that shining afternoon had a quality of incontinent pleasure that I can still recall as vividly as though it were yesterday. The jubilant meeting with Lester and Miss Fishbein, the fusillade of congratulations and obligatory misgivings when the group forgathered at Rudley's, and that last look at Times Square lighting up for the evening just before I walked down the subway steps to go home; the same subway steps, I reminded myself, that I had darted up to have my first look at Broadway long, long ago.

I looked back at the lighted canyon, its daytime ugliness softened into something approaching beauty by the magic of the October twilight deepening around it. The knowledge that I was going to be part of it at last brought me perilously close to that wonderful mixture of emotions that makes one want to laugh and to cry at the same time. It is a mistake to dismiss such a moment as maudlin. To do so is to rob oneself of one of the few innocent pleasures the theatre offers. I enjoyed that last lingering look unabashed by its sentimentality and unashamed of its bathos. I deserved that moment, it seemed to me, and I allowed myself to enjoy it to the full.

I was wise to have done so, for my family's reception of the news, when I stood in the doorway and announced in ringing tones that I had sold the play, in no way matched my own triumphant glow. They received the news with an air of amazed disbelief and infuriating calm. Even the check, which I unfolded carefully and placed in the center of the dining-room table to be admired by them and by myself all over again, was viewed with an irritating detachment and a quite evident distrust.

"I suppose you know what you're doing, taking all that money," said my mother warily, "but I wouldn't touch it until after you've worked with this Mr. Kaufman for a while—in case he asks you to give it back. I certainly wouldn't go around spending it with Eddie Chodorov."

I lost my temper, picked up the check and what remained of my triumphant glow, and spent the rest of the evening on the telephone rekindling the embers of my triumph with Lester, the unsuspecting Eddie, Joe Hyman, and Dore Schary. And as a consequence and in spite of Max Siegel's advice I spent an almost sleepless night, chewing over and sorting out the insistent but contradictory advice I had received from each one on how to meet the first test with George S. Kaufman on the morrow.

THE next morning at five minutes of eleven, I rang the bell of 158 East 63rd Street. The rather modest brownstone house was a little disappointing to my fancy of how a famous playwright should live, but the street was fashionable and the maid who opened the door was a reassuring sight. She was in uniform, a starched white cap perched correctly on her head. More like it, I thought, as she held the door open for me to pass her. I walked in and glanced quickly down the hall at a dining room leading out into a little garden. There was a bowl of flowers on the polished table flanked by silver candlesticks. Just right, I told myself satisfactorily and looked inquiringly at the stairway.

"Mr. Kaufman is waiting for you," said the maid. "The top floor, just go right up."

I walked up the stairs and stopped briefly at the second landing to look at a drawing room and library divided by the stairwell. Both rooms might have come straight out of the movies as far as my innocent eyes were concerned. I knew at once that my first goal the moment the money began to roll in, beyond the taking of taxicabs wherever and whenever I wanted to, would be to live like this. It was an illuminating and expensive moment.

The doors on the third floor—evidently bedrooms—were all tightly closed, and as I reached the fourth-floor landing, Mr. Kaufman stood awaiting me in the doorway of what turned out to be his own bedroom and study combined. After the elegance and style of the drawing room and library, this room was a great blow. It was a small, rather dark room, furnished sparsely with a studio couch, a quite ugly typewriter desk and one easy chair. It was hard for me to believe that a stream of brilliant plays had come out of this monklike interior. I am not certain what I expected the atelier of Kaufman and Connelly would be like, but it most certainly was the opposite of this. There was no hint of any kind that this room was in any way concerned with the theatre. Not a framed photograph or program hung on its walls, and except for an excellent etching of Mark Twain, it might well have been, I thought regretfully, the bedroom and workroom of a certified public accountant. My initial disappointment was to deepen into an active loathing of that room, but at the moment, my eyes after the first quick look were focused on its occupant.

Mr. Kaufman was in the process of greeting me with what turned out to be his daily supply of enthusiasm so far as the social amenities were concerned; that is to say, one finger was being wearily lifted and his voice was managing a tired "Hi." He had moved to the window after this display of cordiality and now stood with his back to the room and to me, staring out at the gardens of the houses on 62nd Street. I had not been asked to sit down, but I was too uncomfortable to remain standing and after a moment of waiting I sat down in the armchair and stared at his back. His arm now reached around his neck to scratch his ear, a gesture I was to come to recognize as a prelude to a rearrangement of a scene or the emergence of a new line; now he remained for a few moments engrossed in the movements of a large cat slowly moving along the garden fence as it contemplated a sparrow on one of the leafless trees. This backyard spectacle seemed to hold him in deep fascination until the cat leaped up into the tree and the bird flew off, whereupon he turned from the window with a large sigh.

I looked at him, eager and alert, but there were still other things of moment that caught and held his attention before he addressed me directly. As he turned from the window, he spied two or three pieces of lint on the floor, and these he carefully removed from the carpet with all the deftness of an expert botanist gathering specimens for the Museum of Natural History. This task completed, he turned his eye toward a mound of sharpened pencils on the desk, found two whose points were not razor-sharp or to his liking, and ground them down in a pencil sharpener attached to the wall. In the process of doing so, he discovered some more lint at the side of the desk and this, too, was carefully picked up, after which he held up and inspected a few sheets of carbon paper, found them still usable, and placed them neatly beside a pile of typewriter paper, which he neatly patted until all its edges were perfectly aligned. His eyes darted dolefully around the room again, seeming to be looking for something else—anything at all, it seemed to me!—to engage his attention, but the carpet being quite free of lint, his gaze finally came to rest on the armchair in which I sat, and he addressed me at last.

"Er . . ." he said, and began to pace rapidly up and down the room. This, too—the word "Er" used as a form of address and followed by a rapid pacing —I was to come to recognize as the actual start of a working session: a signal that lint-picking, cat-watching and pencil-sharpening time was over and that he wanted my attention. During all the time we were engaged together on *Once in a Lifetime*, he never once addressed me by any other name but "Er," even in moments of stress or actual crisis. Perhaps he felt, being the innately shy and private person he was, that "Moss" was too intimate a name to call me; and to address me as "Mr. Hart" seemed a little silly, considering the difference in our ages and positions. But somehow or other I recognized at this first meeting that "Er" meant me and not a clearing of the throat, and I waited attentively until Mr. Kaufman stopped his pacing and stood in front of the armchair looking down at me.

"The trouble begins in the third scene of the first act," he said. "It's messy and unclear and goes off in the wrong direction. Suppose we start with that."

I nodded, trying to look agreeable and knowing at the same time; but this, like my disappointment with the workshop of the master, was my second blow of the morning. After the brilliant peroration on satire in the modern theatre that I had heard from Jed Harris, I had been looking forward with great eagerness to that first talk on play-writing by the celebrated Mr. Kaufman. I had expected to make mental notes on everything he said each day and put it all down every evening in a loose-leaf folder I had bought expressly for that purpose. But this flat, unvarnished statement that something was wrong with the third scene of the first act seemed to be all I was going to get, for Mr. Kaufman was already moving past me now on his way to the bathroom. I turned in my chair and looked at him as he stood by the washbasin and slowly and meticulously washed his hands, and I was struck then and forever afterward by the fact that his hands were what one imagines the hands of a great surgeon to be like.

This impression was further implemented by the odd circumstance that he invariably began the day's work by first washing his hands—a ritual that was, of course, unconscious on his part, but which he would sometimes perform two or three times more during each working session, usually at the beginning of attacking a new scene, as though the anatomy of a play were a living thing whose internal organs were to be explored surgically. I watched him dry his hands and forearms carefully—he took the trouble, I noticed, to undo the cuffs of his shirt and roll them up—and as he came back into the room, walked briskly toward the desk and selected a pencil with just the right pointed sharpness, I was again startled by the inescapable impression that the pencil held poised over the manuscript in those long tensile fingers was a scalpel.

The pencil suddenly darted down onto the paper and moved swiftly along the page, crossing out a line here and there, making a large X through a solid speech, fusing two long sentences into one short one, indicating by an arrow or a question mark the condensation or transference of a section of dialogue so that its point was highlighted and its emphasis sharpened; the operation was repeated with lightning-like precision on the next page and the next, until the end of the scene. Then he picked up the manuscript from the desk and brought it over to me.

"Just cutting away the underbrush," he said. "See what you think." I took the manuscript and read with astonishment. The content of the scene remained the same, but its point was unmuddied by repetition, and the economy and clarity with which everything necessary was now said gave the scene a new urgency. The effect of what he had done seemed to me so magical that I could hardly believe I had been so downright repetitive and verbose. I looked up from the manuscript and stared admiringly at the waiting figure by the desk.

Mr. Kaufman evidently mistook my chagrined and admiring silence for pique. "I may have cut too deeply, of course," he said apologetically. "Is there something you want to have go back?"

"Oh, no," I replied hastily, "not a word. It's just wonderful now. Just great! I don't understand how I could have been so stupid. The scene really works now, doesn't it?"

It was Mr. Kaufman's turn to stare at me in silence for a moment, and he looked at me quizzically over the rims of his glasses before he spoke again. "No, it doesn't work at all," he said gently. "I thought the cuts would show you why it *wouldn't* work." He sighed and scratched his ear. "Perhaps the trouble starts earlier than I thought."

He took the play from my lap and placed it on the desk again. "All right. Page one—Scene One. I guess we might as well face it." He picked up a pencil and held it poised over the manuscript, and I watched fascinated and awestruck as the pencil swooped down on page after page.

If it is possible for a book of this sort to have a hero, then that hero is George S. Kaufman. In the months that followed that first day's work, however, my waking nightmare was of a glittering steel pencil suspended over my head that sometimes turned into a scalpel, or a baleful stare over the rims of a huge pair of disembodied tortoise-shell glasses. I do not think it far-fetched to say that such success as I have had in the theatre is due in large part to George Kaufman. I cannot pretend that I was without talent, but such gifts as I possessed were raw and undisciplined. It is one thing to have a flair for play-writing or even a ready wit with dialogue. It is quite another to apply these gifts in the strict and demanding terms of a fully articulated play so that they emerge with explicitness, precision and form. All of this and a great deal more I learned from George Kaufman. And if it is true that no more eager disciple ever sat at the feet of a teacher, it is equally true that no disciple was ever treated with more infinite patience and understanding.

The debt I owe is a large one, for it could not have been easy for him to deal with some of my initial blunderings and gaucheries, particularly in those first early days of our collaboration. He was not at heart a patient man or a man who bothered to tolerate or maintain the fiction of graceful social behavior in the face of other people's infelicities. In particular, easy admiration distressed him, and any display of emotion filled him with dismay; the aroma of a cigar physically sickened him. I was guilty of all three of these things in daily and constant succession, and since he was too shy or possibly too fearful of hurting my feelings to mention his distress to me, I continued to compound the felony day after day: filling the room with clouds of cigar smoke, being inordinately admiring of everything he did, and in spite of myself, unable to forbear each evening before I left the making of a little speech of gratitude or thanks. His suffering at these moments was acute, but I construed his odd behavior at these times as being merely one more manifestation of the eccentricities that all celebrated people seem to have in such abundance. And the next morning, as I sat down, I would cheerfully light a cigar without pausing to wonder even briefly why Mr. Kaufman was walking as quickly and as far away from me as it was possible for him to get within the confines of that small room.

It did not occur to me, I cannot think why, to be either astonished or confounded by the fact that each time I rose from the armchair and came toward him to speak, he retreated with something akin to terror to the window and stood breathing deeply of such air as was not already swirling with blue cigar smoke. Nor could I understand why, after I fulsomely admired a new line or an acid turn of phrase that he had just suggested that seemed to me downright inspired, he would scratch his ear until I thought it would drop off and stare at me malignantly over the top of his glasses, his face contorted with an emotion that seemed too painful to find expression. Even his passion to remove each dead cigar butt from the room almost before my hand had reached the ashtray with it, and his obsession with keeping the windows wide open on even the most frigid days, did nothing to alert me to his suffering, and I was, seemingly, deaf as well as dense when his diatribes against people who made speeches at each other took on added strength and fervor with each passing day.

I suppose his worst moment of the day came at my leave-taking, when he could sense another little speech coming on. I know now that he evolved various stratagems of his own to escape these eulogies, such as rushing into the bathroom and with the water taps turned full on calling out a good-bye through the closed door, or going to the telephone and with his back to me hurriedly calling a number; but with something approximating genius I nearly always managed to find the moment to have my say. He seldom escaped!

Mr. Kaufman spent a good deal of his time, particularly in the late afternoons, stretched out full length on the floor, and it was usually at one of these unwary moments when he was at his lowest ebb and stretched helplessly below me, that I would stand over him and deliver my captivating compendium of the day's work. Something like a small moan, which I misinterpreted as agreement, would escape from his lips and he would turn his head away from the sight of my face, much the way a man whose arm is about to be jabbed with a needle averts his gaze to spare himself the extra pain of seeing the needle descend.

All unknowing and delighted with my eloquence, I would light a new cigar, puff a last fresh aromatic cloud of smoke down into his face, and cheerfully reminding him of the splendid ideas he had had for the scene we were going to work on tomorrow, I would take my leave. I have never allowed myself to think of some of the imprecations that must have followed my retreating figure down the stairway, but if I was torturing Mr. Kaufman all unknowingly, the score was not exactly one-sided. Quite unaware that he was doing so, he was on his part providing me with a daily Gethsemane of my own that grew more agonizing with each passing day, and though his suffering was of the spirit and mine was of the flesh, I think our pain in the end was about equal, for I was as incapable of mentioning my distress to him as he was of mentioning his to me.

The cause of my agony was simple enough. Mr. Kaufman cared very little about food. His appetite was not the demanding and capricious one mine was—indeed, his lack of concern with food was quite unlike anyone else's I have ever known. The joys and pleasures of the table seemed simply to have passed him by in the way that a dazzling sunset must escape the color-blind. He apparently needed very little food to sustain him and cared even less when and how it was served. He had his breakfast at ten o'clock in the morning, and work was enough to nourish him thereafter until evening. His energy, unlike my own, seemed to be attached not to his stomach but to his brain; and his capacity for work, which was enormous, seemed to flourish and grow in ratio to the rattle of a typewriter.

True, every afternoon at about four o'clock, apparently as a concession to some base need he knew existed in other human beings but did not quite understand himself, tea would be brought in by the maid. Six cookies, no more and no less, and on gala occasions two slices of homemade chocolate cake would lie on a plate naked and shimmering to my hunger-glazed eyes; and, as I could sniff the tea coming up the stairs or hear the teacups rattling on the tray outside the door, my stomach would rumble so loudly and my ravenousness would be so mouth-watering, that I would get up and walk about the room, pretending to stretch my arms and legs, in order to control myself, for it was all I could do not to grab and stuff the minute the maid set the tray down.

My predicament was further complicated by the fact that Mr. Kaufman was always scrupulously polite and devilishly insistent that I help myself first, and since I was only too aware that he took only a sip or two of tea and never more than one cookie, which he absent-mindedly nibbled at, I could never bring myself to do more than slavishly follow his example for fear of being thought ill-mannered or unused to high life—until one day, maddened by hunger, I gobbled up every single cookie and the two slices of chocolate cake while he was in the bathroom washing his hands. Whether it was the mutely empty plate or my guilt-ridden and embarrassed face staring up at him as he approached the tea tray, I do not know; but from that day onward, little sandwiches began to appear, and tea time to my vast relief was moved up an hour earlier.

Meanwhile, in spite of the separate and unwitting mortifications which we daily afflicted on each other, work proceeded with a grueling regularity and an unswerving disregard of endurance, health, well-being or personal life that left me at first flabbergasted and then chastened and awestruck at his unrivaled dedication to the task in hand. It was a kind of unflagging industry and imperturbable concentration that anyone, not just myself, might well marvel at, for this eminently successful man labored each day quite as though our positions had been reversed and this were *his* first play, not mine; his great chance to make his mark as a Broadway playwright, not my own. There was an element of the demoniacal in his tireless search for just the right word to round a sentence into its proper unity, for the exact juxtaposition of words and movement that would slyly lead the audience along the periphery of a scene to its turning point and then propel them effortlessly to its climax.

His ear for a comedic line was faultless and his zeal for the precise effect he wanted boundless. No moment, however small, seemed unimportant enough to escape his almost fierce attention, and his grasp of the play's latent values was immediate and complete. My eyes and ears were opened anew each day to the thousand-and-one endless details that go to make up the subtle and infinitely fragile clockwork of a play's interior mechanism, and to the slow cultivation of its subsoil that gradually makes it blossom into something vital and alive. I watched and listened with the consecration of a yogi, and yet in awe of him though I was, it never occurred to me not to disagree when I thought he was wrong, whether on the reshaping of a scene or even on a newly coined line which he liked and I did not. This was not a special bravery on my part or some noble effort at keeping my own identity intact—it had simply never entered my mind to be timorous with him or to be in any way discomforted by his manner.

I was all the more amazed to discover later on that this gentle man with whom I had been at once thoroughly at ease and completely comfortable, this same kindly and understanding man at whose side I worked each day, could instantly succeed in disquieting the most formidable men in the theatre or out of it and, by his mere presence in a room, frighten the daylights out of half the people there. There could be no doubt about the effect his presence created. Head waiters cowered and the wits of the town watched their tongues as he loomed up in a doorway, the eyes over those tortoise-shell rims seeming to examine the room for a sign of the inept, the fake or the pompous.

Famous raconteurs seemed to wither and dwindle under that penetrating glance, for he could puncture pretense or bombast with an acid verbal thrust that would be repeated with malicious glee in every corner of the so-called charmed circle before the sun set. Even such rugged specimens as New York taxi drivers or talkative barbers quailed at his stare and were silent until he was safely deposited out of the cab or the chair, and so fearsome a practitioner of the art of discomfiture as Alexander Woollcott admitted that

George Kaufman was the one person who could always make him uncomfortable and ill at ease.

This side of him at first bewildered and astonished me. I never ceased being surprised at the startling and sometimes numbing effect he created among even the most seemingly secure and self-assured people, for unquestionably he did indeed intimidate even his close friends. But the result, though trying on the more timid of them, was not without its compensations. People took pains to be at their best with him, and just as a mediocre tennis player will sometimes play above his game when he is matched with a superior opponent, people were generally stimulated into their level best when he was about. It is my own guess that his somewhat terrifying manner, far from being any sort of pose, stemmed from the fact that he more than most men simply refused to resort to the banalities of what usually passes for polite conversation; faced with some of the cant and nonsense that a good deal of theatre talk consists of, he allowed himself the luxury of saying exactly what came into his mind as the only proper answer to the extravagant claptrap and twaddle he was often forced to listen to. It is not difficult to acquire a reputation for asperity and irascibility, particularly if one has the courage to indulge this luxury as a matter of principle and it is accompanied by a tart and ready wit.

These he had and the audacity to use them, for unlike most of us, he was not driven by a savage necessity to be liked. He cared little for the good opinion or the admiration of the special world he moved in and was a celebrated part of. He adhered strictly to his own standards and judgments, and they were stern ones. The most striking characteristic of the personality he presented to the world at large was an almost studied aloofness and indifference, and it struck me as remarkable how the world at large continually tried to break through this wall and win his approval on any terms he chose to make. Indifference can be a wonderful weapon—whether it is used as ammunition in a warfare between lovers or as a mask for timidity and shyness, for behind that mask of disdain and unconcern lay the diffident and modest man whom it never entered my mind to be afraid of.

Perhaps better than most I came to know that this seeming indifference was the protective coloring of a temperament whose secret and inmost recesses held a deep reservoir of emotion; that it was the superficial exterior of a man who chose to reveal himself only to a very few, but whose emotions could be fervent and profound. I knew how quickly he could be seized and touched emotionally and how susceptible he was to the dark doubts that licked at other men's souls. Somehow or other, I do not know why, or quite understand how, I seemed to have managed from the very beginning to bypass both the façade and the legend and immediately to fall into a warmhearted and gay relationship in which he bore no resemblance to the tales I heard or to the scenes I witnessed of his cantankerous behavior with other people.

He was not, of course, without his own mischievous and annoying qualities, even for me. He could be willfully stubborn on small things with a

dogged and inflexible obstinacy, and perversely fair and just on large issues
to the point of exasperating saintliness; and he had an abundant share of
inconsistent and crotchety prejudices that extended over a wide area and
included, most particularly and actively, waiters who never seemed to be
able to take down his order correctly, people who tried to tell him jokes,
and any fellow passenger he happened to find himself next to when he was
in an elevator or on a train and who had the misfortune to recognize him
and attempt to engage him in conversation. If I was with him at one of
these awful moments, his churlishness would make me cringe and I would
move away and pretend we were not together, but to my unfailing amazement it was always him they apologized to and me they glared at. Like
"the man who came to dinner," whom he resembled in a muted way more
than he ever suspected, he suffered daily from the gross inadequacies of the
human race; but these failings, however infuriating, were seldom sufficient
—after a small but satisfactory explosion of irritation—to keep him from
walking toward the typewriter with alacrity. Nothing in the world, as far as
I could tell, ever stopped him from doing that—and as he walked toward
the desk I would marshal my wits and try to think of a bright line to begin
the day's work.

By the end of the first month of our working together, however, I was in
a state of constant weariness. I attributed a great deal of my brain fag to
simple malnutrition, but actually what I was suffering from was insufficient
sleep. Our working hours were from eleven o'clock in the morning until
five thirty or six in the evening, at which time I would eat a walloping
dinner and rush off to Newark or Brooklyn for my little-theatre rehearsals,
which began at seven thirty and usually continued until midnight and
sometimes past. By the time I reached home again, after the obligatory
socializing with the cast over coffee and cake, it was usually three or four in
the morning. Since I had to be up shortly after eight o'clock in order to
allow enough time for the long subway ride, which would get me to 158
East 63rd Street at five minutes of eleven, by the end of the month I was
desperately trying, in those archaic days before Benzedrine and Dexamyl,
not to let Mr. Kaufman notice that my brilliance seemed to diminish with
startling abruptness at about two o'clock in the afternoon.

I did not dare, however, give up my little-theatre work. Apart from the
necessary weekly income that it provided, the basket I carried most of my
eggs in was too precariously balanced to shake, even with a Broadway production in the offing. I knew well enough that failure is the norm of the
theatre, not success.

It was fortunate for me that Mr. Kaufman was the most incurious of
men. The state of my health or the vagaries of my personal life held little
interest for him, nor did he seem to connect my afternoon lassitude with
either one or the other. It did not seem to surprise him that I grasped the
smallest opportunities to take quick cat naps, sometimes even while he was
washing his hands in the bathroom or taking a telephone call, and though

he was vaguely aware that I was engaged in some sort of amateur theatricals in the evenings, it never seemed to occur to him to ask exactly what it was that I did. How he imagined I earned a living I do not know; but it was just as well that he was without curiosity on that score, for I had dropped Shaw and O'Neill from my repertoire and was now enthusiastically rehearsing the pirated works of Kaufman and Connelly.

I had switched to Kaufman and Connelly shortly after seeing *June Moon* and before I had the faintest idea that I myself would be working with one-half of the famous team. Now that I miraculously was, there was no way of changing back even if I wanted to. I breathed a sigh of relief, nevertheless, as each day passed and Mr. Kaufman's lack of interest in my personal life remained untouched, for it was the practice in those days for directors of little-theatre groups to escape, by any means they could devise, the payment of royalties to authors, for the good enough reason that no royalties to an author meant more money to the director, and I had long since hit upon the simple expedient of taking whatever play I wanted to do and giving it a new title of my own. Thus, *Beggar on Horseback*, *Dulcy* and *To the Ladies*, all three of which I was busily rehearsing each evening after I finished the day's work with Mr. Kaufman, were being presented as: *Dreams for Sale*, *Mrs. Fixit* and *The Superior Sex*, by James L. Baker and Michael Crane.

I had never dared face what I would say if he ever questioned me about my evening activities; only once, when I asked if we might stop work early that particular afternoon because I had a dress rehearsal in Newark, was Mr. Kaufman's interest sufficiently aroused to inquire, "What play are you doing?" I was able to gulp an answer, "*Dreams for Sale*," and as I saw his eyebrows arch questioningly at the title of a play he had never heard of, and as my heart began to race with the lie I was about to tell him—at that same moment his eye, luckily, spied a new piece of lint on the carpet and his interest in my personal life vanished.

As best I could and as much as I dared, I tried to end my nightly rehearsals earlier, but my weariness persisted. I had about reached the decision that I would have to borrow money enough to live on from Joe Hyman until *Once in a Lifetime* was produced, when the weariness disappeared as if by magic, never to return in quite the same degree. The magic was accomplished by two events that took place one after the other on the same day, and they instantly banished not only weariness, but also any idea I may have been cherishing of how hard my lot was. In quick succession, I met Beatrice Kaufman and I took a headlong plunge into the off-stage private world of the theatre that I had read about and mooned over for so long and of which I longed to be a part. Even the brief glimpse that I had of it was sufficient to keep me awake for quite a while afterward, for it came at just the right moment.

One morning, as I reached the fourth-floor landing at eleven o'clock as usual, I was surprised to see Mr. Kaufman in conversation with a handsome woman whose luxuriant hair, brushed straight back from her forehead in a high pompadour, was tinted a bluish-gray. I was aware, of course, that other people occupied and moved about in the rooms below us, but I had no idea who they might be. Mr. Kaufman had never spoken of a wife or child, and he did not, to me at least, appear to be a married man—but then it was hard for me to conceive of Mr. Kaufman as a man who had ever had a mother or a father, much less a wife! He seemed like a being who sprang full-grown out of the typewriter each morning and went back into it at the end of each day. I had as little knowledge of his personal life as he had of mine. Once the door closed behind us at eleven o'clock, no person other than the maid who brought up tea ever appeared and I had never glimpsed anyone other than the same maid as I walked down the stairs in the evening and let myself out the door.

I must have stared at them both in open-mouthed surprise, for their conversation ceased as I appeared on the landing and they both turned toward me. Mr. Kaufman lifted the usual one finger in greeting, and then seeming to summon up all the social graces he possessed for the effort, he said, "Moss Hart—Beatrice Kaufman." We smiled at each other and I stood uneasily on the landing, uncertain as to whether I should go into the room. I am a little loath to record that I at once took it for granted that Beatrice Kaufman was Mr. Kaufman's sister, but that, indeed, is what I did assume. For one thing, I had never heard anyone introduced in that fashion before. In the Bronx or Brooklyn, introductions always took the form of, "This is my wife, Mrs. So-and-So," or even more simply, just, "My wife." For another thing, in Brooklyn or the Bronx, a man and wife always occupied the same bedroom, and I knew Mr. Kaufman did not share his room with anyone else. Incredibly simple-minded though it seems, I did not discover that Beatrice Kaufman was Mrs. George Kaufman until a good deal later on, so that the mildly confused look that came into Mr. Kaufman's eyes when I politely inquired now and then how his sister was, is easily accounted for.

They picked up the threads of their interrupted conversation after that somewhat less than revealing introduction, and I stood watching Beatrice Kaufman admiringly. She was not in the conventional sense a beautiful woman, but she had uncommon distinction, an individual style, and a unique and singular quality of her own that lent to everything she said and did a special radiance. She had the gift of imbuing even the smallest of daily undertakings with an enkindling gaiety and an intoxicating flavor. It was a gift which was peculiarly hers and hers alone. I had never listened to or looked at, at such close quarters, anyone quite like her. I eavesdropped shamelessly. To ears used to listening to the female chatter of the Bronx and Brooklyn, her talk seemed to come straight out of Somerset Maugham, and though I could make little of what she was saying in terms of the people she was talking about, I knew she was recounting some tale of the world I had read about for so long in F.P.A.'s column. I marveled at the grace and ease with which she sent Mr. Kaufman into willing and ready laughter—no small feat in itself—and I was fascinated and charmed by the vibrancy and force of the woman herself.

This is the kind of woman I will get to know, I thought, when I become a part of that world myself. It was worth any sort of weariness a thousand times over.

I stared at them enviously and thought, How wonderful to have a sister like that—and as I watched and listened, hoping she would not finish the conversation too soon, to my surprise she suddenly turned to me and said, "I've left strict orders with George, and I'm depending upon you to see that they're carried out. He's to stop work early today and come down to tea. You're to come with him to make sure he gets there." She gave me a quick conspiratorial smile and then she was gone. I looked after her and then at Mr. Kaufman, who was already making his way toward the type-writer.

"Beatrice is having people for tea," he said grumpily as he removed the cover. "And of course the world is supposed to come to a full stop." Not, "My wife is giving a tea this afternoon," mind you—just, "Beatrice is having people for tea." I took it for granted anew that his sister was having a cousin or an elderly aunt, whom he was reluctant to see, in for a family tea —but that she was arranging it, nevertheless, in a devoted, sisterly fashion.

The sparkling flood of light her presence seemed to create remained in the room like an afterglow long after she had gone. It took me a while to settle down to work after the door closed behind her, and then I was brighter for having caught even that fleeting glimpse of her than I had been in days. The creative impulse is a mysterious one. It ignites and flourishes under the strangest of stimuli. I do not know precisely why the sight of Beatrice Kaufman should have unlocked my creative mechanism and set it wildly in motion, except that she seemed to be so striking a symbol of the world which lay just behind success in the theatre that she made the goal itself seem tantalizingly nearer and the drudgery and the weariness worth while. Both drudgery and weariness seemed to have vanished now. I could have worked right through the night.

It came as something of a shock when Mr. Kaufman glanced at his watch and said, "It's quarter of five." The day had sped by without my usual battle to keep awake or of my even being aware that no battle had taken place. He walked to the door and opened it. A babble of voices came up the stairway from the rooms below. "They're here," he sighed. "We'd better go down." He ran a comb through his hair, adjusted his tie, and motioned me to follow him. I was mystified by the number of voices that came more clearly now as we walked down the stairs. It did not sound at all like a family tea party. With some little alarm I realized I was not dressed for anything more than that—indeed, I was hardly dressed suitably for even that. I was wearing my ordinary working and rehearsal clothes, an old sport coat with brass buttons, and a pair of faded, unpressed brown flannel trousers. It was too late to think about the way I looked, however, for we were on the second-floor landing now and I was following Mr. Kaufman toward the drawing room. I drew back at the threshold and stopped dead. The room was alive with people and I recognized every single one of them. It seemed

to my dumfounded eyes as if one of those double-page murals of the great
figures of the theatre and literary world that *Vanity Fair* was always running
had suddenly come to life.

Everyone I had ever read about or hero-worshipped from afar seemed
to be contained within my awestruck gaze, from Ethel Barrymore and Harpo
Marx to Heywood Broun and Edna Ferber, from Helen Hayes and George
Gershwin to F.P.A. and Alexander Woollcott—as though some guardian
angel of the stage-struck had waved a wand and assembled a galaxy luminous
enough to make the most insatiable hero-worshipper's hair stand on end. I
had the feeling that mine was doing exactly that, for I was seized with a kind
of stage fright that made my tongue cleave to the roof of my mouth, and I
was horribly conscious of my clothes. Only a stare from over those tortoise-
shell rims made me move forward into the room.

"Alfred Lunt—Moss Hart," said Mr. Kaufman. Alfred Lunt held out his
hand and I managed to shake it. "Leslie Howard—Moss Hart," and again
I smiled and shook hands, not yet daring to trust my tongue to come un-
stuck. "Get yourself a drink and bring Miss Parker one, will you?" said Mr.
Kaufman. "Dorothy Parker—Moss Hart." I presented Miss Parker with the
same glazed smile and stood grinning crazily at her, unable to get my upper
lip down over my teeth. Neysa McNein—it was unmistakably she—called to
Mr. Kaufman, and he turned away, mercifully releasing me from any more
introductions.

"Don't bother about the drink," said Miss Parker. "Mr. Benchley and Mr.
Sherwood are arriving with reinforcements." Her own slight smile seemed
to indicate a willingness to talk, but Mr. Benchley, arriving with the drinks
at that moment, came between us, and someone I could not see was putting
a pair of arms around her in an embrace. With an inward sigh of relief, I
moved toward the center of the room and stood by myself, watching and
listening. To my further relief, no one paid the slightest attention to me,
and the room was so jammed I felt my clothes would not be much noticed
if I made myself as unobtrusive as possible.

A butler nudged my arm and said, "Tea or a drink, sir?" "A drink, thank
you," I replied and took one from the tray. I took a long swallow and looked
around me delightedly. Six months ago, I thought contentedly, even six
weeks ago, this would have been pure fantasy. Maybe this time next year I'll
be talking to everybody here. A group of people in front of the tea table
moved away, and Beatrice Kaufman seated behind it suddenly caught sight
of me, smiled brightly and waved her hand. I smiled and waved back.

At the far end of the room someone began to play the piano, and though
I could not see who was at the keyboard, I knew that it was probably
George Gershwin. I smiled to myself. I remembered how I had stolen some
of the songs from *Lady Be Good* to use in camp, and I listened to him play
with a special pleasure of my own. I began to enjoy myself hugely. It was
far better, this secret enjoyment, I thought, than any kind of chatter could
possibly be, even if I could manage to bring myself to talk to someone.
The butler moved by me again and I relinquished my empty glass and took

a fresh drink. Herbert Bayard Swope, on his way to join a group near the fireplace, found me directly in his path and said with great heartiness, "Hello, there, how *are* you?" He had obviously mistaken me for someone he thought he knew; but I smiled back and said, "Fine, how are *you?*" Speech had not only returned, but I was able to match his own heartiness in reply. I took a long swallow of the drink and looked around the room carefully. Why not talk to someone after all? What a fine, juicy bit it would make to report to the group at Rudley's. I could already hear myself artfully working a celebrated name into the conversation and then casually remarking, "Oh, yes, I was talking to him just the other afternoon." It would be a gratifying moment. Whom could I talk to, I wondered, that would impress them the most? There was almost too great a selection of the celebrated to choose from; for nearly all of the figures, which were damned and envied at the table at Rudley's every afternoon, were scattered around the room.

There was no question, however, as to who would impress them most. I had noticed him at once, even while I stood gaping at the threshold. And my eyes had searched him out several times since then, but always he was the center of a group that seemed to ring him in and roar with laughter at whatever he was saying. I looked around the room once more, and this time to my surprise Alexander Woollcott was alone. He had moved as far away from the piano as he could get and was sitting in a chair in the opposite corner of the room, calmly reading a book amidst all the hubbub. It seemed to me an astonishing thing to be doing at such a time, but then the celebrated seemed to be full of endless and varied eccentricities. By the same token, I reasoned, taking another large swallow of whiskey, he probably would not think it strange if I interrupted his reading and engaged him in conversation.

I made my way slowly over to where he sat and stood for a moment gathering my courage and my wits for the proper opening gambit. I glanced sideways at the title of the book he was reading and saw that it was a new mystery novel that I had just finished reading a few days ago myself. What better opening than that could I possibly have? Alexander Woollcott was a famous connoisseur of murder and mayhem and I was also an *aficionado* of this particular form of literature. We had that in common to start with, anyway, and then we could branch off into the theatre and all his various enthusiasms, every one of which I knew by heart. I moved closer until I was right beside him, then coughed discreetly to attract his attention.

"You'll like that very much, Mr. Woollcott," I said, pointing to the book, and smiled engagingly down at him.

Mr. Woollcott withdrew his gaze slowly from the page, and his eyes, owlish behind the thick spectacles, fixed themselves on mine. "How would *you* know?" he said.

The tone was so acid that the words seemed to ferment as he delivered them. The owlish eyes gleamed fiercely behind the glasses for a moment more and then removed themselves from mine and returned to the book, quite as though I had splattered against the walls and was no longer visible.

I devoutly wished I could have done so. I would indeed have given anything to be able to vanish into thin air in front of him, but I could only stand for still another harrowing moment, rigid with embarrassment, until my legs were able to move me away. I retreated to the center of the room in a cold sweat of self-consciousness. There are moments so mortifying that one's inner sense of confusion and shame seem completely exposed to the eyes of every passing stranger. I knew well enough that no one had overheard this passage with Woollcott, but I began to tremble with apprehension lest anyone else speak to me. Suddenly, I began to be painfully aware of how raw and unqualified I was to move among these people, and how ludicrous it was to fancy myself ever becoming a part of this exclusive, tight little world. As quickly as I could, I threaded my way through the jammed room and fled down the stairs.

The next morning, my determination to be part of Woollcott's world more firmly strengthened than ever by the preposterous beginning I had made, I was galvanized into a kind of working fury. Out of just such ignoble moments and motives, do plays and novels sometimes emerge. For I do not think that these vain and foolish spurs to creativity obtained only in my own case. On the contrary, I am inclined to believe that just such petty considerations often seductively quicken the wheels of creation. If we could ever glimpse the inner workings of the creative impulse, coldly and without pretense, I am afraid that to a larger degree than we choose to admit of so exalted a process, we would discover that more often the siren enticements of worldly pleasures and rewards spark it into life than the heroic and consecrated goals we are told inspire it.

I have noticed that the lofty and lonely pinnacles inhabited by the purely creative are sometimes surprisingly and most comfortably furnished by Westinghouse, and a new convertible generally waits outside. There is nothing necessarily unacceptable or unworthy about this, but the pious nonsense that regularly issues from those domiciles—about the lacerations to the spirit that the throes of selfless creation impose and the unworldliness of the rewards these artists seek—is irritating to listen to. I knew what I wanted and why, at any rate. And crass as it may sound, it not only left my creative spirit unblemished but it heightened my capacity to enjoy unashamed the inglorious but satisfying mess of pottage that success offers to the less honorably inspired of us.

I SET such a furious pace in the weeks following Beatrice Kaufman's tea party that to my own amazement and to Mr. Kaufman's as well, I think, the second act was completed and the structure of the third act was planned and roughly committed to paper in scenario form. To my further surprise, Mr. Kaufman called a halt. I had begun to think of ourselves as a great force of nature, like Victoria Falls, pouring forth and stopping for nothing. "I think a little breather is indicated before we plunge into the third act," said Mr. Kaufman. "We'll take tomorrow off." And then, accurately gauging the expression on my face to be the onset of a forthcoming burst of eloquence to commemorate the completion of the second act, he added wickedly, "There must be *somebody* else you want to say a few words to," and he rushed into the bathroom and turned the water taps full on!

While he was washing his hands, I eased my way over to the desk and stealthily turned over an envelope lying on top of the pile of manuscript to steal a look at the notations typed on the back of it. Mr. Kaufman's appointments and reminders to himself, which he typed out daily and later stuck in his breast pocket, always fascinated me, and whenever I could, I would shamelessly rubberneck, for they invariably listed meetings with a number of people whose juxtaposition on the same day never ceased to tickle my fancy. The list for tomorrow, freshly and neatly typed, with three dots between appointments, said in part: "Francis Fox . . . Scalp Treatment"; "Aunt Sidonia . . . Gloria Swanson." The jump from Aunt Sidonia to Gloria Swanson was just the kind of unlikely contiguity that delighted me, and there was an even more satisfying conjunction farther down on the envelope, for later in the day, which read: "Inlay . . . Croquet mallet . . . Norma Shearer." Satisfied that Mr. Kaufman's day would be as piquant and provocative as I had hoped it would, I turned the envelope over again and moved away to consider what my own one-day's respite would be. It took no great amount of searching to know what would give me the most pleasure. My day would not be as colorful as Mr. Kaufman's, but it would from my own point of view be equally diverting. I planned simply to stay in bed all day and eat! I would eat until I fell asleep, and when I awoke I would eat again until I dozed off. The very thought of the amount of food I would down filled me with content; but Mr. Kaufman, emerging from the bathroom, put an end to it.

"By the way," he said, "Sam Harris is back from California and he wants to meet you. I told him we wouldn't be working tomorrow, and he'd like you to come to the Music Box at eleven o'clock. Is that all right? I'm going to call Max Siegel now."

I nodded agreeably but seethed inwardly, and instantly made another solemn resolve. From the very first moment I could arrange to do so, I would never put a foot out of bed until noon. The solemn vows of our youth are fervently pledged but usually kept with inconstant faithfulness. This one, however, along with my resolve never to ride in the subway again once I had money enough to take taxis, I have had no trouble in remaining faithful to—and with no little pleasure and profit to myself.

There is ample evidence, I am certain, that the early-morning hours are the golden ones for work, and the testimony of such loiterers as myself on the enduring joys of late-rising carries little weight with folk who are up and about at dawn, busily improving those shining early hours. They continue to have my blessing from the depths of a warm and skeptical bed. I accept their data on the beauties of the early morning along with their thinly veiled scorn of my own pitiable indolence; but the truth is, I have never been able to understand the full extent of my loss. The Bay of Naples and the harbor at Rio de Janeiro were still there at one o'clock in the afternoon when I first laid eyes on them, and were even more beautiful, it seemed to me, for my being wide awake and thoroughly refreshed when I did look upon them. So far as I know, anything worth hearing is not usually uttered at seven o'clock in the morning; and if it is, it will generally be repeated at a more reasonable hour for a larger and more wakeful audience. Much more likely, if it is worth hearing at all, it will be set down in print where it can be decently enjoyed by dawdling souls, like myself, who lumpishly resist the golden glow of dawn.

I was not, therefore, in the best of moods for a first meeting with Sam Harris as I climbed the steps to his office the next morning at a little before eleven o'clock, and it is not a small compliment I pay him when I say that after a few minutes in his presence, I no longer regretted that my dream of stuffing and sleeping had come to nothing. Sam Harris was an irresistible human being. From the moment Max Siegel offered his usual introduction, "This is the young author, Mr. Harris," and Sam Harris came from behind the desk with his hand extended and said, "Hello, kid," I was in love with him and his willing slave.

This was not, I was to discover, an unusual occurrence. Few people in the theatre or out of it remained aloof to the wise and tender sense of life that seemed to envelop Sam Harris and to touch everything about him. The extraordinary effect he produced on people was somehow made all the more striking by the fact that at first glance he gave the impression of being a most ordinary little man. He was short and chunky, with a pushed-in face that was saved from downright ugliness by a pair of the brightest and kindliest eyes I had ever seen, and a smile of such warm-heartedness and amiability that words like "goodness" and "humanity" leaped foolishly into the mind.

Most amazing of all, perhaps, was how immediately one was persuaded that this ordinary-appearing little man, of obviously little education or learning, was a man of impeccable taste, with a mind of vigor, clarity and freshness. He was elegantly turned out, from the pearl stickpin in his chastely hued tie to the fine linen cuffs appearing with studied correctness from under the sleeves of his beautifully tailored suit. He spoke softly, but with a pithy and trenchant conciseness, and his replies to a question were sometimes startlingly laconic. It made the first few moments with him difficult, for neither Mr. Kaufman nor Max Siegel had forewarned me before this first meeting that Sam Harris was more than a little deaf. He pretended, however, to hear everything, and some of the elliptical conversation that I was puzzled by on that first day was due to the fact that he was as vain about his growing deafness as he was about his appearance. It was the only vice, if vanity is indeed a vice, that I ever discovered he possessed.

He was exceptional also in the sense that a man without vices is usually humdrum and dull, and Sam Harris was anything but dull. He had color and gaiety and humor, and a most marvelous bonhomie with theatre people that extended all the way from stagehands to stars. Everyone in the theatre adored him. In a jungle profession, where the petty snipings of envy and mean-spiritedness are the passports to everyday conversation, the reverence in which he was held was a little awesome. So, too, was his renown for the way he could handle the most difficult of stars. On these vulnerable and trigger-tempered creatures the effect he produced was especially astonishing. An actor locked in a tantrum of rage and frustration at the end of a disastrous dress rehearsal would fall into sweet reasonableness at the sound of the first soft-spoken words uttered by Sam Harris. In a twinkling the hoarse words of rage would be muffled and the gentle voice of Sam Harris would take over. His secret, I think, was a simple one. Violence is strongly attracted by serenity, and Sam Harris was by all odds the most tranquil human being I have ever known. The world he lived and worked in was a world whose daily climate was governed by the uproar of hysteria and turmoil, and against this howling calliope of egomania he moved with a calm and a quietude that instantly subdued the most savage and ungovernable outbursts of temper and temperament. No matter how loud the blast or how extravagant the explosion, his untroubled serenity was the balm that allowed the bluster to die down and the bellowing to slacken into something that approached a common ground peaceable enough for rehearsals to continue.

I would be doing him a disservice to suggest that his nature was entirely saintlike or that he did not possess a good-sized temper of his own. He was too merry a fellow to accommodate much of saintliness, and when his temper flared, as it did occasionally, it was marvelous to see him wrestle with it, for it was a rip-snorting affair while it lasted. Actors themselves seldom provoked it, for he was excessively sentimental about theatre people and notoriously soft-hearted about actors in particular. Their lawyers or agents, however, were the worm in the heart of the rose, and about these he would fulminate with unsentimental gusto. Other than that, little else about the theatre daunted him. He was a gambler of unwavering courage, once he placed his bet on an author or star he believed in; and his single-minded passion to give a good play a fine production remained undiminished to the end of his life. He was a great gentleman of the theatre and, so far as I am concerned, its last aristocrat.

We got along famously, once the first moment or two of stiffness had passed and my enjoyment of him outran my shyness. "How are you two fellows getting along?" he asked. And when I replied, "I'm starving most of the time, but I think we've got a good second act," he roared with laughter. After that, I rattled on unrestrained, telling him all sorts of things about myself I could not recall ever having told anyone else; for it was quite evident that he liked me immediately, and there is nothing that so quickly opens the floodgates of friendship and intimacy as that light in the other person's eye that unmistakably signals a delight and pleasure in one's company.

I must have talked on interminably, for Max Siegel finally reappeared and, surprised to see me still chattering away, said, "You got an appointment at the booking office, haven't you, Mr. Harris?" Sam Harris nodded and came from behind the desk. He led me toward the door and rested a hand affectionately on my shoulder. "We'll be seeing more of each other, kid," he said. "I hope a lot more. I think you're going to write some interesting plays." He smiled that special smile of his and waved as I started down the steps. I waved and smiled back and walked out of the Music Box lobby curiously jubilant and elated, though I could not understand why until a few minutes later. Suddenly I knew. Sam Harris had made up my mind for me.

For some two or three weeks past I had been shirking the making of a decision that had to be made, and now, still without knowing quite why I was doing so, I knew that I had made it. This hour with Sam Harris had pushed me over the brink. The decision was not an easy one to make. It was already March, and the owners of the Flagler Hotel had been pressing me since early February to sign a new contract as social director for the coming summer at the largest salary I had ever received and one which they claimed, truthfully I believe, to be the largest sum ever to be offered a social director in the history of the Borscht Circuit. I had backed and filled and excused and put them off in every way I could think of, but eager as I was to put that part of my life behind me, I had to face the possibility of what I would do if the spring tryout of *Once in a Lifetime*, which was planned for the last two weeks in May, was a failure. No camp or hotel, of course, could wait until the end of May to engage a social director, no matter how sought-after he was—March, indeed, was the very latest they dared wait and they had so informed me. But suppose *Once in a Lifetime* was only half-good and needed to be rewritten over the summer—what then? Some plays—in fact, a major proportion of them as I well knew—were summarily abandoned in Asbury Park or Atlantic City and never came to New York at all. If *Once in a Lifetime* were to meet this same fate on its tryout, how would I get through the summer and what would we live on until the little-theatre groups started up again in November? For though I was earning a good deal more money now, both summers and winters, than I ever had, it seemed to disappear with annoying swiftness—a phenomenon, I might add, that has plagued me down the years with dogged persistence. That morning, however, I had finally come to a decision of sorts—a safe compromise, so it seemed to me: the bright idea of having Dore Schary substitute for me as social director until mid-June, when I would certainly know which way the wind was blowing; and then I could take over myself.

This was actually what I was on my way to try to do as I walked out of the Music Box. I was fairly certain the proprietors of the Flagler, anxious to have me as they were, would agree to these terms, and I had made the appointment to meet them and sign the contract at two o'clock this afternoon. Instead, I turned into the Piccadilly Hotel, next door to the Music Box, and marched resolutely toward a telephone booth. I dropped a nickel nervously into the slot, and as I closed the door of the booth, I knew I was going to burn the last bridge behind me. Fresh from the presence of Sam Harris, it seemed a simple and easy thing to do—and somewhat shakily I did it. I emerged from the booth and walked out into 45th Street again, a social director no longer, but a playwright come hell or high water—though no one on the street seemed to notice the startling change in me.

The next morning, arriving for work, I was conscious of a subtle difference in the atmosphere. Even before I had settled myself into the armchair and surreptitiously unwrapped the first Hershey bar in my pocket, Mr. Kaufman said, "Er . . ." and was pacing rapidly up and down the room. Cat-watching, lint-picking, ear-scratching and the straightening out of typewriter and carbon paper seemed to have been dispensed with. Even the pencils had all been sharpened before my arrival, and though Mr. Kaufman proceeded to wash his hands as usual before opening the pile of manuscript on the desk, he washed them hurriedly and kept up a running fire of comment about the third act from within the bathroom. We had long since agreed upon the opening scene and he quickly typed a description of the set, read it aloud, and then turned toward me with a tentative opening line of dialogue. I nodded and suggested a following line, and the opening pages of the third act began to spin from the typewriter.

I have always been more than a little puzzled by the fascination that the mechanics of collaboration seem to hold for most people, fellow playwrights and laymen alike. I have been endlessly questioned about how one proceeds to write a play in collaboration, a good deal of it on the basis, I am sure, of trying to ferret out just who wrote which particular amusing line in what particular play. But since I considered that no one's business but our own, I have always deepened the mystery by smiling inscrutably and pointedly turning the conversation into other channels. Actually, the process of collaboration is exactly what the dictionary says it is: a union of two people working in agreement on a common project.

It requires no special gift except the necessary patience to accommodate one's own working method harmoniously to that of one's collaborator. In *Once in a Lifetime*, it is true, there was a complete play to start from; but other plays were started from scratch and every line and idea, including the idea of the play itself, was so tightly woven into the mosaic of collaboration that it would be impossible to tell who suggested which or what, or how one line sprang full-blown from another. When the basic idea of a play was a good one, our collaboration worked well, and when it was not, it did not work at all. The mechanics of collaboration in the plays we did together remained as simple as putting a fresh sheet of paper into the typewriter and laboriously plugging away until that page satisfied both of us. It pleased me to make a mystery of our play-writing partnership, for the sole reason that the mechanics of two people writing together are no less dull and flat than the mechanics of one person writing alone, and I preferred to let the inquisitive lady on my right drink her demitasse with the idea still intact in her mind that I was a young man of rare and mysterious gifts.

There can be no mystery, however, about the fact that collaboration is an infinitely more pleasurable way of working than working alone. Most human beings fear loneliness, and writing is the loneliest of the professions. Writers agonize a great deal about the loneliness of their craft, and though the wailing is apt to be a little deafening at times, they are telling the truth. The hardest part of writing by far is the seeming exclusion from all humankind while work is under way, for the writer at work cannot be gregarious. If he is not alone, if he is with so much as one other person, he is not at work, and it is this feeling of being cut off from his fellows that drives most writers to invent the most elaborate and ingenious excuses to put work aside and escape back into the world again. Collaboration cuts this loneliness in half. When one is at a low point of discouragement, the very presence in the room of another human being, even though he too may be sunk in the same state of gloom, very often gives that dash of valor to the spirit that allows confidence to return and work to resume. Except on the rarest of occasions, writing is a cheerless business. I have not the least doubt that some young writers of promise have retreated to Hollywood or television simply because they hated being alone. I do not blame them, just as I am never unmoved by the suffering of a fellow writer when he cries out that he is "blocked." It is a protest, I think, against his unalterable fate of being alone, and it is a desperation I can understand and give full sympathy to. When later on I went back to writing plays by myself, I looked back to the warmth and companionship of collaboration with the nostalgia of the exile for his homeland, and I confess that I have moments of missing it still.

Some of the formal quality of our collaboration began to thaw slightly as we approached the end of the third act. For one thing, Mr. Kaufman suddenly grew talkative as he picked lint off the carpet or watched the cats in the backyard gardens across the way. This was formerly a silent business and I generally used the time to stuff Life Savers and bits of Hershey bars into my mouth, for I knew that nothing was expected of me until Mr. Kaufman was ready to say, "Er . . ." and begin his pacing. Now, however, he grew downright loquacious for a man of his taciturn bent, and to my vast surprise, I discovered that he loved gossip, the more indiscreet the better. It was a most unlikely side for a man of his nature to have, but there could be no question that he relished and delighted in the peccadilloes and indiscretions that float about the world of theatre folk like motes in the air on a hot summer's afternoon. He was aware that I was personally unacquainted with most of the people he gossiped about; but I knew the names, of course, and that seemed to be enough for him.

To my further surprise, he turned abruptly toward me one morning and said, "Let's have lunch out today. There seems to be a slight household crisis going on at the moment."

Lunch! I stared at him—we had never had lunch, as I understood lunch, in the four months I had been sitting starved in that chair. He must have caught my look, and completely misunderstood it, for he added, "You'll be able to eat something by about one thirty or so, won't you?" I nodded slowly at him and wondered what in the world he thought the constant chomp-chomp of Hershey bars in my jaws could have meant all through those long afternoons. Obviously, he was still totally unaware that some form of food was a necessity to most ordinary human or animal organisms. A dog, I reflected bitterly, would have slim pickings in Mr. Kaufman's house if he could not provide himself with a few Hershey bars on the side, or whatever the equivalent of Hershey bars is in dogdom.

The lunch he provided that afternoon, however, was a full one. During the course of it, I was somewhat startled to sense that he wanted to ask me a question but that he was embarrassed to do so and was hesitating. He seemed to dismiss it from his mind for a moment, but I could see he was going to ask it after all.

"What would you think," he finally said, "if I were to play the part of Lawrence Vail? We ought to begin to think about casting pretty soon, now."

In spite of myself, I laughed. Scratch a playwright and you find a frustrated actor!

He joined in my laughter, then added hastily, "Of course, it's a bit of a trick because I've never acted professionally, but I think I can do it and it would give that part the kind of authenticity it should have."

"It's a *wonderful* idea," I said, "it couldn't be cast better." I meant what I said. The part of Lawrence Vail was that of a famous Broadway playwright who is brought to Hollywood with frantic pleas and pressures for his immediate arrival, and then is kept waiting for six months without being able to see anyone at all or to find anybody who seems to know what he is even there for. The part, though it appeared in the second act only, provided a Greek chorus of sanity to the lunacy prevailing all around it, and it was important to the play that it be played well. Some of my favorite lines in the play were contained in that part, and I knew they would never be acted better than the way Mr. Kaufman had read them in the privacy of his bedroom when he tried some of the scenes aloud for himself and for me. Not all but certainly some playwrights can give a better performance of their plays in a bedroom or study than those plays ever receive on the stage; just as some composers can sing their own songs far better sitting alone at the piano than any great star of the musical stage can sing them with a full orchestra at her feet.

Mr. Kaufman seemed inordinately pleased at my enthusiasm. So much so, that he seemed to want to hurry me through my cheese and apple pie in order to get back to the typewriter, but I was not to be pushed! I rightly guessed that the next full-sized lunch would be a long time in coming, and I took my own sweet time with each mouthful—in spite of the fact that he called the usual terrorized waiter for the check, paid it, and sat impatiently piling up little blocks of sugar all around the sugar bowl.

"If you take larger bites," he finally remarked, "we could finish the third act in a week."

He was right to the exact day. A week later he typed "The curtain falls on Act Three" and quickly dashed into the bathroom to escape what he correctly surmised would be a few grandiloquent words from me to set the occasion more firmly in his mind. This time, evidently suspecting a whopper, he turned not only the washbasin taps on full, but the bathtub faucets as well, and began to take off his shirt and tie. He smiled and lifted one finger in farewell, knowing it was impossible even for me to make a speech to a man who was stripping down to get into a tub.

"The usual time tomorrow," he called out over the noise of the running water. "We'll have to let Sam Harris know what we'll want in the way of actors. We'll go over the list together up here and then go down to the Music Box," and a little too pleased with himself, he nudged the door with his foot and carefully closed it.

MR. KAUFMAN and Sam Harris, in the days that followed, seemed to me to be casting the play a little too quickly for comfort, but as the inexperienced member of the trio I kept my reservations to myself. They were scrupulous about consulting me on every final selection, but I could sense when they both agreed completely on an actor or actress, and for the most part I remained silent or agreed with them. The fact was, I was enjoying these days of preparation for rehearsals far too much to worry over anything. These days were the dividends I had awaited with growing impatience to collect.

A play for me never really takes on an aspect of reality until it has left the dry air of the study and begins to sniff the musty breezes of a bare stage, with actors reading aloud at auditions. Only then does it begin to come alive. I have never quite understood playwrights who find auditions and rehearsals a grueling bore, or whose real pleasure in their work ends as it leaves their typewriters. For me, the excitement of auditions, the camaraderie of actors in rehearsal, the tight and secret conspiracy against the world, which begins to grow between actors and authors and directors and is the essence of putting on a play—this, to me at any rate, is the really satisfying part of the whole process, and the only thing, I think, that ever persuades me to walk toward a typewriter once again.

After the grind and imprisonment of those months in 63rd Street, the lazy freedom of sitting through auditions at the Music Box was glorious, to say nothing of the bliss of being able to dash into the little drug store next to the theatre between readings and gorge myself on chocolate malteds and hamburgers. I more than made up for the Spartan diet of tea and cookies I had been on for so long. Each day was a holiday so far as I was concerned, and almost before I was aware of it, or would have dreamed it possible, the play was cast and I was walking toward the Music Box for the first rehearsal. My excitement was intense. The bits and pieces of scenes I had heard read aloud at auditions had whetted my appetite to the bursting point to hear the play read in its entirety and in sequence.

My impatience was such that I was, unhappily, the first person to arrive. The stage was empty except for the two stage managers who were setting out chairs in a wide semicircle and placing a table in front of the chairs where Mr. Kaufman, Sam Harris and I would sit. They stared at me, surprised at my undignified promptness, and I thought I saw a good-humored wink pass between them, for I had evidently violated by my early arrival one of the major tenets of the code of first rehearsals. There seems to be a rigid code of behavior for the day of a first rehearsal that is as stately and as set in its pattern as a minuet. The minor actors are always the first ones to arrive. Then the principals stroll casually in, depending upon the order of their billing, timing their arrival by some inner clockwork of their own. Just before the appearance of the author, director and producer, the star appears —or if the star is of sufficient magnitude, she will appear last. The wink between the stage managers was a testimony to my newness as an author, but I did not mind. This was where I wanted to be, and it was a mark of what patience I had left that I had not arrived even before the stage managers themselves!

Gradually, the bit players and minor principals began to arrive; then, since there were no stars in *Once in a Lifetime*, the leading players—Aline MacMahon, Hugh O'Connell, Blanche Ring and Grant Mills—came onto the stage and took their places in the semicircle of chairs, all of them shining with that false brightness that actors seem to bring to a first rehearsal along with their cigarettes. I could hear Sam Harris and Mr. Kaufman talking in the back of the theatre, and now they came down the aisle together and up onto the stage, Sam Harris greeting all of the company even to the bit players, with a word or two or a pat on the shoulder. Mr. Kaufman muttered something to the first stage manager, and then sat down at the table and motioned me to sit beside him. Sam Harris sat down on the other side of Mr. Kaufman, with Max Siegel in the chair next to him. The stage manager called out, "All right, ladies and gentlemen—will you please be sure to use the fire buckets next to your chairs for your cigarettes. Thank you." He sat down again and turned toward Mr. Kaufman. I found it difficult to breathe; I cleared my throat with what sounded to my own ears like an artillery barrage.

Mr. Kaufman opened the manuscript on the table before him and quietly pronounced what have always seemed to me to be the four most dramatic words in the English language: "Act One—Scene One." There was a fractional pause and then the first line of the play came from the semicircle of chairs. It came rather listlessly and quite flatly, and so did the second and third lines. My own nervousness is affecting my hearing, I thought—and I brushed aside the impression I was receiving of the way the play was being read and tried to listen less nervously. It was not, however, just my own taut nerves that were making the opening lines sound so trite. The lines that followed were coming out dull and flat as well, and the play itself sounded entirely lifeless even in this opening scene. It seemed increasingly lifeless as the second scene droned on. I glanced sideways at Mr. Kaufman to see if his face was mirroring my own disturbance, but he seemed to be unaware of how badly the play was emerging. He was busily making notations on each page of the manuscript and seemed not to be listening at all. I looked past him at Sam Harris and Max Siegel, but they too seemed undisturbed. I could not understand it. Surely they were hearing what I was hearing—the sogginess and downright dullness of the play must certainly have been as apparent to them as it was to me. How, then, could they sit there so placidly unconcerned while my own ears were rejecting every line as it was read!

What I did not know, of course, was that all plays sound frightful at the first reading. It appears that still another aspect of the code of behavior of a first rehearsal is that actors, for reasons known only to themselves, consider it a breach of professional etiquette to read the play well the first time through. The stars or the principals mumble through their parts in a hopeless monotone, and if one of the minor players, new like myself to the proper procedure, reads his one or two speeches with a semblance of performance peeping through, he is stared at and contemptuously dismissed as a "good reader" or "radio actor," and the mumbling goes agonizingly on. The result of this witless but unshakable convention is that a new playwright will listen to his play being read for the first time by the company that is going to perform it and quake in his boots, wondering as he suffers through it what in the world he has wasted two years of his life on. Actors, of course, maintain that no such code exists at all and that their own nervousness and nothing else makes them read so execrably, but I have never quite believed it. They may well be telling the truth, but twice I have listened to a first reading in which the stars gave as brilliant a performance at the first reading as they subsequently gave on the stage, and I have never ceased to be grateful to them for it.

Gertrude Lawrence, at the first reading of *Lady in the Dark*, and Rex Harrison, at the first reading of *My Fair Lady*, plunged into their parts with an electric excitement, from the first line onward, that was contagious enough to make their own excitement spread through the rest of the cast like a forest fire; it made this usually dispiriting experience a thing to be set apart and remembered with gratitude.

As the end of the first act of *Once in a Lifetime* ground down to what seemed to me to be a slow death rattle, not only my undergarments were drenched with perspiration but my suit as well. I could feel my jacket sticking wetly to the back of the chair. The stage manager finally called, "Ten minutes, ladies and gentlemen," and I rose from the chair and looked miserably at Max Siegel, not daring to look at either Mr. Kaufman or Sam Harris. Max Siegel came over to me.

"What's the matter," he asked. "Not feeling well?"

"It sounded so terrible," I said, "so plain *awful.*"

He laughed and his laugh never sounded more reassuring. "But it always sounds terrible at a first reading," he replied. "Didn't you know that? The second act will sound a little better, and by the third act they'll begin to forget themselves and even act it a little bit. You watch."

He was correct. The second act did indeed sound like something that mildly approximated a play, and the third act even began to have a hint of amusement in it. I began to breathe again instead of wheezing, and when the stage manager dismissed the company for lunch at the end of the third act, I was amazed to find I even had an unmistakable sign of an appetite. It had seemed to me in the middle of the first act that I would never touch a morsel of food again, and I knew that to be a sign of how badly I had thought things were going.

By the time the company reassembled for the afternoon rehearsal at two o'clock, I was in high spirits once more and considered myself a hardy veteran of rehearsal behavior. Nothing would throw me now, I thought. But I still had two other disappointments to face that afternoon, one after the other in quick succession, and these I did not recover from as quickly. Mr. Kaufman was famed as a topnotch director and I had been eagerly looking forward to the moment when I would see him in action. I considered I had been cheated out of those little talks on play-writing I had expected to have from him and on which he had remained silent through all the months of working together. I could not see how he could very well do me out of the obligatory discussions he would now have with the cast, however. A day or two of these informal but enlightening talks from the director to the actors, on characterization, motivation and the level of performance that would best express the tone and attitude of the play itself, were what I had been given to understand every noted director did as a matter of course, and I had again come armed with a little notebook in which I intended to jot down the salient points he made while I sat in the back of the darkened theatre. I was an old hand at taking down my own homemade brand of shorthand at the back of dark theatres, and I expected to store up a good deal of valuable information for further use from these first rehearsal seminars.

To my surprise, the floor of the stage was already marked out with chalk, and the chairs and an old sofa were set out to represent the first scene of the play when the cast returned from the luncheon break. There was, apparently, to be no discussion at all! I could hardly believe what was taking place, but without so much as a word to the actors Mr. Kaufman already had the script in his hand and with no further ado was staging the opening scene of the play. Nor was this all. He spoke in so muted a tone that I could gather nothing of what he was saying—not that he was saying much of anything. He seemed mainly to be seeing that the actors did not bump into each other. The first scene, though not a long one, was nevertheless a scene which I took for granted would take at least two full days to stage, but it was staged in a little less than an hour. I watched astonished and disgruntled. The movement of the first scene marked out, Mr. Kaufman came from the stage down into the auditorium and asked for the scene to be run again so that he could see it from the front. The actors ran through the scene and he walked back up onto the stage once more. Aha, I thought, *this* is his method, to stage it roughly and *then* have his talk with the actors.

It was merely a question of approach. Now, with the mechanics out of the way, would come the discussion of the playing of it. The motivations of the movement, the psychological background of each character in relationship to the actor himself, and all the rest of it.

Nothing of the sort occurred. Mr. Kaufman sidled up to Aline MacMahon in what seemed to be some slight embarrassment and began a whispered colloquy with her. She nodded in agreement to whatever he was whispering; then he moved to Hugh O'Connell and began to whisper in *his* ear. I began to squirm around in my seat with irritation. I had carefully sat myself down about three rows from the back, well over to one side of the theatre, so as not to have Mr. Kaufman feel that I was breathing down the back of his neck while he worked, but now I got up and moved down to the third row on the aisle. He had walked over to Grant Mills and was now whispering into his ear in the same infuriating fashion. Even in the third row I could not hear one word of what was being said. It would not have done me any good, either, to move up onto the stage itself, for he spoke so quietly that not a word of what he was saying could be overheard even at arm's length away.

He proceeded in just this fashion not only for the rest of that afternoon, but for the rest of the three weeks' period of rehearsal. By the third day I glumly put my notebook away before I left the house to go and sit morosely through still another day of watching what might well have been a silent movie of a man directing a play—directing the first play, moreover, about the "talkies," I thought resentfully.

Gradually, however, and in spite of my annoyance, I could begin to see the pattern of his direction emerge. He gave no lessons in acting nor did he use the power some directors wield to hold a cast helpless before him while he discusses his own interpretation of the playwright's meaning, or with becoming modesty performs each part for each actor in turn to show how easily it might be played to perfection with just a modicum of his own talent. Instead, he seemed to allow the actors to use him as a sounding board. He watched and listened and without seeming to impose his own preconceived ideas of how a scene should be played, he let each actor find a way of his own that was best for him; and slowly, with no more than a whispered word here and there, the scenes began to take on a directorial quality and flavor that was unmistakably his. The sovereign motif of his direction seemed to be an artful mixture of allowing actors the freedom to follow their own instinctive intelligence and taste, and then trusting his own ear for comedic values—an ear that had the unerring exactness of a tuning fork. With no directorial vanity or ego of his own, he was able to indulge the actors in theirs, and an actor's ego in the early days of rehearsal is like a blade of new spring grass that will grow and reseed itself if it is not mowed down too quickly by a power-driven lawn mower—the lawn mower in most cases being the overenthusiastic imposition of a famed directorial hand. Unlike a newer school of directors, he made no pretense of being either a built-in psychoanalyst, a father figure or a professor in residence of dramatic literature—a combination of roles which is sometimes assumed by directors and which always plays havoc with the stern business of getting a play ready to open.

The results of what seemed to be his detached and reticent direction were remarkably effective. The actors, a little at sea at first, gradually found their own balance; and since it was theirs and not a false one imposed by the director, they flourished and blossomed, and the play quickly began to establish an architecture of its own. All too often, or so it seems to me, a play has been so minutely directed to within an inch of its life early on in rehearsal, that some of its more simple and basic values are sacrificed to a showy but costly series of brilliant directorial moments, and these values are never thereafter recaptured. To my jaundiced eye, the best-directed play is the one in which the hand of the director remains unnoticed—where the play seems not to have been directed at all, but merely mirrors the over-all perception and sensitivity of a hidden hand that has been the custodian of the proceedings on the stage, not the star of them. Though it was dull to watch and I continued to feel that I had somehow been cheated out of my just due, I could not deny that each day he accomplished more than I would have thought possible, and on the evening of the eighth day of rehearsals, the first complete run-through of the play was given for Sam Harris.

Max Siegel, as usual, accompanied him, but no other person was allowed in the theatre. Mr. Kaufman did not hold with the theory or the practice of having run-throughs for his friends or friends of the cast, or even for people whose judgment he respected and trusted. He held firmly to the idea that no one person or collection of persons, no matter how wise in the ways of the theatre, could ever be as sound in their reactions as a regulation audience that had planked down their money at the box-office window, and in the main I think he was correct. There is perhaps something to be learned from a run-through for friends or associates; but more often than not, it can be as fooling in one way as it is in another. I have witnessed too many run-throughs on a bare stage with nothing but kitchen chairs and a stark pilot light and seen them go beautifully, and then watched these same plays disappear into the backdrop the moment the scenery and footlights hit them, to place too much reliance on either the enthusiasm or the misgivings of a well-attended run-through. The reverse can be equally true. However well or ill a play may go at a run-through, there are bound to be both some pleasant and some unpleasant surprises in store for the author when it hits its first real audience.

We received neither enthusiasm nor misgivings from Sam Harris at the end of the first run-through of *Once in a Lifetime* that evening. I was disturbed by his silence, but his curious non-communicativeness did not seem to disturb Mr. Kaufman at all. "You'll seldom hear praise from Sam Harris," he explained, "you'll only hear what he *doesn't* like. I don't think he was too displeased tonight or we'd have heard a little more from him. I imagine he's waiting until the play shakes down into a better performance before he says anything much." And with that I had to be content. Mr. Kaufman was too

busily engaged with all the many details of production that engulf a director from that moment onward to give much time to the business of
reassuring an increasingly nervous collaborator. The end of the afternoon
rehearsal usually saw him in conference with the scenic designer, the costume
designer, the prop man or the electrician, and the same conference with one
or more of these same gentlemen took place again at the end of the evening
rehearsal.

*Once in a Lifetime* was a large production. It called for six elaborate
sets, a flood of costumes and a quantity of rather bizarre props, including a
half-dozen live pigeons and two Russian wolfhounds. The pigeons and the
wolfhounds were already being used in rehearsal to allow the actors to grow
used to them, or to allow them to grow used to the actors. But since neither
the pigeons nor the two wolfhounds seemed to respond as readily to Mr.
Kaufman's whispered murmurings as the actors did, and as his patience
with humans did not spill over into the animal world, I thought it politic
under the circumstances not to add to his burdens by voicing my own moments of uncertainty. Part of the daily panic I was feeling, I suppose, was
due to the fact that after the first easygoing week, the production of a
play suddenly increases in tempo until it becomes a headlong rush to meet
the deadline of opening night, and with a complicated production there is
never enough time to do the necessary little things—mainly because of some
impossible rulings by the unions that hedge the theatre in on every side and
effectively strangle the concentrated and creative work a play should be allowed to have in rehearsal.

It was all going too fast; there were a hundred things still undone that I
knew could not be done now before we opened. What I had not yet learned,
and would have to learn the hard way, was that once in rehearsal a play—
and everyone and everything connected with it—is sent spinning down a
toboggan slide on which there is no stopping or turning back. Whirling down
the slope one can only take the twists and turns as they come and hope to
have sufficient luck to land safely. It is a marvel to me that so many do, for
there are no exceptions made—the same rule applies to everyone—and the
toboggan slide is especially iced for each new play.

Before I could believe it was happening, I was dazedly packing my suitcase to go to Atlantic City for the dress rehearsals and the opening. My own
numbing anxiety was in no way helped by the attitude of my family, all of
whom had made a complete turnabout. After their early conviction that
the $500 I had received as advance royalty on *Once in a Lifetime* was
highly suspicious and that eventually I would be asked to give it back, they
were now as firmly convinced that the rosiest of futures awaited only the
rising of the curtain. My mother in particular was in a state of blissful
certainty that somehow I had at last stumbled into a profession which,
while she did not profess to understand it, at least gave the appearance of
being respectable; and in the eyes of her friends, a profession that was perhaps only a rung or two below that of lawyer or dentist. For quite some years

now she had labored under the burden of being unable to explain to her friends exactly what it was her elder son did for a living. My summers were not too difficult to explain, though nothing, God knows, to be proud of, measured against sons who were studying medicine or dentistry or the law; but the work I did in the wintertime completely defied explanation or understanding. She had maintained for a while that I gave "speech" lessons in the evenings; but a son who lay around the house all day and did something so outlandish at night was obviously nothing to boast about. She had, I knew, always refrained from any mention of my "homework" as seeming to put an official stamp on my difference from other people's sons, but now suddenly she could point to that difference with pride.

*Once in a Lifetime* was booked to play a week in Atlantic City and a week in Brighton Beach, and the theatre in Brighton Beach was not too far from where we lived. The neighborhood was already well plastered with billboard posters announcing its coming, and my name, along with George Kaufman's, was prominently displayed. My name had also appeared in newspaper announcements of the play, and even the more theatrically obtuse of her friends could no longer be unaware that her son might be of some consequence at last! I truly believe that it was not the possibility of anything so unbelievable as riches coming out of all this, but simply the fact that my activities, always so mysterious and faintly spurious in the eyes of her friends, had taken on the aura of respectability. I knew very well that, having now seen my name on those billboards, she would be unable to accept the fact that my brand-new "respectable" profession might easily vanish within the space of two weeks, and I did not mention it. Her pleasure and her satisfaction were so apparent that I could not bear to disillusion her, and for much the same reason I said nothing to discourage my father's and my brother's equally unrealistic optimism and high expectations.

I kissed them all good-bye and took the subway to Pennsylvania Station, where I joined the company on the Atlantic City train. The "opening night" glaze already filming my eyes was apparent enough to make Max Siegel take one look at me, laugh, take a flask from his hip pocket and usher me quickly into the club car for a stiff drink.

ATLANTIC CITY in the spring of 1930 was bursting at the seams. Every hotel seemed to be filled to capacity and overflowing into the boarding houses that dotted all the side streets. The boardwalk, always crowded during the fashionable strolling hours, was even jam-packed during the late afternoons, so that the people on its outer edges seemed in some danger of being pushed onto the sands below.

I stared down from my hotel window at the sparkling ocean and at the pleasant pattern the strollers made along the sun-splashed boardwalk, and alert as always for omens, good or bad, I told myself that these holiday-minded folk were bound to be a good audience for a new comedy. Though I could not see their faces clearly, I preferred to imagine them as already wreathed in smiles of good will. After all, I thought reassuringly, Atlantic

City was the top tryout town of the Eastern Seaboard, and the audience that would file into the Apollo Theatre on Tuesday night would not only be a knowledgeable one but an understanding and forgiving one as well, for they were used to tryouts here and did not expect a new play to be airtight. They would accept its lacks as part of the whole holiday spirit that pervaded the resort itself. And unlike that bitter winter's day in Rochester that ushered in the opening of *The Beloved Bandit*, today was mild and balmy and sweet with a lovely tang of freshness as the breeze rolled in from the ocean.

I stood by the open window breathing in the day and looking down at the bright panorama spread out below me, and for a few moments my spirits soared and my faith in omens worked its usual magic. Yet as I turned away from the window and walked toward the bed to unpack my suitcase, I could begin to feel gloom settle over me once more, and try as I would, I could not shake it off. It was a misery as unreasoning and persistent as it was unshakable. I had wrestled with it all through the last week of rehearsal, through the wakeful hours of each night, on the train coming down, and now I could feel the same unmistakable flicks of anxiety and panic uncoiling and welling up within me.

"No one," I said aloud to the empty room as I slammed my things furiously into the bureau, "no one is worried but *you*, and they all know a hundred times more than *you* do, so stop it!" Saying it out loud helped for a moment, but for no more than a moment. The gloom deepened into the frozen panic that Max Siegel had seen clearly mirrored in my eyes as I stepped onto the train a few hours earlier. I threw myself on the bed and lay staring up at the ceiling. I knew little of psychoanalysis—its methods and its meaning were unknown to me—but instinctively I felt that I must make a final effort to try to understand the state of terror I was locked in, or it would take over and immobilize me completely. I lay on the bed for almost an hour, and the conclusion I came to, while not a very satisfactory one, at least had the virtue of presenting me with a calmer exterior and the ability to get out of the room and go to the theatre to face whatever I might have to face with some degree of composure.

What I was finding it impossible to face, I concluded, was the possibility of failure. Too much was riding on the success of *Once in a Lifetime* for me to be able to bear the idea of its failure with ordinary fortitude or even common sense. I was discounting the dread possibility in a way that Dr. Freud would have understood at once. I was obviously arranging an unconscious barter with the gods—offering up, as it were, my pain as a token of worthiness, making my suffering a silent plea for their clemency. It is not, I believe, uncommon behavior for people under strain and tension awaiting the outcome of an event upon which all their hopes are based; but as I dimly perceived that this was what I might be doing, some of the pain eased, and consumed with the idea that I had divined a startling new truth, I walked out of the hotel and toward the theatre. Like all major discoveries made in a hotel room on the eve of an opening, however, this one lasted exactly the same amount of time—that is, it survived until I reached the theatre and walked through the stage door, where it evaporated and merged into the anxiety-ridden atmosphere backstage.

The first dress rehearsal, already well under way by the time I reached the theatre, although no one seemed to have noticed my absence, was going badly. The actors, without make-up and in their street clothes, sat numbly in their dressing rooms or hung about in disconsolate silent little groups in the wings, waiting to be called on stage when and if the stagehands had changed a set or after the electricians had adjusted and focused the lights. Little mounds of cardboard coffee containers, of half-eaten sandwiches and stale doughnuts had already begun to pile up in odd corners of the stage, in the dressing rooms and on the empty seats of the dark theatre. A false gaiety, as depressing and as soggy as the doughnuts themselves, punctuated intervals of equally false camaraderie between the actors and the stagehands, and finally disintegrated into a hollow shell of silence in which no one spoke at all.

The first dress rehearsal, in short, was proceeding in quite the usual way, being neither better nor worse than it usually is, for a large production in the throes of a first dress rehearsal is a dispirited and agonizing process. With it begins the age-old battle to allow the play to emerge in spite of the production, for at this stage of the game each bit of technical virtuosity or stagecraft—that extravagant effort by the lighting expert to suggest a pearly dawn, which takes a good three hours to achieve, and is thoroughly disturbing to the scene being played in front of it; that charming but useless conceit of the scenic artist to have a terrace where none should be, thereby limiting the acting area to a cramped boxlike space in front of the footlights; the extraordinary concoction by the costume designer that does not allow the leading lady to sit down in her evening gown, or a hat that completely covers her face from all but the first three rows of the orchestra—all of these in the first hours of putting a large production together seem to matter more than the play itself, and unless the battle is met head-on with a tough mind and an iron will and the sheer physical endurance to keep constantly alert, fiercely watchful and thoroughly ruthless, a play may be smothered or defeated by the intricacy, the trickiness or even the downright beauty of a production.

Perhaps sheer physical endurance is the prime requisite. It is almost impossible to convey to an outsider the atmosphere of a theatre during those endless hours of unrelieved tedium. The dismal waiting about, the awesome hopelessness of shouting at stagehands who can hear nothing and are obviously blind as well, the whispered but venomous arguments in the back of the theatre with the scenic artist, the lighting expert and the costume designer—all of this, strung out over a period of three days and nights, is my own private conception of what hell or eternal damnation must be like. There exists among the laity a mistaken idea that dress rehearsals are exciting and glamorous. It needs correction. They are pure hell! This particular hell, fortunately, was Mr. Kaufman's, not mine, although as an anguished onlooker I seemed to be doing a good deal more turning on the spit than he was.

I prowled uneasily around the theatre, moved about in the wings among the little groups of weary actors, wandered back and forth between the auditorium and the dressing rooms, finding little comfort on either side of the footlights and growing increasingly more certain that the play would never open by Tuesday, if at all. Mr. Kaufman walked silently up and down the aisle, a dim blue-suited figure, talking softly now and then over the apparatus that connected him with the stage manager backstage; or sat quietly in a seat in the very last row of the theatre, seemingly undisturbed by the chaos that was taking place in front of his eyes; and when I hoarsely whispered to him that the change from the first scene into the second had taken twelve minutes instead of two, he looked at me over the rims of his glasses and replied with a kind of lunatic logic, "I know. I've been right here all the time," and let his unconcerned gaze wander back to the stage again.

The comforting figure of Sam Harris was nowhere to be seen. I learned from Max Siegel, smiling as usual, that Mr. Harris had cast an experienced eye on what was obviously going to be a rocky series of dress rehearsals and had retreated to a chair on the boardwalk or to his hotel room and would not be visible now until curtain time on opening night. "He likes to keep himself fresh," said Max Siegel. "Why don't you do the same thing?" he added. "You can't do any good here standing around and looking green. You're just scaring yourself and the actors. Why don't you go out and get some air?"

I turned away without answering and wandered backstage again. In a little while I wandered listlessly back into the auditorium and slumped down into a seat for what I thought was to be five minutes of closing my eyes against the mayhem that was taking place on the stage, but which turned out to be two hours of the best sleep I had had in two weeks.

I seem to have no clear recollection of the next forty-eight hours. The scenic and light rehearsals went on, the dress parade took place, the actors began to appear in their proper costumes in the right scenes and at the right time. My memory of those hours is actually of a feeling or a sensation—of a curious illusion which is still vivid and remains remarkably clear in my mind to this very day. During those last two days before the opening I seemed to be under a constant hallucination that I was floating down an underground stream whose dark waters seethed and eddied with the faces of actors, stagehands and Mr. Kaufman—where the shore was lined with endless mounds of discolored coffee containers, half-eaten sandwiches and doughnuts—and that I was being borne swiftly and implacably toward an improbable island over which the precise, invariable voice of Mr. Kaufman echoed and re-echoed with a sepulchral clarity, although I could not always understand what he was saying.

I returned to reality, if indeed it may be called that, with the arrival of Joe Hyman in my hotel room at six thirty on the night of the opening. He found me standing in my underpants in front of the washbasin in the bathroom, with my hands outstretched beneath the electric light bulb over the washbasin mirror; I had pulled the cord of the light bulb, then fallen into some bemusement of my own, and instead of turning on the water taps I had remained standing with my palms upturned under the bulb waiting for water to gush forth. "Of all nights for the water to be turned off without warning," I said bitterly to him by way of greeting. "How am I going to shave? I can't go to the opening looking like this!"

Joe Hyman turned on the water tap and said, "Hurry up and shave and I'll buy you a good dinner. If things are as terrible as you look, you'll need one."

There was always a gentle hint of mockery in everything Joe Hyman said, even when he was being most grave. It was the most immediate and personal thing about him and it either attracted or repelled people who knew him only slightly. It was just what I needed right then. It cleared the air of actors, stagehands, even of Mr. Kaufman himself, and brought the real world back into focus. To my surprise, I ate and thoroughly enjoyed the large lobster dinner he bought me, and aided by his brisk matter-of-fact presence I even talked sensibly for the first time in weeks about the play. I had been right to allow him and no one else to come down to the opening. By urgent pleadings and a few not so veiled threats, I had persuaded all of my little coterie—Eddie Chodorov, Dore Schary, Lester Sweyd, et al.—not to come down to Atlantic City for the opening, but to wait until the following week at Brighton Beach. I wanted Joe Hyman and no one else with me tonight.

The initial performance, the raising of a curtain on a play before its very first audience, is for me at least the worst two hours of that play's existence, whatever its subsequent fate may be. No one really knows anything much about a play until it meets its first audience; not its director, its actors, its producers, and least of all its author. The scenes he has counted on most strongly, his favorite bits of fine writing—the delicately balanced emotional or comedic thrusts, the witty, ironic summing up, the wry third-act curtain with its caustic stinging last line that adroitly illuminates the theme—these are the things that are most likely to go down the drain first, sometimes with an audible thud. The big scene in the second act, or the touching speech that reflects all of the author's personal philosophy—that cherished mosaic of words on which he has secretly based his hopes for the Pulitzer Prize or at the very least the Drama Critics Award—such things the audience invariably will sit silently but politely through, patiently waiting for the reappearance of that delightful minor character, who was tossed in only to highlight the speech, or for an echo of that delicious little scene which was written only as a transition to the big one.

It is a humbling process, and the truculent author whose pride or vanity seduces him into believing that his play is above the heads of its out-of-town audience, is due for a rude surprise when his play reaches New York. There are, of course, plays that have withered out of town and then blossomed in New York, but they are the exceptions rather than the rule. By and large, an audience is an audience is an audience, as Gertrude Stein might have said, and the acid test of a play is usually its very first one. It is that first audience that I most fear, for regardless of what miracles of rewriting may be undertaken and even brilliantly carried out, the actual fate of a play is almost always sealed by its first audience.

A New York opening night is not something to be borne with equanimity, but after four weeks out of town, unless one is willfully blind and deaf to the unmistakable signs that an audience gives to even the most sanguine of authors, the ballots are already in and counted—the ball game has already been played and lost. Audiences do not vary that widely, nor for that matter, do critics. The New York notices will generally be more perceptive of the author's intent, more astute in distinguishing the first-rate from the cleverly contrived, but they will fasten on the weakness of a play or a performance with the same kind of exasperating genius that out-of-town audiences have shown from the first performance onward. It is permissible, of course, to believe in miracles as one makes one's way to the theatre on the night of a New York opening; but it is safer and less painful in the end, I have found, to continue to believe that miracles, like taxi accidents, are something that happen to other people, not oneself.

We strolled slowly along the boardwalk to the theatre, my dinner-table calm suddenly giving way to a mounting excitement and dread, distributed in equal parts at the pit of my stomach. Even Joe Hyman, walking beside me, lapsed into a strange loquaciousness to cover, I realized, his own excitement. Neither of us said one word about the play. I discoursed learnedly and at length on one of my favorite topics, the evils of poverty; and Joe Hyman, paying no attention whatever to what I was saying, held forth on the superior taste and chewing consistency of salt-water taffy in the days of his childhood over the present poor makeshift specimens that we passed in store after store as we walked along. The lobby of the Apollo Theatre, when we reached it, was a reassuring sight. It contained within its jammed confines that happy buzz that I had come to associate with an audience about to enter a theatre for an evening of already assured pleasure. Pushing my way through, I heard "George S. Kaufman" and "He always writes hits" with punctuated regularity, and just before I reached the ticket taker a man behind me announced loudly, "I'll lay you two-to-one right now this show is a hit—I'll put my money on Kaufman any day of the week."

Joe Hyman presented his stub to the ticket taker, who nodded his head to me in recognition as I passed through. Joe and I shook hands silently, and I watched him proceed to his seat in the fourth row on the aisle, with the lingering, beseeching look a child gives to its parents when he is about to have his tonsils removed, but Joe did not look back. I turned and looked over the heads of the crowd at the back of the theatre for a glimpse of Mr. Kaufman. Mr. Kaufman, Max Siegel had informed me, never sat for the performance of a play—the first performance or any other one. He stood at the back of the theatre, not looking at the stage, but pacing furiously up and down and listening. Under the mistaken idea that he might expect me to do the same thing, I had not arranged for a seat, but stood dutifully waiting, anxiously casting about for him to make his appearance.

The house lights dimmed to the halfway mark, warning latecomers to get to their seats. There was still no sign of Mr. Kaufman. I wondered if I had misunderstood Max Siegel—I had not been understanding more than half of what was said to me these last few days—and I had a moment of wild panic, feeling certain Mr. Kaufman had met with an accident on his way to the theatre and that the curtain would rise without him, leaving only me in charge. Then, from somewhere over my shoulder quite close by, came an unmistakable snarling voice: "Stop talking and sit down, you son-of-a-bitches." A group of latecomers, rather a large group, gave one startled glance at the grim figure staring at them over the rims of his glasses and scurried silently down the aisle. If Mr. Kaufman saw me, he gave no indication of it.

His wild pacing had already started. Back and forth across the back of the theatre he paced at a tremendous clip, staring down at the carpet and heedless of what or who might be in front of him. The ushers threw him a sidelong look and gave him a wide berth. He paced up and down like a man possessed, as indeed he was possessed at those moments, by a demon that only the laughter of an audience in the proper places could exorcise. For an uncertain moment I considered falling into step beside him, but another look at that formidable figure made me think better of it. Instead, I started my own pacing from the opposite side, so that we passed and repassed each other as we both reached center.

Thus began accidentally, for me, at any rate, a ritual that has persisted ever since. I have never since that night sat in a seat for a performance of one of my own plays. How many hundreds of miles I have paced in how many countless out-of-town theatres I hesitate to think. The mileage, to say nothing of the wear and tear, has been considerable. Moreover, my ear and my brain, attuned since that first memorable pacing, have never had the enjoyment of hearing the audience laugh—they are trained to hear only the silences when laughter is supposed to come but does not. It may account for my look of very real surprise when people have said to me, "It must be wonderful to hear a theatre full of people roar with laughter at something you have written, isn't it?" I have always answered, "Yes, it is," but actually I have never really heard it. I have always been listening ahead for the next line or the next scene, when laughter may not come.

The theatre went dark and the audience fell silent as the footlights glowed on. The curtain rose to a spatter of polite, obligatory applause, but I resolutely kept my face from the stage, fiercely determined to emulate my hero, whose eyes were glued to the carpet and whose legs were taking even longer strides as he came toward me. Aline MacMahon made her entrance and a second or so later, with her third line, the entire audience broke into a roar of laughter. It marked the first time I had ever heard an audience laugh at something I had written.

I stopped dead in my tracks as though someone had struck me hard across the mouth, and the Lobster Newburg resting fitfully in my stomach took a fearful heave and turn. I was near the stairway fortunately, and I raced down to the men's room, making it only just in time, and there I remained for the next fifteen or twenty minutes. I could hear applause and knew that the first scene had ended, and could tell by the other kind of applause that Blanche Ring had made her entrance in the second scene, but I dared not go upstairs. Each time I tried to leave I got only as far as the bottom of the stairway, and then returned to be sick again.

Finally, in the middle of the second scene, I could bear it no longer. The audience was laughing almost continuously now and it was intolerable not to be able to drink it all in. I raced up the stairs and for a few seconds stood gaping at the stage, grinning foolishly and then breaking into delighted laughter myself as the audience laughed.

I might have stayed that way for the rest of the act, or indeed the whole show, but for the figure that loomed up suddenly beside me and interrupted his pacing just long enough to remark thinly, "There were plenty of places where they didn't laugh while you were doing whatever the hell you were doing." He made a grenadier-turn and was off like a whippet to the opposite side of the theatre. Thoroughly ashamed of myself, I resumed my own pacing; and we passed and repassed each other without a word until the curtain fell on the end of the first act.

I could barely wait for Joe Hyman to get up the aisle, but I could tell from the applause and from that wonderful buzz that came from the audience itself on all sides as the house lights went on, that the first act had gone wonderfully. Joe Hyman did not stint. For once he "gave satisfaction," as my mother would have said. "If the rest of it keeps up like this, my boy, you can give up the lecture on the evils of poverty," he said, his face wreathed in one big satisfied grin. I looked around for Mr. Kaufman, but of course he had gone backstage. He was to be discovered already seated as the curtain rose on the second act, and he would be putting on his make-up now. I moved about trying to find Max Siegel or Sam Harris; but Max Siegel was nowhere to be found and Sam Harris was surrounded by a large group of people. He caught sight of me over the edge of the group and winked broadly. There could be no doubt that he was immensely pleased.

The ushers began to shout, "Curtain going up, second act . . . Curtain going up . . ." and the audience started to stream back down the aisles with avidity. The pace with which an audience returns to its seats after an intermission is always a dead giveaway on how the play is going. If they linger to chatter in the lobby or sip their orangeades at the back of the theatre, it is always a fairly good sign that things are not going any too well. I am always infuriated by stragglers, but one cannot blame an audience for being reluctant to return for more of the same if what they have already sat through has been dreary and dull. It seemed to me that this audience could hardly wait to get back to their seats.

Mr. Kaufman's reception, when the curtain rose on the second act, was the biggest of the evening. That gaunt, saturnine figure, his eyes peering malignantly over the rims of his glasses, seemed to amuse them before he even spoke—and the very first line he uttered got the biggest laugh in the play so far. Indeed, they laughed twice at it, so to speak—once a great roar, and as the roar died down they gave another burst of delighted laughter. Then they broke into applause, completely drowning out his next line, but he craftily waited them out, then signaled with his eyes to Leona Maricle, to give him the cue again. He was quite wonderful in the part and in complete control of the audience. His timing was perfect, he looked exactly what he was supposed to be—a New York playwright venomously dedicated against all things Hollywood—and he played with the resourcefulness and skill of an actor who had been all his life on the stage. In my opinion he never received enough credit for his performance. Not being a "real" actor, he was received by the critics with the good-humored tolerance reserved for a theatrical trick or a parochial joke; but it was far above anything of the sort. Every line he uttered, even some of his pantomime, drew huge laughs, and when he made his exit in the middle of the second act a resounding round of applause followed him off.

And then a terrible thing happened. An extraordinary quiet settled over that eager, willing audience!

There were laughs, of course, during the rest of the act but they were scattered and thinnish and sounded as though the audience were forcing themselves to laugh at things they didn't quite find really funny. It was as though they wanted the play to keep on being as good as it had been and were eager to help as much as they could by playing the part of a still delighted audience. The second-act curtain, nevertheless, descended to a polite but disappointed hand.

I did not wait for Joe Hyman to come up the aisle this time. With grim foreboding I made my cowardly way to the stage alley around the corner, where I stood miserably biting my nails and saying silently over and over, "Oh, God, is it going to be like Chicago again?"

I went back to the theatre after the curtain had risen on the third act, to find Mr. Kaufman already pacing furiously up and down. I resumed my own pacing and we passed and repassed each other, though he did not speak to me nor I to him. The third act played more or less like the latter half of the second—scattered thinnish laughs—and finally in the last scene, a scene made all the more lethal because the scene itself was more elaborate in decor and lavish in costume than any other in the play, no laughs at all. It was the scene we had labored hardest on, and true to form, the scene which we both liked the best and were secretly the proudest of. With a silent and disgruntled audience watching it, the elaborate set looked ridiculous and the expensive costumes foolish and a little vulgar.

A deadly cough or two began to echo hollowly through the auditorium—that telltale tocsin that pierces the playwright's eardrums, those sounds that penetrate his heart like carefully aimed poison darts—and after the first few tentative coughs a sudden epidemic of respiratory ailments seemed to spread through every chest in the audience as though a long-awaited signal had been given. Great clearings of the throat, prodigious nose-blowings, Gargantuan sneezes came from all parts of the theatre both upstairs and down, all of them gradually blending until the odious sound emerged as one great and constant cough that drowned out every line that was being uttered on the stage.

I stopped pacing and stared balefully at the serried rows of heads and the backs of necks that stretched straight down to the footlights, as if my fury could spray itself over those heads and throats like an insecticide and make them stop. And my eye was immediately struck by the changed postures of that audience. In the first act they had sat erect in their seats and leaned forward a little, attentive and eager for every word coming over the footlights. Now they sprawled every which way. Some of them had even slumped down in their seats as far as they could get, and their heads rested on the backs of the seats. I have watched the same silent spectacle since then, and even without coughs, it is as good and grim an illustration of a disappointed audience as I know of, and another excellent reason why a playwright should never sit through one of his own works. Looking at the heads of an audience from the back of the orchestra will tell him a good deal more than sitting in a welter of well-wishing friends in the third row. I walked away and leaned against the wall, waiting for the coughing to stop, but of course it did not stop. It continued growing in volume for the rest of that lumpish and hulking scene. The curtain finally and at last came down on what at best could only be described as reluctant and somewhat fugitive applause.

Mr. Kaufman had disappeared at least five minutes before the curtain fell, and I remained where I was at the back of the theatre waiting for Joe Hyman to come up the aisle. I could see his face long before he reached me. It looked sad, sullen, and somehow five years older than when he had come up the aisle at the end of the first act. He reached my side and, never a man to mind putting the obvious into words, said, "You got an act and a half of a hit. What you need pretty badly is the other half." I stared dumbly back at him without replying. "Shall I wait for you back at the hotel and go home tomorrow morning, or would you rather I went home tonight?" he asked.

I found my voice, though it sounded squeaky and high-pitched and the words came out almost like a bleat. "Better go home," I said. "There's a conference in Mr. Kaufman's room right away and I think he'll want to go right to work after we finish. Looks like there's quite a lot to do, doesn't it?" I asked needlessly.

Joe Hyman nodded, and the gentle note of mockery was in his voice again. "While you're working tonight, just keep thinking 'Well, at least I'm not up at camp doing "Mrs. Cohen at the Beach."' That'll help." He held out his hand and I took it. "It's an awful good act and a half, though," he said. "I'll call you from New York tomorrow or the next day. I better run now if I'm going to catch that train back." And he was gone.

I waited until the last stragglers had left the lobby and then walked slowly up the boardwalk toward the hotel. I was in no hurry to get there, even at the risk of keeping Mr. Kaufman waiting. Had it really gone as badly as I feared it had, and if so, what would Mr. Harris and Mr. Kaufman do? Sam Harris was no Augustus Pitou, but I remembered I had heard him say to someone or other during rehearsals, "You can't pinch pennies in show business, but the great secret is to know when to cut your losses. Make up your mind quickly, take your loss and run. Just not doing that little thing has caused a good many managers to die broke." I shivered a little in the warm night air and found that I was already in front of the hotel.

Inevitably some of the other passengers were talking about the show as the elevator ascended. "What did you think of that thing tonight?" said a fat suntanned man addressing another fat suntanned man standing next to me. "I saw you in the lobby, didn't I?"

"Yeah," said the man at my side, "after the first act everyone could have stayed in the lobby. They got a big juicy flop on their hands if you ask me."

Who's asking you, you fat, overfed, overdressed son-of-a-bitch, I thought sullenly as he pressed himself against me.

"You're Beacon Sportswear Sweaters, aren't you?" said the first man to the man at my side. "I'm Ladies Cashmere Woolens."

"Yeah, Beacon Sportswear. You know the line?" the man next to me asked.

I longed to answer him myself, but I lacked the courage. "I know the line," I ached to say; "and your sweaters are lousy—lousier than our third act. I'm wearing one of them right now. They stretch and they unravel. And if you know so much about plays, why don't you make better sweaters, you pompous bastard?" I added silently and illogically as I pushed past him to get off at my floor.

I made my way miserably down the corridor, but in front of Mr. Kaufman's room I turned away and walked a few doors further down to my own room. Whether because of the tension of the evening or because of what Mr. Sportswear had just said in the elevator, my face and forehead and eyes were burning as if with a high fever. I let myself into my room, and without turning on the lights—I had no wish to be mocked by the little pile of telegrams, stacked neatly on the bureau, which I had opened with such amusement and pleasure earlier in the evening—I walked through the dark room to the bathroom. I filled the washbowl with water as cold as I could get it to run and dipped my face and finally my whole head into it. In the dark bedroom I changed my shirt, which was limp and dank with perspiration, and as I stood buttoning it the telephone rang. With a pang I remembered I had told the family to call me in my room at eleven thirty sharp, before I went to the conference, so that I could tell them how the opening had gone. It rang again, and I let it ring without moving to answer it. There was no point in giving them bad news until I knew just how bad the news might be. Still less point in trying to put a good face on it or attempting to whitewash the evening's calamity—my mother would catch me out at once. Better to let them think they had missed me.

I walked out of the room, with the telephone still ringing, and down the hall to Mr. Kaufman's room again and knocked on the door. Mr. Kaufman's voice called, "Come in, come in," and I walked into the room to find no one there, surprisingly enough, but Mr. Kaufman himself. I had expected to see Sam Harris, Max Siegel, the stage manager, the company manager, and even some of the group I had seen talking to Sam Harris during the intermission. Mr. Kaufman's conferences were evidently not going to follow the prescribed ritual. The wrecking crew and even Sam Harris were apparently barred.

Mr. Kaufman, in pajamas and bathrobe, was seated on the sofa, the script already on his knees, a pencil poised above it, and a sheet of yellow paper and carbon stood ready at the typewriter. He did not look up but gestured toward a table on which stood a Thermos of coffee and two thin sandwiches. "Those are for you," he said. "We'll be working all night, and room service closes at one o'clock." I stared hungrily at the sandwiches, but another gesture had motioned me over to the sofa. I sat down beside him.

"You know what didn't go as well as I do," he said. "Curing it is another matter. We'll get to that later. Let's cut right down to the bone first, to give us a clean look at what we've got. It won't fix what's wrong, but at least it will improve the good stuff that's there." Nothing in his tone or manner indicated that there was any thought of abandoning the play. I could easily have thrown my arms around him and hugged him, and my sigh of relief must have been so audible that he turned to me and said, "Did you say something?" I shook my head. The pencil in his hand began to make quick, darting marks on the manuscript, bracketing the cuts on page after page. It was astonishing to find how much of what we had written was unnecessary, how we had underestimated an audience's ability to grasp what was needful for them to know without restating it not once but sometimes two or even three times. It was reassuring to find that so meticulous a craftsman as George Kaufman himself still had to learn the hard way the ever-constant lesson of economy.

There was a knock at the door and I opened it to find Max Siegel standing in the doorway with a number of typewritten sheets in his hand. "Mr. Harris' notes," he said, handing them over. "How's the young author? Not discouraged, I hope." He waved to Mr. Kaufman over my shoulder and walked away. I presented the notes to Mr. Kaufman. He placed them on the table beside him without so much as a glance. "Later," he remarked, without looking up from the manuscript, and the pencil darted surgically over the pages.

I could only guess at the passage of time by the increasingly loud rumblings of my stomach. That large lobster dinner I had eaten with Joe Hyman seemed some years away. Moreover, I had returned it to the sea early in the evening and I was beginning to grow a little dizzy with hunger. I waited until Mr. Kaufman found it necessary to go to the bathroom and then dived for the sandwiches and coffee, stealing a look at my watch at the same time. It was almost four thirty in the morning and we were only just past the middle of the second act.

Mr. Kaufman, returning from the bathroom, walked toward the bureau instead of going back to the sofa, and rummaging under a pile of shirts he brought out a large brown paper bag. "Fudge," he said casually, "for energy. Have some." He held the bag out in front of me and I tentatively picked out the daintiest piece I could find, conscious as always in his presence of my undisciplined appetite. "Have a good-sized piece," he said sharply, "you won't even taste it that way. I make it myself," he added, with a satisfied chuckle.

I looked up at him in surprise. What was even more surprising was the fact that his eyes were shining with the first hint of pride I had ever seen glisten in them. I had tried once or twice to discuss some of his work that I particularly admired, but careful as I had been to keep any hint of admiration out of my voice, his replies had been so lackluster and his indifference so obvious that I had quickly dropped any mention of the plays and never returned to it. To my astonishment, he was now standing over me, waiting as eagerly for me to taste the piece of fudge in my fingers as he might wait for a notice in the *Times* the morning after an opening night. I bit into it and carefully let it melt in my mouth before I gave my report, for his eyes were intent on mine and the expression on his face was so childishly expectant that I knew my judgment must be a considered one before I pronounced it.

The very first bite told the whole story! It was awful fudge—gummy and sickly sweet. I did not have the heart to tell him so. "It's just wonderful," I lied. He smiled delightedly and popped a large piece into his own mouth, still looking at me with the look of fevered expectancy that a favored relative fixes on the family lawyer about to read the will. Evidently "just wonderful" wasn't going to be enough. "I didn't know you could make fudge," I said thickly, trying to make the words sound enthusiastic, for the horrible stuff was sticking to the roof of my mouth and had worked its way around my back molars and gums.

"Can't buy it *this* way anywhere," he said, deeply pleased with himself. "Never the right consistency or not sweet enough. Matter of fact"—he went on chewing contentedly—"This isn't quite sweet enough either. I'll make a new batch to take to Brighton Beach next week."

Oh, God, I thought . . . not sweet enough! If he makes me take another piece I'll be sick right in front of him. "Have some more," said Mr. Kaufman, helping himself to another piece and holding the bag out in front of me. "Best thing I know of to keep you awake."

It'll keep me awake all right, I thought, as I plunged my hand in the bag and tried to pick out the smallest possible piece. Just keeping it down will keep me awake. "Thanks," I said brightly, "it certainly does seem to give you energy, doesn't it?" And I walked into the bathroom. I flushed the lump of wretched stuff down the toilet and emerged from the bathroom falsely chewing away like the traitor I was.

Through the years the brown paper bag full of that terrible fudge emerged from a good many other bureau drawers. Mr. Kaufman rarely traveled without it. It was as much a part of his traveling equipment as the sharpened pencils, the carbon paper, the typewriter and the special hand soap. And the memory of that brown paper bag coming toward me at four or five in the morning is still enough to engender a slight feeling of queasiness. His staunch belief in the energy-giving properties of his own fudge, however, worked like magic—at least, for him—for he worked through the rest of the night without so much as a pause or a single yawn.

It was just after seven thirty in the morning when he closed the manuscript and walked to the windows to draw the curtains and pull up the shades. The bright sunlight made me blink my eyes and made me realize that I ached all over with weariness. "I've called rehearsal for eleven o'clock. We never got to Sam Harris' notes," he added with a regretful sigh. "Oh, well, we'll get a chance to go through them between the morning and afternoon rehearsal. Good night—or good morning—whichever you prefer." He opened the windows, then pulled the curtain and shades to once again and was taking off his bathrobe and making for the bed as I murmured a good night and closed the door after me.

The rest of that work-filled week in Atlantic City was a testimony to the remarkable continuity with which George Kaufman functioned—to the unity of purpose and dogged persistence with which he cut away every superfluous word of the play until its bare bones lay exposed. It was a striking illustration of his dictum "First things first," for he refused to be swerved or stampeded by anyone, Sam Harris and Beatrice Kaufman included, until he had achieved what he chose to call "A naked look at the play itself—I don't care if the curtain comes down at ten o'clock." Indeed, at the Friday evening performance, the final curtain actually did come down at ten fifteen—he had cut a little too deeply, he grudgingly conceded—and some of the cuts were quickly restored for the Saturday matinée; but for that one alarming evening the play must have given the impression to the bewildered and stunned audience of being hardly a play at all, but merely a series of loosely connected scenes strung causelessly together.

There is always one performance in the life of a play that is in trouble out of town, where the entire enterprise, from the idea of the play itself right down to its settings and its actors, succeeds in looking utterly ridiculous and gives to everyone connected with it a sense of deep and complete humiliation. We had apparently reached that terminal point in record time. It was on that black evening also that both Sam Harris and Beatrice Kaufman returned to New York, leaving behind them, or so it seemed to my apprehensive ears, an impression of extremely cautious and guarded optimism as to the play's ultimate chances, in spite of the careful way they phrased everything they said. Nevertheless, that savage and ruthless cutting job accomplished exactly what he had meant it to do: it revealed as nothing else could have the deep trouble we were in, for stripped of its excess verbiage *Once in a Lifetime* emerged as a play of sound satiric viewpoint but very little substance. It was possible, it seemed, for an audience to laugh long and loud at a play, and yet leave the theatre dissatisfied and disappointed—a phenomenon that I have noted in a good many other plays through the years, sometimes in plays of sound enough ideas, but which remained unhappy casualties because of this fundamental lack of what an audience compellingly demands.

I was learning in that memorable week still another aspect of how baffling a quarry an audience can be. Some basic human element or ingredient was missing in *Once in a Lifetime*, and in spite of its high sense of fun and rollicking good spirits, the sum total of the evening did not add up to that magical sense of enjoyment that sends an audience out of the theatre completely satisfied and breeds long lines at the box office afterward. Each night after the labor of cutting was over, we sat in Mr. Kaufman's room and discussed the nature of the disease, but curing it, as he had tartly remarked after the opening performance, was another matter. The gravity of the trouble we were in was obvious enough; the remedy was not so easily come by. We discussed and quickly discarded any number of devices which we sensed were palliatives rather than the pure oxygen the play needed, and as I watched Mr. Kaufman stride toward the windows at the end of each night to pull aside the curtain and let the dawn streak in, I marveled anew at his resiliency—at his uncommon ability to stand up under the punishing load of work he was carrying and still retain his full zest and vigor.

I had ceased to be astonished by the freshness with which he would attack each new day's rehearsal after a night of little or no sleep, but as I made my own weary way down the corridor to my room, my befuddled brain continued to marvel at him. I still do, and I continue to wonder why I have allowed myself to follow the same foolish path. The playwright who directs his own work is playing a fool's game. The schedule he must keep and the load he must carry is an inhuman one and it does not always work to the advantage of his play. If the play is in trouble—and trouble is the out-of-town norm—he will more often than not be forced to rewrite whole scenes during the night, have the rewrite typed and ready for an eleven o'clock rehearsal, rehearse throughout the day, watch the performance that evening, making his notes to give to the actors after the curtain comes down, as well as judging how well or ill the new scenes played, and then go back to his room to repeat the same procedure over again every night until such time as he is lucky enough or clever enough to have rescued his play. Apart from the labor and tension of the original rehearsals, after two or three weeks of this grueling schedule on the road, the playwright who is his own director would be wise not to go to a doctor for a checkup at the end of it. He is very likely to be unpleasantly surprised at the results of his cardiogram. Yet there is no recovery, it is only fair to say, as quick as the recovery from a hit. The roses appear in the playwright's cheeks again with amazing swiftness, and the sparkle of health in his eye gives the lie to the lunatic battering he has just put his physical and nervous system through.

Perhaps it is precisely this unholy knowledge that has caused me to persist in continuing to direct my own plays against all the dictates of common sense, considering that I have teetered along the edge of that porcupine path so many times before. Vanity, I can only presume, inevitably triumphs over plain common sense, for I am certain that some of my plays have suffered at my own hands as director. I have long since reached the conclusion that I am a better director of another's work than of my own—yet I very much doubt if my egoistic sense of pleasure in directing my own plays would allow me to let another man stage them. It is strange that this should be so, for the rewards to a playwright as the director of his own plays are minor compared to the awareness he has of the price he must pay for this indulgence, but vanity is part of a writer's strength as well as his weakness. Without vanity a writer's work is tepid, and he must accept his vanity as part of his stock in trade and live with it as one of the hazards of his profession.

Something of the sort must have held true for George Kaufman, for as I saw him toil under the grind of rewriting and rehearsals I wondered why he usually chose to bear the double burden of play-writing and directing at the same time. It seemed to me a sleeveless errand that vanity alone could explain. More than once as I watched him labor, the thought crossed my mind, "What a social director he would have made," for he was seemingly immune to weariness and his capacity for working around the clock would have made him the loved and envied of the entire Borscht Circuit. By the end of the first week's tryout of *Once in a Lifetime* at Atlantic City, the rigors of social directing seemed to me in retrospect like so much child's play.

On the journey back to New York, I wondered sleepily not if or how we were going to be able to fix the play—my brain seemed to go dry and my wits to scatter if I attempted to focus on it—I wondered instead if the new social director at the Flagler was as dog-tired as I was! There was one salutary thing about social directing, I morosely concluded. "Mrs. Cohen at the Beach" did not need a second act, and if I had to pick up social directing again next season, I would remember it. It was cold comfort, and the sight of Max Siegel, unsmiling for the first time, did not make it a particularly warming journey.

For the first time in my life I found myself walking down to the subway at Times Square with a sense of actual relief. I needed to be alone, to escape from *Once in a Lifetime*—to look at no one connected with it, to have no one ask me about it, or ask me to think about it. I needed to shut it out of my mind and psyche, if only for the measure of a subway ride back to Brooklyn. Brooklyn, however, was holding a surprise in store that I had not quite reckoned with and one that was hardly likely to promote forgetfulness.

I know of no group of people as idiotically confident of success as a playwright's family while his play is still in its tryout stage. In spite of everything I had said over the telephone to my mother from Atlantic City, in spite of my insistence that they must all think of the play as still "trying out" and not as an assured success, I was welcomed home on a note of unqualified triumph. Everything short of flags and a brass band greeted a returning hero, whose own doubts about the play jangled like sleighbells in his ears as he listened to the neighbors' fulsome congratulations and their repeated assurances that they could hardly wait to get to the theatre. My mother could barely wait to get me inside the apartment to proudly parade for my inspection the two new dresses she had bought to celebrate. These twin purchases were explained by the fact that since she expected to attend every performance throughout the week, as well as the opening one, it was hardly to be expected that she could appear all week in the same dress. My father and brother had settled for new ties and shirts and would wear their best blue suits every night, but since different neighbors would be attending the play on different nights it was no more than seemly that she be dressed as the occasion merited. I could only gather that she meant to alternate the dresses, as alternate neighbors attended the performance, for at the end of an hour of listening to lightheaded plans and dreams of the rich, full life we were going to live, I nodded "yes" to everything. It was plainly hopeless to try to persuade her or my father or brother, for that matter, that *Once in a Lifetime* might turn out to be a little less than the shower of gold they had already concluded it was.

To do them justice, this conviction, which seemed so firmly rooted and fixed in all of their minds, was not entirely without a basis in reality. For one thing, the notice in *Variety* had been a surprisingly good one. If one took the trouble to read the notice carefully, however, the reviewer's certainty that a hit was in store for Broadway the following season was based almost entirely on George Kaufman's accepted wizardry of being able to pull a large number of rabbits out of his play-doctor's hat. For another, Dore Schary, Eddie Chodorov, Lester Sweyd, in fact everyone who should have known better and curbed his tongue, had called and offered congratulations in my absence. To my vast surprise, they continued to misread the *Variety* notice when I talked to them myself on the telephone, and they put down my reservations and rumblings to what they laughingly termed, "success modesty." Obviously, the reports that had seeped back to Broadway from Atlantic City had all been good: "Kaufman is working on it night and day," the grapevine had reported—and that was enough for Broadway to know.

By Monday afternoon, the day after my return and the day of the opening at Brighton Beach, I too had succumbed to the general elation. The same self-delusion that had enveloped everyone connected with *The Beloved Bandit*, as it transferred from Rochester to Chicago, fell into place again and operated with equal magic. I reread the *Variety* notice and managed to translate what it plainly stated into something it did not say at all. By the time I left the house that evening and took a trolley car to Brighton Beach, I was in high spirits. I got off the car four or five blocks before I reached the theatre, for I was early and I wanted to enjoy this sudden and unexpected tranquillity. I wanted also, in my usual way, to seek some omen that would make secure my high hopes for tonight. Reason or logic has little to do with these moments of self-deception, which come into play at moments of crisis. We all wear these atavistic wishing caps in one form or another. I still search for opening-night omens, good ones or bad ones, and I invariably find one. I found one now.

Hurrying along the boardwalk I came suddenly upon the bathhouse that had once been the night club my grandfather had taken us all to on that far-off midsummer night. The façade had been altered almost beyond recognition, but there could be no doubt that it was the same building. That night and this place had been too sharply etched in my memory for me to mistake it. I stopped and stood in front of it for a few moments. Everything else but the memory of that night and of my grandfather vanished from my mind. It had been a long time since I had consciously thought of him or of my Aunt Kate, but they came back sharply now. Much of what I was and what I had done, this very journey that was taking me along this boardwalk and past this bathhouse, to a theatre where a play of mine was to raise its curtain in less than an hour—a great deal of both of them was embedded in every step of that journey. And if I needed an omen for tonight, there could scarcely be a better one. This shabby relic of middle-class gaiety had been for my grandfather a cry from the heart against his lot. He would be pleased at the journey I was making, no matter what happened tonight. I hurried past it, my spirits soaring higher than ever.

The crowd that filled the lobby of the Brighton Beach Theatre looked surprisingly like a cross section of a Broadway opening night. I was startled by the turnout. It was stupid of me to have forgotten that the Broadway regulars would of course have waited to test themselves against the play at Brighton Beach, rather than make the journey to Atlantic City. The sight of them lowered my spirits by a good fifty per cent. Agents whose clients had been turned down for parts in the play buzzed softly to scenic and costume designers, who likewise had lost out on their own bids. Even some of the very actors who had auditioned for us, unsuccessfully, were present, to prove to themselves, I suppose, how prejudiced and unseeing authors and managers can be. They would be bringing no great good will down the aisles with them when they went to their seats. Rival managers whose agenda for the new season also included a topical comedy had come to have an appraising look at the possible competition. They would judge and compare silently, without benefit, if possible, of laughter. The jungle drum beaters were also represented in almost their full strength—those faceless folk on the periphery of the theatre to whom it is all-important to be in the know and to know in advance just how good or how bad the incoming merchandise is likely to be.

I stared resentfully at the ones I knew and realized with something of a start that I myself had been an enthusiastic member of the same club, though it did not seem possible that my own eyes could ever have glistened with the same cannibalistic glee that seemed to shine from every countenance at the possibility of imminent failure. This same anticipatory buzz would have sounded equally in key, it seemed to my ears, rising from the throats of a group of savages grouped around a tribal pot, over whose rim rose the steaming heads of George Kaufman and myself. Ticket brokers, columnists, a delegation of some of Mr. Kaufman's Algonquin set, as well as the faces of some of my own friends, appeared and disappeared in the throng. One heart-sinking look was enough to send me quivering backstage, my pulses pounding. I crouched against a piece of furniture that I knew would not be used until the third act and I remained there until I heard the curtain rise and the first laugh waft backstage.

Mr. Kaufman was already pacing furiously when I stole back into the theatre and he did not recognize my presence by even that one lifted finger in traditional greeting. His race across the carpet was if anything more frenzied than it had been at Atlantic City. His long strides had a hint of the pursued in them and his head seemed sunk into his shoulders. He knew, of course, far better than I did, the composition of tonight's audience, and that the closer one drew to Broadway, the larger the lacks in a play loomed. Tonight was as close as one could get without actually opening on Broadway, and this audience would pounce on every lack. I listened for a moment or two and then stopped my own pacing and stared at him. The actors were giving a nervous and strained performance—cutting into their own and each other's laughs, their timing sky-high, and their voices pitched at that taut level that always heralds a shaky performance. Yet the audience, even this audience, was responding to the play with unrestrained laughter. "They like it," I whispered to him as he passed me. He did not reply, but continued his pacing.

As he passed me again a moment or two later, he stopped long enough to state flatly, "They'll like it better when they stop laughing. They haven't long to wait." I looked after him wonderingly. Was he never satisfied? What more could he want or ask? He was right, however. The ethics of the wrecking crew, curiously enough, are as strong as their malice. They adhere to a strict code of theatre behavior that contains its own kind of rough justice. The two things are not mutually exclusive, though they may seem so. In operation it is unfailing. If in the first fifteen minutes a play begins to play like a hit, no matter what ill will or personal animus they may have brought to it as single members of the audience, they give it as an entity their unalloyed blessing and reward it with laughter. This does not deny the fact that individually they might be better pleased if the opposite were true, but once the indications are clear that a hit is about to be revealed before them, the excitement of being present and part of the event itself is enough to outlaw their personal feelings and make them a good audience—sometimes better, in fact, than an audience of friends and well-wishers. For one thing, they are sharper and more acutely aware of the skills of the playwright and the actor, and their very malice creates an electricity of its own. It heightens and sparks both play and performance, so that a positive crackle of wills and wits pervades both sides of the footlights, and when the battle is joined, the evening is a memorable one for all concerned.

The first act of *Once in a Lifetime* played like a hit of vintage rare, and when the curtain descended at the end of it, it was greeted with spontaneous and ungrudging applause. As Mr. Kaufman had prophesied, the faces coming up the aisle were not particularly happy faces. It was as though a hundred pairs of shoulders had shrugged in unison with the unspoken message: "A hit is a hit. You can't stop it. Might as well get on the bandwagon early." But their faces relayed in the same silent fashion that they didn't have to be happy about it either, by God. "Just be patient—it won't be too long," I thought, paraphrasing Mr. Kaufman's cynical assessment of their laughter and their applause, and scurried backstage to avoid the folly of the premature congratulations I saw plainly mirrored on the faces of some of my friends as they struggled up the aisle toward me. They caught a glimpse of me and raised their arms above their heads in congratulation, but I turned on my heel and ran. Let them put it down to nerves, mock modesty, or what they would—I preferred not to face them just yet.

The second act played exactly as it had in Atlantic City, with the exception that from Mr. Kaufman's exit onward the silence was deadlier. There were no willing, scattered laughs now. There was instead a kind of rapt attention, as though they must make thoroughly certain that no sound disturbed the passengers while the crew sank the ship. This, in a sense, was what they had come for, and their silence had the breathless hushed quality of a death watch. The curtain fell to a thin round of obligatory applause, but the faces coming up the aisle were relieved and smiling this time. It did not comfort me or make me feel any the less bitter to know that I had been guilty of exactly the same behavior at other people's plays. The theatre breeds its own kind of cruelty, and its sadism takes on a keener edge since it can be enjoyed under the innocent guise of critical judgment. Charity in the theatre usually begins and ends with people who have a play opening the week following one's own. Their unlikely benevolence is not so much a purity of heart as the knowledge that they face a firing line with rifles aimed in exactly the same direction.

I waited now for Eddie and Dore and the others to come up the aisle. They, at least, wished me well and I wanted desperately to hear something good about the play, no matter what, in spite of what my eyes and ears so plainly told me. They were slower this time in coming up the aisle and their faces were the unsmiling ones. For a brief moment I felt sorry for them. Greeting an author on the opening night of a play that is going badly is in some ways comparable to taking a marriage vow. You are damned if you do and you are damned if you don't. Not to greet him if he catches your eye is impossible as well as painfully obvious, and to murmur evasively when one stands face to face with him is nothing short of outright cruelty. Yet the truth is too painful for him to hear, even if one has the courage to state it, and the truth is exactly what he least wishes to know. It is an impossible moment. Politeness does not suffice and good manners are somehow an affront. I have evolved a credo of my own which serves the occasion but does not attempt to solve the insoluble. Simply stated, I tell the truth to an author on an opening night out of town, and on an opening night in New York I do not. The truth is not always a virtue. There are times when the truth is unnecessary as well as needlessly cruel, and a New York opening night is one of those times. By then the die is cast, and at that moment the author is at his most vulnerable. It is unfriendly not to tell him the truth out of town when it may yet do some good, but by the same token it is nonsense to do so at a time when it can be of no service whatever. The truth at that moment can only succeed in giving the teller the smug satisfaction of virtuous honesty and do the author no good at all. The truth will be his soon enough and he will nourish it for a long time to come.

My friends cushioned the truth and made it as palatable as they could—there was no way of making it pleasant and I did not press them. What, after all, was there to say after that painfully weak second act? It was Joe Hyman, as it turned out, who bore the brunt of my explosive behavior that evening, when he gravely remarked, with that edge of mockery in his voice, "What happened to all that work you were supposed to be doing? This is the same play I saw in Atlantic City." My rage found a target. The defeat of my hopes uncoiled like a cobra within me and I lashed out at him with almost a sense of relief at no longer having to repress the black sense of fury and defeat I had kept concealed from everyone, myself included, until that moment. He did not answer, nor did anyone else interrupt me. When I finished I turned and walked out of the theatre. I felt strangely better. The worst had become true and there was only one more act to live through. I had the courage not to return to the theatre for the third act. Not until I had seen the last of the audience, including my family, leave the theatre and the lights on the marquee go out, did I venture to go backstage to find out what Mr. Kaufman's working plans might be for the following day.

Mr. Kaufman was not there nor had he left a message for me. Neither Sam Harris nor Max Siegel was to be seen either, all three of them, it seemed, having driven back to New York together immediately after the third-act curtain had fallen.

As usual, there was that minor player, about to deposit his dressing-room key with the stage doorman, who informed me brightly that he thought the play had gone wonderfully and that all of *his* friends were certain we were in for a long run on Broadway. I am ashamed to record that my ego was so limp and my spirit so impoverished that I walked him to the subway to hear in greater detail just how wonderful his friends had thought it was. I willingly paid the blackmail of having to listen to how his own part could be strengthened to the greater good of the play. At that particular moment it was worth it.

There is this much to be said for the value of out-of-town notices. If they are good, they can be acknowledged as good for business and for the morale of the actors. If they are bad, they can be brushed aside as out-of-town notices and what do out-of-town critics know anyway? My mother achieved this solid professional viewpoint in exactly one night, or by the time I had awakened the next morning. Standing over me she announced that she had read the local papers and compared their notices to the review in *Variety*. Her pronouncement was professional and exact. "What do Brooklyn papers know about a play, anyway? If they were real critics they wouldn't be here in Brooklyn!" She handed them over, and my own professionalism being neither as steadfast nor as flourishing as her own, I read them avidly and not without a painful twinge or two. The worst, naturally, was the paper I happened to pick up first. "It is probably unfair," the notice ran, "to infer that the good parts of a play are written by one man and the inferior parts by another, but judging by the records of both names listed on the program last night, the first act and a half of *Once in a Lifetime*, which is very good indeed, was written by George S. Kaufman, and the rest by Moss Hart. Mr. Kaufman's witty hand is everywhere in evidence during the hilarious first part, but he seems to have left the typewriter in the custody of Mr. Hart for the rest of the play. He had better get back to it as fast as he can, if the lavish Sam H. Harris production unveiled at the Brighton Beach Theatre last evening, etc., etc." The other Brooklyn papers were less damning, but meager indeed in their praise, which consisted mainly of listing the actors and saying they were all good. "Well, bully for the actors' morale," I thought briefly. "I hope it's in better shape than my own."

I glanced sourly up at my mother, who stood rereading the *Variety* notice and smiling and nodding her head in agreement, and got out of bed and out of the house as fast as I could. I had no wish to hear how much the neighbors had liked it or how violently they disagreed with what the local papers said, which I could see she was firmly determined to tell me, neighbor by neighbor. I went to the drug store on the corner and telephoned Mr. Kaufman from there. If the news was going to be bad, I wanted to be alone to hear it. "Were you planning to work today, Mr. Kaufman?" I asked with as much casualness as I could summon into my voice when his hello came through the receiver.

"I think we both need a respite for a couple of days before we tackle it again," he replied. "By the way," he went on, "don't let yourself be upset by what that silly bastard said. How the hell would he or anyone else know who wrote which parts of a play? It's damned infuriating."

"I'm not upset," I said almost jubilantly. As long as we *were* going to tackle it again, what difference did it make what anyone said?

"Good," he said. "See you there tonight." And the connection clicked off.

I made another telephone call to apologize to Joe Hyman and then returned home to eat a huge breakfast, my mind tumbling with ideas about the play and as refreshed as though I had returned from a month in the country. It is possible that fear in one form or another is as much responsible for that occupational illness, writer's block, as any of the traumatic experiences a writer may have gathered in his childhood.

The second night's performance of a comedy is generally a letdown for both actors and audience. It is a letdown, that is, unless the second-night audience has been told by the reviewers in their morning newspapers that the play is funny. Having thus been relieved of having to exercise their own judgment, they then enter the theatre laughing at the ushers as they receive their programs, and the actors have only to stroll through their parts to be hilariously accepted and applauded. It is a sheeplike exhibition and a dispiriting one to watch. The second-night audience of *Once in a Lifetime*, having been told what to expect, entered the theatre feeling already cheated. One could almost feel them stiffen against the play as they settled into their seats. They opened their programs with an air of preparing themselves not to be amused. Actors can do little with a disgruntled audience. They can win over a cold audience, but not a disapproving one. Even the first act, which contained genuine laughter if an audience met it halfway, played soggily. Moreover, the actors, keyed to the quick perception of the audience of the night before, suddenly found themselves adrift in a sea of unknowing silence, where before waves of laughter had always safely borne them along. Perhaps even more disconcerting than this unexpected stillness was the sound of a single laugh that kept staunchly and hollowly resounding through the silences. It was my mother's laugh, and I could easily have throttled her! The actors gave up when the biggest laugh in the first act was again met with a thudding silence, and played from that point onward with an air of undisguised martyrdom that made the play seem endless.

Mr. Kaufman, other than giving me his traditional single finger lifted in silent greeting, spoke not a word during the first act nor throughout the rest of the evening. If he was dismayed by the dismal reception the play was receiving, he gave no sign of it. His pacing continued, but it was neither more nor less fervent than it had been on any of the other evenings I had watched him. I chose to interpret his silence as a tacit agreement that this was one of those evenings and one of those audiences that must somehow be lived through and on which comment was superfluous. One could only blot it out and hope that by tomorrow evening the memory of those notices would be partially dimmed. Not everyone in Brooklyn, I thought grimly, reads the newspapers or they would vote more sensibly and spend less time at the ball park.

To a large degree this was true. As the week wore on, the audiences grew noticeably better, though increasingly smaller in number. There were, it seemed, just so many friends and neighbors of my mother and they apparently all sat in the balcony. Her faith in the play remained unshaken and her ringing laughter cut through each silence, but her influence on the Brooklyn theatregoing public was obviously negligible. By Thursday evening the gaps in the back rows of the orchestra were alarming. I had another and deeper cause for alarm by Thursday evening, however. Sam Harris and Max Siegel had appeared only once since the opening night at Brighton Beach.

They sat through the second performance, but I had purposely evaded meeting them on that depressing evening. Their absence was unsettling, but I refused to let it or the fact that Mr. Kaufman had given no sign of being ready to go to work yet disquiet me unduly. Perhaps it was pointless for them to keep coming back to look at the play until we knew how we were going to fix it, and Mr. Kaufman had said he had wanted a respite before we tackled the play again. He was not a man to equivocate or to give his word lightly where work was concerned. I could not completely down, however, a feeling of haunting uneasiness as each night's performance came to an end and there was no suggestion of a meeting for the following day, and I took what comfort I could in the fact that he still gave notes to the actors after each performance and continued to make little cuts in scenes. There was, moreover, the solid certainty of his presence in the theatre each night as the curtain rose and the reassuring sight of his pacing back and forth until the last curtain fell.

When he did not appear as the house lights dimmed for the final performance on Saturday night, my stomach took a nasty turn. The absence of that familiar figure pacing to and fro in the dark suddenly exploded all the gnawing doubts I had been able to keep within bounds until now. I paced back and forth alone for a while and then gave it up. I realized that I was hearing not one word that came across the footlights. I left the theatre and scanned the street outside.

The street had that special emptiness of streets outside of theatres after the curtain has risen. For some inexplicable reason no one seems to pass by after curtain time. The street goes as silent and dead as it might in the middle of the night. The only sign of life now on either side of the street was the Negro attendant sweeping up the ticket envelopes and cigarette stubs in the lobby behind me. I walked to the corner and stood there aimlessly, chilled by the emptiness around me but unable to go back into the theatre until I could stem the sense of unease Mr. Kaufman's absence had stirred up. He would have to be there, I knew, in time for his appearance in the second act, but his failure to turn up in time for the first act took on a growing but deadly significance in my mind. It was unlike him not to appear tonight of all nights. He was a bitter-ender, for one thing, and for another he was scrupulous about watching each performance from the beginning, no matter how well or how badly the play might be going. Short of a traffic accident, I could not account for his absence, and the longer I waited the more forbidding his lateness seemed to become.

I did not see a car pull up and stop in front of the theatre until I became aware that the figure helping someone alight from the car was Mr. Kaufman himself and the woman he was helping out was Beatrice Kaufman. He looked quite startled, as well he might have, when my own figure dashed out of the shadows and ran toward him yelling, "The curtain's up," in a tone of wild jubilation. I stood in front of them both, grinning foolishly, so relieved at seeing him that I was unconscious of how idiotic my behavior must seem.

Beatrice Kaufman gave me a puzzled hello, and after a moment Mr. Kaufman recovered himself sufficiently to ask, "How is it going?"

"Great," I found myself unexpectedly replying, though I had barely seen any of it.

"Well, that'll be a nice change," he remarked and started toward the lobby.

Fortunately, they entered the theatre on a burst of laughter, so that I was not made out a complete fool—but laughter, even with this easily pleased Saturday night audience, stopped exactly where it had always stopped before. At Mr. Kaufman's exit, dead center in the middle of the second act—almost as though some hand had pulled a hidden switch that controlled the audience's mirth—all laughter ceased abruptly. For the first time, however, I listened for the expected silence, and when it came I did not, as I had done throughout every other performance, quail inwardly. That long-awaited signal from Mr. Kaufman had been given and it remained in my ears now, filling in the silence. At the end of the first act he had approached me and said, "Come back to the dressing room at the end of the show so that we can talk for a few minutes, will you?" And from that point onward I had hardly bothered to listen to the play at all.

In the middle of the third act, a portion of the evening's listening that was always the hardest for me to bear, I walked out into the lobby for a smoke. Now that I knew we were actually going to work I could spare myself the needless pain of watching scenes that were going to be tossed out or completely rewritten.

A playwright is almost invariably to be found in the lobby throughout one of the bad scenes of his play—during the very scenes, in fact, that warrant his most serious attention; but these are the scenes, of course, that he finds the most painful to watch. No matter how inveterate a smoker he may be, he will somehow manage to contain his longing for a cigarette through the good scenes. Indeed, it would be hard to drag him out of the theatre then under any pretext. Ten lines before a bad scene approaches, however, his need to smoke becomes savage beyond endurance and he gives way to it. He remains puffing away in the lobby until the scene is over, timing his re-entrance with a splendid ingenuity. He can somehow manage to escape the scenes most in need of work until the last possible moment. His excuse to himself and to others is a valid one—he needs the solace of a smoke. It is hard after all to deny a man the steadying influence of a cigarette. The practiced "out-of-town" eye, however, can tell to a nicety just how badly a play is still in need of fixing by the length of time an author spends smoking in the lobby.

I felt no sense of guilt about stealing out to the lobby, for we obviously were going to arrive at an entirely new last act, and I began to sort out some possibilities in my mind. I have had the good fortune of being able to work almost anywhere at all. I have written in subways, on shipboard with people chattering away in deck chairs on either side of me, in theatre lounges with actors rehearsing on the stage above, in kitchens, in automobiles, and on beaches or beside swimming pools with children cavorting about in the water. No particular exercise of discipline is inherent in this ability to work in whatever setting happens to fall my way—it is a lucky or accidental gift of concentration and I have always been grateful for it.

I walked up and down the empty lobby, hardly conscious of where I was, and when one of the doors of the theatre opened, I was so immersed in a tangle of thoughts for a new last act that I stared unseeingly at Beatrice Kaufman for a good thirty seconds before I recognized her and smiled back. She stopped to light a cigarette before she moved toward me, and I was conscious once again that she somehow managed to infuse even so small an action as the lighting of a cigarette with a distinctive quality of her own—just as the way she puffed on the cigarette in its green paper holder was peculiarly hers, fastidious and feminine, yet with a delicate sensuality. The gray smoke curled lazily around her face until it blended with the color of her hair, and she seldom removed the holder from her lips while she talked, so that her entire head was usually haloed in a haze of smoke that made her own bluish-white hair seem to rise out of the smoke and become a part of it. It lent a frisky and rakish air to everything she said and made it sound faintly reckless.

We talked for a few moments about the play, easily and lightly. Her very presence was enlivening after the dreariness of this past week—there had been little chance to talk to her in Atlantic City—and as always, her effect on people and certainly on myself was to induce a sense of exhilaration and gaiety.

I heard myself saying now with the intimacy of old acquaintance, "We'll probably be seeing a good deal of each other during the rewrite this summer."

She did not pause in her reply, but her expression changed slightly. "I won't be here this summer," she said. "We've taken a villa in France for three months—in Antibes—Woollcott and Harpo and Alice Miller and I. I'm leaving next week." I sensed she was about to go on, but my face must have shown such open mouth-watering envy that she burst into laughter instead, and said, "I hope it's as good as all that! Will you tell George I've gone on to the Dietzes' and that I'll send the car back for him?" She held out her hand. "Good-bye," she said and started for the street door.

She had half opened the door when she turned and came back. She hesitated and seemed to be searching for the right words, but they eluded her, for she sighed and somewhat nervously, I thought, lit another cigarette. She smiled uncertainly for a moment before she spoke. "You'll be spending summers in Europe yourself some day," she said. "You're going to be a very successful playwright. You'll be writing other plays."

Again it seemed to me she seemed to be regretting the impulse that had made her return and speak at all. She moved quickly to the door, smiled another good-bye over her shoulder, and was gone.

I looked after her for a moment, a little warning flick of panic beginning to flutter once more. I suppose the difference between the chronic worrier,

the man who seizes on words or even nuances of voice to feed the main-
stream of his fears, and the man who worries not at all until catastrophe is
full upon him, is only an apparent difference, since both attitudes are aspects
of the same neurosis. Given a choice, I should unhesitatingly choose the
latter kind, for if catastrophe is inevitable it is at least less painful to meet
it in one piece rather than in sections, but one is given little choice in such
matters. I seem to have been born a chronic and fretful worrier with an
antenna capable of picking up stray words and looks that to a nature other
than my own would be imperceptible or nonexistent. I picked up the phrase,
"You'll be writing other plays," and bit into it, turning it over and over,
screening it from every angle of the disquiet that I felt mounting within me.
I seized on the word "other" and could not let it go. The word had an ugly
connotation. What did it mean? There were no "other" plays but this one, so
far as I was concerned. Why had Beatrice Kaufman turned back, and having
decided to speak, why had she been reluctant to say what she evidently
had meant to say, except in those veiled and shadowy terms? There had
been an undercurrent of downright compassion in her tone that I did not
like. I liked it less and less, the more I thought about it.

I waited impatiently for the third act to end. I watched Mr. Kaufman
take his bow and then hurried backstage. Actually, I think I knew what he
was going to say before he spoke. He was experiencing the same difficulty
finding the right words that Beatrice Kaufman had encountered, and his
first words confirmed the truth that I was already half prepared for.

"This has not been an easy decision for me to make," he said slowly and
then paused. "It's taken me all week to come to it," he went on, "but I'm
certain now that I haven't anything more to offer to this play. Someone
else, or maybe you alone, would be better than I would be from here on.
I've gone dry on it or maybe I've lost my taste for it. That happens sometimes."

He picked up a towel and began to wipe the cold cream from his face,
waiting for some kind of response from me. I stared at his image in the
mirror, unable to utter a sound.

"I'm sure you'll get it done again," he said finally. "There's a lot of good
stuff there and you may suddenly get an idea that will crack the second
and third acts. I wanted you to know that I want no part of any rights or
royalties for whatever work I've done. It's yours free and clear. I've spoken to
Sam Harris and he'll make a very generous arrangement on the scenery and
costumes with any producer who wants to do it. Sam Harris would like
you to come in and see him on Monday, by the way. I imagine he wants to
tell you himself that . . ."

He left the sentence eloquently unfinished. I had my breath and my wits
back again and I could see he was embarrassed and unhappy. He was waiting
for me to speak but I could still find nothing to say. At least he had spared
us both such grubby phrases as, "I'm sorry it had to turn out this way," or, "I
hope you'll call me some time," and I was silently grateful to him for it.

"You're sure you've gone dry on it, Mr. Kaufman?" I finally asked.

He nodded slowly. "I'd be no use to you any more," he said and looked longingly at the door.

"I see," I said and moved toward the doorway. He looked grateful in his turn that there were to be no speeches on my part, and he solved the question of how to have the agony over and done with as quickly as possible by raising that one finger in a gesture of good-bye. I murmured, "Good-bye," and closed the door behind me.

There is a certain excitement about bad news that is curiously sustaining and in a strange way almost stimulating. Until the shock of it has worn off and reality comes back into focus again, there is a heightened sense of being alive, almost a buoyancy of the spirit, until its import reaches through the walls of self-defense and what has seemed impossible to accept becomes an actuality. I walked along the boardwalk surprised and then astonished to find that I was not feeling bad at all. Other than that first crushing moment in the dressing room, I had felt nothing except the pressing necessity of getting out of the room and the theatre as fast as possible. Now I was conscious only of a weariness that held something akin to boredom in it. If *Once in a Lifetime* had reached a point of no return, so had I. It was almost a relief to know at last that it was over, for there was no doubt in my mind that this was the end of it.

Mr. Kaufman had colored the truth more than a little when he said that there would doubtless be another production under a different management. It was understandable that he should do so under the stress of the moment, but it was not true and he must have known it was not true with the same certainty that I did. If George Kaufman and Sam Harris relinquished a play as unfixable, there was little or no likelihood of another management's picking up the challenge. George Kaufman was usually the man they called in to fix the unfixable. His reason for dropping *Once in a Lifetime* was obvious, and since there are no secrets in the world of the theatre, this one would be common gossip up and down Broadway by Monday morning, no matter what carefully worded announcement from the Harris office appeared in the theatre columns of the *Times*. I leaned over the railing and looked out at the ocean and began to whistle an old camp song. I would be back in camp next summer no doubt, but by the following winter I might have another play. *Once in a Lifetime* had ended, but the world hadn't and neither had I. It was the mark of a professional, I decided, to be able to take it this easily.

It was not until I sat down on a bench and, for want of anything better to do, began idly to watch the passers-by, that my mood changed, with a swiftness that at first startled and then overwhelmed me, from one of relief to one of black despair. The charge that detonates the explosions of rage or bitterness which occur within us is often disguised quite innocently. The boardwalk that evening was full of couples my own age and younger, for though it was only the end of May, it was like a midsummer night. They strolled slowly and happily along, hand in hand or arms around each other's waists, heads pressed closely together. Without knowing that I was doing so, I must have made a bitter identification with them and with my own youth. I stared at these strangers passing in front of me, and all the hopelessness I had been unable to feel before welled up now, transformed into a rage that was like pain. I had had no youth as these young people were having it—no idle sweet time to savor the illusion that life was beginning and that love was the key to its mystery and its flavor. I had let the theatre rob me of mine. With a stab of grinding jealousy I realized I had never gone "steady" with a girl—the small fugitive attempts I had made had always ended quickly, with the knowledge that I had neither the time nor the money necessary for it. Time that was free I had hoarded as something to be used only for work, and money that could be spared was already earmarked for plays that must be seen. I had walked through the years, single-minded, shutting out everything but the goal I had seen shining so steadily in front of me—averting my eyes from everything but the glow of footlights—and now those years were over and done with, as irretrievably finished as *Once in a Lifetime.* These light-hearted couples seemed to crystallize the waste I had made of them—a waste that seemed to have led me nowhere but to this boardwalk tonight.

In the bleakness of that realization it seemed to me that this lifelong intoxication with the theatre had been a barren and unprofitable waste. I could hardly bear to look at those unconcerned carefree figures. Regret and even self-recrimination are bearable emotions. The unbearable one, for me at least, is the hatred of one's self that follows waste, the waste of one's talent or one's affections. The self-hatred that destroys is the waste of unfulfilled promise—the sterility of a thankless affection. I leaned over the back of the bench and turned toward the sea again to shut out the sight of those couples passing before me.

I have no idea how long I remained there, staring out at the ocean, but if I were asked to pinpoint the exact moment or moments that have marked a turning point for me, I should unhesitatingly choose this as one of the decisive ones. In every career, in every profession, there must occur a like moment: when the will to survive falters and almost ceases to exist—when the last reserves of ability to pick up and go on seem to have been used up. This was that moment for me, and its saving grace was a strongly developed sense of irony that began to break through and give me a glimpse of the truth. It rescued me then, and it has come to my rescue many times since. A sharp sense of the ironic can be the equivalent of the faith that moves mountains. Far more quickly than reason or logic, irony can penetrate rage and puncture self-pity. It can be, as it was for me then, the beginning of the first small steps toward clarity; for the truth, of course, as I began to glimpse it slowly, was that it was more than a little ironic for me to envy now what I had never envied before and nonsense to consider as wasted the years in which I had chosen to do exactly what I wanted to do.

It was not accidental that I was sitting on this bench, nor would I have had it otherwise. I had never wanted any idle sweet time to savor anything other than the mystery of how to get through a stage door. I had what I wanted even now, just as I had always had what I wanted, and just as these boys and girls had exactly what they wanted. I would be no whit happier in their shoes, and never would have been, than they would have been in mine. The true waste of these years would be to let them slip through my fingers tonight—to accept as final the decision that George Kaufman had lost his faith in the play or had gone dry on it. If he had gone dry, he must be led to the well again—if he had gone stale, he must be refreshed. Just how this was to be accomplished I had no idea, but it must be done speedily. Delay would produce a finality of its own. I got up from the bench, walked back along the boardwalk to where the streetcar stopped, and waited for one to take me home. The streetcar was full of the same young couples, but I looked at them now with neither envy nor jealousy. I could hardly keep my eyes open. I wanted a good night's sleep more than anything in the world right now, and fortunately I got one. I slept as though someone had hit me over the head.

My relationship with George Kaufman did not include intimacy. His nature did not allow him those easy interchanges between people that ripen into swift friendship. The paradox was that he had a quick sympathy and understanding that made one feel at times that one was on the brink of intimacy, but he invariably retreated behind a barrier of cool detachment that he either chose to maintain or could do nothing about. I had sensed this quickly and had respected it, and I had never tried to pass beyond the limits he himself set. Ours was purely a working relationship that was comfortable and friendly during working hours, but remained aloof and distant away from the typewriter. It precluded any personal appeal to him on my part on the basis of sentiment. Mr. Kaufman would be reached, if indeed he could be reached, on the specific level of work or not at all. Anything else was a waste of time or plain wishful thinking.

Early the following morning I walked back to the little beach where I had written *Once in a Lifetime* and arranged to go to work—a supply of yellow pads in one hand and a bag of sandwiches and soda pop in the other. The one good chance of winning Mr. Kaufman back to the play was to devise new second and third acts that might strike him as worth the extra gamble of picking up the pieces again, considering the time and effort he had already put into it. The difficulty lay in the fact that they must be invented today and presented to him if possible not later than tomorrow, or it might well be too late. He was the most sought-after director in the theatre, and for all I knew might already have embarked on some other venture. He usually went from one play right on to another, sometimes being represented by two or even three plays in the same season. It was unlikely that he would remain inactive with the new season stretching this far in front of him. His telephone was probably jingling with offers right now. It was an unpleasant thought and I did not allow myself to linger on it. I put it firmly out of my mind and stared down at the yellow pad resting on my knees. I had enough to think about otherwise. To ask him to rewrite two full acts, even if I were lucky enough to come up with them, was rather a large order, but there was time enough to do it if I could get him to agree. It had been done before—that was what spring tryouts were for, or some of the solid hits of every other season would never have reached Broadway, and a number of new playwrights would have expired with them.

The formula of the spring tryout was a boon to a new playwright. The two or three months' layoff for rewriting, after which the play was re-opened, was economically possible to the theatre of those days; and it gave the playwright a decent chance to redo his play and, more important, to learn his craft without the shadow of theatre party dates that must be met, booking jams on the road and the scarcity of New York theatres looming constantly over his shoulder. There are plays that can be rewritten in two or three weeks on the road and there are plays that cannot. It takes time to unravel the mechanism of a play without destroying its over-all structure, time to think through and select the good and bad of audience reaction and friendly advice, and more time still to reach a fresh viewpoint or attitude on the work to be done if one is not to make the same mistakes all over again. It is difficult for the new or even the practiced playwright to work well under conditions which include the inevitable deadline of a New York opening only two weeks away, let alone to learn anything worth know-ing in the only laboratory where the art of play-writing can be successfully taught, which is back of the proscenium. I was fortunate to have been a new playwright in a time when the theatre contained a reasonable continuity and did not resemble a wild game of roulette played on the lucky chance that a play either opened in not too great trouble or closed a month later in New York. In the theatre of today, it would have been impossible to do what needed to be done within the limits of the lunatic immediate-hit or immediate-flop procedure that now prevails; nor would I have had the ir-replaceable opportunity of learning my profession with the proper tools, the most important of which is not a pencil or a typewriter, but the necessary time to think before using them.

It was almost dark when I started for home, my pockets stuffed with pages of yellow paper scribbled over with a rough scenario of new second and third acts. That there were still great unresolved holes in it, I knew, but what it lacked in finesse it made up for, I thought, in new invention. Of necessity I had had to leave certain troublesome areas untouched and plunge ahead, but I had had a bit of luck now and then along the way—enough at any rate to make me feel that there was an outside chance that Mr. Kauf-man might accept it. The trick now was to smooth it out and be able to present it to him as skillfully as possible. There is nothing deadlier than having someone read aloud the outline of a play, and it is equally deadly to read a typed résumé full of careful omissions that only serve to high-light the weaknesses and bury the good points. It was far better, I knew, to memorize the scenario completely and rely on my ability to present it sharply and adroitly, covering its lacks and taking advantage of every one of its virtues. I was convinced it had several, and I did not intend to ad lib them tomorrow or trust to the inspiration of the moment.

I chased my mother out of the kitchen, with the supper dishes still unwashed in the sink, put a chair against the door to bar any interruptions and sat down to memorize the outline incident by incident, strengthening its weak spots and heightening its strong points as I went along. It held up well, even under my anxious testing. The thinking was fresh, the invention seemed amusing and the construction was sound. If only I could tell it to Mr. Kaufman tomorrow as well as I was telling it to the kitchen sink now, all would be well.

I presented myself to the maid who opened the door of 158 East 63rd Street at ten o'clock the next morning, and smilingly walked past her into the house. She had no reason to suppose that I was not simply reporting again for work with Mr. Kaufman as I had done all winter, and this, of course, was what I had counted on. I had decided it was much too risky to telephone for an appointment first, and I had come early enough to insure his being in. She returned my good morning and indicated that Mr. Kaufman was upstairs as usual, and I walked up the stairs and into his room without knocking.

He was having his breakfast and in the middle of a phone call, and he was very surprised indeed to see me. The startled look he gave me over his glasses was quite as though he had seen a ghost or some forgotten figure out of the dim past. While he finished his telephone conversation I walked over and stole a sideways glance at the pile of manuscripts on his night table. The top one was titled *Grand Hotel*, and the pile was thick enough to make me feel I had been wise not to let another day pass in getting here. He hung up and said, "Good morning," pleasantly enough, though his voice still held a tone of puzzled surprise in it.

I knew better now than to make any kind of prefacing speech. Instead, I took out an envelope from my inside pocket, much like the one he himself used each day, and glanced briefly at the notes I had typed on one side of it as a guide to help me begin. "I worked out a new second and third act, Mr. Kaufman," I said, "and I'd like you to hear it."

"Right now?" he asked, looking quickly at his watch.

"It won't take long," I lied, knowing full well it would take at least an hour or as long as I needed to finish.

"Mind if I keep eating?" he said.

"Not at all," I answered. "I'll just keep talking."

I started right off. The crackle of cornflakes followed by the crunch of toast is not the most helpful of accompaniments to the telling of a story, particularly of so crucial a story as this one represented to me. The sound was terribly disconcerting, but there was no help for it. I was lucky to catch him and have him listen, and the very fact that he was willing to listen I took as a sign that he was still uncommitted to any one of those manuscripts on the night table. I consciously slowed down until he had finished the second cup of coffee, though he was giving me all of his attention, and mentally noted that memorizing the scenario had been a stroke of absolute genius! I could watch him intently now, the outline thoroughly in my head, hastening the telling when his interest seemed to flag or matching the glint of interest that came into his eyes occasionally with an excitement of my own. He smiled once or twice and laughed outright at an old line of dialogue we had discarded and which I had purposely stuck back in a new place when it fitted perfectly. It had been a favorite line of his which had never worked, and I used it craftily. I knew it would please him. Had there been other little wiles I could have thought of or used I would have used them all shamelessly. Sometimes play-writing only begins when "End of Act Three" is typed on the manuscript.

I finished at last, flushed and a little breathless. I looked at my watch. It had taken just over an hour, even rushing it a bit now and then. Toward the end Mr. Kaufman had retreated to his favorite position, stretched out flat on the floor, and now he slowly and silently arose. He walked to the window and stood staring out at that damned cat which seemed to hold such fascination for him. He turned back toward the room and picked a few bits of lint off the carpet before he looked directly at me.

"What's the matter?" he asked suddenly, giving me a strange look.

I must have been holding my breath without being aware of it and I imagine it gave my eyes a somewhat bug-eyed expression. "Nothing is the matter," I answered. "I'm just waiting."

"How soon could you move in here?" he said.

"In here—with you?" I asked stupidly.

"Not in this room, no," he said not unkindly. "In the house. Beatrice goes to Europe today and Ann is leaving for camp. I meant Ann's room. That's a full summer's work you've laid out, you know, with evenings included. We could get into rehearsal by August, I think, if you moved in here and we worked straight through."

"I'll go home and pack a suitcase and be right back," I said and started for the door.

"Tomorrow morning will do," he called sharply after me. "I'll be looking at you all summer."

"You had a whole day off yesterday," I called back and closed the door behind me.

It was done—and I had also achieved the first moment of intimacy I had ever been able to allow myself with him. I celebrated both victories by having a full-course steak dinner as a second breakfast. The occasion seemed to call for nothing short of that.

PLAY-WRITING, like begging in India, is an honorable but humbling profession. I had privately decided that with an outline before us and armed with the knowledge those two weeks of playing before audiences had given us, we could finish the revision in a month or very little more. I soon saw, however, that Mr. Kaufman was not far wrong in his estimate. He did indeed look at me almost all summer long, including most of the evenings.

What I failed to take into account was that an outline or scenario is an imprecise instrument at best. It cannot be followed slavishly, for as the outline is translated into dialogue, it shifts mercurially under one's fingers, and the emphasis of a scene or sometimes a whole act will twist out of control, taking with it large parts of the carefully plotted scenario that follows after.

We spent the first few days painstakingly setting down and enlarging the outline I had memorized, but by the third day of actual work many of the things that had seemed so promising on yellow paper disappeared under the harsh glare of the sheet of white paper in the typewriter. Nevertheless, some of the better invention remained and even what was unusable served a purpose; but it was apparent not only that there was a full summer's work ahead but that we would actually be lucky to complete it by August. Mr. Kaufman accepted the fact without complaint, and for my own part I was too pleased and grateful to be back at work to mind, however long it took. What I minded, as we settled down into a daily grind, was not work, but the heat and hunger, one or the other of which seemed to be ever present, and which in combination became my chief concern. New York, that summer, was teaching those unlucky enough to have to remain in the city that the Upper Reaches of the Amazon, though not in the same latitude, were perhaps no hotter than the Jewel of the East could be if it chose to rub its inhabitants' noses into a bit of subtropical weather. Heat wave after heat wave broiled the buildings and the pavements with almost no respite, so that even in the evenings the baked brick and stone seemed to give off a heat much like that of a baker's oven that had not yet cooled. The tar in the asphalt paving melted each day and oozed blackly from the cracks, and the parched people still trapped in the city walked heavily along the streets looking wilted and beaten. The weather made the headlines in every edition, and the heat headache I awoke with every morning seemed to throb a little more dully as I read, "Heat Wave Unbroken" or "No Relief in Sight."

The heat became a living and evil thing, for air conditioning, that most glorious of mankind's inventions since the discovery of the wheel, was not in general use—and if it had been, I doubt whether Mr. Kaufman would have considered it anything more than an unnecessary or unworkable toy. He seemed impervious to the heat, and other than washing his hands more often than usual, his only concession to it—made, I think, more for my sake than for his own—was a small electric fan that tiredly plop-plopped around in an uneven contest with the waves of hot air that came in through the windows from the furnace outside. This useless object was placed on the floor in a far corner of the room so as not to ruffle the papers on the desk. Once, *in extremis*, I moved it to a chair where I fancied some of the slight air it circulated might blow directly on me. Instead, it blew the papers from the desk all over the room and four or five pages blew right out the window and skittered into the adjoining yard. I had to hurry downstairs and retrieve them under Mr. Kaufman's baleful eye, and to make matters worse, I got stuck trying to climb back over the fence of the house next door and had to call for the maid to help me down, while Mr. Kaufman watched from the upstairs window. It was an ignominious performance, and after that I let the fan remain where it was and sat as still as I could in the leather chair trying not to think of either the heat or food.

Heat, of course, is supposed to diminish or even rob one entirely of appetite, but my unfortunate appetite was apparently sturdy or robust enough to defy, like the United States mails, heat or sleet or snow and let nothing deter it! There were even times when I grew hungry enough to forget about the heat and to see mirages of food heaped in front of me, for Mr. Kaufman's delicate appetite, slim enough in the winter, seemed to all but disappear with the first robin. With warm weather, long before the first heat wave enveloped the city, a salad and a not too lavish plate of thinly sliced cold meat became the unvarying menu of each day's main meal, and when on a coolish day lamb chops occasionally appeared, my old struggle not to grab and stuff was like a man wrestling with his faith. I had made the terrible mistake, when he asked me the first evening of my arrival what I took each morning for breakfast, to reply genteelly, "Oh, just orange juice, toast and coffee." And I had watched him write it down on a slip of paper and hand it to the maid to give to the cook, knowing even as the words left my lips that I had made a fatal error. It was impossible after that to fill up with a decent breakfast to fortify myself against the rest of a day where lunch remained as always tea and cookies and little cucumber or watercress sandwiches served in the middle of the afternoon, and though cookies and a full pitcher of iced tea were left on the desk, when evening came and that tidy little salad and platter of cold meats stared up at me from the table I was always ravenous.

By the third week of my sojourn, when I was not lying awake all night cursing the heat and my ungovernable appetite, I sat staring during the day at Mr. Kaufman from the depths of the leather chair, not thinking of the next line or scene, but torturing myself with fantasies of thick roast-beef sandwiches or chicken soup with the chicken still floating around in it. He must at times have thought I had taken leave of my senses, for I caught him once or twice staring at me malignantly over his glasses. My own eyes were glazed, not with inattention or boredom, but with hunger.

By Thursday evening of each week, which was the evening Mr. Kaufman played poker and I returned to Brooklyn to visit my family, even my mother's cooking, ordinary at best, seemed positively Lucullan, and the relish and appetite with which I ate everything set before me must have given her the impression that she had turned into Escoffier, or at the very least the best cook in Brooklyn. I was always sprightlier and more nimble-witted on Friday morning than on any other day during the week, a fact which seemed to puzzle Mr. Kaufman considerably.

By the middle of July, Mr. Kaufman became aware that something was wrong with the weather. Even an extra washing of the hands did not quite do the trick, and toward the end of an unbroken two-week stretch of scorching days and nights he suddenly announced that he was taking the weekend off to play in a croquet tournament in Long Island. I could hardly believe my ears. I had been sitting glassy-eyed all that day, watching the perspiration from his forehead drip slowly onto the typewriter and marveling at the fact that he would pass his limp handkerchief over his face and never once make the slightest reference to the weather. It was positively inhuman, I had been thinking to myself just before he spoke, not only to be nobly above man's baser appetites, but to be hermetically sealed in against the weather as well! I was human enough to be meanly delighted that the heat had finally got him. He was pale and drawn, and looking at him, I decided I probably looked even worse. I had not realized that after six years of camp—of being out of the city all summer long—I was now starving for the feel of grass under my feet instead of pavement and longing for the sight of trees and water and an expanse of sky. I could barely wait for the day's work to end.

Five minutes after he placed the cover over the typewriter I telephoned the Flagler and asked if they would have me as guest performer for the weekend. They would be delighted, it seemed, and I managed to catch the evening train for the Catskills.

That weekend was the last time I did a boy-and-girl number in a revue, "To be or not to be" at the campfire, "Mrs. Cohen at the Beach" in the Saturday night musical, and used my full bag of social-director tricks in the dining room, at the indoor games and around the swimming pool. I was welcomed back like a reigning opera star and I did my stint gladly to pay for my free weekend; but even while I performed, and afterward when I mingled with the guests and staff, I wondered how I had ever lasted through six summers of it. I shuddered to think that I might have to come back and do it again, if *Once in a Lifetime* failed. The things that are bearable at a certain period of one's life, out of necessity or made possible by youth itself, are unbearable to contemplate doing again when that time is over. By Sunday night I was champing to return to the city. Those three days, though I did not realize it at the time, did more than just rescue me from the city's heat—they were a blessing in disguise. That weekend, and all that it implied, was just what I needed to see me down the home stretch, for without wanting to or meaning to, I had been faltering and dragging my heels.

As a rule, the writing of a second act seems to drag on forever. It is the danger spot of every play—the soft underbelly of play-writing, as Mr. Churchill might put it—and it is well to be aware of it. A first act carries an impetus of its own that is almost sufficient to carry the writer along with it—the excitement of a new play seems to supply the energy and freshness needed for each day's work at the typewriter, and there are some first acts that literally seem to write themselves. That is why, perhaps, Bernard Shaw is said to have remarked, "Anyone who cannot write a good first act might just as well give up play-writing entirely." It is second acts that separate the men from the boys. We were still mired in the second act when Mr. Kaufman gave way to the heat, and I suspect his giving way to it may have been partly due to his sensing that a point had been reached where a halt might be not only helpful but downright necessary.

Whatever the reason, he returned from his own weekend refreshed and fired as I was with brand-new first-act energy. Cooler weather also coincided with our return—an omen I was quick to seize on as a good one and which was borne out by the fact that lamb chops as well as dessert appeared on the table twice that week. By the middle of the following week, the second act was finished and we both seemed to breathe more freely.

With the beginning of the third act the pace accelerated. We were due to go into rehearsal the beginning of the second week in August, and Mr. Kaufman passed up several of his poker evenings and worked straight through. We were losing part of each day's working time now for recasting and sessions with the scenic artist and costume designer. Two new scenes had been added, one of them quite elaborate and calling for the interior of a Hollywood night club called the Pigeon's Egg, where the patrons sat at tables encased in huge cracked eggs and the waitresses were attired as pigeons, feathers and all. This was one of the new inventions I had concocted during my solitary day on the beach.

There was some doubt now in both our minds that we would finish in time, and Mr. Kaufman grew noticeably edgy. But four days before rehearsals were scheduled to begin he turned toward me and said, "I think you ought to stand up or lie down or shut up or go away or something— I'm about to type 'The End.'" He typed the two words and grinned. "No farewell speech to the troops?" he asked. He was delighted, I could tell, to have finished with a few days to spare.

I shook my head and grinned back, but I did not share his pleasure. I had secretly hoped that we might have to work right through until the evening before rehearsal. The truth was, I hated the idea of this four-day wait, for eager as I had been before to have rehearsals start, as each day brought them closer, I pushed the thought firmly out of my mind and tried to maintain the illusion that they were still far off. While one is in the throes of work it is easy to hold to the fantasy that success is almost certain to crown so sterling an effort, but as the day of rehearsal relentlessly approaches, the fantasy begins to chip away around the edges and the certainty seems to grow slimmer and slimmer until it is swallowed up by a new dogmatism—the certainty of failure. It is commonly called "rehearsal jitters" and I evidently had a severe case of it. I packed my suitcase reluctantly and went back to Brooklyn to wait.

It is not the best time in the world to be around one's family, and I mooned about the house for those four days, succeeding in making both my family and myself utterly miserable. Only those who have lived at close quarters with a bad case of pre-rehearsal nerves understand in some measure the unbalanced behavior of the schizophrenic. Brooklyn is a large borough, but it seemed to me that I walked over most of it in those four days, for there was not enough money to do much else but walk, and when I could no longer stay in my skin and remain in the apartment I got out and walked. In the evenings I twisted the dial of the radio from station to station until it drove them all crazy, or flew out of the house in a temper when I was asked to stop. In a decently arranged world playwrights would be allowed, or even made, to go, a week before rehearsals begin, to some isolated spot not even within flying distance of their families, where their wants would be attended to in silence and their lunacy understood.

I think even my mother was glad to see me leave for rehearsal on Monday morning. She reminded me that a mother's heart went with me, but its balm did not last out the subway ride to Times Square, and I walked through the stage door of the Music Box with that age-old mixture of foreboding and cowardice that marks the true professional. It seemed to me I was some light-years removed from the wide-eyed hopeful who had walked shyly through this same stage door last spring, overawed by the stage managers, embarrassed at being too early, and ridiculously eager for a sniff of the excitement and glamor of a first rehearsal. I was arriving now not ahead of the actors but with the management this time, and I would not panic at that mumbled first reading of the play, but behind my professional manner lay the cowardice gained by a knowledge I had not had before. I knew now that beyond this first rehearsal lay those minutes alone in the hotel room before going down to the theatre to face the first performance. I knew the torment of pacing up and down in the dark, waiting for the sting of an audience's silence when laughter did not come, and the pain of watching those faces come up the aisle. I could almost feel the fatigue of night-long revisions and the weariness of waiting for dawn to come through the blinds so that we could stop rewriting and get some sleep before the next day's rehearsal—and I shrank from facing it all again. I longed to settle back into my ignorance of last spring. It was all to be gone through once more, but this time there was the added knowledge of knowing that the stakes were higher. I had had my second chance.

Sam Harris, coming through the stage door just behind me, phrased it neatly with that facility he had for putting everything there was to say into a short sentence. "Hi, kid," he greeted me, "we're playing for keeps this time, eh?" I nodded glumly and walked to the table where Mr. Kaufman already sat waiting, and a few moments later the stage manager rapped on the table and called the company to attention.

All the little absurdities and affectations of a first rehearsal were again present, but I did not suffer from them too greatly. The actors heaved and mumbled, and Max Siegel smiled sunnily at everything. Mr. Kaufman made his coded chicken marks on the manuscript, seeming not to listen to a word that was being said, and Sam Harris sat rigidly in his chair, his face inscrutable. There were the usual long pauses that had maddened me before, where the parts had been typed incorrectly, and the resultant frenzied search for a pencil by the actor whose part was wrong and who had apparently never thought of bringing a pencil to rehearsal, though he had been in the theatre for forty years. An actor's pained surprise at the need of a pencil at a first rehearsal runs parallel to his bewilderment at having to open a door or a window for the first time at a dress rehearsal in the actual set. He seems never to have opened a door or a window in his life, or even to have seen one before, and he will fiddle with one or the other and delay the proceedings until one has the impulse to leap over the footlights and hit him —or better still, push him straight through it. The rococo politeness and hoary theatrical jokes that always accompany the search for a pencil, while the sense and meaning of the scene being read is lost entirely, is hard to bear, for of course the actor who now has a pencil cannot then find his place.

I sat patiently through it all. My chief interest was in listening, or trying to listen, to Jean Dixon, who had replaced Aline MacMahon in the leading role, and Spring Byington, who had taken over the role of the Hollywood gossip columnist played in the tryout by Blanche Ring. Miss Dixon was a prime mumbler and nervous as a cocker spaniel to boot, but every so often in spite of her mumbling an incisive manner and a corrosive delivery of a line with just the right emphasis shone brilliantly through, and Spring Byington's motherly, wide-eyed mendacity hit the exact fraudulent key the part called for.

I tried now and then to gauge how the new second and third acts might be going by darting overt glances at Sam Harris' face, but I might have spared myself the trouble. It remained throughout like something carved out of stone on Mount Rushmore, nor could I much blame him. It was hard to tell from the way it was being read whether those two acts had been improved or were even worse than they had been, though the actors laughed helpfully as actors always do. They had laughed just as appreciatively last spring and were just as surprised as we were when the audience did not laugh after the curtain was up. Reliance on actors' laughter is the furthest reach in self-deceit, and I shut my ears to it. The second act actually did seem better, but I could tell nothing whatever about the new third act because the typist's errors were so numerous and the scrambling for pencils and the hemming and hawing of correcting parts so distracting that it made any kind of judgment impossible. I gave up listening entirely and made chicken marks of my own on the stage manager's pad until the reading was finished. I would have to contain myself as best I could until the play was roughly staged. The typist had either been typing some other play or we had worked badly. What little I heard sounded terrible.

The rehearsal period of *Once in a Lifetime*'s reopening was perhaps the worst three weeks I have ever spent in rehearsal in the theatre. I knew well enough by now that Mr. Kaufman's directorial method of whispered consultation with each separate actor was unendurable to watch for more than one or two days at the most, and where before I had been content to watch the play grow slowly, sitting through the false starts and the fumblings until play and performance developed, now I wandered restlessly in and out of the theatre and even tried staying away from rehearsals for two full days, in order, so I told myself, to get a fresher look. It was a useless dodge. I was unhappy in the theatre and miserable away from it. The truth of the matter was that I was no longer willing or able to trust my own theatrical instinct or judgment—it had been wrong before, so my reasoning went, therefore how could I judge what was good or bad now? I had not thought the old second and third acts were bad originally—ergo, how could I tell now if they were any better? I walked to rehearsals under an umbrella of disquietude and held it open over my head in the theatre through every rehearsal that I watched. When this happens, the playwright is incapable of judging a baby contest at Asbury Park, much less a play. Everything takes on the coloration of his own anxiety, and what he sees invariably looks not better but worse. I longed for Mr. Kaufman to break his rule and allow a few friends in for the first run-through, but I did not have the courage to suggest such a thing—indeed, I barely had enough courage to come to it myself!

At the end of the first week, the same slim audience of Sam Harris, Max Siegel, Mr. Kaufman and myself sat solemnly through the first run-through and solemnly said good night afterward. It was a little more than I could bear, and I found enough courage when Mr. Kaufman was out of earshot to grab Max Siegel firmly by the lapels and whisper, "What did Mr. Harris think of it?"

"He didn't say," was Max Siegel's unsatisfactory reply. "But I think he liked it or he would have said something. I liked it, if that's any consolation."

It was not—and I realized dully that it would not have mattered if Sam Harris had gone out of his way to praise it, for his praise in my present state of mind would have lasted only long enough for me to tell myself that neither he nor anybody else would really know anything until the curtain rose in front of that first audience in Philadelphia.

I seemed to have spent the final two weeks of rehearsal almost continuously in the company of Max Siegel. I would dutifully appear at the beginning of each day's rehearsal, remain long enough to make Mr. Kaufman aware of my presence, and then streak upstairs to the Sam Harris office and by hook or crook inveigle Max Siegel to come with me to the drug store next door. I used his sunny nature and God-given optimism the way a dentist uses novocaine on a throbbing molar. Max Siegel had apparently emerged from the womb liking the world and everything in it, and he liked everything we had done to the play. He liked everything he saw at every run-through, and every actor in the cast; and seated on a stool next to him at the drug store counter I ate hamburger after hamburger and let him dull my pain. Each day I increased the amount of anesthesia he provided, so that finally not only was he having lunch and dinner with me, but he was walking me around the streets at night after rehearsals were over and until he had to go home to his wife. I think if he had not been married I would have insisted that he come home with me, and the night of the last run-through in New York I almost asked him to take me home with him!

THERE is a phrase that has gone out of fashion now, but it aptly describes the mood of my leave-taking for Philadelphia: the "white feather" was not painted on my suitcase, but it might just as well have been, or stuck in the band of my hat. I said good-bye to my family, a far soberer good-bye on their part this time than the roseate good wishes that had sped me off to Atlantic City. Even my mother now dimly realized that my new profession was largely a gamble in uncertainties so far as eating and paying the rent were concerned, for we were once again coming to a dangerously low ebb financially. Indeed, without my brother, who had his first job that summer, I doubt that we could have managed at all. It seemed to me that the white feather fluttered in the breeze for all to see as I walked down the subway steps to take the train to Pennsylvania Station.

This time I did not need Max Siegel's invitation to join him in a drink. I borrowed his flask and had two stiff drinks before the train was well out of the tunnel. They helped considerably; and the atmosphere of a company on the way to an out-of-town opening is always so sanguine and high-spirited that it is hard to remain downcast, surrounded by so much good cheer and hopeful expectation. Apart from the buoyant spirits actors carry with them on any journey, they usually carry along as well for these three or four weeks out of town their cats, their dogs, their parakeets and canaries, and sometimes even their tropical fish, all of which lend a carnival air to even a journey to Philadelphia. By the time the train pulled into the Broad Street Station I was feeling surprisingly cheerful. I had been too greatly dispirited during rehearsals to try to restore my lack of confidence by searching for a good omen, but I felt so much better now that I began the search as the train slowly moved into the station. I did not have to search far or for long. The heat, as we stepped down from the train onto the station platform, was grisly. The dogs and cats began to pant at once, and their owners drooped visibly, along with my new-found cheerfulness. The true believer does not pick and choose his omens. The range is limited and the selection strict. The first one is the one that counts, and according to the rules of the game this was it.

I picked up my suitcase and followed Mr. Kaufman heavily toward the taxi stand, my shirt already beginning to stick to my back. Cool and unwilted, Mr. Kaufman ordered our bags dropped with the doorman at the hotel, then drove straight on to the theatre to have a look at the new set which he had ordered to be put up first. I could not believe, as the taxicab stopped in front of what looked to me like an armory, that this was the theatre we were going to play, in spite of the posters outside. It seemed to cover a square block. The Lyric Theatre in Philadelphia, now mercifully torn down, was a great barn of a place, about as appropriate for the playing of a comedy as the interior of a steel mill in Pittsburgh and just about as hot. It was, in fact, where large touring musicals generally played, but it was the only theatre on the road at this time that was free and Sam Harris had taken it.

It seems incredible now that theatres in New York and all the other major cities of the East remained open all summer long without benefit of air conditioning, but they did, and people astonishingly enough went to them uncomplainingly. Two giant-sized electric fans on either side of every theatre proscenium were kept running until the house lights dimmed, and were turned on again for each intermission, but the heat generated by an audience on a hot night was still formidable. The make-up ran down the actors' faces, and the audience itself was a sea of waving programs and palm-leaf fans, the rustle of which sometimes drowned out the actors altogether. Nevertheless, summer-long runs in Philadelphia, Boston, Washington and Chicago, with every theatre in full swing, were an accepted fact, and the new season in New York actually began on August 15, or at the latest Labor Day, heat waves or no heat waves.

I followed Mr. Kaufman through the stage door and wandered aimlessly about while he conferred with the carpenter and electrician. The Lyric Theatre backstage smelled stalely of that last touring musical, and the auditorium, of its last perspiring audience. I looked up and counted what seemed to me to be at least seven balconies running clear up to the roof, and I wondered briefly why anyone would climb up there in the heat and how they would manage to hear anything if they got there. The back rows of the huge orchestra seemed difficult enough to reach with the loudest human voice, and my heart sank as I visualized subtle comedy lines being shouted into that vastness. I slid down into a seat and stared at the asbestos curtain. It would have been far better, it seemed to me, to open cold in New York and take our chances than to try the play out in this monstrous cave. It would not have astonished me to see a covey of bats fly down from the balcony or out of one of the boxes. As if to illustrate my thoughts, two moths rose slowly from the red plush a few seats away from me and flew languidly off. I watched them settle on the back of the seat in the row in front and was suddenly in good humor again. I think the idea of the animal or insect world ultimately taking over this rookery delighted me. It was certainly the last place for humans to witness a sparkling new satirical comedy, but my cheerfulness had returned.

A good many of the company had wandered into the auditorium from backstage to have a first look at the Pigeon's Egg from out front, and in a few minutes Mr. Kaufman came through the fire door and the asbestos curtain was taken up. The company burst into laughter and then into applause. It was a remarkable set—an immense baroque affair that in terms of decor and good taste might have been termed Early Frankenstein—and a wonderful conception of Hollywood extravagance at its wildest. Even without the actors in it, it was preposterous enough to be amusing all by itself. I was delighted with it. It seemed to me that every funny line in the scene would be enhanced by this setting, and fortunately it was the last scene in the play. Everything seemed suddenly and miraculously better. Though it was tempting fate to switch omens, I decided that those two moths were the omen I had been looking for and moreover that it would be foolish to dampen my sudden good spirits by sitting through hours of scenic and light rehearsals where nothing much happened except the slow rotting of my mind. I got up from my seat and walked out of the theatre, leaving Mr. Kaufman in full charge of the drudgery that lay ahead. I had read somewhere that some playwrights filled in these useless hours by visiting a museum or even going to a movie, and while I was incapable of such blithe behavior, I had a pleasing enough prospect of my own in view. An author's living expenses out of town are always paid for by the management, including the food he eats, as long as he eats it at the hotel, and the hotel was just where I was going. I could do nothing about the heat, but this time at least I would not go hungry.

Some of the world's pleasantest reading is contained in a good hotel menu, and I sent for one before I even unpacked my suitcase; I also found out just how late room service remained open at night. I had eaten scarcely anything through the four days and nights of dress rehearsals in Atlantic City, though I had known that Sam Harris was footing the bill, and I was not going to be the same kind of fool again. Fresh from Mr. Kaufman's Spartan teas of watercress and cucumber sandwiches, I ordered an afternoon tea of my own. It was extraordinary how much smaller the Lyric Theatre seemed in my mind's eye after Lobster Newburg and Baked Alaska, and I took care to see to it that my mind's eye remained on that same crystal-clear level.

I ate my way through four days and nights of dress rehearsals in Philadelphia and slept beautifully in spite of the heat. Everyone noticed my changed demeanor, and Max Siegel commented on it, but I could hardly explain that a midnight snack each night, and a waiter staggering through the door with a loaded breakfast tray every morning, was the source of my wholesale enthusiasm for everything about the play and the performance. The company manager might have a nasty moment when he looked at my bill, but it was certainly to Sam Harris' advantage to have me as fresh as possible for whatever work needed to be done after we opened. My soaring good spirits had even dissipated my fears about facing the opening—never, in fact, had the play's chances seemed so bright. This almost fatuous optimism was not entirely due to food, I suppose, but to the fact that anxiety had taken a manic swing, as anxiety has a way of doing, but I have an idea that a full stomach was not unhelpful in keeping the swing upward.

I was not even particularly unhappy when Joe Hyman telephoned on the morning of the opening to say that he had a bad summer cold and would have to come down to Philadelphia later in the week. He was surprised at how cheerful and well I sounded, and indeed it was hard for me to recall the abject terror in which I had spent the hours waiting for his arrival in Atlantic City. I felt entirely capable of going through this opening alone and actually impatient of the hours that remained until it was time to go to the theatre and see the curtain rise.

I sat pleasantly through a final light rehearsal and spent the rest of the afternoon trying to find a dozen different ways of working the title of the play into those traditionally funny telegrams to the cast. I was surprised to find that it was suddenly six o'clock and time to get ready. I looked out the window and saw, of all things, a rainbow. To a man who was willing to believe that moths constituted a good omen, that rainbow seemed to be the ultimate sign that everything now seemed to be conspiring in our favor, including the weather. A fierce thunderstorm late in the afternoon had bathed the city in coolness and I leaned out the window and felt the first breeze that hinted of fall. That fresh cool air would certainly put any audience in the best of possible moods, and while I was not yet ready to accept such a heresy as a painless opening, I could not deny the fact that contrary to the way I'd expected to feel, I was not only feeling no pain at all but a distinctly pleasant excitement. The rainbow seemed to call for something more than just staring at it, and obeying a sudden impulse, I went to the telephone and asked the bell captain if he could get me a bottle of Scotch. Rich people in the movies were always sipping Scotch highballs while they dressed for dinner, and though Sam Harris was paying for this one, I sipped it slowly in the bathtub and mused on how pleasant might be the shape of things to come—large sums of money in particular. I was sorry now that Joe Hyman was not here to lift a glass to the future with me and then walk serenely off to the opening.

Even Mr. Kaufman seemed to have an unwonted air of gaiety when I ran into him backstage on my rounds of wishing the cast good luck, and Sam Harris in the lobby gaily reported that the absence of a full quorum of the wrecking crew tonight was due to the fact that so many plays were opening out of town all at once that they had to make a choice of the one that would give them the most pleasure to see fail. "Looks like they've written us off already." He laughed. "But I have an idea we may fool them." It seemed to me that he exuded a note of confidence tonight that had not been there before, and the Lyric Theatre, with its orchestra almost entirely filled, did not seem nearly so barnlike or impossible to play in. I looked impatiently at the last stragglers going down the aisle. I wanted not so much for the play to begin as to have the first act over and done with. I knew they would laugh at the first act. What happened after Mr. Kaufman's exit in the second act would be the test of how well we had worked. I kept watching the giant fans on each side of the proscenium, and at last they slowed down to a whirr and the house lights dimmed and the footlights came on.

I don't know whether it was because this was the largest audience we had ever played to or because it was an uncommonly generous one, but the volume of laughter was greater than it had ever been before, even for the first act. The revisions we had made in it to make it of a piece with the new second and third acts had tightened some of the arid spots and made the laughter almost continuous. It had always played well, but now it played thunderously. The applause lasted a good half-minute after the curtain came down. It was a little too early to gloat; but if the second act was right, it was going to have its best chance with this audience, and I could hardly wait for them to get back to their seats. Sam Harris made no comment other than a laconic, "That act's been improved, kid." Like myself, he was marking time.

It seemed an unconscionably long intermission until the house lights dimmed again. Mr. Kaufman received his usual reception as the curtain rose on the second act and his usual round of applause as he made his exit. I held my breath—the next few minutes would tell the story.

I did not have to hold it for long. They were laughing loudly now in all the places where there had been only silence before, and as the laughter kept on without any sign of diminishing I began to bang delightedly on the back of the orchestra railing with my fists. A blue-suited figure was immediately at my side. "Don't interrupt them, you fool," hissed Mr. Kaufman, but I could tell he was as delighted as I was. The wonderful sound of laughter kept coming in wave after wave, and in spite of that pacing figure nearby, I began to laugh with them myself. It seemed impossible not to. I was, I suppose, a little light-headed with relief. The second act came down to even greater applause than the first and an unmistakable buzz filled the theatre even before the house lights came up.

There is something almost touching about the way an audience comes up the aisles when it has been thoroughly satisfied with a play. They beam at each other with pleasure, as though they had been given an unexpected present. It is a rewarding sight. Sam Harris, caught in the crush coming up the aisle, saw me and winked broadly, and right behind him Max Siegel's smile seemed to be running straight off his face and into his ears. I waved and indicated I would meet them in the lobby.

I was eager to eavesdrop and hear what the audience was saying about the play, though lobby-listening is a dangerous occupation. A playwright is likely to hear last night's bridge game being discussed instead of his play, or how well little Robert is doing since he changed schools. Lobby-listening even at an acknowledged hit in New York is likely to yield no more than, "I don't know what they're raving about, do you?" or, "It's just an evening's entertainment, that's all," to a playwright's outraged ears. But tonight they were actually talking about the play. I threaded my way from group to group and heard them saying, "Funniest play I've seen in years," and, "Wait until this hits Broadway," and reminded myself that this was the time I usually spent in the stage alley, afraid of what I might hear if I remained in the lobby.

I listened so avidly that I failed to meet Sam Harris and Max Siegel—the ushers were already calling out "Curtain going up" by the time I had had my fill. I followed the audience back into the theatre, gathering up the last morsel of comment and relishing every word. I suddenly realized I had also neglected to say a word to Mr. Kaufman, until I saw him beginning to pace back and forth as the house lights began to dim. I went over to him and tried to modulate my excitement to a pitch that would match his own usual conservatism. "They seem to like it, Mr. Kaufman," I said.

To my surprise, he put a hand on my shoulder and said, "You deserve it," and then quickly walked away. Only the rising of the curtain saved him from one of my commemorative speeches.

The audience's response to their first sight of the Pigeon's Egg was almost excessive. They gave a great whoop of laughter and then broke into applause that lasted through the first few lines of dialogue. I took my place at the back of the orchestra rail, prepared to behave with a little more decorum this time and not laugh along with them, even though this was the act we were both certain contained the funniest moments of the play.

Their laughter came promptly as the applause died and the scene went on, but it was not, I quickly noticed, of the same kind. The ear could tell the difference almost immediately. It was a little forced, as though they were unwilling to believe that so good an evening might be going downhill and were perfectly prepared to laugh at costumes and props until the play came to life again. But the play was not coming to life again, even with the best of intentions on the part of this eager-to-laugh-at-anything audience. In spite of themselves, their laughter was growing weaker and more fitful, and finally at about the middle of the act it ceased altogether. I looked around for Mr. Kaufman. For once he had stopped his pacing and was standing staring at the stage as aghast as I was. We had gone terribly wrong somewhere and there was no point in going over and asking him how or why.

He came over to me just before the third act ended and whispered, "We're too close to a hit now not to get this right. Meet me in the room in half an hour."

I watched a bewildered and disappointed audience file out of the theatre, and on my way back to the hotel I walked behind a man and a woman discussing something in so aggrieved a tone that I knew they must be talking about the play.

"It sure as hell didn't hold up, did it?" I heard him say.

And the woman, equally offended, replied, "I don't understand how the same two people could have written that last act, for the life of me."

I was tempted to join them and say, "May I introduce one of the idiots, madam?" In a way I felt quite as victimized as they did.

We had both largely recovered, however, from our own shock and disappointment with the third act by the time we sat facing each other in Mr. Kaufman's room half an hour later. One thing was inescapable. Two acts were right now, where only one had been right before. It seemed impossible not to be able to lick a last act that was all that seemed to stand in the way of a smashing success. That had been Sam Harris' sanguine conclusion, Mr. Kaufman reported, and he was staying right on in Philadelphia, a sure sign that he believed it could be done. Mr. Kaufman's own belief that we could do it was tonic.

He brought out a new box of fudge, placed the manuscript on his knees, poised a pencil above it for the first cuts, and went right to work without further discussion. It was the same old method—cuts down to the bare bones

of the last act to get a clean look at it, until we could glimpse what was
wrong and had an idea of how to solve it. It was dawn as usual before we
finished, for although there was only one act to cut, we spent the last two
hours writing a new scene that might get the act off to a better start, and
we were encouraged the next evening to find that it did.

We worked through the following night on another scene, and that, too,
was an improvement; but nothing we wrote seemed to provide a clue for
that straight line we were seeking. New scenes, even if they are wrong, will
sometimes point out the direction in which a play should move, but nothing
seemed to offer us the slightest hint that we were on the right track. There
was something stubbornly wrong with the basic idea of the last act that
evaded all our efforts to fix it.

Mr. Kaufman, never a man to spare himself or his collaborator where
work was concerned, worked like a man possessed. Something more than
just a play seemed to be at stake. His professional pride was involved now
and made insupportable the fact that he was this tantalizingly close to a hit
and not quite able to achieve it. He drove himself, and me along with him,
at a merciless pace and to a point where each night we worked until it appeared that not another word could be dredged up, yet the night's work was
far from being ended. After flinging himself on the sofa for a few minutes
and closing his eyes in exhaustion, he would get up and walk to the typewriter again. I lost count of the number of new scenes that were written
every night, staged the next day, and played, rough or not, that same evening, only to be tossed out after one performance.

The actors accomplished prodigious feats of memory, learning and un-
learning new scenes for performance after performance, but as a consequence
the first two acts were becoming a little shaky and were not playing nearly
as well as they had played. When actors walk into a first act with a new last
act in their heads almost every night, it is not unnatural that it should play
havoc with their over-all performance. Actors cannot be expected to remember new lines each night and still give the old ones their proper value.

By the end of the first week the first two acts had begun to lose that
wonderful sheen and precision of the opening performance. On Monday
night of the second week there was scarcely a third of the orchestra filled,
and the theatre again began to take on that cavelike quality which had
appalled me so when I had had my first look at it. A week of disappointed
audiences and uncertain performances was beginning to take its toll at the
box office. Out-of-town audiences are extremely sensitive and well aware of
the role they play. They do not resent being used as guinea pigs to test out
a new play, but they pride themselves on their ability to pick winners. Word
is passed around rapidly among out-of-town theatregoers, and they can stay
away from a play on which the report is bad with an obstinacy that borders
on the sinister. The word had evidently gone out on *Once in a Lifetime*,
although we told each other that the heat was actually the villain that had
caused our business to drop with such frightening swiftness. A new heat
wave had engulfed Philadelphia with such scorching intensity that it

dwarfed the New York heat waves I had grumbled about and made them seem almost elfin by comparison. The city emptied under our eyes. By the third day of it, offices and shops were sending their employees home at one o'clock in the afternoon, and the baking streets seemed to be bare of everything except traffic policemen, children dousing themselves under fire hydrants, and water sprinklers endlessly sloshing water over the dusty pavements.

No one could work through such heat and remain unaffected by it, but I began to doubt that the heat was the sole cause of Mr. Kaufman's moody and restive manner with the company as he rehearsed during the day or his increasingly pessimistic air as he watched the play each night. Imperceptibly at first, and then unmistakably, I began to detect little telltale signs of discouragement which seemed to grow larger as I watched for them. He worked through the nights and days without letup, but he was strangely silent now when the result of all our labors was being played night after night to audiences of sometimes less than a hundred people. It was disheartening to watch a new scene that had seemed promising in rehearsal spin itself out before rows of empty seats, and programs waving listlessly to and fro in the heat. Laughter is contagious and does not spread easily among people huddled together as if in self-protection against the emptiness around them. We were literally working in the dark—it was impossible to tell from these audiences what was good and should be saved or what was bad and should be tossed out. What little laughter there was came strangely and in curiously isolated spots, and sometimes laughter came where none at all was called for. Though I would not have admitted it to anyone, I began to mistrust everything we were doing. We had either lost control of the play or the last act was incurable. Mr. Kaufman's silence might very well mean that he had come to the same conclusion and was as loath to put it into words as I was, but while it remained unspoken, miracles were still possible. Self-deception is sometimes as necessary a tool as a crowbar.

As our third and last week in Philadelphia began, however, I could sense that whatever his thoughts might be they were not too far from my own. Very few plays are without faults of one kind or another, but few plays succeed with a bad last act. The best kind of fault for a play to have is first-act trouble, and the worst kind last-act trouble. An audience will forgive a slow or even a weak first act, if the second act grows progressively better; and a third act that sends the audience up the aisles and out of the theatre with the impression of a fully rounded evening, can sometimes make that hairsbreadth difference between failure and success. A bad third act or even a poor last fifteen minutes of a play can be ruinous. It can somehow wipe the slate clean of all that has gone on before and completely negate the two acts preceding it, and if a playwright is not in control of his last act in the final week of the tryout, it is unlikely that he ever will be.

Mr. Kaufman brought it out into the open finally on the Tuesday night of that last week. He was taking the midnight train to New York to meet the boat that was bringing Beatrice Kaufman back from Europe the following morning, and he would return in time for the matinée tomorrow. He tossed the new scene we had played that evening into a wastebasket in the corner of the dressing room and removed the last of the make-up from his face before he turned to me directly.

"I think we ought to face the fact that we may have to settle for what we've got," he said. "We must give the company a chance to play the same show four nights in a row before we open in New York," he went on, "and I've got to have a good crack at getting back the performance of the first two acts to where it was when we opened here or we'll stand no chance at all. I'm going to freeze the show as it stands on Thursday night—no more changes—that's it. Hot or cold. That all right with you?"

"What do you think our chances are in New York with this last act, Mr. Kaufman?" I asked.

"Not wonderful," he replied, "if you have to have my honest opinion." He was silent for a moment and then continued. "Comedies usually have to be ninety-five per cent airtight—at least that's been my experience. You can squeak by with ninety per cent once in a while, but not with eighty-five, and according to my figures, not to keep any secrets from you, this one just inches over the seventy mark. I don't know what son-of-a-bitch set up those figures, but there you are. Well, no one can say we didn't try. We're freezing the show Thursday night, Sam," he called over my shoulder to Sam Harris, who had appeared in the doorway. "And good-bye—I'm just going to make that train."

Sam Harris looked after the figure hurrying down the stairs and laughed. "You know, I think he's glad to duck out of town, kid. He runs down those stairs like he just heard tonight's receipts." He laughed again. "A hundred and four dollars and eighty-five cents," he said. "We jumped eighty-five cents over last night. That just about pays for what the actors eat in that night-club scene." He glanced briefly at the wastebasket and the typed pages scattered over the floor around it. "Come on out with me and have a beer, kid. This is your first night off, isn't it?" I nodded. "Do you good to forget the show," he said and started down the stairs. "Never saw two guys work harder. That last act's a little bastard. I've sat through quite a few tough ones in my time but this one is something special. A couple of beers will do us both good."

Serendipity is a word that has fallen into disuse, but there are few words in the language that so graphically characterize the combinations of fortuitous and random circumstances that make up the behind-the-scenes history of almost every play. It describes precisely what happened that night and afterward as a result of my evening with Sam Harris. In the little speakeasy just around the corner from the Ritz Hotel, we sat drinking beer after beer, our tongues loosened and our minds, a little drunkenly after a while, going over the play, scene by scene and almost line by line.

I was surprised in the beginning at Sam Harris' loquaciousness, for I had never before heard him talk at such length. His comments on the play were usually tersely worded typewritten notes, delivered to Mr. Kaufman's room by Max Siegel every evening after the performance. Mr. Kaufman did not suffer gladly a nightly conference with a producer, even if that producer was Sam Harris. It occurred to me for the first time to wonder if even Sam Harris might not be a little intimidated by George Kaufman. Tonight, with Mr. Kaufman on a train bound for New York, Sam Harris' criticism of the play was far more explicit than his notes had ever been, and I listened as intently as my fuzzy-mindedness would allow after the third bottle of beer. He was a sound and shrewd judge of a play and an old and crafty campaigner in evaluating its chances, but his talk—pithy though it was, and full of the insight of his years in the theatre—did not always make clear his meaning. His turn of phrase was somewhat cryptic and his conversation followed an enigmatic and circuitous course. Though I kept nodding my head in agreement, I was not always certain that I had grasped the significance of what he was saying.

Just before the place closed, when the waiters were piling the chairs up on top of the tables all around us in a last despairing gesture of getting us to leave, my ear caught a phrase he had used once or twice before, but whose meaning had escaped me. "I wish, kid," he sighed, "that this weren't such a noisy play."

"Noisy, Mr. Harris?" I said, determined to understand what he meant by that word. "What do you mean by a noisy play?"

"It's a noisy play, kid," he reiterated without explanation. "One of the noisiest plays I've ever been around."

"But why, Mr. Harris?" I persisted. "It's no noisier than any other play."

"Oh, yes, it is," he replied. "Just think about it. Except for those two minutes at the beginning of the first act, there isn't another spot in this whole play where two people sit down and talk quietly to each other. Is that right, or isn't it?"

I looked at him, a little stunned, and said, "Is that what you mean by noisy?"

"Maybe *noisy* is the wrong word," he said. "But I've watched this play through maybe a hundred times, and I think one of the main things wrong with it is that it tires an audience out. It's a tiring play to sit through, kid . . . I can almost feel them begin to get tired all around me. That stage is so damn full of actors and scenery and costumes and props all the time they never get a chance to catch their breath and listen to the play. Sure they laugh, but I think they're longing to see that stage just once with maybe two or three people on it quietly talking the whole thing over. Give them a chance to sit back themselves and kind of add the whole thing up." He signaled the waiter for the check, then laughed. "Once this show gets under way nobody ever talks to each other. They just keep pounding away like hell and running in and out of that scenery. It's a noisy play, kid, you take my word for it."

I stared at him silently, my mind racing back and forth over what he had said, an odd excitement beginning to take possession of me. He got out of the elevator at his own floor a little tipsily, but I was wide awake now. I took the elevator down again and began to walk. Far from clutching at straws, it seemed to me that Sam Harris in his own paradoxical fashion had put his finger straight on that unfathomable fault in the third act that had defied all our efforts. The more I thought of it, the more certain I became that he was correct, though I could not define why. A curious kind of interpenetration occurs when one watches a play night after night. Impressions are registered unconsciously that emerge as full-blown concepts—sometimes when a chance word or phrase is spoken by someone else. What Sam Harris felt, so closely matched some of my own unconscious thinking, though I had not been able to put it into words, that it had almost a quality of revelation about it.

I was much too stimulated now to think of going to sleep. It was a fine moonlit night and I kept walking. I tried to find my way toward the park, for the air in the streets was still stifling, but I stumbled instead upon a children's playground. It looked a little weird in the moonlight, but it was an open space among the buildings and something approximating a breeze seemed to be blowing through it. I walked to a swing and sat down in it. I swung back and forth, and the higher and more wildly I made the swing go, the greater impression of coolness it created. I was a little apprehensive that a policeman might happen by and wonder what a grown man was doing in a child's swing at four o'clock in the morning. I became absorbed in threading my way through the labyrinth of that third act, and with a shock of recognition I thought I saw clearly where we had gone wrong, and then, in a sudden flash of improvisation, exactly the right way to resolve it. I let the swing come to a full stop and sat there transfixed by the rightness of the idea, but a little staggered at the audacity of it, or at what it would entail.

It called for tossing the Pigeon's Egg out of the show entirely—the specially constructed tables, feathered costumes and all—and bringing the part of the New York playwright, which Mr. Kaufman played and which disappeared from the play after the second act, back into the third act, for a quiet scene with Jean Dixon. The train scene of the first act, which had brought them all out to Hollywood, could be repeated and was the logical setting for it.

I began to examine it slowly and meticulously, fearful that like most four-o'clock-in-the-morning inspirations, it would explode in my face, but it did not. Its very simplicity was its virtue, for while at first glance it seemed like a deceptively simple idea—if tossing $20,000 worth of scenery into the alley may be termed simple—it was, like all simple ideas, startling in how much it would accomplish by its very simplicity. Everything clicked into place with an almost mathematical accuracy. New lines began tumbling into my mind faster than I could remember them, and the new scene on the train began to blossom and grow in a way that not only convinced me of its rightness, but made me itch to call Mr. Kaufman in New York and get him out of bed to tell it to him, but my audacity had limits and common sense told me to wait and present it to him face to face. It would be difficult enough even then, I suspected, to persuade him to make so drastic a change at this stage of the game; but it seemed so singularly right that I could barely wait for his return.

I WAS waiting for Mr. Kaufman in his dressing room when he came back the next afternoon. He was late and the first act was almost over, but there was no time to waste and I talked quickly while he put on his make-up. It would have been better perhaps to wait until after the matinée and to be able to tell it to him less hastily, but if he agreed to do it, every moment was going to count. Simple idea or not, it still had to be written, and I had had time enough to realize that more work was involved than at first met the eye. He listened attentively, but I could tell he was rejecting it long before I had finished. Sensing his rejection, I presented the idea in the worst possible manner—it began to sound lame and foolish, even to my own ears.

"I see what you mean," he said when I had come to the end, "and I see what Sam Harris meant, but it's too risky. It's too big a change to make with only three days left. Suppose we did it and it didn't work? We could never go back to a third act we had so little faith in that we discarded it the last three days in Philadelphia, and ask the company to open with it in New York. We've unsettled this cast enough as it is. Whatever chance we've got is going to depend on how good a show the company gives on the opening night. I don't think we dare take this kind of a gamble now. It's too late."

I had no ready answer, and even if I had been prepared to argue, the stage manager was already knocking at the door and calling out, "Second act, Mr. Kaufman." I followed him down the stairs and went straight back to the hotel. It seemed to me doubtful that even if my very life depended upon it I could watch that third act again. At four o'clock in the morning I had seen a new third act playing brilliantly, and it was still lodged hopelessly in my mind.

I threw myself on the bed and stared up at the ceiling, turning over bit by bit everything Mr. Kaufman had said. I was no longer so certain of my own brilliance or that I had found an inspired way of snatching victory from defeat. In the excitement and enthusiasm of last night I had never stopped to consider the possibility of the idea's not working and the consequences if it did not. There was no guarantee that it would, however right it seemed to me, and everything he had said was true, of course, but I was stubbornly sure that the consequence of not taking the gamble would be equally disastrous. I looked at my watch and decided to take a final gamble of my own. The matinée had been over for half an hour and Mr. Kaufman would be in his room. He was not an easy man to tackle once he had said no to anything, but there was little to be lost now in trying to make him change his mind. I was certain that unless we at least made the attempt, the fate of the play was already sealed.

I walked down the hall and knocked on his door. For a moment there was no answer, but then his voice called out, "Who is it?" and I called back, "It's me." "Come in—I'm in the tub," his voice called again, and I walked through the suite to the bathroom. For once he looked beaten and exhausted, as though my old enemy, the heat, had finally claimed even him. He lay in the tub, his head resting on the back of it; his eyes were closed, and he barely opened them when I came in. They remained closed all the while I talked, a small boon for which I was grateful, for I could not judge how well or how badly I was succeeding, and I took my time. I went over the same ground I had covered in the dressing room, but I presented it well this time—so well, in fact, that I convinced myself all over again—and was making an impassioned plea for taking the gamble, in spite of everything, at the end.

When I had finished he did not move, but reached for his glasses on the edge of the tub and put them on; he seemed reluctant to stir even an arm from the coolness of the water. Now he regarded me silently over the rims of the glasses. "You have as much right to say yes to anything about this play as I have to say no," he said slowly. "It may be that my timidity at making this big a change, in the time we've got left, is too great," he went on. "You know what's at stake as well as I do, but if you feel this strongly, why don't you skip the show tonight and stay here and make a rough draft that we can work on when I get back. Maybe I'll be able to see what you see—or at least see it more clearly than I'm able to see it now." He sighed. "I'd like to play my part of the show tonight right from this tub. Might help business, too." He closed his eyes wearily again.

I forgot about dinner and went right to work. When an idea is sound it writes easily, and I struck pay-dirt early. All the old stumbling blocks that we had uselessly battered our heads against seemed to resolve themselves smoothly and naturally once the Pigeon's Egg had been pried loose from the play. The price we had paid for an audience's momentary laughter and applause at a set had been enormous. Freed from the inflexibility of that scene, exposition that had lacked subtlety became manageable and scenes that had remained lumbering and clumsy seemed suddenly skillful. A play can be blackmailed by its scenery more often than anyone connected with it is likely to realize.

The rearrangement of the third act was too involved to do anything more than attempt the sketchiest of rough drafts, but by the time Mr. Kaufman returned from the theatre I had something ready to show him. A good deal of it had to be indicated in a kind of code, with arrows pointing from my own yellow sheets of paper to the manuscript, but he was reading it with more than just polite interest, and when he had finished he carried the yellow sheets and the manuscript with him toward the typewriter. "Well, here goes twenty thousand dollars' worth of scenery," he said and inserted a new piece of paper in the roller.

I sat staring at him, mesmerized. Instead of the elation I had expected to feel, I was seized by a sudden panic at the enormity of what I had started and of what we were about to do. "If this doesn't work and we can't go back to the old third act, Mr. Kaufman, what happens then?" I asked.

He looked at me quizzically over the glasses. "I sue you," he replied. "Hand me that box of fudge and let's get to work."

I watched the rehearsal the next day with feelings not unlike, I suspected, those held by the company itself. The company received the news of the change in glum silence and went about the business of rehearsing it as though each new line brought them closer to a bog of quicksand. It was a messy job of restaging, and I admired more than ever Mr. Kaufman's forbearance and patience, with time running against him and a reluctant and dissatisfied company to rehearse. The combination of old and new was confusing and there was no question but that the cast was seriously disturbed and its morale at a low ebb.

The morale of a company is one of a play's hidden assets and sometimes its most valuable one. If it remains high in spite of a rocky time out of town, an electric opening-night performance in New York can cover a multitude of sins. A company with high morale, whose faith remains unshaken in its author and director, can accomplish incredible feats of memorizing new lines and business overnight, but it asks in return, and rightfully so, sufficient time afterward to perfect the performance. Nothing contributes more strongly to a company's insecurity than desperate last-minute changes that rob them of the chance of being at their best on an opening night. Their faith in Mr. Kaufman did not waver, but their alarm at being asked to make so drastic a change, with a New York opening less than a week away, was quite evident. It made itself apparent in a dozen different ways, and I could not tell whether the new scheme had any real merit or was just a hodgepodge of the old and new that might play less well than what we were discarding.

The company's unease seemed to fill the theatre and communicate itself even to the stage managers, who took forever placing the chairs for each new scene. It was a long rehearsal and rough on everyone, Mr. Kaufman included. He had to learn new lines himself, as well as redirect some of the old stuff, and stage the new train scene—and all of it had to be done for the evening's performance. Everything had to be tried this night or not at all. The next day was Saturday matinée and the last performance but one in front of an audience before we opened in New York the following Wednesday night. I did not blame the actors for feeling that the old third act with all its faults was less hazardous for them than running the gantlet of a New York opening night with untried material. At least they had played the other and knew all of its pitfalls.

As the afternoon wore on I slumped farther and farther down in my seat, and finally I could sit still no longer. I made for my usual refuge, the stage alley, but after one grim look at the Pigeon's Egg set stacked up against the wall waiting to be carted to the storehouse, I beat a hasty retreat back into the theatre. I had looked at the set triumphantly on my way in to rehearsal

this morning, happy to be seeing the last of it; but this morning's courage
seemed to be oozing out of my finger tips, and there was no Max Siegel
this time to anesthetize me for these next few hours of waiting.

Along with Sam Harris he had been in New York for the last two days
wrestling with the opening-night ticket list, for the laws by which the theatre
is governed remain immutable. Hallowed by time they are not susceptible
to change—and the two most inviolate are opening-night tickets and pictures
in the lobby. However dire the straits a play may be in, they take precedence
above all else, and although they seem almost purposely absurd, any appeal
from their divinity is useless. A company is kept up until five or six in the
morning during one day of the out-of-town tour—thereby making a rehearsal
call, however urgent, impossible the following day—so that pictures may be
had in time to fill the lobby frames on the opening night; and management
and author alike must rid their minds—at this most vital time and no matter
how critical the state of the play—of everything but the crucial dilemma of
who shall be seated next to whom and where on the opening night. Since
not one person out of a hundred ever bothers to look at the pictures in the
lobby on opening night and almost no one at all is ever satisfied with his
opening-night's seats, it is difficult to understand why these rites remain
undisputed, but they are as reverently preserved and as imperishable an
idea as the Kingdom of Heaven.

I would have given much for a Max Siegel smile right then, no matter
how illusory or mistaken, and Sam Harris' presence would have halved the
burden of guilt I was beginning to feel, since in a way he was as much to
blame for that set sitting in the alley as I was, but they would not be
back until curtain time, and then only with luck. I did not believe my taut
nerves would stretch the distance until then, and I did the first two things
that occurred to me. I telephoned Joe Hyman and asked him to get on the
six o'clock train for Philadelphia, and I sneaked back to the hotel and ordered the largest dinner even I had ever had the gall to order. Terror, as
always, had increased my appetite, and the amount of time it would take
to consume that mass of food would fill in the waiting until it was necessary
to go to the theatre and face what had to be faced.

I was almost comatose with food by eight o'clock. I walked to the theatre
swaying slightly and hiccuping as though I were drunk. I stopped at a drug
store and slowly sipped two glasses of plain soda water, but the spasms
seemed to grow worse instead of better. I have since learned that a serious
attack of hiccups can be caused by anxiety or fear, and this must have been
true in my case, for by the time I reached the theatre I could barely talk. I
wheezed a few words to Joe Hyman and Sam Harris, but the hiccups were
coming with such intensity and with so few spaces to breathe in between
that I fled gasping back to the drug store. I gulped some paregoric under
instructions from the pharmacist and then held my breath while he pressed
his fingers behind my ears, and even blew into a paper bag while I counted
slowly up to one hundred—but to no avail. I had drawn an interested little
group of bystanders during these experiments; an old lady at the drug

counter offered the suggestion that the best way to cure hiccups was to scare the living daylights out of the victim, a method which had invariably worked, she insisted, when she was a little girl. Since I was not a little girl, and frightened enough already, it seemed to me, I left the drug store and returned to the theatre.

The first act was nearing its end by the time I arrived and not going too badly so far as I was able to make out, but each body-shaking hiccup I gave, no matter how hard I tried to strangle it before it emerged, echoed with such resonance in the emptiness of the theatre that it seemed to roll down the unfilled rows, across the footlights, and punctuate every other line the actors were speaking. To my horror, a few people in the audience began to laugh at the unearthly sound I was making, for by this time my wheezing and whistling must have sounded like a dog baying at the moon. I ran out of the theatre and walked around the corner to the stage alley. One look at the Pigeon's Egg set, which had not yet been carted away, set me off again and I fled the alley to the street. I walked up and down, cursing the heat, the hiccups, Philadelphia, the food I had eaten, the Lyric Theatre, and anything else that came into my mind. I was growing frantic that I might have to miss the new third act if the spasms did not subside, but they gave little sign of doing so and I dared not go back into the theatre. It seemed to me I was roaring like a calliope. Every few minutes I kept glancing at my watch, knowing by the time exactly what portion of the second act was being played, and finally I could bear it no longer. I walked in the balcony entrance and ran up the stairs.

The exit doors on each landing were dimly lit but I saw no sign of an usher anywhere, and I kept on going. I came out into what must have been the topmost gallery; there was not a soul in it, and it was so far from the stage that I could well believe that even my hurricane gusts would not echo down. I took a seat in the last row and watched the puppet-like creatures on the stage playing out the last scene of the second act. I knew by heart every line they were mouthing, of course, so it mattered little that I could not hear much of what they were saying—and if I could not hear them they probably could not hear me. Looking down from my aerie there seemed to be not more than twenty or thirty people in the orchestra. Actually there must have been a hundred or so, and we might well have jumped another eighty-five cents, but I was well past caring about the nightly receipts.

During the intermission I opened an exit door and walked back and forth along the platform of the iron stairway outside the gallery, taking deep breaths of air. I came back inside and sat down, hiccuping as noiselessly as I could, and waited for the house lights to dim. I was terrified when the fans stopped whirring and in the sudden silence I gave the loudest and longest series of hiccups I had given vent to all evening. But nothing, I was now determined, was going to get me out of the theatre. The audience must have been talking among themselves as they settled back into their seats after the intermission, for there was no sign that anyone had heard me, and I was thankful that in the new arrangement of the third act Mr. Kaufman was already safely backstage. The third act opened now, not with the Pigeon's Egg, but in the Hollywood film studio, and the second scene of the third act was the new train scene with Mr. Kaufman and Jean Dixon. The first scene seemed to be playing better without the Pigeon's Egg, but the train scene, of course, would tell the whole story.

The first scene ended, and as I waited for the lights to come up on the train scene I began to wonder if the old lady at the drug counter might not have been correct; for at that moment I felt as though the daylights had indeed been scared out of me—the palms of my hands were icy and wet with perspiration and my stomach had twisted into a hard knot—but my hiccups had miraculously subsided.

The curtain rose on the train set, and immediately that most accurate of all barometers gave an unmistakable sign that we were on the right track at long last. The audience broke into understanding and appreciative laughter—not the whoop of laughter that the Pigeon's Egg always dazzled them into giving, but the more valuable laughter of an audience that was taking the play into its own hands and carrying it along with them. Jean Dixon was seated alone in the Pullman car, but her aloneness in a train that was obviously headed back to New York told them all they needed to know without a line's being spoken. They made the leap for us themselves without a word of exposition, and the stage, quiet and silent for once, seemed to create by its wordlessness the exact sense of drama and climax that we had previously tried so hard to achieve, without success. The vital scenes of a play are played as much by the audience, I suppose, as they are by the actors on the stage. As surely as one can sense that an audience is lost, I could tell that this one had been captured. The Pullman porter entered and a moment later Mr. Kaufman followed him on. The biggest laugh that tiny audience was capable of giving greeted his appearance, and I knew that our search for the right last act had ended.

I could barely hear the words being spoken on the stage, but I did not need to. I sat back and listened to the audience. The quiet scene Sam Harris had asked for was playing line after line to the biggest laughs in the play. Even some of the perfectly straight lines seemed to evoke laughter, and the laughter mounted until it became one continuous roar. I closed my eyes and just listened until the scene was over, then I walked downstairs and watched the final scene of the play from the back of the orchestra. With the momentum of the train scene behind it, it played flawlessly. That small audience actually broke into applause once or twice. Those crucial last few minutes had been redeemed. *Once in a Lifetime,* in Philadelphia at least, was playing like a hit right up to the curtain.

I left the orchestra rail and leaned against the back wall. The exhaustion I felt was due in large part no doubt to that violent attack of hiccups, but neither hiccups nor the strain of sweating out the last act could entirely account for the almost overpowering weariness that had taken possession of my mind as well as my body. It was a strange inner tiredness of a kind I had never experienced before. I watched Sam Harris and Max Siegel applauding along with the rest of the audience as though they were seeing the play for the first time, and I saw Joe Hyman leave his seat and dash up the aisle in search of me. But I was suddenly too tired to want to hear what they had to say, or to care. I had finally touched bottom so far as *Once in a Lifetime* was concerned. I wanted the New York opening and *Once in a Lifetime* itself over and done with, whatever the outcome. For the first time, success or failure seemed not to matter. Without any sense of elation or triumph, I stared at the curtain going up and down and listened to the audience applauding. I seemed to have used up the last reserve of response or emotion. I wanted of all things to go home, and I wanted to go home with the passionate unreasonableness of a six-year-old.

It is always a little dismaying to discover that the truth, as one explores it, consists largely of a collection of platitudes. More often than we suspect, the old wives' tales are not merely a caricature of the truth, but its faithful echo; and among the most banal in a profession where old wives' tales are commonplace are the proverbial tales of the anguish and frenzy of the last few days before a New York opening. These hours have been portrayed in movies, in novels, and even upon the stage itself, in such hackneyed and platitudinous terms that their banality grates upon the ear with the brassy clink of a worn-out cliché. The distraught playwright, the nerve-torn actress, the harried stage manager, the tight-lipped director, the stubbornly optimistic producer, all are such familiar and stock figures that their anguish has been robbed of reality and their frenzy skirts the edge of farce. Yet the truth in this instance is substantially the same as the parody of itself it has become.

As the train from Boston or Philadelphia pulls into Grand Central or Pennsylvania Station, returning a company from its tryout tour for the New York opening, each member in this changeless drama relinquishes his sanity, takes his place as a stereotype, and begins to live out his own cliché with almost clocklike precision. The uneasy discovery that the truth bears a strong resemblance to travesty, or to every bad movie or play about the stage one has ever seen, does not alter the nature of the role each performs or the misery which he feels while he performs it. However trite the sufferings of the last few days before a New York opening may seem to the outsider, they usually contain enough real anguish to make them the Book of Common Prayer of the Theatre—and I began to learn it chapter and verse even before the train from Philadelphia reached New York.

I had watched the last two performances of the play in Philadelphia with a detachment and self-possession that I had never been capable of before. I had been able to look at the matinée and then the night performance, not with indifference, but with so great a loosening of the emotional tie between the play and myself that it made the turmoil of my usual watching seem foolish and remote. It was an experience so new and so enjoyable that I boarded the midnight train for New York convinced that I had come of age. No one, however, comes of age in the theatre. If he does, he takes his place among the disenchanted—or joins the ranks of those Philistines who mistake the theatre's incoherence and fanaticism for muddle and moonshine. My self-delusion lasted as long as it took me to walk the length of the Pullman car to my seat. Almost every member of the company had bought an early Sunday edition of the *New York Times* at the station news-stand, and they had the drama section spread out on their laps, revealing, as I walked by, the pictures of the opening on the front page, or the large opening advertisement on the inside page. My detachment and self-pos-session vanished after the first quick glance, never to return. By the time I turned the key in the lock of our apartment in Brooklyn, I had taken my rightful place in the old wives' tale, and I played my part exactly as it had always been played—with every platitude intact!

One thing, however, was never to be the same again. My brother and I became friends at last, and that simple fact did much to see me through the time-honored anguish and frenzy of the next few days. It is hard to estimate the way or the moment in which two human beings are able to reach one another. The process, of course, is a gradual one, and perhaps my own unreadiness had always been as great as his; but the moment of my homecoming from Philadelphia marked the beginning of closeness be-tween us. Perhaps events themselves create their own readiness, for I was immediately conscious the moment I opened the door, that this homecom-ing was different from any other. I had lived for so long as a stranger with my family that it had never occurred to me to seek counsel or comfort among them, but tonight I was secretly pleased to find them all waiting up for me. I am by no means certain that blood is thicker than water, but an opening the following week can thicken it as nothing else can. I warmed my hands and my heart in their affection and wondered why I had never found solace with them before. There is nothing like tasting the grit of fear for rediscovering that the umbilical cord is made of piano wire.

I felt closer to my mother and father than I had in years, and my brother in particular was a surprising source of comfort. I began to look at him and to listen to him with a sense of wonder and discovery. The last year had changed him greatly, and it was the year, of course, that I had seen the least of him. His diffidence had vanished and with it his withdrawal from me and his silence. We sat at the kitchen table talking together for almost an hour after my mother and father had gone to bed, drinking the last of the coffee and finishing off the sandwiches. It was the first time such a thing had happened between us, and as we talked, I became slowly aware that behind his unusual talkativeness, behind his innumerable questions about the play, lay a secret pride in me. He had cut out all the picture spreads and ads from the Sunday papers, and presumably as a joke, had tacked them all over the kitchen walls for my homecoming. He had also collected every word that had appeared anywhere about *Once in a Lifetime*, and as I turned the pages of the neatly pasted scrapbook he presented to me, it was my turn to be silent. I, who was never at a loss for words, sud-denly could not find my tongue. The stranger at whose side I had slept for

so many years was offering his friendship and I did not know how to bridge
the gulf between us. I managed to thank him, after a moment, and we
talked on easily enough, but behind the casual words we spoke, each of us
in his own way was reaching out across the years to the other. I lay awake
for a while in the dark after he had gone to sleep, relishing the new idea
of having a brother. It was enjoyable enough to send me off to sleep for
the first time in many a long night without thinking about George Kaufman.

The golden rule for the last three days before an opening is that a company must be kept together as constantly as possible, even if some of the
rehearsals that are called are purely trumped-up ones and fool nobody, including the company itself. If it is impossible to rehearse on the stage because the scenery is not yet set up, or the scenic designer is still lighting
it as he always interminably is, then the rehearsal is held in the lounge of
the theatre or in a rehearsal hall. Almost nothing is accomplished, for the
actors walk through these rehearsals in a state approximating somnambu-
lism, but the rule and the theory behind it is a sound one. Left to their
own devices, a company might conceivably gain the impression that the
world had not stopped in its tracks for these three days and that all life did
not hang in the balance of those two and a half hours three nights hence.
Moreover, misery does indeed love company, and there is nothing so soothing, not to say downright invigorating, as the shared misery of people in
the same boat. Tempers may flare and patience reach the vanishing point,
but temper or even the drudgery of walking through the play in an empty
rehearsal hall can be a safety valve for taut nerves, can prevent the panic
that can rise in a company left to wander too loosely in these last days.

If I had been inclined to doubt the rightness of this procedure, all of
my reservations would have vanished by the afternoon of the day following
my return from Philadelphia. I had passed the morning easily enough in
telephoning, but by mid-afternoon I could scarcely stay in my skin. Though
I knew no rehearsal was scheduled until the next morning at eleven, I
could not remain away from the theatre. I had no idea why I felt it imperative to be there, but I took the subway into town, and at the first
glimpse of the scenery piled up on the street outside the Music Box as I
turned the corner of 45th Street I felt immediately better. I moved toward
it with a lift of the heart and hurried through the stage door as though I
were leaving enemy territory for the safety of the U. S. Marines. There are
few things duller to watch than scenery being set up on a stage, but that
afternoon I found this dull business comforting beyond measure. I watched
every bit of it with pleasure and even fascination. I sat or walked up and
down in the aisles of the empty theatre hour after hour, or wandered backstage and swilled coffee with the stagehands, and knew that this peace I
felt would last only as long as I remained here.

It must have been eight or nine o'clock in the evening when to my surprise I saw Mr. Kaufman wander slowly across the stage, and I immediately
rushed back to talk to him. He seemed equally surprised and a shade embarrassed to see me and quickly mumbled something about wanting to ask

the stage manager if we could use some hand props at tomorrow morning's rehearsal, but I knew at once that he, like myself, had been impelled to seek such comfort as he could find, and the only place to find it was here. We had been talking for only a moment or two, when Sam Harris appeared suddenly from behind a piece of scenery, and our presence was evidently as disconcerting to him as mine had been to Mr. Kaufman. He muttered something about stopping by on his way to dinner and beat a hasty retreat. Mr. Kaufman disappeared shortly afterward, but I was delighted to know that as the time drew near for each one to take his place on the firing line, veteran and neophyte alike was affected in much the same way; I had merely arrived earlier in the afternoon.

The company, when they assembled for rehearsal the next morning, greeted each other with the hungry affection of exiles returning to their native land. They had evidently spent a completely miserable day with their husbands, their wives, their cats or their tropical fish, and were happy to be back among their own kind, amidst people who were using the only language they cared to hear spoken at this particular moment.

Unfortunately, it was also the moment that saw the end of Mr. Kaufman's forbearance and patience. The frenzy, in other words, was starting exactly on schedule. Its cause was simple enough. Though the stagehands had worked through the night, it now turned out we could not get the stage, although more than enough time had been allowed and a free stage had been promised for eleven o'clock this morning. The lighting as usual had held everything up, and Mr. Kaufman, who hated to rehearse in a hall or in the lounge, was furious. This was just the sort of small crisis that threw him into a temper—and Mr. Kaufman in temper was a formidable figure. A genuine crisis he met head-on and with enviable calm, but small irritations he had no capacity whatever to meet. In addition, his chief weakness, even beyond inept waiters and people who insisted on telling him jokes, was what may be best described as "inanimate object trouble," and a rehearsal hall or a theatre lounge inevitably brought out the worst in him. His difficulty with inanimate objects seemed to be that all kinds of furniture contrived to take on a malevolent and almost human design the moment he entered the room. Chairs, lamps, ashtrays and tables seemed to move imperceptibly out of line and craftily place themselves in his path. His progress through a room would begin peaceably enough, but by the time he had stumbled against a chair, knocked against a lamp and banged his elbow against the ashtray as he sank down onto the sofa, his threshold of irritation had been breached. He would sit muttering oaths under his breath and stare malignantly at the furniture, and the same pattern more or less would be repeated when he left the room. It put him in foul humor for a good while afterward, and I had learned to steer clear of him until he had rubbed the bruised knee or elbow sufficiently and was out in an open space where no furniture could move toward him.

I held my breath now as we all filed into the rehearsal hall, for a rehearsal hall is just that—a large empty hall with nothing but chairs in it, and usu-

ally old and rickety chairs at that. Every one of them seemed to perk up
and form an invisible phalanx of enmity as Mr. Kaufman entered the room,
and then move quickly into position. I cannot swear that I saw them move,
but they seemed to tremble with anticipatory glee. Mr. Kaufman usually
surveyed the furniture in a strange room with equal enmity and distrust,
trying to gauge, I always thought, from which side the attack would come
or which chair he would bang himself against first. But he was deeply engaged in conversation at the moment with the two stage managers and he
passed through the doorway without looking up. He did not go very far.
Though the stage manager on either side of him did not so much as even
brush against a chair, Mr. Kaufman ran smack into one before he was ten
steps into the room. He gave a howl of surprise and rage and kicked the
offending chair clear across the room, stubbing his toe, of course, in the
process. He snarled viciously at one of the stage managers who tried to help
him and limped toward the table, where he promptly banged his elbow as
he sat down; and, as he sat, there was a sound of ripping cloth and one and
all knew that a protruding nail in the seat of the chair had torn a hole in
his trousers. Not a soul laughed. Indeed, everyone looked stricken. His
whole aspect in these moments was so terrifying that I firmly believe that
if he had ever slipped on a banana peel in Times Square the entire area
would have been clear of people before he rose to his feet again, for he
somehow managed to convey a sense of individual blame to anyone who
happened to witness this unending warfare with inanimate objects.

There was complete silence in the hall now, for there was every indication of heavy weather ahead, and to make matters worse, Mr. Kaufman
began to sneeze and could not stop. He was susceptible to drafts and convinced that the merest puff of air could lay him low, and a great scurrying
took place to close the offending windows. Some of them would not close,
others were too high to reach, a window pole could not be found, and the
two stage managers were wet with perspiration by the time the windows
were wrestled with and all the chairs shifted to the far end of the hall away
from the draft.

It was not the best of circumstances in which to start the final days of
rehearsal, and Mr. Kaufman's mood was not improved by the news which
arrived in midafternoon that the stage would not be available until tomorrow. It was the company's turn now to lose their tempers, and they proceeded to do so each in turn and according to the size of their billing in the
program. It was hard to blame them. Actors like to adjust their voices and
pitch their performance to the size of the theatre they are going to play
in, and the sooner they are able to do so, the more secure they feel. They
are correct, of course, for a performance suited to the Lyric in Philadelphia
might well be out of scale in the Music Box. The news that they would
have only one day on the stage of the Music Box, instead of the two days
they had every right to expect, cut through, for good and all, the heavy
cream of false politeness that had so far acted as a cover for panic and
nerves.

Miss Dixon promptly broke out in hives, Miss Byington grew waspish, Hugh O'Connell sulked, and Grant Mills could not remember a line. Mr. Kaufman, with a real crisis at hand, was instantly all patience again and at his most winning and understanding; but even he could not save the evening rehearsal from the depressing and unmistakable walk-through that it was. I rode home with the uncomfortable knowledge that tomorrow's rehearsal, though it would take place on the stage of the Music Box, might not be very much better. Everything was obviously proceeding according to schedule. Frenzy had arrived on time. The next step, according to the timetable, was anguish. There was evidently going to be plenty of it around, or enough, it seemed to me, to justify those foolish plays and movies about the theatre that I would never laugh at so easily again.

On the day before a New York opening, a company moves within a solar system of its own. It is a planet in outer space, detached from the moon and stars, and its orbit is the stairway from the dressing rooms to the stage. Each actor sits at his make-up table, staring into the brilliantly lit mirror at his own image, making the proscribed movements that will detach him still further from the world of reality and allow him to achieve the anonymity of complete disguise. The more he becomes at one with the part he is to play, the less of himself that peeps through it, the further he sinks into the atmosphere of make-believe and unreality, the safer he feels. He is seeking a judgment from the real world, not of himself but of the hidden image he carries within him that is both his goal and his refuge. The general conception that all actors are born exhibitionists is far from the truth. They are quite the opposite. They are shy, frightened people in hiding from themselves—people who have found a way of concealing their secret by footlights, make-up and the parts they play. Their own self-rejection is what has made most of them actors. What better way to solve the problem or to evade it than to be someone other than the self one has rejected, and to be accepted and applauded for it every night. They have solved the problem, but not its torment. It is what makes every opening night so painful an experience. Little wonder that on the day before an opening the atmosphere backstage reflects each actor's anxiety at meeting the test anew, for the judgment does not lessen but is compounded by the years, and it is always agonizing no matter how many times an actor has walked out onto the stage to meet it.

It was just as well that I had reconciled myself to a bad rehearsal, for the proceedings on the stage of the Music Box were more like a series of nervous explosions than anything else. Hats and dresses that had fit perfectly well in Philadelphia seemed to have come back from the cleaners a size too small. Entrances were missed or exits bungled, and doors that had opened with ease and props that handled without difficulty before, now presented mysterious problems each time one was opened or picked up. Mr. Kaufman rode out the storm like a pilot searching out the eye of a hurricane—unruffled, detached and ready to report back to the weather bureau that the storm was not a dangerous one. But by the end of the afternoon rehearsal I was in no such state of calm. If the final run-through tonight emerged looking anything like this one, I doubted my capacity to sit through it, or perhaps even to live through it. Mr. Kaufman's composure would have to do for both of us. I intended to hijack Max Siegel and make him walk the streets with me at the first flash of thunder.

There is no need to try to understand the eternal perverseness of the theatre, or to attempt to explain why an afternoon rehearsal can be a shambles and an evening rehearsal on the same day be orderly, smooth and perfect in every detail. Like a good deal of the theatre's disorderliness, it defies explanation. It is simpler to say that the evening run-through of *Once in a Lifetime* was flawless. Every mistake of the afternoon had corrected itself; every error in light cues, every blunder in props, every imperfection in costume had vanished. The rehearsal was faultless except in one particular: the acting was completely hollow. Its emptiness may have been due to the difficulty of playing comedy in an empty theatre, for a preview audience the night before an opening was the exception, not the rule, in those days. But granting this difficulty and making all allowances for it, it was hard not to be aware of the falsity of the playing. Not one performance carried conviction. Each actor seemed to lack fluidity, bounce or humor, and in consequence the play very soon took on the patina of its acting. By the time the final curtain fell, the play seemed to me to be as brittle and humorless as the performance. I walked up the aisle and stood a little away from where Mr. Kaufman and Sam Harris were talking, not eager to have my judgment corroborated. I was more than willing to attribute my feelings about the play to my own unsteady nerves. It would be small comfort to know that they were steadier than I gave them credit for being and that the play was as frail as it looked.

Mr. Kaufman started backstage with his notes for the cast, and Sam Harris was about to follow him when his eye fell upon me. He walked over to where I stood and peered at me closely before he spoke. "I think you need a drink, kid," he said. "Come on up to the office." I followed him meekly, though I did not want or need a drink, and had it been anyone other than Sam Harris I would have refused. What I wanted was to crawl into the subway and get home as fast as possible. I hated the play and every actor in it, and my mood was far too truculent to chance talking to anybody, Mr. Kaufman included. I did not, as it turned out, utter a word for the next four hours. Mr. Harris' intentions were kindly and I have no doubt that the color of my face must have seemed ashen even in the semi-darkness of the theatre, but it was very soon apparent that Mr. Harris' invitation was not altogether altruistic. Mr. Harris badly needed a drink himself for his own reasons. He wanted someone to have it with him, and what was more to the point, he had evidently been having a few drinks on his own all through the evening.

It occurred to me that he walked up the stairs a little strangely, and now he seemed to be having considerable trouble finding the ice and the glasses.

As I watched the amount of liquor he was pouring into each glass I realized he was determined to find a happy oblivion for these next few hours and that it was to consist largely of his self-conceived mission of cheering me up. Though his movements were uncertain, his sense of dedication was not. He plunged immediately into the task at hand. "You worried about this play, kid?" he asked.

I nodded, deciding that the quicker I let him cheer me up the sooner I would be on the subway. Unfortunately, there is almost no protection against being cheered up and I have always been sadly unfitted for dealing with people who have had a drop too much. My nodded agreement to his question was unwise. He mistook my silence for emotion too deep to be expressed and changed his tactics accordingly. I could tell by the way he looked at me that he felt that stronger medicine was going to be needed, and with the first spoonful I knew I was going to get the full dose.

"Did I ever tell you about George M. Cohan and the first play he ever wrote?" he began. "Felt just the way you do now, kid. He was just about your age, I think, and I was still managing Terry McGovern, the prize fighter. The theatre was easier in those days, but the people got just as scared. Let me tell you first how George Cohan and I happened to meet . . ."

He settled back comfortably in the large chair behind the desk, clinked the ice merrily against the glass for a moment, and told the tale with loving attention to detail. The theatre may have been easier in those days, but everything apparently took a great deal longer, for by the time Mr. Harris reached George M. Cohan's first play and Mr. Cohan's triumph over his fears, a good hour had gone by, two or three more drinks had been consumed by Mr. Harris in the telling, and we were only just approaching the beginnings of the famous partnership of Cohan and Harris, which I could sense I was going to receive a full account of. I dared not look at my watch or appear to be restive, for Mr. Harris' mind was completely unclouded and his eye, like the eye of most deaf people, was an inordinately keen one. Obviously, the only attitude to assume was to indicate that some of Mr. Harris' cheerfulness had communicated itself to me and that I was no longer so much in need of his ministrations.

It was a second fatal error! Like my silence, my sudden cheerfulness again decided him on a new tactic. He stopped the Cohan and Harris saga abruptly, mixed himself another drink, and sat down next to me on the sofa. He fixed his eyes rather sternly on mine and said, "All of this stuff I've been telling you was just to take your mind off things so you could listen to what I really wanted to say." He cleared his throat importantly and paused before he continued. "Now, I'm going to tell you why you shouldn't worry too much about this play, kid."

I returned his gaze hopefully and for a few moments it seemed that we would be leaving the office very shortly, for after a preamble on why most dress rehearsals are bound to be disappointing to the author, he stopped as if to marshal his thoughts. I was so certain that this would be his final few words of wisdom and cheer, I was already calculating whether or not I had missed the last express to Brooklyn and would have to take the long ride by local.

To my amazement he rose from the sofa, planted himself in front of me, and announced firmly, "The reason you shouldn't worry about this play, kid, is because it's got a good story. Let me tell it to you . . ."

I stared helplessly up at him, convinced that I must now say something even at the risk of hurting his feelings, but he had already moved away to the center of the room and was launched into telling me the full story of *Once in a Lifetime*. He was not a man to skimp, and liquor seemed to sharpen his memory rather than curtail it. He started with the rise of the first curtain, described the set and the lighting meticulously, and then proceeded to act out each part with every bit of stage business intact. Where he did not remember the exact line, he ad libbed his own interpretation of it, and since he was his own audience and enjoying his own performance immensely, he laughed loudly at all the appropriate places. I sank back into the sofa, horror-struck, as it dawned on me that nothing could prevent him from going through the entire play, scene by scene and line by line, and that I would sit here trapped until the final curtain. At the end of the first act he took an intermission by mixing himself another drink and describing why the audience would like what they had seen up until then, and after a refreshing swallow he placed the glass on the desk and said, "Second act. Now, listen to what happens now!"

There was little else to do but listen with awe-struck attention. In spite of the fact that my eyes occasionally closed, it was somehow fascinating to watch Sam Harris pretending to be Jean Dixon and George Kaufman, mimicking their readings and even falling into a good facsimile of Miss Dixon's slouching walk and Mr. Kaufman's grim leer over the tops of his eyeglasses. His performance was giving him such unalloyed pleasure that at another time I might actually have enjoyed watching him, for all of the sweetness of his nature shone through his innocent enjoyment of himself.

By the time he approached the end of the second act, however, I could keep awake only with enormous effort. I dared not lean back on the sofa, for I would have gone promptly to sleep, and though I shifted my position constantly, my head kept dropping down onto my chest. Only the fact that one of my feet kept going to sleep, sending shooting pains up and down my leg, saved me from drifting off. I roused myself for the intermission, and while Mr. Harris explained why the audience was still liking it, I stood up and stretched discreetly. It helped a little, but not enough. As I watched him fill his glass and get ready for the third act, his enthusiasm and vitality not one bit abated, I was overcome anew with sleepiness. I gave a terrible shudder and so loud a sigh when he announced, "Third act; here's what happens now," that he looked at me sharply and asked, "Not getting a chill, are you, kid?"

I shook my head and went back to my seat. I sat on the very edge of the sofa this time, planted my elbows firmly on my knees and placed one hand at each temple for the double purpose of keeping my head upright and holding my eyelids open with my finger tips. I could do nothing about the enormous yawns that were issuing from my mouth, one after the other; but Sam Harris was so deeply immersed in his attempt to do full justice to the third act that he seemed not to notice or even to be aware of my presence.

He was in full swing again, roaring through the train scene with tremendous verve and gusto, and that last drink seemed to have unleashed a hitherto unrealized athletic capacity for playing comedy. He bounced from one chair to the other as he switched parts, and finally, to illustrate Hugh O'Connell's moment of triumph just before the final curtain, he leaped onto a stool in front of the fireplace with the agility of a mountain goat. I had noticed that the light was changing through the curtained windows behind the desk, and now I saw the first faint streaks of daylight beginning to filter through them. There was silence suddenly and the silence startled me into wakefulness. Sam Harris was standing in front of me, placing his straw hat on his head.

"Go on home and get a good night's sleep, kid," he said. "I think you'll sleep better now."

I got up stiffly from the sofa and followed him out of the office and down the stairs. As we came into the street, he stopped dead and blinked with surprise at the daylight. "What the hell time is it?" he asked.

I glanced at my watch. It was just a few minutes short of five o'clock. "It doesn't matter, Mr. Harris," I said. "I wouldn't have slept much tonight anyway."

He shook his head ruefully and laughed. "That play still needs cutting. That's all I can say, kid," he said, and we started toward Broadway.

Even in my close to sleepwalking state I could see we were going to have a fine day for the opening. The morning sky was cloudless and there was a hint in the air that the day would be warm but not too hot. It was pleasant to know that much about tonight anyway. We stood silently at the corner of 45th Street, waiting for a taxi to appear. It was strange to look up and down a Broadway whose every square foot I thought I knew and find it looking completely different. The long ugly thoroughfare looked clean and friendly. I thought I had seen Broadway in all of its various guises, but I had never seen it like this. It looked, of all things, sleepy and innocent. The tawdriness and the glitter were gone. It seemed to stand hushed and waiting—as if eager to welcome all the new actors and playwrights struggling to reach it.

"Well, you can't go home now, kid," said Mr. Harris, breaking the silence. "By the time you get to Brooklyn you'll just have time to turn around and get back to rehearsal. What time did George call rehearsal for?"

"Eleven o'clock," I replied.

"There you are," he said, "no use going home. Better go to a hotel."

"No," I said, "I'd better go home."

"What for, kid?" he persisted. "What's wrong with going to a hotel? You'll get a few hours' sleep, anyway."

"I'd rather go home, Mr. Harris," I replied carefully and with emphasis, and stepped away from him to signal a taxi I saw in the distance. I could feel him looking at me, and as the taxi drew up he came toward me and held out his hand.

"So long, kid," he said, "see you at rehearsal," and stepped quickly into the cab.

I looked down at my hand and stared at what he had slipped into it. It was a one-hundred-dollar bill! He had, it appeared, gathered the reason for my insistence on going home. I stared down at the lovely banknote in my hand for a long moment before I made my decision. After tomorrow night, I might well be able to afford to stay at the best hotel in town; but then again, I might not. After tomorrow night—or rather tonight, I suddenly realized as the dawn grew brighter—it might be a very long time before I even saw a hundred-dollar bill again. Now was the time to live richly and fully, if only for a few hours, and not waste this lovely windfall of fate on a small side-street hotel. It might actually be an excellent omen for the opening if I had the good sense to make full use of it.

I crossed the street and walked up the steps into the Astor Hotel. There was no question that I had chosen the right omen the moment I entered the lobby. I felt better in every stiff joint. The night clerk looked at me suspiciously, but I was ready for him.

"I want a suite on the Forty-fifth Street side—just until tomorrow morning. My play is opening tomorrow night at the Music Box and I've got a rehearsal at eleven—we had a longer dress rehearsal than I expected. By the way," I added, with the proper touch of casualness, "could you change this for me? I seem to have nothing small to give the bellboy." I handed the hundred-dollar bill to him across the desk.

His attitude made a quick turnabout from the suspicious to the reverential. He pushed the register card toward me respectfully and held the pen out deferentially.

"Would you like to leave a call and your breakfast order with me, sir?" he asked as he brought me the change.

"Yes," I replied. "And is there a masseur in the hotel, by the way?" He nodded. "Have him come in at nine o'clock and wake me up for a massage, and I want a barber and a manicurist at a quarter of ten. I'll have breakfast at ten thirty—orange juice, toast, coffee, bacon and eggs. I think that will be all."

"Thank you, sir," he said, and pressed a buzzer under the desk. "Take Mr. Hart to ten-fourteen," he said as he handed a key to the bellboy, "and wait and find out if the suite is satisfactory. I think you'll like it, sir—it's one of our best. If not, the bellboy will show you another. Good night, sir. I'll take care of all of this for you." We bowed slightly to each other and I followed the bellboy toward the elevator.

There can be no false economies in the rich full life. Excess is the keynote or it cannot be enjoyed at all. I gave the bellboy two brand-new one-dollar bills and was rewarded by a rich full bellboy smile. We both knew that I was overtipping outrageously and we both enjoyed it, each for his own reasons. The bellboy bowed himself out and closed the door, and I walked to the window, opened it and then leaned over the sill staring at the marquee of the Music Box across the street. There was an impersonality about my name looked at from this height. This is the way my name would look to strangers. I stared down at it with the utmost pleasure. Only three short city blocks separated the New Amsterdam Theatre from the Music Box, but the journey between them had been a long one. Whatever the outcome of tonight, my name next to George Kaufman's on that marquee represented triumph. I remained at the window for quite a while. I lowered the shade reluctantly, afraid that I would have trouble getting to sleep now, but my head had barely touched the pillow before I was off into the kind of sleep that only babies and old dogs in front of fires are supposed to enjoy.

THERE are more expert masseurs, I have since found out, than the gentleman who woke me up at nine o'clock the next morning and proceeded to go to work on me, but it was the first massage I had ever had and I have never enjoyed any since then as much. Every twist and stroke of his fingers represented part of that hundred-dollar bill, and my muscles seemed to know it and respond with pleasure. The barber and the manicurist timed their arrival perfectly to his departure, and I sat contentedly for my first manicure and my first shave in a private suite. The barber and the manicurist were somewhat startled to find their client with a bedsheet wrapped around himself toga-fashion, but I explained that I had needed to have my suit pressed immediately, and the reason for my overnight stay. They were at once all solicitude and understanding. Barbers and manicurists who cater to theatre folk are a special breed—they know how to be silent after failure and talkative following success, and the Astor made a specialty of caring for theatre people. Those two knew all about every new play coming in. They had taken care of Sam Harris, Arthur Hopkins, Charles Dillingham and practically everybody else for years. The barber insisted on calling down to the men's shop in the lobby and ordering me a new shirt for the opening, once he caught a glimpse of my wrinkled and soiled one hanging over the chair, and after they had finished, all three of us stood by the window and looked down at the marquee of the Music Box as they wished me good luck.

No day of an opening, it seemed to me, could possibly be starting better than this one.

I could easily have eaten two full breakfasts, but there was barely time to get downstairs, pay my bill, and be across the street for rehearsal at eleven. I took a last look out the window and a quick glimpse at myself in the mirror before I closed the door. There was no question but that the rich full life agreed with me. I looked as smoothed out and as fresh as I felt. Whatever I had spent, I had had more than full value in return. It did not occur to me until I was going down in the elevator that what with overtipping the barber, the manicurist, the valet and the masseur, I might very well have overspent, but I had not. I had fifteen dollars left, and I walked through the stage door of the Music Box the most relaxed and satisfied of mortals. Appropriately enough, Sam Harris was the first person I saw.

"Get any sleep, kid?" he greeted me, and grinned.

"Best sleep I've had in years, Mr. Harris," I replied truthfully enough.

George Kaufman, standing beside him, remarked, "That's the time to sleep—before the notices."

But nothing could shake my eighty-five dollars' worth of well-being. I turned a Max Siegel smile on everyone in sight.

The rehearsal was a short one—a last unnecessary running over of lines in the lounge of the theatre. Actually, there was no reason for a rehearsal at all, except to provide a common meeting ground for opening-night nerves, and the cast was dismissed at one o'clock. It left a long afternoon stretching ominously in front of me and my high spirits, which I was determined not to lose. Once again I turned to Joe Hyman. I called him and asked him to please drop everything and meet me in front of the Plaza Hotel at two o'clock.

There are certain days when everything one touches, when every idea that comes to mind, is completely right, just as there are certain years in the theatre when one can seemingly do no wrong. They are balanced by those other years when it seems impossible to do anything except to do it badly; but I did not know this then. Today anything I chose to do seemed inspired. I had often longed to take a hansom cab for a ride through the park, and it had always seemed a ridiculous indulgence, but I had fifteen dollars left out of that hundred-dollar bill, it was a beautiful September afternoon, and this of all days seemed the proper time for extravagance. I could not have hit upon a better way of weathering these hours of waiting.

We rode around the park together, Joe Hyman and I, by turns talkative and silent, but the awareness in each of our minds of the opening just a few hours away seemed to heighten the color of the leaves on the trees and etch the buildings more sharply against the sky. There is a kind of inner excitement, of pain that is somehow pleasurable, that adds an extra dimension to our awareness of the visible world—the eye seems to look at old scenes and see them with a new depth and clarity. I looked at the Central Park I had always taken for granted and watched it unfold before me with unexpected and surprising beauty. We rode four times around the park and might easily have gone round a fifth time, for Joe Hyman refused to let me pay for anything today and the time seemed to flash by with unnecessary speed. It was suddenly time to send telegrams to the company and to meet the family for dinner, and just as suddenly, in the way time seemed to be rushing headlong toward eight thirty, it was time to leave them in Joe's charge and go on ahead to the theatre to wish the company good luck. Time seems to quicken on opening nights and take on a velocity of its own, just as, I imagine, time must seem to hasten for the very old, accelerating with a swiftness imperceptible to the rest of us.

I walked toward *Once in a Lifetime* for the last time—that final walk every playwright takes toward his play, knowing that it is no longer his, that it belongs to the actors and the audience now, that a part of himself is to be judged by strangers and that he can only watch it as a stranger himself. The main consideration of his day, the keystone that has dictated his every waking moment, the cause that has enlisted his being for all these months, is at an end. He moves toward his destination with mixed emotions—it is the completion he has sought, but there is the ache of finality in it. He is at last a spectator—a spectator with the largest stake in the gamble of the evening, but a spectator nonetheless.

There was already quite a sizable crowd of first-night gawkers and autograph hounds in front of the Music Box as I hurried toward it, and the two mounted policemen trying to herd them to the opposite side of the street were having rather a hard time of it. The crowd ducked out of the way of the policemen and their horses with practiced skill, and the few who were pushed to the opposite curb were smartly back at their old positions in front of the theatre in no time at all. It had the brisk and innocent liveliness of a children's game, with no malice on either side, and as I pushed my own way through the crowd to the stage door I was tempted to turn and shout, "It's not so wonderful being on the inside as you think—you're better off out here!" The panic I had managed to postpone all through the day had suddenly caught up with me. The timetable of the theatre is never very far off. It may vary a little, but opening-night nerves always arrive more or less as promised. Mine had merely been delayed.

I took the bundle of telegrams the stage doorman handed me as though he had put a red-hot poker in my hands and then promptly dropped them on the floor. He picked them up and stuffed them into my pocket without a word, as though he had performed the same service several times before this evening and expected to do it a few more times as well, and I started up the stairway for the dressing rooms on legs that seemed to have no relationship whatever to my body. Two sticks carried me along, and the hand with which I tried to open the first dressing-room door shook so that I could not turn the knob. Hugh O'Connell opened the door from the inside and then stood there looking at me like a rabbit trapped in the glare of automobile headlights. He kept wetting his lips to speak, but no words emerged, or it may be that I did not hear them, for my ears had gone the way of my legs.

It was just as well that my high spirits had vanished in one fell swoop. Even false cheerfulness would have withered quickly in those dressing rooms. The atmosphere in each varied from calm to controlled hysteria, depending upon the opening-night temperature of its occupant. Jean Dixon, vacant-eyed and pale in spite of her make-up, stared at me for a long moment as if trying to focus on who I was, nodded abstractedly, and then resumed a panther-like stalk up and down her dressing room.

Next door, Grant Mills sat looking at himself in the mirror and grinning idiotically. He kept bobbing his head up and down and rubbing his hands together in some silent colloquy with himself. Spring Byington looked so near to being embalmed as she sat solemn and still amidst the mounds of flowers in her dressing room, that I decided to go downstairs and sit on the stage for a while before continuing the rounds.

I seemed to be having a little difficulty breathing myself. I sat on a chair in the stage manager's corner and took the bundle of telegrams out of my pocket, and by purest accident the first two telegrams I opened were from the barber and the manicurist of the Astor Hotel. It was just the sort of happy coincidence to steady the nerves and to restore the faith of a believer in omens. Immediately some of the bright promise of the morning, some of the buoyancy of that ride around the park, began to return.

My spirits lifted with each telegram that I opened. Opening-night telegrams may seem a foolish and perfunctory convention, but they are not. However naïve or fatuous their phrasing may be, those words are the only ones likely to penetrate the minds and warm the hearts of the people who receive them at this particular moment. They may seem dull-witted and senseless the next morning, but opened backstage in that chill interval of waiting for the house lights to darken and the curtain to rise, they perform the admirable function of saying that hope still runs high. Far-fetched little jokes seem uncommonly humorous in opening-night telegrams, and ten words with an unexpected name signed to them can be strangely touching.

There were a good many unexpected names in the telegrams I opened now, as touching to me as those two from the barber and the manicurist. That bundle of telegrams seemed to contain a cross section of the years: the names scrambled the years in wild disorder—George Steinberg and Irving Morrison; the box-office man at the Mayfair Theatre, where I had played *The Emperor Jones*; guests from camp I had all but forgotten; Augustus Pitou; a group of the boys to whom I had told those stories on the stoop outside the candy store, who carefully explained who they were; Priestly Morrison and Mrs. Henry B. Harris; some old neighbors in the Bronx; all the little-theatre groups; Mr. Neuburger of my fur-vault days; Mr. Perleman of the Labor Temple; the tongue-tied athletic instructor who had taught me how to swim, Herb of the Half Moon Country Club . . . The years leaped out of each envelope with quicksilver flashes of memory, the old jumbled with the new. Time seemed to stop as I looked at each name and the years each name recalled, and something like calm began to settle over me.

In the darkness of the stage manager's corner the years that I held in my hand seemed somehow to have been arranged in a design of marvelous felicity, all of them taking me to this hidden corner tonight. I looked around me with an air of wonder and of disbelief. The green shade of the electric-light bulb on the stage manager's stand was focused not only on the prompt script of a play, but on what had once been an impossible dream and was now a reality. The muted sound of the audience out front, the muffled gabble of the stagehands as they called a reminder to each other of a changed light cue or prop, the colored gelatins in the banks of the lights above me, the stage manager's checking the set for the last time, the minor players already beginning to hover in the wings, the voiceless hum of excitement all around me—these were the sights and sounds that no longer belonged to an old dream, but to this corner where I sat and was part of them. I sat on in the chair, riffling through the telegrams again, forgetting that I had not wished the rest of the cast good luck, that I had not yet seen Sam Harris or Mr. Kaufman—I sat on, unwilling to relinquish the serenity this spot seemed to give me.

Not until I heard Max Siegel's voice saying to the stage manager, "They're all in; take the house lights down," could I bring myself to move. I walked through the pass door into the theatre, and in the half-light I peeked through the curtain below the stage box to steal a quick look at the audience—that foolish and hopeful look a playwright sometimes takes in those last few minutes before the curtain rises. What he sees is almost always the same sea of faces—the same well-wishers and ill-wishers, the same critics, the same agents, the same columnists, the very same first-night faces in exactly the same seats they have always sat in, the old faces a little older, the young faces a little stonier—and why he expects some miracle to have changed them into tender and benevolent faces I do not know, but he does. Perhaps the miracle lies in the fact that he should persist in thinking that tonight, for this opening, the miracle will have occurred; but as he anxiously scans row after flinty row, he sees that no miracle has taken place, except the dubious one that the same people have managed to be sitting in the same seats again, and he closes the curtains hastily. No group of people can look as hard and unyielding as first-nighters seem to look, viewed from that vantage point. Even the faces of one's friends seem to be set in concrete, and each critic as one spots him appears to be hewn from the same block of granite as his heart.

I fled up the aisle and almost collided with Mr. Kaufman, whose pacing had already begun. He muttered something that might have been either "Good luck" or "God damn it" and was on his way again. Applause turned me toward the stage. The curtain was rising, and Hugh O'Connell and the set were receiving their regulation round of applause. Jean Dixon made her entrance, the applause swelled, and as it died down she spoke the opening lines. I held my breath to wait for the first laugh, which always came on her second or third line. No sound, however, appeared to be issuing from her lips. One could see her lips moving, but that was all. No sound came forth. Hugh O'Connell spoke, but no sound came from his lips, either. They seemed to be two people talking to each other behind a glass wall.

The audience began to murmur and turn to each other in their seats. My heart skipped a beat and I looked wildly toward Mr. Kaufman. He stood frozen in his tracks, staring at the stage. Jean Dixon and Hugh O'Connell were talking steadily on, unaware that they could not be heard, but aware that something was gravely wrong, for the murmur from the audience was loud enough for them to hear it now and I could see Jean Dixon's hand shake as she lit a cigarette. Still no sound came from the stage, and in the silence a man's voice from the balcony rang out loud and clear: "It's the fans—turn off the fans!"

The audience broke into relieved laughter and applause. I saw Mr. Kaufman make a dash for the pass door that led backstage, but before he was halfway down the aisle, the fans on either side of the proscenium began to slow down. In the opening-night excitement, the electrician had simply forgotten to turn off the fans—one of those simple little opening-night mistakes that lessen the life span of everyone concerned by five or ten years! The nightmare had lasted no more than a minute in all, but it is not one of the minutes I should choose to live over again. Invariably, when horrors of this kind occur, the audience behaves admirably and they did so now. They not only applauded that unknown hero in the balcony, but they rewarded Jean Dixon with a generous round of applause when she went back and started the scene all over again. She could not, of course, go off the stage and re-enter, but aware that not a word of the scene had been heard, she calmly took a puff or two of her cigarette, waited until the fans had stopped, and began the scene anew.

From that moment onward, both play and audience took on something of the quality of fantasy—it was being played and received like a playwright's dream of a perfect opening night. The performance was brilliant and the audience matched it in their response. One of the theatre's most steadfast beliefs is that there is never again a sound of trumpets like the sound of a New York opening-night audience giving a play its unreserved approval. It is a valid belief. Bitter words have been written about the first-night audience, but the fact remains that there is no audience ever again like it—no audience as keen, as alive, as exciting and as overwhelmingly satisfactory as a first-night audience taking a play to its heart. It can unfurl the tricolor of its acclamation and make flags seem to wave from every box; just as in reverse its dissent can seem to dangle the Jolly Roger from the center chandelier and blanket the auditorium in leaden disapproval.

The sound of the audience's approval was unmistakable, even to my own anxious ears. At the end of each act the applause broke before the curtain had quite touched the floor. The second act played better than the first, and the third act—that vulnerable, exasperating third act, the act which had held the play in jeopardy for so long—seemed to have written itself, so effortlessly and winningly was it playing. It was almost irritating to watch it play with such inevitable rightness and ease, remembering the bitter struggle it had given us. The final lines of the play were being spoken now, and then it came—an explosive crash of applause as the curtain fell. It came like a thunderclap, full and tumultuous. I tried to disengage myself and measure the kind of applause it was, but I could not. It sounded like hit applause to me, and it was keeping up. Except for one or two critics with early deadlines dashing up the aisle, the entire audience was remaining in its seats and keeping the curtain going up and down. The cast stood bowing and smiling—they had taken their individual calls and the entire company was lined up on the stage. No other calls had been set, and the company was bowing and smiling somewhat awkwardly now, in the way actors do when they are no longer in the frame of the play; but still the applause showed no sign of diminishing.

To my amazement, I saw Mr. Kaufman step forward and signal the stage manager to keep the curtain up. I stared at the stage in disbelief. He was about to do something so implausible that I could hardly conceive of his doing it—he was about to make a curtain speech. I could not believe my eyes. More than once he had expressed his scorn for authors who made opening-night speeches, and he had expressed it in such scathing terms that it seemed impossible that he was about to make one himself. The audience seemed almost as surprised as I was. The applause stilled immediately and an eager "shushing" took its place. He came forward another step, peered at them over his glasses, and waited for complete quiet.

"I would like this audience to know," he said carefully and slowly, "that eighty per cent of this play is Moss Hart." That was all. He stepped back and signaled the stage manager to lower the curtain. The audience sat bewildered for a full moment and then broke into perfunctory applause. They had expected a witty speech in the manner of the play—or in the caustic tradition of George S. Kaufman. Their disappointment and their lack of interest in what he said was clear, but they obligingly applauded for another curtain.

I stood staring at the stage and at George Kaufman. Generosity does not flower easily or often in the rocky soil of the theatre. Few are uncorrupted by its ceaseless warfare over credit and billing, its jealousies and envies, its constant temptations toward pettiness and mean-spiritedness. It is not only a hard and exacting profession but the most public one as well. It does not breed magnanimity, and unselfishness is not one of its strong points. Not often is a young playwright welcomed into it with a *beau geste* as gallant and selfless as the one that had just come over those footlights.

A hand was tugging at my sleeve and Max Siegel was whispering some words in my ear, but I moved quickly away without answering. I did not trust my voice, and I was ashamed to have him see that my eyes were blurred.

# The Devil and Daniel Webster

## STEPHEN VINCENT BENÉT

### I

IT'S a story they tell in the border country, where Massachusetts joins Vermont and New Hampshire.

Yes, Dan'l Webster's dead—or, at least, they buried him. But every time there's a thunderstorm around Marshfield, they say you can hear his rolling voice in the hollows of the sky. And they say that if you go to his grave and speak loud and clear, "Dan'l Webster—Dan'l Webster!" the ground'll begin to shiver and the trees begin to shake. And after a while you'll hear a deep voice saying, "Neighbor, how stands the Union?" Then you better answer the Union stands as she stood, rock-bottomed and copper-sheathed, one and indivisible, or he's liable to rear right out of the ground. At least, that's what I was told when I was a youngster.

You see, for a while, he was the biggest man in the country. He never got to be President, but he was the biggest man. There were thousands that trusted in him right next to God Almighty, and they told stories about him and all the things that belonged to him that were like the stories of patriarchs and such. They said, when he stood up to speak, stars and stripes came right out in the sky, and once he spoke against a river and made it sink into the ground. They said, when he walked the woods with his fishing rod, Killall, the trout would jump out of the streams right into his pockets, for they knew it was no use putting up a fight against him; and, when he argued a case, he could turn on the harps of the blessed and the shaking of the earth underground. That was the kind of man he was, and his big farm up at Marshfield was suitable to him. The chickens he raised were all white meat down through the drumsticks, the cows were tended like children, and the big ram he called Goliath had horns with a curl like a morning-glory vine and could butt through an iron door. But Dan'l wasn't one of your gentlemen farmers; he knew all the ways of the land, and he'd be up by candlelight to see that the chores got done. A man with a mouth like a mastiff, a brow like a mountain and eyes like burning anthracite—that was Dan'l Webster in his prime. And the biggest case he argued never got written down in the books, for he argued it against the devil, nip and tuck and no holds barred. And this is the way I used to hear it told.

There was a man named Jabez Stone, lived at Cross Corners, New Hampshire. He wasn't a bad man to start with, but he was an unlucky man. If he planted corn, he got borers; if he planted potatoes, he got blight. He had good-enough land, but it didn't prosper him; he had a decent wife and children, but the more children he had, the less there was to feed them. If stones cropped up in his neighbor's field, boulders boiled up in his; if he had a horse with the spavins, he'd trade it for one with the staggers and give something extra. There's some folks bound to be like that, apparently. But one day Jabez Stone got sick of the whole business.

He'd been plowing that morning and he'd just broke the plowshare on a rock that he could have sworn hadn't been there yesterday. And, as he stood looking at the plowshare, the off horse began to cough—that ropy kind of cough that means sickness and horse doctors. There were two children down with the measles, his wife was ailing, and he had a whitlow on his thumb. It was about the last straw for Jabez Stone. "I vow," he said, and he looked around him kind of desperate—"I vow it's enough to make a man want to sell his soul to the devil! And I would, too, for two cents!"

Then he felt a kind of queerness come over him at having said what he'd said; though, naturally, being a New Hampshireman, he wouldn't take it back. But, all the same, when it got to be evening and, as far as he could see, no notice had been taken, he felt relieved in his mind, for he was a religious man. But notice is always taken, sooner or later, just like the Good Book says. And, sure enough, next day, about suppertime, a soft-spoken, dark-dressed stranger drove up in a handsome buggy and asked for Jabez Stone.

Well, Jabez told his family it was a lawyer, come to see him about a legacy. But he knew who it was. He didn't like the looks of the stranger, nor the way he smiled with his teeth. They were white teeth, and plentiful —some say they were filed to a point, but I wouldn't vouch for that. And he didn't like it when the dog took one look at the stranger and ran away howling, with his tail between his legs. But having passed his word, more or less, he stuck to it, and they went out behind the barn and made their bargain. Jabez Stone had to prick his finger to sign, and the stranger lent him a silver pin. The wound healed clean, but it left a little white scar.

II

After that, all of a sudden, things began to pick up and prosper for Jabez Stone. His cows got fat and his horses sleek, his crops were the envy of the neighborhood, and lightning might strike all over the valley, but it wouldn't strike his barn. Pretty soon, he was one of the prosperous people of the county; they asked him to stand for selectman, and he stood for it; there began to be talk of running him for state senate. All in all, you might say the Stone family was as happy and contented as cats in a dairy. And so they were, except for Jabez Stone.

He'd been contented enough, the first few years. It's a great thing when bad luck turns; it drives most other things out of your head. True, every now and then, especially in rainy weather, the little white scar on his finger would give him a twinge. And once a year, punctual as clockwork, the stranger with the handsome buggy would come driving by. But the sixth year, the stranger lighted, and, after that, his peace was over for Jabez Stone.

The stranger came up through the lower field, switching his boots with a cane—they were handsome black boots, but Jabez Stone never liked the look of them, particularly the toes. And, after he'd passed the time of day, he said, "Well, Mr. Stone, you're a hummer! It's a very pretty property you've got here, Mr. Stone."

"Well, some might favor it and others might not," said Jabez Stone, for he was a New Hampshireman.

"Oh, no need to decry your industry!" said the stranger, very easy, showing his teeth in a smile. "After all, we know what's been done, and it's been according to contract and specifications. So when—ahem—the mortgage falls due next year, you shouldn't have any regrets."

"Speaking of that mortgage, mister," said Jabez Stone, and he looked around for help to the earth and the sky, "I'm beginning to have one or two doubts about it."

"Doubts?" said the stranger, not quite so pleasantly.

"Why, yes," said Jabez Stone. "This being the U. S. A. and me always having been a religious man." He cleared his throat and got bolder. "Yes, sir," he said, "I'm beginning to have considerable doubts as to that mortgage holding in court."

"There's courts and courts," said the stranger, clicking his teeth. "Still, we might as well have a look at the original document." And he hauled out a big black pocketbook, full of papers. "Sherwin, Slater, Stevens, Stone," he muttered. "I, Jabez Stone, for a term of seven years—Oh, it's quite in order, I think."

But Jabez Stone wasn't listening, for he saw something else flutter out of the black pocketbook. It was something that looked like a moth, but it wasn't a moth. And as Jabez Stone stared at it, it seemed to speak to him in a small sort of piping voice, terrible small and thin, but terrible human.

"Neighbor Stone!" it squeaked. "Neighbor Stone! Help me! For God's sake, help me!"

But before Jabez Stone could stir hand or foot, the stranger whipped out a big bandanna handkerchief, caught the creature in it, just like a butterfly, and started tying up the ends of the bandanna.

"Sorry for the interruption," he said. "As I was saying—"

But Jabez Stone was shaking all over like a scared horse.

"That's Miser Stevens' voice!" he said, in a croak. "And you've got him in your handkerchief!"

The stranger looked a little embarrassed.

"Yes, I really should have transferred him to the collecting box," he said with a simper, "but there were some rather unusual specimens there and I didn't want them crowded. Well, well, these little contretemps will occur."

"I don't know what you mean by contertan," said Jabez Stone, "but that was Miser Stevens' voice! And he ain't dead! You can't tell me he is! He was just as spry and mean as a woodchuck, Tuesday!"

"In the midst of life—" said the stranger, kind of pious. "Listen!" Then a bell began to toll in the valley and Jabez Stone listened, with the sweat running down his face. For he knew it was tolled for Miser Stevens and that he was dead.

"These long-standing accounts," said the stranger with a sigh; "one really hates to close them. But business is business."

He still had the bandanna in his hand, and Jabez Stone felt sick as he saw the cloth struggle and flutter.

"Are they all as small as that?" he asked hoarsely.

"Small?" said the stranger. "Oh, I see what you mean. Why, they vary." He measured Jabez Stone with his eyes, and his teeth showed. "Don't worry, Mr. Stone," he said. "You'll go with a very good grade. I wouldn't trust you outside the collecting box. Now, a man like Dan'l Webster, of course—well, we'd have to build a special box for him, and even at that, I imagine the wing spread would astonish you. He'd certainly be a prize. I wish we could see our way clear to him. But, in your case, as I was saying—"

"Put that handkerchief away!" said Jabez Stone, and he began to beg and to pray. But the best he could get at the end was a three years' extension, with conditions.

But till you make a bargain like that, you've got no idea of how fast four years can run. By the last months of those years, Jabez Stone's known all over the state and there's talk of running him for governor—and it's dust and ashes in his mouth. For every day, when he gets up, he thinks, "There's one more night gone," and every night when he lies down, he thinks of the black pocketbook and the soul of Miser Stevens, and it makes him sick at heart. Till, finally, he can't bear it any longer, and, in the last days of the last year, he hitches up his horse and drives off to seek Dan'l Webster. For Dan'l was born in New Hampshire, only a few miles from Cross Corners, and it's well known that he has a particular soft spot for old neighbors.

## III

It was early in the morning when he got to Marshfield, but Dan'l was up already, talking Latin to the farm hands and wrestling with the ram, Goliath, and trying out a new trotter and working up speeches to make against John C. Calhoun. But when he heard a New Hampshireman had come to see him, he dropped everything else he was doing, for that was Dan'l's way. He gave Jabez Stone a breakfast that five men couldn't eat, went into the living history of every man and woman in Cross Corners, and finally asked him how he could serve him.

Jabez Stone allowed that it was a kind of mortgage case.

"Well, I haven't pleaded a mortgage case in a long time, and I don't generally plead now, except before the Supreme Court," said Dan'l, "but if I can, I'll help you."

"Then I've got hope for the first time in ten years," said Jabez Stone, and told him the details.

Dan'l walked up and down as he listened, hands behind his back, now and then asking a question, now and then plunging his eyes at the floor, as if they'd bore through it like gimlets. When Jabez Stone had finished, Dan'l puffed out his cheeks and blew. Then he turned to Jabez Stone and a smile broke over his face like the sunrise over Monadnock.

"You've certainly given yourself the devil's own row to hoe, Neighbor Stone," he said, "but I'll take your case."

"You'll take it?" said Jabez Stone, hardly daring to believe.

"Yes," said Dan'l Webster. "I've got about seventy-five other things to do and the Missouri Compromise to straighten out, but I'll take your case. For if two New Hampshiremen aren't a match for the devil, we might as well give the country back to the Indians."

Then he shook Jabez Stone by the hand and said, "Did you come down here in a hurry?"

"Well, I admit I made time," said Jabez Stone.

"You'll go back faster," said Dan'l Webster, and he told 'em to hitch up Constitution and Constellation to the carriage. They were matched grays with one white forefoot, and they stepped like greased lightning.

Well, I won't describe how excited and pleased the whole Stone family was to have the great Dan'l Webster for a guest, when they finally got there. Jabez Stone had lost his hat on the way, blown off when they overtook a wind, but he didn't take much account of that. But after supper he sent the family off to bed, for he had most particular business with Mr. Webster. Mrs. Stone wanted them to sit in the front parlor, but Dan'l Webster knew front parlors and said he preferred the kitchen. So it was there they sat, waiting for the stranger, with a jug on the table between them and a bright fire on the hearth—the stranger being scheduled to show up on the stroke of midnight, according to specification.

Well, most men wouldn't have asked for better company than Dan'l Webster and a jug. But with every tick of the clock Jabez Stone got sadder and sadder. His eyes roved round, and though he sampled the jug you could see he couldn't taste it. Finally, on the stroke of 11:30 he reached over and grabbed Dan'l Webster by the arm.

"Mr. Webster, Mr. Webster!" he said, and his voice was shaking with fear and a desperate courage. "For God's sake, Mr. Webster, harness your horses and get away from this place while you can!"

"You've brought me a long way, neighbor, to tell me you don't like my company," said Dan'l Webster, quite peaceable, pulling at the jug.

"Miserable wretch that I am!" groaned Jabez Stone. "I've brought you a devilish way, and now I see my folly. Let him take me if he wills. I don't hanker after it, I must say, but I can stand it. But you're the Union's stay and New Hampshire's pride! He mustn't get you, Mr. Webster! He mustn't get you!"

Dan'l Webster looked at the distracted man, all gray and shaking in the firelight, and laid a hand on his shoulder.

"I'm obliged to you, Neighbor Stone," he said gently. "It's kindly thought of. But there's a jug on the table and a case in hand. And I never left a jug or a case half finished in my life."

And just at that moment there was a sharp rap on the door.

"Ah," said Dan'l Webster, very coolly, "I thought your clock was a trifle slow, Neighbor Stone." He stepped to the door and opened it. "Come in!" he said.

The stranger came in—very dark and tall he looked in the firelight. He was carrying a box under his arm—a black, japanned box with little air holes in the lid. At the sight of the box, Jabez Stone gave a low cry and shrank into a corner of the room.

"Mr. Webster, I presume," said the stranger, very polite, but with his eyes glowing like a fox's deep in the woods.

"Attorney of record for Jabez Stone," said Dan'l Webster, but his eyes were glowing too. "Might I ask your name?"

"I've gone by a good many," said the stranger carelessly. "Perhaps Scratch will do for the evening. I'm often called that in these regions."

Then he sat down at the table and poured himself a drink from the jug. The liquor was cold in the jug, but it came steaming into the glass.

"And now," said the stranger, smiling and showing his teeth, "I shall call upon you, as a law-abiding citizen, to assist me in taking possession of my property."

Well, with that the argument began—and it went hot and heavy. At first, Jabez Stone had a flicker of hope, but when he saw Dan'l Webster being forced back at point after point, he just sat scrunched in his corner, with his eyes on that japanned box. For there wasn't any doubt as to the deed or the signature—that was the worst of it. Dan'l Webster twisted and turned and thumped his fist on the table, but he couldn't get away from that. He offered to compromise the case; the stranger wouldn't hear of it. He pointed out the property had increased in value, and state senators ought to be worth more; the stranger stuck to the letter of the law. He was a great lawyer, Dan'l Webster, but we know who's the King of Lawyers, as the Good Book tells us, and it seemed as if, for the first time, Dan'l Webster had met his match.

Finally, the stranger yawned a little. "Your spirited efforts on behalf of your client do you credit, Mr. Webster," he said, "but if you have no more arguments to adduce, I'm rather pressed for time—" and Jabez Stone shuddered.

Dan'l Webster's brow looked dark as a thundercloud. "Pressed or not, you shall not have this man!" he thundered. "Mr. Stone is an American citizen, and no American citizen may be forced into the service of a foreign prince. We fought England for that in '12 and we'll fight all hell for it again!"

"Foreign?" said the stranger. "And who calls me a foreigner?"

"Well, I never yet heard of the dev—of your claiming American citizenship," said Dan'l Webster with surprise.

"And who with better right?" said the stranger, with one of his terrible smiles. "When the first wrong was done to the first Indian, I was there. When the first slaver put out for the Congo, I stood on her deck. Am I not in your books and stories and beliefs, from the first settlements on? Am I not spoken of, still, in every church in New England? 'Tis true the North claims me for a Southerner, and the South for a Northerner, but I am neither. I am merely an honest American like yourself—and of the best descent—for, to tell the truth, Mr. Webster, though I don't like to boast of it, my name is older in this country than yours."

"Aha!" said Dan'l Webster, with the veins standing out in his forehead. "Then I stand on the Constitution! I demand a trial for my client!"

"The case is hardly one for an ordinary court," said the stranger, his eyes flickering. "And, indeed, the lateness of the hour—"

"Let it be any court you choose, so it is an American judge and an American jury!" said Dan'l Webster in his pride. "Let it be the quick or the dead; I'll abide the issue!"

"You have said it," said the stranger, and pointed his finger at the door. And with that, and all of a sudden, there was a rushing of wind outside and a noise of footsteps. They came, clear and distinct, through the night. And yet, they were not like the footsteps of living men.

"In God's name, who comes by so late?" cried Jabez Stone, in an ague of fear.

"The jury Mr. Webster demands," said the stranger, sipping at his boiling glass. "You must pardon the rough appearance of one or two; they will have come a long way."

## IV

And with that the fire burned blue and the door blew open and twelve men entered, one by one.

If Jabez Stone had been sick with terror before, he was blind with terror now. For there was Walter Butler, the loyalist, who spread fire and horror through the Mohawk Valley in the times of the Revolution; and there was Simon Girty, the renegade, who saw white men burned at the stake and whooped with the Indians to see them burn. His eyes were green, like a catamount's, and the stains on his hunting shirt did not come from the blood of the deer. King Philip was there, wild and proud as he had been in life, with the great gash in his head that gave him his death wound, and cruel Governor Dale, who broke men on the wheel. There was Morton of Merry Mount, who so vexed the Plymouth Colony, with his flushed, loose, handsome face and his hate of the godly. There was Teach, the bloody pirate, with his black beard curling on his breast. The Reverend John

Smeet, with his strangler's hands and his Geneva gown, walked as daintily as he had to the gallows. The red print of the rope was still around his neck, but he carried a perfumed handkerchief in one hand. One and all, they came into the room with the fires of hell still upon them, and the stranger named their names and their deeds as they came, till the tale of twelve was told. Yet the stranger had told the truth—they had all played a part in America.

"Are you satisfied with the jury, Mr. Webster?" said the stranger mockingly, when they had taken their places.

The sweat stood upon Dan'l Webster's brow, but his voice was clear.

"Quite satisfied," he said. "Though I miss General Arnold from the company."

"Benedict Arnold is engaged upon other business," said the stranger, with a glower. "Ah, you asked for a justice, I believe."

He pointed his finger once more, and a tall man, soberly clad in Puritan garb, with the burning gaze of the fanatic, stalked into the room and took his judge's place.

"Justice Hathorne is a jurist of experience," said the stranger. "He presided at certain witch trials once held in Salem. There were others who repented of the business later, but not he."

"Repent of such notable wonders and undertakings?" said the stern old justice. "Nay, hang them—hang them all!" And he muttered to himself in a way that struck ice into the soul of Jabez Stone.

Then the trial began, and, as you might expect, it didn't look anyways good for the defense. And Jabez Stone didn't make much of a witness in his own behalf. He took one look at Simon Girty and screeched, and they had to put him back in his corner in a kind of swoon.

It didn't halt the trial, though; the trial went on, as trials do. Dan'l Webster had faced some hard juries and hanging judges in his time, but this was the hardest he'd ever faced, and he knew it. They sat there with a kind of glitter in their eyes, and the stranger's smooth voice went on and on. Every time he'd raise an objection, it'd be "Objection sustained," but whenever Dan'l objected, it'd be "Objection denied." Well, you couldn't expect fair play from a fellow like this Mr. Scratch.

It got to Dan'l in the end, and he began to heat, like iron in the forge. When he got up to speak he was going to flay that stranger with every trick known to the law, and the judge and jury too. He didn't care if it was contempt of court or what would happen to him for it. He didn't care any more what happened to Jabez Stone. He just got madder and madder, thinking of what he'd say. And yet, curiously enough, the more he thought about it, the less he was able to arrange his speech in his mind.

Till, finally, it was time for him to get up on his feet, and he did so, all ready to bust out with lightnings and denunciations. But before he started he looked over the judge and jury for a moment, such being his custom. And he noticed the glitter in their eyes was twice as strong as before, and they all leaned forward. Like hounds just before they get the fox, they looked, and the blue mist of evil in the room thickened as he watched them. Then he saw what he'd been about to do, and he wiped his forehead, as a man might who's just escaped falling into a pit in the dark.

For it was him they'd come for, not only Jabez Stone. He read it in the glitter of their eyes and in the way the stranger hid his mouth with one hand. And if he fought them with their own weapons, he'd fall into their power; he knew that, though he couldn't have told you how. It was his own anger and horror that burned in their eyes; and he'd have to wipe that out or the case was lost. He stood there for a moment, his black eyes burning like anthracite. And then he began to speak.

He started off in a low voice, though you could hear every word. They say he could call on the harps of the blessed when he chose. And this was just as simple and easy as a man could talk. But he didn't start out by condemning or reviling. He was talking about the things that make a country a country, and a man a man.

And he began with the simple things that everybody's known and felt —the freshness of a fine morning when you're young, and the taste of food when you're hungry, and the new day that's every day when you're a child. He took them up and he turned them in his hands. They were good things for any man. But without freedom, they sickened. And when he talked of those enslaved, and the sorrows of slavery, his voice got like a big bell. He talked of the early days of America and the men who had made those days. It wasn't a spread-eagle speech, but he made you see it. He admitted all the wrong that had ever been done. But he showed how, out of the wrong and the right, the suffering and the starvations, something new had come. And everybody had played a part in it, even the traitors.

Then he turned to Jabez Stone and showed him as he was—an ordinary man who'd had hard luck and wanted to change it. And, because he'd wanted to change it, now he was going to be punished for all eternity. And yet there was good in Jabez Stone, and he showed that good. He was hard and mean, in some ways, but he was a man. There was sadness in being a man, but it was a proud thing too. And he showed what the pride of it was till you couldn't help feeling it. Yes, even in hell, if a man was a man, you'd know it. And he wasn't pleading for any one person any more, though his voice rang like an organ. He was telling the story and the failures and the endless journey of mankind. They got tricked and trapped and bamboozled, but it was a great journey. And no demon that was ever foaled could know the inwardness of it—it took a man to do that.

v

The fire began to die on the hearth and the wind before morning to blow. The light was getting gray in the room when Dan'l Webster finished. And his words came back at the end to New Hampshire ground, and the one spot of land that each man loves and clings to. He painted a picture of that, and to each one of that jury he spoke of things long forgotten. For his voice could search the heart, and that was his gift and his strength. And to one, his voice was like the forest and its secrecy, and to another like the sea and the storms of the sea; and one heard the cry of his lost nation in it, and another saw a little harmless scene he hadn't remembered for years. But each saw something. And when Dan'l Webster finished he didn't know whether or not he'd saved Jabez Stone. But he knew he'd done a miracle. For the glitter was gone from the eyes of judge and jury, and, for the moment, they were men again, and knew they were men.

"The defense rests," said Dan'l Webster, and stood there like a mountain. His ears were still ringing with his speech, and he didn't hear anything else till he heard Judge Hathorne say, "The jury will retire to consider its verdict."

Walter Butler rose in his place and his face had a dark, gay pride on it.

"The jury has considered its verdict," he said, and looked the stranger full in the eye. "We find for the defendant, Jabez Stone."

With that, the smile left the stranger's face, but Walter Butler did not flinch.

"Perhaps 'tis not strictly in accordance with the evidence," he said, "but even the damned may salute the eloquence of Mr. Webster."

With that, the long crow of a rooster split the gray morning sky, and judge and jury were gone from the room like a puff of smoke and as if they had never been there. The stranger turned to Dan'l Webster, smiling wryly. "Major Butler was always a bold man," he said. "I had not thought him quite so bold. Nevertheless, my congratulations, as between two gentlemen."

"I'll have that paper first, if you please," said Dan'l Webster, and he took it and tore it into four pieces. It was queerly warm to the touch. "And now," he said, "I'll have you!" and his hand came down like a bear trap on the stranger's arm. For he knew that once you bested anybody like Mr. Scratch in fair fight, his power on you was gone. And he could see that Mr. Scratch knew it too.

The stranger twisted and wriggled, but he couldn't get out of that grip. "Come, come, Mr. Webster," he said, smiling palely. "This sort of thing is ridic—ouch!—is ridiculous. If you're worried about the costs of the case, naturally, I'd be glad to pay—"

"And so you shall!" said Dan'l Webster, shaking him till his teeth rattled. "For you'll sit right down at that table and draw up a document, promising never to bother Jabez Stone nor his heirs or assigns nor any other New Hampshireman till doomsday! For any hades we want to raise in this state, we can raise ourselves, without assistance from strangers."

"Ouch!" said the stranger. "Ouch! Well, they never did run very big to the barrel, but—ouch!—I agree!"

So he sat down and drew up the document. But Dan'l Webster kept his hand on his coat collar all the time.

"And, now, may I go?" said the stranger, quite humble, when Dan'l'd seen the document was in proper and legal form.

"Go?" said Dan'l, giving him another shake. "I'm still trying to figure out what I'll do with you. For you've settled the costs of the case, but you haven't settled with me. I think I'll take you back to Marshfield," he said, kind of reflective. "I've got a ram there named Goliath that can butt through an iron door. I'd kind of like to turn you loose in his field and see what he'd do."

Well, with that the stranger began to beg and to plead. And he begged and he pled so humble that finally Dan'l, who was naturally kindhearted, agreed to let him go. The stranger seemed terrible grateful for that and said, just to show they were friends, he'd tell Dan'l's fortune before leaving. So Dan'l agreed to that, though he didn't take much stock in fortunetellers ordinarily.

But, naturally, the stranger was a little different. Well, he pried and he peered at the lines in Dan'l's hands. And he told him one thing and another that was quite remarkable. But they were all in the past.

"Yes, all that's true, and it happened," said Dan'l Webster. "But what's to come in the future?"

The stranger grinned, kind of happily, and shook his head. "The future's not as you think it," he said. "It's dark. You have a great ambition, Mr. Webster."

"I have," said Dan'l firmly, for everybody knew he wanted to be President.

"It seems almost within your grasp," said the stranger, "but you will not attain it. Lesser men will be made President and you will be passed over."

"And, if I am, I'll still be Daniel Webster," said Dan'l. "Say on."

"You have two strong sons," said the stranger, shaking his head. "You look to found a line. But each will die in war and neither reach greatness."

"Live or die, they are still my sons," said Dan'l Webster. "Say on."

"You have made great speeches," said the stranger. "You will make more."

"Ah," said Dan'l Webster.

"But the last great speech you make will turn many of your own against you," said the stranger. "They will call you Ichabod; they will call you by other names. Even in New England some will say you have turned your coat and sold your country, and their voices will be loud against you till you die."

"So it is an honest speech, it does not matter what men say," said Dan'l Webster. Then he looked at the stranger and their glances locked.

"One question," he said. "I have fought for the Union all my life. Will I see that fight won against those who would tear it apart?"

"Not while you live," said the stranger, grimly, "but it will be won. And after you are dead, there are thousands who will fight for your cause, because of words that you spoke."

"Why, then, you long-barreled, slab-sided, lantern-jawed, fortune-telling note shaver!" said Dan'l Webster, with a great roar of laughter, "be off with you to your own place before I put my mark on you! For, by the thirteen original colonies, I'd go to the Pit itself to save the Union!"

And with that he drew back his foot for a kick that would have stunned a horse. It was only the tip of his shoe that caught the stranger, but he went flying out of the door with his collecting box under his arm.

"And now," said Dan'l Webster, seeing Jabez Stone beginning to rouse from his swoon, "let's see what's left in the jug, for it's dry work talking all night. I hope there's pie for breakfast, Neighbor Stone."

But they say that whenever the devil comes near Marshfield, even now, he gives it a wide berth. And he hasn't been seen in the state of New Hampshire from that day to this. I'm not talking about Massachusetts or Vermont.

# Gigi

## COLETTE

### (*Translated by Roger Senhouse*)

"DON'T forget you are going to Aunt Alicia's. Do you hear me, Gilberte? Come here and let me do your curls. Gilberte, do you hear me?"

"Couldn't I go there without having my hair curled, Grandmamma?"

"I should think not," said Madame Alvarez, quietly. She took an old pair of curling-irons, with prongs ending in little round metal knobs, and put them to heat over the blue flame of a spirit-lamp while she prepared the tissue-papers.

"Grandmamma, couldn't you crimp my hair in waves down the side of my head for a change?"

"Out of the question. Ringlets at the very ends—that's as far as a girl of your age can possibly go. Now sit down on the footstool."

To do so, Gilberte folded up under her the heron-like legs of a girl of fifteen. Below her tartan skirt, she revealed ribbed cotton stockings to just above the knees, unconscious of the perfect oval shape of her knee-caps. Slender calf and high arched instep—Madame Alvarez never let her eyes run over these fine points without regretting that her granddaughter had not studied dancing professionally. At the moment, she was thinking only of the girl's hair. She had corkscrewed the ends and fixed them in tissue-paper, and was now compressing the ash-blonde ringlets between the heated knobs. With patient soft-fingered skill, she gathered up the full magnificent weight of finely kept hair into sleek ripples which fell to just below Gilberte's shoulders. The girl sat quite still. The smell of the heated tongs, and the whiff of vanilla in the curling-papers, made her feel drowsy. Besides, Gilberte knew that resistance would be useless. She hardly ever tried to elude the authority exercised by her family.

"Is Mamma singing Frasquita today?"

"Yes. And this evening in *Si j'étais Roi*. I have told you before, when you're sitting on a low seat you must keep your knees close to each other, and lean both of them together, either to the right or to the left, for the sake of decorum."

"But, Grandmamma, I've got on my drawers and my petticoat."

"Drawers are one thing, decorum is another," said Madame Alvarez. "Everything depends on the attitude."

"Yes, I know. Aunt Alicia has told me often enough," Gilberte murmured from under her tent of hair.

"I do not require the help of my sister," said Madame Alvarez testily, "to instruct you in the elements of propriety. On that subject, thank goodness, I know rather more than she does."

"Supposing you let me stay here with you today, Grandmamma, couldn't I go and see Aunt Alicia next Sunday?"

"What next!" said Madame Alvarez haughtily. "Have you any other *purposal* to make to me?"

"Yes, I have," said Gilberte. "Have my skirts made a little longer, so I don't have to fold myself up in a Z every time I sit down. You see, Grandmamma, with my skirts too short, I have to keep thinking of my you-know-what."

"Silence! Aren't you ashamed to call it your you-know-what?"

"I don't mind calling it by any other name, only . . ."

Madame Alvarez blew out the spirit-lamp, looked at the reflection of her heavy Spanish face in the looking-glass above the mantelpiece, and then laid down the law.

"There is no other name."

A skeptical look passed across the girl's eyes. Beneath the cockle-shells of fair hair they showed a lovely dark blue, the color of glistening slate. Gilberte unfolded with a bound.

"But, Grandmamma, all the same, do look! If only my skirts were just that much longer! Or if a small frill could be added!"

"That *would* be nice for your mother, to be seen with a great gawk looking at least eighteen! In her profession! Where are your brains!"

"In my head," said Gilberte. "Since I hardly ever go out with Mamma, what would it matter?"

She pulled down her skirt, which had rucked up towards her slim waist, and asked, "Can I go in my everyday coat? It's quite good enough."

"That wouldn't show that it's Sunday! Put on your serge coat and blue sailor-hat. When will you learn what's what?"

When on her feet, Gilberte was as tall as her grandmother. Madame Alvarez had taken the name of a Spanish lover now dead, and accordingly had acquired a creamy complexion, an ample bust, and hair lustrous with brilliantine. She used too white a powder, her heavy cheeks had begun to draw down her lower eyelids a little, and so eventually she took to calling herself Inez. Her family pursued their fixed orbit around her. Her unmarried daughter Andrée, forsaken by Gilberte's father, now preferred the sober life of a second-lead singer in a State-controlled theatre to the fitful opulence of a life of gallantry. Aunt Alicia—none of her admirers, it seemed, had ever mentioned marriage—lived alone, on an income she pretended was modest. The family had a high opinion of Alicia's judgment, and of her jewels.

Madame Alvarez looked her granddaughter up and down, from the felt sailor-hat trimmed with a quill to the ready-made cavalier shoes.

"Can't you ever manage to keep your legs together? When you stand like that, the Seine could flow between them. You haven't the shadow of a stomach, and yet you somehow contrive to stick it out. And don't forget your gloves, I beg of you."

Gilberte's every posture was still governed by the unconcern of childish innocence. At times she looked like Robin Hood, at others like a carved angel, or again like a boy in skirts; but she seldom resembled a nearly grown-up girl. "How can you expect to be put into long skirts, when you haven't the sense of a child of eight?" Madame Alvarez asked. And Andrée sighed, "I find Gilberte so discouraging." To which Gilberte answered quietly, "If you didn't find *me* discouraging, then you'd find something else." For she was sweet and gentle, resigned to a stay-at-home life and seeing few people outside the family. As for her features, no one could yet predict their final mould. A large mouth, which showed beautiful strong white teeth when she laughed, no chin to speak of, and, between high cheekbones, a nose—"Heavens, where did she get that button?" whispered her mother under her breath. "If you can't answer that question, my girl, who can?" retorted Madame Alvarez. Whereupon Andrée, who had become prudish too late in life and disgruntled too soon, relapsed into silence, automatically stroking her sensitive larynx. "Gigi is just a bundle of raw material," Aunt Alicia affirmed, "it may turn out very well—and, just as easily, all wrong."

"Grandmamma, there's the bell! I'll open the door on my way out. Grandmamma," Gigi shouted from the passage, "It's Uncle Gaston!"

She came back into the room with a tall, youngish looking man, her arm linked through his, chattering to him with the childish pomposity of a school-girl out of class.

"What a pity it is, Tonton, that I've got to desert you so soon! Grandmamma wishes me to pay a call on Aunt Alicia. Which motor-car are you using today? Did you come in the new four-seater de Dion-Bouton with the collapsible hood? I hear it can be driven simply with one hand! Goodness, Tonton, those are smart gloves, and no mistake! So you've had a row with Liane, Tonton?"

"Gilberte," scolded Madame Alvarez, "what business of yours can that be?"

"But, Grandmamma, everybody knows about it. The whole story was in the *Gil Blas*. It began: A *secret bitterness is seeping into the sweet product of the sugarbeet.* . . . At school all the girls were asking me about it, for of course they know I know you. And I can tell you, Tonton, there's not a soul at school who takes Liane's side! They all agree that she's behaved disgracefully!"

"Gilberte!" repeated Madame Alvarez, "Say goodbye to Monsieur Lachaille, and run along!"

"Leave her alone, poor child," Gaston Lachaille sighed. "She, at any rate, intends no harm. And it's perfectly true that all's over between Liane and me. You're off to Aunt Alicia's, Gigi? Take my motor-car and send it back for me."

Gilberte gave a little cry, a jump of joy, and hugged Lachaille.

"Thank you, Tonton! Just think of Aunt Alicia's face! The concierge's eyes will be popping from her head!"

Off she went, with the chatter of a young filly not yet shod.

"You spoil her, Gaston," said Madame Alvarez.

But in this she was not altogether speaking the truth. Gaston Lachaille did not know how to "spoil" anyone—even himself. His luxuries were cut and dried: motor-cars, a dreary mansion on the Parc Monceau, Liane's monthly allowance and birthday jewels, champagne and baccarat at Deauville in the summer, at Monte Carlo in the winter. From time to time he would drop a fat check into some charity fund, or finance a new daily paper, or buy a yacht only to resell it almost at once to some Central European monarch: yet from none of this did he get any fun. He would say, as he looked at himself in the glass, "That's the face of a man who is branded." Because of his rather long nose and large dark eyes he was regarded on all sides as easy game. His commercial instinct and rich man's caution stood him in good stead, however; no one had succeeded in robbing him of his pearl studs, of his massive gold or silver cigarette-cases encrusted with precious stones, of his dark sable-lined topcoat.

From the window he watched his motor-car start up. That year, fashionable automobiles were being built with a slightly higher body and a rather wider top, to accommodate the exaggerated hats affected by Caroline Otero, Liane de Pougy, and other conspicuous figures of 1899: and, in consequence, they would sway gently at every turn of the wheel.

"Mamita," said Gaston Lachaille, "you wouldn't make me a cup of camomile?"

"Two rather than one," answered Madame Alvarez. "Sit down, my poor Gaston."

From the depths of a dilapidated armchair she removed some crumpled illustrated papers, a stocking waiting to be darned, and a box of liquorice candies known as *agents de change*. The jilted man settled down into the chair luxuriously, while his hostess put out the tray and two cups.

"Why does the camomile they brew at home always smell of faded chrysanthemums?" sighed Gaston.

"It's simply a matter of taking pains. You may not believe it, Gaston, but I often pick my best camomile flowers in Paris, growing on waste ground, insignificant little flowers you would hardly notice. But they have a taste that is *unesteemable*. My goodness, what beautiful cloth your suit is made of! That deep-woven stripe is as smart as can be. Just the sort of material your father liked! But, I must confess, he would never have carried it so elegantly."

Never more than once during the course of a conversation did Madame Alvarez evoke the memory of an elder Lachaille, whom she claimed to have known intimately. From her former relationship, real or invented, she drew no advantage other than the close relationship of Gaston Lachaille, and the pleasure to be derived from watching a rich man enjoying the comforts of the poor when he made himself at home in her old armchair. Under their gas-blackened ceiling, these three feminine creatures never asked him for pearls, chinchillas, or solitaire diamonds, and they knew how to converse with tact and due solemnity on scandalous topics traditional and recondite. From the age of twelve, Gigi had known that Madame Otero's string of large black pearls were "dipped," that is to say, artificially tinted, while the three strings of her matchlessly graded pearl necklace were worth "a king's ransom"; that Madame de Pougy's seven rows lacked "life"; that Eugénie Fougère's famous diamond bolero was quite worthless; and that no self-respecting woman gadded about, like Madame Antokolski, in a coupé upholstered in mauve satin. She had obediently broken her friendship with a school friend, Lydia Poret, after the girl had shown her a solitaire, set as a ring, presented by the Baron Ephraim.

"A solitaire!" Madame Alvarez had exclaimed. "For a girl of fifteen! Her mother must be mad!"

"But, Grandmamma," pleaded Gigi, "it's not Lydia's fault if the Baron gave it to her!"

"Silence! I'm not blaming the Baron. The Baron knows what is expected of him. But plain common sense should have told the mother to put the ring in a safe at the bank, while waiting."

"While waiting for what, Grandmamma?"

"To see how things turn out."

"Why not in her jewel-case?"

"Because one never knows. Especially as the Baron is the sort of man who might change his mind. If, on the other hand, he has declared himself openly, Madame Poret has only to withdraw her daughter from her studies. Until the matter has been properly cleared up, you will oblige me by not walking home with that little Poret. Who ever heard of such a thing!"

"But supposing she marries, Grandmamma?"

"Marries? Marries whom, pray?"

"Why, the Baron!"

Madame Alvarez and her daughter exchanged glances of stupefaction. "I find the child so discouraging," Andrée had murmured. "She comes from another planet."

"My poor Gaston," said Madame Alvarez, "is it really true, then, that you have broken with her? In some way, it may be the best thing for you; but in others, I'm sure you must find it most upsetting. Whom can one trust, I ask you!"

Poor Gaston listened while he drank the scalding camomile. The taste of it gave him as much comfort as the sight of the plaster-rose on the ceiling, still black from the hanging lamp now "converted to electricity," still faithfully retaining its shade—a vast frilly bell of palest green. Half the contents of a work-basket lay strewn over the dining-room table, from which Gilberte had forgotten to remove her copy-book. Above the upright piano hung an enlarged photograph of Gilberte at eight months, as a pendant to a portrait in oils of Andrée, dressed for her part in *Si j'étais Roi*. The perfectly inoffensive untidiness, the ray of spring sunshine coming through the point-lace curtains, the warmth given out by a little stove kept at a low heat,—all these homely things were like so many soothing potions to the nerves of a jilted and lonely millionaire.

"Are you positively in torment, my poor Gaston?"

"To be exact, I'm not in torment. I'm just very upset, as you say."

"I have no wish to appear inquisitive," said Madame Alvarez, "but how did it all happen? I've read the papers, of course; but can one believe what they say?"

Lachaille tugged at his small waxed moustache, and ran his fingers over his thick, cropped hair.

"Oh, much the same as on previous occasions. She waited for the birthday present, then off she trotted. And, into the bargain, she must needs go and bury herself in such a wretched little hole in Normandy—so stupid of her! Any fool could have discovered that there were only two rooms at the inn, one occupied by Liane, the other by Sandomir, a skating-instructor from the *Palais de Glace*."

"He's Polaire's tea-time waltzing partner, isn't he? Oh, women don't know where to draw the line nowadays! And just after her birthday, too! Oh! it's so tactless! What could be more unladylike!"

Madame Alvarez stirred the teaspoon round and round in her cup, her little finger in the air. When she lowered her gaze, her lids did not quite cover her protuberant eyeballs, and her resemblance to George Sand became marked.

"I'd given her a rope," said Gaston Lachaille. "What you might call a rope—thirty-seven pearls. The middle one as big as the ball of my thumb."

He held out his white, beautifully manicured thumb, to which Madame Alvarez accorded the admiration due to a middle pearl.

"You certainly know how to do things in style," she said. "You came out of it extremely well, Gaston."

"I came out of it with a pair of horns, certainly."

Madame Alvarez did not seem to have heard him.

"If I were you, Gaston, I should try to get your own back on her. I should take up with some society lady."

"That's a nice pill to offer me," said Lachaille, who was absent-mindedly helping himself to the *agents de change*.

"Yes, indeed, I might even say that sometimes the cure may prove worse than the disease," Madame Alvarez continued, tactfully agreeing with him. "Out of the frying-pan into the fire." After which she respected Gaston Lachaille's silence.

The muffled sounds of a piano penetrated through the ceiling. Without a word, the visitor held out his empty cup, and Madame Alvarez refilled it.

"Is the family all right? What news of Aunt Alicia?"

"Oh, my sister, you know, is always the same. She's smart enough to keep herself to herself. She says she would rather live in a splendid past than an ugly present. Her King of Spain, her Milan of Serbia, her Khedive, her rajahs by the half-dozen—or so she would have you believe! She is very considerate to Gigi. She finds her a trifle backward for her age, as indeed she is, and puts her through her paces. Last week, for instance, she taught her how to eat *homard a l'Américaine* in faultless style."

"Whatever for?"

"Alicia says it will be extremely useful. The three great difficulties in a girl's education, she maintains, are *homard a l'Américaine*, a boiled egg, and asparagus. Bad table manners, she says, have broken up many a happy home."

"That can happen," said Lachaille dreamily.

"Oh, Alicia is no fool! And it's just what Gigi requires—she is so greedy! If only her brain worked as well as her jaws! But she might well be a child of ten! And what breathtaking scheme have you got for the Battle of Flowers? Are you going to dazzle us again this year?"

"O Lord no!" groaned Gaston. "I shall take advantage of my misfortune, and save on the red roses."

Madame Alvarez wrung her hands.

"Oh, Gaston, you mustn't do that! If you're not there, the procession will look like a funeral!"

"I don't care what it looks like," said Gaston gloomily.

"You're never going to leave the prize banner to people like Valérie Cheniaguine? Oh, Gaston, we can't allow that!"

"You will have to. Valérie can very well afford it."

"Especially since she does it on the cheap. Gaston, do you know where she went for the ten thousand bunches thrown last year? She had three women tying them up for two days and two nights, and the flowers were bought in the flower market! In the market! Only the four wheels, and the coachman's whip, and the harness trappings bore the label of Lachaume."

"That's a dodge to remember!" said Lachaille, cheering up. "Good Lord! I've finished the liquorice!"

The tap-tap of Gilberte's marching footsteps could be heard crossing the outer room.

"Back already!" said Madame Alvarez. "What's the meaning of this?"

"The meaning," said the girl, "is that Aunt Alicia wasn't in good form. But I've been out in Tonton's 'tuf-tuf.' "

Her lips parted in a bright smile.

"You know, Tonton, all the time I was in your automobile, I put on a martyred expression—like this—as if I was bored to death with every luxury under the sun. I had the time of my life."

She sent her hat flying across the room, and her hair fell tumbling over her forehead and cheeks. She perched herself on a rather high stool, and tucked her knees up under her chin.

"Well, Tonton? You look as if you were dying of boredom. What about

a game of piquet? It's Sunday, and Mamma doesn't come back between
the two performances. Who's been eating all my liquorice? Oh, Tonton,
you can't get away with that! The least you can do is to send me some more
to make up for it."

"Gilberte, your manners!" scolded Madame Alvarez. "Your knees! Gaston
hasn't the time to bother about your liquorice. Pull down your skirts. Gaston,
would you like me to send her to her room?"

Young Lachaille, with one eye on the dirty pack of cards in Gilberte's
hand, was longing simultaneously to give way to tears, to confide his sorrows,
to go to sleep in the old armchair, and to play piquet.

"Let the child stay! In this room I can relax. It's restful. Gigi, I'll play
you for twenty pounds of sugar."

"Your sugar's not very tempting. I much prefer sweets."

"It's the same thing. And sugar is better for you than sweets."

"You only say that because you make it."

"Gilberte, you forget yourself!"

A smile enlivened the mournful eyes of Gaston Lachaille.

"Let her say what she likes, Mamita. And if I lose, Gigi, what would
you like? A pair of silk stockings?"

The corners of Gilberte's big childish mouth fell.

"Silk stockings make my legs itch. I would rather. . . ."

She raised the snub-nosed face of an angel towards the ceiling, put her
head on one side, and tossed her curls from one cheek to the other.

"I would rather have an *eau-de-nil* Persephone corset, with rococo roses
embroidered on the garters. No, I'd rather have a music-case."

"Are you studying music now?"

"No, but my older friends at school carry their copy-books in music-cases,
because it makes them look like students at the Conservatoire."

"Gilberte, you are making too free!" said Madame Alvarez.

"You shall have your case, and your liquorice. Cut, Gigi."

The next moment, the heir of Lachaille-Sugar was deep in the game. His
prominent nose, large enough to appear false, and his slightly negroid eyes
did not in the least intimidate his opponent. With her elbows on the table,
her shoulders on a level with her ears, and her blue eyes and red cheeks at
their most vivid, she looked like a tipsy page. They both played passionately, almost in silence, exchanging occasional insults under their breath.
"*You spindly spider! you sorrel run to seed!*" Lachaille muttered. "*You old
crow's beak!*" the girl countered. The March twilight deepened over the narrow street.

"Please don't think I want you to go, Gaston," said Madame Alvarez,
"but it's half-past seven. Will you excuse me while I just see about our
dinner?"

"Half-past seven!" cried Lachaille, "and I'm supposed to be dining at
Larue with de Dion, Feydeau, and one of the Barthous! This must be the
last hand, Gigi."

"Why one of the Barthous?" asked Gilberte. "Are there several of them?"

"Two. One handsome and the other less so. The best known is the least handsome."

"That's not fair," said Gilberte. "And Feydeau, who's he?"

Lachaille plopped down his cards in amazement.

"Well, I declare! She doesn't know who Feydeau is! Don't you ever go to a play?"

"Hardly ever, Tonton."

"Don't you like the theatre?"

"I'm not mad about it. And Grandmamma and Aunt Alicia both say that going to plays prevents one from thinking about the serious side of life. Don't tell Grandmamma I told you."

She lifted the weight of her hair away from her ears, and let it fall forward again. "Phew!" she sighed. "This mane does make me hot!"

"And what do they mean by the serious side of life?"

"Oh, I don't know it all off by heart, Uncle Gaston. And, what's more, they don't always agree about it. Grandmamma says: 'Don't read novels, they only depress you. Don't put on powder, it ruins the complexion. Don't wear stays, they spoil the figure. Don't dawdle and gaze at shop windows when you're by yourself. Don't get to know the families of your school friends, especially not the fathers who wait at the gates to fetch their daughters home from school.'"

She spoke very rapidly, panting between words like a child who has been running.

"And on top of that, Aunt Alicia goes off on another tack! I've reached the age when I can wear stays, and I should take lessons in dancing and deportment, and I should be aware of what's going on, and know the meaning of 'caret,' and not be taken in by the clothes that actresses wear. 'It's quite simple,' she tells me, 'of all the dresses you see on the stage, nineteen out of twenty would look ridiculous in the paddock.' In fact, my head is fit to split with it all! What will you be eating at Larue this evening, Tonton?"

"How should I know! *Filets de sole aux moules,* for a change. And of course, saddle of lamb with truffles. Do get on with the game, Gigi! I've got a point of five."

"That won't get you anywhere. I've got all the cards in the pack. Here, at home, we're having the warmed up remains of the *cassoulet.* I'm very fond of *cassoulet.*"

"A plain dish of *cassoulet* with bacon rind," said Inez Alvarez modestly, as she came in. "Goose was exorbitant this week."

"I'll have one sent to you from Bon-Abri," said Gaston.

"Thank you very much, Gaston. Gigi, help Monsieur Lachaille on with his overcoat. Fetch him his hat and stick!"

When Lachaille had gone, rather sulky after a regretful sniff at the warmed up *cassoulet,* Madame Alvarez turned to her granddaughter.

"Will you please inform me, Gilberte, why it was you returned so early from Aunt Alicia's? I didn't ask you in front of Gaston. Family matters must never be discussed in front of a third person, remember that!"

"There's no mystery about it, Grandmamma. Aunt Alicia was wearing her little lace cap to show me she had a headache. She said to me, 'I'm not very well.' I said to her, 'Oh! Then I mustn't tire you out, I'll go home again.' She said to me, 'Sit down and rest for five minutes.' 'Oh!' I said to her, 'I'm not tired. I drove here.' 'You drove here!' she said to me, raising her hands like this. As you may imagine, I had kept the motor-car waiting a few minutes, to show Aunt Alicia. 'Yes,' I said to her, 'the four-seater de-Dion-Bouton-with-the-collapsible-hood, which Tonton lent me while he was paying a call on us. He has had a rumpus with Liane.' 'Who do you think you're talking to?' she says to me, 'I've not yet got one foot in the grave! I'm still kept informed about public events when they're important. I know that he has had a rumpus with that great lamp-post of a woman. Well, you'd better run along home, and not bother about a poor ill old creature like me.' She waved to me from the window as I got into the motor-car."

Madame Alvarez pursed her lips.

"A poor ill old creature! She has never suffered so much as a cold in her life! I like that! What . . ."

"Grandmamma, do you think he'll remember my liquorice and the music-case?"

Madame Alvarez slowly lifted her heavy eyes towards the ceiling.

"Perhaps, my child, perhaps."

"But, as he lost, he owes them to me, doesn't he?"

"Yes, yes, he owes them to you. Perhaps you'll get them after all. Slip on your pinafore, and set the table. Put away your cards."

"Yes, Grandmamma. Grandmamma, what did he tell you about Madame Liane? Is it true she ran out on him with Sandomir and the rope of pearls?"

"In the first place, one doesn't say 'ran out on' anyone. In the second, come here and let me tighten your ribbon, so that your curls won't get soaked in the soup. And finally, the sayings and doings of a person who has broken the rules of etiquette are not for your ears. These happen to be Gaston's private affairs."

"But, Grandmamma, they are no longer private, since everyone's talking about them, and the whole thing came out in *Gil Blas*."

"Silence! All you need to know is that the conduct of Madame Liane d'Exelmans has been the reverse of sensible. The ham for your mother is between two plates: you will put it in the larder."

Gilberte was asleep when her mother—Andrée Alvar, in small type on the Opéra-Comique play-bills—returned home. Madame Alvarez, the elder, seated at a game of patience, inquired from force of habit whether she was not too tired. Following polite family custom, Andrée reproached her mother for having waited up, and Madame Alvarez made her ritual reply.

"I shouldn't sleep in peace unless I knew you were in. There is some ham, and a little bowl of warm *cassoulet*. And some stewed prunes. The beer is on the window-sill."

"The child is in bed?"

"Of course."

Andrée Alvar made a solid meal—pessimists have good appetites. She still looked pretty in theatrical make-up. Without it, the rims of her eyes were pink and her lips colorless. For this reason, Aunt Alicia declared, Andrée never met with the admiration in real life that she gained on the stage.

"Did you sing well, my child?"

"Yes, I sang well. But where does it get me? All the applause goes to Tiphaine, as you may well imagine. Oh dear, oh dear, I really don't think I can bear to go on with this sort of life."

"It was your own choice. But you would bear it much better," said Madame Alvarez sententiously, "if you had someone! It's your loneliness that gets on your nerves, and you take such black views. You're behaving contrary to nature."

"Oh, Mother, don't start that all over again, I'm tired enough as it is. What news is there?"

"None. Everyone's talking of Gaston's break with Liane."

"Yes, they certainly are! Even in the green room at the Opéra-Comique, which can hardly be called up-to-date."

"It's an event of world-wide interest," said Madame Alvarez.

"Is there talk of who's in the running?"

"I should think not! It's far too recent. He is in full mourning, so to speak. Can you believe it, at a quarter to eight he was sitting exactly where you are now, playing a game of piquet with Gigi? He says he has no wish to attend the Battle of Flowers."

"Not really!"

"Yes. If he doesn't go, it will cause a great deal of talk. I advised him to think twice before taking such a decision."

"They were saying at the *Théâtre* that a certain music-hall artiste might stand a chance," said Andrée. "The one billed as the Cobra at the Olympia. It seems she does an acrobatic turn, and is brought on in a basket hardly big enough for a fox-terrier, and from this she uncurls like a snake."

Madame Alvarez protruded her heavy lower lip in contempt.

"What an idea! Gaston Lachaille has not sunk to that level! A music-hall performer! Do him the justice to admit that, as befits a bachelor of his standing, he has always confined himself to the great ladies of the profession."

"A fine pack of bitches!" murmured Andrée.

"Be more careful how you express yourself, my child. Calling people and things by their names has never done anyone any good. Gaston's mistresses have all had an air about them. A liaison with a great professional lady is the only suitable way for him to wait for a great marriage, always supposing that some day he does marry. Whatever may happen, we're in the front row when anything fresh turns up. Gaston has such confidence in me! I wish you had seen him asking me for camomile! A boy, a regular boy! Indeed, he is only thirty-three. And all that wealth weighs so heavily on his shoulders."

Andrée's pink eyelids blinked ironically.

"Pity him, Mother, if you like. I'm not complaining, but all the time we've known Gaston, he has never given you anything except his confidence."

"He owes us nothing. And thanks to him we've always had sugar for our jams, and, from time to time, for my *curaçao*; and birds from his farm, and odds and ends for the child."

"If you're satisfied with that!"

Madame Alvarez held high her majestic head.

"Perfectly satisfied. And even if I was not, what difference would it make?"

"In fact, as far as we're concerned, Gaston Lachaille, rich as he is, behaves as if he wasn't rich at all. Supposing we were in real straits! Would he come to our rescue, do you suppose?"

Madame Alvarez placed her hand on her heart.

"I'm convinced that he would," she said. And after a pause, she added, "But I would rather not have to ask him."

Andrée picked up the *Journal* again, in which there was a photograph of Liane the ex-mistress. "When you take a good look at her, she's not so extraordinary."

"You're wrong," retorted Madame Alvarez, "she is extraordinary. Otherwise she would not be so famous. Successes and celebrity are not a matter of luck. You talk like those scatterbrains who say, 'Seven rows of pearls would look every bit as well on me as on Madame de Pougy. She certainly cuts a dash—but so could I.' Such nonsense makes me laugh. Take what's left of the camomile to bathe your eyes."

"Thank you, Mother. Did the child go to Aunt Alicia's?"

"She did indeed, and in Gaston's motor-car, what's more! He lent it to her. It can go forty miles an hour, I believe! She was in seventh heaven."

"Poor lamb, I wonder what she'll make of her life. She's quite capable of ending up as a mannequin or a saleswoman. She's so backward. At her age, I—"

There was no indulgence in the glance Madame Alvarez gave her daughter.

"Don't boast too much about what you were doing when you were her age. If I remember rightly, at her age you were snapping your fingers at Monsieur Mennesson and all his flour-mills, though he was perfectly ready to make you your fortune. Instead, you must needs bolt with a wretched music master."

Andrée Alvar kissed her mother's lustrous plaits.

"My darling mother, don't curse me at this hour, I'm so sleepy. Goodnight, Mother. I've a rehearsal tomorrow at a quarter to one. I'll eat at the dairy during the entr'acte; don't bother about me."

She yawned and walked in the dark through the little room where her daughter was asleep. All she could see of Gilberte in the obscurity was a bush of hair and the Russian braid of her nightdress. She locked herself into the exiguous bathroom and, late though it was, lit the gas under a kettle. Madame Alvarez had instilled into her progeny, among other virtues, a respect for certain rites. One of her maxims was, "You can, at a pinch, leave the face till the morning, when travelling or pressed for time. For a woman, attention to the lower parts is the first law of self-respect."

The last to go to bed, Madame Alvarez was the first to rise, and allowed the daily cleaning woman no hand in preparing the breakfast coffee. She slept in the dining-sitting room, on a divan-bed, and, at the stroke of half-past seven, she opened the door to the papers, the quart of milk, and the daily maid—who was carrying the others. By eight o'clock she had taken out her curling-pins, and her beautiful coils of hair were dressed and smooth. At ten minutes to nine, Gilberte left for school, clean and tidy, her hair well-brushed. At ten o'clock Madame Alvarez was "thinking about" the mid-day meal, that is, she got into her mackintosh, slipped her arm through the handle of her shopping net, and set off to market.

Today, as on all other days, she made sure that her granddaughter would not be late; she placed the coffee-pot and the jug of milk piping hot on the table, and unfolded the newspaper while waiting for her. Gilberte came in fresh as a flower, smelling of lavender-water, with some vestiges of sleep still clinging to her. A cry from Madame Alvarez made her fully wide awake.

"Call your mother, Gigi! Liane d'Exelmans has committed suicide."

The child replied with a long drawn-out "Oooh!" and asked, "Is she dead?"

"Of course not. She knows what she's about."

"How did she do it, Grandmamma? A revolver?"

Madame Alvarez looked pityingly at her granddaughter.

"The idea! Laudanum, as usual. '*Doctors Morèze and Pelledoux, who have never left the heart-broken beauty's bedside, cannot yet answer for her life, but their diagnosis is reassuring . . .*' My own diagnosis is that if Madame d'Exelmans goes on playing that game, she'll end by ruining her stomach."

"The last time she killed herself, Grandmamma, was for the sake of Prince Georgevitch, wasn't it?"

"Where are your brains, my darling? It was for Count Berthou de Sauveterre."

"Oh, so it was. And what will Tonton do now, do you think?"

A dreamy look passed across the huge eyes of Madame Alvarez.

"It's a toss-up, my child. We shall know everything in good time, even if he starts by refusing to give an interview to anybody. You must always start by refusing to give an interview to anybody. Then later you can fill the front page. Tell the concierge, by the way, to get us the evening papers. Have you had enough to eat? Did you have your second cup of milk, and your two pieces of bread and butter? Put on your gloves before you go out. Don't dawdle on the way. I'm going to call your mother. What a story! Andrée, are you asleep? Oh, so you're out of bed! Andrée, Liane has committed suicide!"

"That's a nice change," muttered Andrée. "She has only the one idea in her head, that woman, but she sticks to it."

"You've not taken out your curlers yet, Andrée?"

"And have my hair go limp in the middle of rehearsal? No thank you!"

Madame Alvarez ran her eyes over her daughter, from the spiky tips of her curlers to the felt slippers. "It's plain that there's no man here for you to bother about, my child! A man in the house soon cures a woman of traipsing about in dressing-gown and slippers. What an excitement, this suicide! Unsuccessful, of course."

Andrée's pallid lips parted in a contemptuous smile: "It's getting too boring—the way she takes laudanum as if it was castor oil!"

"Anyhow, who cares about her? It's the Lachaille heir who matters. This is the first time such a thing has happened to him. He's already had—let me see. He's had Gentiane, who stole his private papers; then that foreigner, who tried to force him into marriage, but Liane is his first suicide. In such circumstances, a man so much in the public eye has to be extremely careful about what line he takes."

"Hm! He'll be bursting with pride, you may be sure."

"And with good reason, too," said Madame Alvarez. "We shall be seeing great things before very long. I wonder what Alicia will have to say about the situation."

"She'll do her best to make a mountain of a molehill."

"Alicia is no angel. But I must confess that she is long-sighted. And that without ever leaving her room!"

"She's no need to, since she has the telephone. Mother, won't you have one put in here?"

"It's expensive," said Madame Alvarez, thoughtfully. "We only just manage to make both ends meet, as it is. The telephone is of real use only to important businessmen, or to women who have something to hide. Now, if you were to change your mode of life—and I'm only putting it forward as a supposition—and if Gigi were to start on a life of her own, I should be the first to say, 'We'll have the telephone put in.' But we haven't reached that point yet, unfortunately."

She allowed herself a single sigh, pulled on her rubber gloves, and coolly set about her household chores. Thanks to her care, the modest flat was growing old without too many signs of deterioration. She retained, from her past life, the honorable habits of women who have lost their honor, and these she taught to her daughter and her daughter's daughter. Sheets never stayed on the beds longer than ten days, and the combination char- and washerwoman told everyone that the chemises and drawers of the ladies of Madame Alvarez' household were changed more often than she could count, and so were the table napkins. At any moment, at the cry of "Gigi, take off your shoes!" Gilberte had to remove shoes and stockings, exhibit white feet to the closest inspection, and announce the least suspicion of a corn.

During the week following Madame d'Exelmans' suicide, Lachaille's reactions were somewhat incoherent. He engaged the stars of the National Musical Academy to dance at a midnight fête held at his own house, and, wishing to give a supper party at the Pré-Catalan, he arranged for that restaurant to open a fortnight earlier than was their custom. The clowns, Footit *et* Chocolat, did a turn: Rita del Erido caracoled on horseback between the supper tables, wearing a divided skirt of white lace flounces, a white hat on her black hair with white ostrich feathers frothing round the relentless beauty of her face. Indeed, Paris mistakenly proclaimed, such was her beauty, that Gaston Lachaille was hoisting her astride a throne of sugar. Twenty-four hours later, Paris was undeceived. For in the false prophecies it had published, *Gil Blas* nearly lost the subsidy it received from Gaston Lachaille. A specialized weekly, *Paris en amour*, provided another red herring, under the headline: "Young Yankee millionairess makes no secret of weakness for French sugar."

Madame Alvarez' ample bust shook with incredulous laughter when she read the daily papers: she had received her information from none other than Gaston Lachaille in person. Twice in ten days, he had found time to drop in for a cup of camomile, to sink into the depths of the now sagging conch-shaped armchair, and there forget his business worries and his dislike of being unattached. He even brought Gigi an absurd Russian leather music-case with a silver-gilt clasp, and twenty boxes of liquorice. Madame Alvarez was given a *pâté de foie gras* and six bottles of champagne, and of these bounties Tonton Lachaille partook by inviting himself to dinner. Throughout the meal, Gilberte regaled them rather tipsily with tittle-tattle about her school, and later won Gaston's gold pencil at piquet. He lost with good grace, recovered his spirits, laughed, and, pointing to the child, said to Madame Alvarez, "There's my best pal!" Madame Alvarez' Spanish eyes moved with slow watchfulness from Gigi's reddened cheeks and white teeth to Lachaille, who was pulling her hair by the fistful. "You little devil, you had the fourth king up your sleeve all the time!"

It was at this moment that Andrée, coming back from the Opéra-Comique, looked at Gigi's disheveled head rolling against Lachaille's sleeve, and saw the tears of excited laughter in her lovely slate-blue eyes. She said nothing, and accepted a glass of champagne, then another, and yet another. After her third glass, Gaston Lachaille was threatened with the Bell Song from *Lakmé*, at which point Andrée's mother led her away to bed.

The following day, no one spoke of this family party except Gilberte, who exclaimed, "Never, never in all my life, have I laughed so much! And the pencil is real gold!" Her unreserved chatter met with a strange silence, or rather with "Now then, Gigi, try to be a little more serious!" thrown out almost absent-mindedly.

After that, Gaston Lachaille let a fortnight go by without giving a sign of life, and the Alvarez family gathered its information from the papers only.

"Did you see, Andrée? In the Gossip Column it says that Monsieur

Gaston Lachaille has left for Monte Carlo. *The reason for this seems to be of a sentimental nature—a secret that we respect.* What next!"

"Would you believe it, Grandmamma, Lydia Poret was saying at the dancing class that Liane travelled on the same train as Tonton, but in another compartment! Grandmamma, do you think it can be true?"

Madame Alvarez shrugged her shoulders.

"If it was true, how on earth would those Porets know? Have they become friends with Monsieur Lachaille all of a sudden?"

"No, but Lydia Poret heard the story in her aunt's dressing room at the Comédie Française."

Madame Alvarez exchanged looks with her daughter.

"In her dressing room! That explains everything!" she exclaimed, for she held the theatrical profession in contempt, although Andrée worked so hard. When Madame Emilienne d'Alençon had decided to present performing rabbits, and Madame de Pougy—shyer on the stage than any young girl—had amused herself by miming the part of Columbine in spangled black tulle, Madame Alvarez had stigmatised them both in a single phrase, "What! have they sunk to that?"

"Grandmamma, tell me, Grandmamma, do you know him, this Prince Radziwill?" Gilberte went on again.

"What's come over the child today? Has she been bitten by a flea? Which Prince Radziwill, to begin with? There's more than one."

"I don't know," said Gigi. "The one who's getting married. Among the list of presents, it says here, '*are three writing-sets in malachite.*' What is malachite?"

"Oh, you're being tiresome, child. If he's getting married, he's no longer interesting."

"But if Tonton got married, wouldn't he be interesting either?"

"It all depends. It would be interesting if he were to marry his mistress. When Prince Cheniaguine married Valérie d'Aigreville, it was obvious that the life she had led him for the past fifteen years was all he wanted; scenes, plates flung across the room, and reconciliations in the middle of the restaurant Durand, Place de la Madeleine. Clearly, she was a woman who knew how to make herself valued. But all that is too complicated for you, my poor Gigi."

"And do you think it's to marry Liane that they've gone away together?"

Madame Alvarez pressed her forehead against the window pane, and seemed to be consulting the spring sunshine, which bestowed upon the street a sunny side and one with shade.

"No," she said, "not if I know anything about anything. I must have a word with Alicia. Gigi, come with me as far as her house; you can leave me there and find your way back along the quais. It will give you some fresh air, since, it would seem, one must have fresh air nowadays. I have never been in the habit of taking the air more than twice a year, myself, at Cabourg and at Monte Carlo. And I am none the worse for that."

That evening Madame Alvarez came in so late that the family dined off tepid soup, cold meat, and some cakes sent round by Aunt Alicia. To Gilberte's "Well, what did she have to say?" she presented an icy front, and answered in clarion tones.

"She says that she is going to teach you how to eat ortolans."

"Lovely!" cried Gilberte. "And what did she say about the summer frock she promised me?"

"She said she would see. And that there's no reason why you should be displeased with the result."

"Oh!" said Gilberte, gloomily.

"She also wants you to go to luncheon with her on Thursday, sharp at twelve."

"With you, too, Grandmamma?"

Madame Alvarez looked at the willowy slip of a girl facing her across the table, at her high, rosy cheekbones beneath eyes as blue as an evening sky, at her strong even teeth biting a fresh-colored but slightly chapped lip, and at the primitive splendor of her ash-gold hair.

"No," she said at last. "Without me."

Gilberte got up and wound an arm about her grandmother's neck.

"The way you said that, Grandmamma, surely doesn't mean that you're going to send me to live with Aunt Alicia? I don't want to leave here, Grandmamma!"

Madame Alvarez cleared her throat, gave a little cough, and smiled.

"Goodness gracious! what a foolish creature you are! Leave here! Why, my poor Gigi, I'm not scolding you, but you've not reached the first stage towards leaving."

For a bell-pull, Aunt Alicia had hung from her front door a length of bead-embroidered braid on a background of twining green vine-leaves and purple grapes. The door itself, varnished and revarnished till it glistened, shone with the glow of a dark brown caramel. From the very threshold, where she was admitted by a "man-servant," Gilberte enjoyed in her undiscriminating way an atmosphere of discreet luxury. The carpet, spread with Persian rugs, seemed to lend her wings. After hearing Madame Alvarez pronounce her sister's Louis XV little drawing room to be "boredom itself," Gilberte echoed her words by saying: "Aunt Alicia's drawing room is very pretty, but it's boredom itself!" reserving her admiration for the dining room, furnished in pale almost golden lemon wood dating from the Directoire, quite plain but for the grain of a wood as transparent as wax. "I shall buy myself a set like that one day," Gigi had once said in all innocence.

"In the Faubourg Antoine, I dare say," Aunt Alicia had answered teasingly, with a smile of her cupid's bow mouth and a flash of small teeth.

She was seventy years old. Her fastidious taste was everywhere apparent: in her silver-grey bedroom with its red Chinese vases, in her narrow white bathroom as warm as a hot-house, and in her robust health, concealed by a pretence of delicacy. The men of her generation, when trying to describe Alicia de Saint-Efflam, fumbled for words and could only exclaim, "Ah, my deah fellow!" or "Nothing could give you the faintest idea . . ." Those who had known her intimately produced photographs which younger men found ordinary enough. "Was she really so lovely? You wouldn't think so from her photographs!" Looking at portraits of her, old admirers would pause for an instant, recollecting the turn of a wrist like a swan's neck, the tiny ear, the profile revealing a delicious kinship between the heart-shaped mouth and the wide-cut eyelids with their long lashes.

Gilberte kissed the pretty old lady, who was wearing a peak of black Chantilly lace on her white hair, and, on her slightly dumpy figure, a tea-gown of shot taffeta.

"You have one of your headaches, Aunt Alicia?"

"I'm not sure yet," replied Aunt Alicia, "it depends on the luncheon. Come quickly, the eggs are ready! Take off your coat! What on earth is that dress?"

"One of Mamma's, altered to fit me. Are they difficult eggs today?"

"Not at all. *Oeufs brouillés aux croutons*. The ortolans are not difficult, either. And you shall have chocolate cream. So shall I."

With her young voice, a touch of pink on her amiable wrinkles, and lace on her white hair, Aunt Alicia was the perfect stage marquise. Gilberte had the greatest reverence for her aunt. In sitting down to table in her presence, she would pull her skirt up behind, join her knees, hold her elbows close to her sides, straighten her shoulder blades, and to all appearances become the perfect young lady. She would remember what she had been taught, break her bread quickly, eat with her mouth shut, and take care, when cutting her meat, not to let her forefinger reach the blade of her knife.

Today her hair, severely tied back in a heavy knot at the nape of her neck, disclosed the fresh line of her forehead and ears, and a very powerful throat, rising from the rather ill-cut opening of her altered dress. This was a dingy blue, the bodice pleated about a let-in piece, and to cheer up this patchwork, three rows of mohair braid had been sewn round the hem of the skirt, and three times three rows of mohair braid round the sleeves, between the wrist and the elbow.

Aunt Alicia, sitting opposite her niece and examining her through fine dark eyes, could find no fault.

"How old are you?" she asked suddenly.

"The same as I was the other day, Aunt. Fifteen and a half. Aunt, what do you really think of this business of Tonton Gaston?"

"Why? Does it interest you?"

"Of course, Aunt. It worries me. If Tonton takes up with another lady, he won't come and play piquet with us any more or drink camomile tea—at least not for some time. That would be a shame."

"That's one way of looking at it, certainly."

Aunt Alicia examined her niece critically, through narrowed eyelids.

"Do you work hard, in class? Who are your friends? Ortolans should be cut in two, with one quick stroke of the knife, and no grating of the blade on the plate. Bite up each half. The bones don't matter. Go on eating while you answer my question, but don't talk with your mouth full. You must manage it. If I can, you can. What friends have you made?"

"None, Aunt. Grandmamma won't even let me have tea with the families of my school friends."

"She is quite right. Apart from that, there is no one who follows you, no little clerk hanging round your skirts? No schoolboy? No older man? I warn you, I shall know at once if you lie to me."

Gilberte gazed at the bright face of the imperious old lady who was questioning her so sharply.

"Why, no, Aunt, no one. Has somebody been telling you tales about me? I am always on my own. And why does Grandmamma stop me from accepting invitations?"

"She is right, for once. You would only be invited by ordinary people, that is to say, useless people."

"And what about us? Aren't we ordinary people ourselves?"

"No."

"What makes these ordinary people inferior to us?"

"They have weak heads and dissolute bodies. Besides, they are married. But I don't think you understand."

"Yes, Aunt, I understand that we don't marry."

"Marriage is not forbidden to us. Instead of marrying 'at once,' it sometimes happens that we marry 'at last.'"

"But does that prevent me from seeing girls of my own age?"

"Yes. Are you bored at home? Well, be a little bored. It's not a bad thing. Boredom helps one to make decisions. What is the matter? Tears? The tears of a silly child who is backward for her age. Have another ortolan."

Aunt Alicia, with three glittering fingers, grasped the stem of her glass and raised it in a toast.

"To you and me, Gigi! You shall have an Egyptian cigarette with your coffee. On condition that you do not wet the end of your cigarette, and that you don't spit out specks of tobacco—going *ptu, ptu.* I shall also give you a note to the *première vendeuse* at Béchoff-David, an old friend of mine who was not a success. Your wardrobe is going to be changed. Nothing venture, nothing gain."

The dark blue eyes gleamed. Gilberte stammered with joy.

"Aunt! Aunt! I'm going to . . . to Bé—"

"—choff-David. But I thought you weren't interested in clothes?" Gilberte blushed.

"Aunt, I'm not interested in home-made clothes."

"I sympathize with you. Can it be that you have taste? When you think of looking your best, how do you see yourself dressed?"

"Oh, but I know just what would suit me, Aunt! I've seen—"

"Explain yourself without gestures. The moment you gesticulate you look common."

"I've seen a dress . . . oh, a dress created for Madame Lucy Gérard! Hundreds of tiny ruffles of pearl-grey silk muslin from top to bottom. And then a dress of lavender-blue cloth cut out on a black velvet foundation, the cut-out design making a sort of peacock's tail on the train."

The small hand with its precious stones flashed through the air.

"Enough! Enough! I see your fancy is to be dressed like a leading *comédienne* at the Théâtre Français,—and don't take that as a compliment! Come and pour out the coffee. And without jerking up the lip of the coffee-pot to prevent the drop from falling. I'd rather have a foot-bath in my saucer than see you juggling like a waiter in a café."

The next hour passed very quickly for Gilberte: Aunt Alicia had unlocked a casket of jewels to use for a lesson that dazzled her.

"What is that, Gigi?"

"A marquise diamond."

"We say, a marquise-shaped brilliant. And that?"

"A topaz."

Aunt Alicia threw up her hands and the sunlight, glancing off her rings, set off a myriad scintillations.

"A topaz! I have suffered many humiliations, but this surpasses them all. A topaz among my jewels! Why not an aquamarine or a chrysolite? It's a yellow diamond, little goose, and you won't often see its like. And this?"

Gilberte half opened her mouth, as if in a dream.

"Oh! That's an emerald. Oh, how beautiful it is!"

Aunt Alicia slipped the large square-cut emerald on one of her thin fingers and was lost in silence.

"Do you see," she said in a hushed voice, "that almost blue flame darting about in the depths of the green light? Only the most beautiful emeralds contain that miracle of elusive blue."

"Who gave it to you, Aunt?" Gilberte dared to ask.

"A king," said Aunt Alicia simply.

"A great king?"

"No. A little one. Great kings do not give very fine stones."

"Why not?"

For a fleeting moment, Aunt Alicia proffered a glimpse of her tiny white teeth.

"If you want my opinion, it's because they don't want to. Between ourselves, the little ones don't either."

"Then who does give great big stones?"

"Who? The shy. The proud, too. And the bounders, because they think that to give a monster jewel is a sign of good breeding. Sometimes a woman does, to humiliate a man. Never wear second-rate jewels, wait till the really good ones come to you."

"And if they don't?"

"Well, then it can't be helped. Rather than a wretched little diamond full of flaws, wear a simple, plainly inexpensive ring. In that case you can say, 'It's a memento. I never part with it, day or night.' Don't ever wear artistic jewelry, it wrecks a woman's reputation."

"What is an artistic jewel?"

"It all depends. A mermaid in gold with eyes of chrysoprase. An Egyptian scarab. A large engraved amethyst. A not very heavy bracelet said to have been chased by a master-hand. A lyre or star, mounted as a brooch. A studded tortoise. In a word, all of them, frightful. Never wear baroque pearls, not even as hat-pins. Beware, above all things, of family jewels!"

"But Grandmamma has a beautiful cameo, set as a medallion."

"There are no beautiful cameos," said Alicia, with a toss of the head. "There are precious stones and pearls. There are white, yellow, blue, blue-white or pink diamonds. We won't speak of black diamonds, they're not worth mentioning. Then there are rubies—when you can be sure of them; sapphires, when they come from Kashmir; emeralds, provided they have no fatal flaw, or are not too light in color, or have a yellowish tint."

"Aunt, I'm very fond of opals, too."

"I am very sorry, but you are not to wear them. I won't allow it."

Dumbfounded, Gilberte remained for a moment open-mouthed.

"Oh! Do you too, Aunt, really believe that they bring bad luck?"

"Why in the world not? You silly little creature," Alicia went bubbling on, "you must pretend to believe in such things. Believe in opals, believe— let's see, what can I suggest—in turquoises that die, in the evil eye . . ."

"But," said Gigi, haltingly, "those are . . . are superstitions!"

"Of course they are, child. They also go by the name of weaknesses. A pretty little collection of weaknesses, and a terror of spiders, are indispensable stock-in-trade with men."

"Why, Aunt?"

The old lady closed the casket, and kept Gilberte kneeling before her.

"Because nine men out of ten are superstitious, nineteen out of twenty believe in the evil eye, and ninety-eight out of a hundred are afraid of spiders. They forgive us—oh! for many things, but not for the absence in us of their own failings," she said. "What makes you sigh?"

"I shall never remember all that!"

"The important thing is not for *you* to remember, but for me to know it."

"Aunt, what is a writing-set in . . . in malachite?"

"Always a calamity. But where on earth did you pick up such terms?"

"From the list of presents at grand weddings, Aunt, printed in the papers."

"Nice reading! But, at least you can gather from it what kind of presents you should never give, or accept."

While speaking, she began to touch here and there the young face on a level with her own, with the sharp pointed nail of her index finger. She lifted one slightly chapped lip, inspected the spotless enamel of the teeth.

"A fine jaw, my girl! With such teeth, I should have gobbled up Paris, and the rest of the world into the bargain. As it was, I had a good bite out of it. What's this you've got here? A small pimple? You shouldn't have a small pimple near your nose. And this? You've pinched a blackhead. You've no business to have such things, or to pinch them. I'll give you some of my astringent lotion. You mustn't eat anything from the pork-butchers' except cooked ham. You don't put on powder?"

"Grandmamma won't let me."

"I should hope not. You go you-know-where regularly? Let me smell your breath. Not that it means anything at this hour, you've just had luncheon."

She laid her hands on Gigi's shoulders.

"Pay attention to what I'm going to say. You have it in your power to please. You have an impossible little nose, a nondescript mouth, cheeks rather like the wife of a moujik—"

"Oh, Aunt!" sighed Gilberte.

"But, with your eyes and eyelashes, your teeth, and your hair, you can get away with it, if you're not a perfect fool. As for the rest—"

She cupped her hands like conch-shells over Gigi's bosom and smiled.

"A promise, but a pretty promise, neatly moulded. Don't eat too many almonds, they add weight to the breasts. Ah! remind me to teach you how to choose cigars."

Gilberte opened her eyes so wide that the tips of her lashes touched her eyebrows.

"Why?"

She received a little tap on the cheek.

"Because—because I do nothing without good reason. If I take you in hand at all, I must do it thoroughly. Once a woman understands the tastes of a man, cigars included, and once a man knows what pleases a woman, they may be said to be well matched."

"And then they fight," concluded Gigi with a knowing air.

"What do you mean, they fight?"

The old lady looked at Gigi in consternation.

"Ah!" she added, "You certainly never invented the triple mirror! Come, you little psychologist! Let me give you a note for Madame Henriette at Béchoff."

While her aunt was writing at a miniature rose-pink escritoire, Gilberte breathed in the scent of the fastidiously furnished room. Without wanting them for herself, she examined the objects she knew so well but hardly appreciated: Cupid, the Archer, pointing to the hours on the mantelpiece; two rather daring pictures; a bed like the basin of a fountain and its chinchilla coverlet; a rosary of small seed pearls and the New Testament on the bedside table; two red Chinese vases fitted as lamps—a happy note against the grey of the walls.

"Run along, my little one. I shall send for you again quite soon. Don't forget to ask Victor for the cake you're to take home. Gently, don't disarrange my hair! And remember, I shall have my eye on you as you leave the house. Woe betide you if you march like a guardsman, or drag your feet behind you!"

The month of May fetched Gaston Lachaille back to Paris, and brought to Gilberte two well-cut dresses and a light-weight coat—"a sack-coat like

Cléo de Mérode's" she called it—as well as hats and boots and shoes. To these she added, on her own account, a few curls over the forehead, which cheapened her appearance. She paraded in front of Gaston in a blue and white dress reaching almost to the ground. "A full seven and a half yards round, Tonton, my skirt measures!" She was more than proud of her slender waist, held in by a grosgrain sash with a silver buckle; but she tried every dodge to free her lovely strong neck from its whale-bone collar of "imitation Venetian point" which matched the tucks of the bodice. The full sleeves and wide flounced skirt of blue and white striped silk rustled deliciously, and Gilberte delighted in picking at the sleeves, to puff them out just below the shoulder.

"You remind me of a performing monkey," Lachaille said to her. "I liked you much better in your old tartan dress. In that uncomfortable collar you look just like a hen with a full crop. Take a peep at yourself!"

Feeling a little ruffled, Gilberte turned round to face the looking-glass. She had a lump in one of her cheeks caused by a large caramel, out of a box sent all the way from Nice at Gaston's order.

"I've heard a good deal about you, Tonton," she retorted, "but I've never heard it said that you had any taste in clothes."

He stared, almost choking, at this newly fledged young woman, then turned to Madame Alvarez.

"Charming manners you've taught her! I congratulate you!"

Whereupon he left the house without drinking his camomile tea, and Madame Alvarez wrung her hands.

"Look what you've done to us now, my poor Gigi!"

"I know," said Gigi, "but then why does he fly at me? He must know by now, I should think, that I can give as good as I get!"

Her grandmother shook her by the arm.

"But think what you've done, you wretched child! Good heavens! when will you learn to think? You've mortally offended the man, as likely as not. Just when we are doing our utmost to—"

"To do what, Grandmamma?"

"Why! to do everything, to make an elegant young lady of you, to show you off to advantage."

"For whose benefit, Grandmamma? You must admit that one doesn't have to turn oneself inside out for an old friend like Tonton!"

But Madame Alvarez admitted nothing; not even to her astonishment, when, the following day, Gaston Lachaille arrived in the best of spirits, wearing a light colored suit.

"Put on your hat, Gigi! I'm taking you out to tea."

"Where?" cried Gigi.

"To the *Réservoirs*, at Versailles!"

"Hurrah! Hurrah! Hurrah!" chanted Gilberte.

She turned towards the kitchen.

"Grandmamma, I'm having tea at the *Réservoirs*, with Tonton!"

Madame Alvarez appeared, and without stopping to untie the flowered satinette apron across her stomach, interposed her soft hand between Gilberte's arm and that of Gaston Lachaille.

"No, Gaston," she said simply.

"What do you mean, No?"

"Oh! Grandmamma!" wailed Gigi.

Madame Alvarez seemed not to hear her.

"Go to your room a minute, Gigi. I should like to talk to Monsieur Lachaille in private."

She watched Gilberte leave the room and close the door behind her; then, returning to Gaston, she met his dark, rather brutal stare without flinching.

"What is the meaning of all this, Mamita? Ever since yesterday, I find quite a change here. What's going on?"

"I shall be glad if you will sit down, Gaston, I'm tired," said Madame Alvarez. "Oh, my poor legs!"

She sighed, waited for a response that did not come, and then untied her apron, under which she was wearing a black dress with a large cameo pinned upon it. She motioned her guest to a high-backed chair, keeping the armchair for herself. Then she sat down heavily, smoothed her greying black coils, and folded her hands on her lap. The unhurried movement of her large dark lambent eyes, and the ease with which she remained motionless, were sure signs of her self-control.

"Gaston, you cannot doubt my friendship for you!" Lachaille emitted a short, businesslike laugh, and tugged at his moustache. "My friendship and my gratitude. Nevertheless, I must never forget that I have a soul entrusted to my care. Andrée, as you know, has neither the time nor the inclination to look after the girl. Our Gilberte has not got the gumption to make her own way in the world, like so many. She is just a child."

"Of sixteen," said Lachaille.

"Of nearly sixteen," consented Madame Alvarez. "For years you have been giving her sweets and playthings. She swears by Tonton, and by him alone. And now you want to take her out to tea, in your automobile, to the *Réservoirs!*"

Madame Alvarez placed a hand on her heart.

"Upon my soul and conscience, Gaston, if there were only you and me, I should say to you, 'Take Gilberte anywhere you like, I entrust her to you blindly.' But there are always the others. The eyes of the world are on you. To be seen tête-à-tête with you, is, for a woman—"

Gaston Lachaille lost patience.

"All right, all right, I understand. You want me to believe that once she is seen having tea with me, Gilberte is compromised! A slip of a girl, a flapper, a chit whom no one knows, whom no one notices!"

"Let us say, rather," interrupted Madame Alvarez gently, "that she will be labeled. No matter where you put in an appearance, Gaston, your presence is remarked upon. A young girl who goes out alone with you is no longer an ordinary girl, or even—to put it bluntly—a respectable girl. Now our little Gilberte must not, above all things, cease to be an ordinary young girl, at least not by that method. So far as it concerns you, it will simply end in one more story to be added to the long list already in existence but, personally, when I read of it in *Gil Blas*, I shall not be amused."

Gaston Lachaille rose, paced from the table to the door, then from the door to the window, before replying.

"Very good, Mamita, I have no wish to vex you. I shan't argue," he said coldly. "Keep your precious child."

He turned round again to face Madame Alvarez, his chin held high.

"I can't help wondering, as a matter of interest, whom you are keeping her for! A clerk earning a hundred a year, who'll marry her and give her four children in three years?"

"I know the duty of a mother better than that," said Madame Alvarez composedly. "I shall do my best to entrust Gigi only to the care of a man capable of saying, 'I take charge of her and answer for her future.' May I have the pleasure of brewing you some camomile tea, Gaston?"

"No, thank you. I'm late already."

"Would you like Gigi to come and say goodbye?"

"Don't bother, I'll see her another time. I can't say when, I'm sure. I'm very much taken up these days."

"Never mind, Gaston, don't worry about her. Have a good time, Gaston."

Once alone, Madame Alvarez mopped her forehead, and went to open the door of Gilberte's room.

"You were listening at the door, Gigi!"

"No, Grandmamma."

"Yes, you had your ear to the key-hole. You must never listen at key-holes. You don't hear properly and so you get things all wrong. Monsieur Lachaille has gone."

"So I can see," said Gilberte.

"Now you must rub the new potatoes in a cloth. I'll sauté them when I come in."

"Are you going out, Grandmamma?"

"I'm going round to see Alicia."

"Again?"

"Is it your place to object?" said Madame Alvarez severely. "You had better bathe your eyes in cold water, since you have been silly enough to cry."

"Grandmamma!"

"What?"

"What difference could it make to you, if you'd let me go out with Tonton Gaston in my new dress?"

"Silence! If you can't understand anything about anything, at least let those who are capable of using their reason do so for you. And put on my rubber gloves before you touch the potatoes!"

Throughout the whole of the following week, silence reigned over the Alvarez household, except for a surprise visit, one day, from Aunt Alicia. She arrived in a hired brougham, all black lace and dull silk with a rose at her shoulder, and carried on an anxious conversation, strictly between themselves, with her younger sister. As she was leaving, she bestowed only a moment's attention on Gilberte, pecked at her cheek with a fleeting kiss, and was gone.

"What did she want?" Gilberte asked Madame Alvarez.

"Oh, nothing . . . the address of the heart specialist who treated Madame Buffetery."

Gilberte reflected for a moment.

"It was a long one," she said.

"What was long?"

"The address of the heart specialist. Grandmamma, I should like a *cachet*. I have a headache."

"But you had one yesterday. A headache doesn't last forty-eight hours!"

"Presumably my headaches are different from other people's," said Gilberte, offended.

She was losing some of her sweetness, and, on her return from school, would make some such remark as "My teacher has it in for me!" or complain of not being able to sleep. She was gradually slipping into a state of idleness, which her grandmother noticed, but did nothing to overcome.

One day Gigi was busy applying liquid chalk to her white canvas button boots, when Gaston Lachaille put in an appearance without ringing the bell. His hair was too long, his complexion sun-tanned, and he was wearing a broad check summer suit. He stopped short in front of Gilberte, who was perched high on a kitchen stool, her left hand shod with a boot.

"Oh! Grandmamma left the key in the door, that's just like her!"

As Gaston Lachaille looked at her without saying a word, she began to blush, put down the boot on the table and pulled her skirt down over her knees.

"So, Tonton, you slip in like a burglar! I believe you're thinner. Aren't you fed properly by that famous chef of yours who used to be with the Prince of Wales? Being thinner makes your eyes look larger, and at the same time makes your nose longer, and—"

"I have something to say to your grandmother," interrupted Gaston Lachaille. "Run into your room, Gigi."

For a moment she remained open-mouthed, then she jumped off her stool. The strong column of her neck, like an archangel's, swelled with anger as she advanced on Lachaille.

"Run into your room! Run into your room! And suppose I said the same to you? Who do you think you are here, ordering me to run into my room? All right, I'm going to my room! And I can tell you one thing; so long as you're in the house, I shan't come out of it!"

She slammed the door behind her, and there was a dramatic click of the bolt.

"Gaston," breathed Madame Alvarez, "I shall insist on the child apologising, yes, I shall insist; if necessary, I'll. . . ."

Gaston was not listening to her, and stood staring at the closed door. "Now, Mamita," said he, "let us talk briefly and to the point."

"Let us go over it all once again," said Aunt Alicia. "To begin with, you are quite sure he said, 'She shall be spoiled, more than—' "

"Than any woman before her!"

"Yes, but that's the sort of vague phrase that every man comes out with. I like things cut and dried."

"Just what they were, Alicia, for he said that he would guarantee Gigi against every imaginable mishap, even against himself, by an insurance policy; and that he regarded himself more or less as her godfather."

"Yes, hmm . . . Not bad, not bad. But vague, vague as ever."

She was still in bed, her white hair arranged in curls against the pink pillow. She was absent-mindedly tying and untying the ribbon of her nightdress. Madame Alvarez, pale and wan under her morning hat as the moon behind passing clouds, was leaning cross-armed against the bedside.

"And he added, 'I don't wish to rush anything. Above all, I am Gigi's best pal. I shall give her all the time she wants to get used to me.' There were tears in his eyes. And he also said, 'After all, she won't have to deal with a savage.' A gentleman, in fact. A perfect gentleman."

"Yes, yes. Rather a vague gentleman. And the child, have you spoken frankly to her?"

"As was my duty, Alicia. This is no time for us to be treating her like a child from whom the cakes have to be hidden. Yes, I spoke frankly. I referred to Gaston as a miracle, as a god, as—"

"Tut, tut, tut," criticised Alicia, "I should have stressed the difficulties rather: the cards to be played, the fury of all those ladies, the conquest represented by so conspicuous a man."

Madame Alvarez wrung her hands.

"The difficulties! The cards to be played! Do you imagine she's like you? Don't you know her at all? She's very far from calculating, she's—"

"Thank you."

"I mean she has no ambition. I was even struck by the fact that she did not react either one way or the other. No cries of joy, no tears of emotion! All I got from her was, 'Oh, yes! Oh, it's very considerate of him.' Then, only at the very end, did she lay down, as her conditions—"

"Conditions, indeed!" murmured Alicia.

"—that she would answer Monsieur Lachaille's proposals herself, and discuss the matter alone with him. In other words, it was her business, and hers only."

"Let us be prepared for the worst! You've brought a nitwit into the world. She will ask for the moon and, if I know him, she won't get it. He is coming at four o'clock?"

"Yes."

"Hasn't he sent anything? No flowers? No little present?"

"Nothing. Do you think that's a bad sign?"

"No. It's what one would expect. See that the child is nicely dressed. How is she looking?"

"Not too well, today. Poor little lamb—"

"Come, come!" said Alicia heartlessly. "You'll have time for tears another day—when she's succeeded in ruining the whole affair."

"You've eaten scarcely anything, Gigi."

"I wasn't too hungry, Grandmamma. May I have a little more coffee?"

"Of course."

"And a drop of Combier?"

"Why, yes. There's nothing in the world better than Combier for settling the stomach."

Through the open window rose the noise and heat from the street below. Gigi let the tip of her tongue lick round the bottom of her liqueur glass.

"If Aunt Alicia could see you, Gigi!" said Madame Alvarez lightheartedly.

Gigi's only reply was a disillusioned little smile. Her old plaid dress was too tight across the breast, and under the table she stretched out her long legs well beyond the limits of her skirt.

"What can Mamma be rehearsing today that's kept her from coming back to eat with us, Grandmamma? Do you think there really is a rehearsal going on at her Opéra-Comique?"

"She said so, didn't she?"

"Personally, I don't think she wanted to eat here."

"What makes you think that?"

Without taking her eyes off the sunny window, Gigi simply shrugged her shoulders.

"Oh, nothing, Grandmamma."

When she had drained the last drop of her Combier, she rose and began to clear the table.

"Leave all that, Gigi, I'll do it."

"Why, Grandmamma? I do it as a rule."

She looked Madame Alvarez straight in the face, with an expression the old lady could not meet.

"We began our meal late, it's almost three o'clock and you're not dressed yet; do pull yourself together, Gigi."

"It's never before taken me a whole hour to change my clothes."

"Won't you need my help? Are you satisfied your hair's all right?"

"It will do, Grandmamma. When the door bell rings, don't bother, I'll go and open it."

On the stroke of four, Gaston Lachaille rang three times. A childish, wistful face looked out from the bedroom door, listening. After three more impatient rings, Gilberte advanced as far as the middle of the hall. She still had on her old plaid dress and cotton stockings. She rubbed her cheeks with both fists, then ran to open the door.

"Good afternoon, Uncle Gaston."

"Didn't you want to let me in, you bad girl?"

They bumped shoulders in passing through the door, said "Oh, sorry!" a little too self-consciously, then laughed awkwardly.

"Please sit down, Tonton. D' you know, I didn't have time to change. Not like you! That navy blue serge couldn't look better!"

"You don't know what you're talking about! It's tweed."

"Of course. How silly of me!"

She sat down facing him, pulled her skirt over her knees, and they stared at each other. Gilberte's tomboy assurance deserted her; a strange woebegone look made her blue eyes seem twice their natural size.

"What's the matter with you, Gigi?" asked Lachaille softly. "Tell me something! Do you know why I'm here?"

She assented with an exaggerated nod.

"Do you want to, or don't you?" he asked, lowering his voice.

She pushed a curl behind her ear, and swallowed bravely.

"I don't want to."

Lachaille twirled the tips of his moustache between two fingers, and for a moment looked away from a pair of darkened blue eyes, a pink cheek with a single freckle, curved lashes, a mouth unaware of its power, a heavy mass of ash-gold hair, and a neck as straight as a column, strong, hardly feminine, all of a piece, innocent of jewelry.

"I don't want what you want," Gilberte began again. "You said to Grandmamma . . ."

He put out his hand to stop her. His mouth was slightly twisted to one side, as if he had the toothache.

"I know what I said to your grandmother. It's not worth repeating. Just tell me what it is you don't want. You can then tell me what you do want. I shall give it to you."

"You mean that?" cried Gilberte.

He nodded, letting his shoulders droop, as if tired out. She watched, with surprise, these signs of exhaustion and torment.

"Tonton, you told Grandmamma you wanted to make me my fortune."

"A very fine one," said Lachaille firmly.

"It will be fine if I like it," said Gilberte, no less firmly. "They've drummed into my ears that I am backward for my age, but all the same I know the meaning of words. 'Make me my fortune,' that means I should go away from here with you, and that I should sleep in your bed."

"Gigi, I beg of you!"

She stopped, because of the strong note of appeal in his voice.

"But, Tonton, why should I mind speaking of it to you? You didn't mind speaking of it to Grandmamma. Neither did Grandmamma mind speaking of it to me. Grandmamma wanted me to see nothing but the bright side. But I know more than she told me. I know very well that if you make me my fortune, then I must have my photograph in the papers, go to the Battle of Flowers and to the races at Deauville. When we quarrel, *Gil Blas* and *Paris en amour* will tell the whole story. When you throw me over once and for all, as you did Gentiane des Cevennes when you'd had enough of her—"

"What! You've heard about that? They've bothered you with all those old stories?"

She gave a solemn little nod.

"Grandmamma and Aunt Alicia. They've taught me that you're world-famous. I know too that Maryse Chuquet stole your letters, and you brought an action against her. I know that Countess Pariewsky was angry with you, because you didn't want to marry a *divorcée*, and she tried to shoot you. I know what all the world knows."

Lachaille put his hand on Gilberte's knee.

"Those are not the things we have to talk about together, Gigi. All that's in the past. All that's over and done with."

"Of course, Tonton, until it begins again. It's not your fault if you're world-famous. But I haven't got a world-famous sort of nature. So it won't do for me."

In pulling at the hem of her skirt, she caused Lachaille's hand to slip off her knee.

"Aunt Alicia and Grandmamma are on your side. But as it concerns me a little, after all, I think you must allow me to say a word on the subject. And my word is, that it won't do for me."

She got up and walked about the room. Gaston Lachaille's silence seemed to embarrass her. She punctuated her wanderings with, "After all, it's true, I suppose! No, it really won't do!"

"I should like to know," said Gaston at last, "whether you're not just trying to hide from me the fact that you dislike me. If you dislike me, you had better say so at once."

"Oh no, Tonton, I don't dislike you at all! I'm always delighted to see you! I'll prove it by making a suggestion in my turn. You could go on coming here as usual, even more often. No one would see any harm in it, since you're a friend of the family. You could go on bringing me liquorice, champagne on my birthdays, and on Sunday we should have an extra special game of piquet. Wouldn't that be a pleasant little life? A life without all this business of sleeping in your bed and everybody knowing about it, losing strings of pearls, being photographed all the time and having to be so careful."

She was absent-mindedly twisting a strand of hair round her nose, and pulled it so tight that she snuffled and the tip of her nose turned purple.

"A very pretty little life, as you say," interrupted Gaston Lachaille. "You're forgetting one thing only, Gigi, and that is, I'm in love with you."

"Oh!" she cried, "you never told me that."

"Well," he owned uneasily, "I'm telling you now."

She remained standing before him, silent and breathing fast. There was no concealing her embarrassment; the rise and fall of her bosom under the tight bodice, the hectic flush high on her cheeks, and the quivering of her close pressed lips—albeit ready to open again and taste of life.

"That's quite another thing!" she cried at last. "But then you are a terrible man! You're in love with me, and you want to drag me into a life where I'll have nothing but worries, where everyone gossips about everyone else, where the papers print nasty stories. You're in love with me, and you don't care a fig if you let me in for all sorts of horrible adventures, ending in separations, quarrels, Sandomirs, revolvers, and lau . . . and laudanum."

She burst into violent sobs, which made as much noise as a fit of coughing. Gaston put his arms round her to bend her towards him like a branch, but she escaped and took refuge between the wall and the piano.

"But listen, Gigi! Listen to me!"

"Never! I never want to see you again! I should never have believed it of you. You're not in love with me, you're a wicked man! Go away from here!"

She shut him out from sight by rubbing her eyes with closed fists. Gaston had moved over to her and was trying to discover some place on her well guarded face where he could kiss her. But his lips found only the point of a small chin wet with tears. At the sound of sobbing, Madame Alvarez had hurried in. Pale and circumspect, she had stopped in hesitation at the door to the kitchen.

"Good gracious, Gaston!" she said. "What on earth's the matter with her?"

"The matter!" said Lachaille. "The matter is that she doesn't want to."

"She doesn't want to!" repeated Madame Alvarez. "What do you mean, she doesn't want to?"

"No, she doesn't want to. I speak plainly enough, don't I?"

"No. I don't want to," whimpered Gigi.

Madame Alvarez looked at her granddaughter in a sort of terror.

"Gigi! It's enough to drive one raving mad! But I told you, Gigi. Gaston, as God is my witness, I told her—"

"You have told her too much!" cried Lachaille.

He turned his face towards the child, looking just a poor, sad, lovesick creature, but all he saw of her was a slim back shaken by sobs and a disheveled head of hair.

"Oh!" he exclaimed hoarsely, "I've had enough of this!" and he went out, banging the door.

The next day, at three o'clock, Aunt Alicia, summoned by *pneumatique,* stepped out from her hired brougham. She climbed the stairs up to the Alvarez' floor—pretending to the shortness of breath proper to someone with a weak heart—and noiselessly pushed open the door which her sister had left on the latch.

"Where's the child?"

"In her room. Do you want to see her?"

"There's plenty of time. How is she?"

"Very calm."

Alicia shook two angry little fists.

"Very calm! She has pulled the roof down about our heads, and she is very calm! These young people of today!"

Once again she raised her spotted veil and withered her sister with a single glance.

"And you, standing there, what do you propose doing?"

With a face like a crumpled rose, she sternly confronted the large pallid face of her sister, whose retort was mild in the extreme.

"What do I propose doing? How do you mean? I can't, after all, tie the child up!" Her burdened shoulders rose on a long sigh. "I surely have not deserved such children as these!"

"While you stand there wringing your hands, Lachaille has rushed away from here and in such a state that he may do something idiotic!"

"And even without his straw hat," said Madame Alvarez. "He got into his motor bare-headed! The whole street might have seen him!"

"If I were to be told that by this time he's already become engaged, or is busy making it up with Liane, it would not surprise me in the least!"

"It is a moment fraught with destiny," said Madame Alvarez lugubriously.

"And afterwards, how did you speak to that little brat?"

Madame Alvarez pursed her lips.

"Gigi may be a bit scatter-brained in certain things and backward for her age, but she's not what you say. A young girl who has held the attention of Monsieur Lachaille is not a little brat."

A furious shrug of the shoulders set Alicia's black lace quivering.

"All right, all right! With all due respect, then, how did you handle your precious princess?"

"I talked sense to her. I spoke to her of the family. I tried to make her understand that we sink or swim together. I enumerated all the things she could do for herself and for us."

"And what about nonsense? Did you talk nonsense to her? Didn't you talk to her of love, travel, moonlight, Italy? You must know how to harp on every string. Didn't you tell her that on the other side of the world the sea is phosphorescent, that there are humming-birds in all the flowers, and that you make love under gardenias in full bloom beside a moonlit fountain?"

Madame Alvarez looked at her spirited elder sister with sadness in her eyes.

"I couldn't tell her all that, Alicia, because I know nothing about it. I've never been further afield than Cabourg and Monte Carlo."

"Aren't you capable of inventing it?"

"No, Alicia."

Both fell silent. Alicia, with a gesture, made up her mind.

"Call the chit in to me. We shall see."

When Gilberte came in, Aunt Alicia had resumed all the airs and graces of a frivolous old lady and was smelling the tea-rose pinned near her chin.

"Good afternoon, my little Gigi."

"Good afternoon, Aunt Alicia."

"What is this Inez has been telling me? You have an admirer? And *what* an admirer! For your first attempt, it's a master-stroke!"

Gilberte acquiesced with a guarded, resigned little smile. She offered to Alicia's darting curiosity a fresh young face, to which the violet-blue shadow on her eyelids and the high color of her mouth gave an almost artificial effect. For coolness' sake, she had dragged back the hair off her temples with the help of two combs, and this drew up the corners of her eyes.

"And it seems you have been playing the naughty girl, and tried your claws on Monsieur Lachaille! Bravo, my brave little girl!"

Gilberte raised incredulous eyes to her aunt.

"Yes, indeed! Bravo! It will only make him all the happier when you are nice to him again."

"But I am nice to him, Aunt. Only, I don't want to, that's all."

"Yes, yes, we know. You've sent him packing to his sugar refinery, that's perfect. But don't send him to the Devil, he's quite capable of going. The fact is, you don't love him."

Gilberte gave a little childish shrug.

"Yes, Aunt, I'm very fond of him."

"Just what I said, you don't love him. Mind you, there's no harm in that, it leaves you free to act as you please. Ah, if you'd been head over heels in love with him, then I should have been a little anxious. Lachaille is a fine figure of a man. Well built—you've only to look at the photographs of him taken at Deauville in bathing costume. He's famous for that. Yes, I should feel sorry for you, my poor Gigi. To start by having a passionate love-affair—to go away all by your two selves to the other side of the world, forgetting everything in the arms of the man who adores you, listening to the song of love in an eternal spring—surely things of that sort must touch your heart! What does all that say to you?"

"It says to me that when the eternal spring is over Monsieur Lachaille will go off with another lady. Or else that the lady—me if you like—will leave Monsieur Lachaille, and Monsieur Lachaille will hurry off to blab the whole story. And then the lady, still me if you like, will have nothing else to do but get into another gentleman's bed. I don't want that. I'm not changeable by nature, indeed I'm not."

She crossed her arms over her breasts and shivered slightly.

"Grandmamma, may I have a *cachet faivre?* I want to go to bed, I feel cold."

"You great goose!" burst out Aunt Alicia, "a silly little milliner's shop is all you deserve! Be off, go and marry a bank clerk!"

"If you wish it, Aunt. But I want to go to bed."

Madame Alvarez put her hand on Gigi's forehead.

"Don't you feel well?"

"I'm all right, Grandmamma. Only I'm sad."

She leaned her head on Madame Alvarez' shoulder, and, for the first time in her life, closed her eyes pathetically like a grown woman. The two sisters exchanged glances.

"You must know, my Gigi," said Madame Alvarez, "that we won't torment you to that extent. If you say you really don't want to—"

"A failure is a failure," said Alicia caustically. "We can't go on discussing it for ever."

"You'll never be able to say you didn't have good advice and the very best at that," said Madame Alvarez.

"I know, Grandmamma, but I'm sad, all the same."

"Why?"

A tear trickled over Gilberte's downy cheek without wetting it, but she did not answer. A brisk peel of the door bell made her jump where she stood.

"Oh, it must be him," she said. "It is him! Grandmamma, I don't want to see him! Hide me, Grandmamma!"

At the low, passionate tone of her voice, Aunt Alicia raised an attentive head, and pricked an expert ear. Then she ran to open the door and came back a moment later. Gaston Lachaille, haggard, his eyes bloodshot, followed close behind her.

"Good afternoon, Mamita. Good afternoon, Gigi!" he said airily. "Please don't move, I've come to retrieve my straw hat."

None of the three women replied, and his assurance left him.

"Well, you might at least say a word to me, even if it's only How-d'you-do?"

Gilberte took a step towards him.

"No," she said, "you've not come to retrieve your straw hat. You have another one in your hand. And you would never bother about a hat. You've come to make me more miserable than ever."

"Really!" burst out Madame Alvarez. "This is more than I can stomach. How can you, Gigi! Here is a man who, out of the goodness of his generous heart—"

"If you please, Grandmamma, just a moment, and I shall have finished."

Instinctively she straightened her dress, adjusted the buckle of her sash, and marched up to Gaston.

"I've been thinking, Gaston. In fact, I've been thinking a great deal—"

He interrupted her, to stop her saying what he was afraid to hear.

"I swear to you, my darling—"

"No, don't swear to me. I've been thinking I would rather be miserable with you than without you. So . . ."

She tried twice to go on.

"So . . . There you are. How d'you do, Gaston, how d'you do?"

She offered him her cheek, in her usual way. He held her, a little longer than usual, until he felt her relax, and become calm and gentle in his arms. Madame Alvarez seemed about to hurry forward, but Alicia's impatient little hand restrained her.

"Leave well alone. Don't meddle any more. Can't you see she is far beyond us?"

She pointed to Gigi, who was resting a trusting head and the rich abundance of her hair on Lachaille's shoulder.

The happy man turned to Madame Alvarez.

"Mamita," he said, "will you do me the honor, the favor, give me the infinite joy of bestowing on me the hand. . . ."

# The Little Minister

(an extract from the novel)

## SIR JAMES M. BARRIE

GAVIN took the path to Caddam Wood, because Sanders told him the Wild Lindsays were there, a gypsy family that threatened the farmers by day and danced devilishly, it was said, at night. The little minister knew them by repute as a race of giants, and that not many persons would have cared to face them alone at midnight; but he was feeling as one wound up to heavy duties, and meant to admonish them severely.

Sanders, an old man who lived with his sister Nanny on the edge of the wood, went with him, and for a time both were silent. But Sanders had something to say.

"Was you ever at the Spittal, Mr. Dishart?" he asked.

"Lord Rintoul's house at the top of Glen Quharity? No."

"Hae you ever looked on a lord?"

"No."

"Or on an auld lord's young leddyship? I have."

"What is she?"

"You surely ken that Rintoul's auld, and is to be married on a young leddyship. She's no' a leddyship yet, but they're to be married soon, so I may say I've seen a leddyship. Ay, an impressive sicht. It was yestreen."

"Is there a great difference in their ages?"

"As muckle as atween auld Peter Spens and his wife, wha was saxteen when he was saxty, and she was playing at dumps in the street when her man was waiting for her to make his porridge. Ay, sic a differ doesna suit wi' common folk, but of course earls can please themsels. Rintoul's so fond o' the leddyship 'at is to be, that when she was at the school in Edinbury he wrote to her ilka day. Kaytherine Crummie told me that, and she says aince you're used to it, writing letters is as easy as skinning moles. I dinna ken what they can write sic a heap about, but I daur say he gies her his views on the Chartist agitation and the potato disease, and she'll write back about the romantic sichts o' Edinbury and the sermons o' the grand preachers she hears. Sal, though, thae grand folk has no religion to speak o', for they're a' English kirk. You're no' speiring what her leddyship said to me?"

"What did she say?"

"Weel, you see, there was a dancing ball on, and Kaytherine Crummie took me to a window whaur I could stand on a flower-pot and watch the critturs whirling round in the ball like teetotums. What's mair, she pointed out the leddyship that's to be to me, and I just glowered at her, for thinks I, 'Take your fill, Sanders, and whaur there's lords and leddyships, dinna waste a minute on colonels and honourable misses and sic like dirt.' Ay, but what wi' my een blinking at the blaze o' candles, I lost sicht o' her till all at aince somebody says at my lug, 'Well, my man, and who is the prettiest lady in the room?' Mr. Dishart, it was her leddyship. She looked like a star."

"And what did you do?"

"The first thing I did was to fall aff the flower-pot; but syne I came to, and says I, wi' a polite smirk, 'I'm thinking, your leddyship,' says I, 'as you're the bonniest yourself.' "

"I see you are a cute man, Sanders."

"Ay, but that's no' a'. She lauched in a pleased way and tapped me wi' her fan, and says she, 'Why do you think me the prettiest?' I dinna deny but what that staggered me, but I thocht a minute, and took a look at the other dancers again, and syne I says, michty sly like, 'The other leddies,' I says, 'has sic sma' feet.' "

Sanders stopped here and looked doubtingly at Gavin.

"I canna make up my mind," he said, "whether she liked that, for she rapped my knuckles wi' her fan fell sair, and aff she gaed. Ay, I consulted Tammas Haggart about it, and he says, 'The flirty crittur,' he says. What would you say, Mr. Dishart?"

Gavin managed to escape without giving an answer, for here their roads separated. He did not find the Wild Lindsays, however. Children of whim, of prodigious strength while in the open, but destined to wither quickly in the hot air of towns, they had gone from Caddam, leaving nothing of themselves behind but a black mark burned by their fires into the ground. Thus they branded the earth through many counties until some hour when the spirit of wandering again fell on them, and they forsook their hearths with as little compunction as the bird leaves its nest.

Gavin had walked quickly, and he now stood silently in the wood, his hat in his hand. In the moonlight the grass seemed tipped with hoar frost. Most of the beeches were already bare, but the shoots, clustering round them, like children at their mother's skirts, still retained their leaves red and brown. Among the pines these leaves were as incongruous as a wedding-dress at a funeral. Gavin was standing on grass, but there were patches of heather within sight, and broom, and the leaf of the blaeberry. Where the beeches had drawn up the earth with them as they grew, their roots ran this way and that, slippery to the feet and looking like disinterred bones. A squirrel appeared suddenly on the charred ground, looked doubtfully at Gavin to see if he was growing there, and then glided up a tree, where it sat eyeing him, and forgetting to conceal its shadow. Caddam was very still. At long intervals came from far away the whack of an axe on wood. Gavin was in a world by himself, and this might be some one breaking into it.

The mystery of woods by moonlight thrilled the little minister. His eyes rested on the shining roots, and he remembered what had been told him of the legend of Caddam, how once on a time it was a mighty wood, and a maiden most beautiful stood on its confines, panting and afraid, for a wicked man pursued her; how he drew near, and she ran a little way into the wood, and he followed her, and she still ran, and still he followed, until both were for ever lost, and the bones of her pursuer lie beneath a beech, but the lady may still be heard singing in the woods if the night be fine, for then she is a glad spirit, but weeping when there is wild wind, for then she is but a mortal seeking a way out of the wood.

The squirrel slid down the fir and was gone. The axe's blows ceased. Nothing that moved was in sight. The wind that has its nest in trees was circling round with many voices, that never rose above a whisper, and were often but the echo of a sigh.

Gavin was in the Caddam of past days, where the beautiful maiden wanders ever, waiting for him who is so pure that he may find her. He will wander over the tree-tops looking for her, with the moon for his lamp, and some night he will hear her singing. The little minister drew a deep breath, and his foot snapped a brittle twig. Then he remembered who and where he was, and stooped to pick up his staff. But he did not pick it up, for as his fingers were closing on it the lady began to sing.

For perhaps a minute Gavin stood stock-still, like an intruder. Then he ran towards the singing, which seemed to come from Windyghoul, a straight road through Caddam that farmers use in summer, but leave in the back end of the year to leaves and pools. In Windyghoul there is either no wind or so much that it rushes down the sieve like an army, entering with a shriek of terror, and escaping with a derisive howl. The moon was crossing the avenue. But Gavin only saw the singer.

She was still fifty yards away, sometimes singing gleefully, and again letting her body sway lightly as she came dancing up Windyghoul. Soon she was within a few feet of the little minister, to whom singing, except when out of tune, was a suspicious thing, and dancing a device of the devil. His arm went out wrathfully, and his intention was to pronounce sentence on this woman.

But she passed, unconscious of his presence, and he had not moved nor spoken. Though really of the average height, she was a little thing to the eyes of Gavin, who always felt tall and stout except when he looked down. The grace of her swaying figure was a new thing in the world to him. Only while she passed did he see her as a gleam of colour, a gypsy elf poorly clad, her bare feet flashing beneath a short green skirt, a twig of rowan berries stuck carelessly into her black hair. Her face was pale. She had an angel's loveliness. Gavin shook.

Still she danced onwards, but she was very human, for when she came to muddy water she let her feet linger in it, and flung up her arms, dancing more wantonly than before. A diamond on her finger shot a thread of fire over the pool. Undoubtedly she was the devil.

Gavin leaped into the avenue, and she heard him and looked behind. He tried to cry "Woman!" sternly but lost the word, for now she saw him, and laughed with her shoulders, and beckoned to him, so that he shook his fist at her. She tripped on, but often turning her head beckoned and mocked him, and he forgot his dignity and his pulpit and all other things, and ran after her. Up Windyghoul did he pursue her, and it was well that the precentor was not there to see. She reached the mouth of the avenue, and, kissing her hand to Gavin, so that the ring gleamed again, was gone.

The minister's one thought was to find her, but he searched in vain. She might be crossing the hill on her way to Thrums, or perhaps she was still laughing at him from behind a tree. After a longer time than he was aware of, Gavin realised that his boots were chirping and his trousers streaked with mud. Then he abandoned the search and hastened homewards in a rage.

From the hill to the manse the nearest way is down two fields, and the little minister descended them rapidly. Thrums, which is red in daylight, was gray and still as the cemetery. He had glimpses of several of its deserted streets. To the south the watch-light showed brightly, but no other was visible. So it seemed to Gavin, and then—suddenly—he lost the power to move. He had heard the horn. Thrice it sounded, and thrice it struck him to the heart. He looked again and saw a shadow stealing along the Tenements, then another, then half a dozen. He remembered Mr. Carfrae's words, "If you ever hear that horn, I implore you to hasten to the square," and in another minute he had reached the Tenements.

Now again he saw the gypsy. She ran past him, half a score of men, armed with staves and pikes, at her heels. At first he thought they were chasing her, but they were following her as a leader. Her eyes sparkled as she waved them to the square with her arms.

"The soldiers, the soldiers!" was the universal cry.

"Who is that woman?" demanded Gavin, catching hold of a frightened old man.

"Curse the Egyptian limmer," the man answered, "she's egging my laddie on to fecht."

"Bless her rather," the son cried, "for warning us that the sojers is coming. Put your ear to the ground, Mr. Dishart, and you'll hear the dirl o' their feet."

The young man rushed away to the square, flinging his father from him. Gavin followed. As he turned into the school wynd, the town drum began to beat, windows were thrown open, and sullen men ran out of closes where women were screaming and trying to hold them back. At the foot of the wynd Gavin passed Sanders Webster.

"Mr. Dishart," the mole-catcher cried, "hae you seen that Egyptian? May I be struck dead if it's no' her little leddyship."

But Gavin did not hear him.

2

Men nearly naked ran past Gavin, seeking to escape from Thrums by the fields he had descended. When he shouted to them they only ran faster. A Tillyloss weaver whom he tried to stop struck him savagely and sped past to the square. In Bank Street, which was full of people at one moment and empty the next, the minister stumbled over old Charles Yuill.

"Take me and welcome," Yuill cried, mistaking Gavin for the enemy. He had only one arm through the sleeve of his jacket, and his feet were bare.

"I am Mr. Dishart. Are the soldiers already in the square, Yuill?"

"They'll be there in a minute."

The man was so weak that Gavin had to hold him.

"Be a man, Charles. You have nothing to fear. It is not such as you the soldiers have come for. If need be, I can swear that you had not the strength, even if you had the will, to join in the weavers' riot."

"For Godsake, Mr. Dishart," Yuill cried, his hands chattering on Gavin's coat, "dinna swear that. My laddie was in the thick o' the riot; and if he's ta'en there's the poor's-house gaping for Kitty and me, for I couldna weave half a web a week. If there's a warrant agin onybody o' the name of Yuill, swear it's me; swear I'm a desperate character, swear I'm michty strong for all I look palsied; and if when they take me, my courage breaks down, swear the mair, swear I confessed my guilt to you on the Book."

As Yuill spoke the quick rub-a-dub of a drum was heard.

"The soldiers!" Gavin let go his hold of the old man, who hastened away to give himself up.

"That's no the sojers," said a woman; "it's the folk gathering in the square. This'll be a watery Sabbath in Thrums."

"Rob Dow," shouted Gavin, as Dow flung past with a scythe in his hand, "lay down that scythe."

"To hell wi' religion!" Rob retorted, fiercely; "it spoils a' thing."

"Lay down that scythe; I command you."

Rob stopped undecidedly, then cast the scythe from him, but its rattle on the stones was more than he could bear.

"I winna," he cried, and, picking it up, ran to the square.

An upper window in Bank Street opened, and Doctor McQueen put out his head. He was smoking as usual.

"Mr. Dishart," he said, "you will return home at once if you are a wise man; or, better still, come in here. You can do nothing with these people to-night."

"I can stop their fighting."

"You will only make black blood between them and you."

"Dinna heed him, Mr. Dishart," cried some women.

"You had better heed him," cried a man.

"I will not desert my people," Gavin said.

"Listen, then, to my prescription," the doctor replied. "Drive that gypsy lassie out of the town before the soldiers reach it. She is firing the men to a red heat through sheer devilry."

"She brocht the news, or we would have been nipped in our beds," some people cried.

"Does any one know who she is?" Gavin demanded, but all shook their heads. The Egyptian, as they called her, had never been seen in these parts before.

"Has any other person seen the soldiers?" he asked. "Perhaps this is a false alarm."

"Several have seen them within the last few minutes," the doctor answered. "They came from Tilliedrum, and were advancing on us from the south, but when they heard that we had got the alarm they stopped at the top of the brae, near T'nowhead's farm. Man, you would take these things more coolly if you smoked."

"Show me this woman," Gavin said, sternly, to those who had been listening. Then a stream of people carried him into the square.

To Gavin, who never before had seen a score of people in the square at once, here was a sight strange and terrible. Andrew Struthers, an old soldier, stood on the outside stair of the town-house, shouting words of command to some fifty weavers, many of them scantily clad, but all armed with pikes and poles. Most were known to the little minister, but they wore faces that were new to him. Newcomers joined the body every moment. If the drill was clumsy the men were fierce. Hundreds of people gathered round, some screaming, some shaking their fists at the old soldier, many trying to pluck their relatives out of danger. Gavin could not see the Egyptian. Women and old men, fighting for the possession of his ear, implored him to disperse the armed band. He ran up the town-house stair, and in a moment it had become a pulpit.

"Dinna dare to interfere, Mr. Dishart," Struthers said, savagely.

"Andrew Struthers," said Gavin, solemnly, "in the name of God I order you to leave me alone. If you don't," he added, ferociously, "I'll fling you over the stair."

"Dinna heed him, Andrew," some one shouted, and another cried, "He canna understand our sufferings; he has dinner ilka day."

Struthers faltered, however, and Gavin cast his eye over the armed men.

"Rob Dow," he said, "William Carmichael, Thomas Whamond, William Munn, Alexander Hobart, Henders Haggart, step forward."

These were Auld Lichts, and when they found that the minister would not take his eyes off them, they obeyed, all save Rob Dow.

"Never mind him, Rob," said the atheist, Cruickshanks, "it's better playing cards in hell than singing psalms in heaven."

"Joseph Cruickshanks," responded Gavin, grimly, "you will find no cards down there."

Then Rob also came to the foot of the stair. There was some angry muttering from the crowd, and young Charles Yuill exclaimed, "Curse you, would you lord it ower us on week-days as weel as on Sabbaths?"

"Lay down your weapons," Gavin said to the six men.

They looked at each other. Hobart slipped his pike behind his back. "I hae no weapon," he said, slily.

"Let me hae my fling this nicht," Dow entreated, "and I'll promise to bide sober for a twelvemonth."

"Oh, Rob, Rob!" the minister said, bitterly, "are you the man I prayed with a few hours ago?"

The scythe fell from Rob's hands.

"Down wi' your pikes," he roared to his companions, "or I'll brain you wi' them."

"Ay, lay them down," the precentor whispered, "but keep your feet on them."

Then the minister, who was shaking with excitement, though he did not know it, stretched forth his arms for silence, and it came so suddenly as to frighten the people in the neighbouring streets.

"If he prays we're done for," cried young Charles Yuill, but even in that hour many of the people were unbonneted.

"Oh, Thou who art the Lord of Hosts," Gavin prayed, "we are in Thy hands this night. These are Thy people, and they have sinned; but Thou art a merciful God, and they were sore tried, and knew not what they did. To Thee, our God, we turn for deliverance, for without Thee we are lost."

The little minister's prayer was heard all round the square, and many weapons were dropped as an Amen to it.

"If you fight," cried Gavin, brightening as he heard the clatter of the iron on the stones, "your wives and children may be shot in the streets. These soldiers have come for a dozen of you; will you be benefited if they take away a hundred?"

"Oh, hearken to him," cried many women.

"I winna," answered a man, "for I'm ane o' the dozen. Whaur's the Egyptian?"

"Here."

Gavin saw the crowd open, and the woman of Windyghoul come out of it, and, while he should have denounced her, he only blinked, for once more her loveliness struck him full in the eyes. She was beside him on the stair before he became a minister again.

"How dare you, woman?" he cried; but she flung a rowan berry at him.

"If I were a man," she exclaimed, addressing the people, "I wouldna let myself be catched like a mouse in a trap."

"We winna," some answered.

"What kind o' women are you," cried the Egyptian, her face gleaming as she turned to her own sex, "that bid your men-folk gang to gaol when a bold front would lead them to safety? Do you want to be husbandless and hameless?"

"Disperse, I command you!" cried Gavin. "This abandoned woman is inciting you to riot."

"Dinna heed this little man," the Egyptian retorted.

It is curious to know that even at that anxious moment Gavin winced because she called him little.

"She has the face of a mischief-maker," he shouted, "and her words are evil."

"You men and women o' Thrums," she responded, "ken that I wish you weel by the service I hae done you this nicht. Wha telled you the sojers was coming?"

"It was you; it was you!"

"Ay, and mony a mile I ran to bring the news. Listen, and I'll tell you mair."

"She has a false tongue," Gavin cried; "listen not to the brazen woman."

"What I have to tell," she said, "is as true as what I've telled already, and how true that is you a' ken. You're wondering how the sojers has come to a stop at the tap o' the brae instead o' marching on the town. Here's the reason. They agreed to march straucht to the square if the alarm wasna given, but if it was they were to break into small bodies and surround the town so that you couldna get out. That's what they're doing now."

At this the screams were redoubled, and many men lifted the weapons they had dropped.

"Believe her not," cried Gavin. "How could a wandering gypsy know all this?"

"Ay, how can you ken?" some demanded.

"It's enough that I do ken," the Egyptian answered. "And this mair I ken, that the captain of the soldiers is confident he'll nab every one o' you that's wanted unless you do one thing."

"What is 't?"

"If you a' run different ways you're lost, but if you keep thegither you'll be able to force a road into the country whaur you can scatter. That's what he's fleid you'll do."

"Then it's what we will do."

"It is what you will not do," Gavin said, passionately. "The truth is not in this wicked woman."

But scarcely had he spoken when he knew that startling news had reached the square. A murmur arose on the skirts of the mob, and swept with the roar of the sea towards the town-house. A detachment of the soldiers were marching down the Roods from the north.

"There's some coming frae the east-town end," was the next intelligence; "and they've gripped Sanders Webster, and auld Charles Yuill has given himsel' up."

"You see, you see," the gypsy said, flashing triumph at Gavin.

"Lay down your weapons," Gavin cried, but his power over the people had gone.

"The Egyptian spoke true," they shouted; "dinna heed the minister."

Gavin tried to seize the gypsy by the shoulders, but she slipped past him down the stair, and crying "Follow me!" ran round the town-house and down the brae.

"Woman!" he shouted after her, but she only waved her arms scornfully. The people followed her, many of the men still grasping their weapons, but all in disorder. Within a minute after Gavin saw the gleam of the ring on her finger, as she waved her hands, he and Dow were alone in the square.

"She's an awfu' woman that," Rob said. "I saw her lauching."

Gavin ground his teeth.

"Rob Dow," he said, slowly, "if I had not found Christ I would have throttled that woman. You saw how she flouted me?"

### 3

Dow looked shamefacedly at the minister, and then set off up the square.

"Where are you going, Rob?"

"To gie myself up. I maun do something to let you see there's one man in Thrums that has mair faith in you than in a fliskmahoy."

"And only one, Rob. But I don't know that they want to arrest you."

"Ay, I had a hand in tying the polissman to the—"

"I want to hear nothing about that," Gavin said, quickly.

"Will I hide, then?"

"I dare not advise you to do that. It would be wrong."

Half a score of fugitives tore past the town-house, and were out of sight without a cry. There was a tread of heavier feet, and a dozen soldiers, with several policemen and two prisoners, appeared suddenly on the north side of the square.

"Rob," cried the minister in desperation, "run!"

When the soldiers reached the town-house, where they locked up their prisoners, Dow was skulking eastward, and Gavin running down the brae.

"They're fechting," he was told, "they're fechting on the brae, the sojers is firing, a man's killed!"

But this was an exaggeration.

The brae, though short, is very steep. There is a hedge on one side of it, from which the land falls away, and on the other side a hillock. Gavin reached the scene to see the soldiers marching down the brae, guarding a small body of policemen. The armed weavers were retreating before them. A hundred women or more were on the hillock, shrieking and gesticulating. Gavin joined them, calling on them not to fling the stones they had begun to gather.

The armed men broke into a rabble, flung down their weapons, and fled back towards the town-house. Here they almost ran against the soldiers in the square, who again forced them into the brae. Finding themselves about to be wedged between the two forces, some crawled through the hedge, where they were instantly seized by policemen. Others sought to climb up the hillock and then escape into the country. The policemen clambered after them. The men were too frightened to fight, but a woman seized a policeman by the waist and flung him head foremost among the soldiers. One of these shouted "Fire!" but the captain cried "No." Then came showers of missiles from the women. They stood their ground and defended the retreat of the scared men.

Who flung the first stone is not known, but it is believed to have been the Egyptian. The policemen were recalled, and the whole body ordered to advance down the brae. Thus the weavers who had not escaped at once were driven before them, and soon hemmed in between the two bodies of soldiers, when they were easily captured. But for two minutes there was a thick shower of stones and clods of earth.

It was ever afterwards painful to Gavin to recall this scene, but less on account of the shower of stones than because of the flight of one divit in it. He had been watching the handsome young captain, Halliwell, riding with his men; admiring him, too, for his coolness. This coolness exasperated the gypsy, who twice flung at Halliwell and missed him. He rode on, smiling contemptuously.

"Oh, if I could only fling straight!" the Egyptian moaned.

Then she saw the minister by her side, and in the tick of a clock something happened that can never be explained. For the moment Gavin was so lost in misery over the probable effect of the night's rioting that he had forgotten where he was. Suddenly the Egyptian's beautiful face was close to his, and she pressed a divit into his hand, at the same time pointing at the officer, and whispering "Hit him."

Gavin flung the clod of earth, and hit Halliwell on the head.

I say I cannot explain this. I tell what happened, and add with thankfulness that only the Egyptian witnessed the deed. Gavin, I suppose, had flung the divit before he could stay his hand. Then he shrank in horror.

"Woman!" he cried again.

"You are a dear," she said, and vanished.

By the time Gavin was breathing freely again the lock-up was crammed with prisoners, and the Riot Act had been read from the town-house stair. It is still remembered that the baron-bailie, to whom this duty fell, had got no further than "Victoria, by the Grace of God," when the paper was struck out of his hands.

While Gavin was with the families whose breadwinners were now in the lock-up, a cell that was usually crammed on fair nights and empty for the rest of the year, the sheriff and Halliwell were in the round-room of the town-house, not in a good temper. They spoke loudly, and some of their words sank into the cell below.

"The whole thing has been a fiasco," the sheriff was heard saying, "owing to our failing to take them by surprise. Why, three-fourths of those taken will have to be liberated, and we have let the worst offenders slip through our hands."

"Well," answered Halliwell, who was wearing a heavy cloak, "I have brought your policemen into the place, and that is all I undertook to do."

"You brought them, but at the expense of alarming the country-side. I wish we had come without you."

"Nonsense! My men advanced like ghosts. Could your police have come down that brae alone to-night?"

"Yes, because it would have been deserted. Your soldiers, I tell you, have done the mischief. This woman, who, so many of our prisoners admit, brought the news of our coming, must either have got it from one of your men or have seen them on the march."

"The men did not know their destination. True, she might have seen us despite our precautions, but you forget that she told them how we were to act in the event of our being seen. That is what perplexes me."

"Yes, and me too, for it was a close secret between you and me and Lord Rintoul and not half a dozen others."

"Well, find the woman, and we shall get the explanation. If she is still in the town she cannot escape, for my men are everywhere."

"She was seen ten minutes ago."

"Then she is ours. I say, Riach, if I were you I would set all my prisoners free and take away a cartload of their wives instead. I have only seen the backs of the men of Thrums, but, on my word, I very nearly ran away from the women."

Wearyworld entered cheerfully.

"This is the local policeman," a Tilliedrum officer said; "we have been searching for him everywhere, and only found him now."

"Where have you been?" asked the sheriff, wrathfully.

"Whaur maist honest men is at this hour," replied Wearyworld: "in my bed."

"How dared you ignore your duty at such a time?"

"It's a long story," the policeman answered, pleasantly, in anticipation of a talk at last.

"Answer me in a word."

"In a word!" cried the policeman, quite crestfallen. "It canna be done. You'll need to cross-examine me, too. It's my lawful richt."

"I'll take you to the Tilliedrum gaol for your share in this night's work if you do not speak to the purpose. Why did you not hasten to our assistance?"

"As sure as death I never kent you was here. I was up the Roods on my rounds when I heard an awfu' din down in the square, and thinks I, there's rough characters about, and the place for honest folk is their bed. So to my bed I gaed, and I was in't when your men gripped me."

"We must see into this before we leave. In the meantime you will act as a guide to my searchers. Stop! Do you know anything of this Egyptian?"

"What Egyptian? Is't a lassie wi' rowans in her hair?"

"The same. Have you seen her?"

"That I have. There's nothing agin her, is there? Whatever it is, I'll up-haud she didna do't, for a simpler, franker-spoken crittur couldna be."

"Never mind what I want her for. When did you see her?"

"It would be about twal o'clock," began Wearyworld, unctuously, "when I was in the Roods, ay, no lang afore I heard the disturbance in the square. I was standing in the middle o' the road, wondering how the door o' the windmill was swinging open, when she came up to me.

"'A fine nicht for the time o' year,' I says to her, for nobody but the minister had spoken to me a' day.

"'A very fine nicht,' says she, very frank, though she was breathing quick like as if she had been running. 'You'll be police?' says she.

"'I am,' says I, 'and wha be you?'

"'I'm just a puir gypsy lassie,' she says.

"'And what's that in your hand?' says I.

"'It's a horn I found in the wood,' says she, 'but it's rusty and winna blaw.'

"I laughed at her ignorance, and says I, 'I warrant I could blaw it.'

"'I dinna believe you,' says she.

"'Gie me haud o't,' says I, and she gae it to me, and I blew some bonny blasts on't. Ay, you see she didna ken the way o't. 'Thank you kindly,' says she, and she ran awa without even minding to take the horn back again."

"You incredible idiot!" cried the sheriff. "Then it was you who gave the alarm?"

"What hae I done to madden you?" honest Wearyworld asked, in perplexity.

"Get out of my sight, sir!" roared the sheriff.

In the round-room (which is oblong), there is a throne on which the bailie sits when he dispenses justice. It is swathed in red cloths that give it the appearance of a pulpit. Left to himself, Halliwell flung off his cloak, and taking a chair near this dais rested his legs on the bare wooden table, one on each side of the lamp. He was still in this position when the door opened, and two policemen thrust the Egyptian into the room.

4

"This is the woman, captain," one of the policemen said, in triumph; "and, begging your pardon, will you keep a grip of her till the sheriff comes back?"

Halliwell did not turn his head.

"You can leave her here," he said, carelessly. "Three of us are not needed to guard a woman."

"But she's a slippery customer."

"You can go," said Halliwell; and the policemen withdrew slowly, eyeing their prisoner doubtfully until the door closed. Then the officer wheeled round languidly, expecting to find the Egyptian gaunt and muscular.

"Now then," he drawled, "why—By Jove!"

The gallant soldier was as much taken aback as if he had turned to find a pistol at his ear. He took his feet off the table. Yet he only saw the gypsy's girlish figure in its red and green, for she had covered her face with her hands. She was looking at him intently between her fingers, but he did not know this. All he did want to know just then was what was behind the hands.

Before he spoke again she had perhaps made up her mind about him, for she began to sob bitterly. At the same time she slipped a finger over her ring.

"Why don't you look at me?" asked Halliwell, selfishly.

"I daurna."

"Am I so fearsome?"

"You're a sojer, and you would shoot me like a craw."

Halliwell laughed, and, taking her wrists in his hands, uncovered her face.

"Oh, by Jove!" he said again, but this time to himself.

As for the Egyptian, she slid the ring into her pocket, and fell back before the officer's magnificence.

"Oh," she cried, "is all sojers like you?"

There was such admiration in her eyes that it would have been self-contempt to doubt her. Yet having smiled complacently, Halliwell became uneasy.

"Who on earth are you?" he asked, finding it wise not to look her in the face. "Why do you not answer me more quickly?"

"Dinna be angry at that, captain," the Egyptian implored. "I promised my mither aye to count twenty afore I spoke, because she thocht I was ower glib. Captain, how is't that you're so fleid to look at me?"

Thus put on his mettle, Halliwell again faced her, with the result that his question changed to "Where did you get those eyes?" Then was he indignant with himself.

"What I want to know," he explained, severely, "is how you were able to acquaint the Thrums people with our movements? That you must tell me at once, for the sheriff blames my soldiers. Come now, no counting twenty!"

He was pacing the room now, and she had her face to herself. It said several things, among them that the officer evidently did not like this charge against his men.

"Does the shirra blame the sojers?" exclaimed this quick-witted Egyptian. "Weel, that cows, for he has nane to blame but himsel'."

"What!" cried Halliwell, delighted. "It was the sheriff who told tales? Answer me. You are counting a hundred this time."

Perhaps the gypsy had two reasons for withholding her answer. If so, one of them was that, as the sheriff had told nothing, she had a story to make up. The other was that she wanted to strike a bargain with the officer.

"If I tell you," she said, eagerly, "will you set me free?"

"I may ask the sheriff to do so."

"But he mauna see me," the Egyptian said, in distress. "There's reasons, captain."

"Why, surely you have not been before him on other occasions," said Halliwell, surprised.

"No in the way you mean," muttered the gypsy, and for the moment her eyes twinkled. But the light in them went out when she remembered that the sheriff was near, and she looked desperately at the window as if ready to fling herself from it. She had very good reasons for not wishing to be seen by Riach, though fear that he would put her in gaol was not one of them.

Halliwell thought it was the one cause of her woe, and great was his desire to turn the tables on the sheriff.

"Tell me the truth," he said, "and I promise to befriend you."

"Weel, then," the gypsy said, hoping still to soften his heart, and making up her story as she told it, "yestreen I met the shirra, and he telled me a' I hae telled the Thrums folk this nicht."

"You can scarcely expect me to believe that. Where did you meet him?"

"In Glen Quharity. He was riding on a horse."

"Well, I allow he was there yesterday, and on horseback. He was on his way back to Tilliedrum from Lord Rintoul's place. But don't tell me that he took a gypsy girl into his confidence."

"Ay, he did, without kenning. He was gieing his horse a drink when I met him, and he let me tell him his fortune. He said he would gaol me for an impostor if I didna tell him true, so I gaed about it cautiously, and after a minute or twa I telled him he was coming to Thrums the nicht to nab the rioters."

"You are trifling with me," interposed the indignant soldier. "You promised to tell me not what you said to the sheriff, but how he disclosed our movements to you."

"And that's just what I am telling you, only you hinna the rumelgumption to see it. How do you think fortunes is telled? First we get out o' the man, without his seeing what we're after, a' about himsel', and syne we repeat it to him. That's what I did wi' the shirra."

"You drew the whole thing out of him without his knowing?"

" 'Deed I did, and he rode awa' saying I was a witch."

The soldier heard with the delight of a schoolboy.

"Now if the sheriff does not liberate you at my request," he said, "I will never let him hear the end of this story. He was right; you are a witch. You deceived the sheriff; yes, undoubtedly you are a witch."

He looked at her with fun in his face, but the fun disappeared, and a wondering admiration took its place.

"By Jove!" he said, "I don't wonder you bewitched the sheriff. I must take care or you will bewitch the captain, too."

At this notion he smiled, but he also ceased looking at her. Suddenly the Egyptian again began to cry.

"You're angry wi' me," she sobbed. "I wish I had never set een on you."

"Why do you wish that?" Halliwell asked.

"Fine you ken," she answered, and again covered her face with her hands.

He looked at her undecidedly.

"I am not angry with you," he said, gently. "You are an extraordinary girl."

Had he really made a conquest of this beautiful creature? Her words said so, but had he? The captain could not make up his mind. He gnawed his moustache in doubt.

There was silence, save for the Egyptian's sobs. Halliwell's heart was touched, and he drew nearer her.

"My poor girl—"

He stopped. Was she crying? Was she not laughing at him rather? He became red.

The gypsy peeped at him between her fingers, and saw that he was of two minds. She let her hands fall from her face, and undoubtedly there were tears on her cheeks.

"If you're no angry wi' me," she said, sadly, "how will you no look at me?"

"I am looking at you now."

He was very close to her, and staring into her wonderful eyes. I am older than the captain, and those eyes have dazzled me.

"Captain dear."

She put her hand in his. His chest rose. He knew she was seeking to beguile him, but he could not take his eyes off hers. He was in a worse plight than a woman listening to the first whisper of love.

Now she was further from him, but the spell held. She reached the door, without taking her eyes from his face. For several seconds he had been as a man mesmerised.

Just in time he came to. It was when she turned from him to find the handle of the door. She was turning it when his hand fell on hers so suddenly that she screamed. He twisted her round.

"Sit down there," he said, hoarsely, pointing to the chair upon which he had flung his cloak. She dared not disobey. Then he leant against the door, his back to her, for just then he wanted no one to see his face. The gypsy sat very still and a little frightened.

Halliwell opened the door presently, and called to the soldier on duty below:

"Davidson, see if you can find the sheriff. I want him. And Davidson—"

The captain paused.

"Yes," he muttered, and the old soldier marvelled at his words, "it is better. Davidson, lock this door on the outside."

Davidson did as he was ordered, and again the Egyptian was left alone with Halliwell.

"Afraid of a woman!" she said, contemptuously, though her heart sank when she heard the key turn in the lock.

"I admit it," he answered, calmly.

He walked up and down the room, and she sat silently watching him.

"That story of yours about the sheriff was not true," he said at last.

"I suspect it wasna," answered the Egyptian, coolly. "Hae you been thinking about it a' this time? Captain, I could tell you what you are thinking now. You're wishing it had been true, so that the ane o' you could not lauch at the other."

"Silence!" said the captain, and not another word would he speak until he heard the sheriff coming up the stair. The Egyptian trembled at his step, and rose in desperation.

"Why is the door locked?" cried the sheriff, shaking it.

"All right," answered Halliwell; "the key is on your side."

At that moment the Egyptian knocked the lamp off the table, and the room was at once in darkness. The officer sprang at her, and, catching her by the skirt, held on.

"Why are you in darkness?" asked the sheriff, as he entered.

"Shut the door," cried Halliwell. "Put your back to it."

"Don't tell me the woman has escaped?"

"I have her! I have her! She capsized the lamp, the little jade. Shut the door."

Still keeping firm hold of her, as he thought, the captain relit the lamp with his other hand. It showed an extraordinary scene. The door was shut, and the sheriff was guarding it. Halliwell was clutching the cloth of the bailie's seat. There was no Egyptian.

A moment passed before either man found his tongue.

"Open the door. After her!" cried Halliwell.

But the door would not open. The Egyptian had fled, and locked it behind her.

What the two men said to each other, it would not be fitting to tell. When Davidson, who had been gossiping at the corner of the town-house, released his captain and the sheriff, the gypsy had been gone for some minutes.

"But she sha'n't escape us," Riach cried, and hastened out to assist in the pursuit.

Halliwell was in such a furious temper that he called up Davidson, and admonished him for neglect of duty.

5

Not till the stroke of three did Gavin turn homeward, with the legs of a ploughman, and eyes rebelling against overwork. Seeking to comfort his dejected people, whose courage lay spilt on the brae, he had been in as many houses as the policemen. The soldiers marching through the wynds came frequently upon him, and found it hard to believe that he was always the same one. They told afterwards that Thrums was remarkable for the ferocity of its women, and the number of its little ministers. The morning was nipping cold, and the streets were deserted, for the people had been ordered within doors. As he crossed the Roods, Gavin saw a gleam of redcoats. In the back wynd he heard a bugle blown. A stir in the Banker's close spoke of another seizure. At the top of the school wynd two policemen, of whom one was Wearyworld, stopped the minister with the flash of a lantern.

"We dauredna let you pass, sir," the Tilliedrum man said, "without a good look at you. That's the orders."

"I hereby swear," said Wearyworld, authoritatively, "that this is no the Egyptian. Signed, Peter Spens, policeman, called by the vulgar Wearyworld. Mr. Dishart, you can pass, unless you'll bide a wee and gie us your crack."

"You have not found the gypsy, then?" Gavin asked.

"No," the other policeman said, "but we ken she's within cry o' this very spot, and escape she canna."

"What mortal man can do," Wearyworld said, "we're doing; ay, and mair, but she's auld wecht, and may find bilbie in queer places. Mr. Dishart, my official opinion is that this Egyptian is fearsomely like my snuff-spoon. I've kent me drap that spoon on the fender, and be beat to find it in an hour. And yet, a' the time I was sure it was there. This is a gey mysterious world, and women's the uncanniest things in't. It's hardly mous to think how uncanny they are."

"This one deserves to be punished," Gavin said, firmly; "she incited the people to riot."

"She did," agreed Wearyworld, who was supping ravenously on sociability; "ay, she even tried her tricks on me, so that them that kens no better thinks she fooled me. But she's cracky. To gie her her due, she's cracky, and as for her being a cuttie, you've said yoursel', Mr. Dishart, that we're all desperately wicked. But we're sair tried. Has it ever struck you that the trouts bites best on the Sabbath? God's critturs tempting decent men."

"Come alang," cried the Tilliedrum man, impatiently.

"I'm coming, but I maun give Mr. Dishart permission to pass first. Hae you heard, Mr. Dishart," Wearyworld whispered, "that the Egyptian diddled baith the captain and the shirra? It's my official opinion that she's no better than a roasted onion, the which, if you grip it firm, jumps out o' sicht, leaving its coat in your fingers. Mr. Dishart, you can pass."

The policeman turned down the school wynd, and Gavin, who had already heard exaggerated accounts of the strange woman's escape from the town-house, proceeded along the Tenements. He walked in the black shadows of the houses, though across the way there was the morning light.

In talking of the gypsy, the little minister had, as it were, put on the black cap; but now, even though he shook his head angrily with every thought of her, the scene in Windyghoul glimmered before his eyes. Sometimes when he meant to frown he only sighed, and then having sighed he shook himself. He was unpleasantly conscious of his right hand, which had flung the divit. Ah, she was shameless, and it would be a bright day for Thrums that saw the last of her. He hoped the policemen would succeed in— It was the gladsomeness of innocence that he had seen dancing in the moonlight. A mere woman could not be like that. How soft— And she had derided him; he, the Auld Licht minister of Thrums, had been flouted before his people by a hussy. She was without reverence, she knew no dif-

ference between an Auld Licht minister, whose duty it was to speak and
hers to listen, and herself. This woman deserved to be— And the look she
cast behind her as she danced and sang! It was sweet, so wistful; the presence of purity had silenced him. Purity! Who had made him fling that
divit? He would think no more of her. Let it suffice that he knew what she
was. He would put her from his thoughts. Was it a ring on her finger?

Fifty yards in front of him Gavin saw the road end in a wall of soldiers.
They were between him and the manse, and he was still in darkness. No
sound reached him, save the echo of his own feet. But was it an echo? He
stopped, and turned round sharply. Now he heard nothing, he saw nothing.
Yet was not that a human figure standing motionless in the shadow behind?

He walked on, and again heard the sound. Again he looked behind, but
this time without stopping. The figure was following him. He stopped.
So did it. He turned back, but it did not move. It was the Egyptian!

Gavin knew her, despite the lane of darkness, despite the long cloak that
now concealed even her feet, despite the hood over her head. She was
looking quite respectable, but he knew her.

He neither advanced to her nor retreated. Could the unhappy girl not
see that she was walking into the arms of the soldiers? But doubtless she
had been driven from all her hiding-places. For a moment Gavin had it in
his heart to warn her. But it was only for a moment. The next a sudden
horror shot through him. She was stealing towards him, so softly that he
had not seen her start. The woman had designs on him! Gavin turned from
her. He walked so quickly that judges would have said he ran.

The soldiers, I have said, stood in the dim light. Gavin had almost reached
them, when a little hand touched his arm.

"Stop," cried the sergeant, hearing some one approaching, and then
Gavin stepped out of the darkness with the gypsy on his arm.

"It is you, Mr. Dishart," said the sergeant, "and your lady?"

"I—" said Gavin.

His lady pinched his arm.

"Yes," she answered, in an elegant English voice that made Gavin stare
at her, "but, indeed, I am sorry I ventured into the streets to-night. I
thought I might be able to comfort some of these unhappy people, captain,
but I could do little, sadly little."

"It is no scene for a lady, ma'am, but your husband has— Did you speak,
Mr. Dishart?"

"Yes, I must inf—"

"My dear," said the Egyptian, "I quite agree with you, so we need not
detain the captain."

"I'm only a sergeant, ma'am."

"Indeed!" said the Egyptian, raising her pretty eyebrows, "and how long
are you to remain in Thrums, sergeant?"

"Only for a few hours, Mrs. Dishart. If this gypsy lassie had not given
us so much trouble, we might have been gone by now."

"Ah, yes, I hope you will catch her, sergeant."

"Sergeant," said Gavin, firmly, "I must—"

"You must indeed, dear," said the Egyptian, "for you are sadly tired. Good night, sergeant."

"Your servant, Mrs. Dishart. Your servant, sir."

"But—" cried Gavin.

"Come, love," said the Egyptian, and she walked the distracted minister through the soldiers, and up the manse road.

The soldiers left behind, Gavin flung her arm from him, and, standing still, shook his fist in her face.

"You—you—woman!" he said.

This, I think, was the last time he called her a woman.

But she was clapping her hands merrily.

"It was beautiful!" she exclaimed.

"It was iniquitous!" he answered. "And I a minister!"

"You can't help that," said the Egyptian, who pitied all ministers heartily.

"No," Gavin said, misunderstanding her. "I could not help it. No blame attaches to me."

"I meant that you could not help being a minister. You could have helped saving me, and I thank you so much."

"Do not dare to thank me. I forbid you to say that I saved you. I did my best to hand you over to the authorities."

"Then why did you not hand me over?"

Gavin groaned.

"All you had to say," continued the merciless Egyptian, "was, 'This is the person you are in search of.' I did not have my hand over your mouth. Why did you not say it?"

"Forbear!" said Gavin, wofully.

"It must have been," the gypsy said, "because you really wanted to help me."

"Then it was against my better judgment," said Gavin.

"I am glad of that," said the gypsy. "Mr. Dishart, I do believe you like me all the time."

"Can a man like a woman against his will?" Gavin blurted out.

"Of course he can," said the Egyptian, speaking as one who knew. "That is the very nicest way to be liked."

Seeing how agitated Gavin was, remorse filled her, and she said, in a wheedling voice:

"It is all over, and no one will know."

Passion sat on the minister's brow, but he said nothing, for the gypsy's face had changed with her voice, and the audacious woman was become a child.

"I am very sorry," she said, as if he had caught her stealing jam. The hood had fallen back, and she looked pleadingly at him. She had the appearance of one who was entirely in his hands.

There was a torrent of words in Gavin, but only these trickled forth:

"I don't understand you."

"You are not angry any more?" pleaded the Egyptian.

"Angry!" he cried, with the righteous rage of one who, when his leg is being sawn off, is asked gently if it hurts him.

"I know you are," she sighed, and the sigh meant that men are strange.

"Have you no respect for law and order?" demanded Gavin.

"Not much," she answered, honestly.

He looked down the road to where the redcoats were still visible, and his face became hard. She read his thoughts.

"No," she said, becoming a woman again, "it is not yet too late. Why don't you shout to them?"

"I do not understand you," Gavin repeated, weakly, and the gypsy bent her head under this terrible charge.

"Only a few hours ago," he continued, "you were a gypsy girl in a fantastic dress, barefooted—"

The Egyptian's bare foot at once peeped out mischievously from beneath the cloak, then again retired into hiding.

"You spoke as broadly," complained the minister, somewhat taken aback by this apparition, "as any woman in Thrums, and now you fling a cloak over your shoulders, and immediately become a fine lady. Who are you?"

"Perhaps," answered the Egyptian, "it is the cloak that has bewitched me." She slipped out of it. "Ay, ay, ou losh!" she said, as if surprised, "it was just the cloak that did it, for now I'm a puir ignorant bit lassie again. My, certie, but claithes does make a differ to a woman!"

This was sheer levity, and Gavin walked scornfully away from it.

"Yet, if you will not tell me who you are," he said, looking over his shoulder, "tell me where you got the cloak."

"Na faags," replied the gypsy out of the cloak. "Really, Mr. Dishart, you had better not ask," she added, replacing it over her.

She followed him, meaning to gain the open by the fields to the north of the manse.

"Good-bye," she said, holding out her hand, "if you are not to give me up."

"I am not a policeman," replied Gavin, but he would not take her hand.

"Surely, we part friends, then?" said the Egyptian, sweetly.

"No," Gavin answered. "I hope never to see your face again."

"I cannot help," the Egyptian said, with dignity, "your not liking my face." Then, with less dignity, she added, "There is a splotch of mud on your own, little minister; it came off the divit you flung at the captain."

With this parting shot she tripped past him, and Gavin would not let his eyes follow her.

Margaret was at her window, looking for him, and he saw her, though she did not see him. He was stepping into the middle of the road to wave his hand to her, when some sudden weakness made him look towards the fields instead. The Egyptian saw him and nodded thanks for his interest in her, but he scowled and pretended to be studying the sky. Next moment he saw her running back to him.

"There are soldiers at the top of the field," she cried. "I cannot escape that way."

"There is no other way," Gavin answered.

"Will you not help me again?" she entreated.

She should not have said "again." Gavin shook his head, but pulled her closer to the manse dyke, for his mother was still in sight.

"Why do you do that?" the girl asked, quickly, looking round to see if she were pursued. "Oh, I see," she said, as her eyes fell on the figure at the window.

"It is my mother," Gavin said, though he need not have explained, unless he wanted the gypsy to know that he was a bachelor.

"Only your mother?"

"Only! Let me tell you she may suffer more than you for your behaviour to-night!"

"How can she?"

"If you are caught, will it not be discovered that I helped you to escape?"

"But you said you did not."

"Yes, I helped you," Gavin admitted. "My God! what would my congregation say if they knew I had let you pass yourself off as—as my wife?"

He struck his brow, and the Egyptian had the propriety to blush.

"It is not the punishment from men I am afraid of," Gavin said, bitterly, "but from my conscience. No, that is not true. I do fear exposure, but for my mother's sake. Look at her; she is happy, because she thinks me good and true; she has had such trials as you cannot know of, and now, when at last I seemed able to do something for her, you destroy her happiness. You have her life in your hands."

The Egyptian turned her back upon him, and one of her feet tapped angrily on the dry ground. Then, child of impulse as she always was, she flashed an indignant glance at him, and walked quickly down the road.

"Where are you going?" he cried.

"To give myself up. You need not be alarmed; I will clear you."

There was not a shake in her voice, and she spoke without looking back.

"Stop!" Gavin called, but she would not, until his hand touched her shoulder.

"What do you want?" she asked.

"Why—" whispered Gavin, giddily, "why—why do you not hide in the manse garden? No one will look for you there."

There were genuine tears in the gypsy's eyes now.

"You are a good man," she said; "I like you."

"Don't say that," Gavin cried, in horror. "There is a summer-seat in the garden."

Then he hurried from her, and, without looking to see if she took his advice, hastened to the manse. Once inside, he snibbed the door.

# The Alien Corn

### W. SOMERSET MAUGHAM

I HAD known the Blands a long time before I discovered that they had any connection with Ferdy Rabenstein. Ferdy must have been nearly fifty when I first knew him, and at the time of which I write he was well over seventy. He had altered little. His hair, coarse but abundant and curly, was white, but he had kept his figure and held himself as gallantly as ever. It was not hard to believe that in youth he had been as beautiful as people said. He had still his fine Semitic profile and the lustrous black eyes that had caused havoc in so many a Gentile breast. He was very tall, lean, with an oval face and a clear skin. He wore his clothes very well, and in evening dress, even now, he was one of the handsomest men I had ever seen. He wore then large black pearls in his shirt front and platinum and sapphire rings on his fingers. Perhaps he was rather flashy, but you felt it was so much in character that it would have ill become him to be anything else.

"After all, I am an Oriental," he said. "I can carry a certain barbaric magnificence."

I have often thought that Ferdy Rabenstein would make an admirable subject for a biography. He was not a great man, but within the limits he set himself he made of his life a work of art. It was a masterpiece in little, like a Persian miniature, and derived its interest from its perfection. Unfortunately the materials are scanty. They would consist of letters that may very well have been destroyed and the recollections of people who are old now and will soon be dead. His memory is extraordinary, but he would never write his memoirs, for he looks upon his past as a source of purely private entertainment; and he is a man of the most perfect discretion. Nor do I know anyone who could do justice to the subject but Max Beerbohm. There is no one else in this hard world of to-day who can look upon the trivial with such tender sympathy and wring such a delicate pathos from futility. I wonder that Max, who must have known Ferdy much better than I, and long before, was never tempted to exercise his exquisite fancy on such a theme. He was born for Max to write about. And who should have illustrated the elegant book that I see in my mind's eye but Aubrey Beardsley? Thus would have been erected a monument of triple brass and the ephemera imprisoned to succeeding ages in the amber's exquisite translucency.

Ferdy's conquests were social and his venue was the great world. He was born in South Africa and did not come to England till he was twenty. For some time he was on the Stock Exchange, but on the death of his father he inherited a considerable fortune, and retiring from business devoted himself to the life of a man about town. At that period English society was still a closed body and it was not easy for a Jew to force its barriers, but to Ferdy they fell like the walls of Jericho. He was handsome, he was rich, he was a sportsman and he was good company. He had a house in Curzon Street, furnished with the most beautiful French furniture, and a French chef, and a brougham. It would be interesting to know the first steps in his wonderful career: they are lost in the dark abysm of time. When I first met him he had been long established as one of the smartest men in London: this was at a very grand house in Norfolk to which I had been asked as a promising young novelist by the hostess who took an interest in letters, but the company was very distinguished and I was overawed. We were sixteen, and I felt shy and alone among these cabinet ministers, great ladies and peers of the realm who talked of people and things of which I knew nothing. They were civil to me, but indifferent, and I was conscious that I was somewhat of a burden to my hostess. Ferdy saved me. He sat with me, walked with me and talked with me. He discovered that I was a writer and we discussed the drama and the novel; he learnt that I had lived much on the continent and he talked to me pleasantly of France, Germany and Spain. He seemed really to seek my society. He gave me the flattering impression that he and I stood apart from the other members of the company and by our conversation upon affairs of the spirit made that of the rest of them, the political situation, the scandal of somebody's divorce and the growing disinclination of pheasants to be killed, seem a little ridiculous. But if Ferdy had at the bottom of his heart a feeling of ever so faint a contempt for the hearty British gentry that surrounded us I am sure that it was only to me that he allowed an inkling of it to appear, and looking back I cannot but wonder whether it was not after all a suave and very delicate compliment that he paid me. I think of course that he liked to exercise his charm, and I daresay the obvious pleasure his conversation gave me gratified him, but he could have had no motive for taking so much trouble over an obscure novelist other than his real interest in art and letters. I felt that he and I at bottom were equally alien in that company, I because I was a writer and he because he was a Jew, but I envied the ease with which he bore himself. He was completely at home. Everyone called him Ferdy. He seemed to be always in good spirits. He was never at a loss for a quip, a jest or a repartee. They liked him in that house because he made them laugh but never made them uncomfortable by talking above their heads. He brought a faint savour of Oriental romance into their lives, but so cleverly that they only felt more English. You could never be dull when he was by and with him present you were safe from the fear of the devastating silences that sometimes overwhelm a British company. A pause looked inevitable and Ferdy Rabenstein had broken into a topic that interested everyone. An invaluable asset to any party. He had an inexhaustible fund of Jewish stories. He was a very good mimic and he assumed the Yiddish accent and reproduced the Jewish gestures to perfection; his head sank into his body, his face grew cunning, his voice oily, and he was a rabbi or an old-clothes merchant or a smart commercial traveller or a fat procuress in Frankfort. It was as good as a play. Because he was himself a Jew and insisted on it you laughed without reserve, but for my own part not without an undercurrent of discomfort. I was not quite sure of a sense of humour that made such cruel fun of his own race. I discovered afterwards that Jewish stories were his speciality, and I seldom met him anywhere without hearing him tell sooner or later the last he had heard.

But the best story he told me on this occasion was not a Jewish one. It struck me so that I have never forgotten it, but for one reason or another I have never had occasion to tell it again. I give it here because it is a curious little incident concerning persons whose names at least will live in the social history of the Victorian Era and I think it would be a pity if it were lost. He told me then that once when quite a young man he was staying in the country in a house where Mrs. Langtry, at that time at the height of her beauty and astounding reputation, was also a guest. It happened to be within driving distance of that in which lived the Duchess of Somerset, who had been Queen of Beauty at the Eglinton Tournament, and knowing her slightly, it occurred to him that it would be interesting to bring the two women together. He suggested it to Mrs. Langtry, who was willing, and forthwith wrote to the Duchess asking if he might bring the celebrated beauty to call on her. It was fitting, he said, that the loveliest woman of this generation (this was in the eighties) should pay her respects to the loveliest woman of the last. 'Bring her by all means,' answered the Duchess, 'but I warn you that it will be a shock to her.' They drove over in a carriage and pair, Mrs. Langtry in a close-fitting blue bonnet with long satin strings, which showed the exquisite shape of her head and made her blue eyes even bluer, and were received by a little ugly old hag who looked with irony out of her beady eyes at the radiant beauty who had come to see her. They had tea, they talked and they drove home again. Mrs. Langtry was very silent and when Ferdy looked at her he saw that she was quietly weeping. When they got back to the house she went to her room and would not come down to dinner that night. For the first time she had realized that beauty dies.

Ferdy asked me for my address and a few days after I got back to London invited me to dinner. There were only six of us, an American woman married to an English peer, a Swedish painter, an actress and a well-known critic. We ate very good food and drank excellent wine. The conversation was easy and intelligent. After dinner Ferdy was persuaded to play the piano. He only played Viennese waltzes—I discovered later that they were his speciality—and the light, tuneful and sensual music seemed to accord well with his discreet flamboyance. He played without affectation, with a lilt, and he had a graceful touch. This was the first of a good many dinners I had with him; he would ask me two or three times a year, and as time passed I met him more and more frequently at other people's houses. I rose in the world and perhaps he came down a little. Of late years I had sometimes found him at parties where other Jews were, and I fancied that I read in his shining liquid eyes, resting for a moment on these members of his race, a certain good-natured amusement at the thought of what the world was coming to. There were people who said he was a snob, but I do not think he was; it just happened that in his early days he had never met any but the great. He had a real passion for art, and in his commerce with those that produced it was at his best. With them he had never that faint air of persiflage which when he was with very grand persons made you suspect that he was never quite the dupe of their grandeur. His taste was exquisite and many of his friends were glad to avail themselves of his knowledge. He was one of the first to value old furniture, and he rescued many an exquisite piece from the attics of ancestral mansions and gave it an honourable place in the drawing-room. It amused him to saunter round the auction rooms, and he was always willing to give his advice to great ladies who desired at once to acquire a beautiful thing and make a profitable investment. He was rich and good-natured. He liked to patronize the arts and would take a great deal of trouble to get commissions for some young painter whose talent he admired or an engagement to play at a rich man's house for a violinist who could in no other way get a hearing. But he never let his rich man down. His taste was too good to deceive, and civil though he might be to the mediocre he would not lift a finger to help him. His own musical parties, very small and carefully chosen, were a treat.

He never married.

"I am a man of the world," he said, "and I flatter myself that I have no prejudices, *tous les goûts sont dans la nature*, but I do not think I could bring myself to marry a Gentile. There's no harm in going to the opera in a dinner-jacket, but it just would never occur to me to do so."

"Then why didn't you marry a Jewess?"

(I did not hear this conversation, but the lively and audacious creature who thus tackled him told me of it.)

"Oh, my dear, our women are so prolific. I could not bear the thought of peopling the world with a little Ikey and a little Jacob and a little Rebecca and a little Leah and a little Rachel."

But he had had affairs of note and the glamour of past romance still clung to him. He was in his youth of an amorous complexion. I have met old ladies who told me that he was irresistible, and when in reminiscent mood they talked to me of this woman and that who had completely lost her head over him, I divined that, such was his beauty, they could not find it in their hearts to blame them. It was interesting to hear of great ladies that I had read of in the memoirs of the day or had met as respectable dowagers garrulous over their grandsons at Eton or making a mess of a hand at bridge and bethink myself that they had been consumed with sinful passion for the handsome Jew. Ferdy's most notorious amour was with the Duchess of Hereford, the loveliest, the most gallant and dashing of the beauties of the end of Queen Victoria's reign. It lasted for twenty years. He had doubtless flirtations meanwhile, but their relations were stable and recognized. It was proof of his marvellous tact that when at last they ended he exchanged an aging mistress for a loyal friend. I remember meeting the pair not so very long ago at luncheon. She was an old woman, tall and of a commanding presence, but with a mask of paint on a ravaged face. We were lunching at the Carlton and Ferdy, our host, came a few minutes late. He offered us a cocktail and the Duchess told him we had already had one.

"Ah, I wondered why your eyes were so doubly bright," he said.

The old rattled woman flushed with pleasure.

My youth passed, I grew middle-aged, I wondered how soon I must begin to describe myself as elderly; I wrote books and plays, I travelled, I underwent experiences, I fell in love and out of it; and still I kept meeting Ferdy at parties. War broke out and was waged, millions of men were killed and the face of the world was changed. Ferdy did not like the war. He was too old to take part in it, and his German name was awkward, but he was discreet and took care not to expose himself to humiliation. His old friends were faithful to him, and he lived in a dignified but not too strict seclusion. But then peace came and with courage he set himself to making the best of changed conditions. Society was mixed now, parties were rowdy, but Ferdy fitted himself to the new life. He still told his funny Jewish stories, he still played charmingly the waltzes of Strauss, he still went round auction rooms and told the new rich what they ought to buy. I went to live abroad, but whenever I was in London I saw Ferdy, and now there was something a little uncanny in him. He did not give in. He had never known a day's illness. He seemed never to grow tired. He still dressed beautifully. He was interested in everybody. His mind was alert and people asked him to dinner, not for old times' sake, but because he was worth his salt. He still gave charming little concerts at his house in Curzon Street.

It was when he invited me to one of these that I made the discovery that started the recollections of him I have here set down. We were dining at a house in Hill Street, a large party, and the women having gone upstairs Ferdy and I found ourselves side by side. He told me that Lea Makart was coming to play for him on the following Friday evening and he would be glad if I would come.

"I'm awfully sorry," I said, "but I'm going down to the Blands."

"What Blands?"

"They live in Sussex at a place called Tilby."

"I didn't know you knew them."

He looked at me rather strangely. He smiled. I didn't know what amused him.

"Oh, yes, I've known them for years. It's a very nice house to stay at."

"Adolph is my nephew."

"Sir Adolphus?"

"It suggests one of the bucks of the Regency, doesn't it? But I will not conceal from you that he was named Adolph."

"Everyone I know calls him Freddy."

"I know, and I understand that Miriam, his wife, only answers to the name of Muriel."

"How does he happen to be your nephew?"

"Because Hannah Rabenstein, my sister, married Alphonse Bleikogel, who ended life as Sir Alfred Bland, first baronet and Adolph, their only son, in due course became Sir Adolphus Bland, second baronet."

"Then Freddy Bland's mother, the Lady Bland who lives in Portland Place, is your sister?"

"Yes, my sister Hannah. She was the eldest of the family. She's eighty, but in full possession of her faculties and a remarkable woman."

"I've never met her."

"I think your friends the Blands would just as soon you didn't. She has never lost her German accent."

"Do you never see them?" I asked.

"I haven't spoken to them for twenty years. I am such a Jew and they are so English." He smiled. "I could never remember that their names were Freddy and Muriel. I used to come out with an Adolph or a Miriam at awkward moments. And they didn't like my stories. It was better that we should not meet. When the war broke out and I would not change my name it was the last straw. It was too late. I could never have accustomed my friends to think of me as anything but Ferdy Rabenstein. I was quite content. I was not ambitious to be a Smith, a Brown, or a Robinson."

Though he spoke facetiously, there was in his tone the faintest possible derision and I felt, hardly felt even, the sensation was so shadowy, that, as it had often vaguely seemed to me before, there was in the depth of his impenetrable heart a cynical contempt for the Gentiles he had conquered.

"Then you don't know the two boys?" I said.

"No."

"The eldest is called George, you know. I don't think he's so clever as Harry, the other one, but he's an engaging youth. I think you'd like him."

"Where is he now?"

"Well, he's just been sent down from Oxford. I suppose he's at home. Harry's still at Eton."

"Why don't you bring George to lunch with me?"

"I'll ask him. I should think he'd love to come."

"It has reached my ears that he's been a little troublesome."

"Oh, I don't know. He wouldn't go into the army, which is what they wanted. They rather fancied the Guards. And so he went to Oxford instead. He didn't work and he spent a great deal of money and he painted the town red. It was all quite normal."

"What was he sent down for?"

"I don't know. Nothing of any consequence."

At that moment our host rose and we went upstairs. When Ferdy bade me good-night he asked me not to forget about his great-nephew.

"Ring me up," he said. "Wednesday would suit me. Or Friday."

Next day I went down to Tilby. It was an Elizabethan mansion standing in a spacious park, in which roamed fallow deer, and from its windows you had wide views of rolling downs. It seemed to me that as far as the eye could reach the land belonged to the Blands. His tenants must have found Sir Adolphus a wonderful landlord, for I never saw farms kept in such order, the barns and cow-sheds were spick and span and the pigsties were a picture; the public-houses looked like old English water-colours and the cottages he had built on the estate combined admirably picturesqueness and convenience. It must have cost him a pot of money to run the place on these lines. Fortunately he had it. The park with its grand old trees (and its nine-hole golf course) was tended like a garden, and the wide-stretching gardens were the pride of the neighbourhood. The magnificent house, with its steep roofs and mullioned windows, had been restored by the most celebrated architect in England and furnished by Lady Bland, with taste and knowledge, in a style that perfectly fitted it.

"Of course it's very simple," she said. "Just an English house in the country."

The dining-room was adorned with old English sporting pictures, and the Chippendale chairs were of incredible value. In the drawing-room were portraits by Reynolds and Gainsborough and landscapes by Old Crome and Richard Wilson. Even in my bedroom with its four-post bed were water-colours by Birket Foster. It was very beautiful and a treat to stay there, but though it would have distressed Muriel Bland beyond anything to know it, it missed oddly enough entirely the effect she had sought. It did not give you for a moment the impression of an English house. You had the feeling that every object had been bought with a careful eye to the general scheme. You missed the dull Academy portraits that hung in the dining-room beside a Carlo Dolci that an ancestor had brought back from the grand tour, and the water-colours painted by a great-aunt that cluttered up the drawing-room so engagingly. There was no ugly Victorian sofa that had always been there and that it never occurred to anybody to take away, and no needlework chairs that an unmarried daughter had so painstakingly worked at about the time of the Great Exhibition. There was beauty but no sentiment.

And yet how comfortable it was and how well looked after you were! And what a cordial greeting the Blands gave you! They seemed really to like people. They were generous and kindly. They were never happier than when they were entertaining the county, and though they had not owned the property for more than twenty years they had established themselves firmly in the favour of their neighbours. Except perhaps in their splendour and the competent way in which the estate was run there was nothing to suggest that they had not been settled there for centuries.

Freddy had been at Eton and Oxford. He was now in the early fifties. He was quiet in manner, courtly, very clever, I imagine, but a trifle reserved. He had great elegance, but it was not an English elegance; he had grey hair and a short pointed grey beard, fine dark eyes and an aquiline nose. He was just above middle height; I don't think you would have taken him for a Jew, but rather for a foreign diplomat of some distinction. He was a man of character, but gave you, strangely enough, notwithstanding the success he had had in life, an impression of faint melancholy. His successes had been financial and political; in the world of sport, for all his perseverance, he had never shone. For many years he had followed hounds, but he was a bad rider and I think it must have been a relief to him when he could persuade himself that middle-age and pressure of business forced him to give up hunting. He had excellent shooting and gave grand parties for it, but he was a poor shot; and despite the course in his park he never succeeded in being more than an indifferent golfer. He knew only too well how much these things meant in England, and his incapacity was a bitter disappointment to him. However, George would make up for it.

George was scratch at golf, and though tennis was not his game he played much better than the average; the Blands had had him taught to shoot as soon as he was old enough to hold a gun, and he was a fine shot; they had put him on a pony when he was two, and Freddy, watching him mount his horse, knew that out hunting when the boy came to a fence he felt exhilaration and not that sickening feeling in the pit of his stomach which, though he had chased the fox with such grim determination, had always made the sport a torture to him. George was so tall and slim, his curly hair, of a palish brown, was so fine, his eyes were so blue, he was the perfect type of the young Englishman. He had the engaging candour of the breed. His nose was straight, though perhaps a trifle fleshy, and his lips were perhaps a little full and sensual, but he had beautiful teeth, and his smooth skin was like ivory. George was the apple of his father's eye. He did not like Harry, his second son, so well. He was rather stocky, broad-shouldered and strong for his age, but his black eyes, shining with cleverness, his coarse dark hair and his big nose revealed his race. Freddy was severe with him, and often impatient, but with George he was all indulgence. Harry would go into the business, he had brains and push, but George was the heir. George would be an English gentleman.

George had offered to motor me down in the roadster his father had given him as a birthday present. He drove very fast and we arrived before the rest of the guests. The Blands were sitting on the lawn and tea was laid out under a magnificent cedar.

"By the way," I said presently, "I saw Ferdy Rabenstein the other day and he wants me to bring George to lunch with him."

I had not mentioned the invitation to George on the way because I thought that if there had been a family coldness I had better address his parents as well.

"Who in God's name is Ferdy Rabenstein?" said George.

How brief is human glory! A generation back such a question would have seemed grotesque.

"He's by way of being your great-uncle," I replied.

A glance had passed from father to mother when I first spoke. "He's a horrid old man," said Muriel.

"I don't think it's in the least necessary for George to resume relationships that were definitely severed before he was born," said Freddy with decision.

"Anyhow I've delivered the message," said I, feeling somewhat snubbed.

"I don't want to see the old blighter," said George.

The conversation was broken off by the arrival of other guests, and in a little while George went off to play golf with one of his Oxford friends.

It was not till next day that the matter was referred to again. I had played an indifferent round with Freddy Bland in the morning, and several sets of what is known as country-house tennis in the afternoon, and was sitting alone with Muriel on the terrace. In England we have so much bad weather that it is only fair that a beautiful day should be more beautiful than anywhere in the world, and this June evening was perfect. The blue sky was cloudless and the air was balmy; before us stretched green rolling downs, and woods, and in the distance you saw red roofs of a little village and the grey tower of the village church. It was a day when to be alive was sufficient happiness. Detached lines of poetry hovered vaguely in my memory. Muriel and I had been chatting desultorily.

"I hope you didn't think it rather horrid of us to refuse to let George lunch with Ferdy," she said suddenly. "He's such a fearful snob, isn't he?"

"D'you think so? He's always been very nice to me."

"We haven't been on speaking terms for twenty years. Freddy never forgave him for his behaviour during the war. So unpatriotic, I thought, and one really must draw the line somewhere. You know, he absolutely refused to drop his horrible German name. With Freddy in Parliament and running munitions and all that sort of thing it was quite impossible. I don't know why he should want to see George. He can't mean anything to him."

"He's an old man. George and Harry are his great-nephews. He must leave his money to some one."

"We'd rather not have his money," said Muriel coldly.

Of course I didn't care a row of pins whether George went to lunch with Ferdy Rabenstein, and I was quite willing to let the matter drop, but evidently the Blands had talked it over and Muriel felt that some explanation was due to me.

"Of course you know that Freddy has Jewish blood in him," she said.

She looked at me sharply. Muriel was rather a big blonde woman and she spent a great deal of time trying to keep down the corpulence to which she was predisposed. She had been very pretty when young and even now was a comely person; but her round blue eyes, slightly prominent, her fleshy nose, the shape of her face and the back of her neck, her exuberant manner, betrayed her race. No Englishwoman, however fair-haired, ever looked like that. And yet her observation was designed to make me take it for granted that she was a Gentile. I answered discreetly.

"So many people have nowadays."

"I know. But there's no reason to dwell on it, is there? After all, we're absolutely English; no one could be more English than George, in appearance and manner and everything; I mean, he's such a fine sportsman and all that sort of thing. I can't see any object in his knowing Jews just because they happen to be distant connections of his."

"It's very difficult in England now not to know Jews, isn't it?"

"Oh, I know, in London one does meet a good many, and I think some of them are very nice. They're so artistic. I don't go so far as to say that Freddy and I deliberately avoid them—of course I wouldn't do that—but it just happens that we don't really know any of them very well. And down here, there simply aren't any to know."

I could not but admire the convincing manner in which she spoke. It would not have surprised me to be told that she really believed every word she said.

"You say that Ferdy might leave George his money. Well, I don't believe it's so very much anyway; it was quite a comfortable fortune before the war, but that's nothing nowadays. Besides, we're hoping that George will go in for politics when he's a little older, and I don't think it would do him any good in the constituency to inherit money from a Mr. Rabenstein."

"Is George interested in politics?" I asked, to change the conversation.

"Oh, I hope so. After all, there's the family constituency waiting for him. It's a safe Conservative seat and one can't expect Freddy to go on with the grind of the House of Commons indefinitely."

Muriel was grand. She talked already of the constituency as though twenty generations of Blands had sat for it. Her remark, however, was my first intimation that Freddy's ambition was not satisfied.

"I suppose Freddy would go to the House of Lords when George was old enough to stand."

"We've done a good deal for the party," said Muriel.

Muriel was a Catholic and she often told you that she had been educated in a convent—"Such sweet women, those nuns. I always said that if I had a daughter I should have sent her to a convent too"—but she liked her servants to be Church of England, and on Sunday evenings we had what was called supper because the fish was cold and there was ice cream, so that they could go to church, and we were waited on by two footmen instead of four. It was still light when we finished, and Freddy and I, smoking our cigars, walked up and down the terrace in the gloaming. I suppose Muriel had told him of her conversation with me, and it may be that his refusal to let George see his great-uncle still troubled him, but being subtler than she he attacked the question more indirectly. He told me that he had been very much worried about George. It had been a great disappointment that he had refused to go into the army.

"I should have thought he'd have loved the life," he said.

"And he would certainly have looked marvellous in his Guards' uniform."

"He would, wouldn't he?" returned Freddy, ingenuously. "I wonder he could resist that."

He had been completely idle at Oxford; although his father had given him a very large allowance, he had got monstrously into debt; and now he had been sent down. But though he spoke so tartly I could see that he was not a little proud of his scapegrace son, he loved him with, oh, such an un-English love, and in his heart it flattered him that George had cut such a dash.

"Why should you worry?" I said. "You don't really care if George has a degree or not."

Freddy chuckled.

"No, I don't suppose I do really. I always think the only important thing about Oxford is that people know you were there, and I daresay that George isn't any wilder than the other young men in his set. It's the future I'm thinking of. He's so damned idle. He doesn't seem to want to do anything but have a good time."

"He's young, you know."

"He's not interested in politics, and though he's so good at games he's not even very keen on sport. He seems to spend most of his time strumming the piano."

"That's a harmless amusement."

"Oh, yes, I don't mind that, but he can't go on loafing indefinitely. You see, all this will be his one day." Freddy gave a sweeping gesture that seemed to embrace the whole country, but I knew that he did not own it all yet. "I'm very anxious that he should be fit to assume his responsibilities. His mother is very ambitious for him, but I only want him to be an English gentleman."

Freddy gave me a sidelong glance as though he wanted to say something but hesitated in case I thought it ridiculous; but there is one advantage in being a writer, that, since people look upon you as of no account, they will often say things to you that they would not to their equals. He thought he would risk it.

"You know, I've got an idea that nowhere in the world now is the Greek ideal of life so perfectly cultivated as by the English country gentleman living on his estates. I think his life has the beauty of a work of art."

I could not but smile when I reflected that it was impossible for the English country gentleman in these days to do anything of the sort without a packet of money safely invested in American bonds, but I smiled with sympathy. I thought it rather touching that this Jewish financier should cherish so romantic a dream.

"I want him to be a good landlord. I want him to take his part in the affairs of the country. I want him to be a thorough sportsman."

"Poor mutt," I thought, but said: "Well, what are your plans for George now?"

"I think he has a fancy for the diplomatic service. He's suggested going to Germany to learn the language."

"A very good idea, I should have thought."

"For some reason he's got it into his head that he wants to go to Munich."

"A nice place."

Next day I went back to London and shortly after my arrival rang up Ferdy.

"I'm sorry, but George isn't able to come to lunch on Wednesday."

"What about Friday?"

"Friday's no good either." I thought it useless to beat about the bush. "The fact is, his people aren't keen on his lunching with you."

There was a moment's silence. Then:

"I see. Well, will you come on Wednesday anyway?"

"Yes, I'd like to," I answered.

So on Wednesday at half-past one I strolled round to Curzon Street. Ferdy received me with the somewhat elaborate graciousness that he cultivated. He made no reference to the Blands. We sat in the drawing-room and I could not help reflecting what an eye for beautiful objects that family had. The room was more crowded than the fashion of to-day approves and the gold snuff-boxes in vitrines, the French china, appealed to a taste that was not mine; but they were no doubt choice pieces; and the Louis XV suite, with its beautiful *petit point*, must have been worth an enormous lot of money. The pictures on the walls by Lancret, Pater and Watteau did not greatly interest me, but I recognized their intrinsic excellence. It was a proper setting for this aged man of the world. It fitted his period. Suddenly the door opened and George was announced. Ferdy saw my surprise and gave me a little smile of triumph.

"I'm very glad you were able to come after all," he said as he shook George's hand.

I saw him in a glance take in his great-nephew whom he saw to-day for the first time. George was very elegantly dressed. He wore a short black coat, striped trousers and the grey double-breasted waistcoat which at that time was the mode. You could only wear it with elegance if you were tall and thin and your belly was slightly concave. I felt sure that Ferdy knew exactly who George's tailor was and what haberdasher he went to, and approved of them. George, so smart and trim, wearing his clothes so beautifully, certainly looked very handsome. We went down to luncheon. Ferdy had the social graces at his fingers' ends and he put the boy at his ease, but I saw that he was carefully appraising him; then, I do not know why, he began to tell some of his Jewish stories. He told them with gusto and with his wonderful mimicry. I saw George flush, and though he laughed at them, I could see that it was with embarrassment. I wondered what on earth had induced Ferdy to be so tactless. But he was watching George and he told story after story. It looked as though he would never stop. I wondered if for some reason I could not grasp he was taking a malicious pleasure in the boy's obvious discomfiture. At last we went upstairs, and to make things easier I asked Ferdy to play the piano. He played us three or four little waltzes. He had lost none of his exquisite lightness nor his sense of their lilting rhythm. Then he turned to George.

"Do you play?" he asked him.

"A little."

"Won't you play something?"

"I'm afraid I only play classical music. I don't think it would interest you."

Ferdy smiled slightly, but did not insist. I said it was time for me to go and George accompanied me.

"What a filthy old Jew," he said as soon as we were in the street. "I hated those stories of his."

"They're his great stunt. He always tells them."

"Would you if you were a Jew?"

I shrugged my shoulders.

"How is it you came to lunch after all?" I asked George.

He chuckled. He was a light-hearted creature, with a sense of humour, and he shook off the slight irritation his great-uncle had caused him.

"He went to see Granny. You don't know Granny, do you?"

"No."

"She treats Daddy like a kid in Etons. Granny said I was to go to lunch with Great-uncle Ferdy, and what Granny says goes."

"I see."

A week or two later George went to Munich to learn German. I happened then to go on a journey, and it was not till the following spring that I was again in London. Soon after my arrival I found myself sitting next to Muriel Bland at dinner. I asked after George.

"He's still in Germany," she said.

"I see in the papers that you're going to have a great beano at Tilby for his coming of age."

"We're going to entertain the tenants and they're making George a presentation."

She was less exuberant than usual, but I did not pay much attention to the fact. She led a strenuous life and it might be that she was tired. I knew she liked to talk of her son, so I continued.

"I suppose George has been having a grand time in Germany," I said.

She did not answer for a moment and I gave her a glance. I was surprised to see that her eyes were filled with tears.

"I'm afraid George has gone mad," she said.

"What do you mean?"

"We've been so frightfully worried. Freddy's so angry, he won't even discuss it. I don't know what we're going to do."

Of course it immediately occurred to me that George, who, I supposed, like most young Englishmen sent to learn the language, had been put with a German family, had fallen in love with the daughter of the house and wanted to marry her. I had a pretty strong suspicion that the Blands were intent on his making a very grand marriage.

"Why, what's happened?" I asked.

"He wants to become a pianist."

"A what?"

"A professional pianist."

"What on earth put that idea in his head?"

"Heaven knows. We didn't know anything about it. We thought he was working for his exam. I went out to see him. I thought I'd like to know that he was getting on all right. Oh, my dear. He looks like nothing on earth. And he used to be so smart; I could have cried. He told me he wasn't going in for the exam and had never had any intention of doing so; he'd only suggested the diplomatic service so that we'd let him go to Germany and he'd be able to study music."

"But has he any talent?"

"Oh, that's neither here nor there. Even if he had the genius of Paderewski we couldn't have George traipsing around the country playing at concerts. No one can deny that I'm very artistic, and so is Freddy—we love music and we've always known a lot of artists—but George will have a very great position; it's out of the question. We've set our hearts on his going into Parliament. He'll be very rich one day. There's nothing he can't aspire to."

"Did you point all that out to him?"

"Of course I did. He laughed at me. I told him he'd break his father's heart. He said his father could always fall back on Harry. Of course I'm devoted to Harry, and he's as clever as a monkey, but it was always understood that he was to go into the business; even though I am his mother I can see that he hasn't got the advantages that George has. Do you know what he said to me? He said that if his father would settle five pounds a week on him he would resign everything in Harry's favour and Harry could be his father's heir and succeed to the baronetcy and everything. It's too ridiculous. He said that if the Crown Prince of Roumania could abdicate a throne he didn't see why he couldn't abdicate a baronetcy. But you can't do that. Nothing can prevent him from being third baronet and, if Freddy should be granted a peerage, from succeeding to it at Freddy's death. Do you know, he even wants to drop the name of Bland and take some horrible German name."

I could not help asking what.

"Bleikogel or something like that," she answered.

That was a name I recognized. I remembered Ferdy telling me that Hannah Rabenstein had married Alphonse Bleikogel, who became eventually Sir Alfred Bland, first baronet. It was all very strange. I wondered what had happened to the charming and so typically English boy whom I had seen only a few months before.

"Of course when I came home and told Freddy he was furious. I've never seen him so angry. He foamed at the mouth. He wired to George to come back immediately, and George wired back to say he couldn't on account of his work."

"Is he working?"

"From morning till night. That's the maddening part of it. He never did a stroke of work in his life. Freddy used to say he was born idle."

"H'm."

"Then Freddy wired to say that if he didn't come he'd stop his allowance, and George wired back: 'Stop it.' That put the lid on. You don't know what Freddy can be when his back is up."

I knew that Freddy had inherited a large fortune, but I knew also that he had immensely increased it, and I could well imagine that behind the courteous and amiable Squire of Tilby there was a ruthless man of affairs. He had been used to having his own way, and I could believe that when crossed he would be hard and cruel.

"We'd been making George a very handsome allowance, but you know how frightfully extravagant he was. We didn't think he'd be able to hold out long, and in point of fact within a month he wrote to Ferdy and asked him to lend him a hundred pounds. Ferdy went to my mother-in-law—she's his sister, you know—and asked her what it meant. Though they hadn't spoken for twenty years Freddy went to see him and begged him not to send George a penny, and he promised he wouldn't. I don't know how George has been making both ends meet. I'm sure Freddy's right, but I can't help being rather worried. If I hadn't given Freddy my word of honour that I wouldn't send him anything I think I'd have slipped a few notes in a letter in case of accident. I mean, it's awful to think that perhaps he hasn't got enough to eat."

"It'll do him no harm to go short for a bit."

"We were in an awful hole, you know. We'd made all sorts of preparations for his coming of age, and I'd issued hundreds of invitations. Suddenly George said he wouldn't come. I was simply frantic. I wrote and wired. I would have gone over to Germany, only Freddy wouldn't let me. I practically went down on my bended knees to George. I begged him not to put us in such a humiliating position. I mean, it's the sort of thing it's so difficult to explain. Then my mother-in-law stepped in. You don't know her, do you? She's an extraordinary old woman. You'd never think she was Freddy's mother. She was German originally but of very good family."

"Oh?"

"To tell you the truth I'm rather frightened of her. She tackled Freddy and then she wrote to George herself. She said that if he'd come home for his twenty-first birthday she'd pay any debts he had in Munich and we'd all give a patient hearing to anything he had to say. He agreed to that and we're expecting him one day next week. But I'm not looking forward to it I can tell you."

She gave a deep sigh. When we were walking upstairs after dinner Freddy addressed me.

"I see Muriel has been telling you about George. The damned fool! I have no patience with him. Fancy wanting to be a pianist! It's so un-gentlemanly."

"He's very young, you know," I said soothingly.

"He's had things too easy for him. I've been much too indulgent. There's never been a thing he wanted that I haven't given him. I'll learn him."

The Blands had a discreet apprehension of the uses of advertisement, and I gathered from the papers that the celebrations at Tilby of George's twenty-first birthday were conducted in accordance with the usage of English county families. There were a dinner party and ball for the gentry and a collation and a dance in marquees on the lawn for the tenants. Expensive bands were brought down from London. In the illustrated papers were pictures of George, surrounded by his family being presented with a solid silver tea set by the tenantry. They had subscribed to have his portrait painted, but since his absence from the country had made it impossible for him to sit, the tea service had been substituted. I read in the columns of the gossip writers that his father had given him a hunter, his mother a gramophone that changed its own records, his grandmother the dowager Lady Bland an Encyclopædia Britannica and his great-uncle Ferdinand Rabenstein a Virgin and Child by Pellegrino da Modena. I could not help observing that these gifts were bulky and not readily convertible into cash. From Ferdy's presence at the festivities I concluded that George's unaccountable vagary had effected a reconciliation between uncle and nephew. I was right. Ferdy did not at all like the notion of his great-nephew becoming a professional pianist. At the first hint of danger to its prestige the family drew together and a united front was presented to oppose George's designs. Since I was not there I only know from hearsay what happened when the birthday celebrations were over. Ferdy told me something and so did Muriel, and later George gave me his version. The Blands had very much the impression that when George came home and found himself occupying the centre of the stage, when, surrounded by splendour, he saw for himself once more how much it meant to be the heir of a great estate, he would weaken. They surrounded him with love. They flattered him. They hung on his words. They counted on the goodness of his heart and thought that if they were very kind to him he would not have the courage to cause them pain. They seemed to take it for granted that he had no intention of going back to Germany, and in conversation included him in all their plans. George did not say very much. He seemed to be enjoying himself. He did not open a piano. Things looked as though they were going very well. Peace descended on the troubled house. Then one day at luncheon when they were discussing a garden party to which they had all been asked for one day of the following week, George said pleasantly:

"Don't count on me. I shan't be here."

"Oh, George, why not?" asked his mother.

"I must get back to my work. I'm leaving for Munich on Monday."

There was an awful pause. Everyone looked for something to say, but was afraid of saying the wrong thing, and at last it seemed impossible to break it. Luncheon was finished in silence. Then George went into the garden and the others, old Lady Bland and Ferdy, Muriel and Sir Adolphus, into the morning-room. There was a family council. Muriel wept. Freddy flew into a temper. Presently from the drawing-room they heard the sound of someone playing a nocturne of Chopin. It was George. It was as though, now he had announced his decision, he had gone for comfort, rest and strength to the instrument he loved. Freddy sprang to his feet.

"Stop that noise," he cried. "I won't have him play the piano in my house."

Muriel rang for a servant and gave him a message.

"Will you tell Mr. Bland that her ladyship has a bad headache and would he mind not playing the piano."

Ferdy, the man of the world, was deputed to have a talk with George. He was authorized to make him certain promises if he would give up the idea of becoming a pianist. If he did not wish to go into the diplomatic service his father would not insist, but if he would stand for Parliament he was prepared to pay his election expenses, give him a flat in London and make him an allowance of five thousand a year. I must say it was a handsome offer. I do not know what Ferdy said to the boy. I suppose he painted to him the life that a young man could lead in London on such an income. I am sure he made it very alluring. It availed nothing. All George asked was five pounds a week to be able to continue his studies and to be left alone. He was indifferent to the position that he might some day enjoy. He didn't want to hunt. He didn't want to shoot. He didn't want to be a Member of Parliament. He didn't want to be a millionaire. He didn't want to be a baronet. He didn't want to be a peer. Ferdy left him, defeated and in a state of considerable exasperation.

After dinner that evening there was a battle royal. Freddy was a quick-tempered man, unused to opposition, and he gave George the rough side of his tongue. I gather that it was very rough indeed. The women who sought to restrain his violence were sternly silenced. Perhaps for the first time in his life Freddy would not listen to his mother. George was obstinate and sullen. He had made up his mind and if his father didn't like it he could lump it. Freddy was peremptory. He forbade George to go back to Germany. George answered that he was twenty-one and his own master. He would go where he chose. Freddy swore he would not give him a penny.

"All right, I'll earn money."

"You! You've never done a stroke of work in your life. What do you expect to do to earn money?"

"Sell old clothes," grinned George.

There was a gasp from all of them. Muriel was so taken aback that she said a stupid thing.

"Like a Jew?"

"Well, aren't I a Jew? And aren't you a Jewess and isn't Daddy a Jew?

We're all Jews, the whole gang of us, and everyone knows it and what the hell's the good of pretending we're not?"

Then a very dreadful thing happened. Freddy burst suddenly into tears. I'm afraid he didn't behave very much like Sir Adolphus Bland, Bart., M.P., and the good old English gentleman he so much wanted to be, but like an emotional Adolph Bleikogel who loved his son and wept with mortification because the great hopes he had set on him were brought to nothing and the ambition of his life was frustrated. He cried noisily with great loud sobs and pulled his beard and beat his breast and rocked to and fro. Then they all began to cry, old Lady Bland and Muriel, and Ferdy, who sniffed and blew his nose and wiped the tears streaming down his face, and even George cried. Of course it was very painful, but to our rough Anglo-Saxon temperament I am afraid it must seem also a trifle ridiculous. No one tried to console anybody else. They just sobbed and sobbed. It broke up the party.

But it had no result on the situation. George remained obdurate. His father would not speak to him. There were more scenes. Muriel sought to excite his pity; he was deaf to her piteous entreaties, he did not seem to mind if he broke her heart, he did not care two hoots if he killed his father. Ferdy appealed to him as a sportsman and a man of the world. George was flippant and indeed personally offensive. Old Lady Bland with her guttural German accent and strong common sense argued with him, but he would not listen to reason. It was she, however, who at last found a way out. She made George acknowledge that it was no use to throw away all the beautiful things the world laid at his feet unless he had talent. Of course he thought he had, but he might be mistaken. It was not worth while to be a second-rate pianist. His only excuse, his only justification, was genius. If he had genius his family had no right to stand in his way.

"You can't expect me to show genius already," said George. "I shall have to work for years."

"Are you sure you are prepared for that?"

"It's my only wish in the world. I'll work like a dog. I only want to be given my chance."

This was the proposition she made. His father was determined to give him nothing, and obviously they could not let the boy starve. He had mentioned five pounds a week. Well, she was willing to give him that herself. He could go back to Germany and study for two years. At the end of that time he must come back and they would get some competent and disinterested person to hear him play, and if then that person said he showed promise of becoming a first-rate pianist no further obstacles would be placed in his way. He would be given every advantage, help and encouragement. If on the other hand that person decided that his natural gifts were not such as to ensure ultimate success he must promise faithfully to give up all thoughts of making music his profession and in every way accede to his father's wishes. George could hardly believe his ears.

"Do you mean that, Granny?"

"I do."

"But will Daddy agree?"

"I vill see dat he does," she answered.

George seized her in his arms and impetuously kissed her on both cheeks.

"Darling," he cried.

"Ah, but de promise?"

He gave her his solemn word of honour that he would faithfully abide by the terms of the arrangement. Two days later he went back to Germany. Though his father consented unwillingly to his going, and indeed could not help doing so, he would not be reconciled to him and when he left refused to say good-bye to him. I imagine that in no other manner could he have caused himself such pain. I permit myself a trite remark. It is strange that men, inhabitants for so short a while of an alien and inhuman world, should go out of their way to cause themselves so much unhappiness.

George had stipulated that during his two years of study his family should not visit him, so that when Muriel heard some months before he was due to come home that I was passing through Munich on my way to Vienna, whither business called me, it was not unnatural that she should ask me to look him up. She was anxious to have first-hand information about him. She gave me George's address and I wrote ahead, telling him I was spending a day in Munich, and asked him to lunch with me. His answer awaited me at the hotel. He said he worked all day and could not spare the time to lunch with me, but if I would come to his studio about six he would like to show me that and if I had nothing better to do would love to spend the evening with me. So soon after six I went to the address he gave me. He lived on the second floor of a large block of flats and when I came to his door I heard the sound of piano-playing. It stopped when I rang and George opened the door for me. I hardly recognized him. He had grown very fat. His hair was extremely long, it curled all over his head in picturesque confusion; and he had certainly not shaved for three days. He wore a grimy pair of Oxford bags, a tennis shirt and slippers. He was not very clean and his fingernails were rimmed with black. It was a startling change from the spruce, slim youth so elegantly dressed in such beautiful clothes that I had last seen. I could not but think it would be a shock to Ferdy to see him now. The studio was large and bare; on the walls were three or four unframed canvases of a highly cubist nature; there were several armchairs much the worse for wear, and a grand piano. Books were littered about and old newspapers and art magazines. It was dirty and untidy and there was a frousty smell of stale beer and stale smoke.

"Do you live here alone?" I asked.

"Yes, I have a woman who comes in twice a week and cleans up. But I make my own breakfast and lunch."

"Can you cook?"

"Oh, I only have bread and cheese and a bottle of beer for lunch. I dine at a *bier stube*."

It was pleasant to discover that he was very glad to see me. He seemed in great spirits and extremely happy. He asked after his relations and we talked of one thing and another. He had a lesson twice a week and for the rest of the time practised. He told me that he worked ten hours a day.

"That's a change," I said.

He laughed.

"Daddy said I was born tired. I wasn't really lazy. I didn't see the use of working at things that bored me."

I asked him how he was getting on with the piano. He seemed to be satisfied with his progress and I begged him to play to me.

"Oh, not now. I'm all in, I've been at it all day. Let's go out and dine and come back here later and then I'll play. I generally go to the same place; there are several students I know there, and it's rather fun."

Presently we set out. He put on socks and shoes and a very old golf coat, and we walked together through the wide quiet streets. It was a brisk cold day. His step was buoyant. He looked round him with a sigh of delight.

"I love Munich," he said. "It's the only city in the world where there's art in the very air you breathe. After all, art is the only thing that matters, isn't it? I loathe the idea of going home."

"All the same I'm afraid you'll have to."

"I know. I'll go all right, but I'm not going to think about it till the time comes."

"When you do, you might do worse than get a haircut. If you don't mind my saying so you look almost too artistic to be convincing."

"You English, you're such Philistines," he said.

He took me to a rather large restaurant in a side street, crowded even at that early hour with people dining and furnished heavily in the German medieval style. A table covered with a red cloth, well away from the air, was reserved for George and his friends, and when we went to it four or five youths were at it. There was a Pole studying Oriental languages, a student of philosophy, a painter—I suppose the author of George's cubist picture—a Swede, and a young man who introduced himself to me, clicking his heels, as Hans Reiting, *dichter*, namely Hans Reiting, poet. Not one of them was more than twenty-two and I felt a trifle out of it. They all addressed George as *du* and I noticed that his German was extremely fluent. I had not spoken it for some time and mine was rusty, so that I could not take much part in the lively conversation. But nevertheless I thoroughly enjoyed myself. They ate sparingly, but drank a good deal of beer. They talked of art and literature and life and ethics and motor-cars and women. They were very revolutionary, and though gay very much in earnest. They were contemptuous of everyone you had ever heard of, and the only point on which they all agreed was that in this topsy-turvy world only the vulgar could hope for success. They argued points of technique with animation, and contradicted one another, and shouted and were obscene. They had a grand time.

At about eleven George and I walked back to his studio. Munich is a

city that frolics demurely, and except about the Marienplatz the streets
were still and empty. When we got in he took off his coat and said:

"Now I'll play to you."

I sat in one of the dilapidated armchairs, and a broken spring stuck into
my behind, but I made myself as comfortable as I could. George played
Chopin. I know very little of music, and that is one of the reasons for
which I have found this story difficult to write. When I go to a concert at
the Queen's Hall and in the intervals read the programme it is all Greek to
me. I know nothing of harmony and counterpoint. I shall never forget how
humiliated I felt once when, having come to Munich for a Wagner Festival,
I went to a wonderful performance of *Tristan und Isolde* and never heard
a note of it. The first few bars sent me off and I began to think of what I
was writing, my characters leapt into life and I heard their long conversations, I suffered their pains and was a party to their joy; the years swept by
and all sorts of things happened to me, the spring brought me its rapture
and in the winter I was cold and hungry; and I loved and I hated and I
died. I suppose there were intervals in which I walked round and round the
garden and probably ate *schinken brödchen* and drank beer, but I have no
recollection of them. The only thing I know is that when the curtain for the
last time fell I woke with a start. I had had a wonderful time, but I could
not help thinking it was very stupid of me to come such a long way and
spend so much money if I couldn't pay attention to what I heard and saw.

I knew most of the things George played. They were the familiar pieces
of concert programmes. He played with a great deal of dash. Then he played
Beethoven's *Appassionata*. I used to play it myself when I played the piano
(very badly) in my far distant youth and I still knew every note of it. Of
course it is a classic and a great work, it would be foolish to deny it, but I
confess that at this time of day it leaves me cold. It is like *Paradise Lost*,
splendid, but a trifle stolid. This too George played with vigour. He sweated
profusely. At first I could not make out what was the matter with his playing, something did not seem to me quite right, and then it struck me that
the two hands did not exactly synchronize, so that there was ever so slight
an interval between the bass and the treble; but I repeat, I am ignorant of
these things; what disconcerted me might have been merely the effect of
his having drunk a good deal of beer that evening, or indeed only my fancy.
I said all I could think of to praise him.

"Of course I know I need a lot more work. I'm only a beginner, but I
know I can do it. I feel it in my bones. It'll take me ten years, but then I
shall be a pianist."

He was tired and came away from the piano. It was after midnight and I
suggested going, but he would not hear of it. He opened a couple of bottles
of beer and lit his pipe. He wanted to talk.

"Are you happy here?" I asked him.

"Very," he answered gravely. "I'd like to stay for ever. I've never had
such fun in my life. This evening for instance. Wasn't it grand?"

"It was very jolly. But one can't go on leading the student's life. Your friends here will grow older and go away."

"Others'll come. There are always students here and people like that."

"Yes, but you'll grow older too. Is there anything more lamentable than the middle-aged man who tries to go on living the undergraduate's life? The old fellow who wants to be a boy among boys, and tries to persuade himself that they'll accept him as one of themselves—how ridiculous he is. It can't be done."

"I feel so at home here. My poor father wants me to be an English gentleman. It gives me gooseflesh. I'm not a sportsman. I don't care a damn for hunting and shooting and playing cricket. I was only acting."

"You gave a very natural performance."

"It wasn't till I came here that I knew it wasn't real. I loved Eton and Oxford was a riot, but all the same I knew I didn't belong. I played the part all right, because acting's in my blood, but there was always something in me that wasn't satisfied. The house in Grosvenor Square is a freehold, and Daddy paid a hundred and eighty thousand pounds for Tilby; I don't know if you understand what I mean, I felt they were just furnished houses we'd taken for the season and one of these days we'd pack up and the real owners would come back."

I listened to him attentively, but I wondered how much he was describing what he had obscurely felt and how much he imagined now in his changed circumstances that he had felt.

"I used to hate hearing Great-uncle Ferdy tell his Jewish stories. I thought it so damned mean. I understand now; it was a safety valve. My God, the strain of being a man about town. It's easier for Daddy, he can play the old English squire at Tilby, but in the city he can be himself. He's all right. I've taken the make-up off and my stage clothes and at last I can be my real self too. What a relief! You know, I don't like English people. I never really know where I am with you. You're so dull and conventional. You never let yourselves go. There's no freedom in you, freedom of the soul, and you're such funks. There's nothing in the world you're so frightened of as doing the wrong thing."

"Don't forget that you're English yourself, George," I murmured.

He laughed.

"I? I'm not English. I haven't got a drop of English blood in me. I'm a Jew and you know it, and a German Jew into the bargain. I don't want to be English. I want to be a Jew. My friends are Jews. You don't know how much more easy I feel with them. I can be myself. We did everything we could to avoid Jews at home; Mummy because she was blonde thought she could get away with it and pretended she was a Gentile. What rot! D'you know, I have a lot of fun wandering about the Jewish parts of Munich and looking at the people. I went to Frankfort once—there are a lot of them there—and I walked about and looked at the frowsy old men with their hooked noses and the fat women with their false hair. I felt such a sympathy for them, I felt I belonged to them, I could have kissed them. When they looked at me I wondered if they knew that I was one of them. I wish to God I knew Yiddish. I'd like to become friends with them, and go into their houses and eat Kosher food and all that sort of thing. I wanted to go to a synagogue, but I was afraid I'd do the wrong thing and be kicked out. I like the smell of the Ghetto and the sense of life, and the mystery and the dust and the squalor and the romance. I shall never get the longing for it out of my head now. That's the real thing. All the rest is only pretence."

"You'll break your father's heart," I said.

"It's his or mine. Why can't he let me go? There's Harry. Harry would love to be squire of Tilby. He'd be an English gentleman all right. You know, Mummy's set her heart on my marrying a Christian. Harry would love to. He'll found the good old English family all right. After all, I ask so little. I only want five pounds a week, and they can keep the title and the park and the Gainsboroughs and the whole bag of tricks."

"Well, the fact remains that you gave your solemn word of honour to go back after two years."

"I'll go back all right," he said sullenly. "Lea Makart has promised to come and hear me play."

"What'll you do if she says you're no good?"

"Shoot myself," he said gaily.

"What nonsense," I answered in the same tone.

"Do *you* feel at home in England?"

"No," I said, "but then I don't feel at home anywhere else."

But he was quite naturally not interested in me.

"I loathe the idea of going back. Now that I know what life has to offer I wouldn't be an English country gentleman for anything in the world. My God, the boredom of it!"

"Money's a very nice thing and I've always understood it's very pleasant to be an English peer."

"Money means nothing to me. I want none of the things it can buy, and I don't happen to be a snob."

It was growing very late and I had to get up early next day. It seemed unnecessary for me to pay too much attention to what George said. It was the sort of nonsense a young man might very well indulge in when thrown suddenly among painters and poets. Art is strong wine and needs a strong head to carry. The divine fire burns most efficiently in those who temper its fury with horse sense. After all, George was not twenty-three yet. Time teaches. And when all was said and done his future was no concern of mine. I bade him good-night and walked back to my hotel. The stars were shining in the indifferent sky. I left Munich in the morning.

I did not tell Muriel on my return to London what George had said to me, or what he looked like, but contented myself with assuring her that he was well and happy, working very hard, and seemed to be leading a virtuous and sober life. Six months later he came home. Muriel asked me to go down to Tilby for the week-end: Ferdy was bringing Lea Makart to hear George play and he particularly wished me to be there. I accepted. Muriel met me at the station.

"How did you find George?" I asked.

"He's very fat, but he seems in great spirits. I think he's pleased to be back again. He's been very sweet to his father."

"I'm glad of that."

"Oh, my dear, I do hope Lea Makart will say he's no good. It'll be such a relief to all of us."

"I'm afraid it'll be a terrible disappointment to him."

"Life is full of disappointments," said Muriel crisply. "But one learns to put up with them."

I gave her a smile of amusement. We were sitting in a Rolls, and there was a footman as well as a chauffeur on the box. She wore a string of pearls that had probably cost forty thousand pounds. I recollected that in the birthday honours Sir Adolphus Bland had not been one of the three gentlemen on whom the King had been pleased to confer a peerage.

Lea Makart was able to make only a flying visit. She was playing that evening at Brighton and would motor over to Tilby on the Sunday morning for luncheon. She was returning to London the same day because she had a concert in Manchester on the Monday. George was to play in the course of the afternoon.

"He's practising very hard," his mother told me. "That's why he didn't come with me to meet you."

We turned in at the park gates and drove up the imposing avenue of elms that led to the house. I found that there was no party.

I met the dowager Lady Bland for the first time. I had always been curious to see her. I had had in my mind's eye a somewhat sensational picture of an old, old Jewish woman who lived alone in her grand house in Portland Place and, with a finger in every pie, ruled her family with a despotic hand. She did not disappoint me. She was of a commanding presence, rather tall, and stout without being corpulent. Her countenance was markedly Hebraic. She wore a rather heavy moustache and a wig of a peculiarly metallic brown. Her dress was very grand, of black brocade, and she had a row of large diamond stars on her breast and round her neck a chain of diamonds. Diamond rings gleamed on her wrinkled hands. She spoke in a rather loud harsh voice and with a strong German accent. When I was introduced to her she fixed me with shining eyes. She summed me up with despatch and to my fancy at all events made no attempt to conceal from me that the judgment she formed was unfavourable.

"You have known my brother Ferdinand for many years, is it not so?" she said, rolling a guttural *r*. "My brother Ferdinand has always moved in very good society. Where is Sir Adolphus, Muriel? Does he know your guest is arrived? And will you not send for George? If he does not know his pieces by now he will not know them by to-morrow."

Muriel explained that Freddy was finishing a round of golf with his secretary and that she had had George told I was there. Lady Bland looked as though she thought Muriel's replies highly unsatisfactory and turned again to me.

"My daughter tells me you have been in Italy?"

"Yes, I've only just come back."

"It is a beautiful country. How is the King?"

I said I did not know.

"I used to know him when he was a little boy. He was not very strong then. His mother, Queen Margarita, was a great friend of mine. They thought he would never marry. The Duchess of Aosta was very angry when he fell in love with that Princess of Montenegro."

She seemed to belong to some long past period of history, but she was very alert and I imagine that little escaped her beady eyes. Freddy, very spruce in plus fours, presently came in. It was amusing and yet a little touching to see this grey-bearded man, as a rule somewhat domineering, so obviously on his best behaviour with the old lady. He called her Mamma. Then George came in. He was as fat as ever, but he had taken my advice and had his hair cut; he was losing his boyish looks, but he was a powerful and well-set-up young man. It was good to see the pleasure he took in his tea. He ate quantities of sandwiches and great hunks of cake. He had still a boy's appetite. His father watched him with a tender smile, and as I looked at him I could not be surprised at the attachment which they all so obviously felt for him. He had an ingenuousness, a charm and an enthusiasm which were certainly very pleasant. There was about him a generosity of demeanour, a frankness and a natural cordiality which could not but make people take to him. I do not know whether it was owing to a hint from his grandmother or merely of his own good nature, but it was plain that he was going out of his way to be nice to his father; and in his father's soft eyes, in the way he hung upon the boy's words, in his pleased, proud and happy look, you felt how bitterly the estrangement of the last two years had weighed on him. He adored George.

We played golf in the morning, a three-ball match, since Muriel, having to go to Mass, could not join us, and at one Ferdy arrived in Lea Makart's car. We sat down to luncheon. Of course Lea Makart's reputation was well-known to me. She was acknowledged to be the greatest woman pianist in Europe. She was a very old friend of Ferdy's, who with his interest and patronage had greatly helped her at the beginning of her career, and it was he who had arranged for her to come and give her opinion of George's chances. At one time I went as often as I could to hear her play. She had no affectations; she played as a bird sings, without any appearance of effort, very naturally, and the silvery notes dripped from her light fingers in a curiously spontaneous manner, so that it gave you the impression that she was improvising those complicated rhythms. They used to tell me that her technique was wonderful. I could never make up my mind how much the delight her playing gave me was due to her person. In those days she was the most ethereal thing you could imagine, and it was surprising that a creature so sylphlike should be capable of so much power. She was very slight, pale, with enormous eyes and magnificent black hair, and at the piano she had a childlike wistfulness that was most appealing. She was very beautiful in a hardly human way, and when she played, a little smile on her closed lips, she seemed to be remembering things she had heard in another world. Now, however, a woman in the early forties, she was sylphlike no more; she was stout and her face had broadened; she had no longer that lovely remoteness, but the authority of her long succession of triumphs. She was brisk, businesslike and somewhat overwhelming. Her vitality lit her with a natural spotlight as his sanctity surrounds the saint with a halo. She was not interested in anything very much but her own affairs, but since she had humour and knew the world she was able to invest them with gaiety. She held the conversation, but did not absorb it. George talked little. Every now and then she gave him a glance, but did not try to draw him in. I was the only Gentile at the table. All but old Lady Bland spoke perfect English, yet I could not help feeling that they did not speak like English people; I think they rounded their vowels more than we do, they certainly spoke louder, and the words seemed not to fall, but to gush from their lips. I think if I had been in another room where I could hear the tone but not the words of their speech I should have thought it was in a foreign language that they were conversing. The effect was slightly disconcerting.

Lea Makart wished to set out for London at about six, so it was arranged that George should play at four. Whatever the result of the audition, I felt that I, a stranger in the circle which her departure must render exclusively domestic, would be in the way and so, pretexting an early engagement in town next morning, I asked her if she would take me with her in her car.

At a little before four we all wandered into the drawing-room. Old Lady Bland sat on a sofa with Ferdy; Freddy, Muriel and I made ourselves comfortable in armchairs; and Lea Makart sat by herself. She chose instinctively a high-backed Jacobean chair that had somewhat the air of a throne, and in a yellow dress, with her olive skin, she looked very handsome. She had magnificent eyes. She was very much made up and her mouth was scarlet.

George gave no sign of nervousness. He was already seated at the piano when I went in with his father and mother, and he watched us quietly settling ourselves down. He gave me the shadow of a smile. When he saw that we were all at our ease he began to play. He played Chopin. He played two waltzes that were familiar to me, a polonaise and an *étude*. He played with a great deal of *brio*. I wish I knew music well enough to give an exact description of his playing. It had strength and a youthful exuberance, but I felt that he missed what to me is the peculiar charm of Chopin, the tenderness, the nervous melancholy, the wistful gaiety and the slightly faded romance that reminds me always of an early Victorian keepsake. And again I had the vague sensation, so slight that it almost escaped me, that the two hands did not quite synchronize. I looked at Ferdy and saw him give his sister a look of faint surprise. Muriel's eyes were fixed on the pianist, but presently she dropped them and for the rest of the time stared at the floor. His father looked at him too, and his eyes were steadfast, but unless I was much mistaken he went pale and his face betrayed something like dismay. Music was in the blood of all of them, all their lives they had heard the greatest pianists in the world, and they judged with instinctive precision. The only person whose face betrayed no emotion was Lea Makart. She listened very attentively. She was as still as an image in a niche.

At last he stopped and turning round on his seat faced her. He did not speak.

"What is it you want me to tell you?" she asked.

They looked into one another's eyes.

"I want you to tell me whether I have any chance of becoming in time a pianist in the first rank."

"Not in a thousand years."

For a moment there was a dead silence. Freddy's head sank and he looked down at the carpet at his feet. His wife put out her hand and took his. But George continued to look steadily at Lea Makart.

"Ferdy has told me the circumstances," she said at last. "Don't think I'm influenced by them. Nothing of this is very important." She made a great sweeping gesture that took in the magnificent room with the beautiful things it contained and all of us. "If I thought you had in you the makings of an artist I shouldn't hesitate to beseech you to give up everything for art's sake. Art is the only thing that matters. In comparison with art, wealth and rank and power are not worth a row of pins." She gave us a look so sincere that it was void of insolence. "We are the only people who count. We give the world significance. You are only our raw material."

I was not too pleased to be included with the rest under that heading, but that is neither here nor there.

"Of course I can see that you've worked very hard. Don't think it's been wasted. It will always be a pleasure to you to be able to play the piano, and it will enable you to appreciate great playing as no ordinary person can hope to do. Look at your hands. They're not a pianist's hands."

Involuntarily I glanced at George's hands. I had never noticed them before. I was astounded to see how podgy they were and how short and stumpy the fingers.

"Your ear is not quite perfect. I don't think you can ever hope to be more than a very competent amateur. In art the difference between the amateur and the professional is immeasurable."

George did not reply. Except for his pallor no one would have known that he was listening to the blasting of all his hopes. The silence that fell was quite awful. Lea Makart's eyes suddenly filled with tears.

"But don't take my opinion alone," she said. "After all, I'm not infallible. Ask somebody else. You know how good and generous Paderewski is. I'll write to him about you and you can go down and play to him. I'm sure he'll hear you."

George now gave a little smile. He had very good manners and, whatever he was feeling, did not want to make the situation too difficult for others.

"I don't think that's necessary. I am content to accept your verdict. To tell you the truth it's not so very different from my master's in Munich."

He got up from the piano and lit a cigarette. It eased the strain. The others moved a little in their chairs. Lea Makart smiled at George.

"Shall I play to you?" she said.

"Yes, do."

She got up and went to the piano. She took off the rings with which her fingers were laden. She played Bach. I do not know the names of the pieces, but I recognized the stiff ceremonial of the frenchified little German courts and the sober, thrifty comfort of the burghers, and the dancing on the village green, the green trees that looked like Christmas trees, and the sunlight on the wide German country, and a tender coziness; and in my nostrils there was a warm scent of the soil and I was conscious of a sturdy strength that seemed to have its roots deep in mother earth, and of an elemental power that was timeless and had no home in space. She played exquisitely, with a soft brilliance that made you think of the full moon shining at dusk in the summer sky. With another part of me I watched the others and I saw how intensely they were conscious of the experience. They were rapt. I wished with all my heart that I could get from music the wonderful exaltation that possessed them. She stopped, a smile hovered on her lips, and she put on her rings. George gave a little chuckle.

"That clinches it, I fancy," he said.

The servants brought in tea, and after tea Lea Makart and I bade the company farewell and got into the car. We drove up to London. She talked all the way, if not brilliantly at all events with immense gusto, she told me of her early years in Manchester and of the struggle of her beginnings. She was very interesting. She never even mentioned George; the episode was of no consequence; it was finished and she thought of it no more.

We little knew what was happening at Tilby. When we left, George went out on the terrace and presently his father joined him. Freddy had won the day, but he was not happy. With his more than feminine sensitiveness he felt all that George was feeling, and George's anguish simply broke his heart. He had never loved his son more than then. When he appeared George greeted him with a little smile. Freddy's voice broke. In a sudden and overwhelming emotion he found it in him to surrender the fruits of his victory.

"Look here, old boy," he said, "I can't bear to think that you've had such a disappointment. Would you like to go back to Munich for another year and then see?"

George shook his head.

"No, it wouldn't be any good. I've had my chance. Let's call it a day."

"Try not to take it too hard."

"You see, the only thing in the world I want is to be a pianist. And there's nothing doing. It's a bit thick if you come to think of it."

George, trying so hard to be brave, smiled wanly.

"Would you like to go round the world? You can get one of your Oxford pals to go with you and I'll pay all the expenses. You've been working very hard for a long time."

"Thanks awfully, Daddy, we'll talk about it. I'm just going for a stroll now."

"Shall I come with you?"

"I'd rather go alone."

Then George did a strange thing. He put his arm round his father's neck and kissed him on the lips. He gave a funny little moved laugh and walked away. Freddy went back to the drawing-room. His mother, Ferdy and Muriel were sitting there.

"Freddy, why don't you marry the boy?" said the old lady. "He is twenty-three. It would take his mind off his troubles and when he is married and has a baby he will soon settle down like everybody else."

"Who is he to marry, Mamma?" asked Sir Adolphus, smiling.

"That's not so difficult. Lady Frielinghausen came to see me the other day with her daughter Violet. She is a very nice maiden and she will have money of her own. Lady Frielinghausen gave me to understand that her Sir Jacob would come down very handsome if Violet made a good match."

Muriel flushed.

"I hate Lady Frielinghausen. George is much too young to marry. He can afford to marry anyone he likes."

Old Lady Bland gave her daughter a strange look.

"You are a very foolish girl, Miriam," she said, using the name Muriel had long discarded. "As long as I am here I shall not allow you to commit a foolishness."

She knew as well as if Muriel had said it in so many words that she wanted George to marry a Gentile, but she knew also that so long as she was alive neither Freddy nor his wife would dare to suggest it.

But George did not go for a walk. Perhaps because the shooting season was about to open he took it into his head to go into the gun-room. He began to clean the gun that his mother had given him on his twentieth birthday. No one had used it since he went to Germany. Suddenly the servants were startled by a report. When they went into the gun-room they found George lying on the floor shot through the heart. Apparently the gun had been loaded and George while playing about with it had accidentally shot himself. One reads of such accidents in the paper often.

# A Profile in Courage

(from *Profiles in Courage*)

## JOHN F. KENNEDY

*"I looked down into my open grave . . ."*
—EDMUND G. ROSS

IN a lonely grave, forgotten and unknown, lies "the man who saved a President," and who as a result may well have preserved for ourselves and posterity constitutional government in the United States—the man who performed in 1868 what one historian has called "the most heroic act in American history, incomparably more difficult than any deed of valor upon the field of battle"—but a United States Senator whose name no one recalls: Edmund G. Ross of Kansas.

The impeachment of President Andrew Johnson, the event in which the obscure Ross was to play such a dramatic role, was the sensational climax to the bitter struggle between the President, determined to carry out Abraham Lincoln's policies of reconciliation with the defeated South, and the more radical Republican leaders in Congress, who sought to administer the downtrodden Southern states as conquered provinces which had forfeited their rights under the Constitution. It was, moreover, a struggle between Executive and Legislative authority. Andrew Johnson, the courageous if untactful Tennessean who had been the only Southern Member of Congress to refuse to secede with his state, had committed himself to the policies of the Great Emancipator to whose high station he had succeeded only by the course of an assassin's bullet. He knew that Lincoln prior to his death had already clashed with the extremists in Congress, who had opposed his approach to reconstruction in a constitutional and charitable manner and sought to make the Legislative Branch of the government supreme. And his own belligerent temperament soon destroyed any hope that Congress might now join hands in carrying out Lincoln's policies of permitting the South to resume its place in the Union with as little delay and controversy as possible.

By 1866, when Edmund Ross first came to the Senate, the two branches of the government were already at each other's throats, snarling and bristling with anger. Bill after bill was vetoed by the President on the grounds that they were unconstitutional, too harsh in their treatment of the South, an unnecessary prolongation of military rule in peacetime or undue interference with the authority of the Executive Branch. And for the first time in our nation's history, important public measures were passed over a President's veto and became law without his support.

But not all of Andrew Johnson's vetoes were overturned; and the "Radical" Republicans of the Congress promptly realized that one final step was necessary before they could crush their despised foe (and in the heat of political battle their vengeance was turned upon their President far more than their former military enemies of the South). That one remaining step was the assurance of a two-thirds majority in the Senate—for under the Constitution, such a majority was necessary to override a Presidential veto. And more important, such a majority was constitutionally required to accomplish their major ambition, now an ill-kept secret, conviction of the President under an impeachment and his dismissal from office!

The temporary and unstable two-thirds majority which had enabled the Senate Radical Republicans on several occasions to enact legislation over the President's veto was, they knew, insufficiently reliable for an impeachment conviction. To solidify this bloc became the paramount goal of Congress, expressly or impliedly governing its decisions on other issues—particularly the admission of new states, the readmission of Southern states and the determination of senatorial credentials. By extremely dubious methods a pro-Johnson Senator was denied his seat. Over the President's veto Nebraska was admitted to the Union, seating two more anti-administration Senators. Although last minute maneuvers failed to admit Colorado over the President's veto (sparsely populated Colorado had rejected statehood in a referendum), an unexpected tragedy brought false tears and fresh hopes for a new vote, in Kansas.

Senator Jim Lane of Kansas had been a "conservative" Republican sympathetic to Johnson's plans to carry out Lincoln's reconstruction policies. But his frontier state was one of the most "radical" in the Union. When Lane voted to uphold Johnson's veto of the Civil Rights Bill of 1866 and introduced the administration's bill for recognition of the new state government of Arkansas, Kansas had arisen in outraged heat. A mass meeting at Lawrence had vilified the Senator and speedily reported resolutions sharply condemning his position. Humiliated, mentally ailing, broken in health and laboring under charges of financial irregularities, Jim Lane took his own life on July 1, 1866.

With this thorn in their side removed, the Radical Republicans in Washington looked anxiously toward Kansas and the selection of Lane's successor. Their fondest hopes were realized, for the new Senator from Kansas turned out to be Edmund G. Ross, the very man who had introduced the resolutions attacking Lane at Lawrence.

There could be no doubt as to where Ross's sympathies lay, for his entire career was one of determined opposition to the slave states of the South, their practices and their friends. In 1854, when only twenty-eight, he had taken part in the mob rescue of a fugitive slave in Milwaukee. In 1856, he had joined that flood of antislavery immigrants to "bleeding" Kansas who intended to keep it a free territory. Disgusted with the Democratic party of his youth, he had left that party, and volunteered in the Kansas Free State Army to drive back a force of proslavery men invading the territory. In 1862, he had given up his newspaper work to enlist in the Union Army, from which he emerged a Major. His leading role in the condemnation of Lane at Lawrence convinced the Radical Republican leaders in Congress that in Edmund G. Ross they had a solid member of that vital two-thirds.

The stage was now set for the final scene—the removal of Johnson. Early in 1867, Congress enacted over the President's veto the Tenure-of-Office Bill which prevented the President from removing without the consent of the Senate all new officeholders whose appointment required confirmation by that body. At the time nothing more than the cry for more patronage was involved, Cabinet Members having originally been specifically exempt.

On August 5, 1867, President Johnson—convinced that the Secretary of War, whom he had inherited from Lincoln, Edwin M. Stanton, was the surreptitious tool of the Radical Republicans and was seeking to become the almighty dictator of the conquered South—asked for his immediate resignation; and Stanton arrogantly fired back the reply that he declined to resign before the next meeting of Congress. Not one to cower before this kind of effrontery, the President one week later suspended Stanton, and appointed in his place the one man whom Stanton did not dare resist, General Grant. On January 13, 1868, an angry Senate notified the President and Grant that it did not concur in the suspension of Stanton, and Grant vacated the office upon Stanton's return. But the situation was intolerable. The Secretary of War was unable to attend Cabinet meetings or associate with his colleagues in the administration; and on February 21, President Johnson, anxious to obtain a court test of the act he believed obviously unconstitutional, again notified Stanton that he had been summarily removed from the office of Secretary of War.

While Stanton, refusing to yield possession, barricaded himself in his office, public opinion in the nation ran heavily against the President. He had intentionally broken the law and dictatorially thwarted the will of Congress! Although previous resolutions of impeachment had been defeated in the House, both in committee and on the floor, a new resolution was swiftly reported and adopted on February 24 by a tremendous vote. Every single Republican voted in the affirmative, and Thaddeus Stevens of Pennsylvania —the crippled, fanatical personification of the extremes of the Radical Republican movement, master of the House of Representatives, with a mouth like the thin edge of an ax—warned both Houses of the Congress coldly: "Let me see the recreant who would vote to let such a criminal escape. Point me to one who will dare do it and I will show you one who will dare the infamy of posterity."

With the President impeached—in effect, indicted—by the House, the frenzied trial for his conviction or acquittal under the Articles of Impeachment began on March 5 in the Senate, presided over by the Chief Justice. It was a trial to rank with all the great trials in history—Charles I before the High Court of Justice, Louis XVI before the French Convention, and

Warren Hastings before the House of Lords. Two great elements of drama were missing: the actual cause for which the President was being tried was not fundamental to the welfare of the nation; and the defendant himself was at all times absent.

But every other element of the highest courtroom drama was present. To each Senator the Chief Justice administered an oath "to do impartial justice" (including even the hot-headed Radical Senator from Ohio, Benjamin Wade, who as President Pro Tempore of the Senate was next in line for the Presidency). The chief prosecutor for the House was General Benjamin F. Butler, the "butcher of New Orleans," a talented but coarse and demagogic Congressman from Massachusetts. (When he lost his seat in 1874, he was so hated by his own party as well as his opponents that one Republican wired concerning the Democratic sweep, "Butler defeated, everything else lost.") Some one thousand tickets were printed for admission to the Senate galleries during the trial, and every conceivable device was used to obtain one of the four tickets allotted each Senator.

From the fifth of March to the sixteenth of May, the drama continued. Of the eleven Articles of Impeachment adopted by the House, the first eight were based upon the removal of Stanton and the appointment of a new Secretary of War in violation of the Tenure-of-Office Act; the ninth related to Johnson's conversation with a general which was said to induce violations of the Army Appropriations Act; the tenth recited that Johnson had delivered "intemperate, inflammatory and scandalous harangues . . . as well against Congress as the laws of the United States"; and the eleventh was a deliberately obscure conglomeration of all the charges in the preceding articles, which had been designed by Thaddeus Stevens to furnish a common ground for those who favored conviction but were unwilling to identify themselves on basic issues. In opposition to Butler's inflammatory arguments in support of this hastily drawn indictment, Johnson's able and learned counsel replied with considerable effectiveness. They insisted that the Tenure-of-Office Act was null and void as a clear violation of the Constitution; that even if it were valid, it would not apply to Stanton, for the reasons previously mentioned; and that the only way that a judicial test of the law could be obtained was for Stanton to be dismissed and sue for his rights in the courts.

But as the trial progressed, it became increasingly apparent that the impatient Republicans did not intend to give the President a fair trial on the formal issues upon which the impeachment was drawn, but intended instead to depose him from the White House on any grounds, real or imagined, for refusing to accept their policies. Telling evidence in the President's favor was arbitrarily excluded. Prejudgment on the part of most Senators was brazenly announced. Attempted bribery and other forms of pressure were rampant. The chief interest was not in the trial or the evidence, but in the tallying of votes necessary for conviction.

Twenty-seven states (excluding the unrecognized Southern states) in the Union meant fifty-four members of the Senate, and thirty-six votes were required to constitute the two-thirds majority necessary for conviction. All twelve Democratic votes were obviously lost, and the forty-two Republicans knew that they could afford to lose only six of their own members if Johnson were to be ousted. To their dismay, at a preliminary Republican caucus, six courageous Republicans indicated that the evidence so far introduced was not in their opinion sufficient to convict Johnson under the Articles of Impeachment. "Infamy!" cried the Philadelphia *Press*. The Republic has "been betrayed in the house of its friends!"

But if the remaining thirty-six Republicans would hold, there would be no doubt as to the outcome. All must stand together! But one Republican Senator would not announce his verdict in the preliminary poll—Edmund G. Ross of Kansas. The Radicals were outraged that a Senator from such an anti-Johnson stronghold as Kansas could be doubtful. "It was a very clear case," Senator Sumner of Massachusetts fumed, "especially for a Kansas man. I did not think that a Kansas man could quibble against his country."

From the very time Ross had taken his seat, the Radical leaders had been confident of his vote. His entire background, as already indicated, was one of firm support of their cause. One of his first acts in the Senate had been to read a declaration of his adherence to Radical Republican policy, and he had silently voted for all of their measures. He had made it clear that he was not in sympathy with Andrew Johnson personally or politically; and after the removal of Stanton, he had voted with the majority in adopting a resolution declaring such removal unlawful. His colleague from Kansas, Senator Pomeroy, was one of the most Radical leaders of the anti-Johnson group. The Republicans insisted that Ross's crucial vote was rightfully theirs, and they were determined to get it by whatever means available. As stated by DeWitt in his memorable *Impeachment of Andrew Johnson*, "The full brunt of the struggle turned at last on the one remaining doubtful Senator, Edmund G. Ross."

When the impeachment resolution had passed the House, Senator Ross had casually remarked to Senator Sprague of Rhode Island, "Well, Sprague, the thing is here; and, so far as I am concerned, though a Republican and opposed to Mr. Johnson and his policy, he shall have as fair a trial as an accused man ever had on this earth." Immediately the word spread that "Ross was shaky." "From that hour," he later wrote, "not a day passed that did not bring me, by mail and telegraph and in personal intercourse, appeals to stand fast for impeachment, and not a few were the admonitions of condign visitations upon any indication even of lukewarmness."

"Throughout the country, and in all walks of life, as indicated by the correspondence of Members of the Senate, the condition of the public mind was not unlike that preceding a great battle. The dominant party of the nation seemed to occupy the position of public prosecutor, and it was scarcely in the mood to brook delay for trial or to hear defense. Washington had become during the trial the central point of the politically dissatisfied and swarmed with representatives of every state of the Union, demanding in a practically united voice the deposition of the President. The footsteps of the anti-impeaching Republicans were dogged from the day's beginning to its end and far into the night, with entreaties, considerations, and threats. The newspapers came daily filled with not a few threats of violence upon their return to their constituents."

Ross and his fellow doubtful Republicans were daily pestered, spied upon and subjected to every form of pressure. Their residences were carefully watched, their social circles suspiciously scrutinized, and their every move and companions secretly marked in special notebooks. They were warned in the party press, harangued by their constituents, and sent dire warnings threatening political ostracism and even assassination. Stanton himself, from his barricaded headquarters in the War Department, worked day and night to bring to bear upon the doubtful Senators all the weight of his impressive military associations. The Philadelphia *Press* reported "a fearful avalanche of telegrams from every section of the country," a great surge of public opinion from the "common people" who had given their money and lives to the country and would not "willingly or unavenged see their great sacrifice made naught."

The New York *Tribune* reported that Edmund Ross in particular was "mercilessly dragged this way and that by both sides, hunted like a fox night and day and badgered by his own colleague, like the bridge at Arcola now trod upon by one Army and now trampled by the other." His background and life were investigated from top to bottom, and his constituents and colleagues pursued him throughout Washington to gain some inkling of his opinion. He was the target of every eye, his name was on every mouth and his intentions were discussed in every newspaper. Although there is evidence that he gave some hint of agreement to each side, and each attempted to claim him publicly, he actually kept both sides in a state of complete suspense by his judicial silence.

But with no experience in political turmoil, no reputation in the Senate, no independent income and the most radical state in the Union to deal with, Ross was judged to be the most sensitive to criticism and the most certain to be swayed by expert tactics. A committee of Congressmen and Senators sent to Kansas, and to the states of the other doubtful Republicans, this telegram: "Great danger to the peace of the country and the Republican cause if impeachment fails. Send to your Senators public opinion by resolutions, letters, and delegations." A member of the Kansas legislature called upon Ross at the Capitol. A general urged on by Stanton remained at his lodge until four o'clock in the morning determined to see him. His brother received a letter offering $20,000 for revelation of the Senator's intentions. Gruff Ben Butler exclaimed of Ross, "There is a bushel of money! How much does the damned scoundrel want?" The night before the Senate was to take its first vote for the conviction or acquittal of Johnson, Ross received this telegram from home:

"Kansas has heard the evidence and demands the conviction of the President."

(*signed*) D. R. ANTHONY AND 1,000 OTHERS

And on that fateful morning of May 16 Ross replied:

"To D. R. Anthony and 1,000 Others: I do not recognize your right to demand that I vote either for or against conviction. I have taken an oath to do impartial justice according to the Constitution and laws, and trust that I shall have the courage to vote according to the dictates of my judgment and for the highest good of the country."

[signed]–E. G. Ross

That morning spies traced Ross to his breakfast; and ten minutes before the vote was taken his Kansas colleague warned him in the presence of Thaddeus Stevens that a vote for acquittal would mean trumped up charges and his political death.

But now the fateful hour was at hand. Neither escape, delay or indecision was possible. As Ross himself later described it: "The galleries were packed. Tickets of admission were at an enormous premium. The House had adjourned and all of its members were in the Senate chamber. Every chair on the Senate floor was filled with a Senator, a Cabinet Officer, a member of the President's counsel or a member of the House." Every Senator was in his seat, the desperately ill Grimes of Iowa being literally carried in.

It had been decided to take the first vote under that broad Eleventh Article of Impeachment, believed to command the widest support. As the Chief Justice announced the voting would begin, he reminded "the citizens and strangers in the galleries that absolute silence and perfect order are required." But already a deathlike stillness enveloped the Senate chamber. A Congressman later recalled that "Some of the members of the House near me grew pale and sick under the burden of suspense"; and Ross noted that there was even "a subsidence of the shuffling of feet, the rustling of silks, the fluttering of fans, and of conversation."

The voting tensely commenced. By the time the Chief Justice reached the name of Edmund Ross twenty-four "guilties" had been pronounced. Ten more were certain and one other practically certain. Only Ross's vote was needed to obtain the thirty-six votes necessary to convict the President. But not a single person in the room knew how this young Kansan would vote. Unable to conceal the suspense and emotion in his voice, the Chief Justice put the question to him: "Mr. Senator Ross, how say you? Is the respondent Andrew Johnson guilty or not guilty of a high misdemeanor as charged in this Article?" Every voice was still; every eye was upon the freshman Senator from Kansas. The hopes and fears, the hatred and bitterness of past decades were centered upon this one man.

As Ross himself later described it, his "powers of hearing and seeing seemed developed in an abnormal degree."

"Every individual in that great audience seemed distinctly visible, some with lips apart and bending forward in anxious expectancy, others with hand uplifted as if to ward off an apprehended blow . . . and each peering with an intensity that was almost tragic upon the face of him who was about to cast the fateful vote. . . . Every fan was folded, not a foot moved, not the rustle of a garment, not a whisper was heard. . . . Hope and fear seemed blended in every face, instantaneously alternating, some with revengeful hate . . . others lighted with hope. . . . The Senators in their seats leaned over their desks, many with hand to ear. . . . It was a tremendous responsibility, and it was not strange that he upon whom it had been imposed by a fateful combination of conditions should have sought to avoid it, to put it away from him as one shuns, or tries to fight off, a nightmare. . . . I almost literally looked down into my open grave. Friendships, position, fortune, everything that makes life desirable to an ambitious man were about to be swept away by the breath of my mouth, perhaps forever. It is not strange that my answer was carried waveringly over the air and failed to reach the limits of the audience, or that repetition was called for by distant Senators on the opposite side of the Chamber."

Then came the answer again in a voice that could not be misunderstood —full, final, definite, unhesitating and unmistakable: "Not guilty." The deed was done, the President saved, the trial as good as over and the conviction lost. The remainder of the roll call was unimportant, conviction had failed by the margin of a single vote and a general rumbling filled the chamber until the Chief Justice proclaimed that "on this Article thirty-five Senators having voted guilty and nineteen not guilty, a two-thirds majority not having voted for conviction, the President is, therefore, acquitted under this Article."

A ten-day recess followed, ten turbulent days to change votes on the remaining Articles. An attempt was made to rush through bills to readmit six Southern states, whose twelve Senators were guaranteed to vote for conviction. But this could not be accomplished in time. Again Ross was the only one uncommitted on the other Articles, the only one whose vote could not be predicted in advance. And again he was subjected to terrible pressure. From "D. R. Anthony and others," he received a wire informing him that "Kansas repudiates you as she does all perjurers and skunks." Every incident in his life was examined and distorted. Professional witnesses were found by Senator Pomeroy to testify before a special House committee that Ross had indicated a willingness to change his vote for a consideration. (Unfortunately this witness was so delighted in his exciting role that he also swore that Senator Pomeroy had made an offer to produce three votes for acquittal for $40,000.) When Ross, in his capacity as a Committee Chairman, took several bills to the President, James G. Blaine remarked: "There goes the rascal to get his pay." (Long afterward Blaine was to admit: "In the exaggerated denunciation caused by the anger and chagrin of the moment, great injustice was done to statesmen of spotless character.")

Again the wild rumors spread that Ross had been won over on the remaining Articles of Impeachment. As the Senate reassembled, he was the only one of the seven "renegade" Republicans to vote with the majority on preliminary procedural matters. But when the second and third Articles of Impeachment were read, and the name of Ross was reached again with the same intense suspense of ten days earlier, again came the calm answer "Not guilty."

Why did Ross, whose dislike for Johnson continued, vote "Not guilty"? His motives appear clearly from his own writings on the subject years later in articles contributed to *Scribner's* and *Forum* magazines:

"In a large sense, the independence of the executive office as a coordinate branch of the government was on trial. . . . If . . . the President must step down . . . a disgraced man and a political outcast . . . upon insufficient proofs and from partisan considerations, the office of President would be degraded, cease to be a coordinate branch of the government, and ever after subordinated to the legislative will. It would practically have revolutionized our splendid political fabric into a partisan Congressional autocracy. . . . This government had never faced so insidious a danger . . . control by the worst element of American politics. . . . If Andrew Johnson were acquitted by a nonpartisan vote . . . America would pass the danger point of partisan rule and that intolerance which so often characterizes the sway of great majorities and makes them dangerous."

The "open grave" which Edmund Ross had foreseen was hardly an exaggeration. A Justice of the Kansas Supreme Court telegraphed him that "the rope with which Judas Iscariot hanged himself is lost, but Jim Lane's pistol is at your service." An editorial in a Kansas newspaper screamed:

On Saturday last Edmund G. Ross, United States Senator from Kansas, sold himself, and betrayed his constituents; stultified his own record, basely lied to his friends, shamefully violated his solemn pledge . . . and to the utmost of his poor ability signed the death warrant of his country's liberty. This act was done deliberately, because the traitor, like Benedict Arnold, loved money better than he did principle, friends, honor and his country, all combined. Poor, pitiful, shriveled wretch, with a soul so small that a little pelf would outweigh all things else that dignify or ennoble manhood.

Ross's political career was ended. To the New York *Tribune*, he was nothing but "a miserable poltroon and traitor." The Philadelphia *Press* said that in Ross "littleness" had "simply borne its legitimate fruit," and that he and his fellow recalcitrant Republicans had "plunged from a precipice of fame into the groveling depths of infamy and death." The Philadelphia *Inquirer* said that "They had tried, convicted and sentenced themselves." For them there could be "no allowance, no clemency."

Comparative peace returned to Washington as Stanton relinquished his office and Johnson served out the rest of his term, later—unlike his Republican defenders—to return triumphantly to the Senate as Senator from Tennessee. But no one paid attention when Ross tried unsuccessfully to explain his vote, and denounced the falsehoods of Ben Butler's investigating committee, recalling that the General's "well known grovelling instincts and proneness to slime and uncleanness" had led "the public to insult the brute creation by dubbing him 'the beast.'" He clung unhappily to his seat in the Senate until the expiration of his term, frequently referred to as "the traitor Ross," and complaining that his fellow Congressmen, as well as citizens on the street, considered association with him "disreputable and scandalous," and passed him by as if he were "a leper, with averted face and every indication of hatred and disgust."

Neither Ross nor any other Republican who had voted for the acquittal of Johnson was ever re-elected to the Senate, not a one of them retaining the support of their party's organization. When he returned to Kansas in 1871, he and his family suffered social ostracism, physical attack, and near poverty.

Who was Edmund G. Ross? Practically nobody. Not a single public law bears his name, not a single history book includes his picture, not a single list of Senate "greats" mentions his service. His one heroic deed has been all but forgotten. But who might Edmund G. Ross have been? That is the question—for Ross, a man with an excellent command of words, an excellent background for politics and an excellent future in the Senate might well have outstripped his colleagues in prestige and power throughout a long Senate career. Instead, he chose to throw all of this away for one act of conscience.

But the twisting course of human events eventually upheld the faith he expressed to his wife shortly after the trial: "Millions of men cursing me today will bless me tomorrow for having saved the country from the greatest peril through which it has ever passed, though none but God can ever know the struggle it has cost me." For twenty years later Congress repealed the Tenure-of-Office Act, to which every President after Johnson, regardless of party, had objected; and still later the Supreme Court, referring to "the extremes of that episode in our government," held it to be unconstitutional. Ross moved to New Mexico, where in his later years he was to be appointed Territorial Governor. Just prior to his death when he was awarded a special pension by Congress for his service in the Civil War, the press and the country took the opportunity to pay tribute to his fidelity to principle in a trying hour and his courage in saving his government from a devastating reign of terror. They now agreed with Ross's earlier judgment that his vote had "saved the country from . . . a strain that would have wrecked any other form of government." Those Kansas newspapers and political leaders who had bitterly denounced him in earlier years praised Ross for his stand against legislative mob rule: "By the firmness and courage of Senator Ross," it was said, "the country was saved from calamity greater than war, while it consigned him to a political martyrdom, the most cruel in our history. . . .

Ross was the victim of a wild flame of intolerance which swept everything before it. He did his duty knowing that it meant his political death. . . . It was a brave thing for Ross to do, but Ross did it. He acted for his conscience and with a lofty patriotism, regardless of what he knew must be the ruinous consequences to himself. He acted right."

*I could not close the story of Edmund Ross without some more adequate mention of those six courageous Republicans who stood with Ross and braved denunciation to acquit Andrew Johnson. Edmund Ross, more than any of those six colleagues, endured more before and after his vote, reached his conscientious decision with greater difficulty, and aroused the greatest interest and suspense prior to May 16 by his noncommittal silence. His story, like his vote, is the key to the impeachment tragedy. But all seven of the Republicans who voted against conviction should be remembered for their courage. Not a single one of them ever won re-election to the Senate. Not a single one of them escaped the unholy combination of threats, bribes and coercive tactics by which their fellow Republicans attempted to intimidate their votes; and not a single one of them escaped the terrible torture of vicious criticism engendered by their vote to acquit.*

*William Pitt Fessenden of Maine, one of the most eminent Senators, orators and lawyers of his day, and a prominent senior Republican leader, who admired Stanton and disliked Johnson, became convinced early in the game that "the whole thing is a mere madness."*

*The country has so bad an opinion of the President, which he fully deserves, that it expects his condemnation. Whatever may be the consequences to myself personally, whatever I may think and feel as a politician, I will not decide the question against my own judgment. I would rather be confined to planting cabbages the remainder of my days. . . . Make up your mind, if need be, to hear me denounced a traitor and perhaps hanged in effigy. All imaginable abuse has been heaped upon me by the men and papers devoted to the impeachers. I have received several letters from friends warning me that my political grave is dug if I do not vote for conviction, and several threatening assassination. It is rather hard at my time of life, after a long career, to find myself the target of pointed arrows from those whom I have faithfully served. The public, when aroused and excited by passion and prejudice, is little better than a wild beast. I shall at all events retain my own self-respect and a clear conscience, and time will do justice to my motives at least.*

*The Radical Republicans were determined to win over the respected Fessenden, whose name would be the first question mark on the call of the roll, and his mail from Maine was abusive, threatening and pleading. Wendell Phillips scornfully told a hissing crowd that "It takes six months for a statesmanlike idea to find its way into Mr. Fessenden's head. I don't say he is lacking; he is only very slow."*

*Fessenden decided to shun all newspapers and screen his mail. But when one of his oldest political friends in Maine urged him to "hang Johnson up by the heels like a dead crow in a cornfield, to frighten all of his tribe," noting that he was "sure I express the unanimous feeling of every loyal heart and head in this state," Fessenden indignantly replied:*

*I am acting as a judge . . . by what right can any man upon whom no responsibility rests, and who does not even hear the evidence, undertake to advise me as to what the judgment, and even the sentence, should be? I wish all my friends and constituents to understand that I, and not they, am sitting in judgment upon the President. I, not they, have sworn to do impartial justice. I, not they, am responsible to God and man for my action and its consequences.*

On that tragic afternoon of May 16, as Ross described it, Senator Fessenden "was in his place, pale and haggard, yet ready for the political martyrdom which he was about to face, and which not long afterward drove him to his grave."

The first Republican Senator to ring out "not guilty"—and the first of the seven to go to his grave, hounded by the merciless abuse that had dimmed all hope for re-election—was William Pitt Fessenden of Maine.

John B. Henderson of Missouri, one of the Senate's youngest members, had previously demonstrated high courage by introducing the Thirteenth Amendment abolishing slavery, simply because he was convinced that it would pass only if sponsored by a slave-state Senator, whose political death would necessarily follow. But when the full delegation of Republican representatives from his state cornered him in his office to demand that he convict the hated Johnson, warning that Missouri Republicans could stomach no other course, Henderson's usual courage wavered. He meekly offered to wire his resignation to the Governor, enabling a new appointee to vote for conviction; and, when it was doubted whether a new Senator would be permitted to vote, he agreed to ascertain whether his own vote would be crucial.

But an insolent and threatening telegram from Missouri restored his sense of honor, and he swiftly wired his reply: "Say to my friends that I am sworn to do impartial justice according to law and conscience, and I will try to do it like an honest man."

John Henderson voted for acquittal, the last important act of his Senatorial career. Denounced, threatened and burned in effigy in Missouri, he did not even bother to seek re-election to the Senate. Years later his party would realize its debt to him, and return him to lesser offices, but for the Senate, whose integrity he had upheld, he was through.

Peter Van Winkle of West Virginia, the last doubtful Republican name to be called on May 16, was, like Ross, a "nobody"; but his firm "not guilty" extinguished the last faint glimmer of hope which Edmund Ross had already all but destroyed. The Republicans had counted on Van Winkle—West Virginia's first United States Senator, and a critic of Stanton's removal; and for his courage, he was labeled "West Virginia's betrayer" by the Wheeling Intelligencer, who declared to the world that there was not a loyal citizen in the state who had not been misrepresented by his vote. He, too, had insured his permanent withdrawal from politics as soon as his Senate term expired.

The veteran Lyman Trumbull of Illinois, who had defeated Abe Lincoln for the Senate, had drafted much of the major reconstruction legislation which Johnson vetoed, and had voted to censure Johnson upon Stanton's removal.

But, in the eyes of the Philadelphia Press, his "statesmanship drivelled into selfishness," for, resisting tremendous pressure, he voted against conviction. A Republican convention in Chicago had resolved "That any Senator elected by the votes of Union Republicans, who at this time blenches and betrays, is infamous and should be dishonored and execrated while this free government endures." And an Illinois Republican leader had warned the distinguished Trumbull "not to show himself on the streets in Chicago; for I fear that the representatives of an indignant people would hang him to the most convenient lamppost."

But Lyman Trumbull, ending a brilliant career of public service and devotion to the party which would renounce him, filed for the record these enduring words:

The question to be decided is not whether Andrew Johnson is a proper person to fill the Presidential office, nor whether it is fit that he should remain in it. . . . Once set, the example of impeaching a President for what, when the excitement of the House shall have subsided, will be regarded as insufficient cause, no future President will be safe who happens to differ with a majority of the House and two-thirds of the Senate on any measure deemed by them important. . . . What then becomes of the checks and balances of the Constitution so carefully devised and so vital to its perpetuity? They are all gone. . . . I cannot be an instrument to produce such a result, and at the hazard of the ties even of friendship and affection, till calmer times shall do justice to my motives, no alternative is left me but the inflexible discharge of duty.

Joseph Smith Fowler of Tennessee, like Ross, Henderson, and Van Winkle a freshman Senator, at first thought the President impeachable. But the former Nashville professor was horrified by the mad passion of the House in rushing through the impeachment resolution by evidence against Johnson "based on falsehood," and by the "corrupt and dishonorable" Ben Butler, "a wicked man who seeks to convert the Senate of the United States into a political guillotine." He refused to be led by the nose by "politicians, thrown to the surface through the disjointed time . . . keeping alive the embers of the departing revolution." Threatened, investigated and defamed by his fellow Radical Republicans, the nervous Fowler so faltered in his reply on May 16 that it was at first mistaken for the word "guilty." A wave of *triumph swept the Senate—Johnson was convicted, Ross's vote was not needed! But then came the clear and distinct answer: "not guilty."*

His re-election impossible, Fowler quietly retired from the Senate at the close of his term two years later, but not without a single statement in defense of his vote: "I acted for my country and posterity in obedience to the will of God."

James W. Grimes of Iowa, one of Johnson's bitter and influential foes in the Senate, became convinced that the trial was intended only to excite public passions through "lies sent from here by the most worthless and irresponsible creatures on the face of the earth" (an indication, perhaps, of the improved quality of Washington correspondents in the last eighty-seven years).

Unfortunately, the abuse and threats heaped upon him during the trial brought on a stroke of paralysis only two days before the vote was to be taken, and he was confined to his bed. The Radical Republicans, refusing any postponement, were delightedly certain that Grimes would either be too sick in fact to attend on May 16, or would plead that his illness prevented him from attending to cast the vote that would end his career. In the galleries, the crowd sang, "Old Grimes is dead, that bad old man, we ne'er shall see him more." And in the New York Tribune, Horace Greeley was writing: "It seems as if no generation could pass without giving us one man to live among the Warnings of history. We have had Benedict Arnold, Aaron Burr, Jefferson Davis, and now we have James W. Grimes."

But James W. Grimes was a man of great physical as well as moral courage, and just before the balloting was to begin on May 16, four men carried the pale and withered Senator from Iowa into his seat. He later wrote that Fessenden had grasped his hand and given him a "glorified smile. . . . I would not today exchange that recollection for the highest distinction of life." The Chief Justice suggested that it would be permissible for him to remain seated while voting—but with the assistance of his friends, Senator Grimes struggled to his feet and in a surprisingly firm voice called out "not guilty."

Burned in effigy, accused in the press of "idiocy and impotency," and repudiated by his state and friends, Grimes never recovered—but before he died he declared to a friend:

I shall ever thank God that in that troubled hour of trial, when many privately confessed that they had sacrificed their judgment and their conscience at the behests of party newspapers and party hate, I had the courage to be true to my oath and my conscience. . . . Perhaps I did wrong not to commit perjury by order of a party; but I cannot see it that way. . . . I became a judge acting on my own responsibility and accountable only to my own conscience and my Maker; and no power could force me to decide on such a case contrary to my convictions, whether that party was composed of my friends or my enemies.

# The Company of the Marjolaine

## JOHN BUCHAN

*"Qu'est-c' qui passe ici si tard,*
*Compagnons de la Marjolaine?"*

—CHANSONS DE FRANCE.

## I

I CAME down from the mountains and into the pleasing valley
of the Adige in as pelting a heat as ever mortal suffered under.
• • • The way underfoot was parched and white; I had newly come
out of a wilderness of white limestone crags, and a sun of Italy blazed blind-
ingly in an azure Italian sky. You are to suppose, my dear aunt, that I had
had enough and something more of my craze for foot-marching. A fortnight
ago I had gone to Belluno in a postchaise, dismissed my fellow to carry my
baggage by way of Verona, and with no more than a valise on my back
plunged into the fastnesses of those mountains. I had a fancy to see the
little sculptured hills which made backgrounds for Gianbellin, and there
were rumours of great mountains built wholly of marble which shone like
the battlements of the Celestial City. So at any rate reported young Mr.
Wyndham, who had travelled with me from Milan to Venice. I lay the
first night at Pieve, where Titian had the fortune to be born, and the
landlord at the inn displayed a set of villainous daubs which he swore were
the early works of that master. Thence up a toilsome valley I journeyed
to the Ampezzan country, where indeed I saw my white mountains, but,
alas! no longer Celestial. For it rained like Westmoreland for five endless
days, while I kicked my heels in an inn and turned a canto of Ariosto into
halting English couplets. By-and-by it cleared, and I headed westward
towards Bozen, among the tangle of wild rocks where the Dwarf King had
once his rose-garden. The first night I had no inn, but slept in the vile
cabin of a forester, who spoke a tongue half Latin, half Dutch, which I
failed to master. The next day was a blaze of heat, the mountain-paths lay
thick with dust, and I had no wine from sunrise to sunset. Can you wonder
that, when the following noon I saw Santa Chiara sleeping in its green
circlet of meadows, my thought was only of a deep draught and a cool
chamber? I protest that I am a great lover of natural beauty, of rock and
cascade, and all the properties of the poet; but the enthusiasm of M.
Rousseau himself would sink from the stars to earth if he had marched

since breakfast in a cloud of dust with a throat like the nether millstone.

Yet I had not entered the place before Romance revived. The little town—a mere wayside halting-place on the great mountain-road to the North —had the air of mystery which foretells adventure. Why is it that a dwelling or a countenance catches the fancy with the promise of some strange destiny? I have houses in my mind which I know will some day and somehow be intertwined oddly with my life; and I have faces in memory of which I know nothing save that I shall undoubtedly cast eyes again upon them. My first glimpses of Santa Chiara gave me this earnest of romance. It was walled and fortified, the streets were narrow pits of shade, old tenements with bent fronts swayed to meet each other. Melons lay drying on flat roofs, and yet now and then would come a high-pitched northern gable. Latin and Teuton met and mingled in the place, and, as Mr. Gibbon has taught us, the offspring of this admixture is something fantastic and unpredictable. I forgot my grievous thirst and my tired feet in admiration and a certain vague expectation of wonders. Here, ran my thought, it is fated, maybe, that Romance and I shall at last compass a meeting. Perchance some princess is in need of my arm, or some affair of high policy is afoot in this jumble of old masonry. You will laugh at my folly, but I had an excuse for it. A fortnight in strange mountains disposes a man to look for something at his next encounter with his kind, and the sight of Santa Chiara would have fired the imagination of a judge in Chancery.

I strode happily into the courtyard of the Tre Croci, and presently had my expectation confirmed. For I found my fellow, Gianbattista,—a faithful rogue I got in Rome on a Cardinal's recommendation,—hot in dispute with a lady's-maid. The woman was old, harsh-featured—no Italian clearly, though she spoke fluently in the tongue. She rated my man like a pickpocket, and the dispute was over a room.

"The signor will bear me out," said Gianbattista. "Was not I sent to Verona with his baggage, and thence to this place of ill manners? Was I not bidden engage for him a suite of apartments? Did I not duly choose these fronting on the gallery, and dispose therein the signor's baggage? And lo! an hour ago I found it all turned into the yard and this woman installed in its place. It is monstrous, unbearable! Is this an inn for travellers, or haply the private mansion of these Magnificences?"

"My servant speaks truly," I said firmly yet with courtesy, having no mind to spoil adventure by urging rights. "He had orders to take these rooms for me, and I know not what higher power can countermand me."

The woman had been staring at me scornfully, for no doubt in my dusty habit I was a figure of small count; but at the sound of my voice she started, and cried out, "You are English, signor?"

I bowed an admission.

"Then my mistress shall speak with you," she said, and dived into the inn like an elderly rabbit.

Gianbattista was for sending for the landlord and making a riot in that hostelry; but I stayed him, and bidding him fetch me a flask of white wine, three lemons, and a glass of *eau de vie*, I sat down peaceably at one of the little tables in the courtyard and prepared for the quenching of my thirst. Presently, as I sat drinking that excellent compound of my own invention, my shoulder was touched, and I turned to find the maid and her mistress. Alas for my hopes of a glorious being, young and lissom and bright with the warm riches of the south! I saw a short, stout little lady, well on the wrong side of thirty. She had plump red cheeks, and fair hair dressed indifferently in the Roman fashion. Two candid blue eyes redeemed her plainness, and a certain grave and gentle dignity. She was notably a gentlewoman, so I got up, doffed my hat, and awaited her commands.

She spoke in Italian. "Your pardon, signor, but I fear my good Cristine has done you unwittingly a wrong."

Cristine snorted at this premature plea of guilty, while I hastened to assure the fair apologist that any rooms I might have taken were freely at her service.

I spoke unconsciously in English, and she replied in a halting parody of that tongue. "I understand him," she said, "but I do not speak him happily. I will discourse, if the signor pleases, in our first speech."

She and her father, it appeared, had come over the Brenner, and arrived that morning at the Tre Croci, where they purposed to lie for some days. He was an old man, very feeble, and much depending upon her constant care. Wherefore it was necessary that the rooms of all the party should adjoin, and there was no suite of the size in the inn save that which I had taken. Would I therefore consent to forego my right, and place her under an eternal debt?

I agreed most readily, being at all times careless where I sleep, so the bed be clean, or where I eat, so the meal be good. I bade my servant see the landlord and have my belongings carried to other rooms. Madame thanked me sweetly, and would have gone, when a thought detained her.

"It is but courteous," she said, "that you should know the names of those whom you have befriended. My father is called the Count d'Albani, and I am his only daughter. We travel to Florence, where we have a villa in the environs."

"My name," said I, "is Hervey-Townshend, an Englishman travelling abroad for his entertainment."

"Hervey?" she repeated. "Are you one of the family of Miladi Hervey?"

"My worthy aunt," I replied, with a tender recollection of that preposterous woman.

Madame turned to Cristine, and spoke rapidly in a whisper.

"My father, sir," she said, addressing me, "is an old frail man, little used to the company of strangers; but in former days he has had kindness from members of your house, and it would be a satisfaction to him, I think, to have the privilege of your acquaintance."

She spoke with the air of a vizier who promises a traveller a sight of the Grand Turk. I murmured my gratitude, and hastened after Gianbattista. In an hour I had bathed, rid myself of my beard, and arrayed myself in decent clothing. Then I strolled out to inspect the little city, admired an altar-piece, chaffered with a Jew for a cameo, purchased some small necessaries, and returned early in the afternoon with a noble appetite for dinner.

The Tre Croci had been in happier days a bishop's lodging, and possessed a dining-hall ceiled with black oak and adorned with frescoes. It was used as a general *salle à manger* for all dwellers in the inn, and there accordingly I sat down to my long-deferred meal. At first there were no other diners, and I had two maids, as well as Gianbattista, to attend on my wants. Presently Madame d'Albani entered, escorted by Cristine and by a tall gaunt serving-man, who seemed no part of the hostelry. The landlord followed, bowing civilly, and the two women seated themselves at the little table at the farther end. "Il Signor Conte dines in his room," said Madame to the host, who withdrew to see to that gentleman's needs.

I found my eyes straying often to the little party in the cool twilight of that refectory. The man-servant was so old and battered, and yet of such a dignity, that he lent a touch of intrigue to the thing. He stood stiffly behind Madame's chair, handing dishes with an air of silent reverence—the lackey of a great noble, if ever I had seen the type. Madame never glanced towards me, but conversed sparingly with Cristine, while she pecked delicately at her food. Her name ran in my head with a tantalising flavour of the familiar. Albani! D'Albani! It was a name not uncommon in the Roman States, but I had never heard it linked to a noble family. And yet I had,—somehow, somewhere; and in the vain effort at recollection I had almost forgotten my hunger. There was nothing bourgeois in the little lady. The austere servants, the high manner of condescension, spake of a stock used to deference, though, maybe, pitifully decayed in its fortunes. There was a mystery in these quiet folk which tickled my curiosity. Romance after all was not destined to fail me at Santa Chiara.

My doings of the afternoon were of interest to myself alone. Suffice it to say that when I returned at nightfall I found Gianbattista the trustee of a letter. It was from Madame, written in a fine thin hand on a delicate paper, and it invited me to wait upon the signor, her father, that evening at eight o'clock. What caught my eye was a coronet stamped in a corner. A coronet, I say, but in truth it was a crown, the same as surmounts the Arms Royal of England on the signboard of a Court tradesman. I marvelled at the ways of foreign heraldry. Either this family of d'Albani had higher pretensions than I had given it credit for, or it employed an unlearned and imaginative stationer. I scribbled a line of acceptance and went to dress.

The hour of eight found me knocking at the Count's door. The grim serving-man admitted me to the pleasant chamber which should have been mine own. A dozen wax candles burned in sconces, and on the table among fruits and the remains of supper stood a handsome candelabra of silver. A small fire of logs had been lit on the hearth, and before it in an armchair sat a strange figure of a man. He seemed not so much old as aged. I should have put him at sixty, but the marks he bore were clearly less those of Time than of Life. There sprawled before me the relics of noble looks. The fleshy nose, the pendulous cheek, the drooping mouth, had once been cast in the lines of manly beauty. Heavy eyebrows above and heavy bags beneath spoiled the effect of a choleric blue eye, which age had not dimmed. The man was gross and yet haggard; it was not the padding of good living which clothed his bones, but a heaviness as of some dropsical malady. I could picture him in health a gaunt loose-limbed being, high-featured and swift and eager. He was dressed wholly in black velvet, with fresh ruffles and wristbands, and he wore heeled shoes with antique silver buckles. It was a figure of an older age which rose slowly to greet me, in one hand a snuff-box and a purple handkerchief, and in the other a book with finger marking place. He made me a great bow as Madame uttered my name, and held out a hand with a kindly smile.

"Mr. Hervey-Townshend," he said, "we will speak English, if you please. I am fain to hear it again, for 'tis a tongue I love. I make you welcome, sir, for your own sake and for the sake of your kin. How is her honourable ladyship, your aunt? A week ago she sent me a letter."

I answered that she did famously, and wondered what cause of correspondence my worthy aunt could have with wandering nobles of Italy.

He motioned me to a chair between Madame and himself, while a servant set a candle on a shelf behind him. Then he proceeded to catechise me in excellent English, with now and then a phrase of French, as to the doings in my own land. Admirably informed this Italian gentleman proved himself. I defy you to find in Almack's more intelligent gossip. He inquired as to the chances of my Lord North and the mind of my Lord Rockingham. He had my Lord Shelburne's foibles at his fingers' ends. The habits of the Prince, the aims of their ladyships of Dorset and Buckingham, the extravagance of this noble Duke and that right honourable gentleman were not hid from him. I answered discreetly yet frankly, for there was no ill-breeding in his curiosity. Rather it seemed like the inquiries of some fine lady, now buried deep in the country, as to the doings of a forsaken Mayfair. There was humour in it and something of pathos.

"My aunt must be a voluminous correspondent, sir," I said.

He laughed, "I have many friends in England who write to me, but I have seen none of them for long, and I doubt I may never see them again. Also in my youth I have been in England." And he sighed as at a sorrowful recollection.

Then he showed the book in his hand. "See," he said, "here is one of your English writings, the greatest book I have ever happened on." It was a volume of Mr. Fielding.

For a little he talked of books and poets. He admired Mr. Fielding profoundly, Dr. Smollett somewhat less, Mr. Richardson not at all. But he was clear that England had a monopoly of good writers, saving only my friend M. Rousseau, whom he valued, yet with reservations. Of the Italians he had no opinion. I instanced against him the plays of Signor Alfieri. He groaned, shook his head, and grew moody.

"Know you Scotland?" he asked suddenly.

I replied that I had visited Scotch cousins, but had no great estimation for the country. "It is too poor and jagged," I said, "for the taste of one who loves colour and sunshine and suave outlines."

He sighed. "It is indeed a bleak land, but a kindly. When the sun shines at all he shines on the truest hearts in the world. I love its bleakness too. There is a spirit in the misty hills, and the harsh seawind which inspires men to great deeds. Poverty and courage go often together, and my Scots, if they are poor, are as untamable as their mountains."

"You know the land, sir?" I asked.

"I have seen it, and I have known many Scots. You will find them in Paris and Avignon and Rome, with never a plack in their pockets. I have a feeling for exiles, sir, and I have pitied these poor people. They gave their all for the cause they followed."

Clearly the Count shared my aunt's views of history—those views which have made such sport for us often at Carteron. Stalwart Whig as I am, there was something in the tone of the old gentleman which made me feel a certain majesty in the lost cause.

"I am Whig in blood and Whig in principle," I said, "but I have never denied that those Scots who followed the Chevalier were too good to waste on so trumpery a leader."

I had no sooner spoken the words than I felt that somehow I had been guilty of a *bêtise*.

"It may be so," said the Count. "I did not bid you here, sir, to argue on politics, on which I am assured we should differ. But I will ask you one question. The King of England is a stout upholder of the right of kings. How does he face the defection of his American possessions?"

"The nation takes it well enough, and as for his Majesty's feelings, there is small inclination to inquire into them. I conceive of the whole war as a blunder out of which we have come as we deserved. The day is gone by for the assertion of monarchic rights against the will of a people."

"May be. But take note that the King of England is suffering to-day as—how do you call him?—the Chevalier suffered forty years ago. 'The wheel has come full circle,' as your Shakespeare says. Time has wrought his revenge."

He was staring into a fire, which burned small and smokily.

"You think the day for kings is ended. I read it differently. The world will ever have need of kings. If a nation cast out one it will have to find another. And mark you, those later kings, created by the people, will bear a harsher hand than the old race who ruled as of right. Some day the world will regret having destroyed the kindly and legitimate line of monarchs and put in their place tyrants who govern by the sword or by flattering an idle mob."

This belated dogma would at other times have set me laughing, but the strange figure before me gave no impulse to merriment. I glanced at Madame, and saw her face grave and perplexed, and I thought I read a warning gleam in her eye. There was a mystery about the party which irritated me, but good breeding forbade me to seek a clue.

"You will permit me to retire, sir," I said. "I have but this morning come down from a long march among the mountains east of this valley. Sleeping in wayside huts and tramping those sultry paths make a man think pleasantly of bed."

The Count seemed to brighten at my words. "You are a marcher, sir, and love the mountains? Once I would gladly have joined you, for in my youth I was a great walker in hilly places. Tell me, now, how many miles will you cover in a day?"

I told him thirty at a stretch.

"Ah," he said, "I have done fifty, without food, over the roughest and mossiest mountains. I lived on what I shot, and for drink I had springwater. Nay, I am forgetting. There was another beverage, which I wager you have never tasted. Heard you ever, sir, of that *eau de vie* which the Scots call *usquebagh*? It will comfort a traveller as no thin Italian wine will comfort him. By my soul, you shall taste it. Charlotte, my dear, bid Oliphant fetch glasses and hot water and lemons. I will give Mr. Hervey-Townshend a sample of the brew. You English are all *têtes-de-fer*, sir, and are worthy of it."

The old man's face had lighted up, and for the moment his air had the jollity of youth. I would have accepted the entertainment had I not again caught Madame's eye. It said, unmistakably and with serious pleading, "Decline." I therefore made my excuses, urged fatigue, drowsiness, and a delicate stomach, bade my host good-night, and in deep mystification left the room.

Enlightenment came upon me as the door closed. There on the threshold stood the man-servant whom they called Oliphant, erect as a sentry on guard. The sight reminded me of what I had once seen at Basle when by chance a Rhenish Grand Duke had shared the inn with me. Of a sudden a dozen clues linked together—the crowned notepaper, Scotland, my aunt Hervey's politics, the tale of old wanderings.

"Tell me," I said in a whisper, "who is the Count d'Albani, your master?" and I whistled softly a bar of "Charlie is my darling."

"Ay," said the man, without relaxing a muscle of his grim face. "It is the King of England—my king and yours."

II

In the small hours of the next morning I was awoke by a most unearthly sound. It was as if all the cats on all the roofs of Santa Chiara were sharpening their claws and wailing their battle-cries. Presently out of the noise came a kind of music—very slow, solemn, and melancholy. The notes ran up in great flights of ecstasy, and sunk anon to the tragic deeps. In spite of my sleepiness I was held spellbound, and the musician had concluded with certain barbaric grunts before I had the curiosity to rise. It came from somewhere in the gallery of the inn, and as I stuck my head out of my door I had a glimpse of Oliphant, nightcap on head and a great bagpipe below his arm, stalking down the corridor.

The incident, for all the gravity of the music, seemed to give a touch of farce to my interview of the past evening. I had gone to bed with my mind full of sad stories of the deaths of kings. Magnificence in tatters has always affected my pity more deeply than tatters with no such antecedent, and a monarch out at elbows stood for me as the last irony of our mortal life. Here was a king whose misfortunes could find no parallel. He had been in his youth the hero of a high adventure, and his middle age had been spent in fleeting among the courts of Europe, and waiting as pensioner on the whims of his foolish but regnant brethren. I had heard tales of a growing sottishness, a decline in spirit, a squalid taste in pleasures. Small blame, I had always thought, to so ill-fated a princeling. And now I had chanced upon the gentleman in his dotage, travelling with a barren effort at mystery, attended by a sad-faced daughter and two ancient domestics. It was a lesson in the vanity of human wishes which the shallowest moralist would have noted. Nay, I felt more than the moral. Something human and kindly in the old fellow had caught my fancy. The decadence was too tragic to prose about, the decadent too human to moralise on. I had left the chamber of the—shall I say *de jure* King of England?—a sentimental adherent of the cause. But this business of the bagpipes touched the comic. To harry an old valet out of bed and set him droning on pipes in the small hours smacked of a theatrical taste, or at least of an undignified fancy. Kings in exile, if they wish to keep the tragic air, should not indulge in such fantastic serenades.

My mind changed again when after breakfast I fell in with Madame on the stair. She drew aside to let me pass, and then made as if she would speak to me. I gave her good-morning, and, my mind being full of her story, addressed her as "Excellency."

"I see, sir," she said, "that you know the truth. I have to ask your forbearance for the concealment I practised yesterday. It was a poor requital for your generosity, but is it one of the shifts of our sad fortune. An uncrowned king must go in disguise or risk the laughter of every stable-boy. Besides, we are too poor to travel in state, even if we desired it."

Honestly, I knew not what to say. I was not asked to sympathise, having already revealed my politics, and yet the case cried out for sympathy. You remember, my dear aunt, the good Lady Culham, who was our Dorsetshire neighbour, and tried hard to mend my ways at Carteron? This poor Duchess —for so she called herself—was just such another. A woman made for comfort, housewifery, and motherhood, and by no means for racing about Europe in charge of a disreputable parent. I could picture her settled equably on a garden seat with a lapdog and needlework, blinking happily over green lawns and mildly rating an errant gardener. I could fancy her sitting in a summer parlour, very orderly and dainty, writing lengthy epistles to a tribe of nieces. I could see her marshalling a household in the family pew, or riding serenely in the family coach behind fat bay horses. But here, on an inn staircase, with a false name and a sad air of mystery, she was wofully out of place. I noted little wrinkles forming in the corners of her eyes, and the ravages of care beginning in the plump rosiness of her face. Be sure there was nothing appealing in her mien. She spoke with the air of a great lady, to whom the world is matter only for an afterthought. It was the facts that appealed and grew poignant from her courage.

"There is another claim upon your good-nature," she said. "Doubtless you were awoke last night by Oliphant's playing upon the pipes. I rebuked the landlord for his insolence in protesting, but to you, a gentleman and a friend, an explanation is due. My father sleeps ill, and your conversation seems to have cast him into a train of sad memories. It has been his habit on such occasions to have the pipes played to him, since they remind him of friends and happier days. It is a small privilege for an old man, and he does not claim it often."

I declared that the music had only pleased, and that I would welcome its repetition. Where upon she left me with a little bow and an invitation to join them that day at dinner, while I departed into the town on my own errands. I returned before midday, and was seated at an arbour in the garden, busy with letters, when there hove in sight the gaunt figure of Oliphant. He hovered around me, if such a figure can be said to hover, with the obvious intention of addressing me. The fellow had caught my fancy, and I was willing to see more of him. His face might have been hacked out of grey granite, his clothes hung loosely on his spare bones, and his stockinged shanks would have done no discredit to Don Quixote. There was no dignity in his air, only a steady and enduring sadness. Here, thought I, is the one of the establishment who most commonly meets the shock of the world's buffets. I called him by name and asked him his desires.

It appeared that he took me for a Jacobite, for he began a rigmarole about loyalty and hard fortune. I hastened to correct him, and he took the correction with the same patient despair with which he took all things. 'Twas but another of the blows of Fate.

"At any rate," he said in a broad Scotch accent, "ye come of kin that has helpit my maister afore this. I've many times heard tell o' Herveys and Townshends in England, and a' folk said they were on the richt side. Ye're maybe no a freend, but ye're a freend's freend, or I wadna be speirin' at ye."

I was amused at the prologue, and waited on the tale. It soon came. Oliphant, it appeared, was the purse-bearer of the household, and woful straits that poor purse-bearer must have been often put to. I questioned him as to his master's revenues, but could get no clear answer. There were payments due next month in Florence which would solve the difficulties for the winter, but in the meantime expenditure had beaten income. Travelling had cost much, and the Count must have his small comforts. The result in plain words was that Oliphant had not the wherewithal to frank the company to Florence; indeed, I doubted if he could have paid the reckoning in Santa Chiara. A loan was therefore sought from a friend's friend, meaning myself.

I was very really embarrassed. Not that I would not have given willingly, for I had ample resources at the moment and was mightily concerned about the sad household. But I knew that the little Duchess would take Oliphant's ears from his head if she guessed that he had dared to borrow from me, and that, if I lent, her back would for ever be turned against me. And yet, what would follow on my refusal? In a day or two there would be a pitiful scene with mine host, and as like as not some of their baggage detained as security for payment. I did not love the task of conspiring behind the lady's back, but if it could be contrived 'twas indubitably the kindest course. I glared sternly at Oliphant, who met me with his pathetic, dog-like eyes.

"You know that your mistress would never consent to the request you have made of me?"

"I ken," he said humbly. "But payin' is *my* job, and I simply havena the siller. It's no' the first time it has happened, and it's a sair trial for them both to be flung out o' doors by a foreign hostler because they canna meet his charges. But, sir, if ye can lend to me, ye may be certain that her leddyship will never hear a word o't. Puir thing, she takes nae thocht o' where the siller comes frae, ony mair than the lilies o' the field."

I became a conspirator. "You swear, Oliphant, by all you hold sacred, to breathe nothing of this to your mistress, and if she should suspect, to lie like a Privy Councillor?"

A flicker of a smile crossed his face. "I'll lee like a Scotch packman, and the Father o' lees could do nae mair. You need have no fear for your siller, sir. I've aye repaid when I borrowed, though you may have to wait a bittock." And the strange fellow strolled off.

At dinner no Duchess appeared till long after the appointed hour, nor was there any sign of Oliphant. When she came at last with Cristine, her eyes looked as if she had been crying, and she greeted me with remote courtesy. My first thought was that Oliphant had revealed the matter of the loan, but presently I found that the lady's trouble was far different. Her father, it seemed, was ill again with his old complaint. What that was I did not ask, nor did the Duchess reveal it.

We spoke in French, for I had discovered that this was her favourite speech. There was no Oliphant to wait on us, and the inn servants were always about, so it was well to have a tongue they did not comprehend. The lady was distracted and sad. When I inquired feelingly as to the general condition of her father's health she parried the question, and when I offered my services she disregarded my words. It was in truth a doleful meal, while the faded Cristine sat like a sphinx staring into vacancy. I spoke of England and of her friends, of Paris and Versailles, of Avignon where she had spent some years, and of the amenities of Florence, which she considered her home. But it was like talking to a nunnery door. I got nothing but "It is indeed true, sir," or "Do you say so, sir?" till my energy began to sink. Madame perceived my discomfort, and, as she rose, murmured an apology. "Pray forgive my distraction, but I am poor company when my father is ill. I have a foolish mind, easily frightened. Nay, nay!" she went on when I again offered help, "the illness is trifling. It will pass off by tomorrow, or at the latest the next day. Only I had looked forward to some ease at Santa Chiara, and the promise is belied."

As it chanced that evening, returning to the inn, I passed by the north side where the windows of the Count's room looked over a little flowergarden abutting on the courtyard. The dusk was falling, and a lamp had been lit which gave a glimpse into the interior. The sick man was standing by the window, his figure flung into relief by the lamplight. If he was sick, his sickness was of a curious type. His face was ruddy, his eye wild, and, his wig being off, his scanty hair stood up oddly round his head. He seemed to be singing, but I could not catch the sound through the shut casement. Another figure in the room, probably Oliphant, laid a hand on the Count's shoulder, drew him from the window, and closed the shutter.

It needed only the recollection of stories which were the property of all Europe to reach a conclusion on the gentleman's illness. The legitimate King of England was very drunk.

As I went to my room that night I passed the Count's door. There stood Oliphant as sentry, more grim and haggard than ever, and I thought that his eye met mine with a certain intelligence. From inside the room came a great racket. There was the sound of glasses falling, then a string of oaths, English, French, and for all I know, Irish, rapped out in a loud drunken voice. A pause, and then came the sound of maudlin singing. It pursued me along the gallery, an old childish song, delivered as if 'twere a pot-house catch—

> "*Qu'est-c' qui passe ici si tard,*
> *Compagnons de la Marjolaine—*"

One of the late-going company of the Marjolaine hastened to bed. This king in exile, with his melancholy daughter, was becoming too much for him.

### III

It was just before noon next day that the travellers arrived. I was sitting in the shady loggia of the inn, reading a volume of De Thou, when there drove up to the door two coaches. Out of the first descended very slowly and stiffly four gentlemen; out of the second four servants and a quantity of baggage. As it chanced there was no one about, the courtyard slept its sunny noontide sleep, and the only movement was a lizard on the wall and a buzz of flies by the fountain. Seeing no sign of the landlord, one of the travellers approached me with a grave inclination.

"This is the inn called the Tre Croci, sir?" he asked.

I said it was, and shouted on my own account for the host. Presently that personage arrived with a red face and a short wind, having ascended rapidly from his own cellar. He was awed by the dignity of the travellers, and made none of his usual protests of incapacity. The servants filed off solemnly with the baggage, and the four gentlemen set themselves down beside me in the loggia and ordered each a modest flask of wine.

At first I took them for our countrymen, but as I watched them the conviction vanished. All four were tall and lean beyond the average of mankind. They wore suits of black, with antique starched frills to their shirts; their hair was their own and unpowdered. Massive buckles of an ancient pattern adorned their square-toed shoes, and the canes they carried were like the yards of a small vessel. They were four merchants, I had guessed, of Scotland, maybe, or of Newcastle, but their voices were not Scotch, and their air had no touch of commerce. Take the heavy-browed preoccupation of a Secretary of State, add the dignity of a bishop, the sunburn of a fox-hunter, and something of the disciplined erectness of a soldier, and you may perceive the manner of these four gentlemen. By the side of them my assurance vanished. Compared with their Olympian serenity my person seemed fussy and servile. Even so, I mused, must Mr. Franklin have looked when baited in Parliament by the Tory pack. The reflection gave me the cue. Presently I caught from their conversation the word "Washington," and the truth flashed upon me. I was in the presence of four of Mr. Franklin's countrymen. Having never seen an American in the flesh, I rejoiced at the chance of enlarging my acquaintance.

They brought me into the circle by a polite question as to the length of road to Verona. Soon introductions followed. My name intrigued them, and they were eager to learn of my kinship to Uncle Charles. The eldest of the four, it appeared, was Mr. Galloway out of Maryland. Then came two brothers, Sylvester by name, of Pennsylvania, and last Mr. Fish, a lawyer of New York. All four had campaigned in the late war, and all four were members of the Convention, or whatever they call their rough-and-ready parliament. They were modest in their behaviour, much disinclined to speak of their past, as great men might be whose reputation was worldwide. Somehow the names stuck in my memory. I was certain that I had heard them linked with some stalwart fight or some moving civil deed or some defiant manifesto. The making of history was in their steadfast eye and the grave lines of the mouth. Our friendship flourished mightily in a brief hour, and brought me the invitation, willingly accepted, to sit with them at dinner.

There was no sign of the Duchess or Cristine or Oliphant. Whatever had happened, that household to-day required all hands on deck, and I was left alone with the Americans. In my day I have supped with the Macaronies, I have held up my head at the Cocoa Tree, I have avoided the floor at hunt dinners, I have drunk glass to glass with Tom Carteron. But never before have I seen such noble consumers of good liquor as those four gentlemen from beyond the Atlantic. They drank the strong red Cyprus as if it had been spring-water. "The dust of your Italian roads takes some cleansing,

Mr. Townshend," was their only excuse, but in truth none was needed. The wine seemed only to thaw their iron decorum. Without any surcease of dignity they grew communicative, and passed from lands to peoples and from peoples to constitutions. Before we knew it we were embarked upon high politics.

Naturally we did not differ on the war. Like me, they held it to have been a grievous necessity. They had no bitterness against England, only regrets for her blunders. Of his Majesty they spoke with respect, of his Majesty's advisers with dignified condemnation. They thought highly of our troops in America; less highly of our generals.

"Look you, sir," said Mr. Galloway, "in a war such as we have witnessed the Almighty is the only strategist. You fight against the forces of Nature, and a newcomer little knows that the success or failure of every operation he can conceive depends not upon generalship, but upon the confirmation of a vast country. Our generals, with this in mind and with fewer men, could make all your schemes miscarry. Had the English soldiery not been of such stubborn stuff, we should have been victors from the first. Our leader was not General Washington, but General America, and his brigadiers were forests, swamps, lakes, rivers, and high mountains."

"And now," I said, "having won, you have the greatest of human experiments before you. Your business is to show that the Saxon stock is adaptable to a republic."

It seemed to me that they exchanged glances.

"We are not pedants," said Mr. Fish, "and have no desire to dispute about the form of a constitution. A people may be as free under a king as under a senate. Liberty is not the lackey of any type of government."

These were strange words from a member of a race whom I had thought wedded to the republicanism of Helvidius Priscus.

"As a loyal subject of a monarchy," I said, "I must agree with you. But your hands are tied, for I cannot picture the establishment of a House of Washington, and—if not, where are you to turn for your sovereign?"

Again a smile seemed to pass among the four.

"We are experimenters, as you say, sir, and must go slowly. In the meantime, we have an authority which keeps peace and property safe. We are at leisure to cast our eyes round and meditate on the future."

"Then, gentlemen," said I, "you take an excellent way of meditation in visiting this museum of old sovereignties. Here you have the relics of any government you please—a dozen republics, tyrannies, theocracies, merchant confederations, kingdoms, and more than one empire. You have your choice. I am tolerably familiar with the land, and if I can assist you I am at your service."

They thanked me gravely. "We have letters," said Mr. Galloway; "one in especial is to a gentleman whom we hope to meet in this place. Have you heard in your travels of the Count of Albany?"

"He has arrived," said I, "two days ago. Even now he is in the chamber above us at dinner."

The news interested them hugely.

"You have seen him?" they cried. "What is he like?"

"An elderly gentleman in poor health, a man who has travelled much, and, I judge, has suffered something from fortune. He has a fondness for the English, so you will be welcome, sirs; but he was indisposed yesterday, and may still be unable to receive you. His daughter travels with him and tends his old age."

"And you—you have spoken with him?"

"The night before last I was in his company. We talked of many things, including the late war. He is somewhat of your opinion on matters of government."

The four looked at each other, and then Mr. Galloway rose.

"I ask your permission, Mr. Townshend, to consult for a moment with my friends. The matter is of some importance, and I would beg you to await us." So saying, he led the others out of doors, and I heard them withdraw to a corner of the loggia. Now, thought I, there is something afoot, and my long-sought romance approaches fruition. The company of the Marjolaine, whom the Count had sung of, have arrived at last.

Presently they returned and seated themselves at the table.

"You can be of great assistance to us, Mr. Townshend, and we would fain take you into our confidence. Are you aware who is this Count of Albany?"

I nodded. "It is a thin disguise to one familiar with history."

"Have you reached any estimate of his character or capabilities? You speak to friends, and, let me tell you, it is a matter which deeply concerns the Count's interests."

"I think him a kindly and pathetic old gentleman. He naturally bears the mark of forty years' sojourn in the wilderness."

Mr. Galloway took snuff.

"We have business with him, but it is business which stands in need of an agent. There is no one in the Count's suite with whom we could discuss affairs?"

"There is his daughter."

"Ah, but she would scarcely suit the case. Is there no man—a friend, and yet not a member of the family who can treat with us?"

I replied that I thought that I was the only being in Santa Chiara who answered the description.

"If you will accept the task, Mr. Townshend, you are amply qualified. We will be frank with you and reveal our business. We are on no less an errand than to offer the Count of Albany a crown."

I suppose I must have had some suspicion of their purpose, and yet the revelation of it fell on me like a thunderclap. I could only stare owlishly at my four grave gentlemen.

Mr. Galloway went on unperturbed. "I have told you that in America we are not yet republicans. There are those among us who favour a republic, but they are by no means a majority. We have got rid of a king who misgoverned us, but we have no wish to get rid of kingship. We want a king of our own choosing, and we would get with him all the ancient sanctions of monarchy. The Count of Albany is of the most illustrious royal stock in Europe,—he is, if legitimacy goes for anything, the rightful King of Britain. Now, if the republican party among us is to be worsted, we must come before the nation with a powerful candidate for their favour. You perceive my drift? What more potent appeal to American pride than to say: 'We have got rid of King George; we choose of our own free will the older line and King Charles'?"

I said foolishly that I thought monarchy had had its day, and that 'twas idle to revive it.

"That is a sentiment well enough under a monarchical government; but we, with a clean page to write upon, do not share it. You know your ancient historians. Has not the repository of the chief power always been the rock on which republicanism has shipwrecked? If that power is given to the chief citizen, the way is prepared for the tyrant. If it abides peacefully in a royal house, it abides with cyphers who dignify, without obstructing, a popular constitution. Do not mistake me, Mr. Townshend. This is no whim of a sentimental girl, but the reasoned conclusion of the men who achieved our liberty. There is every reason to believe that General Washington shares our views, and Mr. Hamilton, whose name you may know, is the inspirer of our mission."

"But the Count is an old man," I urged; for I knew not where to begin in my exposition of the hopelessness of their errand.

"By so much the better. We do not wish a young king who may be fractious. An old man tempered by misfortune is what our purpose demands."

"He has also his failings. A man cannot lead his life for forty years and retain all the virtues."

At that one of the Sylvesters spoke sharply. "I have heard such gossip, but I do not credit it. I have not forgotten Preston and Derby."

I made my last objection. "He has no posterity—legitimate posterity—to carry on his line."

The four gentlemen smiled. "That happens to be his chiefest recommendation," said Mr. Galloway. "It enables us to take the House of Stuart on trial. We need a breathing-space and leisure to look around; but unless we establish the principle of monarchy at once the republicans will forestall us. Let us get our king at all costs, and during the remaining years of his life we shall have time to settle the succession problem. We have no wish to saddle ourselves for good with a race who might prove burdensome. If King Charles fails he has no son, and we can look elsewhere for a better monarch. You perceive the reason of my view?"

I did, and I also perceived the colossal absurdity of the whole business. But I could not convince them of it, for they met my objections with excellent arguments. Nothing save a sight of the Count would, I feared, disillusion them.

"You wish me to make this proposal on your behalf?" I asked.

"We shall make the proposal ourselves, but we desire you to prepare the way for us. He is an elderly man, and should first be informed of our purpose."

"There is one person whom I beg leave to consult—the Duchess, his daughter. It may be that the present is an ill moment for approaching the Count, and the affair requires her sanction."

They agreed, and with a very perplexed mind I went forth to seek the lady. The irony of the thing was too cruel, and my heart ached for her. In the gallery I found Oliphant packing some very shabby trunks, and when I questioned him he told me that the family were to leave Santa Chiara on the morrow. Perchance the Duchess had awakened to the true state of their exchequer, or perchance she thought it well to get her father on the road again as a cure for his ailment.

I discovered Cristine, and begged for an interview with her mistress on an urgent matter. She led me to the Duchess's room, and there the evidence of poverty greeted me openly. All the little luxuries of the menage had gone to the Count. The poor lady's room was no better than a servant's garret, and the lady herself sat stitching a rent in a travelling cloak. She rose to greet me with alarm in her eyes.

As briefly as I could I set out the facts of my amazing mission. At first she seemed scarcely to hear me. "What do they want with him?" she asked. "He can give them nothing. He is no friend to the Americans or to any people who have deposed their sovereign." Then, as she grasped my meaning, her face flushed.

"It is a heartless trick, Mr. Townshend. I would fain think you no party to it."

"Believe me, dear madame, it is no trick. The men below are in sober earnest. You have but to see their faces to know that theirs is no wild adventure. I believe sincerely that they have the power to implement their promise."

"But it is madness. He is old and worn and sick. His day is long past for winning a crown."

"All this I have said, but it does not move them." And I told her rapidly Mr. Galloway's argument.

She fell into a muse. "At the eleventh hour! Nay, too late, too late. Had he been twenty years younger, what a stroke of fortune! Fate bears too hard on us, too hard!"

Then she turned to me fiercely. "You have no doubt heard, sir, the gossip about my father, which is on the lips of every fool in Europe. Let us have done with this pitiful make-believe. My father is a sot. Nay, I do not blame him. I blame his enemies and his miserable destiny. But there is the fact. Were he not old, he would still be unfit to grasp a crown and rule over a turbulent people. He flees from one city to another, but he cannot flee from himself. That is his illness on which you condoled with me yesterday."

The lady's control was at breaking-point. Another moment and I expected a torrent of tears. But they did not come. With a great effort she regained her composure.

"Well, the gentlemen must have an answer. You will tell them that the Count, my father—nay, give him his true title if you care—is vastly obliged to them for the honour they have done him, but would decline on account of his age and infirmities. You know how to phrase a decent refusal."

"Pardon me," said I, "but I might give them that answer till doomsday and never content them. They have not travelled many thousand miles to be put off by hearsay evidence. Nothing will satisfy them but an interview with your father himself."

"It is impossible," she said sharply.

"Then we must expect the renewed attentions of our American friends. They will wait till they see him."

She rose and paced the room.

"They must go," she repeated many times. "If they see him sober he will accept with joy, and we shall be the laughing-stock of the world. I tell you it cannot be. I alone know how immense is the impossibility. He cannot afford to lose the last rags of his dignity, the last dregs of his ease. They must not see him. I will speak with them myself."

"They will be honoured, madame, but I do not think they will be convinced. They are what we call in my land 'men of business.' They will not be content till they get the Count's reply from his own lips."

A new Duchess seemed to have arisen, a woman of quick action and sharp words.

"So be it. They shall see him. Oh, I am sick to death of fine sentiments and high loyalty and all the vapouring stuff I have lived among for years. All I ask for myself and my father is a little peace, and, by Heaven! I shall secure it. If nothing will kill your gentlemen's folly but truth, why, truth they shall have. They shall see my father, and this very minute. Bring them up, Mr. Townshend, and usher them into the presence of the rightful King of England. You will find him alone." She stopped her walk and looked out of the window.

I went back in a hurry to the Americans. "I am bidden to bring you to the Count's chamber. He is alone and will see you. These are the commands of madame his daughter."

"Good!" said Mr. Galloway, and all four, grave gentlemen as they were, seemed to brace themselves to a special dignity as befitted ambassadors to a king. I led them upstairs, tapped at the Count's door, and, getting no answer, opened it and admitted them.

And this was what we saw. The furniture was in disorder, and on a couch lay an old man sleeping a heavy drunken sleep. His mouth was open and his breath came stertorously. The face was purple, and large purple veins stood out on the mottled forehead. His scanty white hair was draggled over his cheek. On the floor was a broken glass, wet stains still lay on the boards, and the place reeked of spirits.

The four looked for a second—I do not think longer—at him whom they

would have made their king. They did not look at each other. With one
accord they moved out, and Mr. Fish, who was last, closed the door very
gently behind him.

In the hall below Mr. Galloway turned to me. "Our mission is ended,
Mr. Townshend. I have to thank you for your courtesy." Then to the others,
"If we order the coaches now, we may get well on the way to Verona ere
sundown."

An hour later two coaches rolled out of the courtyard of the Tre Croci.
As they passed, a window was half-opened on the upper floor, and a head
looked out. A line of a song came down, a song sung in a strange quavering
voice. It was the catch I had heard the night before:

> *"Qu'est-c' qui passe ici si tard.*
> *Compagnons de la Marjolaine—e?"*

It was true. The company came late indeed—too late by forty years. . . .

# First Day Finish

(from *The Friendly Persuasion*)

### JESSAMYN WEST

"THEE'S home, Lady," Jess told his mare.

They had made the trip in jig time. The sun was still up, catalpa shadows long across the grass, and mud daubers still busy about the horse trough, gathering a few last loads before nightfall, when Lady turned in the home driveway.

Jess loosened the reins, so that on their first homecoming together they could round the curve to the barn with a little flourish of arrival. It was a short-lived flourish, quickly subsiding when Jess caught sight of the Reverend Marcus Augustus Godley's Black Prince tied to the hitching rack.

"Look who's here," Jess told his mare and they came in slow and seemly as befitted travelers with forty weary miles behind them.

The Reverend Godley himself, shading his eyes from the low sun, stepped to the barn door when his Black Prince nickered.

Jess lit stiffly down and was standing at Lady's head when the Reverend Marcus Augustus reached them.

"Good evening, Marcus," said Jess. "Thee run short of something over at thy place?"

"Welcome home," said the Reverend Godley, never flinching. "I was hunting, with Enoch's help, a bolt to fit my seeder," he told Jess, but he never took his eyes off Lady.

He was a big man, fat but not pursy, with a full red face preaching had kept supple and limber. A variety of feelings, mostly painful, flickered across it now as he gazed at Jess' mare.

He opened and shut his mouth a couple of times, but all he managed to say was, "Where'd you come across that animal, Friend Birdwell?"

"Kentucky," Jess said shortly.

"I'm a Kentuckian myself." The Reverend Godley marveled that the state that had fathered him could have produced such horseflesh.

"You trade Red Rover for this?" he asked.

Jess rubbed his hand along Lady's neck. "The mare's name is Lady," he said.

"Lady!" The preacher gulped, then threw back his big head and disturbed the evening air with laughter.

"Friend," Jess said, watching the big bulk heave, "thy risibilities are mighty near the surface this evening."

The Reverend Godley wiped the tears from his face and ventured another look. "It's just the cleavage," he said. "The rift between the name and looks."

"That's a matter of opinion," Jess told him, "but Lady is the name."

The preacher stepped off a pace or two as if to try the advantage of a new perspective on the mare's appearance, clapped a handful of hoar-hound drops into his mouth, and chewed reflectively.

"I figure it this way," he told Jess. "You bought that animal Red Rover. Flashy as sin and twice as unreliable. First little brush you have with me and my cob, Red Rover curdles on you—goes sourer than a crock of cream in a June storm. What's the natural thing to do?"

The Reverend Godley gave his talk a pulpit pause and rested his big thumbs in his curving watch chain.

"The natural thing to do? Why, just what you done. Give speed the go-by. Say farewell to looks. Get yourself a beast sound in wind and limb and at home behind a plow. Friend," he commended Jess, "you done the right thing, though I'm free to admit I never laid eyes before on a beast of such dimensions. Have some hoar-hound drops?" he asked amiably. "Does wonders for the throat."

Jess shook his head.

"Well," he continued, "I want you to know—Sunday mornings on the way to church, when I pass you, there's nothing personal in it. That morning when I went round you and Red Rover, I somehow got the idea you's taking it personal. Speed's an eternal verity, friend, an eternal verity. Nothing personal. Rain falls. The stars shine. The grass withereth. The race is to the swift. A fast horse passes a slow one. An eternal verity, Friend Birdwell. You're no preacher, but your wife is. She understands these things. Nothing personal. Like gravitation, like life, like death. A law of God. Nothing personal.

"The good woman will be hallooing for me," he said, gazing up the pike toward his own farm a quarter of a mile away. He took another look at Jess' new mare.

"Name's Lady," he said, as if reminding himself. "Much obliged for the bolt, Friend Birdwell. Me and my cob'll see you Sunday."

Enoch stepped out from the barn door as the Reverend Godley turned down the driveway.

"Figure I heard my sermon for the week," he said.

"He's got an endurin' flock," Jess told his hired man.

"Cob?" Enoch asked. "What's he mean always calling that animal of his a cob? He ignorant?"

"Not ignorant—smooth," Jess said. "Cob's just his way of saying Black Prince's no ordinary beast without coming straight out with so undraped a word as stallion."

The two men turned with one accord from Godley's cob to Jess' Lady. Enoch's green eyes flickered knowingly; his long freckled hand touched Lady's muscled shoulder lightly, ran down the powerful legs, explored the deep chest.

"There's more here, Mr. Birdwell, than meets the eye?"

Jess nodded.

"As far as looks goes," Enoch said, "the Reverend called the turn."

"As far as looks goes," Jess agreed.

"She part Morgan?"

"Half," Jess said proudly.

Enoch swallowed. "How'd you swing it?"

"Providence," Jess said. "Pure Providence. Widow woman wanted a pretty horse and one that could be passed."

"Red Rover," Enoch agreed and added softly, "The Reverend was took in."

"He's a smart man," said Jess. "We'd best not bank on it. But, by sugar, Enoch, I tell thee I was getting tired of taking Eliza down the pike to Meeting every First Day like a tail to Godley's comet. Have him start late, go round me, then slow down so's we'd eat dust. Riled me so I was arriving at Meeting in no fit state to worship."

"You give her a tryout—coming home?" Enoch asked guardedly.

"I did, Enoch," Jess said solemnly. "This horse, this Morgan mare named Lady's got the heart of a lion and the wings of a bird. Nothing without pinfeathers is going to pass her."

"It's like Mr. Emerson says," said Enoch earnestly.

Jess nodded. "Compensation," he agreed. "A clear case of it and her pure due considering the looks she's got."

"You figure on this Sunday?" Enoch asked.

"Well," Jess said, "I plan to figure on nothing. Thee heard the Reverend Marcus Augustus. A fast horse goes round a slow one. Eternal law. If Black Prince tries to pass us First Day—and don't—it's just a law, just something eternal. And mighty pretty, Enoch, like the stars."

"A pity," Enoch said, reflecting, "the Reverend's young'uns all so piddling and yours such busters. Pity Steve and Jane's so well set up and chunky. It'll tell on your mare."

"A pity," Jess acquiesced, "but there it is. Eliza'd never agree to leave the children home from Meeting."

Enoch ruminated, his fingers busy with Lady's harness. "What'll your wife say to this mare? Been a considerable amount of trading lately."

"Say?" said Jess. "Thee heard her. 'Exchange Red Rover for a horse not racy-looking.' This mare racy-looking?"

"You have to look twice to see it," Enoch admitted.

"Eliza don't look twice at a horse. I'll just lead Lady up now for Eliza to see. She don't hold with coming down to the barn while men's about."

Jess took Lady from the shafts and led her between the rows of currant bushes up to the house. Dusk was come now, lamps were lit. Inside, Eliza and the children were waiting for their greeting until the men had had their talk.

"Lady," Jess said fondly, "I want thee to see thy mistress."

The rest of the week went by, mild and very fair, one of those spells in autumn when time seems to stand still. Clear days with a wind which would die down by afternoon. The faraway smoke-colored ridges seemed to have moved up to the orchard's edge. The purple ironweed, the farewell summer, the goldenrod, stood untrembling beneath an unclouded sky. Onto the corn standing shocked in the fields, gold light softer than arrows, but as pointed, fell. A single crow at dusk would drop in a slow arc against the distant wood to show that not all had died. Indian summer can be a time of great content.

First Day turned up pretty. Just before the start for Meeting, Jess discovered a hub cap missing off the surrey.

"Lost?" asked Eliza.

"I wouldn't say lost," Jess told her. "Missing."

Odd thing, a pity to be sure, but there it was. Nothing for it but for him and Eliza to ride to Meeting in the cut-down buggy and leave the children behind. Great pity, but there it was.

Eliza stood in the yard in her First Day silk. "Jess," she said in a balky voice, "this isn't my idea of what's seemly. A preacher going to Meeting in a cut-down rig like this. Looks more like heading for the trotting races at the county fair than preaching."

Jess said, "Thee surprises me, Eliza. Thee was used to put duty before appearance. Friend Fox was content to tramp the roads to reach his people. Thee asks for thy surrey, fresh blacking on the dashboard and a new whip in the socket."

He turned away sadly. "The Lord's people are everywhere grown more worldly," he said, looking dismally at the ground.

It didn't set good with Jess, pushing Eliza against her will that way—and he wasn't any too sure it was going to work. But the name Fox got her. When she was a girl she'd set out to bring the Word to people, the way Fox had done, and he'd have gone, she knew, to Meeting in a barrow, if need be.

So that's the way they started out, and in spite of the rig, Eliza was lighthearted and holy-feeling. When they pulled out on the pike, she was pleased to note the mare's gait was better than her looks. Lady picked up her feet like she knew what to do with them.

"Thee's got a good-pulling mare, Jess," she said kindly.

"She'll get us there, I don't misdoubt," Jess said.

They'd rounded the first curve below the clump of maples that gave the Maple Grove Nursery its name when the Reverend Godley bore down upon them. Neither bothered to look back; both knew the heavy, steady beat of Black Prince's hoofs.

Eliza settled herself in the cut-down rig, her Bible held comfortably in her lap. "It taxes the imagination," she said, "how a man church-bound can have his mind so set on besting another. Don't thee think so, Jess?"

"It don't tax mine," Jess said, thinking honesty might be the only virtue he'd get credit for that day.

Eliza was surprised not to see Black Prince pulling abreast them. It was here on the long stretch of level road that Black Prince usually showed them his heels.

"Thee'd best pull over, Jess," she said.

"I got no call to pull out in the ditch," Jess said. "The law allows me half the road."

The mare hadn't made any fuss about it—no head-shaking, no fancy foot-work—but she'd settled down in her harness, she was traveling. It was plain to Eliza they were eating up the road.

"Don't thee think we'd better pull up, Jess?" Eliza said it easy, so as not to stir up the contrary streak that wasn't buried very deep in her husband.

"By sugar," Jess said, "I don't see why."

As soon as Eliza heard that "by sugar" spoken as bold-faced as if it were a weekday, she knew it was too late for soft words. "By sugar," Jess said again, "I don't see why. The Reverend Godley's got half the road and I ain't urging my mare."

It depended on what you called urging. He hadn't taken to lambasting Lady with his hat yet, the way he had Red Rover, but he was sitting on the edge of the seat—and sitting mighty light, it was plain to see—driving the mare with an easy rein and talking to her like a weanling.

"Thee's a fine mare. Thee's a tryer. Thee's a credit to thy dam. Never have to think twice about thy looks again."

Maybe, strictly speaking, that was just encouraging, not urging, but Eliza wasn't in a hairsplitting mood.

She looked back at the Reverend Marcus Augustus, and no two ways about it: he was urging Black Prince. The Reverend Godley's cob wasn't a length behind them and the Reverend himself was half standing, slapping the reins across Black Prince's rump and exhorting him like a sinner newly come to the mourners' bench.

This was a pass to which Eliza hadn't thought to come twice in a life-time—twice in a lifetime to be heading for Meeting like a county fair racer in a checkered shirt.

"Nothing lacking now," she thought bitterly, "but for bets to be laid on us."

That wasn't lacking either, if Eliza had only known it. They'd come in view of the Bethel Church now, and more than one of Godley's flock had got so carried away by the race as to try for odds on their own preacher. It didn't seem loyal not to back up their Kentucky brother with hard cash. Two to one the odds were—with no takers.

The Bethel Church sat atop a long, low rise, not much to the eye—but it told on a light mare pulling against a heavy stallion, and it was here Black Prince began to close in; before the rise was half covered, the stallion's nose was pressing toward the buggy's back near wheel.

Jess had given up encouraging. He was urging now. Eliza lifted the hat off his head. Come what might, there wasn't going to be any more hat-whacking if she could help it—but Jess was beyond knowing whether his head was bare or covered. He was pulling with his mare now, sweating with her, sucking the air into scalding lungs with her. Lady had slowed on the rise—she'd have been dead if she hadn't—but she was still a-going, still trying hard. Only the Quaker blood in Jess' veins kept him from shouting with pride at his mare's performance.

The Reverend Godley didn't have Quaker blood in his veins. What he had was Kentucky horse-racing blood, and when Black Prince got his nose opposite Lady's rump Godley's racing blood got the best of him. He began to talk to his cob in a voice that got its volume from camp-meeting practice —and its vocabulary, too, as a matter of fact—but he was using it in a fashion his camp-meeting congregations had never heard.

They were almost opposite the Bethel Church now; Black Prince had nosed up an inch or two more on Lady and the Reverend Godley was still strongly exhorting—getting mighty personal, for a man of his convictions.

But Lady was a stayer and so was Jess. And Eliza, too, for that matter. Jess spared her a glance out of the corner of his eye to see how she was faring. She was faring mighty well—sitting bolt upright, her Bible tightly clasped, and clucking to the mare. Jess couldn't credit what he heard. But there was no doubt about it—Eliza was counseling Lady. "Thee keep a-going, Lady," she called. Eliza hadn't camp-meeting experience, but she had a good clear pulpit voice and Lady heard her.

She kept a-going. She did better. She unloosed a spurt of speed Jess hadn't known was in her. Lady was used to being held back, not yelled at in a brush. Yelling got her dander up. She stretched out her long neck, lengthened her powerful stride, and pulled away from Black Prince just as they reached the Bethel Church grounds.

Jess thought the race was won and over, that from here on the pace to Meeting could be more suitable to First Day travel. But the Reverend Godley had no mind to stop at so critical a juncture. He'd wrestled with sinners too long to give up at the first setback. He figured the mare was weakening. He figured that with a strong stayer like his Black Prince he'd settle the matter easy in the half mile that lay between the Bethel Church and the Quaker Meeting House at the grove. He kept a-coming.

But one thing he didn't figure—that was that the slope from Bethel to the Meeting House was against him. Lady had a downhill grade now. It was all she needed. She didn't pull away from Black Prince in any whirlwind style, but stride by stride she pulled away.

It was a great pity Jess' joy in that brush had to be marred. He'd eaten humble pie some time now, and he was pleasured through and through to be doing the dishing up himself. And he was pleasured for the mare's sake.

But neither winning nor his mare's pleasure was first with Jess. Eliza was. There she sat, white and suffering, holding her Bible like it was the Rock of Ages from which she'd come mighty near to clean slipping off. Jess knew Eliza had a forgiving heart when it came to others—but whether she could forgive herself for getting heated over a horse race the way she'd done, he couldn't say.

And the worst for Eliza was yet to come. Jess saw that clear enough. When Lady and Black Prince had pounded past Godley's church, a number of the Bethel brethren, who had arrived early and were still in their rigs, set out behind the Reverend Marcus Augustus to be in at the finish. And they were going to be. Their brother was losing, but they were for him still, close behind and encouraging him in a wholehearted way. The whole caboodle was going to sweep behind Jess and Eliza into the Quaker churchyard. They wouldn't linger, but Jess feared they'd turn around there before heading back again. And that's the way it was.

Lady was three lengths ahead of Black Prince when they reached the Grove Meeting House. Jess eased her for the turn, made it on two wheels, and drew in close to the church. The Bethelites swooped in behind him and on out—plainly beat but not subdued. The Reverend Marcus Augustus was the only man among them without a word to say. He was as silent as a tombstone and considerably grimmer. Even his fancy vest looked to have faded.

The Quakers waiting in the yard for Meeting to begin were quiet, too. Jess couldn't tell from their faces what they were feeling; but there was no use thinking that they considered what they'd just witnessed an edifying sight. Not for a weekday even, that mess of rigs hitting it down the pike with all that hullabaloo—let alone to First Day and their preacher up front, leading it.

Jess asked a boy to look after Lady. He was so taken up with Eliza he no more than laid a fond hand on Lady's hot flank in passing. He helped Eliza light down, and set his hat on his head when she handed it to him. Eliza looked mighty peaked and withdrawn, like a woman communing with the Lord.

She bowed to the congregation and they bowed back and she led them out of the sunshine into the Meeting House with no word being spoken on either side. She walked to the preacher's bench, laid her Bible quietly down, and untied her bonnet strings.

Jess sat rigid in his seat among the men. Jess was a birthright Quaker—and his father and grandfathers before him—and he'd known Quakers to be read out of Meeting for less.

Eliza laid her little plump hands on her Bible and bowed her head in silent prayer. Jess didn't know how long it lasted—sometimes it seemed stretching out into eternity, but Quakers were used to silent worship and he was the only one who seemed restive. About the time the ice round Jess' heart was hardening past his enduring, Eliza's sweet, cool, carrying voice said, "If the spirit leads any of you to speak, will you speak now?"

Then Eliza lowered her head again—but Jess peered round the Meeting House. He thought he saw a contented look on most of the faces—nothing that went so far as to warm into a smile, but a look that said they were satisfied the way the Lord had handled things. And the spirit didn't move any member of the congregation to speak that day except for the prayers of two elderly Friends in closing.

The ride home was mighty quiet. They drove past the Bethel Church, where the sermon had been short—for all the hitching racks were empty. Lady carried them along proud and untired. Enoch, Steve and Jane met them down the pike a ways from home and Emanuela waited on the doorstep, but Jess could only nod the good news to them; he couldn't glory in it the way he'd like because of Eliza.

Eliza was kind, but silent. Very silent. She spoke when spoken to, did her whole duty by the children and Jess, but in all the ways that made Eliza most herself, she was absent and withdrawn.

Toward evening Jess felt a little dauncy—a pain beneath the ribs, heart, or stomach, he couldn't say which. He thought he'd brew himself a cup of sassafras tea, take it to bed and drink it there, and maybe find a little ease.

It was past nightfall when Jess entered his and Eliza's chamber, but there was a full moon and by its light he saw Eliza sitting at the east window in her white nightdress, plaiting her black hair.

"Jess," asked Eliza, noting the cup he carried, "has thee been taken ill?"

"No," Jess said, "no," his pain easing off of itself when he heard by the tones of Eliza's voice that she was restored to him—forgiving and gentle, letting bygones be bygones.

"Eliza," he asked, "wouldn't thee like a nice hot cup of sassafras tea?"

"Why, yes, Jess," Eliza said. "That'd be real refreshing."

Jess carried Eliza her cup of tea walking down a path of roses the moon had lit up in the ingrain carpet.

He stood, while she drank it, with his hand on her chair, gazing out the window: the whole upcurve and embowered sweep of the earth soaked in moonlight—hill and wood lot, orchard and silent river. And beneath that sheen his own rooftree, and all beneath it, peaceful and at rest. Lady in her stall, Enoch reading Emerson, the children long abed.

" 'Sweet day,' " he said, " 'so cool, so calm, so bright, The bridal of the earth and sky.' "

And though he felt so pensive and reposeful, still the bridge of his big nose wrinkled up, his ribs shook with laughter.

Eliza felt the movement of his laughing in her chair. "What is it, Jess?" she asked.

Jess stopped laughing, but said nothing. He figured Eliza had gone about as far in one day as a woman could in enlarging her appreciation of horse-flesh; still he couldn't help smiling when he thought of the sermon that might have been preached that morning in the Bethel Church upon the eternal verities.

# The Adventure of the Priory School

### SIR ARTHUR CONAN DOYLE

W E have had some dramatic entrances and exits upon our small stage at Baker Street, but I cannot recollect anything more sudden and startling than the first appearance of Thorneycroft Huxtable, M.A., Ph.D., etc. His card, which seemed too small to carry the weight of his academic distinctions, preceded him by a few seconds, and then he entered himself—so large, so pompous, and so dignified that he was the very embodiment of self-possession and solidity. And yet his first action, when the door had closed behind him, was to stagger against the table, whence he slipped down upon the floor, and there was that majestic figure prostrate and insensible upon our bearskin hearthrug.

We had sprung to our feet, and for a few moments we stared in silent amazement at this ponderous piece of wreckage, which told of some sudden and fatal storm far out on the ocean of life. Then Holmes hurried with a cushion for his head, and I with brandy for his lips. The heavy, white face was seamed with lines of trouble, the hanging pouches under the closed eyes were leaden in colour, the loose mouth drooped dolorously at the corners, the rolling chins were unshaven. Collar and shirt bore the grime of a long journey, and the hair bristled unkempt from the well-shaped head. It was a sorely stricken man who lay before us.

"What is it, Watson?" asked Holmes.

"Absolute exhaustion—possibly mere hunger and fatigue," said I, with my finger on the thready pulse, where the stream of life trickled thin and small.

"Return ticket from Mackleton, in the north of England," said Holmes, drawing it from the watch-pocket. "It is not twelve o'clock yet. He has certainly been an early starter."

The puckered eyelids had begun to quiver, and now a pair of vacant gray eyes looked up at us. An instant later the man had scrambled on to his feet, his face crimson with shame.

"Forgive this weakness, Mr. Holmes, I have been a little overwrought. Thank you, if I might have a glass of milk and a biscuit, I have no doubt that I should be better. I came personally, Mr. Holmes, in order to insure that you would return with me. I feared that no telegram would convince you of the absolute urgency of the case."

"When you are quite restored——"

"I am quite well again. I cannot imagine how I came to be so weak. I wish you, Mr. Holmes, to come to Mackleton with me by the next train."

My friend shook his head.

"My colleague, Dr. Watson, could tell you that we are very busy at present. I am retained in this case of the Ferrers Documents, and the Abergavenny murder is coming up for trial. Only a very important issue could call me from London at present."

"Important!" Our visitor threw up his hands. "Have you heard nothing of the abduction of the only son of the Duke of Holdernesse?"

"What! the late Cabinet Minister?"

"Exactly. We had tried to keep it out of the papers, but there was some rumor in the *Globe* last night. I thought it might have reached your ears."

Holmes shot out his long, thin arm and picked out Volume "H" in his encyclopædia of reference.

"'Holdernesse, 6th Duke, K.G., P.C.'—half the alphabet! 'Baron Beverley, Earl of Carston'—dear me, what a list! 'Lord Lieutenant of Hallamshire since 1900. Married Edith, daughter of Sir Charles Appledore, 1888. Heir and only child, Lord Saltire. Owns about two hundred and fifty thousand acres. Minerals in Lancashire and Wales. Address: Carlton House Terrace; Holdernesse Hall, Hallamshire; Carston Castle, Bangor, Wales. Lord of the Admiralty, 1872; Chief Secretary of State for——' Well, well, this man is certainly one of the greatest subjects of the Crown!"

"The greatest and perhaps the wealthiest. I am aware, Mr. Holmes, that you take a very high line in professional matters, and that you are prepared to work for the work's sake. I may tell you, however, that his Grace has already intimated that a check for five thousand pounds will be handed over to the person who can tell him where his son is, and another thousand to him who can name the man or men who have taken him."

"It is a princely offer," said Holmes. "Watson, I think that we shall accompany Dr. Huxtable back to the north of England. And now, Dr. Huxtable, when you have consumed that milk, you will kindly tell me what has happened, when it happened, how it happened, and, finally, what Dr. Thorneycroft Huxtable, of the Priory School, near Mackleton, has to do with the matter, and why he comes three days after an event—the state of your chin gives the date—to ask for my humble services."

Our visitor had consumed his milk and biscuits. The light had come back to his eyes and the colour to his cheeks, as he set himself with great vigour and lucidity to explain the situation.

"I must inform you, gentlemen, that the Priory is a preparatory school, of which I am the founder and principal. *Huxtable's Sidelights on Horace* may possibly recall my name to your memories. The Priory is, without exception, the best and most select preparatory school in England. Lord Leverstoke, the Earl of Blackwater, Sir Cathcart Soames—they all have intrusted their sons to me. But I felt that my school had reached its zenith when, three weeks ago, the Duke of Holdernesse sent Mr. James Wilder, his secretary, with the intimation that young Lord Saltire, ten years old, his only son and heir, was about to be committed to my charge. Little did I think that this would be the prelude to the most crushing misfortune of my life.

"On May 1st the boy arrived, that being the beginning of the summer term. He was a charming youth, and he soon fell into our ways. I may tell you—I trust that I am not indiscreet, but half-confidences are absurd in such a case—that he was not entirely happy at home. It is an open secret that the Duke's married life had not been a peaceful one, and the matter had ended in a separation by mutual consent, the Duchess taking up her residence in the south of France. This had occurred very shortly before, and the boy's sympathies are known to have been strongly with his mother. He moped after her departure from Holdernesse Hall, and it was for this reason that the Duke desired to send him to my establishment. In a fortnight the boy was quite at home with us and was apparently absolutely happy.

"He was last seen on the night of May 13th—that is, the night of last Monday. His room was on the second floor and was approached through another larger room, in which two boys were sleeping. These boys saw and heard nothing, so that it is certain that young Saltire did not pass out that way. His window was open, and there is a stout ivy plant leading to the ground. We could trace no footmarks below, but it is sure that this is the only possible exit.

"His absence was discovered at seven o'clock on Tuesday morning. His bed had been slept in. He had dressed himself fully, before going off, in his usual school suit of black Eton jacket and dark gray trousers. There were no signs that anyone had entered the room, and it is quite certain that anything in the nature of cries or a struggle would have been heard, since Caunter, the elder boy in the inner room, is a very light sleeper.

"When Lord Saltire's disappearance was discovered, I at once called a roll of the whole establishment—boys, masters, and servants. It was then that we ascertained that Lord Saltire had not been alone in his flight. Heidegger, the German master, was missing. His room was on the second floor, at the farther end of the building, facing the same way as Lord Saltire's. His bed had also been slept in, but he had apparently gone away partly dressed, since his shirt and socks were lying on the floor. He had undoubtedly let himself down by the ivy, for we could see the marks of his feet where he had landed on the lawn. His bicycle was kept in a small shed beside this lawn, and it also was gone.

"He had been with me for two years, and came with the best references, but he was a silent, morose man, not very popular either with masters or boys. No trace could be found of the fugitives, and now, on Thursday morning, we are as ignorant as we were on Tuesday. Inquiry was, of course, made at once at Holdernesse Hall. It is only a few miles away, and we imagined that, in some sudden attack of homesickness, he had gone back to his father, but nothing had been heard of him. The Duke is greatly agitated, and, as to me, you have seen yourselves the state of nervous prostration to which the suspense and the responsibility have reduced me. Mr. Holmes, if ever you put forward your full powers, I implore you to do so now, for never in your life could you have a case which is more worthy of them."

Sherlock Holmes had listened with the utmost intentness to the statement of the unhappy schoolmaster. His drawn brows and the deep furrow between them showed that he needed no exhortation to concentrate all his attention upon a problem which, apart from the tremendous interests involved, must appeal so directly to his love of the complex and the unusual. He now drew out his notebook and jotted down one or two memoranda.

"You have been very remiss in not coming to me sooner," said he, severely. "You start me on my investigation with a very serious handicap. It is inconceivable, for example, that this ivy and this lawn would have yielded nothing to an expert observer."

"I am not to blame, Mr. Holmes. His Grace was extremely desirous to avoid all public scandal. He was afraid of his family unhappiness being dragged before the world. He has a deep horror of anything of the kind."

"But there has been some official investigation?"

"Yes, sir, and it has proved most disappointing. An apparent clue was at once obtained, since a boy and a young man were reported to have been seen leaving a neighbouring station by an early train. Only last night we had news that the couple had been hunted down in Liverpool, and they prove to have no connection whatever with the matter in hand. Then it was that in my despair and disappointment, after a sleepless night, I came straight to you by the early train."

"I suppose the local investigation was relaxed while this false clue was being followed up?"

"It was entirely dropped."

"So that three days have been wasted. The affair has been most deplorably handled."

"I feel it and admit it."

"And yet the problem should be capable of ultimate solution. I shall be very happy to look into it. Have you been able to trace any connection between the missing boy and this German master?"

"None at all."

"Was he in the master's class?"

"No, he never exchanged a word with him, so far as I know."

"That is certainly very singular. Had the boy a bicycle?"

"No."

"Was any other bicycle missing?"

"No."

"Is that certain?"

"Quite."

"Well, now, you do not mean to seriously suggest that this German rode off upon a bicycle in the dead of the night, bearing the boy in his arms?"

"Certainly not."

"Then what is the theory in your mind?"

"The bicycle may have been a blind. It may have been hidden somewhere, and the pair gone off on foot."

"Quite so, but it seems rather an absurd blind, does it not? Were there other bicycles in this shed?"

"Several."

"Would he not have hidden *a couple*, had he desired to give the idea that they had gone off upon them?"

"I suppose he would."

"Of course he would. The blind theory won't do. But the incident is an admirable starting-point for an investigation. After all, a bicycle is not an easy thing to conceal or to destroy. One other question. Did anyone call to see the boy on the day before he disappeared?"

"No."

"Did he get any letters?"

"Yes, one letter."

"From whom?"

"From his father."

"Do you open the boys' letters?"

"No."

"How do you know it was from the father?"

"The coat of arms was on the envelope, and it was addressed in the Duke's peculiar stiff hand. Besides, the Duke remembers having written."

"When had he a letter before that?"

"Not for several days."

"Had he ever one from France?"

"No, never."

"You see the point of my questions, of course. Either the boy was carried off by force or he went of his own free will. In the latter case, you would expect that some prompting from outside would be needed to make so young a lad do such a thing. If he has had no visitors, that prompting must have come in letters; hence I try to find out who were his correspondents."

"I fear I cannot help you much. His only correspondent, so far as I know, was his own father."

"Who wrote to him on the very day of his disappearance. Were the relations between father and son very friendly?"

"His Grace is never very friendly with anyone. He is completely immersed in large public questions, and is rather inaccessible to all ordinary emotions. But he was always kind to the boy in his own way."

"But the sympathies of the latter were with the mother?"

"Yes."

"Did he say so?"

"No."

"The Duke, then?"

"Good heaven, no!"

"Then how could you know?"

"I have had some confidential talks with Mr. James Wilder, his Grace's secretary. It was he who gave me the information about Lord Saltire's feelings."

"I see. By the way, that last letter of the Duke's—was it found in the boy's room after he was gone?"

"No, he had taken it with him. I think, Mr. Holmes, it is time that we were leaving for Euston."

"I will order a four-wheeler. In a quarter of an hour, we shall be at your service. If you are telegraphing home, Mr. Huxtable, it would be well to allow the people in your neighbourhood to imagine that the inquiry is still going on in Liverpool, or wherever else that red herring led your pack. In the meantime I will do a little quiet work at your own doors, and perhaps the scent is not so cold but that two old hounds like Watson and myself may get a sniff of it."

That evening found us in the cold, bracing atmosphere of the Peak country, in which Dr. Huxtable's famous school is situated. It was already dark when we reached it. A card was lying on the hall table, and the butler whispered something to his master, who turned to us with agitation in every heavy feature.

"The Duke is here," said he. "The Duke and Mr. Wilder are in the study. Come, gentlemen, and I will introduce you."

I was, of course, familiar with the pictures of the famous statesman, but the man himself was very different from his representation. He was a tall and stately person, scrupulously dressed, with a drawn, thin face, and a nose which was grotesquely curved and long. His complexion was of a dead pallor, which was more startling by contrast with a long, dwindling beard of vivid red, which flowed down over his white waistcoat, with his watch-chain gleaming through its fringe. Such was the stately presence who looked stonily at us from the centre of Dr. Huxtable's hearthrug. Beside him stood a very young man, whom I understood to be Wilder, the private secretary. He was small, nervous, alert, with intelligent light-blue eyes and mobile features. It was he who at once, in an incisive and positive tone, opened the conversation.

"I called this morning, Dr. Huxtable, too late to prevent you from starting for London. I learned that your object was to invite Mr. Sherlock Holmes to undertake the conduct of this case. His Grace is surprised, Dr. Huxtable, that you should have taken such a step without consulting him."

"When I learned that the police had failed——"

"His Grace is by no means convinced that the police have failed."

"But surely, Mr. Wilder——"

"You are well aware, Dr. Huxtable, that his Grace is particularly anxious to avoid all public scandal. He prefers to take as few people as possible into his confidence."

"The matter can be easily remedied," said the browbeaten doctor; "Mr. Sherlock Holmes can return to London by the morning train."

"Hardly that, Doctor, hardly that," said Holmes, in his blandest voice. "This northern air is invigorating and pleasant, so I   propose to spend a few days upon your moors, and to occupy my mind as best I may. Whether I have the shelter of your roof or of the village inn is, of course, for you to decide."

I could see that the unfortunate doctor was in the last stage of indecision, from which he was rescued by the deep, sonorous voice of the red-bearded Duke, which boomed out like a dinner-gong.

"I agree with Mr. Wilder, Dr. Huxtable, that you would have done wisely to consult me. But since Mr. Holmes has already been taken into your confidence, it would indeed be absurd that we should not avail ourselves of his services. Far from going to the inn, Mr. Holmes, I should be pleased if you would come and stay with me at Holdernesse Hall."

"I thank your Grace. For the purposes of my investigation, I think that it would be wiser for me to remain at the scene of the mystery."

"Just as you like, Mr. Holmes. Any information which Mr. Wilder or I can give you is, of course, at your disposal."

"It will probably be necessary for me to see you at the Hall," said Holmes. "I would only ask you now, sir, whether you have formed any explanation in your own mind as to the mysterious disappearance of your son?"

"No, sir, I have not."

"Excuse me if I allude to that which is painful to you, but I have no alternative. Do you think that the Duchess had anything to do with the matter?"

The great minister showed perceptible hesitation.

"I do not think so," he said, at last.

"The other most obvious explanation is that the child has been kidnapped for the purpose of levying ransom. You have not had any demand of the sort?"

"No, sir."

"One more question, your Grace. I understand that you wrote to your son upon the day when this incident occurred."

"No, I wrote upon the day before."

"Exactly. But he received it on that day?"

"Yes."

"Was there anything in your letter which might have unbalanced him or induced him to take such a step?"

"No, sir, certainly not."

"Did you post that letter yourself?"

The nobleman's reply was interrupted by his secretary, who broke in with some heat.

"His Grace is not in the habit of posting letters himself," said he. "This letter was laid with others upon the study table, and I myself put them in the post-bag."

"You are sure this one was among them?"

"Yes, I observed it."

"How many letters did your Grace write that day?"

"Twenty or thirty. I have a large correspondence. But surely this is somewhat irrelevant?"

"Not entirely," said Holmes.

"For my own part," the Duke continued, "I have advised the police to turn their attention to the south of France. I have already said that I do not believe that the Duchess would encourage so monstrous an action, but the lad had the most wrongheaded opinions, and it is possible that he may have fled to her, aided and abetted by this German. I think, Dr. Huxtable, that we will now return to the Hall."

I could see that there were other questions which Holmes would have wished to put, but the nobleman's abrupt manner showed that the interview was at an end. It was evident that to his intensely aristocratic nature this discussion of his intimate family affairs with a stranger was most abhorrent, and that he feared lest every fresh question would throw a fiercer light into the discreetly shadowed corners of his ducal history.

When the nobleman and his secretary had left, my friend flung himself at once with characteristic eagerness into the investigation.

The boy's chamber was carefully examined, and yielded nothing save the absolute conviction that it was only through the window that he could have escaped. The German master's room and effects gave no further clue. In his case a trailer of ivy had given way under his weight, and we saw by the light of a lantern the mark on the lawn where his heels had come down. That one dint in the short, green grass was the only material witness left of this inexplicable nocturnal flight.

Sherlock Holmes left the house alone, and only returned after eleven. He had obtained a large ordnance map of the neighbourhood, and this he brought into my room, where he laid it out on the bed, and, having balanced the lamp in the middle of it, he began to smoke over it, and occasionally to point out objects of interest with the reeking amber of his pipe.

"This case grows upon me, Watson," said he. "There are decidedly some points of interest in connection with it. In this early stage, I want you to realize those geographical features which may have a good deal to do with our investigation.

"Look at this map. This dark square is the Priory School. I'll put a pin in it. Now, this line is the main road. You see that it runs east and west past the school, and you see also that there is no side road for a mile either way. If these two folk passed away by road, it was *this* road."

"Exactly."

"By a singular and happy chance, we are able to some extent to check what passed along this road during the night in question. At this point, where my pipe is now resting, a county constable was on duty from twelve to six. It is, as you perceive, the first cross-road on the east side. This man declares that he was not absent from his post for an instant, and he is positive that neither boy nor man could have gone that way unseen. I have spoken with this policeman to-night, and he appears to me to be a perfectly reliable person. That blocks this end. We have now to deal with the other. There is an inn here, the Red Bull, the landlady of which was ill. She had sent to Mackleton for a doctor, but he did not arrive until morning, being absent at another case. The people at the inn were alert all night, awaiting his coming, and one or other of them seems to have continually had an eye upon the road. They declare that no one passed. If their evidence is good, then we are fortunate enough to be able to block the west, and also to be able to say that the fugitives did *not* use the road at all."

"But the bicycle?" I objected.

"Quite so. We will come to the bicycle presently. To continue our reasoning: if these people did not go by the road, they must have traversed the country to the north of the house or to the south of the house. That is certain. Let us weigh the one against the other. On the south of the house is, as you perceive, a large district of arable land, cut up into small fields, with stone walls between them. There, I admit that a bicycle is impossible. We can dismiss the idea. We turn to the country on the north. Here there lies a grove of trees, marked as the 'Ragged Shaw,' and on the farther side stretches a great rolling moor, Lower Gill Moor, extending for ten miles and sloping gradually upward. Here, at one side of this wilderness, is Holdernesse Hall, ten miles by road, but only six across the moor. It is a peculiarly desolate plain. A few moor farmers have small holdings, where they rear sheep and cattle. Except these, the plover and the curlew are the only inhabitants until you come to the Chesterfield high road. There is a church there, you see, a few cottages, and an inn. Beyond that the hills become precipitous. Surely it is here to the north that our quest must lie."

"But the bicycle?" I persisted.

"Well, well!" said Holmes, impatiently. "A good cyclist does not need a high road. The moor is intersected with paths, and the moon was at the full. Halloa! what is this?"

There was an agitated knock at the door, and an instant afterwards Dr. Huxtable was in the room. In his hand he held a blue cricket-cap with a white chevron on the peak.

"At last we have a clue!" he cried. "Thank heaven! at last we are on the dear boy's track! It is his cap."

"Where was it found?"

"In the van of the gipsies who camped on the moor. They left on Tuesday. To-day the police traced them down and examined their caravan. This was found."

"How do they account for it?"

"They shuffled and lied—said that they found it on the moor on Tuesday morning. They know where he is, the rascals! Thank goodness, they are all safe under lock and key. Either the fear of the law or the Duke's purse will certainly get out of them all that they know."

"So far, so good," said Holmes, when the doctor had at last left the room. "It at least bears out the theory that it is on the side of the Lower Gill Moor that we must hope for results. The police have really done nothing locally, save the arrest of these gipsies. Look here, Watson! There is a watercourse across the moor. You see it marked here in the map. In some parts it widens into a morass. This is particularly so in the region between Holdernesse Hall and the school. It is vain to look elsewhere for tracks in this dry weather, but at *that* point there is certainly a chance of some record being left. I will call you early to-morrow morning, and you and I will try if we can throw some little light upon the mystery."

The day was just breaking when I woke to find the long, thin form of Holmes by my bedside. He was fully dressed, and had apparently already been out.

"I have done the lawn and the bicycle shed," said he. "I have also had a ramble through the Ragged Shaw. Now, Watson, there is cocoa ready in the next room. I must beg you to hurry, for we have a great day before us."

His eyes shone, and his cheek was flushed with the exhilaration of the master workman who sees his work lie ready before him. A very different Holmes, this active, alert man, from the introspective and pallid dreamer of Baker Street. I felt, as I looked upon that supple figure, alive with nervous energy, that it was indeed a strenuous day that awaited us.

And yet it opened in the blackest disappointment. With high hopes we struck across the peaty, russet moor, intersected with a thousand sheep paths, until we came to the broad, light-green belt which marked the morass between us and Holdernesse. Certainly, if the lad had gone homeward, he must have passed this, and he could not pass it without leaving his traces. But no sign of him or the German could be seen. With a darkening face my friend strode along the margin, eagerly observant of every muddy stain upon the mossy surface. Sheep-marks there were in profusion, and at one place, some miles down, cows had left their tracks. Nothing more.

"Check number one," said Holmes, looking gloomily over the rolling expanse of the moor. "There is another morass down yonder, and a narrow neck between. Halloa! halloa! halloa! what have we here?"

We had come on a small black ribbon of pathway. In the middle of it, clearly marked on the sodden soil, was the track of a bicycle.

"Hurrah!" I cried. "We have it."

But Holmes was shaking his head, and his face was puzzled and expectant rather than joyous.

"A bicycle, certainly, but not *the* bicycle," said he. "I am familiar with forty-two different impressions left by tyres. This, as you perceive, is a Dunlop, with a patch upon the outer cover. Heidegger's tyres were Palmer's, leaving longitudinal stripes. Aveling, the mathematical master, was sure upon the point. Therefore, it is not Heidegger's track."

"The boy's, then?"

"Possibly, if we could prove a bicycle to have been in his possession. But this we have utterly failed to do. This track, as you perceive, was made by a rider who was going from the direction of the school."

"Or towards it?"

"No, no, my dear Watson. The more deeply sunk impression is, of course, the hind wheel, upon which the weight rests. You perceive several places where it has passed across and obliterated the more shallow mark of the front one. It was undoubtedly heading away from the school. It may or may not be connected with our inquiry, but we will follow it backwards before we go any farther."

We did so, and at the end of a few hundred yards lost the tracks as we emerged from the boggy portion of the moor. Following the path backwards, we picked out another spot, where a spring trickled across it. Here, once again, was the mark of the bicycle, though nearly obliterated by the hoofs of cows. After that there was no sign, but the path ran right on into Ragged Shaw, the wood which backed on to the school. From this wood the cycle must have emerged. Holmes sat down on a boulder and rested his chin in his hands. I had smoked two cigarettes before he moved.

"Well, well," said he, at last. "It is, of course, possible that a cunning man might change the tyres of his bicycle in order to leave unfamiliar tracks. A criminal who was capable of such a thought is a man whom I should be proud to do business with. We will leave this question undecided and hark back to our morass again, for we have left a good deal unexplored."

We continued our systematic survey of the edge of the sodden portion of the moor, and soon our perseverance was gloriously rewarded. Right across the lower part of the bog lay a miry path. Holmes gave a cry of delight as he approached it. An impression like a fine bundle of telegraph wires ran down the centre of it. It was the Palmer tyres.

"Here is Herr Heidegger, sure enough!" cried Holmes, exultantly. "My reasoning seems to have been pretty sound, Watson."

"I congratulate you."

"But we have a long way still to go. Kindly walk clear of the path. Now let us follow the trail. I fear that it will not lead very far."

We found, however, as we advanced that this portion of the moor is intersected with soft patches, and, though we frequently lost sight of the track, we always succeeded in picking it up once more.

"Do you observe," said Holmes, "that the rider is now undoubtedly forcing the pace? There can be no doubt of it. Look at this impression, where you get both tyres clear. The one is as deep as the other. That can only mean that the rider is throwing his weight on to the handle-bar, as a man does when he is sprinting. By Jove! he has had a fall."

There was a broad, irregular smudge covering some yards of the track. Then there were a few footmarks, and the tyres reappeared once more.

"A side-slip," I suggested.

Holmes held up a crumpled branch of flowering gorse. To my horror I perceived that the yellow blossoms were all dabbled with crimson. On the path, too, and among the heather were dark stains of clotted blood.

"Bad!" said Holmes. "Bad! Stand clear, Watson! Not an unnecessary footstep! What do I read here? He fell wounded—he stood up—he remounted —he proceeded. But there is no other track. Cattle on this side path. He was surely not gored by a bull? Impossible! But I see no traces of anyone else. We must push on, Watson. Surely, with stains as well as the track to guide us, he cannot escape us now."

Our search was not a very long one. The tracks of the tyre began to curve fantastically upon the wet and shining path. Suddenly, as I looked ahead, the gleam of metal caught my eye from amid the thick gorse-bushes. Out of them we dragged a bicycle, Palmer-tyred, one pedal bent, and the whole front of it horribly smeared and slobbered with blood. On the other side of the bushes, a shoe was projecting. We ran round, and there lay the unfortunate rider. He was a tall man, full-bearded, with spectacles, one glass of which had been knocked out. The cause of his death was a frightful blow upon the head, which had crushed in part of his skull. That he could have gone on after receiving such an injury said much for the vitality and courage of the man. He wore shoes, but no socks, and his open coat disclosed a night-shirt beneath it. It was undoubtedly the German master.

Holmes turned the body over reverently, and examined it with great attention. He then sat in deep thought for a time, and I could see by his ruffled brow that this grim discovery had not, in his opinion, advanced us much in our inquiry.

"It is a little difficult to know what to do, Watson," said he, at last. "My own inclinations are to push this inquiry on, for we have already lost so much time that we cannot afford to waste another hour. On the other hand, we are bound to inform the police of the discovery, and to see that this poor fellow's body is looked after."

"I could take a note back."

"But I need your company and assistance. Wait a bit! There is a fellow cutting peat up yonder. Bring him over here, and he will guide the police."

I brought the peasant across, and Holmes dispatched the frightened man with a note to Dr. Huxtable.

"Now, Watson," said he, "we have picked up two clues this morning. One is the bicycle with the Palmer tyre, and we see what that has led to. The other is the bicycle with the patched Dunlop. Before we start to investigate that, let us try to realize what we *do* know, so as to make the most of it, and to separate the essential from the accidental."

"First of all, I wish to impress upon you that the boy certainly left of his own free will. He got down from his window and he went off, either alone or with someone. That is sure."

I assented.

"Well, now, let us turn to this unfortunate German master. The boy was fully dressed when he fled. Therefore, he foresaw what he would do. But the German went without his socks. He certainly acted on very short notice."

"Undoubtedly."

"Why did he go? Because, from his bedroom window, he saw the flight of the boy; because he wished to overtake him and bring him back. He seized his bicycle, pursued the lad, and in pursuing him met his death."

"So it would seem."

"Now I come to the critical part of my argument. The natural action of a man in pursuing a little boy would be to run after him. He would know that he could overtake him. But the German does not do so. He turns to his bicycle. I am told that he was an excellent cyclist. He would not do this, if he did not see that the boy had some swift means of escape."

"The other bicycle."

"Let us continue our reconstruction. He meets his death five miles from the school—not by a bullet, mark you, which even a lad might conceivably discharge, but by a savage blow dealt by a vigorous arm. The lad, then, *had* a companion in his flight. And the flight was a swift one, since it took five miles before an expert cyclist could overtake them. Yet we survey the ground round the scene of the tragedy. What do we find? A few cattle-tracks, nothing more. I took a wide sweep round, and there is no path within fifty yards. Another cyclist could have had nothing to do with the actual murder, nor were there any human footmarks."

"Holmes," I cried, "this is impossible."

"Admirable!" he said. "A most illuminating remark. It *is* impossible as

I state it, and therefore I must in some respect have stated it wrong. Yet you saw for yourself. Can you suggest any fallacy?"

"He could not have fractured his skull in a fall?"

"In a morass, Watson?"

"I am at my wit's end."

"Tut, tut, we have solved some worse problems. At least we have plenty of material, if we can only use it. Come, then, and, having exhausted the Palmer, let us see what the Dunlop with the patched cover has to offer us."

We picked up the track and followed it onward for some distance, but soon the moor rose into a long, heather-tufted curve, and we left the watercourse behind us. No further help from tracks could be hoped for. At the spot where we saw the last of the Dunlop tyre it might equally have led to Holdernesse Hall, the stately towers of which rose some miles to our left, or to a low, gray village which lay in front of us and marked the position of the Chesterfield high road.

As we approached the forbidding and squalid inn, with the sign of a game-cock above the door, Holmes gave a sudden groan, and clutched me by the shoulder to save himself from falling. He had had one of those violent strains of the ankle which leave a man helpless. With difficulty he limped up to the door, where a squat, dark, elderly man was smoking a black clay pipe.

"How are you, Mr. Reuben Hayes?" said Holmes.

"Who are you, and how do you get my name so pat?" the countryman answered, with a suspicious flash of a pair of cunning eyes.

"Well, it's printed on the board above your head. It's easy to see a man who is master of his own house. I suppose you haven't such a thing as a carriage in your stables?"

"No, I have not."

"I can hardly put my foot to the ground."

"Don't put it to the ground."

"But I can't walk."

"Well, then, hop."

Mr. Reuben Hayes's manner was far from gracious, but Holmes took it with admirable good-humour.

"Look here, my man," said he. "This is really rather an awkward fix for me. I don't mind how I get on."

"Neither do I," said the morose landlord.

"The matter is very important. I would offer you a sovereign for the use of a bicycle."

The landlord pricked up his ears.

"Where do you want to go?"

"To Holdernesse Hall."

"Pals of the Dook, I suppose?" said the landlord, surveying our mud-stained garments with ironical eyes.

Holmes laughed good-naturedly.

"He'll be glad to see us, anyhow."

"Why?"

"Because we bring him news of his lost son."

The landlord gave a very visible start.

"What, you're on his track?"

"He has been heard of in Liverpool. They expect to get him every hour."

Again a swift change passed over the heavy, unshaven face. His manner was suddenly genial.

"I've less reason to wish the Dook well than most men," said he, "for I was his head coachman once, and cruel bad he treated me. It was him that sacked me without a character on the word of a lying corn-chandler. But I'm glad to hear that the young lord was heard of in Liverpool, and I'll help you to take the news to the Hall."

"Thank you," said Holmes. "We'll have some food first. Then you can bring round the bicycle."

"I haven't got a bicycle."

Holmes held up a sovereign.

"I tell you, man, that I haven't got one. I'll let you have two horses as far as the Hall."

"Well, well," said Holmes, "we'll talk about it when we've had something to eat."

When we were left alone in the stone-flagged kitchen, it was astonishing how rapidly that sprained ankle recovered. It was nearly nightfall, and we had eaten nothing since early morning, so that we spent some time over our meal. Holmes was lost in thought, and once or twice he walked over to the window and stared earnestly out. It opened on to a squalid courtyard. In the far corner was a smithy, where a grimy lad was at work. On the other side were the stables. Holmes had sat down again after one of these excursions, when he suddenly sprang out of his chair with a loud exclamation.

"By heaven, Watson, I believe that I've got it!" he cried. "Yes, yes, it must be so. Watson, do you remember seeing any cow-tracks to-day?"

"Yes, several."

"Where?"

"Well, everywhere. They were at the morass, and again on the path, and again near where poor Heidegger met his death."

"Exactly. Well, now, Watson, how many cows did you see on the moor?"

"I don't remember seeing any."

"Strange, Watson, that we should see tracks all along our line, but never a cow on the whole moor. Very strange, Watson, eh?"

"Yes, it is strange."

"Now, Watson, make an effort, throw your mind back. Can you see those tracks upon the path?"

"Yes, I can."

"Can you recall that the tracks were sometimes like that, Watson"—he arranged a number of bread-crumbs in this fashion— : : : : : —"and sometimes like this"— : . : . : . : . —"and occasionally like this"— . · . · . · . "Can you remember that?"

"No, I cannot."

"But I can. I could swear to it. However, we will go back at our leisure and verify it. What a blind beetle I have been, not to draw my conclusion."

"And what is your conclusion?"

"Only that it is a remarkable cow which walks, canters, and gallops. By George! Watson, it was no brain of a country publican that thought out such a blind as that. The coast seems to be clear, save for that lad in the smithy. Let us slip out and see what we can see."

There were two rough-haired, unkempt horses in the tumble-down stable. Holmes raised the hind leg of one of them and laughed aloud.

"Old shoes, but newly shod—old shoes, but new nails. This case deserves to be a classic. Let us go across to the smithy."

The lad continued his work without regarding us. I saw Holmes's eye darting to right and left among the litter of iron and wood which was scattered about the floor. Suddenly, however, we heard a step behind us, and there was the landlord, his heavy eyebrows drawn over his savage eyes, his swarthy features convulsed with passion. He held a short, metal-headed stick in his hand, and he advanced in so menacing a fashion that I was right glad to feel the revolver in my pocket.

"You infernal spies!" the man cried. "What are you doing there?"

"Why, Mr. Reuben Hayes," said Holmes, coolly, "one might think that you were afraid of our finding something out."

The man mastered himself with a violent effort, and his grim mouth loosened into a false laugh, which was more menacing than his frown.

"You're welcome to all you can find out in my smithy," said he. "But look here, mister, I don't care for folk poking about my place without my leave, so the sooner you pay your score and get out of this the better I shall be pleased."

"All right, Mr. Hayes, no harm meant," said Holmes. "We have been having a look at your horses, but I think I'll walk, after all. It's not far, I believe."

"Not more than two miles to the Hall gates. That's the road to the left." He watched us with sullen eyes until we had left his premises.

We did not go very far along the road, for Holmes stopped the instant that the curve hid us from the landlord's view.

"We were warm, as the children say, at that inn," said he. "I seem to grow colder every step that I take away from it. No, no, I can't possibly leave it."

"I am convinced," said I, "that this Reuben Hayes knows all about it. A more self-evident villain I never saw."

"Oh! he impressed you in that way, did he? There are the horses, there is the smithy. Yes, it is an interesting place, this Fighting Cock. I think we shall have another look at it in an unobtrusive way."

A long, sloping hillside, dotted with gray limestone boulders, stretched behind us. We had turned off the road, and were making our way up the hill, when, looking in the direction of Holdernesse Hall, I saw a cyclist coming swiftly along.

"Get down, Watson!" cried Holmes, with a heavy hand upon my shoulder. We had hardly sunk from view when the man flew past us on the road.

Amid a rolling cloud of dust, I caught a glimpse of a pale, agitated face—a face with horror in every lineament, the mouth open, the eyes staring wildly in front. It was like some strange caricature of the dapper James Wilder whom we had seen the night before.

"The Duke's secretary!" cried Holmes. "Come, Watson, let us see what he does."

We scrambled from rock to rock, until in a few moments we had made our way to a point from which we could see the front door of the inn. Wilder's bicycle was leaning against the wall beside it. No one was moving about the house, nor could we catch a glimpse of any faces at the windows. Slowly the twilight crept down as the sun sank behind the high towers of Holdernesse Hall. Then, in the gloom, we saw the two side-lamps of a trap light up in the stable-yard of the inn, and shortly afterwards heard the rattle of hoofs, as it wheeled out into the road and tore off at a furious pace in the direction of Chesterfield.

"What do you make of that, Watson?" Holmes whispered.

"It looks like a flight."

"A single man in a dog-cart, so far as I could see. Well, it certainly was not Mr. James Wilder, for there he is at the door."

A red square of light had sprung out of the darkness. In the middle of it was the black figure of the secretary, his head advanced, peering out into the night. It was evident that he was expecting someone. Then at last there were steps in the road, a second figure was visible for an instant against the light, the door shut, and all was black once more. Five minutes later a lamp was lit in a room upon the first floor.

"It seems to be a curious class of custom that is done by the Fighting Cock," said Holmes.

"The bar is on the other side."

"Quite so. These are what one may call the private guests. Now, what in the world is Mr. James Wilder doing in that den at this hour of night, and who is the companion who comes to meet him there? Come, Watson, we must really take a risk and try to investigate this a little more closely."

Together we stole down to the road and crept across to the door of the inn. The bicycle still leaned against the wall. Holmes struck a match and held it to the back wheel, and I heard him chuckle as the light fell upon a patched Dunlop tyre. Up above us was the lighted window.

"I must have a peep through that, Watson. If you bend your back and support yourself upon the wall, I think that I can manage."

An instant later, his feet were on my shoulders, but he was hardly up before he was down again.

"Come, my friend," said he, "our day's work has been quite long enough. I think that we have gathered all that we can. It's a long walk to the school, and the sooner we get started the better."

He hardly opened his lips during that weary trudge across the moor, nor would he enter the school when he reached it, but went on to Mackleton Station, whence he could send some telegrams. Late at night I heard him consoling Dr. Huxtable, prostrated by the tragedy of his master's death, and later still he entered my room as alert and vigorous as he had been when he started in the morning. "All goes well, my friend," said he. "I promise that before to-morrow evening we shall have reached the solution of the mystery."

At eleven o'clock next morning my friend and I were walking up the famous yew avenue of Holdernesse Hall. We were ushered through the magnificent Elizabethan doorway and into his Grace's study. There we found Mr. James Wilder, demure and courtly, but with some trace of that wild terror of the night before still lurking in his furtive eyes and in his twitching features.

"You have come to see his Grace? I am sorry, but the fact is that the Duke is far from well. He has been very much upset by the tragic news. We received a telegram from Dr. Huxtable yesterday afternoon, which told us of your discovery."

"I must see the Duke, Mr. Wilder."

"But he is in his room."

"Then I must go to his room."

"I believe he is in his bed."

"I will see him there."

Holmes's cold and inexorable manner showed the secretary that it was useless to argue with him.

"Very good, Mr. Holmes, I will tell him that you are here."

After an hour's delay, the great nobleman appeared. His face was more cadaverous than ever, his shoulders had rounded, and he seemed to me to be an altogether older man than he had been the morning before. He greeted us with a stately courtesy and seated himself at his desk, his red beard streaming down on the table.

"Well, Mr. Holmes?" said he.

But my friend's eyes were fixed upon the secretary, who stood by his master's chair.

"I think, your Grace, that I could speak more freely in Mr. Wilder's absence."

The man turned a shade paler and cast a malignant glance at Holmes.

"If your Grace wishes——"

"Yes, yes, you had better go. Now, Mr. Holmes, what have you to say?"

My friend waited until the door had closed behind the retreating secretary.

"The fact is, your Grace," said he, "that my colleague, Dr. Watson, and myself had an assurance from Dr. Huxtable that a reward had been offered in this case. I should like to have this confirmed from your own lips."

"Certainly, Mr. Holmes."

"It amounted, if I am correctly informed, to five thousand pounds to any-one who will tell you where your son is?"

"Exactly."

"And another thousand to the man who will name the person or persons who keep him in custody?"

"Exactly."

"Under the latter heading is included, no doubt, not only those who may have taken him away, but also those who conspire to keep him in his present position?"

"Yes, yes," cried the Duke, impatiently. "If you do your work well, Mr. Sherlock Holmes, you will have no reason to complain of niggardly treatment."

My friend rubbed his thin hands together with an appearance of avidity which was a surprise to me, who knew his frugal tastes.

"I fancy that I see your Grace's check-book upon the table," said he. "I should be glad if you would make me out a check for six thousand pounds. It would be as well, perhaps, for you to cross it. The Capital and Counties Bank, Oxford Street branch, are my agents."

His Grace sat very stern and upright in his chair and looked stonily at my friend.

"Is this a joke, Mr. Holmes? It is hardly a subject for pleasantry."

"Not at all, your Grace. I was never more earnest in my life."

"What do you mean, then?"

"I mean that I have earned the reward. I know where your son is, and I know some, at least, of those who are holding him."

The Duke's beard had turned more aggressively red than ever against his ghastly white face.

"Where is he?" he gasped.

"He is, or was last night, at the Fighting Cock Inn, about two miles from your park gate."

The Duke fell back in his chair.

"And whom do you accuse?"

Sherlock Holmes's answer was an astounding one. He stepped swiftly forward and touched the Duke upon the shoulder.

"I accuse *you*," said he. "And now, your Grace, I'll trouble you for that check."

Never shall I forget the Duke's appearance as he sprang up and clawed with his hands, like one who is sinking into an abyss. Then, with an extraordinary effort of aristocratic self-command, he sat down and sank his face in his hands. It was some minutes before he spoke.

"How much do you know?" he asked at last, without raising his head.

"I saw you together last night."

"Does anyone else beside your friend know?"

"I have spoken to no one."

The Duke took a pen in his quivering fingers and opened his check-book.

"I shall be as good as my word, Mr. Holmes. I am about to write your check, however unwelcome the information which you have gained may be to me. When the offer was first made, I little thought the turn which events might take. But you and your friend are men of discretion, Mr. Holmes?"

"I hardly understand your Grace."

"I must put it plainly, Mr. Holmes. If only you two know of this incident, there is no reason why it should go any farther. I think twelve thousand pounds is the sum that I owe you, is it not?"

But Holmes smiled and shook his head.

"I fear, your Grace, that matters can hardly be arranged so easily. There is the death of this schoolmaster to be accounted for."

"But James knew nothing of that. You cannot hold him responsible for that. It was the work of this brutal ruffian whom he had the misfortune to employ."

"I must take the view, your Grace, that when a man embarks upon a crime, he is morally guilty of any other crime which may spring from it."

"Morally, Mr. Holmes. No doubt you are right. But surely not in the eyes of the law. A man cannot be condemned for a murder at which he was not present, and which he loathes and abhors as much as you do. The instant that he heard of it he made a complete confession to me, so filled was he with horror and remorse. He lost not an hour in breaking entirely with the murderer. Oh, Mr. Holmes, you must save him—you must save him! I tell you that you must save him!" The Duke had dropped the last attempt at self-command, and was pacing the room with a convulsed face and with his clenched hands raving in the air. At last he mastered himself and sat down once more at his desk. "I appreciate your conduct in coming here before you spoke to anyone else," said he. "At least, we may take counsel how far we can minimize this hideous scandal."

"Exactly," said Holmes. "I think, your Grace, that this can only be done by absolute frankness between us. I am disposed to help your Grace to the best of my ability, but, in order to do so, I must understand to the last detail how the matter stands. I realize that your words applied to Mr. James Wilder, and that he is not the murderer."

"No, the murderer has escaped."

Sherlock Holmes smiled demurely.

"Your Grace can hardly have heard of any small reputation which I possess, or you would not imagine that it is so easy to escape me. Mr. Reuben Hayes was arrested at Chesterfield, on my information, at eleven o'clock last night. I had a telegram from the head of the local police before I left the school this morning."

The Duke leaned back in his chair and stared with amazement at my friend.

"You seem to have powers that are hardly human," said he. "So Reuben Hayes is taken? I am right glad to hear it, if it will not react upon the fate of James."

"Your secretary?"

"No, sir, my son."

It was Holmes's turn to look astonished.

"I confess that this is entirely new to me, your Grace. I must beg you to be more explicit."

"I will conceal nothing from you. I agree with you that complete frankness, however painful it may be to me, is the best policy in this desperate situation to which James's folly and jealousy have reduced us. When I was a very young man, Mr. Holmes, I loved with such a love as comes only once in a lifetime. I offered the lady marriage, but she refused it on the grounds that such a match might mar my career. Had she lived, I would certainly never have married anyone else. She died, and left this one child, whom for her sake I have cherished and cared for. I could not acknowledge the paternity to the world, but I gave him the best of educations, and since he came to manhood I have kept him near my person. He surprised my secret, and has presumed ever since upon the claim which he has upon me, and upon his power of provoking a scandal which would be abhorrent to me. His presence had something to do with the unhappy issue of my marriage. Above all, he hated my young legitimate heir from the first with a persistent hatred. You may well ask me why, under these circumstances, I still kept James under my roof. I answer that it was because I could see his mother's face in his, and that for her dear sake there was no end to my long-suffering. All her pretty ways too—there was not one of them which he could not suggest and bring back to my memory. I *could* not send him away. But I feared so much lest he should do Arthur—that is, Lord Saltire—a mischief, that I dispatched him for safety to Dr. Huxtable's school.

"James came into contact with this fellow Hayes, because the man was a tenant of mine, and James acted as agent. The fellow was a rascal from the beginning, but, in some extraordinary way, James became intimate with him. He had always a taste for low company. When James determined to kidnap Lord Saltire, it was of this man's service that he availed himself. You remember that I wrote to Arthur upon that last day. Well, James opened the letter and inserted a note asking Arthur to meet him in a little wood called the Ragged Shaw, which is near to the school. He used the Duchess's name, and in that way got the boy to come. That evening James bicycled over—I am telling you what he has himself confessed to me—and he told Arthur, whom he met in the wood, that his mother longed to see him, that she was awaiting him on the moor, and that if he would come back into the wood at midnight he would find a man with a horse, who would take him to her. Poor Arthur fell into the trap. He came to the appointment, and found this fellow Hayes with a led pony. Arthur mounted, and they set off together. It appears—though this James only heard yesterday —that they were pursued, that Hayes struck the pursuer with his stick, and that the man died of his injuries. Hayes brought Arthur to his public-house, the Fighting Cock, where he was confined in an upper room, under the care of Mrs. Hayes, who is a kindly woman, but entirely under the control of her brutal husband.

"Well, Mr. Holmes, that was the state of affairs when I first saw you two days ago. I had no more idea of the truth than you. You will ask me what was James's motive in doing such a deed. I answer that there was a great deal which was unreasoning and fanatical in the hatred which he bore my heir. In his view he should himself have been heir of all my estates, and he deeply resented those social laws which made it impossible. At the same time, he had a definite motive also. He was eager that I should break the entail, and he was of opinion that it lay in my power to do so. He intended to make a bargain with me—to restore Arthur if I would break the entail, and so make it possible for the estate to be left to him by will. He knew well that I should never willingly invoke the aid of the police against him. I say that he would have proposed such a bargain to me; but he did not actually do so, for events moved too quickly for him, and he had not time to put his plans into practice.

"What brought all his wicked scheme to wreck was your discovery of this man Heidegger's dead body. James was seized with horror at the news. It came to us yesterday, as we sat together in this study. Dr. Huxtable had sent a telegram. James was so overwhelmed with grief and agitation that my suspicions, which had never been entirely absent, rose instantly to a certainty, and I taxed him with the deed. He made a complete voluntary confession. Then he implored me to keep his secret for three days longer, so as to give his wretched accomplice a chance of saving his guilty life. I yielded—as I have always yielded—to his prayers, and instantly James hurried off to the Fighting Cock to warn Hayes and give him the means of flight. I could not go there by daylight without provoking comment, but as soon as night fell I hurried off to see my dear Arthur. I found him safe and well, but horrified beyond expression by the dreadful deed he had witnessed. In deference to my promise, and much against my will, I consented to leave him there for three days, under the charge of Mrs. Hayes, since it was evident that it was impossible to inform the police where he was without telling them also who was the murderer, and I could not see how that murderer could be punished without ruin to my unfortunate James. You asked for frankness, Mr. Holmes, and I have taken you at your word, for I have now told you everything without an attempt at circumlocution or concealment. Do you in turn be as frank with me."

"I will," said Holmes. "In the first place, your Grace, I am bound to tell you that you have placed yourself in a most serious position in the eyes of the law. You have condoned a felony, and you have aided the escape of a murderer, for I cannot doubt that any money which was taken by James Wilder to aid his accomplice in his flight came from your Grace's purse."

The Duke bowed his assent.

"This is, indeed, a most serious matter. Even more culpable in my opinion, your Grace, is your attitude towards your younger son. You leave him in this den for three days."

"Under solemn promises——"

"What are promises to such people as these? You have no guarantee that he will not be spirited away again. To humour your guilty elder son, you have exposed your innocent younger son to imminent and unnecessary danger. It was a most unjustifiable action."

The proud lord of Holdernesse was not accustomed to be so rated in his own ducal hall. The blood flushed into his high forehead, but his conscience held him dumb.

"I will help you, but on one condition only. It is that you ring for the footman and let me give such orders as I like."

Without a word, the Duke pressed the electric bell. A servant entered.

"You will be glad to hear," said Holmes, "that your young master is found.

It is the Duke's desire that the carriage shall go at once to the Fighting Cock Inn to bring Lord Saltire home.

"Now," said Holmes, when the rejoicing lackey had disappeared, "having secured the future, we can afford to be more lenient with the past. I am not in an official position, and there is no reason, so long as the ends of justice are served, why I should disclose all that I know. As to Hayes, I say nothing. The gallows awaits him, and I would do nothing to save him from it. What he will divulge I cannot tell, but I have no doubt that your Grace could make him understand that it is to his interest to be silent. From the police point of view he will have kidnapped the boy for the purpose of ransom. If they do not themselves find it out, I see no reason why I should prompt them to take a broader point of view. I would warn your Grace, however, that the continued presence of Mr. James Wilder in your household can only lead to misfortune."

"I understand that, Mr. Holmes, and it is already settled that he shall leave me forever, and go to seek his fortune in Australia."

"In that case, your Grace, since you have yourself stated that any unhappiness in your married life was caused by his presence, I would suggest that you make such amends as you can to the Duchess, and that you try to resume those relations which have been so unhappily interrupted."

"That also I have arranged, Mr. Holmes. I wrote to the Duchess this morning."

"In that case," said Holmes, rising, "I think that my friend and I can congratulate ourselves upon several most happy results from our little visit to the North. There is one other small point upon which I desire some light. This fellow Hayes had shod his horses with shoes which counterfeited the tracks of cows. Was it from Mr. Wilder that he learned so extraordinary a device?"

The Duke stood in thought for a moment, with a look of intense surprise on his face. Then he opened a door and showed us into a large room furnished as a museum. He led the way to a glass case in a corner, and pointed to the inscription.

"These shoes," it ran, "were dug up in the moat of Holdernesse Hall. They are for the use of horses, but they are shaped below with a cloven foot of iron, so as to throw pursuers off the track. They are supposed to have belonged to some of the marauding Barons of Holdernesse in the Middle Ages."

Holmes opened the case, and moistening his finger he passed it along the shoe. A thin film of recent mud was left upon his skin.

"Thank you," said he, as he replaced the glass. "It is the second most interesting object that I have seen in the North."

"And the first?"

Holmes folded up his check and placed it carefully in his notebook. "I am a poor man," said he, as he patted it affectionately, and thrust it into the depths of his inner pocket.

# A Christmas Memory

TRUMAN CAPOTE

IMAGINE a morning in late November. A coming of winter morning more than twenty years ago. Consider the kitchen of a spreading old house in a country town. A great black stove is its main feature; but there is also a big round table and a fireplace with two rocking chairs placed in front of it. Just today the fireplace commenced its seasonal roar.

A woman with shorn white hair is standing at the kitchen window. She is wearing tennis shoes and a shapeless gray sweater over a summery calico dress. She is small and sprightly, like a bantam hen; but, due to a long youthful illness, her shoulders are pitifully hunched. Her face is remarkable —not unlike Lincoln's, craggy like that, and tinted by sun and wind; but it is delicate too, finely boned, and her eyes are sherry-colored and timid. "Oh my," she exclaims, her breath smoking the windowpane, "it's fruitcake weather!"

The person to whom she is speaking is myself. I am seven; she is sixty-something. We are cousins, very distant ones, and we have lived together— well, as long as I can remember. Other people inhabit the house, relatives; and though they have power over us, and frequently make us cry, we are not, on the whole, too much aware of them. We are each other's best friend. She calls me Buddy, in memory of a boy who was formerly her best friend. The other Buddy died in the 1880's, when she was still a child. She is still a child.

"I knew it before I got out of bed," she says, turning away from the window with a purposeful excitement in her eyes. "The courthouse bell sounded so cold and clear. And there were no birds singing; they've gone to warmer country, yes indeed. Oh, Buddy, stop stuffing biscuit and fetch our buggy. Help me find my hat. We've thirty cakes to bake."

It's always the same: a morning arrives in November, and my friend, as though officially inaugurating the Christmas time of year that exhilarates her imagination and fuels the blaze of her heart, announces: "It's fruitcake weather! Fetch our buggy. Help me find my hat."

The hat is found, a straw cartwheel corsaged with velvet roses out-of-doors has faded: it once belonged to a more fashionable relative. Together, we guide our buggy, a dilapidated baby carriage, out to the garden and into a grove of pecan trees. The buggy is mine; that is, it was bought for me when I was born. It is made of wicker, rather unraveled, and the wheels wobble like a drunkard's legs. But it is a faithful object; springtimes, we take it to the woods and fill it with flowers, herbs, wild fern for our porch pots; in the summer, we pile it with picnic paraphernalia and sugar-cane fishing poles and roll it down to the edge of a creek; it has its winter uses, too: as a truck for hauling firewood from the yard to the kitchen, as a warm bed for Queenie, our tough little orange and white rat terrier who has survived distemper and two rattlesnake bites. Queenie is trotting beside it now.

Three hours later we are back in the kitchen hulling a heaping buggyload of windfall pecans. Our backs hurt from gathering them: how hard they were to find (the main crop having been shaken off the trees and sold by the orchard's owners, who are not us) among the concealing leaves, the frosted, deceiving grass. Caaracklel A cheery crunch, scraps of miniature thunder sound as the shells collapse and the golden mound of sweet oily ivory meat mounts in the milk-glass bowl. Queenie begs to taste, and now and again my friend sneaks her a mite, though insisting we deprive ourselves. "We mustn't, Buddy. If we start, we won't stop. And there's scarcely enough as there is. For thirty cakes." The kitchen is growing dark. Dusk turns the window into a mirror: our reflections mingle with the rising moon as we work by the fireside in the firelight. At last, when the moon is quite high, we toss the final hull into the fire and, with joined sighs, watch it catch flame. The buggy is empty, the bowl is brimful.

We eat our supper (cold biscuits, bacon, blackberry jam) and discuss tomorrow. Tomorrow the kind of work I like best begins: buying. Cherries and citron, ginger and vanilla and canned Hawaiian pineapple, rinds and raisins and walnuts and whiskey and oh, so much flour, butter, so many eggs, spices, flavorings: why, we'll need a pony to pull the buggy home.

But before these purchases can be made, there is the question of money. Neither of us has any. Except for skinflint sums persons in the house occasionally provide (a dime is considered very big money); or what we earn ourselves from various activities: holding rummage sales, selling buckets of hand-picked blackberries, jars of homemade jam and apple jelly and peach preserves, rounding up flowers for funerals and weddings. Once we won seventy-ninth prize, five dollars, in a national football contest. Not that we know a fool thing about football. It's just that we enter any contest we hear about: at the moment our hopes are centered on the fifty-thousand-dollar Grand Prize being offered to name a new brand of coffee (we suggested "A.M."; and, after some hesitation, for my friend thought it perhaps sacrilegious, the slogan "A.M.! Amen!"). To tell the truth, our only *really* profitable enterprise was the Fun and Freak Museum we conducted in a backyard woodshed two summers ago. The Fun was a stereopticon with slide views of Washington and New York lent us by a relative who had been to those places (she was furious when she discovered why we'd borrowed it); the Freak was a three-legged biddy chicken hatched by one of our own hens. Everybody hereabouts wanted to see that biddy: we charged grownups a nickel, kids two cents. And took in a good twenty dollars before the museum shut down due to the decease of the main attraction.

But one way and another we do each year accumulate Christmas savings, a Fruitcake Fund. These moneys we keep hidden in an ancient bead purse under a loose board under the floor under a chamber pot under my friend's bed. The purse is seldom removed from this safe location except to make a deposit, or, as happens every Saturday, a withdrawal; for on Saturdays I am allowed ten cents to go to the picture show. My friend has never been to a picture show, nor does she intend to: "I'd rather hear you tell the story, Buddy. That way I can imagine it more. Besides, a person my age shouldn't squander their eyes. When the Lord comes, let me see him clear." In addition to never having seen a movie, she has never: eaten in a restaurant, traveled more than five miles from home, received or sent a telegram, read anything except funny papers and the Bible, worn cosmetics, cursed, wished someone harm, told a lie on purpose, let a hungry dog go hungry. Here are a few things she has done, does do: killed with a hoe the biggest rattlesnake ever seen in this county (sixteen rattles), dip snuff (secretly), tame hummingbirds (just try it) till they balance on her finger, tell ghost stories (we both believe in ghosts) so tingling they chill you in July, talk to herself, take walks in the rain, grow the prettiest japonicas in town, know the recipe for every sort of old-time Indian cure, including a magical wart-remover.

Now, with supper finished, we retire to the room in a faraway part of the house where my friend sleeps in a scrap-quilt-covered iron bed painted rose pink, her favorite color. Silently, wallowing in the pleasures of conspiracy, we take the bead purse from its secret place and spill its contents on the scrap quilt. Dollar bills, tightly rolled and green as May buds. Somber fifty-cent pieces, heavy enough to weight a dead man's eyes. Lovely dimes, the liveliest coin, the one that really jingles. Nickels and quarters, worn smooth as creek pebbles. But mostly a hateful heap of bitter-odored pennies. Last summer others in the house contracted to pay us a penny for every twenty-five flies we killed. Oh, the carnage of August: the flies that flew to heaven! Yet it was not work in which we took pride. And, as we sit counting pennies, it is as though we were back tabulating dead flies. Neither of us has a head for figures; we count slowly, lose track, start again. According to her calculations, we have $12.73. According to mine, exactly $13. "I do hope you're wrong, Buddy. We can't mess around with thirteen. The cakes will fall. Or put somebody in the cemetery. Why, I wouldn't dream of getting out of bed on the thirteenth." This is true: she always spends thirteenths in bed. So, to be on the safe side, we subtract a penny and toss it out the window.

Of the ingredients that go into our fruitcakes, whiskey is the most expensive, as well as the hardest to obtain: State laws forbid its sale. But everybody knows you can buy a bottle from Mr. Haha Jones. And the next day, having completed our more prosaic shopping, we set out for Mr. Haha's business address, a "sinful" (to quote public opinion) fish-fry and dancing café down by the river. We've been there before, and on the same errand; but in previous years our dealings have been with Haha's wife, an iodine-dark Indian woman with brassy peroxided hair and a dead-tired disposition. Actually, we've never laid eyes on her husband, though we've heard that he's an Indian too. A giant with razor scars across his cheeks. They call him Haha because he's so gloomy, a man who never laughs. As we approach his café (a large log cabin festooned inside and out with chains of garish-gay naked light bulbs and standing by the river's muddy edge under the shade of river trees where moss drifts through the branches like gray mist) our steps slow down. Even Queenie stops prancing and sticks close by. People have been murdered in Haha's café. Cut to pieces. Hit on the head. There's a case coming up in court next month. Naturally these goings-on happen at night when the colored lights cast crazy patterns and the victrola wails. In the daytime Haha's is shabby and deserted. I knock at the door, Queenie barks, my friend calls: "Mrs. Haha, ma'am? Anyone to home?"

Footsteps. The door opens. Our hearts overturn. It's Mr. Haha Jones himself! And he *is* a giant; he *does* have scars; he *doesn't* smile. No, he glowers at us through Satan-tilted eyes and demands to know: "What you want with Haha?"

For a moment we are too paralyzed to tell. Presently my friend half-finds her voice, a whispery voice at best: "If you please, Mr. Haha, we'd like a quart of your finest whiskey."

His eyes tilt more. Would you believe it? Haha is smiling! Laughing, too. "Which one of you is a drinkin' man?"

"It's for making fruitcakes, Mr. Haha. Cooking."

This sobers him. He frowns. "That's no way to waste good whiskey." Nevertheless, he retreats into the shadowed café and seconds later appears carrying a bottle of daisy yellow unlabeled liquor. He demonstrates its sparkle in the sunlight and says: "Two dollars."

We pay him with nickels and dimes and pennies. Suddenly, jangling the coins in his hand like a fistful of dice, his face softens. "Tell you what," he proposes, pouring the money back into our bead purse, "just send me one of them fruitcakes instead."

"Well," my friend remarks on our way home, "there's a lovely man. We'll put an extra cup of raisins in *his* cake."

The black stove, stoked with coal and firewood, glows like a lighted pumpkin. Eggbeaters whirl, spoons spin round in bowls of butter and sugar, vanilla sweetens the air, ginger spices it; melting, nose-tingling odors saturate the kitchen, suffuse the house, drift out to the world on puffs of chimney smoke. In four days our work is done. Thirty-one cakes, dampened with whiskey, bask on window sills and shelves.

Who are they for?

Friends. Not necessarily neighbor friends: indeed, the larger share are intended for persons we've met maybe once, perhaps not at all. People who've struck our fancy. Like President Roosevelt. Like the Reverend and Mrs. J. C. Lucey, Baptist missionaries to Borneo who lectured here last winter. Or the little knife grinder who comes through town twice a year. Or Abner Packer, the driver of the six o'clock bus from Mobile, who exchanges waves with us every day as he passes in a dust-cloud whoosh. Or the young Wistons, a California couple whose car one afternoon broke down outside the house and who spent a pleasant hour chatting with us on the porch (young Mr.

Wiston snapped our picture, the only one we've ever had taken). Is it because my friend is shy with everyone *except* strangers that these strangers, and merest acquaintances, seem to us our truest friends? I think yes. Also, the scrapbooks we keep of thank-you's on White House stationery, time-to-time communications from California and Borneo, the knife grinder's penny post cards, make us feel connected to eventful worlds beyond the kitchen with its view of a sky that stops.

Now a nude December fig branch grates against the window. The kitchen is empty, the cakes are gone; yesterday we carted the last of them to the post office, where the cost of stamps turned our purse inside out. We're broke. That rather depresses me, but my friend insists on celebrating—with two inches of whiskey left in Haha's bottle. Queenie has a spoonful in a bowl of coffee (she likes her coffee chicory-flavored and strong). The rest we divide between a pair of jelly glasses. We're both quite awed at the prospect of drinking straight whiskey; the taste of it brings screwed-up expressions and sour shudders. But by and by we begin to sing, the two of us singing different songs simultaneously. I don't know the words to mine, just: *Come on along, come on along, to the dark-town strutters' ball.* But I can dance: that's what I mean to be, a tap dancer in the movies. My dancing shadow rollicks on the walls; our voices rock the chinaware; we giggle: as if unseen hands were tickling us. Queenie rolls on her back, her paws plow the air, something like a grin stretches her black lips. Inside myself, I feel warm and sparky as those crumbling logs, carefree as the wind in the chimney. My friend waltzes round the stove, the hem of her poor calico skirt pinched between her fingers as though it were a party dress: *Show me the way to go home,* she sings, her tennis shoes squeaking on the floor. *Show me the way to go home.*

Enter: two relatives. Very angry. Potent with eyes that scold, tongues that scald. Listen to what they have to say, the words tumbling together into a wrathful tune: "A child of seven! whiskey on his breath! are you out of your mind? feeding a child of seven! must be loony! road to ruination! remember Cousin Kate? Uncle Charlie? Uncle Charlie's brother-in-law? shame! scandal! humiliation! kneel, pray, beg the Lord!"

Queenie sneaks under the stove. My friend gazes at her shoes, her chin quivers, she lifts her skirt and blows her nose and runs to her room. Long after the town has gone to sleep and the house is silent except for the chimings of clocks and the sputter of fading fires, she is weeping into a pillow already as wet as a widow's handkerchief.

"Don't cry," I say, sitting at the bottom of her bed and shivering despite my flannel nightgown that smells of last winter's cough syrup, "don't cry," I beg, teasing her toes, tickling her feet, "you're too old for that."

"It's because," she hiccups, "I *am* too old. Old and funny."

"Not funny. Fun. More fun than anybody. Listen. If you don't stop crying you'll be so tired tomorrow we can't go cut a tree."

She straightens up. Queenie jumps on the bed (where Queenie is not allowed) to lick her cheeks. "I know where we'll find real pretty trees, Buddy. And holly, too. With berries big as your eyes. It's way off in the woods. Farther than we've ever been. Papa used to bring us Christmas trees from there: carry them on his shoulder. That's fifty years ago. Well, now: I can't wait for morning."

Morning. Frozen rime lusters the grass; the sun, round as an orange and orange as hot-weather moons, balances on the horizon, burnishes the silvered winter woods. A wild turkey calls. A renegade hog grunts in the undergrowth. Soon, by the edge of knee-deep, rapid-running water, we have to abandon the buggy. Queenie wades the stream first, paddles across barking complaints at the swiftness of the current, the pneumonia-making coldness of it. We follow, holding our shoes and equipment (a hatchet, a burlap sack) above our heads. A mile more: of chastising thorns, burs and briers that catch at our clothes; of rusty pine needles brilliant with gaudy fungus and molted feathers. Here, there, a flash, a flutter, an ecstasy of shrillings remind us that not all the birds have flown south. Always, the path unwinds through lemony sun pools and pitch vine tunnels. Another creek to cross: a disturbed armada of speckled trout froths the water round us, and frogs the size of plates practice belly flops; beaver workmen are building a dam. On the farther shore, Queenie shakes herself and trembles. My friend shivers, too: not with cold but enthusiasm. One of her hat's ragged roses sheds a petal as she lifts her head and inhales the pine-heavy air. "We're almost there; can you smell it, Buddy?" she says, as though we were approaching an ocean.

And, indeed, it is a kind of ocean. Scented acres of holiday trees, prickly-leafed holly. Red berries shiny as Chinese bells: black crows swoop upon them screaming. Having stuffed our burlap sacks with enough greenery and crimson to garland a dozen windows, we set about choosing a tree. "It should be," muses my friend, "twice as tall as a boy. So a boy can't steal the star." The one we pick is twice as tall as me. A brave handsome brute that survives thirty hatchet strokes before it keels with a creaking rending cry. Lugging it like a kill, we commence the long trek out. Every few yards we abondon the struggle, sit down and pant. But we have the strength of triumphant huntsmen; that and the tree's virile, icy perfume revive us, goad us on. Many compliments accompany our sunset return along the red clay road to town; but my friend is sly and noncommittal when passers-by praise the treasure perched in our buggy: what a fine tree and where did it come from? "Yonderways," she murmurs vaguely. Once a car stops and the rich mill owner's lazy wife leans out and whines: "Giveya two-bits cash for that ol tree." Ordinarily my friend is afraid of saying no; but on this occasion she promptly shakes her head: "We wouldn't take a dollar." The mill owner's wife persists. "A dollar, my foot! Fifty cents. That's my last offer. Goodness, woman, you can get another one." In answer, my friend gently reflects: "I doubt it. There's never two of anything."

Home: Queenie slumps by the fire and sleeps till tomorrow, snoring loud as a human.

A trunk in the attic contains: a shoebox of ermine tails (off the opera cape of a curious lady who once rented a room in the house), coils of frazzled tinsel gone gold with age, one silver star, a brief rope of dilapidated, undoubtedly dangerous candy-like light bulbs. Excellent decorations, as far as they go, which isn't far enough: my friend wants our tree to blaze "like a Baptist window," droop with weighty snows of ornament. But we can't afford the made-in-Japan splendors at the five-and-dime. So we do what we've always done: sit for days at the kitchen table with scissors and crayons and stacks of colored paper. I make sketches and my friend cuts them out: lots of cats, fish too (because they're easy to draw), some apples, some watermelons, a few winged angels devised from saved-up sheets of Hershey-bar tin foil. We use safety pins to attach these creations to the tree; as a final touch, we sprinkle the branches with shredded cotton (picked in August for this purpose). My friend, surveying the effect, clasps her hands together. "Now honest, Buddy. Doesn't it look good enough to eat?" Queenie tries to eat an angel.

After weaving and ribboning holly wreaths for all the front windows, our next project is the fashioning of family gifts. Tie-dye scarves for the ladies, for the men a home-brewed lemon and licorice and aspirin syrup to be taken "at the first Symptoms of a Cold and after Hunting." But when it comes time for making each other's gift, my friend and I separate to work secretly. I would like to buy her a pearl-handled knife, a radio, a whole pound of chocolate-covered cherries (we tasted some once, and she always swears: "I could live on them, Buddy, Lord yes I could—and that's not taking His name in vain"). Instead, I am building her a kite. She would like to give me a bicycle (she's said so on several million occasions: "If only I could, Buddy. It's bad enough in life to do without something *you* want; but confound it, what gets my goat is not being able to give somebody something you want *them* to have. Only one of these days I will, Buddy. Locate you a bike. Don't ask how. Steal it, maybe"). Instead, I'm fairly certain that she is building me a kite—the same as last year, and the year before: the year before that we exchanged slingshots. All of which is fine by me. For we are champion kite-fliers who study the wind like sailors; my friend, more accomplished than I, can get a kite aloft when there isn't enough breeze to carry clouds.

Christmas Eve afternoon we scrape together a nickel and go to the butcher's to buy Queenie's traditional gift, a good gnawable beef bone. The bone, wrapped in funny paper, is placed high in the tree near the silver star. Queenie knows it's there. She squats at the foot of the tree staring up in a trance of greed: when bedtime arrives she refuses to budge. Her excitement is equaled by my own. I kick the covers and turn my pillow as though it were a scorching summer's night. Somewhere a rooster crows: falsely, for the sun is still on the other side of the world.

"Buddy, are you awake?" It is my friend, calling from her room, which is next to mine; and an instant later she is sitting on my bed holding a candle. "Well, I can't sleep a hoot," she declares. "My mind's jumping like a jack rabbit. Buddy, do you think Mrs. Roosevelt will serve our cake at dinner?" We huddle in the bed, and she squeezes my hand I-love-you. "Seems like your hand used to be so much smaller. I guess I hate to see you grow up. When you're grown up, will we still be friends?" I say always. "But I feel so bad, Buddy. I wanted so bad to give you a bike. I tried to sell my cameo Papa gave me. Buddy—" she hesitates, as though embarrassed—"I made you another kite." Then I confess that I made her one, too; and we laugh. The candle burns too short to hold. Out it goes, exposing the starlight, the stars spinning at the window like a visible caroling that slowly, slowly daybreak silences. Possibly we doze; but the beginnings of dawn splash us like cold water: we're up, wide-eyed and wandering while we wait for others to waken. Quite deliberately my friend drops a kettle on the kitchen floor. I tap-dance in front of closed doors. One by one the household emerges, looking as though they'd like to kill us both; but it's Christmas, so they can't. First, a gorgeous breakfast: just everything you can imagine— from flapjacks and fried squirrel to hominy grits and honey-in-the-comb. Which puts everyone in a good humor except my friend and I. Frankly, we're so impatient to get at the presents we can't eat a mouthful.

Well, I'm disappointed. Who wouldn't be? With socks, a Sunday school shirt, some handkerchiefs, a hand-me-down sweater and a year's subscription to a religious magazine for children. *The Little Shepherd*. It makes me boil. It really does.

My friend has a better haul. A sack of Satsumas, that's her best present. She is proudest, however, of a white wool shawl knitted by her married sister. But she *says* her favorite gift is the kite I built her. And it *is* very beautiful; though not as beautiful as the one she made me, which is blue and scattered with gold and green Good Conduct stars; moreover, my name is painted on it, "Buddy."

"Buddy, the wind is blowing."

The wind is blowing, and nothing will do till we've run to a pasture below the house where Queenie has scooted to bury her bone (and where, a winter hence, Queenie will be buried, too.) There, plunging through the healthy waist-high grass, we unreel our kites, feel them twitching at the string like sky fish as they swim into the wind. Satisfied, sun-warmed, we sprawl in the grass and peel Satsumas and watch our kites cavort. Soon I forget the socks and hand-me-down sweater. I'm as happy as if we'd already won the fifty-thousand-dollar Grand Prize in that coffee-naming contest.

"My, how foolish I am!" my friend cries, suddenly alert, like a woman remembering too late she has biscuits in the oven. "You know what I've always thought?" she asks in a tone of discovery, and not smiling at me but a point beyond. "I've always thought a body would have to be sick and dying before they saw the Lord. And I imagined that when He came it would be like looking at the Baptist window: pretty as colored glass with the sun pouring through, such a shine you don't know it's getting dark. And it's been a comfort: to think of that shine taking away all the spooky feeling. But I'll wager it never happens. I'll wager at the very end a body realizes the Lord has already shown Himself. That things as they are"—her hand circles in a gesture that gathers clouds and kites and grass and Queenie pawing earth over her bone—"just what they've always seen, was seeing Him. As for me, I could leave the world with today in my eyes."

This is our last Christmas together.

Life separates us. Those who Know Best decide that I belong in a military school. And so follows a miserable succession of bugle-blowing prisons, grim reveille-ridden summer camps. I have a new home too. But it doesn't count. Home is where my friend is, and there I never go.

And there she remains, puttering around the kitchen. Alone with Queenie. Then alone. ("Buddy dear," she writes in her wild hard-to-read script, "yesterday Jim Macy's horse kicked Queenie bad. Be thankful she didn't feel much. I wrapped her in a Fine Linen sheet and rode her in the buggy down to Simpson's pasture where she can be with all her Bones . . ."). For a few Novembers she continues to bake her fruitcakes singlehanded; not as many, but some: and, of course, she always sends me "the best of the batch." Also, in every letter she encloses a dime wadded in toilet paper: "See a picture show and write me the story." But gradually in her letters she tends to confuse me with her other friend, the Buddy who died in the 1880's; more and more thirteenths are not the only days she stays in bed: a morning arrives in November, a leafless birdless coming of winter morning, when she cannot rouse herself to exclaim: "Oh my, it's fruitcake weather!"

And when that happens, I know it. A message saying so merely confirms a piece of news some secret vein had already received, severing from me an irreplaceable part of myself, letting it loose like a kite on a broken string. That is why, walking across a school campus on this particular December morning, I keep searching the sky. As if I expected to see, rather like hearts, a lost pair of kites hurrying toward heaven.

# Death and Professor Raikes

### ALICE DUER MILLER

## I

MILLICENT CHESTER was discontented, and discontent hath its tragedies no less profound than grief. But as she was pretty, healthy and assured by her parents' finances of a roof over her head and three meals a day, most people thought her merely wicked. They said: "A girl like that who has everything to make life agreeable—" and thought how wonderful they were to be happy with so much less. Yet Millicent had good grounds for discontent—grounds which, in a man of her age —that is, twenty-five—would have been thought not only good but creditable; she was energetic, intelligent, executive, and she had no possible outlet for any of these qualities.

She looked elegant, almost overelaborate. Her beauty was of the delicate, slender sort. People said it was impossible to imagine Millie where she couldn't get her hair waved and her nails manicured. As a matter of fact, she needed such accessories far less than other people. Her gold-brown hair could not be prevented from waving and arranged itself in those deep furrows almost without guidance. Her smooth white skin was kept white and smooth, not by eastern unguents—which was the way it looked—but by Millie's excellent natural good health. Her body—a little too slender for her height—was stronger than many thicker-set bodies. And her hands, which seemed to drip with idleness, were extremely competent and could even in an emergency hammer a nail.

To this confusing effect Millie consciously contributed, since, like most of us, she wished to enjoy the rewards of both her types; and as in the life she was leading exotic elegance was more rewarded than executive ability, Millie was more often exotically elegant. She had two voices too—one crisp and decisive; the other soft, with a gasp in it, and that melted hearts. And two ways of looking at you out of her slate-blue eyes—one very straight and honest—what some one had called her "let's get our riding boots on and be off" look, and the other, slanting and veiled and disturbing to a degree.

She had been educated—in name, at least—in a country boarding school— "one of our best schools," it was called by those people who thought she had everything to make life agreeable; a school which flourished under the old idea that, for women at least, culture and accuracy are natural foes. Mathematics was necessarily taught, but with smiling appreciation of those who were too artistic by nature to understand it; science was dealt with in one general undifferentiated course, called, not inappropriately, science. Most of the attention of the teachers turned to English and French litera- ture, history and art. When, at fifteen, Millicent had shown an embarrassing desire to be prepared for college, Miss Rudge, the head of the school, who had had this problem to meet before, knew perfectly the way to deal with it. She sent for Millicent's parents and explained to them that it would be easy for the Southside School to prepare the child for college; that, in fact, they did that already, except that the last year at Southside was the equivalent of four years at college; only she must warn Mr. and Mrs. Ches- ter that in her experience college utterly unfitted a girl for home life—it made her discontented. So Mr. and Mrs. Chester, devoted parents as they were, and looking forward eagerly to the time when Millie would be at home again, instantly decided against a college education and supposed somehow that they had a guaranty that their child would be happy at home.

And for a year or so she was. Immediately after she finished school she was taken abroad, and then she came back to New York and began to go out. Naturally she was a great social success. Her skin was white as some thick-leaved flowers are white—pure and unsullied—her eyes were an intense, clouded gray blue, and her manner was one of almost tremulous depend- ence on the opinion of whoever it was she was speaking to. The first year she went to every party she was asked to, content in the simple glory of being more cut in on than any other débutante. She slept till noon, and then all day long either hung on the telephone making and breaking dates with her partners of the evening before, or else dashed out to tea or the movies with them, while her father said: "I don't see how she tells them apart," and her mother murmured: "I'm not sure I ought to let her go to the movies with them."

The second year she became more discriminating—went only to parties where she was sure of meeting the people she already knew best, and spoke with some scorn of débutantes and sophomores. That year romance began to raise its ugly head. Mr. and Mrs. Chester, who were now in the neighbor- hood of fifty—she just under and he just over that fatal decade—took the first of these affairs most seriously. They themselves had married early and they supposed that Millie would. When, instead of a dozen young men calling her up at meals, it began to be always the same one, they looked at each other with intense significance when she had left the room. Hardly making any sound, but moving her lips so as to be well understood, Mrs. Chester said: "I don't like him." That was enough for Mr. Chester; he did not like the fellow either. They decided, however, not to offer open oppo- sition, which would only make Millie more determined. A few weeks later they even suggested asking him to a dinner they were having, but Millie refused; she said she did not wish to dictate their guests to them, but, frankly, the man bored her.

After this the Chesters' attitude relaxed a little; too much perhaps, for one evening after Mrs. Chester had praised an utterly unknown dark young man who had turned up and eaten a family dinner, Millie observed quietly, "Yes, he is attractive, isn't he? He's sailing for Senegambia on Saturday, and I may go with him. . . . Oh, I'd marry him first, mother dear, of course." She did not marry him, or, as far as her parents could tell, ever think of him again after his departure for Senegambia.

The Chesters said the things that parents do say under the circumstances. They were still deeply—Millie would have thought, "reprehensibly"—interested in their own lives. Mr. Chester was rapidly amassing a fortune at the law, and Mrs. Chester, who had known poverty in the early days of her marriage, was immensely excited and amused with the possession of wealth. They were not people who lived wholly in the next generation. They said to each other that Millie had got through the worst phase; that she would soon marry and settle down and forget all this nonsense. They little knew what was ahead of them.

For it was the next year, when the number and violence of her love affairs had waned, that Millie began to be discontented, and for her parents this was the worst phase of all. After all, when a new young man had appeared on the scene during the former stage, she was gay and amusing, but now her entrance into a room of happy, laughing people was like the sweeping of an icy blast over a flower garden. Her parents, chatting to each other about something that seemed vital to them—politics or buying a country place, or a great lawsuit of Mr. Chester's—would find the words dying on their lips as Millie's slate-blue eyes passed over them as if she were saying: "Can it be such things interest sane people?"

It would not be a gross exaggeration to say that at this time Mr. Chester disliked his only child. Her mother, more understanding, explained to him that what Millie wanted was something to do.

"She ought to get married," said he.

"And find out what real trouble is," replied his wife.

But now the extremely poor quality of the education which they had so trustingly bestowed upon her began to be evident. There was nothing that Millie was fitted to do. Her natural abilities—a gift for languages and some practical dexterity—did not seem to be commercially salable. Most of her friends were going into interior decoration, but Millie, noting that in the earlier stages this profession seemed to consist principally of matching samples for clients who did not mean to buy, decided that this was no activity for her.

Mr. Chester, feeling a little guilty now, offered Millie a job in his office—to keep it looking tidy and attractive and receive clients. But after three days of it Millie saw that it was not a real job at all. She tried to explain herself to him.

"Because I want to do something, it doesn't mean I want to do anything," she said. "It must have something real about it."

"Charitable work is real, isn't it?" said her father. "I should think a girl like you, with plenty of money, if she wanted to do anything would want to do it for charity."

But Millie didn't want to work in charitable institutions. She was not noble enough to do it for a good motive and not egotistical enough to do it for a bad one.

She did not really want to, but, nevertheless, in her great agony for some activity, she did go on the board of a charity—a rich old-fashioned organization which had been wasting money with the least possible trouble to the executives in a dignified and correct manner for fifty years. It never occurred to them that a girl of twenty-three would upset their régime; would, in fact, do anything at all, except what she was told to do, and probably very little of that. But they did not know Millie. She saw in the twinkling of an eye that the whole thing was wrong—was mismanaged and extravagant—and she decided to change it.

She failed. She failed because fourteen lazy people, eager to do nothing, can usually block one intelligent person, eager to act. Millie showed herself intelligent, hard working, direct and executive, but she was ruthless, and thus alienated the small number of her fellow board members who might have helped her.

She failed and resigned in a rage, much to every one's relief, but she had tasted blood. She knew now that she had ability; if only she could have found some field in which to exercise it.

The next two years were very bad for Millie. She learnt the secret that makes people criminals—namely, that you can break laws and pay no penalty. The laws that Millie broke were not the laws of the state, not even the more obvious moral laws; they were the codes of social amenities and coöperation. She learnt, for instance, that she could be insolent to her father, and that he was absolutely helpless under his surprise and awkwardness; that she could withdraw into an icy mist and force her mother to do anything; that she could be rude to the hostess of a dull dinner, and instead of being ignored, the next time would find she had been better placed; that she could play cards for high stakes, and instead of getting into debt, make a comfortable income; that she could take married men away from devoted wives by a few long, sweet, sliding glances, and when they became troublesome return them like a wrongly addressed package. In fact, in two years, from having been a naïve, wondering, sunny-tempered girl, she became a bitter-tongued, insolent and strong-willed woman. Except for the bitter erosion of her own spirit, she seemed to pay no price. People spoke ill of her, it is true, and many cordially disliked her, but she was always a member of whatever group she wished to be a member of. Her loneliness and bitterness and desperation had developed, for good or evil, that rare power of the will which there seems to be no mechanical method of developing. And then she remained very lovely to look at—harder, but not less beautiful.

Her mother, who had been happily married at twenty-two, was incapable of understanding Millie's state of mind, and yet was wise enough to see that they were dealing not with wickedness but with tragedy; only she made the mistake of trying to soothe and placate Millie, and to try to be soothing to Millie at this time was as safe as to try to be soothing to a wounded tiger.

The whole situation culminated in a family scene. It was Mr. Chester's habit to take his annual holiday in the autumn—in October or November —when his partners had come back from theirs. This year he and his wife were going to the Arizona desert and the Grand Canyon, riding and walking and camping out. They were very eager about it, and as pleased with the prospect of an uninterrupted month of each other's society as if they had been married three instead of almost thirty years. That was one of Millie's complaints—her parents were sufficient to each other. Chester was all for leaving Millie alone in New York, but Mrs. Chester said that the trip would be good for Millie and that she would enjoy it, and that she must be included—cordially included. Much to her father's relief, Millie absolutely refused to go.

"What will you do while we are gone?" he asked.

Millie suppressed a smile at the idea that their going or coming could make any difference to her, and replied that she would probably stay where she was.

"Alone?" said her mother, as if it wouldn't do.

"Alone, dear mother," answered Millie. She was standing on the hearth rug between her parents, sunk in deep armchairs on either side of her. Her hands were clasped behind her and she turned from one to the other as she spoke: "Do you really think you are a great protection to me?"

Mrs. Chester was fond, but spunky, and she retorted, "Yes, I think, as far as mere parents can be, we are a conventional protection."

Millie shook her head. "No, my dear," she said, "really you're not. In fact, I might be more of a protection to you. I certainly know more about the world as it is to-day than you do. I couldn't even tell you about it, for fear of shocking you."

Mr. Chester suddenly lost his temper, and said: "You certainly are the most disagreeable, insolent, impossible young woman I ever knew."

Millie bowed slightly from the waist. "I quite agree with you, father," she said. "I can't imagine a greater disaster than I am as a person, and yet I wasn't such bad material to work with." Her father did not instantly see her meaning, but her mother knew that an attack was being made upon them.

"You mean," she said, "that, as your father and I are responsible for bringing you into the world—"

"No, I don't mean that," the girl answered. "I mean that since you got me here you have destroyed me."

"Destroyed you?" said her father with a shout, and he pushed back his chair and began to stamp his feet as if about to rise and do something terrible, but he didn't as Millie went on:

"Yes, destroyed me. Look at me. I'm twenty-five. I have not an interest or a responsibility. There is not a single thing I ought to do at any time. Oh, yes, you'll say, make myself agreeable to you and mother, but really what you like best is to be alone together."

"Who will give an idle, ignorant girl responsibilities? Responsibilities come to those who—"

"Exactly," Millie interrupted him. "And who made me idle? Who took me out of school and told me to go to parties every night and sleep as late as ever I wanted in the morning? I did not particularly want to come out and lead that kind of life; it was mother who thought it was the right thing for a girl to do. What a silly, empty sort of an experience it is. Do you think a boy would come through it so well—dancing every night and sleeping every morning? Would he be ready, after two or three years of it, to take up great responsibilities? No. But it doesn't matter about girls."

"All your friends have done it, dear," said Mrs. Chester.

"And many of them feel as I do, only they haven't sense enough to know it, or they are too kind-hearted to tell the truth."

"That doesn't trouble you much—kind-heartedness," said her father.

"No," she answered, "I'm as hard as a stone."

"You're a silly, cruel, ignorant girl," said her father.

She turned her head slowly toward him. "That," she returned, "is the second time you have called me ignorant. I am. But how could I help being with the education you have given me?"

"We sent you to the best school in—"

"You sent me to a school that taught me nothing except to be idle."

"Oh, if you'd wanted to study—"

"I did want to study. I wanted to go to college—not, heaven knows, that you learn so much there, but at least you learn how to find out what you want to know. But you wouldn't have it. You were afraid, and rightly, that it would unfit me for a life of complete idleness. I'm just what you especially designed me to be, father. I'm idle, useless, good-looking, well-dressed, ignorant, and I should think, by this time, absolutely worthless to any one. I'm not even bad."

Conversations of this sort never can be said to end, and this went on and on—between Mr. and Mrs. Chester alone, Mrs. Chester crying, and her husband frankly swearing; between Millie and her father, he furious and she coldly driving home her points in spite of his abuse; then between Millie and her mother, Mrs. Chester trying to reach this cool, remote judge and Millie receding further and further away from her.

It was Mrs. Chester who, with some affection left in her bruised heart, finally succeeded in bringing a little light to the situation.

"Millie," she asked, "if you had been trained—if it were possible—is there anything in the world you would like to do?"

Mr. Chester permitted himself a faint sneer, anticipating that his child would be obliged to confess that there was not, but she annoyed him even here by having a perfectly definite desire.

"Yes," she answered. "Oh, yes. I should love to be an archeologist—to go and dig in Central America or Yucatan."

"What do you know about such things?" he inquired contemptuously, since, for the duration of this discussion, he was her enemy.

"I know a great deal," said Millie, and strange to say, she spoke no more than the truth.

"Where did you learn anything about Central American archeology?" he asked, still hostile.

"I learned it," said Millie with a faint smile, "in the only two ways you have made it possible for me to learn—by reading in a ladylike way in my own room, and through a man who was in love with me." It was true.

Two or three years before, one of the most enduring of Millie's fancies had been for a young Harvard graduate student who was writing his Ph.D. thesis on the difference between the construction of Central American and Egyptian pyramids. Like most girls, Millie could get more information in five minutes from a young man who loved her than she could in four years' study at school. She and he wandered many hours in the Central American and Mexican rooms of the Museum of Natural History, and when she went to Boston for football games they would manage to wedge in a little time at the Peabody Museum. The subject thrilled her even without the additional stimulus of the young man's adoration, and she contrived, before the final parting, to acquire a little more than a smattering of knowledge.

About the time that this romance was at its height rubber cutters in the republic of Gatacosta had begun to come in with gossip of ten masonry hills set in a deep valley in the continental range, masonry which, examined, turned out to be stepped pyramids with ruins on the top. Bentham College had immediately sent a man to investigate, with a result that the little college was now sending out a serious expedition.

Mr. Chester was an alumnus of Bentham, although he had become more identified in the public mind with Harvard, where he had taken his law degree. Still Bentham did not allow him to forget his allegiance; particularly as he became one of the prominent corporation lawyers of New York. Lately a determined effort had been made to make him go on the board of trustees. If Millie had really set her heart on joining this expedition, there seemed to be a promise of her father's being able to exert some pressure on her behalf. There was a time, of course, when Mr. Chester would have looked with horror on the suggestion that his only child should go off into the jungle for many months, but four years of discontent had taught him much, and when his wife asked him if he could ask President Norwich of Bentham to help poor Millie in her ambition to go and dig in Gatacosta, he replied promptly:

"No, I'm not such a fool. We'll have the old boy here to dinner and let Millie put in some of her fine work herself."

The President of Bentham college had, as every college president ought to have, a magnificent façade, and some people said he had nothing else, but then, college presidents always have foes of their own household. He had a delicate, egotistical face, bushy white hair, jet-black—suspiciously jet-black—eyebrows, and he wore an eyeglass on a heavy black ribbon.

Sitting down at a small dinner party at his old friends', the Chesters, he found himself next to a slim fairylike creature, dressed in white, looking up at him with a pair of wide-open slate-blue eyes.

"Bless me!" he said. "Don't tell me my friend Chester has got anything as beautiful as you for a daughter."

"Oh, beauty doesn't get you very far, except, perhaps, as far as the presidency of colleges," she returned. Both reckoned this a pretty good beginning.

Millie began to use that voice she used whenever she wanted to charm any one; it was so soft that an ear had to be literally inclined toward her; it panted, it trembled, it seemed to swoon with admiration. The president felt all his male ego expand and glow under the tone. But the matter, too, was flattering. He had very little time for the lady he had taken in to dinner—the hard, handsome, important wife of an important alumnus—for Millie, in this thrilling voice of hers, was explaining to him that since her childhood she had had a thwarted passion for American archeology. Having first satisfied herself that he was not himself an archeologist—he had been professor of homiletics in a theological seminary before he became president of Bentham, and though Millie did not know what homiletics might be, she was sure it wasn't archeological—she went on interlarding her conversation with the names of the best known of the buried cities, with such phrases as "popularly called Aztec," and with such words as "squeezes" and "orientation"—all learned in the period of her interest in the young Harvard man— until the president actually believed that he was in the presence of real knowledge.

He drew away and stared at her. "You seem to me a very remarkable young woman," he said, "to look as you do and to have such a hobby as this."

"And what good does it do me?" said Millie. "I dare say I know as much as many young men who are given every chance, but just because I haven't got a college degree—" And then she painted the picture—not much heightened, either—of how as a girl she had wanted to go to college, but had been prevented by her parents and teachers, and suddenly a belated wave of feminism rose in the heart of the president and he thought how he spent his life trying to bring and keep young men in college, while this lovely girl had been kept out.

"You would be interested in our expedition to Central America," he said, and was sorry to find she thought he meant that there was a chance that she might be allowed to go. He hastened to say that he had not meant that —oh, no!

"Do women never go?" asked Millie.

He could not truthfully say that they never did. Three years before, that remarkable woman, Professor Laureletta Briggs, the expert on orchids, had gone with the last expedition Bentham had sent out and had done some remarkable classifications.

"But, my dear child, Professor Briggs is sixty, and monstrously plain."

Millie would not smile at his compliment. "Are youth and good looks always to be a curse?" she said.

"A curse most people would give a good deal to possess."

But he was not to get off with any such evasion as that. Indeed, he was soon to learn that Millie had a persistence and a strength of will that many a college president might envy. At first he could hardly believe it; it was as if a gardenia turned out to be made of steel. He knew, or thought he knew, that it was out of the question for her to accompany the Bentham expedition, but two motives made him deal gently with her hopes: First, he wished to retain Chester's friendship. Chester, though not yet such a rich man himself, as a lawyer had the control of many estates and trust funds from which endowments might flow, to say nothing of being present when wills were drawn. Then, too, the president cherished a certain humorous dislike of the head of the expedition—Professor Raikes. Why should not Raikes deal with the situation? Why should not Raikes be the one to refuse? Ah, ah, there would be an interview—Greek meeting Greek. He would like to be there to hear. Many a wound received in faculty meeting from the insolent and irritable head of the archeological department would be avenged if matters ever got as far as an interview. But the president was obliged to admit things probably never would, for of course the Chesters would not dream of allowing their only daughter to go off to Central America with a party of scientists—a lovely, sheltered, young creature, the apple of their eye. If his daughter— But the idea of his elderly spinster daughter plunging off into the jungle was impossible.

He came and dropped into a chair beside Mrs. Chester after dinner. "That's a very remarkable young person—your daughter. How old is she?"

"Twenty-five," said her mother.

"Good gracious! I took her for seventeen."

"Slender people always seem younger and gentler than they are," replied Mrs. Chester, but the president did not note the warning.

"Do you know what she has been talking to me about all the evening?"

"I can imagine—about her passion for going on this expedition of yours."

"It's quite out of the question, you know."

He explained the organization of such an expedition. It consisted only of Professor Raikes and the assistant, Professor Thorley, and a young graduate student whose name at the moment escaped the president. Mrs. Thorley, an experienced traveler, went with them, but was usually left before they went into the deep jungle.

"If your daughter did go her fate would be to be cached with Mrs. Thorley, probably, and left for weeks in some steaming jungle village."

"That would, of course, be very disappointing," said Mrs. Chester. In her mind's eye, however, she did not see her Millie submitting to this treatment.

"To speak frankly," said the president, slightly lowering his voice, "the most serious objection of the whole thing is the character of Professor Raikes."

"Good heavens!" cried Mrs. Chester, suddenly becoming every inch a mother. "You mean he isn't respectable?"

"I mean he has the most disagreeable disposition I have ever encountered —to the degree that it is actually a faculty problem. A brilliant, a very brilliant man; perhaps the foremost man in America to-day in his line. Why is he with us instead of one of the great universities? Because it is well known that no one can coöperate with him. . . . This in strict confidence, of course. . . . He uses his brilliant mind simply to make other people feel inferior. He has—something I never saw combined before—all the petty irritability of a weak nature and all the intense violence of a strong one. He is known to have shaken a student in the classroom, and there's a story—not true—that he once tried to kill a man many years ago."

Mrs. Chester settled back in her chair again. "Oh," she said, "I think Millie could manage him all right."

"If she can," said the president, "I will have a monument put up to her on our campus."

When, after the last guest had gone, he himself got up rather reluctantly to go—he had had a very pleasant evening—he was urged by his host to stay.

"Come back into my study," said Chester, "and smoke one last cigar. . . . Oh, you don't smoke. Well, watch me then while I do."

Some people might have felt a little embarrassed at offering a noble-faced college president what amounted, in everything but name, to a bribe. But Chester was not embarrassed, nor, as a matter of fact, was Doctor Norwich. In fact he was so far from it that he merely raised his price.

It happened very decently like this.

"Look here, sir," said Chester. "I don't suppose this child of mine would be of any enormous assistance on an expedition of this kind, but she is so passionately eager to go that I can't see that she would be of any detriment to it, and as to the expense to the college, of course I'd stand that, and a little more—say twenty-five thousand to the endowment fund."

The president laughed heartily. "Thy money perish with thee, Chester," he said. "It's quite out of my hands. Professor Raikes has the say as to the make-up of his expedition. As an old Bentham man, you know the policy of the trustees—departmental freedom. Personally, if I were going on the trip, there is no one I should so much like to have as a traveling companion as this lovely little daughter of yours, Chester. . . . What an enchanting child! . . . And as for your endowment offer, my dear fellow, all of us college presidents must go about begging, of course; only, I will tell you that I would far rather have your consent to go on our board than give us five times the sum."

Chester did not want to go on the board; it meant several long journeys every year to board meetings, and always at times when he was busiest; it meant giving money steadily instead of at odd moments when he felt rich. But: "Go on the board, doctor!" he cried with gladness in his tone, quite as if he had not been unofficially approached a dozen times. "What man would not go on the board of his own college? I should be very proud, very proud indeed."

They understood each other perfectly. Before the president left, it was arranged that Millie should come up to Bentham and have an interview with Professor Raikes.

"Of course the matter lies entirely with Raikes. I can promise nothing," said the president.

"Oh, I understand. Of course, of course," said Chester.

In his bedroom he told his wife rather boastfully that he had turned the trick.

"I hope it didn't cost you a fortune," said Mrs. Chester, immediately beginning to make her plans for Canada.

"It didn't cost me a penny," said her husband. "You know this is my thirtieth anniversary and I had promised twenty-five thousand to the endowment fund. I just made that twenty-five thousand do a little work for me first."

Both parents informed Millie of all they had heard about the terrifying quality in Professor Raikes, but Millie was not a girl to be terrified.

"I don't believe much in ogres," she said. What she really meant was that ogres were sometimes the easiest of all to tame. And so, as so often happens, the battle between these two was joined before they had ever met face to face.

One morning two or three weeks later Professor Raikes was dealing with his correspondence before the opening of his first morning lecture. He was walking up and down his long sunny study—for space was no object at Bentham—and dictating to his stenographer, Miss Barnes. None of the other stenographers about the college would work for Professor Raikes, and indeed Miss Barnes sometimes thought the strain too great, not only the long words, the rapidity of his diction, but the constant threat of his irritability. Her hands were always cold with nervousness and she made more mistakes than she did under other circumstances. He was walking with long, quick strides, his hands in his pockets and his head tilted back so that he could stare at the ceiling. The result of this position was that every now and then he fell over a piece of furniture or at least barked his shins, at which he swore, kicked the object aside and continued in the same pose. He was a man not much under six feet, so thin that he looked boyish at a distance, although he was thirty-seven and his smooth black hair was getting gray. His eyes were set deeply in his head and, being almost true black, were hard to read; hard to see, even. His skin would have been naturally a dead even white, but long years in the tropics had tanned it to a light brown. He was clean shaven, and the pleasantest feature in his face was his mouth, firm, with a funny delicate little flicker about the corners.

"—as I shall already have sailed, I am obliged to decline your courteous [the sudden sound of wooden legs sliding on the bare floor—blankety-blankety-blank. "Who the devil put that chair there?"]—invitation to speak at your annual dinner. . . . Wherever it is, Miss Barnes. Finish that when I've gone. Take another. Mr. Ephraim F. . . . Well, you have his address. . . . Dear Sir: The belief on the part of parents that their children fail in examinations only owing to the dishonorable machinations of those who are supposed to instruct them— Come in. Come in. Come in! . . . God, how I hate to have to yell 'come in' a dozen times. . . . Oh, Jimmy, is it you? Come in. . . . No, I'm not busy."

It was the graduate student whose name had escaped the president, who was to make the third member of the expedition. The minute Raikes saw his face he exclaimed, with that rapidity of perception possessed by the irritable; the cause, perhaps, of their irritability: "What's the matter, Jimmy? You've been doing something you oughtn't to do. What is it?"

"I've been talking to the prettiest girl you ever saw," said Jimmy, coloring, though his tone was casual.

"You're in love!" cried Raikes. "Oh, if I could only get away once without taking lovesick assistants to mope in the jungle and be sent home with fever because they want to be. Shall I ever forget Thorley when he was engaged—"

"One moment, please. I have only been talking to her about ten minutes, and it's you she's after."

"Me?" cried Raikes with a sort of whoop. He was silent a moment, evidently running over the list of pretty girls who might conceivably want to see him. His memory seemed to yield nothing.

"Who is she?" he asked.

"Her name is Chester."

"I don't know any one called Chester."

"She's the prettiest girl I ever saw."

"A book agent, I bet. They're getting them pretty nowadays."

"She gave me this letter for you."

Raikes seized it and tore it open; it was a letter of introduction from one of the trustees. He looked up.

"You say she's pretty?"

"Divine."

Professor Raikes was usually supposed to be a woman hater. This was quite untrue—the opposite of the truth. He was subject to very gusty emotions, but one quality in the fair sex had always shocked and annoyed him, and that was what he called their tendency to take everything personally; that is to say, to be upset when sworn at. Several early love affairs of his had ended in stupendous rows, and so, gradually, he had come to the conclusion that women, at least as wives, were a difficult, entangling luxury, utterly unsuited to a busy, frank-spoken man like himself. He always said that he feared he was unfit for matrimony, but what he really thought was that the fault lay in the ridiculous unintelligible sensitiveness of women. He of course rather encouraged the legend that he hated them for its obvious advantages; it at once interested them, kept them at arm's length and added a peculiar flattery to his friendship when he did bestow it.

"Well, we'll let her in," said Raikes, and so Jimmy went back to the outer office, where he had left Millie sitting on a high stool with her hands folded in her lap, like a good child waiting for her nurse to come and take her home. He had left her staring up at the great photographs of Chichen-Itza and Copan, and when he came back she was in exactly the same attitude. She looked so good he felt he ought to save her or at least warn her of what might befall her.

"Don't be afraid of him," he said impulsively. "He can't really hurt you."

Millie smiled a little. "I'm not afraid," she said. "I never am—of people, at least."

"What are you afraid of?"

"Only of snakes and high places," she answered, and she got down off her stool, smoothed her dress with an infantile gesture and moved toward the door, which he opened and closed behind her. Bentham was a religious college, and a dim recollection of a verse in the Bible about his darling among the lions hung in the young man's mind.

And so Millie, a very sweet Daniel, walked into the den. Raikes, still with his hands in his pockets, but now rocking slightly to and fro from his heels to his toes, stared at her silently; it was his method—the greetingless entrance; it drove many visitors mad immediately and saved a long interview.

"Are you Professor Raikes?"

That low, pulsating voice affected him as it had affected less susceptible men; it affected him not through the consciousness, but speaking in some mysterious way directly to his emotions, as some singing voices make you cry without your experiencing the least emotion of sadness. He did not betray emotion—at least not this one. He merely said:

"Yes, yes. Of course—of course—of course."

"Don't frighten me to death before I've even told what I want," said Millie.

"Frighten you? How absurd! Who the hell— I beg your pardon Miss Barnes. I know you don't like swearing. . . . The hour for you to go to the president? Then go—go by all means. I have never made any effort to detain you beyond my legitimate time. Go, go, go. . . . Now, Miss Chester, I am entirely at your disposal."

Millie, like Cæsar, was not susceptible to fear. She was not in the least alarmed by Raikes. Moreover, she felt, superstitiously, that luck was with her. She had spoken to Jimmy Salisbury because he was the first person she had seen on the steps of the archeology building, and it was nice to have some one smooth the way. The probability was that, standing there, he was a student of the department, but it was great luck that he should be the special student who was going on the expedition, and who, moreover, was a favorite of Professor Raikes and knew how to manage him. She was glad, too, that he as well as Miss Barnes had gone; she was always more effective in tête-à-tête.

"And what can I do for you?" said Raikes, as if his life were one long series of benevolent deeds; and then he added, fearing he might be imposed upon: "At least in the few minutes I have at your disposal."

"Professor Raikes, I want to go on your expedition to Central America."

Raikes looked at her a second and then frankly laughed. His laugh was pleasant and ought to have been the ruin of all her hopes, for if he had thought there was the least possibility of her going he would have been in a frenzy of bad temper.

"Why do you laugh?"

"It amuses me that you should have such an absurd wish, for I can assure you, you wouldn't enjoy it."

"Why is it absurd?"

"Ah—ah," said Raikes. "The well-known Socratic method." He folded his arms and began a lecture. "The Socratic method, having come down to us through the mentality of a great genius, has gained a prestige which, when it is administered, as it usually is, by slow and prejudiced minds—"

"Professor Raikes, if we have only a few minutes, do not let us spend it entirely on Socrates." Millie's tone was not quite so gaspingly admiring as it had been.

Raikes smiled. "That was my plan, I must admit," he replied.

"Will you tell me why it is absurd that I wish to go on your expedition."

"We do not take utterly untrained people on scientific expeditions."

"But why do you assume that I am utterly untrained?"

"Because not being a mathematician, thank fortune, I usually do assume the obvious. Why is it obvious? Because promising graduate students in archeology are so rare that if one of your sex, and may I add, appearance, had shown any ability, I should most certainly have heard of you, and I must tell you that the name of Chester has never come into my consciousness, except as the middle name of a president, and a town where a classmate of mine was married once among scenes of rather indecent revelry —but as you may imagine, that was a good many years ago."

"I have not been trained in any college, but I do know something of the subject."

"What?" he answered. "That the ten tribes of Israel built the Central American cities, or the inhabitants of the lost Atlantis? Apparently, to dig for buried treasure is one of the great cravings of the human heart. We cannot take every one with us who would like to go, Miss Chester, and therefore we are obliged to select those who seem best fitted to be of service to us."

"I want so very much to go," said Millie simply.

"You wouldn't if you had ever been," said Raikes grimly. "Do you know what the outstanding feature of these trips is? Not golden treasures and scientific joy. Fleas, insects of all kinds—mosquitoes, cockroaches, aniguas —but constantly and worst, fleas; heat and fever and fleas."

Millie smiled. "I thought you were going to say snakes," she said.

"Oh, yes, snakes; there are lots of them, of course," said Raikes, not knowing that he was throwing away his most powerful argument, "but they want to get out of your way if they can, but fleas—"

"Fleas don't bite me," said Millie again, with a really angelic smile.

"You have probably never been where they were."

"I've been all over Italy and Spain, with my parents going nearly mad, poor dears," she answered. "They won't touch me, nor mosquitoes either."

For the first time since their interview got going, Raikes showed signs of irritation. "Good heavens!" he exclaimed. "Good heavens!" He stopped himself with an effort, and then added: "And that brings us to another reason why it would be impossible to take a girl like you on such an expedition— my temper. It may surprise you to learn, Miss Chester, but such is the fact, that I am not a good-tempered man."

"I don't see why that should affect me in any way," said Millie.

"I don't see why either," he returned, "but it would; it always does. I regret to say that I cannot be ten minutes in the company of one of your sex, and be natural, without reducing them to tears."

"You seem to be rather proud of it," said Millie.

"I am not in the least proud of it. It is extremely inconvenient. I should be ashamed of it if I did not really think it was ridiculous sensitiveness on their part, rather than anything really offensive in me."

"Well," said Millie, "you would not reduce me to tears."

"We shall never know," said Raikes, standing up. "And now, as I have a class impatiently waiting for me not to come—"

"Shall I wait here?"

She succeeded in surprising him. "What for?"

"So that we can discuss this a little more fully and, if you will let me say so, a little more rationally."

Raikes' brow began to lower. "You have at least the virtue of persistence," he said. "We have nothing further to discuss."

"I should think," returned Millie, "that before deciding whether you would take me or not you would wish to inquire into my qualification for going. I am extremely healthy, very calm and good-tempered—"

"I do not mean to take you on this expedition. I will go further. I should think that any man who did take you was a fool."

She looked at him gravely. "I don't think you've made out a very good case for yourself," she said dispassionately.

He walked to a chair near the door where his battered gray felt hat was lying. "Miss Chester," he said, "I think you presume on your sex; really I do," and he went out, shutting the door behind him.

Presently the door opened and Salisbury came stealing in to see what was left of the radiant being whom he had admitted only a short time before. He was astonished to see her looking very much the same.

"Well, what happened?" he asked.

"He said he wouldn't take me." She glanced up at him brightly.

"Well, you didn't expect he would, did you?"

Millie did not answer this question directly. "He's very amusing, isn't he?" she said reflectively. "Very amusing—almost witty."

"His wit is rather cruel, I think."

"All wit is that's any good," said Millie decisively. She rose to her feet, and he asked, as she meant him to ask: "Where are you going now?"

"I'm to lunch with Doctor Norwich," said Millie, "but there's a good deal of time between now and luncheon."

"Would you—would you let me show you about a little?" said Salisbury timidly. "There are some quite pretty walks about here."

"Oh, I couldn't," said Millie. "I know you must be busy."

But no, it appeared that Mr. Salisbury was not busy; nothing, at least, that could not wait, and so presently they were walking through the autumn woods, and Millie was punctuating an intelligent and attentive silence with such phrases as: "Oh, of course, not cuneiform in the right sense," "the squeezes in the Peabody Museum," "such orientation as we have in the Egyptian pyramids." Salisbury was sure she knew as much as he did—an opinion which Millie comfortably knew he would impart to Raikes at the first opportunity.

In the meantime the professor was giving one of the early lectures in a course of which he heartily disapproved—an outline of archeology. In faculty meeting the president had been enthusiastic about such a course. "Give the students a general idea of the subject," he had said.

"Give them a general idea they know something about a subject of which they are densely ignorant," said Raikes; at which every one present voted for the course and he found himself obliged to inaugurate it. As he lectured he found that he was more irritated about Miss Chester's not being bitten by fleas than about her desire to go on his expedition. How absurd for Nature to bestow this priceless immunity on a girl to whom it was of no practical value, while he, Raikes, a scientist, whose work was of positive value to the world—

At the end of the lecture he received a message that the president wished to speak to him at his "early convenience"—the sort of phrase the president loved. Raikes groaned on general principles. It did not occur to him that the interview would have anything to do with the girl with the gasp in her voice. Being naturally of a pessimistic habit of mind, induced probably by the fact that he had great art in luring enmity in his direction, he ran over all the disagreeable possibilities and came to the conclusion as he crossed the campus toward the president's house that the old man was going to cut down the money for the Gatacosta expedition. In which case—in which case —Raikes thought bitterly of some revenge on his part—resignation, first of all. He would not do the thing on the cheap; he would not endanger some of the best years of his life to save money for some damned business course. He would not!

The president met him, beaming: "Well," he said, "I have some good news for you, Raikes—good with a little bad in it."

There are two schools for the executive anticipating opposition in his subordinates. One is to maneuver so that they never have the opportunity of putting themselves on record as opposed, and the other is to allow them to get "no" thoroughly out of their systems. The president used both methods, but always the latter with Raikes. Doctor Norwich was not a very strong or noble character, but he had a great deal of experience in dealing with men of letters and science. He knew just about what Raikes' interview with Millie would have been—that he would have refused and that she would have been persistent; that he would have become too rough and would now very slightly regret, not his refusal but a lack of suavity in his refusal.

"Sit down," he said. "I think I'm on the track of twenty-five thousand dollars additional for your expedition."

Raikes' eyes grew dark and burning with excitement. "That means I can do the whole job at one clip," he said.

The president nodded. "But there's a condition attached to it," he said, "and I'm afraid you may feel, a prohibitive one."

Raikes thought loyally. "What a fool the old boy is to think I would find anything prohibitive that made the whole thing perfect from my point of view."

"It would have to be pretty steep," said Raikes. "What is it?"

"The necessity of including an outsider in your personnel," said the president.

"Oh," said Raikes, seeing the whole thing in a minute. Twenty-five thousand dollars against the annoyance of a girl like that; it was a nice balance. He scowled, staring at the floor. "What do you wish me to do, sir?" he asked. His tone sounded respectful, but his thought was: "If it's another plant of the old man's I won't do it. I'm free to run my own department."

But the old man was too clever to be caught by that trap. "It's entirely for you to say, Raikes. It's your expedition. I must confess I should not care to chaperon and manage that young lady myself."

"Oh, I don't think I shall find much trouble in that," said the professor, almost automatically. "I believe it might be a salutary experience for that young lady; and it is always pleasant, doctor, as you must know, to be a salutary influence. There is nothing in the contract that calls for her enjoying the trip, is there?"

"No, nothing whatsoever," said the president. "In fact, there is no understanding about taking her into the interior at all. If you should find it better to leave her where Mrs. Thorley is usually left—"

Raikes laughed gayly. "Oh, of course I shall do that," he said. "I was only thinking it would be a bore to have a girl like that on your hands on the boat and at the port and as far into the jungle as we take her."

The president nodded sympathetically. "I must warn you of one thing," he said—"that her father, Carter Chester, has been elected to the board of trustees, so that when you come back—"

"He may ask for my resignation. Well, you know, Doctor Norwich, my resignation is always ready. In fact, if I am required to give many more lectures like the one I have just come from, it will be given in anyhow. I must say that, of all courses designed to teach nothing—"

They plunged into the problem of the curriculum, and Doctor Norwich saw with some surprise that he was thus easily to have his own way about Millie.

When she arrived—a little late—for luncheon, he told her the good news.

"Well, well," he said, "what did you do to our stern aloof professor of archeology? He agrees to take you on the trip."

The speech was not so utterly insincere as it sounds, for seeing her suddenly, so lovely, and flushed both from her walk and the open adoration of Salisbury, she appeared to the president so desirable that he thought any man in his senses would take her anywhere without the bribe of twenty-five thousand dollars. To be candid, Millie thought so too. Her life had been too full of admiration for that explanation to seem unnatural.

"He said very plainly that he wouldn't take me," she answered. "I'm so glad he's changed his mind."

The talk at luncheon turned, of course, on Raikes. Miss Norwich, the third person at table, observed quietly that she hoped Miss Chester would not fall in love with him. The remark came oddly from the lips of a rather withered blond spinster of fifty—or so it seemed to Millie—who was already considering the possibility that Raikes was in love with her, and engaged at odd moments when her mind was free in composing romantic episodes with him in the jungle.

The president was annoyed at his daughter, as indeed he often was. The extreme neutrality of her appearance and conduct was often contradicted by the freedom of her mind and speech.

"Really, my dear Livia," he said, "I should think that that was the least danger Miss Chester ran—a man old enough to be her father."

"I should think it quite the greatest," said Miss Norwich, and leaning forward politely, she asked: "Will you have some tea? We have tea with luncheon here, though in New York, I know, you don't."

Millie declined tea, and added: "No, Miss Norwich, I don't think I shall fall in love with Professor Raikes, but I do see he may need a little management."

The president smiled at his little guest. "I'm sure you could do it if any one could."

"But no one can," answered Miss Norwich. "The only person who can manage any one is some one who is utterly indifferent. Any woman who isn't in love with Timmy Raikes hates him."

"I never heard of any woman being in love with him," said the president, frowning a little.

"No?" said his daughter. She wondered if her father really did not know that his younger daughter had married a tiresome professor of English and gone to California simply to get away from the agony of her love for Raikes.

Millie was amused by the shrewdness of Miss Norwich's analysis. She thought to herself that very likely she was the instrument selected by heaven to discipline Raikes. Stranger things had been.

"Anyhow," she said, "I promise not to fall in love with him."


II


The boat that was to take the Bentham expedition to the port of Gatacosta was a small steamship, dedicated to the proposition that bananas were more important than passengers. At each trip it brought its cargo of that pale rather mushy fruit to whatever Gulf city promised the speediest sale. This time it happened to be Mobile. The party assembled separately. The Thorleys had been in Mobile several days attending to getting the equipment on board. Raikes had stopped in Washington to make some final arrangement with the State Department and the minister of the rather turbulent government of Gatacosta; Salisbury had gone to Ohio to say good-by to his family, and had approached down the Mississippi; and last of all, Millie had taken the best drawing-room on the New Orleans express and arrived in the dark hours between midnight and dawn, only a few hours before the *Stella* was scheduled to sail.

She had scouted the idea of her parents coming as far as Mobile with her, or even of their sending any one, but when she stepped off on the deserted platform of the Mobile station she had a momentary sensation of loneliness.

A man in a seaman's cap and jacket came up to her almost at once and said: "Miss Chester, for the *Stella*." He took her bag. "I'm the purser. Delisle's the name."

He turned sharply away and Millie followed as best she could. It was not easy to keep up with his long strides. They entered a covered wharf, smelling of harbor water and musty fruit. How was she to know, she thought, that she was boarding the *Stella?* Tales of white slavery in China and Argentina came to her mind. Her guide turned to the right and stepped down into the waist of a tiny ship. Surely it couldn't be the *Stella.* No one would actually put to sea— A tender perhaps; a small copy of those that come out at Cherbourg. "New York Society Girl Disappears in Mobile Docks."

She drew back, hesitating, and then a voice spoke to her: "Oh, you did come after all." Jimmy Salisbury was watching for her from the upper deck.

"Deck cabin C, starboard side," said the purser.

"I'll take Miss Chester's bag," said Jimmy.

"I have it," said the purser. For an instant both men laid firm hands on Millie's Russian-leather dressing case. Then the purser, seeing his advantage, let Jimmy have the bag while he walked ahead, piloting Millie. He was a pale sandy-haired young Southerner who had had an unfortunate disagreement with a negro, which in the North would have led to a criminal trial, and in his own state led to his finding an occupation designed to keep him away from home for a year or so.

Both men attempted to induce Millie to sit up and watch the moonlight on the great round area of Mobile Bay, but she was firm; she wasn't going to begin her trip that way.

It was no great wonder that the officers of a vessel accustomed to carrying no passengers except malarious planters and large Spanish-American ladies disposed to seasickness should all fall in love with Millie. The purser had spread the report of her beauty to unbelieving ears—Delisle was considered romantic about women—but when Millie appeared at luncheon in a simple gray-blue dress the color of her eyes he was entirely vindicated.

She had slept very late, and when at length she got on deck she found that the *Stella* had passed beyond the silt that the Mississippi carries into the Gulf, and was riding the waves of a sapphire sea. It was half-past twelve and every one had been at luncheon some time when she entered. The captain, a stout jovial New Englander, at the head of the table, with Mrs. Thorley on his right and a grizzled Gatacostan official, returning from Washington, on his left. Millie sat down between the purser and the chief engineer, and found she was immediately opposite to Raikes and Jimmy. Raikes bowed to her with a face as blank as a statue's.

The chief engineer was a black-haired, brown-eyed young Scotchman, always struggling against a craving for whisky as the only anodyne to his acute dislike and disapprobation of the general scheme of mortality. He was not of the type who are rendered happier or more hopeful even by the early stages of love. He cast one glance at Millie and became more aware than ever of the futility of life and the cruelty of death. He faced the fact that he could never hope to possess her, and after a few minutes of deep silence he sent the steward to his cabin for a bottle of whisky.

The captain found himself affected by a desire to tell Millie about his wife and children, whom he had left in a small wooden house in South Boston. The purser would have liked to prance before her on a coal-black steed, sweeping a feathered hat to the ground, but was obliged to content himself with telling her legends of the South in its great days. The Gatacostan looked at her continually, with his head tilted back so that his great magnifying spectacles focused upon her. He did not speak but amused himself by thinking how much better men of his race appeared in this first approach to beauty than blundering Anglo-Saxons and romantic Celts.

Raikes had put on his stone-image face and did not look at her at all; only now and then he gave vent to a low sound like an etherealized snort, indicating contempt or dissatisfaction with something that had been said; at which Jimmy would attempt to engage his chief's attention or distract his mind, and often bring down wrath upon his head—which was perhaps Jimmy's object.

The trip should have taken four days, but seemed on this occasion likely to take five, owing—or so the story went about the ship—to the chief engineer's slowing down the engines; but actually because the old engines, pounding themselves each trip nearer to dissolution, required an attention which MacPherson was no longer in any condition to give them. Raikes was furious at the idea of losing a day and would not speak to any one.

He had preëmpted a part of the upper deck to his own use and sat there all day long in the only real steamer chair the little boat possessed—all the others were of canvas—with his hat pulled over his eyes and a pile of books and papers beside him. Thorley, never a good sailor and particularly ill affected by the bounding motion of a small, empty vessel on the swells of the Caribbean, lay all day long on the sofa in the saloon or strolled on deck with a forced smile that tried to give the lie to the luminous green of his complexion. Mrs. Thorley sat under the awning on the after deck, stitching flannel bands to keep her husband from dysentery. There, too, Millie held her court. They came and went—the captain with anecdotes about his little Zillah; the purser with his tales of the War of Secession; Jimmy, too humble and admiring to be jealous; and at meals—only at meals—MacPherson, with his eyes getting to be more and more like live embers every day.

Sometimes Don Manuel, the Gatacostan official, would invite her to walk with him on the deck, and would flatter her in words, while examining her with perfectly cold, curious eyes. She was glad of an opportunity to practice her Spanish, and heard in return that American women were very cold— not to be borne or understood by Latin males. He was now burnt out, an old man, but in his youth had been very fiery. Millie probably bore out the evil name of her compatriots, for she showed she was more interested when he spoke of the ruins of his native land.

The only person who never came near her and never spoke to her except at table, to ask her to hand him a dish, was Raikes. The vanity of a girl with less cause for self-confidence than Millie might have been wounded by his neglect, but Millie could not accept such indifference as completely natural, and as soon as she admitted that it was a mask she was free to let her imagination run wild as to what the mask covered. She smiled to herself. After three or four weeks in the jungle she would know. It would be amusing, it would be exciting, when the breakdown of that fine high-strung nature finally came. Her heart beat a little faster in just thinking about it.

"And you were the man," she would say, "who did not want me to come."

And all the time, in her own strange way, she was honestly trying to fit herself to be a member of the expedition, reading Spanish, studying the irregular verbs, talking to Mrs. Thorley about clothes and health, examining Don Manuel about the ruins of his native country, and steadily learning everything that Jimmy knew on the whole subject.

The third morning out the captain came down the narrow stairs that led from the bridge to that part of the deck that Raikes preëmpted, and stood leaning his back on the railing. His eyes traveled over the ship, up to masthead and over the horizon, as seafaring people's eyes are always traveling, and then he remarked:

"I'm worried about my chief engineer." Raikes, who would have scowled at Millie and sworn at Jimmy for interrupting his train of thought, looked up at the great fat captain with calm and friendliness, and thus encouraged, the captain went on: "He hasn't touched a drop since he's been with me —that's two years—and now he's been drunk almost ever since we cleared."

"I've noticed it," said Raikes dryly.

"Well, what am I going to do about it?" said the captain.

"What were you thinking of doing about it?"

"Maybe it's a bad idea," said the captain, "but I was thinking—with your approval—of asking Miss Chester to say a word of warning to him. Sometimes a man sees himself different in a woman's eyes, and I've a notion— Well, maybe I'm wrong."

"No, you're not wrong," said Raikes. "Only she won't do it. She will be very much surprised, and say that she doesn't know Mr. Mac—whatever it is—well enough."

The captain sighed. "Well, there's no reason why she should if she doesn't want to."

"Not unless you threatened to put her in irons if she doesn't."

The captain laughed, taking this as more of a joke than it was meant to be. "I'm not much of a believer in threats," he said.

"I'm not much of a believer in anything else," replied Raikes, and added as the captain moved away with his rolling step: "Let me know if you fail, and I'll try my hand."

He had been reading about half an hour, when a shadow fell upon his book, and looking up, he saw the captain was back.

"Well, you win," he said. "She said just what you said she would, and of course she's right." Then, as Raikes gave a sort of snort, he added: "She made me feel pretty cheap—not being able to run my own ship." And the captain rolled away again, up the companionway to the bridge.

Raikes glanced after him and murmured to himself: "What fools men are about women—especially my countrymen." Presently he stopped the steward, who was passing, and asked him to tell Miss Chester that he wanted to speak to her.

Millie, who had been digging away at Spanish all the morning, had just paused long enough to confide the story of her interview with the captain to Jimmy, who, surprising to relate, thought exactly as she did about it—

that it was a strange and impertinent thing for the captain to ask her to enter into such a personal discussion with a man of this sort, whom she had never seen before and would never see again. Then the steward brought her the message from Raikes. Clever, Millie was, but it never crossed her mind that the message had anything to do with MacPherson. It seemed to her merely that the long-expected moment had come; the moment when Raikes admitted that he knew of her existence. It was an exciting prospect. She rose slowly and stood very straight and smiled down at Jimmy.

"Am I not learning?" she said. "To any one else I would answer that if he wanted to speak to me he could come and find me, but I go. I know my master's voice." And thus leaving Jimmy more dissatisfied with Raikes than he had ever been in his life, she went gayly up to the upper deck.

The weather had become hot and she was dressed in the simplest white —white that made her eyes as blue as a patch of sky on a cloudy day. Looking at her secretly, under the rim of his hat, Raikes had an instant's sympathy with MacPherson, not with her.

There was no chair near but his own, and Raikes did not offer it to her. He did, however, get up and lean on the back of it as he observed:

"The captain tells me he spoke to you about the chief engineer."

Millie opened her eyes. "Yes, he did," she answered. Her manner was perfect. She merely admitted a peculiar fact. If only she would have let it go at that, but she couldn't. She added: "Wasn't it strange?"

"Very," said Raikes, "very strange that a simple seaman should have put his finger on a not too obvious psychological situation."

"I wonder," said Millie very sweetly, "whether I understand you?"

"I don't know," said Raikes, "but I guarantee that you will before I've finished." He looked at her sternly. "I wish you to stop fascinating the chief engineer of this ship," he announced.

"I?" said Millie. She laid her hand on her bosom and looked rapidly from side to side, as if seeking on the surface of the blue Caribbean some explanation of Raikes' words. "I have hardly spoken to the man." She was enjoying herself enormously.

"Great heavens!" said Raikes. "I think pretty women are the greatest cheats in the world. Murderers and forgers and confidence men have to learn their dirty trade and take chances, but pretty women have this utterly irresponsible power handed to them, and nobody can ever go into a court of law and swear it was unjustly used."

Millie drew herself up and said with a good deal of dignity: "Professor Raikes, I really can't let you speak to me like that."

"Why not?"

She found the question a difficult one to answer but replied: "Because, as you must know, you're talking like a madman. I have hardly spoken to this unfortunate man. I have sat next to him at three or four meals."

Raikes brushed all that aside. "You are perfectly aware of what you are doing to MacPherson," he said.

"And will you tell me what it is?"

"Yes and no," he answered. "I can't tell you what gravitation is, but I know some of its laws. I can't explain electricity, but I can describe some of its manifestations. You come in always a little late, knowing that your looks and your proximity and that damned perfume you use shake the poor fellow, and you sit down and begin to let this great braggart of a purser absorb all your attention, while MacPherson sits there rolling bread crumbs and trying to think of some simple sentence that will make you turn your head so that at least he can see you. Then all of a sudden he sees you are going to speak to him of yourself—what joy!—that your head is turning, slowly turning toward him, that in a minute those blue eyes of yours are going to be looking at him, and then you say to him in a special voice you have, with a catch in the middle: 'Did we make a good run to-day?' No, I don't know how it is done, but without moving an inch you suddenly put yourself into his hands, as if you trusted him beyond any one in the world, and it makes him faint with adoration. I don't know how it's done, but I know it is done."

Millie was surprised to find herself trembling very slightly. Of course it is exciting to be the subject of serious, even if hostile, conversation; it is flattering to be told that you are fascinating, but the most flattering element of all was the fact that she had been so closely observed. It was a perfect description of her method—one of her methods—but she was too excited to admit this.

Aloud she said: "But it's fantastic—what you are saying. Why in the world should I want to charm this young man, who—well, I don't want to say anything disagreeable about him, but he really isn't—" Her voice died away.

"Well, I think I know that too."

"Why?"

"Do you really want me to tell you?"

"Indeed I do."

"I think you do it to show off before me."

Show off? This is one of the great fighting words, and Millie at once lost her temper. "How dare you say such a thing to me?" she exclaimed, her eyes blazing at him.

Show off, indeed! She had not had such a thing said to her since she was out of the nursery. She wanted to hurt him just as much as she possibly could.

So she said almost sweetly, like a person really seeking information: "And do you think yourself so attractive that every one wishes to—what is it?—show off for your benefit?" She laughed gayly at the joke which she had all to herself. "Tell me, Professor Raikes; honestly, do you think yourself attractive?"

Raikes did not appear to be angry. He was leaning his elbows on the back of the chair, and he rocked slowly to and fro as he answered reflectively: "Attractive? Well, that's a woman's word—a schoolgirl's word, rather. Men don't think like that; don't ask themselves whether they are attractive or not. They ask themselves whether, if they wanted a woman, they could go out and get her."

Millie was annoyed afterward to remember that she had glanced at him to ask if she were that woman, and that his face had been as impersonal as a stone god's.

"I gather," she said, "that you feel no harassing doubt that you could."

"And to go back to what we were saying about the chief engineer," said Raikes, exactly as if she had not spoken at all; "really, he must stop drinking."

"It is much to be hoped for, as the captain was saying."

He went on in the same tone, "I leave it to you to arrange."

"What do you mean?"

"I mean that I will not dictate your method. I merely insist on the result. We often find it the best way with intelligent students."

"I think one of us is crazy," said Millie. "What have I to do with the man's drinking?"

"We went into that a moment ago."

"How can I stop him?"

"I don't have to tell you that," he answered. "Only this: That if he does not stop, if he is not back on duty to-morrow morning you will go back to New York by the first steamer out."

Millie's heart stopped a second in fear and then leaped forward a beat in anger. This was the most unjust, the most insanely unjust. Was she to be sent home because a man, almost a total stranger to her— Raikes drew himself up, patiently folded his arms, once even shut his eyes, as the torrent of her protest swept over him. She went on and on. To hold her responsible for something over which she had no control. He might as well threaten to send her home if the sea were not calm. What could she do about it, except perhaps pray?

"Well," he said, "that has been favorably considered as a method."

"How could you justify such an arbitrary and tyrannical action?" she demanded. He smiled at her long words.

"I don't have to justify myself. But I might in private explain to Doctor Norwich that you had already shown yourself to be a trouble maker."

"I a trouble maker! What trouble have I made?"

"Oh, dear me," said Raikes. "Let me think. In two days you have changed a harmless and inefficient young purser into an offensive braggart; you have started this unfortunate engineer drinking again—and that will make us a day late when every day is priceless to me; you have made Mrs. Thorley feel so inferior that I can't get an opinion from her on any of the practical matters that she really knows about; and as for Jimmy Salisbury, whose only claim was that he was docile and devoted, you have made him so critical and mutinous that he hardly consents to do what I tell him to do. Well, you may say, that I should have known just what sort of a person you were when I consented to take you. I did, but I thought you had enough intelligence to adapt yourself." He struck one fist into his open hand. "By heaven," he said, "I still think you have intelligence! That is why I am giving you this one chance!"

But Millie could not let it end there, for something was happening that had never happened before—she was being coerced by an individual. She had experienced a little impersonal coercion at school; she hadn't minded it much. The discipline exerted by an organization is bearable, but, to Millie at least, the discipline attempted by an individual was insulting, unbearable—a challenge.

"You are a little inaccurate in something you just said, Professor Raikes," she observed. "You spoke of sending me home. You can, of course, prevent my being a member of your expedition, but you really cannot send me home."

"I doubt," he replied, "whether you would enjoy knocking about Gatacosta with nothing to do."

She moved her shoulders. "I don't know that," she answered. "I might find some thing to do. I might even find some archeological work of my own."

He looked at her reflectively for an instant and then said: "I feel inclined to do something I don't often do—and that is, to offer you a piece of advice."

She gave him a slightly insolent smile, as if to say she was curious rather than interested in what he might have to say.

"It's this," Raikes went on: "Try behaving as if you were a very plain woman who wanted to make herself useful."

"I don't know what you mean."

"Think it over," he answered, and then he added: "Oh, and to save myself from the accusation of making threats which I cannot carry out, I must explain that I could have you sent home if I wanted to; at least I believe I could. The country that we are going to is somewhat different from our native land. The president of Gatacosta has the right to order any one deported whom he has reason to believe threatens the welfare of the state."

Millie laughed. "It would be difficult to persuade him, I think, that I was a danger to the state."

"Well," said Raikes, "it is true that the law was designed against revolutionists from across the borders, but he is a good friend of mine—old Munoz is—and deeply interested in the archeology of his country. If I told him that a girl had forced herself into my party, was of no use and was destroying the morale—"

"It wouldn't be true—I mean, you haven't tried me yet."

Raikes sat down in the only chair, thus ending the interview, as he replied. "Well, you have tried me—a lot."

Millie went away without answering. They were to be enemies, then. Well, she did not hate him; she rather admired his methods; only, when he did succumb, she would be obliged to make him suffer a little. And he would succumb. Of that she felt no doubt, and on that point she had rarely been mistaken. It was not just general vanity and belief in her own charms that made her think it. She knew when she exercised power over a man—knew it, often, long before he did. Sometimes, of course, the creatures freed themselves by flight or by some accident, such as the opportune arrival of a woman to whom they owed an earlier allegiance, or of a man in whom she was more interested. But there was no such chance for Raikes.

Six weeks alone—well, practically alone—with her in the jungle. Yes, she would make him suffer for some of the things he had said.

In the meantime she would remember his advice: To behave like a plain woman who wanted to make herself useful. It was a good idea.

That night at dinner her place was empty, and the chief engineer, for the first time in three nights, left his whisky untasted.

Millie would have been avenged if she had known the keenness of Raikes' curiosity to know how she had done it. He felt pleased with his own judgment. Everything, from his point of view, improved with Millie absent. The captain told not one anecdote of his children, the purser ceased to boast, Jimmy became again dutiful and humble minded, even Mrs. Thorley hazarded an opinion about the number of tins of baked beans they would need. Yet it was a little like being at home again after an exciting play; he missed the spectacle. He contented himself by arguing with Don Manuel about the legendary treasure in the so-called temple of the sun; though, as Raikes pointed out, it was more likely a moon temple. Don Manuel thought he made a mistake to waste his time digging in the Casas Viejas, when it was well known that only a few miles farther in a great treasure awaited discovery under the temple of the sun. Raikes could not tell him that he knew positively that Jenkinson had smuggled the whole thing out of the country in 1903 and that it was now in a certain museum, wrongly marked so that it could not be claimed by the government. Clever fellow, Jenkinson—dishonest, but clever. He had put the earth and stones back so that no one could guess it had been disturbed, and the jungle had grown over it in a year as if no one had ever touched it.

He did not see Millie again until the next day, their fourth at sea, when she came down to luncheon a little late. This time it was the chief engineer who wasn't there. It was understood that he was pressing the engine in order to get in early the next morning. Raikes wondered if Millie were going to sulk, but she gave him a brilliant, friendly smile.

He thought to himself: "I wonder what she has up her sleeve now. Something, I'll be bound. She has spirit and is not altogether a fool."

He settled back in his chair with a pleased feeling that the curtain was about to go up again. Then almost at once he began to be annoyed. Millie had hardly taken her seat before the captain began once more to hand out kodaks of his little family, the purser to boast, and Jimmy to explain Raikes' remarks in an apologetic tone. "What the boss means, Millie—"

The second time he did it Raikes turned on him. "Why must I be interpreted to Miss Chester, Jimmy?" he asked mildly. "Am I so unintelligible or is she unintelligent?"

Jimmy sank into a crimson sulk and did not speak again.

Mrs. Thorley, vaguely feeling something was wrong, turned to the captain and inquired how old his little girl was—a harmless question.

Raikes threw his napkin on the table and left the saloon.

Early next morning they steamed into the little harbor between the islands and the coral reefs. Fortunately there was no wind, and landing in wide rowboats was not dangerous. Millie had heard dreadful stories of high surf on the bar.

The party was to take the morning train for the interior, not to delay in the port, but there was a good deal of business with the customs and in the process of unloading the steamer and getting the stuff on the train; those long periods of waiting that seem to extend themselves especially under tropical skies. No one seemed to be really active except Jimmy Salisbury and a small, clever, brown-faced policeman from the hill country.

Once, as she sat swinging her feet on the edge of an empty freight car, Raikes came up to her with his hands in his pockets and his hat tipped well over his sharp nose.

"Like to see some sharks?" he asked, as if he were offering a great and deserved treat. What would a plain woman wanting to be useful reply?

"Oh, yes, indeed, sir," said Millie, slipping off her car and looking up at him with a sort of brilliant docility. Would he guess she was making fun of him?

He led her to the sea wall and looked over, where the water, not turquoise colored as it was farther out, but dark green, was swinging up and down on great stones, and just beyond these he pointed out dark fins weaving to and fro.

He stared at them. "Sinister creatures," he said.

Somebody called her to come and identify her trunk, and she left him staring at the water.

At one time it seemed as if they would be obliged to miss the train, though it was obligingly delaying its departure for their sakes, and then everything changed. A slim smart figure in dark blue and gold appeared, asking for the *el jefe*. It was the president's aide, come to facilitate their arrival. He was a pale handsome young man, with jet-black eyes and mustaches, arched eyebrows that rose higher at the sight of Millie. His glittering eyes kept flashing across her again and again, and then coming to rest upon her. With his arrival things began to move; motion-picture cameras were snatched from the blundering hands of curious custom officials, tins of plaster of Paris were allowed to remain unopened, a file of soldiers in dark blue duck began to pile everything they could lay their hands on—even luggage belonging to the planter and the two officials who had been on the steamer—into the best seats in the train. The conductor, in a dark brown suit and an official cap, came very courteously to ask if Raikes would like the regular train to start now; Raikes gave his assent, and after a due interval they were all in their places and the train started, the president's aide standing at attention on the platform.

The car was of the American type, and Jimmy managed to save himself a place beside Millie. She noticed at once that there was a cloud on his brow, and they had hardly left the town and plunged into the palm jungle which fringed it before he explained to her that the gold-braided fellow had stared at her very boldly and had asked whether she were Raikes' wife. No. His fiancée perhaps? No. Ah, well, they were very fortunate in having so beautiful a companion in the jungle. Jimmy thought Raikes had been angered, too, for he had offered such a fantastic explanation of her presence. He had agreed very gravely that they were fortunate; she was a witch, he said, who had the power of finding treasure; she understood, in fact, the use of the divining rod.

"I don't suppose that sophisticated young man in gold braid believed him," said Millie, but for some undefined reason she was pleased at Raikes' having said it.

"I don't suppose so," said Jimmy, "and yet the chief looked at him so sternly when he said it that he did not dare show disbelief."

The train began to puff slowly up the steep incline of the first hills. The Bentham expedition would alight in the next valley. Sometimes the train simply split itself in two and the engine hauled first one half and then the other, but this day it managed to make the grade as a unit. Presently it was jingling riotously down on the other side.

"Valverde," said the conductor. It was their station. Everything began to be taken out again—the cameras, the plaster of Paris, the canned food, the insect powder. It was now loaded on mules and small ponies. The noonday sun was incredibly hot. A dilapidated-looking motor car was waiting for the members of the party. It held four, including the driver; they were five. They wedged themselves into it, Thorley and the two women at the back, Raikes and Jimmy in front with the driver, an Indian boy. Driving half an hour over a very bad road to a wooden shed on stilts. Luncheon. Every one got out. The train of mules was far away behind them. Luncheon consisted of oranges, fried eggs, bread and Danish butter out of a tin, frijoles, and coffee with condensed milk. Then on again, up the narrowing valley over a worse and worse road, driven with a great deal of dash by the native boy, and suddenly in the forest a village—a flat-faced pink church and a square of one-storied white adobe houses—San Roberto. Their first stop, their permanent headquarters.

Here the expedition owned or rented a house, and it was still full of the equipment left from Raikes' short visit of the previous year. Millie was surprised to find it possible to spend a comfortable night, in spite of mud floors and the absence of running water. The bathroom was a room of a cemented floor with a hole in it, where it was possible to stand and throw pails of water over yourself. She slept on a canvas cot and woke in the morning to find, to her surprise, that at dawn Thorley and Jimmy had been sent forward, while Raikes stayed over a day, unpacking, collecting and making final arrangements.

All that day Millie and Mrs. Thorley worked hard, getting the house in order, selecting and to a great degree cooking the food, giving out the wash, to see it later being pounded by stones in the river and hung on barbed wire to dry.

Then Millie volunteered to arrange the storeroom—to unpack all the equipment and range it on shelves, scattering about a kind of white powder, which cockroaches—the foe, in those latitudes, to household cleanliness, as flies are in ours—refrained from crossing. Mrs. Thorley said they eat the bindings of cloth books, particularly brown books. Millie repressed a shudder.

She had never worked so hard in all her life. It was great fun. Strange how much easier it was to play a part than merely to do your duty. She tried to think of herself as a very plain girl. It was as if a fairy princess had laid aside her fairy ring or wand or rose, and had stepped down to find out what it was like to be a mere mortal. Yes, she got the idea perfectly—you thought what Mrs. Thorley would like, and if she were too tired, and where it would be most convenient for Professor Raikes to find the extra films. Of course, one would not want to do it all one's life, but for a day or so it was amusing.

Late in the afternoon she heard Mrs. Thorley say to Raikes, "Do get Millie to stop working. She'll wear herself out."

Presently, when she looked up, he was standing in the doorway watching her. She did not know quite how long he had been there. She felt a little resentful, as every one does at being watched, especially as she had been doing something rather ridiculous—lining up the cans of soup with a ruler, so that they looked very neat, like soldiers on parade. She saw he was smiling at her, but not in ridicule—not that slight one-sided smile that she hated—but the way people who like children smile when they watch them. But he went away again without a word, even of praise.

She had worked hard and felt herself to be approved, yet still she was not sure he meant to take her with him when, the next morning, he was to start for the site of the digging. But now luck was with her. An Indian who came in from camp mentioned casually that Thorley had cut his hand with his machete. Badly? *Bastante!* Mrs. Thorley took fright and announced her intention of going to see about it. Raikes obviously thought her solicitude exaggerated but could not forbid her to go, and as she was going, there was no reason for leaving Millie behind all by herself.

At three o'clock the following afternoon they were on their way. First Raikes in old khaki riding breeches, a panama hat and high-laced boots. Then Millie, riding, like him, astride, in white crash breeches and coat, with a large rough straw hat like a native woman, tied under her chin. Then Mrs. Thorley, on a Spanish sidesaddle like an armchair; then the Indian in blue overalls and nothing else.

They rode three hours through narrow paths in the forest which looked now old and worn, now as if they were merely the tracks of animals, and now as if they had been cut the day before. It was very hot. At intervals, without warning, a sheet of rain would fall perpendicularly upon them, and a moment afterward the sun would be shining so brightly that Millie would watch with interest the steam rising from Raikes' soaked khaki shirt. He had already warned her not to touch any of the branches of trees or giant leaves of plants that projected over the path. Why not? Oh, you never knew what you were disturbing. She had determined to put the idea of snakes out of her head, not to think about them unless she actually saw one. Still she could not help looking in likely places. She saw none.

Just before the short twilight of the tropics they saw a spire of gray smoke by the river they were following, and came into camp. Never were two women more warmly welcomed. Thorley, who had been a little too heroic over his accident when it first happened, had begun to worry about his wound and did not quite like to say so. Jimmy, after twenty-four hours of absence from Millie, felt that he had endured all a man could endure for the love of science. A new can of beans was opened, more oranges brought out, more coffee. The tents were rearranged.

Except on the river side, the tropical forest was like a wall about them—a terraced wall. First the line of undergrowth, then the impenetrable line of the vines, then the line of trees, and shooting through these here and there, the giant trees, whose tops were among the stars. There was something terrifying about the density of the forest. Millie felt an impulse she had never known before—the impulse to cling, to Jimmy, to Raikes, to Thorley, even to Mrs. Thorley. It occurred to her that of them all Raikes was the only one who seemed entirely at home in his surroundings; from that point of view, the best person to cling to.

She said this to Jimmy, not meaning it wholly as a compliment to Raikes. "There is something wild about him," she said—"wild in the sense of eerie and untrained."

But Jimmy wasn't amused. He shook his head gravely. "Do you know what I've been tormenting myself about these last two days—that you'd fall in love with Raikes?" and he gave her the quick, appealing glance of a person who wants to be contradicted.

"Why, Jimmy," she said, laughing, "how rude of you. I thought you were going to say because he would fall in love with me."

She expected to hear him answer that that was a matter of course, and then she was ready to explain how, really, it wasn't. But much to her surprise, when she looked at Jimmy she found he was shaking his head.

"Oh, no," he said, "I never thought he would fall in love with you. He doesn't like clever women, or—or—" Jimmy did not like to say, "ladies."

"He doesn't like equals," said Millie. "Oh, how I dislike people who get all their sense of superiority from selecting their associates from inferiors." She looked at Jimmy and suddenly thought that he ought to be freed from his bondage to Raikes. "You know, Jimmy," she said, "he rules every one by making us feel that we are all perfect fools."

Jimmy laughed nervously. He never enjoyed talking about Raikes with Millie, and yet somehow they never talked of anything else.

"Well, you know," he said gently, "he is ever so much ahead of Thorley and me—even of you, Millie," he added loyally.

"That isn't the point," the girl answered. "The point is that he deliberately makes you feel inferior; he tries to paralyze you, when a real leader, a great man, would give you a sense of your own power."

Jimmy writhed. It was perfectly true. It had always been Raikes' fault as a leader, but the boy did not want to hear it put into words.

"I somehow wish you wouldn't abuse him, Millie," he said. "I think he's a great man in spite of his irritability and scorn."

"I'm not abusing him," she answered promptly. "But I must confess,

Jimmy, I find it painful to see you so much on your knees to him. It isn't
dignified; it isn't good for you."

Jimmy answered gently that he did not think it a bad thing for a young
man to admire, even slavishly, the ability of an older one. Nevertheless, he
was aware that Millie would approve a more rebellious attitude on his part.
Was she right? Ought he to be more rebellious? It was the sort of problem
that he usually took direct to Raikes for solution. He sighed.

The next morning Mrs. Thorley announced herself dissatisfied with the
appearance of Thorley's wound. There were traces of inflammation about
the edges, she decided. In any case, she thought it should have some stitches
taken, and she took him off to see the railroad doctor who would be coming
through the village of San Roberto the next day. Thorley's departure would
leave the expedition short-handed. It was assumed without a word that
Millie should stay.

She was amused to see that Raikes disapproved of Thorley's going, although he refrained from opposing it.

"These wives," he said to Jimmy. "They love to make men behave like
babies." Jimmy was wise enough not to answer.

The ruin of their city, which still, to an untrained eye, appeared like
natural hills in the forest, began here and there to show its true character.
There was lots of work; Millie was praised for the celerity with which she
cut down a small tree while the ax was lying idle.

"But for goodness' sake don't cut off your foot or hand. We don't want to
send any more patients back to the railroad's doctor," said Raikes crossly.

Their routine was this: To get up long before it was light, to breakfast in
camp, and then begin work at the first light and take advantage of the
coolness of early morning. By half-past ten they were back in camp for
luncheon—"almuerzo," as the Indians called it—and slept and rested and
wrote notes and prepared cameras. Then, as the sun began again to decline,
they went back to work for another three hours before dark.

It was real work. Physical work. Raikes not only directed the Indians in
their digging and hewing down of trees but he worked with them. So did
Jimmy. So, to a less extent, did Millie.

She did a great deal in scraping long flat plaques of decoration free from
vines and small verdure, showing beautiful festoons of overlapping circles
and serpents and tapirs' heads. Her Spanish, less correct than Raikes', was
infinitely more flowing and understandable. She and the headman had endless talks. He told that over the shoulder of the hill was the great temple,
very rich, a buried treasure with a curse on it.

It was an idea to fire the imagination—the silver and gold cups of feasts
long over, and the gold and turquoise ornaments of women long dead. Millie
thought of it a great deal and almost every day she and the head Indian
had a few words about it. Why hadn't he dug for it himself? Oh, he had—he
and his father before him. His father had found a god—a little god, a *deosito*
—in gold. He would bring it to show the *señorita* some day. But they had
found nothing else; they were not like the *señorita*—they had no magic.

Millie disclaimed magic, too, but not finally. Who knows? One might be a sorceress without knowing it.

They had been ten days in the jungle, and though the work was interesting—oh, very interesting—Millie had begun to ask herself whether it was going to be nothing but this—getting up before dawn, working like slaves and going to bed just after sunset. They did not—though the statement would have seemed almost incredible to her—see a great deal of one another, and hardly talked at all, except she and Jimmy for a few minutes between supper and bedtime; only Jimmy was always so tired he could hardly keep his eyes open even for her. Nothing much had happened. Jimmy had been badly stung by nothing more exotic than a wasp, a lintel had almost fallen on three of the Indians, and Raikes had shot a beautiful little jaguar that had prowled round the camp at night. He had manifested none of those symptoms of hopeless passion which Millie had expected to see within a week. Now and then she found him staring at her, but more as if he were appraising than worshiping.

At first he, too, had sat with Millie and Jimmy after supper, but lately he had removed himself to a rock in the river, where he sat, smoking to keep the mosquitoes away. Millie asked Jimmy what the chief was always thinking so much about. But Jimmy explained that he didn't think he was thinking.

"He's just trying to smooth himself out so as to go through another day," he said.

"And does he need any more smoothing out than the rest of us?" she asked.

"Mercy, yes," answered Jimmy. Millie was irritated at this new habit. She wanted to talk to him about the treasure, to suggest digging there instead of here. She finally decided one evening to send Jimmy to the rock with a message. He was to say that he had been talking with the Indians and had reason to believe—

Jimmy was not gone long. He returned with the report that the boss said there was nothing in it.

Millie's straight golden-brown eyebrows drew slightly together.

"How does he know that, Jimmy?" Jimmy did not know. "You didn't ask his reasons?"

"No."

"But it doesn't make sense," answered Millie. "Go back and find out." Then, as the boy obviously hesitated, she added: "Are you afraid?"

"You might call it that. I know it would annoy him, and after all, it isn't my business. I'm here to work under him, you know, not to run the expedition."

"You are here because you have ability, which you ought to put at his disposal. There is every reason, it seems to me, Jimmy, to believe that these Indians and Don Manuel—everybody who knows the country—are right. Why should Raikes ignore it? It isn't a difficult thing to do—to investigate. And think what a help from the point of view of publicity, if he dug up a great treasure. He—the chief—would never have any more trouble raising money for his expeditions."

Jimmy was obliged to admit that every word she said was true. But he still refused to urge the plan on Raikes.

"Then I will," said Millie.

Anything rather than that. He preferred to be crushed between his two beloved millstones rather than see them grinding each other to pieces.

The next evening at supper he said, with the false ease of the timid: "You never gave me your reasons, boss, why you are so opposed to digging in the sun temple. It can't be more than ten or twelve miles away."

Raikes was surprisingly pleasant. "Didn't I, Jimmy?" he answered. "I meant to. I am not doing it because there is nothing of interest in the temple and the treasure isn't there."

"You know that?"

"Yes."

Jimmy forced himself another step: "How do you know, sir?"

Raikes was lighting a cigarette, and answered with it between his lips: "That's neither here nor there."

Jimmy was silent. Not so Millie.

"How do you mean, it's neither here nor there?" she said, speaking a little faster than she wanted to. "Jimmy and I are not fools. We have very good reasons for believing it is there. You are the leader, you have a right to decide—even if you are wrong—but we have a right to know your reasons."

Raikes had lit his cigarette, the smoke of which was curling up into his left eye; he regarded Millie malignly out of the other.

"I disagree with you," he said, and got up and left the circle.

Millie was in a fury; he was an arbitrary, tyrannical man, a second-rate nature that enjoyed the exercise of power for its own sake. No wonder he was an unknown professor in a third-rate college. "I'm sorry, Jimmy, but you know Bentham is third-rate." She believed it was their duty to make gesture of freedom, to take the two horses and go themselves and investigate. What fun it would be if they found the treasure. He'd probably steal all the glory and persuade himself it had been his plan. Would Jimmy go with her?

No, Jimmy would not.

So she quarreled with Jimmy, too, and went to bed. She did not sleep for a long time. If she could only get Raikes out of the way for a day, she knew she could persuade Jimmy to go; if Raikes would cut his hand like Thorley— She lay on her canvas cot tense with excitement, half arranging the details, half imagining the triumph.

Early in the next day's work, Raikes and Jimmy broke into a small, brightly painted room. The colors shown by flash lights were as clear as the day they had been put on—terra cotta and Nile green and lapislazuli blue. Now, indeed, Thorley, the official photographer, was missed. Suppose something went wrong; suppose they faded or the rain got at them. Millie suggested she could paint a copy of them.

It was a great success. She did it beautifully. Raikes was delighted; he hung over her paper praising her. It seemed to Millie as if she had never been praised in all her life before. This was a new sensation, flattering beyond anything that had ever been. She tried to laugh about it to Jimmy, but even from him she could not hide her beaming joy.

"This is better than any photograph!" Raikes had cried.

It was like a crown of laurel on her brow.

Perhaps after all he wasn't such a bad leader, for undoubtedly she valued his praise much more than she would have done if it had been a commoner commodity. He began to talk with her, to listen to her, to admit her to the fellowship of trained workers. She saw, with the most naïve surprise, that hard work and ability had done something with a man that beauty and charm had not been able to do. It was a turning point in her life. Contrary to her training, to her previous experience, to her reading of fiction, she found there was another aspect of her personality more valuable than her beauty. That was what he had meant by saying that pretty women were cheats. It was true—she had been cheating all her life. She had gloried in getting what she wanted by use of her money and her beauty. She called it knowing her way about. She could park her car, in the Chesters' summer place, where no one else was allowed to, because she was so sweet and had known the policeman since her childhood; she knew how to bribe Pullman conductors so that she got the compartment on a crowded train that some one else had engaged weeks before. So it was when she wanted to go to the theater at the last moment—yes, she cheated. And when she needed a partner at a dance or found herself in a tiresome house party, she looked about and took some one else's property with a smile. She cheated. But the point was not so much that she did it as that she was pleased with herself for doing it. She had cheated in coming on this expedition—her father, the president. Well, here she was. Now, for the first time in her life, she found that, with one person at least, it would be necessary to make good. With Jimmy she could go on cheating; he would think everything she did wonderful and her mere presence a benediction. But Raikes would accept nothing but the best. That was stimulating. She was extraordinarily happy; happier than she had ever been in all her life. Happy because she was using every faculty— her physical powers in the daily work, her mental abilities, for no one could be with Raikes and not use his mind—and now this other great faculty, the will, the strangest and most exciting of all.

For this she had Raikes to thank, and she was grateful to him. Not slavishly grateful like Jimmy; at least she hoped not. But how different life was. All her discontent gone. Instead of asking herself, as she unclosed her eyes, what she could do with the empty hours of the day, or why she was living at all, she sprang up in the pale dawn, with the sky overhead the color of dark silver and the stars like diamond points, knowing that there was a hard, interesting and—most important—appreciated, work to be done.

They were excavating a long series of rock-built rooms, with a façade consisting of a heavily decorated band above the lintels, and wonderfully complex pillars between the openings. Jimmy had taken the Indians round to mount to the top and cut down a huge tree which was growing on the roof, for the roots curled about the stones made clearing the stones difficult.

Millie, at some distance outside, was cleaning a stone that must have fallen from the lintels, turning it over gingerly to give the scorpions time to get away. Millie did not like scorpions and centipedes, and even little harmless lizards that moved too quick for her eye to follow them. She had just cleared the stone enough to see with interest the very gap in the decoration from which it had fallen, when she heard Raikes call from inside the first cave-like opening:

"Come here, Jimmy. This is interesting."

"He's not come back yet," she answered. "What is it?"

"This room has been painted too."

She went to him. "Mayn't I see?" she said.

She could see he was less interested in showing it to her than he would have been in showing it to an expert, but he was civil. He was standing three or four feet below her, with his flash light in one hand, and he held out the other to help her to step down over the débris of excavation to the floor of the room on which he was standing. She had just given him her hand and was stooping to step down, when something of a gray-brown color moved beside her, very quickly, and yet like a procession taking an appreciable time to pass a given point; a great snake, larger round than Millie's arm, glided out of the inner depths of the cave and hid itself in the jungle.

Strange to say, it was the first Millie had seen. She felt as if her whole body was made of a shaking, icy substance, like water just before it freezes. She gave a series of shrill little cries and hid her face in Raikes' shoulder and clung to him with all her strength, and that was a great deal. In the extremity of her terror she would have clung to Mrs. Thorley or the head Indian with the same convulsive clutch.

"Don't be frightened," said Raikes. "It's a perfectly harmless snake, and it's gone anyhow."

She answered with a little animal moan, not at all like Millie.

With the arm that he had put round her, he gave her a little shake: "Don't be a fool," he said crossly. She did not raise her head. "Don't be a fool," he repeated, this time less crossly, and Millie became aware that it was Raikes she was holding so tightly. "Don't be a fool," he said a third time, quite gently, and lifting her head, he kissed her mouth.

He had certainly succeeded in distracting her mind from her terrors. There had never been anything like it. But he gave her no time to speak; he set her on her feet outside the cave just as Jimmy came running up.

"Did you call?" he said. "I thought I heard a scream."

"You did," said Raikes. "Our lady assistant has seen a snake." He spoke in his flattest voice—the voice of a man who has never had an emotion in his life—and picking up his tools, went off to the farther side of the hill.

Jimmy was in that unfortunate stage of unrequited love when he felt personally responsible for everything disagreeable that happened to the object of his affections. He behaved now as if he had created all the snakes of the tropics.

"Oh, Millie," he said, "I'm so sorry. Oh, dear, I wish I had been here. The chief has no understanding or sympathy for that sort of fear."

"He was not unsympathetic," said Millie.

She wished passionately that Jimmy would go away and leave her in possession of this great secret, this precious and exciting possession. Raikes loved her. She was no baby; when a man kissed you like that he was yours to do with what you liked. He might not know it, but it was true. What did she like? It was for her to say. This was her triumph, and she felt triumphant as if she could have shouted and danced and flung her arms in the air, only there was Jimmy repeating that really there were not many snakes, and ten to one she would not see another, but that he would stay there until she quieted down.

"Quieted down?" she said. "I'm perfectly quiet. Do go back to your work, Jimmy, and let me finish this drawing before the light fades."

He went obediently, not knowing that her hands were shaking so that she could hardly hold the brush with which she was pretending to paint.

When he had disappeared round the corner she gave up the pretense of work and sat waiting for Raikes' return. She had no doubt of his coming. But she was glad he was giving her time to conquer this wild, surging excitement, like ultimate chaos, which was going on inside of her. She had many insults to avenge; she recalled them one by one—this was the man who had not wanted her to come, who had threatened to have her deported, who had told her to behave like a plain woman who wanted to be useful. Well, she had, and see what had come of it. She listened. She could not hear the sound of his spade. No, he would not be working; he was thinking or already softly making his way back to her. She wondered what he would say. She would look at him steadily, calmly. He would not be able to tell if it were anger, reproach or injured pride. Perhaps he would apologize abjectly—an undefended girl, and under his care. Her lips curved cruelly. And yet she almost hoped he wouldn't be abject. If, on the other hand, he came to her and took her in his arms again— Ah, that would be more difficult. In that case—

The light was failing fast. Why didn't he come? At any minute now the others would be coming back, would get there before him. His only chance. Was he a fool?

Evidently he was, for now it was too late. Jimmy was coming home too. She could hear him singing far off. He must have sung in his school choir, for he was familiar with many hymn tunes, and he was singing one now:

> "Now the day is over,
>   Night is drawing nigh,
>   Shadows of the evening
>   Steal across the sky."

He wandered away into the second in a good bass.

The other one was coming too. She could see him now. He had his spade over his shoulder and had hung his hat on it. She saw that he would have time for a word, nothing more than that, before Jimmy was within earshot. She sat up straight, waiting, wondering what that word would be. He stopped. Her eyes met his expectantly.

"Well," he said, "aren't we going to have any supper to-night?" He spoke in a tone of courteous irritation; one of the most trying of all his tones.

III

It took Millie fully twenty-four hours to be sure that Raikes intended to ignore the incident—ignore it more thoroughly than was involved in not speaking of it. He had apparently wiped it out of his consciousness. His eye met hers as steadily, his voice was as even when he spoke to her, his whole manner was as completely impersonal as if his lips and hers had never met. Strange to say that of all the possibilities she had thought of in the hour she sat waiting for his return she had never thought of this.

Did he imagine she was the sort of girl to whom it made no difference whether you kissed or not? It was the insolence of the attitude that maddened her. Perhaps he thought he had done her an honor. And she was so helpless. If he did not speak of it, pride and strategy alike prevented her doing so. If she could have thought of some cutting phrase in which to bring the subject up she would have had work finding an opportunity. They were never alone. She could not pursue him to his work to ask him—what? His intentions? They had already been made clear. His intention was to forget.

She was driven to the eminently unsatisfactory revenge of secretly despising him. She called him "chief" in a voice like honey, and a look that challenged him to notice its contempt. He managed to ignore both. So did Jimmy, who thought things had never gone so well.

"I knew you'd get to like the chief," he said one evening.

"Like him?" said Millie. She thought, if Jimmy weren't such a goose that sentence might have alarmed her.

"It's wonderful that he's so much interested in your painting. He respects you as a fellow worker. That's grand." The boy laughed with some embarrassment as he went on: "To be honest, Millie, I was awfully nervous when you said that about expecting me to expect him to fall in love with you. Do you remember?"

"It was indeed a mad thought," answered Millie.

Jimmy did not quite like her tone. "I don't mean it sounded mad to me, as you know very well. I only meant that I was pretty sure that Raikes wouldn't see it like that. I mean, because he never seems to be much interested in women."

"No?"

"And anyhow, it's better this way, isn't it?" Jimmy went on. "More flattering too. Any fellow might fall in love with your beauty, Millie, but to have a man like Raikes accept you as an assistant—"

"It quite turns one's head," said Millie.

That evening the Indian, who had gone back to San Roberto, where he lived, showed her a small gold god, which he had brought to convince her skepticism. His father, he said, had found it twenty years ago in the ground below the steep side of the pyramid of the sun temple. He knew there was more where that came from. Would she not speak to the patron and tell him, persuade him? A day's work might make them all rich.

Millie took up the heavy little haloed figure, with its crude upturned feet, its square shoulders, and stared at it. It was an almost irrefutable piece of evidence. She thought of showing it to Raikes, but she couldn't do it; she could not reopen that subject. Jimmy could though. She would speak again to Jimmy.

It was inevitable that, feeling as she did to Raikes, she and Jimmy should have been drawn closer together. Every evening now, after supper, they sat an hour or so by the fire, smoldering to keep mosquitoes away, and talked of their work and themselves, but for the most part, of Raikes.

"Now, Jimmy, what is the use of saying there isn't any treasure there when there was this?" she said, and put the heavy little image into his hand and closed his fingers on it. Her touch was persuasive. Jimmy opened his hand reluctantly and stared at the god, lying on its back in such an ungodlike manner.

Yes, he admitted there was no doubt of the authenticity of that. Well, then, would Jimmy show it to the chief? Jimmy shook his head; not so much in refusal as indicating that she didn't know what she was asking of him.

"Don't you think that he might admit for once in a lifetime that he was wrong? No? He must never, never be wrong, never have made the slightest error of judgment from the cradle to the grave?"

She knew that she made Jimmy suffer when she talked like this, but, she said to herself, it was for his good if she could free him, could make him more of a person, less timidly subservient. But he would not meet her in the open, and she chivvied him from vagueness to vagueness, from ambush to ambush, as strong natures will chivvy weak ones. It did not occur to her that if she succeeded in making him do her will it was only a shift of masters for him.

"Oh, Jimmy," she exclaimed at last in desperation, "will you never look at the thing honestly? Do you or do you not believe that there is treasure under the sun temple?"

Jimmy, like a man being led to execution, admitted that he thought it likely. Well, probable. Well, almost certain now.

"Then this is the situation," said Millie: "You believe that there is treasure there—you hold the proof of it in your hand—but you do not intend to tell the leader of your expedition of your knowledge. Why? Because you dread an outbreak of bad temper. That is cowardly, Jimmy, my dear—cowardly—and if you will let me say so, really disloyal. You were talking about loyalty a few minutes ago—that I wasn't loyal to him as chief—but I assure you I should consider it treacherous to do what you're doing. Suppose, after we go home, some one else finds it—as of course they will—and gets a huge appropriation from the Carnegie people or from one of the great universities. How will he feel if he finds we knew about it all the time, but were afraid to tell him for fear of his irritability?"

"It isn't just like that, Millie," the boy answered, speaking with some difficulty. "I'm afraid of his outbursts, but more because they wreck him so afterward. He hates being like that more than we hate it. Yes, I know— I know that's saying a great deal, but it's true. I really think he's a genius, Millie, but he's utterly unfit for dealing with stupid things and idiotic people, and the world is made up of them. The only way he can get on at all is for some stupid person like me to make everything as easy as possible for him to go his way; not to question, but just to coöperate. I know he's irritable and unreasonable, but I feel sorrier for him than for any one I ever saw, and I won't create a situation in which I know he is going to behave badly."

She tried to stop him, but too late; Raikes had been within earshot and had heard all of the last sentence—only the last, not all the admiration and affection that had gone before.

"Has it come to this—to be pitied by Jimmy Salisbury!" said Raikes, standing scowling at them in the firelight. "For I am afraid there is no doubt that this unreasonable individual who must be saved from behaving badly is my unhappy self."

As Millie looked at him a feeling like repulsion swept over her, not at the man himself but at the evil spirit that had suddenly taken possession of him. She had seen people in wild fits of temper before and had not minded, but there exhaled from Raikes at this moment a bitterness of hate that was like an icy, impenetrable cloud about him. There was something terrible, almost indecent, about it. If this was what Jimmy meant by his behaving badly he was fully justified.

"Might I ask you to explain why you feel sorry for me?" he went on.

Jimmy, almost incapable of speech and quite incapable of thought, stammered that he was sorry for him because he wasn't happy.

"Happy!" said Raikes with a sort of shout. "Of course I'm not happy! Did you ever know any one with the least intelligence who was—any one who could look forward, or back, for that matter? If you're going about ignorantly pitying every one who isn't happy you'll have your hands full."

One of the qualities that differentiated Millie from a million other girls like her was a certain ideal of courage that she kept before her. Because she was now afraid of the poison in the air, she made up her mind to speak, especially as Jimmy was in a despair that rendered him mute.

"You would understand better," she said, "if you had heard all that Jimmy—"

The sunken, piercing eyes turned on her for an instant. "Would you be good enough to stop trying to interpret Jimmy to me and me to Jimmy?" he said. "We have neither of us, I think, asked for your good offices and they have not, so far, been very successful." Then he went on addressing Jimmy alone: "I don't suppose you know how much opposition I met with when I proposed taking you on this expedition. It was said that you were actually the worst student in the department—dull and industrious, the most hopeless material of all. But I insisted, not so much because I differed with the opinion of my colleagues as because I found in you something solid, docile and obedient, something I could count on—or so I thought. And now I find you gossiping about me behind my back, frightened into idiocy by my approach. Fearing I shall behave badly! According to whose standards? Yours?"

Jimmy was suffering horribly. It was terrible to see, and yet it was not in order to save Jimmy that Millie now rose to her feet. Jimmy was suffering, yes, but Raikes was like a man destroying himself. She could not bear it. She, who had always been the first to throw a little tow on any fire already burning, suddenly felt she would do or say anything to stop this scene. She got up and, going to Raikes, she put one hand on his shoulder, and with her other she took his hand, which was clenched at his side.

"Don't talk to him like that," she said gently.

He withdrew his shoulder from her touch, and opening his fist, cast off her hand as if his fingers had been entangled in a spider's web. Otherwise he did not notice her at all, but went on to Jimmy:

"Of course I know why you are making an idiot of yourself, whose influence is guiding your uncertain steps toward liberty, but what a fool—what a fool you are to have let a woman like that destroy you. I don't mean, destroy you as a flaming sword destroys." He cast one glance at her over his shoulder. "I mean, destroy you in the sense that a clumsy baby destroys its toys without knowing that it's doing any mischief at all."

With this he left the firelit circle as quickly as he had appeared in it, and going into his own tent, dropped the flap. Jimmy did not move. He sat still with his elbows on his knees and his hands on each side of his brow. Millie stood erect with her head back and her eyes closed. She felt strangely tired. Yes, that was it—poisoned by all this hate and bitterness.

Then she heard Jimmy speaking to her: "Thank you, Millie. You did your best. It was brave of you."

"Brave of me! I'm not afraid of this man."

He did not answer in words, but took her limp hand hanging at her side and kissed it. Suddenly Millie found herself shaking off his hands as if her fingers had become entangled with a spider's web, and heard her voice saying: "I'm sorry, Jimmy, but I can't bear men who cry."

"Oh," said Jimmy with a gasp. It was his first knowledge that his face was wet. Millie turned away and went into her tent and dropped the flap. It only needed that—that she, too, should be brutal to poor Jimmy. It was Raikes who had made her like that. How dreadful to go through the world exhaling a poison that made every one bitter and cruel! How she hated him! She could not sleep thinking of wild, stinging sentences to tell him what she thought of him, nor was it much better when this phase passed and she found herself crying with pity for him, who, as Jimmy had said, was suffering more than they. He must be so lonely, he must be so wretched. It was a long time since Millie had either cried or spent a sleepless night.

They were all up and at breakfast at their usual hour, each manifesting their distress according to their physical temperament—Jimmy looking pasty; Millie looking pale eyed and faded, but faded as a child is faded, looking younger than usual; Raikes was the color of old ivory, and his eyes, sunk farther than ever in his head, blazed sullenly.

They went about their work in silence, like sick people or people under some doom. In civilization they would have parted and each one gone his separate path, seeking comfort of forgetfulness in his own way. But buried in the jungle, pledged to do a piece of work, they could only withdraw themselves mentally one from the other.

This went on for two days. The third day Millie saw with surprise that Raikes was beginning to pick up the pieces. He did it in the only way possible to him—by rousing their intellectual interest. He began talking at luncheon that day about the legendary aura that surrounds all science, but especially the science of archeology. He went over the whole field of the origins of the race, from the myth of Atlantis to the indigenous prehistoric culture, to the caves of Western China and the deserts of Tibet. Jimmy listened, revived, responded and forgot his injuries. Millie listened, too, with interest, but she could not forget, not so much his insults as the fact that he destroyed something new and wonderful in her, something kind and noble that could, she felt, never rise again. She felt as if she were made of stone.

The morning of the fourth day, Thorley appeared, cheerful, eager for work and absolutely insensitive to atmosphere. It was just what was needed. Raikes lost all his gloom showing Thorley the new, painted rooms. The three men drew intellectually together. Once more Millie found herself an outsider.

After the noonday meal, when Thorley and Jimmy had already gone back to work, Raikes approached her. He said very simply: "I think you had better go back to San Roberto with the Indian who guided Thorley in."

"He's started already," answered Millie.

"Yes, but on one of the horses you could catch him in five minutes. It won't take you long to get your things together?"

"Oh, no." He was evidently surprised at her acquiescence. She was surprised herself. She moved toward her tent to get her saddlebags, and then turned to him. "Is there anything special you want me to do in San Roberto?"

"No. Whatever Mrs. Thorley suggests. We shall be in and out, you know. Go home, if you want to, or stay with her—either one."

"I see," said Millie, and went into her tent. When, a few minutes later, she came out again he had gone. She heard the sound of a spade where he usually worked.

She was entirely alone in the camp. Far, far up over her head, like a blue eye looking down a green well, she could see the heavy cerulean of the sky, and a few yards away she could hear the hurrying, rippling river. Well, she was a failure and was being sent ignominiously home, she who had come out so confident of victory. Strange to say, she felt no protest, no revolt at the humiliation; it was all swallowed up in a general despair. She loved Raikes; at least that was probably the nearest word. She had always thought of herself as having the priceless gift for the right man—her love. But it was no gift at all to him, and to her it was just a pain and weakness and involvement. If she could get away from his physical presence it would be a different kind of pain, and that would be a sort of rest. No, she was not sorry to go.

She untied one of the horses, and mounted, throwing her saddlebags across his withers. The path home was along the river. So, she suddenly thought, was the path to the sun temple, only in the opposite direction.

She paused, thinking it over while her horse rubbed his nose on his knee. It was not much after noon. It took three hours to get to San Roberto; she had two hours extra before dark—an hour to go and an hour to come. No harm would be done by her riding an hour up the river instead of down. She might be able to satisfy herself; she could at least see the temples; she would lose some of this sense of the flatness of the whole thing, now that she was going home. She turned her horse's head away from the trail home.

The river curved away from the site of the city in a great flat arc, and along the near side of this the water was shallow and made a pathway. Millie had understood very clearly from the Indian that you rode four hundred varas along the river and then turned in through the jungle where there was a path. Except for the rippling of the water, everything was quiet; there was no wind even in the high, remote tops of the trees, which she could see when she looked along the alley of the river. Now and then a monkey would chatter, but except for this there was no sound. She was not afraid, not conscious of any real danger, yet just enough conscious of the adventure of her action to restore her self-respect. She knew that the risk she took was the risk of being lost; at least, that is what every one would say, but going this way—along the river—she would only need to find the river again—not a difficult task—and then ride back along it to the camp.

If only she had not made such a fool of herself about that snake. "Don't be a fool—don't be a fool—don't be a fool," and then he had kissed her. If it were only to be done again she could say quite calmly, "Oh, look at that dear little brown snake. How quickly it moves," but she had seen it so suddenly, as she was stepping down with her hand in his. What had been his emotion when he kissed her—pity, contempt? How did he dare go about as if it had never happened?

Every now and then she passed little trails into the jungle, but very small and overgrown; made, she thought, by the small animals of the jungle —red deer, or even perhaps tapir. She would not call them paths. She went on and on, and then at last—yes, a real path and the traces of bare feet in the sands of the river. This was what the Indian had meant. Four hundred varas? More like a mile. She turned her horse's head and entered a narrow path inclosed like a green corridor.

The beauty of her scheme was its simplicity. The temple of the sun stood alone on its pyramid, approached by stairs on three sides, but the fourth, the Indian told her, was a sheer descent to a well or a pit, where the victims of sacrifice, in all their gold and feathers and jewels, had been thrown. The gold and jewels, he said, were still there. You did not need to climb the pyramid, to cut a slow way up the ruined steps. You went to the foot of that sheer side and dug—that was all. It was not impossible that she herself, feeling about with the machete that she had stuck in her saddle straps, might turn up some little object of clay or copper or even gold which would serve to change Raikes' stiff unbelief and make him praise her once more.

Again she thought she heard something moving near her. But there were no fourfooted beasts to be feared. The timid little deers, the jaguar, most unlikely to attack in the daylight, tapirs, running away in herds. What could be following her? A gigantic snake? That happened only in dreams. Still, her heart began to beat thickly. The tropical forest is always more or less menacing, hardly more when she was alone like this on an adventure than when doing her work in camp. It is a thick wall about you that does not protect but does cut you off; it does not screen you but myriads of unseen enemies, the denizens of the forest, while the forest itself waits, when the deadly work is done, to roll over you, to strangle, poison and, finally, bury you in verdure.

Yes, something was coming. She turned her horse to meet it. Raikes rode round a bend in the path, and the two horses neighed cheerfully at each other.

"You're going the wrong way," he said. It was impossible to tell from his tone whether he meant to give her directions for the road or reproof for disobedience.

To avoid all danger of appearing caught doing wrong, she explained her plans. She had two hours; she believed in the existence of the treasure—

He cut her short. "Listen to me," he said. "I know the man who found it, who took it out of the country. I know where it is at home. I have gone all over it. I know from his reports that there is nothing left, unless, possibly, at a level we could not reach in a month. Will nothing persuade you that I know my business?" She was silent, taking in the fact that she had been wrong once more, and he added less pleasantly: "And now, will you be so good as to go back to San Roberto at once?"

"Yes, yes, yes," she returned, but without moving. "I can imagine how well pleased you feel with yourself. Everything has worked out exactly as you thought. What confidence you must have gained in your own judgment. You said I would not be useful to your expedition, and now you are sending me back, a complete failure. You said I would not learn, and it appears I haven't. I opposed you about this treasure and I was utterly ignorant and wrong about it. You must be triumphant."

"Triumphant?" he said. He was looking at her steadily, with his head a little back and his eyes even more like embers than the young engineer's on the boat.

"But in your place," she went on, "I shouldn't be triumphant; I should be ashamed, utterly ashamed of myself. You destroy good things in every one in order to protect and nourish this uncontrolled, egotistical irritability of yours. I don't say I'm very valuable, but for the first time in my life I was doing something, happier than I have ever been, better, if you like, than I have ever been, and because you overhear something that wounds your pride you come slashing down like a big man with a sword among children, and cut us all down—Jimmy, who will never really regain his self-respect after all those horrors you said to him, and I, who will have to go home now and tell all the people who wanted me to fail that I have failed. Any one with a trace of human kindness would have helped me, or would at least have let me alone, but you have always wanted me to fail, and now that you have accomplished it, you are triumphant—triumphant."

"You think I feel triumphant?"

"Yes, I do."

He turned his head away from her and stared out into the forest, and she noticed for the first time how white and worn and thin he looked, like a man who had just been through some illness or long anxiety.

"Well," he said, "for a woman who understands wounding the human heart, you don't understand reading it very accurately. I am not, believe me, triumphant." He paused, and then he added: "Jimmy's self-respect can be restored, I think. He is very sane and generous minded. And as for you, life will be all opportunities for you. You need not worry."

"Easy for you to say," she retorted. "It is the only one that I ever have had that I cared for, and you have ruined it."

"Perhaps," he said, "you will find it different when you go home; perhaps better things will come to you."

Her golden-brown eyebrows ran up. "Oh, you have molded me, you mean? You have taught me these better things?" Her tone was like steel. He blinked his eyes and for an instant gave her the impression of a man in pain; then it was gone, and she went on: "You might have taught me. Why not? You are older and presumably wiser, but—"

"Almost old enough to be your father."

"But you are too cruel to teach."

"I am not cruel," he said. "I can be exceedingly kind and tender-hearted when great events are stirring." He suddenly smiled, as if he knew how absurd a plea this was, even before Millie answered quickly:

"But great events so seldom stir."

"Well, that's the fault of the general scheme, not mine," he returned. She felt, without understanding why, he had the tone of a man "jesting, as martyrs do, upon the sword that slays them." She was silent, and in the pause they both heard the sound of movement in the dense growth about them. Their eyes met, their faces grew tense. Raikes raised himself in his stirrups, craning his neck, and his hand went back to his belt where his revolver was strapped in its case. But he never drew it. Out of the forest all about them darted small, ragged, unshaven men, a dozen or more. They seized the bridles of the horses; they caught Raikes' hand and disarmed him.

It happened so quickly, it was all so strange; the men were so little, like gnomes or children dressed up as bandits, that Millie was more startled than frightened. Some of them were obviously Spanish, some Indians, most of mixed blood. Some were in torn uniforms, some in blue overalls, some in the checked trousers and short jacket of the peon's Sunday wear, some were barefooted and some wore wooden shoes. All were armed, and cartridge belts strapped about their waists were filled.

"What are they?" said Millie over their heads to Raikes.

"I wish I knew," he answered.

"Do you suppose we are in danger?"

"I rather fancy we are," he answered. "It seems absurd, though, doesn't it?"

Raikes was made to dismount, and one of the men climbed proudly into his saddle. Millie was allowed to ride, two men at her bridle. The horses' heads were turned inland and the procession moved on. They were going, if Millie's information was correct, straight for the pyramid of the sun.

Raikes walked along, turning the whole strange incident over in his mind, and at last addressed the man beside him in his most courteous Spanish.

"Do me the favor of telling me, señor," he said. "Are you not the men of Avilla?"

The form of speech seemed to be right, for the man replied that the señor had the right of it. Well, Raikes reflected, for good or evil, he now knew the truth. Avilla was a bandit. He had heard the president speak of him. He had been an army officer, had been in an unsuccessful revolution under Munoz's predecessor, and made his living by blackmail, raiding lonely haciendas and by an occasional murder. A disagreeable situation, not desperate, if it were not for Millie. He wished they did not all admire blondes so much. If she'd been dark-haired and ten times as beautiful he'd have felt safer. He did not like to talk too freely to her; there was always the chance that some of the men might have picked up enough English to understand. Yet he ought to warn her to stick by him if she could, and not to try and charm the bandit into letting her go. She ought to be remote and dignified; perhaps she had better be his wife. That might be safer for her, or possibly not. He turned the possibilities over in his mind. It wasn't going to be easy.

They went on and on; the pace was slow. In about an hour they came to a great open space in the midst of which rose the majestic ruin of the temple of the sun—a great green mound on which, here and there, the masonry of the stairs could be seen through the mantel of green. Under the sheer wall were several huts of bamboo thatched with banana leaves, and as they approached they could see a man standing in front of one of these—obviously Avilla.

He was a small man according to northern standards, dressed in worn riding breeches, puttees and low shoes, showing a triangle of bare insteps. He wore a khaki tunic which had probably once belonged to an American officer in some earlier military style. Belted about his waist was the inevitable machete—the fork and knife, the ax, the walking stick of the American tropics. Avilla was standing with one small hand on his hip and the other shielding his eyes while he stared along the path. Raikes was halted with most of the little band at a distance of perhaps twenty yards, just out of earshot, but Millie, still on her horse, was led up to where the bandit was standing. Raikes watched the scene in an agony of apprehension.

Avilla stood motionless for several seconds, a proud, rigid little figure;

then he swept off his hat. Raikes could see his small neat features, his pale oval face, the long black mustache and bright beadlike black eyes—a man probably counted very handsome by the women of his race. He had the manner of a man who believes himself successful with women. Like most criminals in most countries, he was evidently intensely vain, but Millie, of course, would never think of that. If she wounded his male vanity they were lost.

Straining his ears, he could not hear a word. They were of course speaking Spanish. Avilla was saying something that surprised Millie but did not apparently alarm her. What could it be? She was refusing, denying, shaking her head; he was insisting.

Raikes made up his mind this must not go on. Heaven only knew what a girl like Millie might say or do toward her own destruction. He decided to join the conference.

"*Venga conmi,*" he said to his captors, and strode forward, carrying them with him. He succeeded in getting within speaking distance of Avilla, and began loudly, with as much dignity as a man can display who has three men almost tearing off his shirt and a fourth clinging about his neck: "What does this mean, Señor Avilla?"

"Ah," said Avilla, his bright eyes flashing. "You know me. Men still speak of Avilla, do they?"

"What do you want with us?" said Raikes. The four little bandits had dropped off him now and were engaged in holding his arms back, two on each side.

Avilla smiled, showing beautiful even teeth. "I do not want you at all, *señor*; I want only *blanchita.*"

Raikes' heart sank at this news. In a country where courtship is carried on mostly with the eyes, sudden passions are common. He had only a second to make his decision, and he made it.

"You do not expect me to allow my wife to be captured without coming to her assistance?" he said. Well, it might be a protection to her.

"She is your wife?"

Raikes bowed and, as he bent his head, caught a distinct twinkle in the eyes of Millie.

"You are a brave man," said Avilla. Millie almost laughed at this, but Raikes scowled at her. And then at Avilla.

"What do you mean?" he asked angrily.

"I would not marry a witch, however beautiful," said Avilla. "But since she is your woman, tell her to exercise her power."

"I don't know what you mean."

Avilla made the quick gesture with his forefinger before his nose which indicates the desire to clear away all clouds of misunderstanding.

"Ah, *señor,*" he exclaimed, "let us have no more of that. I know the *blanchita* has the power of finding gold. Under our feet there is gold, much treasure. Let her find it and she shall go free."

Raikes laughed. "You are too much of a man of the world to believe such tales," he said.

"I have your word. You have said it yourself," answered Avilla, beginning to scowl in his turn.

"It was a joke," answered Raikes, cursing, as he had so often had occasion to do before, his effort of amusing himself when talking to dull people.

"And was it a joke that she found gold already, digging. A snake came and brought her the secret and then she found the gold. We know. I know," said Avilla, drawing himself up until his little heels almost left the solid earth.

"Listen to me," said Raikes sternly. "This is all to no purpose. You cannot imagine that you can detain two American citizens, people of position"— "*Gente conicidá*" was his phrase—"and not suffer for it."

Avilla threw back his head and gave a sort of bark. "I suffer!" he exclaimed, striking his breast once sharply. "How can I suffer? Who talks any more of Avilla? I hear everywhere that he has ceased to exist, that his band is no more, that under the good rule of that black pork Munoz, he has emigrated to Costa Rica, has been seen in Honduras."

"And if this lady and I are not back to-morrow," said Raikes, "the United States Government—"

"Will be sorry to learn that two of their citizens have wandered into the jungle and lost themselves. You will be searched for, *señor*, but your bodies will never, never be found. You know the Indian proverb: Who can find what the jungle desires to hide? Your horses—though, God knows, we need horses—they may be found, riderless, but you will have disappeared."

"People do not disappear," said Raikes.

"Many have disappeared into our jungle, leaving no trace. But even if a trace should be found, there is nothing to connect it with me. Indeed, Munoz struts about priding himself that he has rid his country of me; he cannot now admit that I have been here."

"*Mira, señor*," said Raikes, interrupting. "If this lady and I are not back in camp to-morrow the United States Government—"

"Will act—will act in time," said Avilla; "will send marines and guns and demand reparation. Of whom? Of that black pork who now destroys this country with his cruelty. It will destroy him. Let it. Then I shall return."

"Do not think that you and your band will go free—" Raikes began, but Avilla raised his hands like a priest blessing a congregation, and interrupted:

"All this talk is for nothing, *señor*," he said. "If the *blanchita* will find gold for me I will pledge my word you shall be free in twenty-four hours. I shall have what I need to go away. If she will not you will both die. I give you until the dawn to think about it."

Raikes saw Millie give them each in turn a quick look, as if for the first time she saw some hint of danger in the situation.

"You are mad; you are destroying yourself," Raikes began, but Avilla would not listen. He flung his right hand across his face and turned on his heel. "*Es finito*," he said.

"I don't suppose he means what he says," Millie whispered.

"I hope not," he answered. It had always been his belief that the truth was best, and he could not bring himself to deceive her now. Then he was dragged back, so that, though he was not out of sight of Millie, still on her horse, further conversation was impossible.

He felt not the least doubt that Avilla would have them shot in the morning. Human life was unimportant to a man like that, and to Raikes himself it was clear that it was safer for the bandit to kill them and go, leaving no trace, than to let them go free, with the inevitable sequence of his own pursuit. Really, as a logical man, he had not been able to argue against it. He felt doom in the air.

There seemed to him only one possible chance—the arrival of Thorley with some sort of supporting force. That Jimmy and Thorley would follow them, he felt sure, but probably not until daylight the next day—an hour, perhaps, after their death. Even if he came at once—and Raikes really could not see why he should—if he came alone, as would be most natural, he would be captured, as they had been. If, on the other hand, he followed and came upon evidence that there had been a number of men involved, he would go back and attempt to get help from the president or the local police, but that would all be much too late. They would not be easy to follow anyhow, for he and Millie had both ridden their horses through the shallow water at the river's edge and there were no footmarks. And then Jimmy would have no reason to think of this particular danger; there had been no talk whatsoever of bandits. Three years before, when he, Raikes, had been in Gatacosta, there had been talk of Avilla and his raids, but lately no one had mentioned him. What would Jimmy think? Probably that he and Millie had ridden off together—back to the town perhaps—and the boy would be uncomfortable and resist an impulse to follow them. Or if he began to suspect something wrong he would think that they had fallen into a subterranean well, like that German fellow in 1880. Thorley would certainly think that, if he were consulted, for it was one of his nightmares. All too late, all too late.

The only chance was to make an escape in the darkness, and as he thought this—for the short dusk of the tropics was almost over—he saw that a great white three-quarters moon was riding over the tree tops as bright as a searchlight.

Avilla's plan for keeping them safe was simple. He made them mount the sixty feet of steep and partly ruined stairs that led to the remains of the old temple on the top of the pyramid. None of his men would venture on this haunted ground, but it was not necessary. The prisoners could not have descended unobserved in the flooding moonlight, and if they could have been invisible the noise of falling stones would have betrayed them. A better prison could hardly have been devised.

Avilla did not even trouble to convey these orders to them himself. Raikes saw him wrapping himself in an enormous cloak, throwing it over his shoulder with a graceful swing, preparatory, apparently, to retiring to his hut. The second in command ordered them up the steps; hard going it would have been even by daylight. Millie went up easily, touching her hands now and then. Raikes noticed how conspicuous she was in her light-colored riding clothes. Halfway up he glanced back, to see that two men with rifles had taken up a position at the foot of the stairs. The sky overhead was cloudless, the rich deep blue of the tropical sky by moonlight; not a chance that clouds would rise to put out that moon.

"Can you do it?" he asked.

She didn't trouble to answer but asked instead: "Do you think there are any snakes up there?" He looked toward the three low lozenges of black that were the entrances to the temple, and replied that he was sure there were not.

"I wish I were," said Millie.

He had matches in his pocket, and when they reached the platform on which the little temple opened he was able to reassure her. The space was small and damp, hardly five feet high, but it had been cleaned out recently, and the bare stones were still tightly fitted and admitted no possibility of snakes.

They sat down in silence in the shadow of the overhanging cornice of the temple, with their feet on the top step. The night was mild and very still. A smell of rich damp earth came to them from the jungle, of wet green growth. The tall trees shut out their view, high as they were, but the higher peaks of the volcanoes in the interior thrust themselves above even the tallest trees, a translucent gray in the moonlight.

"Well," said Raikes in his coolest, flattest voice, "I must say the world is making a very fine farewell appearance."

"You think he really means it?" she asked.

"I can't lie to you. I think he really does."

There was a silence, and in the dark she knew that he was listening for the faintest sign that would give him a clew to her state of mind.

"Isn't it queer?" she said. "I'm not frightened. I always thought I would be when I read about queens—Anne Boleyn and Mary Stuart—but I'm not. I used to think I couldn't stand it, I couldn't face it. I'm only excited terribly—terribly excited."

"Yes." He stretched out his long legs straight in front of him. "Death is exciting, even other people's."

"I hope it won't come over me at the last moment. I hope I shall behave well," she murmured.

"Oh, you'll behave perfectly, just to annoy them. It's about the only fun left. Just ignore them, the swine. I may allow myself to laugh at them."

Another long silence. The moon came out over the tall umbrella-topped trees, and Raikes, looking up at the stars, not wholly extinguished by the flood of light, found himself thinking of his own subject and how cleverly the old builders had managed to orient their temples—this one to the rising sun of midsummer, but some to the more complex movements of the evening star.

"Do you think we really go on?" said Millie. "That our souls live?"

"I can't see it," he answered. "I hope to heaven I don't. I never have been able to see how such common, base animal processes as birth and death can be the links with eternity. At the same time"—he paused—that gesture Millie knew so well—reached back for a cigarette, lit it, and went on—"at the same time, I have always been inclined to the belief that time is not a sequence as it appears, that it is a complete static whole. In which case, of course—"

"I can't get much comfort out of that," said Millie.

"My poor child."

Her breath trembled a little at his pity, and they both knew it was dangerous. The great excitement of approaching death was like an intoxication and made her long to tell everything that came through her mind, and what was always in her mind was the fact that she loved him. She wanted to tell him. She remembered years ago, when she was seventeen, at a house party a game had been played: What would you do if you knew you were going to die to-morrow? No one had played it honestly except one girl; the boys had all shaken their heads and intimated that they would do things too terrible to tell, and the girls spent their time trying to make them tell; all but one girl, who said simply she would tell the man she loved that she loved him. There had been an idea that he was present and was indeed actually being told. Millie hadn't thought of that girl for years, but she thought of her now. For she wanted passionately to tell Raikes that she loved him, but she knew she must not do it.

In the first place, with her mind racing, as it was, like a disordered engine, she wouldn't tell him right, and then she knew he wanted peace; he wanted to sit there in a godlike calm, awaiting death. In this moment he wanted an equal companion, not a groveling lovesick girl. It would be to him a painful scene, possibly even an ugly one. This way she would have something; the other way, nothing. Nothing, at least, except for her the comfort of his physical touch, for then she could cling to him and put her head on his shoulder. He could hardly refuse her that, but he would not like it; he would not respect her as much as he did now. A meaningless physical contact, or this immensely significant spiritual communion? She firmly chose the latter, but her heart ached for the other. She remembered how, as a child, she had been comforted from imaginary terrors at night by the mere feeling of her mother's arms about her. That was really all she wanted now. Well, she wouldn't take it. She set her will against it. She took her decision. She was a woman who could abide by a decision.

She thought of her parents. Oh, dear, so much to regret there, such senseless sinful cruelty on her part. What a hard, horrible shell had overlaid her love for them so that she had never shown it at all, had never felt as she felt it now, too late, too late.

She said aloud, "I want to write to my mother."

He gave a sound between a groan and a laugh. "You think they'll forward it?"

No, of course not. Her heart gave a sickening drop. No one would ever know what had happened to them. Why did it make it worse?

"I'm sorry," she said simply. "It seems to me now that I've always been terrible to my parents."

"I shouldn't worry about that," said Raikes. "They probably loved you all the more because you were difficult, and you know the people who get the fun out of a relation are the people who love, not the ones who are loved." She wanted desperately to ask how he knew that, and after a minute she did, but he did not answer.

Instead he said, "I believe there might be a chance, if you left a paper up here, that some day it would be sent to your family. I doubt if these fellows would have sense enough to search the place after us. Write it anyhow."

He had no paper in his pocket, but a used envelope on which he had written a list, which said: "Pair of stockings, bottle of iodine and have knife sharpened." But cutting the envelope open, the wrong side was available.

"Isn't it funny?" said Millie. "My mind isn't frightened at all, but my body is. I feel sick and light, as if I were floating—a horrible feeling—and I want to talk and talk. . . . Have you got a pencil?"

He produced one, and she wrote, partly by moonlight, partly feeling her way, that she wasn't much afraid, that she loved them both, that they had done everything always to make her happy, and she had done so little for them.

When it was finished they arranged it neatly with stones to weight it down and draw attention to it.

As they did she looked up and asked suddenly: "Where is the east?"

"We face it."

"Isn't the horizon lightening?" Her voice shook, an electric tremor of fear ran through her.

"Oh, no," he answered, "it is not yet near day." Neither of them noticed that he used the words of Juliet. "It isn't even midnight yet." He stretched his wrist out as so often Millie had watched him do; one of those little gestures we get to know and hug to our breasts when we love a person. "It isn't ten o'clock."

Another silence fell upon them, and then Millie said: "I suppose there is no use in my trying to tell you how sorry, how bitterly sorry I am. Of course it is all my fault. I mean, I got you into this—my silly adventure to see the temple."

"Oh, don't worry about me," he answered. "As a matter of fact, my comic flight about your being a witch is just as responsible as your exploring impulse. But as far as I'm concerned I'm quite content to die. A little more than that. Life as a whole has not been a great success to me; for the most part a bitter, ugly contention—as you have probably noticed. My own doing, my own nature; no easier for that knowledge. I've so often been on the point of ending it; but one doesn't. One doesn't like to confess defeat. Only when it's settled like this— I give you my word of honor I feel happier and more at peace this moment than I have for twenty years, except, of course, for you. It maddens me that I can't think of any way out for you."

"Don't worry about me," said Millie mechanically, not knowing she had used his words.

"But I do, of course, worry about you. You have everything to live for—beauty, youth, brains. If I can get you out—"

His voice died away in thought, and Millie found herself wondering if this were mere frivolity that at the point of death she could feel so elated by his calling her beautiful. If he had only said so before she might not have been so rebellious, might not have come adventuring here at all. There was no use of thinking along those lines. No, she mustn't tell him she loved him; he wouldn't even be flattered by it. He wanted peace, and so did she; just the peace and dignity of an equal relationship; two brave people, almost strangers, about to go hence and be seen no more. Why did she think of the burial service? There would be no burial service for her. The sun would be shining hotly on this very spot and she would not be here at all—anywhere. Did she really want peace? Wasn't it only this wild whirling excitement that kept her from panic?

His voice broke in: "I believe there is a chance of getting you out of this. If I made an attack on Avilla—there must be about fourteen of these fellows, and they would get me in the end—but there would be some minutes of turmoil and excitement, and you might have an opportunity of grabbing one of the horses and getting off. The gray horse is faster. They'd shoot at you, but they are probably very bad shots, and the only person who could pursue you would be the man on the other horse, and he could not catch you."

But she was already saying, "No, no, no, I couldn't do it—couldn't escape and leave you to be killed."

She wanted to tell him that there was some comfort—a wild sort of secret joy—in dying with him, but to be killed away from him, running away—she couldn't face it.

He argued with her—that she owed it to her parents; he was alone in the world, there was no one to care whether he was killed or not; she had much to live for; it was better for the expedition if the facts were known at once, it would save valuable time, nothing was gained by her staying. But she shook her head. She knew she must seem obstinate and stupid. After a few minutes he gave it up.

A meteor shot across overhead and disappeared behind the fringed edges of the trees; and a bird, under their feet, woke up and gave a long, throaty, dreamy note and went to sleep again. He lit another cigarette, and this time offered her one. She put out her hand mechanically to take it, and then drew back.

"Oh, no," she said. "I don't really want one and you haven't many left."

He laughed. "All I shall need, I assure you," he said.

She suddenly covered her face with her hands. "Oh, why did you say that; it made it so near and clear," she gasped.

"Come, come," he said. "Pull yourself together. You've been so brave. Quite the bravest person I ever saw."

"Well, you're rather bracing, you know," she answered, trying to take his tone.

"I? Not at all. I'm not being brave. I'm just natural. I give you my word, I never felt happier. Twenty years more of annihilation than I had hoped for—all velvet to me." She gave a little moan, and he saw something must be done quickly. "I never was happy as a child," he said quickly. "Were you? What is the earliest thing you remember?"

She had his complete attention. His voice seemed to say that no story had ever been so absorbing. Terror retreated again like an exorcised ghost. A few minutes later she was telling him about her childhood—about the house she had lived in in summer, by the sea, how she had always loved the sea and yet had never failed to dream, the first night she slept near it, that it was slowly rising into a solid wall hundreds of feet high and sweeping over the dunes, with a little foam on the crest of it. Great things and little she told him—of dresses she had loved, and beautiful proud sights she had seen, and men who had loved her, and poetry and music she had loved. She was carried on and on by the fever of excitement she was in and by his alert attention. She thought to herself, after all, if they could not live together in the future, there was a certain comfort in sharing the past. She stopped, remembering suddenly that it was only her past. She had been talking almost uninterruptedly for an hour or more. She felt abashed.

"Forgive me," she said, "going on like this. I told you I felt this insane impulse to talk. And I suppose you want to be quiet and think about the people who really matter to you who you'll never see again."

"No, really not," he answered. "I would rather listen to you than do anything."

His cool flat tone kept the statement from being a compliment; it was merely, she thought, his expression of a rather odd taste.

"And I took your only scrap of paper," she went on. "I am mad not to have thought there must be some one you would want to leave a word for."

"There isn't." He hesitated a moment and went on: "No, I live very much alone, for reasons which you thoroughly understand."

"That I understand?"

"You gave a masterly exposition of them this very afternoon." For a second she really could not remember. One of the confusing aspects of the man was that he was so different at different times that you could not remember, not merely what he had been but what you had thought of him. He went on: "You were quite right. I do destroy any one who trusts to me. So as I grow older and wiser I encourage fewer and fewer people to do so. And as it is more painful to destroy things you love, the better I like people the farther off I keep. So that means living alone."

She began to remember things she had said. "Those things I said," she began—"they were not true, not what I really felt."

He held up his hand. "Don't go back on them," he said. "They were accurately observed and well expressed."

"They were bitter, and bitterness is never quite true."

"Ah, I know all about that"—and he smiled at her. She could see his teeth flash so very white in the moonlight. "All that you said was true," he went on, his voice growing suddenly deeper. "It inflicted that peculiar agony that only truth inflicts."

She remembered the look on his face as he had turned it into profile. That was pain, then? She had tried so many times to hurt him during their brief acquaintance, and now that she knew she had, she could hardly bear her remorse for having done it.

He was apparently distrustful of silence, for he said rather briskly, "Tell me of the things you were telling me just now—tell me about your parents. What sort of people are they?"

She shook her head. "No, I've lost interest in myself," she answered. "I want you to tell me something about yourself."

"What, in heaven's name?"

"Anything that you think would interest me to hear and you to tell."

There was another long silence. She knew, from the fact that he did not refuse, that he was going to speak, going to tell her something or other. In the dark she bent her head and came near to prayer—that whatever he told her would be real, would bring them nearer, even if it were his love for another woman; nothing horrible, bitter, no cruel experience that had ruined his youth. She heard him draw a long breath, and her whole being trembled at it.

"Well," he said, "I can only think of one thing about myself that would interest you, at least. Yes, I'm sure it would interest you to hear."

He put out his hand and covered hers where it lay on her lap in the moonlight. Hers was trembling as a leaf trembles, but his was vibrating as heavy wires vibrate in strong winds.

"Did you know that I am insanely in love with you? Speak to me, Millie. What is it? Are you crying? Do you hate me to love you?"

Far down below them a drowsy sentinel thought he heard a laugh, and sprang to attention. A laugh. What did that mean? These crazy foreigners were mad, of course, and yet to laugh when they were to die at dawn. Had they magic to escape? Ought he report it? Or was it, after all, a wakeful owl in some high tree or some little forest creature, disturbed by the radiance of the moon. He looked up to the top of the pyramid. Well, they were not trying to escape, for he could see nothing; nothing but the three black lozenges that were the black entrances to the temple, and he leaned his forehead once more on his hands clasped on his rifle, and dozed again.

IV

When at last, behind the gray volcanoes, Millie did detect the first pale lightening of the sky, she did not mention it, for she was just hearing what every woman must hear from her lover—when it was he first knew that he loved her. She was not going to be the only girl in history to die without that information.

She was hearing how, when she first came into his study at Bentham, he had said to himself: "Well, I am definitely old. Here is a girl, exactly the physical type I have always admired, and for that type, peculiarly alluring, and yet she does not give me an emotion."

And he had gone about his work for weeks thinking how strange it was that he thought of her without emotion, and never observing that he thought of her constantly. Then, on the ship, his hatred of the purser and desire to make her suffer for the attentions of the other men—it did not occur to him that that was a sort of jealousy. No, it was not until the day in the storeroom, when she had been so tired, with a long smut across her face and didn't care about it, that, as he looked at her, he had felt something. Still, he had managed to deceive himself until he had kissed her. It was then he had made up his mind to send her away, only he did not want it to be too obvious. He had waited a few days, and the coming of Thorley had made it easy. He had supposed her docility about going had meant that she understood and was glad to be out of it.

"Do you mean," said Millie, "you would never have told me, if it had not been for this?"

"Of course not."

"I think I bless Avilla then, Tim. No, don't laugh; I really do. But I can't understand at all. Why wouldn't you have told me?"

Raikes shook his head. "It's strange," he said, "but women never understand renouncing love. They are so much more given to self-sacrifice than men are in most things, but not in that."

"I should say not," said Millie.

"Yet, can't you see that we should have been wretched? I'm twenty years older than you—"

"No, you're not."

"—hard-up, utterly absorbed in my own work, accustomed to having things all my own way within my own walls. Well, perhaps none of that would matter, as your groanings and gruntings are suggesting, if it were not for what I do to people who trust themselves to me. You said it yourself. I destroy them, Millie."

"Oh, how I wish I'd had my silly tongue torn out before I said such a thing to you."

He put his arm about her. "Your saying it didn't make it true," he answered. "I knew it and acted on it before you called it to my attention. I meant to send you off and never see you again, and break my heart for you in comfortable bitterness. Oh, imagine my doing to you what I did to poor Jimmy the other day. Jimmy, thank fortune, is made of resilient material, but you—you, my darling Millie—how should I feel when I realized that I had tortured you and tormented you and made you hate me?"

"You never would."

"Ah, don't believe it, my dear."

"And if you did I would not let it hurt me—not so terribly. I should understand."

"And perhaps you think that wouldn't make me worse. It is, you know, as if I were possessed with a devil."

"It wouldn't happen if I loved you enough. Oh," she cried, "it will be too cruel if I can never prove to you that I am right."

"Death isn't as cruel as life. I give you my word, Millie."

"Oh, Tim," she said softly, "wasn't that a bird?"

They listened, and now from one corner of the forest, now from another, came faint peeps and chirps echoed back and forth, so strangely like Wagner's representation of it.

"Yes," said Raikes slowly, "it's getting light."

Millie hid her eyes for an instant against his shoulder, and then, reflecting that she would probably never see another sunrise in his company, she lifted her head and looked proudly before her.

The magnificent pageant of tropical dawn began to happen; a little too quickly to eyes accustomed to the leisurely sunrises of northern latitudes. Millie remembered that Raikes had said, under less dramatic conditions, when they all got up before dawn in order to dig, not to die, that it was like noble music played a little too fast.

There had already been sounds of activity from the camp below, and as soon as it was light enough to see, Avilla himself, still wrapped in his Napoleonic cloak, appeared at the foot of the stairs and asked in a high voice and a Spanish accent from which every guttural had been eliminated, whether the *blanchita* had made her decision.

It was Raikes who stepped out to answer, looking as tall as a giant at the top of the long steps.

"*Sí, señor*," he answered in ringing tones.

A murmur of satisfaction went up from the group of men; they turned and spoke to one another. Millie, watching them from the shadow of the temple, could almost hear that they were arranging how to spend their part of the treasure.

Raikes folded his arms and looked down at them. "The *blanchita*," he said, "consents to search for your treasure, and will find it if it is there."

Many cries that it was there—"Oh, *seguro!*" "*Esta! Esta!*"—went up.

"But," Raikes went on, "she cannot find what is not there, and I believe it is there no longer."

Avilla, who had mounted a few steps, clambering with less dignity than heretofore, now observed that it was much to be hoped for their sakes that the treasure was there, as otherwise—

"Do you think," murmured Millie, "that it is wise to discourage them too much?"

"I don't want them to think we are too eager to do this stunt," he answered.

Then, turning to Avilla again, he requested, in his most courteous Spanish, the privilege of borrowing his cloak for the *blanchita*. Avilla, with the gesture of a Sir Walter Raleigh, swung it off his shoulders. Raikes turned it about in his hand. It was not, he said, the sort of cloak the *blanchita* was accustomed to doing magic in, but better than nothing.

Below, the men questioned one another. Some had heard, some had not. You must have a cloak to do magic? They all nodded their small unshaven heads. "Oh, *sí, Como no.*" They seemed for the moment the friendliest audience, and yet Raikes knew that the instant Millie failed to find them gold they would obey orders to shoot without the slightest hesitation. He came back up the temple steps to where, in the shadows, she was waiting for him.

"It seems a silly plan we made," she said. "I wonder if it wouldn't be better just to go down and die quietly."

"Come, come," he said sternly, dropping the cloak on her shoulders. "This is what we decided last night, and we are going to go through with it now, for better or worse."

Something in his tone chilled her heart. Was it true that he really did not want to escape? That only certain death had made him reveal his love, and that if they did escape he would send her away and, as he had said, break his heart in comfortable bitterness? She would not allow it. But could she prevent it? She could imagine his saying, in that peculiarly remote, flat voice of his: "No, no, my dear Millie, I die very prettily with young ladies, but I cannot live with them." Yes, she would almost rather die at once. And yet she could hardly bargain with him, ask him his intentions. And as for that flat voice, he could do strange things with it, as she knew, making it sound like a New England parson's at the moment when he was most deeply moved.

There was a shout from below.

"The curtain's up, Millie," he said.

Millie, now wrapped in Avilla's cloak from chin to heels, came out of the temple and held out both her hands for silence. She was bareheaded and a faint early breeze just lifted her hair and made it light and golden.

"Listen," she said. "Listen carefully that everything may be done in order. I must find and cut for myself a magic wand, and if it turns in my hand, there will be treasure of silver or gold. I cannot tell which or what. It may turn at once, it may take time. But while I am seeking it no one must speak; there must be no sound at all. The horses must be taken away to a little distance"—and she waved her hand up the path they had ridden the day before—"so that they may not neigh, as horses will sometimes do at the approach of spirits. You must all stand in a circle about me, but sufficiently apart for me to pass to and fro between you. But most important of all is this: The method by which the treasure is to be divided." She paused and noticed that she was holding the interest of her audience. This point seemed to them, too, the most important. "The chief must have his half share," she said, and Avilla nodded. "After that, it must be divided in halves according to the order in which you men actually touch it; the first man who touches it must have half of what is left, the next man half of what is left."

A great hubbub of talk rose among the band as the meaning of her words penetrated. A lame man shouted that it was unfair, whereas the fleet of foot were delighted; the man who had been told off to take care of the horses demanded whether or not he was to have his place.

Raikes looked down at them with folded arms. "The dragon's teeth," he said to Millie. "Maybe they'll tear one another to pieces and save us all further trouble."

"I'm getting waves of being frightened, Tim," she said. "I think I feel faint or something."

"Oh, not of these vermin," said Raikes.

Millie now descended the last few steps, trailing Avilla's sable cloak from the tips of her shoulders. Indeed, love and death had done something superb to her young face, so that it was exalted and ethereal.

Years ago, when she was a child, she remembered that in a little country place where her father had rented a house there had been trouble about water. In a dry season the well had gone dry and the landlord had sent a local man—"a dowser," he was called—to look for subterranean water with a willow wand. She could see the whole scene before her, as people are supposed to see all their life before they drown. She could see the respectful villager, and the contemptuous New York servants, and the old man himself, holding the wand before him with both his hands, the thumbs up, his slow pontifical walk. And then she could see how suddenly the wand had twisted like a live animal and turned itself until it pointed straight downward, and how the old man had drawn a circle and told them to dig there, and they had dug and found water. She had been very eager to try it herself, and the old man had shown her how to hold the wand, though he warned it might be of no use; she might not be a dowser.

It appeared that she was not, for the prong would not turn for her, though once as she walked she thought she felt a quiver run along the wand, like a shiver of life. It had frightened her, but it had gone no further. Fortunately she remembered the whole experience very clearly—the way of holding it, the length and appearance of the wand, and above everything, the slow impressive step.

She walked toward the jungle, seeking for a cleft twig, not at once easy to find among the branchless trunks of tall trees and the huge, waving leaves of mammoth plants. Several curious little men crept after her. She took her time; she was acting the sorceress.

Raikes remained on the steps, aloof, but well placed to observe everything that was happening. Millie stooped and stretched and sought, allowing herself to be very witchlike, and at last said with a great cry, "Al fin!" She had found something that might do. She asked for a machete to cut it with, and rather to her surprise a dozen were offered to her. She chose one after a long deliberation; there must be nothing quick and eager and likely to excite suspicion.

She cut her forked wand, trimmed it and walked slowly toward the flat open place under the steep back wall of the pyramid. As she did so her cloak fell over her hands and she stuck the machete into her boot without any one noticing her action. Her two hands were now free for her experiment.

With the docility of young children, the bandits formed themselves into a great circle about her, leaving room for her to pass between them, while she, very slowly, imitating that pontifical step of the dowser, walked slowly to and fro before them holding her wand before her, with her two hands thrown up.

The plan that Raikes had made was this: That she was to go back and forth, weaving her way among them until they grew used to her being now behind and now before them; that she was gradually to draw them on until they were all behind the pyramid and facing the blank wall, when she was to announce that the wand had turned—to turn it, in fact—and then, in the wild excitement of digging, she and Raikes would make a bolt to where the horses were tied—the only two horses in the whole company—and take their chance of being shot by any one who was not wholly absorbed in getting his part of the treasure.

But, as almost every one finds who plays with magic for their own base purposes, magic plays with them. Millie had not been walking up and down nearly as long as she intended to walk when she felt strange little tremors begin to go through her wand. Was it her imagination that it had moved in her firm grasp? She had never thought of its turning of itself. The plan had been that she would tell them it had turned, that she would turn it downward at a convenient spot. But now—yes, it certainly was moving. An excited murmur began to go up from the circle of sharp, watching eyes. She came to a standstill almost in the exact center, just where the sheer wall of the pyramid cast the darkest shadow, and there the wand twisted like a live snake and pointed straight down.

She stood quite dazed, staring at it. A cry went up from all the band: "*El tesoro! El oro!*" They flung themselves forward with spades and pick-axes and the inevitable machete, with tin cups and even with their bare hands. They were all on their knees digging, digging; they thrust her aside; they got in front of her.

She turned toward the steps and saw that one person had not forgotten. Avilla, whose portion was secure without effort, was standing motionless at the foot of the steps, watching not the diggers but Raikes, and he had a revolver in his right hand.

She hesitated a moment, not knowing what to do. She was free as air, except for this one little figure on guard. The crisis had come more quickly than they had expected. She looked up at Raikes, standing four or five feet above Avilla on the temple steps. She meant to ask him what must be done now, and as she looked she saw him fling himself like a catapult, full at the little man below him, so straight, so quickly, that Avilla did not have time to fire. They came to the ground together, landing on a welter of vines and plants, unnoticed by any one but Millie. All the others were digging, digging only a few feet away, but utterly absorbed; even the man who had been holding the horses had tied them to a tree at the first shout of gold and was now digging with the rest.

She stood rooted, wondering what Raikes was going to do to Avilla—gag him, tie him up? But there was no rope. Then she saw Raikes' long body bend and his knee go up until it rested on Avilla's chest, and his thin strong hands closed about the little man's throat. Oh, yes, of course, naturally he was going to kill him. She felt not the slightest shock or repulsion —she who was too delicate to look at a galled horse in the street; she felt only an intense absorbed interest. Would it go this way or that? The bodies of the two men moved and heaved together, but always Raikes was on top of the other.

She did not suppose he saw her, for he had not glanced in her direction, but suddenly she was aware he was speaking to her. He said: "Go—to—the—horses!" He panted a little, and at each word she could see the rolling head of Avilla nod a little, as if confirming the order. Still she could not move, still she wanted to watch. How difficult it was to kill a man.

Then Raikes spoke again: "Go on, I tell you!" he said.

She woke from her trance of interest and ran toward the horses. She cut the rope that tied them with her machete, mounted one of them and had both heads turned down the path by the time Raikes came running toward her. He mounted as he started both horses at a run. Jungles are so thickly carpeted that even galloping feet do not reverberate.

"Did you kill him?" she asked.

"Yes. I was sorry you had to see it."

She was surprised to think how little she had minded.

Not a shot had been fired, not a head had been turned. They went on past the spot where less than twenty-four hours before they had talked so bitterly, on down the green tunnel of the path, and came out on the river. The horses went splashing through the shallow water, clattering and striking fire from the stones. But there was no danger, no one on foot could catch them now. They were free, they were safe. Still they pushed the horses on. Little red deer, hardly as large as goats, which had come down for their morning drink at the river, fled, alarmed, and fawn-colored iguanas which had crept out on fawn-colored rocks for the first morning sun wriggled off and into the forest again, but there was no sound of pursuit.

At last they saw ahead of them a column of gray smoke rising from the camp, gray against the green, and blue in the sunlight. A little way off the familiar sound of an ax could be heard, but breakfast for one was still untouched on the table. Through the open flap of his tent Jimmy could be seen still asleep, oversleeping in the absence of his chief.

"Lazy dog," said Raikes angrily.

Oh, yes, they were back again. That was the other Raikes speaking.

He flung himself off his horse. "Don't get off," he said. "I want you to go straight on to San Roberto. You can't tell. I don't trust our own Indians yet." He poured out Jimmy's coffee and handed her up a cup where she sat on the horse, looking very young and illumined, with her hair still standing on end and her face like alabaster. "Jimmy!" he shouted, while he made her a sandwich of bread and bacon. An alarmed grunt from the tent. Then to her: "Be off. Be off," he said.

"Without you?" she wailed.

"I'll follow at once. I must speak to Thorley."

"You promise that you will follow me at once?" she repeated. Somehow there seemed more menace in this separation than in the whole past night.

"Oh, of course—of course." He turned her horse and started it on its way.

She rode alone down the path in the glorious blue and green of the early morning, safe, happy—well, almost happy. A little strain of homesickness for their lost companionship. Why had he left her so soon? How absurd! He would be with her now at any moment. She looked over her shoulder. There was no one coming.

Then at last the rustling of some one behind her. At last—at last. Round the bend of the path came the brown horse, and on its back was Jimmy.

She felt sick with disappointment. "Where's—where's—" She made that fatal hesitation for a name. Really, after all that had occurred, she could not say "Professor Raikes." Nor would she stoop to the comedy of "the boss."

Jimmy was too much excited to hear her, however.

"Oh, Millie," he cried, "for heaven's sake, tell me what happened! To think I was sleeping like a pig while you were in danger of your life. I thought you had gone to San Roberto, and when Raikes didn't appear I thought he had followed you. I was jealous, Millie, and said to myself there was no use in working for a fellow who went off like that without a word, and I pictured you both—"

"Where is he, Jimmy?"

"Coming in a few minutes. He sent me on in case you felt nervous. Oh, Millie, he says you were so brave. Tell me everything that happened."

That, Millie thought, would be going a little too far, but she was not above enjoying living her "battles o'er," and Jimmy was not aware of great gaps in her narrative.

"You know you look different, Millie—like some one who has been through something great. Weren't you even frightened?"

"Oh, I won't say that, Jimmy, but he—Professor Raikes—is very bracing. He seemed to feel so entirely calm about dying."

"Oh, no, he doesn't mind dying; he always says so."

"Did he say so this morning?" she asked sharply.

"Oh, he's always said so."

Millie sighed. It was difficult to get a straight answer from one who does not see the importance of the question. She glanced back over her shoulder and wondered why he did not come. Could he be avoiding her? In his place she would not have let this time elapse.

Jimmy chattered on, almost more excited about it than she was. "Wouldn't you know," he said, "that if something romantic was going to happen I wouldn't be in it. But then, of course, if I had, we would both be dead by this time, I suppose. I should never be able to think of a plan like that. He's so clever. It must, in a way, Millie, have been a wonderful experience to go through something like that with Raikes."

"Well, in a way it was," said Millie. Her voice sounded as if it came over a bad telephone from an immense distance.

Something—not exactly a suspicion—made Jimmy say, "I suppose it will always be a great bond between you—a thing like that."

Her doubt suddenly became an agony as she answered, "Oh, you can't tell. It may not be at all."

In due time they reached San Roberto, where, in the little *sala* of the house, Mrs. Thorley was rocking and stitching flannel bands, as if nothing dangerous or dramatic had ever been known to happen.

"Why," she said, looking up, "what brings you into town?"

Jimmy, glancing apologetically at Millie for stealing her story, allowed Mrs. Thorley to hear a little of the reason. But Millie had reached a point of exhaustion and despair in which even the narration of her own adventures could not rouse her. She said that all she wanted was a hot bath and to sleep.

Well, a hot bath could be obtained, but not in five minutes. A little Indian servant went padding about on bare feet, stoking the stove with coffee wood, filling all the receptacles in the house from kettles to tin boilers for washing clothes. Meantime Jimmy, who had become official historian of the night's events, explained what had happened, and Millie sat waiting, with her eyes fixed on the path that led down from the jungle.

Once in her steaming bath, however, she felt that nothing else mattered—nothing but sleep. She was too exhausted to care whether he came or not, too exhausted and too wise, for now she knew it would mean nothing for her. But when, an instant later, she actually did hear his voice in the *sala*, a thrill like an electric shock went through her and she sprang out of her bath and began to dress as rapidly as trembling hands would allow. She must see him at once.

When she emerged, there was Mrs. Thorley, rocking as before, who said: "Why, Millie, I thought you were going to bed, and there you are all dressed."

Millie looked all round the room. "I wanted to speak to Professor Raikes," she said. Her throat felt dry.

"Well, now, isn't that too bad," said Mrs. Thorley, alarmingly sympathetic.

"Too bad?"

"I mean you just missed him; he's just gone. He sent Jimmy back to the Casas Viejas. After all, my poor husband can't do all the work, willing as he is to do more than—"

"Then where did Professor Raikes go?"

"To the capital to report the whole thing. You don't kill a man, my dear, without mentioning it to the authorities."

Of course. He had killed Avilla; she had forgotten. Mrs. Thorley settled back in her chair, rocking as she sewed. "Fortunately the president is a friend of Professor Raikes. I don't think there will be any real trouble. My husband says that human life—"

"Did he say when he would be back?" asked Millie, hardly troubling to make her tone sound casual.

"I didn't ask him," answered Mrs. Thorley almost proudly. "I don't think people like to be forever pinned down about what they are going to do. When I got married I made it a rule I would never ask Mr. Thorley any questions I could avoid. I do the same with other men. But let me see. He'll get there this evening. I suppose he'll take all to-morrow with his business, and be back the next day or the day after."

That being so, Millie thought she would go to bed. She turned at the door.

"Did he ask for me?" she said. This time she did achieve a wonderfully casual tone.

"Oh, yes," said Mrs. Thorley. "Yes, indeed, he asked for you, and I told him you had had a bath and had gone to bed, and he said it was a good thing you had—gone to bed, I mean. He seemed to think you needed rest."

Probably she did, but did not seem likely at the moment to get it. She undressed and lay down on her canvas cot, not bothering to shut out the uncompromising light of the early afternoon. She felt a deep, reasonable conviction that, as far as she was concerned, he had gone forever. Incredible but true. She remembered every tone of his voice when he had spoken of renouncing love, that they would never be married, that he would not destroy the woman he loved. That was the voice of the real man speaking. His love for her was real too; she could not remember the night and doubt it. She knew now it was only death that had given him to her, and life was going to take him away.

Strangely enough, she had no thought of trying to change his decision, partly because she knew she couldn't and that all she would do was to render them both wretched by a scene—she pleading, he refusing. Oh, no, she wouldn't go through that—but partly because she had no wish to do so. All her will had gone. Now, if she had been facing a death sentence, it would have made very little difference to her. He had been right when he suggested that perhaps it was a mistake to escape. All reality seemed very remote. Perhaps, she thought, having looked so closely at the face of death releases you of some of your allegiance to life. She did not care now whether she lived or died. Professor Raikes? A man she had not known existed two months ago. How was it possible he could make her happy or unhappy? He couldn't—all a fancy, a dream. Her parents? If she knew they were in the next room she would not get up to meet them. Nothing mattered—nothing.

Just as the light began to fade into the short gray dusk of the tropics she fell asleep.

She was waked by a bright light shining on the blue adobe wall of the room, which she was facing. Some one must have turned on the relentless electricity. No. And yet, could that light be sunlight? Even in the tropics the sun does not return a few minutes after setting, and certainly she had only been asleep a few minutes. She turned over with a flounce and found it broad midmorning, and Raikes, sitting with one leg thrown over the other and his arms crossed, looking at her. She stared at him. All her lethargy of will was gone; she felt with agony that she could not let him go without a struggle—that no sacrifice of pride was too great.

He whispered, just forming the words: "She can hear every word and she's sitting there listening."

Millie colored. He had guessed that she was about to say something more intimate than he wished to hear.

Then, very loud and casually, he said, "Well, how do you feel?"

"I hardly know yet. I'm just awake." Then lower: "Where have you been?"

"I went up to the capital to explain to the president why I had murdered one of his countrymen." Then, to prove that he was right, Mrs. Thorley came hurrying in.

"Is she awake?" she said benevolently. . . . "How do you feel?"

"Hungry," said Millie. It was not true, but she knew what would appeal to the older woman.

"Yes, it's nearly lunchtime," said Mrs. Thorley, leaning against the lintel of the door and beaming at her. "We've got a good meal for you."

Raikes uncrossed his legs. Millie thought: "If he goes before Mrs. Thorley does I shall scream. I shall go mad." He crossed his legs the other way. He looked at her. Mrs. Thorley could not see his face, and his look meant something, but Millie wasn't sure what.

She said aloud, "I should love a cup of coffee, Mrs. Thorley, now, this minute. Do you think I could have it?"

"I don't know about now this minute," Mrs. Thorley replied; she was a person who liked to make fun of any form of expression not her own, "but I can get it for you in a short time." She disappeared from the doorway. Millie sat up.

"Where have you been?" she asked.

He put out his hand, and withdrew it as Mrs. Thorley returned.

"I wondered," she said, "whether you'd like a piece of toast with your coffee."

"I should," returned Millie gently, "very, very much."

"You don't think it will spoil your luncheon?"

"I'm sure it wouldn't."

She had gone again, and Millie's hand was inclosed.

"I went to the capital."

"To see the president?"

"To see the American minister . . . and a clergyman."

"A clergyman, Tim?"

"Aren't you going to marry me, Millie?" Her hand was almost tossed in her face. "You haven't gone back on me?"

"Oh, Tim, I've been persuading myself, after all you said, that you had decided not to marry me."

"Good heavens," cried Raikes, "I've got myself tangled up with a moron!"

# Leiningen versus the Ants

## CARL STEPHENSON

U NLESS they alter their course and there's no reason why they should, they'll reach your plantation in two days at the latest."
Leiningen sucked placidly at a cigar about the size of a corncob and for a few seconds gazed without answering at the agitated District Commissioner. Then he took the cigar from his lips, and leaned slightly forward. With his bristling grey hair, bulky nose, and lucid eyes, he had the look of an aging and shabby eagle.

"Decent of you," he murmured, "paddling all this way just to give me the tip. But you're pulling my leg of course when you say I must do a bunk. Why, even a herd of saurians couldn't drive me from this plantation of mine."

The Brazilian official threw up lean and lanky arms and clawed the air with wildly distended fingers. "Leiningen!" he shouted. "You're insane! They're not creatures you can fight—they're an elemental—an 'act of God!' Ten miles long, two miles wide—ants, nothing but ants! And every single one of them a fiend from hell; before you can spit three times they'll eat a full-grown buffalo to the bones. I tell you if you don't clear out at once there'll be nothing left of you but a skeleton picked as clean as your own plantation."

Leiningen grinned. "Act of God, my eye! Anyway, I'm not an old woman; I'm not going to run for it just because an elemental's on the way. And don't think I'm the kind of fathead who tries to fend off lightning with his fists, either. I use my intelligence, old man. With me, the brain isn't a second blindgut; I know what it's there for. When I began this model farm and plantation three years ago, I took into account all that could conceivably happen to it. And now I'm ready for anything and everything —including your ants."

The Brazilian rose heavily to his feet. "I've done my best," he gasped. "Your obstinacy endangers not only yourself, but the lives of your four hundred workers. You don't know these ants!"

Leiningen accompanied him down to the river, where the Government launch was moored. The vessel cast off. As it moved downstream, the exclamation mark neared the rail and began waving its arms frantically. Long after the launch had disappeared round the bend, Leiningen thought he could still hear that dimming, imploring voice, "You don't know them, I tell you! *You don't know them!*"

But the reported enemy was by no means unfamiliar to the planter. Before he started work on his settlement, he had lived long enough in the country to see for himself the fearful devastations sometimes wrought by these ravenous insects in their campaigns for food. But since then he had planned measures of defence accordingly, and these, he was convinced, were in every way adequate to withstand the approaching peril.

Moreover, during his three years as a planter, Leiningen had met and defeated drought, flood, plague and all other "acts of God" which had come against him—unlike his fellow-settlers in the district, who had made little or no resistance. This unbroken success he attributed solely to the observance of his lifelong motto: *The human brain needs only to become fully aware of its powers to conquer even the elements.* Dullards reeled senselessly and aimlessly into the abyss; cranks, however brilliant, lost their heads when circumstances suddenly altered or accelerated and ran into stone walls, sluggards drifted with the current until they were caught in whirlpools and dragged under. But such disasters, Leiningen contended, merely strengthened his argument that intelligence, directed aright, invariably makes man the master of his fate.

Yes, Leiningen had always known how to grapple with life. Even here, in this Brazilian wilderness, his brain had triumphed over every difficulty and danger it had so far encountered. First he had vanquished primal forces by cunning and organization, then he had enlisted the resources of modern science to increase miraculously the yield of his plantation. And now he was sure he would prove more than a match for the "irresistible" ants.

That same evening, however, Leiningen assembled his workers. He had no intention of waiting till the news reached their ears from other sources. Most of them had been born in the district; the cry "The ants are coming!" was to them an imperative signal for instant, panic-stricken flight, a spring for life itself. But so great was the Indians' trust in Leiningen, in Leiningen's word, and in Leiningen's wisdom, that they received his curt tidings, and his orders for the imminent struggle, with the calmness with which they were given. They waited, unafraid, alert, as if for the beginning of a new game or hunt which he had just described to them. The ants were indeed mighty, but not so mighty as the boss. Let them come!

They came at noon the second day. Their approach was announced by the wild unrest of the horses, scarcely controllable now either in stall or under rider, scenting from afar a vapor instinct with horror.

It was announced by a stampede of animals, timid and savage, hurtling past each other; jaguars and pumas flashing by nimble stags of the pampas, bulky tapirs, no longer hunters, themselves hunted, outpacing fleet kinkajous, maddened herds of cattle, heads lowered, nostrils snorting, rushing through tribes of loping monkeys, chattering in a dementia of terror; then followed the creeping and springing denizens of bush and steppe, big and little rodents, snakes, and lizards.

Pell-mell the rabble swarmed down the hill to the plantation, scattered right and left before the barrier of the water-filled ditch, then sped onwards to the river, where, again hindered, they fled along its bank out of sight.

This water-filled ditch was one of the defence measures which Leiningen had long since prepared against the advent of the ants. It encompassed three sides of the plantation like a huge horseshoe. Twelve feet across, but not very deep, when dry it could hardly be described as an obstacle to either man or beast. But the ends of the "horseshoe" ran into the river which formed the northern boundary, and fourth side, of the plantation. And at the end nearer the house and outbuildings in the middle of the plantation, Leiningen had constructed a dam by means of which water from the river could be diverted into the ditch.

So now, by opening the dam, he was able to fling an imposing girdle of water, a huge quadrilateral with the river as its base, completely around the plantation, like the moat encircling a medieval city. Unless the ants were clever enough to build rafts, they had no hope of reaching the planta-tion, Leiningen concluded.

The twelve-foot water ditch seemed to afford in itself all the security needed. But while awaiting the arrival of the ants, Leiningen made a fur-ther improvement. The western section of the ditch ran along the edge of a tamarind wood, and the branches of some great trees reached over the water. Leiningen now had them lopped so that ants could not descend from them within the "moat."

The women and children, then the herds of cattle, were escorted by peons on rafts over the river, to remain on the other side in absolute safety until the plunderers had departed. Leiningen gave this instruction, not be-cause he believed the non-combatants were in any danger, but in order to avoid hampering the efficiency of the defenders. "Critical situations first become crises," he explained to his men, "when oxen or women get excited."

Finally, he made a careful inspection of the "inner moat"—a smaller ditch lined with concrete, which extended around the hill on which stood the ranch house, barns, stables and other buildings. Into this concrete ditch emptied the inflow pipes from three great petrol tanks. If by some miracle the ants managed to cross the water and reached the plantation, this "ram-part of petrol" would be an absolutely impassable protection for the be-seiged and their dwellings and stock. Such, at least, was Leiningen's opinion.

He stationed his men at irregular distances along the water ditch, the first line of defence. Then he lay down in his hammock and puffed drowsily away at his pipe until a peon came with the report that the ants had been observed far away in the South.

Leiningen mounted his horse, which at the feel of its master seemed to forget its uneasiness, and rode leisurely in the direction of the threatening offensive. The southern stretch of ditch—the upper side of the quadrilateral —was nearly three miles long; from its center one could survey the entire countryside. This was destined to be the scene of the outbreak of war be-tween Leiningen's brain and twenty square miles of life-destroying ants.

It was a sight one could never forget. Over the range of hills, as far as eye could see, crept a darkening hem, ever longer and broader, until the shadow spread across the slope from east to west, then downwards, downwards, uncannily swift, and all the green herbage of that wide vista was being mown as by a giant sickle, leaving only the vast moving shadow, extending, deepening, and moving rapidly nearer.

When Leiningen's men, behind their barrier of water, perceived the approach of the long-expected foe, they gave vent to their suspense in screams and imprecations. But as the distance began to lessen between the "sons of hell" and the water ditch, they relapsed into silence. Before the advance of that awe-inspiring throng, their belief in the powers of the boss began to steadily dwindle.

Even Leiningen himself, who had ridden up just in time to restore their loss of heart by a display of unshakable calm, even he could not free himself from a qualm of malaise. Yonder were thousands of millions of voracious jaws bearing down upon him and only a suddenly insignificant, narrow ditch lay between him and his men and being gnawed to the bones "before you can spit three times."

Hadn't this brain for once taken on more than it could manage? If the blighters decided to rush the ditch, fill it to the brim with their corpses, there'd still be more than enough to destroy every trace of that cranium of his. The planter's chin jutted; they hadn't got him yet, and he'd see to it they never would. While he could think at all, he'd flout both death and the devil.

The hostile army was approaching in perfect formation; no human battalions, however well-drilled, could ever hope to rival the precision of that advance. Along a front that moved forward as uniformly as a straight line, the ants drew nearer and nearer to the water ditch. Then, when they learned through their scouts the nature of the obstacle, the two outlying wings of the army detached themselves from the main body and marched down the western and eastern sides of the ditch.

This surrounding maneuver took rather more than an hour to accomplish; no doubt the ants expected that at some point they would find a crossing.

During this outflanking movement by the wings, the army on the center and southern front remained still. The besieged were therefore able to contemplate at their leisure the thumb-long, reddish black, long-legged insects; some of the Indians believed they could see, too, intent on them, the brilliant, cold eyes, and the razor-edged mandibles, of this host of infinity.

It is not easy for the average person to imagine that an animal, not to mention an insect, can *think*. But now both the European brain of Leiningen and the primitive brains of the Indians began to stir with the unpleasant foreboding that inside every single one of that deluge of insects dwelt a thought. And that thought was: Ditch or no ditch, we'll get to your flesh!

Not until four o'clock did the wings reach the "horseshoe" ends of the ditch, only to find these ran into the great river. Through some kind of secret telegraphy, the report must then have flashed very swiftly indeed along the entire enemy line. And Leiningen, riding—no longer casually—along his side of the ditch, noticed by energetic and widespread movements of troops that for some unknown reason the news of the check had its greatest effect on the southern front, where the main army was massed. Perhaps the failure to find a way over the ditch was persuading the ants to withdraw from the plantation in search of spoils more easily attainable.

An immense flood of ants, about a hundred yards in width, was pouring in a glimmering-black cataract down the far slope of the ditch. Many thousands were already drowning in the sluggish creeping flow, but they were followed by troop after troop, who clambered over their sinking comrades, and then themselves served as dying bridges to the reserves hurrying on in their rear.

Shoals of ants were being carried away by the current into the middle of the ditch, where gradually they broke asunder and then, exhausted by their struggles, vanished below the surface. Nevertheless, the wavering, floundering hundred-yard front was remorselessly if slowly advancing towards the beseiged on the other bank. Leiningen had been wrong when he supposed the enemy would first have to fill the ditch with their bodies before they could cross; instead, they merely needed to act as stepping-stones, as they swam and sank, to the hordes ever pressing onwards from behind.

Near Leiningen a few mounted herdsmen awaited his orders. He sent one to the weir—the river must be dammed more strongly to increase the speed and power of the water coursing through the ditch.

A second peon was dispatched to the outhouses to bring spades and petrol sprinklers. A third rode away to summon to the zone of the offensive all the men, except the observation posts, on the near-by sections of the ditch, which were not yet actively threatened.

The ants were getting across far more quickly than Leiningen would have deemed possible. Impelled by the mighty cascade behind them, they struggled nearer and nearer to the inner bank. The momentum of the attack was so great that neither the tardy flow of the stream nor its downward pull could exert its proper force; and into the gap left by every submerging insect, hastened forward a dozen more.

When reinforcements reached Leiningen, the invaders were halfway over. The planter had to admit to himself that it was only by a stroke of luck for him that the ants were attempting the crossing on a relatively short front: had they assaulted simultaneously along the entire length of the ditch, the outlook for the defenders would have been black indeed.

Even as it was, it could hardly be described as rosy, though the planter seemed quite unaware that death in a gruesome form was drawing closer and closer. As the war between his brain and the "act of God" reached its climax, the very shadow of annihilation began to pale to Leiningen, who now felt like a champion in a new Olympic game, a gigantic and thrilling contest, from which he was determined to emerge victor. Such, indeed, was his aura of confidence that the Indians forgot their stupefied fear of the peril only a yard or two away; under the planter's supervision, they began fervidly digging up to the edge of the bank and throwing clods of earth and spadefuls of sand into the midst of the hostile fleet.

The petrol sprinklers, hitherto used to destroy pests and blights on the plantation, were also brought into action. Streams of evil-reeking oil now soared and fell over an enemy already in disorder through the bombardment of earth and sand.

The ants responded to these vigorous and successful measures of defence by further developments of their offensive. Entire clumps of huddling insects began to roll down the opposite bank into the water. At the same time, Leiningen noticed that the ants were now attacking along an ever-widening front. As the numbers both of his men and his petrol sprinklers were severely limited, this rapid extension of the line of battle was becoming an overwhelming danger.

To add to his difficulties, the very clods of earth they flung into that black floating carpet often whirled fragments toward the defenders' side, and here and there dark ribbons were already mounting the inner bank. True, wherever a man saw these they could still be driven back into the water by spadefuls of earth or jets of petrol. But the file of defenders was too sparse and scattered to hold off at all points these landing parties, and though the peons toiled like madmen, their plight became momentarily more perilous.

One man struck with his spade at an enemy clump, did not draw it back quickly enough from the water; in a trice the wooden haft swarmed with upward scurrying insects. With a curse, he dropped the spade into the ditch; too late, they were already on his body. They lost no time; wherever they encountered bare flesh they bit deeply; a few, bigger than the rest, carried in their hind-quarters a sting which injected a burning and paralyzing venom. Screaming, frantic with pain, the peon danced and twirled like a dervish.

Realizing that another such casualty, yes, perhaps this alone, might plunge his men into confusion and destroy their morale, Leiningen roared in a bellow louder than the yells of the victim: "Into the petrol, idiot! Douse your paws in the petrol!" The dervish ceased his pirouette as if transfixed, then tore off his shirt and plunged his arm and the ants hanging to it up to the shoulder in one of the large open tins of petrol. But even then the fierce mandibles did not slacken; another peon had to help him squash and detach each separate insect.

Distracted by the episode, some defenders had turned away from the ditch. And now cries of fury, a thudding of spades, and a wild trampling to and fro, showed that the ants had made full use of the interval, though luckily only a few had managed to get across. The men set to work again desperately with the barrage of earth and sand. Meanwhile an old Indian, who acted as medicine-man to the plantation workers, gave the bitten peon a drink he had prepared some hours before, which, he claimed, possessed the virtue of dissolving and weakening ants' venom.

Leiningen surveyed his position. A dispassionate observer would have estimated the odds against him at a thousand to one. But then such an onlooker would have reckoned only by what he saw—the advance of myriad battalions of ants against the futile efforts of a few defenders—and not by the unseen activity that can go on in a man's brain.

For Leiningen had not erred when he decided he would fight elemental with elemental. The water in the ditch was beginning to rise; the stronger damming of the river was making itself apparent.

Visibly the swiftness and power of the masses of water increased, swirling into quicker and quicker movement its living black surface, dispersing its pattern, carrying away more and more of it on the hastening current.

Victory had been snatched from the very jaws of defeat. With a hysterical shout of joy, the peons feverishly intensified their bombardment of earth clods and sand.

And now the wide cataract down the opposite bank was thinning and ceasing, as if the ants were becoming aware that they could not attain their aim. They were scurrying back up the slope to safety.

All the troops so far hurled into the ditch had been sacrificed in vain. Drowned and floundering insects eddied in thousands along the flow, while Indians running on the bank destroyed every swimmer that reached the side.

Not until the ditch curved towards the east did the scattered ranks assemble again in a coherent mass. And now, exhausted and half-numbed, they were in no condition to ascend the bank. Fusillades of clods drove them round the bend towards the mouth of the ditch and then into the river, wherein they vanished without leaving a trace.

The news ran swiftly along the entire chain of outposts, and soon a long scattered line of laughing men could be seen hastening along the ditch towards the scene of victory.

For once they seemed to have lost all their native reserve, for it was in wild abandon now they celebrated the triumph—as if there were no longer thousands of millions of merciless, cold and hungry eyes watching them from the opposite bank, watching and waiting.

The sun sank behind the rim of the tamarind wood and twilight deepened into night. It was not only hoped but expected that the ants would remain quiet until dawn. But to defeat any forlorn attempt at a crossing, the flow of water through the ditch was powerfully increased by opening the dam still further.

In spite of this impregnable barrier, Leiningen was not yet altogether convinced that the ants would not venture another surprise attack. He ordered his men to camp along the bank overnight. He also detailed parties of them to patrol the ditch in two of his motor cars and ceaselessly to illuminate the surface of the water with headlights and electric torches.

After having taken all the precautions he deemed necessary, the farmer ate his supper with considerable appetite and went to bed. His slumbers were in no wise disturbed by the memory of the waiting, live, twenty square miles.

Dawn found a thoroughly refreshed and active Leiningen riding along the edge of the ditch. The planter saw before him a motionless and unaltered throng of besiegers. He studied the wide belt of water between them and the plantation, and for a moment almost regretted that the fight had ended so soon and so simply. In the comforting, matter-of-fact light of morning, it seemed to him now that the ants hadn't the ghost of a chance to cross the ditch. Even if they plunged headlong into it on all three fronts at once, the force of the now powerful current would inevitably sweep them away. He had got quite a thrill out of the fight—a pity it was already over.

He rode along the eastern and southern sections of the ditch and found everything in order. He reached the western section, opposite the tamarind wood, and here, contrary to the other battle fronts, he found the enemy very busy indeed. The trunks and branches of the trees and the creepers of the lianas, on the far bank of the ditch, fairly swarmed with industrious insects. But instead of eating the leaves there and then, they were merely gnawing through the stalks, so that a thick green shower fell steadily to the ground.

No doubt they were victualing columns sent out to obtain provender for the rest of the army. The discovery did not surprise Leiningen. He did not need to be told that ants are intelligent, that certain species even use others as milch cows, watchdogs and slaves. He was well aware of their power of adaptation, their sense of discipline, their marvelous talent for organization.

His belief that a foray to supply the army was in progress was strengthened when he saw the leaves that fell to the ground being dragged to the troops waiting outside the wood. Then all at once he realized the aim that rain of green was intended to serve.

Each single leaf, pulled or pushed by dozens of toiling insects, was borne straight to the edge of the ditch. Even as Macbeth watched the approach of Birnam Wood in the hands of his enemies, Leiningen saw the tamarind wood move nearer and nearer in the mandibles of the ants. Unlike the fey Scot, however, he did not lose his nerve; no witches had prophesied his doom, and if they had he would have slept just as soundly. All the same, he was forced to admit to himself that the situation was far more ominous than that of the day before.

He had thought it impossible for the ants to build rafts for themselves—well, here they were, coming in thousands, more than enough to bridge the ditch. Leaves after leaves rustled down the slope into the water, where the current drew them away from the bank and carried them into midstream. And every single leaf carried several ants. This time the farmer did not trust to the alacrity of his messengers. He galloped away, leaning from his saddle and yelling orders as he rushed past outpost after outpost: "Bring petrol pumps to the southwest front! Issue spades to every man along the line facing the wood!" And arrived at the eastern and southern sections, he dispatched very man except the observation posts to the menaced west.

Then, as he rode past the stretch where the ants had failed to cross the day before, he witnessed a brief but impressive scene. Down the slope of the distant hill there came towards him a singular being, writhing rather than running, an animal-like blackened statue with shapeless head and four quivering feet that knuckled under almost ceaselessly. When the creature reached the far bank of the ditch and collapsed opposite Leiningen, he recognized it as a pampas stag, covered over and over with ants.

It had strayed near the zone of the army. As usual, they had attacked its eyes first. Blinded, it had reeled in the madness of hideous torment straight into the ranks of its persecutors, and now the beast swayed to and fro in its death agony.

With a shot from his rifle Leiningen put it out of its misery. Then he pulled out his watch. He hadn't a second to lose, but for life itself he could not have denied his curiosity the satisfaction of knowing how long the ants would take—for personal reasons, so to speak. After six minutes the white polished bones alone remained. That's how he himself would look before you can—Leiningen spat once, and put spurs to his horse.

The sporting zest with which the excitement of the novel contest had inspired him the day before had now vanished; in its place was a cold and violent purpose. He would send these vermin back to the hell where they belonged, somehow, anyhow. Yes, but how was indeed the question; as things stood at present it looked as if the devils would raze him and his men from the earth instead. He had underestimated the might of the enemy; he really would have to bestir himself if he hoped to outwit them.

The biggest danger now, he decided, was the point where the western section of the ditch curved southwards. And arrived there, he found his worst expectations justified. The very power of the current had huddled the leaves and their crews of ants so close together at the bend that the bridge was almost ready.

True, streams of petrol and clumps of earth still prevented a landing. But the number of floating leaves was increasing ever more swiftly. It could not be long now before a stretch of water a mile in length was decked by a green pontoon over which the ants could rush in millions.

Leiningen galloped to the weir. The damming of the river was controlled by a wheel on its bank. The planter ordered the man at the wheel first to lower the water in the ditch almost to vanishing point, next to wait a moment, then suddenly to let the river in again. This maneuver of lowering and raising the surface, of decreasing then increasing the flow of water through the ditch was to be repeated over and over again until further notice.

This tactic was at first successful. The water in the ditch sank, and with it the film of leaves. The green fleet nearly reached the bed and the troops on the far bank swarmed down the slope to it. Then a violent flow of water at the original depth raced through the ditch, overwhelming leaves and ants, and sweeping them along.

This intermittent rapid flushing prevented just in time the almost completed fording of the ditch. But it also flung here and there squads of the enemy vanguard simultaneously up the inner bank. These seemed to know their duty only too well, and lost no time accomplishing it. The air rang with the curses of bitten Indians. They had removed their shirts and pants to detect the quicker the upwards-hastening insects; when they saw one, they crushed it; and fortunately the onslaught as yet was only by skirmishers.

Again and again, the water sank and rose, carrying leaves and drowned ants away with it. It lowered once more nearly to its bed; but this time the exhausted defenders waited in vain for the flush of destruction. Leiningen sensed disaster; something must have gone wrong with the machinery of the dam. Then a sweating peon tore up to him—

"They're over!"

While the besieged were concentrating upon the defence of the stretch opposite the wood, the seemingly unaffected line beyond the wood had become the theatre of decisive action. Here the defenders' front was sparse and scattered; everyone who could be spared had hurried away to the south.

Just as the man at the weir had lowered the water almost to the bed of the ditch, the ants on a wide front began another attempt at a direct crossing like that of the preceding day. Into the emptied bed poured an irresistible throng. Rushing across the ditch, they attained the inner bank before the slow-witted Indians fully grasped the situation. Their frantic screams dumfounded the man at the weir. Before he could direct the river anew into the safeguarding bed he saw himself surrounded by raging ants. He ran like the others, ran for his life.

When Leiningen heard this, he knew the plantation was doomed. He wasted no time bemoaning the inevitable. For as long as there was the slightest chance of success, he had stood his ground, and now any further resistance was both useless and dangerous. He fired three revolver shots into the air—the prearranged signal for his men to retreat instantly within the "inner moat." Then he rode towards the ranch house.

This was two miles from the point of invasion. There was therefore time enough to prepare the second line of defence against the advent of the ants. Of the three great petrol cisterns near the house, one had already been half emptied by the constant withdrawals needed for the pumps during the fight at the water ditch. The remaining petrol in it was now drawn off through underground pipes into the concrete trench which encircled the ranch house and its outbuildings.

And there, drifting in twos and threes, Leiningen's men reached him. Most of them were obviously trying to preserve an air of calm and indifference, belied, however, by their restless glances and knitted brows. One could see their belief in a favorable outcome of the struggle was already considerably shaken.

The planter called his peons around him.

"Well, lads," he began, "we've lost the first round. But we'll smash the beggars yet, don't you worry. Anyone who thinks otherwise can draw his pay here and now and push off. There are rafts enough and to spare on the river and plenty of time still to reach 'em."

Not a man stirred.

Leiningen acknowledged his silent vote of confidence with a laugh that was half a grunt. "That's the stuff, lads. Too bad if you'd missed the rest of the show, eh? Well, the fun won't start till morning. Once these blighters turn tail, there'll be plenty of work for everyone and higher wages all round.

And now run along and get something to eat; you've earned it all right."

In the excitement of the fight the greater part of the day had passed without the men once pausing to snatch a bite. Now that the ants were for the time being out of sight, and the "wall of petrol" gave a stronger feeling of security, hungry stomachs began to assert their claims.

The bridges over the concrete ditch were removed. Here and there solitary ants had reached the ditch; they gazed at the petrol meditatively, then scurried back again. Apparently they had little interest at the moment for what lay beyond the evil-reeking barrier; the abundant spoils of the plantation were the main attraction. Soon the trees, shrubs and beds for miles around were hulled with ants zealously gobbling the yield of long weary months of strenuous toil.

As twilight began to fall, a cordon of ants marched around the petrol trench, but as yet made no move towards its brink. Leiningen posted sentries with headlights and electric torches, then withdrew to his office, and began to reckon up his losses. He estimated these as large, but, in comparison with his bank balance, by no means unbearable. He worked out in some detail a scheme of intensive cultivation which would enable him, before very long, to more than compensate himself for the damage now being wrought to his crops. It was with a contented mind that he finally betook himself to bed where he slept deeply until dawn, undisturbed by any thought that next day little more might be left of him than a glistening skeleton.

He rose with the sun and went out on the flat roof of his house. And a scene like one from Dante lay around him; for miles in every direction there was nothing but a black, glittering multitude, a multitude of rested, sated, but none the less voracious ants: yes, look as far as one might, one could see nothing but that rustling black throng, except in the north, where the great river drew a boundary they could not hope to pass. But even the high stone breakwater, along the bank of the river, which Leiningen had built as a defence against inundations, was, like the paths, the shorn trees and shrubs, the ground itself, black with ants.

So their greed was not glutted in razing that vast plantation? Not by a long chalk; they were all the more eager now on a rich and certain booty—four hundred men, numerous horses, and bursting granaries.

At first it seemed that the petrol trench would serve its purpose. The besiegers sensed the peril of swimming it, and made no move to plunge blindly over its brink. Instead they devised a better maneuver; they began to collect shreds of bark, twigs and dried leaves and dropped these into the petrol. Everything green, which could have been similarly used, had long since been eaten. After a time, though, a long procession could be seen bringing from the west the tamarind leaves used as rafts the day before.

Since the petrol, unlike the water in the outer ditch, was perfectly still, the refuse stayed where it was thrown. It was several hours before the ants succeeded in covering an appreciable part of the surface. At length, however, they were ready to proceed to a direct attack.

Their storm troops swarmed down the concrete side, scrambled over the supporting surface of twigs and leaves, and impelled these over the few remaining streaks of open petrol until they reached the other side. Then they began to climb up this to make straight for the helpless garrison.

During the entire offensive, the planter sat peacefully, watching them with interest, but not stirring a muscle. Moreover, he had ordered his men not to disturb in any way whatever the advancing horde. So they squatted listlessly along the bank of the ditch and waited for a sign from the boss.

The petrol was now covered with ants. A few had climbed the inner concrete wall and were scurrying towards the defenders.

"Everyone back from the ditch!" roared Leiningen. The men rushed away, without the slightest idea of his plan. He stooped forward and cautiously dropped into the ditch a stone which split the floating carpet and its living freight, to reveal a gleaming patch of petrol. A match spurted, sank down to the oily surface—Leiningen sprang back; in a flash a towering rampart of fire encompassed the garrison.

This spectacular and instant repulse threw the Indians into ecstasy. They applauded, yelled and stamped, like children at a pantomime. Had it not been for the awe in which they held the boss, they would infallibly have carried him shoulder high.

It was some time before the petrol burned down to the bed of the ditch, and the wall of smoke and flame began to lower. The ants had retreated in a wide circle from the devastation, and innumerable charred fragments along the outer bank showed that the flames had spread from the holocaust in the ditch well into the ranks beyond, where they had wrought havoc far and wide.

Yet the perseverance of the ants was by no means broken; indeed, each setback seemed only to whet it. The concrete cooled, the flicker of the dying flames wavered and vanished, petrol from the second tank poured into the trench—and the ants marched forward anew to the attack.

The foregoing scene repeated itself in every detail, except that on this occasion less time was needed to bridge the ditch, for the petrol was now already filmed by a layer of ash. Once again they withdrew; once again petrol flowed into the ditch. Would the creatures never learn that their self-sacrifice was utterly senseless? It really was senseless, wasn't it? Yes, of course it was senseless—provided the defenders had an *unlimited* supply of petrol.

When Leiningen reached this stage of reasoning, he felt for the first time since the arrival of the ants that his confidence was deserting him. His skin began to creep; he loosened his collar. Once the devils were over the trench there wasn't a chance in hell for him and his men. God, what a prospect, to be eaten alive like that!

For the third time the flames immolated the attacking troops, and burned down to extinction. Yet the ants were coming on again as if nothing had happened. And meanwhile Leiningen had made a discovery that chilled him to the bone—petrol was no longer flowing into the ditch. Something must be blocking the outflow pipe of the third and last cistern—a snake or a dead rat? Whatever it was, the ants could be held off no longer, unless petrol could by some method be led from the cistern into the ditch.

Then Leiningen remembered that in an outhouse nearby were two old disused fire engines. Spry as never before in their lives, the peons dragged them out of the shed, connected their pumps to the cistern, uncoiled and laid the hose. They were just in time to aim a stream of petrol at a column of ants that had already crossed and drive them back down the incline into the ditch. Once more an oily girdle surrounded the garrison, once more it was possible to hold the position—for the moment.

It was obvious, however, that this last resource meant only the postponement of defeat and death. A few of the peons fell on their knees and began to pray; others, shrieking insanely, fired their revolvers at the black, advancing masses, as if they felt their despair was pitiful enough to sway fate itself to mercy.

At length, two of the men's nerves broke: Leiningen saw a naked Indian leap over the north side of the petrol trench, quickly followed by a second. They sprinted with incredible speed towards the river. But their fleetness did not save them; long before they could attain the rafts, the enemy covered their bodies from head to foot.

In the agony of their torment, both sprang blindly into the wide river, where enemies no less sinister awaited them. Wild screams of mortal anguish informed the breathless onlookers that crocodiles and sword-toothed piranhas were no less ravenous than ants, and even nimbler in reaching their prey.

In spite of this bloody warning, more and more men showed they were making up their minds to run the blockade. Anything, even a fight midstream against alligators, seemed better than powerlessly waiting for death to come and slowly consume their living bodies.

Leiningen flogged his brain till it reeled. Was there nothing on earth could sweep this devil's spawn back into the hell from which it came?

Then out of the inferno of his bewilderment rose a terrifying inspiration. Yes, one hope remained, and one alone. It might be possible to dam the great river completely, so that its waters would fill not only the water ditch but overflow into the entire gigantic "saucer" of land in which lay the plantation.

The far bank of the river was too high for the waters to escape that way. The stone breakwater ran between the river and the plantation; its only gaps occurred where the "horseshoe" ends of the water ditch passed into the river. So its waters would not only be forced to inundate into the plantation, they would also be held there by the breakwater until they rose to its own high level. In half an hour, perhaps even earlier, the plantation and its hostile army of occupation would be flooded.

The ranch house and outbuildings stood upon rising ground. Their foundations were higher than the breakwater, so the flood would not reach them. And any remaining ants trying to ascend the slope could be repulsed by petrol.

It was possible—yes, if one could only get to the dam! A distance of nearly two miles lay between the ranch house and the weir—two miles of ants. Those two peons had managed only a fifth of that distance at the cost of their lives. Was there an Indian daring enough after that to run the gauntlet five times as far? Hardly likely; and if there were, his prospect of getting back was almost nil.

No, there was only one thing for it, he'd have to make the attempt himself; he might just as well be running as sitting still, anyway, when the ants finally got him. Besides, there was a bit of a chance. Perhaps the ants weren't so almighty, after all; perhaps he had allowed the mass suggestion of that evil black throng to hypnotize him, just as a snake fascinates and overpowers.

The ants were building their bridges. Leiningen got up on a chair. "Hey, lads, listen to me!" he cried. Slowly and listlessly, from all sides of the trench, the men began to shuffle towards him, the apathy of death already stamped on their faces.

"Listen, lads!" he shouted. "You're frightened of those beggars, but you're a damn sight more frightened of me, and I'm proud of you. There's still a chance to save our lives—by flooding the plantation from the river. Now one of you might manage to get as far as the weir—but he'd never come back. Well, I'm not going to let you try it; if I did I'd be worse than one of those ants. No, I called the tune, and now I'm going to pay the piper.

"The moment I'm over the ditch, set fire to the petrol. That'll allow time for the flood to do the trick. Then all you have to do is wait here all snug and quiet till I'm back. Yes, I'm coming back, trust me"—he grinned—"when I've finished my slimming-cure."

He pulled on high leather boots, drew heavy gauntlets over his hands, and stuffed the spaces between breeches and boots, gauntlets and arms, shirt and neck, with rags soaked in petrol. With close-fitting mosquito goggles he shielded his eyes, knowing too well the ants' dodge of first robbing their victim of sight. Finally, he plugged his nostrils and ears with cotton-wool, and let the peons drench his clothes with petrol.

He was about to set off, when the old Indian medicine man came up to him; he had a wondrous salve, he said, prepared from a species of chafer whose odor was intolerable to ants. Yes, this odor protected these chafers from the attacks of even the most murderous ants. The Indian smeared the boss' boots, his gauntlets, and his face over and over with the extract.

Leiningen then remembered the paralyzing effect of ants' venom, and the Indian gave him a gourd full of the medicine he had administered to the bitten peon at the water ditch. The planter drank it down without noticing its bitter taste; his mind was already at the weir.

He started off towards the northwest corner of the trench. With a bound he was over—and among the ants.

The beleaguered garrison had no opportunity to watch Leiningen's race against death. The ants were climbing the inner bank again—the lurid ring of petrol blazed aloft. For the fourth time that day the reflection from the fire shone on the sweating faces of the imprisoned men, and on the reddish-black cuirasses of their oppressors. The red and blue, dark-edged flames leaped vividly now, celebrating what? The funeral pyre of the four hundred, or of the hosts of destruction?

Leiningen ran. He ran in long, equal strides, with only one thought, one sensation, in his being—he *must* get through. He dodged all trees and shrubs; except for the split seconds his soles touched the ground the ants should have no opportunity to alight on him. That they would get to him soon, despite the salve on his boots, the petrol in his clothes, he realized only too well, but he knew even more surely that he must, and that he would, get to the weir.

Apparently the salve was some use after all; not until he reached halfway did he feel ants under his clothes, and a few on his face. Mechanically, in his stride, he struck at them, scarcely conscious of their bites. He saw he was drawing appreciably nearer the weir—the distance grew less and less— sank to five hundred—three—two—one hundred yards.

Then he was at the weir and gripping the ant-hulled wheel. Hardly had he seized it when a horde of infuriated ants flowed over his hands, arms and shoulders. He started the wheel—before it turned once on its axis the swarm covered his face. Leiningen strained like a madman, his lips pressed tight; if he opened them to draw breath. . . .

He turned and turned; slowly the dam lowered until it reached the bed of the river. Already the water was overflowing the ditch. Another minute, and the river was pouring through the near-by gap in the breakwater. The flooding of the plantation had begun.

Leiningen let go the wheel. Now, for the first time, he realized he was coated from head to foot with a layer of ants. In spite of the petrol, his clothes were full of them, several had got to his body or were clinging to his face. Now that he had completed his task, he felt the smart raging over his flesh from the bites of sawing and piercing insects.

Frantic with pain, he almost plunged into the river. To be ripped and splashed to shreds by piranhas? Already he was running the return journey, knocking ants from his gloves and jacket, brushing them from his bloodied face, squashing them to death under his clothes.

One of the creatures bit him just below the rim of his goggles; he managed to tear it away, but the agony of the bite and its etching acid drilled into the eye nerves; he saw now through circles of fire into a milky mist, then he ran for a time almost blinded, knowing that if he once tripped and fell. . . . The old Indian's brew didn't seem much good; it weakened the poison a bit, but didn't get rid of it. His heart pounded as if it would burst; blood roared in his ears; a giant's fist battered his lungs.

Then he could see again, but the burning girdle of petrol appeared infinitely far away; he could not last half that distance. Swift-changing pictures flashed through his head, episodes in his life, while in another part of his brain a cool and impartial onlooker informed this ant-blurred, gasping, exhausted bundle named Leiningen that such a rushing panorama of scenes from one's past is seen only in the moment before death.

A stone in the path . . . too weak to avoid it . . . the planter stumbled and collapsed. He tried to rise . . . he must be pinned under a rock . . . it was impossible . . . the slightest movement was impossible. . . .

Then all at once he saw, starkly clear and huge, and, right before his eyes, furred with ants, towering and swaying in its death agony, the pampas stag. In six minutes—gnawed to the bones. God, he *couldn't* die like that! And something outside him seemed to drag him to his feet. He tottered. He began to stagger forward again.

Through the blazing ring hurtled an apparition which, as soon as it reached the ground on the inner side, fell full length and did not move. Leiningen, at the moment he made that leap through the flames, lost consciousness for the first time in his life. As he lay there, with glazing eyes and lacerated face, he appeared a man returned from the grave. The peons rushed to him, stripped off his clothes, tore away the ants from a body that seemed almost one open wound; in some places the bones were showing. They carried him into the ranch house.

As the curtain of flames lowered, one could see in place of the illimitable host of ants an extensive vista of water. The thwarted river had swept over the plantation, carrying with it the entire army. The water had collected and mounted in the great "saucer," while the ants had in vain attempted to reach the hill on which stood the ranch house. The girdle of flames held them back.

And so imprisoned between water and fire, they had been delivered into the annihilation that was their god. And near the farther mouth of the water ditch, where the stone mole had its second gap, the ocean swept the lost battalions into the river, to vanish forever.

The ring of fire dwindled as the water mounted to the petrol trench, and quenched the dimming flames. The inundation rose higher and higher: because its outflow was impeded by the timber and underbrush it had carried along with it, its surface required some time to reach the top of the high stone breakwater and discharge over it the rest of the shattered army.

It swelled over ant-stippled shrubs and bushes, until it washed against the foot of the knoll whereon the besieged had taken refuge. For a while an alluvial of ants tried again and again to attain this dry land, only to be repulsed by streams of petrol back into the merciless flood.

Leiningen lay on his bed, his body swathed from head to foot in bandages. With fomentations and salves, they had managed to stop the bleeding, and had dressed his many wounds. Now they thronged around him, one question in every face. Would he recover? "He won't die," said the old man who had bandaged him, "if he doesn't want to."

The planter opened his eyes. "Everything in order?" he asked.

"They're gone," said his nurse. "To hell." He held out to his master a gourd full of a powerful sleeping draught. Leiningen gulped it down.

"I told you I'd come back," he murmured, "even if I am a bit streamlined." He grinned and shut his eyes. He slept.

# Mrs. 'Arris Goes to Paris

### PAUL GALLICO

*one*

THE small, slender woman with apple-red cheeks, graying hair, and shrewd, almost naughty little eyes sat with her face pressed against the cabin window of the BEA Viscount morning flight from London to Paris. As with a rush and a roar the steel bird lifted itself from the runway and the wheels, still revolving, began to retract into its belly, her spirits soared aloft with it. She was nervous, but not at all frightened, for she was convinced that nothing could happen to her now. Hers was the bliss of one who knew that at last she was off upon the adventure at the end of which lay heart's desire.

She was neatly dressed in a somewhat shabby tan twill topcoat with clean tan cotton gloves, and she carried a battered imitation leather brown handbag which she hugged close to her. And well she might do so, for it contained not only ten one-pound notes, the legal limit of currency that could be exported from the British Isles, and a round-trip air ticket to Paris and back, but likewise the sum of fourteen hundred dollars in American currency, a thick roll of five-, ten- and twenty-dollar bills, held together by a rubber band. Only in the hat she wore did her ebullient nature manifest itself. It was of green straw, and to the front of it was attached a huge and preposterous rose on a flexible stem and which leaned this way and that, seemingly following the hand of the pilot upon the wheel as the plane tilted and circled for altitude.

Any knowledgeable London housewife who had ever availed herself of the services of that unique breed of "daily women," who come in to scrub and tidy up by the hour, or for that matter any Britisher, would have said: "The woman under that hat could only be a London char," and what is more, she would have been right.

On the passenger manifest of the airliner she appeared as Mrs. Ada Harris, though she invariably pronounced it as "Mrs. 'Arris," No. 5 Willis Gardens, Battersea, London, S.W. 11, and she was indeed a charwoman, a widow, who "did" hours for a clientèle who lived in and on the fringes of the fashionable Eaton Square and Belgravia.

Up to that magic moment of finding herself hoisted off the face of the earth hers had been a life of never ending drudgery, relieved by nothing more than an occasional visit to the flicks, the corner pub, or an evening at the music hall.

The world in which Mrs. Harris, now approaching her sixties, moved was one of a perpetual mess, slop and untidiness. Not once, but half a dozen times a day she opened the doors of homes or flats with the keys entrusted to her, to face the litter of dirty dishes and greasy pans in the sink, areas of stale, rumpled, unmade beds, articles of clothing scattered about, wet towels on the bathroom floor, mouthwash water left in the glass, dirty laundry to be filed away and, of course, cigarette stubs in the ash trays, dust on tables and mirrors, and all the other litter that human pigs are capable of leaving behind them when they leave their homes in the morning.

Mrs. Harris cleaned up these messes because it was her profession, a way of gaining a livelihood and keeping body and soul together. And yet with some chars there was more to it than just that, and particularly with Mrs. Harris—a kind of perpetual house-proudness. And it was a creative effort as well, something in which a person might take pride and satisfaction. She came to these rooms to find them pigsties, she left them neat, clean, sparkling and sweet-smelling. The fact that when she returned the next day they would be pigsties all over again did not bother her. She was paid her three shillings an hour and she would again leave them immaculate. This was the life and profession of the little woman, one of thirty assorted passengers on the huge airplane bound for Paris.

The green-and-brown-checkered relief map of British soil slipped beneath the wings of the aircraft and gave way suddenly to the wind-ruffled blue of the English Channel. Where previously she had looked down with interest at the novelty of the tiny houses and farms below, these were now exchanged for the slender shapes of tankers and freighters plowing the surface of the sea. For the first time Mrs. Harris realized that she was leaving England behind her and was about to enter into a foreign country, to be amongst foreign people who spoke a foreign language and who, from all she had ever heard about them, were immoral, grasping, ate snails and frogs, and were particularly inclined to crimes of passion and dismembered bodies in trunks. She was still not afraid, for fear has no place in the vocabulary of the British char, but she was now all the more determined to be on her guard and not stand for any nonsense. It was a tremendous errand that was taking her to Paris, but she hoped in the accomplishing of it to have as little to do with the French people as possible.

The airplane flew on and a wholesome British steward served her a wholesome British breakfast and then would take no money for it, saying that it came with the compliments of the airline, a little bit of all right.

Mrs. Harris kept her face pressed to the window and her purse to her side. The steward came through, saying: "You will see the Eiffel Tower in the distance on your right."

"Lumme," said Mrs. Harris to herself when a moment later she discovered its pin point upthrust from what seemed to be an old patchwork quilt of gray roofs and chimney pots, with a single snakelike blue thread of a river running through it. "It don't look as big as in the pictures."

A minute or so later the machine set down without so much as a bump on the concrete of the French airport. Mrs. Harris' spirits rose still further. None of her friend Mrs. Butterfield's gloomy prognostications that the thing would either blow up in the sky or plunge with her to the bottom of the sea had been borne out. Paris perhaps might not prove so formidable after all. Nevertheless, from now on she was inclined to be suspicious and careful, a precaution not lessened by the long bus ride from Le Bourget through strange streets lined with strange houses and shops offering strange wares in a strange and unintelligible language.

The British European Airways man assigned to assist travelers confused by the hurly-burly of the Invalides Air Station in Paris took one look at the hat, the bag, the outsize shoes and, of course, the inimitable saucy little eyes, and recognized her immediately for what she was. "Good heavens," he said to himself under his breath, "a London char! What on earth is she doing here in Paris? The domestic help situation here can't be *that* bad."

He noted her uncertainty, quickly consulted his manifest, and guessed right again. Moving smoothly to her side, he touched his cap and asked: "Can I help you in any way, Mrs. Harris?"

The clever, roguish eyes inspected him carefully for any signs of moral depravity or a foreign monkey business. Somewhat to her disappointment, he seemed just like any Englishman. Since his approach was polite and harmless, she said cautiously: "Ow, so they can speak the Queen's English over 'ere."

The Airways man said: "Well, ma'am, I ought to, I *am* British. But I think you will find most people over here speak a little English and you can get along. I see you are returning with us on the eleven o'clock plane this evening. Is there any particular place you wish to go to now?"

Mrs. Harris reflected upon just how much she was prepared to tell a stranger and then replied firmly: "I'll just 'ave a taxi, if it's all the same to you. I've got me ten quid."

"Ah, well then," the Airways man continued, "you'd better have some of it in French money. One pound comes to roughly a thousand francs."

At the *Bureau de change* a few of Mrs. Harris' green pound notes were translated into flimsy, tattered, dirty, blue paper with the figure 1000 on them and some greasy metal hundred-franc coins.

Mrs. Harris was justly indignant. "What's all this?" she demanded. "Call this 'ere stuff money? Them coins feel like duds."

The Airways man smiled. "Well, in a sense they are, but only the government's allowed to make them. The fact just hasn't caught up with the French yet. Still, they continue to pass." He guided her through the crowd and up the ramp and placed her in a taxi. "Where shall I tell him to take you?"

Mrs. Harris sat up with her slender back, thin from hard work, ramrod straight, the pink rose pointing due north, her face as calm and composed as that of a duchess. Only the little eyes were dancing with excitement. "Tell him to take me to the dress shop of Christian Dior," she said.

The Airways man stared at her, refusing the evidence of his ears. "I beg your pardon, ma'am?"

"The dress shop of Dior, you 'eard me?"

The Airways man had heard her all right, but his brain, used to dealing with all kind of emergencies and queer cases, could just not make the connection between a London daily woman, one of that vast army that sallied forth every morning to scrub up the city's dirt in office and home, and the most exclusive fashion center in the world, and he still hesitated.

"Come on then, get on with it," commanded Mrs. Harris sharply, "what's so strange about a lydy going to buy 'erself a dress in Paris?"

Shaken to the marrow, the Airways man spoke to the driver in French. "Take Madame to the House of Christian Dior in the Avenue Montaigne. If you try to skin her out of so much as a sou, I'll take care you never get back on this rank again."

As Mrs. Harris was driven off he went back inside shaking his head. He felt he had seen everything now.

Riding along in the taxi, her heart beating with excitement, Mrs. Harris' thoughts went back to London and she hoped that Mrs. Butterfield would be able to cope.

Mrs. Harris' list of clients, whilst subject to change without notice—that is to say she might suddenly dismiss one of them, never they her—remained fairly static. There were some to whom she gave several hours every day and others who desired her services only three times a week. She worked ten hours a day, her labors beginning at eight in the morning and ending at six o'clock in the night, with a half day devoted to certain favored customers on Saturdays. This schedule she maintained fifty-two weeks in the year. Since there were just so many hours in a day her patrons were limited to some six or eight and she herself organized that the area of her labors was restricted to the fashionable sector of Eaton and Belgrave squares known as Belgravia. For once she had arrived in that neighborhood in the morning she was then able to walk quickly from house to flat to mews.

There was a Major Wallace, her bachelor, whom naturally she spoiled and in whose frequent and changing love affairs she took an avid interest.

She was fond of a Mrs. Schreiber, a somewhat muddled person, the wife of a Hollywood film representative living in London, for her American warmth and generosity which displayed itself in many ways, but chiefly by her interest in and consideration for Mrs. Harris.

She "did" for fashionable Lady Dant, the wife of a wealthy industrial baron, who maintained a flat in London as well as a country manor—Lady Dant was always getting her picture in The Queen or The Tatler at hunt balls and charity affairs, and this made Mrs. Harris proud.

There were others: a White Russian Countess Wyszcinska, whom Mrs. Harris liked because she was divinely mad; a young married couple; a second son, whose charming flat she loved because there were pretty things in it; Mrs. Fford Foulks, a divorcée, who was a valuable mine of gossip as to what the idle rich were up to; and several others, including a little actress, Miss Pamela Penrose, who was struggling to gain recognition from her base in a two-room mews flat.

All of these establishments Mrs. Harris looked after quite on her own.

Yet she was not without assistance and someone to fall back on in case of emergency in the person of her friend and alter ego Mrs. Violet Butterfield, like herself a widow and a char, and inclined to take the gloomy aspect of life and affairs wherever there was any choice.

Mrs. Butterfield, who was as large and stout as Mrs. Harris appeared to be thin and frail, naturally had her own set of clients, fortunately likewise in the same neighborhood. But they helped one another out with a nice bit of teamwork whenever the necessity arose.

If either one of them was ill or had pressing business elsewhere, the other would manage to pinch enough time from her clients to make the rounds of the other's customers sufficiently to keep them quiet and satisfied. Were Mrs. Harris to be bedded with some malaise, as rarely happened, she would telephone her clients to advise them of this catastrophe and add: "But don't you worry. Me friend Mrs. Butterfield will look in on you and I'll be around again tomorrow," and vice versa. Although they were different as night and day in character, they were firm, loving and loyal friends, and considered covering one another a part of their duty in life. A friend was a friend and that was that. Mrs. Harris' basement flat was at No. 5 Willis Gardens, Mrs. Butterfield lived in No. 7, and rare was the day that they did not meet or visit one another to exchange news or confidences.

The taxicab crossed a big river, the one Mrs. Harris had seen from the air, now gray instead of blue. On the bridge the driver got himself into a violent altercation with another chauffeur. They shouted and screamed at one another. Mrs. Harris did not understand the words but guessed at the language and the import and smiled happily to herself. This time her thoughts returned to Miss Pamela Penrose and the fuss she had kicked up when informed of Mrs. Harris' intention to take a day off. Mrs. Harris had made it a special point with Mrs. Butterfield to see that the aspiring actress was not neglected.

Curiously, for all her shrewdness and judgment of character, Mrs. Harris' favorite of all her clients was Miss Penrose.

The girl—whose real name, as Mrs. Harris had gleaned from superficially inspecting letters that occasionally came so addressed, was Enid Snite—lived untidily in a one-story walk-up mews flat, the headquarters for her precarious existence.

She was a small, smooth blonde with a tight mouth and curiously static eyes that seemed fixed greedily upon but one thing—herself. She had an exquisite figure and clever tiny feet that never once had tripped upon the corpses she had climbed over on her way up the ladder of success. There was nothing she would not do to further what she was pleased to call her career, which up to that time had included a year or two in the chorus line, some bit parts in a few pictures and several appearances on television. She was mean, hard, selfish and ruthless, and, of course, her manners were abominable as well.

One would have thought that Mrs. Harris would have penetrated the false front of this little beast and abandoned her, for it was so that when something about a client displeased Mrs. Harris she simply dropped the key through the mailbox and did not return. Like so many of her sisters who did not char for charring's sake alone, even though it was her living, she also brought a certain warmth to it. She had to like either the person or the person's home where she worked.

But it was just the fact that Mrs. Harris had pierced the front of Miss Snite to a certain extent that made her stick to her, for she understood the fierce, wild, hungry craving of the girl to be something, to be somebody, to lift herself out of the ruck of everyday struggle and acquire some of the good things of life for herself.

Prior to her own extraordinary craving which had brought her to Paris, Mrs. Harris had not experienced this in herself though she understood it very well. With her it had not been so much the endeavor to make something of herself as it had been the battle to survive, and in that sense these two were not unalike. When Mrs. Harris' husband had died some twenty years past and left her penniless, she simply had to make a go of things, her widow's pension being insufficient.

And then too there was the glamour of the theater which surrounded Miss Snite, or rather Penrose, as Mrs. Harris chose to think of her, and this was irresistible.

Mrs. Harris was not impressed by titles, wealth, position, or family, but she was susceptible to the enchantment that enveloped anything or anyone that had to do with the stage, the television, or the flicks.

She had no way of knowing how tenuous and sketchy was Miss Penrose's connection with these, that she was not only a bad little girl but a mediocre actress. It was sufficient for Mrs. Harris that from time to time her voice was heard on the wireless or she would pass across the television screen wearing an apron and carrying a tray. Mrs. Harris respected the lone battle the girl was waging, humored her, cosseted her, and took from her what she would not from anyone else.

The taxicab entered a broad street lined with beautiful buildings, but Mrs. Harris had no eye or time for architecture.

"'Ow far is it?" she shouted at the cab driver, who replied, not slowing down one whit, by taking both hands off the steering wheel, waving his arms in the air, turning around and shouting back at her. Mrs. Harris, of course, understood not a word, but his smile beneath a walrus mustache was engaging and friendly enough, and so she settled back to endure the ride until she should reach the so-long-coveted destination. She reflected upon the strange series of events that led to her being there.

*two*

It had all begun that day several years back when, during the course of her duties at the apartment of Lady Dant, Mrs. Harris had opened a wardrobe which she was wont to tidy and had come upon the two dresses hanging there. One was a bit of heaven in cream, ivory, lace and chiffon, the other an explosion in crimson satin and taffeta, adorned with great red bows and a huge red flower. She stood there as though struck dumb, for never in all her life had she seen anything quite as thrilling and beautiful.

Drab and colorless as her existence would seem to have been, Mrs. Harris had always felt a craving for beauty and color and which up to this moment had manifested itself in a love for flowers. She had the proverbial green thumb, coupled with no little skill, and plants flourished for her where they would not, quite possibly, for any other.

Outside the windows of her basement flat were two window boxes of geraniums, her favorite flower, and inside, wherever there was room, there was a little pot containing a geranium struggling desperately to conquer its environment, or a single hyacinth or tulip, bought from a barrow for a hard-earned shilling.

Then too, the people for whom she worked would sometimes present her with the leavings of their cut flowers which in their wilted state she would take home and try to nurse back to health, and once in a while, particularly in the spring, she would buy herself a little box of pansies, primroses or anemones. As long as she had flowers Mrs. Harris had no serious complaints concerning the life she led. They were her escape from the somber stone desert in which she lived. These bright flashes of color satisfied her. They were something to return to in the evening, something to wake up to in the morning.

But now as she stood before the stunning creations hanging in the closet she found herself face to face with a new kind of beauty—an artificial one created by the hand of man the artist, but aimed directly and cunningly at the heart of woman. In that very instant she fell victim to the artist; at that very moment there was born within her the craving to possess such a garment.

There was no rhyme or reason for it; she would never wear such a creation; there was no place in her life for one. Her reaction was purely feminine. She saw it and she wanted it dreadfully. Something inside her yearned and reached for it as instinctively as an infant in the crib snatches at a bright object. How deeply this craving went, how powerful it was, Mrs. Harris herself did not even know at that moment. She could only stand there enthralled, rapt and enchanted, gazing at the dresses, leaning upon her mop, in her music-hall shoes, soiled overall, and wispy hair down about her ears, the classic figure of the cleaning woman.

It was thus that Lady Dant found her when she happened to come in from her writing room. "Oh!" she exclaimed. "My dresses!" And then noting Mrs. Harris' attitude and the expression on her face, said: "Do you like them? I haven't made up my mind yet which one I am going to wear tonight."

Mrs. Harris was hardly conscious that Lady Dant was speaking, she was still so engrossed in these living creations of silks and taffetas and chiffons in heart-lifting colors, daring cut and stiff with cunning internal construction so that they appeared to stand almost by themselves like creatures with a life of their own. "Coo," she gasped finally, "ain't they beauties. I'll bet they didn't 'arf cost a packet."

Lady Dant had been unable to resist the temptation to impress Mrs. Harris. London chars do not impress easily, in fact are the least impressionable people in the world. She had always been a little afraid of Mrs. Harris, and here was her chance to score. She laughed her brittle laugh and said: "Well, yes, in a way. This one here—'Ivoire'—cost three hundred fifty pounds and the big one, the red—it's called 'Ravishing'—came to around four hundred fifty. I always go to Dior, don't you think? Then, of course, you know you're right."

"Four hundred fifty quid," echoed Mrs. Harris, "'ow would anyone ever get that much money?" She was not unfamiliar with Paris styles, for she was an assiduous reader of old fashion magazines sometimes presented to her by clients, and she had heard of Fath, Chanel and Balenciaga, Carpentier, Lanvin and Dior, and the last-named now rang like a bell through her beauty-starved person.

For it was one thing to encounter photographs of dresses, leafing through the slick pages of *Vogue* or *Elle*, where, whether in color or black and white, they were impersonal and as out of her world and her reach as the moon or the stars. It was quite another to come face to face with the real article, to feast one's eyes upon its every clever stitch, to touch it, smell it, love it, and suddenly to become consumed with the fires of desire.

Mrs. Harris was quite unaware that in her reply to Lady Dant she had already given voice to a determination to possess a dress such as this. She had not meant "How would anyone get that much money?" but "How would *I* get that much money?" There, of course, was no answer to this, or rather only one. One would have to win it. But the chances of this were likewise as remote as the planets.

Lady Dant was quite well pleased with the impression she seemed to have created and even took each one down and held it up to her so that Mrs. Harris could get some idea of the effect. And since the char's hands were spotless from the soap and water in which they were immersed most of the time, she let her touch the material, which the little drudge did as though it were the Grail.

"Ain't it loverly," she whispered again. Lady Dant did not know that at that instant Mrs. Harris had made up her mind that what she desired above all else on earth, and in Heaven thereafter, was a Dior dress of her own to have hanging in her closet.

Smiling slyly, pleased with herself, Lady Dant shut the closet door, but she could not shut out from the mind of Mrs. Harris what she had seen there: beauty, perfection, the ultimate in adornment that a woman could desire. Mrs. Harris was no less a woman than Lady Dant or any other. She wanted, she wanted, she wanted a dress from what must be surely the most expensive store in the world, that of Mr. Dior in Paris.

Mrs. Harris was no fool. Not so much as a thought of ever wearing such a garment in public ever entered her head. If there was one thing Mrs. Harris knew, it was her place. She kept to it herself, and woe to anyone else who tried to encroach upon it. Her place was a world of unremitting toil, but it was illuminated by her independence. There was no room in it for extravagance and pretty clothes.

But it was possession she desired now, feminine physical possession: to have it hanging in her cupboard, to know that it was there when she was away, to open the door when she returned and find it waiting for her, exquisite to touch, to see and to own. It was as though all she had missed through the poverty, the circumstances of her birth and class in life could be made up by becoming the holder of this one glorious bit of feminine finery. The same vast, unthinkable amount of money could be represented as well by a piece of jewelry, or a single diamond which would last forever. Mrs. Harris had no interest in diamonds. The very fact that one dress could represent such a huge sum increased its desirability and her yearning for it. She was well aware that her wanting it made no sense whatsoever, but that did not prevent her one whit from doing so.

All through the rest of that day, a damp, miserable and foggy one, she was warmed by the images of the creations she had seen, and the more she thought of them the more the desire and the craving grew upon her.

That evening as the rain dripped from the thick London fog, Mrs. Harris sat in the cozy warmth of Mrs. Butterfield's kitchen for the important ceremony of making out their coupons for the weekly football pool.

Ever since she could remember, it seemed that she and Mrs. Butterfield had been contributing their thruppence a week to this fascinating national lottery. It was cheap at the price, the hope and excitement and the suspense that could be bought for no more than three pennies each. For once the coupon was filled out and dropped into the postbox it represented untold wealth until the arrival of the newspapers with the results and disillusionment, but never really disappointment since they actually did not expect to win. Once Mrs. Harris had achieved a prize of thirty shillings and several times Mrs. Butterfield had got her money back, or rather a free play for the following week, but, of course, that was all. The fantastic major prizes remained glamorous and ambition-inspiring, fairy tales that occasionally found their way into the newspapers.

Since Mrs. Harris was not sports-minded, nor had the time to follow the fortunes of the football teams, and since as well the possible combinations and permutations ran into the millions, she was accustomed to making out her selections by guess and by God. The results of some thirty games, win, lose, or draw, had to be predicted, and Mrs. Harris' method was to pause with her pencil poised over each line and to wait for some inner or outer message to arrive and tell her what to put down. Luck, she felt, was something tangible that floated around in the air and sometimes settled on people in large chunks. Luck was something that could be felt, grabbed at, bitten off; luck could be all around one at one moment and vanish in the next. And so, at the moment of wooing good fortune in the guise of the football pools, Mrs. Harris tried to attune herself to the unknown. Usually as she paused if she experienced no violent hunches or felt nothing at all, she would mark it down as a draw.

On this particular evening as they sat in the pool of lamplight, their coupons and steaming cups of hot tea before them, Mrs. Harris felt the presence of luck as thickly about her as the fog without. As she poised her pencil over the first line—"Aston Villa vs. Bolton Wanderers"—she looked up and said intensely to Mrs. Butterfield: "This is for me Dior dress."

"Your what, dearie?" queried Mrs. Butterfield, who had but half heard what her friend said, for she herself was addicted to the trance method of filling out her list and was already entering into that state where something clicked in her head and she wrote her selections down one after the other without even stopping for a breath.

"Me Dior dress," repeated Mrs. Harris, and then said fiercely, as though by her very vehemence to force it to happen: "I'm going to 'ave me a Dior dress."

"Are you now?" murmured Mrs. Butterfield, unwilling to emerge entirely from the state of catalepsy she had been about to enter. "Something new at Marks & Sparks?"

"Marks & Sparks me eye," said Mrs. Harris. "'Aven't you ever heard of Dior?"

"Can't say I 'ave, love," Mrs. Butterfield murmured, still half betwixt and between.

"It's the most expensive shop in the world. It's in Paris. The dresses cost four hundred fifty quid."

Mrs. Butterfield came out of it with a bang. Her jaw dropped, her chins folded into one another like the sections of a collapsible drinking cup.

"Four hundred fifty what?" she gasped. "'Ave you gone barmy, dearie?"

For a moment even Mrs. Harris was shocked by the figure, but then its very outrageousness, coupled with the force of the desire that had been born within her, restored her conviction. She said: "Lady Dant 'as one of them in 'er cupboard. She brought it up for the charity ball tonight. I've never seen anything like it in me life before except maybe in a dream or in a book." Her voice lowered for a moment as she became reflective. "Why, even the Queen ain't got a dress like that," she said, and then loudly and firmly, "and I mean to 'ave one."

The shock waves had now begun to subside in Mrs. Butterfield and she returned to her practical pessimism. "Where're you going to get the money, ducks?" she queried.

"Right 'ere," replied Mrs. Harris, tapping her coupon with her pencil so as to leave the fates in no doubt as to what was expected of them.

Mrs. Butterfield accepted this since she herself had a long list of articles she expected to acquire immediately should *her* ticket come home. But she had another idea. "Dresses like that ain't for the likes of us, dearie," she gloomed.

Mrs. Harris reacted passionately: "What do I care what is or isn't for a likes of us; it's the most beautiful thing I've ever laid me eyes on and I mean to 'ave it."

Mrs. Butterfield persisted: "What would you do with it when you got it?"

This brought Mrs. Harris up short, for she had not even thought beyond the possession of such a wonderful creation. All she knew was that she craved it most fearfully, and so to Mrs. Butterfield's question she could not make other reply than " 'Ave it! Just 'ave it!"

Her pencil was resting on the first line of the pool coupon. She turned her attention to it and said: "Now then, 'ere goes for it." And without another moment's hesitation, almost as though her fingers were working outside her own volition, she filled in line after line, win, lose, draw, win, win, draw, draw, draw, lose, and win, until the entire blank was completed. She had never done it like that before. "There," she said.

"Good luck to you, love," said Mrs. Butterfield. She was so fascinated by her friend's performance that she paid only perfunctory attention to her own and soon had it completed.

Still in the grip of something, Mrs. Harris said hoarsely: "Let's post them now, right now while me luck is running."

They put on coats, bound scarfs about their heads and went off into the rain and the dripping fog to the red pillar box gleaming faintly on the corner beneath the street lamp. Mrs. Harris pressed the envelope to her lips for a moment, said " 'Ere's for me Dior dress," and slipped the letter through the slit, listening for its fall. Mrs. Butterfield posted hers with less confidence. "Don't expect nuffink and you won't get disappointed. This's my motto," she said. They returned to their tea.

*three*

The marvelous and universe-shattering discovery was made that weekend not by Mrs. Harris, but by Mrs. Butterfield, who, flesh a-quivering, came storming into the former's kitchen in such a state that she was hardly able to speak and indeed seemed to be on the verge of apoplexy.

"D-d-d-ducks," she stammered, "ducks, it's 'APPENED!"

Mrs. Harris, who was engaged in ironing Major Wallace's shirts after washing them—this was one of the ways in which she spoiled him—said without looking up from the nicety of turning the neckband: "Take it easy, dear, or you'll 'ave yerself an attack. W*ot*'s 'appened?"

Panting and snorting like a hippopotamus, Mrs. Butterfield waved the newspaper. "You've won!"

The full import of what her friend was saying did not reach Mrs. Harris at once, for having placed her ultimate fate in the hands of the powerful feeling of luck, she had then temporarily put the matter from her mind. But at last the meaning of what Mrs. Butterfield was shouting came home to her and she dropped her iron to the floor with a crash. "Me Dior dress!" she cried, and the next moment she had seized her stout friend about the waist and the two of them were dancing like children about the kitchen.

Then, lest there be a mistake, they had to sit down, and minutely, score by score, figure by figure (for, of course, they kept duplicates of their selections), she and Mrs. Butterfield pored over the results of that Saturday's contests. It was true. But for two games, Mrs. Harris had tallied a perfect score. There would be a prize, a rich one, certainly, perhaps even the jackpot, depending upon whether anyone else had surpassed or matched Mrs. Harris' effort.

One thing seemed certain, however, the Dior dress, or at least the money for it, was assured, for neither could conceive that the prize for achieving twenty-eight out of thirty games could be less. But there was one great trial yet to be undergone by both. They would have to wait until Wednesday before they would be advised by telegram of the amount of Mrs. Harris' swag.

"Whatever's over from what I need for me dress, I'll split with you," the little charwoman told her stout friend in a moment of warm generosity, and meant every word of it. In the first flush of excitement over the winning Mrs. Harris saw herself marching through this Dior's emporium, flanked by scraping and bowing sales personnel. Her handbag would be crammed to bursting with the stuff. She would walk down aisle after aisle, pass rack after rack of wondrous garments standing stiff with satin, lace, velvets and brocades to make her choice finally and say: "I'll 'ave *that* one."

And yet—and yet—naturally gay optimist that she was, Mrs. Harris could not help harboring a suspicion gleaned from the precarious task of the living of daily life and making a go of things that it might not be all that easy. To crave something exquisite but useless, a luxury wholly out of one's reach, to pin one's faith in getting it on a lottery and to draw immediately the winning number, this was storybook stuff.

Still, it did seem to happen to people from time to time. One kept reading of such events in the newspapers every other day. Well, there was nothing to do but wait until Wednesday. But there was no gainsaying the facts and figures, or that she was a winner, for she had checked them over time and time again. The Dior dress would be hers, and perhaps much, much more, even when she split with Mrs. Butterfield. A top pool had been known to yield as much as a hundred and fifty thousand pounds.

Thus she dithered for three days until Wednesday morning, when the fateful telegram from the pool headquarters arrived. It was the measure of her affection for her friend that she did not tear it open at once to learn its contents, but held back until she was fully dressed and could run over to Mrs. Butterfield, who sat herself braced in a chair for the big moment, fanning herself with her apron, crying: "For the Lor's sake, love, open it. I'm like to die of excitement."

At last, with trembling fingers, Mrs. Harris breached the seal and unfolded the message. It advised her briefly that her coupon had been a winning one and that her share would be one hundred and two pounds, seven shillings and ninepence ha'penny. It was well in a way that Mrs. Harris had entertained the possibility of a letdown, for the sum was so much less than what she needed to become the possessor of a dress from Dior that the realization of her dream was as far away and seemingly impossible as ever. Not even Mrs. Butterfield's Job's comforting "Well, it's better than nothing; a lot of folks would be glad of the money" could help her to overcome her initial disappointment, even though she knew in her heart of hearts that that was what life was like.

What had happened? A list of winners sent to Mrs. Harris a few days later made it plain enough. It had been a weird week in the football leagues, with many upsets. While no one had tabbed all games correctly, quite a few had tied Mrs. Harris' effort, shrinking the cut for each one to the above figure.

One hundred and two pounds, seven and ninepence ha'penny was a sum not to be sneezed at, and yet for several days thereafter it left Mrs. Harris with rather a numb feeling about the region of her heart and at night she would awaken with a feeling of sadness and unshed tears, and then she would remember why.

Once the disappointment was over, Mrs. Harris would have thought that the excitement of winning a hundred pounds in the football pool—a hundred pounds to be spent upon anything she liked—would have put an end to her desire for the Dior dress. Yet the contrary proved to be the case. Her yearning was as strong as ever. She could not put it out of her mind. In the morning when she woke up, it was to a feeling of sadness and emptiness, as though something unpleasant had happened to her, or something was missing which sleep had temporarily obliterated. Then she would realize that it was the Dior dress, or *a* Dior dress—just one, once in her lifetime, that she was still craving and would never have.

And at night, when after her final cup of tea and chat with Mrs. Butterfield she repaired to her old friends the hot water bottles in her bed and pulled the covers up about her chin, there would begin a desperate struggle to think of something else—Major Wallace's new girl, introduced this time as his niece from South Africa (they were always either nieces, wards, secretaries or friends of the family), or the latest oddity of the Countess Wyszcinska, who had taken to smoking a pipe. She tried to concentrate upon her favorite apartment, or upon the language Miss Pamela Penrose had used because she had broken an ash tray. She tried to invent and concentrate upon a flower garden. But it was no use. The more she tried to think of other things the more the Dior dress intruded into her consciousness, and she lay there in the darkness, shivering and craving it.

Even with the light out and no more than the glimmer of the street lamp filtering into the basement window, she could look right through the closet door and imagine it hanging there. The color and the materials kept changing, sometimes she saw it in gold brocade, others in pink, or crimson satin, or white with ivory laces. But always it was the most beautiful and expensive thing of its kind.

The originals that had started this strange desire had disappeared from the cupboard of Lady Dant and were no longer there to tantalize her. (Later there was a picture in *The Tatler* of Lady Dant wearing the one known as "Ravishing.") But Mrs. Harris did not need to see them any longer. The craving to possess such a thing was indelibly imbedded in her mind. Sometimes the longing was so strong it would bring tears to her eyes before she fell asleep, often to continue thereafter with some distorted dream.

But one night, a week or so later, Mrs. Harris' thoughts took a new tack. She reflected upon the evening she had made out the football coupon with Mrs. Butterfield and the curious sense of certainty she had experienced that this would win her the coveted dress. The results, it is true, had been in line with what she knew by experience were the disappointments of life, and yet, after all, had they? She had won a hundred pounds, nay, more, a hundred and two pounds, seven shillings and ninepence ha'penny.

Why then this curious sum, what was the message or the meaning it held for her? For Mrs. Harris' world was filled with signals, signs, messages, and portents from on High. With the price of a Dior dress of four hundred fifty pounds, three hundred fifty pounds was still wholly out of her reach. But wait! A flash of insight and inspiration came to her, and she snapped on the light and sat up in bed with the sheer excitement of it. It was not really three hundred fifty pounds any longer. She had not only her hundred pounds in the bank, but a start of two pounds, seven shillings, ninepence ha'penny on the second hundred, and once she had achieved that the third hundred pounds would no longer be so difficult.

"That's it," said Mrs. Harris to herself aloud, "I'll 'ave it if it is the last thing I do and it takes the rest of me life." She got out of bed, secured pencil and paper, and began to figure.

Mrs. Harris had never in her life paid more than five pounds, roughly the equivalent of fourteen dollars, for a dress, a sum she noted down on the paper opposite the utterly fantastic figure of four hundred fifty pounds. Had Lady Dant named some such sum as fifty of sixty pounds as the price of the marvelous creations in her closet it is quite possible that Mrs. Harris would have put the entire matter out of her head immediately as not only a gap in price she was not prepared to consider, but also a matter of a class into which she preferred not to encroach.

But the very outrageousness of the sum put it all into a wholly different category. What is it that makes a woman yearn for chinchilla, or Russian sables, a Rolls-Royce, or jewels from Cartier, or Van Cleef & Arpels, or the most expensive perfume, restaurant, neighborhood, etc.? It is this very pinnacle and preposterousness of price that is the guarantee of the value of her femininity and person. Mrs. Harris simply felt that if one owned a dress so beautiful that it cost four hundred fifty pounds there was then nothing left upon earth to be desired. Her pencil began to move across the paper.

She earned three shillings, approximately forty-five cents, an hour. She worked ten hours a day, six days a week, fifty-two weeks in the year. Mrs. Harris screwed her tongue into her cheek and applied the multiplication table, reaching the figure of four hundred sixty-eight pounds per annum, close to fourteen hundred dollars, just the price of a Dior gala ball dress plus the amount of the fare to Paris and back.

Now, with equal determination and vigor, Mrs. Harris initiated a second column: rent, taxes, food, medicines, shoes, and all the little incidentals of living of which she could think. The task was a staggering one when she subtracted debits from credits. Years of savings lay ahead of her, two at the very least, if not three, unless she had some other stroke of luck or a windfall of tips. But the figures shook neither her confidence nor her determination. On the contrary, they steeled them. "I'll 'ave it," she said once more, and snapped out the light. She went to sleep immediately, peacefully as a child, and when she awoke the following morning felt no longer sad, but only eager and excited as one who is about to embark upon a great and unknown adventure.

The matter came out into the open the next evening, their regular night to go to the cinema, when Mrs. Butterfield appeared as usual shortly after eight, swathed against the cold, and was surprised to find Mrs. Harris in her kitchen unprepared for any expedition and examining some kind of prospectus entitled EARN MONEY IN YOUR LEISURE TIME AT HOME.

"We'll be late, ducks," admonished Mrs. Butterfield.

Mrs. Harris looked at her friend guiltily. "I ain't going," she said.

"Ain't going to the flicks?" echoed the astounded Mrs. Butterfield. "But it's Marilyn Monroe."

"I carn't 'elp it. I carn't go. I'm syvin' me money."

"Lor' bless us," said Mrs. Butterfield, who occasionally herself submitted to a temporary economy wave. "Whatever for?"

Mrs. Harris gulped before she replied: "Me Dior dress."

"Lor' love you, ducks, you 'ave gone barmy. I thought you said the dress cost a ruddy four hundred and fifty quid."

"I've already got a hundred and two poun', seven and ninepence ha'penny," Mrs. Harris said. "I'm syvin' up for the rest."

Mrs. Butterfield's chins quivered as she shook her head in admiration. "Character, that's what you've got," she said. "I could never do it meself. Tell you what, dear; you come along with me. I'll stand treat."

But Mrs. Harris was adamant. "I carn't," she said, "I wouldn't be able to stand treat back."

Mrs. Butterfield sighed a heavy sigh and began to divest herself of her outer clothing. "Oh well," she said, "I guess Marilyn Monroe ain't everything. I'd just as soon 'ave a cup of tea and a quiet chat. 'Ave you seen where Lord Klepper 'as been arrested again? Syme thing. It's 'is nephew I do for in Halker Street. As nice a lad as you could ever wish to know. Nothing wrong about 'im."

Mrs. Harris accepted the sacrifice her friend was making, but her glance traveled guiltily to the tea box. It was full enough now, but soon would be inhospitably empty. For this was one of the things on her list to cut down. She put the kettle on.

Thus began a long, hard period of scrimping, saving and privation, none of which in the least interfered with Mrs. Harris' good humor, with the exception that she denied herself the occasional pot of flowers in season and more than ever watched over the health of her beloved geraniums lest she not be able to replace them.

She went without cigarettes—and a quiet smoke used to be a solace—and without gin. She walked instead of taking the bus or the underground and when holes appeared in her shoes she wadded them with newsprint. She gave up her cherished evening papers and got her news and gossip a day late out of the wastebaskets of her clients. She scrimped on food and clothing. The former might have been injurious, except that Mrs. Schreiber, the American woman, at whose apartment she was usually working around lunch time, was generous and always offered her an egg or something cold from the frige. This she now accepted.

But the cinema saw her no more, nor did the King's Crown, the pub on the corner; she went herself almost tealess so that there might be some in the canister when it was Mrs. Butterfield's turn to visit her. And she came near to ruining her eyes with some badly paid homework which she did at night, sewing zippers onto the backs of cheap blouses. The only thing Mrs. Harris did not give up was the thruppence a week for the football pool, but, of course, lightning had no intention whatsoever of striking twice in this same place. Nevertheless, she felt she could not afford not to continue playing it.

Through discarded six-month-old fashion magazines she kept up with the doings of Christian Dior, for all this took place before the sudden and lamented passing of the master, and always before her eyes, buoying her up and stiffening her backbone, was the knowledge that one of these days in the not too distant future one of these unique creations would be hers.

And while Mrs. Butterfield did not change her opinion that no good could come from wanting things above one's station and somewhere along the line Mrs. Harris would encounter disaster, she nevertheless admired her friend's determination and courage and stoutly supported her, helping her wherever she could and, of course, keeping her secret, for Mrs. Harris told no one else of her plans and ambitions.

*four*

Mrs. Harris jangled the bell pull of the flat of her friend Mrs. Butterfield one night in midsummer during this period in a state of considerable excitement. Her apple cheeks were flushed and pinker than usual, and her little eyes were electric with excitement. She was in the grip of something bigger than herself, "a 'unch," as she called it. The 'unch was guiding her to the Dog Track at White City, and she was calling upon Mrs. Butterfield to accompany her.

"Going to take a flyer, are you, dearie?" queried Mrs. Butterfield. "I don't mind a night out meself. 'Ow're you coming on with your syvings?"

The excitement under which she was laboring made Mrs. Harris' voice hoarse. "I've got two hundred and fifty quid laid away. If I could double it I'd have me dress next week."

"Double it or lose it, dearie?" said Mrs. Butterfield, the confirmed pessimist of the pair, who enjoyed looking upon the darker side of life.

"I've a 'unch," whispered Mrs. Harris. "Come on then, the treat's on me."

Indeed, to Mrs. Harris it seemed almost more than a hunch—in fact, more like a message from Above. She had awakened that morning with the feeling that the day was most propitious, and that her God was looking down upon her with a friendly and co-operative eye.

Mrs. Harris' Deity had been acquired at Sunday school at an early age, and had never changed in her mind from a Being who combined the characteristics of a nannie, a policeman, a magistrate, and Santa Claus, an Omnipotence of many moods, who was at all times concerned with Mrs. Harris' business. She could always tell which phase was uppermost in the Almighty by what was happening to her. She accepted her punishments from Above when she had been naughty without quibbling, as she would have accepted a verdict from the Bench. Likewise, when she was good she expected rewards; when she was in distress she asked for assistance, and expected service; when things went well she was always prepared to share the credit with the Good Lord. Jehova was a personal friend and protector, yet she was also a little wary of Him, as she might be of an elderly gentleman who occasionally went into fits of inexplicable tantrums.

That morning when she was awakened by the feeling that something wonderful was about to happen to her, she was convinced it could only have to do with her desire to own the dress, and that on this occasion she was to be brought nearer to the fulfillment of her wishes.

All day at her labors she had attuned herself to receive further communications as to what form the expected bounty would take. When she arrived at the flat of Miss Pamela Penrose to cope with the usual mess of untidiness left by the struggling actress, a copy of the *Evening Standard* was lying on the floor, and as she glanced at it lines of black print conveyed the intelligence to her that the dogs were running at White City that evening. That was it! The message had been delivered and received. Thereafter there was nothing to do but to find the right dog, the right price, collect her winnings and be off to Paris.

Neither Mrs. Harris nor Mrs. Butterfield was a stranger to the paradise that was White City, but that night the *mise-en-scène* that otherwise would have enthralled them—the oval track outlined in electric light, the rush and roar of the mechanical rabbit, the pulsating ribbon of the dogs streaming behind in its wake, the bustling crowds in the betting queues and the packed stands—was no more than the means to an end. Mrs. Butterfield too, by this time, had caught the fever, and went waddling in Mrs. Harris' wake from paddock to stands and back again without protest. They did not even pause for a cup of tea and a sausage at the refreshment booth, so intent were they upon attuning themselves to the work in hand.

They searched the race cards for clues, they examined the long, thin, stringy animals, they kept their ears flapping for possible tidbits of information, and it was this last precaution that eventually yielded results—results of such stunning portent that there could be no question of either authenticity or outcome.

Crushed in the crowd at the paddock where the entrants for the fourth race were being paraded, Mrs. Harris listened to the conversation of two sporty-looking gentlemen standing just beside them.

The first gentleman was engaged in digging into his ear with his little finger and studying his card at the same time. "Haut Coutoure, that's the one."

The other gentleman, who was conducting similar operations on his nose, glanced sharply along the line of dogs and said: "Number six. What the devil does 'Haut Coutourie' mean?"

The first gentleman was knowledgeable. "She's a French bitch," he said, consulting his card again, "owned by Marcel Duval. I dunno—ain't Haut Coutoure got something to do with dressmaking, or something like that?"

Mrs. Harris and Mrs. Butterfield felt cold chills run down their spines as they turned and looked at one another. There was no question, this was it. They stared at their cards, and sure enough there was the name of the dog, "Haute Couture," and her French owner, and some of her record. A glance at the board showed them that her price was five to one.

"Come along," cried Mrs. Harris, making for the betting windows. She, like a tiny destroyer escorting the huge battleship of Mrs. Butterfield, parted the crowds on either side of them and arrived breathless at the queue.

"What will you put on her, dearie—five quid?" panted Mrs. Butterfield.

"Five quid," echoed Mrs. Harris, "after a 'unch like that? Fifty!"

At the mention of this sum Mrs. Butterfield looked as though she were going to faint. Pallor spread from chin to chin, until it covered all three. She quivered with emotion. "Fifty quid," she whispered, in case anyone should be listening to such folly. "Fifty quid!"

"At five to one that would be two hundred fifty pounds," asserted Mrs. Harris calmly.

Mrs. Butterfield's normal pessimism assailed her again. "But what if she loses?"

"It carn't," said Mrs. Harris imperturbably. " 'Ow can it?"

By this time they were at the window. While Mrs. Butterfield's eyes threatened to pop out of the folds of her face, Mrs. Harris opened her battered brown pocketbook, extracted a sheaf of money and said: "Fifty quid on Howt Cowter, number six, to win."

Mechanically the ticket seller repeated: "Haute Couture, number six, fifty pounds, to win," and then, startled by the amount, bent down to look through the wire screen at the heavy bettor. His eyes looked into the glowing blue beads of Mrs. Harris, and the apparition of the little char startled him into an exclamation of "Blimey," which he quickly corrected into "Good luck, madam," and pushed the ticket to her. Mrs. Harris' hand was not even trembling as she took it, but Mrs. Butterfield stared at it as though it were a snake that might bite her. The two went off to the trackside to attend the fulfillment of the promised miracle.

The tragedy that they then witnessed was brief and conclusive. Haute Couture led the first time around, running easily and smoothly, like the thoroughbred lady she was, but at the last turn she was assailed suddenly by an uncontrollable itch. She ran out into the middle of the track, sat down and scratched it to her relief and satisfaction. When she had finished, so was the race—and Mrs. Harris.

It was not so much the loss of her hard-earned, hard-saved, so-valued fifty pounds that upset Mrs. Harris and darkened her otherwise ebullient spirits in the following days, as the evidence that the policeman-magistrate God was uppermost, and that He was out of sorts with her. She had evidently misread His intentions, or perhaps it was only her own idea to take a flyer, and the Creator did not hold with this. He had sent swift and sure punishment in the form of a heavenly flea. Did it mean that He was not going to allow Mrs. Harris to have her dress after all? Was she wishing for something so foolish and out of keeping with her position that He had chosen this method to indicate His disapproval?

She went about her work torn by this new problem, moody and preoccupied, and, of course, just because her Preceptor seemed to be against the idea it made desire for the dress all the greater. She was of the breed who could defy even her Maker if it was necessary, though, of course, she had no notion that one could win out over Him. He was all-powerful, and His decisions final, but that did not say that Mrs. Harris had to like them, or take them lying down.

The following week, as she returned one evening from her labors, her eyes cast down due to the oppression that sat upon her, they were caught by a glitter in the gutter, as of a piece of glass reflecting in the lamplight overhead. But when she bent down, it was not a piece of glass at all, but a diamond clip, and one, as she saw at once, from the platinum frame and the size of the stones, of considerable value.

This time she had no truck either with hunches or communications. The thought that this piece of jewelry might be ten times the worth of the dress she longed for never even entered her head. Because she was who she was and what she was, she responded almost automatically; she wended her way to the nearest police station and turned the article in, leaving her name and address, and a description of where she had found it. Within a week she was summoned back to the police station, where she received the sum of twenty-five pounds' reward from the grateful owner of the lost clip.

And now all oppression was lifted from the soul of Mrs. Harris, for the stern Magistrate Above had taken off His wig, reversed it and donned it as the beard of Santa Claus, and she was able to interpret both that which had happened to her and the Divine Intention. He had returned half her money to show that He was no longer angry with her, and that if she were faithful and steadfast she might have her dress—but she was no longer to gamble; the missing twenty-five pounds said that. It was to be earned by work, sweat and self-denial. Well, in the joy that filled her, she was prepared to give all that.

*five*

Somewhere along the line without really trying—for Mrs. Harris believed that by looking into things too energetically one could sometimes learn too much—the little charwoman had come across two pertinent bits of information. There were currency restrictions which forbade exporting more than ten pounds out of Great Britain, and ergo no French shop would accept a large sum of money in pounds, but demanded another currency. So it would have done her no good to have smuggled out such a sum as four hundred fifty pounds, nor would she have done so.

For Mrs. Harris' code of ethics was both strict and practical. She would tell a fib but not a lie. She would not break the law, but she was not averse to bending it as far as it would go. She was scrupulously honest, but at the same time was not to be considered a mug.

Since pounds were forbidden as well as useless in quantities in Paris, she needed some other medium of exchange and hit upon dollars. And for dollars there was one person to whom she could turn, the friendly, kind and not too bright American lady, Mrs. Schreiber.

Mrs. Harris conveniently invented a nephew in America who was apparently constitutionally impecunious, a kind of half-wit, unable to support himself and to whom, on a blood-is-thicker-than-water basis, she was compelled to send money. The name Mrs. Harris cooked up for him was Albert, and he lived in Chattanooga, a place she had picked out of the daily America column in the *Express*. She often held long conversations with Mrs. Schreiber about this derelict relative. "A good boy, my poor dead sister's son, but a bit weak in the 'ead, he is."

Mrs. Schreiber, who was more than a bit muzzy herself with regard to British currency laws, saw no reason why she should not aid such a good-hearted person as Mrs. Harris, and since she was herself wealthy and possessed an almost limitless supply of dollars, or could get fresh ones whenever she wanted them, Mrs. Harris' slowly accumulating hoard of pounds got themselves translated into American currency. It became an accepted thing week by week, this exchange. Mrs. Schreiber likewise paid her in dollars and tipped her in dollars, and nobody was any the wiser.

Slowly but surely over a period of two years the wad of five-, ten- and twenty-dollar bills grew in girth and vigor until one fresh morning, early in January, counting her hoard and thumbing her bankbook, Mrs. Harris knew that she was not any longer too far away from the realization of her dream.

She was well aware that anyone leaving the British Isles to travel abroad must hold a valid British passport, and she consulted Major Wallace as to what was necessary to obtain such a document, receiving explicit information as to where, how and to whom she must apply in writing.

"Thinking of going abroad?" he asked with some amazement and no little alarm, since he considered Mrs. Harris' ministrations indispensable to his comfort and well-being.

Mrs. Harris tittered: "'Oo me? Where would I be going?" She hastily invented another relative. "It's for me niece. She is going out to Germany to get married. Nice boy stationed in the Army there."

And here you can see how Mrs. Harris differentiated between a fib and a lie. A fib such as the above did nobody any harm, while a lie was a deliberate untruth, told to save yourself or gain an unfair advantage.

Thus a never to be forgotten moment of preparation was the day the instructions arrived from the Passport Office, a formidable blank to be filled out with "4 photographs of the applicant 2 inches by 2 inches in size," etc.

"Whatever do you think," Mrs. Harris confided to her friend Mrs. Butterfield in a state of high excitement, "I've got to 'ave me photograff tyken. They want it for me passport. You'd better come along and hold me 'and."

The one and only time that Mrs. Harris had ever faced the camera lens was upon the occasion of her wedding to Mr. Harris, and then she had the stout arm of that stout plumber to support her during the ordeal.

That picture in a flower-painted frame now adorned the table of her little flat. It showed Mrs. Harris of thirty years ago, a tiny, thin-looking girl whose plain features were enhanced by the freshness of youth. Her hair was short-bobbed, the fashion of the day, and she wore a white muslin wedding dress tiered somewhat in the manner of a Chinese pagoda. In her posture there was already some hint of the courage and independence she was to display later when she became widowed. The expression on her face was one of pride in the man she had captured and who stood beside her, a nice-looking boy somewhat on the short side, wearing a dark suit and his hair carefully plastered down. As was becoming to his new status, he looked terrified. And thereafter nobody had ever again troubled to reproduce Mrs. Harris, nor had she so much as thought about it.

"Won't it cost a packet?" was Mrs. Butterfield's reaction to the dark side of things.

"Ten bob for 'arf a dozen," Mrs. Harris reported. "I saw an ad in the paper. I'll give you one of the extra ones if you like."

"That's good of you, dearie," said Mrs. Butterfield, and meant it.

"Ow Lor'!" The exclamation was torn from Mrs. Harris as she was suddenly riven by a new thought. "Ow Lor'!" she repeated. "If I'm going to 'ave me photograff tyken I'll 'ave to 'ave a new 'at."

Two of Mrs. Butterfield's chins quivered at the impact of this revelation. "Of course you will, dearie, and that *will* cost a packet."

Mrs. Harris accepted the fact philosophically and even with some pleasure. It had been years since she had invested in a new hat. "It carn't be 'elped. Just as well I've got some of the stuff."

The pair selected the following Saturday afternoon, invading the King's Road to accomplish both errands, beginning, of course, with the choice of the hat. There was no doubt but that Mrs. Harris fell in love with it immediately she saw it in the window, but at first turned resolutely away for it was priced at a guinea, while all about it were others on sale, specials at ten and six, and even some at seven and six.

But Mrs. Harris would not have been a true London char had she not favored the one at a guinea, for it had been thought of, designed and made for members of her profession. The hat was a kind of flat sailor affair of green straw, but what made it distinguished was the pink rose on a short but flexible stem that was affixed to the front. It was, of course, her fondness for flowers and the rose that got Mrs. Harris. They went into the shop and Mrs. Harris dutifully tried on shapes and materials considered to be within her price range, but her thoughts and her eyes kept roving to the window where the hat was displayed. Finally she could contain herself no longer and asked for it.

Mrs. Butterfield examined the price tag with horror. "Coo," she said, "a guinea! It's a waste of money, you that's been syving for so long."

Mrs. Harris set it upon her head and was lost. "I don't care," she said fiercely. "I can go a week later."

If a camera was to fix her features and person for all time, to be carried in her passport, to be shown to her friends, to be preserved in a little frame on Mrs. Butterfield's dresser, that was how she wanted it, with that hat and no other. "I'll 'ave it," she said to the sales girl, and produced the twenty-one shillings. She left the shop wearing it contentedly. After all, what was one guinea to someone who was about to invest four hundred fifty pounds in a dress.

The passport photographer was not busy when they arrived and soon had Mrs. Harris posed before the cold eye of his camera while hump-backed he inspected her from beneath the concealment of his black cloth. He then turned on a hot battery of floodlights which illuminated Mrs. Harris' every fold, line and wrinkle etched into her shrewd and merry little face by the years of toil.

"And now, madam," he said, "if you would kindly remove that hat——"

"Not b— likely," said Mrs. Harris succinctly. "What the 'ell do you think I've bought this 'at for if not to wear it in me photograff."

The photographer said: "Sorry, madam, against regulations. The Passport Office won't accept any photographs with hats on. I can make some specials at two guineas a dozen for you later, with the hat on, if you like."

Mrs. Harris told the photographer a naughty thing to do with his two-guinea specials, but Mrs. Butterfield consoled her. "Never mind, dearie," she said, "you'll have it to wear when you go to Paris. You'll be right in with the fashion."

It was on a hazy May morning, four months later, or to be exact two years, seven months, three weeks and one day following her resolve to own a Dior dress, that Mrs. Harris, firm and fully equipped beneath the green hat with the pink rose, was seen off on the bus to the air station by a tremulous and nervous Mrs. Butterfield. Besides the long and arduously hoarded fortune, the price of the dress, she was equipped with passport, round-trip ticket to Paris and sufficient funds to get there and back.

The intended schedule of her day included the selection and purchase of her dress, lunch in Paris, a bit of sight-seeing and return by the evening plane.

The clients had all been warned of the unusual event of Mrs. Harris' taking a day off, with Mrs. Butterfield substituting, and had reacted in accordance with their characters and natures. Major Wallace was, of course, dubious since he could not so much as find a clean towel or a pair of socks without the assistance of Mrs. Harris, but it was the actress, Miss Pamela Penrose, who kicked up the ugliest fuss, storming at the little char. "But that's horrid of you. You can't. I won't hear of it. I pay you, don't I? I've a most important producer coming for drinks here tomorrow. You charwomen are all alike. Never think of anybody but yourselves. I do think, after all I've done for you, you might show me a little consideration."

For a moment, in extenuation, Mrs. Harris was tempted to reveal where she was off to and why—and resisted. The love affair between herself and the Dior dress was private. Instead she said soothingly: "Now, now, ducks, no need for you to get shirty. Me friend Mrs. Butterfield will look in on you on her way home tomorrow and give the place a good tidying up. Your producer friend won't know the difference. Well, dearie, 'ere's 'oping 'e gives you a good job," she concluded cheerily, and left Miss Penrose glowering and sulking.

*six*

All thoughts of the actress, and for that matter all of her meandering back into the past, were driven out of Mrs. Harris' head when with a jerk and a squeal of brakes the cab came to a halt at what must be her destination.

The great gray building that is the House of Christian Dior occupies an entire corner of the spacious Avenue Montaigne leading off the Rond-Point of the Champs-Elysées. It has two entrances, one off the avenue proper which leads through the Boutique, where knickknacks and accessories are sold at prices ranging from five to several hundreds of dollars, and another more demure and exclusive one.

The cab driver chose to deposit Mrs. Harris at the latter, reserved for the genuinely loaded clièntèle, figuring his passenger to be at the very least an English countess or milady. He charged her no more than the amount registered on the clock and forbore to tip himself more than fifty francs, mindful of the warning of the Airways man. Then crying to her gaily the only English he knew, which was " 'Ow do you do," he drove off, leaving her standing on the sidewalk before the place that had occupied her yearnings and dreams and ambitions for the past three years.

And a strange misgiving stirred in the thin breast beneath the tan twill coat. It was no store at all, like Selfridge's on Oxford Street, or Harrod's, or Marks & Spencer, where she did her shopping and which was the S. J. Klein of London, not a proper store at all, with windows for display and wax figures with pearly smiles and pink cheeks, arms outstretched in elegant attitudes to show off the clothes that were for sale. There was nothing, nothing at all, but some windows shaded by ruffled gray curtains and a door with an iron grille behind the glass. True, in the keystone above the arch of the entrance were chiseled the words CHRISTIAN DIOR, but no other identification.

When you have desired something as deeply as Mrs. Harris had longed for her Paris dress, and for such a time, and when at last that deep-rooted feminine yearning is about to taste the sweetness of fulfillment, every moment attending its achievement becomes acute and indelibly memorable.

Standing alone now on the pave in a foreign city, assailed by the foreign roar of foreign traffic and the foreign bustle of foreign passers-by, outside the great gray mansion that was like a private house and not a store at all, Mrs.

Harris suddenly felt lonely, frightened and forlorn, and in spite of the great roll of silver-green American dollars in her handbag she wished for a moment that she had not come, or that she had asked the young man from the Airways to accompany her, or that the taxi driver had not driven away, leaving her standing there.

And then, as luck would have it, a car from the British Embassy drove by and the sight of the tiny Union Jack fluttering from the mudguard stiffened her spine and brought determination to her mouth and eyes. She reminded herself who and what she was, drew in a deep breath of the balmy Paris air laced with petrol fumes and resolutely pushed open the door and entered.

She was almost driven back by the powerful odor of elegance that assailed her once she was inside. It was the same that she smelled when Lady Dant opened the doors to her wardrobe, the same that clung to the fur coat and clothes of the Countess Wyszcinska, for whom she cleaned from four to six in the afternoons, the same she sometimes sniffed in the streets when as she passed someone opened the door of a luxurious motorcar. It was compounded of perfume and fur and satins, silks and leather, jewelry and face powder. It seemed to arise from the thick gray carpets and hangings, and fill the air of the grand staircase before her.

It was the odor of the rich, and it made her tremble once more and wonder what she, Ada 'Arris, was doing there instead of washing up the luncheon dishes for Mrs. Ffbrd Foulks back home, or furthering the career of a real theatrical star like Pamela Penrose by seeing that her flat was neat and tidy when her producer friends came to call.

She hesitated, her feet sinking into the pile of the carpet seemingly up to her ankles. Then her fingers crept into her handbag and tested the smooth feel of the roll of American bills. "That's why you're 'ere, Ada 'Arris. That says you're ruddy well as rich as any of 'em. Get on with it then, my girl."

She mounted the imposing and deserted staircase, it then being half past eleven in the morning. On the first half landing there was but a single silver slipper in a glass showcase let into the wall, on the second turn there was a similar showcase housing an outsize bottle of Dior perfume. But otherwise there were no goods of any kind on display, nor were there crowds of people rushing up and down the stairs as in such emporiums back home as Marks & Spencer's or Selfridge's. Nowhere was there any sign of anything that so much as resembled the shops to which she was accustomed.

On the contrary, the elegance and atmosphere of the deserted staircase gave her the feeling of a private house, and one on a most grand scale at that. Was she really in the right place? Her courage threatened to ooze again, but she told herself that sooner or later she must come upon some human being who would be able to direct her to the dresses, or at least put her right if she were in the wrong building. She pressed on, and indeed on the first-floor landing came upon a dark handsome woman in her early forties who was seated at a desk writing. She was clad in a simple black dress relieved by three rows of pearls at the neck, her coiffure was neat and glossy; her features were refined, her skin exquisite, but closer inspection would have revealed that she looked tired and careworn, and that there were dark hollows beneath her eyes.

Behind her Mrs. Harris noted a fair-sized room opening into a second one, gray-carpeted like the stairs, with fine silk hangings at the windows, and furnished only with several rows of gray and golden chairs around the perimeter. A few floor-to-ceiling pier mirrors completed the décor, but of anything to sell or even so much as to look at, there was not a sign.

Mme. Colbert, the manageress, had had a bad morning. Ordinarily a kind and gracious lady, she had let herself into a quarrel with M. Fauvel, the young and handsome chief of the auditing department, of whom otherwise she was rather fond, and had sent him upstairs again to his domaine with his ears reddening.

It was merely a matter of his inquiring about a client whose bills seemed to run too long without payment. On any other day Mme. Colbert might have favored the auditor with a penetrating and not unhumorous run-down of the clients' characteristics, idiosyncrasies and trustworthiness since sooner or later they all bared themselves to her. Instead of which she railed angrily at him that it was her business to sell dresses and his to collect the money and she had not the time to inspect the bank accounts of clients. That was his affair.

Besides giving short answers all morning, she had ticked off several of the sales girls and even permitted herself to scold Natasha, the star model of the house, for being late for a fitting, when, as she knew well, the Métro and the buses were engaging in a slow-down strike. What made it worse was that the exquisite Natasha had responded to the sharp words in a most un-prima-donna-like manner: she didn't argue or snap back, only two large tears formed at her eyes and rolled down her cheeks.

And then besides, Mme. Colbert was not at all sure that she had not muddled the invitations and seating for the afternoon's review of the collection. As head of the department she was an important and all-powerful person. It was she who issued or denied invitations to see the collection, sorted out spies and curiosity seekers and barred the undesirables. She was in charge of the seating arrangements, as complicated as faced any headwaiter of a fashionable restaurant, as clients must be placed in accordance with importance, rank, title and bank roll. She was the directress of a fashion parade, having something to say as to the order in which the creations appeared, and likewise she was the commander-in-chief of a battalion of black-garbed salesladies, deploying them on the staircase and taking great care to match them psychologically to their clients—a gay and gossipy sales girl for a gay and gossipy woman, a silent and respectful salesperson for a mature and important customer, an English-speaking girl with a persuasive line for an American, a good bully with a commanding aspect for a German, etc.

When such a powerful person was out of sorts or ill-humored, repercussions would ring far and wide. The *crise* which Mme. Colbert was suffering had to do with her husband Jules and the love, respect and affection for him which had grown over the twenty years they had been together. Dear, good, decent, clever Jules, who had more knowledge in one fingertip than all the rest of them in the Foreign Office, with their striped trousers and morning coats and political connections. But one thing Jules lacked, or rather two—he had not the ability to push himself, and he had no political friends or affiliations.

He had achieved his position, beginning as a poor boy, by brilliance and application. Yet whenever there was a better or higher position opening he was rejected in favor of someone of lesser intellect but greater affiliations who then from his new position of eminence used Jules' brains to conduct his post. As his wife, and herself an intelligent woman *au courant* affairs in France, Mme. Colbert knew that many a difficult problem had been solved by her husband's brains and intuition. Yet time and time again he had been passed over for promotion, time and time again his eager optimism and enthusiasm had been shattered. In the past year for the first time Mme. Colbert had become aware of a growing hopelessness and misanthropy in her husband. A man of fifty now, he felt he could look forward to nothing but the existence of a Foreign Office hack. He had all but given up, and it broke her heart to see the changes in the man to whom she had given her devotion.

Recently there had been a sudden death at the Quai d'Orsay; the chief of an important department had succumbed to a heart failure. Speculation was rife as to who would replace him. Jules Colbert was one of those in line for the job and yet—

It saddened Mme. Colbert almost to the point of desperation to see how her husband's buoyancy from his younger days struggled to break through the weight of pessimism that experience had laid upon his shoulders. He dared to hope again, even against all of the political corruption which would shatter his hopes and this time leave him an old and broken man.

This then was the burden that Mme. Colbert carried about with her. She had helped her husband by working and taking financial strain off him and so had built herself into her position in the great dressmaking house. But she realized now that this was not enough and that in another way she had failed. The wife of a diplomat or a politician must herself be a diplomat or a politician, conduct a salon to which the great and the might-be great would be invited; she would wheedle, flatter, intrigue, even if need be give herself to advance her husband's interests. Here was the ideal situation for such assistance; a plum was ready to fall to the right man and there was no way she could influence it into the lap of her Jules. There was no one in those circles who cared so much as a fig for her or her husband.

This knowledge drove Mme. Colbert almost frantic with unhappiness for she loved her husband and could not bear to see him destroyed, but neither could she do anything to prevent it and break the ugly pattern of his being shunted aside in favor of someone who had the right connections of money, family or political power. Nights she lay awake racking her brains for some means to help him. By day she could only become more and more convinced of the futility of her efforts, and thus her bitterness was carried off into the life of her daily work and began to affect those about her. She was not unaware of the change in herself; she seemed to be going about in some kind of nightmare from which she could not awake.

Seated now at her desk on the first-floor landing and trying to concentrate on the placing of the guests for the afternoon show, Mme. Colbert looked up to see an apparition ascending the stairs which caused a shudder to pass through her frame and led her to brush her hand across her brow and eyes as though to clear away a hallucination, if it was one. But it was not. She was real enough.

One of Mme. Colbert's assets was her unvarying judgment in estimating the quality of would-be customers or clients, divining the genuine article from the time-wasters, penetrating the exterior of eccentrics to the bank rolls within. But this woman ascending the stairs in the worn, shabby coat, gloves of the wrong color, shoes that advertised only too plainly her origin, the dreadful glazed imitation leather handbag, and the wholly preposterous hat with its jiggling rose defied her.

Swiftly Mme. Colbert's mind raced through all the categories of clients she had ever seen and known. If the creature had been what she looked like, a cleaning woman (and here you see how marvelous Mme. Colbert's instincts were), she would have been entering by the back way. But, of course, this was absurd since all of the cleaning was done there at night, after hours. It was impossible that this could be a client of or for the House of Dior.

And yet she waited for the woman to speak, for she realized that she was so upset by her own personal problems that her judgment might be warped. She had not long to wait.

"Ah, there you are, dearie," the woman said. "Could you tell me which way to the dresses?"

Mme. Colbert no longer had any doubts as to her judgment. Such a voice and such an accent had not been heard inside the walls of the House of Dior since its inception.

"The dresses?" inquired Mme. Colbert in chilled and flawless English. "What dresses?"

"Oh, come now, ducksie," admonished Mrs. Harris, "aren't you a bit on the slow side this morning? Where is it they 'angs up the dresses for sale?"

For one moment Mme. Colbert thought that this weird person might have strayed from looking for the little shop below. "If you mean the Boutique——"

Mrs. Harris cocked an ear. "Bou—what? I didn't arsk for any booties. It's them dresses I want, the expensive ones. Pull yourself together, dearie. I've come all the way from London to buy me one of your dresses and 'aven't any time to waste."

All was as clear as day to Mme. Colbert now. Every so often an error came marching up the grand staircase, though never before one quite so obvious and ghastly as this one, and had to be dealt with firmly. Her own troubles and frustrations rendered the manageress colder and more unsympathetic than usual in such circumstances. "I am afraid you have come to the wrong place. We do not display dresses here. The collection is only shown privately here in the afternoons. Perhaps if you go to the Galeries Lafayette——"

Mrs. Harris was completely bewildered. "Wot Galleries?" she asked. "I don't want no galleries. Is this Dior or ain't it?" Then before the woman could reply she remembered something. She used to encounter the word "collections" in the fashion magazines, but thought they had something to do with charity, such as the collection in the church on Sunday. Now her native shrewdness cut through the mystery. "Look 'ere," she said, "maybe it's this 'ere collection I want to see, what about it?"

Impatience seized Mme. Colbert, who was anxious to return to the miseries of her own thoughts. "I am sorry," she said coldly, "the salon is filled for this afternoon and the rest of the week." To get rid of her finally she repeated the usual formula: "If you will leave the name of your hotel. Perhaps next week sometime we can send you an invitation."

Righteous anger inflamed the bosom of Mrs. Harris. She moved a step nearer to Mme. Colbert and the pink rose attached to the front of the hat bobbed vigorously as she cried: "Coo, that's a good one. You'll send me a invitytion to spend me hard-earned money dusting and mopping and ruinin' me 'ands in dirty dish water, next week, maybe—me that's got to be back in London tonight. 'Ow do you like that?"

The rose bobbed menacingly a foot from Mme. Colbert's face. "See 'ere, Miss Snooty-at-the-Desk, if yer don't think I've got the money to pay for what I want—'ERE!" And with this Mrs. Harris opened the imitation leather bag and upended it. The rubber band about her roll chose that moment to burst, dramatically showering a green cascade of American five-, ten- and twenty-dollar bills. "There!" at which point Mrs. Harris raised her indignant voice to roof level: "What's the matter with that? Ain't my money as good as anybody else's?"

Caught by surprise, Mme. Colbert stared at the astonishing and, truth to tell, beautiful sight, murmuring to herself "*Mon Dieu!* Better than most." Her mind had turned suddenly to her recent quarrel with young André Fauvel, who had complained about the fall of the French franc and clients not paying their bills and she thought ironically that here was a genuine cash customer and how would he like that. There was no gainsaying that the mound of dollars on the desk was real money.

But Mme. Colbert was now confused as well as taken aback by the appearance and manner of this weird customer. How had she, who professed to scrubbing floors and washing dishes for her living, come by so much money, and in dollars at that? And what on earth did she want with a Dior dress? The whole business smacked of irregularity leading to trouble. Nowhere did it add up or make any sense, and Mme. Colbert felt she had enough trouble as it was without becoming involved with this impossible British visitor who had more money on her person than she ought.

Adamantly, in spite of the sea of green dollars covering her desk, Mme. Colbert repeated: "I am sorry, the salon is full this afternoon."

Mrs. Harris' lip began to tremble and her little eyes screwed up as the implications of the disaster became clear. Here, in this apparently empty, hostile building, before cold hostile eyes, the unimaginable seemed about to happen. They didn't seem to want her; more, they didn't even appear to want her money. They were going to send her away and back to London without her Dior dress.

"Lummel" she cried. "Ain't you Frenchies got any 'eart? You there, so smooth and cool! Didn't you ever want anything so bad you could cry every time you thought about it? Ain't you never stayed awake nights wanting somefink and shivering, because maybe you couldn't never 'ave it?"

Her words struck like a knife to the heart of Mme. Colbert, who night after night had been doing just that, lying awake and shivering from the wanting to be able to do something for her man. And the pain of the thrust forced a little cry from the manageress. "How did you know? How ever could you guess?"

Her own dark unhappy eyes suddenly became caught up in the small vivid blue ones of Mrs. Harris, which were revealing the first glint of tears. Woman looked into woman, and what Mme. Colbert saw filled her first with horror and then a sudden rush of compassion and understanding.

The horror was directed at herself, at her own coldness and lack of sympathy. In one moment it seemed this odd little woman facing her had held a mirror up to her and let her see herself as she had become through self-indulgence and yielding to her personal difficulties. She thought with shame how she had behaved towards M. Fauvel, and with even more contrition her feckless scolding of the sales girls and even Natasha, the model, who was one of her pets.

But above all she was appalled at the realization that she had let herself be so encrusted, so hardened by the thoughts with which she lived daily that she had become both blind and deaf to human needs and cries emanating from the human heart. Wherever she came from, whatever her walk in life, the person opposite her was a woman, with all of a woman's desires, and as the scales fell thus from her own eyes, she whispered: "My dear, you've set your heart on a Dior dress."

Mrs. Harris would not have been a veteran member in good standing of her profession had she forborne to reply: "Well now, 'ow did *you* know?"

Mme. Colbert ignored the sarcasm. She was looking now at the pile of money and shaking her head in amazement. "But however did you——?"

"Scrimped and syved," said Mrs. Harris. "It's took me three years. But if you wants somefink bad enough, there's always ways. Mind you, you got to 'ave a bit o' luck as well. Now tyke me, after I won a hundred pounds on a football pool I said to meself, 'That's a sign, Ada 'Arris,' so I started syving and 'ere I am."

Mme. Colbert had a flash of intuition as to what "syving" meant to such a person, and a wave of admiration for the courage and gallantry of the little woman passed through her. Perhaps if she herself had shown more of this kind of courage and tenacity, instead of taking out her frustration on innocent and helpless sales girls, she might have been able to accomplish something for her husband. She passed her hand over her brow again and came to a quick decision. "What is your name, my dear?" When Mrs. Harris told her she filled it in quickly on an engraved card that said that M. Christian Dior, no less, would be honored by her presence at the showing of his collection that afternoon. "Come back at three," she said, and handed it to her. "There really *is* no room, but I will make a place for you on the stairs from where you will be able to see the collection."

All rancor and sarcasm vanished from the voice of Mrs. Harris as she gazed in ecstasy at her admission to Paradise. "Now that's kind of you, love," she said. "It looks like me luck is 'olding out."

A curious feeling of peace pervaded Mme. Colbert and a strange smile illuminated her countenance as she said: "Who can say, perhaps you will be lucky for me too."

*seven*

At five minutes to three that afternoon three people whose lives were to become strangely entangled found themselves within a whisper of one another by the grand staircase in the House of Dior, now crowded with visitors, clients, sales girls, staff and members of the press, all milling about.

The first of these was M. André Fauvel, the young chief auditor. He was well set up and handsome in a blond way, in spite of a scar upon his cheek honorably acquired and the source of a military medal won during his army service in Algeria.

It was sometimes necessary for him to descend from the chilling regions of his account books on the fourth floor to the warmth of the atmosphere of perfumes, silks and satins and the females they encased on the second. He welcomed these occasions and even sought excuses for them in the expectation of catching a glimpse of his goddess, the star model, with whom he was desperately and, of course, quite hopelessly in love.

For Mlle. Natasha, as she was known to press and public in the fashion world, was the toast of Paris, a dark-haired, dark-eyed beauty of extraordinary attraction and one who surely had a brilliant career before her either in films or a rich and titled marriage. Every important bachelor in Paris, not to mention a considerable quota of married men, were paying her court.

M. Fauvel came from a good middle-class family; his was a good position with a good wage, and he had a little money besides, but his world was as far removed from the brilliant star of Natasha as was the planet earth from the great Sirius.

He was fortunate, for that moment he did catch a sight of her in the doorway of the dressing room, already encased in the first number she was to model, a frock of flame-colored wool, and on her glossy head perched a flame-colored hat. A diamond snowflake sparkled at her throat, and a sable stole was draped carelessly over one arm. M. Fauvel thought that his heart would stop and never beat again, so beautiful was she and so unattainable.

Glancing out of her sweet grave eyes set wide apart in narrowing lids, Mlle. Natasha saw M. Fauvel and yet saw him not as, showing a sliver of pink tongue, she stifled a yawn. For, truth to tell, she was prodigiously bored. None but a few at Dior's knew the real identity, much less the real personality, of the long-limbed, high-waisted, raven-haired Niobe who attracted the rich and famous to her side like flies.

Her real name then was Suzanne Petitpierre. Her origin was a simple bourgeois family in Lyon and she was desperately weary of the life her profession forced her to lead, the endless rounds of cocktail parties, dinners, theaters and cabarets, as companion to film men, automobile men, steel men, titled men, all of whom wished to be seen with the most glamorous and photographed model in the city. Mlle. Petitpierre wanted nothing of any of them. She had no ambition for a career in films, or on the stage, or to take her place as the châtelaine of some noble château. What she desired more than anything else was somehow to be able to rejoin that middle class from which she had temporarily escaped, marry someone for love, some good, simple man, who was not too beautiful or clever, settle down in a comfortable bourgeois home and produce a great many little bourgeois offspring. Such men existed, she knew, men who were not consistently vain, boastful, or superintellectual to the point where she could not keep up with them. But they were somehow now all outside of her orbit. Even at that very moment when she was beneath the gaze of many admiring eyes she felt lost and unhappy. She remembered vaguely having seen the young man who was regarding her so intensely somewhere before, but could not place him.

Finally Mrs. Harris of 5 Willis Gardens, Battersea, London, came bustling up the staircase already crowded with recumbent figures, to be received by Mme. Colbert. And then and there an astonishing thing took place.

For to the regulars and cognoscenti the staircase at Christian Dior's is Siberia, as humiliating a spot as when the headwaiter of a fashionable restaurant seats you among the yahoos by the swinging doors leading to the kitchen. It was reserved strictly for boobs, nosies, unimportant people and the minor press.

Mme. Colbert regarded Mrs. Harris standing there in all her cheap clothing, and she looked right through them and saw only the gallant woman and sister beneath. She reflected upon the simplicity and the courage that had led her thither in pursuit of a dream, the wholly feminine yearning for an out-of-reach bit of finery, the touching desire, once in her drab cheerless life, to possess the ultimate in a creation. And she felt that somehow Mrs. Harris was quite the most important and worth-while person in the gathering there of chattering females waiting to view the collection that day.

"No," she said to Mrs. Harris. "Not on the staircase. I will not have it. Come. I have a seat for you inside."

She threaded Mrs. Harris through the throng, holding her by the hand, and took her into the main salon, where all but two of the gold chairs in the double rows were occupied. Mme. Colbert always kept one or two seats in reserve for the possible unexpected arrival of some VIP or a favored customer bringing a friend.

She towed Mrs. Harris across the floor and seated her on a vacant chair in the front row. "There," said Mme. Colbert. "You will be able to see everything from here. Have you your invitation? Here is a little pencil. When the models enter, the girl at the door will call out the name and number of the dress—in English. Write down the numbers of the ones you like the best, and I will see you afterwards."

Mrs. Harris settled herself noisily and comfortably on the gray and gold chair. The awful handbag she parked on the vacant seat at her left, the card and pencil she prepared for action. Then with a pleased and happy smile she began taking stock of her neighbors.

Although she had no means of identifying them, the main salon contained a cross section of the haut monde of the world, including a scattering of the nobility, ladies and honorables from England, marquises and countesses from France, baronesses from Germany, principessas from Italy, new-rich wives of French industrialists, veteran-rich wives of South American millionaires, buyers from New York, Los Angeles and Dallas, stage actresses, film stars, playwrights, playboys, diplomats, etc.

The seat to Mrs. Harris' right was occupied by a fierce-looking old gentleman with snow-white hair and mustaches, tufted eyebrows that stood out like feathers from his face and dark pouches under his eyes which were, however, of a penetrating blue and astonishingly alert and young-looking. His hair was combed down over his brow in a sort of fringe; his boots were magnificently polished; his vest was edged with white, and in the lapel of his dark jacket was fastened what seemed to Mrs. Harris to be a small rosebud which both fascinated and startled her, since she had never seen a gentleman wearing such before, and so she was caught by him staring at it.

The thin beak nose aimed itself at her; the keen blue eyes scrutinized her, but the voice that addressed her in perfect English was sere and tired. "Is there something wrong, madame?"

It was not in the nature of Mrs. Harris to be abashed or put out of countenance by anyone, but the thought that she might have been rude stirred her to contrition and she favored the old gentleman with a self-deprecating smile.

"Fancy me gawking at you like you was a waxworks," she apologized. "Where's me manners? I thought that was a rose in yer button 'ole. Jolly good idea, too." Then in explanation she added: "I'm very fond of flowers."

"Are you," said the gentleman. "That is good." Whatever hostility had been engendered by her stare was dispelled by the engaging innocence of her reply. He looked upon his neighbor with a new interest and saw now that she was a most extraordinary creature and one he could not immediately place. "Perhaps," he added, "it would be better if this were indeed a rose instead of a—rosette."

Mrs. Harris did not understand this remark at all, but the pleasant manner in which it had been delivered showed her that she had been forgiven for her rudeness and the tiny shadow that had fallen across her mood was dispelled. "Ain't it loverly 'ere?" she said by way of keeping the conversation going.

"Ah, you feel the atmosphere too." Puzzled, the old gentleman was racking his brain, trying to catch or connect with something that was stirring there, something that seemed to be connected vaguely with his youth and his education, which had been rounded out by two years at a British university. He was remembering a dark and dingy closet, dark-paneled, that had been his bedroom and study, cold and austere, opening off a dark hallway, and incongruously, as the picture formed in his mind, there was a slop pail standing in the hall at the head of the stairs.

Mrs. Harris' alert little eyes now dared to engage those of the old gentleman. They penetrated the fierceness of his exterior, peering through the fringe of white hair and menacing eyebrows and the immaculate front of his clothing to a warmth that she felt within. She wondered what he was doing there, for his attitude of hands folded over a gold-headed cane was of one who was unaccompanied. Probably looking for a dress for his granddaughter, she thought, and, as always, with her kind, resorted to the direct question to satisfy her curiosity. She did, however, as a gesture of benevolence advance the prospective recipient a generation.

"Are you looking for a dress for your daughter?" Mrs. Harris inquired.

The old man shook his head, for his children were scattered and far removed. "No," he replied, "I come here from time to time because I like to see beautiful clothes and beautiful women. It refreshes me and makes me feel young again."

Mrs. Harris nodded assent so that the pink rose affixed to her hat jiggled vigorously. "Ain't it the truth!" she agreed. Then with the pleasant feeling that she had found someone else in whom she might confide she leaned towards him and whispered: "I've come all the way from London to buy me a Dior dress."

A flash of insight, half a Frenchman's marvelous perspicacity, half the completion of the memory he had been trying to dredge up, illuminated the old gentleman, and he knew now who and what she was. The old picture of the dark-stained hallway and creaking stairs with the slop pail at the top returned, but now a figure stood beside the bucket, a large slatternly woman in a bedraggled overall, outsize shoes, reddish-gray hair and freckled skin, sole commander of a battery of brooms, mops, dusting cloths and brushes. She had been for him the only cheerful note throughout the gloomy precincts of the college dormitory.

A slattern whose husband had deserted her, the sole support of five children, she exuded unfailing good humor and a kind of waspish but authentic and matter-of-fact philosophy sandwiched in between comments upon the weather, the government, the cost of living and the vicissitudes of life. "Tyke what you can get and don't look no gift 'orse in the eye," was one of her sayings. He remembered that her name had been Mrs. Maddox, but to him and another French boy in the dormitory she had always been Madame Mops, and as such had been their friend, counselor, bearer of tidings, source of gossip and intramural news.

He remembered too that beneath the brash and comic exterior he had recognized the intrepid bravery of women who lived out lives of hardship and ceaseless toil to render their simple duties to their own, leavened with no more than the sprinkling of the salt of minor grumbling and acid commentary upon the scoundrels and scallywags who ran things. He could see her again now, the reddish-gray hair down about her eyes, a cigarette tucked behind one ear, her head bobbing with concentrated energy as she charred the premises. He could almost hear her speak again. And then he realized that he *had*.

For seated next him in the most exclusive and sophisticated dress salon in Paris was the reincarnation of his Madame Mops of half a century ago.

True, there was no physical resemblance, for his neighbor was slight and worn thin by work—the old gentleman's eyes dropping to her hands confirmed the guess—but that was not how he recognized her; it was by the bearing, the speech, of course, and the naughty little eyes, but above all by the aura of indomitable courage and independence and impudence that surrounded her.

"A Dior dress," he echoed her, "a splendid idea. Let us hope that you will find here this afternoon what you desire."

There was no need in him to question her as to *how* it was possible for her to fulfill such a wish. He knew from his own experience something of the nature of these special Englishwomen and simply assumed that she had been left a legacy, or had suddenly acquired a large sum of money through one of those massive and extraordinary football lotteries he was always reading about in the papers as conferring untold wealth upon British railroad porters, coal miners or grocery clerks. But had he known just how Mrs. Harris had come by the entire sum needed to satisfy her ambition he would not have been surprised either.

They now understood one another as did old friends who had much in life behind them.

"I wouldn't let on to anyone else," Mrs. Harris confessed from the comfort of her new-found friendship, "but I was frightened to death to come 'ere."

The old man looked at her in astonishment. "You? Frightened?"

"Well," Mrs. Harris confided, "you know, the French . . ."

The gentleman emitted a sigh. "Ah yes. I know them very well. Still, there is nothing now but for you to choose the gown that you like the best. It is said the collection this spring is superb."

There was a stir and a rustle. A chic, expensively dressed woman came in acolyted by two salesladies and made for the seat beside Mrs. Harris where the shabby handbag containing the latter's fortune reposed momentarily.

Mrs. Harris snatched it away with an "Oops, dearie, sorry!" then brushed the seat of the chair with her hand and, smiling cheerily, said: "There you are now. All ready for you."

The woman, who had close-set eyes and a too small mouth, sat down with a jangle of gold bracelets, and immediately Mrs. Harris felt herself enveloped in a cloud of the most delectable and intoxicating perfume. She leaned closer to the woman for a better sniff and said with sincere admiration: "My, you do smell good."

The newcomer made a testy motion of withdrawal and a line appeared between the narrow eyes. She was looking towards the door as though searching for someone.

It would be time to begin soon. Mrs. Harris felt as eager and excited as a child and mentally apostrophized herself: "Look at you, Ada 'Arris! Whoever would have thought you'd be sitting in the parlor at Dior's in Paris one day, buying a dress with all the toffs? And yet 'ere you are, and noffink can stop you now——"

But the woman next her, the wife of a speculator, had found whom she sought—Madame Colbert, who had just emerged from the dressing rooms leading off from the stairs, and she beckoned her over, speaking sharply and loudly to her in French as she neared. "What do you mean by seating a vulgar creature like this next to me? I wish her removed at once. I have a friend coming later who will occupy her chair."

Mme. Colbert's heart sank. She knew the woman and the breed. She bought not for love of clothes, but for the ostentation of it. Nevertheless, she spent money. To temporize Mme. Colbert said: "I am sorry, madame, but I have no recollection of reserving this seat for a friend of yours, but I will look."

"It is not necessary to look. I told you I wished this seat for a friend. Do as I say at once. You must be out of your mind to place such a person next to me."

The old gentleman next to Mrs. Harris was beginning to color, the crimson rising from the neckline of his collar and spreading to his ears. His blue eyes were turning as frosty as his white fringe.

For a moment Mme. Colbert was tempted. Surely the little cleaning woman from London would understand if she explained to her that there had been an error in the reservations and the seat was taken. She would be able to see just as much from the head of the stairs. Her glance traveled to Mrs. Harris sitting there in her shabby coat and preposterous hat. And the object of this contretemps, not understanding a word of the conversation, looked up at her with her sunniest and most trusting apple-cheeked smile. "Ain't you the dear to put me 'ere with all these nice people," she said. "I couldn't be 'appier if I was a millionaire."

A worried-looking man in striped trousers and frock coat appeared at the head of the salon. The angry woman called to him: "Monsieur Armand, come here at once, I wish to speak to you. Madame Colbert has had the impertinence to seat me next to this vulgar woman. Am I to be forced to put up with this?"

Flustered by the vehemence of the attack, M. Armand took one look at Mrs. Harris and then to Mme. Colbert he made secret ousting movements with his hands and said: "Well, well. You heard. Get rid of her at once."

The angry red in the face of the fierce old gentleman turned to purple, he half arose from his chair, his mouth opening to speak when Mme. Colbert preceded him.

Many thoughts and fears had raced through the Frenchwoman's mind: her job, prestige of the firm, possible loss of a wealthy client, consequences of defiance of authority. Yet she also knew that though M. Armand was her superior, on this floor she was in supreme command. And now that the unwitting Mrs. Harris was the subject of a cruel attack, the head saleswoman experienced more than ever the feeling of kinship and sisterhood with this strange little visitor from across the Channel returning overpoweringly. Whatever happened, oust her she could not and would not. It would be like beating an innocent child. She thrust out her firm round chin at M. Armand and declared: "Madame has every right to be seated there. She has journeyed here from London especially to buy a dress. If you wish her removed, do it yourself, for I will not."

Mrs. Harris guessed she was being discussed and identified too the city of her birth, but took no hint as to the import of the discussion. She gathered that Mme. Colbert had acquainted the gentleman in the frock coat with the story of her ambitions. She therefore favored him with her most engaging smile and, in addition, tipped him a large and knowing wink.

The old gentleman had in the meantime resumed both his seat and his normal color, but he was staring at Mme. Colbert, his face lit up with a kind of fierce and angry joy. He had momentarily forgotten Mrs. Harris in his discovery of something new, or rather on the contrary, something very old and almost forgotten—a Frenchwoman of selfless courage, honor and integrity.

As for M. Armand, he hesitated—and was lost. Mme. Colbert's firm stand as well as Mrs. Harris' wink had unnerved him. Some of Dior's best clients, he was aware, were frequently most odd-appearing and eccentric women. Mme. Colbert was supposed to know what she was doing. Throwing up his hands in a gesture of surrender, he fled the battlefield.

The wife of the speculator snapped: "You will hear further about this. I think, Madame Colbert, this will cost you your position," got up and stalked from the room.

"Ah, but this I think it will not!" The speaker was now the old gentleman with the tufted eyebrows, fiercely prominent nose and the rosette of the Légion d'Honneur in his buttonhole. He arose and declaimed somewhat dramatically: "I am proud to have been a witness that the spirit of true democracy is not entirely extinguished in France and that decency and honor still have some adherents. If there are any difficulties over this I will speak to the Patron myself."

Mme. Colbert glanced at him and murmured: "Monsieur is very kind." She was bewildered, sick at heart and not a little frightened as she peered momentarily into the dark abyss of the future—Jules passed over again, a broken man, she dismissed from her job and no doubt blacklisted by a malicious woman.

A girl stationed at the door called out: "Number wan, 'Nocturne'" as a model in a beige suit with wide lapels and flaring skirt minced into the room.

A little shriek of excitement was torn from Mrs. Harris. "Lumme. It's begun!"

In spite of her state of mind Mme. Colbert felt suddenly an inexplicable welling up in her of love for the charwoman and, bending over her, she gave her a little squeeze. "Look well now," she said, "so that you may recognize your heart's desire."

### eight

Thereafter, for the next hour and a half, before the enthralled eyes of Mrs. Harris, some ten models paraded one hundred and twenty specimens of the highest dressmaker's art to be found in the most degenerately civilized city in the world.

They came in satins, silks, laces, wools, jerseys, cottons, brocades, velvets, twills, broadcloths, tweeds, nets, organzas and muslins.

They showed frocks, suits, coats, capes, gowns, clothes for cocktails, for the morning, the afternoon, for dinner parties and formal and stately balls and receptions.

They entered trimmed with fur, bugle beads, sequins, embroidery with gold and silver thread, or stiff with brocades; the colors were wonderfully gay and clashed in daring combinations; the sleeves were long, short, medium, or missing altogether. Necklines ranged from choke to plunge, hemlines wandered at the whim of the designer. Some hips were high, others low, sometimes the breasts were emphasized, sometimes neglected or wholly concealed. The theme of the show was the high waist and hidden hips. There were hints and forecasts of the sack and trapeze to come. Every known fur from Persian lamb, mink and nutria to Russian baum marten and sable were used in trim or in the shape of stoles or jackets.

It was not long before Mrs. Harris began to become accustomed to this bewildering array of richness and finery and soon came to recognize the various models upon their appearance in rotation.

There was the girl who walked slinky sly—with her stomach protruded a good six inches before her, and the petite one with the come-hither eyes and provocative mouth. There was the model who seemed to be plain until Mrs. Harris noted her carriage and quiet air of elegance, and another who was on the plump side just sufficiently to convey the idea to a stout customer. There was the girl with her nose in the air and disdain at her lips, and an opposite type, a red-haired minx who wooed the whole salon as she made her rounds.

And then, of course, there was the one and only Natasha, the star. It was the custom in the salon to applaud when a creation made a particular hit, and Mrs. Harris' palms, horny from application to scrubbing brush and mop, led the appreciation each time Natasha appeared, looking lovelier than the last. Once, during one of her appearances, the charwoman noticed a tall, blond, pale young man with an odd scar on his face standing outside, staring hungrily as Natasha made an entrance, and said to herself: "Coo, he ain't arf in love with her, he ain't. . . ."

She was in love herself, was Mrs. Harris, with Natasha, with Mme. Colbert, but above all with life and the wonderful thing it had become. The back of her card was already covered with penciled numbers of frocks and dresses and frantic notes, messages and reminders to herself that she would never be able to decipher. How could one choose between them all?

And then Natasha glided into the salon wearing an evening gown, number eighty-nine, called "Temptation." Mrs. Harris had just a fleeting instant in which to note the enraptured expression on the face of the young man by the door before he turned away quickly, as though that was what he had come for, and then it was all up with her. She was lost, dazzled, blinded, overwhelmed by the beauty of the creation. This was IT! Thereafter there were yet to come further stunning examples of evening gowns until the traditional appearance of the bridal costume brought the show to a close, but the char saw none of them. Her choice was made. Feverish excitement accelerated her heartbeat. Desire coursed like fire in her veins.

"Temptation" was a black velvet gown, floor-length, encrusted halfway from the bottom up with a unique design picked out in beads of jet that gave to the skirt weight and movement. The top was a froth of cream, delicate pink and white chiffon, tulle and lace from which arose the ivory shoulders and neck and dreamy-eyed dark head of Natasha.

Rarely had a creation been better named. The wearer appeared like Venus arising from the pearly sea, and likewise she presented the seductive figure of a woman emerging from tousled bedclothes. Never had the upper portion of the female form been more alluringly framed.

The salon burst into spontaneous applause at Natasha's appearance and the clacking of Mrs. Harris' palms sounded like the beating upon boards with a broomstick.

Cries and murmurs of "La, la!" and "Voyez, c'est formidable!" arose on all sides from the males present while the fierce old gentleman thumped his cane upon the floor and beamed with ineffable pleasure. The garment covered Natasha most decently and morally and yet was wholly indecent and overwhelmingly alluring.

Mrs. Harris was not aware that there was anything extraordinary as to the choice she had made. For she was and eternally would be a woman. She had been young once and in love. She had had a husband to whom her young heart had gone out and to whom she had wished to give and be everything. Life in that sense had not passed her by. He had been shy, embarrassed, tongue-tied, yet she had heard the love words forced haltingly from his lips whispered into her ear. Incongruously at that moment she thought of the photograph upon her dresser with herself in the tiered muslin dress that had seemed so grand then, only now she saw herself clad in "Temptation" in the picture instead.

The bridal model showed herself perfunctorily; the gathering, buzzing as it emerged from the two salons, were sucked towards the exit leading to the grand staircase, where, lined up like ravens, the vendeuses, the black-clad saleswomen with their little sales books under their arms, waited to pounce upon their customers.

Mrs. Harris, her small blue eyes glittering like aquamarines, found Mme. Colbert. "Number eighty-nine, 'Temptytion,'" she cried, and then added, "oh Lor', I 'ope it don't cost more'n what I've got."

Mme. Colbert smiled a thin, sad smile. She might almost have guessed it. "Temptation" was a poem created in materials by a poet of women, for a young girl in celebration of her freshness and beauty and awakening to the mysterious power of her sex. It was invariably demanded by the faded, the middle-aged, the verging-on-passé women. "Come," she said, "we will go in back and I will have it brought to you."

She led her through gray doors into another part of the building, through endless meadows of the soft gray carpeting until at last Mrs. Harris came into yet another world that was almost stifling with excitement.

She found herself in a curtained-off cubicle on a corridor that seemed to be a part of an endless maze of similar corridors and cubicles. Each cubicle held a woman, like a queen bee in a cell, and through the corridors rushed the worker bees with the honey—arms full of frilly, frothy garments in colors of plum, raspberry, tamarind and peach, gentian flower, cowslip, damask rose and orchid, to present them where they had been ordered for trial and further inspection.

Here was indeed woman's secret world, where gossip and the latest scandal were exchanged, the battlefield where the struggle against the ravages of age was carried on with the weapons of the dressmaker's art and where fortunes of money were spent in a single afternoon.

Here, attended by saleswomen, seamstresses, cutters, fitters and designers, who hovered about them with tape, scissors, basting needle and thread and mouths full of pins, rich Frenchwomen, rich American women, rich German women, super-rich South American women, titled women from England, maharanees from India, and even, it was rumored, the wife or two of an ambassador or commissar from Russia, spent their afternoons—and their husbands' money.

And here too, in the midst of this thrilling and entrancing hive, surrounded by her own entourage, stood the London charwoman, encased in "Temptation"—whom it fitted astonishingly, yet logically, since she too was slender, thinned by occupational exercise and too little food.

She issued from the wondrous, frothy foam of seashell pink, sea cream and pearl white like—Ada 'Arris from Battersea. The creation worked no miracles except in her soul. The scrawny neck and graying head that emerged from the shoulder décolleté of the gown, the weathered skin, small button-bright blue eyes and apple cheeks contrasted with the classic fall of jet-encrusted black velvet panels were grotesque—but still not wholly so, for the beautiful gown as well as the radiance of the person in it yet managed to lend an odd kind of dignity to this extraordinary figure.

For Mrs. Harris had attained her Paradise. She was in a state of dreamed-of and longed-for bliss. All of the hardships, the sacrifices, the economies and hungers and doings-without she had undergone faded into insignificance. Buying a Paris dress was surely the most wonderful thing that could happen to a woman.

Mme. Colbert was consulting a list. "Ah, *oui*," she murmured, "the price is five hundred thousand francs." The apple cheeks of Mrs. Harris paled at this announcement. There was not that much money in the whole world. "That is five hundred British pounds," Mme. Colbert continued, "which is one thousand four hundred American dollars, and with our little discount for cash——"

Mrs. Harris' yell of triumph interrupted her. "Blimey! That's exactly what I've got. I'll 'ave it! Can I pye for it now?" and moving stiffly beneath the crinolines, jet and interior reinforcements of the dress, she reached for her purse.

"Of course—if you wish. But I do not like to handle such an amount of cash. I will ask M. Fauvel to descend," Mme. Colbert replied, and reached for a telephone.

A few minutes later the young, blond, M. André Fauvel appeared in the cubicle, where the shrewd appraising eyes recognized him at once as the man who had gazed with such a hopelessly lovelorn expression upon Natasha.

As for M. Fauvel, he looked upon Mrs. Harris rising out of "Temptation" registering sheer and almost unconcealed horror at the picture of this earthy person desecrating the gown modeled in the collection by his goddess. To the inflamed mind of young Fauvel it was as though one of the girls from the Rue Blanche or the Place Pigalle had wrapped herself in the flag of France.

The creature smiled at him, revealing missing and imperfect teeth and wrinkling the cheeks so that they looked like fruit shrunken by frost, as she said, "It's all 'ere, ducks. Fourteen hundred dollars, and that's me last penny. 'Strewth'!" And she handed him the sheaf of dollars.

Mme. Colbert caught the look upon the face of the young auditor. She could have told him this was something they went through a hundred times each week, watching exquisite creations meant for beautiful women carried off by raddled old frumps. She touched his arm gently, distracting him, and explained in a few swift sentences in French. It failed to abate his anger at seeing the outer shell of his beloved so mocked and burlesqued.

"It don't need no altering," Mrs. Harris was saying. "I'll take it just as it is. 'Ave it wrapped for me."

Mme. Colbert smiled. "But, my dear, surely you must know we cannot let you have *this* dress. This is the model and there is yet another month of summer showings. We will make you one, of course, exactly like——"

Alarm squeezed the heart of Mrs. Harris as the import of what Mme. Colbert was saying struck home. "Lumme! Myke me one——" she repeated, and suddenly looking like an older travesty of herself, asked, " 'Ow long does it take?"

Mme. Colbert felt alarm now too. "Ten days to two weeks ordinarily—but for you we would make an exception and rush it through in a week——"

The awful silence following upon this revelation was broken by the cry torn from the depth of Mrs. Harris. "But don't you understand? I can't stay in Paris. I've just enough money to get me 'ome! It means I can't 'ave it!" She saw herself back in the gloomy Battersea flat, empty-handed, possessed only of her useless money. What did she want with all that money? It was ownership of "Temptation" for which she craved, body and soul, even though she never again put it on her back.

"*Horrible, dreadful, common woman,*" thought M. André. "*Serves you right, and I shall enjoy handing your vulgar money back to you.*"

Thereupon, to the horror of all, they saw two tears form at the corners of the little eyes, followed by others that coursed down the red-veined cheeks as Mrs. Harris stood there in the midst of them, in the exquisite ball gown, miserable, abandoned, desperately unhappy.

And M. André Fauvel, auditor and money man, supposedly with heart of stone, suddenly felt himself moved as he had never thought possible, deeply and unbearably touched, and, with one of those flashes of insight of which the French are so capable, knew that it was the hopeless love he felt for the girl Natasha whose sweet and dear body had inhabited this garment that had brought him so suddenly to an understanding of the tragedy of this stranger who, on the brink of realizing her greatest desire, was to suffer frustration.

Thereupon he dedicated his next remark to that girl who would never know how much or greatly he had loved her, or that he had loved her at all, for that matter. He presented himself to Mrs. Harris with a formal little bow. "If Madame would care, I invite her to come to my home and remain with me during this period as my guest. It is not much—only a small house, but my sister has had to go to Lille and there would be room——"

His reward was almost immediate in the expression that came over the little woman's face and her cry of "Oh, Lor' love yer! Do yer really mean it?" and the odd gesture of Mme. Colbert which might have been the brushing away of something from the corner of her eyes as she said: "*Oh, André, vous êtes un ange!*"

But then Mrs. Harris gave a little shriek. "Oh lumme—my jobs——"

"Haven't you a friend," suggested Mme. Colbert helpfully, "someone who would help you out while you were away?"

"Mrs. Butterfield," Mrs. Harris replied immediately. "But a whole week——"

"If she is a real friend she will not mind," Mme. Colbert counseled. "We could send her a telegram from you."

Mrs. Butterfield would not mind, particularly when she heard all about it, Mrs. Harris felt certain. Her conscience smote her when she thought of Pamela Penrose and her important producer friends and her career. Yet there was "Temptation." "I'll do it," she cried. "I've got to 'ave it."

Thereupon, to her excitement and delight, *her* horde of fitters, cutters, dressmakers and seamstresses descended upon her with tape, pattern muslin, pins, basting thread, scissors and all the wondrous exciting paraphernalia that was connected with making up the most expensive dress in the world.

By late afternoon, when at last Mrs. Harris was done with measuring and fitting, the most remote corner of the establishment had heard the tale of the London charwoman who had saved her wages and journeyed to Paris to buy herself a Dior dress and she was in the way of becoming something of a celebrity. Members of the staff from the lowest to the highest, including the Patron himself, had managed an excuse to pass by the cubicle to catch a glimpse of this remarkable Englishwoman.

And later, while for the last time Mrs. Harris was encased in the model, Natasha herself, clad in a neat cocktail frock, for she was about to start out on a round of evening engagements, came and saw nothing unusual or grotesque in the figure of the charwoman in the beautiful creation, for she had heard the story and felt herself touched by it. She understood Mrs. Harris. "I am so glad you have chosen that one," she said simply.

When the latter suddenly said: "Coo, 'owever am I going to get to this Mr. Fauvel? He gave me 'is address, but I wouldn't know where it was," Natasha was the first to offer to take her thither.

"I have a leetle car; I will drive you there myself. Let me see where it is."

Mrs. Harris handed her the card M. Fauvel had given her with the address, "No. 18 Rue Dennequin." Natasha wrinkled her pretty forehead over the name. "Monsieur André Fauvel," she repeated. "Now where have I heard that name before?"

Mme. Colbert smiled indulgently. "It is only the auditor of our company, chérie," she said. "He is the one who pays out your salary."

"Oh la!" laughed Natasha. "One might love such a one. Very well, Madame Harris, when you are ready I will take you to heem."


*nine*


Thus it was that shortly after six Mrs. Harris found herself in Natasha's sporty little Simca, negotiating the traffic rapids of the Etoile and then sailing down the broad stream of the Avenue Wagram, bound for the home of M. Fauvel. A telegram had already been dispatched to London, asking her friend to cope with her clients as best she could until her return; a telegram calculated to shake Mrs. Butterfield to her very marrow, emanating from Paris as it did. But Mrs. Harris cared not. She was still exploring Paradise.

No. 18 Rue Dennequin was a small, two-story gray house with mansard roof, built in the nineteenth century. When they rang the doorbell, M. Fauvel cried: "*Entrez, entrez*—come in," from within, believing it to be Mrs. Harris by herself. They pushed through the door that was ajar and found themselves in a home in exactly that state of chaos to be expected when a bachelor's sister has gone away leaving explicit instructions with the daily cleaning woman, who would naturally choose that moment to become ill.

Dust lay thick; nothing had been touched for a week; books and clothes were scattered about. It took no trick of the imagination to estimate the piled-up dishes in the kitchen sink, the greasy pans on the stove, as well as the condition of the bathroom and the unmade beds above.

Never was a man in such confusion. His honorable scar gleaming white in a face crimson with shame—the cicatrice rather made him attractive-looking—M. Fauvel appeared before them stammering: "Oh, no—no—Mademoiselle Natasha—you of all people—I cannot permit you to enter—I, who would have given anything to have welcomed—I mean, I have been living alone here for a week—I am disgraced——"

Mrs. Harris saw nothing unusual in the condition of the place. If anything, it was comfortably like old times, for it was exactly the same as greeted her in every house, flat or room when she came to work daily in London.

"'Ere, 'ere, ducksie," she called out genially. "What's all the fuss about? I'll 'ave all this put right in a jiffy. Just you show me where the mop closet is, and get me a bucket and a brush——"

As for Natasha—she was looking right through and past the dirt and disorder to the solid bourgeois furniture she saw beneath it, the plush sofa, the whatnot cabinet, the huge portrait-size framed photographs of M. Fauvel's grandfather and -mother in stiff, beginning-of-the-century clothes, the harpsichord in one corner, the great tub with the plant in another, the lace on the sofa pillows, the chenille curtains and the overstuffed chairs—comfort without elegance—and her heart yearned towards it. This was a home, and she had not been in one like it since she had left her own in Lyon.

"Oh please," she cried, "may I remain and help? Would you permit it, monsieur?"

M. Fauvel went into a perfect hysteria of abject apologies—"But, mademoiselle—you of all people—in this pigpen, for which I could die of shame—to soil those little hands—never in a thousand years could I permit——"

"Ow—come off it, dearie," ordered Mrs. Harris succinctly. "Blimey, but all the thick 'eads ain't on our side of the Channel. Carn't you see the girl WANTS to? Run along now and keep out of the way and let us get at it."

*Dear me*, Mrs. Harris thought to herself as she and Natasha donned headcloths and aprons and seized upon brooms and dustcloths, *French people are just like anyone else, plain and kind, only maybe a little dirtier. Now 'oo would have thought it after all one 'ears?*

That particular evening, Natasha had a rendezvous for drinks with a count, an appointment for dinner with a duke, and a late evening date with an important politico. It gave her the most intense pleasure she had known since she came to Paris to leave the count standing and, with the professional and efficient Mrs. Harris, make the dirt fly at No. 18 Rue Dennequin as it had never flown before.

It seemed no time at all before everything was in order again. The mantelpieces and furniture gleamed, the plant was watered, the beds stiff with clean sheets and pillowcases, the ring around the bath tub banished, pots, pans, dishes, glasses and knives and forks washed up.

*Oh, it is good to be inside a home again, where one can be a woman and not just a silly little doll*, Natasha said to herself as she attacked the dust and cobweb salients in the corners and contemplated the horrors that M. Fauvel, manlike, had brushed under the carpet.

And as she stood there for a moment, reflecting upon the general hopelessness of the male species, she found herself suddenly touched by the plight of M. Fauvel and thought, *That must be a fine sister he has, poor boy, and he is SO ashamed,* and suddenly in her mind's eye she saw herself holding this blond head with the blushing face and the white scar—surely acquired in some noble manner—to her breast while she murmured, *Now, now, my little one, do not take on so. Now that I am here everything will be all right again.* And this to a perfect stranger she had seen only vaguely before as he appeared occasionally in the background of the establishment for which she worked. She stood stock-still for a moment with astonishment at herself, leaning upon her broom, the very picture of housewifely grace, to be discovered so by the sudden return of the enchanted M. Fauvel himself.

So busy had been the two women that neither had noticed the absence of the auditor until he suddenly reappeared but half visible behind the mountain of parcels with which he was laden.

"I thought that after such exhausting labors you might be hungry," he explained. Then, regarding a disheveled, smudged, but thoroughly contented Natasha, he stammered: "Would you—could you—dare I hope that you might remain?"

The count and his date were already dead pigeons. Bang, bang went both barrels, and the duke and the politico joined him. With the utmost simplicity and naturalness, and quite forgetting herself, Natasha, or rather Mlle. Petitpierre of Lyon, threw her arms about M. Fauvel's neck and kissed him. "But you are an angel to have thought of this, André. I am ravenous. First I will allow myself a bath in that wonderful deep old tub upstairs and then we will eat and eat and eat."

M. Fauvel thought too that he had never been so happy in his life. What an astonishing turn things had taken ever since—why, ever since that wonderful little Englishwoman had come to Dior's to buy herself a dress.

Mrs. Harris had never tasted caviar before, or *pâté de foie gras* fresh from Strasbourg, but she very quickly got used to them both, as well as the lobster from the Pas-de-Calais and the eels from Lorraine in jelly. There was *charcuterie* from Normandy, a whole cold roast *poulet de Bresse* along with a crispy skinned duck from Nantes. There was a Chassagne-Montrachet with the lobster and hors d'oeuvres, champagne with the caviar and Beaune Romanée with the fowl, while an Yquem decorated the chocolate cake.

Mrs. Harris ate for the week before, for this and the next as well. There had never been a meal like it before and probably never would be again. Her little eyes gleamed with delight as she crowed: "Lumme, if there's anything I like it's a good tuck-in."

"The night without is heavenly," said M. Fauvel, his eyes meltingly upon the sweet, well-fed-pussycat face of Natasha. "Perhaps afterwards we will let Paris show herself to us——"

"Ooof!" grunted Mrs. Harris, stuffed to her wispy eyebrows. "You two go.

I've 'ad a day to end all days. I'll just stay 'ome 'ere and do the dishes and then 'get into me bed and try not to wake up back in Battersea."

But now a feeling of restraint and embarrassment seemed suddenly to descend upon the two young people and which Mrs. Harris in her state of repletion failed to notice. Had his guest consented to go, M. Fauvel was thinking, all would have been different and the exuberance of the party plus the glorious presence of Natasha might have been maintained. But, of course, without this extraordinary person the thought of his showing Dior's star model the sights of Paris suddenly seemed utterly ridiculous.

To Natasha, Paris at night was the interior of a series of smoky boîtes or expensive night clubs, such as Dinazard or Shéhérazade, and of which she was heartily sick. She would have given much to be able to stand on the Grande Terrasse of Le Sacré-Coeur under the starry night and look out over these stars reflected in the sea of the lights of Paris—and in particular with M. Fauvel at her side.

But with Mrs. Harris' plumping for bed there seemed no further excuse for her presence. She had already intruded too much into his privacy. She had shamelessly pried into his quarters with broom and duster, seen the squalor in his sink and permitted herself the almost unthinkable intimacy of washing out his bath tub, and in her exuberance the even more unpardonable one of bathing in it herself.

She was suddenly overcome with confusion and blushing murmured: "Oh, no, no, no. I cannot, it is impossible. I am afraid I have an appointment. I must be going."

M. Fauvel accepted the blow, which was expected. *Ah, yes,* he thought, *you must return, little butterfly, to the life you love best. Some count, marquis, duke or even prince will be waiting for you. But at least I have had this one night of bliss and I should be content.* Aloud he murmured: "Yes, yes, of course, Mademoiselle has been too kind."

He bowed, they touched hands lightly, and their glances met and for a moment lingered. And this time the sharp knowing eyes of Mrs. Harris twigged. *Oho,* she said to herself, *so that's 'ow it is. I should have went with them.*

But it was too late to do anything about it now and the fact was that she really was too stuffed to move. "Well, good night, dears," she said loudly and pointedly, and tramped up the stairs, hoping that with her presence removed they might still get together on an evening out. But a moment later she heard the front door open and shut and then the clatter as the motor of Natasha's Simca came to life. Thus ended Mrs. Ada 'Arris' first day in a foreign land and amidst a foreign people.

The following morning, however, when M. Fauvel proposed that in the evening he show her something of Paris, Mrs. Harris lost no time in suggesting that Natasha be included in the party. Flustered, M. Fauvel protested that sight-seeing was not for such exalted creatures as Mlle. Natasha.

"Garn," scoffed Mrs. Harris. "What makes you think she is different from any other young girl when there is an 'andsome man about? She'd 'ave gone with you last night if you 'ad 'ad the brains to ask her. You just tell 'er I said she was to come."

That morning the two of them encountered briefly upon the gray carpeted stairs at Dior. They paused for an instant uncomfortably. M. Fauvel managed to stammer: "Tonight I shall be showing Mrs. Harris something of Paris. She has begged that you would accompany us."

"Oh," murmured Natasha, "Madame Harris has asked? She wishes it? Only she?"

M. Fauvel could only nod dumbly. How could he in the chill austerity of the grand staircase of the House of Christian Dior cry out: "Ah, no, it is I who wish it, crave it, desire it, with all my being. It is I who worship the very nap of the carpet on which you stand."

Natasha finally said: "If she desires it then, I will come. She is adorable, that little woman."

"At eight then."

"I will be there."

They continued on their routes, he up, she down.

The enchanted night duly took place. It began for the three of them with a ride up the Seine on a *bâteaumouche* to a riverside restaurant in a tiny suburb. With a wonderful sense of tact and feeling M. Fauvel avoided those places where Mrs. Harris might have felt uncomfortable, the expensive luxury and glitter spots, and never knew how happy Natasha herself felt in this more modest environment.

This was a little family restaurant. The tables were of iron, the tablecloths checkered, and the bread wonderfully crisp and fresh. Mrs. Harris took it all in, the simple people at neighboring tables, the glassy, shimmering surface of the river with boating parties gliding about and the strains of accordion music drifting over from the water, with a deep sigh of satisfaction. She said: "Lumme, if it ain't just like 'ome. Sometimes, on an hot night, me friend Mrs. Butterfield and I go for a ride up the river and drop in for a pint at a little plyce near the brewery."

But at the eating of a snail she firmly balked. She examined them with interest in their steaming fragrant shells. The spirit was willing but her stomach said no.

"I carn't," she finally confessed, "not arfter seeing them walking about."

From that time on, unspoken, the nightly gathering of the three for roamings about Paris became taken for granted. In the daytime, while they worked, except for her fittings, which took place at eleven-thirty in the mornings, and her tidying of Fauvel's premises, Mrs. Harris was free to explore the city on her own, but the evenings were heralded by the arrival of Natasha in her Simca, and they would be off.

Thus Mrs. Harris saw Paris by twilight from the second landing of the Tour Eiffel, by milky moonlight from the Sacré-Coeur, and waking up in the morning at dawn when the market bustle at Les Halles began, and after a night of visiting this or that part of the city of never ending wonder they breakfasted there on eggs and garlic sausages, surrounded by workmen, produce handlers and lorry drivers.

Once, instigated somewhat in a spirit of mischief by Natasha, they took Mrs. Harris to the "Revue des Nudes," a cabaret in the Rue Blanche, but she was neither shocked nor impressed. There is a curiously cozy kind of family atmosphere at some of these displays: whole groups, including grandmothers, fathers, mothers and the young, come up from the country for a celebration or anniversary of some kind, bringing along a picnic hamper; they order wine and settle down to enjoy the fun.

Mrs. Harris felt right at home in this milieu. She did not consider the parade of stitchless young ladies immoral. Immoral in her code was doing someone the dirty. She peered interestedly at the somewhat beefy naiads and remarked: "Coo, some of them don't arf want a bit o' slimming, what?" Later when an artiste adorned with no more than a *cache sexe* consisting of a silver fig leaf performed rather a strenuous dance, Mrs. Harris murmured: "Lumme, I don't see 'ow she does it."

"Does which?" queried M. Fauvel absent-mindedly, for his attention was riveted upon Natasha.

"Keeps that thing on 'oppin' about like that."

M. Fauvel blushed crimson and Natasha shouted with laughter, but forbore to explain.

And in this manner Mrs. Harris lost all fear of the great foreign capital, for they showed her a life and a city teeming with her own kind of people—simple, rough, realistic and hard-working and engaged all of them in the same kind of struggle to get along as she herself back home.

*ten*

Free to wander where she would during the day in Paris except for her fittings, Mrs. Harris never quite knew where her footsteps would lead her. It was not the glittering shopping sections of the Champs-Elysées, the Faubourg St.-Honoré and the Place Vendôme that interested her, for there were equally shimmering and expensive shopping sections in London which she never visited. But she loved people and odd *quartiers*, the beautiful parks, the river and the manner in which life was lived in the poorer section by the inhabitants of the city.

She explored thus the Left Bank and the Right and eventually through accident stumbled upon a certain paradise in the middle, the Flower Market, located by the Quai de Corse on the Ile de la Cité.

Often back home Mrs. Harris had peered longingly into the windows of flower shops, at the display of hothouse blooms, orchids, roses, gardenias, etc., on her way to and from her labors, but never in her life had she found herself in the midst of such an intoxicating profusion of blossoms of every kind, color and shape, ranged upon the sidewalks and filling booths and stands of the Flower Market within sight of the twin towers of Notre-Dame.

Here were streets that were nothing but a mass of azaleas, in pots; plants in pink, white, red, purple, mingling with huge bunches of cream, crimson and yellow carnations. There seemed to be acres of boxes of pansies smiling up into the sun, blue irises, red roses, and huge fronds of gladioli forced into early bud in hothouses.

There were many plants and flowers Mrs. Harris did not even know the names of, small rubbery-looking pink blooms, or flowers with yellow centers and deep blue petals, every conceivable kind of daisy and marguerite, bushy-headed peonies and, of course, row upon row of Mrs. Harris' own very dearest potted geraniums.

But not only were her visual senses enthralled and overwhelmed by the masses of shapes and colors, but on the soft breeze that blew from the Seine came as well the intoxication of scent to transport the true lover of flowers into his or her particular heaven, and such a one was Mrs. Harris. All the beauty that she had ever really known in her life until she saw the Dior dress had been flowers. Now her nostrils were filled with the scent of lilies and tuberoses, the ineffable fragrance of freesias. From every quarter came beautiful odors, and through this profusion of color and scent Mrs. Harris wandered as if in a dream.

Yet another and familiar figure was promenading in that same dream, none other than the fierce old gentleman who had been Mrs. Harris' neighbor at the Dior show and whose name was the Marquis de Chassagne, of an ancient family. He was wearing a light tan spring coat, a tan-colored homburg and fawn-colored gloves. There was no fierceness in his face now, and even his tufted wild-flung eyebrows seemed at peace as he strolled through the lanes of fresh, dewy blossoms and breathed deeply and with satisfaction of the perfumes that mounted from them.

His path crossed that of the charwoman, a smile broke out over his countenance and he raised his homburg with the same gesture he would have employed doffing it to a queen. "Ah," he said, "our neighbor from London who likes flowers. So you have found your way here."

Mrs. Harris said: "It's like a bit of 'Eaven, ain't it? I wouldn't have believed it if I 'adn't seen it with me own eyes." She looked down at a huge jar bulging with crisp white lilies and another with firm, smooth, yet un-opened gladioli with but a gleam of mauve, crimson, lemon or pink showing at the stalks to indicate what colors they would be. Drops of fresh water glistened on them. "Oh Lor'!" murmured Mrs. Harris, "I do 'ope Mrs. Butter-field won't forget to water me geraniums."

"Ah, madame, you cultivate geraniums?" the marquis inquired politely.

"Two window boxes full and a dozen or so pots wherever I can find a place to put one. You might say as it was me 'obby."

"*Epatant!*" the marquis murmured to himself, and then inquired: "And the dress you came here to seek. Did you find it?"

Mrs. Harris grinned like a little imp. "Didn't I just! It's the one called 'Temptytion,' remember? It's black velvet trimmed wiv black bugle beads and the top is some sort of pink soft stuff."

The marquis reflected for a moment and then nodded. "Ah yes, I do remember. It was worn by that exquisite young creature——"

"Natasha," Mrs. Harris concluded for him. "She's me friend. It's being myde for me. I've got three more days to wait."

"And so, with infinite good sense, you acquaint yourself with the genuine attractions of our city."

"And you——" Mrs. Harris began, and broke off in the middle of her sentence, for intuitively she knew the answer to the question she had been about to ask.

But the Marquis de Chassagne was not at all put out, and only remarked gravely: "You have guessed it. There is so little time left for me to enjoy the beauties of the earth. Come, let us sit on this seat in the sun a little, you and I, and talk."

They sat then, side by side on the green wooden bench, in the midst of the sensuous colors and ravishing perfumes, the aristocrat and the charwoman, and conversed. They were worlds apart in everything but the simplicity of their humanity, and so they were really not apart at all. For all of his title and eminent position, the marquis was a lonely widower, his children married and scattered. And what was Mrs. Harris but an equally lonely widow, but with the courage to embark upon one great adventure to satisfy her own craving for beauty and elegance. They had much in common, these two.

Besides her geraniums, Mrs. Harris remarked, she also received cut flowers from time to time with which to brighten her little basement flat from clients about to leave for a week-end in the country, or who received presents of fresh flowers and would make it a point to present Mrs. Harris with their old and half-wilted blooms. "I get them 'ome as fast as ever I can," she explained, "cut off their stems and put them in a fresh jug of water with a penny at the bottom."

The marquis looked astounded at this piece of intelligence.

"Ow, didn't you know?" Mrs. Harris said. "If you put a copper in the water with wilted flowers it brings them right back."

The marquis, full of interest, said: "Well now, it is indeed true that one is never too old to learn." He went on to another subject that had interested him. "And you say that Mademoiselle Natasha has become your friend?"

"She's a dear," said Mrs. Harris, "not at all like you might expect, high and mighty with all the fuss that's made over her. She's as unspoiled as your own daughter would be. They're all me friends, I do believe—that nice young Monsieur Fauvel, the cashier—it's his 'ouse I am stopping at—and that poor Madame Colbert——"

"Eh," said the marquis, "and who is Madame Colbert?"

It was Mrs. Harris' turn to look surprised. "Ow, surely you know Madame Colbert—the manageress—the one who tells you whether you can come in or not. She's a real love. Imagine putting Ada 'Arris right in with all the toffs."

"Ah yes," said the marquis with renewed interest, "that one. A rare person, a woman of courage and integrity. But why poor?"

Mrs. Harris waggled her rear end more comfortably into the bench to enjoy a jolly good gossip. Why, this French gentleman was just like anybody when it came to interest in tidbits about other people's trouble and miseries. Her voice became happily confidential as she tapped him on the arm and answered: "Ow, but of course you wouldn't know about her poor 'usband."

"Oh," said the marquis, "she has a husband then? What is the difficulty, is he ill?"

"Not exactly," replied Mrs. Harris. "Madame Colbert wouldn't dream of telling anybody about it but, of course, she's told me. A woman who's buried a husband as I 'ave can understand things. Twenty-five years in the same office 'e was——"

"Your husband?" asked the marquis.

"No, no, Madame Colbert's, the brains of his office he is. But every time he comes up for a big job they give it to some count or some rich man's son until his 'eart is near broken, and Madame Colbert's, too."

The marquis felt a curious tingling at the base of his scalp as a faint glimmer of light began to dawn. Mrs. Harris' voice for a moment mimicked some of the bitterness contained in that of Mme. Colbert's as she said: "There's another chance for him now and no one to speak up for him or give him a 'and. Madame Colbert's crying her poor dear eyes out."

A little smile that was almost boyish illuminated the stern mouth of the old marquis. "Would Madame Colbert's husband by any chance have the name of Jules?"

Mrs. Harris stared at him in blank amazement, as though he were a magician. "Go on!" she cried. " 'Ow did *you* know? That's 'is name, Jules. Do you know him? Madame Colbert says 'e's got more brains in his little finger than all the rest of them in their striped pants."

The marquis suppressed a chuckle and said: "Madame Colbert may be right. There can be no question as to the intelligence of a man who has the good sense to marry such a woman." He sat in silent thought for a moment and then, fishing into an inside pocket, produced a card case from which he extracted a finely engraved card, upon the back of which he wrote a brief message with an old-fashioned fountain pen. He waved the card dry and then presented it to Mrs. Harris. "Will you remember to give this to Madame Colbert the next time you see her."

Mrs. Harris inspected the card with frank and unabashed interest. The engraved portion read: "Le Marquis Hypolite de Chassagne, Chef des Affaires Etrangères, Quai d'Orsay," which meant nothing to her except that her friend was a nob with a title. She turned it over, but the message thereon was scribbled in French and she did not understand that either. "Right-o," she said, "I've got a 'ead like a sieve, but I won't forget."

A church clock struck eleven. "Lor'!" she exclaimed. "I 'aven't been watching the time. I'll be lyte for me fitting." She leaped up from the bench, cried: "So long, ducks, don't forget to put the penny in the jug for the flowers," and was off. The marquis remained sitting on the bench in the sun looking after her, an expression of rapt and total admiration on his countenance.

During Mrs. Harris' fitting that morning Mme. Colbert dropped into the cubicle to see how things were going and assisted the seamstress with a hint here and a suggestion there when Mrs. Harris suddenly gave a little shriek. "Lumme! I almost forgot. 'Ere, 'e said I was to give you this." She secured her ancient handbag, rummaged in it and finally produced the card and handed it to Mme. Colbert.

The manageress turned first red and then deathly pale as she examined the pasteboard and the message on the reverse. The fingers holding the card began to shake. "Where did you get this?" she whispered. "Who gave it to you?"

Mrs. Harris looked concerned. "The old gent. The one that was sitting next to me with the red thing in 'is button'ole that day at the collection. I met 'im in the Flower Market and 'ad a bit of a chat with 'im. It ain't bad news, is it?"

"Oh, no, no," murmured Mme. Colbert, her voice trembling with emotion and hardly able to hold back the tears. Suddenly and inexplicably she went to Mrs. Harris, took her in her arms and held her tightly for a moment. "Oh, you wonderful, wonderful woman," she cried, and then turned and fled from the cubicle. She went into another booth, an empty one, where she could be alone to put her head down upon her arms and cry unashamedly with the joy of the message which had read: "Please ask your husband to come to see me tomorrow. I may be able to help him—Chassagne."

*eleven*

On the last night of Mrs. Harris' magical stay in Paris, M. Fauvel had planned a wonderful party for her and Natasha, an evening out with dinner at the famous restaurant Pré-Catelan in the Bois de Boulogne. Here in the most romantic setting in the world, seated in the open air beneath the spreading boughs of a venerable hundred-and-sixty-year-old beech tree, illuminated by fairy lights strung between the leafy branches, and with gay music in the background, they were to feast on the most delicious and luxurious of foods and drink the finest wines that M. Fauvel could procure.

And yet what should have been the happiest of times for the three started out as an evening of peculiar and penetrating sadness.

M. Fauvel looked distinguished and handsome in dinner jacket with the ribbon of the military medal he had won in his lapel. Natasha had never looked more ravishing, in an evening dress of pink, gray and black, cut to show off her sweet shoulders and exquisite back. Mrs. Harris came as she was except for a fresh, somewhat daringly peek-a-boo lace blouse she had bought with some of her remaining British pounds.

Her sadness was only an overlay on the delight and excitement of the place and the hour and the most thrilling thing of all that was to happen tomorrow. It was due to the fact that all good things must come to an end and that she must be leaving these people of whom in a short time she had grown so extraordinarily fond.

But the unhappiness that gripped M. Fauvel and Mlle. Petitpierre was of heavier, gloomier and thicker stuff. Each had reached the conclusion that once Mrs. Harris departed, this idyll which had brought them together and thrown them for a week into one another's company would be at an end.

Natasha was no stranger to the Pré-Catelan. Countless times she had been taken there to dine and dance by wealthy admirers who meant nothing to her, who held her clutched to them in close embrace upon the dance floor and who talked interminably of themselves over their food. There was only one person now she wished to dance with ever again, whom she desired to hold her close, and this was the unhappy-looking young man who sat opposite her and did not offer to do so.

Ordinarily in any country two young people have little difficulty in exchanging signals, messages and eventually finding one another, but when in France they have emerged, so to speak, from the same class and yet are still constrained by the echoes of this class strange obstacles can put themselves in the way of an understanding. For all of the night, the lights, the stars and the music, M. Fauvel and Mlle. Petitpierre were in danger of passing one another by.

For as he gazed upon the girl, his eyes misty with love, M. Fauvel knew that this was the proper setting for Natasha—here she belonged amidst the gay, lighthearted and the wealthy. She was not for him. He had never been to this colorful restaurant before in the course of the modest life he led and he was now more than ever convinced that it was only because of Madame Harris that Natasha endured him. He was aware that a curious affection had grown up between that glamorous creature, Dior's star model, and the little cleaning woman. But then he had grown very fond of Mrs. Harris himself. There was something about this Englishwoman that seemed to drive straight to the heart.

As for Natasha, she felt herself pushed out of André Fauvel's life by the very thing for which she so much yearned, his middle-class respectability. He would never dream of marrying one such as her, presumably spoiled, flighty, steeped in publicity, dowerless. No, never. He would choose some good, simple, middle-class daughter of a friend or acquaintance, or perhaps his absent sister would choose her for him. He would settle down to the tranquillity of an unexciting married life and raise many children. How she wished that she could be that wife and lead that tranquil life by his side and bear for him those children.

The band beat out a tingling cha-cha-cha. A bottle of champagne stood opened by the table. They were between courses, awaiting the arrival of a super Châteaubriand. All about them voices were raised in merriment and laughter, and the three sat enveloped in thick silence.

Shaking off the shadow that had fallen athwart her and feeling the wonderful excitement of life and beauty that was all about them, Mrs. Harris suddenly became aware of the condition of her two companions and tried to do something about it. "Ain't you two going to dance?" she asked.

M. Fauvel blushed and mumbled something about not having danced for a long time. He would have loved nothing better, but he had no wish to compel Natasha to endure an embrace that must be repulsive to her.

"I do not feel like dancing," said Mlle. Petitpierre. She would have given everything to have been on the floor with him at that moment, but would not embarrass him after his obvious reluctance to have anything to do with her beyond the normal requirements of duty and politeness.

But Mrs. Harris' keen ears had already caught the hollowness of their voices with the unmistakable note of misery contained therein, and her shrewd little eyes darted from one to the other, appraising them.

"Look 'ere," she said, "wot's the matter wiv you two?"

"But nothing."

"Of course, nothing."

In their efforts to prove this M. Fauvel and Mlle. Petitpierre simultaneously broke into bright and brittle chatter aimed at Mrs. Harris while they avoided one another's eyes and which they kept up for a minute until it suddenly petered out and the silence resettled itself more thickly.

"Blimey," said Mrs. Harris, "of all the fools me. I thought you two 'ad it settled between you long ago." She turned to M. Fauvel and asked: "Ain't you got no tongue in your 'ead? What are you waitin' for?"

M. Fauvel flushed as brightly crimson as the electric light bulb above his head. "But—but—I—I—" he stammered. "She would never—"

Mrs. Harris turned to Natasha. "Can't you 'elp 'im a bit? In my day when a young lydy had her 'eart set on a fellow she'd let him know soon enough. 'Ow do you think I got me own 'usband?"

There was a white light above the beautiful, dark, glossy head of the girl, and now she turned as pale as its incandescence.

"But André does not—" she whispered.

"Garn," said Mrs. Harris. "'E does, too—and so do you. I've got eyes in me 'ead. You're both in love, what's keepin' you apart?"

Simultaneously M. Fauvel and Mlle. Petitpierre began:

"He wouldn't—"

"She couldn't—"

Mrs. Harris chuckled wickedly. "You're in love, ain't you? 'Oo carn't do wot?"

For the first time the two young people looked one another directly in the eyes and saw what lay there. Caught up in one another's gaze which they could not relinquish, into their faces, at last came the clarifying expressions of hope and love. Two tears formed at the corners of Natasha's exquisite eyes and glistened there.

"And now, if you'll excuse me for a minute," Mrs. Harris announced significantly, "I'll just go and pay a little visit to me aunt." She arose and went off in the direction of the pavillon.

When she returned a good fifteen minutes later, Natasha was locked in M. Fauvel's arms on the dance floor, her head pillowed on his chest and her face was wet with tears. But when they saw she had returned to the table they came running to her and threw their arms about her. M. Fauvel kissed one withered apple cheek, Natasha the other, and then the girl put both arms around Mrs. Harris' neck and wept there for a moment murmuring: "My dear, I am so happy, André and I are going to—"

"Go on," said Mrs. Harris, "what a surprise! 'Ow about a bit of bubbly to celebrate?"

They all lifted their glasses and thereafter it was the gayest, brightest, happiest night that Mrs. Harris had ever known in her whole life.

*twelve*

And so the day dawned at last when "Temptation" was finished and it came time for Mrs. Harris to take possession of her treasure swathed in reams of tissue paper and packed in a glamorous cardboard box with the name DIOR printed on it in golden letters as large as life.

There was quite a little gathering for her in the salon of Dior's in the late morning—she was leaving on an afternoon plane—and from somewhere a bottle of champagne had appeared. Mme. Colbert was there, Natasha and M. Fauvel, and all of the fitters, cutters and seamstresses who had worked so hard and faithfully to finish her dress in record time.

They drank her health and safe journey, and there were gifts for her: a genuine crocodile leather handbag from a grateful Mme. Colbert, a wrist watch from an equally grateful M. Fauvel and gloves and perfume from the more than grateful Natasha.

The manageress took Mrs. Harris in her arms, held her closely for a moment, kissed her and whispered in her ear: "You have been very, very lucky for me, my dear. Soon perhaps I shall be able to write you of a big announcement concerning my husband."

Natasha hugged her too and said: "I shall never forget you, or that I shall owe all my happiness to you. André and I will marry in the fall. I shall make you godmother to our first child."

M. André Fauvel kissed her on the cheek and fussed over her, advising her to take good care of herself on the return trip, and then with the true concern of a man whose business is with cash asked: "You are sure now that you have your money to pay the duty in a safe place? You have it well hidden away, no? It is better you have it not in the purse, where it might be snatched."

Mrs. Harris grinned her wonderfully jagged and impish grin. Well fed for the first time in her life, rested and happy, she looked younger by decades. She opened her new crocodile bag to show the air ticket and passport therein, with one single green pound note, a bill of five hundred francs and a few leftover French coins to see her to the airport. "That's the lot," she said. "But it's plenty to get me back to me duties. There's nuffink for no one to snatch."

"Oh la la! But no!" cried M. Fauvel, his voice shaken by sudden anguish while a fearful silence fell upon the group in the salon as the shadow of impending disaster made itself felt. "I mean the customs duty at the British *douane. Mon Dieu!* Have you not provided? At six shillings in the pound"—he made a swift calculation—"that would be one hundred and fifty pounds. Did you not know you must pay this?"

Mrs. Harris looked at him stunned—and aged twenty years. "Gor," she croaked, "hundred and fifty quid. I couldn't raise a bob to me nyme! Ow, why didn't somebody tell me? 'Ow was I to know?"

Mme. Colbert reached fiercely. "La, what nonsense are you talking, André? Who pays duty any more to customs? You think those titled ladies and rich Americans do? All, all is smuggle, and you too, my little Ada, shall smuggle yours——"

The little blue eyes of Mrs. Harris became filled with fear, alarm, suspicion. "That would be telling a lie, wouldn't it?" she said, looking helplessly from one to the other. "I don't mind telling a fib or two, but I don't tell lies. That would be bryking the law. I could go to jail for that——" Then as the true and ghastly import of what M. Fauvel said dawned upon her she quite suddenly sank down into the pile of the gray carpet, covered her face with her workworn hands and sent up a wail of despair that penetrated through the establishment so that the Great Patron himself came running in. "I can't 'ave it. It ain't for such as me. I should 'ave known me place. Tyke it away—give it away, do anything. I'll go 'ome and forget about it."

The story of the dilemma ran like wildfire through the building. Experts appeared from all sides to give advice, including that there be a petition directed to the British Ambassador, until it was pointed out that so stern was the British regard for the law that not even the Ambassador or the Queen herself could intervene to have it set aside, even in so worthy a cause——

It was the Patron himself, familiar with Mrs. Harris' story, who solved the dilemma, severing the Gordian knot with one swift, generous stroke—or thought he had. "Reduce the price of the dress to this good woman," he ordered auditor Fauvel, "and give her the balance in cash to pay the duty."

"But, sir," protested the horrified Fauvel, who now for the first time himself saw the trap into which his benefactress had fallen, "it is impossible!"

They all stared at him as though he were a poisonous reptile. "Do you not see? Madame has already unwittingly broken British law by exporting the one thousand four hundred dollars, illegally exchanged by her American friend in the United Kingdom. If now she, poor woman, appears at British customs at the airport declaring a dress worth five hundred pounds and offers a further hundred and fifty pounds in cash to pay the duty, there would be inquiries how she, a British subject, had come by these monies; there would be a scandal——"

They continued to look at the unfortunate auditor as though he were a king cobra, but they also knew that he was right. "Let me go 'ome and die," wailed Mrs. Harris.

Natasha was at her side, her arms about her. Voices rose in a babel of sympathy. Mme. Colbert had an inspiration. "Wait," she cried, "I have it." She too dropped to her knees at Mrs. Harris' side. "My dear, will you listen to me? I can help you. I shall be lucky for you, as you have been for me——"

Mrs. Harris removed her hands to reveal the face of an old and frightened Capucin monkey. "I won't do nuffink dishonest—or tell no lies."

"No, no. Trust me. You shall say nothing but the absolute truth. But you must do exactly how and what I say for, my dear, we ALL wish you to have your beautiful dress to take home. Now listen." And Mme. Colbert, placing her lips close to Mrs. Harris' little monkey ear so that no one else might hear, whispered her instructions.

As she stood in the customs hall of London Airport, Mrs. Harris felt sure that her thumping heart must be audible to all, yet by the time the pleasant-looking young customs officer reached her, her native-born courage and cheerfulness buoyed her up, and her naughty little eyes were even twinkling with an odd kind of anticipatory pleasure.

On the counter before her rested not the glamorous Dior box, but a large and well-worn plastic suitcase of the cheapest kind. The officer handed her a card on which was printed the list of dutiable articles purchased abroad.

"You read it to me, duckie," Mrs. Harris grinned impudently, "I left me specs at 'ome."

The inspector glanced at her sharply once to see whether he was being had; the pink rose on the green hat bobbed at him; he recognized the breed at once. "Hullo," he smiled. "What have *you* been doing over in Paris?"

"'Aving a bit of a 'oliday on me own."

The customs man grinned. This was a new one on him. The British char abroad. The mop-and-broom business must be good, he reflected, then inquired routinely: "Bring anything back with you?"

Mrs. Harris grinned at him. "'Aven't I just? A genuine Dior dress called 'Temptytion' in me bag 'ere. Five 'undred quid it cost. 'Ow's that?"

The inspector laughed. It was not the first time he had encountered the London char's sense of humor. "You'll be the belle of the ball with it, I'll wager," he said, and made a mark with a piece of chalk on the side of the case. Then he sauntered off and presented his card to the next passenger whose luggage was ready.

Mrs. Harris picked up her bag and walked—not ran, though it was a great effort not to bolt—to the exit and down the escalator to freedom. She was filled not only with a sense of relief, but righteousness as well. She had told the truth. If, as Mme. Colbert had said, the customs officer chose not to believe her, that was not her fault.

### *thirteen*

Thus it was that at four o'clock in the afternoon of a lovely London spring day, the last obstacle hurdled, and with "Temptation" safe and sound in her possession, Mrs. Harris found herself standing outside of Waterloo Air Station home at last. And but one thing was troubling her conscience. It was the little matter of Miss Pamela Penrose, the actress, and her flat.

Her other clients were all wealthy, but Miss Penrose was poor and struggling. What if Mrs. Butterfield hadn't coped properly? It was yet early. The keys to the flat were in her new crocodile handbag, now emerged from the suitcase. Mrs. Harris said to herself: "Lord love the poor dear. It's early yet.

Maybe she's got to entertyne some nobs. I'll just drop by 'er flat and surprise
'er by tidying up a bit." She caught the proper bus and shortly afterwards
was in the mews, inserting her key in the door.

No sooner had she the street door open than the sound of the girl's sobs
reached to her, causing Mrs. Harris to hurry up the stairs and into the tiny
living room, where she came upon Miss Penrose lying face down upon her
couch crying her eyes out.

Mrs. Harris went to her, laid a sympathetic hand upon a shaking shoulder
and said: "Now, now, dearie, what's the matter? It can't be as bad as all
that. If you're in trouble maybe I can help you."

Miss Penrose sat up. "YOU help me!" she repeated, looking through tear-
swollen eyes. Then in a kindlier tone she said: "Oh, it's you, Mrs. Harris.
Nobody in the whole world could help me. Oh, I could die. If you must
know, I've been invited to dine at the Caprice with Mr. Korngold the producer. It's my one and only chance to impress him and get ahead. Nearly
ALL of Mr. Korngold's girls—I mean friends—have become stars——"

"Well, now I don't see anything to cry about there," declared Mrs. Harris.
"You ought to be a star, I'm sure."

Miss Penrose's heart-rending grief turned momentarily to rage. "Oh,
don't be STUPID!" she stormed. "Don't you see? I can't go. I haven't anything to wear. My one good dress is at the cleaner's and my other one has a
stain. Mr. Korngold is absolutely particular about what the girls wear he
takes out."

Could you, had you been Mrs. Harris, with what she had in her plastic
suitcase on the landing, have been able to resist the temptation to play
fairy godmother? Particularly if you were still under the spell of the sweet
gentleness and simplicity of Natasha, and the crusted kindness of Mme.
Colbert and all their people, and knew what it was like to want something
dreadfully, something you did not think you were ever going to get?

Before Mrs. Harris quite realized what she was saying, the words popped
out: "See 'ere. Maybe I can 'elp you after all. I could lend you me Dior
dress."

"Your WHAT? Oh, you—you odious creature. How DARE you make fun
of me?" Miss Penrose's small mouth was twisted and her eyes cloudy with
rage.

"But I ain't. 'Strewth, so 'elp me, I've just come back from Paris, where
I bought me a Dior dress. I'd let you wear it tonight if it would 'elp you
with Mr. Korngold."

Somehow Miss Penrose, née Snite, brought herself under control as some
guardian instinct warned her that with these charwomen one never really
knew what to expect. She said: "I'm sorry. I didn't mean—but of course
you couldn't—— Where is it?"

"'Ere," said Mrs. Harris, and opened the suitcase. The intense gasp of
wonder and excitement and the joy that came into the girl's eyes made it
worth the gesture. "Oh—oh—oh!" she cried. "I can't *believe* it." In an instant
she had the dress out of its tissue wrappings, holding it up, then hugging it
to her, she searched out the label with greedy fingers. "Oh! It really IS a

Dior. May I try it on right away, Mrs. Harris? We are about the same size, are we not? Oh, I could die with excitement."

In a moment she was stripping off her clothes, Mrs. Harris was helping her into the dress, and a few minutes later it was again fulfilling the destiny for which it had been designed. With her lovely bare shoulders and blonde head rising from the chiffon and tulle, Miss Penrose was both Venus appearing from the sea and Miss Snite emerging from the bedclothes.

Mrs. Harris and the girl gazed raptly at the image reflected from the full-length mirror in the closet door. The actress said: "Oh, you are a dear to let me wear it. I'll be ever so careful. You don't KNOW what it means to me."

But Mrs. Harris knew very well. And it seemed almost as though fate wished this beautiful creation to be worn and shown off and not hung away in a closet. This perhaps being so, she had a request: "Would you mind very much if I came to the restaurant where you are 'aving dinner and stood outside to watch you go in? Of course, I wouldn't speak to you or anything——"

Miss Penrose said graciously: "Of course I wouldn't mind. If you'll be standing at the right side of the door as I get out of Mr. Korngold's Rolls-Royce, I can sort of turn to you so that you can see me better."

"Oh," said Mrs. Harris. "You *are* kind, dearie." And meant it.

Miss Penrose kept her promise, or half kept it, for a storm came up and suddenly it was a thundery, blustery, rain-swept night when at half past nine Mr. Korngold's Rolls-Royce drew up at the entrance to Caprice. Mrs. Harris was standing to the right of the door, somewhat protected from the rain by the canopy.

A rumble of thunder and a swooping wind accompanied the arrival; Miss Penrose paused for one instant, turning towards Mrs. Harris, her head graciously inclined, her evening wrap parted. Then with a toss of her golden hair she ran swiftly into the doorway. Mrs. Harris had had no more than a glimpse of jet beads beneath an evening wrap, a flash of foamy pink, white cream chiffon and tulle, and then it was over.

But she was quite happy and remained there a little longer, contented and lost in imaginings. For now the headwaiter would be bowing low to *her* dress and leading IT to a favored and conspicuous table. Every woman in the room would recognize it at once as one from Dior; all heads would be turning as the creation moved through the aisles of tables, the velvet skirt, heavy with jet beads swinging enticingly while above, the sweet young bosom, shoulders, arms and pink and white face emerged from the lovely bodice. Mr. Korngold would be pleased and proud and would surely decide to give so well dressed and beautiful a girl an important part in his next production.

And no one there, not a single, solitary soul outside the girl herself would know that the exquisite gown which had done it all and had made every eye brighten with envy or admiration was the sole and exclusive property of Mrs. Ada Harris, char, of No. 5 Willis Gardens, Battersea.

And thither she went now, smiling to herself all the way during the long bus ride home. There remained only the problem of Mrs. Butterfield, who would be anxiously awaiting her, to be dealt with. She would wish to see the dress of course and hear all about it. For some reason she could not fathom, Mrs. Harris felt that she did not care for Mrs. Butterfield to know that she had loaned her dress to the actress.

But by the time she had arrived at her destination she had the solution. A little fib and the fatigue that had collected in her bones would serve to put her off.

"Lor'!" she said from the depths of Mrs. Butterfield's billowy bosom, where she found herself enveloped, "I'm that fagged I've got to 'old me eyelids open with me fingers. It's so late, I won't even stay for a cup o' tea."

"You poor dear," sympathized Mrs. Butterfield, "I won't keep you. You can show me the dress——"

"It's coming tomorrow," Mrs. Harris demi-fibbed. "I'll tell you all about it then."

Once more in her own bed, she gave herself up to the sweet, delicious sense of accomplishment and with not so much as a single foreboding as to what the morrow might bring was soon fast asleep.

### fourteen

The hour that Mrs. Harris devoted to Miss Penrose was from five to six and all the next day, as she worked in the various homes and made her peace with her clients, who were too happy to see her back to grouse about her prolonged absence, she lived in tingling anticipation of that moment. At last it came, and she hurried to the little flat that had once been a stables behind the great house in the square and, opening the door, stood for a moment at the foot of the narrow staircase.

At first it was only disappointment that she experienced for the place was dark and silent. Mrs. Harris would have liked to hear from the girl's own lips the story of the triumph scored by the Dior dress and its effect upon Mr. Korngold.

But it was the strange, unfamiliar odor that assailed her nostrils that turned her cold with alarm and set the skin of her scalp to pricking with terror. And yet, on second thought, the odor was *not* unfamiliar. Why did it awaken memories of the war she had lived through in London—the rain of high explosives and the deluge of fire?

At the top of the stairs Mrs. Harris turned on the lights in the vestibule and the living room and went in. The next instant she was staring down, frozen with horror, at the ruins of her dress. And then she knew what the odor was that had assailed her nostrils and made her think of the nights when the incendiaries had poured down upon London.

The Dior dress had been tossed carelessly upon the disordered couch with the burned-out velvet panel where the fire had eaten into it showing shockingly in a fearful gap of melted beadwork, burned and singed cloth.

Beside it lay a pound and a hastily scrawled note. Mrs. Harris' fingers were trembling so that she could hardly read it at first, but at last its contents became clear.

"Dear Mrs. Harris, I am terribly sorry I could not stay to explain in person, but I have to go away for a little while. I am most awfully sorry about what happened to the dress, but it wasn't my fault, and if Mr. Korngold had not been so quick I might have burned to death. He said I had a very narrow escape. After dinner we went to the 30 Club, where I stopped to comb my hair in front of a mirror, and there was an electric heater right underneath, and all of a sudden I was burning—I mean the dress, and I could have burned to death. I am sure they will be able to repair it and your insurance will take care of the damage, which is not as bad as it looks as it is only the one panel. I am going away for the week. Please look after the flat as usual. I am leaving a pound for your wages in the meantime."

It was astonishing that when Mrs. Harris had finished reading the letter she did not cry out, or even murmur, or say anything at all. Instead she took up the damaged garment and, folding it carefully, packed it once more into the old plastic suitcase Mme. Colbert had given her and which she retrieved from the closet where she had stowed it the night before. She left the letter and the money lying on the couch, went downstairs and into the street.

When she had closed the outside door she paused only long enough to remove the key to the flat from her chain, since she would not be needing it any more, and push it through the slot of the mail drop in the door. Then she walked the five minutes to Sloane Square, where she caught a bus for home.

It was damp and chilly in her flat. She put the kettle on for tea and then, guided by habit, she did all of the things she was used to doing, even to eating, though she hardly knew what food she tasted. She washed up the dishes and put everything away. But there the mechanism ended, and she turned to the unpacking of the ruins of the Dior dress.

She fingered the charred edges of the velvet and the burned and melted jet. She knew night clubs, for she had cleaned in them. She thought she could see it happening—the girl, half drunken, coming down the stairs from without, on the arm of her escort, thoughtless, heedless of all but that which concerned herself, pausing before the first mirror to study herself and apply a comb.

Then the sudden ascent of smoke from her feet, the little shriek of fright, perhaps an orange line of fire in the dress and the man beating at it with his hands until it was extinguished and only the smoldering wreck of the most beautiful and expensive frock in the world remained.

And here it was in her hands now, still with the stink of charred cloth rising from it and which all the perfume given to her by Natasha would not suffice to blot out. A thing once as perfect and beautiful as human hands could make it was destroyed.

She tried to tell herself that it was not the fault of the girl, that it had been an accident and that only she herself was to blame for trying to play fairy godmother to this spoiled brat of a bad actress who had not even the grace to be grateful to her for her foolish gesture.

Mrs. Harris was a sensible person, a realist who had lived an exacting life and was not given to self-delusion. Looking now upon this singed and tragic wreck of her desires, she was well aware of her own foolish pride and vanity, not only involved in the possession of such a treasure, but in the displaying of it.

She had savored the casual way she might say to her landlady, when queried as to where she had been: "Oh, I was only over in Paris, dearie, to look at the collection and buy me a Dior dress. It's called 'Temptytion.'" And, of course, she had visualized a hundred times the reaction of Mrs. Butterfield when she unveiled her prize. There would be no calling in of her friend now—or anyone else—for she would only croak: "Didn't I tell yer something orful would 'appen? Things like that ain't for the likes of us! What was you going to do with it, anyway?"

What indeed had she been meaning to do with it? Hang it away in an old, stale closet next to her aprons, overall, and one poor Sunday frock, secretly to gloat over when she came home at night? The dress had not been designed and created to languish in the dark of a cupboard. It was meant to be out where there was gaiety, lights, music and admiring eyes.

Quite suddenly she could not bear to look upon it any longer. She was at the end of her resistance to grief. She reinterred it in the plastic suitcase, hurriedly blotting out the sight of it with the crumpled tissue paper and then, flinging herself upon her bed, buried her face in her pillow and commenced to cry. She wept silently, inconsolably and interminably, after the fashion of women whose hearts have been broken.

She wept for her own foolishness, and too for her self-acknowledged guilt of the sin of pride and the swift, sure punishment that had followed upon its heels, but mostly she wept simply and miserably for her lost dress and the destruction of this so dear possession.

She might have wept thus into eternity, but for the insistent ringing of her doorbell, which at last penetrated grief and into her consciousness. She raised her tear-swollen face momentarily and then decided to ignore it. It could be none other than Mrs. Butterfield, eager to see and discuss her Paris dress and hear of her adventures amongst the heathen. What was there to show her now for the long wait, the hard work, the sacrifice and the foolish determination? A burned-out rag. Worse than Mrs. Butterfield's croakings of "I told you so" would be the sympathy that would follow, the tuttings and cluckings and the warm but clumsy attempts to comfort her and which Mrs. Harris felt she could not bear. She wanted only to get on with her crying—to be allowed to weep alone until she died.

She pulled the damp pillow about her ears to shut out the sound of the ringing, but now, somewhat to her alarm, heard it replaced by a loud knocking and thumping on the door, something rather more strenuous and imperative than she could connect with Mrs. Butterfield. Perhaps there was something wrong somewhere, an emergency, and she was needed. She arose quickly, brushed the wisps of disheveled hair out of her eyes and opened the door to reveal a B.E.A. messenger standing there goggling at her as though he had seen a ghost.

He croaked forth a kind of bilious "Mrs. 'Arris, is it?"

" 'Oo else did you expect? Princess Margaret? Bangin' and thumpin' like the 'ouse was afire . . ."

"Phew!" he said, mopping his brow with relief. "You didn't arf give me a turn, you did. I thought maybe you was dead. You not answering the door-bell, and all these flowers to deliver. I thought they might be for the corpse."

"Eh?" Mrs. Harris asked. "Wot flowers?"

The postman grinned. "Flown over especial from France, and express delivery. 'Ere now. Leave the door open while I bring 'em in."

Swinging wide the rear doors of the van, he began to produce them, white box upon long white box marked: AIR EXPRESS—FRAGILE—PERISH-ABLE, looming shapes of objects packed first in straw, then in cartons, then in paper—it seemed to the mystified Mrs. Harris that he would never end his trips from the van to her living room and that there must be some mistake.

But there was none. "Sign 'ere," he said, his task at last ended, and shoving his book under her nose. It was her name and address right enough —Madame Ada Harris, 5 Willis Gardens, Battersea. "There's six bob cus-toms charges to pay."

In a daze she paid him and was alone again. Then she turned to opening her boxes and packages and in an instant found herself transported back to Paris again, for the dingy little room suddenly vanished beneath the garden bower of flowers that overwhelmed it, dark, deep red roses by the dozen, cream-white lilies, bunches of pink and yellow carnations and sheaves of gladioli ready to burst into every color from deep mauve to palest lemon. There were azaleas, salmon-colored, white and crimson, and a great tub of geraniums, bundles of sweet-smelling freesias and one great bouquet of vio-lets a foot in span with six white gardenias centered.

In an instant her dwelling seemed changed into a stall of the Marché aux Fleurs, for market-fresh, the crisp, smooth petals were still dewed with pearls of water.

Was this coincidence or some magic foresight that this sweet, healing gift should reach her in her moment of deepest anguish? She detached the cards from the blossoms and read the messages thereon. They were a welcome home, a simultaneous outpouring of remembrance and affection from her friends, laced with good news.

"Welcome home. We could not wait. André and I were married today. God bless you. Natasha."

"I am the happiest man in the world thanks to you. André Fauvel."

"A welcome back to the lady who loves geraniums. I have not forgotten the copper penny. Hypolite de Chassagne."

"Compliments of M. Christian Dior." (This with the violets.)

"Greetings on your return. The Staff of Christian Dior."

"Good luck to you. Cutters, Fitters and Seamstresses, Maison Christian Dior."

And finally: "Jules was named First Secretary of the Department for

Anglo-Saxon Relations at the Quai d'Orsay today. What can I say, my dear, but thank you. Claudine Colbert."

Her knees trembling beneath her, Mrs. Harris sank to the floor, leaned her cheek against the tight, smooth, cool, heavily fragrant petals of the roses Mme. Colbert had sent her, tears filling her eyes again, her mind thrown into a turmoil of memories by the messages, the colors and the fragrance of the flowers that filled her little living room.

Once again she saw the understanding, womanly Mme. Colbert, with her dark, glossy, perfectly groomed hair and pure skin, the lithe, exquisite laughing Natasha and the blond serious-minded, grave-faced and scarred M. Fauvel, who overnight had changed from an adding machine into a boy and a lover.

All manner of memories and isolated pictures crowded into her thoughts. For an instant she saw the furrowed brows and concentrated expressions of the fitters kneeling before her, their mouths bristling with pins. She felt once more the pile of the thick gray carpet beneath her feet and smelled the sweet, thrilling odor of the interior of the House of Dior.

The hubbub and murmur of the voices of the audience and patrons in the gray and white salon seemed to come back to her, and immediately, blinking through her tears, she was there again as each model more beautiful than the last clad in the loveliest frocks, suits, ensembles, gowns and furs came thrusting, swaying or gliding into the room—three steps and a twirl—three more steps and another twirl—then off with the pastel mink or dark marten coat to be dragged behind on the soft carpet, off with the jacket—a toss of the head, another twirl and she was gone to be replaced by yet another.

From there it was but a flash for her to be back in the hive of the cubicles, a part of the delicious atmosphere of woman world compounded of the rustle of silks and satins, the variegated perfumes carried thither by the clients, the murmuring voices of saleswomen and dressmakers like the droning of bees and the sound of whispering from neighboring booths and smothered laughter.

Then she was sitting in the sunlight beneath a sky of a peculiar blue, on a bench in the Flower Market, surrounded by nature's own fashion creations, flowers in their matchless shapes and colors and emanating perfumes of their own. And next to her was a handsome aristocratic old gentleman who had understood her and treated her as an equal.

But it was the people she had met who kept returning to her thoughts, and she remembered the expressions on the faces of Fauvel and Natasha as they had embraced her the night of the Pré-Catelan and seemed to feel once again the warm pressure of Mme. Colbert's arms about her as she had kissed her before her departure and whispered: "You have been very lucky for me, my dear. . . ."

Reflecting now upon Mme. Colbert, Mrs. Harris thought how the Frenchwoman had worked and schemed to help her to realize her vain, foolish wish to possess a Dior dress. Had it not been for her and her clever plan at the end it would never have reached England. And Mrs. Harris thought that even the damage to "Temptation" might not be irreparable. A letter to Mme. Colbert would result in the immediate dispatch of another beaded panel such as had been destroyed. A clever seamstress could insert it so that the dress would be as good as new. And yet would it ever be the same again?

This ephemeral question had a most curious effect upon Mrs. Harris. It stopped the flow of tears from her eyes and brought her to her feet once more as she looked about the flower-laden room and the answer came to her in one shrewd, inspired burst of insight.

It would not. It would never be the same again. But then neither would she.

For it had not been a dress she had bought so much as an adventure and an experience that would last her to the end of her days. She would never again feel lonely or unwanted. She had ventured into a foreign country and a foreign people she had been taught to suspect and despise. She had found them to be warm and human, men and women to whom human love and understanding was a mainspring of life. They had made her feel that they loved her for herself.

Mrs. Harris opened the suitcase and took out "Temptation." Once more she fingered the burnt place and saw how easily the panel could be replaced and the damage repaired. But she would not have it so. She would keep it as it was, untouched by any other fingers than those which had expedited every stitch because of love and feeling for another woman's heart.

Mrs. Harris hugged the dress to her thin bosom, hugged it hard, as though it were alive and human, nestling her face to the soft folds of the material. Tears flowed again from the small, shrewd blue eyes and furrowed down the apple cheeks, but they were no longer tears of misery.

She stood there rocking back and forth, holding and embracing her dress, and with it she was hugging them all, Mme. Colbert, Natasha, André Fauvel, down to the last anonymous worker, seamstress and cutter, as well as the city that had bestowed upon her such a priceless memory treasure of understanding, friendship and humanity.

# 'They'

## RUDYARD KIPLING

ONE view called me to another; one hill-top to its fellow, half across the county, and since I could answer at no more trouble than the snapping forward of a lever, I let the county flow under my wheels. The orchid-studded flats of the East gave way to the thyme, ilex, and grey grass of the Downs; these again to the rich cornland and fig-trees of the lower coast, where you carry the beat of the tide on your left hand for fifteen level miles; and when at last I turned inland through a huddle of rounded hills and woods I had run myself clean out of my known marks. Beyond that precise hamlet which stands godmother to the capital of the United States, I found hidden villages where bees, the only things awake, boomed in eighty-foot lindens that overhung grey Norman churches; miraculous brooks diving under stone bridges built for heavier traffic than would ever vex them again; tithe-barns larger than their churches, and an old smithy that cried out aloud how it had once been a hall of the Knights of the Temple. Gipsies I found on a common where the gorse, bracken, and heath fought it out together up a mile of Roman road; and a little farther on I disturbed a red fox rolling dog-fashion in the naked sunlight.

As the wooded hills closed about me I stood up in the car to take the bearings of that great Down whose ringed head is a landmark for fifty miles across the low countries. I judged that the lie of the country would bring me across some westward-running road that went to his feet, but I did not allow for the confusing veils of the woods. A quick turn plunged me first into a green cutting brim-full of liquid sunshine, next into a gloomy tunnel where last year's dead leaves whispered and scuffled about my tyres. The strong hazel stuff meeting overhead had not been cut for a couple of generations at least, nor had any axe helped the moss-cankered oak and beech to spring above them. Here the road changed frankly into a carpeted ride on whose brown velvet spent primrose-clumps showed like jade, and a few sickly, white-stalked bluebells nodded together. As the slope favoured I shut off the power and slid over the whirled leaves, expecting every moment to meet a keeper; but I only heard a jay, far off, arguing against the silence under the twilight of the trees.

Still the track descended. I was on the point of reversing and working my way back on the second speed ere I ended in some swamp, when I saw sunshine through the tangle ahead and lifted the brake.

It was down again at once. As the light beat across my face my fore-wheels took the turf of a great still lawn from which sprang horsemen ten feet high with levelled lances, monstrous peacocks, and sleek round-headed maids of honour—blue, black, and glistening—all of clipped yew. Across the lawn—the marshalled woods besieged it on three sides—stood an ancient house of lichened and weather-worn stone, with mullioned windows and roofs of rose-red tile. It was flanked by semi-circular walls, also rose-red, that closed the lawn on the fourth side, and at their feet a box hedge grew man-high. There were doves on the roof about the slim brick chimneys, and I caught a glimpse of an octagonal dove-house behind the screening wall.

Here, then, I stayed; a horseman's green spear laid at my breast; held by the exceeding beauty of that jewel in that setting.

'If I am not packed off for a trespasser, or if this knight does not ride a wallop at me,' thought I, 'Shakespeare and Queen Elizabeth at least must come out of that half-open garden door and ask me to tea.'

A child appeared at an upper window, and I thought the little thing waved a friendly hand. But it was to call a companion, for presently another bright head showed. Then I heard a laugh among the yew-peacocks, and turning to make sure (till then I had been watching the house only) I saw the silver of a fountain behind a hedge thrown up against the sun. The doves on the roof cooed to the cooing water; but between the two notes I caught the utterly happy chuckle of a child absorbed in some light mischief.

The garden door—heavy oak sunk deep in the thickness of the wall—opened further: a woman in a big garden hat set her foot slowly on the time-hollowed stone step and as slowly walked across the turf. I was form-ing some apology when she lifted up her head and I saw that she was blind.

'I heard you,' she said. 'Isn't that a motor car?'

'I'm afraid I've made a mistake in my road. I should have turned off up above—I never dreamed——' I began.

'But I'm very glad. Fancy a motor car coming into the garden! It will be such a treat——' She turned and made as though looking about her. 'You—you haven't seen any one, have you—perhaps?'

'No one to speak to, but the children seemed interested at a distance.'

'Which?'

'I saw a couple up at the window just now, and I think I heard a little chap in the grounds.'

'Oh, lucky you!' she cried, and her face brightened. 'I hear them, of course, but that's all. You've seen them and heard them?'

'Yes,' I answered. 'And if I know anything of children, one of them's having a beautiful time by the fountain yonder. Escaped, I should imagine.'

'You're fond of children?'

I gave her one or two reasons why I did not altogether hate them.

'Of course, of course,' she said. 'Then you understand. Then you won't think it foolish if I ask you to take your car through the gardens, once or twice—quite slowly. I'm sure they'd like to see it. They see so little, poor things. One tries to make their life pleasant, but——' she threw out her hands towards the woods. 'We're so out of the world here.'

'That will be splendid,' I said. 'But I can't cut up your grass.'

She faced to the right. 'Wait a minute,' she said. 'We're at the South gate, aren't we? Behind those peacocks there's a flagged path. We call it the Peacocks' Walk. You can't see it from here, they tell me, but if you squeeze along by the edge of the wood you can turn at the first peacock and get on to the flags.'

It was sacrilege to wake that dreaming house-front with the clatter of machinery, but I swung the car to clear the turf, brushed along the edge of the wood and turned in on the broad stone path where the fountain-basin lay like one star-sapphire.

'May I come too?' she cried. 'No, please don't help me. They'll like it better if they see me.'

She felt her way lightly to the front of the car, and with one foot on the step she called: 'Children, oh, children! Look and see what's going to happen!'

The voice would have drawn lost souls from the Pit, for the yearning that underlay its sweetness, and I was not surprised to hear an answering shout behind the yews. It must have been the child by the fountain, but he fled at our approach, leaving a little toy boat in the water. I saw the glint of his blue blouse among the still horsemen.

Very disposedly we paraded the length of the walk and at her request backed again. This time the child had got the better of his panic, but stood far off and doubting.

'The little fellow's watching us,' I said. 'I wonder if he'd like a ride.'

'They're very shy still. Very shy. But, oh, lucky you to be able to see them! Let's listen.'

I stopped the machine at once, and the humid stillness, heavy with the scent of box, cloaked us deep. Shears I could hear where some gardener was clipping; a mumble of bees and broken voices that might have been the doves.

'Oh, unkind!' she said weariedly.

'Perhaps they're only shy of the motor. The little maid at the window looks tremendously interested.'

'Yes?' She raised her head. 'It was wrong of me to say that. They are really fond of me. It's the only thing that makes life worth living—when they're fond of you, isn't it? I daren't think what the place would be without them. By the way, is it beautiful?'

'I think it is the most beautiful place I have ever seen.'

'So they all tell me. I can feel it, of course, but that isn't quite the same thing.'

'Then have you never——?' I began, but stopped abashed.

'Not since I can remember. It happened when I was only a few months old, they tell me. And yet I must remember something, else how could I dream about colours? I see light in my dreams, and colours, but I never see *them*. I only hear them just as I do when I'm awake.'

'It's difficult to see faces in dreams. Some people can, but most of us haven't the gift,' I went on, looking up at the window where the child stood all but hidden.

'I've heard that too,' she said. 'And they tell me that one never sees a dead person's face in a dream. Is that true?'

'I believe it is—now I come to think of it.'

'But how is it with yourself—yourself?' The blind eyes turned towards me.

'I have never seen the faces of my dead in any dream,' I answered.

'Then it must be as bad as being blind.'

The sun had dipped behind the woods and the long shades were possessing the insolent horsemen one by one. I saw the light die from off the top of a glossy-leafed lance and all the brave hard green turn to soft black. The house, accepting another day at end, as it had accepted an hundred thousand gone, seemed to settle deeper into its rest among the shadows.

'Have you ever wanted to?' she said after the silence.

'Very much sometimes,' I replied. The child had left the window as the shadows closed upon it.

'Ah! So've I, but I don't suppose it's allowed. . . . Where d'you live?'

'Quite the other side of the county—sixty miles and more, and I must be going back. I've come without my big lamps.'

'But it's not dark yet. I can feel it.'

'I'm afraid it will be by the time I get home. Could you lend me someone to set me on my road at first? I've utterly lost myself.'

'I'll send Madden with you to the cross-roads. We are so out of the world, I don't wonder you were lost! I'll guide you round to the front of the house; but you will go slowly, won't you, till you're out of the grounds? It isn't foolish, do you think?'

'I promise you I'll go like this,' I said, and let the car start herself down the flagged path.

We skirted the left wing of the house, whose elaborately cast lead guttering alone was worth a day's journey; passed under a great rose-grown gate in the red wall, and so round to the high front of the house, which in beauty and stateliness as much excelled the back as that all others I had seen.

'Is it so very beautiful?' she said wistfully when she heard my raptures. 'And you like the lead figures too? There's the old azalea garden behind. They say that this place must have been made for children. Will you help me out, please? I should like to come with you as far as the cross-roads, but I mustn't leave them. Is that you, Madden? I want you to show this gentleman the way to the cross-roads. He has lost his way, but—he has seen them.'

A butler appeared noiselessly at the miracle of old oak that must be called the front door, and slipped aside to put on his hat. She stood looking at me with open blue eyes in which no sight lay, and I saw for the first time that she was beautiful.

'Remember,' she said quietly, 'if you are fond of them you will come again,' and disappeared within the house.

The butler in the car said nothing till we were nearly at the lodge gates, where catching a glimpse of a blue blouse in a shrubbery I swerved amply lest the devil that leads little boys to play should drag me into child-murder.

'Excuse me,' he asked of a sudden, 'but why did you do that, sir?'

'The child yonder.'

'Our young gentleman in blue?'

'Of course.'

'He runs about a good deal. Did you see him by the fountain, sir?'

'Oh, yes, several times. Do we turn here?'

'Yes, sir. And did you 'appen to see them upstairs too?'

'At the upper window? Yes.'

'Was that before the mistress come out to speak to you, sir?'

'A little before that. Why d'you want to know?'

He paused a little. 'Only to make sure that—that they had seen the car, sir, because with children running about, though I'm sure you're driving particularly careful, there might be an accident. That was all, sir. Here are the cross-roads. You can't miss your way from now on. Thank you, sir, but that isn't *our* custom, not with——'

'I beg your pardon,' I said, and thrust away the British silver.

'Oh, it's quite right with the rest of 'em as a rule. Good-bye, sir.'

He retired into the armour-plated conning-tower of his caste and walked away. Evidently a butler solicitous for the honour of his house, and interested, probably through a maid, in the nursery.

Once beyond the signposts at the cross-roads I looked back, but the crumpled hills interlaced so jealously that I could not see where the house had lain. When I asked its name at a cottage along the road, the fat woman who sold sweetmeats there gave me to understand that people with motor cars had small right to live—much less to 'go about talking like carriage folk.' They were not a pleasant-mannered community.

When I retraced my route on the map that evening I was little wiser. Hawkin's Old Farm appeared to be the Survey title of the place, and the old County Gazetteer, generally so ample, did not allude to it. The big house of those parts was Hodnington Hall, Georgian with early Victorian embellishments, as an atrocious steel engraving attested. I carried my difficulty to a neighbour—a deep-rooted tree of that soil—and he gave me a name of a family which conveyed no meaning.

A month or so later—I went again, or it may have been that my car took the road of her own volition. She over-ran the fruitless Downs, threaded every turn of the maze of lanes below the hills, drew through the high-walled woods, impenetrable in their full leaf, came out at the cross-roads where the butler had left me, and a little farther on developed an internal trouble which forced me to turn her in on a grass way-waste that cut into a summer-silent hazel wood. So far as I could make sure by the sun and a six-inch Ordnance map, this should be the road flank of that wood which I had first explored from the heights above. I made a mighty serious business of my repairs and a glittering shop of my repair kit, spanners, pump, and the like, which I spread out orderly upon a rug. It was a trap to catch all childhood, for on such a day, I argued, the children would not be far off. When I paused in my work I listened, but the wood was so full of the noises of summer (though the birds had mated) that I could not at first distinguish these from the tread of small cautious feet stealing across the dead leaves. I rang my bell in an alluring manner, but the feet fled, and I repented, for to a child a sudden noise is very real terror. I must have been at work half an hour when I heard in the wood the voice of the blind woman crying: 'Children, oh, children! Where are you?' and the stillness made slow to close on the perfection of that cry. She came towards me, half feeling her way between the tree boles, and though a child, it seemed, clung to her skirt, it swerved into the leafage like a rabbit as she drew nearer.

'Is that you?' she said, 'from the other side of the county?'

'Yes, it's me from the other side of the county.'

'Then why didn't you come through the upper woods? They were there just now.'

'They were here a few minutes ago. I expect they knew my car had broken down, and came to see the fun.'

'Nothing serious, I hope? How do cars break down?'

'In fifty different ways. Only mine has chosen the fifty-first.'

She laughed merrily at the tiny joke, cooed with delicious laughter, and pushed her hat back.

'Let me hear,' she said.

'Wait a moment,' I cried, 'and I'll get you a cushion.'

She set her foot on the rug all covered with spare parts, and stooped above it eagerly. 'What delightful things!' The hands through which she saw glanced in the chequered sunlight. 'A box here—another box! Why, you've arranged them like playing shop!'

'I confess now that I put it out to attract them. I don't need half those things really.'

'How nice of you! I heard your bell in the upper wood. You say they were here before that?'

'I'm sure of it. Why are they so shy? That little fellow in blue who was with you just now ought to have got over his fright. He's been watching me like a Red Indian.'

'It must have been your bell,' she said. 'I heard one of them go past me in trouble when I was coming down. They're shy—so shy even with me.' She turned her face over her shoulder and cried again: 'Children, oh, children! Look and see!'

'They must have gone off together on their own affairs,' I suggested, for there was a murmur behind us of lowered voices broken by the sudden squeaking giggles of childhood. I returned to my tinkerings and she leaned forward, her chin on her hand, listening interestedly.

'How many are they?' I said at last. The work was finished, but I saw no reason to go.

Her forehead puckered a little in thought. 'I don't quite know,' she said simply. 'Sometimes more—sometimes less. They come and stay with me because I love them, you see.'

'That must be very jolly,' I said, replacing a drawer, and as I spoke I heard the inanity of my answer.

'You—you aren't laughing at me?' she cried. 'I—I haven't any of my own. I never married. People laugh at me sometimes about them because—because——'

'Because they're savages,' I returned. 'It's nothing to fret for. That sort laugh at everything that isn't in their own fat lives.'

'I don't know. How should I? I only don't like being laughed at about *them*. It hurts; and when one can't see. . . . I don't want to seem silly,' her chin quivered like a child's as she spoke, 'but we blindies have only one skin, I think. Everything outside hits straight at our souls. It's different with you. You've such good defences in your eyes—looking out—before anyone can really pain you in your soul. People forget that with us.'

I was silent, reviewing that inexhaustible matter—the more than inherited (since it is also carefully taught) brutality of the Christian peoples, beside which the mere heathendom of the West Coast nigger is clean and restrained. It led me a long distance into myself.

'Don't do that!' she said of a sudden, putting her hands before her eyes.

'What?'

She made a gesture with her hand.

'That! It's—it's all purple and black. Don't! That colour hurts.'

'But how in the world do you know about colours?' I exclaimed, for here was a revelation indeed.

'Colours as colours?' she asked.

'No. *Those* Colours which you saw just now.'

'You know as well as I do,' she laughed, 'else you wouldn't have asked that question. They aren't in the world at all. They're in *you*—when you went so angry.'

'D'you mean a dull purplish patch, like port wine mixed with ink?' I said.

'I've never seen ink or port wine, but the colours aren't mixed. They are separate—all separate.'

'Do you mean black streaks and jags across the purple?'

She nodded. 'Yes—if they are like this,' and zig-zagged her finger again, 'but it's more red than purple—that bad colour.'

'And what are the colours at the top of the—whatever you see?'

Slowly she leaned forward and traced on the rug the figure of the Egg itself.

'I see them so,' she said, pointing with a grass stem, 'white, green, yellow, red, purple, and when people are angry or bad, black across the red—as you were just now.'

'Who told you anything about it—in the beginning?' I demanded.

'About the Colours? No one. I used to ask what Colours were when I was little—in table-covers and curtains and carpets, you see—because some colours hurt me and some made me happy. People told me; and when I got older that was how I saw people.' Again she traced the outline of the Egg which it is given to very few of us to see.

'All by yourself?' I repeated.

'All by myself. There wasn't anyone else. I only found out afterwards that other people did not see the Colours.'

She leaned against the tree-bole plaiting and unplaiting chance-plucked grass stems. The children in the wood had drawn nearer. I could see them with the tail of my eye frolicking like squirrels.

'Now I am sure you will never laugh at me,' she went on after a long silence. 'Nor at *them*.'

'Goodness! No!' I cried, jolted out of my train of thought. 'A man who laughs at a child—unless the child is laughing too—is a heathen!'

'I didn't mean that, of course. You'd never laugh *at* children, but I thought—I used to think—that perhaps you might laugh about *them*. So now I beg your pardon. . . . What are you going to laugh at?'

I had made no sound, but she knew.

'At the notion of your begging my pardon. If you had done your duty as a pillar of the State and a landed proprietress you ought to have summoned me for trespass when I barged through your woods the other day. It was disgraceful of me—inexcusable.'

She looked at me, her head against the tree-trunk—long and steadfastly —this woman who could see the naked soul.

'How curious,' she half whispered. 'How very curious.'

'Why, what have I done?'

'You don't understand . . . and yet you understood about the Colours. Don't you understand?'

She spoke with a passion that nothing had justified, and I faced her bewilderedly as she rose. The children had gathered themselves in a roundel behind a bramble bush. One sleek head bent over something smaller, and the set of the little shoulders told me that fingers were on lips. They, too, had some child's tremendous secret. I alone was hopelessly astray there in the broad sunlight.

'No,' I said, and shook my head as though the dead eyes could note. 'Whatever it is, I don't understand yet. Perhaps I shall later—if you'll let me come again.'

'You will come again,' she answered. 'You will surely come again and walk in the wood.'

'Perhaps the children will know me well enough by that time to let me play with them—as a favour. You know what children are like.'

'It isn't a matter of favour but of right,' she replied, and while I wondered what she meant, a dishevelled woman plunged round the bend of the road, loose-haired, purple, almost lowing with agony as she ran. It was my rude, fat friend of the sweetmeat shop. The blind woman heard and stepped forward. 'What is it, Mrs. Madehurst?' she asked.

The woman flung her apron over her head and literally grovelled in the dust, crying that her grandchild was sick to death, that the local doctor was away fishing, that Jenny the mother was at her wits' end, and so forth, with repetitions and bellowings.

'Where's the next nearest doctor?' I asked between paroxysms.

'Madden will tell you. Go round to the house and take him with you.

I'll attend to this. Be quick!' She half supported the fat woman into the shade. In two minutes I was blowing all the horns of Jericho under the front of the House Beautiful, and Madden, in the pantry, rose to the crisis like a butler and a man.

A quarter of an hour at illegal speeds caught us a doctor five miles away. Within the half-hour we had decanted him, much interested in motors, at the door of the sweetmeat shop, and drew up the road to await the verdict.

'Useful things cars,' said Madden, all man and no butler. 'If I'd had one when mine took sick she wouldn't have died.'

'How was it?' I asked.

'Croup. Mrs. Madden was away. No one knew what to do. I drove eight miles in a tax-cart for the doctor. She was choked when we came back. This car 'd ha' saved her. She'd have been close on ten now.'

'I'm sorry,' I said. 'I thought you were rather fond of children from what you told me going to the cross-roads the other day.'

'Have you seen 'em again, sir—this mornin'?'

'Yes, but they're well broke to cars. I couldn't get any of them within twenty yards of it.'

He looked at me carefully as a scout considers a stranger—not as a menial should lift his eyes to his divinely appointed superior.

'I wonder why,' he said just above the breath that he drew.

We waited on. A light wind from the sea wandered up and down the long lines of the woods, and the wayside grasses, whitened already with summer dust, rose and bowed in sallow waves.

A woman, wiping the suds off her arms, came out of the cottage next the sweetmeat shop.

'I've be'n listenin' in de back-yard,' she said cheerily. 'He says Arthur's unaccountable bad. Did ye hear him shruck just now? Unaccountable bad. I reckon t'will come Jenny's turn to walk in de wood nex' week along, Mr. Madden.'

'Excuse me, sir, but your lap-robe is slipping,' said Madden deferentially. The woman started, dropped a curtsey, and hurried away.

'What does she mean by "walking in the wood"?' I asked.

'It must be some saying they use hereabouts. I'm from Norfolk myself,' said Madden. 'They're an independent lot in this county. She took you for a chauffeur, sir.'

I saw the Doctor come out of the cottage followed by a draggle-tailed wench who clung to his arm as though he could make treaty for her with Death. 'Dat sort,' she wailed—'dey're just as much to us dat has 'em as if dey was lawful born. Just as much—just as much! An' God, He'd be just as pleased if you saved 'un, Doctor. Don't take it from me. Miss Florence will tell ye de very same. Don't leave 'im, Doctor!'

'I know, I know,' said the man; 'but he'll be quiet for a while now. We'll get the nurse and the medicine as fast as we can.' He signalled me to come forward with the car, and I strove not to be privy to what followed; but I saw the girl's face, blotched and frozen with grief, and I felt the hand without a ring clutching at my knees when we moved away.

The Doctor was a man of some humour, for I remember he claimed my car under the Oath of Æsculapius, and used it and me without mercy. First we convoyed Mrs. Madehurst and the blind woman to wait by the sick-bed till the nurse should come. Next we invaded a neat county town for prescriptions (the Doctor said the trouble was cerebrospinal meningitis), and when the County Institute, banked and flanked with scared market cattle, reported itself out of nurses for the moment we literally flung ourselves loose upon the county. We conferred with the owners of great houses —magnates at the ends of overarching avenues whose big-boned womenfolk strode away from their tea-tables to listen to the imperious Doctor. At last a white-haired lady sitting under a cedar of Lebanon and surrounded by a court of magnificent Borzois—all hostile to motors—gave the Doctor, who received them as from a princess, written orders which we bore many miles at top speed, through a park, to a French nunnery, where we took over in exchange a pallid-faced and trembling Sister. She knelt at the bottom of the tonneau telling her beads without pause till, by short cuts of the Doctor's invention, we had her to the sweetmeat shop once more. It was a long afternoon crowded with mad episodes that rose and dissolved like the dust of our wheels; cross-sections of remote and incomprehensible lives through which we raced at right angles; and I went home in the dusk, wearied out, to dream of the clashing horns of cattle; round-eyed nuns walking in a garden of graves; pleasant tea-parties beneath shady trees; the carbolic-scented, grey-painted corridors of the County Institute; the steps of shy children in the wood, and the hands that clung to my knees as the motor began to move.

I had intended to return in a day or two, but it pleased Fate to hold me from that side of the county, on many pretexts, till the elder and the wild rose had fruited. There came at last a brilliant day, swept clear from the south-west, that brought the hills within hand's reach—a day of unstable airs and high filmy clouds. Through no merit of my own I was free, and set the car for the third time on that known road. As I reached the crest of the Downs I felt the soft air change, saw it glaze under the sun; and, looking down at the sea, in that instant beheld the blue of the Channel turn through polished silver and dulled steel to dingy pewter. A laden collier hugging the coast steered outward for deeper water, and, across copper-coloured haze, I saw sails rise one by one on the anchored fishing-fleet. In a deep dene behind me an eddy of sudden wind drummed through sheltered oaks, and spun aloft the first dry sample of autumn leaves. When I reached the beach road the sea-fog fumed over the brickfields, and the tide was telling all the groynes of the gale beyond Ushant. In less than an hour summer England vanished in chill grey. We were again the shut island of the North, all the ships of the world bellowing at our perilous gates; and between their outcries ran the piping of bewildered gulls. My cap dripped moisture, the folds of the rug held it in pools or sluiced it away in runnels, and the salt-rime stuck to my lips.

Inland the smell of autumn loaded the thickened fog among the trees, and the drip became a continuous shower. Yet the late flowers—mallow of the wayside, scabious of the field, and dahlia of the garden—showed gay in the mist, and beyond the sea's breath there was little sign of decay in the leaf. Yet in the villages the house doors were all open, and bare-legged, bare-headed children sat at ease on the damp doorsteps to shout 'pip-pip' at the stranger.

I made bold to call at the sweetmeat shop, where Mrs. Madehurst met me with a fat woman's hospitable tears. Jenny's child, she said, had died two days after the nun had come. It was, she felt, best out of the way, even though insurance offices, for reasons which she did not pretend to follow, would not willingly insure such stray lives. 'Not but what Jenny didn't tend to Arthur as though he'd come all proper at de end of de first year—like Jenny herself.' Thanks to Miss Florence, the child had been buried with a pomp which, in Mrs. Madehurst's opinion, more than covered the small irregularity of its birth. She described the coffin, within and without, the glass hearse, and the evergreen lining of the grave.

'But how's the mother?' I asked.

'Jenny? Oh, she'll get over it. I've felt dat way with one or two o' my own. She'll get over. She's walkin' in de wood now.'

'In this weather?'

Mrs. Madehurst looked at me with narrowed eyes across the counter.

'I dunno but it opens de 'eart like. Yes, it opens de 'eart. Dat's where losin' and bearin' comes so alike in de long run, we do say.'

Now the wisdom of the old wives is greater than that of all the Fathers, and this last oracle sent me thinking so extendedly as I went up the road, that I nearly ran over a woman and a child at the wooded corner by the lodge gates of the House Beautiful.

'Awful weather!' I cried, as I slowed dead for the turn.

'Not so bad,' she answered placidly out of the fog. 'Mine's used to 'un. You'll find yours indoors, I reckon.'

Indoors, Madden received me with professional courtesy, and kind inquiries for the health of the motor, which he would put under cover.

I waited in a still, nut-brown hall, pleasant with late flowers and warmed with a delicious wood fire—a place of good influence and great peace. (Men and women may sometimes, after great effort, achieve a creditable lie; but the house, which is their temple, cannot say anything save the truth of those who have lived in it.) A child's cart and a doll lay on the black-and-white floor, where a rug had been kicked back. I felt that the children had only just hurried away—to hide themselves, most like—in the many turns of the great adzed staircase that climbed statelily out of the hall, or to crouch and gaze behind the lions and roses of the carven gallery above. Then I heard her voice above me, singing as the blind sing—from the soul:—

'In the pleasant orchard-closes.'

And all my early summer came back at the call.

> 'In the pleasant orchard-closes,
> God bless all our gains, say we—
> But may God bless all our losses,
> Better suits with our degree.'

She dropped the marring fifth line, and repeated—

> 'Better suits with our degree!'

I saw her lean over the gallery, her linked hands white as pearl against the oak.

'Is that you—from the other side of the county?' she called.

'Yes, me—from the other side of the county,' I answered, laughing.

'What a long time before you had to come here again.' She ran down the stairs, one hand lightly touching the broad rail. 'It's two months and four days. Summer's gone!'

'I meant to come before, but Fate prevented.'

'I knew it. Please do something to that fire. They won't let me play with it, but I can feel it's behaving badly. Hit it!'

I looked on either side of the deep fireplace, and found but a half-charred hedge-stake with which I punched a black log into flame.

'It never goes out, day or night,' she said, as though explaining. 'In case any one comes in with cold toes, you see.'

'It's even lovelier inside than it was out,' I murmured. The red light poured itself along the age-polished dusky panels till the Tudor roses and lions of the gallery took colour and motion. An old eagle-topped convex mirror gathered the picture into its mysterious heart, distorting afresh the distorted shadows, and curving the gallery lines into the curves of a ship. The day was shutting down in half a gale as the fog turned to stringy scud. Through the uncurtained mullions of the broad window I could see the valiant horsemen of the lawn rear and recover against the wind that taunted them with legions of dead leaves.

'Yes, it must be beautiful,' she said. 'Would you like to go over it? There's still light enough upstairs.'

I followed her up the unflinching, wagon-wide staircase to the gallery whence opened the thin fluted Elizabethan doors.

'Feel how they put the latch low down for the sake of the children.' She swung a light door inward.

'By the way, where are they?' I asked. 'I haven't even heard them today.'

She did not answer at once. Then, 'I can only hear them,' she replied softly. 'This is one of their rooms—everything ready, you see.'

She pointed into a heavily-timbered room. There were little low gate tables and children's chairs. A dolls' house, its hooked front half open, faced a great dappled rocking-horse, from whose padded saddle it was but a child's scramble to the broad window-seat overlooking the lawn. A toy gun lay in a corner beside a gilt wooden cannon.

'Surely they've only just gone,' I whispered. In the failing light a door creaked cautiously. I heard the rustle of a frock and the patter of feet—quick feet through a room beyond.

'I heard that,' she cried triumphantly. 'Did you? Children, oh, children! Where are you?'

The voice filled the walls that held it lovingly to the last perfect note, but there came no answering shout such as I had heard in the garden. We hurried on from room to oak-floored room; up a step here, down three steps there; among a maze of passages; always mocked by our quarry. One might as well have tried to work an unstopped warren with a single ferret. There were bolt-holes innumerable—recesses in walls, embrasures of deep-slitted windows now darkened, whence they could start up behind us; and abandoned fireplaces, six feet deep in the masonry, as well as the tangle of communicating doors. Above all, they had the twilight for their helper in our game. I had caught one or two joyous chuckles of evasion, and once or twice had seen the silhouette of a child's frock against some darkening window at the end of a passage; but we returned empty-handed to the gallery, just as a middle-aged woman was setting a lamp in its niche.

'No, I haven't seen her either this evening, Miss Florence,' I heard her say, 'but that Turpin he says he wants to see you about his shed.'

'Oh, Mr. Turpin must want to see me very badly. Tell him to come to the hall, Mrs. Madden.'

I looked down into the hall whose only light was the dulled fire, and deep in the shadow I saw them at last. They must have slipped down while we were in the passages, and now thought themselves perfectly hidden behind an old gilt leather screen. By child's law, my fruitless chase was as good as an introduction, but since I had taken so much trouble I resolved to force them to come forward later by the simple trick, which children detest, of pretending not to notice them. They lay close, in a little huddle, no more than shadows except when a quick flame betrayed an outline.

'And now we'll have some tea,' she said. 'I believe I ought to have offered it you at first, but one doesn't arrive at manners somehow when one lives alone and is considered—h'm—peculiar.' Then with very pretty scorn, 'Would you like a lamp to see to eat by?'

'The firelight's much pleasanter, I think.' We descended into that delicious gloom and Madden brought tea.

I took my chair in the direction of the screen ready to surprise or be surprised as the game should go, and at her permission, since a hearth is always sacred, bent forward to play with the fire.

'Where do you get these beautiful short faggots from?' I asked idly. 'Why, they are tallies!'

'Of course,' she said. 'As I can't read or write I'm driven back on the early English tally for my accounts. Give me one and I'll tell you what it meant.'

I passed her an unburned hazel-tally, about a foot long, and she ran her thumb down the nicks.

'This is the milk-record for the home farm for the month of April last year, in gallons,' said she. 'I don't know what I should have done without tallies. An old forester of mine taught me the system. It's out of date now for every one else; but my tenants respect it. One of them's coming now to see me. Oh, it doesn't matter. He has no business here out of office hours. He's a greedy, ignorant man—very greedy, or—he wouldn't come here after dark.'

'Have you much land then?'

'Only a couple of hundred acres in hand, thank goodness. The other six hundred are nearly all let to folk who knew my folk before me, but this Turpin is quite a new man—and a highway robber.'

'But are you sure I shan't be——?'

'Certainly not. You have the right. He hasn't any children.'

'Ah, the children!' I said, and slid my low chair back till it nearly touched the screen that hid them. 'I wonder whether they'll come out for me.'

There was a murmur of voices—Madden's and a deeper note—at the low, dark side door, and a ginger-headed, canvas-gaitered giant of the unmistakable tenant-farmer type stumbled or was pushed in.

'Come to the fire, Mr. Turpin,' she said.

'If—if you please, Miss, I'll—I'll be quite as well by the door.' He clung to the latch as he spoke like a frightened child. Of a sudden I realised that he was in the grip of some almost overpowering fear.

'Well?'

'About that new shed for the young stock—that was all. These first autumn storms settin' in . . . but I'll come again, Miss.' His teeth did not chatter much more than the door-latch.

'I think not,' she answered levelly. 'The new shed—m'm. What did my agent write you on the 15th?'

'I—fancied p'raps that if I came to see you—ma—man to man like, Miss. But——'

His eyes rolled into every corner of the room wide with horror. He half opened the door through which he had entered, but I noticed it shut again —from without and firmly.

'He wrote what I told him,' she went on. 'You are overstocked already. Dunnett's Farm never carried more than fifty bullocks—even in Mr. Wright's time. And *he* used cake. You've sixty-seven and you don't cake. You've broken the lease in that respect. You're dragging the heart out of the farm.'

'I'm—I'm getting some minerals—superphosphates—next week. I've as good as ordered a truck-load already. I'll go down to the station tomorrow about 'em. Then I can come and see you man to man like, Miss, in the daylight. . . . That gentleman's not going away, is he?' He almost shrieked.

I had only slid the chair a little farther back, reaching behind me to tap on the leather of the screen, but he jumped like a rat.

'No. Please attend to me, Mr. Turpin.' She turned in her chair and faced him with his back to the door. It was an old and sordid little piece of scheming that she forced from him—his plea for the new cow-shed at his landlady's expense, that he might with the covered manure pay his next year's rent out of the valuation after, as she made clear, he had bled the enriched pastures to the bone. I could not but admire the intensity of his greed, when I saw him outfacing for its sake whatever terror it was that ran wet on his forehead.

I ceased to tap the leather—was, indeed, calculating the cost of the shed —when I felt my relaxed hand taken and turned softly between the soft hands of a child. So at last I had triumphed. In a moment I would turn and acquaint myself with those quick-footed wanderers. . . .

The little brushing kiss fell in the centre of my palm—as a gift on which the fingers were, once, expected, to close: as the all-faithful, half-reproachful signal of a waiting child not used to neglect even when grown-ups were busiest—a fragment of the mute code devised very long ago.

Then I knew. And it was as though I had known from the first day when I looked across the lawn at the high window.

I heard the door shut. The woman turned to me in silence, and I felt that she knew.

What time passed after this I cannot say. I was roused by the fall of a log, and mechanically rose to put it back. Then I returned to my place in the chair very close to the screen.

'Now you understand,' she whispered, across the packed shadows.

'Yes, I understand—now. Thank you.'

'I—I only hear them.' She bowed her head in her hands. 'I have no right, you know—no other right. I have neither borne nor lost—neither borne nor lost!'

'Be very glad then,' said I, for my soul was torn open within me.

'Forgive me!'

She was still, and I went back to my sorrow and my joy.

'It was because I loved them so,' she said at last, brokenly. 'That was why it was, even from the first—even before I knew that they—they were all I should ever have. And I loved them so!'

She stretched out her arms to the shadows and the shadows within the shadow.

'They came because I loved them—because I needed them. I—I must have made them come. Was that wrong, think you?'

'No—no.'

'I—I grant you that the toys and—and all that sort of thing were nonsense, but—but I used to so hate empty rooms myself when I was little.' She pointed to the gallery. 'And the passages all empty. . . . And how could I ever bear the garden door shut? Suppose——'

'Don't! For pity's sake, don't!' I cried. The twilight had brought a cold rain with gusty squalls that plucked at the leaded windows.

'And the same thing with keeping the fire in all night. I don't think it so foolish—do you?'

I looked at the broad brick hearth, saw, through tears, I believe, that there was no unpassable iron on or near it, and bowed my head.

'I did all that and lots of other things—just to make believe. Then they came. I heard them, but I didn't know that they were not mine by right till Mrs. Madden told me——'

'The butler's wife? What?'

'One of them—I heard—she saw. And knew Hers! Not for me. I didn't know at first. Perhaps I was jealous. Afterwards, I began to understand that it was only because I loved them, not because— . . . Oh, you *must* bear or lose,' she said piteously. 'There is no other way—and yet they love me. They must! Don't they?'

There was no sound in the room except the lapping voices of the fire, but we two listened intently, and she at least took comfort from what she heard. She recovered herself and half rose. I sat still in my chair by the screen.

'Don't think me a wretch to whine about myself like this, but—but I'm all in the dark, you know, and *you* can see.'

In truth I could see, and my vision confirmed me in my resolve, though that was like the very parting of spirit and flesh. Yet a little longer I would stay since it was the last time.

'You think it is wrong, then?' she cried sharply, though I had said nothing.

'Not for you. A thousand times no. For you it is right. . . . I am grateful to you beyond words. For me it would be wrong. For me only. . . .'

'Why?' she said, but passed her hand before her face as she had done at our second meeting in the wood. 'Oh, I see,' she went on simply as a child. 'For you it would be wrong.' Then with a little indrawn laugh, 'And, d'you remember, I called you lucky—once—at first. You who must never come here again!'

She left me to sit a little longer by the screen, and I heard the sound of her feet die out along the gallery above.

# Son of a Tinker

## MAURICE WALSH

### I

OWEN OGE O'CALLAGHAN was his name, and he was incredibly tough in body and spirit. He was a smallish, wiry, supple-shouldered lad, with a high-cheekboned, tanned face, a bush of crisp black hair, and blue long-lashed eyes with a devil in them. Any woman at all, gentle or simple, might turn to look at him with a woman's eye, unless she knew the tribe he belonged to, and if she did she would pretend that he was one of the invisible men.

For he was a tinker born and bred, and, so, an outcast by race amongst settled men. Mind you, when Owen Oge was young, his father, the Old Man of the tribe, had ambitions for him, and belted him to school—as long as he was beltable—four days a week from November to March, while the caravan was in winter quarters. And it could be that the little scrap of education he picked up set him apart from his roystering kinsmen.

But Owen Oge was a warrior by race too, and when the Big War came to shatter the world, Owen Oge, at the age of eighteen, sallied forth, carefree, to see what war was like. He saw it. My word! he saw it: from North Africa to the plains of the Po. And, moreover, he came through it unscathed in body, and if his mind was unscathed we may be seeing.

Owen Oge came back from war to a changed world, and for him a lonely and a hungry world. His father was dead and his tribe scattered, and it is possible that the dead-end, devil-me-care life of the broken clans no longer appealed to a grown man who had won some distinction in a famous regiment and had carried the authority of two stripes on his sleeve.

He had his trade, of course, his father's trade, the tinker's trade, the making of tin cans, the mending of pots and kettles and saucepans, anything that a soldering-iron would hold together. So he strapped on his father's budget—the ancient leather bag holding the tinsman's tools—and went out into the province of Munster to ply his wandering trade.

He found the hoeing hard. The age of the cheap store and aluminium ware had come to Ireland, and repairing was no longer worth while. Owen Oge began to know want; not hunger, for no man need go hungry in Ireland as long as he has a foot under him and a tongue in his head; but a free man must have a pound or two for a pint for his thrapple, a shirt to his back, boots to his feet, and a bed to lie on once in a while.

*By the gor!* said Owen Oge, *at this bloody rate I'll be forced to look for a job and a man for a master.*

No tinker, anywhere, has been known to fall so low in the tinkers' scale as to hire himself out. Soldiering yes, but not servile labour. But Owen Oge fell so low as to take to plain peddling, the tinker-woman's trade beneath the dignity of the male craftsman. He sold his tinsman's tools, and half-filled the leather bag with all the small gadgets to wheedle a farmer's wife out of her egg money.

But still want pursued him and slept with him many a night under a haycock. For the travelling shop had also found its way into Ireland: stocked motor-vans covering Owen Oge's territory with dispatch, and selling at a figure he could not touch, and live. But he put up a good fight.

The country people, old and young, liked him. He was gay-hearted, live-eyed, tongued with honey and gall, and many a farmer's wife bought a shilling's worth from him and she not needing it. The men liked him because he was a man's man back of all. He could play handball with the best of them, putt the light shot to their best mark, take a point and stand a pint, and tell a story to make a cat laugh. And he was not a quarrelsome man, drunk or sober, but when it came to the bit he would back down from no man that ever drew breath.

*I can keep this up, but for how long?* he asked himself. *Maybe five years pullin' the divil by the tail, and after that a hobo of a tramp on every road. Very well so! Better for me to be enjoyin' life wide and aisy while I'm young, robbin' my way through Ireland, spendin' the cold weather in jail, and dyin' in a ditch when my time comes.*

He had summed up the tinkers' life, and did not like it, for he had a sound core in him, and he did not want it sapped by a slow and inevitable degradation. And, perhaps, he knew that degradation had already taken its first nibble.

*No, be the Powers!* He decided grimly. *Give everything its wan chance, and I'll give a job o' work its wan chance too. A job o' work to suit the wanderin' foot, and the man for me is Matthew Murnahan and Son. And may the divil melt the same son!*

Murnahan and Son ran a store in the town of Cairnglass. Their motor-vans covered Owen Oge's circuit and seemed to swish about him ten times a day. And Ignatius Murnahan, the son, had a habit of hooting his motor-horn derisively in Owen Oge's coat-tails.

II

Owen Oge circled his way into the town of Cairnglass, and marched up the main street to the Murnahan store. There it was covering four numbers, with a plate-glass window at each side of the main entrance, and a long sign flaunting above: MATTHEW MURNAHAN AND SON, GENERAL EMPORIUM. And it was a general emporium at that: grocery, bakery, drapery, iron-mongery, haberdashery, furniture, boots and shoes—with a public bar and a saloon bar on the side: an astonishing store run on ball-bearings by old Matthew, with son Ignatius blustering along behind.

Owen Oge, bold-fronted, strode straight in and through till he came to where a big fellow, behind a counter, was slicing bacon. This was son Ignatius himself, and big he was: a tow-haired, buck-toothed, thick-waisted young fellow, with hands on him like the hams he handled.

"Hello, tinker me lad!" he greeted Owen Oge. "Is it a drink you're after—with the price of it?"

"I'm after a job," said Owen Oge quietly. "Where is your ould fellow?"

Young Murnahan threw back his head and roared mocking laughter, and Owen Oge, his face as open as the day, let him have his laugh out. A man past his middle years came out of an office close by. He was loosely fat, but a jut of strong jaw stood out between dewlaps, and small keen eyes looked out under a penthouse roof of brow.

"Stop that bull's bellow, Natty!" he ordered. "Is it a customer you'd be making fun of?"

"A customer!" cried Natty. "A tinker lookin' for a job! Did you ever hear the like, da?" And he laughed again.

Old Matt Murnahan silenced him with a contemptuous hand, and turned the small, keen eyes on Owen Oge.

"Who are you, young fellow?"

"Owen Oge O'Callaghan is my name—"

"Ah-ha! You're the lad cutting into my business out Moynaspig way?"

"The cut don't keep my teeth in practice," said Owen Oge.

"And you're wanting a job?"

"I am," said Owen Oge. "A job worth three square meals a day, and a few bob in my pocket come Saturday."

"Not much you're wanting, the dear knows!" said old Matt. "But most men I know have to root hard for the same."

"And I'll root me share." Owen Oge swung his empty budget to the front. "Fill that for me off your shelves, give me a fair run in the country, and I'll empty it once a day for you on a fair commission."

"Chickenfeed!" mocked Ignatius. "Don't mind him, da! I'll have him out of Moynaspig before Christmas."

"Is that all you can promise me, young Callaghan?" said old Matt.

"No, nor half," said Owen Oge boldly. "I know the people, and the people know me, and I'll get orders for you—on the same commission. I'll get orders for heavy goods I can't horse myself. You are losing them now to shops in Limerick, because the agent you have"—he gestured thumb towards Ignatius —"is no damn good. Look! don't take my word for it, but give me a week's trial—and you won't if you are your son's father."

"Shut up, Natty!" old Matt ordered his exploding son. He tapped on the counter, and contemplated the young tinker. The frank devil spoke truth: a country agent was needed for the business, and Natty was not popular amongst the people. He pointed a finger at Owen Oge.

"Give me time, young fellow! Come in to-morrow morning and I'll talk to you. Shut your gob, Natty, and give the lad a pint o' stout." And he sidled back to his cubby of an office where his young daughter kept the books.

Natty, growling, gave Owen Oge a pot of stale porter, and Owen Oge, after one mouthful, turned a cold eye on Natty, and walked out of the store.

But next morning, bright and early, he was back with his empty budget.

"Leave your bag with me, boy," said old Matt, "and go in to your breakfast in the kitchen. My daughter, Roisin, has the tea ready."

The breakfast of bacon and eggs was more to his mind than the daughter Roisin, who poured his tea. She was a young, hobbledehoy sort of girl, with no great looks on her, and red hair. Owen Oge, who looked at every girl twice, and courted one here and there for devilment, looked at her only once, and went on eating. She looked at him too, but kept her thoughts to herself. Ten words did not pass between them that time.

When he got back to the store, old Matt had the budget filled with a nice assortment of small articles to take a housewife's eye.

"Very well, young Callaghan!" he said. "I'll try you out. The commission is ten per cent. on what you sell, and seven and a half on orders."

"You're a fair man," said Owen Oge softly.

"The first time I was called that," said old Matt.

Owen Oge emptied his budget four or, maybe, five times that first week, and, besides, he got orders and the promise of orders, for he was a popular young devil, and knew his people.

On Saturday evening old Matt called him into the office and took an itemised fold of paper from his daughter's hand. He totted it up slowly and surely. Roisin could tot ten times better than he could, but in a matter of shillings and pence he would trust no slip of a girl. Then he looked over the top of his spectacles at Owen Oge.

"Good work, Callaghan me boy!" he said quietly.

"I'll do better when I'm organised proper," boasted Owen Oge. "How much am I getting?"

The old man counted out thirty-two shillings and seven coppers on a corner of the desk.

"By the gor!" cried Owen Oge. "I didn't see as much at one time since I got me gratuity."

"And you'll see more if you keep on disremembering the blood that runs in you," said old Matt. "Listen now, boy! don't be wasting your bit of money on drink."

"I will not," said Owen Oge; "but, all the same, I'll have a single solitary pint to take the taste of the country dust out o' me mouth. What's more, I'll pay for it, and if it's stale I'll leave someone with his eye in his fist."

"Leave you Natty alone!" warned the old man. "He might hurt you bad, and no man likes to see his son hurted—much."

Owen Oge had his pint of stout, and it was not stale, but there was the taste of dust still in his throat, so he had another; and then a man he knew came into the bar, and that meant two more pints, and two more after that. And after that the deluge.

When he waked up on Sunday afternoon his throat was like a limekiln, and he walked three miles to a shebeen and got drunk on villainous new poteen. And when he waked early on Tuesday morning in a hayshed there was not as much as a brass farthing in his pockets. He was as unkempt as a bush, and there was white hayseed in his black hair, but his face was not haggard, nor were his eyes bloodshot, for he was a tough and seasoned man. But he knew he was slipping all the same, and he shook his head at the bleak truth.

*What's the use o' tryin'?* said he. *Once a tinker always a tinker, and there's only the one road for the likes o' me.*

But the road he took that day was the direct one to Murnahan's store.

"So there you are at last," said old Matt, sadly stern.

"Here I am," said Owen Oge evenly. "I' been drunk since Saturday, and I'm here now to get the sack out of your own mouth."

Old Matt shook his massive head. "What do you think I expected from the son and the grandson and the great-grandson of a tinker? No, me boy! You'll get sacked for one thing only: cheat me out of a penny and you'll know what that thing is. Give me that budget, and away in to your breakfast."

"My sowl to the devil!" swore Owen Oge. "You're the man for me, Matthew Murnahan."

III

Matthew Murnahan, the settled man, and Owen Oge O'Callaghan, son of a tinker, pulled amicably together for all of three years.

Owen Oge was no longer a peddler of small articles; he was a commercial agent on foot over a territory that took him five days to cover, and his budget was now stocked only with an assortment of samples. He not only took orders for the whole range of Murnahan's goods, he also bartered for eggs and poultry, fruit and vegetables, goose feathers and duck's down. He was many times a better businessman than son Ignatius, who, in the end, was no more than a carrier of the orders that Owen Oge had secured. Ignatius knew that, and hated Owen Oge accordingly.

In his private life he became more or less civilised. He had week-end quarters of his own in the attic above the stores; in the country he had midday dinner in any farmhouse where dinner-time found him; and slept, mostly indoors, where night fell on him. And always he had sweets for the children.

He was even saving a little money—the first tinker that ever did in all history. He no longer drank—like a tinker—while he had money in his pocket. But, indeed, he sometimes got drunk, and sometimes slept under a hedge, but, always, he pulled himself up in time, and the thing that helped him was the memory of what Matt Murnahan had said: *What would I expect from the son of a tinker?*

And then—and it is a pity that the so-obvious has to be stated—Owen Oge noticed that Matthew Murnahan had a daughter. Roisin—little rose—was her name, and devil the rose was she! Owen Oge had been seeing her for all of three years before he noticed her; she was callow, and she was bony under a thin freckled skin, and her red hair had no sheen. He might run over a book of patterns with her, and take his week's commission from her hands, and say a pleasant bantering word now and then, but, as soon as he turned his back, he forgot that she even existed. And old Mother Nature, the devil she is, with a rod in pickle for him all the time.

Matthew Murnahan could have given his daughter a college education, and a finishing course in a Brussels convent, to make her a governess in Spain or High Peruvia—God save the mark! *"I' hell with that!"* said Matt. *"She'll be like her mother before her—God rest her soul—good behind the counter, better in her kitchen, and best of all we know where."*

So at the age of sixteen, after getting her leaving certificate from secondary school, she was installed behind the office window, and had her education completed the hard way.

She took to the life of the store like a duck to water, for she was her father's daughter. In no time at all she was running the office, and soon she was doing all the ordering for the business, and on busy market-days she was not above giving a hand behind the counter. She, and not Ignatius, was her father's right hand; Natty had a vice in him, and his father knew that if the whelp got a chance he would make ducks and drakes of the business.

And then, almost overnight, Roisin Murnahan was a young woman. She blossomed like the rose her name, and old Mother Nature stood back brushing her hands as much as to say: *A neat job, my daughter! Off with you now, and do a neat job for me!* And begobs! the job was close to hand.

Owen Oge really looked at her for the first time. He blinked and looked again, and it was the man's look this time. She was lank no longer, and, somehow, no longer did her freckles show, but her hair was redder than ever, only now it had a sheen to it like polished copper. Her skin was delicately fine, and the fineness of it was a translucency over her nicely padded and shapely bones; her eyes had the virgin, dreaming lustre, and when she smiled, her smile went back to Eve—ay! or even Lilith.

Let it be said that, though Owen Oge had not noticed Roisin for three years, Roisin had been observing him off and on, and was a point or two up in the game. He had that something in him that took a girl's eye—or fancy: the set and poise of his head, his grave face lighting up, his lashed devil's eyes, the cadences of his voice—or, maybe, none of these, but something else altogether. How would a man know? But, anyway, she was ready to show this tinker lad his place, and keep him in it—if she could.

So now, when he looked at her with that new look, she blushed most entrancing to behold, and Owen Oge was knocked clean off his perch.

"Why, Roisin Rhu!" said he, and he put a husky twist into that "Roisin Rhu"—his little red rose—that made the blood mantle again. But in her own mind she said *Time for you!* and proceeded with her woman's work.

Now, more than ever, Owen Oge consulted her about his work. He was into the office every chance he got, cheek by cheek with her over a book of patterns, his brown dry hand sometimes resting on hers, to hold a sample in place as it were; or haggling hot and strong—and the hotter the better—over his commission, and she not yielding him a penny more than his due; or, sometimes, teasing her with a new meaning in every word, and she, the quick learner, paying him back in his own coin and one or two of her own. But, always and nevertheless, he could bring the colour to her face and the shyness to her eyes with his tongue round "Roisin Rhu"; but that blade was double-edged.

He grew civilised altogether. Barring a friendly glass of beer on occasion, he gave up drink as a pastime; his shapely jowl was blue-shaven four mornings a week; he sported an elegant worsted trousers that he creased under his mattress, and a homespun sports-jacket of seventeen colours; and his tie was a brilliant red against a shirt of dark green. Any woman at all would (and did) look at him twice, and forget the blood that flowed in him. But whatever he said, and he said plenty, he had eyes for only one woman, and her name is known.

One evening in May, Owen Oge, sort of by accident, encountered Roisin Rhu coming home from a Mission sermon. He turned and walked home with her through the lovers' twilight, and had a pot of tea with her in the kitchen, and a gay bit of badinage that skirted courting by the shaving of an eyelash.

That religious revival damn near made a Christian out of Owen Oge. It lasted ten days, and he attended every evening, and listened to hour-long sermons deploring the company-keeping of the young under the shades of the gloaming. But for all that he walked home every evening with Roisin Rhu, who might not have been very attentive to the sermons either. And on the tenth evening, a sickle of moon in the sky and a thrush singing, his arm was round her waist; and at the gable-end of the house he kissed her ear, and then her chin, and at last her mouth. And there they were.

It could be that Owen Oge started that philandering out of natural devilment, but, indeed, it might be that Roisin Rhu led him on out of the very same thing. They were young and alive, and why shouldn't they have a bit of fun and a kiss or two in the bygoing? And, sure, they could stop when they wanted! They would have to stop sometime; for how could a tinker lad aspire to his boss's daughter, and how could a merchant's daughter stoop to a tinker's son?

They were in no hurry to stop all the same; maybe they knew they couldn't stop, and, knowing it, were very circumspect in keeping their courting secret. The first time they were careless they were caught.

IV

It was a night in the fall, with a full harvest moon—the lovers' moon—and they paused for a last kiss in the yard back of the kitchen. And as bad luck—or good—would have it, Ignatius came bustling round the corner; and there was his sister in the arms of a tinker, and her red head under the tinker's ear. He let a bellow out of him and leaped.

One huge hand clutched the tinker by the collar, and squeezed so hard that Owen Oge would have strangled if a stud had not given way.

"Into the house, you slut!" Natty roared. He shook Owen Oge. "The tinker at his tricks! Come on, you bastar'! and let me da talk to you!"

Roisin looked at Owen Oge, and saw his hands loose and idle at his side. "Owen Oge!" she cried at him, a bugle in her voice.

"I will not, Roisin Rhu," said he firmly. "What good would it do beltin' the gom now? Wait for me in the kitchen! I'll talk to your da."

"You will so," growled Natty, "and after that meself will kick you a mile o' the road."

Roisin, her hands to her hair, went into the kitchen then, and Owen Oge, jerking himself free with a sudden virility, went into the store by the side door. Natty came close behind, pounding the floor, but not too eager to pounce.

Old Matt was in the front office looking over his day-book under an electric bulb. He looked up, and one hairy eyebrow came down.

"Look at him, da!" cried his son exultingly. "Him and Roisin coortin' outside the back door, and he kissin' her to bate a band!"

The other eyebrow came down, and the small eyes gimleted into Owen Oge, who nodded his head and spoke quickly.

"There was nothing wrong, Matt Murnahan. Your daughter is a dacent girl."

"Dacent!" cried Natty, "and she kissin' a tinker."

"I can't say that this is the surprise o' my life," said old Matt equably. "I noticed the pair o' them, and they circlin' about each other, but I was hoping Roisin would come to her senses before the canoodlin' stage. I dunno about you, young Callaghan. Is this thing serious between you and Roisin?"

"Stop your blatherin', Matt Murnahan!" said Owen Oge, savage enough. "I'm here to get the order o' the boot."

Matt nodded heavily. "I'm not fooling you, I can see that," he said. "You know what's in my mind: I wouldn't have my only daughter the wife of a tinker's son."

"I'd have her in spite of you if I could keep her decently," said Owen Oge, the devil lifting in him.

"Not while I have a foot on me," growled Natty.

Old Matt pointed a finger, and his voice was stern. "To your bed, Natty! This is my business." And Natty went, still growling.

Owen Oge put his hands in his pockets, and held hard to his temper. The old man tapped on the desk, and his crafty mind was busy. He knew that he could not browbeat this tinker lad, and he knew that he must get round him in some way that would look reasonable and above board. After a time he spoke slowly. "I am a fair man, I do hope. I want to be fair now too, and dambut! I will be fair. Listen to me, Owen Oge Callaghan! When my Roisin marries, I'll put five hundred pounds into her hand." He tapped the desk again. "When you are ready, put five hundred pounds down there, and I'll talk matchmaking with you, tinker's son or no tinker's son—and that's my last word, and a fair word."

"Fair as hell," said Owen Oge. "Say another last word now, and I've lost a job."

"Business has nothing to do with a bit of foolish coortin'," said old Matt calmly, "and you are the business getter for me."

Owen Oge looked at him keenly. "You're not for sackin' me?"

"Sack yourself if you want to, but I'd be advising you to try a bit patience first. Didn't you ever hear of the lad that worked seven years for a father's daughter?"

"That's only an ould story," said Owen Oge, the pagan.

"An ould story is often a true story," said old Matt, and shooed him away with a hand. "Off with you now, and Roisin will have supper ready for you in the kitchen—and a word or two of advice, maybe. I'll talk to the both of ye later."

Owen Oge found Roisin in the kitchen, but she had no supper ready for him. She sat at the end of the table, her chin in her hands, and looked unsmilingly at his set face.

"What did my father say, Owen Oge?" she came to the point at once.

Owen Oge spoke as lightly as he could. "He offered to sell you for five hundred quid."

"You've got sixty only," said Roisin.

"Well you know, you rogue!" He sat on the table near her. "He talked, as well, of a lad that worked seven years for a father's daughter."

"Fourteen for the one he wanted," said Roisin, and slapped the table with her father's gesture. "You could save a hundred a year, Owen Oge?"

He put his hand over hers on the table. "Would you wait five years for me, Roisin Rhu?"

"I would." She put her other hand over his. "I would do more than that. God help me!" Her hand tightened. "Say the word, and I'll go away with you this very night. And amn't I the fool o' the world?"

"You are." His heart stirred, but he kept his voice steady. "You know what you are saying, girl?"

"We'd be together—"

"With hunger and want in a tenement house," he stopped her. "No, Roisin Rhu! A rogue I am, but I'll not do that sort of tinker roguery on you." He pushed her hands away roughly, and rose from the table.

She rose to her feet and turned close to him. But before they could put a hand on each other, Matt Murnahan opened the door from the store. He looked and saw, but all he said was:

"It is time for your bed, Roisin."

She turned at him like a spring, and, in another draw of breath, would have flared. But Owen Oge spoke quietly behind her.

"Go to your bed, Roisin Rhu!"

And Roisin Rhu let one bolt fly. "May the devil melt the pair of ye!" and flounced out of the kitchen.

"Her mother's temper, by glory!" said old Matt, "and no supper for aither of us."

"To hell with supper!" said Owen Oge. "I'm for my bed too."

He moved quiet-footed to the back door, and the old man went with him, and put a staying hand on his arm.

"I' been thinking back there, Owen Oge," he said, "and I'll not deceive you any longer—"

"I'd deceive you if I could, you ould devil," said Owen Oge, and let his temper go a hand's breadth. "By the Lord God! if I had five hundred pounds, I'd have me own van, and my wife an' myself would take away half your business, Matt Murnahan."

"Maybe so, maybe so!" said the old man coolly. "You haven't the five hundred, and I'll not trust a man of your breed with it. Listen to me, young Callaghan! There are three things you can do: you can steal Roisin from me, and I know it—and that will be the end of her; you can save your money, hoping to get her in time, and that is where I was deceiving you. Listen again, boy! I am going to marry Roisin off before two months are over your head. I have the man in my eye, and him ready and willing."

Old Matt paused for the storm, but no storm came.

"And there's the third thing?" said Owen Oge softly.

Old Matt opened the back door. "You'll have to work that out for yourself," he said, pushed Owen Oge out into the night, and banged the door between them.

Owen Oge stood and stared up at the full harvest moon and the sky behind it where the stars were faint and few.

*Ayso! Ayso, indeed!* he addressed himself. *Three things to do: I can steal her away as many a tinker stole before me; I can hang on and gamble, the cards packed agin me; and—yes!—I know the third way too, and it is the way for me.* He thudded a brown brogue on the cobbles. *Face it, you son of a tinker—face it!* He threw his head back, and suppled his shoulders, and faced his forlornness. *A man forgets always, and a woman forgets late or airly, and Roisin Rhu will forget me lost in the twisty roads of Ireland. Very well so! To-morrow I will tie all my loose ends, and then away I go, and fare-you-well, Mr. O'Callaghan, travellin' agent.*

v

Early in the afternoon Owen Oge was footing it back to Cairnglass from Moynaspig way. His budget was empty, and all his loose ends had been tied.

He was leg-weary who was seldom leg-weary, and at the cross of Curraheen he sat on the fence for a rest and a smoke before facing the final three miles into Cairnglass. Inside the fence, a farmer and his son, who were heading corn stooks, worked across towards him, and paused to pass the time of day. They lit two pipes and a cigarette with one match, and Owen Oge, in his pleasant way, retailed the news of the country further afield.

After ten minutes or so the purr of a motor engine came from the left-hand road, where a green van was coming at a fast lick, and not slowing enough for the turn.

"Big Natty Murnahan!" remarked the farmer's son.

"Begobs! you'll get a lift in, Owen Oge," said the farmer.

"I mightn't, but there's no harm in tryin'," said Owen Oge.

He hopped off the fence, stepped out into the road, and lifted a hand. Natty saw him, hooted his horn, but did not slow down; in fact, he seemed to accelerate. The van took the turn on a wide, tyre-protesting curve, came over to the wrong side of the road, and—

Owen Oge had to leap for his life. He had time enough to leap, there is no doubt about that. But in the very act his foot twisted on a loose stone and he went down on his hands. He was as active as a cat, and, like a cat, propelled himself sideways and back, and just made it. The front mudguard barely brushed his shoulder. But, alas! his empty budget had leaped above his head, and the strap of it hooked the handle of the driving-cab as it flashed past. Owen Oge took the air.

Luckily the strap broke at the wrench, and Owen Oge took only one clean somersault. He landed on his heels with a jarring, brain-searing shock, and fell forward on his face. He lay flat for a moment, half-lifted himself on his elbows, saw the van sliding to a halt, and fell on his face again.

When Natty came lumbering back, savage dismay in his eyes, the farmer was on his knees over Owen Oge, and his son faced round on Natty. He held a two-pronged fork at the attack, and was angry to the point of bloodletting. Natty Murnahan was nearer death, then, than Owen Oge had been a few seconds before.

"I got a good mind to bed the pike in your yalla gizzard," the lad threatened fiercely.

Natty flung guarding arms. "I never touched him," he roared. "He threw himself under the wheels, and I twisted away from him."

"Look where your wheel-marks are, you bloody liar!" the boy shouted back. "You tried to kill him, and I'll swear you to the gallows if killed he is."

The farmer was turning Owen Oge carefully over. Owen Oge's face was white, and blood was trickling from his nose. His eyelids flickered open and shut.

"Am I kill't dead?" he wanted to know faintly.

"Glory be to God!" cried the farmer. "The stim of life is still in him."

"I can't move my legs—me back is broke," whispered Owen Oge.

"I barely touched him, I tell ye," wailed Natty desperately.

The farmer looked up sternly. "Keep that for the judge," he said. "We saw what you were at, and we'll swear to it."

"But amn't I telling you—"

"Shut up!" The farmer was a prompt man. "Come on! you're taking him to hospital, and we're coming with you to make our statement. Get a move on, you *thulkeragh!*"

Owen Oge was still unconscious—or comatose—when they got him to the hospital at Cairnglass.

VI

The house surgeon came into the waiting-room, and looked cold-eyed at Matthew Murnahan slumped on a bench. Every citizen in Cairnglass had looked cold-eyed at Murnahan and son for the past ten days. The old man got stiffly to his feet.

"Is he any better, doctor?"

"He'll be a lot worse," said the doctor shortly.

"Mother o' God! he's not dying on us?"

"Not yet, but I fear he is in for spastic paralysis."

"Paralysed! Oh, murdher! A cripple for life?"

"Possibly. He jarred his whole spinal column, and has very little feeling from the hips down. He may have none later on."

"Can't he be cured at all?"

"He may be. A process of re-education. We may know in three months."

*Three months!* old Murnahan mused to himself. *Three months tied to his bed—and time enough to get Roisin safely married.* He looked keenly at the surgeon. "I have a bit business—could I talk to him?"

"Why not? His brain is clear enough." The surgeon smiled with some sarcasm. "He used it yesterday in a way that may not please you."

"I know he saw Moran, the lawyer. That's why I'm here." The old man grumbled. "Dammit! everyone in this town is against me."

"No, Murnahan!" the doctor corrected him. "They are all for Owen Oge O'Callaghan. Come this way."

Owen Oge was in a semi-private ward of three beds, but he was the only occupant. His still body was outlined below the covers, and his brown hands, outside the coverlet, were clasped over his flat stomach. He was still pallid, but his blue eyes were intensely alive below their thatch of black brow.

Matthew Murnahan sat on a hard chair, and placed a strangely gentle hand over Owen Oge's. "I'm sorry to see you like this, boy," he said sincerely.

Owen Oge looked at him unsmilingly. He liked the old man, but when it came to a showdown he would not trust him as far as he could throw a cow by the tail. Only his lips moved.

"How is Roisin Rhu?"

"Plain hell, that's what she is. She came to see you?"

Owen Oge did not answer that, but, instead, he gave old Matt a wallop between wind and water.

"You got me tied here all right, Mr Murnahan, sir, and I'm wonderin' to myself if no one bribed Natty to run me down."

"God'llmighty!" exploded old Matt.

"You got me where you wanted me, anyway."

"No, begod!" said old Matt spiritedly. "'Tis you has got me. I'm not blaming you at all. You got Natty, the gom, and I'll pay. You saw Moran, the lawyer, yesterday? I don't want this case to go into court, young Callaghan. I'll pay any damages in reason."

Owen Oge turned a live eye on him. "You talked to Moran?"

"I did, and I'm talking to you, man to man. Any damages in reason, that's what I said."

"Would two thousand pounds be in reason?"

"Make it half and I'll tell you."

"I don't take half."

"What will you take?"

"I'll take five hundred."

Some of the wind spilled from old Matt's sails.

"Five hundred?"

"Five hundred pounds—no more and no less."

Old Matt looked at him shrewdly and shook his head.

"My poor, foolish lad! Is that wild notion still in your mind: five hundred pounds, a van of your own, and my daughter wife to a cripple?"

"Cripple your granny! For all you know I'll be cured out of here in a week."

"I hope to God you will!" lied old Matt fervently.

"I will, and for that week my offer stands. After that, Moran will fight you for all we can get."

"Is that your last word?"

"Take it or leave it."

"Very well so," said old Matt, and he was worried in his mind. He levered himself to his feet, and moved slowly to the door. There he turned to have the last word.

"God bless you, ladeen! Stay you snug in your bed—for three months—and after that there might be a job, and a van as well."

Owen Oge, having said his say, would not be drawn.

## VII

Ignatius Murnahan was having his tea in the kitchen. His sister Roisin thumped the teapot down on its stand, and hot, brown liquid shattered the fellow's fleshy hands. He shouted at her.

"Damn your eyes! Get out o' here!"

Roisin lashed him back. "I'll not get out of here. I want to see the bite choke you."

He sought in his mind for something to hurt her, and found it.

"The man you want to choke is Benjy Gallon."

"What is Benjy Gallon to me?"

"Don't you know? My da and his da, they were matchmaking all day yesterday for you. Ha-ha!"

"They were wasting their time," she said coldly.

He stabbed a finger at her. "And where is the coortin' tinker to help you now? Thanks be to the good God! I put him on his back for three months."

It was at that very moment a scrape came at the back door. The latch lifted, the door opened, and there stood Owen Oge O'Callaghan his own self. There was a crutch under his left oxter, and a hazel stick in his right hand.

"God save all here!" he gave the customary salute, and, glancing at Natty, added, "I'm asking too much, maybe."

"Owen—Owen—Owen!" cried Roisin deep in her throat, and made as if to drive towards him. But her brother, on his feet, caught at her arm. His mouth had fallen open, but he shut it to roar.

"Get out o' my kitchen, you robber!"

Owen Oge shut the door with his shoulder and stumped two steps forward.

"Get out yourself, you slob!" he said, quietly stern. "I want to talk to Roisin."

Natty tried to move Roisin out of his way, but she stiffened against him.

"Would you dare hurt a crippled man?" she cried.

"Crippled or not, out he goes." But the poltroon in him was not yet spurred to action, and a wallop from a crutch in a tinker's hand was no birthday present.

"Wo—oh wo!" said Owen Oge. "This thing had to be, and now is the time. You will be notin', Roisin, that I have no hard feelings. Your big brother has been askin' for a lesson this many a day, and I'm not denyin' him any longer. Wait you!"

He stumped to the door into the store and locked it, and came back to the end of the table. Natty kept a wary eye on the crutch, hoping for a chance to snatch it.

"I am doing a foolish thing, Roisin," Owen Oge said regretfully, "for I'll never make a man of him. He's yalla at bottom, and how in the world am I going to give him a false courage for two minutes? By the gor! I have it. Take a look at these boyos, Roisin!"

He put his hazel stick on the table, extracted a wad of notes from an inside breast-pocket, and ruffled the edges with his thumb.

"Fifty ten-pound notes we took off your da, Roisin."

"You tricked him, you—" roared Natty.

"Maybe it was a trick, Roisin, and we'll give Natty his chance of turnin' the trick back on us. See! I am puttin' the whole five hunderd down here on the bread-board. There it is! Now let Natty throw me out the door and the money is his, and Owen Oge O'Callaghan is done forever and a day." There was a fine daredevil challenge in his voice.

"Owen Oge, you fool!" cried Roisin, wild with dismay.

"We have to settle our conscience some way, girleen," said Owen Oge, "and isn't this killin' two birds with one stone? Is Natty ready? Be the gor! I do believe he's afraid o' the crutch. Very well so! There goes the crutch on the table, and I'm his meat."

Natty flung his sister aside so forcefully that she brought up against the dresser, and saved her face with her hands.

"I got you at last," he shouted, and leaped, his huge hands clutching.

Owen Oge slipped away from the table, and he was no longer a cripple. He slid forward and under the pawing hands, and pulled the trigger on his right hand. Natty's thick jowl jerked up, his buck teeth clicked, and his knees yielded for an instant.

"That was too hard, I'm thinkin'," said Owen Oge easily, "so we'll go soft for a bit." He slid in again, gave Natty a swift jab in the diaphragm, and Natty's head came down. "And here's one to addle him," and he clouted

Natty roundarm over an ear. "And a mark where it won't show," and he bent Natty the other way with a swing to the short ribs.

The big fellow was not able to launch one real blow, and merely pawed with his hands looking for a hold. Owen Oge, moving in and out on his boxer's feet, thumped him back and fore, this way and that way, but generally in the direction of the back door.

"Time is short, and is that his da kickin' the door?" said Owen Oge at last. "So here goes! not forgetting the bloody nose," and he gave Natty one real up-drive on his fleshy proboscis. Blood spurted, and Natty sat down hard against the back door.

Owen Oge dragged him aside by the back of the neck, and flung the door wide. But he did not need to throw the big poltroon out, for Natty tore free, and went out-of-doors in a frog's leap.

Owen Oge shut the door and brushed his hands. He wasn't even breathing hard.

"I didn't hurt him—much, Roisin, did I?" he enquired.

Roisin had barricaded herself behind the table.

"Oh, you little black divil!" she cried, half in pride and half in expostulation. "You didn't think of me at all, risking our good money!"

"The poor gom! Your money was safe as in a bank." He gestured head towards the store door. "Your da will have that door off the hinges."

The rattling at the door was supplemented by bangings.

"Let him stay there!" said Roisin unfeelingly.

"No, my girl! A thing or two has to be said. But let us not astonish the dacent man for a start." He again propped the crutch under oxter. "Let him in now."

Matthew Murnahan, starting to swear, checked short in the doorway when he saw Owen Oge, and then let his eyes slide past him.

"Where is Natty?" he demanded. "I heard him bellowin'."

"He was here a minute ago," said Owen Oge.

"Where is Natty, I'm askin'?" The old man raised his voice.

"Lying on his back to stop his nose bleeding," his daughter told him with satisfaction.

"I didn't hit him with the crutch aither," said Owen Oge. "He is not hurted—much."

The old man waddled across the kitchen and sat in the chair at the table end. His mood suddenly changed.

"Roisin, pour me a cup o' tea, and stop bitin' your fingers."

She hurried to do that, and the two men watched her deft hands. The old man took a deep gulp.

"Blast it! could as bedamn!" he complained.

"I thought your temper would warm it," his daughter told him.

Old Matt shrugged his shoulders. "There is a time for temper, but this is not it." Without lifting his head he addressed Owen Oge. "I'm glad to see you on your feet, young fellow. Are you feeling better?"

"I am better," said Owen Oge. "Doctors only know what they're told— and didn't I promise to be here in a week?"

Old Matt's question was casual. "And you cashed my bit of a cheque?"

"Look at them notes on the bread-board—Holy japers! they've gone."

Roisin laughed half-embarrassedly. "You poor gambling fool! Did you think I would let Natty take our money?—and I was afraid he would. I have it here safe for you." And she touched below her young bosom.

Old Matt leaned back in his chair, and laughed, at first growlingly and then heartily—and he could hardly stop.

"It was her own money anyway," declared Owen Oge, and laughed shamefacedly.

Old Matt wiped his eyes. "Up the Murnahans at the end of the game! You took the money off me, Owen Oge, and my daughter slipped it away from you, and what is she going to do next?"

Roisin was round in a whirl of skirts, and placed her hands firmly on the table.

"I'll tell you what I'll do, father, and you may as well know it now: I'll marry Owen Oge O'Callaghan." She slapped the board under his nose. "And then—and then—"

Her father put a hand over hers. "Wait, my girl! Wait! Don't go too far. Let me say it. If I was in Owen Oge's place I'd marry you, and buy that van too—and cut into the business if I was driven to it. But I'm not driving you—"

"What are you doing then?" she asked succinctly.

"Taking my medicine, girl." He rubbed his hands through his mop of grizzled hair. "Let us keep our tempers, and try for a fresh start." He turned to Owen Oge. "I'll talk to a man, and a man I need, and a man I've proved. I'll do business with you, Owen Oge O'Callaghan. Look! for a start I'll buy that van, put you in charge, and pay you twenty per cent. commission."

"And you're the man for me, Matthew Murnahan!" and Owen Oge reached a binding hand towards him.

But Roisin slapped his hand aside firmly, and her voice was firm and dominant.

"Listen to me! I am in this, for my life depends on it—and other lives, too." She bent to her father. "Stop scheming for the fun of it, and do the fair thing now. There's you, and there's Ignatius, and there will be my husband and myself. You will assign—Owen Oge and me—our proper share in the business, and if you are the man I know you are it will be a share that will keep Natty in his place." She smiled, and her voice held a caress, but her eyes were watchful. "Sure that is what is in your mind, and don't I know it?"

Matthew Murnahan shoved his tea-cup away and rose to his feet. His voice was that of a man whose own plans had blossomed.

"Damn cold tea anyway! Owen Oge, I have it in my heart to be sorry for you, and the wife you're getting. Come on out and have a drink with me—and bring the crutch, for I wouldn't like to be laughed at outside the family."

"One drink only," said Roisin.

"Whatever you say, Mrs O'Callaghan, ma'am," said Owen Oge softly.

# History Lesson

## ARTHUR C. CLARKE

NO ONE could remember when the tribe had begun its long journey. The land of great rolling plains that had been its first home was now no more than a half-forgotten dream.

For many years Shann and his people had been fleeing through a country of low hills and sparkling lakes, and now the mountains lay ahead. This summer they must cross them to the southern lands. There was little time to lose. The white terror that had come down from the Poles, grinding continents to dust and freezing the very air before it, was less than a day's march behind.

Shann wondered if the glaciers could climb the mountains ahead, and within his heart he dared to kindle a little flame of hope. This might prove a barrier against which even the remorseless ice would batter in vain. In the southern lands of which the legends spoke, his people might find refuge at last.

It took weeks to discover a pass through which the tribe and the animals could travel. When midsummer came, they had camped in a lonely valley where the air was thin and the stars shone with a brilliance no one had ever seen before.

The summer was waning when Shann took his two sons and went ahead to explore the way. For three days they climbed, and for three nights slept as best they could on the freezing rocks, and on the fourth morning there was nothing ahead but a gentle rise to a cairn of gray stones built by other travelers, centuries ago.

Shann felt himself trembling, and not with cold, as they walked toward the little pyramid of stones. His sons had fallen behind. No one spoke, for too much was at stake. In a little while they would know if all their hopes had been betrayed.

To east and west, the wall of mountains curved away as if embracing the land beneath. Below lay endless miles of undulating plain, with a great river swinging across it in tremendous loops. It was a fertile land; one in which the tribe could raise crops knowing that there would be no need to flee before the harvest came.

Then Shann lifted his eyes to the south, and saw the doom of all his hopes. For there at the edge of the world glimmered that deadly light he had seen so often to the north—the glint of ice below the horizon.

There was no way forward. Through all the years of flight, the glaciers from the south had been advancing to meet them. Soon they would be crushed beneath the moving walls of ice . . .

Southern glaciers did not reach the mountains until a generation later. In that last summer the sons of Shann carried the sacred treasures of the tribe to the lonely cairn overlooking the plain. The ice that had once gleamed below the horizon was now almost at their feet. By spring it would be splintering against the mountain walls.

No one understood the treasures now. They were from a past too distant for the understanding of any man alive. Their origins were lost in the mists that surrounded the Golden Age, and how they had come at last into the possession of this wandering tribe was a story that now would never be told. For it was the story of a civilization that had passed beyond recall.

Once, all these pitiful relics had been treasured for some good reason, and now they had become sacred though their meaning had long been lost. The print in the old books had faded centuries ago though much of the lettering was still visible—if there had been any to read it. But many generations had passed since anyone had had a use for a set of seven-figure logarithms, an atlas of the world, and the score of Sibelius' Seventh Symphony printed, according to the flyleaf, by H. K. Chu and Sons, at the City of Pekin in the year 2371 A.D.

The old books were placed reverently in the little crypt that had been made to receive them. There followed a motley collection of fragments—gold and platinum coins, a broken telephoto lens, a watch, a cold-light lamp, a microphone, the cutter from an electric razor, some midget radio tubes, the flotsam that had been left behind when the great tide of civilization had ebbed forever.

All these treasures were carefully stowed away in their resting place. Then came three more relics, the most sacred of all because the least understood.

The first was a strangely shaped piece of metal, showing the coloration of intense heat. It was, in its way, the most pathetic of all these symbols from the past, for it told of man's greatest achievement and of the future he might have known. The mahogany stand on which it was mounted bore a silver plate with the inscription:

> Auxiliary Igniter from Starboard Jet
> Spaceship "Morning Star"
> Earth-Moon, A.D. 1985

Next followed another miracle of the ancient science—a sphere of transparent plastic with strangely shaped pieces of metal imbedded in it. At its center was a tiny capsule of synthetic radio-element, surrounded by the converting screens that shifted its radiation far down the spectrum. As long as the material remained active, the sphere would be a tiny radio transmitter, broadcasting power in all directions. Only a few of these spheres had ever been made. They had been designed as perpetual beacons to mark the orbits of the asteroids. But man had never reached the asteroids and the beacons had never been used.

Last of all was a flat, circular tin, wide in comparison with its depth. It was heavily sealed, and rattled when shaken. The tribal lore predicted that disaster would follow if it was ever opened, and no one knew that it held one of the great works of art of nearly a thousand years before.

The work was finished. The two men rolled the stones back into place and slowly began to descend the mountainside. Even to the last, man had given some thought to the future and had tried to preserve something for posterity.

That winter the great waves of ice began their first assault on the mountains, attacking from north and south. The foothills were overwhelmed in the first onslaught, and the glaciers ground them into dust. But the mountains stood firm, and when the summer came the ice retreated for a while.

So, winter after winter, the battle continued, and the roar of the avalanches, the grinding of rock and the explosions of splintering ice filled the air with tumult. No war of man's had been fiercer than this, and even man's battles had not quite engulfed the globe as this had done.

At last the tidal waves of ice began to subside and to creep slowly down the flanks of the mountains they had never quite subdued. The valleys and passes were still firmly in their grip. It was stalemate. The glaciers had met their match, but their defeat was too late to be of any use to man.

So the centuries passed, and presently there happened something that must occur once at least in the history of every world in the universe, no matter how remote and lonely it may be.

The ship from Venus came five thousand years too late, but its crew knew nothing of this. While still many millions of miles away, the telescopes had seen the great shroud of ice that made Earth the most brilliant object in the sky next to the sun itself.

Here and there the dazzling sheet was marred by black specks that revealed the presence of almost buried mountains. That was all. The rolling oceans, the plains and forests, the deserts and lakes—all that had been the world of man was sealed beneath the ice, perhaps forever.

The ship closed in to Earth and established an orbit less than a thousand miles away. For five days it circled the planet, while cameras recorded all that was left to see and a hundred instruments gathered information that would give the Venusian scientists many years of work.

An actual landing was not intended. There seemed little purpose in it. But on the sixth day the picture changed. A panoramic monitor, driven to the limit of its amplification, detected the dying radiation of the five-thousand-year-old beacon. Through all the centuries, it had been sending out its signals with ever-failing strength as its radioactive heart steadily weakened.

The monitor locked on the beacon frequency. In the control room, a bell clamored for attention. A little later, the Venusian ship broke free from its orbit and slanted down toward Earth, toward a range of mountains that still towered proudly above the ice, and to a cairn of gray stones that the years had scarcely touched. . . .

The great disk of the sun blazed fiercely in a sky no longer veiled with mist, for the clouds that had once hidden Venus had now completely gone. Whatever force had caused the change in the sun's radiation had doomed one civilization, but had given birth to another. Less than five thousand years before, the half-savage people of Venus had seen sun and stars for the first time. Just as the science of Earth had begun with astronomy, so had that of Venus, and on the warm, rich world that man had never seen progress had been incredibly rapid.

Perhaps the Venusians had been lucky. They never knew the Dark Age that held man enchained for a thousand years. They missed the long detour into chemistry and mechanics but came at once to the more fundamental laws of radiation physics. In the time that man had taken to progress from the Pyramids to the rocket-propelled spaceship, the Venusians had passed from the discovery of agriculture to antigravity itself—the ultimate secret that man had never learned.

The warm ocean that still bore most of the young planet's life rolled its breakers languidly against the sandy shore. So new was this continent that the very sands were coarse and gritty. There had not yet been time enough for the sea to wear them smooth.

The scientists lay half in the water, their beautiful reptilian bodies gleaming in the sunlight. The greatest minds of Venus had gathered on this shore from all the islands of the planet. What they were going to hear they did not know, except that it concerned the Third World and the mysterious race that had peopled it before the coming of the ice.

The Historian was standing on the land, for the instruments he wished to use had no love of water. By his side was a large machine which attracted many curious glances from his colleagues. It was clearly concerned with optics, for a lens system projected from it toward a screen of white material a dozen yards away.

The Historian began to speak. Briefly he recapitulated what little had been discovered concerning the Third Planet and its people.

He mentioned the centuries of fruitless research that had failed to interpret a single word of the writings of Earth. The planet had been inhabited by a race of great technical ability. That, at least, was proved by the few pieces of machinery that had been found in the cairn upon the mountain.

"We do not know why so advanced a civilization came to an end," he observed. "Almost certainly, it had sufficient knowledge to survive an Ice Age. There must have been some other factor of which we know nothing. Possibly disease or racial degeneration may have been responsible. It has even been suggested that the tribal conflicts endemic to our own species in prehistoric times may have continued on the Third Planet after the coming of technology.

"Some philosophers maintain that knowledge of machinery does not necessarily imply a high degree of civilization, and it is theoretically possible to have wars in a society possessing mechanical power, flight, and even radio. Such a conception is alien to our thoughts, but we must admit its possibility. It would certainly account for the downfall of the lost race.

"It has always been assumed that we should never know anything of the physical form of the creatures who lived on Planet Three. For centuries our artists have been depicting scenes from the history of the dead world, peopling it with all manner of fantastic beings. Most of these creations have resembled us more or less closely, though it has often been pointed out that because *we* are reptiles it does not follow that all intelligent life must necessarily be reptilian.

"We now know the answer to one of the most baffling problems of history. At last, after hundreds of years of research, we have discovered the exact form and nature of the ruling life on the Third Planet."

There was a murmur of astonishment from the assembled scientists. Some were so taken aback that they disappeared for a while into the comfort of the ocean, as all Venusians were apt to do in moments of stress. The Historian waited until his colleagues re-emerged into the element they so disliked. He himself was quite comfortable, thanks to the tiny sprays that were continually playing over his body. With their help he could live on land for many hours before having to return to the ocean.

The excitement slowly subsided and the lecturer continued:

"One of the most puzzling of the objects found on Planet Three was a flat metal container holding a great length of transparent plastic material, perforated at the edges and wound tightly into a spool. This transparent tape at first seemed quite featureless, but an examination with the new sub-electronic microscope had shown that this is not the case. Along the surface of the material, invisible to our eyes but perfectly clear under the correct radiation, are literally thousands of tiny pictures. It is believed that they were imprinted on the material by some chemical means, and have faded with the passage of time.

"These pictures apparently form a record of life as it was on the Third Planet at the height of its civilization. They are not independent. Consecutive pictures are almost identical, differing only in the detail of movement. The purpose of such a record is obvious. It is only necessary to project the scenes in rapid succession to give an illusion of continuous movement. We have made a machine to do this, and I have here an exact reproduction of the picture sequence.

"The scenes you are now going to witness take us back many thousands of years, to the great days of our sister planet. They show a complex civilization, many of whose activities we can only dimly understand. Life seems to have been very violent and energetic, and much that you will see is quite baffling.

"It is clear that the Third Plant was inhabited by a number of different species, none of them reptilian. That is a blow to our pride, but the conclusion is inescapable. The dominant type of life appears to have been a two-armed biped. It walked upright and covered its body with some flexible material, possibly for protection against the cold, since even before the Ice

Age the planet was at a much lower temperature than our own world. But I will not try your patience any further. You will now see the record of which I have been speaking."

A brilliant light flashed from the projector. There was a gentle whirring, and on the screen appeared hundreds of strange beings moving rather jerkily to and fro. The picture expanded to embrace one of the creatures, and the scientists could see that the Historian's description had been correct.

The creature possessed two eyes, set rather close together, but the other facial adornments were a little obscure. There was a large orifice in the lower portion of the head that was continually opening and closing. Possibly it had something to do with the creature's breathing.

The scientists watched spellbound as the strange being became involved in a series of fantastic adventures. There was an incredibly violent conflict with another, slightly different creature. It seemed certain that they must both be killed, but when it was all over neither seemed any the worse.

Then came a furious drive over miles of country in a four-wheeled mechanical device which was capable of extraordinary feats of locomotion. The ride ended in a city packed with other vehicles moving in all directions at breathtaking speeds. No one was surprised to see two of the machines meet head-on with devastating results.

After that, events became even more complicated. It was now quite obvious that it would take many years of research to analyze and understand all that was happening. It was also clear that the record was a work of art, somewhat stylized, rather than an exact reproduction of life as it actually had been on the Third Planet.

Most of the scientists felt themselves completely dazed when the sequence of pictures came to an end. There was a final flurry of motion, in which the creature that had been the center of interest became involved in some tremendous but incomprehensible catastrophe. The picture contracted to a circle, centered on the creature's head.

The last scene of all was an expanded view of its face, obviously expressing some powerful emotion. But whether it was rage, grief, defiance, resignation or some other feeling could not be guessed. The picture vanished. For a moment some lettering appeared on the screen, then it was all over.

For several minutes there was complete silence, save for the lapping of the waves upon the sand. The scientists were too stunned to speak. The fleeting glimpse of Earth's civilization had had a shattering effect on their minds. Then little groups began to start talking together, first in whispers and then more and more loudly as the implications of what they had seen became clearer. Presently the Historian called for attention and addressed the meeting again.

"We are now planning," he said, "a vast program of research to extract all available knowledge from this record. Thousands of copies are being made for distribution to all workers. You will appreciate the problems involved. The psychologists in particular have an immense task confronting them.

"But I do not doubt that we shall succeed. In another generation, who can say what we may not have learned of this wonderful race? Before we leave, let us look again at our remote cousins, whose wisdom may have surpassed our own but of whom so little has survived."

Once more the final picture flashed on the screen, motionless this time, for the projector had been stopped. With something like awe, the scientists gazed at the still figure from the past, while in turn the little biped stared back at them with its characteristic expression of arrogant bad temper.

For the rest of time it would symbolize the human race. The psychologists of Venus would analyze its actions and watch its every movement until they could reconstruct its mind. Thousands of books would be written about it. Intricate philosophies would be contrived to account for its behavior.

But all this labor, all this research, would be utterly in vain. Perhaps the proud and lonely figure on the screen was smiling sardonically at the scientists who were starting on their age-long fruitless quest.

Its secret would be safe as long as the universe endured, for no one now would ever read the lost language of Earth. Millions of times in the ages to come those last few words would flash across the screen, and none could ever guess their meaning:

## A Walt Disney Production.

# The Truth about the Flood

## (from *The Bible as History*)

### WERNER KELLER

AND THE LORD SAID UNTO NOAH, COME THOU AND ALL THY HOUSE INTO
THE ARK. . . . FOR YET SEVEN DAYS, AND I WILL CAUSE IT TO RAIN UPON THE
EARTH FORTY DAYS AND FORTY NIGHTS; AND EVERY LIVING SUBSTANCE THAT
I HAVE MADE WILL I DESTROY FROM OFF THE FACE OF THE EARTH. . . . AND
IT CAME TO PASS AFTER SEVEN DAYS THAT THE WATERS OF THE FLOOD WERE
UPON THE EARTH. (Gen. 7:1, 4, 10)

WHEN we hear the word "flood," almost immediately we think of the Bible and the story of Noah's Ark. This wonderful Old Testament story has traveled round the world with Christianity. But although this is the best known tradition of the flood, it is by no means the only one. Among people of all races there is a variety of traditions of a gigantic and catastrophic flood. The Greeks told a flood story and connected it with Deucalion; long before Columbus many stories told among the natives of the continent of America kept the memory of a great flood alive; in Australia, India, Polynesia, Tibet, Kashmir, and Lithuania tales of a flood have been handed down from generation to generation to the present day. Are they all fairy tales and legends? Are they all inventions?

It is highly probable that all flood stories reflect the same world-wide catastrophe. This frightful occurrence must, however, have taken place at a time when there were human beings on earth who could experience it, survive it, and then pass on an account of it. Geologists thought that they could solve this ancient mystery by pointing to the warm periods in the earth's history between the Ice Ages. They suggested that when the huge ice caps covering the continents, some of them many thousand feet high, gradually began to melt, the level of the sea rose to four times its normal height all over the world. This great additional volume of water altered land contours, flooded low-lying coastal areas and plains, and annihilated their population, their animals, and their vegetation. But all these attempts at explanation ended in speculation and theory. Possible hypotheses satisfy the historian least of all. He constantly demands unambiguous factual evidence. But there was none; no scientist, whatever his line, could produce any. Actually it was by a coincidence, during research into something quite different, that unmistakable evidence of the Flood appeared, as it were, of its own accord. And that happened at a place with which we are already familiar —at the excavations at Ur.

For six years American and British archaeologists had been examining the ground at Tell al Muqayyar, which by that time looked like one vast building site. When the Baghdad railway stopped there for a moment, travelers looked with amazement at the soaring sandhills that had resulted from the diggings. Wagonloads of soil were removed, carefully searched, and put through the riddle. Rubbish thousands of years old was treated like precious cargo. Perseverance, conscientiousness, and painstaking effort had in six years yielded a handsome dividend. Discovery of the Sumerian temples with their warehouses, workshops, and law courts and of the villa type of dwellings was followed, between 1926 and 1928, by discoveries of such magnificence and splendor that everything uncovered thus far paled into insignificance.

"The graves of the kings of Ur"—so Woolley, in the exuberance of his delight at discovering them, had dubbed the tombs of Sumerian nobles whose truly regal splendor had been exposed when the spades of the archaeologists attacked a fifty-foot mound south of the temple and found a long row of superimposed graves. The stone vaults were veritable treasure chests, for they were filled with all the costly things that Ur in its heyday possessed. Golden drinking cups and goblets, wonderfully shaped jugs and vases, bronze tableware, mother of pearl mosaics, lapis lazuli, and silver surrounded these bodies which had moldered into dust. Harps and lyres rested against the walls. A young man, "Hero of the land of God," as an inscription described him, wore a golden helmet. A golden comb decorated with blossoms in lapis lazuli adorned the hair of the beautiful Sumerian Lady Shubad. Even the famous tombs of Nofretete and Tutankhamen contained no more beautiful objects. Moreover, "the graves of the kings of Ur" are 1000 years older at least.

The graves of the kings had, as well as these precious contents, another more grisly and depressing experience in store for the discoverers, enough to send a slight shiver down the spine. In the vaults were found teams of oxen with the skeletons still in harness, and each of the great wagons was laden with artistic household furniture. The whole retinue had clearly accompanied the nobleman in death, as could be gathered from the richly clad and ornamented skeletons with which they were surrounded. The tomb of the Lady Shubad had twenty such skeletons; other vaults had as many as seventy.

What can have happened here so long ago? There was not the slightest indication that they were victims of a violent death. In solemn procession, it would seem, the attendants with the ox-drawn treasure wagons accompanied the body to the tomb. And while the grave was being sealed outside they composed their dead master for his last rest within. Then they took some drug, gathered round him for the last time and died of their own free will in order to be able to serve him in his future existence.

For two centuries the citizens of Ur had buried their eminent men in these tombs. When they came to open the lowest and last tomb, the archaeologists of the twentieth century A.D. found themselves transported into the world of 2800 B.C.

As the summer of 1929 approached, the sixth season of digging at Tell al Muqayyar was drawing to a close. Woolley had put his native diggers once more onto the hill of "the graves of the kings." It left him no peace. He wanted to determine whether the ground under the deepest royal grave had fresh discoveries in store for the next season's excavation.

After the foundations of the tomb had been removed, a few hundred thrusts of the spade made it quite plain that further layers of rubble lay below. How far into the past could these silent chronometers take them?

When had the very first human settlement arisen on virgin soil under this mound? Woolley had to know. To make certain he very slowly and carefully sank shafts and stood over them to examine the soil which came up from the underlying strata. "Almost at once," he wrote later in his diary, "discoveries were made which confirmed our suspicions. Directly under the floor of one of the tombs of the kings we found in a layer of charred wood ash numerous clay tablets, which were covered with characters of a much older type than the inscriptions on the graves. Judging by the nature of the writing the tablets could be assigned to about 3000 B.C. They were therefore two or three centuries earlier than the tombs."

The shafts went deeper and deeper. New strata, with fragments of jars, pots, and bowls, kept appearing. The experts noticed that the pottery remained surprisingly enough unchanged. It looked exactly like that which had been found in the graves of the kings. Therefore, it seemed that for centuries Sumerian civilization had undergone no radical change. They must, according to this conclusion, have reached a high level of development astonishingly early.

When after several days some of Woolley's workmen called out to him, "We are on ground level," he let himself down onto the floor of the shaft to satisfy himself. Traces of any kind of settlement did in fact break off abruptly in the shaft. The last fragments of household utensils lay on the smooth flat surface of the base of the pit. Here and there were charred remains. Woolley's first thought was, "This is it at last." He carefully prodded the ground on the floor of the shaft and stopped short. It was sand, pure sand of a kind that could only have been deposited by water. Mud in a place like that? Woolley tried to find an explanation: it must be the accumulated silt of the Euphrates in bygone days. This stratum must have come into existence when the great river thrust its delta far out into the Persian Gulf, just as it still does, creating new land out of the sea at the river mouth at the rate of seventy-five feet a year. When Ur was in its heyday, the Euphrates flowed so close to it that the great staged tower was reflected in its waters and the Gulf was visible from the temple on its summit. The first buildings must therefore have sprung up on the mud flats of the delta.

Measurements of the adjacent area and more careful calculations, however, brought Woolley eventually to a quite different conclusion. "I saw that we were much too high up. It was most unlikely that the island on which the first settlement was built stood up so far out of the marsh."

The foot of the shaft, where the layer of mud began, was several yards above the river level. The mud, therefore, could not be river deposit. What then was the meaning of this remarkable stratum? Where did it come from? None of his associates could give him a satisfactory answer. They decided to dig on and make the shaft deeper. Woolley gazed intently as once more basket after basket came out of the trench and their contents were examined. Deeper and deeper went the spades into the ground: three feet, six feet— still pure mud. Suddenly, at nearly ten feet, the layer of mud stopped as abruptly as it had started. What would come now?

The next baskets that came to the surface gave an answer that none of the expedition would have dreamed of. They could hardly believe their eyes. They had expected pure virgin soil, but what now emerged into the glaring sunshine was rubble and more rubble, ancient rubbish, and countless potsherds. Under this clay deposit almost ten feet thick, they had struck fresh evidence of human habitation. The appearance and quality of the pottery had noticeably altered. Above the mud stratum were jars and bowls that had obviously been turned on a potter's wheel; here, on the contrary, they were handmade. No matter how carefully the contents of the baskets were sifted, amid increasing excitement, metal remains were nowhere to be found. The primitive implement that did emerge was made of hewn flint. It must belong to the Stone Age!

That day a telegram from Mesopotamia flashed what was perhaps the most extraordinary message that had ever stirred men's imaginations: "We have found the Flood." The incredible discovery at Ur made headline news in the United States and in Britain.

The Flood—that was the only possible explanation of this great clay deposit beneath the hill at Ur, which quite clearly separated two epochs of settlement. The sea had left its unmistakable traces in the shape of remains of little marine organisms embedded in the mud. Woolley had to confirm his conclusions without delay; a chance coincidence—although the odds were against it—might conceivably have been making fools of them. Therefore, 300 yards from the first shaft he sank a second one.

The spades produced the same result: shards, mud, fragments of handmade pottery.

Finally, to remove all doubt, Woolley made his men dig a shaft through the rubble where the old settlement lay on a natural hill, that is to say, on a considerably higher level than the stratum of mud.

At just about the same level as in the two other shafts the shards of wheel-turned vessels ended suddenly. Immediately beneath them came handmade clay pots. It was exactly as Woolley had supposed and expected. Naturally the intermediate layer of mud was missing. "About sixteen feet below a brick pavement," noted Woolley, "which we could with reasonable certainty date about 2700 B.C., we were among the ruins of that Ur which had existed before the Flood."

How far did the layer of clay extend? What area was affected by the disaster? A proper hunt now started for traces of the Flood in other parts of Mesopotamia. Other archaeologists discovered a further important check point near Kish, northeast of Babylon, where the Euphrates and the Tigris flow in a great bend toward each other. There they found a similar band of clay, but only eighteen inches thick. Gradually, by a variety of tests, the limits of the Flood waters could be established. According to Woolley the disaster engulfed an area northwest of the Persian Gulf 400 miles long and 100 miles wide. Looking at the map today we should call it "a local occurrence," but for the inhabitants of the river plains it was, in those days, their whole world.

After endless inquiry and attempts at explanation, without achieving any concrete results, hope of solving the great riddle of the Flood had long since been given up. It seemed to lie in a dark and distant region of time which we could never hope to penetrate. Now Woolley and his associates had, through their tireless and patient efforts, made a discovery that shattered even the experts. A vast catastrophic inundation, resembling the Biblical Flood, which had regularly been described by skeptics as either a fairy tale or a legend, not only had taken place but was, moreover, an event within the compass of history.

At the foot of the old staged tower of the Sumerians, at Ur on the lower Euphrates, anyone could climb down a ladder into a narrow shaft and see and touch the remains of a gigantic and catastrophic flood which had deposited a layer of clay almost ten feet thick. Reckoning by the age of the strata containing traces of human habitation, and in this respect they are as reliable as a calendar, it can also be ascertained when the great Flood took place.

It happened about 4000 B.C.

# A Candle for St. Jude

## RUMER GODDEN

1

THIRTY years ago Madame Holbein had seen the wistaria and taken the house. "I didn't look at anything else," she said. "I didn't need to."

"You didn't look at the drains and *look* at the drains!" said Miss Ilse. The wistaria grew over the coach-house that Madame had converted into the theatre. "It is a perfect setting. Perrfect! Those shutters! That scrolled-iron balcony above it! The wistaria!" It was, truthfully, like a stage wistaria; Madame almost felt indignant with it for not being in flower for her winter season in December. "There is not another like it in the whole of London," she said.

The theatre was the reason for the existence of the school. Madame had started it when she had retired from ballet those thirty years ago. It had been her brother Jan's idea, his dream that he did not live to see. "And he was spared a lot of trrouble, not?" said Madame. She had planned it as a self-contained unit, a theatre with its own company trained in its own school, self-contained, though small. "Then I shall have it exactly as I want," Madame had said at the beginning. She was still discovering how wrong she had been. "It will be a nest-egg of ballet," she had said. "Something valuable."

"Valuable! How will you pay for it?" asked Miss Ilse.

Madame did not know. "Somehow," she said, and that was how it had been paid for ever since. The prudent Miss Ilse had often tried to make her lease it for other purposes. "You could have plays, small productions, Anna."

"Only ballet."

"Or films. Films pay."

"Only ballet."

"They could be French films, Anna."

"Only ballet."

"But, Anna, we shall be ruined."

"How can we be?" asked Madame. "I made the theatre small so that the expenses could be small."

"But they are not small. You take such risks."

"You don't understand," said Madame with dignity, and with more dignity she said, "It is economically necessary that I take risks." It might be said that it was. At all events, the theatre had survived. Its course had not been smooth, but then nothing with Madame was smooth. Like all theatrical enterprises it had had its storms and quarrels and mistakes and mishaps and opportunities taken and opportunities missed and accidents and triumphs and tears. A theatre is blooded in triumphs and tears. The thing that had held the slippery, rudimentary structure of this one together was the unshaken belief of Madame. It had not occurred to her to doubt. "You always were conceited, Anna," Miss Ilse said often. "Yes, I olways was," agreed Madame. She might tirade at the moment but she took little notice of those triumphs or of tears. She made mistakes—"Ah! hundreds of them!" said Madame, but immediately added, "And most people would have made hundreds more!"—but on the whole, through the years, she had been miraculously right. " 'Miraculously' is correct," said Madame gravely. "Olways at the eleventh minute something comes along to save me, not?" "I don't know how you do it!" people exclaimed to Madame. Often she did not know either.

Her theatre was a miniature one, her company young, from her own school. "But they take me seriously," said Madame. "It is not a pupils' show." Twice every year, in May, "when the wistaria is out, full," said Madame, and before Christmas, a little part of London came to Hampstead and she gathered her small influential public. She never took her company to other theatres, she never took it on tour. "No. It was designed for this small stage," she said. "It shall stay where it is, at home."

She complained that her pupils used her, that they left just as she had matured them: "Oll the years of worrk and care, one season and then, tchk-tchk!" said Madame. " 'Good-bye, Madame, thank you verry much,' and off they go."

"That is your reward," said Mr. Felix.

Madame looked at him. Was he speaking bitterly or stating a fact? It was bitter and it was a fact; that was her reward. She still complained.

"But, Madame, wouldn't you have felt cramped and cheated if you had had to dance always on such a tiny stage?" That was Lion.

"I should have been glad to have the chance," said Madame haughtily. "To begin with, yes . . ."

"Besides, my dearr Lion, you can't compare me. That is rridiculous! I needed a big company, a big audience, a big stage. I could fill it."

"Doesn't every dancer feel that?"

"But often it is not trrue."

"Sometimes it is," said Lion.

Of course they used her. Everyone who came near her used her. "Everyone wants something," she would sometimes say when she had grown exhausted, and nowadays she was frail. "Keep them away, Ilse. Shut the door. Let me not see anyone today. They are oll selfish, inconsiderate. Oll of them want—want—want! None of them have anything to give." Miss Ilse was happy when Madame needed her but, of course, none of it was quite true. Madame gave, but she was an arch-taker; she took from them all, from Miss Ilse, Mr. Felix, from Lion; particularly and skilfully from every male she knew, from Leonid Gustave, the giant of the ballet world, down to her smallest pupil, Archie, whom she called Khokhlik[1] because of his tuft of hair. She took from the whole of life. How else was she to give?

Miss Ilse Holbein was not a participant in the Holbein Theatre and Ballet School; she was a part.

To make confusion worse, Miss Ilse was Madame Holbein, while Madame was Miss; Miss Ilse had married Jan Holbein, Madame's elder brother; Anna, Madame, had not married at all. "I did not need to," said Madame.

"No," agreed Miss Ilse, and said no more.

"One must be adult in these things," Madame said. "Besides," she said with a twinkle in her otherwise grave eyes, "I have olways said you can have your cake and eat it."

On a table in Miss Ilse's office in the school was a pair of Jan Holbein's shoes under a glass dome, and his death mask. The small pupils in the school dared not be left alone with that still marble face, and they wondered how Miss Ilse could turn her back on it and sit calmly at her desk writing Madame's notes and adding up the household accounts. The truth was that Miss Ilse felt he was scarcely to do with her; if she had been married to Jan, both of them had been married to Madame's career; Jan had been Anna Holbein's teacher and adviser till the day of his death, though he was a fine dancer and choreographer in his own right. "He never was mine. He was all for Anna," said Miss Ilse. She said it without rancour; she belonged to Madame too. Her heart and body and mind were given to Madame; her soul, firmly, to God through the medium of the Catholic Church, in particular the Church and Convent of the Presentation, opposite the school; it did not occur to her that she had nothing left for herself, but moments of depression came on Miss Ilse when everything she had been taught to believe seemed to her wrong. She had tried to be the things she felt she should be: gentle, considerate, unselfish, patient, and as truthful as she could, and yet she had little of life while Madame, who was wilful, inconsiderate, passionate, and not always strictly truthful, had life in abundance.

"I like life whole, in the rround," said Madame. "I . . . welcome it. Oll! I don't want to, how do you say, *dodge* any of it. I think that is important."

"Then why are you always grumbling?" asked Miss Ilse.

"My grumbling is part of the whole," said Madame haughtily. "Besides, I don't agree. I don't grumble."

"But you do, Anna. You grumble at everything: at the east wind, at the soup, at your time-table, at your exercises, at the children."

"Then I have to. To balance what I love. I love so many things."

"What things?" asked Miss Ilse suspiciously.

"Universal things," said Madame dreamily. "You would not understand, but I shall explain to you. Universal things that are for everybody and things that are for me, personally," said Madame with dignity. "I olways feel, for instance, that red and white roses together are for me. Don't ask me why. They are for me. Yes, red and white roses, and then, the Gulf Stream."

[1] *Russian for a crest or tuft. Also used as an endearment.*

"The Gulf Stream, Anna?"

"Yes. We in England ought to love the Gulf Stream. It keeps us from being frozen . . . quite. And I love spires and may trees, and views, some views; and houses, some houses; I love mahogany and the smell of spices; *peculiarly* I love the smell of spices, and food, the taste of that salmon at lunch, out of season, not? And poems. I love that poem about the deer by . . . by? . . . We had wine at lunch and that is why I think of him (and tomorrow we shall lunch on poached eggs and coffee, not? That is life) . . . Drrinkwater, that is his name. I love his poem. I love so much, everything; this minute. And today . . ." She shut her eyes. "Today, say, anemones in flower."

"But anemones are not in flower. They are over long ago."

"That makes not the slightest difference," said Madame.

"Sometimes, Anna, you behave like a child. Or a young girl."

"I am a young girl," said Madame, with her eyes still shut. "I am what I was for ever. So are you, Ilse, but you have forgotten. I don't forrget. I am what I am, each moment, for ever." . . . Time passes, that is what they say, thought Madame, but that is what it cannot do . . .

Above the fireplace in the first-class room downstairs was a photograph in a large oval frame, one among the hundreds of photographs all through the house. This was of a girl with dark ringlets in a small-waisted, full-skirted, scallop-flounced white dress painted with cherries: Madame, the dancer Anna Holbein, as Columbine in *Carnaval*.

"But they do *Carnaval now!*" one of the smallest pupils exclaimed.

"Yes . . . and I saw a company here in London use a blue painted backdrrop instead of the Bakst frieze and curtains," snapped Madame.

"But . . . if they couldn't get them, Anna? Things are difficult since the war," said Miss Ilse.

"Then don't do it at oll. Better to let it be lost than turned to a trravesty. Where is the poetry? Where is the rrichness? I ask you."

"Anna, I beg you. Don't get excited."

"I am not in the *least* excited. I am perrfectly calm."

Even Madame's illusions were personal. For instance, she believed that she was serene. "A dancer should give serenity," she told each pupil. "She must set her audience at rrest, dear child. She must be calm."

"Then why isn't she?" the pupil might have said.

Madame loved and cherished her little theatre.

It was at the side of the house, opening on the Avenue; it ran back into the garden and here she had built the stage. Its frontage was only the width of old stables, and its glassed entrance had been made where the harness-room door had been, with the scrolled-iron balcony above it on which the wistaria had spread along the front and on to the wall.

The theatre had been blasted in the war and all its glass broken. "But there never was much glass," said Madame obstinately.

"Yes. It always was a stuffy little hole," agreed Lion.

"Stuffy—little—hole!"

But it had had to close. Now Lion had arranged for the glass to be mended and the cracks in the walls to be repaired. He made Madame apply for a permit, "and for redecorating as well," said Lion.

"Not redecorating," contradicted Madame. "It is to stay exactly as it is. Repainting, that is oll."

"You will need a permit for that."

"A permit! To paint my own theatre!" Finally he, and Glancy, who for years had been stage carpenter and electrician, and some of the male students, painted it themselves.

A whisper began to run through the school. The theatre was to be lent to the Spanish Dancers, to the Harlem Ballets Nègres, to the Balmont Company. "To anyone but ourselves," the pupils said disconsolately.

"How could we open? We haven't a company," said Alma.

"We are the beginnings of a company ourselves." That was the ambitious restless Hilda.

"You are mad about that theatre," said Alma.

"Yes I am," said Hilda broodingly. She looked across the garden to the private door from the school to the theatre that was still locked. "We have Liuba Rayevskaya. We have John," she argued. "They are quite ready—and Lion would get the Metropolitan to release him to dance with us for a short season."

"It would have to be Lion and Caroline," Alma reminded her, and Hilda was silent.

"We are ready," she whispered rebelliously. She was more than ready. She was overdue.

Then Madame made an announcement. She was reopening the theatre for a five weeks' season, "My usual weeks in May," and the opening night was to coincide with the anniversary of her debut, fifty years ago. "It will be my jubilee," Madame explained. "Only I do not like that worrd. And you will give me a very special performance, not?" As special as you can, she thought, you are oll young untried dancers, though Lion and Caroline will be here. "Fifty years ago I made my debut," said Madame, "though I had danced many times before that at the Maryinsky but, of course, unnamed, and we were olways taken strraight home after we had done our parrt. Once I was named," said Madame, and she smiled. "But I was so small you would hardly notice me. That was before even I went to Russia, when I was with Jan, my brother, in Buenos Aires, and I danced the Humming-Bird in a ballet he had arranged there and that I shall revive for you this season, perhaps even on the opening night. Yes, I think on the opening night," said Madame. "It will be my diamond jubilee, if you must say jubilee, of that. I was seven," said Madame, and she added, with a twinkle, "Now at last you know how old I am."

Rehearsals had begun. "But we shan't be in it," said the youngest ones in the Beginners' Class. They had not been told any of this. It did not concern them, but they knew. News did not filter down to the Beginners' Class; they had a telegraph system of their own which knew everything long before their elders; its wires kept buzzing and humming and tapping and vibrating; the most startling messages were delivered continually and, if there had been any envelopes, they would have been the brightest possible orange. Now it was flashed through the class that one of them was to be chosen for that part of Madame's, the Humming-Bird in Jan Holbein's ballet *Cat Among the Pigeons*. "It will be Archie," said the Intelligence Department in the Beginners' Class. It was Archie.

Though the theatre was miniature, it was real. The old coach-house was the auditorium. Lion had repainted its walls; they were cream with small gilt sconces that Madame had had regretfully to electrify. "But it's better," said Miss Ilse. "Those candles were far too hot; and they had to be snuffed and relighted."

"That was part of the fascination."

"And their smell was horrid."

"Their smell was lovely and exciting," said Madame. "I infinitely regret those candles."

At first she had been afraid that the seating must be chairs. "It will look like a school hall or a chapel," she had said. But Miss Ilse, staying away at the seaside, as she liked to do and Madame did not, had heard of a pier theatre closing down and had sent an urgent message to Madame, who had come down from London and bought thirty rows of seats, red plush with red arms. Madame adored those seats.

Cream walls, gilt sconces, red plush seats; she added a small orchestra pit with a brass rail and curtains of Indian cotton that hung in heavy pleats and were garishly patterned in blue and crimson on a cream ground. She had her own Bechstein from the drawing-room moved in. "But the upright would have done," wailed Miss Ilse. The stage curtains were blue velvet, worn and faded now, their cords and fringes red. The stage itself was fitted with side curtains and a back-drop of plain greenish grey, "Because often we must do without sets," Madame had said, but, so far, she had never done without sets. The stage, built out into the garden, was properly fitted, of suitable height, and had a sloped floor of soft pine. "As good to dance on as any anywhere," declared Madame. She knew. She had had to dance on every kind of floor. There was a full range of lights from the first old-fashioned battens and footlights to the recently imported spots and floods. Lion had found a young man, Edwin, and Madame had coaxed him into doing the lights; now he did little else. Besides Edwin there was Glancy, the stage carpenter, electrician, and house gardener, though Madame gave him little time for gardening, and Emile, Zanny's husband, who helped in the house and acted as porter and commissionaire when the theatre was open. Then, too, there was a girl for the box-office, and Miss Parkes the secretary's married sister who came as a programme-seller and usherette; there was an extra hand to help Glancy on the stage itself, and behind the scenes there were Zanny and Miss Porteus, the timid little red-nosed dressmaker who made many of the dresses and, between times, was expert in making tutus for the girls in the school.

The stables themselves had been converted into dressing-rooms, a loose-box for the men, another for the girls, while the stalls made cubicles for two principals. The flat and loft above had been turned into a wardrobe-room, with dresses hung along rods behind green curtains and properties in dress baskets down the centre. A big sewing table was pushed against the window and beside it stood a treadle sewing-machine and ironing-boards; the girls helped Zanny and Miss Porteus iron and mend the dresses. The floor was always littered with snippets and ends of tarlatan and gauze. Here Miss Porteus spent most of her day. Here she and Zanny had often worked far into the night before the seasons. "That has not happened for five years now," said Zanny. "No," said Miss Porteus with her perpetual little sniff. "I don't know how I should do it now, I am sure. My arthritis wasn't bad then. When it gets into my hands I shan't be able to sew." Miss Porteus wore a little hard black velvet pincushion pinned to the left breast of her dress in the shape of a heart. To her niece, Lollie, it seemed that it was Miss Porteus' heart, withered and worn, stuck with sharp pins. Madame would have added, "Filled with sawdust instead of good red blood," but that was too old a thought for Lollie, who worried about her aunt. Lollie had come to live with Miss Porteus so that she could work with Madame; Madame had seen her for the sake of Miss Porteus; she kept her for her own. "I wonder what she will become," said Madame. "She may end up with a rabbit face like Miss Porteus or she may have beauty."

The theatre box-office was in what had been the harness-room, that, painted and given a deep red carpet and gilt chairs, made a foyer.

As well as the drawing-room piano, Madame had taken the drawing-room chandelier; it hung in the foyer and made Miss Ilse feel sad every time she saw it. As soon as they found anything for a home, Madame took it away. "How can we ever hope to have a home?" said Miss Ilse.

The chandelier, to Madame, gave the last right finish. "Yes, I was rright about it," she said. "Ab-so-lute-ly right."

In May, the smell of the wistaria came in over the smell of wax and gauze and canvas and dust and grease-paint on to the stage itself; the mauve pendulums hung over the balcony and along the wall. "And that wistaria can change its character," said Madame. "It can be Japanese, tantalizing, hanging like lanterns; it can be the Rhine and love-songs and *Carnaval*; it can be English of cool green summers and meadows; it can grow on old brick walls, by the river, or on London sooted stone. I was ab-so-lute-ly rright about the wistaria," said Madame.

With the coach-house, of course, went the house. The house was always secondary to the theatre. "But . . . we want a home," said Miss Ilse.

"Anyone can have a home," said Madame.

"Anyone but I," Miss Ilse might have said.

Miss Ilse loved orderliness and light and white curtains and the more delicate flowers. Sometimes she could not bear the very richness of the big dark house. Other people did not have houses like this, with its size and the dirtiness that came from its size, "And never enough servants," said Miss Ilse, "and the windows are so big they are *impossible* to keep clean." She was distressed by the crowd in it, the heterogeneous tongues and customs, the continual noise and hurry, and Madame's swift changes of mind, and the children leaving their shoes on the stairs and Zanny, Madame's old dresser, now her maid and despot wardrobe-mistress in the little theatre, who never did as she was asked or told. No, the house had never succeeded in establishing itself as a house; it was wiped out, first by the theatre, then by its characters.

It stood on its high North London ridge looking down on other roofs and streets, in tiers and crescents below it. It stood in trees. There was a recreation ground on one side that in spring had lilac and laburnum and pink may and chestnut trees, and on its other was the Avenue, with stucco houses that had flights of steps leading up to their front doors and laurels and shrubs in their front gardens. The house itself was grey and mammoth, with a double line of full-length windows that had wooden shutters from which all the paint had peeled and that had now the look of decay seen on the wood of some old river houses.

When Madame bought it, its garden had been neglected. Miss Ilse had cherished all kinds of plans for the garden but it was neglected still. It had a rough circular lawn in the middle of which stood a leaden basin with a fountain; it was useful for posing photographs but the fountain was broken. A path ran round the lawn, its asphalt was cracked and green with moss. By the house there were holly bushes; above them creepers hung from the balcony and the steps that led from the ground floor to the garden; they made the dark basement dressing-rooms under them darker still. Along the walls was a tangle of shrubs and plants. Glancy was supposed to take care of them, but Glancy had no time. If he kept the front in reasonable order, that was as much as he could do and, Miss Ilse had to admit, Madame was always calling him away for something else. The students ate their sandwiches in the garden in summer and were allowed to sit on the grass and sun-bathe if there were any sun and if Madame were out. Madame liked to look down from her windows and see its green; it was green, even if it had no flowers, and she preferred to see it empty. She liked to open the windows in spring to let in the smell of lilac even though it was always blended with the smell of cinders and cats.

Along the end and front walls there were plane trees and poplar trees that shed their different sizes of leaves in the garden and on the pavements; the plane-tree leaves turned brown or mottled brown and green, the poplars a bright clear yellow. "They are like bass and treble notes," said Hilda.

Music from the dancing school went over the wall into the road and the sounds of the road broke into the music: cars passed, buses, horses, footsteps on the pavement, voices, and the voices of sparrows, but the children's voices on the stairs often sounded like sparrows.

Madame and Miss Ilse were so conditioned to living with music that neither of them heard it but, if Madame had listened, each piece or repeat or motive or end or tag had its association.

"You don't hear music as music any more," Mr. Felix accused her.

"I do!"

"No, it isn't possible for you . . . You never did," said Mr. Felix. "You understand nothing about music at all."

"What nonsense!" cried the indignant Madame. "It was brred in me."

"You should have been bred in it," said Mr. Felix. "No. You distort it, and colour it until it isn't music. You would have driven me mad," said Mr. Felix, "if I had been anyone else . . . and if you had been anyone else," he added under his breath.

"I know you," said Mr. Felix sternly to Madame. "You like the conventional, the pretty, the traditional, only you exaggerate it and say 'trra-ditional.'"

"You are very rrude," said Madame.

"The evening breeze," said Mr. Felix, "the pastorale; the ball, the petite; the white wreath, the Glinka waltz; and you can *not* free it from association."

She had to admit it. To associate is to be with another, with someone, something else. "Yes, to me music is the dance; that is trrue," said Madame. Sometimes it was a dance, simply; sometimes, someone in a dance; sometimes, very often, that other was herself. That is my *Impromptu*, said Madame, listening. *The Folly Impromptu.* I remember the little pink gloves I wore, apple-blossom pink. That is Bianca's *Tarantella*, with those red petticoats. That *Tarantella* belonged to Bianca. I could never give it to anyone else, but, perhaps, one day, someday, I shall find someone for it. That is the dance of the Wilis from *Giselle*, second act, and that is my *pas de deux* with Jan; I remember it in Madrid with Serge too. I taught it to Lydia and Paul; that hurt me, but I couldn't bear it to be lost. They are dancing it still in New York. I might give it to Francis and Liuba. It would suit Liuba, not? Caroline is not . . . saucy enough, said Madame. That is *Clair de Lune*, but I call it a cascade. Yes. I have olways the idea of a waterfall from that. Why a waterfall from moonlight? I don't know, but it comes from a thread of sound, like a question, like a source. Or do I mean a stream? asked Madame but no, her mind was obstinate, she meant a source that grew to a cascade. That is the laurel-wreath dance I taught to the children, thought Madame, listening. That is *Epiphany Hymn*. That ballet was a failure. It was Lion's first and only attempt at choreography. "It failed," said Madame. "And it cost you five hundred pounds," said Miss Ilse.

"Lion doesn't understand music. He shouldn't write ballets," said Mr. Felix. "He can dance them . . . if they are explained to him," he said not very kindly.

"Nonsense. Lion is quite musical."

"Quite musical people shouldn't experiment with music," said Mr. Felix acidly, and he added, "There is only one of you here who has that understanding."

"Caroline has exceptional feeling."

"None of Caroline's feelings are exceptional. I was talking of Hilda."

"Hilda! She plays, yes, but she doesn't play so very well."

"She knows more than she plays, then. I have never heard her play. She doesn't know yet what she knows." He paused and then said, "She is old. I call her the Egyptian."

"That isn't in the least like Hilda. Egyptian is another name for gypsy."

"Not that kind of an Egyptian. It is odd, sometimes, that you should be so stupid," said Mr. Felix most politely.

The house vibrated from the passing of the buses in the road and vibrated from the thud-leap-thud of the classes in its rooms. The buses were reflected in its mirrors, with the sky and leaves and the dancers in the rooms. The buses passed horizontally across while the leaves fell longitudinally, in and out of the mirrors' compass, in and out. Nothing had an end in those mirrors. Their frames were tarnished now, some of them were fly-blown, but they had kept their clarity. They reflected the rooms over and over again, as they reflected the dancers, as they had reflected other dancers, and others before them, one to another, and one to another again, and again: feet and legs and hands and arms and hips and waists and shoulders and heads; each, in its turn, was sharp, defined, and clear in the mirrors. "But you shouldn't look in the mirrors too much," said Madame. "You must feel. Feel to the tips of your fingers."

She said this to the small ones of the low division of the Beginners' Class, struggling with their five positions with Rebecca Clarke, her assistant.

"Your positions are like do, re, mi, fa that you sing in a scale; all your dancing will be based on them. You must learn them," said Rebecca.

"You must *feel* them," corrected Madame. "Zoël why are you waving your hands like that? It is very prretty but it is not dancing. What are you thinking? You are thinking of something else, not of your *fouetté* at all."

She said it to her Advanced pupils, most of them taller than herself. "What you are doing now is verry likely more difficult than anything you will be called to do on the stage," she told them. "But it is far more difficult to feel it on the stage, I warn you. You not only have to prresent your dance, you have to give yourself to it as well. You must have temperrament." Madame's eyes would look along their ranks as if searching for that temperament among them. "Your audience should remember you when they have forrgotten how you danced." It was Hilda who heard the sadness in Madame's voice as she said that.

A dancer shouldn't grow old, thought Hilda. It is better if they die young; but, if Madame had died, thought Hilda, there would have been no Ballet Holbein and no theatre. Both were extremely necessary to Hilda at this time.

The front door of the dancing school was not the front door of the house. It was found by a process of elimination or divination. It was not the side door, nor the door to the left of the side door that led into the cellars; many mothers had found themselves first in the cellars; "And I wish some of them could have stayed there," said Madame. It was a door round at the back that had once been the garden door of the house. Here was a bell-pull that was broken. "Really, we must get the bell mended," said Miss Ilse, but, every time, Madame put it off. Miss Ilse suspected she preferred the bell broken. "Well, it is less disturbing," said Madame.

New pupils, new mothers, and visitors stood on the doorstep timidly expectant, wondering why nobody heard them and if they dared walk in.

They could have walked in, almost at any time, because, in winter, as in summer, the door was nearly always open. "What a drraught! Go and shut the outside door!" was one of Madame's most frequent commands, but, however often it was shut, it was sure, almost immediately, to be left open again.

It opened into the dressing-rooms, three grimy crowded dark basement rooms with windows on the garden that were overhung by the creepers from the balcony above. One dressing-room was for the boys and young men, one for girls, and one for little girls. Men and boys were supposed to use the flight of steps that led up into the hall above, but they liked to slip through the girls' room to the back staircase where the oilcloth was worn away to strands and only the brass treads were left. Here they all sat, and read, or learnt their notes or ate buns and sweets and chattered. They were not supposed to talk, but they talked, and every evening Miss Ilse picked up toffee papers and newspapers and tufts of the wool the girls used in their blocked shoes and often two or three pairs of shoes as well. "Very dangerous!" Miss Ilse would say, "with all the ribbons left hanging," and she would pin them on the notice-board she had put up in the hall, though Madame usually left her notices on the piano or in her pocket.

Each room had a big table in the centre and pegs and pigeon-holes along the walls with benches under them; on the tables, in the pigeon-holes, on the pegs, was always a conglomeration of objects: hats and coats and gloves and bags and tunics and scarves and socks and tights; sandwiches in paper bags, buns, bottles of milk and lemonade; parts of costumes; tambourines, newspapers, music, cheap *attaché* cases, powder puffs; and shoes, always shoes, pink, white, black, green, blocked, unblocked; red character shoes, black shoes with red heels; and always shoe ribbons, entangled on the tables, under the tables, and hanging from the pigeon-holes. The air smelled of soot and powder and rosin, of garlic from the sausage the Italian boys, Lippi and Giacomo, brought in for lunch; of acid-drops and gas. The whole big old-fashioned house smelled of gas.

There were two classrooms on the ground floor, huge rooms that had been the dining- and drawing-rooms. They ran the width of the house, from front to back, with windows looking over the front wall through the plane trees to the buses, and to the garden over the balcony at the back.

The rooms were old now. Three decades of dancers had taken their steps on the floors that now had an imperishable dust compounded of rosin and of old wood that was never polished. The ceilings had kept their gilt but their white paint had yellowed and cracked, and the old embossed paper on the walls had relapsed into uniform brownness. The light in the rooms, made greenish and soft by the trees outside, was darkened still more by the walls and struck the glass in the photograph frames as gently as it struck the mirrors.

No house ever had as many photographs. They were five or six deep in each room along the walls, over the mantelpieces, some even high up over the doors . . . But those must be the ones Madame thought nothing of, thought Hilda. . . . They were in the hall, in the office, up the stairs. Some, very old and yellow, were in the dressing-rooms. Archie had drawn beards and moustaches on some of the women and given breasts to some of the men. When he came to a Columbine in the corner he saw that someone, long ago, had been before him and given her whiskers round her mouth in Prussian blue.

The *barres* were blackened and smoothed by those three decades of hands, the stuffing had split the red rep in the seats under the windows, the pianos had become kettledrums, and still the work went on. "No! We are too shabby. It is disgraceful," said Madame. "We must have the rrooms redone." And then, when Miss Ilse had made the arrangements, she said in surprise, "But how can I, *now*, while we are so busy?"

Madame's colours were red and gold and, like Miss Ilse, white, but the difference was the difference between muslin and snow.

On the first floor were Madame's own rooms. Miss Ilse shared Madame's, which meant she herself had none. Here were Madame's colours in the white and gilt papers, red carpets, and gilt frames of mirrors. "Don't you have enough of mirrors downstairs?" asked Miss Ilse. "I am used to mirrors," said Madame.

There was gilt on handles and doorplates and more red in the flowers Madame liked to buy herself. "The money you spend on those flowers, we could have bought a little house for ourselves with it!" "I am used to flowers," said Madame, "and I don't like little houses." The white was in the flowers too, and in the long net curtains; the furniture was of Madame's favorite wood, mahogany.

Miss Ilse polished it herself with a cloth wrung out in boiling water and vinegar. "My mother taught me that, *not* to use furniture polish," said Miss Ilse. One day she read that that was how good wood was treated in old Japan and China. It made her curiously happy. Now, when she looked at the wistaria, which anyhow made her think always of Japan, she felt she had a defiant little secret of her own.

Madame's rooms had a collection of what the students called "relics." There was a great frame of newspaper cuttings from all over the world, another of programmes. There were Madame's first blocked shoes, kept like Jan's, and looking like two soiled pink sugar mice under their glass dome. There was a cast, in bronze, of her foot; in a cabinet, the cloak and swansdown muff she had worn in *Snowflakes*; a lace frill off a bouquet, and the filigree holder that had held it; a chocolate box that the Tsar had given her as a child at the Imperial School, "Oll the children had one, but I kept mine"; a fan from the Empress of Austria; an opal from the people of Sydney; and, among all these, the white kid collar of her dead cat, Pomponette.

Each was a memento of something that had happened, tender, triumphant, sorrowful, or gay, but always exciting, in her life. She could not bear to part with one of them. The students called them her "relics": *that which is left after loss or decay of the rest*—but, more than they knew, they were relics in another sense: *personal memorials to be held in reverence and an incentive to faith*. If they had had them they would have treasured them equally. Only they would not have had so many, said Madame.

2

The sound of the evening Angelus fell with a gentle peremptoriness into the office where Miss Ilse sat answering Madame's personal notes. Miss Parkes, the secretary, answered the rest, but so many of Madame's notes were personal. "To be imperrsonal is to be dull," said Madame. But to be very personal can be wearisome. Miss Ilse sighed.

"*Dear General Cook Yarborough,*" she wrote, "*Madame Holbein asks me to tell you she has not the least intention . . .*"

"Ding. Ding-dong," went the bell. Miss Ilse underlined *least*, it made it sound more like Madame, and laid down her pen and stood up.

"*Hail Mary, full of grace . . .*" She shut her eyes, her lips moved.

"*Blessed art Thou . . .*" The words and thought were like dew to someone parched with the heat of the day, and the day had been at white-heat with Madame. "*And blessed is the fruit . . .*"

The telephone rang.

"*Of Thy womb, Jesus.*" Miss Ilse continued steadily.

"Ding. Ding-dong." "*Hail Mary . . .*"

The telephone rang again.

"Ilse, can't you not answer that telephone?"

"*The Lord is with Thee.*" Miss Ilse put out her hand and laid the receiver down beside the telephone on the desk. "*Blessed art Thou . . .*"

Madame came in angrily but stopped when she saw Miss Ilse standing with her eyes shut and her lips moving. Though so gentle, Miss Ilse was like a stone in her religion. She would admit no other.

"But oll are good," argued Madame. "The Buddhists . . ." She saw a Buddhist as a little man, not unlike Mr. Felix, her old pianist, with a Buddha face, smooth and ageless; a little man sitting on a remote mountain, above cloud, watching the world turning below, as complete and detached from him as the circle of his prayer-wheel. "How restful!" said Madame. "But naturally. It is olways easier to do anything without emotion . . . if you can, but then, emotion is so interresting," said Madame. She loved the fire and singleness of the Mohammedans. "Islam, one God, the mosque that is empty of everything but prayer, the whole world of faith in a prayer-mat; the sword; the discipline of the month of fast. It is a man's faith," said Madame. "And Hinduism is rrich and intangible and strange, not easily to be understood, and that is intriguing; and in Confucius there is such sense. I can understand fire-worship," said Madame, who was always shivering. "And sun-worship; and the worship of ancestors. That is trradition," said Madame. "A dancer reverences tradition, *peculiarly,*" said Madame. "And my own Russian Orthodox Church, so old and filled with beauty; but to hear Ilse," said Madame, "you would think that there is only one in the whole wide world, her own."

"Only one," said Miss Ilse.

"You are narrow. Bigoted."

"I can't help it. That is what I believe."

"I don't understand you."

It had not occurred to Madame that dancing was her religion and she was remarkably intolerant about it. "Ilse, and her Saints and her prayers," said Madame, but she who ruled Miss Ilse had not been able to stop her slipping over the way to see the nuns or light a candle or say a prayer at one time or another, for one thing or another, in all the ups and downs of their life; to St. Anthony, on all the occasions that Madame lost her purse, or the key of the safe; to St. Michael when she was ill; to the Little Flower. The Saints, their merits and attributes, were clear and consistent, while the people who thronged the house and school and theatre, these balletomanes and dancers and artists and actors and poets, from the producers to the pupils, were all so muddled and unhappy, so feverish and contradictory, that Miss Ilse could never arrive at understanding one of them; and Madame . . . "But then," said Miss Ilse, "she is always the same, or never the same for ten minutes together!" Miss Ilse said prayers for a great many people, but the most of her candles and prayers were for Madame.

Once, long ago, for instance, in Copenhagen . . . "Yes, it was in Copenhagen," said Miss Ilse, who often told this to the children, "the winter of nineteen-eleven, just after Christmas. I remember how beautiful the snow was, and the Square, and the green spires of the churches, and the sleighs coming in from the country to market, and the early copper sunsets. There was a sleighing party and I asked Anna not to go. I had a foreboding . . .

"Anna. You shouldn't go. I feel it in my bones."

"Don't be a fool, Ilse."

"Don't go, Anna. Don't go. I beg of you. Not on a Gala night."

"I am going with . . ." Miss Ilse could not remember his name, but she saw him clearly still: young brown eyes and brown moustaches and black frogging on his great-coat.

"Anna. He drives so fast."

"They oll drive fast."

"Suppose there is an accident."

"Tchk-tchk! Why should there be an accident?"

"It is a command performance, Anna. Suppose you couldn't dance. Anna . . . if the sleigh overturns!"

"Why should it overturn?" But it did, as Miss Ilse had mysteriously known it would, and Madame's foot was caught and bruised. She stormed and wept and pleaded, but it was hopeless. The placards outside the theatre announcing the Gala performance in the presence of the King and Queen had her name, ANNA HOLBEIN, in large letters, but Madame could not stand on her foot. How could she dance?

Zanny was with them. "Zanny was *always* with us," said Miss Ilse in annoyance; and, of course, Zanny knew best and pushed Miss Ilse aside and ran out to a cabmen's eating-house near by and came back with an apron of hot potatoes. "Hot potatoes for bruises," said Zanny.

"I never heard of such a thing," said Miss Ilse, but Zanny pushed her aside again and opened potato after potato and applied them, like poultices, to the foot. Miss Ilse pressed her lips together . . . she pressed her lips together now . . . and took down her cloak from behind the door where Zanny had hung it out of the way. She remembered it, a dark-blue cloak with a narrow sealskin collar cut from an old muff of Madame's.

"Where are you going, Ilse?" Miss Ilse had preferred not to say in front of Zanny and had gone silently out into the twilit snow. She remembered how foreign the streets had seemed in that half light, how dim and cold, with a hustle that confused her more in the confusion of her worry about Madame, but she had found what she had been looking for, a church, and in it the Saint she was looking for. "St. Jude," said Miss Ilse, and she smiled, remembering. "Yes. I lighted my candle to him there."

"St. Jude. Why St. Jude?" asked Madame scornfully, trying her shoe, and biting her lips with the pain. "It's no good, Ilse. I can't dance."

"St. Jude is the saint of lost causes, Anna. Try again."

"St. Jude!" said Madame more scornfully, but presently, after more poulticing, she was able to stand in her shoe, presently to stand on her *pointes*, to turn, then to warm up a little and, finally, though in pain, to dance. The lace upstairs in the cabinet, the filigree holder, was from a bouquet she had that night. "Was it from the Queen?" asked Miss Ilse. "Or did the Queen send the bracelet? I remember something from the Queen, or was it that young man with the moustaches? Did he send the bracelet or the bouquet?" She did not know, but she knew Madame had danced that night.

"It was the potatoes," said Zanny.

"It was St. Jude," said Miss Ilse.

Now in the office Madame looked at Miss Ilse with irritation and disdain, but she answered the telephone.

"Was it anything important?" asked Miss Ilse when the last sound of the Convent bell had died away and she had stood for a moment as if she were reluctant to let it go. She sighed as she opened her eyes. "The telephone hasn't been quiet all day."

"What do you expect, the day before the opening?" Madame said crossly. "Ilse, you are one of the people who would pray while Jericho was falling."

"It was Edmund White," she said. "You know, *the* Edmund White." Miss Ilse shook her head. "Don't be a fool, Ilse. The prroducer. Broadwood Studios. He says he will give Lollie an audition, here, tomorrow at four. I said he should see her in the theatre."

"In the *theatre!* The *afternoon* of the *opening!* Well, *really*, Anna!"

"It should be empty then."

"They will be doing the flowers."

"They can stop doing the flowers for a little while. I know Edmund. It will only take a few minutes."

"And how do you know you won't want the stage? What a thing to arrange, Anna!"

"I didn't arrange it. It arranged itself. I said any other time but tomorrow, and there was no other time. Edmund is leaving for Nice the day after."

"But, Anna, there is no reason . . ."

"Anything can be a reason," said Madame, and it was true that in her hands it could.

Miss Ilse sighed. "Even if you won't be using it, there is still the cleaning, and the florists will be there, you know the children are having it decorated for you. It isn't as if it were anything important."

"It may be imporrtant for Lollie."

"You may even be rehearsing."

"Surely to God not then, *still*. But we may," said Madame, and she sighed and turned away from Miss Ilse and went to the table and stood looking down at Jan's face. "I'm glad Jan won't be here tomorrow," she said slowly.

Miss Ilse looked up. "Anna. What is wrong?"

"Everything is wrong," said Madame vehemently. "Everything!"

"*Now?*"

"Yes. Now!"

"But, Anna! Things can't be wrong *now*. It's too late for them to be wrong!" cried Miss Ilse.

"They are."

"*Anna!*"

"Yes, *Anna!*" mocked Madame bitterly. "That is what I have been saying oll day, oll this day. This is a terrible day, Ilse. Now at the eleventh minute I know that I, Anna Holbein, have made a mistake. And what am I to do?"

"But . . . what mistake, Anna?"

"It is that ballet of Hilda's. Ah, I wish I had never seen her!" cried Madame. "I listened to Felix, to Lion, when I should have trusted myself. I have never liked it. Never."

"Then . . . why . . . ?"

"I don't know why," said Madame wearily, and shut her eyes. "Don't ask me why. Because we oll, oll of us, do stupid things. I liked the dance of 'Peace' in it. I liked her 'Evocation.'"

"Then . . ."

"I still like them," said Madame. "But I know now it is wrong."

"But . . . if you liked it before . . ." argued Miss Ilse, "perhaps it is just that you are tired . . . depressed, Anna. You know you are easily depressed . . ."

Madame's eyes flew open. "It is *wrrong*, Ilse," she said severely. "Don't you hear me? Ah, don't make me such a storrm in a teapot about accepting one little worrd! It is wrrong. W*rrong!*"

"Then . . . what are you going to do?"

"I don't know."

She walked past Miss Ilse to the window, back to the desk, and then to the table, where she stood and looked down on Jan's still mask. "Tomorrow is an occasion, not?" she said. "I suppose, really, I have waited for it oll my life. Yes, that could be said, Ilse. Fifty years of worrk. Fifty years of success . . . and now!"

"But, Anna . . . You say, often, that you don't understand modern work . . ."

"Nonsense! I understand everything," said Madame. "Now is not the old days," she said slowly. "Then . . . for everything, everyone, there was something, someone, we could put in its place. We had a repertoire. The company was experienced, more or less, but now . . . they are young, untried. I think I have worked too quickly. That is what comes of fitting your work to an occasion, Ilse. And so . . ." said Madame. "Now"—she made a helpless gesture with her hands—"if I cut it, I have no alternative . . . that I care to give, and I have no alternative . . . but to cut it," said Madame.

"If you cut it . . . you will *have* to put something in its place."

"Don't be a fool, Ilse," said Madame tersely. "Send Hilda to me."

"Anna . . . the poor child . . ." Miss Ilse had an inexplicable liking for Hilda, inexplicable to Madame. Hilda, from the first time Madame saw her, had always made her think of a little snake.

Madame Holbein had a propensity for likening her pupils to animals. In an atmosphere where personalities ran high, each was likely to find himself with two, his own and the one Madame had given him. It was in her class that Lion had first become Lion. "And Caroline must be a lamb, an ewe lamb." It was Hilda who said that, slit-tongued Hilda. Some of Madame's names were cruel but all of them were apt: Francis, who was inclined to be stout and pallid and who had pink-rimmed eyes, was a polar bear; Lao-Erh, the Anglo-Chinese child, with her neat eye, smooth head, and broad foot, was a Mandarin duck; John, easily startled, with great eyes and the thin long strength of his legs, was a gazelle; the handsome well-dressed flashy eleven-year-old Zoë was a jaguar, and Archie, both in looks and manners, was a street sparrow.

As if this were catching, Madame herself was like nothing so much as a little foreign monkey, sad in the English climate. If she were tired or excited, and she usually was tired or excited, she shivered and she huddled her purple woollen coat round her like a monkey's jacket. She was thin and small and light and agile and she had beautiful nutshell-shaped eyes, but, if they had a monkey sadness and sharpness, they were not shallow as a monkey's are; they were full of comprehension, sensitive and expressive; as Madame grew older, more and more of her seemed to go into her eyes; and to her students, most of whom were bounded by their teens, Madame was very old indeed.

"Anna, you should retire. You burn yourself out. Surely you have enough of money and prestige?"

"It isn't the money," said Madame. "It isn't the prestige."

"But you are getting older, more frail. You get so tired, Anna."

"Yes. I get tired," admitted Madame.

"A little house, not this great barracks," said Miss Ilse longingly. "Think, you and I, sitting quietly by our own fire!"

"We can sit quietly when we are dead," said Madame. "I hope I shall work until I die."

The school at Holbein's existed for the theatre. "And not the theatre for the school," said Madame sharply to each pupil. "Don't you think it. It is not to be your lazy way in. They use me," said Madame. "What am I but a sprringboard, yes, a springboard, for their careers." No pupil who had passed through her school and company was more implacably bent on using her than Hilda.

Between Madame and everyone she taught was a direct strong personal link; too personal, her critics said. Pupils had either to be in entire submission or in conflict. Hilda was doomed to be in perpetual conflict.

Madame felt Hilda was a snake . . . or something to do with a snake . . . is it Eve? thought Madame. But we have no proof that Eve was an Egyptian. But what am I thinking? asked Madame. It was Felix who said that and not I. . . . The girl was not pretty, though she had a beautiful slender body, exceptional legs, straight and strong, and feet, long but finishing squarely, the toes remarkably even. "A dancer's foot," Madame might have said, but, for some reason, she grudged saying it. "She is like a snake," said Madame, and that was almost all she ever said of Hilda. It was true that Hilda's neck was a little long and that made her small wedge-shaped face look smaller; her hair was sandy brown and thick and fine, spread like a hood in small crinkled waves down to her neck. She had a very white skin: "One of those skins that do not change," said Madame. "They are insensitive." She liked the apple-blossom cheeks of the little Russian, Liuba Rayevskaya, or Caroline's fair colouring. "But Caroline has a beautiful complexion," said Madame. Hilda's eyes were green, faintly slanted; their lids were unusual; the lids were white and heavy and showed their veins in pale-blue markings, hyacinth-blue. If her skin were not sensitive, those eyelids were, but Madame did not look at them.

"Why don't you like her better?" said Miss Ilse.

"I don't like her at all."

"She is talented. Very talented."

"Yes," said Madame. "But . . . her talent is too strong."

"Can talent be too strong?"

Madame did not know the answer to that herself. Hilda puzzled her. She did not know the answer to Hilda.

The list of names of past pupils at Holbein's was illustrious; none of them as illustrious as Madame herself, but illustrious enough.

"But no one is illustrious now," said Madame. "No one. They have forgotten how to be."

"But, Anna, surely . . ."

"They are oll geese," said Madame fiercely.

"But, Anna, some of the children are good."

"Good! What good is good to me?" said Madame.

"I can tell you some names," said Miss Ilse. "Bianca. Michel Boré. Sonia Volskaya. Claudie. The little Lointaine . . ."

"They are oll gone," interrupted Madame.

"There will be more. There always are."

"Where? Where? Show them to me. In oll my life," said Madame, "I have never come across these children, these young girls, who dance by themselves in a passage or the moonlight and you are strruck dumb. I have never been struck dumb," said Madame. "No. Nonsense. Genius, if there is any genius, will discover itself by harrd worrk in its proper place in class. I have had no geniuses," said Madame.

There were too many names. Madame felt there were too many names, but at the same time she felt, as she felt today, that there were not enough. "Because look at what happens to them," said Madame. "Where are they now? Look at Bianca, what she is doing, and who can blame her?" Though Madame blamed her bitterly, Bianca was in Hollywood. "I do not teach for films and musicals," said Madame, but, often, that was where her teaching went. "Claudie has married and left the stage. Michel has grown fat . . ."

"Plump," pleaded Miss Ilse, who had liked Michel.

"Fat," said Madame. "Well, he is in New York now again, so I do not know how fat he is," she conceded. "He is in New York, and so is Sonia. I never see them now. So many go to America," said Madame.

"They dance just as well in America, Anna."

"And Lointaine is in Paris and I never see her either. Paul is back in Russia. Stephen and Edith in Australia."

"All over the world," said Miss Ilse.

"Yes, oll over the worrld," said Madame more cheerfully. She liked to think of that. She often talked of it. "I could paper the walls of the office with the stamps on the letters I have had from abroad this year," said Madame.

"Paper the walls with stamps!" said the literal Lollie Porteus. She worked it out. Allowing for the window and the door and the fireplace, the answer came to one hundred and thirteen thousand, four hundred stamps. "Would even Madame have that many letters in a year?" asked Lollie, but her faith in Madame was unshaken.

It was true that dancers from the Holbein Ballet covered the world. "And you can say they are pedigree dancers," said Madame. "They have been taught by me and I was taught by Marli and Galina Shumskaya herself. I, a pupil of Shumskaya, who was a pupil of Semyenova who was a pupil of Krassouskaya. We are in dirrect tradition. Yes. There are not many like me," said Madame, "and I was not fit to kiss her hand," she said reverently of Marli. "She was verry great artist."

Now she had only this handful of young ones in the school, "and only a school, not a company," said Madame. "We have never been so young, so without experience." Over and over again she would go over their names. "John. Liuba. Yes, Liubochka does very well, but . . . no more than that . . ." said Madame with a sigh. Liuba Rayevskaya was to dance the Eldest Pupil in *Cat Among the Pigeons*, with John as the Interloper. "I am giving them their chance," said Madame. She had hesitated between Rayevskaya and Hilda, but she had finally given Hilda the second part, the Second Pupil, and cast her as the Waiting Maid, second to Caroline, in the last ballet on the programme, *The Noble Life.*

"Then Hilda is not to have anything?" asked Miss Ilse.

"What do you mean, anything? She has two good parts."

"They are not good enough for Hilda," said Miss Ilse, with unaccustomed boldness. "Felix thinks so too."

"Felix can keep his nose out of the pie," said Madame.

"And so does Lion."

"What does Lion know? A boy like that?"

"He isn't a boy. He is a young man. You allow him to help you with rehearsals, more than Rebecca," said Miss Ilse.

"Because he helps more than Rebecca, and that is for his sake, not for mine," said Madame coldly. "I am teaching him," said Madame.

No one, not even Miss Ilse, knew what would induce Madame to take one pupil, or refuse another. Perhaps she did not always know herself. Some that appeared promising, she refused; others, for no apparent reason, she took. It was the same with the fees. "They should pay me hundreds of pounds," said Madame. "For what I teach them they should pay hundreds of pounds." Then she would take someone, like Lollie, for nothing.

Lion had been taken for nothing. Years ago he had come by himself and rung the bell and waited two hours outside the door for an answer. And it was winter, said Madame. What a little gamin he was! An arab from the street, dirty, thin, a ragged little boy. Now he had grown to this immense black-haired gold-skinned young man, muscular, lean, with wide shoulders, narrow-hipped and beautiful. . . . I look at you sometimes, thought Madame, and I don't know where you come from! . . . He was now with Caroline in the Metropolitan Theatre Company. Very often they were cast as partners. Caroline and Lion were Madame's two almost-realized hopes. From her first lesson, Caroline had begun to make a career for herself.

"She had an easy way in," said Miss Ilse. "She has rich parents who give her all she wants."

"That can make no difference to her dancing."

"It can make her path smooth. She has never had to struggle. One day . . ."

"One day I shall show her to Gustave," said Madame dreamily. "Ilse. I have heard that Gustave is in London. Then why hasn't he come? Does he think I have no one now to show him? But one day I shall show him Lion and Caroline."

The students in the school called Lion "Golden-Syrup Lion" from the lion that was a trade-mark on the tin of a certain brand of golden syrup. Madame when she heard it was indignant.

"It is right," said Mr. Felix. "He is too sweet. He agrees with every word you say."

"Lion has sense," said Madame. "Naturally he agrees with me. He knows where I can help him."

"He knows too well. Still . . . he may turn out all right," said Mr. Felix, "but I should watch Caroline. She has sharp elbows."

"It is my plan," said Madame, disregarding him, "that Lion shall have this company when I die, he . . . and Caroline."

"H'mm!" said Mr. Felix.

"Caroline has great personal beauty," said Madame, up in arms. "You can't deny it."

"I don't deny it. I don't like it," said Mr. Felix, and he added, "I have never thought a great deal of Caroline."

"Then you are mistaken."

"So may you be," said Mr. Felix. "Even you."

It was said in the school that Mr. Felix had once upon a time been a concert pianist. Mr. Felix did not say it. He had been musical director of the little Holbein Theatre since it had started and before that been with Madame on her tours and had often acted as her accompanist. He was a small old man with sparse white silky hair; his skin was the colour of yellowed ivory; he was Tartar in physiognomy and had blue eyes as bright as forget-me-nots. He played with dexterity, considering he had lost the tops of three fingers of his right hand. "Considering that, not otherwise," said Mr. Felix.

He played for such of Madame's classes as had music with perfect accuracy, while he read a book propped up in front of him on the music rack. Miss Ilse felt this was rude and tried to remonstrate with him. "You are playing for the children. You should watch them."

"I should if there were anything to watch."

"The mothers don't like it."

"I am not playing for the mothers. I am playing for the children, you just said so."

The book was usually a history book, but not always. "I find history, equally, in a novel," said Mr. Felix. He might have said he found history, equally, in everything and everyone.

"My world should have been music," said Mr. Felix. "But, as that has been prevented, meaning my fingers, the dance does nicely instead; quite nicely, that is." With anyone else, his pause would have been a sigh. "It is more obvious, more poignant, more exciting, and more easy to understand, and, perhaps, it suits me better," said Mr. Felix, "because I am growing old; not nerve-old, excitable-old, like Anna, but bone-old, and I don't want to bother too much. I study this little world," said Mr. Felix. "It has life, death, history, and, like any other world, it turns, unconsidered among other worlds, or almost unconsidered because it is a little famous. . . ." He chuckled. "They think I detach myself from my history book to consider it, but, of course, I don't. It and my history book are exactly the same."

"What would you have done, Mr. Felix, if your fingers had been taken off a little shorter," asked Archie, "so that you couldn't have played the piano at all?"

"I should have been a taxi-driver," said Mr. Felix, "and driven about in my taxi and watched the world from my little seat as I do now."

It was Mr. Felix, more than Lion, who had made Madame direct her attention to Hilda. Madame knew that Lion often danced through these ballets of Hilda's with her, and criticized and helped her. Lion was attracted by Hilda, Madame knew that too and did not want to know it; but Mr. Felix had no reason for praising Hilda except that he thought her worth his praise, "And Felix knows more about dancers than most people have forgotten," said Madame. It seemed that her attention was directed to Hilda, willy-nilly.

Now she said suddenly, "Do you remember, Ilse, when the children gave me the Fête on my birthday, do you remember that *Guy* of Hilda's? Do you remember how clever Felix thought it was?"

"It was clever," said Miss Ilse. "It was horrible. I hated it. I remember wishing I need not see an uncomfortable dance like that. It was a little *Petrouchka.*"

"It wasn't *Petrouchka,*" said Madame. "It wasn't anything but itself. It had its own flavour. It was original. Something good ought to have come from that child." She looked at the clock. "We have only a few minutes before rehearsal. I must make up my mind." She sighed and beat her hands together, one into the palm of the other, in distress. "Don't stand there staring at me, Ilse. Send Hilda to me."

When Hilda came she was not made up but her hair was done in the coils and satin bow of the Second Pupil; she was in tights and her practice dress and she was breathing quickly. "I was . . . warming up," she said breathlessly. Madame could see she was in a glow of excitement. Well, I olways was, thought Madame involuntarily. Each time. Yes. I was arrdent, thought Madame. So is she. . . . But she smothered that thought and returned to the worry over the ballet and her voice was crisp and cold as she said, "Hilda, I have sent for you because I am not satisfied with your *Lyre.*"

Hilda's eyes widened in astonishment. "But . . . I thought . . ."

"Never mind what you thought," said Madame. She did not know why she spoke so cruelly. Hilda's lids fell and her face grew hard.

"I need not tell you, Hilda," said Madame, "that it is quite extraordinary for so young and inexperienced a choreographer—though you are not yet a choreographer, of course—for so young a girl, then, to be allowed to prroduce her worrk on an occasion like tomorrow." Madame did not know herself why she was making this long preamble; she was not given to speeches. "I think I can say that my anniversary is uncommon. It is unique. Isn't it unique, Hilda?"

"Yes, Madame." Hilda hardly opened her lips. She isn't thinking of me at oll, thought Madame with irritation. She is thinking of herself! "It is a chance for you," said Madame severely. "An enormous chance. A girl of only seventeen . . . I ask you?"

But she isn't seventeen, thought Madame irritably. She is as old as the hills. I hate hills, thought Madame. Baffling and steep. Spoiling the view. No good is going to come out of this, said Madame.

She remembered when she had first discussed the ballet with Hilda, how obstinate she had been and how she, Madame, had then a feeling of acting against her better judgment. I ought to have waited, talked to her, encouraged her to write something else, been *sympathetic,* thought Madame, but she could not tell, even now, how she could have brought herself to be sympathetic to Hilda. "Either you are, or you are not," said Madame. "It is no good disguising it, not?"

"Well, what is this ballet?" she had said then. "Tell it to me. Tell it."

"It is called *Lyre with Seven Strings*."

"It isn't Greek, or Chinese, or Irish?" asked Madame with suspicion.

Hilda said distantly that it had no country. "There is Man. Universal Man. You could call him Adam . . . or John Smith."

"Ah! One of those!" said Madame. "Ah well! Well, go on."

Hilda explained that she had taken the idea from a novel of George Sand. She thought that George Sand had taken the idea from . . . "But why does that matter?" interrupted Madame. "It doesn't matter where you got it from, it matters what it is. Well, what is it? Go on."

Man's aspiration was like the lyre, Hilda explained seriously, and he could attain to harmony only after he had learnt to play on all the seven strings.

"Nonsense!" said Madame. "You can have harmony with two or three or four."

"Not full harmony," said Hilda. In the ballet, the strings were dancers who embodied their qualities. "Man dances with each in turn," said Hilda. "The strings are Peace, War, Sorrow, Joy, Evocation, Love, and God."

"You can't have God in a ballet," said Madame.

Hilda explained that when it came to God, Man danced by himself, alone.

"Then how does one know it is God?"

It was certainly hard to tell it to Madame. Hilda found herself wishing that she had chosen something more simple.

"I have the synopsis here, and my notes," she said, and, in spite of herself, her hurt dignity showed in her voice. Madame looked up. She knew how much work and earnestness Hilda had put into this ballet and she curbed her tongue. "Let me look at them," she said, and she gave Hilda the recognition of looking at them carefully. "It is an idea," she said slowly. "Well, I should like to see some of it, one or two of the dances. . . ."

Hilda's lids flew up and her eyes shone with faith and hope. "Would you?" she said. Now her voice is like an ordinary young girl's, thought Madame. She looked at Hilda and she had a sudden and surprising pang of jealousy. Hilda's green eyes were incandescently pure. That is because she is young . . . and untouched, said Madame. My eyes are far more beautiful than hers, even now, said Madame, but they can never look like that because I am old and she is young. . . . Suddenly she hated Hilda for being young.

"What is your music?" she said, and she added sarcastically, "Scriabin?"

Hilda said with dignity that it was not Scriabin, it was Zedek.

"I never heard of him."

A smile flickered at the corners of Hilda's mouth. "He is a contemporary Czech composer," she said gently, but Madame had seen the smile and she did not forgive her.

"Mr. Felix helped you with that."

"No," said Hilda truthfully. Mr. Felix had refused to help her. "If you want to find out music you must find it out for yourself. That will teach you!" said Mr. Felix, though whether he meant it as a threat or a fact Hilda did not know. "If you want to do these ballets, do them by yourself," said Mr. Felix to her later. "Don't let anyone else lay a finger on them."

"I only want advice."

"Advice is the worst kind of help. It is pernicious, and if you don't know what that means," said Mr. Felix, "you should go and look it up in the dictionary." Hilda looked it up and was surprised to find how strong and final its meaning was.

"Once . . . I showed him some music . . ." She hesitated and said, "It was recorded. I found it and showed it to him. He said he thought it should make a good ballet. That was a year ago but I couldn't forget it, and . . ."

"Is there anyone here who knows this? Who has danced any of it?" interrupted Madame. She had not been listening.

"John and Alma know it, and Francis, and Liuba. They are here. I can fetch them in a minute. They will come. I have the records."

It was all arranged promptly. It is surprising how obliging they are when it is something they want, thought Madame.

She did not like the theme. If life were to be a lyre, she thought, its strings, life's attributes, it was her experience that you did not learn to play them one by one as you were ready, but . . . higgledy-piggledy, thought Madame, willy-nilly. . . . Hilda knew better. The ballet was perfectly clear, unusually well arranged. Madame immediately liked the dance of "Peace," with Adam, or John Smith; in Hilda's "peace," the usual roles were reversed and it was the female partner who was the background for the male, who kept the sustaining part; and what surprised Madame was the restraint of its whole conception . . . that is unusual in the work of so young a girl. . . . She did not like "Sorrow," nor "War"; "they are gloomy, heavy." Hilda said she thought they should be gloomy and heavy; after all, she pointed out, they were Sorrow and War. "They are overdone," said Madame. "Sometimes you are too strong, in everything. Why, when you have that restraint? Sometimes you overdance." Hilda did not understand that herself. "It's because you are young," said Madame.

Neither did Madame like "Love." "It is dull and flat and staid," she said. "You had it coming. It was good to begin with, but it should have gone quicker, quicker, quicker, more fast, and then he should have swept her up and taken her away. Not go back to the firrst rhythm like that."

"But that . . . that you are thinking of," said Hilda, "is only one aspect of love. I want to show it all."

"My dearr child! Who are you?" said Madame, and she returned to the argument. "It gets tedious. You should *not* go back to the first theme like that."

"The music does."

"But love doesn't."

"The music does."

"Then change the music."

Hilda answered with austerity that she did not think *she* should change the music.

"But you *should*," said Madame. "You should change it and chop it and twist it and do anything with it rather than spoil your ballet. I olways did," said Madame.

Hilda was superiorly silent. What a little prrig she is, thought Madame, and then "Evocation" made her smile. "I said you had wit, Hilda," she cried. "This is delightful." When Hilda saw that smile she knew that she had succeeded, though, for a long time, it was to be a mystery to Hilda that she, who was so deadly serious about her work—"Yes, deadly," said Madame—should be able to make people smile with scarcely an effort; and still more mysterious why Madame and, later on, other people for whose opinion she had the deepest respect should think that far more clever than her serious work. It would take years for Hilda to discover that it was her serious work.

"You will write a real ballet one day," said Madame when she had seen *Lyre with Seven Strings* through. Hilda did not know whether to be proud or offended.

"But . . . is it good?" she asked. She always remembered Madame's answer.

"Why should it be good?" said Madame. "Think what it takes to make something good, what brrains and knowledge and experience. Who are you? You are oll the same, you young ones. Is it good? You should thank God you can do it at oll."

Hilda still wanted to know if it were good. Now she had to stand before Madame in the office and wait for her to continue this laceration.

"I am sorry I have to tell you this," said Madame. "I blame myself. I don't know where my eyes have been, and my ears, oll my five wits. We must be frank, Hilda, not? This is the truth. I have made a mistake."

"A mistake?" Small white patches showed round Hilda's nostrils, her voice was tight, otherwise she showed no emotion at all.

"We shall have to cut it," said Madame.

Hilda said nothing but Madame could see the breast of her tunic rising tempestuously up and down as she breathed, and she could see a quiver in her throat. But that is only muscles, said Madame scornfully. People should show feeling in their eyes.

"I shall have to cut it," said Madame aloud, "unless . . ."

Hilda's lids flicked up, flicked down. There was a knock on the door and Mr. Felix came in with Lion. Now Hilda felt as if she were facing an inquisition. She did not know which side Mr. Felix was on, if he were on any side; in his brown alpaca coat, with his silky hair brushing his coat collar, he looked a mild old man far removed from this torture, but she felt he would watch gravely to see how she behaved under it. She did not look at Lion but she was acutely aware that he was there.

"I am telling Hilda I am afraid we must cut *Lyre.*"

They all looked at Hilda. She kept her lids down but she knew they must guess she was pressing back tears. Tears would be natural, thought Madame. It would be natural to storm and to cry. It is a disappointment, but you will see. She won't shed a tear. She is sly.

"Cut it? Altogether?" asked Lion, his eyes bright with pity and interest. "All of it?"

Mr. Felix said nothing. He waited.

"Perhaps I need not do that," said Madame slowly. "I have wondered if we couldn't make of it a suite of dances." Hilda's head came up sharply and her eyes opened, looking at Madame with even more astonishment. "A suite of dances," repeated Madame. "We could call them *Meditations* or something like that. *Meditations on the Qualities*, not? We should keep four, I think. 'Peace,' 'Joy,' 'Evocation,' and 'Love' . . . 'Love' with my alterations, of course, yes?"

"No," said Hilda.

There was silence.

"Do you say 'No' to me, Hilda?"

Hilda's eyes were level with Madame's. Now Madame could not have said she looked sly. She looked desperate and defiant. "It won't be my ballet," said Hilda.

"It will be a good deal better than your ballet."

"It will be founded on yours. In fact it will be all yours," said Lion.

Hilda only said again, "It won't be my ballet."

"It will be the best part, with the worst cut away," said Lion. "The dances Madame has chosen *are* the best, and they won't be spoilt by the faults of the others."

Hilda looked past him to Madame. "Isn't it better to have your own faults?" asked Hilda, and Madame knew she was right.

Cut it. Throw it out. Be cruel. Execrate it, misjudge it, but don't persuade her to change it against her will, said something in Madame. . . . As far as it is in her power she has made it complete. If she has no more power that is a pity, but it is none the less complete. Then take it or leave it, said Madame silently to herself. But . . . surely she must be guided, said a second part of Madame. Why should she produce a faulty thing on my stage? . . . Again she contradicted that with the feeling that it would be better to have it faulty than interfere. . . . But I should be ashamed for them to see it, said Madame. What does that matter? her first part said steadily, refusing to be moved. What does that matter? They are lucky to see it at all, if it is interesting. It is the thing she is trying to do that matters, not they . . . the audience. But you can't have ballet without an audience, cried Madame. If I put on ballets like this I should soon have no audience at oll. One must be expedient. . . . She caught herself up. That was a word she had blamed other people for using and said she should never consent to use herself. The word seemed to hang on the air and its after-taste was sour. . . . Words don't have tastes, said Madame, but she felt its sourness and, beginning to be angry, she tapped her foot impatiently and said, "Well, Hilda?"

Hilda could not answer.

Why am I doing this? Madame asked herself. To make up my programme, not because I sincerely believe that, in this form, her ballet will be good. It is good olready, as good as ever it will be; that is, it has the elements of being good. . . . She paused, puzzled herself to know what to say next.

"I like it better like this," said Lion. "I think it sounds terribly attractive."

"Terribly is surely the wrong word," murmured Mr. Felix.

"The dresses are made and the set," said Lion, "and, after all, Hilda, Madame has paid for them. I think you should think of that."

"I do think of it," said Hilda desperately.

"And think of all the work, Mr. Felix's, the company's, mine, and Madame's. Above all, hers. You are under an obligation to Madame Holbein, Hilda."

"She is under no obligation," said Madame coldly. "It's not her fault that I made a mistake."

"Hilda," said Lion with his extraordinary sweetness, "Madame must know better than you."

"Yes. I know, but . . ." said Hilda, trying to find words to defend herself.

"Then . . . ?"

"She doesn't know my ballet as I do. She . . . she can't." It was torn out of her and she knew it sounded young and crude. She turned from them in despair. They were all arraigned against her. She had no choice. Then she looked up and saw Mr. Felix watching her as if he thought she had a choice.

If one looks at the faces of most young girls, they have two halves to their faces; one shows what they are now, the other what they will become. Hilda had only one face and it was set, implacable as a little stone, on what she intended to do.

Long ago Madame could have placed her in one of the ballet companies. She could have gone to the Metropolitan last year. Madame's own Michel Boré on his tour from America had seen her and wanted to take her back with him but she would not go. "What more do you want?" Madame had asked her then.

"That isn't what I want," Hilda had answered and she had said, as if she were talking to herself, "I want more than that."

At Holbein's she was labelled conceited and yet, if one came to examine it, it was a queer conceit that kept her working month after month as a class pupil and nothing more. "Why don't you leave, Hilda?" Lion had urged her.

"I'm not ready to leave."

"But it's ridiculous. You need stage experience, no matter what you want to do."

Hilda shook her head. "Not that stage experience," she said, and, as she looked past him, he thought she saw further than he did. "Where else should I find a possible stage?" asked Hilda.

"Possible?" asked Lion puzzled.

"Possible for me," said Hilda.

Now Hilda was attracted from her path. Lion had drawn her aside and was talking to her, earnestly and quietly, his head bent down close to hers. Madame watched them.

"A lion should have a mane," said Mr. Felix, and Madame saw that Lion's head with its shorn black curls was more like a ram than a lion. A sheep! thought Madame, and caught the thought back, and looked daggers at Mr. Felix.

As Hilda looked up at Lion, Madame saw colour steal slowly up her cheeks. She couldn't blush outright, said Madame. No. She isn't honest enough for that, but she blushes oll the same. It gave Madame a feeling of triumph that Hilda, the superior Hilda, was like any other girl. The same, just the same, said Madame. She was spiteful because she was jealous. "Go and talk it over with Lion," said Madame aloud. "You have a few minutes before rehearsal. Talk it over with Lion," said Madame treacherously.

As she said it, she knew that she knew of a better way; that there was something altogether different, adult and inspired, that she could have said to Hilda to help her, and that no one else but she, Madame, could say . . . because no one else has the knowledge, said Madame; but this second, wilful, jealous, petty part in her would not let it be said. And so, I throw Hilda to the lions, she thought, but she did not laugh. She saw Mr. Felix give her a stern glance. Felix is olways poking his nose in my pie, she thought crossly, and was all the crosser when she remembered that it was she who had asked him to be there. Together they watched while Lion, his hand under Hilda's elbow, took her, still talking earnestly, to the door. Hilda went with him as if mesmerized. And who shall blame her? said Madame with a pang in her heart. Isn't he oll he should be? Big, attractive, gay and sweet and kind? But, she thought involuntarily, he should be more than that. . . . What made her think it? She did not know. Then Hilda, who was at the door, released herself brusquely and turned round and came back to Madame.

Ah, she is like me! thought Madame. At the eleventh minute she saves herself, not? . . . She saw it with admiration but with irritation as well.

Hilda had lost her tinge of colour. She was as pale as ever and her eyes were wide and distraught with unhappiness. "I can't agree," said Hilda. "Madame. I'm sorry, but I can't. I know what you all think and I expect you are right, but . . . you must have it as it is, or not at all."

She stood, her eyes on Madame beseeching her to understand.

"You are arrogant and conceited," said Madame, as she would have killed a fly. "Then . . . not at oll." And she walked out of the office.

Outside the door she almost stepped on a small girl who, instead of backing away, stayed where she was.

"What do you want, Lollie? Who told you to come upstairs? What are you doing up here in my prrivate hall?"

"You sent for me," said Lollie calmly.

She had been in the hall for quite a long time, but she did not mind that. The floor of the hall was in black-and-white marble squares, cool and polished. Lollie remembered the first time she had seen them. "Marble? Is it *real* marble?" she had asked, and tiptoed across it as if her tread might crack it. She liked to be alone with its opulence. Lollie had a capacity for reverence, but not even Madame could have called her a chameleon. For instance, she reverenced Madame but, as Madame had already noticed, she remained firm.

"*Lollie!*" cried Madame when she had first come. "No one is called Lollie."

"I am."

"But it isn't a name."

"It is my name."

It was not her name. She did not intend to tell Madame her name, because she very justly thought that if Madame knew it, she would approve of it and use it. Lollie's name was Ingeborg. It would be years before she would come to appreciate it.

"Now how does Miss Porteus, with her red eyes and her thin bent shoulders and her sniffles and her arthritis, come to have a niece like that?" asked Madame.

"Backgrounds don't matter here." Madame said that often, but it was not true, because every one of the dancers carried something of this background with him like a halo or an aura. Lollie was a refreshing child with an antiquated staid little turn of speech that made people smile though she said nothing that was funny; she had what Madame called a two-edged smile, that sprang joyfully to her eyes while it was woe-begone and curiously touching on her lips. "With a smile like that she is made," said Rebecca. "Even without her dancing." She had a fine slender small physique with the promise of what Madame said might be classical beauty, and she was remarkably gifted, but she showed very clearly the poverty of her upbringing and background, not only in food and clothes and language and knowledge but in ideas.

"Your horizon is no bigger than this saucer," Madame told her once, but Lollie did not even know, then, what a horizon was. Holbein's was making it larger. "I have been moved up in school," she told Madame. "I am learning music now as you said." It was Madame who was paying for the lessons. "And I know the names of the stars."

"What stars? What sort of stars?" asked Madame suspiciously.

"Aldebaran and Sirius and those."

"Six months ago you would have meant film stars."

Madame remembered coming on Lollie standing ignominiously outside the door of Rebecca's class. "She told me to be the wind in a field of corn," said Lollie. "How could I be? I have never seen a field of corn."

So much of my dancing, said Madame, came out of my childhood. . . . Her childhood had been spent in her grandmother's house in the country, or travelling with Jan. . . . At Lollie's age . . . thought Madame, and sighed. However gifted she might be, no one could make that difference up in Lollie.

For everyone there is someone for whom, with whom, they cannot do wrong. Madame was fallible, but she was infallible for Lollie, as she had been for Lion. From the beginning, as she had with him, Madame taught Lollie far more than dancing. She allowed Lollie to talk to her as she allowed none of the others. "They do not need it," said Madame, "they have so much at home, but these lost children need me." They were, to her, lost in the immensity of the world they had to fight and they seemed to her to have no strength to borrow from but hers. She let Lollie be more intimate than the little Lion had been, because, in some curious way, Lollie seemed to her a reflection of herself.

Once Lollie had come to class with dirty finger-nails and Madame had execrated her. Lollie had borne it in silence but afterwards she told Madame that she did not see what finger-nails had to do with dancing. "Oll of you, every little bit, is to do with dancing," Madame had answered and she told Lollie how, long ago, Jan had said that to her.

"What did you say?" asked Lollie.

"I said it was going too far, and Jan said, 'Not nearly far enough. For you, everything you see and hear and touch and taste and smell is to do with dancing, *if* you are a dancer.'"

"If you are a dancer," repeated Lollie thoughtfully. She was not at all sure, at times, that she could be one. It was very arduous. It was only what Auntie called her obstinacy, an obstinate belief in her own dancing, that made her go steadily on.

Madame knew that, but even she did not know what a struggle it was.

Once Lollie had seen Miss Ilse cutting up a dried-looking fruit for Madame; when it was opened on the plate it showed myriads of deep red seeds. "What is it?" asked Lollie.

"A pomegranate. Those are its seeds."

"They look like blood."

"Yes. They call the Martyrs pomegranate seeds," said Miss Ilse absently. "The seed of the blood of the Church."

"What are martyrs?"

"You are a martyr if you believe and suffer for your faith. You can die for it."

"Oh, Saints!"

"Not only Saints. Everyone who believes must prepare to be a martyr more or less," said Madame, who had come in. "You believe you are going to be a dancer. Already you have to do for that, things that other children don't do; give up your playtime, work when you are tired. But you believe you will be a dancer and you must suffer for it."

Miss Ilse arranged the pieces of pomégranate on a Dresden plate and Madame carried them away.

Lollie was a martyr. A new child did not have an easy time among the other children at Holbein's. "They are fiends to one another. Perrfect little fiends," said Madame. She had no myopia about children; because they were small, she did not make excuses for them either as people or dancers; and as dancers, she did not give them any quarter though she knew that, like themselves, their scope was small.

With few exceptions, the orbit of a dancer moves entirely round himself, and the smaller he is, the lower down the scale, the more petty that orbit is. Each pupil in the Beginners' Class at Holbein's, Madame's "eggs" as she called them, "because we don't know what they will hatch into," looked on each new other one as a personal threat. Lollie was new and small but already she had ousted Zoë, the big showy child who was the leader of the class, and she had ousted Archie, who, up till then, had showed the greatest promise. Madame had given no sign of this but the class knew it to the last hair on their little bodies. The only person who did not know it was Lollie. The more Madame valued a pupil, the more she execrated him or her, but Lollie was not to know this, and she was bewildered by the criticisms that were poured on her head when she had obviously done the best *enchaînement* and listened to every word that Madame said.

Now she wondered miserably why she was sent for; though she appeared calm, Lollie's calmness was often the calmness of acceptance. It was no surprise to Lollie to be scolded any more than it was a surprise to be cold or tired or hungry. She had heard the angry voices in the office. It's a funny time to scold, thought Lollie, just before the big rehearsal . . . but she knew what she had done. It's the shoes, thought Lollie, and she burned wearily with guilt and shame.

Shoes were Auntie's and Lollie's nightmare. The shops for ballet shoes were in Soho or far away down the Charing Cross Road, and it was necessary to be there early and to queue for them and that meant being late for school. Lollie needed blocked shoes now, and unblocked shoes and heeled shoes for character dancing, and they were eight-and-six a pair. No matter how carefully she looked after them, they soon became dirty and worn.

"You must practise, Lollie. While you wait for your aunt and the rooms are empty, you must practise." Yes, but if she practised her shoes wore out. The others had mothers and fathers to buy their shoes for them, and so, when they had gone home, Lollie took their shoes out of their pigeon-holes and wore them to practise in and save her own.

"Lollie." Lollie looked up sharply, her eyes stretched with fear, her brow stretched too as if the bows of her turned-up plaits were tied too tightly.

"Why do you look so frightened?" asked Madame. "You look at me with eyes like a hare." Then she softened. Lollie, with her huge scared eyes, as expressive as Madame's own, and her hair strained back and plaited and turned up in bows like ears each side of her face, looked, not like a hare, but a very young caught leveret. "There is nothing to be frightened of," said Madame irritably. She sat down on a chest in the hall. "Lollie," she said, "will you grow up conceited and more clever than your olders? Yes, you will. You are sure to, and use me like a . . . like a cat's paw," said Madame.

"Pardon?" said Lollie politely, and looked so frightened that Madame had to laugh. She laughed unwillingly. There. You see, she thought. I can't even be angry in peace. She remembered now why she had sent for Lollie.

"You have never danced on the stage, have you, Lollie?"

"Yes, I have," said Lollie. (Then it was not the shoes.) "I have danced at the Coliseum, in matinees, twice. I was the Seed Pearl in the *Under-the-Water* ballet, and next time I was a Half Pint of Milk. I wore white for both."

"I see," said Madame. "Did you like it?"

"No," said Lollie. "That is one of my troubles. I get stage fright."

"Every dancer, that is worrth anything, always gets stage fright."

"Doesn't she . . . *ever* get over it?" asked Lollie faintly.

"Never. The greater she is, probably the more she is nervous and strung up, because more is expected of her. She will be in a state of nerves, each time she waits to dance."

"*Each* time?"

"Each time," said Madame firmly.

"Well, I'm too young to get a licence," said Lollie comfortably. "My cousin was in *Puss in Boots* at Croydon last Christmas."

"You have no need to dance in Pantomime," said Madame.

"Three pounds a week," said Lollie, and sighed.

"You have other things to do," said Madame. "Now listen to me. You have worked well this year and I am pleased with you, though I should be more pleased," said Madame with a sudden riposte, "if I had not had to see that *cabriole* you showed me this morning, or what you called a *cabriole*, from the *Arabesque: jeté, glissé, pas de chat*, and off with the *cabriole*. Remember?" Lollie winced and hung her head. She remembered.

"But still, I am pleased with you and I have decided to give you a chance. It will please your auntie, not? It happens that a friend of mine, Mr. Edmund White, of Broadwood Studios, is looking for a child dancer, not for very much, you understand, but to appear and dance in his new film. It is the life of a ballerina, or what they think is the life of a ballerina," said Madame severely. "He has asked me to find him such a child and I have thought of you."

"Me!" cried Lollie aghast.

"Say 'I,' not 'me,' Lollie."

"I? I couldn't do that," said Lollie decidedly.

"You will have to pass a test, of course." Madame went on as if she had not heard her. "A screen test, but first Mr. White will give you an audition. He is coming here, to the theatre at four o'clock tomorrow . . ."

"But, Madame . . ."

"Lollie!" Madame fixed her with a stern eye and Lollie quailed.

"What . . . what shall I dance?" she said weakly.

Madame thought. "The variation I taught you in class. You know that well."

"But . . . it's not even a dance," said Lollie. "Couldn't I do my Polish dance and wear my Polish dress?" The Polish dance was difficult but Lollie mysteriously knew it would be easier to dance at an audition than the variation. Madame took that hope from her.

"No. In a character dance you will be that character, that is if you dance it as you should, which you don't olways, Lollie. He will want to see you as you are. You will dance the variation."

The prelude that accompanied the variation immediately began in Lollie's head, but instead of the steps that went to it she found she was thinking of those she had been wrong in that morning! From the *Arabesque: jeté, glissé, pas de chat*, then off with the *cabriole*. But that isn't it at all, thought Lollie, and she looked at Madame in despair. "I shall never do it," said Lollie.

"You must."

"But . . . I am no good at auditions," said Lollie with conviction.

"You have been prroperly taught. You have only to keep your head," said Madame unsympathetically.

"But . . ."

"Then you would like me to give it to Zoë? Or perhaps to little Miette?"

Lollie flushed. She had suffered from Zoë, and Miette was the newest and youngest and latest joined.

"You cannot have it every way, Lollie. You must choose. Perhaps you would rather be a dressmaker, say, like your aunt?" Then suddenly Madame softened. "Auditions are nothing to be afraid of, any more than a bridge," she said. "They are a means of travelling, that is oll. If you get this parrt, if you don't get it, makes no difference to your dancing, it doesn't matter, but what *does* matter," said Madame severely, "is if you dance well."

"Yes, Madame."

"It is like photographs. Do I mind being photographed, I ask you? It is tiresome, yes, but it is my duty and you must learn what your duty is. The imporrtant thing is . . . Is the pose natural and beautiful as it should be in the dance? I olways photograph perrfectly," said Madame.

"Yes, Madame," said Lollie.

"*Or* an examination. What is an examination? A little stick to measure your technique. Naturally you pass them, coming from here, but they don't mean that you can dance. Ah, dearr no!" said Madame, getting up from the chest. "Now don't let me waste my breath on air, Lollie."

"No, Madame."

*Chassée, arabesque, assemblée* over, *jeté croisée*, repeat, thought Lollie. That was it, but then she was back again: From the *Arabesque*: *jeté, glissé, pas de chat*, off with the *cabriole*. What shall I do if I go off with the *cabriole* in the middle? thought Lollie. And what shall I wear? . . . Her tutu was too short, there was no time for Auntie to make her a new one, and her tunics were darned and old. Lollie had heard enough about auditions to know that one should look attractive, as attractive as one could, but tomorrow was the Opening and no one, Lollie knew very certainly, would have a minute to spare for her. The-Opening-old-darned-tunic-*pas-de-chat-cabriole*, thought Lollie, in the snare.

"Madame . . ."

"What *is* it, Lollie?"

Lollie had not the courage to say what it was; she said instead, "Madame, will . . . you be there?"

Madame paused, looked down at her. "Do you want me to be there?" Lollie nodded. She could not speak, but at that moment, however sharp Madame might be afterwards, she wanted Madame to be there.

"Your teacher can't hold your hand for ever," said Madame, "but I shall be there, I promise you. Now don't look so frightened. A promise is a promise, not? . . .

"And now where is everyone?" cried Madame. "We are late. Everyone is late. Felix. Lion. Is no one here? Where are oll the children? And Rebecca? And Miss Parkes. Ilse? You are never here when I want you. Are we to stand about oll evening? There you are, Miss Parkes. Here I have been standing for hours and hours . . . Is my time nothing? Ah, in the theatre? Why didn't you say so before? Go and tell them I am coming. We must go thrrough everything, not run through, but completely. What hours I wait and no one is ready for me yet!"

Lollie was left standing in the hall.

Madame had to have an audition before she passed into the Imperial School, thought Lollie. She had often heard her tell of that. "So many judges," said Madame, "the management, the teachers, past and present dancers, some famous names, famous even to me, that ignorrant little girl. There were more than a hundred candidates and they oll seemed to me so beautiful and strrong and prrettily dressed, and I had only a small old pale-blue dress that Jan had borrowed for me; we were very poor then, very poor. What chance had I?" said Madame dramatically, "a small pale girl among so many? How wise and clever those judges must have been to see such prromise in her."

Will they see mine in me? asked Lollie bitterly. Me in my old white tunic. She decided they would not and stood, frowning at the marble squares to think what she should do. Madame ought to have known, thought Lollie.

Perhaps Madame was right to overlook the difficulties. Difficulties can be surmounted and they are no excuse.

"Well, you have lost an opportunity," said Lion.

"I know," said Hilda in a tense, proud little voice, and turned her back on him and walked to the window.

When Madame left the office Hilda had walked out after her and blindly past her and Lollie and into the classroom.

"H'm!" said Mr. Felix, and wiped his forehead on his handkerchief. Mr. Felix's handkerchiefs were like himself, thin, old, yellowed, but of a good quality, but Lion did not look at it but at Mr. Felix. Mr. Felix looked as if for once he really cared, and he looked satisfied.

"What a little fool!" said Lion.

"Yes. You can't please God and Mammon," said Mr. Felix politely.

Lion glared at him, hesitated, and went out after Hilda.

He was genuinely astonished at Hilda, astonished and distressed, and he genuinely thought that she was wrong, not perhaps about the ballet but to oppose Madame. Lion went with the stream; he believed there was a tide in the affairs of men, and if he saw it, he promptly took it. People like Madame and Hilda stood against it like rocks and he regretted the waves and collisions that resulted. It had not occurred to him that it is the rocks that change the current of the stream.

Hilda had done what he would not have done, what he could not have done perhaps; that did not attract him—it, rather, shocked him—but more and more Hilda herself attracted him. She drew him like a little magnet. His future appeared to be bound up with Caroline, and up to now he had made no objection; he liked Caroline, he depended on her, in a way he had come to love her, but the tawny-haired Hilda with the lidded eyes acted on him in a strange heady and exhilarating way. It was not only Hilda herself; it was Hilda's dancing. There was a quality in it that was not in Caroline's, that he did not think was in his own. He could imagine Caroline off the stage, out of ballet, in a home, married, with children, teaching or writing poetry or keeping a hat shop; Caroline, but not Hilda. Dancing was a necessity to Hilda. The dancer in Lion recognized that and saluted it, and was drawn to her all the more. He did not want this, he even tried not to encourage it, but if she had been poison it would have been the same.

He had fallen into the habit of staying behind when he came to the school and talking over Hilda's ballets with her. At first he had not been particularly interested in the ballets; then, as Hilda talked to him about them and explained them and they danced excerpts, he had become interested. Hilda was dazzled by Lion's notice. She knew nothing of Lion's feelings for her nor of hers for him. As Mr. Felix said, "She doesn't know what she knows." Then, one evening, in the last week, she had unfolded to him her latest secret, a ballet for two dancers, based on the loud uncanny music she had shown Mr. Felix. It had excited Hilda more than any work she had done, and as she read the notes to Lion she was breathless and flushed; flushed for Hilda, which is to say she had colour below her cheekbones and her eyes were wide open . . . as if, thought Lion, trying to attend, her lids had rolled back and left her eyes unaware. . . . Lion suddenly realized he was in danger; eyes, voice, music, the whole idea of the new ballet, were sweeping him away. "Let's try it," said Hilda, but Lion knew that, then, he did not trust himself to dance with her. He was so overcome that he was rude and abrupt. He stopped the gramophone and put down the book. "I'm going now," he said.

It was like a slap in the face to Hilda. She blanched, and he saw her eyes for a moment before the lids came down; they were so mute with hurt that they had lost all power of expression. Lion's heart turned over in a strange way. He saw that he had made things worse. Till then, Hilda had not been conscious of him, as himself, but now she knew by her own hurt how much she cared. Lion tried to defend his panic. "I'm a busy person you know, my dear. I can't be always on call."

Hilda had not forgotten nor forgiven that. She had meant to be quite implacable to Lion after it, but when he had come to her, in her stress in Madame's office, his nearness and the warmth of his presence and the way he had come in for her, even if it were in the end against her, had touched her in spite of herself; she had been proof against him; she had walked past him and taken her own way. She liked to think of that, but now, in the classroom, she was intensely aware of him in the room behind her as she stood by the window.

"Hilda."

No one, and no one ever again, made her name sound as it did when Lion said it.

"Hilda."

Lion came up to the window behind her and took her elbows into his hands as he pressed them against her sides. Her elbows were warm, rounded, but in their softness he could feel the small hard strong bones.

"What strong bones you have," he said.

"I haven't," said Hilda with a sob in her breath.

"Hilda, dear!"

He heard her catch her breath again and felt the tumult of misery sweep up in her. Emotion is catching and Lion began to be in a tumult too. He pressed her closer, back against him. "Your hair smells of . . . what are those flowers that grow on bushes in London gardens? Syringa."

"London syringa smells of soot," said Hilda with a laugh that was a sob.

"Don't cry, my dear. Madame . . ."

"Madame is too great," said Hilda and her voice burnt with resentment. "She has forgotten how one begins. That one *must* begin."

Lion said nothing. He rested his cheek against her hair. It was not like Caroline's hair that was heavy, like silk; it was not as beautiful hair; it was feathery, almost like a child's, and it brushed his cheek and his eyes very lightly. For no reason he found that he was trembling and he drew back quickly. "Hilda," he began reasonably, "couldn't you . . . ?"

She turned and faced him. For her he had always been Lion, dazzling, overpowering, but since the day he had snubbed her and left her she had known he was human, like herself, like anyone . . . less than some people, thought Hilda. She had grown up; she felt old and serious and tired, because to grow much in a short while is very tiring. She saw Lion, his height and his strong shoulders, the pleasing line of his cheek. She saw the foreign olive glow of his skin, and his dark shorn curly hair. She saw all these things objectively, and for the first time she looked at his eyes. His eyes were like an Indian's, a red Indian's, quick and melting and naïve but cold. . . . I am utterly removed from him, she said proudly, but she was not. His arm came round her with urgency and he held her and said, "Hilda, give in. If you wanted to . . ."

"Do you think I don't want to?" she cried, and gave another, more heartbroken sob.

Before he could answer the others came in.

The news had spread like wildfire through the company. Now, Francis, who was War, May, the scholarship girl from Cardiff, who took Sorrow, the little Italian, Lippi, with the extraordinary *élévation*, who had been inappropriately chosen for John Smith, and Alma, and the Teacher from "Evocation," had come in. Love, Jessica Anderson, had been kept by Madame for a sharp scolding on her make-up. Alma, who was not in the first ballet, the Spanish *Cat Among the Pigeons*, wore her dress as Peace. Hilda looked at it mournfully.

"Why should Peace always be in grey?" she had asked. "In peace there is time to see colours. She should have all the colours there are."

"Then she will look like Joseph," said Madame, but the dress, designed by Mathilde Pascal from Hilda's idea, was beautiful in blue and green and violet with narrow floating petunia ribbons.

The dancers gathered round Hilda, talking, pleading, criticizing, arguing, and quarrelling. The voices beat on her ears. She could only stand in the middle of them and say, "I am sorry."

"Madame could force you, you know," said Lippi with ferocity. He was cruelly disappointed.

"She couldn't."

"She could. She could make you pay for the dresses and the cost," said Lippi spitefully. He was feeling spiteful. It was his first big part.

"We worked on it so hard," said the Teacher. "I think you should have a little consideration for us, Hilda."

"You don't think of us at all."

"I think she is quite right," said Francis. "Madame should give all of it or none."

"You only say that because you were cut. It's better this way, Hilda. Really it is."

"Yes, really Hilda. None of us liked 'War.'"

"You are jealous, Michael, because it made 'Evocation' look weak."

" 'Evocation' couldn't look weak. It's the best thing in the ballet. Madame said so."

"Hilda. Darling. Don't, don't, don't let it be cut."

"Everyone said my 'Prologue' make a sensation, and now no sensation!" cried poor Lippi.

"Hilda, *please!*"

"Please, Hilda."

"Please, Hilda."

"No," said Hilda tight-lipped.

"But why?"

"*Why*, Hilda?"

"Why?"

"Tell them why," said Lion treacherously.

Because . . . If I had given in I should have hated myself. Now you hate me, but I can bear that, Hilda might have flung at them and him, but she said nothing, and stood there among them, tears stinging in her eyes and throat.

"Won't you change your mind?"

"Change your mind, Hilda."

"Hilda, dear."

Then Lion put his arm round her shoulders and pressed her to him and said, "Stop bullying her. She can't do what she thinks wrong. Leave her alone. She shall do exactly what she likes."

Hilda, whose face had been as white and hard as if it were carved in stone, flushed again. Her lips and her eyes and her voice quivered as she called out, "Very well. Have it. Have it as *Meditations* or as anything else that you like."

Lippi and the Teacher wrung her hands, Alma kissed her. Francis and May looked at her as if she were a traitor. But they would have been on the other side if their dances had been chosen, thought Hilda wearily. Everyone has their price. Well, mine isn't very high. The stinging in her eyes and throat grew sharper and she burst into tears.

She was aware that Lion had sent the others away with a jerk of his head. She was intensely aware that his arm was round her and that she hated his arm.

"You have done a wise thing, Hilda," said Lion, and he laid his cheek against her hair. He knew it was dangerous, but he wanted to feel that light brushing again. He felt it and his lips travelled over her hair to her cheek and Hilda was filled with such despair that her tears almost choked her. She jerked her cheek away and turned back to the window.

Sounds, voices, music, the sharp clapping of a pair of hands, reached them through the open garden door of the theatre. The rehearsal had begun. They should both have been there but they did not move. It was beginning to be twilight in the garden; shut in by houses, it had an early dusk. It was twilight in the classroom too, dark on the floor, darker in the corners, dark, broken by light, in the reflections in the mirrors; they reflected Hilda and Lion and glimpses of Hilda and Lion: their hands and faces made moving patches against their dark practice clothes, and the long line of Hilda's legs and feet showed in her pink tights.

"You can't go in to rehearsal like that," said Lion. "Listen, they are playing the *pas de deux*, Liuba's first dance with John. It's such a calm little dance that it will calm you. Come and dance it with me."

"Dance it with me." He could not, at that moment, have said anything better to Hilda. She answered, "No," but, "Come," said Lion, and took her hand and led her into the middle of the floor, and, in the twilight, to the music coming from the theatre, they danced.

Lion would have said before that Hilda was not tall enough for him; now she filled what he could only feel was a womanly place beside him; she seemed exactly the right height. She danced with him, and he took her strong responsive little body in his hands, and could feel her taut against him; he could feel her muscles harden and change under his hand as he held her and supported her and held her against him, swung her, lifted her, and put her down, and held her again, below him, her back arched so that he looked down on the swelling of her breast, her throat, and her face bent back to look up at him. He saw, with a tinge of amusement, what he had not noticed before, that though her nose and brows and chin were all severely straight, her eyes were tilted . . . She is not such a little nun, thought Lion, and then he was not amused. Hilda's eyes had been closed with tears, but now, as they looked backwards up at him, they were wide open and warm and bright. Lion held her more tightly still.

Hilda was shaken out of herself by emotion. She had been angry with Lion because she was disappointed in him; then why was she so helpless and pliant that she let Lion do with her as he wished? She did not know. She had not seen this Hilda in herself before. To dance with Lion was to forget him, all except the fact that he was Lion, the superb young man. The dance between the Eldest Pupil and Interloper was tender as well as calm. "I have never known you dance like this, Hilda," said Lion.

"Haven't you?" said Hilda demurely. They were both breathing a little faster than usual. Then he loosed her and said, "This is a boy's dance. It's too young for me. Hilda, what was that ballet you started to show me last week?"

Hilda flushed.

"You hadn't time to see it," she said crisply.

"Yes. I know, but . . . You wouldn't understand. I remember it. Let's try it now."

Hilda went to the gramophone and took two records off the shelf. She had no need to look for them. They had been there for months. She put the first of them on the turn-table and switched on the gramophone, and released the catch and set the needle. The music swelled out into the room. It began gently. "That is my *adage*," said Hilda. Then it rose. It was not polite music, it was raucous and savage sweeping through the room.

"Yes, that is the one I mean," said Lion.

"Watch," said Hilda. "This is your part." She had begun on the rush of music, where it grew louder. Lion watched. They switched back the gramophone and he went through it again, Hilda beside him. Then they started again, Hilda in the solo *adage* with which the ballet opened. Though she should have been unconscious of him, Hilda was very conscious, but when the opening theme ended and he came, in the savage overbearing rush that she had worked out but never seen, she shrank back in real fear and surprise and cried out, "Lion. No!"

"Why? Why, what is the matter?" Lion was angry at being stopped, angrier than he knew. "Why did you stop me? Isn't that right?"

"Yes . . . only . . ."

"Isn't that what you meant?" said Lion, more angry.

"Yes, but . . ."

"But what? What?"

"It's too . . . strong," said Hilda faintly.

"It can't be," said Lion. "It has to be strong. Begin again," he ordered.

She began and this time, though again she had the giddy feeling of being violently overthrown, borne backwards and mastered, she danced with him. "I don't envy her. I shouldn't like to dance that," said Alma later, watching her. "Nor should I," said Rayevskaya, and a great many of the girls in the company agreed with her. "It's too queer," said Alma, and Liuba Rayevskaya, her eyes solemn and round, said what they many of them felt, "I think it's shocking." As Hilda danced, more and more her power came up to match Lion until she was dancing so much with him that she was almost . . . within him, thought Hilda. It's only a dance, she thought giddily. It's only a dance. . . . Her hands clung, she felt his thigh lift her, force her, his breath came on her cheek and his head bent over hers. She gave a little gasp. His eyes were shut.

"And *what* is the meaning of this *deafening noise?*" asked Madame's voice in the doorway.

## 3

The rehearsal was not going well.

Madame had not come to it in a good mood. The cause of her mood, she thought, was Hilda, but was it Hilda's behaviour to her, or hers to Hilda? Madame covered that question quickly in her mind. It was Hilda.

"Isn't it sufficient, ab-so-lute-ly sufficient, that she should have been allowed to prroduce her little ballet on an occasion like tomorrow without dictating to me? A double anniversary! The reopening of the theatre and my jubilee, only I don't wish to say jubilee, it sounds like the kitchen, not? But, fifty years! Fifty years and a girl of seventeen thinks she can dictate, I ask you?" She said this to Rebecca and Miss Parkes, who neither of them, in any case, would have dared to contradict her.

Madame knew it did not matter if Hilda were young or old, old as the hills. Olways those hills, said Madame. She was also beginning to understand what Mr. Felix meant when he called Hilda an Egyptian. They are old too, thought Madame. An uncomfortable people, stiff and angular, refusing to crumble into dust like others, having themselves preserved for ever, building uncomfortable monumental sharp-edged things like pyramids and having themselves drawn with a one-eyed profile. Yes, single-eyed, said Madame, and for a moment she was arrested. If we could oll be that, and she sighed, but a moment later she said, irritated, I don't like Egyptians. Hilda will have to grow out of it, of being so marked. A dancer should have no country.

*The moon is my country.* Who had said that? She was beginning to be tired, or she would not have such thoughts. I am inconsequential, not? but not as bad as that. *The moon is my country.* Who said it? No one, said Madame, but she knew it was Pierrot. . . . Well, Pierrot is the no one in us oll, olways yearning. "But I don't want the moon," said Madame aloud. "I want the earth and I get what I want because I don't expect something for nothing. I expect something for something," said Madame severely. "Hilda must learn that too."

Miss Parkes and Rebecca, who had looked up in surprise, politely concurred.

Something else was running in her head. It was a sentence and nothing to do with Hilda or the performance, an echo coming from far away. Why should she hear it now? It was a small sentence, utterly detached from anything around her, with no bearing or significance that she could see. It floated detached into her head and said itself over and over again: *Listen, Niura, that is a nightingale.* No one has called me Niura for years, thought Madame. Niura. Anechka. *Listen, Niura, that is a nightingale.* She began to be annoyed. "How stupid," she said aloud. "Stupid! Silly! Obstinate!"

Rebecca and Miss Parkes searched the stage to find who was the unlucky person she was speaking of.

On the stage *Cat Among the Pigeons* had begun. Its music came in a warm sparkling torrent, with the infectious clicking rhythm of castanets, to Madame where she stood in the aisle between the stalls. The Convent Pupils in their white skirts fringed with black were circling, stamping their heels between tubs of orange trees in blossom. "Gently! Crrisply!" called Madame. "You sound like horses in a forge. Carrt horses!" said Madame.

The company knew Madame's mood to a hair. Madame was in a temper.

Not temper, temperrament, she would have said, but to the young dancers on the stage, to every man in the orchestra, to Mr. Felix conducting, to the experienced Rebecca, and to Miss Parkes standing by, it was temper, plain spoiled temper.

It affected them differently. Mr. Felix's conducting became more spontaneous as if he suddenly found it more interesting; his gloved hands moved more lightly; he always wore gloves to conduct. "They draw even more attention to your hands," said Miss Ilse. "Let them," said Mr. Felix. "They look macabre." And Madame had interfered and said, "I like them macabre." Miss Parkes felt cold, tired and helpless. She had just handed Madame the sheaf of letters with which Madame beat the rail. She had typed them that day and she could not go home until Madame had signed them . . . if there is anything left of them to sign, thought Miss Parkes hopelessly. Rebecca thought that, if she dared, she would leave. She wished she had left last Christmas or on any number of the times she had wanted to leave before that. The flautist stopped playing and thoughtfully let a trickle of saliva run out of his flute. "We shall have trouble, I think," he said to the oboe. Of the dancers on the stage, some grew resentful and looked sulky, some became stupid from fright, some danced as though the stage boards were coals and burnt their feet, and some, with stronger nerves, became excited.

In her irritability small things, almost irrelevant things, caught Madame's attention. And that is what should *not* be happening, now, thought Madame. Now I should be seeing it *whole!* This was the time for sight and strength. This is when I should pull it oll together! Have it in my hand! It is now, or never! It looked as if it would be never.

The gay insouciant *Cat Among the Pigeons* was the best of Jan Holbein's ballets. Madame had chosen it for this anniversary because of that and, as she had told the company, because sixty years ago she herself had danced, as a small child, the part that Archie was to take tomorrow, the Humming-Bird.

"A *boy* for the Humming-Bird?" asked Miss Ilse. She said it as if it would be sacrilege.

"He will be perrfect," said Madame. He was. With his extreme lightness and quickness and polish, his crest of hair, and brilliant feathered surcoat, Archie made an impression, all the more because he was a boy. Madame felt she could not have borne it had he been another girl. Every movement, every dart and line of those dances, was in her still.

There was a description of a humming-bird that Jan had read to her from a book he had had as a child . . . *the feathers on its wings and tail were black, those on its body and under its wings were of a greenish brown with a fine red cast or gloss which neither silk nor velvet could imitate. It had a small crest on its head, green at the bottom and gilded at the top, which sparkled in the sun like a little star in the middle of its forehead. Its black eyes appeared like two shining points and its bill was black and slender and about the length of a small pin. Its eggs are about the size of a small pea and white as snow and its nest is not larger than half an apricot and of the same shape and lined with cotton.* Madame read it to Archie. Archie was interested but not bewitched.

The Humming-Bird danced against the green of the Spanish-styled Brazilian garden, the black and white of the nuns, the white and black of the Convent Pupils; the music had the sound of bells dropping from the square bell-tower and was warm like the lax, sun-baked little town beyond the walls, broken by the quivering passage of the Humming-Bird. Now, though it should have had all its old enchanting quality, it was not the same. To Madame it seemed that the music dragged, that the bells were flat, the pupils lumpy; she noted that one of them, Gaby, was not wearing the required coral cross, and that John, leaping from the wall, landed with a thud that would have made any portress turn round, but these were little things. Madame's eager and powerful eye saw them all, but never, at this stage, would she do more than note them and speak about them afterwards; now she found herself wanting to stop the rehearsal. It was ostensibly for them, she did not know where the real trouble lay. She could not see it. She could not see it whole.

"No! No! No!" cried Madame, beating the orchestra rail with Miss Parkes' letters. "No! I will not have it like this. John, you are dancing like a mastodon . . . a lorry-load of bricks. Liuba, you were late on that entrance. Late! Felix! You are taking it too slow. Your tempo is oll wrong."

Mr. Felix said courteously that the tempo was the same as yesterday. "Then yesterday it was too slow. Now start again." She looked along the line of Convent Pupils and said, "you are not oll here. Who isn't here?" Several voices replied that it was Hilda.

"So! She thinks she can disobey me as well as . . . as *flout* me," said Madame, and she turned to speak to someone at her side. There was no one there. She looked into the wings. Then, "Where is Lion?" she asked.

After a pause, a voice said that he was not there. There was a longer pause.

Lion had always been by Madame when she needed him as far as it had been compatible with his own ends; they both knew it was as far as was compatible; Madame would not have had it otherwise; it was necessary for Lion to go away, to the Continent, to America, on tour. It was necessary that he should be a great deal at the Metropolitan and with his own wide circle of useful friends, but tonight there was no excuse; he should have been there when she needed him and what, who, on her ground, could be more compatible with Lion than she? A storm of anger began to come up in Madame. If she could have recognized it, she would have seen that it was the same brand of feeling that had made her choose a boy instead of a girl for the Humming-Bird, but this was stronger.

"Go strraight on! Gaby, go into Hilda's place," she said. Her eyes had a dark glitter and her hand, holding the letters, had crumpled them up. "Oh, don't do that!" Miss Parkes could have cried. "I typed them all so carefully," but Madame was oblivious of Miss Parkes. Then her voice shrilled above the orchestra.

"Liuba! You were late on your beat again. Late!"

The gay small-limbed Liuba Rayevskaya stopped almost in mid-air, turned pale and then red, her eyes bright with fear and dismay.

"Liuba Ivanovna Rayevskaya, have you no earrs?" asked Madame in a deadly small voice across the silenced orchestra. "Can—you—not—hear? I ask you those four little tiny little words. Can—you—not—hear? Ah God!" cried Madame. "Why do I have to waste my time with dolts?"

No one answered her. Mr. Felix began Rayevskaya's introduction again. She went back to her place. She was late again. Mr. Felix stopped the orchestra himself. The dancers held their breath. Rayevskaya burst into tears. Madame threw down her letters and walked out of the theatre.

Outside the theatre door she leant against the wall and closed her eyes. She felt dizzy and sick. "Ah no!" she whispered. "This isn't what I came to do. This is . . . fiasco." Madame Holbein did not have fiascos. Well? "Yes, I know," whispered Madame. "It is in my hands." Her hands were not light and gloved like Mr. Felix's, they were firm and experienced, but sometimes they were too hard. Not many days ago she had caught Archie pinching a little girl in class; Archie liked to pinch the little girls on their chests and small plump hams. "Now I shall pinch you, Archie," Madame had said, "and my fingers are harrd, harrd from playing castanets." Hard from castanets perhaps, but also from pulling, jerking, tweaking, tugging, smoothing, moulding. Experienced hands can mould what is malleable almost to what they will, if they know when they have gone too far. She saw the little Rayevskaya's terrified blue eyes. "Ah! No. No!" cried Madame. "She will never dance like that. Ah no!"

To calm herself she began to walk up and down the garden, where it was not yet dark but where the green was made dim by the lit oblongs and squares thrown on the grass and across the bushes by the lighted windows of the theatre. It was cool in the garden after the crowd and heat inside; its coolness fell on her face and neck and hands, but to her it was cold and she huddled her shoulders in her jacket. "Does she sleep in it?" the children sometimes said. Only Lollie could see nothing wrong in Madame's jacket. "It is the colour of pansies," said Lollie. She had seen pansies.

To teach, to direct, is to correct and criticize, to change and widen vision, to lead, but it is also to know when to leave alone . . . and when to capitulate. That is what Madame Holbein found hardest of all to do. Perhaps she had never quite learnt it.

Now she walked up and down the garden, down and up, trying to bring herself to it, to the moment when she must go back into the theatre and start again.

She began to think of the ballet and now, as she had wanted, she began to see it as a whole, to see what was needful and what she must do. She began to work it out, and, as she thought of it, this work that was her own and utterly familiar began to lay its own quiet and steadiness on her; with all its alarums and fireworks, it was steady and it was quiet, and it was patient. "Madame is so impatient," the pupils, everyone, said, but she was infinitely patient. It was sixty years since she had run in the feathered coat of which Archie's was the replica across that far-off stage in Buenos Aires; fifty since she had made her debut as a finished dancer . . . but a dancer is never finished, never . . . and it seemed to Madame now, truthfully, that she had not rested for a day since . . . because even when I was resting I was planning.

Tomorrow Archie would dart, every nerve alive in a tumultuous effort to please, his eyes hot and dry, his cheeks burning, his heart beating like a clapper with excitement. It happened again, in every season, with every performance, with each entrance of each dance. Time passes, that is what they say, but that is what it doesn't do, said Madame. In each one, with each one, Madame lived through it again. It left her exhausted, but that was why she lived.

"How do you do all you do?" they asked her. "How could I not do it?" she might have answered. She was in Archie, as she was in Rayevskaya and John and Lion and Caroline and Bianca and Michel and Lointaine, all the names, down to the little ones, down to the new little Miette, that crumb of a child. Now, this moment, she was Rayevskaya, whom she had frightened out of her sturdy native wits; she was John who stood beside Rayevskaya, and every dancer in the ballet, Archie, Jessica, Michael, May, Gaby, Hilda . . . Hilda! No, she could not bring herself to be Hilda.

All at once Madame became aware that, while the theatre was muted, waiting, music was streaming from the house, where all but the dressing-room windows were dark. It was blatant loud music of a curious impoliteness.

She stood for a moment, listening, startled. Where is Ilse? she thought. She should have been in the office, but the office was dark. She has gone over to see the nuns, thought Madame furiously. She is never here when I want her, never! Madame could still move quickly; she went through the dressing-rooms and up the back staircase like a whirlwind and threw open the classroom door. "And *what* is the meaning of this *deafening noise?*" asked Madame's voice on the threshold.

Madame did not know what it was that Hilda and Lion were dancing; she saw only that they were dancing together, that Lion was dancing with Hilda while she, Madame, was left to take the rehearsal alone. The whole of her changed to spite. How dare you! she could have cried to Hilda. Let me tell you that oll this, this, is nothing at oll that you think. He is Lion. Lion . . . and you are a crude little girl; crrude and arrogant and conceited and vain and sly. No, he is not for you. Hold your tongue. Don't speak to me, cried Madame as Hilda raised her head, but neither of them had said a word.

Hilda had been standing with her back to the door so that the shock of

Madame's voice had been greater. Lion had seen her and stayed his rush. He did not look very disconcerted. He took a long leap towards Madame and finished in front of her. "I have been talking to Hilda. She has come round," he said triumphantly. "Now we can all agree."

For a moment, Madame was more angry than ever. She felt cheated. I can't even be angry in peace, she thought for the second time that evening. Lion had brought her up too sharply. She felt angry with Lion too. He shows his teeth too much when he smiles, she thought. You wouldn't notice that of course, you little fool, she flung silently at Hilda. He has bewitched you . . . but she knew that, if there had been any bewitching, it was Hilda who had bewitched Lion, and she herself had not noticed his teeth before.

"You are pleased?" said Lion. "Say you are pleased."

She had to be pleased, though she still hardly knew how she had come to be in this position. Hilda, she felt, had turned the tables on her. "I am pleased, if it's trrue," she said grudgingly, and glared at Hilda.

Hilda was angry too. Madame, in the doorway, had given her a shock and a nasty little premonition of knowledge that she would rather have been without. She was angry against Madame, angrier with Lion, and most angry with herself.

"Is this true, Hilda?"

"Yes, Madame," said Hilda, and closed her lips; but she knew she had closed them too late. She felt she was a Judas.

"It is very sudden, not?" said Madame looking at her and keeping her eyes away from Lion.

"Yes, Madame."

"You are quite sure?"

"Yes, Madame."

"Then, if you have finished . . . being talked round," said Madame dryly, "we had better go to the theatre."

As they came into the theatre they were greeted by stricken silence. All the heads came round towards them, Madame could even see Archie's crest under John's arm. Did they think I should never come back? thought Madame. I wonder what they would have done, not? It did not occur to her that they might have gone home, nor to them. Her amusement left her as she saw Rayevskaya's round face nearly haggard with unhappiness. The dancers were grouped ready for a new entrance, the portress was in her place, the two nuns in the garden; Mr. Felix, holding his baton, smoothed a wrinkle from the back of his left glove with his one good right-hand finger; Miss Parkes was flattening the mutilated letters on her knee; Rebecca had evidently been parleying with all of them, she looked hot and tired, but now no word was spoken, no one moved.

Madame came down from the garden door to the orchestra rail. "Liuba," she called. "Liubochka, come here."

John pushed the shrinking Rayevskaya forward.

"Now, dearr child!" said Madame, "I want you to go back from the dance of the two pupils. Hilda, go and dress and take your place. Now, Liubochka, dearr child, from where you brreak away towards John: *attitude . . . pirou-*

ettes . . . *entrechat volée* . . . You remember? So! Yes. Lion, I want you to watch this *particularly*. I have never seen you, Liubochka, do as well before. Now! Do you see, Lion?" Rayevskaya, encouraged, let herself dance. "You see, Lion. Give it a moment longer, Liuba, a little more weight, a little more of the head. So! Ex-cel-lent! Go on from there." Rayevskaya, surprised and dazzled, went on, Madame nodded to Mr. Felix, the others slipped into their places, and the rehearsal began again.

Soon Madame saw it was gathering the impetus it needed; it grew smooth and clear. She was sure that Mr. Felix had quickened his pace. Rayevskaya was heartened and relieved by the praise just as Madame had meant her to be, and began to dance with the grace of a little swallow. How artless they are, thought Madame, and sighed. It was almost boring; then she caught sight of Hilda, come back in her fringed skirts to whirl among the others. Not oll of them, thought Madame. Her smile changed to a frown as she looked at Lion watching in the wings. Exactly as she had guessed, he was watching Hilda. "Tchk-tchk!" said Madame, and turned her attention to the rehearsal. I have other things to think of than about the two of them.

She did not think about them, but she had to think persistently of Hilda's ballet. She had a strong impulse, now that she had won her point, to leave it alone. Leave it altogether or cut it, said Madame's instinct. That means cut it, said her brain. And you have nothing to put in its place. *Cat Among the Pigeons, The Noble Life*, that isn't an adequate programme. Then you must keep it and be expedient, said her brain.

That was that word again, the word she had said she would not consent to use. It tasted no better than it had before. But words do *not* have tastes, thought Madame sharply. She did not know what to do, and again she had a quite unpredicted instinct to do nothing at all. "But I can't, now! At the eleventh minute," cried Madame. "I can't do nothing."

"What is there to do now?" asked Lion who had come down to join her. "Isn't it all settled?"

Madame did not answer. She knew that it was not.

With final quietness in its music *Cat Among the Pigeons* was drawing to its end. The last flick of the heels of the Interloper was gone, the last of his friends had gone back over the wall where he belonged; the Nun read aloud, the Pupils were grouped round her with their round frames and long white pieces of embroidery; the sound of bells fell into the garden, the gate was shut; the Humming-Bird made its last quick flight and each Pupil lifted her head and stole a glance at the next, the Nun continued to read aloud, and the curtain came down.

It immediately went up again for Madame to say what she thought to the company. The dancers waited tensely; each one of them knew, or thought he or she knew, what he or she had done or not done, but Madame said nothing. She looked at them as if she did not see them and then roused herself to say, "That will do. Now go and change, oll of you," and to Rayevskaya, "Bravo!" Then she called Hilda and told her to fetch the dancers who had roles in *Lyre*. They came down off the stage and stood round while Madame explained the new dance order to them.

"Each separate. No attempt to link them. Yes, Hilda?"

"Yes, Madame."

Madame felt Mr. Felix looking at her. She looked back at him. Who said Felix's eyes are like forget-me-nots? she thought irritably. They are. They say *forget me not* as if he were reminding . . . She turned her back on him. Mr. Felix came round and spoke to her. "What about the harpist?" he said. "You won't want him now. He played only for John Smith in the 'Prologue' and 'Epilogue,' and now you have no lyre."

"No. No lyre," said Madame.

"Pity. He was a guinea a rehearsal and he has done six," said Mr. Felix. Hilda followed him back to the orchestra and stood there beside the rail. "Mr. Felix . . ."

"You are an appeaser," said Mr. Felix severely.

"It . . . it is of no use standing up to Madame."

"It is of use," said Mr. Felix, making a huge cross from margin to margin across the page with his blue pencil. "One day we shall get to the end of this music *mince*," said Mr. Felix.

Madame made Hilda try the *Meditations* through, standing at her side. They did not speak to one another, nor to Lion who, as Hilda's co-producer, stood beside them too. When it was finished, there was complete silence.

"Well, what do you think of it?" asked Madame. "Well, is it better or isn't it? Haven't you a tongue? Can't you say?"

Hilda could not say because she did not know. She had only one feeling about it and that was the same she had had in the office that they had called unreasonable: It isn't my ballet. She said it aloud, "It isn't my ballet." She spoke quite unlike Hilda, she spoke stupidly, but Madame again knew that she was right. Before, it had at least been a ballet, now it was not anything; it was meaningless. Hilda looked at Madame. Do *you* like it? her look said. It had been on the tip of Madame's tongue to say, "Very well, put it oll back. At least it was interesting before," but, when she caught that look, she read it as a taunt and her resentment against Hilda flared up again. Before she knew what she had done, she had called the dancers off the stage. "It won't do," said Madame. "I can't have it."

"Then . . . what . . ." began Lion.

"I don't know," said Madame, "but not this. Not this."

"Let me call them tomorrow at ten," said Lion. "We can work on it . . ."

"No."

"Then?"

"I don't know."

"But . . . You must decide. If not now, tomorrow. There *is* only tomorrow," said Lion, and he paused. "There *isn't* tomorrow," he said. "Tomorrow is the day."

But that instinct, more powerful now, told Madame that she must not decide, that she should leave it alone. "No, leave it alone," she said aloud.

"But . . . Madame . . ." Lion looked at her as if she were mad.

"Ah, Lion! Don't conflict me so. I beg you. I am getting tired out. We shall go strraight on to *Noble Life*. Hilda, why are you standing there? Go and change. Everrybody go and change. Are we oll to wait for you, not?"

*The Noble Life* had been arranged as a ballet for Madame at the height of her career. It had been her own idea, taken from the tapestries in the Cluny Museum. She had been helped in the choreography by her old teacher, Bellini, and the music had been arranged for it from chorales and songs of sixteenth-century French music. Even Mr. Felix approved of the music. The sets and dresses had been taken from the tapestries. They had been kept with the same thought and care with which she had kept all her wardrobe. "It is perrfectly possible to conserrve everrything, if you are careful enough," said Madame. She did not pause to think how she would have conserved them without Miss Ilse and Zanny. "Set, dresses, music, choreography, are parts of a single vision, of the whole idea," she said. "They should *not* be changed." Now the clothes had been copied, where necessary, or their originals worn; the sets were faded, but Madame's friend, the disreputable Noel Streete, had repainted them. "He has kept them ex-act-ly the same," said Madame. "They tell me Noel is olways drrunk and gone to pieces, but I tell you he can still paint and he has rrespect," said Madame, "and that is more than some ones have." The sets were from the background of the tapestries, fleurettes on a dark-blue ground.

Madame's dress as the Lady was too small for Caroline. That was disappointing. She had given one of her own parts to Archie, but this was far more personal. She felt that it was only to Caroline that she could have given this, relinquished it, because no one but herself had ever danced the Lady. "There were two or three changes for the Nobleman," she told Caroline, "but the Lady was entirely mine, mine. It was the last part I ever danced." Now, the dress would not fit. "But I was wrrong for the Lady," said Madame generously. "She should have been fair and tall as Caroline is, and I was not." Still, she was disappointed.

Why do I mind about this ballet? she asked herself. Was I perhaps a little in love with my partner? But she could not remember who those partners were, and there had been two or three of them as the Nobleman. No, I wasn't in love . . . not with my parrtner, said Madame. Was I ever in love? I suppose I was, but I can't remember it now. *Niura. That is a nightingale.* It was not a nightingale she heard but the sound of birds, sleepy, hazy, distant, in an English garden. He sent me roses, each time I danced the Lady, said Madame slowly, but who was he? She tried to think but she could think only of Lion. He followed me wherever I went . . . but not for long. One season. No more, but I went on dancing, without him and his roses. Madame lifted her chin. *Listen, Niura . . .* I must be very tired, said Madame.

She turned her attention to the stage. "Tell them we shall go strraight on, Rebecca."

"But we can't go straight on," said Rebecca. "Caroline hasn't come."

Madame asked for Lion.

"He is telephoning, Madame."

Madame knew he was telephoning the Metropolitan. In a few minutes he came back and his face was clouded. Lion hated trouble and here was trouble. "More trouble," said the flautist to the oboe.

"She is on her way, Madame. She will be here directly."

Madame looked at him without pretence, steadily. "What was Caroline dancing at the Metropolitan tonight?"

"*Sylphides,* the 'Prelude.'"

"Only *Sylphides?*"

"Yes."

"She should have been here by now," said Madame. She asked quietly, "Who is her understudy?"

"Hilda," said Rebecca.

Madame frowned. "I should like Liuba to try it," said Madame.

"She doesn't know it, Madame."

"Then Alma."

"Alma!" Lion spoke in surprise. "But . . . you gave the understudy to Hilda."

"Did I?" said Madame. "Yes, I did. Why did I?"

"Alma isn't up to it, Madame," said Lion. "Caroline is on her way," he said diplomatically. "Better wait for her."

"No," said Madame proudly.

"Then let Hilda stand in for her until she comes." He was ready to go on in the Nobleman's silks and velvets. She knew he wanted to dance it with Hilda and that made her struggle all the sharper.

"Call Hilda then," she said.

Hilda came off the stage. She was in her dress as the Waiting Maid with the Mirror in the embroidery scene.

"You will dance Caroline's part."

"Yes, Madame."

"You know it?"

"Yes, Madame."

Madame felt that Lion, beside her, was watching and looking. She herself noticed how, once again, Hilda's eyes were illuminated when she was pleased and she noticed, as Lion had done, that the angle at which they were set was provocative. You are not going to have this quite oll your own way, she could have told Lion then, and to her surprise that gave her a perverse feeling of pleasure. As if women were bonded together, thought Madame, even I and Hilda.

"Gaby must go into your part," she told Hilda. "It will be experience for her."

Gaby's face shone equally with Hilda's. Madame was touched by that. "How good they are! How nice it is to please them!" she said to Lion. "They may be simple, young, not hearrd of, but they are better to work with, Lion, than your ballerinas. They are fresh and earrnest. I should like to give them oll a chance with the good parrts . . . oll that deserve it, that is." Her eye had fallen on a group waiting on the stage. "Jessica! And what are you doing?"

"N-nothing Madame."

"Then to do nothing is to go kicking and twisting about like a bag full of bones? You will stand still, *still*, even if it is for hours while I am talking, not? You will have the manners, the rrespect to wait for me."

The curtain came down and went up on the first scene, "The Walk."

With Lion on the stage there came to Madame a complete sense of rest. Lion, as a dancer, had come into his prime; she had no need to trouble about him, she could take her reward and joy in the sureness of his power. I see you, Lion, Madame might have said. There is no need to magnify you because you are big enough. He was big, strong, and virile; he had none of the air of girlishness, the pallor, of John, or even Francis, or so many male dancers. Lion was male, with male zest and male strength. Yes, you are a lord of creation, thought Madame, watching him.

He was singularly beautiful in the Nobleman's clothes. The dark velvet doublet made his skin look darker. Dark as . . . ivy, thought Madame, or velvet itself, like Romeo, but that is wrrong. In this ballet it is the Lady who should be beautiful. She had a pang of sheer jealousy when she thought of Hilda in her place as the Lady. Hilda won't hold a candle to him, she thought with jealous satisfaction, but when Hilda came on, Madame was surprised to see how well she looked and how she matched Lion. "She has her own beauty, a quality of beauty," Madame was surprised into saying to Rebecca.

"I have always thought so," Rebecca answered.

"She isn't tall enough," said Madame quickly, and surprised herself still more by adding, "Neither was I. But no one noticed it," she chuckled. "I had such dignity."

"So has Hilda," said Rebecca, and, for once, she was unconscious of Madame's frown.

It was true. Though Hilda's head was not on a level with Lion's cheek, she had a dignity that made her tall. "Head and shoulders out of his reach," said Madame, "and that is how she should be."

For a moment the figures of Lion and Hilda swam uncertainly in front of her eyes. She was on the stage, under the lights, the pearls of the head-dress touched her cheek and she tossed back the ermine lappets of her sleeves and saw her hand coming small from the frilled cuff of the embroidered under-sleeve. Watching Caroline's interpretation she had forgotten her own. Now Hilda brought it startlingly to life. She . . . she . . . thought Madame, and she cried, "Who taught her this?"

"No one," said Rebecca.

"No one. The little upstart. How dare she," said Madame.

For the second time that day, Lion danced with Hilda. "Take it calmly. Don't press it," he whispered to her. "Let it happen. Don't take pains now. You can do it, easily." He did not know the half of what Hilda could do and, as he danced with her, he began to be puzzled. It was different from Caroline. As they danced, he felt Hilda draw more and more away from him and he wondered more and more why, until he saw that she was in part; he

was not Lion, he was the importunate Nobleman and she the aloof Lady.
That piqued him.

Lion knew, without a shadow of doubt, of his effect on Hilda. He had
had adulation and flattery, sometimes even adoration. He knew that this
young serious green-eyed girl loved him in spite of herself, and because he
was innately gentle it touched him; he was beginning to have a tender
feeling for Hilda that was quite apart from her attraction for him.

Behind them, the pages were walking with long garlands of leaves and
flowers in the maze dance that linked the scenes. Now Lion had to draw
Hilda on one side, his arm, the Nobleman's arm, round her. "Hilda. We
dance well together, don't we?"

"Hush."

The Attendant, Francis, with the falcon on his wrist, was on in the
opening of "Departure for the Hunt." In a minute Lion would have to leave
her after an embrace, a stage embrace, but Hilda thought of it with quickened breath.

"Hilda . . ."

"Hush."

His arm was holding her, a stage arm it was true, but Lion's arm. She
was pressed against him, his cheek was against her cheek. The stage spun
round her, but it still had an axis on which it could spin and she remained
cool and clear in her head.

"Hilda, you are a little iceberg."

"Hush." But then he had to turn her, hold her, with her face towards
him; before she bent backwards and away from him, she smiled at him from
under her lids, and it was a smile of pure happiness.

Madame clapped her hands. The orchestra stopped and there beside
Madame was Caroline.

> "Egypt's might is tumbled down,
> Down a-down the deeps of thought . . ."

said Mr. Felix to Hilda in the pause while they were waiting for Caroline to
dress. If Mr. Felix had ever been sufficiently interested to be cruel, Hilda
thought, he was cruel then. "I was only standing in for Caroline," she said
with dignity.

Caroline was gracious. She had a wait in the wings and Hilda, as her
Maid, was beside her. She could have ignored Hilda, but Caroline was gracious. "You danced that part very well. Very well, did you know?" she said
kindly.

"I know," said Hilda. That was a queer rude answer for a chit of a pupil
to give to a dancer in Caroline's position and it was accompanied by such a
blaze in those green eyes that Caroline's own, always wide open, opened
wider in astonishment.

Once Caroline was on the stage it became obvious that Hilda had no real
beauty at all. "Now they are in their rright places," said Madame, satisfied.
They were where she would have them be, Caroline partnered with Lion.
Lion drew the circle in the air . . . you are beautiful . . . in front of Caro-

line's face. It could not have been more true. "She has everything in that face," Madame had often said, but now, watching her, it seemed she had not . . . everything. Caroline's every movement was pure, classical . . . arristocratic, said Madame, watching her, and surely that was right for the Lady? But . . . was Caroline's Lady a little moon-faced? Did she lack spice after . . . ? Madame caught herself up, but she could not help remembering the precision and lightness of Hilda's attack.

"What do you think, Rebecca?" she said aloud.

Rebecca was watching and Madame saw she was puzzled. "Hilda has come on tremendously in this last year," said Rebecca.

I asked you what you were thinking of *Caroline*, Madame might have said, but she saw that Rebecca's thoughts matched her own.

But . . . even if Caroline is different, that ought not to matter, thought Madame. There is plenty of room for difference. It makes it more interesting, not? She began to see that the trouble lay, not in the difference, but in Caroline herself. She could not bear that. She covered it quickly. "Look at their two faces," began Madame to Rebecca. Caroline's had a pleasing gentle brow, a smooth fair skin, rounded curves of chin and mouth and nose; Hilda's was straight, severe, though she had those tip-tilted eyes. "Hilda can look ugly," said Madame. "Caroline could never by any chance look ugly."

"Hilda can look anything," said Rebecca, and smiled.

"She is a cold calculating little . . ." But Madame knew that Hilda was not. She was relentless, but she could also be reckless and generous; she would give herself away, over and over again. She gave herself away in her parts. "Overdanced them," Madame had said. Caroline never overdanced. "It is interesting that, in Hilda," said Madame, in spite of herself, "that she should be strrong, headstrong often, and yet she has real restrraint in her ballets."

"Hilda can discipline all except her feelings," said Rebecca, and she added, "That may be hard for her. She has more feeling than most."

Madame saw the difference in their eyes; Hilda's lidded into secrecy perhaps but, in moments, wide open, giving her away, transparent with vision; and Caroline's, always open, larger, finer, with heavy silk lashes, but bland, opaque—and Madame knew, and knew she had always known, that they were slightly too close together. "Caroline's grandfather was a wool merchant who made nearly a million pounds," she said suddenly to Rebecca.

But Madame loved Caroline. For few people Madame felt love; for things, very many things, but few people.

"When Caroline was my age," asked the zealous Lollie, "was she a much better dancer than me?"

"Say 'I,' Lollie."

"But was she?"

"You haven't starrted yet," said Madame. "And you will never starrt if you don't worrk at that *battement, battement-en-ronde*, Lollie. In waves, Lollie; that does not mean to zigzag up and down. Conttrol your foot. Conttrol it.

Caroline? Caroline came to me from the very beginning. She had no faults like these, that I can*not* bear, to erradicate."

"And was she *so* good? So very, very good?"

"Ah!" said Madame with a far-away warm look. "There has only been one Caroline."

Now she was seeing flaws. She watched more closely. Caroline had been away on tour with the Metropolitan Company in Holland. One of the leading dancers had been ill and stayed behind and Caroline had been given some of her roles. She had had a small ovation and notice in the press, and when they came back to London she found herself promoted to them. She had been pleased—"Naturrally," said Madame—and better pleased with herself. Now she had come from her larger world to this small outworn one, and an old monotonous family world . . . and she thinks this will pass, thought Madame and she hunched herself in her jacket and watched with gimlet eyes.

In the Holbein Company all members took their turn in the corps de ballet; Rayevskaya, Hilda, John, Francis, and Alma were its principals, but they were subject to that discipline no less than the others. Lion, producing under Madame, obeyed her, but Caroline had position and dignity, was a guest artiste, dancing for Madame by courtesy of the Metropolitan Company, as indeed was Lion; Caroline was now in no way Madame's pupil; as a member of the Metropolitan Company she was taught by their ballet master. Madame's hands were tied. Worse, her tongue was tied. She could do nothing but stand and watch the girl in whom she had so much belief. What has happened to her? thought Madame. The answer began to be plain. Caroline was not trying. "So," Madame whispered, "she doesn't think it worrth her while to try for me."

Miss Ilse had come in and stood beside her. "This is a terrible evening," she said to Miss Ilse.

"Anna. You want your supper."

"Supper! How can I think about supper?" She put out her hand to Miss Ilse.

"How cold you are! At least let me fetch you a hot drink."

Madame shook her head.

"Some *vin sucré*, hot, Anna."

"No. Don't go. I want you." She wanted Miss Ilse, who was accustomed, intimate. "Is this rehearsal never going to end?" she said.

"You must have nearly finished, Anna."

Madame shook her head, again.

She could not let it end. At the close, when the curtain had come down, gone up, she had to say, "Again. Oll over again."

The girls went back to the opening group; John and Francis, the small Lippi, and the other young men, to the wings right and left. There were murmurs which Madame allowed to go unrebuked.

"Madame . . ."

"Well, Caroline?"

"I have been dancing since this morning. Rehearsal and the performance and now this."

"What do you expect if you take part in two companies?" asked Madame. "Do you think I shouldn't rehearse you, not?"

"Madame . . ." began Lion.

"There is nothing to say, Lion," said Madame.

Caroline's gaze flickered and fell. Mr. Felix polished his baton thoughtfully with his glove.

"What about the orchestra?" asked Lion.

"What about it?" asked Mr. Felix.

"Will you stay?"

"Like you, we will stay as long as it's necessary," said Mr. Felix. It sounded like a snub.

Everyone was tired. There had been an atmosphere of strain and discord in the theatre all evening. It was not only that Madame was cross; they were used to that and, in some ways, they appreciated it because it stimulated them and made them brace themselves for an extra effort, but they knew that something was wrong. "Fundamentally wrong," said John to Hilda, who shrugged her shoulder at him crossly too.

"What do you think will happen?" asked John, as everyone was asking.

"I don't know," said Hilda.

"What do you think she will do?"

"How do I know?" said Hilda.

"Tomorrow?"

No one knew what would happen tomorrow.

Outside, in the Avenue, the theatre doors were open for booking and the bills were displayed:

### HOLBEIN BALLET
#### Gala Anniversary Performance

Cat Among the Pigeons
(Jan Holbein)

The Noble Life
(Holbein-Bellini)

Lyre with Seven Strings
(Hilda French)

They were in the theatre ticket agencies too, in the sides of the moving staircases in the Underground stations, all over London. Would they now have to be changed, all over London? "But there wouldn't be time," said Hilda.

"They could paste those narrow papers over you," said John. "Over your name. But what will they put on them? *Meditations?*"

"My name shouldn't go under that," said Hilda. "It's not mine."

They were all tired. The girls had unusually brilliant eyes, their make-up had run a little, their hair was untidy. The men looked sulky, their faces were sticky and pale. Caroline was cross and even Lion was put out. As he danced with Caroline he was increasingly disappointed. Nonsense, thought Lion. She is my favourite partner. It's a wonderful thing for me to have the chance to dance with her. He still felt disappointed. Mr. Felix had not spoken to his orchestra nor they to him; Miss Parkes drooped in her stall, the valiant Rebecca stood beside Madame, Miss Ilse had gone.

Madame stood there, in front, her jacket wrapped round her; she tottered a little on her feet but her eyes were still quick, they missed nothing. The lights burnt on; if they had been candles they would have burnt down long ago. At last it was over. The curtain fell, went up, everyone waited, and again Madame said nothing.

It was Lion who spoke. "Madame, some of the girls have to catch a bus or a train home. They will miss the last if you don't let them go now."

Madame at last opened her lips and said, "Very well."

"Do you want them tomorrow?"

"No."

"But, Madame . . ."

"No, I tell you. Not before evening." She saw consternation on his face. "I shall see tomorrow," said Madame.

Caroline came to say good night. "Madame, you look so tired."

"I am not tirred. I don't allow myself to be tired until I have things right." Her eyes had a look of disdain that Hilda knew well but that Caroline had never seen before.

Caroline hesitated. Then she kissed Madame smoothly and went away. Madame's face, as she looked after her, was tired and very old.

All over London they will be pasting out my name. Hilda did not know in the least if this was to be true, but she was too tired to think coherently and John's words had lodged in her head. All over London. She saw those strips, pasted down, blotting her out . . . forever, thought Hilda dramatically. They none of them knew what was to happen, but Hilda knew in her bones that neither *Lyre with Seven Strings* nor *Meditations* would be done. Then why did she say it was good? asked Hilda bitterly. She said more bitterly, And I needn't have given in. It did no good to give in. Why did I give in?

Before, though she was equally desolate, she had had a strong feeling of pride, almost of grandeur, to sustain her in her loneliness. Now that was gone. She was like the rest of them, like anybody else. I can't even despise them now, thought Hilda. That should, of course, have been a good thing; it is not good to be conceited, but for Hilda it was strangely necessary. She was conceited, but for her it was truth.

She had come up to the classroom to put her notes and records away before anybody found them, but now she was too tired even to do that. Let them find them, said Hilda. What do I care? If I stop now I shall miss my bus. She made no effort to go and catch her bus. She stood by the window as she had stood that evening; she had fallen into the same pose but she was far more unhappy. Outside it was dark, though the theatre was still lit. I suppose Madame is still there, tearing me to pieces, thought Hilda. . . . Below the ridge, street after street, tier below tier, was lit. The lights stretched below her in uneven chains of light, from windows upstairs and windows down, but now, mostly, from windows upstairs; there were street lights and the passing lights of buses and cars and, farther away, a ball of light, a dome or bubble in the sky, the brilliant rolling West End world. That is where I thought my name would be, said Hilda, leaning her forehead on the cold glass.

Lion has gone home now, perhaps he has taken Caroline home, or he is with Madame, discussing me. Why did they say it was good? asked Hilda, a tear rolling down her nose. Madame isn't fair. She gives with one hand and takes back with the other. Why did she say it was good?

Madame had not said it was good. "Why should it be good?" said Madame. "Think what it takes to make something good. Who are you?"

That question seemed to go rolling out into the darkness among the lights.

The lights stretched in millions and, for each, there was, not a name in lights, but one little window. Like any other window, said Hilda. And each one is someone, no one. The glass was growing warm now from the pressure of her forehead, but she pressed it against it more tightly.

That is the tragedy, said Hilda, or the comedy . . . and she tried to laugh. Each someone is no one. No one, said Hilda, and the tears splashed down on the window-sill. No one; wanting, yearning, but with no power to do what they want. "Isn't it enough that you can do it at oll?" asked Madame. No, it isn't enough, cried Hilda. Not for me.

"You are very conceited." They all said that.

Yes, I am, said Hilda. I am, and I always shall be. The lights slid together in a blur of tears.

There was a rustle beside her and she looked down. The child Lollie was at her elbow.

"Lollie! You here at this time of night! You ought to have gone home hours ago."

"I can't go home," said Lollie. "Auntie can't have me alone in the flat, and Mrs. Zannger kept her."

"Your aunt is Miss Porteus?"

"Yes," said Lollie without enthusiasm.

Like Hilda, Lollie was oppressed. Like Hilda, it was partly tiredness and, like her, again, the difficulties were real. "There is a way round every difficulty," said Madame. "In dancing they don't exist." She took no excuses. She did not excuse herself.

Lollie was oppressed, but she had boundless tenacity. She had, under her fears and starts, more tenacity than anyone in the school, even Lion. Lollie would have scorned to be as anxious for her own ends as Lion. She had far more tenacity than Hilda, almost more than Madame. She had only to get over her initial fright. Where many of the young dancers gave the impression of being avid, as Madame herself was sometimes avid, Lollie gave the impression of holding back, of a naturally timed restraint that seemed to say that, with the unfolding of time, in her own time Lollie would do everything she promised and that it was her business to do. The grownups liked her. They found her restful and strong. Can a child be restful and strong? Lollie was, and this quality showed clearly in her dancing. Her torments were minor compared to her strength.

"In London today," Madame told them, "there are thousands of girls who learn dancing; in London alone, not counting Paris or New York or other great cities, nor all the towns and little towns. Of those thousands, a few hundreds perhaps think themselves as good as you do. Of those few hundreds, perhaps a hundred are ready, as dancers, for their debut to the public every year; but there are few companies, four or five or six perhaps, and, among them, they may have three, five, or shall we say, eight, places to offer to those hundred dancers."

"Eight could get in," said Lollie.

"Yes, and what happens to the other ninety-two?"

"What happens to the eight?" said Lollie.

None of this feeling communicated itself to Hilda, who stood leaning against the window and then stood back and pushed it up and leant out. The light wind blew from the theatre and brought with it a scent of flowers to the half-open window. "It doesn't smell like London, does it?" said Lollie.

Hilda paid no attention to the flowers. Could I hear talking in the theatre from here? she was wondering. The lights are still on. Is she still thinking or discussing? Or is it decided now? She felt again it was decided. Yes, my ballet is gone, thought Hilda. Gone. Still-born.

She had no inkling of feeling that she would write others; for her, tonight, it was finished. The child was dead. She was even serene in the sad calm that comes after a death. There was no more to do. It was over. The thought that she was still fertile, that there would be others, had not come to her yet, or if it came she discarded it. No, it is too difficult, Hilda might have said. It is too heart-breaking. And what good is it, to do it against the whole world? The world is too big, said Hilda. Anything I can do would make a mark no bigger than a fly's leg, if it made a mark at all. Why sweat and worry and strive and spoil all my life for this? I won't, said Hilda.

"There are thousands of girls," Madame said.

Yes, too many, thought Hilda.

"Eight places to offer to those hundred dancers," said Madame.

Ninety-two don't get in. What happens to those ninety-two? thought Hilda.

Madame . . . Madame doesn't understand, said Hilda. She is too great. Madame looked down from the past. Hilda and the other young ones were thrusting up from the present, and the present she was sure was more difficult than any Madame had known. But is it? Madame might have said, Isn't it olways the same? If it isn't one thing, it is another that makes it difficult. It must be difficult, said Madame. . . . No, said Hilda, it couldn't possibly in any time have been as difficult as it is today. We all think that, said Madame. This was the kind of maddening, monotonous dialogue Hilda often held with Madame. I wish we could cut ourselves off from the past, she said impatiently, but one can never do that. In ballet especially, we have to do this . . . this ancestor-worship! said Hilda. . . .

"Look at the lights," said Lollie.

"Yes," said Hilda. She did not want to look at them.

"It's hard to tell where the lights leave off and the stars begin," said Lollie, and she said, "I have been learning the names of the stars in school."

"I used to hate that," said Hilda. "When they used to say we were a pin-point in the universe, I used to feel as if the whole earth dwindled away and I was lost. It used to frighten me."

"I don't know," said Lollie judiciously. "When they say that, then I think, well, we are a star as well."

"Don't wait for me, Lion," said Madame. "I will put out the lights." Everyone else had left the theatre. Lion, waiting for Madame in the door-way, looked broad-shouldered and heavy and comforting. But I had better not be comforted, thought Madame, I have work to do. "Go," she said to Lion, but he still waited.

"It was a disastrous evening, not?"

"Not disastrous, difficult."

And this was to have been my climax, the crown, thought Madame. She looked round the theatre and it was adept in answering her thought. Yes, it said, you made me ready for this. "I had planned . . ." said Madame, and broke off.

"A bad rehearsal makes a good performance."

"My *dearr* Lion!"

"Anyone can make a mistake," persisted Lion.

"When they are young, not when they are old," said Madame. "It is too late for me to make a mistake."

One mistake is not a tragedy. No, agreed Madame. But what else is it? She was tired, disappointed, worried, and grieved. Tomorrow was close. It was almost here.

"Wait till tomorrow," said Lion, and he said helplessly, "You never know."

"Tchk-tchk!" said Madame. "Go home, Lion, before you drrive me mad."

Lion went home. One by one, lingeringly, she turned out the lights. She locked the outer doors, walking across the stage, which was set again for Jan's Brazilian garden. She walked past the painted flats that vibrated with her tread in her heeled shoes; she stepped over coils of cable, and struts and braces, breathing the smell of paint and canvas and dust and rosin and powder. The smell of powder hung about the dressing-rooms with the smell of cream and grease-paint and gauze from the pupils' dresses hung, wide-skirted ghosts, along their racks; she touched them, and they swung back in a ghost of dancing. She picked up a velvet bow from the floor, and two bus tickets. She took a hand-glass off a stool and blew powder off its glass and put it back on the long dressing-table, where there were tufts of cotton-wool stained with red and blue and flesh-coloured grease-paint, an eyebrow pencil left out; one of the blue skull-caps belonging to the Pages in the *Noble Life* was there, with pins, hair-clips, a piece of a wafer biscuit, and a mascot panda bear. How untidy they are, said Madame. I give them waste-paper baskets, not? She dropped the wafer and the bus tickets and the cotton-wool into a basket and took a shoe off the section of the table next the door. It is bad luck to put shoes on the table, she thought, or is it only new shoes? She hoped it was only new shoes.

She turned out the light and went into the passage where small cubicles made Lion's and Caroline's dressing-rooms opposite each other. Caroline's was immaculate. Well, it should be. She has a dresser, not? It smelled faintly of Caroline's scent. There was an organdie cover on the table and a jar of white lilac. The Lady's dress hung on its hanger, the head-dress was on the table, the shoes on their own rack. Madame went in and touched the fur on the sleeves of the dress. Mine was ermine, she thought. We could not do that for Caroline.

"Let me take it off yours, Madame," Zanny had said, but she would not let her dress be touched.

"But, Anna, you don't want it."

"I do," said Madame.

"But . . ."

"I am going to be buried in it," snapped Madame.

Now it seemed to her cheap and pitiful that Caroline's ermine should be white rabbit fur sewn with black. "It looks as good from the front," said Zanny. That was the whole point, of course, and Madame concurred in it, but it still seemed to her cheap. She still did not think it could be the same. "It is a question of quality," she said. The quality was gone. It was that back-drop in *Carnaval* over again. "And I shall not give *Carnaval* till I can have them," said Madame. That might be the wrong point of view, but it was Madame's.

"Hilda ought to have a dressing-room," Miss Ilse had said.

"Has she said so?" demanded Madame.

"No, but . . . she is a principal."

"And what about Liuba?"

"Hilda is rather more than Liuba. She isn't just a principal."

"There is no dressing-room. She will have to share and share alike. It won't hurrt her. Why shouldn't she?"

Miss Ilse did not answer, but it seemed to her that Hilda was not alike. Sometimes, she thought, Anna is curiously ungrateful.

On Lion's door was a small brass knocker of a lion's head with a ring in its mouth. They put rings in animal noses so that they can be led, thought Madame irrelevantly . . . but the ring was in the lion's mouth. The dressing-rooms were so close to the stage that a rule of silence had to be kept; some-one had tied up the lion's mouth with a piece of silk.

Madame put out the lights and went back into the theatre and through it to the foyer. It was close here and smelled of print and paper. She looked at the booking plans on the ledge of the little box-office. They were full for almost the whole season. She touched the telephone, silent now, but it, like the one in the office, had been ringing all day. The lettering on the hand-bills was clear and large. *Cat Among the Pigeons. The Noble Life. Lyre with Seven Strings.* "Tchk-tchk!" said Madame.

There were photographs along the walls, chiefly of Lion, and Caroline, but also of Rayevskaya, Hilda, John, Francis, Lippi, Alma. On a stand was a large one of Madame as the Humming-Bird in Buenos Aires sixty years ago and, in the corner of the frame, a small one of Archie. Madame had half a mind to take Archie out. There were others of Madame in *Lac des Cygnes, Schéhérazade, Giselle, Snowflakes, Thamar*, as the Princess Aurora, as the Lady. Tomorrow the whole foyer would be heaped with flowers. "They are sure to send me flowers," said Madame.

Emile had swept the carpet here before he went to bed. Its crimson glowed deep and clear against the white walls and gilt frames. It oll looks charming, thought Madame. Just as I should have it look. She looked up at the chandelier and smiled. Its crystal caught the light in its drops and reflected the crimson and white and gleams of gold. I was rright about the chandelier, said Madame.

She turned out the lights here too and went back into the theatre, and at last put out the last light and stood at the garden door looking back into the dark cave of the auditorium, so small compared to any other she had known but, tonight and tomorrow night, much more important. The light from outside, cast into the garden from the street lamps on the pavements, showed a patch of cream wall, the backs of a few rows of seats, a candle sconce. They waited.

Lion had said, "Wait till tomorrow. You never know."

"Something olways saves me at the eleventh minute, not?" Madame said that often, but now she could not think as far as that; she only caught, like a breath from the theatre, what Lion had said, "Wait. Wait till tomorrow."

She stepped outside into the garden and closed the door.

## 4

Madame went upstairs and found Miss Ilse in her bedroom, where she had been feeling the bottle Zanny had put in Madame's bed to see if it were really hot. She thought Madame was Zanny and jumped. "Anna, how late you are! It's very late."

"Where were you? You olways go away just when I want you. You have been over to the Convent, Ilse. What use are you to me?"

"Only for a moment, and when I came in there was your supper to arrange. Zanny was in the theatre. And there have been notes all day and telephone messages." She looked at Madame. "Anna, has it gone worse? Is it still wrong?"

"No. Not at oll!" said Madame bitingly.

"You are tired out," said Miss Ilse. "You will work yourself to death at this rate, Anna."

"Yes, I will," said Madame. "And what do you care? When I am dead you will be able to go to church and pray for me, oll you like, and I shall be wiped out, oll I have done . . . and not done," said Madame. "That is oll you care. Oll!"

"God forgive you, Anna," said Miss Ilse. "You are very unjust." Her voice was trembling. "Your supper is ready in the sitting-room. I am going to bed."

Madame let her go. She went to the window and looked down on the road.

Outside, the last bus had run, the road was empty, the street lamps shed a pool of light on empty pavements. The trees rustled. The wind had again that scent of flowers that Hilda had not noticed. Madame noticed it; it was the town cousin of a country wind. She did not remember a London night as quiet, with this night wind and scent. It gave her a nostalgia but she did not know for what, for whom. She said, forgetting Miss Ilse was not there, "Ilse, do you remember the nightingale?"

Miss Ilse could not remember the nightingale. The nightingale was before Miss Ilse, before even she, Madame, had become Anna Holbein, when she was a child and lived in her grandmother's house in the country, a child called Niura. *Listen, Niura, that is a nightingale.* She remembered the words but not who had spoken them, nor, no matter how she trained her ears, could she hear the least thread of song and surely one should remember, first, its song of a nightingale?

"You always were unpredictable, irresponsible, Anna." Miss Ilse had said that, but it was only half true. Unpredictable, yes, but not irresponsible. Tonight her shoulders were bowed with it; she was old, old in responsibility. Old, but what I was I am forever, said Madame. I am still Niura who heard the nightingale.

She went into the sitting-room, familiar with its colours and comfort and warmth but unfamiliar, too, tonight as if she saw it for the first time. Whom does this belong to? . . . It did not belong to Niura, the little girl. It was too rich for her. . . . You have to get used to this rrichness gradually or it will give you indigestion, said Madame. She shivered. Indigestion? Ilse is right. I need food.

The fire was bright. In front of it, drawn up to it, was a small table with a white lace-edged cloth. It was set for supper and with candles in a two-branched gilt candlestick. Like a little altar, thought Madame. Ilse knows I love candlelight. It was an altar. In all the quarrels in the world Miss Ilse would still consecrate herself to see that Madame had her supper. She must have come in, just before, to light the candles. I should go to her, said Madame, but she did not go.

She sat down by the fire. There was a tumbler with red wine in it, and, balanced across it, a spoon with a lump of sugar; beside it was a hot-water jug wrapped round in a napkin. As Madame lifted its lid, steam came out. She poured in the water and dropped the sugar in and sat stirring it round. Such horrible wine, thought Madame, making a grimace; but Miss Ilse thought it was good for her and put it out for her every evening. It was at any rate warm and comforting. She sat holding it, watching the sugar turn dark. I don't remember my grandmother, thought Madame, but I remember her black skirt turned back from the fire as she sat like this and I remember the glass in her hand and the spoon stirring and the sugar turning dark. What she did I do now, thought Madame. I must be very old.

The house, that house, was wooden with slats and a birch tree at the gate. She remembered the birch leaves in spring, and the gate made a noise, *ouoie-ouoiee-eee*, because its wood had swelled. There was a flat place along the road where there were other trees. Willows, said Madame. . . . In the summer the dust in the road was white, she could feel it between her bare toes, and the frogs croaked all night; unlike the nightingale, she could hear the frogs. Yes, there were frogs and tadpoles and a boy, thought Madame. Nikita? Vaslav? Stanislav? She could not remember his name.

She lifted the dish cover and began her supper; it was one of Zanny's ragouts with a chicken, a few button mushrooms, and very small carrots. She must have made it before Ilse got there. I am glad she did, thought Madame. Zanny, who cooked untidily, was a far better cook than Miss Ilse. "But she isn't clean, Anna. Food should be pure." "I don't like my food pure," said Madame, "I like it to *taste*." Miss Ilse had added brown bread and butter, a salad, and strawberries and cream. Madame left the salad, she knew Miss Ilse's salads, and ate the rest. . . . But she arranged oll this for me and what did she have herself? . . . Nothing. Tea and bread and butter. Care and devotion. Madame sighed. Tonight she did not want care and devotion, she wanted judgment. Someone who could judge for her or help her to judge for herself. That is what I didn't have, thought Madame. No judgment. None at oll. Never. Or did I? she asked. Thinking over her life, backwards, down the years, it seemed to her that she did. She could not possibly have managed as well as she did, without.

It was curious how totally she had forgotten Niura and how refreshing she found it, in her tiredness, to remember her now. There was a river, she thought eating her supper, and there, as well as the frogs and the tadpoles, there was a crane. These things were like footfalls in her memory, she could follow them where they led; she saw the crane now, standing in the water on one leg. But it couldn't have done that oll the time, she argued, but that was how Niura had seen it and for her it stood like that for ever. As she had remembered the feel of the summer dust in the road between her toes, she remembered paddling in the river; she saw her feet, through the water, on the river sand. They look quite ordinary feet, thought Madame, the feet of any little girl, but they were mine. That was the miracle. That one pair of feet should have a power denied to another, that all feet were the same, and all different.

She tried to take herself one step further, where Niura had gone away with Jan, the big brother come from their father's relations in Holland; Jan had taught her there in the country all one summer . . . and I didn't like it. I wept. He was so stern, said Madame, and then he took me away and I wasn't Niura, I was Anna, and then we came back to St. Petersburg and I went to the Maryinsky school. . . . *Among the small pupils that year was the little Anna Holbein,* a great ballerina had written in her memoirs. *I remember the fragile big-eyed little girl with the grasshopper legs, as we used to call them. She was surprisingly naughty. Perhaps no one had ever dared to be naughty there before. We were always surprised when she was*

*forgiven. Looking back on her now, I am no longer surprised. She was ex-*
*traordinarily gifted. I remember her . . .*

Madame could not remember her at all. Instead, into her mind came
Lollie. But she is not at all like I was, said Madame. I never had plaits
turned up in those knobs! Nor that woe-begone smile, she might have added,
nor that name. What a name! said Madame. No one has a name like that.
She will have to use another, said Madame.

"When you were my age," Lollie asked her, "were you much better than
me?"

"Than 'I,' Lollie."

"But were you? Were you?"

Madame could not see the small Anna for Lollie. She could clearly see
her grandmother's house with its birch trees and the wooden gate; she could
see the birds and tadpoles Niura had been interested in . . . and how lucky
I was to have that childhood, thought Madame. How much came out of it
later.

*"I have never seen the wind in a field of corn."*

Madame sighed and put away her plate and took a strawberry. Stars, to
Lollie, might easily mean film stars . . . and yet, she *should* have seen stars,
argued Madame, on the top of a bus, for instance . . . but it would only be
from the top of a bus, not on a hill, open above woods, or through trees,
or in a foreign train, crossing the plain like a little glittering snake under
the glittering sky, or in the mountains where a peak could shut off a whole
galaxy of stars, or on a ship made small by its own loneliness between the
wide sky and sea. But one day she will see it, thought Madame. Even for
Lollie, if she works and has a little luck, it may be. There will be nothing
phenomenal in that, it would be purely natural. It always annoyed her when
they said her own success was phenomenal. "It was not in the least," she
said. "It was only to be expected." I must do more for Lollie, she thought
now. More for all of them. But she knew she could not. Each must get on as
best he might.

She rolled a strawberry in sugar. "Not too much sugar, Anna. We have to
be careful . . ." "Don't you dole my sugar to me," said Madame. "Let me
enjoy it and then, if there is no more, I shall do without. That is the way to
live," said Madame severely. Miss Ilse sighed. Madame made such an issue
of little things. "But little things are the issue," said Madame. "They are
the same as big."

Now she dipped the strawberry whole in sugar and ate it thoughtfully,
slowly, looking into the fire. The summer scents of that garden were not like
their town cousin she had smelled from her window tonight; they were robust and rough but fragrant; she remembered hay-making days, and poppies
and marguerites growing in the rye, the corn Lollie had never seen. Marguerites. Marguerites always made Madame think of *Giselle*. Of all ballets
*Giselle* was unquestionably the one she loved the most. I had marguerites
for it once, marguerites with the white gauze. They said they were not correct, but I think they suited it better than lilies or roses. Marguerites; those
grave-eyed flowers. There is a photograph of me with them, thought Mad-

ame. I must get Ilse to change it for the one in the foyer. I should like to have it there tomorrow night. *Giselle* . . . in the second act, with Albrecht . . . and suddenly she found that she was not thinking of the young Anna Holbein; she was thinking of Hilda. "Tchk-tchk!" said Madame, and pushed the strawberries away.

Why should she think of Hilda? It was not likely that Hilda would ever dance *Giselle*. How many dancers do? Few in each generation. Then I can safely prophesy . . . But can anyone safely prophesy anything? Prophets can, perhaps, but Madame was no prophet. But I don't think she will go as far as that, said Madame.

She thought of the way she herself had come since the days of Niura. It seemed to her like a road winding and winding, round loops and bends and corners and up steep places with precipices and chasms and barriers to make it difficult and longer. And I used to think it would be like a meadow, a panorama meadow with flowers and lawns and a brook to cool it and sun and a blue sky. But it wasn't in the *least*, said Madame.

When she thought of the road, particularly the precipices, she thought of Hilda; when she thought of the meadow, the panorama meadow, she thought of Caroline. Now what is the significance of that? she asked. She felt it had significance, but she did not know what it could be. She was too tired, tired out, too tired to divine. I am no more a witch than a prophet, said Madame crossly. Nor, what do they call it, a delph? A sibyl? She was too tired to think what she was. I am I, I suppose, she said. That seemed to comprehend it all.

The starting point, the freshet, was Lollie. Not Lollie, Niura, she corrected, but, obstinately, it was Lollie. A freshet is a spring, the bubbling, rising, of a spring. Spring. Even while there were snowdrifts, snowdrops—no, snowdrifts—on the ground, the spring wind used to blow in the birch trees. . . . Birch buds, you should make tea of them and drink it in the spring; it makes old blood young again. But that isn't possible, said Madame. I have been through oll the seasons, said Madame. This season, that season; but now it is only winter, winter alone, without a trrace of spring. I am in winter now . . . and she shivered. Why am I shivering? I have my food and my *vin sucré*. I shouldn't be cold. But I am cold. Cold. She drew her chair closer to the fire. I must expect to be cold, said Madame, to feel the frost in me, to be bound and cold as ice. I can't expect to be arrdent, and eager as I was as a young girl, though even now I am more arrdent than most of them, said Madame with a flicker of her self; but the flicker sank down. It is too difficult to be ardent when one is tired. Too tiring, said Madame. You can't make old blood young again.

She thought of herself in the photograph downstairs, that young girl with the ringlets, and other early photographs: the one with the marguerites that was to go into the foyer, the Odile in the black tutu she had innovated, in *Armide*, in *Thamar* . . . all with the same grace of arms and neck and head, the straight beauty of the legs, the face with its iridescent eyes . . . oll me, thought Madame, and found again that she was thinking of Hilda.

This . . . this double memory, cried Madame. Life was exceedingly treacherous. Alone? Alone in winter? Nothing was alone, by itself. She could not remember in peace any more than she could be angry in peace. Everything, everyone, everything, insisted on being with something or somebody else. When she wished to think about herself, she thought of these Lollies and Hildas. It was provoking. And why think of Hilda, when it is Caroline I love? The thought of Caroline gave her a stab. How little she cared for you tonight, it said. Madame lifted her chin. If you love people, you must be prepared to suffer them. I shall speak to Caroline in the morning, said Madame. I shall speak to her privately as I couldn't do with oll of them there in the theatre. She will take it from me. Caroline is olways sweet-tempered, and it is naturral she should get swollen head, not? The wonder is that it hasn't happened before. I shall speak in the morning and it will be oll rright, but Hilda . . . That brought her back to the trouble of the ballet. It isn't oll right, cried Madame in despair. Hilda. Why did I ever see Hilda? It is a fiasco. A fiasco!

Never before, said Madame, have I had nothing new to show; nothing to make them talk, worth while to remember. A young dancer, a new ballet, a new idea. A nest-egg of ballet, said Madame bitterly, with not one single egg in it! Nothing to show. Nothing to bring them to see, only the old, with no new blood in it. Adequate? Ah yes, of course, but that is oll, and it isn't even adequate with a third of the programme gone. Ah, why did I listen to Felix? Why did I listen to Lion? Why didn't I use my own judgment, if I had any judgment, thought Madame.

It was very quiet. Time seemed to be suspended in the house, but, if she listened, she could hear the clocks ticking, her Swiss clock that she had bought not in Switzerland but in New York and her Dresden clock that she had bought not in Dresden but in Paris. They had begun to tick in Berne and Dresden as they ticked here, now, in London; as they had ticked in Paris and New York and all over the world: London, Paris, Dresden, Berlin, St. Petersburg, Petrograd, Milan, Madrid, Johannesburg, Cape Town, Sydney, Adelaide, Brisbane, Buenos Aires, Rio, San Francisco, New York. She saw the labels that were pasted to the slips on the dress baskets. She saw Miss Ilse pasting them freshly on again and again, pinkish labels printed *Ballet Holbein* in large letters; Royal Theatre, Copenhagen: La Scala, Milan: the Colon, Buenos Aires: Zarzuela, Madrid: Civic Opera House, Chicago. Oll over the world, said Madame. And not for one performance, one, have I failed. That is a record, I think, said Madame. . . . That success had not been easy, it was often tedious, troublesome, with bone-breaking work. They forget the work, said Madame. Well, let them. The work is nothing, but . . . even to work isn't enough. One can fail. Ah, what shall I do? What shall I do? said Madame.

Hilda! Hilda! Hilda! ticked the clocks. Time passes, but that is what it doesn't do, said Madame, it goes on and on for ever. You cannot get away from it. She leaned back in her chair and closed her eyes.

*Listen, Niura. That is a nightingale.*

She could not remember the name of that boy. There were others. There was Serge and Paul. She had not thought of them for a long time. And that

French boy, Jean Marie. I called him Médor, he was like a faithful little dog to me. There was that young Englishman, Gerald . . . Gerald? Well, Gerald, said Madame. . . . There was Kuprin, her first partner, and into her mind came a strange old Scotsman who had followed her last tour all through South America, from place to place, never speaking to anyone in the company, never writing or asking to meet her, but always in the theatre to see her dance; I used to bow to him, thought Madame, but he never sent me any flowers. I suppose he thought he had spent enough in following us about, and it must have cost him a good deal, thought Madame fairly. It had made her remember him, that he had never sent her flowers. There had been so many flowers. She remembered the bouquet that had been in the little holder upstairs, the bouquet with the lace frill. . . . It was after the accident in Copenhagen. Ilse said he would drive fast and he did. . . . Like Miss Ilse, she could remember his moustache, but she could not remember his name. She remembered the gala performance, *Swan Lake*. She remembered kissing the Queen's hand in its white glove and she remembered the bouquet. They had stiffened its lace and that had shocked Miss Ilse. She had washed it lovingly. . . . I have it still in the cabinet on the stairs.

Yes. There were many who had loved Anna Holbein, but whom had she loved? I suppose I loved them, thought Madame. Perhaps I loved them oll —or none. A flame came up from the glow of the coals and shone, reflected in the polish of the chairs and tables, in the glass and silver on the table, in the candlestick, in the mirrors and on the walls.

*Anna. My darling. Darling Anna.*

Yes, they said that, said Madame, nodding her head, they felt it . . . and what was one to do when one felt that rush of love? That mastery? What was one to do against that power? Nothing at oll, said Madame. Why make such a fuss of it? Miss Ilse, for instance, always made a fuss. You would think it the ends of the earth, said Madame. "Anna, you should be *ashamed*," Miss Ilse had said. "I am not ashamed," said Madame mildly.

*Anna. Darling Anna.* They were only words . . . and it is a parrt of life, not? said Madame, those words?

The first season she gave *The Noble Life* . . . It is because we do it now that I think of him, because I am tired, but . . . She could not remember him, clearly. It had not been for long, a few weeks from a lifetime, but she should not have forgotten them; she wanted to remember them now. In the morning, before it was really morning, while it was still night, when the first light lay in the angle of the window frames, and the bird song had begun in the garden. "*To hold your hands is like holding two birds in my hands, Anna.*" "*You are thinking of the birds in the garden.*" "*Are they birds, that sleepy noise?*" She was almost with him, then instead she saw Lion.

She thought of Lion. Of Lion's golden skin with olive lights, of his hair that was crinkled with curls like the pelt of a lamb, of his eyes. She saw him in his silks and velvets as the Nobleman, in his street clothes, in his dark tights. I had lovers, said Madame. Yes. Well? I needed a counterpart.

Just as I had to have a partner in the dance. That was oll. No more than that. I was olways busy. I could not give myself away. No, I could not do that. . . . Well, Lion is not for me, she said, but, however firmly she said it, she felt again that rebellious pang of jealousy. Ah. Don't conflict me so, said Madame to herself. You are old. For years you have been old. You should be used to it by now, said Madame severely, and she sighed. It had been peaceful to be old, till now.

She raised her head and listened. The emptiness of the house answered her. Even the mice are asleep, said Madame. How did I come to think such thoughts, thoughts that haven't trroubled me for years? But do they trouble me? Ah no! They give me rrest, and joy, thought Madame, leaning back in her chair, and strength.

In the night, she thought, when everyone is asleep, that is the time, when the moments are emptied of the thoughts of others, cleared, that is the time to think. That is why thought comes as strongly and as truly as it has tonight. I have been awake oll night as I was then, said Madame, but afterwards, in the morning, I slept. . . . There was no arm round her now, no shoulder and breast to pillow her head, she was alone, her little tired body upright in the arm-chair. She shut her eyes, but almost at once, indignantly, they opened. She was thinking of Hilda again.

Into her mind had come the remembrance of Hilda dancing with Lion. They could have their perfect moment, those two children, she had thought involuntarily. They are matched. Nonsense, said Madame. Hilda a match for Lion? That is presumption, and she began to be indignant again, then found she was too tired. I can't bother about them. They must get on as best they can, thought Madame. I am too tired to combat them. Lion must fend for himself. I am too tired.

There was no warmth and support or inspiration or glory now for her, and she had none to give. My day is over, said Madame.

She lifted her head. Under the blinds that Miss Ilse had drawn, the light lay in the angle of the window frames, an angle of light and an angle of darkness, that she had seen before. She could hear the first sound of a chirp in the garden. It isn't night, she said. It is day.

She was reluctant to meet this day. To go into it with its troubles and difficulties and strain and work. I am not fit for it, said Madame. I have had no rest, no sleep, and it will be a calamitous day. I feel it.

Oll over the world and here in London, day after day, year in, year out, what I have done, I have done well, till now. I have been prroud of that, prroud and interested to be proud. I am not interested in failure. I have olways given the best, the very best, said Madame. She looked round bewildered as if she did not know how this had happened, how it was that this day promised her, Madame Holbein, no success. She felt old, beaten, too tired, too cold, to deal with it. Her eyes felt as dry as paper, her body ached. What am I to do? Cancel the season? Put off the performance tonight? Return the seats? How can I? But what else? What else is there to do? I wanted to show them Caroline in a big role, and Caroline doesn't choose to dance. Rayevskaya is charming, but she is nothing, and the ballets are nothing new. As they stand they are not enough. What shall I do? *Have a backbone, not a wishbone, Anna.* Who said that? She remembered. It was Jan. "Yes," said Madame aloud. "Yes." Another feeling came up in her, tough and obstinate with pride, and with a certain excitement of its own. Olways, at the eleventh minute, I save myself, said Madame. She pushed back the chair and stood up. I don't know what I shall do, but something. Something, that is what I shall do.

She began to walk about. She had a hot flush on each cheek, and her eyes, under those paper eyelids, felt hard and glittering. I must have deep wrinkles this morning, she thought. The room, with its blinds drawn, the ashes in the fire, and its used supper table, seemed dead and depressing, closed in by the night. She opened the door and listened and went down to the first classrooms where there were no blinds to pull, no curtains to draw and shut out this necessary day. Here she could meet it, as it had to be met.

Someone had left the window open. A wave of cool, dew-filled air met her and, though it chilled her, it was freshening. The garden was empty and colourless, cold and unfeeling. After a moment she pushed the window down; now the garden was a glass garden with no wind and no birds. That is better, said Madame. Better for me today.

She stood looking at the theatre wall, at the door that would presently open. She thought beyond it, into the theatre, the auditorium that would presently be filled with pleasantly expectant people, of Miss Parkes' sister with the programmes, of the orchestra that would assemble, of Mr. Felix, of Glancy and William on the stage, of the busy hive behind it: Rebecca and Miss Parkes scurrying to and fro, Zanny and Miss Porteus, the dancers; beyond them again to the frontage, and the foyer, where the bills were posted and Emile in his blue uniform would wait to open the car doors. Yes, said Madame, and pressed her hands to her temples. Yes. But what to do? What to do?

Here in this room were all the habits of her life and work; all her discipline, her inspiration. She looked around it as if she were calling to it, asking it to rally to her now. The floor, dusty, dry with the lines of its boards; the wainscot, runway of the mice, with its holes and cracks and blistered paint; the embossed old darkened paper; the *barres* in their iron clamps; the piano shut as Mr. Felix left it shut, music on its top, music under the cushion of the stool, and bursting from the rack: the forms under the windows, the white stuffing showing in the splits of their red seats; a pair of shoes left on the floor under them, their tapes trailing in the dirt of the floor; the gramophone. Madame's eyes stopped.

The gramophone was open, its lid raised, and on it was an open notebook. She walked over to it. On the turn-table was a large record; she could not read its label without lifting it up, but she picked up the notebook; the writing was as large, sprawled, and untidy as her own; she could read it without bringing it too close to her eyes. *Solo, Leda,* she read: *Leda travels backwards on line five to centre: entrechat quatre, relevé passé derrière on alternate feet, arms fifth en bas* . . . Leda? asked Madame, and turned the pages back: *Leda, looking for shells on the lake shore* . . . she read. "Tchk-

tchk!" said Madame, and she carried the book to the light and read on, stooping her nose into the pages: *And now, towards the reeds and the girl, the Swan comes with a rush, the wings beat round her, making her stagger and reel dizzily, bearing her backwards* . . . "Tchk-tchk!" said Madame.

She turned the book over. In the front was written: *Leda and the Swan.* Hm! said Madame. Now, why did no one ever think of making that into a ballet before? It seemed to her now an inevitable theme. She read the notes through and then went to the gramophone. She took off the record and, holding it close to her eyes, was able to read it: *Fantasia and Variations,* Carlorossi. Never heard of it, said Madame, and put it back again, switched the gramophone on, and released the catch. It began quietly, then the raucous impolite music she had heard in the garden burst into the room. "Tchk-tchk!" cried Madame, recoiling in surprise. "Tchk-tchk-tchk!" but she listened.

There was no hiding that music. It broke its way into every corner of the house and woke Miss Ilse and brought her running down the stairs.

"Anna! What are you doing?" But her voice was drowned in sound.

The music rent the air. Miss Ilse had to wait until it was finished.

"Anna? It's only five o'clock. You will wake the whole road."

"Hush," said Madame.

"Hush. After that noise." She looked at Madame. "Anna, you haven't been to bed all night."

"No," Madame agreed abstractedly. Her voice was buoyant and full of life.

Miss Ilse stared at her. "Anna," she said suspiciously, "what have you been doing?"

"What should I have been doing?" asked Madame, not thinking of her.

"You . . . you look like you used to do," said Miss Ilse. "You look almost like a young girl. Anna, what did you do last night?"

"Last night?" Madame could not remember last night. Last night was over. It was today.

### 5

"Ilse, you must get Lion."

"Lion? *Now?* Do you know what the time is, Anna?"

"Yes, you have told me," said Madame, and she said urgently, "There isn't a minute to lose. And Felix. You must get Felix."

"But, Anna . . ."

"And Edwin for lights, and who . . . who for the set? Mathilde? No. Noel for this, but I suppose he has only gone to bed; no, better not Noel perhaps. He is bad-tempered in the morning, and we can't wait. Pierre Moron, perhaps. But no. No. Noel is better; wake Zanny; and Miss Porteus, we shall have to get Miss Porteus . . ."

"But, Anna . . ."

"But nothing can be done without Lion." She turned on Miss Ilse. "Why are you standing there, not even dressed? Why are you waiting? I said you should get Lion. Then get Lion, at once."

"But how shall I get him? He will be in bed. They will all be in bed. No one will answer the telephone."

"Then you must go in a taxi and fetch him."

"Where shall I get a taxi at five in the morning?" Miss Ilse dissolved into tears. "You are so unfeeling, Anna. Last night and now . . . this morning. I don't understand what is happening," sobbed Miss Ilse. "You haven't been to bed all night. You look as if you had been . . . I don't understand. I don't understand what is happening. How do you expect me to understand when you don't explain?"

Madame had a moment of exasperation, then she came and put her arms round Miss Ilse. "Do you remember the time when you went to Milan and fetched my shoes?" she asked, her cheek against Miss Ilse's pale wet one. "It was just at the opening of the Covent Garden season and Baretti had sent my shoes and sent them oll wrrong? I was in despair, remember?"

Miss Ilse nodded. She remembered the despair very well.

"And you went strraight to Milan to get them. No one else but you would have gone."

"There was no one else to go," said Miss Ilse, but she sniffed back her tears.

"There is no one else now," said Madame. "There never has been. You know that, Ilse. You have olways helped me. You must help me now. I haven't time to explain to you more than this: I think I have discovered something that may . . . only may . . . Ilse, solve us for the perrformance tonight. If I have, it will save us from disgrace," said Madame dramatically.

"Is it as bad as that, Anna?"

"Well, no," admitted Madame, "but any fall at our height would be hard to bear, Ilse, not? Everyone would be sorry we were not as good. They would rregret. I refuse to have regrrets. Last night I was wretched. I didn't see how it could be saved, and now I have found, what do you think? A new ballet, Ilse."

"A new ballet! Now! Oh, *Anna!*"

"Don't say 'Oh,' say 'Ah,'" said Madame testily. "'Ah' is big, dramatic, generous . . ."

"But everyone says 'Oh'!"

"Yes, everyone! Ilse, it isn't a ballet, not a complete . . . but I think it *is* complete, and it's more than a dance. It is a ballet, a ballet for two." She paused and went over to the gramophone and picked up the notebook and brought it to Miss Ilse. "Ilse, this book is Hilda's, not? It's her writing."

Miss Ilse, her head in a maze, was able to say that it was.

"It would be!" said Madame.

"Mother of God, a new ballet!" Miss Ilse was praying. "*Now!* Mother of God, Mary, help us. It isn't possible, but she will make it possible. Oh, help us. Give us strength." Panic broke through. "How is it possible?" cried Miss Ilse. "There are only a few hours before the curtain goes up. Who is to dance it, Anna? Learn it, rehearse it in the time? It isn't possible."

"It is," said Madame.

"And it isn't only the rehearsing. There is music. Dresses. Lights. And what will you do for a set? Use curtains . . ."

"You know I never use curtains."

"But you will have to . . ."

"I shan't."

"But . . ."

"Ah, Ilse, don't make me such a storrm in a teapot. We shall never get on."

"And the programmes will have to be altered. What about the *printers?*" cried Miss Ilse.

"Ilse, I beg of you. Before I lose my temper," said Madame blazing, "go and get me Lion."

Lion came.

"I know about it," said Lion. He looked sideways at Madame. "It was that that I was dancing with Hilda when you stopped us yesterday."

"It was that? Why didn't you tell me?" She gave him no time to answer but swept on, looking at him intently. "How good is it, Lion? Is it good?"

"I think so," said Lion.

"Why didn't you tell me about it instead of about that *Lyre?*"

"I didn't know what it was until I danced it with Hilda last night."

"And last night I was in despair and you knew and you still didn't tell me." She stopped. "You wanted it for the Metropolitan, Lion."

"I didn't." Lion flushed.

"You did."

"It never occurred to me."

"You are oll, oll the same," said Madame with scorn. *There is an infinite variety in people.* Who had said that? My mind is full of ends and tags, said Madame, and it's not trrue. There is no variety in people. They are oll the same; oll how do you say it, *clay.* "I don't know what to make of you, Lion," she said sadly.

"No, you don't." Lion was surly and offended.

I don't know in the least if he did it or not, thought Madame. No. I don't know what to make of Lion.

"The Metropolitan is my company," said Lion sourly.

"So is this."

"That must come first."

"This was first."

"I am sorry you should think this of me."

"So am I."

Madame felt angry and hurt and uncertain. There seemed a hiatus that she could not bridge. She looked at Lion helplessly. Lion walked away to the window and whistled. He doesn't seem to care what I think, said Madame, perplexed. What is the matter with him?

"Anna, you want some breakfast," said Miss Ilse.

"No."

"Some good hot coffee . . ." said Miss Ilse, moving towards the door.
"No."

"And you too, Lion. With toast and some fruit . . ."

"No," said Lion.

"You will feel better for it, both of you. Dear goodness, Anna was up all night. Nothing to eat . . . enough to make her ill. I will go and get it at once. You will be better after some breakfast."

Miss Ilse could almost have followed her own loved St. Catherine who lived on salads and water, but Madame had to have food; she liked it and needed it and ate it. "A dancer works on her stomach," she often said that, and, though she did not dance, she was still a dancer. It was almost mortifying to see how much better she felt after the coffee and toast and fruit. "And so does Lion," said Madame. "He isn't nearly as quarrelsome, not?"

"And now," said Miss Ilse content, "I can go and call Mr. Felix and then I shall go on for Miss Porteus and Edwin."

Some people *are* different, said Madame, touched. There are a few, a faithful few, who burn like those altar lamps that never go out, that are olways lit by care and devotion. My supper table was like an altar last night. A lamp olways lit, steady, because it is tended. It is devotion that tends them, not like fitful candles, said Madame looking suspiciously at Lion again. "Ilse . . ." she said with love. Then her tone changed. "*Ilse!*"

Miss Ilse had not gone to fetch Mr. Felix. She was standing just outside the door, her face rapt, her eyes shut, her lips moving.

"Ding. Ding-dong," went the Convent bell. It was the Angelus.

*"Hail Mary, full of grace . . ."*

"Ilse, must you spend time now?"

No answer.

"Ilse would pray when Jericho was falling!" said Madame.

"That would be the time to pray, wouldn't it?" said Lion.

"You must see Hilda before you do anything further," said Lion. "You can't arrange all this without her. You must wait till she comes."

" 'Must,' Lion?"

"Yes, you must."

"Why?"

"Because it's hers."

"She did it in my school, as a member of my company," argued Madame. "What could she possibly have to say?"

"You may not like it when you see it danced."

"I may not. What else?"

"She may not want you to do it." Madame's head came up. "She didn't particularly like the way you treated her over *Lyre*," said Lion.

"Treated her over *Lyre!* To give her a wonderful chance like that! It was a chance even if it didn't happen," said Madame.

"She may prefer the Metropolitan to do it," said Lion smoothly.

"You wouldn't think of it, Lion!"

"You said I would," Lion reminded her.

"Hilda wouldn't trreat me like that. She wouldn't dare. I shouldn't allow her to trreat me like that—nor you, Lion." She said again, "Hilda wouldn't treat me like that." Then she remembered how she had sometimes treated Hilda and was silenced. Oll these birrds come home to roost, she thought angrily. It was, she felt, exactly like Hilda to come home to roost. She paused. "Lion," she said slowly, "Hilda will want to dance Leda herself."

"Who else?" said Lion. "Or do you want her to give it to Caroline? I had better go and fetch Hilda. I have a taxi outside. Zanny is giving the man some breakfast to keep him quiet."

Madame did not answer. She felt as she had felt about the Lady. She did not want to relinquish this part to anyone. Relinquish, cried Madame to herself. I have never had it. If she had to . . . to give it up! thought Madame—and, in spite of sense, she felt she gave it up—then she could bear only to give it up to Caroline, and yet . . . Hilda dancing it was more herself. But I am talking about the Lady, thought Madame. This is another part. Ah, I hate to be old! she cried suddenly, silently. I hate to be old! Where had that feeling come from? She had gone past that long ago, past the age of regrets. I should have died before them oll, thought Madame. That is what a dancer should do, die young. I am old, dried, hideous. And the whole of her cried again, I don't want anyone else to have this part.

"Anyway, Leda doesn't matter," said Lion. "She is only a counterpart to the Swan."

"How can you?" said Madame, up in arms, but Lion only smiled at her quite certainly and went away to fetch Hilda.

This is doing something to Lion, thought Madame, looking after him. Something he needs. He is . . . emerging, said Madame. But is he hard enough, strange enough, for this Swan? It is a strange wild white part. It is bird ferocity, less male, more cruel, than an animal. *The Swan comes with a rush*, a rush of love, said Madame. Lion doesn't know that—or does he? With all her knowledge of him, that was something she could not know; the intimate, the strongest moment is hidden except from one . . . And I am not that one, said Madame, and again she had the feeling of being ousted. "You live on in these children," they said to her. Yes, that is the trrouble, said Madame. I only live in them, and it isn't enough. The old feelings had woken. Ah, don't be so trroublesome, said Madame to herself. There is too much to do for me to be trroubled with you now.

*Bring together the component parts* . . . but if the parts are in conflict, how will they ever compound? "They must compound," said Madame. The conflict began with Hilda.

"You mean . . . you want to have my *Leda and the Swan* if you like it, instead of *Lyre with Seven Strings?*"

"Of course. Of course," said Madame impatiently. "It is oll settled long ago." It annoyed her that Hilda looked startled.

"How can it be long ago, when I saw you late last night and it is only seven o'clock in the morning now?" Hilda's look seemed to say.

"I shall explain it to you later," said Madame haughtily. Hilda knew she never would, but she let it pass. "That isn't the point. The point is *time*, dearr child," said Madame. "Lion is changing. Go and get into your practice things and come back to me here and let me see it."

"Then . . . you think *Leda and the Swan* is good?"

Is she doing this on purpose? thought Madame. "Why should it be . . ." she began aloud, and stopped. "How do I know what it is?" she said instead. "I haven't seen it yet."

"But you like the idea?"

"The idea has possibilities," said Madame as judiciously as she could, then her impatience broke. "Well, what are you waiting for?" she cried. "What more do you want?"

"I'm not sure," said Hilda, and another look came into her face. Madame recognized it. She had seen it on many faces before. It had the beginnings of obstinacy; it was wary and she saw it with irritation and a slight sinking of her heart. Surely, she thought, I shall not have to *flatter* this out of Hilda. That would be too . . . Ah! How can clever people be so stupid! asked Madame impatiently, but she knew quite well they could.

"Listen to me, dearr child," she said, and, all the while, the precious minutes were ticking away. We shall never get done at this rate, thought Madame, and aloud: "Listen to me." She had no idea what she had to say to which Hilda could profitably listen, but she knew it was no use arguing; the more one argued with that look the more embattled it became, but "Listen to me," she said. Inspiration came. "Hilda, it was many years ago Mikhail Mikhailovitch came to my dressing-room . . ."

Hilda's unabated look asked plainly what Mikhail Mikhailovitch was to do with her.

"Mikhail was Mayakovsky, the manager. He came to my dressing-room and he said, 'Anna. Go to Signora Beltrametti and get fitted for Tanya's dress and then go on the stage to Polonsky. You will dance the Doll tonight.' He did not explain to me: Tanya has quarrelled with Polonsky, they have refused to dance together, and I have refused her to stay without it, and such-and-such an arrangement has been made. No. There was no need to. I accepted it without a worrd," said Madame. Lion had come in and she saw him look at her, in that new sideways way. "Without a murmur," said Madame defiantly at Lion. "And that was my success, Hilda. I was second ballerina then, it was trrue; perhaps our cases are not parallel, but after that I was second to nobody, *but* if I had quarrelled and quibbled I should not have had my destiny." She put her hand gently on Hilda's shoulder. "Is this perhaps your destiny, Hilda?" she asked.

Was destiny too large a word to use to Hilda? No, destinies can be oll sizes, said Madame.

Hilda had several things she meant to say to Madame: Are you going to change it and twist it and spoil it? Will you pull this one to pieces too? Is it going to be my ballet or yours? . . . Now she went to change without a word.

"Did Mikhail Mikhailovitch come to your dressing-room?" asked Lion when Hilda had gone.

"Of course he did," said Madame, and with dignity she asked, "Why not?"

"I wondered," said Lion smoothly.

"You can't manage people with lies, my dear Lion," said Madame untruthfully, and added, "At least, not for very long."

Hilda, when she came back again, looked as if she were destined for beauty. That is only an illusion, said Madame. She isn't at all beautiful. Her face is too narrow, her neck is too long, but what has happened to her? thought Madame.

Hilda had not chosen to put on her usual practice dress. With tights, she wore a white tutu and, because it was early and cold, she had wound her bodice and shoulders with an old scarf of poppy-coloured silk sewn with sequins. As she came in, with her sleek small head and scintillating scarf and fine legs in their tights and ribbon-laced shoes, she had a springing radiant vitality that surprised Madame. I seem to be continually surprised at Hilda, she thought, as if she has a fund of life to draw on. But that is what I had, thought Madame jealously. Hilda's eyes were radiant, her skin fresh . . . as dew, thought Madame. That is because she is young . . . and her jealousy grew more biting. "Why a tutu?" asked Madame. "It should have been a tunic for Leda."

Hilda stared at her rebuked. It should have been a tunic for Leda. At this important minute she, Hilda, had been thinking not of Leda, the role, but of herself. That was unlike Hilda. Madame looked at her curiously as she went across the floor and stood in Leda's first pose, waiting for Lion to release the gramophone and set the needle. As she took the pose, Madame saw her smile at Lion. Hilda thought the smile was secret, but it was completely palpable to Madame. She has been kissed in the taxi, that one, said Madame.

Lion set the needle and the music began. *Leda, looking for shells on the lake shore* . . .

Because Madame had liked the theme of the ballet, because it appealed to her, perhaps peculiarly appealed to her, she watched it all the more severely. She would not be betrayed again into overlooking anything . . . no, not even by my personal taste. . . . To be impersonal is to be dull, to be too personal is to make judgment difficult, and Madame, for all her doubts and lapses, still knew how to judge. She stood, a stern scrutator, watching Lion and Hilda dance.

There was no help in the room. The light was bleak and cold, they were in practice dress, though Hilda had the warm colour of the scarf; the room was too small, the music sounded too loud and blatant in its narrow space, and Madame was in no mood to be pleased; she was tired in mind and body, she ached from her eyes to her insteps, and she had a pain in the back of her neck and in her temples that felt stiff and taut with strain. She watched intently. They had several stops; places where Hilda had to stop Lion and explain to him, or read directions; they stopped again and then again. Hilda threw a quick look at Madame, but Madame remained patient. Presently it took shape. They went back to the beginning and it began to move; it moved swiftly. One of the things Madame saw and noted with approval was its pace. Older people, many older, will envy that, she found herself thinking. Where did she get it from? asked Madame.

Choreography, the science and design of dancing, is not to be arrived at easily, in five minutes, or five years, or, for most, not in fifty. How then had this young silent girl achieved it? Madame did not know, but she saw, as the pattern of the ballet unfolded, how deep and firm were the strata of Hilda's knowledge. And so they should be, said Madame. I taught her . . . but she knew that few, perhaps none, of the others had learnt from her like this. Hilda had something Madame had not taught her, and had it in more degree than Madame herself. She had vision. *She knows more than she knows she knows.* Who had said that? Mr. Felix. Felix, said Madame. Felix will say *I told you so.* And he will be right, said Madame.

The ballet was short and as tense and dramatic as even Madame could have wished. Leda, the young unconscious dreaming virgin Leda, is attacked on the lake shore by the Swan in all his force; then in his preening solitary love dance he dances alone until, under his renewed savage force, Leda abandons herself and is carried away. It was an extravagant theme, but Hilda had discarded extravagance; it had no virtuoso, no extravagant lifts or fireworks such as might be expected with the strength of the theme and her slight experience. It had technical strength and it had drama. And it has beauty, said Madame, and she paused. It makes you remember it after . . . said Madame. It's bold, she said, very bold for a young girl's work, and strong. No wonder I felt her too strong in the classroom. And she looked at Hilda with that surprise again. It's a long time since I saw a ballet that is romantic without nostalgia, said Madame. As if romance must be half dead, not? This is alive, said Madame. I feel it, my pulses feel it. I didn't know I had such pulses, said Madame.

Lion and Hilda stood shoulder to shoulder, their cheeks hot and their eyes bright, waiting for Madame's verdict. Her excitement had communicated itself to them as theirs had to her. She said, "Dance it again."

They danced and, watching them then, Madame thought they were never again to dance it quite as they did this time. They were excited, and their feeling for one another was in its first flush and so, after all, was the ballet in its first flush. Afterwards must come the toil of its production when it would become real with properties attached to it; when, built up round its first conception, must come buttresses of *décor*, orchestration, dresses, lights. Now it was itself, still visionary though fledged. I should like it to stay like that, said Madame, though she had no intention of allowing it. I wish it could keep that . . . that pristine quality, but they don't. They don't because they can't; they can't be new again for ever . . . or only a few—a very few. It isn't to be supposed that this is one of the few, but . . . I said her talent was too strong, said Madame. I was right in the wrong way. There is something more than talent here, and she is going to do something for Lion, if he is wise.

It was over in a few minutes. It had gone, but it would come again . . . over and over again if I am not very much mistaken, said Madame. But I wish it could stay as it was then. The last quiver of the last chord, loud and . . . searing, said Madame, there was no other word for it . . . had died away and there was a pause. Then . . . "I think it is beautiful," said Madame gravely. Those five small words meant more to Hilda than anything that would be said to her in her life again. She shone with happiness.

But I was right, thought Madame, she is too dominant for Leda, too strong. . . . At this moment Hilda could dance Leda because, at this moment, she loved Lion and was subservient to love. Now she was in the state of being eager, trembling, pliant . . . as they oll are, thought Madame . . . and, in a curious way, again it pleased her to see that the serious conceited cold little snake Hilda was not exempt. She is ripe for Leda, exactly ripe now, diagnosed Madame, and she wondered how long it could last. I hope it will last the season, she said. It should, not? It is only three weeks, and she thinks it will last for ever. You may lose it in any second, she said silently to Hilda. Any single little thing may spoil it. It's brief, it's brittle. You can break it easily. . . . But in spite of this warning Hilda looked as safe and unconscious as anyone caught up out of the world to a separate pinnacle. But you will have to come down, said Madame jealously.

She tried to turn her thoughts away. "How did you write this? What made you think of it?" she asked Hilda.

"I . . . don't know," said Hilda. "It came to me."

Madame nodded approvingly. She approved of that. "That is rright," she said gravely. "It came to you. You didn't make it up. That is what so many of them say. It came to you, it was *vouchsafed* to you," said Madame severely. Afterwards, when she came to write other ballets, Hilda often thought it was.

"I found the Carlorossi *Fantasia and Variations*," she said slowly. "They gave me the first idea of it. I thought they fitted. I showed them to Mr. Felix. He thought so too. That is how it began."

Mr. Felix came. He heard, listened, and saw. "And when do you want it?" asked Mr. Felix. "*Tonight?* You want to have it in the programme tonight? My dear Anna!"

"I mean to have it in the programme tonight," Madame corrected him.

"It's quite shorrt," Madame argued. "It only takes a few minutes. It is really only a divertissement, only you couldn't call it a divertissement, and Hilda has arranged the music down to the last bar."

"Off records," said Mr. Felix dryly. "Then you will use the records? For tonight?"

"I have an orchestra, not?" said Madame. "Why shouldn't I use it?"

"Because, to begin with, there isn't a score of that Carlorossi in London, or if there is, I don't know where to find it."

"You are not trrying, Felix."

"Anna, there isn't time to try."

"Couldn't you, not, score it from the records?"

"I could, in several days. I thought you wanted it for tonight."

"You are very disagreeable," said Madame.

"But, Anna . . ."

"You are never enthusiast. Never."

"Well, what can I do?" asked Mr. Felix and out of his bright forget-me-not eyes he watched her.

Madame walked away to the end of the room, back again, beating her clenched fist into the palm of her other hand.

"Lion?"

Lion shook his head.

"I tried to get a score as a possibility for Hilda," said Mr. Felix. Hilda looked surprised. "I tried everywhere I know, and I know everywhere."

"The Metropolitan? Great Marlborough Street? B.B.C.?"

"All tried. No one has it."

"But there must have been a score, to make the records. We must go to the makers."

"There wouldn't be time," said Mr. Felix. "It would take all day, perhaps two days, to unearth it, even if they could find it. Still, we might try."

"Miss Parkes, go and ring up. Take the records and see what you can do."

"Could we broadcast for it?" said Hilda.

"We could," said Felix. "If anybody had it it would probably be in Wales or somewhere like that."

"Ilse could go to Wales and fetch it," said Madame.

"Anna . . ."

"You could."

"I could," said Miss Ilse, "but . . ."

"Not in time for tonight," said Mr. Felix. "Still . . . it may not be in Wales. Lion, you will have to go personally, to Broadcasting House."

"That would take me all day," said Lion. "Let's think of something."

"Oll of you think," urged Madame. "Ilse," she accused, "you are thinking of something else. Not of me and this trrouble at oll, not? I know you when your face looks like that . . ."

"Anna," interrupted Miss Ilse. "I was thinking of Madame Rosa."

"Madame Rosa? Yes! Madame Rosa! Get on to her, Ilse, im-me-diat-ely."

"Madame Rosa?" asked Mr. Felix.

"She is Spanish," said Madame. "She is the widow of Miguel, the conjuror."

"If she is Spanish, why is she 'Madame'?"

"Because she is clairvoyant."

"I . . . see. Then she will divine for the score?"

"No, of course not," said Madame crossly. "She has every score that is in existence, prractically. It was not Miguel who was the collector. It was his father. His father was head clerk in Pasqual's in Madrid."

"Pasqual's! They had everything," said Mr. Felix.

"Of course. Why do you think we have been talking? Wasting our breath?" said Madame. "He collected scores, and when he was not a Fascist or a Franco or whatever the others were, he brought them to England. He died, and Madame Rosa has kept them. I hope she has kept them. Ilse, you must go to her at once. She lives in Clapham. You know Clapham, Ilse."

"No," said Miss Ilse.

"Zanny will know, but don't send Zanny or she will quarrel. If she doesn't know, the laundry will know, because it was Madame Rosa who told us about the laundry. Get on to the laundry and you will find out. Don't look so bewildered, Ilse. It's not so far to Clapham."

"Not as far as Wales . . . or Milan," said Miss Ilse, with rare spirit.

"Can we telephone her first?" asked the more merciful Hilda.

Madame Rosa's number was found out from the laundry and Miss Ilse telephoned her. Madame Rosa said she would look for the score but it was early and first she must have her coffee.

"Coffee!" cried Madame. "When have I had coffee?"

"Ages ago," said Lion.

"You must be reasonable, Anna."

"If I am reasonable, this ballet won't go on."

Miss Ilse telephoned again in a few minutes and five minutes after that. Madame Rosa then said she refused to look for the score.

"There," said Miss Ilse. "What did I tell you?"

"You must go to her, Ilse. You must explain to her, beg her, plead her. Do anything. Tell her I am sorry. Tell her anything. Don't pull that face to me. Shouldn't I go myself if I could be spared? Go with her, Felix. After oll it is your business. Please, please go. Ah, what a trroublesome woman! How impatient. Won't wait one little minute. I don't understand how people can be impatient like that," said Madame. "Felix, you must get a taxi and go with Ilse. Ah! What else is to happen this morning!"

A minute later Madame Rosa telephoned to say she had after all, on second thoughts, as a favour to Madame Holbein, looked for the score.

"And she has it?"

"She has it."

"Ah! Ilse! Thank God! Tell her a thousand thanks. A thousand thousand thanks. Say I shall send her tickets, say I shall send her a bottle of good brrandy—when I have one. Say . . ."

"Wait," said Mr. Felix.

"Wait? For what? We have the score. What do you need now more?"

"The parts," said Mr. Felix.

"Parrts? What parts? Ah, the orchestra parts!"

"Yes, the orchestra parts. The score is no use without parts."

"Dear God in Heaven!" said Miss Ilse.

"Stop talking, Ilse! Go. Ask her, has she the parts?"

No. Madame Rosa regretted, but she had not. There was silence.

"You could wrrite them," said Madame.

"By tonight."

"Of course. What else? You could, Felix. There are not so many. We could shut you up oll day by yourself . . ."

"Thank you," said Mr. Felix but he did not say no. He said, "If you have a rehearsal of *Noble Life* . . ."

"We won't have a rehearsal, or, if we do, we can manage. Danielli can conduct. We can manage with him. We can manage anything if you will write those parrts, and get it ready in time. The orchestra can be called for when you wish. Lion and Hilda will stay here to rehearse with you . . ."

"I shall need three copyists," said Mr. Felix. "Pah!" He threw down his pencil. "What is the use of talking, Anna? Where will you get three copyists today? They are all working on films. No, it's impossible I tell you, Anna. Im-poss-i-ble!"

"Lion," said Madame, "go and get me Edmund White on the telephone. Edmund, personally, Lion."

"But . . . shall I get him personally? Won't there be a *battery* of secretaries?"

"Tell them it is Madame Holbein," said Madame grandly, and then her certainty cracked. "Tell them how imporrtant it is, how little time, how urrgent . . ." She stopped herself. "No! Don't tell them any of that. Tell them it is Madame Holbein."

Mr. Felix was dry and refused to become excited, but Madame had not, from the beginning, a moment of doubt that he would do all in his power to help. He had thrown all the cogs he should in her wheels but no others; "It was his duty," said Madame. "They were not cogs, they were knots that had to be untied if he was to do his worrk."

"You make me giddy," said Lion.

The artists were another thing. Noel Streete had no telephone; she sent the unwilling Miss Parkes round to his rooms, but his landlady said he had only just come in and gone to bed and no one dared wake him . . . "'until he has slept it off,' she said," reported Miss Parkes.

"Ah! Why does everyone conflict me so?" cried Madame. "Very well. We must get Moron. Pierre Moron. I don't like his work so well, but it is better for this than Mathilde's, and he is very fashionable."

"He did the re-dress for *Cimarosiana*," said Hilda.

"It wasn't a success," said Lion.

"A re-dress never is," said Madame sweepingly. "I have told you, Lion. It must be one; choreographer, artist, composer must be parrtners, but for this, this ballet, we shall have to contrrive." She looked at Hilda. "Now what is the matter, Hilda?"

"If it isn't to be properly set, I had rather it wasn't done," said Hilda mutinously.

"Who said it shouldn't be properly set?" demanded Madame. "Because I say we shall have to contrrive it doesn't mean that we should compromise, be expedient." Now she could use that word derisively . . . as it is meant to be used, said Madame. "We must use our wits," said Madame, her eyes sparkling. "You don't trust yours. I trrust mine."

Pierre Moron saw the ballet, and was immediately filled with compliments and hope. "It's exquisite, *but* exquisite! And raw. How raw! I like it raw. And that overbearing sexual force that is so rare . . ."

"It isn't rare at oll," said Madame. "It happens oll the time. Now, can you do this, Pierre, do you think? Yes or no?"

"Given time . . ." said Pierre charmingly.

"You know there is no time."

They were in the theatre to give Pierre Moron the proportions of the stage, its height and depth and lighting and fittings. "He ought to know them," said Lion. "As well as *Cimarosiana* he did *Orientales*."

"And just as badly," said Madame. She was beginning to be cross with Pierre. Time was passing every moment and he did nothing but admire and flash his eyes at Hilda. They were fine eyes, black, large, brilliant as diamonds. But too large to be real diamonds, thought Madame. They must be false, and he should leave Hilda alone when I am here, not? It isn't polite to me. "Well, Pierre," she said. "I'm waiting."

"I see it," said Moron, half shutting his eyes.

"What do you see?"

"*Attendez.* I'm telling you. First the Swan. I see the Swan," said Pierre. "A close-fitting all-over costume, like tights, you understand, but all over—arms, head, everything—fitting the whole torso and painted, painted in flaky grey-white, tempera perhaps, to give the idea of coldness, close-fitting over the head, even the hands; non-human, stiff, cold as a shrroud," said Pierre. "We could make a mask to cover the face. A mask of mosquito netting, stiffened with plaster of Paris, perhaps, and plaster of Paris feathers on the shoulders and knees."

"How should I dance?" asked Lion. "How should I breathe?"

Pierre considered. "We should leave holes for you to breathe through," he said kindly. "It would be a little stiff, but very effective."

"The Swan must have wings," said Hilda.

"Wings?"

"I don't see him with wings," Pierre objected.

"I do," said Hilda. "He must have wings."

"Leda should be blue," said Pierre.

"Blue all over?" said Madame caustically.

"She is virginal, yes?" Pierre ignored Madame.

"No," said Hilda. "That isn't her quality."

"She is virgin. You say so."

"It still isn't her quality."

"That is how I see her."

"Then you see her wrong."

Lion stared. If Hilda had been Madame she could not have been more crisp.

"Pierre. Come now. Try," said Madame.

Pierre, injured, opened his eyes. "I *am* trying, but if Miss . . . Miss . . . quarrels with me all the time . . . what can I do?"

"You can do nothing," said Madame fiercely. "Nothing at oll. What they are oll talking about in you I don't know. Miss Parkes, take Monsieur Moron away, and Hilda, if you must be so difficult, you will please to hold your tongue. I am giving you this production, not, and how can I if you upset the cart oll the time?"

"The Swan must have wings," said Hilda.

"Lion, you must go for Noel. You must bring him. You must get him awake somehow and you must make him come."

Noel was still in his evening clothes when Lion brought him. He sagged with illness and tiredness; his face was yellow-green and the whites of his eyes were yellow-brown and bloodshot; he looked at the light obliquely as if it hurt him, and he was sullen and apathetic.

"Noel, I have to ask you . . ."

"Damfool to ask me an'thing now, this bloody time a mornin'. Have y' a black handkerchief?" said Noel.

"A black handkerchief?"

"Yes, want it for m' eyes. M' eyes feel bloody wrong."

"They mustn't feel wrong now. I need your eyes," cried Madame in anguish. Then she rallied herself. "Lion, you have a black scarf. Miss Parkes, fetch Mr. Streete a large whisky and soda."

"No soda," said Noel. Madame was glad Miss Ilse was gone with Mr. Felix to Madame Rosa.

When the whisky came, she guided Noel into a seat, touching him with the tips of her fingers. "Now, Miss Parkes, go and tell Zanny to make a large pot of strong black coffee, hot, verry hot, and bring it back here." She let Noel sit still, let the whisky soak into him before she signalled to Lion.

She did not explain anything. She said, "Look." He should understand that no matter how bad he is, thought Madame.

She had been afraid that the music would hurt Noel's head, but he seemed unmoved by it. He sat by her, his hands hanging loose, his head pushed forward at the stage, his eyelids, that were puffy and red, heavy over his eyes. He smells sodden, thought Madame. His whole body is sodden. And to think of the things that are shut up in that body. Poor Noel. She was angry with him too. He isn't pitiful, he is wicked, she said.

Once he spoke. "What is it?"

"Leda and the Swan."

"Hmmph!"

When it was over he said, "Who did it?"

"The girl. Hilda French."

"Hmmph! You want me to do it for you?"

"Yes, Noel."

"For when?"

Madame took a breath, looked at his face and away again, and said, "For tonight," and waited for his explosion.

But Noel only nodded and said, "I thought so. When you sent for me at this damfool hour of th' morning."

Madame waited.

"I would do it for you, if I could," said Noel.

"You *could*, Noel."

"M' dear, with what? I'm not a bloody conjuror. I can't make a set or dresses out of th' air."

"We can improvise."

"Like a damfool village pageant?"

"No! No! Not at oll," said Madame, in a flash of temper. "Would I ask you? Use your sense, Noel, if you have any left. No. Firrst decide what you want, and then we shall rransack London," said Madame, "the whole of London to find it."

"It takes time to ransack-hic London," said Noel and gave a sudden yawn. "London-is-so-big."

"Noel, you are not to go to sleep. Miss Parkes, where is that coffee? Give Mr. Streete some coffee and then tell Hilda to come here."

Hilda too was tired with a bad night, continual dancing, much emotion, and no breakfast. She did not like the look of Noel. "Why did you bring him? He is drunk," she said, offended, like a little puritan, to Lion.

"He is always drunk," said Lion, as if that were an explanation.

"Then why does Madame let . . ."

"Wait," said Lion. "You will see," and as Hilda looked still unconvinced he said, "You didn't like the Moron, did you?"

"No."

"Noel Streete did the sets for *The Other Island*," said Lion, "and *Collage*."

"Did he?" Hilda's eyes opened. "Is he *that* Noel?"

"That Noel," said Lion. "Wait. Leave him to Madame."

When Hilda came near Noel part of her was offended by his looks and his smell, part of her was interested and instinctively respectful of something she recognized as alive in this sodden heap of a man. It is that Noel, she thought. But how dreadful he looks.

He stood up when Madame introduced him, holding on to the seat in front of him with one hand. "It was clever of you to write that," he said. His voice was husky and bleared, but he looked at her intently from under his weary lids. "How old are you?"

"Seventeen," said Hilda.

"Seventeen. Lucky," said Noel. "Lucky. Don't you go and tie yourself up now with any bloody nonsense. You keep yourself clear and one day . . . one day, hic . . ." He held the back of the seat more tightly and turned away from Hilda. Presently he turned back again and asked, "How do you want it dressed?"

"I want the Swan to have wings," said Hilda immediately.

"How can he dance in wings?" said Madame.

"He can," insisted Hilda.

"What about his lifts?"

"They must be swinging wings," said Hilda. "Not stiffly fixed, fixed so that they can swing."

"I see what you mean," said Noel, brooding. "I . . . see . . . what . . . you mean. Great wings and feathered, like Icarus."

"Even bigger," said Hilda.

"Even bigger," said Noel. "And? What else?"

Hilda, who usually had so many ideas that she could hardly choose among them, hesitated. "Anything I think of seems banal," she said. "Feathers . . .

tights . . . they all give the idea of an imitation, an unreal swan. I . . . haven't been able to think what else he should wear."

"Because he shouldn't wear anything else," said Noel. "He is savage and wild." Her eyes closed to think of that, and then widened, bright with interest. "Isn't he?" said Noel.

"Yes. Yes, he is."

"Except for the wings," said Noel, "he should be naked."

"But he can't be naked . . . on the stage, Noel," said Madame. "Not on my stage."

"It doesn't matter what damfool stage," said Noel irritably. "He must be whitened, his whole skin. He can wear a G-string," he said irritably to Madame, "Feathered, with the feathers just fitting the hipbones. And, like a savage wears, feathers round his wrists. Yes, he must be whitened, his face and his hair . . ."

"A white wig?" said Madame doubtfully.

"A wig won't do. No damfool wig," said Noel violently. "It must be his own hair, whitened with something that thickens it and mats it and makes it stiff, so that it suggests a casque of feathers, but stiff, not soft. Ordinary wet-white whitening should do; if that isn't stiff enough, whitewash. It must be done some time before so that it sets."

"Oh, well, I dance nothing before it," said Lion, "and I can have a bath after, I suppose, in time to dress for *Noble Life*."

"I will do you myself, Lion," said Noel.

"You watch while Joe does it," said Lion prudently. "Go on."

"The webs," said Noel. "Those webs are important. They are a horrifying part of a swan, big, powerful, black. We should paint your legs black to the thighs . . ."

"Paint? Why not tights?"

"The texture," said Noel briefly. "They must be skin, swarthy and matt, but if we do that it will foreshorten you, make you thick-set. No, we shall have to go without it. You must have black shoes and your eyes must be made up to look heavy, painted with that stuff Indians put on their eyes, kohl, and you must have a red spot on your forehead between the brows. We must try it now. There isn't time for maquettes," and he said to Madame as if she were Miss Parkes, "Get wet-white and whitening. Better get whitewash ready as well, in case, and grease-paint, let's see, black and a blue and vermilion, I think, and the trunks, not trunks but a covering, and the feathers . . ."

"Zanny and Miss Porteus can take those off the *Swan Lake* dresses, Miss Parkes. Tell them."

"Yes, Madame."

"And the wings. You must get great white towering wings," said Noel, "almost as high as Lion himself."

Madame, Lion, Hilda, Miss Parkes, looked at one another in silence. "Get wings!"

"But, Noel . . ."

"You said you would get me whatever I wanted," said Noel. "Now you can."

"But, Noel. Can you think . . ."

"How can I think if you go on talking to me? How can I work your bloody thing out? Come here," he said, jerking his head to Hilda, "Listen."

"Call Miss Porteus and Zanny," said Madame. "Lion, would the Metropolitan . . ."

"I can ask them," said Lion doubtfully, "but I don't think so . . ."

"They had wings on the dreamboat in the last act of *Swan Lake*," said Miss Parkes.

"Those were wooden," said Madame witheringly.

"Even paper wouldn't do," said Lion. "It would rustle."

Miss Ilse came in, spent and white, but with a look of secret elation that Madame knew. Like a cat that has been at the cream, said Madame. She has been in, over the way. She turned her back on Miss Ilse. "Zanny. Miss Porteus," she said. "We have to make Lion a pair of wings."

"What is he?" asked Zanny. "A fairy or an aeroplane or a beetle?"

"Zanny, don't be rude to Madame," said Miss Ilse.

"I'm not rude to Madame."

"Ilse, don't interfere. You don't know what we are talking about. You are too *late* to know what we are talking about. You didn't come in with Felix, not? I know where you have been."

"Anna . . ."

"Wings take days, Madame," said Miss Porteus.

"These can't take days. We must have them this morning."

"That isn't possible, Madame."

"It must be possible. It can be possible if you choose."

"Anna."

"Be quiet, Ilse. Anything can be possible, Miss Porteus, if you have enough will. That is what you haven't . . . enough will. You have no courage, Miss Porteus, and that isn't what I like to see in you . . ."

"Anna . . ."

"Ilse, *will* you not interrupt. I say we must get those wings today and we shall get those wings."

"You had better ask Miss Ilse to work a miracle for you," suggested Zanny tartly.

"I can," said Miss Ilse. "Anna, I have been trying to tell you. The Convent has wings. They have most beautiful great feathered wings, shaped right to the ground from the shoulders; all made of long white feathers, on stiffened frames. They use them for the Archangel Gabriel and for angels in the tableaux. They move most beautifully when they walk; the nuns will lend them," said Miss Ilse. "I knew Hilda wanted them, so I went in on my way to ask."

Hilda and Noel were talking of Leda. "She will have to have her dress torn off her," said Noel.

"*Not* on my stage," said Madame again.

"It's difficult to find a suitable dress for that," said Noel moodily, as if he had not heard her.

"There is a picture . . ." said Hilda hesitantly. She was respectfully hesitant with Noel. "You . . . you know it, of course. *The Nativity* of Piero della Francesca in the National Gallery. Do you remember the dresses of the choir of angels?"

"We seem full of angels, not?" said Madame, and she said sharply, "What are they like?"

"They . . . could tear off," said Hilda, "leaving only the underdress. There —there would be a contrast between the high-necked looped gown and the underdress, limp and soft. I think . . . dark deep red, a brown-red for the overdress, and . . ."

"Scarlet underneath. The colour you are wearing," said Noel, his eyes looking down on Hilda in the sequined scarf. "I'm not sure of the shape of the gown. Let's take a taxi to the Gallery and see."

Madame opposed this. She did not want to let Noel out of her sight. She did not want Hilda to go with Noel. "No," she said. "You two needn't go. Hilda mustn't get tired."

"If she wants to have her *décor* done she must get tired," said Noel. "She has to work."

"But you needn't go to the Gallery. I can send Miss Parkes for a copy of the picture. Miss Parkes or anyone." She had a feeling of danger, an antenna that told her that if Hilda went with Noel it would, in some way, destroy her mood for Lion. . . . Why? I don't know. How? *Look* at Noel and then look at Lion. How could it? I don't know, said Madame, but it could.

"Miss Parkes, or whatever her name is, can't bring the colours," argued Noel. "We shan't be long."

"But, Noel . . ."

"Madame, I must. . . ."

"I can't spare Hilda."

"I must have her."

"No, Noel."

"Yes."

Madame was nearly exhausted. Olways . . . when you have things arranged, this, this character crrops up. "Noel, my dearr!" she began, and, discarding her exhaustion, she put her hand under his arm and turned him towards her and began to talk to him.

"Oh, very well," said Noel after a moment or two, and flung away from her. "I suppose we needn't go."

"For colours, no," said Madame. "You have them oll here in your head; and to see Hilda, no. Hilda has other things to do, and so have you, Noel."

"You are a slave-driver," said Noel, but he did not say it crossly. "I must go home for my things."

"I shall send for them," said Madame quickly. No, it would not do for Noel to get away; she might not see him again. "You can work here, Noel. You have to work here, not?"

"Have you a back-cloth without dye on it?" asked Noel. "Get it put down;

and what colour curtains have you? I shall need them to mask in the sides."

"They are grey," said Madame. "Grey-grreen."

"Good," said Noel thoughtfully. "Yes, good. Couldn't be better. Get someone to ring Elibanks. They can probably send two of their boys or a girl along. Tell them to bring two buckets, mixed grey-green, and brushes and a stipple brush."

"I don't want it stippled, Noel."

"Not stippled, to finish it off evenly," said Noel. He was looking at the stage, measuring it with his eyes that were so nearly closed that Madame was afraid he was going to sleep again standing up.

You not only have to light the fires, she said irritably to herself, you have to keep them burrning. She called Miss Parkes and told her to give Noel another cup of coffee. "See that it is hot firrst," she said; she suspected that Miss Parkes was capable of lukewarm coffee.

She was grateful that she had neither jerked Noel nor spoken to him when he looked up. "Was it the *Gossip Review*," he asked, "that showed those French postcards in a cut cloth of paper lace?"

"Postcards? In paper lace?"

"Yes, it was small, quite small." His eyes measured the proscenium again. "I believe it would do . . . if we can get it. If they have still got it. Lion," he called. "Here, Lion. Come here."

"But . . . Noel . . . you are not going to put Leda into a frame of paper lace?"

"Wait," said Noel abstractedly. "Wait. Lion, is Glancy here? Good. Now listen. You must get on to the Gossip, the Gossip Theatre, and ask for Munro Jennings and ask him . . ." he walked away with Lion. ". . . might fit here . . . no time to make it." He was showing Lion what he meant, measuring with his hands; now he did not look shambling, nor as ill, and his voice was clear. "I think he is going to do it," said Madame to Hilda, who was standing near her. "I think he is going to be oll right."

Hilda left Madame and went to them. Glancy joined them. They stood in a group talking, oblivious. Then Edwin, the young electrician, came on the stage. Lion called him down. "Good," said Madame. "They should begin to think of lights." She watched them with growing content. "It's going forward, not?" she said.

Lion went away to telephone and presently came back. "Yes, they have it, but it's torn, and one of the battens is split."

"I can get on to that," said Glancy. "We can patch it."

Miss Porteus came down with a tape measure and measured Lion as he stood talking. She had the velvet heart pinned to her dress; Madame could see the pins gleaming in it as she knelt to pass the tape round Lion's thighs. Madame could hear her sniff as she paused and wrote the measurement down on her little piece of paper. Poor Miss Porteus, thought Madame. I mustn't forget Lollie at four.

"Zanny thinks it a pity to spoil the *Swan Lake* dresses," said Rebecca. "I am going down to Wardour Street, to get some feathers."

"Has anyone gone to the Gallery for Noel's picture?"

"Yes. Alma came in. I sent her."

"And Felix? How is Felix doing?"

"He has shut himself in the classroom. Miss Ilse has put a table for him there. She has taken him some breakfast."

"The copyists should be on their way from Broadwood," said Madame.

"Mr. Felix needs more manuscript paper. Shall I get it?" said Miss Parkes.

"Yes. And who should go to the printers? Miss Parkes, you should go there at once though it won't be any good. Send one of the girls for the paper."

Glancy came up to them. "Please, ma'am. Mr. Streete says can we arrange for a lorry to go to the Gossip."

From a lorry to feathers. What a mixture of things can go to the making of a ballet.

Now Leon went to the gramophone. "Where are the records?"

"Mr. Felix has them," called Hilda.

"Get them from him, Miss Parkes. Say he must give them up for a little while. We shall brring them straight back. Lion and Hilda have to rehearse to show Edwin for the lights."

As they danced, a back-cloth came down and Madame saw Noel with a boy, and a girl in an overall, her hair tied in a handkerchief, come on the stage with buckets and a step-ladder. Behind the dancers she saw Noel explaining to them; he had a sketch on a piece of brown cardboard. He and the girl conferred, went to the buckets, and stirred up the paint. Noel tried it with a brush. Then they began to lay it on in the same grey-green colour as the curtains. Neither boy nor girl paid the slightest attention to the dancers, and Hilda and Lion modified their steps so as not to crash into the buckets.

"Now they are oll working in together, not?" said Madame with growing satisfaction. "I tell you," she said to Miss Ilse, who had come up behind her, "it is worrth oll the pains when you see it grrowing like this. Slowly, slowly grrowing."

"It isn't slow. It's marvellously quick," said Miss Ilse. "I don't know how you have done it, Anna. It's miraculously quick."

"It isn't quick enough," said Madame, her eyes brooding. "I feel anxious about those copyists for Felix."

"They have come," said Miss Ilse, "and I have brought you an egg flip."

"Ah, Ilse, I hate them!"

"It has brandy in it," said Miss Ilse. "I have one too for Hilda. The child must be exhausted."

"Did you put brandy in hers?"

"Yes," said Miss Ilse firmly.

"Madame." It was Noel. "I want something for feathers, drifting down. At the beginning, before the Swan comes, when Leda is alone, gathering shells. Something for a drifting feather, or feathers. The Swan's feathers drifting down. Torn tissue paper looks like snow."

"Real feathers?"

"No. Either too insignificant or too heavy."

"Anna . . ."

"Wait, Ilse. I am trying to *think!*"

"But, Anna . . ."

"*Ilse!*"

"What is it?" asked Noel, turning to Miss Ilse.

"I'm trying to tell her," said Miss Ilse, flushed, "I used to cut paper feathers when I was a child. They wouldn't look like snow because they are shaped. Cut paper feathers would be the right weight," said Miss Ilse.

"They would," said Noel. "They would." He smiled at Miss Ilse, and Miss Ilse smiled back at him. That is currious, said Madame. I had thought Ilse would be shocked at him and she isn't, not at oll, and I have never seen Noel smile at anyone before.

"Here," said Noel. He was holding in front of her the cardboard sketch she had seen him showing to the two young painters. "I have had to do everything roughly," said Noel. "Couldn't make anything but sketches for the dresses, and I roughed out this."

Now she saw what he meant to do with the frame. It was narrow, of white feathers framing the stage . . . feathers? I suppose they are feathers, but they might be white coral or seaweed, but anyhow white. The back-cloth was grey-green, stormy, "We shall make it look more stormy and then change it with the lights," said Noel, but its grey-green was stormy already, deep with a tinge of greengage. "The curtains are the right colour, or as near as," said Noel. "Just as well, I have enough to do with those bloody feathers."

Then they are feathers, thought Madame.

"Well, is it right?" asked Noel.

"I think it's extrremely clever," said Madame. "I don't know how you thought of it. It seems to me, now I have seen it, exactly right . . . which is queer," said Madame, "because I never could have seen it for myself."

"Blue shells . . ." Noel was saying to himself. "Blue shells . . ."

Miss Porteus and Zanny came back about Hilda's dress. The picture had come and from it Noel had sketched a rough design. "We can get the dark red, more maroon it is, from one of the mantles from *Collage*," said Zanny, "but for the scarlet underdress . . . there is only that scarlet gauze sari of yours, the Benares sari, Madame."

"You wouldn't cut *that,*" said Miss Ilse, glaring at Zanny. "That lovely thing!"

"What else then?" said Zanny. "Perhaps you have time to go all round London looking for it, and you can look till you drop and you won't find that colour, and it has to be *made,*" said Zanny.

"Ah, don't quarrel me oll morning, I can't bear it," said Madame. "Is there time to quibble over this and that, I ask you, Ilse? Cut it, Zanny."

She and Miss Ilse stood and watched Hilda and Lion working together on the stage.

"Anna . . ."

"Yes, Ilse."

"Anna, it's not . . . indecent, is it Anna?"

"It's not indecent," said Madame.

"N-no," said Miss Ilse. "The dress *would* tear, with a swan," said Miss Ilse judiciously. "I always think swans are terrifying, but . . . it's very strong, Anna," she said faintly.

"It's strong," said Madame. "This isn't a children's matinee, Ilse. It is for adults, not?"

"I hope it's not too strong," said Miss Ilse.

Mr. Felix had come in. "I shall have to get the harpist back. I need a harp."

"Well, get him then."

"If he will come. He worked six rehearsals without a performance, and now we want him to work a performance without a rehearsal. But perhaps he will come."

"Felix . . ."

"Anna?"

"Felix, Ilse thinks the Swan obscene."

"Anna, I *didn't* say so."

"I can see it by your face. Felix, will it offend their taste? The English taste?"

"It wasn't invented to please it," said Mr. Felix, watching the stage.

"But . . ."

"As that is neither here nor there, I think it will," said Mr. Felix.

"Offend it or please it?"

"Please it."

"There now, Ilse."

"He didn't say it wasn't indecent," said Miss Ilse. She paused. "And, Anna, who is to pay for all this?"

"It won't cost much, hardly anything, Ilse."

"Hardly anything can be a great deal. Noel paid fifty pounds for that framework from the Gossip Theatre. I heard Lion agree to it on the telephone."

"Ah, Ilse, let's do it firrst and count it later."

"But, Anna . . ."

Madame steeled herself. Sometimes it took all her nerves to disregard Miss Ilse.

"Oll my life, whatever I wanted to do, Ilse, you have said 'Don't.' 'Don't.' 'Don't, Anna.' 'Be careful.' 'Don't do it.' 'Don't take a risk.' If I listened to you I should be sitting at home knitting and reading Sunday books. Go away from me. You are a raven, croaking and croaking and croaking. Isn't it oll going perrfectly well? Why do you throw your doubts on it then? It couldn't be better, Ilse."

Miss Ilse was not listening. "Anna," she said, "Caroline is here."

"Caroline?"

"Yes. She is watching Lion and Hilda," said Miss Ilse. "I don't think she is pleased."

Madame had gone to her sitting-room. "I need a few minutes, Ilse. I must think what this oll is, I must reckon it. If anyone wants me I shall be in my room. They can come to me there, and see Miss Parkes about the printers.

They must get it through for us, Ilse . . . and don't let Noel go away." She said that as a parting injunction.

She went up to the sitting-room and sat down at her desk and rested her head on her hands. Now she had time to think of it, her head was spinning. Reckon it! I can't, said Madame. How can one ever? How can anyone tell the cost of doing any little thing? But jubilance filled her. I can't reckon it, but I have done it, she said. I don't know how far it has come, but it has come a considerable way.

She was sitting at her desk that, every day, Miss Ilse arranged tidily and that, in the first five minutes Madame spent at it, she made untidy again. On it were lists, block sheets of designs, letters, a wire basket of bills. These began the day on Miss Parkes' or Miss Ilse's desks but were gradually transferred to Madame's, where there was great difficulty in finding them again. "Madame, please, have you seen Driscoll's bill?" "No, why should I?" "But . . ." "I have never had it, never!" declared Madame, but Miss Parkes found it in her desk. "Anna, that answer to General Cook Yarborough . . ." "What answer?" "I put it on your desk for you to sign." "I never saw it. Wait, I have signed it, not? Where is it? It isn't here. It must be somewhere." Miss Ilse found it pinned to the back of a design, and Madame had drawn a blue-pencil sketch on it.

There was a heterogeneous collection of things among the papers: an illuminated card that Miss Ilse had laid there for her to see; some pressed primulas in a sheet of old yellowed tissue paper that had been sent to her that morning by an admiral who alleged she had thrown them to him in his box from her bouquet years before in Panama. But why primulas? thought Madame. They would be so difficult to throw? And I don't think they have primulas in Panama?

There was an edition of the child's book, *Peter Rabbit*, in French, and there was an oblong red case of which the velvet was worn.

Madame sat idly turning over the pages of *Peter Rabbit*. She had bought it for Lollie.

"Why should dancing be in French?" said Lollie. "Why should we have to learn all these names in French?"

"Because it is the language of dancing, as Latin is the language of the Catholic Church and medicine and plants."

"But why not plain English?"

"You are an English pupil," said Madame, "but in the same class with you is Calliope, who is Greek, and Lao-Erh, who is half Chinese, and Lippi's little brother, who is Italian. Why should they worrk in English?"

"Why should they work in French?"

"Ballet is international, and it must have a language that can be understood by oll. By trradition its language is French and its tradition has been handed down, even to you, Lollie—and to Calliope and Lao-Erh and Archie and Giacomo and Zoë and Miette. I am glad you have asked me. Even the smallest dancer should understand the dignity and history and tradition of her art."

Holding the little book, Madame thought of Lollie and Lollie's class, her "eggs." If she shut her eyes she could hear the scattering sound, between a slither and a scamper, they made as they ran across the floor in their light shoes when she called "Places."

She saw the feet, standing all alike, the arms lifted in unison showing the small armpits that, in the little girls, had a pearly allure that was far older than they; chins were turned dutifully over shoulders, leg muscles strained and swelled in their efforts to please, thighs turned out, each calf, each instep, was held rigid, the toes pointed in black or white or pink shoes laced over socks. They were held, rigid, then moved all together, to the right, to the left, to the right, arms changed, heads turned, all alike, all adroit.

I know them oll, said Madame, not only their bodies, but their charracters, their sulks and smiles, their pluck and . . . no pluck, said Madame. I can read them, their foreheads and legs and minds and hearts. I am not often wrrong, thought Madame. I was even right in a way about Hilda. I kept her in spite of my feeling against her. I had enough judgment for that. I must not forrget Lollie's audition, thought Madame, and she read in the book: *Il fut attrapé et mis en pâté par Madame McGregor.* . . . Poor Lollie, thought Madame, and smiled.

She laid down the book and picked up the red velvet case and held it for a long while in her hand. She pressed the catch slowly, lingeringly, and as the lid came up she saw the old diamonds sparkle from the dark rubies and she smiled. You have hearrd me speak of this, often . . . the words formed themselves in her head. It was given to Marli the great Italian ballerina when she came to St. Petersburg from Milan as guest artiste for a single performance of *Giselle*. It was given to her by the Tsar, with his own hand, when she was presented. She gave it to me when I came back to the Moscow Festival as a guest artiste myself. I had been her pupil while I was in Italy, I went to Milan to study with her, and she was in Moscow when I came there to dance. I had meant to keep it olways, till my death, but I see that I should allow it to go on. Now you have come back to me, as a guest artiste in my little theatre in your little way. It is only a little way, of course, but, because I believe that you are to do great things, I am giving it to you. I want you to have it, Caroline.

She saw Caroline, her head with its plaited bronze hair, the eyes, the curved face, the white neck, soft shoulders, lovely arms; she saw her in the parts she had had . . . so far, said Madame. "Prelude" in *Sylphides*. The golden "Valse" in *Nutcracker*. One of Prince Florestan's sisters in *Aurora's Wedding*. Chosen Virgin in *Sacre du Printemps*. She is coming, thought Madame. Coming fast. She touched the cross with her finger. But you didn't choose to dance for me last night.

She found herself advancing reasons and excuses: she who never allowed excuses. Caroline had been working oll day. Rehearsals and the performance. She was tired. A bad rehearsal makes a good performance . . . but it was Lion who said *that* tarrydiddle, said Madame, and she shut the box with a click. I shall see how you dance, she said, and then she opened it again. No, she said. One must have faith, not? I shall wrap it up and put it on her table in her dressing-room. I *know* she will dance well for me tonight.

There was a knock at the door. It opened. It was Caroline.

"I am sorry to disturb you, Madame."

Madame looked at her with love and indulgence. "You don't disturb me. You give me rrest, dear child. Come in and shut the door. You may sit down."

Caroline did not sit down. She stood opposite Madame, her hands holding the back of the chair. Her face was angry; there was a red patch on each cheek and her knuckles showed white as she held the chair.

"What is it, Caroline?"

"You didn't mean me to come here this morning, did you?"

Madame stared amazed.

"What are you talking of, dear child?"

"You didn't mean me to know anything about this until tonight, till it was too late to change."

The love and indulgence left Madame's face. "It is too late to change," she said evenly.

"I shan't accept that," said Caroline.

"What do you mean?"

"I refuse." Madame did not answer. "I can refuse," said Caroline. "I am not under contract here."

"Certainly you are not under contract," said Madame. "I put none of my dancers under contract. They are free to go whenever they think they must. I don't keep them."

"Madame . . ." Caroline's gaze flickered and fell as it had when she would not face Madame from the stage. "Madame, I can't be treated like this."

"How are you treated? Pre-cise-ly as before."

"That isn't true."

"I don't tell lies, Caroline."

"I came here as prima ballerina . . ."

"Ballerina? What are you thinking of, Caroline? You are far too young, too inexperrienced to . . . to have that honour," said Madame. "Do you know what a ballerina is? You should think before you say, dearr child! We have no ballerinas here. You are our guest. You have gone further, a little further, than the others, so I give you the biggest parrt, the principal role, tonight. My favourrite part. A bigger role than any you have had so far. Then what do you mean?"

"It . . . it's out of all proportion," said Caroline, indignation in her eyes. "First you let Hilda put on Lyre, and I could have told you it wouldn't be a success, and now this . . ."

"You have seen the new ballet, then?"

"Yes."

"You thought it was promising . . . ?"

"It's beautiful," said Caroline. "It's one of the most beautiful things I have ever seen."

"You didn't object to Lyre because you didn't think it would be a success.

You object to this because you think it will. Then am I rright, Caroline, in saying you are jealous of Hilda?"

"Of *course* not."

"Then?"

"She didn't dance herself in *Lyre*, but this . . . It will take everything," said Caroline slowly. "You know it will. It will take the whole programme."

"I hope it will take its place in the programme," said Madame. "We needed it, Caroline."

"You can't put a young untried dancer beside me."

"Not if she puts herself there?"

"It's such an indignity. She is no one."

"Everyone was no one once. I didn't think, in making room for Hilda, I was hurting you," said Madame. "I didn't think you could be hurt by Hilda."

"But—think of who she is and who I am."

"If she is who you say she is, no one, a young untried dancer, how can she hurt you? If she isn't, she is in her rrightful place. Then why are you afraid?"

"I'm *not* afraid." That stung Caroline.

Why is it, how is it, thought Madame, that I should be driven to taking the part of that little serpent Hilda against you, my Caroline? She looked with infinite misery at Caroline. Caroline did not look full of beauty now, she looked fearful and angry . . . and stupid, thought Madame suddenly. Yes . . . and soft. Things have been too easy for you olways, thought Madame. You have had them too much your own way. She thought of that meadow, that panoramic meadow that she had never seen. Caroline is like a meadow, Hilda is like the road . . . that I came on, the hard highway. But who was Hilda to expose Caroline to Madame, to show her these things she did not want to know? She isn't only a serpent, said Madame. I was rright. She is Eve too. Eve with her fruit of knowledge.

"Caroline," said Madame, and her voice was very gentle. "You have gone so high. Are you not going higher? Not?"

"Of . . . of course I am," Caroline stammered. "I hope I am."

"I wonder if you are," said Madame. "I wonder if you are."

"That isn't fair," cried Caroline. "Just because I defend myself. You know we all have to fight, fight hard for our places. If we don't push ourselves, who will? Very well, I am jealous of Hilda. I have to be. All dancers have to be. Hard and jealous. When you were my age I expect you were often jealous yourself."

"I certainly was not," said Madame. "I was far too prroud."

"You kept your position."

"Of courrse I kept it, but not by being hard to other people—by being hard on myself. Of course I kept it. No one could take it from me. You should watch that for yourself, Caroline. Perhaps you are right to feel yourself in danger. I tell you, Hilda gave the better performance of the Lady last night. She danced it with her whole body and soul, you danced it with the tip of your little finger."

They faced one another across the desk. Madame felt she was turning to stone. She had been trembling but now she was not trembling, she was cold

with a numbness that was creeping up from her feet, up her legs and thighs
to her heart.

"I have to be trruthful about these things, Caroline."

"Very well. I shall go," said Caroline. "Then you may have Hilda. Hilda,
body and soul, for the Lady. But you have forgotten one thing," she said,
and she looked at Madame with triumph in her eyes. "If I go . . . Lion will
go too." She saw the instant stricken look on Madame's face, and said with
spite, "He came here as my partner. He will go with me."

"Lion came here as my pupil, firrst," said Madame. "He is still my pupil,
learrning with me."

"Only out of hours," said Caroline. "Only as a hobby," said Caroline
tauntingly. "If I go, he will go too."

"You belong to a Trade Union, then?"

"No, of course not, but he is my partner, not Hilda's. I chose him."

"The Metropolitan lets you choose your partners, not?" said Madame
caustically.

"I am not talking of the Metropolitan, but of something else. Something
I was looking forward to telling you," said Caroline, with a look of the old
Caroline in her eyes.

"What is it, Caroline?"

"I have a chance to get into the Ballets Internationales—with Leonid
Gustave."

"With Gustave?" Madame's voice could not help warming. "Ah, Caroline!
That is what I have olways wanted for you. Olways. There is only one
Gustave. There will never be another. Ah, Caroline! I am *delighted*."

Caroline did not warm or waver. "Lion wants to go with me," said Caroline gently and spitefully. "There is a chance he might, but, of course, if he
stays here without me, I shouldn't dance with him any more."

"I see," said Madame.

"You can't blame Lion. He is only thinking . . ."

"That you are more use to him than I," said Madame. She sprang up,
knocking her chair backwards, and hit the desk top with her open hand.
*Pierre Lapin* was knocked into the waste-paper basket, the red case on to
the floor. "Did Lion think you could come here and say these things for
him? No, he must say them himself. Fetch him. Fetch him here in front of
me."

Lion came. He stood in front of her desk in his dark-blue sweater and
tights, and the sun fell on his face and on his broad shoulders and curled
dark hair, but his face was sullen and his eyes would not look at Madame,
nor at Caroline.

"Lion, is this true? Do you do this to me?"

Lion smiled. "Don't smile," said Madame sharply.

"Do you, Lion?"

Lion looked up angrily as if he were caught and trapped in this nest of
women. "Can't we arrange something?" he said. "Perhaps Hilda would be
content if you gave her her production with Caroline in the part. She should
be. After all, Leda doesn't matter very much, it is the Swan . . . I want to

dance the Swan. I want to dance it," said Lion to Caroline, who made not the slightest response. "Or why shouldn't you double the part, Hilda one night, Caroline the next? You have the Lady," pleaded Lion. Caroline still did not answer.

"There has been enough of this discussion," said Madame. She had to hold to the desk and the coldness was on her neck, in her head, in her lips, so that she could hardly make them speak. "I cannot be told, and not told, what I am to do with my own theatre. By you, you *children!*"

"We are not children."

"Children, that you should trreat me as if I didn't know, as if I were . . . *inutile*; that you should think so little of the thing you do, you would destroy it wantonly. Where is the discipline, the rrespect?" cried Madame. She might have cried, Where is the love? She said, "You have nothing at your hearts but your little cold self-interest." She saw the red case on the floor at her feet and, clumsily and stiffly, because she was so cold, she bent down and picked it up. She stood, looking at it.

Where is the love? she might have said. The discussion is ended. She did not say that either. She said, as she had said at the end of each class that they, either of them, had ever had with her: "Very well, you may go."

"Madame . . ." began Lion.

She never heard what he had to say. The desk and the lists, the red case in her hand, Caroline, Lion, the room, were suddenly swung sideways. A dizzying cold whiteness came up from her knees and hummed in her ears. But colour hasn't a sound, she said, and then she heard Caroline cry out and knew that she was falling.

"Lion!" cried Madame, "Lion." She felt his arms come round her and catch her as she fell.

6

It was Miss Ilse's arm, cold, bony, faithful, that was under her head when she woke. Not woke, opened my eyes, came to . . . to oll this care and trrouble. Opened my eyes to what I must see. "But need I see it, need I?" whispered Madame.

Miss Ilse's arm was faithful but comfortless; those others had been comforting but faithless. What can comfort me now? thought Madame. She turned her face away from all of them and it was, surprisingly, her pillow that she turned it into, her pillow cool against her aching eyes. She had not seen her pillow for a long while . . . "a long long time," she whispered. Miss Ilse was putting a shawl round her, her soft Indian shawl that was large and deeply red . . . "red as roses," whispered Madame. It mitigated the coldness, like sitting near a fire, and the pillow was cool and white as snow. Fire rose red, snow white, white and red olways for me. She was still cold, but the numbness had gone, she was able to shiver, even her teeth were shivering. But teeth don't shiver, they ch-chatter, thought Madame. But no, mine are shivering silently.

Someone came and put hot-water bottles at her feet and sides. From the brown hands, smelling of soap and a little of onion, from the firm wide tread so different from Miss Ilse's flutterings, she knew it was Zanny.

"*T' n' sens pas bien d' tout*," said Zanny, smoothing Madame's hair. "*Petite reine. Mignonne.* Zanny will take care of you."

"I can take care of Madame, thank you, Zanny."

"It appears not," said Zanny.

"You know how headstrong she is . . ."

"Never with me," lied Zanny. Miss Ilse knew she lied, but her fright and worry made her absurdly vulnerable. "There! You see, that is all you can do. Weep and pray. Pray and weep," chanted Zanny. "I . . . I am making in the kitchen a good strrong soup. She will drink that and gain her strength."

"She doesn't like soup."

"Not your soup. She likes mine. A soup with little *croutes* . . ."

"Go away, the both of you," said Madame. "I am not a bone for you to fight over. You make my head worrse. Go away. Take your soup and prayers away. Leave me alone."

"You must try to sleep, Anna."

"How can I sleep? When everything . . . when . . . when . . . the printing is not arranged for, and now it will have to be altered. When Felix's copyists . . . And the wings," cried Madame. "And what about that lorry, Ilse? Has Miss Parkes come back? And Rebecca? Noel wanted us to ring Eli . . . Eli . . . those scene-painter people. . . . Edwin. It's time they thought about lights . . ."

"Hush. Hush," said Miss Ilse. "All that is arranged. It's all arranged . . . at least it was arranged," she said sadly.

"I must get up," said Madame.

"Not yet, Anna. At least for an hour. I have never known you to faint before. I must get a doctor."

"I don't need a doctor. I need to deal with this." She struggled to a sitting position, the shawl fell away and a hot-bottle slumped to the floor, but the humming whirling whiteness came round her again. "I can't . . . get up," said Madame.

"No, no, Anna! You mustn't. Tell us what to do, and we shall do it."

"I don't know what to do," said Madame. She said it flatly and lay back on the pillow and closed her eyes. Shades were closing down on her. She saw, under her lids, the vast shape of Zanny pulling down the blind, and moving out of her line of vision, away. Madame made one more effort. "Tell . . . tell . . ."

"Yes?" said Miss Ilse.

Madame shook her head on the pillow and motioned Miss Ilse to go away.

7

Zanny's hand had drawn the blind so that the room was wiped out in darkness. Madame was left in a pool of quiet where there was no noise, no cold, only the grateful cool and warmth and quiet. She tried to grip her senses . . . my five wits, said Madame, but she was sliding into sleep. She needed sleep as if it were healing and she slept, not deeply but lightly, and in her sleep she was extraordinarily clear.

*Niura, that is a nightingale.* It was so quiet that she could hear it now. The streams of music, raucous impolite disturbing music, were wiped away under it; the demanding, querulous voices had ceased to hammer into her brain. The quiet had wiped them out, and in the quiet she could hear the nightingale. Her eyes were shut; their eyes—Miss Ilse's anxious and easily swimming in tears, Mr. Felix's boring like two little blue weevils, Hilda's hidden by her lids, Lion's bright . . . but not meaning a worrd they say . . . Caroline's fine blue ones that looked only inwards at herself, Noel's with their discoloured yellow-brown bloodshot whites, Moron's false and black, Lollie's young leveret ones—could not look at her now. She could hear the nightingale beyond the birch trees and it was sweet . . . sweet, and, in the garden before dawn, not in Russian woods but in the London dew, birds were singing. *To hold your hands is like holding two birds in my hand. Anna, my darling. Anna.*

"No," said Madame, and she said it aloud in her sleep. "No. Don't disturb me now. Ah no! Let me rest. Rrest."

Rest was not long, any more than love, for her. She was restless. Now she was the Humming-Bird, dancing instead of Archie, as Archie, that night. She was small and she was breaking in her own small shoe in the hot theatre wings. She saw the pan of rosin, her toes were firm, padded, in the shoe, and she worked it and felt the stiffness leaving it. She bent to lace the ribbons; she felt the unaccustomed pull of her tights at the back as she bent forward and the coloured ends of the feathered wings swung from her arms; she was breaking in her shoe and the shoes were under the glass dome like two soiled pink sugar mice. Now she was grown and it was long gauze skirts that fell away from her as she moved, gauze skirts and grave-eyed marguerites, and now she had a little gilt trumpet, and round rouged spots on her cheek; the Queen's hand in the white glove was held out for her to kiss, and the black tutu of Odile tilted round her as she curtsied. Perhaps I am going to die, said Madame. Perhaps at last they have killed me. She felt sorry for herself. I have never fainted before, and, in the last few minutes before you die, the past comes back to you, not? But that happens oll the time, said Madame. Time passes, but that is what it doesn't do. Past, present, and future. Her past and her present, her future if she were not going to die, were all dancing. Dancing-dancing-dancing-dancing-the dance-the dance-the dance—that was like the clocks ticking. They had begun to tick in . . . Berne? was it, or Dresden? (She did not know which clock it was in here) . . . and had gone on ticking ever since as the labels had been pasted on to the baskets and the foreign letters came. I could paper the walls of my sitting-room with the stamps on the letters I have had from abroad this year. Oll over the world. They are pedigree dancers. She fell into another uneasy sleep in which she had Marli's cross, the diamond cross, in her hand, and there was no one to whom she could give it, no breast to which she

could pin it. "But it isn't a medal," cried Madame in her sleep; but, in her
hand, it had become one. All over the world. Madrid, Milan, Cairo, Chicago, and Calcutta, Johannesburg . . . *The moon is my country.* Who had
said that? Pierrot, and Pierrot is the no one in us all, that lonely no one who
is left alone at last. No one. No-one-no-one-no-one, ticked the clock and,
deeply, tired out, Madame slept.

She was woken by Hilda asking, "Is it good?"

"Why should it be good?" she answered exasperated. "How do I know what
it is? I haven't seen it."

She did not know which answer she had given, but she was wide awake.
The coldness and whiteness had gone, she could sit up, on her elbow, and
see the darkened room. The clock was ticking still, very clearly. Something-
for-something-something-for-something, said the clock.

"Ah no!" cried Madame aloud, and lay down again.

It would be Hilda to wake her, even though it were only the thought of
her. Hilda, the serpent, Eve with her fruit. "Go away," said Madame. "Go
away," but Hilda was saying what the clock had said: "Something for something," said Hilda.

Madame's head ached, and her bones. Her eyes felt as if they had not
slept, but the sound of the clock, the thought of Hilda, had come between
her and her pillow and presently she lifted herself and sat up again and
thought, What is the time?

The room was too dark for her to see. Giddy, and beginning to be cold
again, she put back the shawl and swung her feet on to the floor. The electric
fire was on and its glow lay in a circle on the carpet; she stood in its warmth
and shivered. Then in her stockinged feet, giddy and weak, she walked uncertainly, with this new clumsiness, over to the window and pulled up the
blind. The light made pain leap in her head and dazzled her eyes but she
stood there until she grew used to it. She turned to look at the clock. It was
five minutes to four.

Something is to happen at four, said Madame. But what? What?

Where is Ilse? she thought. Why isn't she here? She never is here when I
want her. You would think she didn't understand what had happened. And
*what* is to happen? asked Madame. She called, "Ilse. Ilse," but there was
no answering flutter and rustle. She does nothing at oll, said Madame. Nothing at oll to help me.

She knew that everything was yet to happen, but she could not grasp it.
Her mind, no less than her body, felt weak. She was still in the borders of
her faint and her sleep and the confusion of her distress. She was old, old
and unresilient. Distress and worry surged back in her. Why didn't I die?
she said. I thought I was going to, then why didn't I? It would have saved
so much trouble. With honour, they would have cancelled the perrformance
tonight.

She put her hands to her head that ached so that the temples throbbed
and hurt as she touched them. What will happen? What can I do? Lion
. . . But there was no Lion. No Lion, and Caroline had gone, walked out of
her life . . . because I will never consent to see her again. Never. But what

can I do? She could not think. Thought led into a labyrinthian tangle of all they were doing and not doing: Felix, feathers, harpist, lorry, copyists, lights, Noel, whitening, the Benares sari, Miguel the conjuror, lights . . . I must alter the programme, thought Madame, Ilse must get Driscolls . . . but what is to go in the programme? And who? . . . Who?

She looked down from the window and saw that it was raining; quick rain was driving between her and the road. She felt for her shoes and put them on and went through into the sitting-room. From its windows she could see the theatre, but the rain cut it off; the wistaria looked heavy and sodden, she could see no lights, hear no sound. She stood by the window looking out into the rain, and the clock in this room sounded clearly too, loudly ticking. Something-for-something! ticked in her head.

"If only I could think," she whispered. "If I could find one thing, clear, that I must do. I could start with that. It would lead me in again. Something, however small and unnoticed. It would do to start with, something clear and simple, by itself. What could I do? Speak to Noel? But what is the good if . . . See Lion's wings? But he isn't to wear them. . . . Ah! If I could only think." Her thoughts would not go forward. They went irresistibly back to bed, with the pillow and the shawl and the warmth and quiet when she could sleep and dream and hear the nightingale. Then, into confusion came one small clear thought, by itself. Lollie was the freshet. "Of course," said Madame aloud. "Lollie's audition at four. I promised her I should be there."

A promise is a promise, it is a prrinciple, said Madame. You can *not* go back to bed, she told herself. You will now go down and keep your promise and take Lollie into the theatre to Edmund White. When it's most difficult to keep a promise, that is the time you should, that is its *proof*, said Madame. That I shall go down and keep my prromise to Lollie and then I shall see what I shall do.

She went to the mirror that hung over the fireplace and looked at herself. Better not to look, said Madame quickly, and, without going in to her bedroom to tidy herself, "Not even as much as to pass a comb through your hair!" as Miss Ilse said to her afterwards, she went downstairs. She had caught a glimpse of an old white wrinkled face with dark patches under the eyes and massed untidy hair. I expect I look like a witch, she said. A witch without a potion or a brroomstick to ride away on. I wish I could rride away! Never mind. A promise is a promise, she said, and I have to keep it. I can thank Edmund for the copyists even if they came to no purpose. And after . . . She could not think about after. She ceased to think and went on her way down the stairs.

There was no one in the hall, but, on the chest, two men's hats were lying, a broad white scarf, a stick, and a pair of gloves. Now where have I seen that scarf, that stick, and those gloves before? She picked them up; the scarf was of heavy silk, the stick was malacca with a silver band, and the gloves were fine. Evidently a someone, thought Madame. I know them. Then they can't be Edmund's. I don't know Edmund's stick and scarf and gloves, but I know these. Whose can they be? She looked at the two hats.

Someone else has come with Edmund. Someone I know. They have come and Ilse has taken them over to the theatre. I must go.

She went through the classroom, and there was the table Miss Ilse had put for Mr. Felix. Sheets of Music were strewn on it, his ink bottle, blue pencil, pencils, were there, but Mr. Felix had gone. I expect he went home, thought Madame. It was no good his staying, not?

As she passed the window she saw that the theatre lights were on. They glittered through the rain. Madame did not let people see her weep; "I only crry on the stage," she said, but now she was alone, and when she saw those lights a sob suddenly shook her. Be quiet! Madame said to herself. How can you go and meet Edmund, if you do that? She spoke so sternly that the sob was choked down. She opened the door to the back staircase and met Miss Ilse face to face.

"Oh, Anna!"

"Oh Anna!" mocked Madame. She was suddenly furious. "I could have died up there by myself. Where were you? Where have you been?"

"Anna . . ."

"Answer me. Where have you been oll this time? Letting me sleep as if there were nothing to be done." She looked at Miss Ilse with suspicion. "You have been over to the Church."

"Only for a moment, Anna . . ."

"I am ill!" said Madame bitterly. "And you leave me alone. Ill, beaten down, in trouble, and you go to church. To church! Zanny is quite rright!"

"When we are in trouble," said Miss Ilse with dignity, "naturally I go to church."

"Naturally," mocked Madame.

"Yes, naturally," said Miss Ilse. "I went to light a candle to St. Jude. That seemed to me the best thing to be done. The *best!*" She looked back firmly at Madame. "You see, I believe," said Miss Ilse. "But, Anna, what am I thinking of? I came to tell you . . ."

"Tell me nothing," said Madame rudely. "Keep away from me. Don't speak to me at oll," and she brushed past Miss Ilse and went down the stairs.

Lollie was waiting in the big girls' dressing-room and with every minute she grew more afraid. "What do you do when you are thoroughly frightened?" she had asked Miss Ilse as she came through on her way upstairs.

"Say a Hail Mary, that always helps me," said Miss Ilse kindly as she passed.

Lollie did not know how to say a Hail Mary. She did not know what a Hail Mary was. That was no help to her.

Auntie was no better. Miss Porteus had found time to come from the theatre to "look the child over" as she explained to Zanny. That was exactly what she did do. She looked Lollie over and over despairingly. "Your tunic is too short," she said with her unhappy sniff. "You look all legs. I don't know how you grow so much." She tightened Lollie's bows that were already too tight, but Lollie said nothing, because Auntie had bought the ribbon for those bows. "Real silk ribbon, not rag," said Lollie. "Well, I hope you get it," said Auntie. "But I don't suppose you will. You have never been what I should call a taking child, at all. Seems to me for the cinema they would want curls. You never had the vestige of a curl. Blue eyes are what they like and dimples, and you are downright skinny," said Auntie. "Still, you never know. You may get it. Unlikely things *do* happen. We could do with it with my arthritis. I'm crippled today, crippled! Well," said Auntie with another sniff, "don't let's meet our troubles till we get them."

"No, Auntie."

It seemed to Lollie they had several troubles now. Food, for instance. She was hungry. She thought of what of all the things in the world she would like best to eat, if you could get all the things in the world. "A banana sundae," thought Lollie.

"We are not very hungry, are we?" Auntie would say. "Let's put the kettle on and have a nice cup of tea and some bread and butter, or a bun or a pie from the little shop round the corner, or a kipper." "A dancer must dance on her stomach," Madame said, which made the others giggle. It did not make Lollie giggle. She understood it; she understood it sharply. She had such difficulty to dance on hers.

She heard that in Lion's company, the Metropolitan, the corps de ballet started on five pounds a week.

"Five pounds?" said Lollie. "A *week?*"

"Yes, how little!"

"How—how much!" said Lollie.

"You are too young to understand how little it is," said Madame.

Lollie was silent because she was certain that Madame did not understand how much it was. She knew that Madame did not understand, as she and Auntie did, how to spend a pound . . . or a shilling, or a penny. "The price of a cup of tea." People often said that, but how many of them knew how much it was? Five pounds, thought Lollie. Auntie and I could live on that. I could buy four hundred kippers and one thousand two hundred cups of tea. I could buy fifteen pairs of shoes in one week! Why, I could keep Auntie and she could have arthritis in peace!

As soon as Auntie left her, she took off the tunic that was too short. Lollie did not know much, but she knew it was not wise to look leggy at auditions if it could be avoided. "It pays to dress." That was another of the things that people said. How did one pay? They did not explain that, but there was a way round every difficulty, Madame said. Lollie knew of only one way round hers, and that was to do about the tunic as she had done about the shoes and take someone else's. She stepped over to Zoë's shelf. She chose Zoë because Zoë was the best-dressed child in the school. Yes, Zoë had left her tunic. She shook out Zoë's nicely folded tunic and tried it against herself, looking in the old long mirror that had been relegated here from the classroom. Its fly-brown marks came across her face, but she could see that she looked considerably improved in it. The tunic was rose-coloured, which made her look less pale; it was full and gathered, with far more material than her own, which made her look less skinny; and, given a tunic of the proper length, she did not look leggy at all. Lollie put it on, folded her own away, and sat down on the table to wait till she was fetched.

It isn't stealing, said Lollie, it's only borrowing, and I shall be found out, because Archie may be in the theatre, and if he is, he will tell. Oh, well! said Lollie, and she might have added, Beggars can't be choosers.

To think about money was better than a Hail Mary, whatever that was. Money was the most familiar, the most sobering thing Lollie knew. She decided that, till the moment she had to dance, she would say her money tables.

> Four farthings, one penny,
> Twelve pennies, one shilling,
> One thousand and two hundred cups of tea, five pounds.

She looked up and saw Madame.

"But . . . Miss Ilse said you couldn't come."

"Ilse is a fool," said Madame. "I promised you, not? You must learn, Lollie, that people keep their promises."

Lollie was silent. That had not been her experience, but, certainly, Madame had come. She looked at Madame. Madame looked odd; her clothes were puckered as if they needed what Auntie called "a good pull-down"; her stockings were wrinkled, and her hair looked like a thatch and her skin looked tired and . . . pouched, thought Lollie. "Are you better?" she asked doubtfully.

Madame said she was, but, when she held out her hand to Lollie and said "Come," her hand was colder than Lollie's own. Why should my hands be cold when I am so burning hot?

"They have arrived," said Madame. "We must not keep them waiting."

"N-no," said Lollie and understood that, in Madame's eyes, even the victim was obliged to have good manners. But . . . I don't want to go into the theatre. The time has come and I don't want the time to come. I can't do it! cried Lollie, by Madame's side, without a word.

I don't want to go into the theatre, thought Madame. The moment I do it will start oll over again . . . it will do that because it must, and I am not equal to it, said Madame, but together, hand in hand, she and Lollie walked silently across the garden to the theatre door.

In the garden Madame took a deep breath. The rain fell against her face, quick and soft; it chilled her but it was freshening, and she stopped and lifted her face and saw the width of the sky, between trees and roofs, filled with rain clouds; a rift in the cloud showed a vision of light and grey; the light struck the rooftops and a weathercock on a steeple; the wet slates shone and the gold cock glittered; there was a smell of wet soot and earth and grass, and from the wistaria bunches a wave of scent came out to her, warm and wet with the fresh rain. I pinned my faith to that wistaria, thought Madame. I was a fool. You shouldn't pin your faith to things, or people . . . but you have to, said Madame. If you are to live at oll you have no choice.

As she opened the door, a gust of music swept past them into the garden, welling out from the theatre, which was ablaze with lights.

She could see Mr. Felix's head as he conducted. The light shone on his skull under his white hair, and she could see his hand, in its white glove, lifted as he held his baton. The Carlorossi theme welled past them, over-filling the theatre. "It's too big for here," said Madame aloud. "I was afraid it would not be; orchestrated, it might have been blatant, thin; but it isn't, it is big."

Above the orchestra, on the stage, the curtains were pulled back and Noel's set was there; the frame with its painted white curling feathers set in gold, and the stormy grey-green background lit so that it looked threatening and deep. "But . . . it is perrfect," said Madame.

As she looked, the first white swan-feather floated down and Hilda was on the stage. *Leda, looking for shells on the lake shore.* Madame watched her walk on, always a critical moment to Madame, but she saw that Hilda had it easily in her grasp; she watched, nodding approval as, in the contained little looped maroon gown that, swinging open, showed a sudden line of scarlet, Hilda passed into the opening of her *adage*. Madame did not know how long the passage lasted; she watched enthralled, nodding her head; occasionally she smiled.

Then the music changed to that loud downbearing whirring rush, and Madame suddenly gripped Lollie's shoulder so that Lollie cried out. Lollie, staring, saw an immense white Swan, towering with its wings, with swept-back feathered hair and black-marked eyes; Madame saw that the Swan was Lion.

Lion! "But . . ." said Madame. "But . . ."

Lollie twitched her sleeve.

"Wait, Lollie."

"But, Madame . . ."

"Wait."

"Madame . . . are those them?"

" 'They,' Lollie . . . 'Are those they?' "

"Yes, but are they? Which of them is him?"

" 'He,' Lollie. Who?" Madame reluctantly tore her eyes away from the stage and followed Lollie's gaze, to where two men stood between the stalls talking, with Miss Parkes and Rebecca standing respectfully by. She saw first the one she had expected to see, the flat pink face, grey hair, and monocle of Edmund White.

She looked past him to the other, a little square man with a Mongolian forehead and skin and eyes and small gesticulating hands. She gave a cry, and Lollie quickly moved her shoulder out of reach. "It's Gustave!" cried Madame. "Gustave! Gustave himself!" Now who, thought Madame swiftly, who has Gustave come to see?

8

Hilda had not heard the quarrel between Lion and Caroline. She did not know there had been a quarrel. When Lion had leaped off the stage she had waited for him to come back. She did not understand that he had left her with the ballet half-rehearsed, without warning and without apology. Perhaps Hilda was conceited. It had not occurred to her that Lion could do that.

"Where is Lion?" she said presently to Rebecca. "I'm waiting for him."

"I don't know," said Rebecca helplessly. "Caroline was here, very angry with him and with you."

"With me? Why?"

"She is jealous."

"*Caroline*, jealous of *me*? Don't be absurd, Rebecca."

"Well, she has gone storming off to Madame, and Lion has run after her."

Lion has run after her. The impact of what that meant hit Hilda between the eyes. "Lion, run after Caroline when he . . . when I . . ." and Rebecca saw Hilda blush as she had not known that Hilda could blush, a deep burning painful red.

A kiss can be a very big, or a very little thing. It depends on who you are, thought Hilda. She had let Lion kiss her and she had kissed him and now it seemed to her that, as Madame said she overdanced, as she had overdone herself in *Lyre*, she had given too much away to Lion, been generously reckless or recklessly generous. She blushed now and burned to think how strong she had been, and this was not from modesty but from pride. When am I ever going to learn? thought Hilda despairingly. I hate myself. I hate . . . hate Lion.

However she tried to belittle him, he stayed as Lion. Even as she said she hated him, she felt again the way he lifted her, the way he turned her towards him and let her slip down, her body against his, held firmly and, she could have sworn, loved, in his arms. She felt the warmth and smooth health of his skin, the way his eyes looked into hers, teasing and commanding; Hilda had never been teased or commanded by a man before. She remembered how angry and hurt she had been against him in Madame's office yesterday . . . was it only yesterday? . . . and how, as soon as he touched her, she had melted. But that is purely physical, she said austerely, but was it? Would she have liked Lion to touch her, hold her, kiss her, if she had not loved him? She knew she would not. But . . . it's ignominious to love where you are not loved. He . . . he is a Golden-Syrup Lion. She argued and burned with shame, and still he still was Lion.

But there is a difference, thought Hilda proudly. Nothing I do now will be done willingly. Before, I gave in completely. I capitulated. He has killed that. If ever I give in, it will be with reservations. She saw those reservations as high impenetrable fences that no Lion on earth could hope to scale or look over. She hoped they would stand firm.

"Caroline says she will refuse to dance tonight," said Rebecca.

"Let her." Hilda, naturally, did not mind that in the least. "I can dance the Lady," she said.

"Without Lion?"

"Without *Lion*? Rebecca, you don't mean . . ."

"Caroline says if she goes, Lion will go too."

"But, she couldn't do that. She hasn't the power," said Hilda.

"Caroline has influence and money," said Rebecca. "She has always had Lion under her thumb, and we all know what Lion is."

Except me, thought Hilda bitterly. What a fool I have been . . . but her private troubles were drowned under this greater implication.

"She . . . he . . . they couldn't do that to Madame, now, at the last minute. It's unspeakable. It would be dastardly."

"What words you use, Hilda. It would be dastardly, but they could do it. You don't know yet how mean dancers can be, a great many of them, mean and petty and jealous. Here comes Miss Ilse with the news," said Rebecca, and she said seriously, "It *is* that news, Hilda. She is crying."

"God help us, what shall we do?" wept Miss Ilse. "Anna. Anna. It's the first time I have ever known her to take off her hand for a single moment. Now she . . . she . . . God forgive them!" cried Miss Ilse. "I can't. He went after Caroline without a word."

"The times, the times I have had him in my kitchen and given him a good hot meal," hissed Zanny. "We fed him and taught him and kept him. I wish I had thrown it in his face before I saw him," said Zanny. For once she and Miss Ilse were in complete accord.

"Anna . . . oh, Anna!"

"Madame! Madame!"

"Madame, *ma pauvre, pauvre Madame!*"

"Anna! Anna!"

They reminded Hilda of a Greek chorus. She began to be irritated and that took away some of her dismay. Rebecca was not much better. Rebecca and Miss Parkes were busy calculating the consequences.

"Will they be *allowed* to do this?" Rebecca was saying. "Will the Metropolitan countenance it? To Madame? Madame is someone, after all."

"It will be interesting to see whose part they take."

"Will they back their own dancers or Madame?"

"But . . . Rebecca . . . it won't be a public quarrel?" asked Miss Ilse in a quavering voice.

"Won't it!" said Rebecca. "Of course it will," she said with relish.

Miss Ilse dissolved into tears again. "Such a thing has never happened to us, never."

"It needn't be public unless we tell everybody," said Hilda suddenly and crisply. "The Metropolitan wouldn't want it public either. We can say that Lion and Caroline have been taken ill."

"*Both* of them? That isn't likely. Who would believe that? You will never hide it," said Rebecca and Miss Parkes together. They are like two ghouls, thought Hilda, and she said aloud, "Well, if it can't be hidden, we must win."

"Win, with the performance tonight? How can we? Oh, Anna . . . Anna," cried Miss Ilse, breaking into still fresh tears. "What shall we do with the performance tonight?"

"Give it," said Hilda.

"But . . . how can we do that?"

"We must do that. There is nothing else at all that we can do. You must call an immediate rehearsal," she said to Rebecca.

"I? But I have nothing to do with the theatre and the ballets."

"That doesn't matter. It's the authority that matters. You have authority. I will tell you what to do. If I do it myself there will be quarrels and objections."

"She is right," said Miss Ilse, her tears drying.

"But . . ." said Rebecca to Hilda, "can you take upon yourself, in Madame's absence . . . ?"

"Yes," said Hilda, quite certainly. She saw them stare at her and she said, "What would Madame do? Give in?" she asked Miss Ilse. "Recriminate?" she asked Zanny. "Make a scandal?" she asked Miss Parkes and Rebecca. "She wouldn't do any of those things. She wouldn't waste her time. We shall have to rehearse *Noble Life* and *Leda*. Francis must do the Nobleman. After all, he has been the Attendant all this time, he ought to know it. Lippi can take the Attendant, or Hugh."

"And the Swan . . . ? Who for the Swan?"

Hilda stopped. Her thought had stopped too. To think of anyone else as the Swan was unbearable to her. She had written it for Lion, built it on him, built it round him.

"John?"

"No, John wouldn't do," she said slowly. "He is too slight, John would be wrong. Quite wrong."

"Could Francis do it too?" asked Rebecca doubtfully.

"You can have a plump Nobleman but you can't have a plump Swan," said Hilda seriously. "It must be Lippi," she said suddenly, "and Hugh must be the Attendant."

"Lippi? But he isn't up to the others."

"I know, but he is the most like Lion." That slipped out when she had not meant it to, but Rebecca only nodded. "Miss Parkes and I will get on to the telephones," she said. "I shall get Lippi first, he has the most to learn."

"But Lippi?" Madame said afterwards. "You chose Lippi? He is more like a boisterous young eagle than a swan."

"Whom would you have chosen?" asked Hilda.

Madame had to admit that she would have chosen Lippi.

As Rebecca went to telephone, Hilda suddenly called her back. It was an impulse she could not name. "Rebecca," she said. "Don't tell Lippi it's to dance Lion's part, nor Francis. Tell them it's to understudy."

"Why?" asked Rebecca.

"Because . . ."

"He won't come back, Hilda," said Rebecca gently. Hilda glared. She resented that gentleness.

"Lion" . . . "Lion" . . . "Lion" . . . Hilda heard his name in whispers, in derision, in complaint, in anger. "Lion."

"Ah, forget Lion," she cried impatiently.

No one had a good word to say for him. In spite of all she had hoped it had leaked out that he, "and Caroline," Hilda reminded them fairly, had walked out on Madame. "And no one has ever done that before," they said in awe. "She has walked out on us. Never one of us on her."

"I should hope you would have more sense," said Rebecca.

"But to think that Lion . . ."

"*And* Caroline," said Hilda firmly.

"But Caroline isn't as bad as Lion." That was the general verdict, and it was true. Caroline was high-handed, but at least she had acted for herself. "Lion is a follower," said witty John, and Hilda winced. "Not a lion but a jackal," said John.

"Must we play animal grab?" asked Hilda.

"Rebecca said I was to understudy Lion," said Lippi, when they were resting in the wings, she panting and tired, Lippi fresh and eager. "Lion isn't coming back, is he?"

"We don't know," said Hilda slowly. "We are doing this in case he doesn't."

"Madame wouldn't take him back."

"We don't know what Madame will do. It isn't for us to judge," said Hilda primly.

"But he won't," said Lippi.

Hilda was too tired to argue. She had been dancing since early morning in a rising crisis of emotion, and now nothing seemed left in her but the ability to dance; all anger, all feeling of mortification, had left her, but she had an inescapable yearning for Lion. To dance Leda to Lippi's Swan after Lion's was like dancing with nothing at all. Lippi's rushes were like the rushes of the young eagle with which Madame after compared him; he was not tall enough, nor strong enough, nor big enough. She felt tired out, and tired of heart as well as in body and mind.

She left Lippi and went and stood near Noel. Noel was no comfort but, curiously, when she was with Noel, Lion faded a little, into what she felt was probably his proper place. But was it? Were they all wrong about Lion, even she?

"He won't come back, m' dear. I know Lion."

"Don't you ever leave room for anyone to grow?" snapped Hilda.

"Doesn't happen," said Noel, and stood up and stretched his arms. "That's finished." He was not talking of Hilda and Lion but of his cut cloth of feathers.

Ironically, now that Hilda's whole reason for it was no longer there, the ballet was complete. Elibank's young painters were cleaning their brushes; Noel had finished the painting of the last spine and curl of the last feather. "For Jesus' sake don't touch it. It's still wet." The members of the orchestra had come in long ago and had sat smoking and waiting; now Mr. Felix appeared and called them sharply and began distributing the parts. "The ink is dry on them," he said, "but only just."

Hilda went down to him. "Shall we rehearse with you now, straightaway?"

"Why do you think we are here?" asked Mr. Felix, who was in no amiable mood.

"You know Lion has gone. We are managing," said Hilda, not without pride. "Lippi is dancing the Swan."

"Manage with whom you choose," said Mr. Felix. "It's nothing to do with me. I'm here for the music, and the music is the same. I attend to my business. You attend to yours." Though he was grumpy, Hilda had the feeling that he thought she was attending to it well.

When he started to conduct his arrangement of the Carlorossi music, pride and excitement welled up in her. He has done it beautifully, beautifully, but without Lion . . . Ah, what a waste! cried Hilda. Lion! How *could* you do that to me?

She had been called upstairs to try on her dress and had kept it on to dance in so that Noel could watch it. Noel turned her this way and that, lowered the bodice, cutting it down between her breasts, lifting the underskirt as impersonally as if she were a dummy. "That will do," said Noel, "or I think it will. Can't tell till I have seen it from the front. Come in front and see it," he told Miss Porteus. The task of whitening Lippi had still to come. "But before I do that," said Noel, "let him put on the wings and trunks and come on the stage with Hilda. Better dance it. I can't see what those wings will do until he dances in them."

"But don't stop Mr. Felix," Hilda warned Noel as he went. "We can come in with him. You don't need to see it all through. Let Noel get down in front," she told Lippi. "He wants to see how the wings look as you come on." She listened. The ballet was nearing its end. "It's just before the climax. We can pick it up there. Where I go on and you come after me, and take me in the big lift." Lippi nodded obediently. He was obedient . . . and that is the last thing the Swan should be, thought Hilda in despair. This was where Lion . . .

In all the times she had danced Leda, Hilda had still not lost the terror of this swoop of Lion's when he came down on her from behind and bore her up, higher than his shoulder; the power of his grasp left her almost paralyzed. Lippi could lift adequately, gracefully, but no more than that. "Well," sighed Hilda. "It will have to do.

"Now," she called over her shoulder to Lippi. She had her back to him as she danced.

She had not danced this with the orchestra before; after the gramophone it was new, loud, strong, and hotly alive. It made her dance as if she were new too with fresh life. Ah, if only . . . cried Hilda, but she had to curb that and wonder if Lippi were coming, if he had timed it or would be late; then she was swept off her feet from behind with such a force that she cried out realistically with fear and surprise. She was held high, brought violently down and crushed in Lion's arms, against his breast and shoulder, as he carried her off.

"You have been busy, haven't you?" said Lion as he put her down. He was furious. "Who the hell put Lippi in my part?"

"I did," said Hilda icily, but she was shaking with surprise and joy. "He did it very well," she added.

"Lippi!" said Lion. "You little busy-body!"

"Lippi is at least reliable," said Hilda.

"Shut up!" said Lion. "On again," and he turned her round to the stage.

9

"Gustave!" Lollie did not recognize Madame's voice, flattered and shy. "Leonid!"

"Anna! Dear Anna!" He kissed her hand . . . as if she is a queen, thought Lollie.

"Gustave, now tell me, what has brought you here? What have you heard? Whom have you come to see?"

"Whom? Why, you, Anna. Who else, today? It is today, not?"

"Of course, it is my anniversary," said Madame slowly. "I . . . I had forgotten it. *Forgotten* it. It is today." She felt excitement beginning in her in every vein.

"I have come to pay my respects to you, as they say, Anna. My profound respect. Fifty years, and good years, Anna. I think oll London should be here tonight; the part that counts to us will be, not?"

He says *not* and *oll* like Madame, thought Lollie. He is like Madame. They began to speak in French. Always French, thought Lollie . . . and of course far more quickly than she could follow. As she talked Madame's fingers absently smoothed the hairs on Lollie's neck, between the dragged plaits, but her eyes were looking over Lollie's head to the stage.

Gustave was watching the stage as well.

"That is a very remarkable little girl you have here, my dear Anna. How old is she? And it is her work?" He watched again. "She should have a chance Anna, not?"

Madame, with a pang, answered, "Yes." Noel had painted Lion, made up his eyes, whitened his hair. Gustave did not say anything about Lion in the full panoply of the Swan.

These words fell into the air over Lollie's head and reached her ears. She looked at the gentleman, Gustave, with startled eyes. How did he know she was a remarkable little girl when he had not seen her dance?

When the ballet was ended he said, "Anna. I should like to see that again."

Will he want to see me twice? thought Lollie. Fancy having to do it twice. I didn't know Lion and Hilda were having an audition too.

They began again, and, as suddenly as he had asked for it, Gustave stopped it. He has no manners, thought Lollie. "No, I have seen enough," he said. "I shall come again tonight. Tell me about what time. I want to see this again. I con-grat-u-late you, Anna. I told you, Edmund. I told you, she has olways something up her sleeve." He turned. "Well, we must go until tonight. Then I shall want to meet your little dancer. I think you will let me have her, not? And we shall do her ballet perhaps. The young man too. They are good! I mean it. Well, we must go. Good-bye."

"But . . ." said the other gentleman, Edmund. "I must see my child."

"What child? Where? For what? What child? I have an appointment at five."

"I came here to see a child, for *Starlight*. Why do you think I came all this way, Gustave?"

"Well, Anna, give him what he wants. He wants a child. Anna always has plenty. I'm sure she will give you one. Here," he said, catching Lollie by the shoulders. "This one will do. Here is a complete little child all ready."

> Four sixpences, one florin,
> Five sixpences, half a crown,
> Twenty sixpences . . .

"This is the child, Edmund," said Madame, laughing. How could she laugh? thought Lollie. She thought the gentleman Gustave went far too fast. Who was he to give orders?

"Say 'thank you' and bring her along," said Gustave. "We can put her in the pocket of the car."

"Wait, Gustave," said Madame. "This is important for Edmund and for the child . . . Lollie, this is Mr. Edmund White. Say how do you do."

Lollie stiffly held out her hand. Mr. Edmund White looked down on her doubtfully; she looked up, dazed, at him.

"You are very small," he said.

"Yes," said Lollie in a whisper, and then she rallied herself. "There are plenty smaller than me."

"Than 'I,' Lollie."

He bent down and looked at her closely, holding her hand. "Can I see you smile?"

"Yes," said Lollie, not smiling. She had come prepared to dance, not to smile.

"Smile," he said. It was a command, so definite that Lollie recognized it. She smiled her two-edged smile obediently and immediately.

"Does she smile like that always?" he asked. "Smile again." Lollie smiled.

"She smiles with her eyes," said Edmund White. "That is ve-ry satisfactory. Send her up on the stage."

"Of course," said Madame. "Lollie."

It had come. Lollie felt she had no legs, that she was all forehead and eyes and beating heart but, mysteriously, she was up on the stage. *Forty sixpences, one pound.*

"Don't look at the lights."

"No," said Lollie. She saw Mr. Felix ready for her, and took her stance for the opening of the variation.

"No, not to dance," said Edmund White. "Walk over to the left and look back at me and imagine you are asking for something." That was easy. She imagined she was asking for a banana sundae.

"Superb," said Gustave. "What more do you want, Eddie?"

"Smile again." Lollie smiled. He smiled too.

"But . . . can she dance?"

"Oll Anna's children can dance. Do you think she would have shown her to you else? Anna knows much more than we do about dancing? You can leave that to her."

"I like her," said Edmund White to Madame. "I should like to have her along for a test. I should like George to see her. I love that smile—woe-begone, wonderful! I like her. . . ."

Lollie waited patiently, nerved to dance. Her moment, even if it were a lean little moment, was here. She was ready. *Eight half-crowns, one pound.* She stood ready, her arms ready to lift, her foot in the first *dégagé*, her ear cocked to Mr. Felix, her eyes and her smile waiting for Madame's nod.

"Good-bye."

"Good-bye, Anna. Good-bye."

"Till this evening. You are coming, Eddie?"

"Good-bye."

Mr. White came down to the orchestra rail. "Good-bye Lollie. I shall see you soon. You smiled very nicely."

Lion and Hilda stepped out of the wings. Mr. Felix had stood up and turned round to bow. Madame and Miss Ilse, followed by Rebecca and Miss Parkes, were walking up with them to the entrance. Everyone had turned their backs. Daylight shone in for a moment as the outer door was opened and shut. They were gone.

"They . . . he . . . he hasn't seen me dance!" said Lollie.

No one heard her. Lion and Hilda, full of excitement, had run down to the dressing-rooms. Mr. Felix was arranging his music, and the men were climbing out of the orchestra pit one by one; the flautist emptied his flute into his saucer and put it away and went out wiping his mouth on the back of his hand as if he were thirsty.

Now Glancy and another man in stained blue jeans came on to the stage, pulling on ropes so that the frame slowly lifted up and Lollie saw the weights coming down. The grey-green back-drop was drawn up and the yellow one with the square tower and poinsettias came down for the *Cat Among the Pigeons.* She could see Glancy turning the great iron handle and the ropes moving. The other man brought on the Nun's seat. "Out of the way, Christmas," he said.

"You can't put that here. I have to dance," said Lollie with dignity.

"No more dancing until tonight," said Glancy.

"But . . . they are coming back. They must be."

"Not they. Off to their tea. Seen all they wanted to. They won't come back."

It was true. Emile and Zanny and Mrs. Pilgrim the charwoman from the house had come in and were sweeping between the seats and up the aisles. They wouldn't be sweeping if anyone important . . .

A woman in a dark dress and two girls in green overalls came and began carrying in boxes and tubs of flowers, flowers such as Lollie had only seen in shops; they were all the same—white and red carnations, green ferns, and white jessamine. The air had been full of the dust from the brooms; now it was heavy with scent. Even in her hurt and dismay Lollie breathed it in with reverent admiration. What it must have cost! thought Lollie. In her life, Lollie would have many flowers herself, bouquets and baskets, but she would never lose that instinctive feeling about them. What it must have cost.

"Please, dear," said the woman in the dark dress, coming across the stage and pushing Lollie out of her way. Then Miss Parkes came on with her notebook and pencil. "What are you doing here, Lollie?" she asked. "Run away and change."

"Lion and Hilda danced twice, twice!" said Lollie in a trembling voice. No one answered her.

"The carnations *grouped*," the woman was saying to Miss Parkes, "and the jessamine, like spray, along the edge."

The heads bent over the ropes, over the brooms, over the notebook, over the flowers. Lollie walked slowly off the stage.

"To appear like that before Gustave," said Miss Ilse. "Your clothes all pulled round, not even as much as to pass a comb through your hair. How could you, Anna? I was so ashamed. You looked like a scarecrow, and before Gustave of all people."

"He didn't look at me," said Madame comfortably. "Ilse. I have a feeling he will take them both. He will see Lion thoroughly tonight."

"Lion doesn't deserve it," said Miss Ilse, and pinched in her lips.

"He came back," said Madame.

"Yes, like a lord," said Miss Ilse. "Caroline . . ."

"Caroline." As she said it the happiness and excitement passed out of Madame's face.

"Hilda should move into Caroline's dressing-room," said Miss Ilse.

"She told you to ask for that?" said Madame quickly and suspiciously.

"No, she didn't, Anna."

"Tchk-tchk!" said Madame.

Miss Ilse led the way backstage and into the dressing-rooms. They paused in the narrow passage between the cubicles. As they paused, Lion came out. He was matt white, his eyes darkened and deepened by the kohl, his hair stiff with whitening. It was not dry and he had a towel on his shoulders. He stopped when he saw Madame.

"What are you doing here?" said Madame.

"I am just going on to let Noel see me again under the lights."

"I thought you had left my theatre, not?"

"No."

"No?"

"No."

"You are very firm."

"I am very firm," said Lion. He looked at her with warm deep affection in his eyes. "I carried you upstairs," he said. "Why are you standing about? Why do you let her stand?" he asked Miss Ilse, who gave an indignant little snort and went past them into Caroline's dressing-room.

"Caroline?" asked Madame.

Lion's eyes looked grave. Grave, not clouded as they did before when there was trouble, thought Madame. Grave and sorry.

"It's a pity about Caroline," said Lion. "I tried, but she wouldn't listen. I think she will be sorry," but the old Lion was not gone yet. "Do you know," he said confidentially, "I think Hilda is going farther than Caroline."

Madame went into Caroline's dressing-room. Caroline had taken her things away, but on the dressing-table was a litter of powder dust and face tissues and cotton-wool. There was wool on the floor, too, from her shoes. Miss Porteus was there, unpacking a box that was filled with tissue paper and from which a smell of camphor came. "What is that?" asked Madame.

"It's your dress of the Lady. Caroline's is too big for Hilda. It will need too much alteration. She will have to wear yours," said Miss Ilse.

"You should have asked me first," cried Madame.

They looked at her in astonishment. "Isn't it enough," cried Madame, "that she should oust . . . ?" They thought she meant Caroline, but she did not mean Caroline, or not only Caroline. Caroline was a small part of it. "Hilda is *not* to have my dress," said Madame. "Even if you sew oll night." She went to the box and touched the folded silk, an edge of embroidery, an ermine sleeve. "She is *not* to have my dress," she said. "Put it away."

"Take it upstairs, Miss Porteus," said Miss Ilse and, when Miss Porteus had gone, "You are wicked and ungrateful," she said to Madame. "When you think what Hilda has done."

"She should be grateful to me," flashed Madame. "Gustave . . ."

"Gustave! What would you have shown to Gustave but for Hilda?"

"It works both ways," argued Madame.

"It does indeed. Do you know what Hilda deserves?" asked Miss Ilse.

"She deserves anything I can give her," said Madame with sudden meekness.

"Then you should give her the Tsar's cross that Marli gave to you. *She* should have it, not Caroline."

"Yes," said Madame.

"And I shall fetch Zanny to get this room ready for Hilda," said Miss Ilse, dusting powder off the dressing-table.

"Yes," said Madame.

"Caroline will be sorry when she hears Gustave has been here," said Lion. He did not say it spitefully, but thoughtfully, as a fact to be regretted.

"Caroline deserves all she gets," said Miss Ilse, picking wool up from the floor.

"Yes," said Madame.

"Now I shall get Mrs. Pilgrim to sweep in here, and Zanny can move Hilda's things."

"Wait," said Madame suddenly. Miss Ilse looked up. Madame was standing in the doorway, her hand on Lion's arm. "Hilda doesn't need this dressing-room, Ilse," Madame pleaded. "Don't change anything, Ilse. Wait a little while. Lion, let Noel see you and then take oll this stuff off you and go to Caroline. Tell her what has happened, about Gustave, you understand. Then tell her . . . she is wanted by Madame."

Lion left Caroline with Madame and came back into the theatre. He met Hilda in the passage outside his dressing-room. She was dressed in the petticoats of the Second Pupil, with her sequined scarf wound round her. She was not made up, nor was her hair done, but tied back plainly with a white ribbon. She looked as plain as she had looked well that morning, but Lion did not know if she were plain or not. She was Hilda.

"Where have you been?" asked Lion.

"Having a bath," said Hilda. "I needed it."

Lion hesitated. "You . . . know . . . Caroline has come back?" He watched her to see how she would take it, but it did him no good. Hilda dropped her lids and he could gather nothing of how she felt. Hilda's reservations were up.

"Are you surprised?" he asked.

"Nothing that happens today will surprise me."

"Oh, well! You have plenty," said Lion. "Where are you off to? It's early. Where are you going?"

"Into the theatre."

"Can I come?"

"No."

"Hilda." He put his arm round her and felt her quiver under his touch, the reservations tottered.

"Lion. Please. Let me go."

"Why?"

"Because now, I . . . I want to be alone."

"Why?"

"Please, Lion."

"Kiss me, then."

"Not in the passage."

"In the passage."

She kissed him and suddenly she felt his lips quiver under the kiss; his, not hers. He . . . he cares, thought Hilda.

A new exultant certainty came into her.

"I . . . want to come with you," said Lion. She shook her head.

"I want to come," he said like a child.

"You can't," she said like a grownup, and gave him a gentle push away. She let her hand cling to his a moment and left him.

The florists had gone and the theatre bloomed with flowers, banked along the stage, by the orchestra, and in the niches. Other flowers had been arriving all day and had been handed in to Emile and at the stage door. Except some for Caroline, few were for the company; they were for Madame: bunches and bouquets and baskets, a basket of red roses, a wreath of laurel leaves tied with a white ribbon. Telegrams were opened and pinned up on a notice-board; the telephone rang in the house and the box-office. Emile, Glancy, Mrs. Pilgrim, and the stage-hands came in and out of the theatre placing extra small gilt chairs that Miss Parkes had hastily sent for.

Miss Parkes, Rebecca, anyone that could be spared, were in the office amending the anniversary programmes with their crimson tassels. "First take out *Lyre*, put in those *Meditations*," said Rebecca. "Take out the *Medita-*

*tions.* Put in *Leda and the Swan.* Then take out Caroline. Take out Lion. Put in Hilda. Put in Francis and Lippi. Take out Francis and Lippi. Put in Lion. Take out Hilda. Put in Caroline. I wish I had left at Christmas," said Rebecca.

Now, for a little while, the theatre was empty. Swept, filled with the scent of the flowers, it waited.

The curtain was down. Behind it the stage was set for *Cat Among the Pigeons.* In the dressing-rooms the freshly ironed clothes hung ready on the racks. The irons, still hot, were put to cool on the stands and Miss Porteus and Zanny toiled up and down carrying the dresses to the dressing-room. Wigs and jewellery and hats and caps hung on the mirrors; shoes were put ready in the shoe-holes under each stool. The dancers had brought in their good-luck charms and mascots, some serious, some ridiculous, and some sentimental. Madame's own were sentimental; she had always liked to have one red and one white rose in the vase on her table, and a certain little toy fan of white net with gold sequins that she had had as a child. She would never say who had given it to her. Perhaps she could not, now. The sequins were nearly worn away, but it and the roses were on her table tonight. "Ilse, you remembered them?"

"Of course I remembered them, Anna. We mustn't quarrel tonight."

"Quarrel! We *never* quarrel!" said Madame.

The girls had dolls or golliwoggs; some had teddy-bears; Alma had a Polish marionette and Rayevskaya a little Christmas tree with red wax buds. Gaby had an elephant's-hair bangle, Jessica a gold cross; "But you ought not to use that as a charm," Rayevskaya rebuked her. Francis had a sandalwood carving of Ganesh the Hindu god of success; when he heard Lion had come back, he turned Ganesh round with his face to the wall, but before he went on that evening he would run back and turn him round again . . . just in case. The branches of Rayevskaya's tree came across from her place at the mirror into Hilda's. Hilda had nothing at all. She felt her luck was in the theatre itself.

"How do you feel?" they had all asked her.

"I feel just the same."

"After Gustave . . . and your ballet. A ballet of your own with Gustave!"

She felt the same. She had always had these things in her. She had known that. It was only they who had not known. A week ago, yesterday, she might have said it. It was an older, wiser Hilda who held her tongue.

"But all in one day!" they said.

Not in one day. Years. Seventeen years. Ever since I was born, thought Hilda.

In the orchestra pit the lid was open on the piano, the clavichord for *The Noble Life* behind it; the harp stood to one side uncovered, its gilt strings shining in the one light Emile had left burning. He would come and turn the full lights on presently. It shone on the side of the cello and the bassoon, on the leather violin cases, on a silk handkerchief on one of the violinists' stands. The woodwind places were there, the music ready stacked, Mr. Felix's baton was on his stand. Will he bring his history book tonight? wondered Hilda. Or will he be a tiny bit interested? But then he says it is all history, she thought. Is it history? thought Hilda.

The light made a quiet pool on the cream walls, caught the angle of the blue stage curtains, the gilt rail, the cream and red and blue patternings of the orchestra curtains, a line of plush-backed seats, a gilt chair. It showed the colours of the gilt, the red plush and the flowers, the red and white carnations and the white jessamine. For the rest the theatre was dim, except out in the little foyer, where the chandelier was lit, shining in all its crystal ropes and pendants, reflected in the glass of the photographs on the walls and on the stand. Miss Ilse had changed the one of Giselle for Giselle with marguerites. Hilda's sister had hurriedly brought down more photographs of Hilda. Caroline's and Lion's had been taken down, put up again. Now the foyer was quiet and in order, gleaming with light and filled with flowers. Emile had put the basket of roses under Madame's photograph on the stand; it was from Gustave. Later Gustave would lead her out before the audience on the stage, but now, for a few minutes, the theatre was alone, except for Hilda.

Outside in the road, the late afternoon light was growing richer as it drew towards evening. The rain had stopped and the ground steamed gently and Emile had put away the big canvas umbrella he had taken out. The smell of wet stone and earth and soot and brick and asphalt rose into the air, but the little theatre smelled inside and out of flowers. The sun lay on its façade, on the scrolled-iron balcony, the pendants of wistaria, and the new bills, still wet with printers' ink and limp with paste as Emile had put them up:

### BALLETS HOLBEIN
Tonight at 7:00 and for a limited season

| | |
|---|---|
| *Cat Among the Pigeons* | *The Noble Life* |
| (Holbein) | (Holbein-Bellini) |

*Leda and the Swan*
(Hilda French)
Evenings at 7:00 Wed. Sat. 2:30
Holbein Theatre, Primrose Avenue, N.W. 3

To evoke is to call out, to draw out, and bring forth . . . the dust of other seasons, other summers, other winters that, now they were evoked by this, shed their dust and came to life; other summers in other Mays, but with the same wistaria; winter seasons when Madame felt the wistaria should have been out, and another girl brought in just such a Christmas tree with red wax buds as Rayevskaya brought in now; other Rayevskayas, other Johns and Almas and Archies; other successful disappointed Lollies; other tears and other aspirations; other hates and other loves; other Hildas and other Lions.

Now a small queue began to form outside the gallery door, not yet opened. The dancers were slipping in, in ones and twos and threes, to make themselves up before they came down to warm up with Rebecca as was Madame's rule.

Caroline had come. She came from Madame and went to her dressing-room without a word to anyone, her head high. She too met Lion. Lion stepped back to let her pass and did not speak to her and she went into her dressing-room and shut the door.

On her table was a small package. It was from Madame. She recognized the careless sprawling writing. Caroline was still smarting from the things Madame had said, and she picked it up and put it down. Then she picked it up again and sprung open the lid warily, and diamonds sparkled up at her from rubies and she opened her lips in surprise. She read the note pinned to the velvet: *You have heard me speak of this often. It was given to me . . . Marli . . . the Tsar. . . . I had meant to keep it always . . . now you have come back to me . . . I want you to have it, Caroline. . . .*

Lion met Caroline again. She had come out of her dressing-room in tights and practice dress. He thought she had been crying and he felt peacefully sorry for her. He had a peaceful utter friendliness for Caroline. It was peaceful not to want anything from her, not a place in Gustave's ballet, not even love. Of course I have all these things, he admitted, but it was true that Hilda had immunized him from his old practices. Now he paused. "Hullo," he said.

"Hullo," said Caroline.

"Where are you going?"

"To warm up with Rebecca."

"But . . ." Caroline's face warned him to stop. "But you are not on for nearly two hours."

"All the same," said Caroline, and she argued, "I can rest and warm up again."

Lion did not whistle nor show his surprise. He held out his hand. "I'm going to her too," he said. "Come along."

"Now you see, *if* I had put off Lollie's audition as you wanted me to, Ilse, as you tried to make me, this would never have happened. If I had not sat up oll night . . ."

"If Hilda had not written the ballet," said Miss Ilse dryly.

Candles were lit on Madame's dressing-table above her roses and her fan. "You make yourself up by candlelight and then it is all wrong," said Miss Ilse.

"Never mind. I like what I have to see best by candlelight, now I am old," said Madame.

She touched the roses. "I am old. There is no one to give these to me now, excepting you, Ilse."

"What nonsense," said Miss Ilse. "The whole theatre is overflowing with flowers."

Zanny was busy and Madame had been calling for Miss Ilse to hook her dress. "Where are you, Ilse? You are never, never here when I want you."

Miss Ilse had been going once more all through the theatre to see that it was all well, all arranged. Miss Ilse was not a participant, she was a part; a very necessary part. She had found a chair with a broken leg—"And imagine if anyone had sat on it!" She had had to mediate in a fight between Zanny and Archie's mother; and she had paused to watch the dancers working quietly with Rebecca.

"Can you imagine? Caroline was there!" she told Madame. "Caroline! Working with Rebecca!"

"Ah!" said Madame softly.

"And she was crying."

"Ah!" said Madame more softly still. "We shall have a very good performance from everyone tonight," she said. "I feel it. Sometimes, Ilse, I think, do you know what I think? I think I don't deserve so much goodness, so much happiness. I haven't forgotten how to manage, have I, Ilse? I couldn't manage the printers, but that was to be expected in these days. It is like the hole left to keep out the Evil Eye. There is some life left in me, not? *She always has something up her sleeve.* That was what Gustave said, not? And it is true. But I confess it to you, Ilse, I don't know myself what it was that I did for tonight. I don't know how it happened. It was a miracle, Ilse."

"I lit a candle to St. Jude," said Miss Ilse, to explain the miracle.

"Don't talk such nonsense, Ilse. You are a fool. St. Jude! It might have been Lollie and the audition and Edmund bringing Gustave . . . but if we had not done *Leda and the Swan,* what would he have seen? If I had not sat up oll night and found it, we should not have had *Leda and the Swan.* If Felix had not helped . . . if Noel had not come . . . and we mustn't forget Edwin and Zanny and Miss Porteus and, even, Glancy. They have oll worked well, oll of them; we must not grudge it them. If they call me on the stage tonight, and they *may* call me, Ilse, not? . . ."

"Of course they will call you, Anna."

"Then I shall call them oll. Oll. Every one of them. From Caroline and Lion, down to them oll."

"I think you should call Hilda, first, by herself."

Madame was silent. She said slowly, "I shall have to call Hilda. I shall call her and then . . . I shall leave the stage. To her. By herself. Yes. I shall have to do that. It is rright." It was right, but it was still disagreeable. "Hilda will not stay with us," she said. "There is nothing more for her here. Yes. We have served her purpose," said Madame. It was bitter, but it was a fact. She had thought of Caroline as a meadow and that was right; now she could see the bounds of Caroline, but she could not tell how far Hilda would go; she knew that Hilda had passed her and was going out of sight. "Tonight, for me, is perhaps the end," she said, "but for Hilda it is only a milestone." She had again, and not even finally, that same jealous rebel pang. "Tchk-tchk!" said Madame. "Ilse, will you hook my dress, not? What are you standing there for? It is late and everybody will be waiting. What are you thinking of?" She paused and said, "Still, I don't know what it was. Not one thing by itself, but the way it all turned out, not? I wonder what it was," said Madame.

And Miss Ilse said, as she bent to hook the dress, "It was my candle to St. Jude."